T0089071

The H. P. Lovecraft editions from Del Rey Books

The Best of H. P. Lovecraft:
BLOODCURDLING TALES OF HORROR AND THE MACABRE

The Dream Cycle of H. P. Lovecraft:
DREAMS OF TERROR AND DEATH

The Transition of H. P. Lovecraft:
THE ROAD TO MADNESS

THE HORROR IN THE MUSEUM

THE WATCHERS OUT OF TIME

WAKING UP SCREAMING

SHADOWS OF DEATH

Other stories in the H. P. Lovecraftian World

H. P. Lovecraft and Others:
TALES OF THE CTHULHU MYTHOS

Stories Inspired by H. P. Lovecraft:
CTHULHU 2000

Also available from The Modern Library

AT THE MOUNTAINS OF MADNESS
The Definitive Edition

The Horror in the Museum

minature worlds in which the protecting armour could be dispensed with. They contrived marvellously ingenious things,
so that for a while men persisted in the rusting towers,
thinking [illegible]
and resume existence. Many thought it only a temporary change
which time would remedy; and did not believe the sad astronomers
of that far date. But one day the whole remaining colony of a
large city called in the old days Yuanario failed to respond
to signals, and when explorers came, they were found dead of
the intense heat.

It was then [illegible] realized these cities were lost
to them; knew they must forever abandon them to Nature. The
other colonists in these regions evacuated their brave posts,
and total silence fell upon the great empty cities. Nothing was
[illegible] multitudinous activities [illegible]
[illegible] deserted factories and buildings that reflected
the daily more intolerable heat, the dazzling radiance, and
never felt the vanished rain.

There were still many continents and lands unaffected,
though, and life soon absorbed the refugees; [illegible]
Cities were half forgotten During strangely prosperous centuries
Few thought of these spectral, rotting towers... can you conceive
the great cities of man [illegible] ? Darkly silent ? Deserted ?

Wars came, sinful and prolonged, but the times of peace were
greater, always [illegible], the swollen sun increased its radiance
as earth drew closer to its parent. [illegible]
to its distant origin in that seething chaos.

After a time the same thing happened to the extremes of
Europe, and then Paris and Berlin [illegible] These ancient cities [illegible]
[illegible] centuries [illegible] deserted, [illegible]
British Isles. This steady abandonment was a terrible [illegible]

The Horror in the Museum

H. P. Lovecraft and Others

DEL REY Ballantine Books • New York

The Horror in the Museum is a work of fiction. Names, characters, places, and incidents are the products of the authors' imaginations or are used fictitiously. Any resemblance to actual events, locales, or persons, living or dead, is entirely coincidental.

2007 Del Rey Trade Paperback Edition

Copyright © 1970, 1989 by Arkham House Publishers, Inc.
"A Note on the Texts" copyright © 1970 by S. T. Joshi
"Lovecraft's 'Revisions'" copyright © 1970 by August Derleth
Introduction copyright © 2007 by Stephen Jones

All rights reserved.

Published in the United States by Del Rey Books, an imprint of The Random House Publishing Group, a division of Random House, Inc., New York.

"Two Black Bottles" by Wilfred Blanch Talman, copyright © 1927 by the Popular Fiction Publishing Company; copyright © 1944 by August Derleth. By permission of Wilfred Blanch Talman.
Frontispiece courtesy of Brown University Library

DEL REY is a registered trademark and the Del Rey colophon is a trademark of Random House, Inc.

Originally published in different form in hardcover in the United States by Arkham House Publishers, Inc., in 1970. This edition was first published by Arkham House Publishers, Inc., in 1989.

ISBN 978-0-345-48572-4

www.delreybooks.com

147429898

Contents

SECONDARY REVISIONS

Introduction

Howard Phillips Lovecraft certainly could write. And the many books and stories bearing his byline are ample proof of that.

In a world filled with pastiches, spoofs, and sequels (trust me, I know—I've edited a couple of those volumes myself), Lovecraft is the *real* thing.

Although it has become fashionable by some contemporary critics to decry the author's somewhat archaic and eldritch writing style, there is no doubt that Lovecraft knew exactly what he was doing, and like Edgar Allan Poe—who he both admired and now rivals in influence—he was an American stylist of the highest order.

My own introduction to Lovecraft's work occurred in 1969 when, at the age of sixteen, I came across a paperback edition of *Dagon and Other Macabre Tales* in a local Woolworth's branch. I was initially attracted to the book by the distinctive black-and-white illustration on the cover, but the stories it contained were a revelation to me.

Within a year I had tracked down and read every major story Lovecraft had ever written. And despite having collected the author's work in many rare and original editions over the years, I still have the very same copy of that first paperback on my shelf, almost forty years later.

However, once I had exhausted Lovecraft's relatively small body of work, I started searching around for other stories in a similar vein.

* * *

Born in his grandparents' house in Providence, Rhode Island, on August 20, 1890, H. P. Lovecraft led a somewhat sheltered life as a child. Because of an apparent nervous disorder, he was treated as a semi-invalid by his protective mother and her indulgent family, and this coddled seclusion allowed the young boy to read a great many books.

A lifelong Anglophile as a result of his family's paternal English ancestry, Lovecraft had an old-fashioned writing style that may not have appealed to many contemporary readers, and he was easily discouraged when things did not go his way. Yet, despite all of these tribulations, his work has survived and flourished in the seventy years since his premature death.

This is because Lovecraft had an imagination second-to-none. Most famously, he created a pantheon of ancient Gods and alien deities in a series of loosely connected stories that later came to be called the "Cthulhu Mythos."

Even during his lifetime, Lovecraft's concepts were added to by an ever-widening circle of writers. It has been argued that Lovecraft did not actively encourage these pastiches, although at first they were mostly written by his friends, correspondents, and fellow writers from the legendary pulp magazine *Weird Tales*. These, most notably, included August W. Derleth, Robert E. Howard, Robert Bloch, Clark Ashton Smith, and Frank Belknap Long.

It was also Lovecraft's habit to adopt the inventions of his friends—such as the names of demonic divinities and cursed tomes of eldritch lore—and give them his seal of approval by incorporating them into his own fiction.

However, there also exists a converse group of stories that exhibit a much more personal involvement by the author, even if his name invariably did not appear on the originally published byline.

Despite his devotion to the actual craft of writing, Lovecraft's attitude to his own work often bordered on the dismissive, if not downright lazy. Although he made a meager living as a commercial writer, he rarely considered markets. He was as likely to have his work published in an amateur press publication for little or no reward as he was to see his name on the cover of a newsstand pulp magazine that invariably still only paid its contributors a pittance.

In his early twenties Lovecraft became immersed with the amateur journalism movement. He was also an inveterate letter writer, churning out an average of eight to ten letters a day, each usually four to eight pages in length, to a wide circle of correspondents, when he should have been producing more fiction.

Much of Lovecraft's writing was done in longhand with a fountain pen, and he hated revising or retyping his work (to the extent that others would sometimes do it for him). If a particular story was rejected by a specific market he had submitted it to, Lovecraft would more likely become despondent than try to sell the tale elsewhere: "Rejections are so numerous lately that I think I'll stop writing for a while & use the time in revision," he wrote to correspondent August Derleth.

As an author he wrote what he wanted, and when that did not pay the bills, he turned to rewriting other people's stories—often so extensively that they became wholly his own work.

This was the case with "The Crawling Chaos," an early dream-narrative written with the amateur poet Winifred Virginia Jackson and published under the double pseudonyms Lewis Theobold, Jr., and Elizabeth Neville Berkley in *The United Co-operative,* an amateur magazine.

With money always tight, and as a method of subsidizing his precarious income, Lovecraft provided a literary revision service, giving advice and suggestions where needed, or completely changing the work of some of his less talented clients. In fact, these (usually uncredited) revisions became Lovecraft's major source of income, with his own fiction merely a sideline. Although much of this work consisted of correcting spelling, punctuation and grammar, or copying out manuscript pages, he would sometimes entirely revise and rewrite a story, retaining only its title or the nucleus of the plot if its content inspired his imagination.

Among the amateur authors whose work he substantially rewrote or revised were U.S. consul Adolphe de Castro; family friend and fellow Providence resident C. M. Eddy, Jr.; Lovecraft's future literary executor Robert H. Barlow; writer and editor Wilfred Blanch Talman; midwest journalist and romance writer Zealia B. Bishop; Massachusetts divorcée Hazel Heald; world traveler William Lumley; Lovecraft's future wife Sonia H. Greene (Davis); and even the famous magician and escape artist Harry Houdini (Ehrich Weiss), all of whom went on to sell their fiction to *Weird Tales.*

"He would criticize paragraph after paragraph and pencil remarks beside them," recalled Hazel Heald, "and then make me rewrite them until they pleased him."

It was also through this service that Lovecraft added stories by such writers as Bishop, Heald, Lumley, and Frank Belknap Long to the burgeoning "Cthulhu Mythos."

"The stories I sent him always came back so revised from their basic idea that I felt I was a complete failure as a writer," Zealia Bishop remembered. "As a writer and instructor in the field of supernatural fiction he was an undisputed master, and another's work seldom pleased him when he first saw it. He could always find much to improve, and he was generous with his advice, drawing on a vast store of knowledge quite beyond the capacity of the average man of education of his or our time."

Bishop felt so grateful to Lovecraft that when her story "Medusa's Coil" ultimately appeared in the January 1939 issue of *Weird Tales,* she stipulated that half the fee ($120) should be paid to his surviving aunt, Annie E. P. Gamwell. "My debt to Lovecraft is great," Bishop admitted. "I count myself fortunate that I was one of his epistolary friends and pupils."

The Horror in the Museum contains some of the best of these "revisions" or, as they should more properly be called, "collaborations." If not quite up to the standard of Lovecraft's own finest work, such tales as C. M. Eddy's controversial "The Loved Dead," Robert H. Barlow's "Till A' the Seas," Hazel Heald's "Out of the Aeons" and "The Horror in the Burying-Ground," William Lumley's "The Diary of Alonzo Typer," and Zealia Bishop's "The Curse of Yig," "Medusa's Coil," and the short novel "The Mound," along with the title story itself, are all worthy of being considered minor gems in the canon of weird fiction. This is not really so surprising when you recognize that, as August Derleth so succinctly pointed out, "Lovecraft wrote most of what is memorable in them!"

But for me, the greatest thrill of buying this book when I was still a teenager was discovering that I shared my name (and its particular spelling) with the doomed protagonist of the Lovecraft–Hazel Heald collaboration "The Horror in the Museum." Not only that, but the story is atypically set in London—just across the River Thames from where I was born!

Reading this tale, I have never felt closer to the writer whose work helped shaped my own career in the field of macabre fiction.

* * *

Howard Phillips Lovecraft died on the morning of March 15, 1937, at the ridiculously young age of forty-six. He was buried in the family plot in the Swan Point Cemetery, where his name was inscribed alongside those of his parents. Just four people attended his funeral.

In the intervening years, all of Lovecraft's stories have been kept in print, not least through Del Rey's continuing series of attractive compilations. His work continues to sell millions of copies throughout the world and have been translated into every major language. Anthology editors such as myself continue to draw upon his relatively small cadre of fiction, and there are numerous websites and chat rooms devoted to the man and his work on the Internet.

Perhaps even more important, his stories and concepts have continued to inspire new generations of authors, many of whom have gone on to forge major careers in the weird fiction field.

But when it comes right down to it, there is only one H. P. Lovecraft. Although his style and themes have been copied, expanded, and adapted by countless others, he is genuinely unique among writers of supernatural fiction.

So don't be fooled by the bylines on these stories. For the most part, these are the *real* thing. The source of the nightmares. The ground zero of horror. Yes, H. P. Lovecraft certainly *could* write, no matter where the original concept came from or who received the final credit . . . as this book so aptly proves.

STEPHEN JONES
London, England
February 2007

STEPHEN JONES is one of Britain's most acclaimed anthologists of horror and dark fantasy. He has more than eighty-five books to his credit, including *H. P. Lovecraft's Book of Horror, H. P. Lovecraft's Book of the Supernatural, Shadows Over Innsmouth,* and *Weird Shadows Over Innsmouth*. You can visit his website at www.herebedragons.co.uk/jones.

A Note on the Texts

In this corrected edition of H. P. Lovecraft's revisions and collaborations, we have attempted not merely to restore the texts but to arrange the tales in accordance with the presumed degree of Lovecraft's involvement with them. What we have called "primary" revisions are those that were wholly or almost wholly written by Lovecraft (although a plot-germ or occasionally an actual draft was supplied by the revision client); the "secondary" revisions are those in which Lovecraft merely touched up—albeit sometimes extensively—a preexisting draft.

The two collaborations with Winifred Virginia Jackson, "The Green Meadow" and "The Crawling Chaos," are interesting in that they are among the few works (the others are "Poetry and the Gods," "Through the Gates of the Silver Key," and "In the Walls of Eryx") where Lovecraft affixed his name along with that of his collaborator, even though here both used pseudonyms. Nevertheless, there is little evidence to suggest that Jackson contributed any prose to either tale.

For the two tales revised for Adolphe de Castro, "The Last Test" and "The Electric Executioner," we have de Castro's original versions: they were published in his collection *In the Confessional* (1893), under the titles "A Sacrifice to Science" and "The

Automatic Executioner." Lovecraft has rewritten both stories completely, preserving only the skeleton of each work. It should be noted that in Lovecraft's only reference to the first tale he calls it "Clarendon's Last Test"; it is not certain whether he or someone else made the change. Lovecraft also speaks in letters of a third story revised for de Castro, but this has evidently been lost.

All three stories revised for Zealia Bishop—"The Curse of Yig," "The Mound," and "Medusa's Coil"—were, as Lovecraft notes, based on the scantiest of plot-germs and are accordingly close to original works by Lovecraft. The persistent rumor that Frank Belknap Long assisted in the writing of "The Mound" is false: Long, as Zealia Bishop's agent, merely abridged the story in a vain attempt to place it with a pulp magazine; after these efforts failed, the original version of the story as written by Lovecraft was restored, remaining in manuscript until Lovecraft's death. August Derleth then radically revised and abridged both "The Mound" and "Medusa's Coil" and marketed them to *Weird Tales*. This edition represents the first unadulterated publication of both works.

There is abundant evidence that Lovecraft wrote nearly the entirety of all five stories revised for Hazel Heald; Heald's contention that Lovecraft's role in "The Man of Stone" was somewhat less extensive than in the others does not seem to be borne out by the text.

For "The Diary of Alonzo Typer" we have both a draft by William Lumley (the title is his) and Lovecraft's rewriting. Again Lovecraft has preserved only the nucleus of the plot, and all the prose is his. Lumley's draft was first published (along with the original versions of the two Adolphe de Castro tales) in a special edition of *Crypt of Cthulhu, Ashes and Others* (1982).

Of the secondary revisions, Sonia H. Greene (Davis) reports that Lovecraft "revised and edited" "The Horror at Martin's Beach" (the title "The Invisible Monster" was supplied by *Weird Tales*), hence we can assume a preexisting draft. The other tale by Greene thought to be revised by Lovecraft, "Four O'Clock," was written, as Greene tells us, only at Lovecraft's suggestion and does not seem to bear any Lovecraftian prose or content; it has accordingly been omitted from this edition.

In recent years Lovecraft's revisory hand has been detected in a number of tales by his friends and colleagues, and five stories have been added to this edition. Kenneth W. Faig, Jr., first observed that Lovecraft in letters refers to four tales revised for C. M. Eddy, Jr.; all were probably based on existing drafts by Eddy, who wrote many tales in his own right. "Ashes" appears to be the earliest of these stories, and Lovecraft's hand in it is probably very light. In the other three—"The Ghost-Eater," "The Loved Dead," and "Deaf, Dumb, and Blind"—the two authors probably contributed equally.

It is difficult to ascertain how much of Lovecraft remains in Wilfred Blanch Talman's "Two Black Bottles," as Lovecraft's letters suggest that Talman was annoyed at Lovecraft's extensive revisions in the story and may perhaps have reinstated his own prose in the final draft.

I discovered Lovecraft's role in Henry S. Whitehead's "The Trap"; in a letter to R. H. Barlow (25 February 1932) he reports writing the entire central section of the story. In letters Lovecraft refers to another story by Whitehead, "The Bruise," for which he supplied a synopsis; and although William Fulwiler, who brought this matter to our attention, believes that Lovecraft may have actually written the story (published as "Bothon" in *West India Lights*), I am not convinced that Lovecraft contributed any prose to this work.

Lovecraft's letters to Duane W. Rimel indicate that he was reading and reviewing many of Rimel's tales during the 1930s, and in two of them he seems to have had a hand. Scott Connors noted Lovecraft's involvement in "The Tree on the Hill," and Robert M. Price and I confirmed it. Rimel has stated that Lovecraft wrote the entire third section of the tale, as well as the citation from the mythical *Chronicle of Nath* in the second section. Will Murray first suspected, on internal evidence, Lovecraft's role in "The Disinterment." Rimel maintains that Lovecraft's revisions in the story were very light, and letters by Lovecraft unearthed by Murray and myself appear to confirm that claim.

For R. H. Barlow's "'Till A' the Seas'" we have a typescript by Barlow (apparently a second draft) with exhaustive revisions by Lovecraft in pen. Dirk W. Mosig discovered Lovecraft's hand in Barlow's "The Night Ocean," as cited in a letter to Hyman Bradofsky (4 November 1936). Mosig believed the tale to be nearly entirely written by Lovecraft; but documents subsequently consulted by me suggest that he played a much smaller role in the genesis and writing of the tale. The work was probably largely Barlow's, although with heavy revisions and additions by Lovecraft at random points.

For a more detailed discussion of the degree of Lovecraft's involvement in these stories, see my article "Lovecraft's Revisions:

How Much of Them Did He Write?" *Crypt of Cthulhu* 2 (Candlemas 1983): 3–14.

Our editorial practice for this disparate body of work must of necessity be cautious. Autograph manuscripts (or Lovecraft's autograph corrections) exist for only two tales in this volume—"'Till A' the Seas'" and "The Diary of Alonzo Typer." Typescripts exist only for "The Mound" and "Medusa's Coil," although both were prepared by Frank Belknap Long and contain several errors and incoherencies, the apparent result of Long's inability to read Lovecraft's handwriting. The texts for all other works must be based upon publications in amateur journals or pulp magazines. For the primary revisions we have reinstated Lovecraft's normal punctuational, stylistic, and syntactic usages, on the principle that nearly all the prose in these tales is his; for the secondary revisions we have only corrected obvious misprints or internal inconsistencies of usage in the original publications.

Many colleagues have assisted in the compilation of this volume, and I am especially grateful to Donald R. Burleson, Kenneth R. Johnson, Marc A. Michaud, Dirk W. Mosig, Will Murray, and Robert M. Price. The advice of James Turner has been invaluable both in the overall arrangement of this edition and in countless points of difficulty in the texts themselves.

S. T. Joshi

Lovecraft's "Revisions"

However paradoxical it may seem, in view of his present posthumous fame as a master of the macabre, Howard Phillips Lovecraft made his scant living principally by revising and correcting manuscripts of prose and poetry sent to him by a variety of hopeful writers. The greater number of his clients seldom achieved publication in any but amateur-press magazines, but his revision of the stories by a small group of writers with reasonably strong themes but a concomitant lack of literary skills or prose style enlisted a greater share of his interest and assistance—amounting often to the complete rewriting of a submitted manuscript—and so found their way into print.

Lovecraft's revision work can be divided into two classes. The bulk of it amounted to little more than professional correction of language, syntax, punctuation, and the like, but a minority of tales in the domain of the macabre aroused his personal interest to the extent of active participation. Even this small group of tales was subdivided into areas of lesser and major interest. Some, as in the case of Sonia H. Greene's story, the early work of Hazel Heald, and the tales of his old Providence friend C. M. Eddy, Jr., required less drastic revision and more or less advisory assistance. Writing on 30 September 1944 of one such story, "The Man of Stone," the late

Hazel Heald admitted, "Lovecraft helped me on this story as much as on the others, and did actually rewrite paragraphs. He would criticize paragraph after paragraph and pencil remarks beside them, and then make me rewrite them until they pleased him." But of course Lovecraft did considerably more with Hazel Heald's later stories: he rewrote them from beginning to end so that they are essentially Lovecraft stories, retaining only the plot or central theme of the author whose by-line appeared over the work—and not even this in every case. The kind of revision to which Mrs. Heald here referred is illustrated in the manuscript of R. H. Barlow's tale, "'Till A' the Seas,'" in the Lovecraft Collection of the John Hay Library of Brown University, a specimen page from which appears as the frontispiece to the present volume.

Zealia Bishop, in her 1953 memoir "H. P. Lovecraft: A Pupil's View," sets forth an experience central to the majority of the writers represented in this collection, one shared by only a relatively few of Lovecraft's clients: "The stories I sent him always came back so revised from their basic idea that I felt I was a complete failure as a writer." The extent to which she felt herself indebted to Lovecraft was indicated by her insistence that half the fee paid by *Weird Tales* for "Medusa's Coil," published after Lovecraft's untimely death in 1937, be sent to his surviving aunt, Mrs. Annie E. Phillips Gamwell. "I had learned from him fundamental principles of writing technique and the appreciation of literature. . . . My debt to Lovecraft is great. I count myself fortunate that I was one of his epistolary friends and pupils."

Lovecraft also encouraged his fiction clients to turn a hand to the macabre, since this after all was his specialized field, in which he was far more at home than in the popular contemporary veins of romance or realism; fantasy was the one literary genre in which he could be of greatest service to his patrons. Even the most casual reading of the revisions collected herein offers patent evidence that with Hazel Heald's tale, "The Horror in the Museum," Lovecraft saw himself rather more as collaborator than as revisionist. The story is pure Lovecraft, even to the introduction of names from the Cthulhu Mythos, and the same circumstance obtains with "Out of the Aeons."

And this to some extent is true, too, of many of the other stories: William Lumley's "The Diary of Alonzo Typer," Hazel Heald's "The Horror in the Burying-Ground," Adolphe de Castro's "The Last Test" and "The Electric Executioner," and the three by Zealia

Bishop, "The Curse of Yig," "Medusa's Coil," and the short novel "The Mound," one of the most impressive tales in this book.

One can well imagine the pleasure Lovecraft took in reworking some of these tales, for next to creating a new story of his own, he enjoyed nothing more than giving his vivid imagination free rein in revising fiction that belonged to his favorite field. His letters are crowded with references to his revision work; he wrote about the drudgery of trying to advise amateur poets, of "revising" their poems; he wrote about the difficulties of working with some writers who fancied themselves geniuses and had not a grain of ability—but he never once complained about rewriting a story in the domain of fantasy and the macabre, and there are frequent paragraphs listing stories in current issues of *Weird Tales* in which he "had a hand."

These "revisions," which are either largely or totally by Lovecraft, properly belong in the Lovecraft canon. They are uneven in manner and flavor, but Lovecraft's imagination and writing hand are not to be denied in the pages that follow. The best of these tales are certainly good enough to stand among Lovecraft's stories—and why not?—since he wrote most of what is memorable in them!

AUGUST DERLETH

The Horror in the Museum

Translated by Elizabeth Neville Berkeley
and Lewis Theobald, Jun.

The Green Meadow

INTRODUCTORY NOTE: The following very singular narrative or record of impressions was discovered under circumstances so extraordinary that they deserve careful description. On the evening of Wednesday, August 27, 1913, at about 8:30 o'clock, the population of the small seaside village of Potowonket, Maine, U.S.A., was aroused by a thunderous report accompanied by a blinding flash; and persons near the shore beheld a mammoth ball of fire dart from the heavens into the sea but a short distance out, sending up a prodigious column of water. The following Sunday a fishing party composed of John Richmond, Peter B. Carr, and Simon Canfield caught in their trawl and dragged ashore a mass of metallic rock, weighing 360 pounds, and looking (as Mr. Canfield said) like a piece of slag. Most of the inhabitants agreed that this heavy body was none other than the fireball which had fallen from the sky four days before; and Dr. Richmond M. Jones, the local scientific authority, allowed that it must be an aerolite or meteoric stone. In chipping off specimens to send to an expert Boston analyst, Dr. Jones discovered imbedded in the semimetallic mass the strange book containing the ensuing tale, which is still in his possession.

In form the discovery resembles an ordinary notebook, about 5 × 3 inches in size, and containing thirty leaves. In material, however, it presents marked peculiarities. The covers are apparently of some dark stony substance unknown to geologists, and unbreakable by any mechanical means. No chemical reagent seems to act upon them. The leaves are much the same, save that they are lighter in colour, and so infinitely thin as to be quite flexible. The whole is bound by some process not very clear to those who have observed it; a process involving the adhesion of the leaf substance to the cover substance. These substances cannot now be separated, nor can the leaves be torn by any amount of force. The writing is *Greek of the purest classical quality,* and several students of palaeography declare that the characters are in a cursive hand used about the second century B. C. There is little in the text to determine the date. The mechanical mode of writing cannot be deduced beyond the fact that it must have resembled that of the modern slate and slate-pencil. During the course of analytical efforts made by the late Prof. Chambers of Harvard, several pages, mostly at the conclusion of the narrative, were blurred to the point of utter effacement before being read; a circumstance forming a well-nigh irreparable loss. What remains of the contents was done into modern Greek letters by the palaeographer Rutherford and in this form submitted to the translators.

Prof. Mayfield of the Massachusetts Institute of Technology, who examined samples of the strange stone, declares it a true meteorite; an opinion in which Dr. von Winterfeldt of Heidelberg (interned in 1918 as a dangerous enemy alien) does not concur. Prof. Bradley of Columbia College adopts a less dogmatic ground; pointing out that certain utterly unknown ingredients are present in large quantities, and warning that no classification is as yet possible.

The presence, nature, and message of the strange book form so momentous a problem, that no explanation can even be attempted. The text, as far as preserved, is here rendered as literally as our language permits, in the hope that some reader may eventually hit upon an interpretation and solve one of the greatest scientific mysteries of recent years.

—E.N.B.—L.T., Jun.

(THE STORY)

It was a narrow place, and I was alone. On one side, beyond a margin of vivid waving green, was the sea; blue, bright, and billowy, and sending up vaporous exhalations which intoxicated me. So profuse, indeed, were these exhalations, that they gave me an odd impression of a coalescence of sea and sky; for the heavens were likewise bright and blue. On the other side was the forest, ancient almost as the sea itself, and stretching infinitely inland. It was very dark, for the trees were grotesquely huge and luxuriant, and incredibly numerous. Their giant trunks were of a horrible green which blended weirdly with the narrow green tract whereon I stood. At some distance away, on either side of me, the strange forest extended down to the water's edge; obliterating the shore line and completely hemming in the narrow tract. Some of the trees, I observed, stood in the water itself; as though impatient of any barrier to their progress.

I saw no living thing, nor sign that any living thing save myself had ever existed. The sea and the sky and the wood encircled me, and reached off into regions beyond my imagination. Nor was there any sound save of the wind-tossed wood and of the sea.

As I stood in this silent place, I suddenly commenced to tremble; for though I knew not how I came there, and could scarce remember what my name and rank had been, I felt that I should go mad if I could understand what lurked about me. I recalled things I had learned, things I had dreamed, things I had imagined and yearned for in some other distant life. I thought of long nights when I had gazed up at the stars of heaven and cursed the gods that my free soul could not traverse the vast abysses which were inaccessible to my body. I conjured up ancient blasphemies, and terrible delvings into the papyri of Democritus; but as memories appeared, I shuddered in deeper fear, for I knew that I was alone—horribly alone. Alone, yet close to sentient impulses of vast, vague kind; which I prayed never to comprehend nor encounter. In the voice of the swaying green branches I fancied I could detect a kind of malignant hatred and daemoniac triumph. Sometimes they struck me as being in horrible colloquy with ghastly and unthinkable things which the scaly green bodies of the trees half hid; hid from sight but not from consciousness. The most oppressive of my sensations was a sinister feeling of alienage. Though I saw about me objects which I could name—trees, grass, sea, and sky; I felt that their relation to me was not the same as that of the trees, grass, sea, and sky I knew in another and dimly remembered life. The nature of the difference I could not tell, yet I shook in stark fright as it impressed itself upon me.

And then, in a spot where I had before discerned nothing but the misty sea, I beheld the Green Meadow; separated from me by a vast expanse of blue rippling water with sun-tipped wavelets, yet strangely near. Often I would peep fearfully over my right shoulder at the trees, but I preferred to look at the Green Meadow, which affected me oddly.

It was while my eyes were fixed upon this singular tract, that I first felt the ground in motion beneath me. Beginning with a kind of throbbing agitation which held a fiendish suggestion of conscious action, the bit of bank on which I stood detached itself from the grassy shore and commenced to float away; borne slowly onward as if by some current of resistless force. I did not move, astonished and startled as I was by the unprecedented phenomenon; but stood rigidly still until a wide lane of water yawned betwixt me and the land of trees. Then I sat down in a sort of daze, and again looked at the sun-tipped water and the Green Meadow.

Behind me the trees and the things they may have been hiding seemed to radiate infinite menace. This I knew without turning to view them, for as I grew more used to the scene I became less and less dependent upon the five senses that once had been my sole reliance. I knew the green scaly forest hated me, yet now I was safe from it, for my bit of bank had drifted far from the shore.

But though one peril was past, another loomed up before me. Pieces of earth were constantly crumbling from the floating isle which held me, so that death could not be far distant in any event. Yet even then I seemed to sense that death would be death to me no more, for I turned again to watch the Green Meadow, imbued with a curious feeling of security in strange contrast to my general horror.

Then it was that I heard, at a distance immeasurable, the sound of falling water. Not that of any trivial cascade such as I had known, but that which might be heard in the far Scythian lands if all the Mediterranean were poured down an unfathomable abyss. It was toward this sound that my shrinking island was drifting, yet I was content.

Far in the rear were happening weird and terrible things; things which I turned to view, yet shivered to behold. For in the sky dark vaporous forms hovered fantastically, brooding over trees and seeming to answer the challenge of the waving green branches. Then a thick mist arose from the sea to join the sky-forms, and the shore was erased from my sight. Though the sun—what sun I knew not—shone brightly on the water around me, the land I had left seemed involved in a daemoniac tempest where clashed the will of the hellish trees and what they hid, with that of the sky and the sea.

And when the mist vanished, I saw only the blue sky and the blue sea, for the land and the trees were no more.

It was at this point that my attention was arrested by the *singing* in the Green Meadow. Hitherto, as I have said, I had encountered no sign of human life; but now there arose to my ears a dull chant whose origin and nature were apparently unmistakable. While the words were utterly undistinguishable, the chant awaked in me a peculiar train of associations; and I was reminded of some vaguely disquieting lines I had once translated out of an Egyptian book, which in turn were taken from a papyrus of ancient Meroë. Through my brain ran lines that I fear to repeat; lines telling of very antique things and forms of life in the days when our earth was exceeding young. Of things which thought and moved and were alive, yet which gods and men would not consider alive. It was a strange book.

As I listened, I became gradually conscious of a circumstance which had before puzzled me only subconsciously. At no time had my sight distinguished any definite objects in the Green Meadow, an impression of vivid homogeneous verdure being the sum total of my perception. Now, however, I saw that the current would cause my island to pass the shore at but a little distance; so that I might learn more of the land and of the singing thereon. My curiosity to behold the singers had mounted high, though it was mingled with apprehension.

Bits of sod continued to break away from the tiny tract which carried me, but I heeded not their loss; for I felt that I was not to die with the body (or appearance of a body) which I seemed to possess. That everything about me, even life and death, was illusory; that I had overleaped the bounds of mortality and corporeal entity, becoming a free, detached thing; impressed me as almost certain. Of my location I knew nothing, save that I felt I could not be on the earth-planet once so familiar to me. My sensations, apart from a kind of haunting terror, were those of a traveller just embarked upon an unending voyage of discovery. For a moment I thought of the lands and persons I had left behind; and of strange ways whereby I might some day tell them of my adventurings, even though I might never return.

I had now floated very near the Green Meadow, so that the voices were clear and distinct; but though I knew many languages I could not quite interpret the words of the chanting. Familiar they indeed were, as I had subtly felt when at a greater distance, but beyond a sensation of vague and awesome remembrance I could make nothing of them. A most extraordinary *quality* in the voices —a quality which I cannot describe—at once frightened and fascinated me. My eyes could now discern several things amidst the omnipresent verdure—rocks, covered with bright green moss, shrubs of considerable height, and less definable shapes of great magnitude which seemed to move or vibrate amidst the shrubbery in a peculiar way. The chanting, whose authors I was so anxious to glimpse, seemed loudest at points where these shapes were most numerous and most vigorously in motion.

And then, as my island drifted closer and the sound of the distant waterfall grew louder, I saw clearly the *source* of the chanting, and in one horrible instant remembered everything. Of such things I cannot, dare not tell, for therein was revealed the hideous solution of all which had puzzled me; and that solution would drive you mad, even as it almost drove me. . . . I knew now the change through which I had passed, and through which certain others who once were men had passed! and I knew the endless cycle of the future which none like me may escape. . . . I shall live forever, be conscious forever, though my soul cries out to the gods for the boon of death and oblivion. . . . All is before me: beyond the deafening torrent lies the land of Stethelos, where young men are infinitely old. . . . The Green Meadow . . . I will send a message across the horrible immeasurable abyss. . . .

[*At this point the text becomes illegible.*]

Elizabeth Berkeley and Lewis Theobald, Jun.

The Crawling Chaos

Of the pleasures and pains of opium much has been written. The ecstasies and horrors of De Quincey and the *paradis artificiels* of Baudelaire are preserved and interpreted with an art which makes them immortal, and the world knows well the beauty, the terror, and the mystery of those obscure realms into which the inspired dreamer is transported. But much as has been told, no man has yet dared intimate the *nature* of the phantasms thus unfolded to the mind, or hint at the *direction* of the unheard-of roads along whose ornate and exotic course the partaker of the drug is so irresistibly borne. De Quincey was drawn back into Asia, that teeming land of nebulous shadows whose hideous antiquity is so impressive that "the vast age of the race and name overpowers the sense of youth in the individual", but farther than that he dared not go. Those who *have* gone farther seldom returned; and even when they have, they have been either silent or quite mad. I took opium but once—in the year of the plague, when doctors sought to deaden the agonies they could not cure. There was an overdose—my physician was worn out with horror and exertion—and I travelled very far indeed. In the end I returned and lived, but my nights are filled with strange memories, nor have I ever permitted a doctor to give me opium again.

The pain and pounding in my head had been quite unendurable when the drug was administered. Of the future I had no heed; to escape, whether by cure, unconsciousness, or death, was all that concerned me. I was partly delirious, so that it is hard to place the exact moment of transition, but I think the effect must have begun shortly before the pounding ceased to be painful. As I have said, there was an overdose; so my reactions were probably far from normal. The sensation of falling, curiously dissociated from the idea of gravity or direction, was paramount; though there was a subsidiary impression of unseen throngs in incalculable profusion, throngs of infinitely diverse nature, but all more or less related to me. Sometimes it seemed less as though I were falling, than as though the universe or the ages were falling past me. Suddenly my pain ceased, and I began to associate the pounding with an external rather than internal force. The falling has ceased also, giving place to a sensation of uneasy, temporary rest; and when I listened closely, I fancied the pounding was that of the vast, inscrutable sea as its sinister, colossal breakers lacerated some desolate shore after a storm of titanic magnitude. Then I opened my eyes.

For a moment my surroundings seemed confused, like a projected image hopelessly out of focus, but gradually I realised my solitary presence in a strange and beautiful room lighted by many windows. Of the exact nature of the apartment I could form no idea, for my thoughts were still far from settled; but I noticed vari-coloured rugs and draperies, elaborately fashioned tables, chairs, ottomans, and divans, and delicate vases and ornaments which conveyed a suggestion of the exotic without being actually alien. These things I noticed, yet they were not long uppermost in my mind. Slowly but inexorably crawling upon my consciousness, and rising above every other impression, came a dizzying fear of the unknown; a fear all the greater because I could not analyse it, and seeming to concern a stealthily approaching menace—not death, but some nameless, unheard-of thing inexpressibly more ghastly and abhorrent.

Presently I realised that the direct symbol and excitant of my fear was the hideous pounding whose incessant reverberations throbbed maddeningly against my exhausted brain. It seemed to come from a point outside and below the edifice in which I stood, and to associate itself with the most terrifying mental images. I felt that some horrible scene or object lurked beyond the silk-hung walls, and shrank from glancing through the arched, latticed windows that opened so bewilderingly on every hand. Perceiving shutters attached to these windows, I closed them all, averting my eyes from the exterior as I did so. Then, employing a flint and steel which I found on one of the small tables, I lit the many candles reposing about the walls in Arabesque sconces. The added sense of security brought by closed shutters and artificial light calmed my nerves to some degree, but I could not shut out the monotonous pounding. Now that I was calmer, the sound became as fascinating as it was fearful, and I felt a contradictory desire to seek out its source despite my still powerful shrinking. Opening a portiere at the side of the room nearest the pounding, I beheld a small and richly draped corridor ending in a carven door and large oriel window. To this window I was irresistibly drawn, though my ill-defined apprehensions seemed almost equally bent on holding me back. As I approached it I could see a chaotic whirl of waters in the distance. Then, as I attained it and glanced out on all sides, the stupendous picture of my surroundings burst upon me with full and devastating force.

I beheld such a sight as I had never beheld before, and which no living person can have seen save in the delirium of fever or the inferno of opium. The building stood on a narrow point of land—or what was *now* a narrow point of land—fully 300 feet above what must lately have been a seething vortex of mad waters. On either side of the house there fell a newly washed-out precipice of red earth, whilst ahead of me the hideous waves were still rolling in frightfully, eating away the land with ghastly monotony and deliberation. Out a mile or more there rose and fell menacing breakers at least fifty feet in height, and on the far horizon ghoulish black clouds of grotesque contour were resting and brooding like unwholesome vultures. The waves were dark and purplish, almost black, and clutched at the yielding red mud of the bank as if with uncouth, greedy hands. I could not but feel that some noxious marine mind had declared a war of extermination upon all the solid ground, perhaps abetted by the angry sky.

Recovering at length from the stupor into which this unnatural spectacle had thrown me, I realised that my actual physical danger was acute. Even whilst I gazed the bank had lost many feet, and it could not be long before the house would fall undermined into the awful pit of lashing waves. Accordingly I hastened to the opposite side of the edifice, and finding a door, emerged at once, locking it after me with a curious key which had hung inside. I now beheld more of the strange region about me, and marked a singular division which seemed to exist in the hostile ocean and firmament. On each side of the jutting promontory different conditions held sway. At my left as I faced inland was a gently heaving sea with great green waves rolling peacefully in under a brightly shining sun. Something about that sun's nature and position made me shudder, but I could not then tell, and cannot tell now, what it was. At my right also was the sea, but it was blue, calm, and only gently undulating, while the sky above it was darker and the washed-out bank more nearly white than reddish.

I now turned my attention to the land, and found occasion for fresh surprise; for the vegetation resembled nothing I had ever seen or read about. It was apparently tropical or at least sub-tropical—a conclusion borne out by the intense heat of the air. Sometimes I thought I could trace strange analogies with the flora of my native land, fancying that the well-known plants and shrubs might assume such forms under a radical change of climate; but the gigantic and omnipresent palm trees were plainly foreign. The house I had just left was very small—hardly more than a cottage—but its material was evidently marble, and its architecture was weird and composite, involving a quaint fusion of Western and Eastern forms. At the corners were Corinthian columns, but the red tile roof was like that of a Chinese pagoda. From the door inland there stretched a path of singularly white sand, about four feet wide, and lined on either side with stately palms and unidentifiable flowering shrubs and plants. It lay toward the side of the promontory where the sea was blue and the bank rather whitish. Down this path I felt impelled to flee, as if pursued by some malignant spirit from the pounding ocean. At first it was slightly uphill, then I reached a gentle crest. Behind me I saw the scene I had left; the entire point with the cottage and the black water, with the green sea on one side and the blue sea on the other, and a curse unnamed and unnamable lowering over all. I never saw it again, and often wonder. . . . After this last look I strode ahead and surveyed the inland panorama before me.

The path, as I have intimated, ran along the right-hand shore as one went inland. Ahead and to the left I now viewed a magnificent valley comprising thousands of acres, and covered with a swaying growth of tropical grass higher than my head. Almost at the limit of vision was a colossal palm tree which seemed to fascinate and beckon me. By this time wonder and escape from the imperilled peninsula had largely dissipated my fear, but as I paused and sank fatigued to the path, idly digging with my hands into the warm, whitish-golden sand, a new and acute sense of danger seized me. Some terror in the swishing tall grass seemed added to that of the diabolically pounding sea, and I started up crying aloud and disjointedly, "Tiger? Tiger? Is it Tiger? Beast? Beast? Is it a Beast that I am afraid of?" My mind wandered back to an ancient and classical story of tigers which I had read; I strove to recall the author, but had difficulty. Then in the midst of my fear I remembered that the tale was by Rudyard Kipling; nor did the grotesqueness of deeming him an ancient author occur to me. I wished for the volume containing this story, and had almost started back toward the doomed cottage to procure it when my better sense and the lure of the palm prevented me.

Whether or not I could have resisted the backward beckoning without the counter-fascination of the vast palm tree, I do not know. This attraction was now dominant, and I left the path and crawled on hands and knees down the valley's slope despite my fear of the grass and of the serpents it might contain. I resolved to fight for life and reason as long as possible against all menaces of sea or land, though I sometimes feared defeat as the maddening swish of the uncanny grasses joined the still audible and irritating pounding of the distant breakers. I would frequently pause and put my hands to my ears for relief, but could never quite shut out the detestable sound. It was, as it seemed to me, only after ages that I finally dragged myself to the beckoning palm tree and lay quiet beneath its protecting shade.

There now ensued a series of incidents which transported me to the opposite extremes of ecstasy and horror; incidents which I tremble to recall and dare not seek to interpret. No sooner had I crawled beneath the overhanging foliage of the palm, than there dropped from its branches a young child of such beauty as I never beheld before. Though ragged and dusty, this being bore the features of a faun or demigod, and seemed almost to diffuse a radiance in the dense shadow of the tree. It smiled and extended its hand, but before I could arise and speak I heard in the upper air the exquisite melody of singing; notes high and low blent with a sublime and ethereal harmoniousness. The sun had by this time sunk below the horizon, and in the twilight I saw that an aureola of lambent light encircled the child's head. Then in a tone of silver it addressed me: "It is the end. They have come down through the gloaming from the stars. Now all is over, and beyond the Arinurian streams we shall dwell blissfully in Teloe." As the child spoke, I beheld a soft radiance through the leaves of the palm tree, and rising greeted a pair whom I knew to be the chief singers among those I had heard. A god and goddess they must have been, for such beauty is not mortal; and they took my hands, saying, "Come, child, you have heard the voices, and all is well. In Teloe beyond the Milky Way and the Arinurian streams are cities all of amber and chalcedony. And upon their domes of many facets glisten the images of strange and beautiful stars. Under the ivory bridges of Teloe flow rivers of liquid gold bearing pleasure-barges bound for blossomy Cytharion of the Seven Suns. And in Teloe and Cytharion abide only youth, beauty, and pleasure, nor are any sounds heard, save of laughter, song, and the lute. Only the gods dwell in Teloe of the golden rivers, but among them shalt thou dwell."

As I listened, enchanted, I suddenly became aware of a change in my surroundings. The palm tree, so lately overshadowing my exhausted form, was now some distance to my left and considerably below me. I was obviously floating in the atmosphere; companioned not only by the strange child and the radiant pair, but by a constantly increasing throng of half-luminous, vine-crowned youths and maidens with wind-blown hair and joyful countenance. We slowly ascended together, as if borne on a fragrant breeze which blew not from the earth but from the golden nebulae, and the child whispered in my ear that I must look always upward to the pathways of light, and never backward to the sphere I had just left. The youths and maidens now chaunted mellifluous choriambics to the accompaniment of lutes, and I felt enveloped in a peace and happiness more profound than any I had in life imagined, when the intrusion of a single sound altered my destiny and shattered my soul. Through the ravishing strains of the singers and the lutanists, as if in mocking, daemoniac concord, throbbed from gulfs below the damnable, the detestable pounding of that hideous ocean. And as those black breakers beat their message into my ears I forgot the words of the child and looked back, down upon the doomed scene from which I thought I had escaped.

Down through the aether I saw the accursed earth turning, ever turning, with angry and tempestuous seas gnawing at wild desolate shores and dashing foam against the tottering towers of deserted cities. And under a ghastly moon there gleamed sights I can never describe, sights I can never forget; deserts of corpse-like clay and jungles of ruin and decadence where once stretched the populous plains and villages of my native land, and maelstroms of frothing ocean where once rose the mighty temples of my forefathers. Around the northern pole steamed a morass of noisome growths and miasmal vapours, hissing before the onslaught of the ever-mounting waves that curled and fretted from the shuddering deep. Then a rending report clave the night, and athwart the desert of deserts appeared a smoking rift. Still the black ocean foamed and gnawed, eating away the desert on either side as the rift in the centre widened and widened.

There was now no land left but the desert, and still the fuming ocean ate and ate. All at once I thought even the pounding sea seemed afraid of something, afraid of dark gods of the inner earth that are greater than the evil god of waters, but even if it was it could not turn back; and the desert had suffered too much from those nightmare waves to help them now. So the ocean ate the last of the land and poured into the smoking gulf, thereby giving up all it had ever conquered. From the new-flooded lands it flowed again, uncovering death and decay; and from its ancient and immemorial bed it trickled loathsomely, uncovering nighted secrets of the years when Time was young and the gods unborn. Above the waves rose weedy, remembered spires. The moon laid pale lilies of light on dead London, and Paris stood up from its damp grave to be sanctified with star-dust. Then rose spires and monoliths that were weedy but not remembered; terrible spires and monoliths of lands that men never knew were lands.

There was not any pounding now, but only the unearthly roaring and hissing of waters tumbling into the rift. The smoke of that rift had changed to steam, and almost hid the world as it grew denser and denser. It seared my face and hands, and when I looked to see how it affected my companions I found they had all disappeared. Then very suddenly it ended, and I knew no more till I awaked upon a bed of convalescence. As the cloud of steam from the Plutonic gulf finally concealed the entire surface from my sight, all the firmament shrieked at a sudden agony of mad reverberations which shook the trembling aether. In one delirious flash and burst it happened; one blinding, deafening holocaust of fire, smoke, and thunder that dissolved the wan moon as it sped outward to the void.

And when the smoke cleared away, and I sought to look upon the earth, I beheld against the background of cold, humorous stars only the dying sun and the pale mournful planets searching for their sister.

Adolphe de Castro

The Last Test

I.

Few persons know the inside of the Clarendon story, or even that there is an inside not reached by the newspapers. It was a San Francisco sensation in the days before the fire, both because of the panic and menace that kept it company, and because of its close linkage with the governor of the state. Governor Dalton, it will be recalled, was Clarendon's best friend, and later married his sister. Neither Dalton nor Mrs. Dalton would ever discuss the painful affair, but somehow the facts have leaked out to a limited circle. But for that, and for the years which have given a sort of vagueness and impersonality to the actors, one would still pause before probing into secrets so strictly guarded at the time.

The appointment of Dr. Alfred Clarendon as medical director of San Quentin Penitentiary in 189- was greeted with the keenest enthusiasm throughout California. San Francisco had at last the honour of harbouring one of the greatest biologists and physicians of the period, and solid pathological leaders from all over the world might be expected to flock thither to study his methods, profit by his advice and researches, and learn how to cope with their own local problems. California, almost over night, would become a centre of medical scholarship with earthwide influence and reputation.

Governor Dalton, anxious to spread the news in its fullest significance, saw to it that the press carried ample and dignified accounts of his new appointee. Pictures of Dr. Clarendon and his new home near old Goat Hill, sketches of his career and manifold honours, and popular accounts of his salient scientific discoveries were all presented in the principal California dailies, till the public soon felt a sort of reflected pride in the man whose studies of pyemia in India, of the pest in China, and of every sort of kindred disorder elsewhere would soon enrich the world of medicine with an antitoxin of revolutionary importance—a basic antitoxin combating the whole febrile principle at its very source, and ensuring the ultimate conquest and extirpation of fever in all its diverse forms.

Back of the appointment stretched an extended and not wholly unromantic history of early friendship, long separation, and dramatically renewed acquaintance. James Dalton and the Clarendon family had been friends in New York ten years before—friends and more than friends, since the doctor's only sister, Georgina, was the sweetheart of Dalton's youth, while the doctor himself had been his closest associate and almost his protégé in the days of school and college. The father of Alfred and Georgina, a Wall Street pirate of the ruthless elder breed, had known Dalton's father well; so well, indeed, that he had finally stripped him of all he possessed in a memorable afternoon's fight on the stock exchange. Dalton Senior, hopeless of recuperation and wishing to give his one adored child the benefit of his insurance, had promptly blown out his brains; but James had not sought to retaliate. It was, as he viewed it, all in the game; and he wished no harm to the father of the girl he meant to marry and of the budding young scientist whose admirer and protector he had been throughout their years of fellowship and study. Instead, he turned to the law, established himself in a small way, and in due course of time asked "Old Clarendon" for Georgina's hand.

Old Clarendon had refused very firmly and loudly, vowing that no pauper and upstart lawyer was fit to be his son-in-law; and a scene of considerable violence had occurred. James, telling the wrinkled freebooter at last what he ought to have been told long before, had left the house and the city in a high temper; and was embarked within a month upon the California life which was to lead him to the governorship through many a fight with ring and politician. His farewells to Alfred and Georgina had been brief, and he had never known the aftermath of that scene in the Clarendon library. Only by a day did he miss the news of Old Clarendon's death from apoplexy, and by so missing it, changed the course of his whole career. He had not written Georgina in the decade that followed; knowing her loyalty to her father, and waiting till his own fortune and position might remove all obstacles to the match. Nor had he sent any word to Alfred, whose calm indifference in the face of affection and hero-worship had always savoured of conscious destiny and the self-sufficiency of genius. Secure in the ties of a constancy rare even then, he had worked and risen with thoughts only of the future; still a bachelor, and with a perfect intuitive faith that Georgina also was waiting.

In this faith Dalton was not deceived. Wondering perhaps why no message ever came, Georgina found no romance save in her dreams and expectations; and in the course of time became busy with the new responsibilities brought by her brother's rise to greatness. Alfred's growth had not belied the promise of his youth, and the slim boy had darted quietly up the steps of science with a speed and permanence almost dizzying to contemplate. Lean and ascetic, with steel-rimmed pince-nez and pointed brown beard, Dr. Alfred Clarendon was an authority at twenty-five and an international figure at thirty. Careless of worldly affairs with the negligence of genius, he depended vastly on the care and management of his sister, and was secretly thankful that her memories of James had kept her from other and more tangible alliances.

Georgina conducted the business and household of the great bacteriologist, and was proud of his strides toward the conquest of fever. She bore patiently with his eccentricities, calmed his occasional bursts of fanaticism, and healed those breaches with his friends which now and then resulted from his unconcealed scorn of anything less than a single-minded devotion to pure truth and its progress. Clarendon was undeniably irritating at times to ordinary folk; for he never tired of depreciating the service of the individual as contrasted with the service of mankind as a whole, and in censuring men of learning who mingled domestic life or outside interests with their pursuit of abstract science. His enemies called him a bore; but his admirers, pausing before the white heat of ecstasy into which he would work himself, became almost ashamed of ever having any standards or aspirations outside the one divine sphere of unalloyed knowledge.

The doctor's travels were extensive and Georgina generally accompanied him on the shorter ones. Three times, however, he had taken long, lone jaunts to strange and distant places in his studies of exotic fevers and half-fabulous plagues; for he knew that it is out of the unknown lands of cryptic and immemorial Asia that most of the earth's diseases spring. On each of these occasions he had brought back curious mementoes which added to the eccentricity of his home, not least among which was the needlessly large staff of Thibetan servants picked up somewhere in U-tsang during an epidemic of which the world never heard, but amidst which Clarendon had discovered and isolated the germ of black fever. These men, taller than most Thibetans and clearly belonging to a stock but little investigated in the outside world, were of a skeletonic leanness which made one wonder whether the doctor had sought to symbolise in them the anatomical models of his college years. Their aspect, in the loose black silk robes of Bonpa priests which he chose to give them, was grotesque in the highest degree; and there was an unsmiling silence and stiffness in their motions which enhanced their air of fantasy and gave Georgina a queer, awed feeling of having stumbled into the pages of *Vathek* or the *Arabian Nights*.

But queerest of all was the general factotum or clinic-man, whom Clarendon addressed as Surama, and whom he had brought back with him after a long stay in Northern Africa, during which he had studied certain odd intermittent fevers among the mysterious Saharan Tuaregs, whose descent from the primal race of lost Atlantis is an old archaeological rumour. Surama, a man of great intelligence and seemingly inexhaustible erudition, was as morbidly lean as the Thibetan servants; with swarthy, parchment-like skin drawn so tightly over his bald pate and hairless face that every line of the skull stood out in ghastly prominence—this death's-head effect being heightened by lustrelessly burning black eyes set with a depth which left to common visibility only a pair of dark, vacant sockets. Unlike the ideal subordinate, he seemed despite his impassive features to spend no effort in concealing such emotions as he possessed. Instead, he carried about an insidious atmosphere of irony or amusement, accompanied at certain moments by a deep, guttural chuckle like that of a giant turtle which has just torn to pieces some furry animal and is ambling away toward the sea. His race appeared to be Caucasian, but could not be classified more closely than that. Some of Clarendon's friends thought he looked like a high-caste Hindoo notwithstanding his accentless speech, while many agreed with Georgina—who disliked him—when she gave her opinion that a Pharaoh's mummy, if miraculously brought to life, would form a very apt twin for this sardonic skeleton.

Dalton, absorbed in his uphill political battles and isolated from Eastern interests through the peculiar self-sufficiency of the old West, had not followed the meteoric rise of his former comrade; Clarendon had actually heard nothing of one so far outside his chosen world of science as the governor. Being of independent and even of abundant means, the Clarendons had for many years stuck to their old Manhattan mansion in East Nineteenth Street, whose ghosts must have looked sorely askance at the bizarrerie of Surama and the Thibetans. Then, through the doctor's wish to transfer his base of medical observation, the great change had suddenly come, and they had crossed the continent to take up a secluded life in San Francisco; buying the gloomy old Bannister place near Goat Hill, overlooking the bay, and establishing their strange household in a rambling, French-roofed relic of mid-Victorian design and gold-rush parvenu display, set amidst high-walled grounds in a region still half suburban.

Dr. Clarendon, though better satisfied than in New York, still felt cramped for lack of opportunities to apply and test his pathological theories. Unworldly as he was, he had never thought of using his reputation as an influence to gain public appointment; though more and more he realised that only the medical directorship of a government or a charitable institution—a prison, almshouse, or hospital—would give him a field of sufficient width to complete his researches and make his discoveries of the greatest use to humanity and science at large.

Then he had run into James Dalton by sheer accident one afternoon in Market Street as the governor was swinging out of the Royal Hotel. Georgina had been with him, and an almost instant recognition had heightened the drama of the reunion. Mutual ignorance of one another's progress had bred long explanation and histories, and Clarendon was pleased to find that he had so important an official for a friend. Dalton and Georgina, exchanging many a glance, felt more than a trace of their youthful tenderness; and a friendship was then and there revived which led to frequent calls and a fuller and fuller exchange of confidences.

James Dalton learned of his old protégé's need for political appointment, and sought, true to his protective role of school and college days, to devise some means of giving "Little Alf" the needed position and scope. He had, it is true, wide appointive powers; but the legislature's constant attacks and encroachments forced him to exercise these with the utmost discretion. At length, however, scarcely three months after the sudden reunion, the foremost institutional medical office in the state fell vacant. Weighing all the elements with care, and conscious that his friend's achievements and reputation would justify the most substantial rewards, the governor felt at last able to act. Formalities were few, and on the eighth of November, 189-, Dr. Alfred Schuyler Clarendon became medical director of the California State Penitentiary at San Quentin.

II.

In scarcely more than a month the hopes of Dr. Clarendon's admirers were amply fulfilled. Sweeping changes in methods brought to the prison's medical routine an efficiency never before dreamed of; and though the subordinates were naturally not without jealousy, they were obliged to admit the magical results of a really great man's superintendence. Then came a time where mere appreciation might well have grown to devout thankfulness at a providential conjunction of time, place, and man; for one morning Dr. Jones came to his new chief with a grave face to announce his discovery of a case which he could not but identify as that selfsame black fever whose germ Clarendon had found and classified.

Dr. Clarendon shewed no surprise, but kept on at the writing before him.

"I know," he said evenly; "I came across that case yesterday. I'm glad you recognised it. Put the man in a separate ward, though I don't believe this fever is contagious."

Dr. Jones, with his own opinion of the malady's contagiousness, was glad of this deference to caution; and hastened to execute the order. Upon his return Clarendon rose to leave, declaring that he would himself take charge of the case alone. Disappointed in his wish to study the great man's methods and technique, the junior physician watched his chief stride away toward the lone ward where he had placed the patient, more critical of the new regime than at any time since admiration had displaced his first jealous pangs.

Reaching the ward, Clarendon entered hastily, glancing at the bed and stepping back to see how far Dr. Jones's obvious curiosity might have led him. Then, finding the corridor still vacant, he shut the door and turned to examine the sufferer. The man was a convict of a peculiarly repulsive type, and seemed to be racked by the keenest throes of agony. His features were frightfully contracted, and his knees drawn sharply up in the mute desperation of the stricken. Clarendon studied him closely, raising his tightly shut eyelids, took his pulse and temperature, and finally dissolving a tablet in water, forced the solution between the sufferer's lips. Before long the height of the attack abated, as shewn by the relaxing body and returning normality of expression, and the patient began to breathe more easily. Then, by a soft rubbing of the ears, the doctor caused the man to open his eyes. There was life in them, for they moved from side to side, though they lacked the fine fire which we are wont to deem the image of the soul. Clarendon smiled as he surveyed the peace his help had brought, feeling behind him the power of an all-capable science. He had long known of this case, and had snatched the victim from death with the work of a moment. Another hour and this man would have gone—yet Jones had seen the symptoms for days before discovering them, and having discovered them, did not know what to do.

Man's conquest of disease, however, cannot be perfect. Clarendon, assuring the dubious trusty-nurses that the fever was not contagious, had had the patient bathed, sponged in alcohol, and put to bed; but was told the next morning that the case was lost. The man had died after midnight in the most intense agony, and with such cries and distortions of face that the nurses were driven almost to panic. The doctor took this news with his usual calm, whatever his scientific feelings may have been, and ordered the burial of the patient in quicklime. Then, with a philosophic shrug of the shoulders, he made the usual rounds of the penitentiary.

Two days later the prison was hit again. Three men came down at once this time, and there was no concealing the fact that a black fever epidemic was under way. Clarendon, having adhered so firmly to his theory of non-contagiousness, suffered a distinct loss of prestige, and was handicapped by the refusal of the trusty-nurses to attend the patients. Theirs was not the soul-free devotion of those who sacrifice themselves to science and humanity. They were convicts, serving only because of the privileges they could not otherwise buy, and when the price became too great they preferred to resign the privileges.

But the doctor was still master of the situation. Consulting with the warden and sending urgent messages to his friend the governor, he saw to it that special rewards in cash and in reduced terms were offered to the convicts for the dangerous nursing service; and by this method succeeded in getting a very fair quota of volunteers. He was steeled for action now, and nothing could shake his poise and determination. Additional cases brought only a curt nod, and he seemed a stranger to fatigue as he hastened from bedside to bedside all over the vast stone home of sadness and evil. More than forty cases developed within another week, and nurses had to be brought from the city. Clarendon went home very seldom at this stage, often sleeping on a cot in the warden's quarters, and always giving himself up with typical abandon to the service of medicine and of mankind.

Then came the first mutterings of that storm which was soon to convulse San Francisco. News will out, and the menace of black fever spread over the town like a fog from the bay. Reporters trained in the doctrine of "sensation first" used their imagination without restraint, and gloried when at last they were able to produce a case in the Mexican quarter which a local physician—fonder perhaps of money than of truth or civic welfare—pronounced black fever.

That was the last straw. Frantic at the thought of the crawling death so close upon them, the people of San Francisco went mad en masse, and embarked upon that historic exodus of which all the country was soon to hear over busy wires. Ferries and rowboats, excursion steamers and launches, railways and cable cars, bicycles and carriages, moving-vans and work carts, all were pressed into instant and frenzied service. Sausalito and Tamalpais, as lying in the direction of San Quentin, shared in the flight; while housing space in Oakland, Berkeley, and Alameda rose to fabulous prices. Tent colonies sprang up, and improvised villages lined the crowded southward highways from Millbrae to San Jose. Many sought refuge with friends in Sacramento, while the fright-shaken residue forced by various causes to stay behind could do little more than maintain the basic necessities of a nearly dead city.

Business, save for quack doctors with "sure cures" and "preventives" for use against the fever, fell rapidly to the vanishing-point. At first the saloons offered "medicated drinks", but soon found that the populace preferred to be duped by charlatans of more professional aspect. In strangely noiseless streets persons peered into one another's faces to glimpse possible plague symptoms, and shopkeepers began more and more to refuse admission to their clientele, each customer seeming to them a fresh fever menace. Legal and judicial machinery began to disintegrate as attorneys and county clerks succumbed one by one to the urge for flight. Even the doctors deserted in large numbers, many of them pleading the need of vacations among the mountains and the lakes in the northern part of the state. Schools and colleges, theatres and cafés, restaurants and saloons, all gradually closed their doors; and in a single week San Francisco lay prostrate and inert with only its light, power, and water service even half normal, with newspapers in skeletonic form, and with a crippled parody on transportation maintained by the horse and cable cars.

This was the lowest ebb. It could not last long, for courage and observation are not altogether dead in mankind; and sooner or later the non-existence of any widespread black fever epidemic outside San Quentin became too obvious a fact to deny, notwithstanding several actual cases and the undeniable spread of typhoid in the unsanitary suburban tent colonies. The leaders and editors of the community conferred and took action, enlisting in their service the very reporters whose energies had done so much to bring on the trouble, but now turning their "sensation first" avidity into more constructive channels. Editorials and fictitious interviews appeared, telling of Dr. Clarendon's complete control of the disease, and of the absolute impossibility of its diffusion beyond the prison walls. Reiteration and circulation slowly did their work, and gradually a slim backward trickle of urbanites swelled into a vigorous refluent stream. One of the first healthy symptoms was the start of a newspaper controversy of the approved acrimonious kind, attempting to fix blame for the panic wherever the various participants thought it belonged. The returning doctors, jealously strengthened by their timely vacations, began striking at Clarendon, assuring the public that they as well as he would keep the fever in leash, and censuring him for not doing even more to check its spread within San Quentin.

Clarendon had, they averred, permitted far more deaths than were necessary. The veriest tyro in medicine knew how to check fever contagion; and if this renowned savant did not do it, it was clearly because he chose for scientific reasons to study the final effects of the disease, rather than to prescribe properly and save the victims. This policy, they insinuated, might be proper enough among convicted murderers in a penal institution, but it would not do in San Francisco, where life was still a precious and sacred thing.

Thus they went on, and the papers were glad to publish all they wrote, since the sharpness of the campaign, in which Dr. Clarendon would doubtless join, would help to obliterate confusion and restore confidence among the people.

But Clarendon did not reply. He only smiled, while his singular clinic-man Surama indulged in many a deep, testudinous chuckle. He was at home more nowadays, so that reporters began besieging the gate of the great wall the doctor had built around his house, instead of pestering the warden's office at San Quentin. Results, though, were equally meagre; for Surama formed an impassable barrier between the doctor and the outer world—even after the reporters had got into the grounds. The newspaper men getting access to the front hall had glimpses of Clarendon's singular entourage and made the best they could in a "write-up" of Surama and the queer skeletonic Thibetans. Exaggeration, of course, occurred in every fresh article, and the net effect of the publicity was distinctly adverse to the great physician. Most persons hate the unusual, and hundreds who could have excused heartlessness or incompetence stood ready to condemn the grotesque taste manifested in the chuckling attendant and the eight black-robed Orientals.

Early in January an especially persistent young man from the *Observer* climbed the moated eight-foot brick wall in the rear of the Clarendon grounds and began a survey of the varied outdoor appearances which trees concealed from the front walk. With quick, alert brain he took in everything—the rose-arbour, the aviaries, the animal cages where all sorts of mammalia from monkeys to guinea-pigs might be seen and heard, the stout wooden clinic building with barred windows in the northwest corner of the yard—and bent searching glances throughout the thousand square feet of intramural privacy. A great article was brewing, and he would have escaped unscathed but for the barking of Dick, Georgina Clarendon's gigantic and beloved St. Bernard. Surama, instant in his response, had the youth by the collar before a protest could be uttered, and was presently shaking him as a terrier shakes a rat, and dragging him through the trees to the front yard and the gate.

Breathless explanations and quavering demands to see Dr. Clarendon were useless. Surama only chuckled and dragged his victim on. Suddenly a positive fright crept over the dapper scribe, and he began to wish desperately that this unearthly creature would speak, if only to prove that he really was a being of honest flesh and blood belonging to this planet. He became deathly sick, and strove not to glimpse the eyes which he knew must lie at the base of those gaping black sockets. Soon he heard the gate open and felt himself propelled violently through; in another moment waking rudely to the things of earth as he landed wetly and muddily in the ditch which Clarendon had had dug around the entire length of the wall. Fright gave a place to rage as he heard the massive gate slam shut, and he rose dripping to shake his fist at the forbidding portal. Then, as he turned to go, a soft sound grated behind him, and through a small wicket in the gate he felt the sunken eyes of Surama and heard the echoes of a deep-voiced, blood-freezing chuckle.

This young man, feeling perhaps justly that his handling had been rougher than he deserved, resolved to revenge himself upon the household responsible for his treatment. Accordingly he prepared a fictitious interview with Dr. Clarendon, supposed to be held in the clinic building, during which he was careful to describe the agonies of a dozen black fever patients whom his imagination ranged on orderly rows of couches. His master-stroke was the picture of one especially pathetic sufferer gasping for water, while the doctor held a glass of the sparkling fluid just out of his reach, in a scientific attempt to determine the effect of a tantalising emotion on the course of the disease. This invention was followed by paragraphs of insinuating comment so outwardly respectful that it bore a double venom. Dr. Clarendon was, the article ran, undoubtedly the greatest and most single-minded scientist in the world; but science is no friend to individual welfare, and one would not like to have one's gravest ills drawn out and aggravated merely to satisfy an investigator on some point of abstract truth. Life is too short for that.

Altogether, the article was diabolically skilful, and succeeded in horrifying nine readers out of ten against Dr. Clarendon and his supposed methods. Other papers were quick to copy and enlarge upon its substance, taking the cue it offered, and commencing a series of "faked" interviews which fairly ran the gamut of derogatory fantasy. In no case, however, did the doctor condescend to offer a contradiction. He had no time to waste on fools and liars, and cared little for the esteem of a thoughtless rabble he despised. When James Dalton telegraphed his regrets and offered aid, Clarendon replied with an almost boorish curtness. He did not heed the barking of dogs, and could not bother to muzzle them. Nor would he thank anyone for messing with a matter wholly beneath notice.

Silent and contemptuous, he continued his duties with tranquil evenness.

But the young reporter's spark had done its work. San Francisco was insane again, and this time as much with rage as with fear. Sober judgment became a lost art; and though no second exodus occurred, there ensued a reign of vice and recklessness born of desperation, and suggesting parallel phenomena in mediaeval times of pestilence. Hatred ran riot against the man who had found the disease and was struggling to restrain it, and a light-headed public forgot his great services to knowledge in their efforts to fan the flames of resentment. They seemed, in their blindness, to hate him in person, rather than the plague which had come to their breeze-cleaned and usually healthy city.

Then the young reporter, playing in the Neronic fire he had kindled, added a crowning personal touch of his own. Remembering the indignities he had suffered at the hands of the cadaverous clinic-man, he prepared a masterly article on the home and environment of Dr. Clarendon, giving especial prominence to Surama, whose very aspect he declared sufficient to scare the healthiest person into any sort of fever. He tried to make the gaunt chuckler appear equally ridiculous and terrible, succeeding best, perhaps, in the latter half of his intention, since a tide of horror always welled up whenever he thought of his brief proximity to the creature. He collected all the rumours current about the man, elaborated on the unholy depth of his reputed scholarship, and hinted darkly that it could have been no godly realm of secret and aeon-weighted Africa wherein Dr. Clarendon had found him.

Georgina, who followed the papers closely, felt crushed and hurt by these attacks upon her brother, but James Dalton, who called often at the house, did his best to comfort her. In this he was warm and sincere; for he wished not only to console the woman he loved, but to utter some measure of the reverence he had always felt for the starward-bound genius who had been his youth's closest comrade. He told Georgina how greatness can never be exempted from the shafts of envy, and cited the long, sad list of splendid brains crushed beneath vulgar heels. The attacks, he pointed out, formed the truest of all proofs of Alfred's solid eminence.

"But they hurt just the same," she rejoined, "and all the more because I know that Al really suffers from them, no matter how indifferent he tries to be."

Dalton kissed her hand in a manner not then obsolete among well-born persons.

"And it hurts me a thousand times more, knowing that it hurts you and Alf. But never mind, Georgie, we'll stand together and pull through it!"

Thus it came about that Georgina came more and more to rely on the strength of the steel-firm, square-jawed governor who had been her youthful swain, and more and more to confide in him the things she feared. The press attacks and the epidemic were not quite all. There were aspects of the household which she did not like. Surama, cruel in equal measure to man and beast, filled her with the most unnamable repulsion; and she could not but feel that he meant some vague, indefinable harm to Alfred. She did not like the Thibetans, either, and thought it very peculiar that Surama was able to talk with them. Alfred would not tell her who or what Surama was, but had once explained rather haltingly that he was a much older man than would be commonly thought credible, and that he had mastered secrets and been through experiences calculated to make him a colleague of phenomenal value for any scientist seeking Nature's hidden mysteries.

Urged by her uneasiness, Dalton became a still more frequent visitor at the Clarendon home, though he saw that his presence was deeply resented by Surama. The bony clinic-man formed the habit of glaring peculiarly from those spectral sockets when admitting him, and would often, after closing the gate when he left, chuckle monotonously in a manner that made his flesh creep. Meanwhile Dr. Clarendon seemed oblivious of everything save his work at San Quentin, whither he went each day in his launch—alone save for Surama, who managed the wheel while the doctor read or collated his notes. Dalton welcomed these regular absences, for they gave him constant opportunities to renew his suit for Georgina's hand. When he would overstay and meet Alfred, however, the latter's greeting was always friendly despite his habitual reserve. In time the engagement of James and Georgina grew to be a definite thing, and the two awaited only a favourable chance to speak to Alfred.

The governor, whole-souled in everything and firm in his protective loyalty, spared no pains in spreading propaganda on his old friend's behalf. Press and officialdom both felt his influence, and he even succeeded in interesting scientists in the East, many of whom came to California to study the plague and investigate the anti-fever bacillus which Clarendon was so rapidly isolating and perfecting.

These doctors and biologists, however, did not obtain the information they wished; so that several of them left with a very unfortunate impression. Not a few prepared articles hostile to Clarendon, accusing him of an unscientific and fame-seeking attitude, and intimating that he concealed his methods through a highly unprofessional desire for ultimate personal profit.

Others, fortunately, were more liberal in their judgments, and wrote enthusiastically of Clarendon and his work. They had seen the patients, and could appreciate how marvellously he held the dread disease in leash. His secrecy regarding the antitoxin they deemed quite justifiable, since its public diffusion in unperfected form could not but do more harm than good. Clarendon himself, whom many of their number had met before, impressed them more profoundly than ever, and they did not hesitate to compare him with Jenner, Lister, Koch, Pasteur, Metchnikoff, and the rest of those whose whole lives have served pathology and humanity. Dalton was careful to save for Alfred all the magazines that spoke well of him, bringing them in person as an excuse to see Georgina. They did not, however, produce much effect save a contemptuous smile; and Clarendon would generally throw them to Surama, whose deep, disturbing chuckle upon reading formed a close parallel to the doctor's own ironic amusement.

One Monday evening early in February Dalton called with the definite intention of asking Clarendon for his sister's hand. Georgina herself admitted him to the grounds, and as they walked toward the house he stopped to pat the great dog which rushed up and laid friendly fore paws on his breast. It was Dick, Georgina's cherished St. Bernard, and Dalton was glad to feel that he had the affection of a creature which meant so much to her.

Dick was excited and glad, and turned the governor nearly half about with his vigorous pressure as he gave a soft quick bark and sprang off through the trees toward the clinic. He did not vanish, though, but presently stopped and looked back, softly barking again as if he wished Dalton to follow. Georgina, fond of obeying her huge pet's playful whims, motioned to James to see what he wanted; and they both walked slowly after him as he trotted relievedly to the rear of the yard where the top of the clinic building stood silhouetted against the stars above the great brick wall.

The outline of lights within shewed around the edges of the dark window-curtains, so they knew that Alfred and Surama were at work. Suddenly from the interior came a thin, subdued sound like a cry of a child—a plaintive call of "Mamma! Mamma!" at which Dick barked, while James and Georgina started perceptibly. Then Georgina smiled, remembering the parrots that Clarendon always kept for experimental uses, and patted Dick on the head either to forgive him for having fooled her and Dalton, or to console him for having been fooled himself.

As they turned slowly toward the house Dalton mentioned his resolve to speak to Alfred that evening about their engagement, and Georgina supplied no objection. She knew that her brother would not relish the loss of a faithful manager and companion, but believed his affection would place no barrier in the way of her happiness.

Later that evening Clarendon came into the house with a springy step and aspect less grim than usual. Dalton, seeing a good omen in this easy buoyancy, took heart as the doctor wrung his hand with a jovial "Ah, Jimmy, how's politics this year?" He glanced at Georgina, and she quietly excused herself, while the two men settled down to a chat on general subjects. Little by little, amidst many reminders of their old youthful days, Dalton worked toward his point; till at last he came out plainly with the crucial query.

"Alf, I want to marry Georgina. Have we your blessing?"

Keenly watching his old friend, Dalton saw a shadow steal over his face. The dark eyes flashed for a moment, then veiled themselves as wonted placidity returned. So science or selfishness was at work after all!

"You're asking an impossibility, James. Georgina isn't the aimless butterfly she was years ago. She has a place in the service of truth and mankind now, and that place is here. She's decided to devote her life to my work—to the household that makes my work possible—and there's no room for desertion or personal caprice."

Dalton waited to see if he had finished. The same old fanaticism—humanity versus the individual—and the doctor was going to let it spoil his sister's life! Then he tried to answer.

"But look here, Alf, do you mean to say that Georgina, in particular, is so necessary to your work that you must make a slave and martyr of her? Use your sense of proportion, man! If it were a question of Surama or somebody in the utter thick of your experiments it might be different; but after all, Georgina is only a housekeeper to you in the last analysis. She has promised to be my wife and says that she loves me. Have you the right to cut her off from the life that belongs to her? Have you the right—"

"That'll do, James!" Clarendon's face was set and white. "Whether or not I have the right to govern my own family is no business of an outsider."

"Outsider—you can say that to a man who—" Dalton almost choked as the steely voice of the doctor interrupted him again.

"An outsider to my family, and from now on an outsider to my home. Dalton, your presumption goes just a little too far! Good evening, Governor!"

And Clarendon strode from the room without extending his hand.

Dalton hesitated for a moment, almost at a loss what to do, when presently Georgina entered. Her face shewed that she had spoken with her brother, and Dalton took both her hands impetuously.

"Well, Georgie, what do you say? I'm afraid it's a choice between Alf and me. You know how I feel—you know how I felt before, when it was your father I was up against. What's your answer this time?"

He paused as she responded slowly.

"James, dear, do you believe that I love you?"

He nodded and pressed her hands expectantly.

"Then, if you love me, you'll wait a while. Don't think of Al's rudeness. He's to be pitied. I can't tell you the whole thing now, but you know how worried I am—what with the strain of his work, the criticisms, and the staring and cackling of that horrible creature Surama! I'm afraid he'll break down—he shews the strain more than anyone outside the family could tell. I can see it, for I've watched him all my life. He's changing—slowly bending under his burdens—and he puts on his extra brusqueness to hide it. You can see what I mean, can't you, dear?"

She paused, and Dalton nodded again, pressing one of her hands to his breast. Then she concluded.

"So promise me, dear, to be patient. I must stand by him; I must! I must!"

Dalton did not speak for a while, but his head inclined in what was almost a bow of reverence. There was more of Christ in this devoted woman than he had thought any human being possessed; and in the face of such love and loyalty he could do no urging.

Words of sadness and parting were brief; and James, whose blue eyes were misty, scarcely saw the gaunt clinic-man as the gate to the street was at last opened to him. But when it slammed to behind him he heard that blood-curdling chuckle he had come to recognise so well, and knew that Surama was there—Surama, whom Georgina had called her brother's evil genius. Walking away with a firm step, Dalton resolved to be watchful, and to act at the first sign of trouble.

III.

Meanwhile San Francisco, the epidemic still on the lips of all, seethed with anti-Clarendon feeling. Actually the cases outside the penitentiary were very few, and confined almost wholly to the lower Mexican element whose lack of sanitation was a standing invitation to disease of every kind; but politicians and the people needed no more than this to confirm the attacks made by the doctor's enemies. Seeing that Dalton was immovable in his championship of Clarendon, the malcontents, medical dogmatists, and ward-heelers turned their attention to the state legislature; lining up the anti-Clarendonists and the governor's old enemies with great shrewdness, and preparing to launch a law—with a veto-proof majority—transferring the authority for minor institutional appointments from the chief executive to the various boards or commissions concerned.

In the furtherance of this measure no lobbyist was more active than Clarendon's chief assistant, Dr. Jones. Jealous of his superior from the first, he now saw an opportunity for turning matters to his liking; and he thanked fate for the circumstance—responsible indeed for his present position—of his relationship to the chairman of the prison board. The new law, if passed, would certainly mean the removal of Clarendon and the appointment of himself in his stead; so, mindful of his own interest, he worked hard for it. Jones was all that Clarendon was not—a natural politician and sycophantic opportunist who served his own advancement first and science only incidentally. He was poor, and avid for salaried position, quite in contrast to the wealthy and independent savant he sought to displace. So with a rat-like cunning and persistence he laboured to undermine the great biologist above him, and was one day rewarded by the news that the new law was passed. Thenceforward the governor was powerless to make appointments to the state institutions, and the medical directorship of San Quentin lay at the disposal of the prison board.

Of all this legislative turmoil Clarendon was singularly oblivious. Wrapped wholly in matters of administration and research, he was blind to the treason of "that ass Jones" who worked by his side, and deaf to all the gossip of the warden's office. He had never in his life read the newspapers, and the banishment of Dalton from his house cut off his last real link with the world of outside events. With the naiveté of a recluse, he at no time thought of his position as insecure. In view of Dalton's loyalty, and of his forgiveness of even the greatest wrongs, as shewn in his dealings with the elder Clarendon who had crushed his father to death on the stock exchange, the possibility of a gubernatorial dismissal was, of course, out of the question; nor could the doctor's political ignorance envisage a sudden shift of power which might place the matter of retention or dismissal in very different hands. Thereupon he merely smiled with satisfaction when Dalton left for Sacramento; convinced that his place in San Quentin and his sister's place in his household were alike secure from disturbance. He was accustomed to having what he wanted, and fancied his luck was still holding out.

The first week in March, a day or so after the enactment of the new law, the chairman of the prison board called at San Quentin. Clarendon was out, but Dr. Jones was glad to shew the august visitor—his own uncle, incidentally—through the great infirmary, including the fever ward made so famous by press and panic. By this time converted against his will to Clarendon's belief in the fever's non-contagiousness, Jones smilingly assured his uncle that nothing was to be feared, and encouraged him to inspect the patients in detail—especially a ghastly skeleton, once a very giant of bulk and vigour, who was, he insinuated, slowly and painfully dying because Clarendon would not administer the proper medicine.

"Do you mean to say," cried the chairman, "that Dr. Clarendon refuses to let the man have what he needs, knowing his life could be saved?"

"Just that," snapped Dr. Jones, pausing as the door opened to admit none other than Clarendon himself. Clarendon nodded coldly to Jones and surveyed the visitor, whom he did not know, with disapproval.

"Dr. Jones, I thought you knew this case was not to be disturbed at all. And haven't I said that visitors aren't to be admitted except by special permission?"

But the chairman interrupted before his nephew could introduce him.

"Pardon me, Dr. Clarendon, but am I to understand that you refuse to give this man the medicine that would save him?"

Clarendon glared coldly, and rejoined with steel in his voice.

"That's an impertinent question, sir. I am in authority here, and visitors are not allowed. Please leave the room at once."

The chairman, his sense of drama secretly tickled, answered with greater pomp and hauteur than were necessary.

"You mistake me, sir! I, not you, am master here. You are addressing the chairman of the prison board. I must say, moreover, that I deem your activity a menace to the welfare of the prisoners, and must request your resignation. Henceforth Dr. Jones will be in charge, and if you wish to remain until your formal dismissal you will take your orders from him."

It was Wilfred Jones's great moment. Life never gave him another such climax, and we need not grudge him this one. After all, he was a small rather than a bad man, and he had only obeyed a small man's code of looking to himself at all costs. Clarendon stood still, gazing at the speaker as if he thought him mad, till in another second the look of triumph on Dr. Jones's face convinced him that something important was indeed afoot. He was icily courteous as he replied.

"No doubt you are what you claim to be, sir. But fortunately my appointment came from the governor of the state, and can therefore be revoked only by him."

The chairman and his nephew both stared perplexedly, for they had not realised to what lengths unworldly ignorance can go. Then the older man, grasping the situation, explained at some length.

"Had I found that the current reports did you an injustice," he concluded, "I would have deferred action; but the case of this poor man and your own arrogant manner left me no choice. As it is—"

But Dr. Clarendon interrupted with a new razor-sharpness in his voice.

"As it is, I am the director in charge at present, and I ask you to leave this room at once."

The chairman reddened and exploded.

"Look here, sir, who do you think you're talking to? I'll have you chucked out of here—damn your impertinence!"

But he had time only to finish the sentence. Transformed by the insult to a sudden dynamo of hate, the slender scientist launched out with both fists in a burst of preternatural strength of which no one would have thought him capable. And if his strength was preternatural, his accuracy of aim was no less so; for not even a champion of the ring could have wrought a neater result. Both men—the chairman and Dr. Jones—were squarely hit; the one full in the face and the other on the point of the chin. Going down like felled trees, they lay motionless and unconscious on the floor; while Clarendon, now clear and completely master of himself, took his hat and cane and went out to join Surama in the launch. Only when seated in the moving boat did he at last give audible vent to the frightful rage that consumed him. Then, with face convulsed, he called down imprecations from the stars and the gulfs beyond the stars; so that even Surama shuddered, made an elder sign that no book of history records, and forgot to chuckle.

IV.

Georgina soothed her brother's hurt as best she could. He had come home mentally and physically exhausted and thrown himself on the library lounge; and in that gloomy room, little by little, the faithful sister had taken in the almost incredible news. Her consolations were instantaneous and tender, and she made him realise how vast, though unconscious, a tribute to his greatness the attacks, persecution, and dismissal all were. He had tried to cultivate the indifference she preached, and could have done so had personal dignity alone been involved. But the loss of scientific opportunity was more than he could calmly bear, and he sighed again and again as he repeated how three months more of study in the prison might have given him at last the long-sought bacillus which would make all fever a thing of the past.

Then Georgina tried another mode of cheering, and told him that surely the prison board would send for him again if the fever did not abate, or if it broke out with increased force. But even this was ineffective, and Clarendon answered only in a string of bitter, ironic, and half-meaningless little sentences whose tone shewed all too clearly how deeply despair and resentment had bitten.

"Abate? Break out again? Oh, it'll abate all right! At least, they'll think it has abated. They'd think anything, no matter what happens! Ignorant eyes see nothing, and bunglers are never discoverers. Science never shews her face to that sort. And they call themselves doctors! Best of all, fancy that ass Jones in charge!"

Ceasing with a quick sneer, he laughed so daemoniacally that Georgina shivered.

The days that followed were dismal ones indeed at the Clarendon mansion. Depression, stark and unrelieved, had taken hold of the doctor's usually tireless mind; and he would even have refused food had not Georgina forced it upon him. His great notebook of observations lay unopened on the library table, and his little gold syringe of anti-fever serum—a clever device of his own, with a self-contained reservoir, attached to a broad gold finger ring, and single-pressure action peculiar to itself—rested idly in a small leather case beside it. Vigour, ambition, and the desire for study and observation seemed to have died within him; and he made no inquiries about his clinic, where hundreds of germ cultures stood in their orderly phials awaiting his attention.

The countless animals held for experiments played, lively and well fed, in the early spring sunshine; and as Georgina strolled out through the rose-arbour to the cages she felt a strangely incongruous sense of happiness about her. She knew, though, how tragically transient that happiness must be; since the start of new work would soon make all these small creatures unwilling martyrs to science. Knowing this, she glimpsed a sort of compensating element in her brother's inaction, and encouraged him to keep on in a rest he needed so badly. The eight Thibetan servants moved noiselessly about, each as impeccably effective as usual; and Georgina saw to it that the order of the household did not suffer because of the master's relaxation.

Study and starward ambition laid aside in slippered and dressing-gowned indifference, Clarendon was content to let Georgina treat him as an infant. He met her maternal fussiness with a slow, sad smile, and always obeyed her multitude of orders and precepts. A kind of faint, wistful felicity came over the languid household, amidst which the only dissenting note was supplied by Surama. He indeed was miserable, and looked often with sullen and resentful eyes at the sunny serenity in Georgina's face. His only joy had been the turmoil of experiment, and he missed the routine of seizing the fated animals, bearing them to the clinic in clutching talons, and watching them with hot brooding gaze and evil chuckles as they gradually fell into the final coma with wide-opened, red-rimmed eyes, and swollen tongue lolling from froth-covered mouth.

Now he was seemingly driven to desperation by the sight of the carefree creatures in their cages, and frequently came to ask Clarendon if there were any orders. Finding the doctor apathetic and unwilling to begin work, he would go away muttering under his breath and glaring curses upon everything; stealing with cat-like tread to his own quarters in the basement, where his voice would sometimes ascend in deep, muffled rhythms of blasphemous strangeness and uncomfortably ritualistic suggestion.

All this wore on Georgina's nerves, but not by any means so gravely as her brother's continued lassitude itself. The duration of the state alarmed her, and little by little she lost the air of cheerfulness which had so provoked the clinic-man. Herself skilled in medicine, she found the doctor's condition highly unsatisfactory from an alienist's point of view; and she now feared as much from his absence of interest and activity as she had formerly feared from his fanatical zeal and overstudy. Was lingering melancholy about to turn the once brilliant man of intellect into an innocuous imbecile?

Then, toward the end of May, came the sudden change. Georgina always recalled the smallest details connected with it; details as trivial as the box delivered to Surama the day before, postmarked Algiers, and emitting a most unpleasant odour; and the sharp, sudden thunderstorm, rare in the extreme for California, which sprang up that night as Surama chanted his rituals behind his locked basement door in a droning chest-voice louder and more intense than usual.

It was a sunny day, and she had been in the garden gathering flowers for the dining-room. Re-entering the house, she glimpsed her brother in the library, fully dressed and seated at the table, alternately consulting the notes in his thick observation book, and making fresh entries with brisk assured strokes of the pen. He was alert and vital, and there was a satisfying resilience about his movements as he now and then turned a page, or reached for a book from the rear of the great table. Delighted and relieved, Georgina hastened to deposit her flowers in the dining-room and return; but when she reached the library again she found that her brother was gone.

She knew, of course, that he must be in the clinic at work, and rejoiced to think that his old mind and purpose had snapped back into place. Realising it would be of no use to delay the luncheon for him, she ate alone and set aside a bite to be kept warm in case of his return at an odd moment. But he did not come. He was making up for lost time, and was still in the great stout-planked clinic when she went for a stroll through the rose-arbour.

As she walked among the fragrant blossoms she saw Surama fetching animals for the test. She wished she could notice him less, for he always made her shudder; but her very dread had sharpened her eyes and ears where he was concerned. He always went hatless around the yard, and the total hairlessness of his head enhanced his skeleton-like aspect horribly. Now she heard a faint chuckle as he took a small monkey from its cage against the wall and carried it to the clinic, his long, bony fingers pressing so cruelly into its furry sides that it cried out in frightened anguish. The sight sickened her, and brought her walk to an end. Her inmost soul rebelled at the ascendancy this creature had gained over her brother, and she reflected bitterly that the two had almost changed places as master and servant.

Night came without Clarendon's return to the house, and Georgina concluded that he was absorbed in one of his very longest sessions, which meant total disregard of time. She hated to retire without a talk with him about his sudden recovery; but finally, feeling it would be futile to wait up, she wrote a cheerful note and propped it before his chair on the library table; then started resolutely for bed.

She was not quite asleep when she heard the outer door open and shut. So it had not been an all-night session after all! Determined to see that her brother had a meal before retiring she rose, slipped on a robe, and descended to the library, halting only when she heard voices from behind the half-opened door. Clarendon and Surama were talking, and she waited till the clinic-man might go.

Surama, however, shewed no inclination to depart; and indeed, the whole heated tenor of the discourse seemed to bespeak absorption and promise length. Georgina, though she had not meant to listen, could not help catching a phrase now and then, and presently became aware of a sinister undercurrent which frightened her very much without being wholly clear to her. Her brother's voice, nervous, incisive, held her notice with disquieting persistence.

"But anyway," he was saying, "we haven't enough animals for another day, and you know how hard it is to get a decent supply at short notice. It seems silly to waste so much effort on comparative trash when human specimens could be had with just a little extra care."

Georgina sickened at the possible implication, and caught at the hall rack to steady herself. Surama was replying in that deep, hollow tone which seemed to echo with the evil of a thousand ages and a thousand planets.

"Steady, steady—what a child you are with your haste and impatience! You crowd things so! When you've lived as I have, so that a whole life will seem only an hour, you won't be so fretful about a day or week or month! You work too fast. You've plenty of specimens in the cages for a full week if you'll only go at a sensible rate. You might even begin on the older material if you'd be sure not to overdo it."

"Never mind my haste!" the reply was snapped out sharply; "I have my own methods. I don't want to use our material if I can help it, for I prefer them as they are. And you'd better be careful of them anyway—you know the knives those sly dogs carry."

Surama's deep chuckle came.

"Don't worry about that. The brutes eat, don't they? Well, I can get you one any time you need it. But go slow—with the boy gone, there are only eight, and now that you've lost San Quentin it'll be hard to get new ones by the wholesale. I'd advise you to start in on Tsanpo—he's the least use to you as he is, and—"

But that was all Georgina heard. Transfixed by a hideous dread from the thoughts this talk excited, she nearly sank to the floor where she stood, and was scarcely able to drag herself up the stairs and into her room. What was the evil monster Surama planning? Into what was he guiding her brother? What monstrous circumstances lay behind these cryptic sentences? A thousand phantoms of darkness and menace danced before her eyes, and she flung herself upon the bed without hope of sleep. One thought above the rest stood out with fiendish prominence, and she almost screamed aloud as it beat itself into her brain with renewed force. Then Nature, kinder than she expected, intervened at last. Closing her eyes in a dead faint, she did not awake till morning, nor did any fresh nightmare come to join the lasting one which the overheard words had brought.

With the morning sunshine came a lessening of the tension. What happens in the night when one is tired often reaches the consciousness in distorted forms, and Georgina could see that her brain must have given strange colour to scraps of common medical conversation. To suppose her brother—only son of the gentle Frances Schuyler Clarendon—guilty of savage sacrifices in the name of science would be to do an injustice to their blood, and she decided to omit all mention of her trip downstairs, lest Alfred ridicule her fantastic notions.

When she reached the breakfast table she found that Clarendon was already gone, and regretted that not even this second morning had given her a chance to congratulate him on his revived activity.

Quietly taking the breakfast served by stone-deaf old Margarita, the Mexican cook, she read the morning paper and seated herself with some needlework by the sitting-room window overlooking the great yard. All was silent out there, and she could see that the last of the animal cages had been emptied. Science was served, and the lime-pit held all that was left of the once pretty and lively little creatures. This slaughter had always grieved her, but she had never complained, since she knew it was all for humanity. Being a scientist's sister, she used to say to herself, was like being the sister of a soldier who kills to save his countrymen from their foes.

After luncheon Georgina resumed her post by the window, and had been busily sewing for some time when the sound of a pistol shot from the yard caused her to look out in alarm. There, not far from the clinic, she saw the ghastly form of Surama, a revolver in his hand, and his skull-face twisted into a strange expression as he chuckled at a cowering figure robed in black silk and carrying a long Thibetan knife. It was the servant Tsanpo, and as she recognised the shrivelled face Georgina remembered horribly what she had overheard the night before. The sun flashed on the polished blade, and suddenly Surama's revolver spat once more. This time the knife flew from the Mongol's hand, and Surama glanced greedily at his shaking and bewildered prey.

Then Tsanpo, glancing quickly at his unhurt hand and at the fallen knife, sprang nimbly away from the stealthily approaching clinic-man and made a dash for the house. Surama, however, was too swift for him, and caught him in a single leap, seizing his shoulder and almost crushing him. For a moment the Thibetan tried to struggle, but Surama lifted him like an animal by the scruff of the neck and bore him off toward the clinic. Georgina heard him chuckling and taunting the man in his own tongue, and saw the yellow face of the victim twist and quiver with fright. Suddenly realising against her own will what was taking place, a great horror mastered her and she fainted for the second time within twenty-four hours.

When consciousness returned, the golden light of late afternoon was flooding the room. Georgina, picking up her fallen work-basket and scattered materials, was lost in a daze of doubt; but finally felt convinced that the scene which had overcome her must have been all too tragically real. Her worst fears, then, were horrible truths. What to do about it, nothing in her experience could tell her; and she was vaguely thankful that her brother did not appear. She must talk to him, but not now. She could not talk to anybody now. And, thinking shudderingly of the monstrous happening behind those barred clinic windows, she crept into bed for a long night of anguished sleeplessness.

Rising haggardly on the following day, Georgina saw the doctor for the first time since his recovery. He was bustling about preoccupiedly, circulating between the house and the clinic, and paying little attention to anything besides his work. There was no chance for the dreaded interview, and Clarendon did not even notice his sister's worn-out aspect and hesitant manner.

In the evening she heard him in the library, talking to himself in a fashion most unusual for him, and she felt that he was under a great strain which might culminate in the return of his apathy. Entering the room, she tried to calm him without referring to any trying subject, and forced a steadying cup of bouillon upon him. Finally she asked gently what was distressing him, and waited anxiously for his reply, hoping to hear that Surama's treatment of the poor Thibetan had horrified and outraged him.

There was a note of fretfulness in his voice as he responded.

"What's distressing me? Good God, Georgina, what *isn't?* Look at the cages and see if you have to ask again! Cleaned out—milked dry—not a cursed specimen left; and a line of the most important bacterial cultures incubating in their tubes without a chance to do an ounce of good! Days' work wasted—whole programme set back—it's enough to drive a man mad! How shall I ever get anywhere if I can't scrape up some decent subjects?"

Georgina stroked his forehead.

"I think you ought to rest a while, Al dear."

He moved away.

"Rest? That's good! That's damn good! What else have I been doing but resting and vegetating and staring blankly into space for the last fifty or a hundred or a thousand years? Just as I manage to shake off the clouds, I have to run short of material—and then I'm told to lapse back again into drooling stupefaction! God! And all the while some sneaking thief is probably working with my data and getting ready to come out ahead of me with the credit for my own work. I'll lose by a neck—some fool with the proper specimens will get the prize, when one week more with even half-adequate facilities would see me through with flying colours!"

His voice rose querulously, and there was an overtone of mental strain which Georgina did not like. She answered softly, yet not so softly as to hint at the soothing of a psychopathic case.

"But you're killing yourself with this worry and tension, and if you're dead, how can you do your work?"

He gave a smile that was almost a sneer.

"I guess a week or a month—all the time I need—wouldn't quite finish me, and it doesn't much matter what becomes of me or any other individual in the end. Science is what must be served—science—the austere cause of human knowledge. I'm like the monkeys and birds and guinea-pigs I use—just a cog in the machine, to be used to the advantage of the whole. They had to be killed—I may have to be killed—what of it? Isn't the cause we serve worth that and more?"

Georgina sighed. For a moment she wondered whether, after all, this ceaseless round of slaughter really was worth while.

"But are you absolutely sure your discovery will be enough of a boon to humanity to warrant these sacrifices?"

Clarendon's eyes flashed dangerously.

"Humanity! What the deuce is humanity? Science! Dolts! Just individuals over and over again! Humanity is made for preachers to whom it means the blindly credulous. Humanity is made for the predatory rich to whom it speaks in terms of dollars and cents. Humanity is made for the politician to whom it signifies collective power to be used to his advantage. What is humanity? Nothing! Thank God that crude illusion doesn't last! What a grown man worships is truth—knowledge—science—light—the rending of the veil and the pushing back of the shadow. Knowledge, the juggernaut! There is death in our own ritual. We must kill—dissect—destroy—and all for the sake of discovery—the worship of the ineffable light. The goddess Science demands it. We test a doubtful poison by killing. How else? No thought for self—just knowledge—the effect must be known."

His voice trailed off in a kind of temporary exhaustion, and Georgina shuddered slightly.

"But this is horrible, Al! You shouldn't think of it that way!"

Clarendon cackled sardonically, in a manner which stirred odd and repugnant associations in his sister's mind.

"Horrible? You think what *I* say is horrible? You ought to hear Surama! I tell you, things were known to the priests of Atlantis that would have you drop dead of fright if you heard a hint of them.

Knowledge was knowledge a hundred thousand years ago, when our especial forbears were shambling about Asia as speechless semi-apes! They know something of it in the Hoggar region—there are rumours in the farther uplands of Thibet—and once I heard an old man in China calling on Yog-Sothoth—"

He turned pale, and made a curious sign in the air with his extended forefinger. Georgina felt genuinely alarmed, but became somewhat calmer as his speech took a less fantastic form.

"Yes, it may be horrible, but it's glorious too. The pursuit of knowledge, I mean. Certainly, there's no slovenly sentiment connected with it. Doesn't Nature kill—constantly and remorselessly—and are any but fools horrified at the struggle? Killings are necessary. They are the glory of science. We learn something from them, and we can't sacrifice learning to sentiment. Hear the sentimentalists howl against vaccination! They fear it will kill the child. Well, what if it does? How else can we discover the laws of disease concerned? As a scientist's sister you ought to know better than to prate sentiment. You ought to help my work instead of hindering it!"

"But, Al," protested Georgina, "I haven't the slightest intention of hindering your work. Haven't I always tried to help as much as I could? I am ignorant, I suppose, and can't help very actively; but at least I'm proud of you—proud for my own sake and for the family's sake—and I've always tried to smooth the way. You've given me credit for that many a time."

Clarendon looked at her keenly.

"Yes," he said jerkily as he rose and strode from the room, "you're right. You've always tried to help as best you knew. You may yet have a chance to help still more."

Georgina, seeing him disappear through the front door, followed him into the yard. Some distance away a lantern was shining through the trees, and as they approached it they saw Surama bending over a large object stretched on the ground. Clarendon, advancing, gave a short grunt; but when Georgina saw what it was she rushed up with a shriek. It was Dick, the great St. Bernard, and he was lying still with reddened eyes and protruding tongue.

"He's sick, Al!" she cried. "Do something for him, quick!"

The doctor looked at Surama, who had uttered something in a tongue unknown to Georgina.

"Take him to the clinic," he ordered; "I'm afraid Dick's caught the fever."

Surama took up the dog as he had taken poor Tsanpo the day before, and carried him silently to the building near the mall. He did not chuckle this time, but glanced at Clarendon with what appeared to be real anxiety. It almost seemed to Georgina that Surama was asking the doctor to save her pet.

Clarendon, however, made no move to follow, but stood still for a moment and then sauntered slowly toward the house. Georgina, astonished at such callousness, kept up a running fire of entreaties on Dick's behalf, but it was of no use. Without paying the slightest attention to her pleas he made directly for the library and began to read in a large old book which had lain face down on the table. She put her hand on his shoulder as he sat there, but he did not speak or turn his head. He only kept on reading, and Georgina, glancing curiously over his shoulder, wondered in what strange alphabet this brass-bound tome was written.

In the cavernous parlour across the hall, sitting alone in the dark a quarter of an hour later, Georgina came to her decision. Something was gravely wrong—just what, and to what extent, she scarcely dared formulate to herself—and it was time that she called in some stronger force to help her. Of course it must be James. He was powerful and capable, and his sympathy and affection would shew him the right thing to do. He had known Al always, and would understand.

It was by this time rather late, but Georgina had resolved on action. Across the hall the light still shone from the library, and she looked wistfully at the doorway as she quietly donned a hat and left the house. Outside the gloomy mansion and forbidding grounds, it was only a short walk to Jackson Street, where by good luck she found a carriage to take her to the Western Union telegraph office. There she carefully wrote out a message to James Dalton in Sacramento, asking him to come at once to San Francisco on a matter of the greatest importance to them all.

V.

Dalton was frankly perplexed by Georgina's sudden message. He had had no word from the Clarendons since that stormy February evening when Alfred had declared him an outsider to his home; and he in turn had studiously refrained from communicating, even when he had longed to express sympathy after the doctor's summary ousting from office. He had fought hard to frustrate the politicians and keep the appointive power, and was bitterly sorry to watch the unseating of a man who, despite recent estrangements, still represented to him the ultimate ideal of scientific competence.

Now, with this clearly frightened summons before him, he could not imagine what had happened. He knew, though, that Georgina was not one to lose her head or send forth a needless alarm; hence he wasted no time, but took the Overland which left Sacramento within the hour, going at once to his club and sending word to Georgina by a messenger that he was in town and wholly at her service.

Meanwhile things had been quiescent at the Clarendon home, notwithstanding the doctor's continued taciturnity and his absolute refusal to report on the dog's condition. Shadows of evil seemed omnipresent and thickening, but for the moment there was a lull. Georgina was relieved to get Dalton's message and learn that he was close at hand, and sent back word that she would call him when necessity arose. Amidst all the gathering tension some faint compensating element seemed manifest, and Georgina finally decided that it was the absence of the lean Thibetans, whose stealthy, sinuous ways and disturbing exotic aspect had always annoyed her. They had vanished all at once; and old Margarita, the sole visible servant left in the house, told her they were helping their master and Surama at the clinic.

The following morning—the twenty-eighth of May—long to be remembered—was dark and lowering, and Georgina felt the precarious calm wearing thin. She did not see her brother at all, but knew he was in the clinic hard at work at something despite the lack of specimens he had bewailed. She wondered how poor Tsanpo was getting along, and whether he had really been subjected to any serious inoculation, but it must be confessed that she wondered more about Dick. She longed to know whether Surama had done anything for the faithful dog amidst his master's oddly callous indifference. Surama's apparent solicitude on the night of Dick's seizure had impressed her greatly, giving her perhaps the kindliest feeling she had ever had for the detested clinic-man. Now, as the day advanced, she found herself thinking more and more of Dick; till at last her harassed nerves, finding in this one detail a sort of symbolic summation of the whole horror that lay upon the household, could stand the suspense no longer.

Up to that time she had always respected Alfred's imperious wish that he be never approached or disturbed at the clinic; but as this fateful afternoon advanced, her resolution to break through the barrier grew stronger and stronger. Finally she set out with determined face, crossing the yard and entering the unlocked vestibule of the forbidden structure with the fixed intention of discovering how the dog was or of knowing the reason for her brother's secrecy.

The inner door, as usual, was locked; and behind it she heard voices in heated conversation. When her knocking brought no response she rattled the knob as loudly as possible, but still the voices argued on unheeding. They belonged, of course, to Surama and her brother; and as she stood there trying to attract attention she could not help catch something of their drift. Fate had made her for the second time an eavesdropper, and once more the matter she overheard seemed likely to tax her mental poise and nervous endurance to their ultimate bounds. Alfred and Surama were plainly quarrelling with increasing violence, and the purport of their speech was enough to arouse the wildest fears and confirm the gravest apprehensions. Georgina shivered as her brother's voice mounted shrilly to dangerous heights of fanatical tension.

"You, damn you—you're a fine one to talk defeat and moderation to me! Who started all this, anyway? Did *I* have any idea of your cursed devil-gods and elder world? Did *I* ever in my life think of your damned spaces beyond the stars and your crawling chaos Nyarlathotep? I was a normal scientific man, confound you, till I was fool enough to drag you out of the vaults with your devilish Atlantean secrets. You egged me on, and now you want to cut me off! You loaf around doing nothing and telling me to go slow when you might just as well as not be going out and getting material. You know damn well that I don't know how to go about such things, whereas you must have been an old hand at it before the earth was made. It's like you, you damned walking corpse, to start something you won't or can't finish!"

Surama's evil chuckle came.

"You're insane, Clarendon. That's the only reason I let you rave on when I could send you to hell in three minutes. Enough is enough, and you've certainly had enough material for any novice at your stage. You've had all I'm going to get you, anyhow! You're only a maniac on the subject now—what a cheap, crazy thing to sacrifice even your poor sister's pet dog, when you could have spared him as well as not! You can't look at any living thing now without wanting to jab that gold syringe into it. No—Dick had to go where the Mexican boy went—where Tsanpo and the other seven went—where all the animals went! What a pupil! You're no fun any more—you've lost your nerve. You set out to control things, and they're controlling you. I'm about done with you, Clarendon. I thought you had the stuff in you, but you haven't. It's about time I tried somebody else. I'm afraid you'll have to go!"

In the doctor's shouted reply there was both fear and frenzy.

"Be careful, you ——! There are powers against your powers—I didn't go to China for nothing, and there are things in Alhazred's *Azif* which weren't known in Atlantis! We've both meddled in dangerous things, but you needn't think you know all my resources. How about the Nemesis of Flame? I talked in Yemen with an old man who had come back alive from the Crimson Desert—he had seen Irem, the City of Pillars, and had worshipped at the underground shrines of Nug and Yeb—Iä! Shub-Niggurath!"

Through Clarendon's shrieking falsetto cut the deep chuckle of the clinic-man.

"Shut up, you fool! Do you suppose your grotesque nonsense has any weight with me? Words and formulae—words and formulae—what do they all mean to one who has the substance behind them? We're in a material sphere now, and subject to material laws. You have your fever; I have my revolver. You'll get no specimens, and I'll get no fever so long as I have you in front of me with this gun between!"

That was all Georgina could hear. She felt her senses reeling, and staggered out of the vestibule for a saving breath of the lowering outside air. She saw that the crisis had come at last, and that help must now arrive quickly if her brother was to be saved from the unknown gulfs of madness and mystery. Summoning up all her reserve energy, she managed to reach the house and get to the library, where she scrawled a hasty note for Margarita to take to James Dalton.

When the old woman had gone, Georgina had just strength enough to cross to the lounge and sink weakly down into a sort of semi-stupor. There she lay for what seemed like years, conscious only of the fantastic creeping up of the twilight from the lower corners of the great, dismal room, and plagued by a thousand shadowy shapes of terror which filed with phantasmal, half-limned pageantry through her tortured and stifled brain. Dusk deepened into darkness, and still the spell held. Then a firm tread sounded in the hall, and she heard someone enter the room and fumble at the match-safe. Her heart almost stopped beating as the gas-jets of the chandelier flared up one by one, but then she saw that the arrival was her brother. Relieved to the bottom of her heart that he was still alive, she gave vent to an involuntary sigh, profound, long-drawn, and tremulous, and lapsed at last into kindly oblivion.

At the sound of that sigh Clarendon turned in alarm toward the lounge, and was inexpressibly shocked to see the pale and unconscious form of his sister there. Her face had a death-like quality that frightened his inmost spirit, and he flung himself on his knees by her side, awake to a realisation of what her passing away would mean to him. Long unused to private practice amidst his ceaseless quest for truth, he had lost the physician's instinct of first aid, and could only call out her name and chafe her wrists mechanically as fear and grief possessed him. Then he thought of water, and ran to the dining-room for a carafe. Stumbling about in a darkness which seemed to harbour vague terrors, he was some time in finding what he sought; but at last he clutched it in shaking hand and hastened back to dash the cold fluid in Georgina's face. The method was crude but effective. She stirred, sighed a second time, and finally opened her eyes.

"You are alive!" he cried, and put his cheek to hers as she stroked his head maternally. She was almost glad she fainted, for the circumstance seemed to have dispelled the strange Alfred and brought her own brother back to her. She sat up slowly and tried to reassure him.

"I'm all right, Al. Just give me a glass of water. It's a sin to waste it this way—to say nothing of spoiling my waist! Is that the way to behave every time your sister drops off for a nap? You needn't think I'm going to be sick, for I haven't time for such nonsense!"

Alfred's eyes shewed that her cool, common-sense speech had had its effect. His brotherly panic dissolved in an instant, and instead there came into his face a vague, calculating expression, as if some marvellous possibility had just dawned upon him. As she watched the subtle waves of cunning and appraisal pass fleetingly over his countenance she became less and less certain that her mode of reassurance had been a wise one, and before he spoke she found herself shivering at something she could not define. A keen medical instinct almost told her that his moment of sanity had passed, and that he was now once more the unrestrained fanatic for scientific research. There was something morbid in the quick narrowing of his eyes at her casual mention of good health. What was he thinking? To what unnatural extreme was his passion for experiment about to be pushed? Wherein lay the special significance of her pure blood and absolutely flawless organic state? None of these misgivings, however, troubled Georgina for more than a second, and she was quite natural and unsuspicious as she felt her brother's steady fingers at her pulse.

"You're a bit feverish, Georgie," he said in a precise, elaborately restrained voice as he looked professionally into her eyes.

"Why, nonsense, I'm all right," she replied. "One would think you were on the watch for fever patients just for the sake of shewing off your discovery! It *would* be poetic, though, if you could make your final proof and demonstration by curing your own sister!"

Clarendon started violently and guiltily. Had she suspected his wish? Had he muttered anything aloud? He looked at her closely, and saw that she had no inkling of the truth. She smiled up sweetly into his face and patted his hand as he stood by the side of the lounge. Then he took a small oblong leather case from his vest pocket, and taking out a little gold syringe, he began fingering it thoughtfully, pushing the piston speculatively in and out of the empty cylinder.

"I wonder," he began with suave sententiousness, "whether you would really be willing to help science in—something like that way—if the need arose? Whether you would have the devotion to offer yourself to the cause of medicine as a sort of Jephthah's daughter if you knew it meant the absolute perfection and completion of my work?"

Georgina, catching the odd and unmistakable glitter in her brother's eyes, knew at last that her worst fears were true. There was nothing to do now but keep him quiet at all hazards and to pray that Margarita had found James Dalton at his club.

"You look tired, Al dear," she said gently. "Why not take a little morphia and get some of the sleep you need so badly?"

He replied with a kind of crafty deliberation.

"Yes, you're right. I'm worn out, and so are you. Each of us needs a good sleep. Morphine is just the thing—wait till I go and fill the syringe and we'll both take a proper dose."

Still fingering the empty syringe, he walked softly out of the room. Georgina looked about her with the aimlessness of desperation, ears alert for any sign of possible help. She thought she heard Margarita again in the basement kitchen, and rose to ring the bell, in an effort to learn of the fate of her message. The old servant answered her summons at once, and declared she had given the message at the club hours ago. Governor Dalton had been out, but the clerk had promised to deliver the note at the very moment of his arrival.

Margarita waddled below stairs again, but still Clarendon did not reappear. What was he doing? What was he planning? She had heard the outer door slam, so knew he must be at the clinic. Had he forgotten his original intention with the vacillating mind of madness? The suspense grew almost unbearable, and Georgina had to keep her teeth clenched tightly to avoid screaming.

It was the gate bell, which rang simultaneously in house and clinic, that broke the tension at last. She heard the cat-like tread of Surama on the walk as he left the clinic to answer it; and then, with an almost hysterical sigh of relief, she caught the firm, familiar accents of Dalton in conversation with the sinister attendant. Rising, she almost tottered to meet him as he loomed up in the library doorway; and for a moment no word was spoken while he kissed her hand in his courtly, old-school fashion. Then Georgina burst forth into a torrent of hurried explanation, telling all that had happened, all she had glimpsed and overheard, and all she feared and suspected.

Dalton listened gravely and comprehendingly, his first bewilderment gradually giving place to astonishment, sympathy, and resolution. The message, held by a careless clerk, had been slightly delayed, and had found him appropriately enough in the midst of a warm lounging-room discussion about Clarendon. A fellow-member, Dr. MacNeil, had brought in a medical journal with an article well calculated to disturb the devoted scientist, and Dalton had just asked to keep the paper for future reference when the message was handed him at last. Abandoning his half-formed plan to take Dr. MacNeil into his confidence regarding Alfred, he called at once for his hat and stick, and lost not a moment in getting a cab for the Clarendon home.

Surama, he thought, appeared alarmed at recognising him; though he had chuckled as usual when striding off again toward the clinic. Dalton always recalled Surama's stride and chuckle on this ominous night, for he was never to see the unearthly creature again. As the chuckler entered the clinic vestibule his deep, guttural gurgles seemed to blend with some low mutterings of thunder which troubled the far horizon.

When Dalton had heard all Georgina had to say, and learned

that Alfred was expected back at any moment with an hypodermic dose of morphine, he decided he had better talk with the doctor alone. Advising Georgina to retire to her room and await developments, he walked about the gloomy library, scanning the shelves and listening for Clarendon's nervous footstep on the clinic path outside. The vast room's corners were dismal despite the chandelier, and the closer Dalton looked at his friend's choice of books the less he liked them. It was not the balanced collection of a normal physician, biologist, or man of general culture. There were too many volumes on doubtful borderland themes; dark speculations and forbidden rituals of the Middle Ages, and strange exotic mysteries in alien alphabets both known and unknown.

The great notebook of observations on the table was unwholesome, too. The handwriting had a neurotic cast, and the spirit of the entries was far from reassuring. Long passages were inscribed in crabbed Greek characters, and as Dalton marshalled his linguistic memory for their translation he gave a sudden start, and wished his college struggles with Xenophon and Homer had been more conscientious. There was something wrong—something hideously wrong—here, and the governor sank limply into the chair by the table as he pored more and more closely over the doctor's barbarous Greek. Then a sound came, startlingly near, and he jumped nervously at a hand laid sharply on his shoulder.

"What, may I ask, is the cause of this intrusion? You might have stated your business to Surama."

Clarendon was standing icily by the chair, the little gold syringe in one hand. He seemed very calm and rational, and Dalton fancied for a moment that Georgina must have exaggerated his condition. How, too, could a rusty scholar be absolutely sure about these Greek entries? The governor decided to be very cautious in his interview, and thanked the lucky chance which had placed a specious pretext in his coat pocket. He was very cool and assured as he rose to reply.

"I didn't think you'd care to have things dragged before a subordinate, but I thought you ought to see this article at once."

He drew forth the magazine given him by Dr. MacNeil and handed it to Clarendon.

"On page 542—you see the heading, 'Black Fever Conquered by New Serum.' It's by Dr. Miller of Philadelphia—and he thinks he's got ahead of you with your cure. They were discussing it at the club, and MacNeil thought the exposition very convincing. I, as a layman, couldn't pretend to judge; but at all events I thought you oughtn't to miss a chance to digest the thing while it's fresh. If you're busy, of course, I won't disturb you—"

Clarendon cut in sharply.

"I'm going to give my sister an hypodermic—she's not quite well—but I'll look at what that quack has to say when I get back. I know Miller—a damn sneak and incompetent—and I don't believe he has the brains to steal my methods from the little he's seen of them."

Dalton suddenly felt a wave of intuition warning him that Georgina must not receive that intended dose. There was something sinister about it. From what she had said, Alfred must have been inordinately long preparing it, far longer than was needed for the dissolving of a morphine tablet. He decided to hold his host as long as possible, meanwhile testing his attitude in a more or less subtle way.

"I'm sorry Georgina isn't well. Are you sure that the injection will do her good? That it won't do her any harm?"

Clarendon's spasmodic start shewed that something had been struck home.

"Do her harm?" he cried. "Don't be absurd! You know Georgina must be in the best of health—the very best, I say—in order to serve science as a Clarendon should serve it. She, at least, appreciates the fact that she is my sister. She deems no sacrifice too great in my service. She is a priestess of truth and discovery, as I am a priest."

He paused in his shrill tirade, wild-eyed, and somewhat out of breath. Dalton could see that his attention had been momentarily shifted.

"But let me see what this cursed quack has to say," he continued. "If he thinks his pseudo-medical rhetoric can take a real doctor in, he is even simpler than I thought!"

Clarendon nervously found the right page and began reading as he stood there clutching his syringe. Dalton wondered what the real facts were. MacNeil had assured him that the author was a pathologist of the highest standing, and that whatever errors the article might have, the mind behind it was powerful, erudite, and absolutely honourable and sincere.

Watching the doctor as he read, Dalton saw the thin, bearded face grow pale. The great eyes blazed, and the pages crackled in the tenser grip of the long, lean fingers. A perspiration broke out on the high, ivory-white forehead where the hair was already thinning, and the reader sank gaspingly into the chair his visitor had vacated as he kept on with his devouring of the text. Then came a wild scream as from a haunted beast, and Clarendon lurched forward on the table, his outflung arms sweeping books and paper before them as consciousness went dark like a wind-quenched candle-flame.

Dalton, springing to help his stricken friend, raised the slim form and tilted it back in the chair. Seeing the carafe on the floor near the lounge, he dashed some water into the twisted face, and was rewarded by seeing the large eyes slowly open. They were sane eyes now—deep and sad and unmistakably sane—and Dalton felt awed in the presence of a tragedy whose ultimate depth he could never hope or dare to plumb.

The golden hypodermic was still clutched in the lean left hand, and as Clarendon drew a deep, shuddering breath he unclosed his fingers and studied the glittering thing that rolled about on his palm. Then he spoke—slowly, and with the ineffable sadness of utter, absolute despair.

"Thanks, Jimmy, I'm quite all right. But there's much to be done. You asked me a while back if this shot of morphia would do Georgie any harm. I'm in a position now to tell you that it won't."

He turned a small screw in the syringe and laid a finger on the piston, at the same time pulling with his left hand at the skin of his own neck. Dalton cried out in alarm as a lightning motion of his right hand injected the contents of the cylinder into the ridge of distended flesh.

"Good Lord, Al, what have you done?"

Clarendon smiled gently—a smile almost of peace and resignation, different indeed from the sardonic sneer of the past few weeks.

"You ought to know, Jimmy, if you've still the judgment that made you a governor. You must have pieced together enough from my notes to realise that there's nothing else to do. With your marks in Greek back at Columbia I guess you couldn't have missed much. All I can say is that it's true.

"James, I don't like to pass blame along, but it's only right to tell you that Surama got me into this. I can't tell you who or what he is, for I don't fully know myself, and what I do know is stuff that no sane person ought to know; but I will say that I don't consider him a human being in the fullest sense, and that I'm not sure whether or not he's alive as we know life.

"You think I'm talking nonsense. I wish I were, but the whole hideous mess is damnably real. I started out in life with a clean mind and purpose. I wanted to rid the world of fever. I tried and failed—and I wish to God I had been honest enough to say that I'd failed. Don't let my old talk of science deceive you, James—*I found no antitoxin and was never even half on the track of one!*

"Don't look so shaken up, old fellow! A veteran politician-fighter like you must have seen plenty of unmaskings before. I tell you, I never had even the start of a fever cure. But my studies had taken me into some queer places, and it was just my damned luck to listen to the stories of some still queerer people. James, if you ever wish any man well, tell him to keep clear of the ancient, hidden places of the earth. Old backwaters are dangerous—things are handed down there that don't do healthy people any good. I talked too much with old priests and mystics, and got to hoping I might achieve things in dark ways that I couldn't achieve in lawful ways.

"I shan't tell you just what I mean, for if I did I'd be as bad as the old priests that were the ruin of me. All I need say is that after what I've learned I shudder at the thought of the world and what it's been through. The world is cursed old, James, and there have been whole chapters lived and closed before the dawn of our organic life and the geologic eras connected with it. It's an awful thought—whole forgotten cycles of evolution with beings and races and wisdom and diseases—all lived through and gone before the first amoeba ever stirred in the tropic seas geology tells us about.

"I said gone, but I didn't quite mean that. It would have been better that way, but it wasn't quite so. In places traditions have kept on—I can't tell you how—and certain archaic life-forms have managed to struggle thinly down the aeons in hidden spots. There were cults, you know—bands of evil priests in lands now buried under the sea. Atlantis was the hotbed. That was a terrible place. If heaven is merciful, no one will ever drag up that horror from the deep.

"It had a colony, though, that didn't sink; and when you get too confidential with one of the Tuareg priests in Africa, he's likely to tell you wild tales about it—tales that connect up with whispers you'll hear among the mad lamas and flighty yak-drivers on the secret table-lands of Asia. I'd heard all the common tales and whispers when I came on the big one. What that was, you'll never know—but it pertained to somebody or something that had come down from a blasphemously long time ago, and could be made to live again—or seem alive again—through certain processes that weren't very clear to the man who told me.

"Now, James, in spite of my confession about the fever, you know I'm not bad as a doctor. I plugged hard at medicine, and soaked up about as much as the next man—maybe a little more, because down there in the Hoggar country I did something no priest had ever been able to do. They led me blindfolded to a place that had been sealed up for generations—and I came back with Surama.

"Easy, James! I know what you want to say. How does he know all he knows?—why does he speak English—or any other language, for that matter—without an accent?—why did he come away with me?—and all that. I can't tell you altogether, but I can say that he takes in ideas and images and impressions with something besides his brain and senses. He had a use for me and my science. He told me things, and opened up vistas. He taught me to worship ancient, primordial, and unholy gods, and mapped out a road to a terrible goal which I can't even hint to you. Don't press me, James—it's for the sake of your sanity and the world's sanity!

"The creature is beyond all bounds. He's in league with the stars and all the forces of Nature. Don't think I'm still crazy, James—I swear to you I'm not! I've had too many glimpses to doubt. He gave me new pleasures that were forms of his palaeogean worship, and the greatest of those was the black fever.

"God, James! Haven't you seen through the business by this time? Do you still believe the black fever came out of Thibet, and that I learned about it there? Use your brains, man! Look at Miller's article here! He's found a basic antitoxin that will end all fever within half a century, when other men learn how to modify it for the different forms. He's cut the ground of my youth from under me—done what I'd have given my life to do—taken the wind out of all the honest sails I ever flung to the breeze of science! Do you wonder his article gave me a turn? Do you wonder it shocks me out of my madness back to the old dreams of my youth? Too late! Too late! But not too late to save others!

"I guess I'm rambling a bit now, old man. You know—the hypodermic. I asked you why you didn't tumble to the facts about black fever. How could you, though? Doesn't Miller say he's cured seven cases with his serum? A matter of diagnosis, James. He only thinks it is black fever. I can read between his lines. Here, old chap, on page 551, is the key to the whole thing. Read it again.

"You see, don't you? The fever cases *from the Pacific Coast* didn't respond to his serum. They puzzled him. They didn't even seem like any true fever he knew. Well, those were *my* cases! Those were the *real* black fever cases! And there can't ever be an antitoxin on earth that'll cure black fever!

"How do I know? *Because black fever isn't of this earth!* It's from *somewhere else,* James—and Surama alone knows where, because he brought it here. He *brought it and I spread it!* That's the secret, James! That's all I wanted the appointment for—*that's all I ever did—just spread the fever that I carried in this gold syringe and in the deadlier finger-ring-pump-syringe you see on my index finger!* Science? A blind! I wanted to kill, and kill, and kill! A single pressure on my finger, and the black fever was inoculated. I wanted to see living things writhe and squirm, scream and froth at the mouth. A single pressure of the pump-syringe and I could watch them as they died, and I couldn't live or think unless I had plenty to watch. That's why I jabbed everything in sight with the accursed hollow needle. Animals, criminals, children, servants—and the next would have been—"

Clarendon's voice broke, and he crumpled up perceptibly in his chair.

"That—that, James—was—my life. Surama made it so—he taught me, and kept me at it till I couldn't stop. Then—then it got too much *even for him.* He tried to check me. Fancy—*he* trying to check anybody in that line! But now I've got my last specimen. That is my last test. Good subject, James—I'm healthy—devilish healthy. Deuced ironic, though—the madness has gone now, so there won't be any fun watching the agony! Can't be—can't—"

A violent shiver of fever racked the doctor, and Dalton mourned amidst his horror-stupefaction that he could give no grief. How much of Alfred's story was sheer nonsense, and how much nightmare truth he could not say; but in any case he felt that the man was a victim rather than a criminal, and above all, he was a boyhood comrade and Georgina's brother. Thoughts of the old days came back kaleidoscopically. "Little Alf"—the yard at Phillips Exeter—the quadrangle at Columbia—the fight with Tom Cortland when he saved Alf from a pommeling. . . .

He helped Clarendon to the lounge and asked gently what he could do. There was nothing. Alfred could only whisper now, but he asked forgiveness for all his offences, and commended his sister to the care of his friend.

"You—you'll—make her happy," he gasped. "She deserves it. Martyr—to—a myth! Make it up to her, James. Don't—let—her—know—more—than she has to!"

His voice trailed off in a mumble, and he fell into a stupor. Dalton rang the bell, but Margarita had gone to bed, so he called up the stairs for Georgina. She was firm of step, but very pale. Alfred's scream had tried her sorely, but she had trusted James. She trusted him still as he shewed her the unconscious form on the lounge and asked her to go back to her room and rest, no matter what sounds she might hear. He did not wish her to witness the awful spectacle of delirium certain to come, but bade her kiss her brother a final farewell as he lay there calm and still, very like the delicate boy he had once been. So she left him—the strange, moonstruck, star-reading genius she had mothered so long—and the picture she carried away was a very merciful one.

Dalton must bear to his grave a sterner picture. His fears of delirium were not vain, and all through the black midnight hours his giant strength restrained the frenzied contortions of the mad sufferer. What he heard from those swollen, blackening lips he will never repeat. He has never been quite the same man since, and he knows that no one who hears such things can ever be wholly as he was before. So, for the world's good, he dares not speak, and he thanks God that his layman's ignorance of certain subjects makes many of the revelations cryptic and meaningless to him.

Toward morning Clarendon suddenly woke to a sane consciousness and began to speak in a firm voice.

"James, I didn't tell you what must be done—about everything. Blot out these entries in Greek and send my notebook to Dr. Miller. All my other notes, too, that you'll find in the files. He's the big authority today—his article proves it. Your friend at the club was right.

"But everything in the clinic must go. *Everything without exception, dead or alive or—otherwise.* All the plagues of hell are in those bottles on the shelves. Burn them—burn it all—if one thing escapes, Surama will spread black death throughout the world. *And above all burn Surama!* That—that *thing*—must not breathe the wholesome air of heaven. You know now—what I told you—you know why such an entity can't be allowed on earth. It won't be murder—Surama isn't human—if you're as pious as you used to be, James, I shan't have to urge you. Remember the old text—'Thou shalt not suffer a witch to live'—or something of the sort.

"Burn him, James! Don't let him chuckle again over the torture of mortal flesh! I say, *burn him*—the Nemesis of Flame—that's all that can reach him, James, unless you can catch him asleep and drive a stake through his heart. . . . *Kill him—extirpate him—cleanse the decent universe of its primal taint—the taint I recalled from its age-long sleep. . . ."*

The doctor had risen on his elbow, and his voice was a piercing shriek toward the last. The effort was too much, however, and he lapsed very suddenly into a deep, tranquil coma. Dalton, himself fearless of fever, since he knew the dread germ to be non-contagious, composed Alfred's arms and legs on the lounge and threw a light afghan over the fragile form. After all, mightn't much of this horror be exaggeration and delirium? Mightn't old Doc MacNeil pull him through on a long chance? The governor strove to keep awake, and walked briskly up and down the room, but his energies had been taxed too deeply for such measures. A second's rest in the chair by the table took matters out of his hands, and he was presently sleeping soundly despite his best intentions.

Dalton started up as a fierce light shone in his eyes, and for a moment he thought the dawn had come. But it was not the dawn, and as he rubbed his heavy lids he saw that it was the glare of the burning clinic in the yard, whose stout planks flamed and roared and crackled heavenward in the most stupendous holocaust he had ever seen. It was indeed the "Nemesis of Flame" that Clarendon had wished, and Dalton felt that some strange combustibles must be involved in a blaze so much wilder than anything normal pine or redwood could afford. He glanced alarmedly at the lounge, but Alfred was not there. Starting up, he went to call Georgina, but met her in the hall, roused as he was by the mountain of living fire.

"The clinic's burning down!" she cried. "How is Al now?"

"He's disappeared—disappeared while I dropped asleep!" replied Dalton, reaching out a steadying arm to the form which faintness had begun to sway.

Gently leading her upstairs toward her room, he promised to search at once for Alfred, but Georgina slowly shook her head as the flames from outside cast a weird glow through the window on the landing.

"He must be dead, James—he could never live, sane and knowing what he did. I heard him quarrelling with Surama, and know that awful things were going on. He is my brother, but—it is best as it is."

Her voice had sunk to a whisper.

Suddenly through the open window came the sound of a deep, hideous chuckle, and the flames of the burning clinic took fresh contours till they half resembled some nameless, Cyclopean creatures of nightmare. James and Georgina paused hesitant, and peered out breathlessly through the landing window. Then from the sky came a thunderous peal, as a forked bolt of lightning shot down with terrible directness into the very midst of the blazing ruin. The deep chuckle ceased, and in its place came a frantic, ululant yelp as of a thousand ghouls and werewolves in torment. It died away with long, reverberant echoes, and slowly the flames resumed their normal shape.

The watchers did not move, but waited till the pillar of fire had shrunk to a smouldering glow. They were glad of a half-rusticity which had kept the firemen from trooping out, and of the wall that excluded the curious. What had happened was not for vulgar eyes —it involved too much of the universe's inner secrets for that.

In the pale dawn, James spoke softly to Georgina, who could do no more than put her head on his breast and sob.

"Sweetheart, I think he has atoned. He must have set the fire, you know, while I was asleep. He told me it ought to be burned—the clinic, and everything in it, Surama, too. It was the only way to save the world from the unknown horrors he had loosed upon it. He knew, and he did what was best.

"He was a great man, Georgie. Let's never forget that. We must always be proud of him, for he started out to help mankind, and was titanic even in his sins. I'll tell you more sometime. What he did, be it good or evil, was what no man ever did before. He was the first and last to break through certain veils, and even Apollonius of Tyana takes second place beside him. But we mustn't talk about that. We must remember him only as the Little Alf we knew—as the boy who wanted to master medicine and conquer fever."

In the afternoon the leisurely firemen overhauled the ruins and found two skeletons with bits of blackened flesh adhering—only two, thanks to the undisturbed lime-pits. One was of a man; the other is still a subject of debate among the biologists of the coast. It was not exactly an ape's or a saurian's skeleton, but it had disturbing suggestions of lines of evolution of which palaeontology has revealed no trace. The charred skull, oddly enough, was very human, and reminded people of Surama; but the rest of the bones were beyond conjecture. Only well-cut clothing could have made such a body look like a man.

But the human bones were Clarendon's. No one disputed this, and the world at large still mourns the untimely death of the greatest doctor of his age; the bacteriologist whose universal fever serum would have far eclipsed Dr. Miller's kindred antitoxin had he lived to bring it to perfection. Much of Miller's late success, indeed, is credited to the notes bequeathed him by the hapless victim of the flames. Of the old rivalry and hatred almost none survived, and even Dr. Wilfred Jones has been known to boast of his association with the vanished leader.

James Dalton and his wife Georgina have always preserved a reticence which modesty and family grief might well account for. They published certain notes as a tribute to the great man's memory, but have never confirmed or contradicted either the popular estimate or the rare hints of marvels that a very few keen thinkers have been known to whisper. It was very subtly and slowly that the facts filtered out. Dalton probably gave Dr. MacNeil an inkling of the truth, and that good soul had not many secrets from his son.

The Daltons have led, on the whole, a very happy life; for their cloud of terror lies far in the background, and a strong mutual love has kept the world fresh for them. But there are things which disturb them oddly—little things, of which one would scarcely ever think of complaining. They cannot bear persons who are lean or deep-voiced beyond certain limits, and Georgina turns pale at the sound of any guttural chuckling. Senator Dalton has a mixed horror of occultism, travel, hypodermics, and strange alphabets which most find hard to unify, and there are still those who blame him for the vast proportion of the doctor's library that he destroyed with such painstaking completeness.

MacNeil, though, seemed to realise. He was a simple man, and he said a prayer as the last of Alfred Clarendon's strange books crumbled to ashes. Nor would anyone who had peered understandingly within those books wish a word of that prayer unsaid.

Adolphe de Castro

The Electric Executioner

For one who has never faced the danger of legal execution, I have a rather queer horror of the electric chair as a subject. Indeed, I think the topic gives me more of a shudder than it gives many a man who has been on trial for his life. The reason is that I associate the thing with an incident of forty years ago—a very strange incident which brought me close to the edge of the unknown's black abyss.

In 1889 I was an auditor and investigator connected with the Tlaxcala Mining Company of San Francisco, which operated several small silver and copper properties in the San Mateo Mountains in Mexico. There had been some trouble at Mine No. 3, which had a surly, furtive assistant superintendent named Arthur Feldon; and on August 6th the firm received a telegram saying that Feldon had decamped, taking with him all the stock records, securities, and private papers, and leaving the whole clerical and financial situation in dire confusion.

This development was a severe blow to the company, and late in the afternoon President McComb called me into his office to give orders for the recovery of the papers at any cost. There were, he knew, grave drawbacks. I had never seen Feldon, and there were only very indifferent photographs to go by. Moreover, my own wedding was set for Thursday of the following week—only nine days ahead—so that I was naturally not eager to be hurried off to Mexico on a man-hunt of indefinite length. The need, however, was so great that McComb felt justified in asking me to go at once; and I for my part decided that the effect on my status with the company would make ready acquiescence eminently worth while.

I was to start that night, using the president's private car as far as Mexico City, after which I would have to take a narrow-gauge railway to the mines. Jackson, the superintendent of No. 3, would give me all details and any possible clues upon my arrival; and then the search would begin in earnest—through the mountains, down to the coast, or among the byways of Mexico City, as the case might be. I set out with a grim determination to get the matter done —and successfully done—as swiftly as possible; and tempered my discontent with pictures of an early return with papers and culprit, and of a wedding which would be almost a triumphal ceremony.

Having notified my family, fiancée, and principal friends, and made hasty preparations for the trip, I met President McComb at eight p.m. at the Southern Pacific depot, received from him some written instructions and a check-book, and left in his car attached to the 8:15 eastbound transcontinental train. The journey that followed seemed destined for uneventfulness, and after a good night's sleep I revelled in the ease of the private car so thoughtfully assigned me; reading my instructions with care, and formulating plans for the capture of Feldon and the recovery of the documents. I knew the Tlaxcala country quite well—probably much better than the missing man—hence had a certain amount of advantage in my search unless he had already used the railway.

According to the instructions, Feldon had been a subject of worry to Superintendent Jackson for some time; acting secretively, and working unaccountably in the company's laboratory at odd hours. That he was implicated with a Mexican boss and several peons in some thefts of ore was strongly suspected; but though the natives had been discharged, there was not enough evidence to warrant any positive step regarding the subtle official. Indeed, despite his furtiveness, there seemed to be more of defiance than of guilt in the man's bearing. He wore a chip on his shoulder, and talked as if the company were cheating him instead of his cheating the company. The obvious surveillance of his colleagues, Jackson wrote, appeared to irritate him increasingly; and now he had gone with everything of importance in the office. Of his possible whereabouts no guess could be made; though Jackson's final telegram suggested the wild slopes of the Sierra de Malinche, that tall, myth-surrounded peak with the corpse-shaped silhouette, from whose neighbourhood the thieving natives were said to have come.

At El Paso, which we reached at two a.m. of the night following our start, my private car was detached from the transcontinental train and joined to an engine specially ordered by telegraph to take it southward to Mexico City. I continued to drowse till dawn, and all the next day grew bored on the flat, desert Chihuahua landscape. The crew had told me we were due in Mexico City at noon Friday, but I soon saw that countless delays were wasting precious hours. There were waits on sidings all along the single-tracked route, and now and then a hot-box or other difficulty would further complicate the schedule.

At Torreón we were six hours late, and it was almost eight o'clock on Friday evening—fully twelve hours behind schedule—when the conductor consented to do some speeding in an effort to make up time. My nerves were on edge, and I could do nothing but pace the car in desperation. In the end I found that the speeding had been purchased at a high cost indeed, for within a half-hour the symptoms of a hot-box had developed in my car itself; so that after a maddening wait the crew decided that all the bearings would have to be overhauled after a quarter-speed limp ahead to the next station with shops—the factory town of Querétaro. This was the last straw, and I almost stamped like a child. Actually I sometimes caught myself pushing at my chair-arm as if trying to urge the train forward at a less snail-like pace.

It was almost ten in the evening when we drew into Querétaro, and I spent a fretful hour on the station platform while my car was sidetracked and tinkered at by a dozen native mechanics. At last they told me the job was too much for them, since the forward truck needed new parts which could not be obtained nearer than Mexico City. Everything indeed seemed against me, and I gritted my teeth when I thought of Feldon getting farther and farther away—perhaps to the easy cover of Vera Cruz with its shipping or Mexico City with its varied rail facilities—while fresh delays kept me tied and helpless. Of course Jackson had notified the police in all the cities around, but I knew with sorrow what their efficiency amounted to.

The best I could do, I soon found out, was to take the regular night express for Mexico City, which ran from Aguas Calientes and made a five-minute stop at Querétaro. It would be along at one a.m. if on time, and was due in Mexico City at five o'clock Saturday morning. When I purchased my ticket I found that the train would be made up of European compartment carriages instead of long American cars with rows of two-seat chairs. These had been much used in the early days of Mexican railroading, owing to the European construction interests back of the first lines; and in 1889 the Mexican Central was still running a fair number of them on its shorter trips. Ordinarily I prefer the American coaches, since I hate to have people facing me; but for this once I was glad of the foreign carriage. At such a time of night I stood a good chance of having a whole compartment to myself, and in my tired, nervously hypersensitive state I welcomed the solitude—as well as the comfortably upholstered seat with soft arm-rests and head-cushion, running the whole width of the vehicle. I bought a first-class ticket, obtained my valise from the sidetracked private car, telegraphed both President McComb and Jackson of what had happened, and settled down in the station to wait for the night express as patiently as my strained nerves would let me.

For a wonder, the train was only half an hour late; though even so, the solitary station vigil had about finished my endurance. The conductor, shewing me into a compartment, told me he expected to make up the delay and reach the capital on time; and I stretched myself comfortably on the forward-facing seat in the expectation of a quiet three-and-a-half-hour run. The light from the overhead oil lamp was soothingly dim, and I wondered whether I could snatch some much-needed sleep in spite of my anxiety and nerve-tension. It seemed, as the train jolted into motion, that I was alone; and I was heartily glad of it. My thoughts leaped ahead to my quest, and I nodded with the accelerating rhythm of the speeding string of carriages.

Then suddenly I perceived that I was not alone after all. In the corner diagonally opposite me, slumped down so that his face was invisible, sat a roughly clad man of unusual size, whom the feeble light had failed to reveal before. Beside him on the seat was a huge valise, battered and bulging, and tightly gripped even in his sleep by one of his incongruously slender hands. As the engine whistled sharply at some curve or crossing, the sleeper started nervously into a kind of watchful half-awakening; raising his head and disclosing a handsome face, bearded and clearly Anglo-Saxon, with dark, lustrous eyes. At sight of me his wakefulness became complete, and I wondered at the rather hostile wildness of his glance. No doubt, I thought, he resented my presence when he had hoped to have the compartment alone all the way; just as I was myself disappointed to find strange company in the half-lighted carriage. The best we could do, however, was to accept the situation gracefully; so I began apologising to the man for my intrusion. He seemed to be a fellow-American, and we could both feel more at ease after a few civilities. Then we could leave each other in peace for the balance of the journey.

To my surprise, the stranger did not respond to my courtesies with so much as a word. Instead, he kept staring at me fiercely and almost appraisingly, and brushed aside my embarrassed proffer of a cigar with a nervous lateral movement of his disengaged hand. His other hand still tensely clutched the great, worn valise, and his whole person seemed to radiate some obscure malignity. After a time he abruptly turned his face toward the window, though there was nothing to see in the dense blackness outside. Oddly, he appeared to be looking at something as intently as if there really were something to look at. I decided to leave him to his own curious devices and meditations without further annoyance; so settled back in my seat, drew the brim of my soft hat over my face, and closed my eyes in an effort to snatch the sleep I had half counted on.

I could not have dozed very long or very fully when my eyes fell open as if in response to some external force. Closing them again with some determination, I renewed my quest of a nap, yet wholly without avail. An intangible influence seemed bent on keeping me awake; so raising my head, I looked about the dimly lighted compartment to see if anything were amiss. All appeared normal, but I noticed that the stranger in the opposite corner was looking at me very intently—intently, though without any of the geniality or friendliness which would have implied a change from his former surly attitude. I did not attempt conversation this time, but leaned back in my previous sleepy posture; half closing my eyes if I had dozed off once more, yet continuing to watch him curiously from beneath my down-turned hat brim.

As the train rattled onward through the night I saw a subtle and gradual metamorphosis come over the expression of the staring man. Evidently satisfied that I was asleep, he allowed his face to reflect a curious jumble of emotions, the nature of which seemed anything but reassuring. Hatred, fear, triumph, and fanaticism flickered compositely over the lines of his lips and the angles of his eyes, while his gaze became a glare of really alarming greed and ferocity. Suddenly it dawned upon me that this man was mad, and dangerously so.

I will not pretend that I was anything but deeply and thoroughly frightened when I saw how things stood. Perspiration started out all over me, and I had hard work to maintain my attitude of relaxation and slumber. Life had many attractions for me just then, and the thought of dealing with a homicidal maniac—possibly armed and certainly powerful to a marvellous degree—was a dismaying and terrifying one. My disadvantage in any sort of struggle was enormous; for the man was a virtual giant, evidently in the best of athletic trim, while I have always been rather frail, and was then almost worn out with anxiety, sleeplessness, and nervous tension. It was undeniably a bad moment for me, and I felt pretty close to a horrible death as I recognised the fury of madness in the stranger's eyes. Events from the past came up into my consciousness as if for a farewell—just as a drowning man's whole life is said to resurrect itself before him at the last moment.

Of course I had my revolver in my coat pocket, but any motion of mine to reach and draw it would be instantly obvious. Moreover, if I did secure it, there was no telling what effect it would have on the maniac. Even if I shot him once or twice he might have enough remaining strength to get the gun from me and deal with me in his own way; or if he were armed himself he might shoot or stab without trying to disarm me. One can cow a sane man by covering him with a pistol, but an insane man's complete indifference to consequences gives him a strength and menace quite superhuman for the time being. Even in those pre-Freudian days I had a common-sense realisation of the dangerous power of a person without normal inhibitions. That the stranger in the corner was indeed about to start some murderous action, his burning eyes and twitching facial muscles did not permit me to doubt for a moment.

Suddenly I heard his breath begin to come in excited gasps, and saw his chest heaving with mounting excitement. The time for a showdown was close, and I tried desperately to think of the best thing to do. Without interrupting my pretence of sleep, I began to slide my right hand gradually and inconspicuously toward the pocket containing my pistol; watching the madman closely as I did so, to see if he would detect any move. Unfortunately he did—almost before he had time to register the fact in his expression. With a bound so agile and abrupt as to be almost incredible in a man of his size, he was upon me before I knew what had happened; looming up and swaying forward like a giant ogre of legend, and pinioning me with one powerful hand while with the other he forestalled me in reaching the revolver. Taking it from my pocket and placing it in his own, he released me contemptuously, well knowing how fully his physique placed me at his mercy. Then he stood up at his full height—his head almost touching the roof of the carriage—and stared down at me with eyes whose fury had quickly turned to a look of pitying scorn and ghoulish calculation.

I did not move, and after a moment the man resumed his seat opposite me; smiling a ghastly smile as he opened his great bulging valise and extracted an article of peculiar appearance—a rather large cage of semi-flexible wire, woven somewhat like a baseball catcher's mask, but shaped more like the helmet of a diving-suit. Its top was connected with a cord whose other end remained in the valise. This device he fondled with obvious affection, cradling it in his lap as he looked at me afresh and licked his bearded lips with an almost feline motion of the tongue. Then, for the first time, he spoke—in a deep, mellow voice of softness and cultivation startlingly at variance with his rough corduroy clothes and unkempt aspect.

"You are fortunate, sir. I shall use you first of all. You shall go into history as the first fruits of a remarkable invention. Vast sociological consequences—I shall let my light shine, as it were. I'm radiating all the time, but nobody knows it. Now you shall know. Intelligent guinea-pig. Cats and burros—it worked even with a burro. . . ."

He paused, while his bearded features underwent a convulsive motion closely synchronised with a vigorous gyratory shaking of the whole head. It was as though he were shaking clear of some nebulous obstructing medium, for the gesture was followed by a clarification or subtilisation of expression which hid the more obvious madness in a look of suave composure through which the craftiness gleamed only dimly. I glimpsed the difference at once, and put in a word to see if I could lead his mind into harmless channels.

"You seem to have a marvellously fine instrument, if I'm any judge. Won't you tell me how you came to invent it?"

He nodded.

"Mere logical reflection, dear sir. I consulted the needs of the age and acted upon them. Others might have done the same had their minds been as powerful—that is, as capable of sustained concentration—as mine. I had the sense of conviction—the available will power—that is all. I realised, as no one else has yet realised, how imperative it is to remove everybody from the earth before Quetzalcoatl comes back, and realised also that it must be done elegantly. I hate butchery of any kind, and hanging is barbarously crude. You know last year the New York legislature voted to adopt electric execution for condemned men—but all the apparatus they have in mind is as primitive as Stephenson's 'Rocket' or Davenport's first electric engine. I knew of a better way, and told them so, but they paid no attention to me. God, the fools! As if I didn't know all there is to know about men and death and electricity—student, man, and boy—technologist and engineer—soldier of fortune. . . ."

He leaned back and narrowed his eyes.

"I was in Maximilian's army twenty years and more ago. They were going to make me a nobleman. Then those damned greasers killed him and I had to go home. But I came back—back and forth, back and forth. I live in Rochester, N.Y. . . ."

His eyes grew deeply crafty, and he leaned forward, touching me on the knee with the fingers of a paradoxically delicate hand.

"I came back, I say, and I went deeper than any of them. I hate greasers, but I like Mexicans! A puzzle? Listen to me, young fellow—you don't think Mexico is really Spanish, do you? God, if you knew the tribes I know! In the mountains—in the mountains—Anahuac—Tenochtitlan—the old ones. . . ."

His voice changed to a chanting and not unmelodious howl.

"Iä! Huitzilopotchli! . . . Nahuatlacatl! Seven, seven, seven . . . Xochimilca, Chalca, Tepaneca, Acolhua, Tlahuica, Tlascalteca, Azteca! . . . Iä! Iä! I have been to the Seven Caves of Chicomoztoc, but no one shall ever know! I tell you *because you will never repeat it. . . .*"

He subsided, and resumed a conversational tone.

"It would surprise you to know what things are told in the mountains. Huitzilopotchli is coming back . . . of that there can be no doubt. Any peon south of Mexico City can tell you that. But I meant to do nothing about it. I went home, as I tell you, again and again, and was going to benefit society with my electric executioner when that cursed Albany legislature adopted the other way. A joke, sir, a joke! Grandfather's chair—sit by the fireside—Hawthorne—"

The man was chuckling with a morbid parody of good nature.

"Why, sir, I'd like to be the first man to sit in their damned chair and feel their little two-bit battery current! It wouldn't make a frog's legs dance! And they expect to kill murderers with it—reward of merit—everything! But then, young man, I saw the uselessness—the pointless illogicality, as it were—of killing just a few. Everybody is a murderer—they murder ideas—steal inventions—stole mine by watching, and watching, and watching—"

The man choked and paused, and I spoke soothingly.

"I'm sure your invention was much the better, and probably they'll come to use it in the end."

Evidently my tact was not great enough, for his response shewed fresh irritation.

"'Sure,' are you? Nice, mild, conservative assurance! Cursed lot you care—*but you'll soon know!* Why, damn you, all the good there ever will be in that electric chair will have been stolen from me. The ghost of Nezahualpilli told me that on the sacred mountain. They watched, and watched, and watched—"

He choked again, then gave another of those gestures in which he seemed to shake both his head and his facial expression. That seemed temporarily to steady him.

"What my invention needs is testing. That is it—here. The wire hood or head-net is flexible, and slips on easily. Neckpiece binds but doesn't choke. Electrodes touch forehead and base of cerebellum—all that's necessary. Stop the head, and what else can go? The fools up at Albany, with their carved oak easy-chair, think they've got to make it a head-to-foot affair. Idiots!—don't they know that you don't need to shoot a man through the body after you've plugged him through the brain? I've seen men die in battle—I know better. And then their silly high-power circuit—dynamos—all that. Why didn't they see what I've done with the storage-battery? Not a hearing—nobody knows—I alone have the secret—that's why I and Quetzalcoatl and Huitzilopotchli will rule the world alone—I and they, if I choose to let them. . . . But I must have experimental subjects—subjects—*do you know whom I've chosen for the first?*"

I tried jocoseness, quickly merging into friendly seriousness, as a sedative. Quick thought and apt words might save me yet.

"Well, there are lots of fine subjects among the politicians of San Francisco, where I come from! They need your treatment, and I'd like to help you introduce it! But really, I think I can help you in all truth. I have some influence in Sacramento, and if you'll go back to the States with me after I'm through with my business in Mexico, I'll see that you get a hearing."

He answered soberly and civilly.

"No—I can't go back. I swore not to when those criminals at Albany turned down my invention and set spies to watch me and steal from me. But I must have American subjects. Those greasers are under a curse, and would be too easy; and the full-blood Indians—the real children of the feathered serpent—are sacred and inviolate except for proper sacrificial victims . . . and even those must be slain according to ceremony. I must have Americans without going back—and the first man I choose will be signally honoured. Do you know who he is?"

I temporised desperately.

"Oh, if that's all the trouble, I'll find you a dozen first-rate Yankee specimens as soon as we get to Mexico City! I know where there are lots of small mining men who wouldn't be missed for days—"

But he cut me short with a new and sudden air of authority which had a touch of real dignity in it.

"That'll do—we've trifled long enough. Get up and stand erect like a man. You're the subject I've chosen, and you'll thank me for the honour in the other world, just as the sacrificial victim thanks the priest for transferring him to eternal glory. A new principle—no other man alive has dreamed of such a battery, and it might never again be hit on if the world experimented a thousand years. Do you know that atoms aren't what they seem? Fools! A century after this some dolt would be guessing if I were to let the world live!"

As I arose at his command, he drew additional feet of cord from the valise and stood erect beside me; the wire helmet outstretched toward me in both hands, and a look of real exaltation on his tanned and bearded face. For an instant he seemed like a radiant Hellenic mystagogue or hierophant.

"Here, O Youth—a libation! Wine of the cosmos—nectar of the starry spaces—Linos—Iacchus—Ialmenos—Zagreus—Dionysos—Atys—Hylas—sprung from Apollo and slain by the hounds of Argos—seed of Psamathë—child of the sun—Evoë! Evoë!"

He was chanting again, and this time his mind seemed far back amongst the classic memories of his college days. In my erect posture I noticed the nearness of the signal cord overhead, and wondered whether I could reach it through some gesture of ostensible response to his ceremonial mood. It was worth trying, so with an antiphonal cry of "Evoë!" I put my arms forward and upward toward him in a ritualistic fashion, hoping to give the cord a tug before he could notice the act. But it was useless. He saw my purpose, and moved one hand toward the right-hand coat pocket where my revolver lay. No words were needed, and we stood for a moment like carven figures. Then he quietly said, "Make haste!"

Again my mind rushed frantically about seeking avenues of escape. The doors, I knew, were not locked on Mexican trains; but my companion could easily forestall me if I tried to unlatch one and jump out. Besides, our speed was so great that success in that direction would probably be as fatal as failure. The only thing to do was to play for time. Of the three-and-a-half-hour trip a good slice was already worn away, and once we got to Mexico City the guards and police in the station would provide instant safety.

There would, I thought, be two distinct times for diplomatic stalling. If I could get him to postpone the slipping on of the hood, that much time would be gained. Of course I had no belief that the thing was really deadly; but I knew enough of madmen to understand what would happen when it failed to work. To his disappointment would be added a mad sense of my responsibility for the failure, and the result would be a red chaos of murderous rage. Therefore the experiment must be postponed as long as possible. Yet the second opportunity did exist, for if I planned cleverly I might devise explanations for the failure which would hold his attention and lead him into more or less extended searches for corrective influences. I wondered just how far his credulity went, and whether I could prepare in advance a prophecy of failure which would make the failure itself stamp me as a seer or initiate, or perhaps a god. I had enough of a smattering of Mexican mythology to make it worth trying; though I would try other delaying influences first and let the prophecy come as a sudden revelation. Would he spare me in the end if I could make him think me a prophet or divinity? Could I "get by" as Quetzalcoatl or Huitzilopotchli? Anything to drag matters out till five o'clock, when we were due in Mexico City.

But my opening "stall" was the veteran will-making ruse. As the maniac repeated his command for haste, I told him of my family and intended marriage, and asked for the privilege of leaving a message and disposing of my money and effects. If, I said, he would lend me some paper and agree to mail what I should write, I could die more peacefully and willingly. After some cogitation he gave a favourable verdict and fished in his valise for a pad, which he handed me solemnly as I resumed my seat. I produced a pencil, artfully breaking the point at the outset and causing some delay while he searched for one of his own. When he gave me this, he took my broken pencil and proceeded to sharpen it with a large, horn-handled knife which had been in his belt under his coat. Evidently a second pencil-breaking would not profit me greatly.

What I wrote, I can hardly recall at this date. It was largely gibberish, and composed of random scraps of memorised literature when I could think of nothing else to set down. I made my handwriting as illegible as I could without destroying its nature as writing; for I knew he would be likely to look at the result before commencing his experiment, and realised how he would react to the sight of obvious nonsense. The ordeal was a terrible one, and I chafed each second at the slowness of the train. In the past I had often whistled a brisk gallop to the sprightly "tac" of wheels on rails, but now the tempo seemed slowed down to that of a funeral march—my funeral march, I grimly reflected.

My ruse worked till I had covered over four pages, six by nine; when at last the madman drew out his watch and told me I could have but five minutes more. What should I do next? I was hastily going through the form of concluding the will when a new idea struck me. Ending with a flourish and handing him the finished sheets, which he thrust carelessly into his left-hand coat pocket, I reminded him of my influential Sacramento friends who would be so much interested in his invention.

"Oughtn't I to give you a letter of introduction to them?" I said. "Oughtn't I to make a signed sketch and description of your executioner so that they'll grant you a cordial hearing? They can make you famous, you know—and there's no question at all but that they'll adopt your method for the state of California if they hear of it through someone like me, whom they know and trust."

I was taking this tack on the chance that his thoughts as a disappointed inventor would let him forget the Aztec-religious side of his mania for a while. When he veered to the latter again, I reflected, I would spring the "revelation" and "prophecy". The scheme worked, for his eyes glowed an eager assent, though he brusquely told me to be quick. He further emptied the valise, lifting out a queer-looking congeries of glass cells and coils to which the wire from the helmet was attached, and delivering a fire of running comment too technical for me to follow yet apparently quite plausible and straightforward. I pretended to note down all he said, wondering as I did so whether the queer apparatus was really a battery after all. Would I get a slight shock when he applied the device? The man surely talked as if he were a genuine electrician. Description of his own invention was clearly a congenial task for him, and I saw he was not as impatient as before. The hopeful grey of dawn glimmered red through the windows before he wound up, and I felt at last that my chance of escape had really become tangible.

But he, too, saw the dawn, and began glaring wildly again. He knew the train was due in Mexico City at five, and would certainly force quick action unless I could override all his judgment with engrossing ideas. As he rose with a determined air, setting the battery on the seat beside the open valise, I reminded him that I had not made the needed sketch; and asked him to hold the headpiece so that I could draw it near the battery. He complied and resumed his seat, with many admonitions to me to hurry. After another moment I paused for some information, asking him how the victim was placed for execution, and how his presumable struggles were overcome.

"Why," he replied, "the criminal is securely strapped to a post. It does not matter how much he tosses his head, for the helmet fits tightly and draws even closer when the current comes on. We turn the switch gradually—you see it here, a carefully arranged affair with a rheostat."

A new idea for delay occurred to me as the tilled fields and increasingly frequent houses in the dawnlight outside told of our approach to the capital at last.

"But," I said, "I must draw the helmet in place on a human head as well as beside the battery. Can't you slip it on yourself a moment so that I can sketch you with it? The papers as well as the officials will want all this, and they are strong on completeness."

I had, by chance, made a better shot than I had planned; for at my mention of the press the madman's eyes lit up afresh.

"The papers? Yes—damn them, you can make even the papers give me a hearing! They all laughed at me and wouldn't print a word. Here, you, hurry up! We've not a second to lose!"

He had slipped the headpiece on and was watching my flying pencil avidly. The wire mesh gave him a grotesque, comic look as he sat there with nervously twitching hands.

"Now, curse 'em, they'll print pictures! I'll revise your sketch if you make any blunders—must be accurate at any cost. Police will find you afterward—they'll tell how it works. Associated Press item —back up your letter—immortal fame. . . . Hurry, I say—hurry, confound you!"

The train was lurching over the poorer roadbed near the city, and we swayed disconcertingly now and then. With this excuse I managed to break the pencil again, but of course the maniac at once handed me my own which he had sharpened. My first batch of ruses was about used up, and I felt that I should have to submit to the headpiece in a moment. We were still a good quarter-hour from the terminal, and it was about time for me to divert my companion to his religious side and spring the divine prophecy.

Mustering up my scraps of Nahuan-Aztec mythology, I suddenly threw down pencil and paper and commenced to chant.

"Iä! Iä! Tloquenahuaque, Thou Who Art All In Thyself! Thou, too, Ipalnemoan, By Whom We Live! I hear, I hear! I see, I see! Serpent-bearing Eagle, hail! A message! A message! Huitzilopotchli, in my soul echoes thy thunder!"

At my intonations the maniac stared incredulously through his odd mask, his handsome face shewn in a surprise and perplexity which quickly changed to alarm. His mind seemed to go blank a moment, and then to recrystallise in another pattern. Raising his hands aloft, he chanted as if in a dream.

"Mictlanteuctli, Great Lord, a sign! A sign from within thy black cave! Iä! Tonatiuh-Metztli! Cthulhutl! Command, and I serve!"

Now in all this responsive gibberish there was one word which struck an odd chord in my memory. Odd, because it never occurs in any printed account of Mexican mythology, yet had been overheard by me more than once as an awestruck whisper amongst the peons in my own firm's Tlaxcala mines. It seemed to be part of an exceedingly secret and ancient ritual; for there were characteristic whispered responses which I had caught now and then, and which were as unknown as itself to academic scholarship. This maniac must have spent considerable time with the hill peons and Indians, just as he had said; for surely such unrecorded lore could have come from no mere book-learning. Realising the importance he must attach to this doubly esoteric jargon, I determined to strike at his most vulnerable spot and give him the gibberish responses the natives used.

"Ya-R'lyeh! Ya-R'lyeh!" I shouted. "Cthulhutl fhtaghn! Niguratl-Yig! Yog-Sototl—"

But I never had a chance to finish. Galvanised into a religious epilepsy by the exact response which his subconscious mind had probably not really expected, the madman scrambled down to a kneeling posture on the floor, bowing his wire-helmeted head again and again, and turning it to the right and left as he did so. With each turn his obeisances became more profound, and I could hear his foaming lips repeating the syllable "kill, kill, kill," in a rapidly swelling monotone. It occurred to me that I had overreached myself, and that my response had unloosed a mounting mania which would rouse him to the slaying-point before the train reached the station.

As the arc of the madman's turnings gradually increased, the slack in the cord from his headpiece to the battery had naturally been taken up more and more. Now, in an all-forgetting delirium of ecstasy, he began to magnify his turns to complete circles, so that the cord wound round his neck and began to tug at its moorings to the battery on the seat. I wondered what he would do when the inevitable would happen, and the battery would be dragged to presumable destruction on the floor.

Then came the sudden cataclysm. The battery, yanked over the seat's edge by the maniac's last gesture of orgiastic frenzy, did indeed fall; but it did not seem to have wholly broken. Instead, as my eye caught the spectacle in one too-fleeting instant, the actual impact was borne by the rheostat, so that the switch was jerked over instantly to full current. And the marvellous thing is that there *was* a current. The invention was no mere dream of insanity.

I saw a blinding blue auroral coruscation, heard an ululating shriek more hideous than any of the previous cries of that mad, horrible journey, and smelled the nauseous odour of burning flesh. That was all my overwrought consciousness could bear, and I sank instantly into oblivion.

When the train guard at Mexico City revived me, I found a crowd on the station platform around my compartment door. At my involuntary cry the pressing faces became curious and dubious, and I was glad when the guard shut out all but the trim doctor who had pushed his way through to me. My cry was a very natural thing, but it had been prompted by something more than the shocking sight on the carriage floor which I had expected to see. Or should say, by something *less,* because in truth there was not anything on the floor at all.

Nor, said the guard, had there been when he opened the door and found me unconscious within. My ticket was the only one sold for that compartment, and I was the only person found within it. Just myself and my valise, nothing more. I had been alone all the way from Querétaro. Guard, doctor, and spectators alike tapped their foreheads significantly at my frantic and insistent questions.

Had it all been a dream, or was I indeed mad? I recalled my anxiety and overwrought nerves, and shuddered. Thanking the guard and doctor, and shaking free of the curious crowd, I staggered into a cab and was taken to the Fonda Nacional, where, after telegraphing Jackson at the mine, I slept till afternoon in an effort to get a fresh grip on myself. I had myself called at one o'clock, in time to catch the narrow-gauge for the mining country, but when I got up I found a telegram under the door. It was from Jackson, and said that Feldon had been found dead in the mountains that morning, the news reaching the mine about ten o'clock. The papers were all safe, and the San Francisco office had been duly notified. So the whole trip, with its nervous haste and harrowing mental ordeal, had been for nothing!

Knowing that McComb would expect a personal report despite the course of events, I sent another wire ahead and took the narrow-gauge after all. Four hours later I was rattled and jolted into the station of Mine No. 3, where Jackson was waiting to give a cordial greeting. He was so full of the affair at the mine that he did not notice my still shaken and seedy appearance.

The superintendent's story was brief, and he told me it as he led me toward the shack up the hillside above the *arrastre,* where Feldon's body lay. Feldon, he said, had always been a queer, sullen character, ever since he was hired the year before; working at some secret mechanical device and complaining of constant espionage, and being disgustingly familiar with the native workmen. But he certainly knew the work, the country, and the people. He used to make long trips into the hills where the peons lived, and even to take part in some of their ancient, heathenish ceremonies. He hinted at odd secrets and strange powers as often as he boasted of his mechanical skill. Of late he had disintegrated rapidly; growing morbidly suspicious of his colleagues, and undoubtedly joining his native friends in ore-thieving after his cash got low. He needed unholy amounts of money for something or other—was always having boxes come from laboratories and machine shops in Mexico City or the States.

As for the final absconding with all the papers—it was only a crazy gesture of revenge for what he called "spying". He was certainly stark mad, for he had gone across country to a hidden cave on the wild slope of the haunted Sierra de Malinche, where no white men live, and had done some amazingly queer things. The cave, which would never have been found but for the final tragedy, was full of hideous old Aztec idols and altars; the latter covered with the charred bones of recent burnt-offerings of doubtful nature. The natives would tell nothing—indeed, they swore they knew nothing—but it was easy to see that the cave was an old rendezvous of theirs, and that Feldon had shared their practices to the fullest extent.

The searchers had found the place only because of the chanting and the final cry. It had been close to five that morning, and after an all-night encampment the party had begun to pack up for its empty-handed return to the mines. Then somebody had heard faint rhythms in the distance, and knew that one of the noxious old native rituals was being howled from some lonely spot up the slope of the corpse-shaped mountain. They heard the same old names—Mictlanteuctli, Tonatiuh-Metzli, Cthulhutl, Ya-R'lyeh, and all the rest—but the queer thing was that some English words were mixed with them. Real white man's English, and no greaser patter. Guided by the sound, they had hastened up the weed-entangled mountainside toward it, when after a spell of quiet the shriek had burst upon them. It was a terrible thing—a worse thing than any of them had ever heard before. There seemed to be some smoke, too, and a morbid acrid smell.

Then they stumbled on the cave, its entrance screened by scrub mesquites, but now emitting clouds of foetid smoke. It was lighted within, the horrible altars and grotesque images revealed flickeringly by candles which must have been changed less than a half-hour before; and on the gravelly floor lay the horror that made all the crowd reel backward. It was Feldon, head burned to a crisp by some odd device he had slipped over it—a kind of wire cage connected with a rather shaken-up battery which had evidently fallen to the floor from a nearby altar-pot. When the men saw it they exchanged glances, thinking of the "electric executioner" Feldon had always boasted of inventing—the thing which everyone had rejected, but had tried to steal and copy. The papers were safe in Feldon's open portmanteau which stood close by, and an hour later the column of searchers started back for No. 3 with a grisly burden on an improvised stretcher.

That was all, but it was enough to make me turn pale and falter as Jackson led me up past the *arrastre* to the shed where he said the body lay. For I was not without imagination, and knew only too well into what hellish nightmare this tragedy somehow supernaturally dovetailed. I knew what I should see inside that gaping door around which the curious miners clustered, and did not flinch when my eyes took in the giant form, the rough corduroy clothes, the oddly delicate hands, the wisps of burnt beard, and the hellish machine itself—battery slightly broken, and headpiece blackened by the charring of what was inside. The great, bulging portmanteau did not surprise me, and I quailed only at two things—the folded sheets of paper sticking out of the left-hand pocket, and the queer sagging of the corresponding right-hand pocket. In a moment when no one was looking I reached out and seized the too familiar sheets, crushing them in my hand without daring to look at their penmanship. I ought to be sorry now that a kind of panic fear made me burn them that night with averted eyes. They would have been a positive proof or disproof of something—but for that matter I could still have had proof by asking about the revolver the coroner afterward took from that sagging right-hand coat pocket. I never had the courage to ask about that—because my own revolver was missing after the night on the train. My pocket pencil, too, shewed signs of a crude and hasty sharpening unlike the precise pointing I had given it Friday afternoon on the machine in President McComb's private car.

So in the end I went home still puzzled—mercifully puzzled, perhaps. The private car was repaired when I got back to Querétaro, but my greatest relief was crossing the Rio Grande into El Paso and the States. By the next Friday I was in San Francisco again, and the postponed wedding came off the following week.

As to what really happened that night—as I've said, I simply don't dare to speculate. That chap Feldon was insane to start with, and on top of his insanity he had piled a lot of prehistoric Aztec witch-lore that nobody has any right to know. He was really an inventive genius, and that battery must have been the genuine stuff. I heard later how he had been brushed aside in former years by press, public, and potentates alike. Too much disappointment isn't good for men of a certain kind. Anyhow, some unholy combination of influences was at work. He had really, by the way, been a soldier of Maximilian's.

When I tell my story most people call me a plain liar. Others lay it to abnormal psychology—and heaven knows I *was* overwrought

—while still others talk of "astral projection" of some sort. My zeal to catch Feldon certainly sent my thoughts ahead toward him, and with all his Indian magic he'd be about the first one to recognise and meet them. Was he in the railway carriage or was I in the cave on the corpse-shaped haunted mountain? What would have happened to me, had I not delayed him as I did? I'll confess I don't know, and I'm not sure that I want to know. I've never been in Mexico since—and as I said at the start, I don't enjoy hearing about electric executions.

Zealia Bishop

The Curse of Yig

In 1925 I went into Oklahoma looking for snake lore, and I came out with a fear of snakes that will last me the rest of my life. I admit it is foolish, since there are natural explanations for everything I saw and heard, but it masters me none the less. If the old story had been all there was to it, I would not have been so badly shaken. My work as an American Indian ethnologist has hardened me to all kinds of extravagant legendry, and I know that simple white people can beat the redskins at their own game when it comes to fanciful inventions. But I can't forget what I saw with my own eyes at the insane asylum in Guthrie.

I called at that asylum because a few of the oldest settlers told me I would find something important there. Neither Indians nor white men would discuss the snake-god legends I had come to trace. The oil-boom newcomers, of course, knew nothing of such matters, and the red men and old pioneers were plainly frightened when I spoke of them. Not more than six or seven people mentioned the asylum, and those who did were careful to talk in whispers. But the whisperers said that Dr. McNeill could shew me a very terrible relic and tell me all I wanted to know. He could explain why Yig, the half-human father of serpents, is a shunned and feared object in central Oklahoma, and why old settlers shiver at the secret Indian orgies which make the autumn days and nights hideous with the ceaseless beating of tom-toms in lonely places.

It was with the scent of a hound on the trail that I went to Guthrie, for I had spent many years collecting data on the evolution of serpent-worship among the Indians. I had always felt, from well-defined undertones of legend and archaeology, that great Quetzalcoatl—benign snake-god of the Mexicans—had had an older and darker prototype; and during recent months I had well-nigh proved it in a series of researches stretching from Guatemala to the Oklahoma plains. But everything was tantalising and incomplete, for above the border the cult of the snake was hedged about by fear and furtiveness.

Now it appeared that a new and copious source of data was about to dawn, and I sought the head of the asylum with an eagerness I did not try to cloak. Dr. McNeill was a small, clean-shaven man of somewhat advanced years, and I saw at once from his speech and manner that he was a scholar of no mean attainments in many branches outside his profession. Grave and doubtful when I first made known my errand, his face grew thoughtful as he carefully scanned my credentials and the letter of introduction which a kindly old ex–Indian agent had given me.

"So you've been studying the Yig legend, eh?" he reflected sententiously. "I know that many of our Oklahoma ethnologists have tried to connect it with Quetzalcoatl, but I don't think any of them have traced the intermediate steps so well. You've done remarkable work for a man as young as you seem to be, and you certainly deserve all the data we can give.

"I don't suppose old Major Moore or any of the others told you what it is I have here. They don't like to talk about it, and neither do I. It is very tragic and very horrible, but that is all. I refuse to consider it anything supernatural. There's a story about it that I'll tell you after you see it—a devilish sad story, but one that I won't call magic. It merely shews the potency that belief has over some people. I'll admit there are times when I feel a shiver that's more than physical, but in daylight I set all that down to nerves. I'm not a young fellow any more, alas!

"To come to the point, the thing I have is what you might call a victim of Yig's curse—a physically living victim. We don't let the bulk of the nurses see it, although most of them know it's here. There are just two steady old chaps whom I let feed it and clean out its quarters—used to be three, but good old Stevens passed on a few years ago. I suppose I'll have to break in a new group pretty soon; for the thing doesn't seem to age or change much, and we old boys can't last forever. Maybe the ethics of the near future will let us give it a merciful release, but it's hard to tell.

"Did you see that single ground-glass basement window over in the east wing when you came up the drive? That's where it is. I'll take you there myself now. You needn't make any comment. Just look through the moveable panel in the door and thank God the light isn't any stronger. Then I'll tell you the story—or as much as I've been able to piece together."

We walked downstairs very quietly, and did not talk as we threaded the corridors of the seemingly deserted basement. Dr. McNeill unlocked a grey-painted steel door, but it was only a bulkhead leading to a further stretch of hallway. At length he paused before a door marked B 116, opened a small observation panel which he could use only by standing on tiptoe, and pounded several times upon the painted metal, as if to arouse the occupant, whatever it might be.

A faint stench came from the aperture as the doctor unclosed it, and I fancied his pounding elicited a kind of low, hissing response. Finally he motioned me to replace him at the peep-hole, and I did so with a causeless and increasing tremor. The barred, ground-glass window, close to the earth outside, admitted only a feeble and uncertain pallor; and I had to look into the malodorous den for several seconds before I could see what was crawling and wriggling about on the straw-covered floor, emitting every now and then a weak and vacuous hiss. Then the shadowed outlines began to take shape, and I perceived that the squirming entity bore some remote resemblance to a human form laid flat on its belly. I clutched at the door-handle for support as I tried to keep from fainting.

The moving object was almost of human size, and entirely devoid of clothing. It was absolutely hairless, and its tawny-looking back seemed subtly squamous in the dim, ghoulish light. Around the shoulders it was rather speckled and brownish, and the head was very curiously flat. As it looked up to hiss at me I saw that the beady little black eyes were damnably anthropoid, but I could not bear to study them long. They fastened themselves on me with a horrible persistence, so that I closed the panel gaspingly and left the creature to wriggle about unseen in its matted straw and spectral twilight. I must have reeled a bit, for I saw that the doctor was gently holding my arm as he guided me away. I was stuttering over and over again: "B-but for God's sake, *what is it?*"

Dr. McNeill told me the story in his private office as I sprawled opposite him in an easy-chair. The gold and crimson of late afternoon changed to the violet of early dusk, but still I sat awed and motionless. I resented every ring of the telephone and every whir of the buzzer, and I could have cursed the nurses and internes whose knocks now and then summoned the doctor briefly to the outer office. Night came, and I was glad my host switched on all the lights. Scientist though I was, my zeal for research was half forgotten amidst such breathless ecstasies of fright as a small boy might feel when whispered witch-tales go the rounds of the chimney-corner.

It seems that Yig, the snake-god of the central plains tribes—presumably the primal source of the more southerly Quetzalcoatl or Kukulcan—was an odd, half-anthropomorphic devil of highly arbitrary and capricious nature. He was not wholly evil, and was usually quite well-disposed toward those who gave proper respect to him and his children, the serpents; but in the autumn he became abnormally ravenous, and had to be driven away by means of suitable rites. That was why the tom-toms in the Pawnee, Wichita, and Caddo country pounded ceaselessly week in and week out in August, September, and October; and why the medicine-men made strange noises with rattles and whistles curiously like those of the Aztecs and Mayas.

Yig's chief trait was a relentless devotion to his children—a devotion so great that the redskins almost feared to protect themselves from the venomous rattlesnakes which thronged the region. Frightful clandestine tales hinted of his vengeance upon mortals who flouted him or wreaked harm upon his wriggling progeny; his chosen method being to turn his victim, after suitable tortures, to a spotted snake.

In the old days of the Indian Territory, the doctor went on, there was not quite so much secrecy about Yig. The plains tribes, less cautious than the desert nomads and Pueblos, talked quite freely of their legends and autumn ceremonies with the first Indian agents, and let considerable of the lore spread out through the neighbouring regions of white settlement. The great fear came in the land-rush days of '89, when some extraordinary incidents had been rumoured, and the rumours sustained, by what seemed to be hideously tangible proofs. Indians said that the new white men did not know how to get on with Yig, and afterward the settlers came to take that theory at face value. Now no old-timer in middle Oklahoma, white or red, could be induced to breathe a word about the snake-god except in vague hints. Yet after all, the doctor added with almost needless emphasis, the only truly authenticated horror had been a thing of pitiful tragedy rather than of bewitchment. It was all very material and cruel—even that last phase which had caused so much dispute.

Dr. McNeill paused and cleared his throat before getting down to his special story, and I felt a tingling sensation as when a theatre curtain rises. The thing had begun when Walker Davis and his wife Audrey left Arkansas to settle in the newly opened public lands in the spring of 1889, and the end had come in the country of the Wichitas—north of the Wichita River, in what is at present Caddo County. There is a small village called Binger there now, and the railway goes through; but otherwise the place is less changed than other parts of Oklahoma. It is still a section of farms and ranches—quite productive in these days—since the great oil-fields do not come very close.

Walker and Audrey had come from Franklin County in the Ozarks with a canvas-topped wagon, two mules, an ancient and useless dog called "Wolf", and all their household goods. They were typical hill-folk, youngish and perhaps a little more ambitious than most, and looked forward to a life of better returns for their hard work than they had had in Arkansas. Both were lean, raw-boned specimens; the man tall, sandy, and grey-eyed, and the woman short and rather dark, with a black straightness of hair suggesting a slight Indian admixture.

In general, there was very little of distinction about them, and but for one thing their annals might not have differed from those of thousands of other pioneers who flocked into the new country at that time. That thing was Walker's almost epileptic fear of snakes, which some laid to prenatal causes, and some said came from a dark prophecy about his end with which an old Indian squaw had tried to scare him when he was small. Whatever the cause, the effect was marked indeed; for despite his strong general courage the very mention of a snake would cause him to grow faint and pale, while the sight of even a tiny specimen would produce a shock sometimes bordering on a convulsion seizure.

The Davises started out early in the year, in the hope of being on their new land for the spring ploughing. Travel was slow; for the roads were bad in Arkansas, while in the Territory there were great stretches of rolling hills and red, sandy barrens without any roads whatever. As the terrain grew flatter, the change from their native mountains depressed them more, perhaps, than they realised; but they found the people at the Indian agencies very affable, while most of the settled Indians seemed friendly and civil. Now and then they encountered a fellow-pioneer, with whom crude pleasantries and expressions of amiable rivalry were generally exchanged.

Owing to the season, there were not many snakes in evidence, so Walker did not suffer from his special temperamental weakness. In the earlier stages of the journey, too, there were no Indian snake-legends to trouble him; for the transplanted tribes from the south-east do not share the wilder beliefs of their western neighbours. As fate would have it, it was a white man at Okmulgee in the Creek country who gave the Davises the first hint of Yig beliefs; a hint which had a curiously fascinating effect on Walker, and caused him to ask questions very freely after that.

Before long Walker's fascination had developed into a bad case of fright. He took the most extraordinary precautions at each of the nightly camps, always clearing away whatever vegetation he found, and avoiding stony places whenever he could. Every clump of stunted bushes and every cleft in the great, slab-like rocks seemed to him now to hide malevolent serpents, while every human figure not obviously part of a settlement or emigrant train seemed to him a potential snake-god till nearness had proved the contrary. Fortunately no troublesome encounters came at this stage to shake his nerves still further.

As they approached the Kickapoo country they found it harder and harder to avoid camping near rocks. Finally it was no longer possible, and poor Walker was reduced to the puerile expedient of droning some of the rustic anti-snake charms he had learned in his boyhood. Two or three times a snake was really glimpsed, and these sights did not help the sufferer in his efforts to preserve composure.

On the twenty-second evening of the journey a savage wind made it imperative, for the sake of the mules, to camp in as sheltered a spot as possible; and Audrey persuaded her husband to take advantage of a cliff which rose uncommonly high above the dried bed of a former tributary of the Canadian River. He did not like the rocky cast of the place, but allowed himself to be overruled this once; leading the animals sullenly toward the protecting slope, which the nature of the ground would not allow the wagon to approach.

Audrey, examining the rocks near the wagon, meanwhile noticed a singular sniffing on the part of the feeble old dog. Seizing a rifle, she followed his lead, and presently thanked her stars that she had forestalled Walker in her discovery. For there, snugly nested in the gap between two boulders, was a sight it would have done him no good to see. Visible only as one convoluted expanse, but perhaps comprising as many as three or four separate units, was a mass of lazy wriggling which could not be other than a brood of new-born rattlesnakes.

Anxious to save Walker from a trying shock, Audrey did not hesitate to act, but took the gun firmly by the barrel and brought the butt down again and again upon the writhing objects. Her own sense of loathing was great, but it did not amount to a real fear. Finally she saw that her task was done, and turned to cleanse the improvised bludgeon in the red sand and dry, dead grass near by. She must, she reflected, cover the nest up before Walker got back from tethering the mules. Old Wolf, tottering relic of mixed shepherd and coyote ancestry that he was, had vanished, and she feared he had gone to fetch his master.

Footsteps at that instant proved her fear well founded. A second more, and Walker had seen everything. Audrey made a move to catch him if he should faint, but he did no more than sway. Then the look of pure fright on his bloodless face turned slowly to something like mingled awe and anger, and he began to upbraid his wife in trembling tones.

"Gawd's sake, Aud, but why'd ye go for to do that? Hain't ye heerd all the things they've been tellin' about this snake-devil Yig? Ye'd ought to a told me, and we'd a moved on. Don't ye know they's a devil-god what gets even if ye hurts his children? What for d'ye think the Injuns all dances and beats their drums in the fall about? This land's under a curse, I tell ye—nigh every soul we've a-talked to sence we come in's said the same. Yig rules here, an' he comes out every fall for to git his victims and turn 'em into snakes. Why, Aud, they won't none of them Injuns acrost the Canayjin kill a snake for love nor money!

"Gawd knows what ye done to yourself, gal, a-stompin' out a hull brood o' Yig's chillen. He'll git ye, sure, sooner or later, unlessen I kin buy a charm offen some o' the Injun medicine-men. He'll git ye, Aud, as sure's they's a Gawd in heaven—he'll come outa the night and turn ye into a crawlin' spotted snake!"

All the rest of the journey Walker kept up the frightened reproofs and prophecies. They crossed the Canadian near Newcastle, and soon afterward met with the first of the real plains Indians they had seen—a party of blanketed Wichitas, whose leader talked freely under the spell of the whiskey offered him, and taught poor Walker a long-winded protective charm against Yig in exchange for a quart bottle of the same inspiring fluid. By the end of the week the chosen site in the Wichita country was reached, and the Davises made haste to trace their boundaries and perform the spring ploughing before even beginning the construction of a cabin.

The region was flat, drearily windy, and sparse of natural vegetation, but promised great fertility under cultivation. Occasional outcroppings of granite diversified a soil of decomposed red sandstone, and here and there a great flat rock would stretch along the surface of the ground like a man-made floor. There seemed to be a very few snakes, or possible dens for them; so Audrey at last persuaded Walker to build the one-room cabin over a vast, smooth slab of exposed stone. With such a flooring and with a good-sized fireplace the wettest weather might be defied—though it soon became evident that dampness was no salient quality of the district. Logs were hauled in the wagon from the nearest belt of woods, many miles toward the Wichita Mountains.

Walker built his wide-chimneyed cabin and crude barn with the aid of some of the other settlers, though the nearest one was over a mile away. In turn, he helped his helpers at similar house-raisings, so that many ties of friendship sprang up between the new neighbours. There was no town worthy the name nearer than El Reno, on the railway thirty miles or more to the northeast; and before many weeks had passed, the people of the section had become very cohesive despite the wideness of their scattering. The Indians, a few of whom had begun to settle down on ranches, were for the most part harmless, though somewhat quarrelsome when fired by the liquid stimulation which found its way to them despite all government bans.

Of all the neighbours the Davises found Joe and Sally Compton, who likewise hailed from Arkansas, the most helpful and congenial. Sally is still alive, known now as Grandma Compton; and her son Clyde, then an infant in arms, has become one of the leading men of the state. Sally and Audrey used to visit each other often, for their cabins were only two miles apart; and in the long spring and summer afternoons they exchanged many a tale of old Arkansas and many a rumour about the new country.

Sally was very sympathetic about Walker's weakness regarding snakes, but perhaps did more to aggravate than cure the parallel nervousness which Audrey was acquiring through his incessant praying and prophesying about the curse of Yig. She was uncommonly full of gruesome snake stories, and produced a direfully strong impression with her acknowledged masterpiece—the tale of a man in Scott County who had been bitten by a whole horde of rattlers at once, and had swelled so monstrously from poison that his body had finally burst with a pop. Needless to say, Audrey did not repeat this anecdote to her husband, and she implored the Comptons to beware of starting it on the rounds of the countryside. It is to Joe's and Sally's credit that they heeded this plea with the utmost fidelity.

Walker did his corn-planting early, and in midsummer improved his time by harvesting a fair crop of the native grass of the region. With the help of Joe Compton he dug a well which gave a moderate supply of very good water, though he planned to sink an artesian later on. He did not run into many serious snake scares, and made his land as inhospitable as possible for wriggling visitors. Every now and then he rode over to the cluster of thatched, conical huts which formed the main village of the Wichitas, and talked long with the old men and shamans about the snake-god and how to nullify his wrath. Charms were always ready in exchange for whiskey, but much of the information he got was far from reassuring.

Yig was a great god. He was bad medicine. He did not forget things. In the autumn his children were hungry and wild, and Yig was hungry and wild, too. All the tribes made medicine against Yig when the corn harvest came. They gave him some corn, and danced in proper regalia to the sound of whistle, rattle, and drum. They kept the drums pounding to drive Yig away, and called down the aid of Tiráwa, whose children men are, even as the snakes are Yig's children. It was bad that the squaw of Davis killed the children of Yig. Let Davis say the charms many times when the corn harvest comes. Yig is Yig. Yig is a great god.

By the time the corn harvest did come, Walker had succeeded in getting his wife into a deplorably jumpy state. His prayers and borrowed incantations came to be a nuisance; and when the autumn rites of the Indians began, there was always a distant wind-borne pounding of tom-toms to lend an added background of the sinister. It was maddening to have the muffled clatter always stealing over the wide red plains. Why would it never stop? Day and night, week on week, it was always going in exhaustless relays, as persistently as the red dusty winds that carried it. Audrey loathed it more than her husband did, for he saw in it a compensating element of protection. It was with this sense of a mighty, intangible bulwark against evil that he got in his corn crop and prepared cabin and stable for the coming winter.

The autumn was abnormally warm, and except for their primitive cookery the Davises found scant use for the stone fireplace Walker had built with such care. Something in the unnaturalness of the hot dust-clouds preyed on the nerves of all the settlers, but most of all on Audrey's and Walker's. The notions of a hovering snake-curse and the weird, endless rhythm of the distant Indian drums formed a bad combination which any added element of the bizarre went far to render utterly unendurable.

Notwithstanding this strain, several festive gatherings were held at one or another of the cabins after the crops were reaped; keeping naively alive in modernity those curious rites of the harvest-home which are as old as human agriculture itself. Lafayette Smith, who came from southern Missouri and had a cabin about three miles east of Walker's, was a very passable fiddler; and his tunes did much to make the celebrants forget the monotonous beating of the distant tom-toms. Then Hallowe'en drew near, and the settlers planned another frolic—this time, had they but known it, of a lineage older than even agriculture; the dread Witch-Sabbath of the primal pre-Aryans, kept alive through ages in the midnight blackness of secret woods, and still hinting at vague terrors under its latter-day mask of comedy and lightness. Hallowe'en was to fall on a Thursday, and the neighbours agreed to gather for their first revel at the Davis cabin.

It was on that thirty-first of October that the warm spell broke. The morning was grey and leaden, and by noon the incessant winds had changed from searingness to rawness. People shivered all the more because they were not prepared for the chill, and Walker Davis' old dog Wolf dragged himself wearily indoors to a place beside the hearth. But the distant drums still thumped on, nor were the white citizenry less inclined to pursue their chosen rites. As early as four in the afternoon the wagons began to arrive at Walker's cabin; and in the evening, after a memorable barbecue, Lafayette Smith's fiddle inspired a very fair-sized company to great feats of saltatory grotesqueness in the one good-sized but crowded room. The younger folk indulged in the amiable inanities proper to the season, and now and then old Wolf would howl with doleful and spine-tickling ominousness at some especially spectral strain from Lafayette's squeaky violin—a device he had never heard before. Mostly, though, this battered veteran slept through the merriment; for he was past the age of active interests and lived largely in his dreams. Tom and Jennie Rigby had brought their collie Zeke along, but the canines did not fraternise. Zeke seemed strangely uneasy over something, and nosed around curiously all the evening.

Audrey and Walker made a fine couple on the floor, and Grandma Compton still likes to recall her impression of their dancing that night. Their worries seemed forgotten for the nonce, and Walker was shaved and trimmed into a surprising degree of spruceness. By ten o'clock all hands were healthily tired, and the guests began to depart family by family with many handshakings and bluff assurances of what a fine time everybody had had. Tom and Jennie thought Zeke's eerie howls as he followed them to their wagon were marks of regret at having to go home; though Audrey said it must be the far-away tom-toms which annoyed him, for the distant thumping was surely ghastly enough after the merriment within.

The night was bitterly cold, and for the first time Walker put a great log in the fireplace and banked it with ashes to keep it smouldering till morning. Old Wolf dragged himself within the ruddy glow and lapsed into his customary coma. Audrey and Walker, too tired to think of charms or curses, tumbled into the rough pine bed and were asleep before the cheap alarm-clock on the mantel had ticked out three minutes. And from far away, the rhythmic pounding of those hellish tom-toms still pulsed on the chill night-wind.

Dr. McNeill paused here and removed his glasses, as if a blurring of the objective world might make the reminiscent vision clearer.

"You'll soon appreciate," he said, "that I had a great deal of difficulty in piecing out all that happened after the guests left. There were times, though—at first—when I was able to make a try at it." After a moment of silence he went on with the tale.

Audrey had terrible dreams of Yig, who appeared to her in the guise of Satan as depicted in cheap engravings she had seen. It was, indeed, from an absolute ecstasy of nightmare that she started suddenly awake to find Walker already conscious and sitting up in bed. He seemed to be listening intently to something, and silenced her with a whisper when she began to ask what had roused him.

"Hark, Aud!" he breathed. "Don't ye hear somethin' a-singin' and buzzin' and rustlin'? D'ye reckon it's the fall crickets?"

Certainly, there was distinctly audible within the cabin such a sound as he had described. Audrey tried to analyse it, and was impressed with some element at once horrible and familiar, which hovered just outside the rim of her memory. And beyond it all, waking a hideous thought, the monotonous beating of the distant tom-toms came incessantly across the black plains on which a cloudy half-moon had set.

"Walker—s'pose it's—the—the—curse o' Yig?"

She could feel him tremble.

"No, gal, I don't reckon he comes that away. He's shapen like a man, except ye look at him clost. That's what Chief Grey Eagle says. This here's some varmints come in outen the cold—not crickets, I calc'late, but summat like 'em. I'd orter git up and stomp 'em out afore they make much headway or git at the cupboard."

He rose, felt for the lantern that hung within easy reach, and rattled the tin match-box nailed to the wall beside it. Audrey sat up in bed and watched the flare of the match grow into the steady glow of the lantern. Then, as their eyes began to take in the whole of the room, the crude rafters shook with the frenzy of their simultaneous shriek. For the flat, rocky floor, revealed in the new-born illumination, was one seething, brown-speckled mass of wriggling rattlesnakes, slithering toward the fire, and even now turning their loathsome heads to menace the fright-blasted lantern-bearer.

It was only for an instant that Audrey saw the things. The reptiles were of every size, of uncountable numbers, and apparently of several varieties; and even as she looked, two or three of them reared their heads as if to strike at Walker. She did not faint—it was Walker's crash to the floor that extinguished the lantern and plunged her into blackness. He had not screamed a second time—fright had paralysed him, and he fell as if shot by a silent arrow from no mortal's bow. To Audrey the entire world seemed to whirl about fantastically, mingling with the nightmare from which she had started.

Voluntary motion of any sort was impossible, for will and the sense of reality had left her. She fell back inertly on her pillow, hoping that she would wake soon. No actual sense of what had happened penetrated her mind for some time. Then, little by little, the suspicion that she was really awake began to dawn on her; and she was convulsed with a mounting blend of panic and grief which made her long to shriek out despite the inhibiting spell which kept her mute.

Walker was gone, and she had not been able to help him. He had died of snakes, just as the old witch-woman had predicted when he was a little boy. Poor Wolf had not been able to help, either—probably he had not even awaked from his senile stupor. And now the crawling things must be coming for her, writhing closer and closer every moment in the dark, perhaps even now twining slipperily about the bedposts and oozing up over the coarse woollen blankets. Unconsciously she crept under the clothes and trembled.

It must be the curse of Yig. He had sent his monstrous children on All-Hallows' Night, and they had taken Walker first. Why was that—wasn't he innocent enough? Why not come straight for her—hadn't she killed those little rattlers alone? Then she thought of the curse's form as told by the Indians. She wouldn't be killed—just turned to a spotted snake. Ugh! So she would be like those things she had glimpsed on the floor—those things which Yig had sent to get her and enroll her among their number! She tried to mumble a charm that Walker had taught her, but found she could not utter a single sound.

The noisy ticking of the alarm-clock sounded above the maddening beat of the distant tom-toms. The snakes were taking a long time—did they mean to delay on purpose to play on her nerves? Every now and then she thought she felt a steady, insidious pressure on the bedclothes, but each time it turned out to be only the automatic twitchings of her overwrought nerves. The clock ticked on in the dark, and a change came slowly over her thoughts.

Those snakes *couldn't* have taken so long! They couldn't be Yig's messengers after all, but just natural rattlers that were nested below the rock and had been drawn there by the fire. They weren't coming for her, perhaps—perhaps they had sated themselves on poor Walker. Where were they now? Gone? Coiled by the fire? Still crawling over the prone corpse of their victim? The clock ticked, and the distant drums throbbed on.

At the thought of her husband's body lying there in the pitch blackness a thrill of purely physical horror passed over Audrey. That story of Sally Compton's about the man back in Scott County! He, too, had been bitten by a whole bunch of rattlesnakes, and what had happened to him? The poison had rotted the flesh and swelled the whole corpse, and in the end the bloated thing had *burst* horribly—burst horribly with a detestable *popping* noise. Was that what was happening to Walker down there on the rock floor? Instinctively she felt she had begun to *listen* for something too terrible even to name to herself.

The clock ticked on, keeping a kind of mocking, sardonic time with the far-off drumming that the night-wind brought. She wished it were a striking clock, so that she could know how long this eldritch vigil must last. She cursed the toughness of fibre that kept her from fainting, and wondered what sort of relief the dawn could bring, after all. Probably neighbours would pass—no doubt somebody would call—would they find her still sane? Was she still sane now?

Morbidly listening, Audrey all at once became aware of something which she had to verify with every effort of her will before she could believe it; and which, once verified, she did not know whether to welcome or dread. *The distant beating of the Indian tom-toms had ceased.* They had always maddened her—but had not Walker regarded them as a bulwark against nameless evil from outside the universe? What were some of those things he had repeated to her in whispers after talking with Grey Eagle and the Wichita medicine-men?

She did not relish this new and sudden silence, after all! There was something sinister about it. The loud-ticking clock seemed abnormal in its new loneliness. Capable at last of conscious motion, she shook the covers from her face and looked into the darkness toward the window. It must have cleared after the moon set, for she saw the square aperture distinctly against the background of stars.

Then without warning came that shocking, unutterable sound—ugh!—that dull, putrid *pop* of cleft skin and escaping poison in the dark. God!—Sally's story—that obscene stench, and this gnawing, clawing silence! It was too much. The bonds of muteness snapped, and the black night waxed reverberant with Audrey's screams of stark, unbridled frenzy.

Consciousness did not pass away with the shock. How merciful if only it had! Amidst the echoes of her shrieking Audrey still saw the star-sprinkled square of window ahead, and heard the doom-boding ticking of that frightful clock. Did she hear another sound? Was that square window still a perfect square? She was in no condition to weigh the evidence of her senses or distinguish between fact and hallucination.

No—that window was *not* a perfect square. *Something had encroached on the lower edge.* Nor was the ticking of the clock the only sound in the room. There was, beyond dispute, a heavy breathing neither her own nor poor Wolf's. Wolf slept very silently, and his wakeful wheezing was unmistakable. Then Audrey saw against the stars the black, daemoniac silhouette of something anthropoid—the undulant bulk of a gigantic head and shoulders fumbling slowly toward her.

"Y'aaaah! Y'aaaah! Go away! Go away! Go away, snake-devil! Go 'way, Yig! I didn't mean to kill 'em—I was feared he'd be scairt of 'em. Don't, Yig, don't! I didn't go for to hurt yore chillen—don't come nigh me—don't change me into no spotted snake!"

But the half-formless head and shoulders only lurched onward toward the bed, very silently.

Everything snapped at once inside Audrey's head, and in a second she had turned from a cowering child to a raging madwoman. She knew where the axe was—hung against the wall on those pegs near the lantern. It was within easy reach, and she could find it in the dark. Before she was conscious of anything further it was in her hands, and she was creeping toward the foot of the bed—toward the monstrous head and shoulders that every moment groped their way nearer. Had there been any light, the look on her face would not have been pleasant to see.

"Take *that,* you! And *that,* and *that,* and *that!*"

She was laughing shrilly now, and her cackles mounted higher as she saw that the starlight beyond the window was yielding to the dim prophetic pallor of coming dawn.

Dr. McNeill wiped the perspiration from his forehead and put on his glasses again. I waited for him to resume, and as he kept silent I spoke softly.

"She lived? She was found? Was it ever explained?"

The doctor cleared his throat.

"Yes—she lived, in a way. And it was explained. I told you there was no bewitchment—only cruel, pitiful, material horror."

It was Sally Compton who had made the discovery. She had ridden over to the Davis cabin the next afternoon to talk over the party with Audrey, and had seen no smoke from the chimney. That was queer. It had turned very warm again, yet Audrey was usually cooking something at that hour. The mules were making hungry-sounding noises in the barn, and there was no sign of old Wolf sunning himself in the accustomed spot by the door.

Altogether, Sally did not like the look of the place, so was very timid and hesitant as she dismounted and knocked. She got no answer but waited some time before trying the crude door of split logs. The lock, it appeared, was unfastened; and she slowly pushed her way in. Then, perceiving what was there, she reeled back, gasped, and clung to the jamb to preserve her balance.

A terrible odour had welled out as she opened the door, but that was not what had stunned her. It was what she had seen. For within that shadowy cabin monstrous things had happened and three shocking objects remained on the floor to awe and baffle the beholder.

Near the burned-out fireplace was the great dog—purple decay on the skin left bare by mange and old age, and the whole carcass burst by the puffing effect of rattlesnake poison. It must have been bitten by a veritable legion of the reptiles.

To the right of the door was the axe-hacked remnant of what had been a man—clad in a nightshirt, and with the shattered bulk of a lantern clenched in one hand. *He was totally free from any sign of snake-bite.* Near him lay the ensanguined axe, carelessly discarded.

And wriggling flat on the floor was a loathsome, vacant-eyed thing that had been a woman, but was now only a mute mad caricature. All that this thing could do was to hiss, and hiss, and hiss.

Both the doctor and I were brushing cold drops from our foreheads by this time. He poured something from a flask on his desk, took a nip, and handed another glass to me. I could only suggest tremulously and stupidly:

"So Walker had only fainted that first time—the screams roused him, and the axe did the rest?"

"Yes." Dr. McNeill's voice was low. "But he met his death from snakes just the same. It was his fear working in two ways—it made him faint, and it made him fill his wife with the wild stories that caused her to strike out when she thought she saw the snake-devil."

I thought for a moment.

"And Audrey—wasn't it queer how the curse of Yig seemed to work itself out on her? I suppose the impression of hissing snakes had been fairly ground into her."

"Yes. There were lucid spells at first, but they got to be fewer and fewer. Her hair came white at the roots as it grew, and later began to fall out. The skin grew blotchy, and when she died—"

I interrupted with a start.

"*Died?* Then what was that—that thing downstairs?"

McNeill spoke gravely.

"*That* is what was born to her three-quarters of a year afterward. There were three more of them—two were even worse—but this is the only one that lived."

Zealia Bishop

The Mound

I.

It is only within the last few years that most people have stopped thinking of the West as a *new* land. I suppose the idea gained ground because our own especial civilisation happens to be new there; but nowadays explorers are digging beneath the surface and bringing up whole chapters of life that rose and fell among these plains and mountains before recorded history began. We think nothing of a Pueblo village 2500 years old, and it hardly jolts us when archaeologists put the sub-pedregal culture of Mexico back to 17,000 or 18,000 B. C. We hear rumours of still older things, too—of primitive man contemporaneous with extinct animals and known today only through a few fragmentary bones and artifacts—so that the idea of newness is fading out pretty rapidly. Europeans usually catch the sense of immemorial ancientness and deep deposits from successive life-streams better than we do. Only a couple of years ago a British author spoke of Arizona as a "moon-dim region, very lovely in its way, and stark and old—an ancient, lonely land".

Yet I believe I have a deeper sense of the stupefying—almost horrible—ancientness of the West than any European. It all comes from an incident that happened in 1928; an incident which I'd greatly like to dismiss as three-quarters hallucination, but which has left such a frightfully firm impression on my memory that I can't put it off very easily. It was in Oklahoma, where my work as an American Indian ethnologist constantly takes me and where I had come upon some devilishly strange and disconcerting matters before. Make no mistake—Oklahoma is a lot more than a mere pioneers' and promoters' frontier. There are old, old tribes with old, old memories there; and when the tom-toms beat ceaselessly over brooding plains in the autumn the spirits of men are brought dangerously close to primal, whispered things. I am white and Eastern enough myself, but anybody is welcome to know that the rites of Yig, Father of Snakes, can get a real shudder out of me any day. I have heard and seen too much to be "sophisticated" in such matters. And so it is with this incident of 1928. I'd like to laugh it off—but I can't.

I had gone into Oklahoma to track down and correlate one of the many ghost tales which were current among the white settlers, but which had strong Indian corroboration, and—I felt sure—an ultimate Indian source. They were very curious, these open-air ghost tales; and though they sounded flat and prosaic in the mouths of the white people, they had earmarks of linkage with some of the richest and obscurest phases of native mythology. All of them were woven around the vast, lonely, artificial-looking mounds in the western part of the state, and all of them involved apparitions of exceedingly strange aspect and equipment.

The commonest, and among the oldest, became quite famous in 1892, when a government marshal named John Willis went into the mound region after horse-thieves and came out with a wild yarn of nocturnal cavalry horses in the air between great armies of invisible spectres—battles that involved the rush of hooves and feet, the thud of blows, the clank of metal on metal, the muffled cries of warriors, and the fall of human and equine bodies. These things happened by moonlight, and frightened his horse as well as himself. The sounds persisted an hour at a time; vivid, but subdued as if brought from a distance by a wind, and unaccompanied by any glimpse of the armies themselves. Later on Willis learned that the seat of the sounds was a notoriously haunted spot, shunned by settlers and Indians alike. Many had seen, or half seen, the warring horsemen in the sky, and had furnished dim, ambiguous descriptions. The settlers described the ghostly fighters as Indians, though of no familiar tribe, and having the most singular costumes and weapons. They even went so far as to say that they could not be sure the horses were really horses.

The Indians, on the other hand, did not seem to claim the spectres as kinsfolk. They referred to them as "those people", "the old people", or "they who dwell below", and appeared to hold them in too great a frightened veneration to talk much about them. No ethnologist had been able to pin any tale-teller down to a specific description of the beings, and apparently nobody had ever had a very clear look at them. The Indians had one or two old proverbs about these phenomena, saying that "men very old, make very big spirit; not so old, not so big; older than all time, then spirit he so big he near flesh; those old people and spirits they mix up—get all the same".

Now all of this, of course, is "old stuff" to an ethnologist—of a piece with the persistent legends of rich hidden cities and buried races which abound among the Pueblo and plains Indians, and which lured Coronado centuries ago on his vain search for the fabled Quivira. What took me into western Oklahoma was something far more definite and tangible—a local and distinctive tale which, though really old, was wholly new to the outside world of research, and which involved the first clear descriptions of the ghosts which it treated of. There was an added thrill in the fact that it came from the remote town of Binger, in Caddo County, a place I had long known as the scene of a very terrible and partly inexplicable occurrence connected with the snake-god myth.

The tale, outwardly, was an extremely naive and simple one, and centred in a huge, lone mound or small hill that rose above the plain about a third of a mile west of the village—a mound which some thought a product of Nature, but which others believed to be a burial-place or ceremonial dais constructed by prehistoric tribes. This mound, the villagers said, was constantly haunted by two Indian figures which appeared in alternation; an old man who paced back and forth along the top from dawn till dusk, regardless of the weather and with only brief intervals of disappearance, and a squaw who took his place at night with a blue-flamed torch that glimmered quite continuously till morning. When the moon was bright the squaw's peculiar figure could be seen fairly plainly, and over half the villagers agreed that the apparition was headless.

Local opinion was divided as to the motives and relative ghostliness of the two visions. Some held that the man was not a ghost at all, but a living Indian who had killed and beheaded a squaw for gold and buried her somewhere on the mound. According to these theorists he was pacing the eminence through sheer remorse, bound by the spirit of his victim which took visible shape after dark. But other theorists, more uniform in their spectral beliefs, held that both man and woman were ghosts; the man having killed the squaw and himself as well at some very distant period. These and minor variant versions seemed to have been current ever since the settlement of the Wichita country in 1889, and were, I was told, sustained to an astonishing degree by still-existing phenomena which anyone might observe for himself. Not many ghost tales offer such free and open proof, and I was very eager to see what bizarre wonders might be lurking in this small, obscure village so far from the beaten path of crowds and from the ruthless searchlight of scientific knowledge. So, in the late summer of 1928 I took a train for Binger and brooded on strange mysteries as the cars rattled timidly along their single track through a lonelier and lonelier landscape.

Binger is a modest cluster of frame houses and stores in the midst of a flat windy region full of clouds of red dust. There are about 500 inhabitants besides the Indians on a neighbouring reservation; the principal occupation seeming to be agriculture. The soil is decently fertile, and the oil boom has not reached this part of the state. My train drew in at twilight, and I felt rather lost and uneasy—cut off from wholesome and every-day things—as it puffed away to the southward without me. The station platform was filled with curious loafers, all of whom seemed eager to direct me when I asked for the man to whom I had letters of introduction. I was ushered along a commonplace main street whose rutted surface was red with the sandstone soil of the country, and finally delivered at the door of my prospective host. Those who had arranged things for me had done well; for Mr. Compton was a man of high intelligence and local responsibility, while his mother—who lived with him and was familiarly known as "Grandma Compton"—was one of the first pioneer generation, and a veritable mine of anecdote and folklore.

That evening the Comptons summed up for me all the legends current among the villagers, proving that the phenomenon I had come to study was indeed a baffling and important one. The ghosts, it seems, were accepted almost as a matter of course by everyone in Binger. Two generations had been born and grown up within sight of that queer, lone tumulus and its restless figures. The neighbourhood of the mound was naturally feared and shunned, so that the village and the farms had not spread toward it in all four decades of settlement; yet venturesome individuals had several times visited it. Some had come back to report that they saw no ghosts at all when they neared the dreaded hill; that somehow the lone sentinel had stepped out of sight before they reached the spot, leaving them free to climb the steep slope and explore the flat summit. There was nothing up there, they said—merely a rough expanse of underbrush. Where the Indian watcher could have vanished to, they had no idea. He must, they reflected, have descended the slope and somehow managed to escape unseen along the plain; although there was no convenient cover within sight. At any rate, there did not appear to be any opening into the mound; a conclusion which was reached after considerable exploration of the shrubbery and tall grass on all sides. In a few cases some of the more sensitive searchers declared that they felt a sort of invisible restraining presence; but they could describe nothing more definite than that. It was simply as if the air thickened against them in the direction they wished to move. It is needless to mention that all these daring surveys were conducted by day. Nothing in the universe could have induced any human being, white or red, to approach that sinister elevation after dark; and indeed, no Indian would have thought of going near it even in the brightest sunlight.

But it was not from the tales of these sane, observant seekers that the chief terror of the ghost-mound sprang; indeed, had their experience been typical, the phenomenon would have bulked far less prominently in the local legendry. The most evil thing was the fact that many other seekers had come back strangely impaired in mind and body, or had not come back at all. The first of these cases had occurred in 1891, when a young man named Heaton had gone with a shovel to see what hidden secrets he could unearth. He had heard curious tales from the Indians, and had laughed at the barren report of another youth who had been out to the mound and had found nothing. Heaton had watched the mound with a spy glass from the village while the other youth made his trip; and as the explorer neared the spot, he saw the sentinel Indian walk deliberately down into the tumulus as if a trap-door and staircase existed on the top. The other youth had not noticed how the Indian disappeared, but had merely found him gone upon arriving at the mound.

When Heaton made his own trip he resolved to get to the bottom of the mystery, and watchers from the village saw him hacking diligently at the shrubbery atop the mound. Then they saw his figure melt slowly into invisibility; not to reappear for long hours, till after the dusk drew on, and the torch of the headless squaw glimmered ghoulishly on the distant elevation. About two hours after nightfall he staggered into the village minus his spade and other belongings, and burst into a shrieking monologue of disconnected ravings. He howled of shocking abysses and monsters, of terrible carvings and statues, of inhuman captors and grotesque tortures, and of other fantastic abnormalities too complex and chimerical even to remember. "Old! Old! Old!" he would moan over and over again, "great God, they are older than the earth, and came here from somewhere else—they know what you think, and make you know what they think—they're half-man, half-ghost—crossed the line—melt and take shape again—getting more and more so, yet we're all descended from them in the beginning—children of Tulu—everything made of gold—monstrous animals, half-human—dead slaves—madness—Iä! Shub-Niggurath!—*that white man—oh, my God, what they did to him! . . .*"

Heaton was the village idiot for about eight years, after which he died in an epileptic fit. Since his ordeal there had been two more cases of mound-madness, and eight of total disappearance. Immediately after Heaton's mad return, three desperate and determined men had gone out to the lone hill together; heavily armed, and with spades and pickaxes. Watching villagers saw the Indian ghost melt away as the explorers drew near, and afterward saw the men climb the mound and begin scouting around through the underbrush. All at once they faded into nothingness, and were never seen again. One watcher, with an especially powerful telescope, thought he saw other forms dimly materialise beside the hapless men and drag them down into the mound; but this account remained uncorroborated. It is needless to say that no searching-party went out after the lost ones, and that for many years the mound was wholly unvisited. Only when the incidents of 1891 were largely forgotten did anybody dare to think of further explorations. Then, about 1910, a fellow too young to recall the old horrors made a trip to the shunned spot and found nothing at all.

By 1915 the acute dread and wild legendry of '91 had largely faded into the commonplace and unimaginative ghost-tales at present surviving—that is, had so faded among the white people. On the nearby reservation were old Indians who thought much and kept their own counsel. About this time a second wave of active curiosity and adventuring developed, and several bold searchers made the trip to the mound and returned. Then came a trip of two Eastern visitors with spades and other apparatus—a pair of amateur archaeologists connected with a small college, who had been making studies among the Indians. No one watched this trip from the village, but they never came back. The searching-party that went out after them—among whom was my host Clyde Compton—found nothing whatsoever amiss at the mound.

The next trip was the solitary venture of old Capt. Lawton, a grizzled pioneer who had helped to open up the region in 1889, but who had never been there since. He had recalled the mound and its fascination all through the years; and being now in comfortable retirement, resolved to have a try at solving the ancient riddle. Long familiarity with Indian myth had given him ideas rather stranger than those of the simple villagers, and he had made preparations for some extensive delving. He ascended the mound on the morning of Thursday, May 11, 1916, watched through spy glasses by more than twenty people in the village and on the adjacent plain. His disappearance was very sudden, and occurred as he was hacking at the shrubbery with a brush-cutter. No one could say more than that he was there one moment and absent the next. For over a week no tidings of him reached Binger, and then—in the middle of the night—there dragged itself into the village the object about which dispute still rages.

It said it was—or had been—Capt. Lawton, but it was definitely *younger* by as much as forty years than the old man who had climbed the mound. Its hair was jet black, and its face—now distorted with nameless fright—free from wrinkles. But it did remind Grandma Compton most uncannily of the captain as he had looked back in '89. Its feet were cut off neatly at the ankles, and the stumps were smoothly healed to an extent almost incredible if the being really were the man who had walked upright a week before. It babbled of incomprehensible things, and kept repeating the name "George Lawton, George E. Lawton" as if trying to reassure itself of its own identity. The things it babbled of, Grandma Compton thought, were curiously like the hallucinations of poor young Heaton in '91; though there were minor differences. "The blue light!—the blue light! . . ." muttered the object, "always down there, before there were any living things—older than the dinosaurs—always the same, only weaker—never death—brooding and brooding and brooding—*the same people, half-man and half-gas*—the dead that walk and work—oh, those beasts, those half-human unicorns—houses and cities of gold—old, old, old, older than time

—came down from the stars—Great Tulu—Azathoth—Nyarlathotep—waiting, waiting. . . ." The object died before dawn.

Of course there was an investigation, and the Indians at the reservation were grilled unmercifully. But they knew nothing, and had nothing to say. At least, none of them had anything to say except old Grey Eagle, a Wichita chieftain whose more than a century of age put him above common fears. He alone deigned to grunt some advice.

"You let um 'lone, white man. No good—those people. All under here, all under there, them old ones. Yig, big father of snakes, he there. Yig is Yig. Tiráwa, big father of men, he there. Tiráwa is Tiráwa. No die. No get old. Just same like air. Just live and wait. One time they come out here, live and fight. Build um dirt tepee. Bring up gold—they got plenty. Go off and make new lodges. Me them. You them. Then big waters come. All change. Nobody come out, let nobody in. Get in, no get out. You let um 'lone, you have no bad medicine. Red man know, he no get catch. White man meddle, he no come back. Keep 'way little hills. No good. Grey Eagle say this."

If Joe Norton and Rance Wheelock had taken the old chief's advice, they would probably be here today; but they didn't. They were great readers and materialists, and feared nothing in heaven or earth; and they thought that some Indian fiends had a secret headquarters inside the mound. They had been to the mound before, and now they went again to avenge old Capt. Lawton—boasting that they'd do it if they had to tear the mound down altogether. Clyde Compton watched them with a pair of prism binoculars and saw them round the base of the sinister hill. Evidently they meant to survey their territory very gradually and minutely. Minutes passed, and they did not reappear. Nor were they ever seen again.

Once more the mound was a thing of panic fright, and only the excitement of the Great War served to restore it to the farther background of Binger folklore. It was unvisited from 1916 to 1919, and would have remained so but for the daredeviltry of some of the youths back from service in France. From 1919 to 1920, however, there was a veritable epidemic of mound-visiting among the prematurely hardened young veterans—an epidemic that waxed as one youth after another returned unhurt and contemptuous. By 1920—so short is human memory—the mound was almost a joke;

and the tame story of the murdered squaw began to displace darker whispers on everybody's tongues. Then two reckless young brothers —the especially unimaginative and hard-boiled Clay boys—decided to go and dig up the buried squaw and the gold for which the old Indian had murdered her.

They went out on a September afternoon—about the time the Indian tom-toms begin their incessant annual beating over the flat, red-dusty plains. Nobody watched them, and their parents did not become worried at their non-return for several hours. Then came an alarm and a searching-party, and another resignation to the mystery of silence and doubt.

But one of them came back after all. It was Ed, the elder, and his straw-coloured hair and beard had turned an albino white for two inches from the roots. On his forehead was a queer scar like a branded hieroglyph. Three months after he and his brother Walker had vanished he skulked into his house at night, wearing nothing but a queerly patterned blanket which he thrust into the fire as soon as he had got into a suit of his own clothes. He told his parents that he and Walker had been captured by some strange Indians—not Wichitas or Caddos—and held prisoners somewhere toward the west. Walker had died under torture, but he himself had managed to escape at a high cost. The experience had been particularly terrible, and he could not talk about it just then. He must rest—and anyway, it would do no good to give an alarm and try to find and punish the Indians. They were not of a sort that could be caught or punished, and it was especially important for the good of Binger—for the good of the world—that they be not pursued into their secret lair. As a matter of fact, they were not altogether what one could call real Indians—he would explain about that later. Meanwhile he must rest. Better not to rouse the village with the news of his return—he would go upstairs and sleep. Before he climbed the rickety flight to his room he took a pad and pencil from the living-room table, and an automatic pistol from his father's desk drawer.

Three hours later the shot rang out. Ed Clay had put a bullet neatly through his temples with a pistol clutched in his left hand, leaving a sparsely written sheet of paper on the rickety table near his bed. He had, it later appeared from the whittled pencil-stub and stove full of charred paper, originally written much more; but had finally decided not to tell what he knew beyond vague hints. The surviving fragment was only a mad warning scrawled in a curiously backhanded script—the ravings of a mind obviously deranged by hardships—and it read thus; rather surprisingly for the utterance of one who had always been stolid and matter-of-fact:

> For gods sake never go nere that mound it is part of some kind of a world so devilish and old it cannot be spoke about me and Walker went and was took into the thing just melted at times and made up agen and the whole world outside is helpless alongside of what they can do—they what live forever young as they like and you cant tell if they are really men or just gostes—and what they do cant be spoke about and this is only 1 entrance—you cant tell how big the whole thing is—after what we seen I dont want to live aney more France was nothing besides this—and see that people always keep away o god they wood if they see poor walker like he was in the end.
>
> Yrs truely
> Ed Clay

At the autopsy it was found that all of young Clay's organs were transposed from right to left within his body, as if he had been turned inside out. Whether they had always been so, no one could say at the time, but it was later learned from army records that Ed had been perfectly normal when mustered out of the service in May, 1919. Whether there was a mistake somewhere, or whether some unprecedented metamorphosis had indeed occurred, is still an unsettled question, as is also the origin of the hieroglyph-like scar on the forehead.

That was the end of the explorations of the mound. In the eight intervening years no one had been near the place, and few indeed had even cared to level a spy glass at it. From time to time people continued to glance nervously at the lone hill as it rose starkly from the plain against the western sky, and to shudder at the small dark speck that paraded by day and the glimmering will-o'-the-wisp that danced by night. The thing was accepted at face value as a mystery not to be probed, and by common consent the village shunned the subject. It was, after all, quite easy to avoid the hill; for space was unlimited in every direction, and community life always follows beaten trails. The mound side of the village was simply kept trail-less, as if it had been water or swampland or desert. And it is a curious commentary on the stolidity and imaginative sterility of the human animal that the whispers with which children and strangers were warned away from the mound quickly sank once more into the flat tale of a murderous Indian ghost and his squaw victim. Only the tribesmen on the reservation, and thoughtful old-timers like Grandma Compton, remembered the overtones of unholy vistas and deep cosmic menace which clustered around the ravings of those who had come back changed and shattered.

It was very late, and Grandma Compton had long since gone upstairs to bed, when Clyde finished telling me this. I hardly knew what to think of the frightful puzzle, yet rebelled at any notion to conflict with sane materialism. What influence had brought madness, or the impulse of flight and wandering, to so many who had visited the mound? Though vastly impressed, I was spurred on rather than deterred. Surely I must get to the bottom of this matter, as well I might if I kept a cool head and an unbroken determination. Compton saw my mood and shook his head worriedly. Then he motioned me to follow him outdoors.

We stepped from the frame house to the quiet side street or lane, and walked a few paces in the light of a waning August moon to where the houses were thinner. The half-moon was still low, and had not blotted many stars from the sky; so that I could see not only the westering gleams of Altair and Vega, but the mystic shimmering of the Milky Way, as I looked out over the vast expanse of earth and sky in the direction that Compton pointed. Then all at once I saw a spark that was not a star—a bluish spark that moved and glimmered against the Milky Way near the horizon, and that seemed in a vague way more evil and malevolent than anything in the vault above. In another moment it was clear that this spark came from the top of a long distant rise in the outspread and faintly litten plain; and I turned to Compton with a question.

"Yes," he answered, "it's the blue ghost-light—and that is the mound. There's not a night in history that we haven't seen it—and not a living soul in Binger that would walk out over that plain toward it. It's a bad business, young man, and if you're wise you'll let it rest where it is. Better call your search off, son, and tackle some of the other Injun legends around here. We've plenty to keep you busy, heaven knows!"

II.

But I was in no mood for advice; and though Compton gave me a pleasant room, I could not sleep a wink through eagerness for the next morning with its chances to see the daytime ghost and to question the Indians at the reservation. I meant to go about the whole thing slowly and thoroughly, equipping myself with all available data both white and red before I commenced any actual archaeological investigations. I rose and dressed at dawn, and when I heard others stirring I went downstairs. Compton was building the kitchen fire while his mother was busy in the pantry. When he saw me he nodded, and after a moment invited me out into the glamorous young sunlight. I knew where we were going, and as we walked along the lane I strained my eyes westward over the plains.

There was the mound—far away and very curious in its aspect of artificial regularity. It must have been from thirty to forty feet high, and all of a hundred yards from north to south as I looked at it. It was not as wide as that from east to west, Compton said, but had the contour of a rather thinnish ellipse. He, I knew, had been safely out to it and back several times. As I looked at the rim silhouetted against the deep blue of the west I tried to follow its minor irregularities, and became impressed with a sense of something moving upon it. My pulse mounted a bit feverishly, and I seized quickly on the high-powered binoculars which Compton had quietly offered me. Focussing them hastily, I saw at first only a tangle of underbrush on the distant mound's rim—and then something stalked into the field.

It was unmistakably a human shape, and I knew at once that I was seeing the daytime "Indian ghost". I did not wonder at the description, for surely the tall, lean, darkly robed being with the filleted black hair and seamed, coppery, expressionless, aquiline face looked more like an Indian than anything else in my previous experience. And yet my trained ethnologist's eye told me at once that this was no redskin of any sort hitherto known to history, but a creature of vast racial variation and of a wholly different culture-stream. Modern Indians are brachycephalic—round-headed—and you can't find any dolichocephalic or long-headed skulls except in ancient Pueblo deposits dating back 2500 years or more; yet this man's long-headedness was so pronounced that I recognised it at once, even at his vast distance and in the uncertain field of the binoculars. I saw, too, that the pattern of his robe represented a decorative tradition utterly remote from anything we recognise in southwestern native art. There were shining metal trappings, likewise, and a short sword or kindred weapon at his side, all wrought in a fashion wholly alien to anything I had ever heard of.

As he paced back and forth along the top of the mound I followed him for several minutes with the glass, noting the kinaesthetic quality of his stride and the poised way he carried his head; and there was borne in upon me the strong, persistent conviction that this man, whoever or whatever he might be, was certainly *not a savage.* He was the product of a *civilisation,* I felt instinctively, though of what civilisation I could not guess. At length he disappeared beyond the farther edge of the mound, as if descending the opposite and unseen slope; and I lowered the glass with a curious mixture of puzzled feelings. Compton was looking quizzically at me, and I nodded non-committally. "What do you make of that?" he ventured. "This is what we've seen here in Binger every day of our lives."

That noon found me at the Indian reservation talking with old Grey Eagle—who, through some miracle, was still alive; though he must have been close to a hundred and fifty years old. He was a strange, impressive figure—this stern, fearless leader of his kind who had talked with outlaws and traders in fringed buckskin and French officials in knee-breeches and three-cornered hats—and I was glad to see that, because of my air of deference toward him, he appeared to like me. His liking, however, took an unfortunately obstructive form as soon as he learned what I wanted; for all he would do was to warn me against the search I was about to make.

"You good boy—you no bother that hill. Bad medicine. Plenty devil under there—catchum when you dig. No dig, no hurt. Go and dig, no come back. Just same when me boy, just same when my father and he father boy. All time buck he walk in day, squaw with no head she walk in night. All time since white man with tin coats they come from sunset and below big river—long way back—three, four times more back than Grey Eagle—two times more back than Frenchmen—all same after then. More back than that, nobody go near little hills nor deep valleys with stone caves. Still more back, those old ones no hide, come out and make villages. Bring plenty gold. Me them. You them. Then big waters come. All change. Nobody come out, let nobody in. Get in, no get out. They no die—no get old like Grey Eagle with valleys in face and snow on head. Just same like air—some man, some spirit. Bad medicine. Sometimes at night spirit come out on half-man–half-horse-with-horn and fight where men once fight. Keep 'way them place. No good. You good boy—go 'way and let them old ones 'lone."

That was all I could get out of the ancient chief, and the rest of the Indians would say nothing at all. But if I was troubled, Grey Eagle was clearly more so; for he obviously felt a real regret at the thought of my invading the region he feared so abjectly. As I turned to leave the reservation he stopped me for a final ceremonial farewell, and once more tried to get my promise to abandon my search. When he saw that he could not, he produced something half-timidly from a buckskin pouch he wore, and extended it toward me very solemnly. It was a worn but finely minted metal disc about two inches in diameter, oddly figured and perforated, and suspended from a leathern cord.

"You no promise, then Grey Eagle no can tell what get you. But if anything help um, this good medicine. Come from my father—he get from he father—he get from he father—all way back, close to Tiráwa, all men's father. My father say, 'You keep 'way from those old ones, keep 'way from little hills and valleys with stone caves. But if old ones they come out to get you, then you shew um this medicine. They know. They make him long way back. They look, then they no do such bad medicine maybe. But no can tell. You keep 'way, just same. Them no good. No tell what they do.'"

As he spoke, Grey Eagle was hanging the thing around my neck, and I saw it was a very curious object indeed. The more I looked at it, the more I marvelled; for not only was its heavy, darkish, lustrous, and richly mottled substance an absolutely strange metal to me, but what was left of its design seemed to be of a marvellously artistic and utterly unknown workmanship. One side, so far as I could see, had borne an exquisitely modelled serpent design; whilst the other side had depicted a kind of octopus or other tentacled monster. There were some half-effaced hieroglyphs, too, of a kind which no archaeologist could identify or even place conjecturally. With Grey Eagle's permission I later had expert historians, anthropologists, geologists, and chemists pass carefully upon the disc, but from them I obtained only a chorus of bafflement. It defied either classification or analysis. The chemists called it an amalgam of unknown metallic elements of heavy atomic weight, and one geologist suggested that the substance must be of meteoric origin, shot from unknown gulfs of interstellar space. Whether it really saved my life or sanity or existence as a human being I cannot attempt to say, but Grey Eagle is sure of it. He has it again, now, and I wonder if it has any connexion with his inordinate age. All his fathers who had it lived far beyond the century mark, perishing only in battle. Is it possible that Grey Eagle, if kept from accidents, will *never die?* But I am ahead of my story.

When I returned to the village I tried to secure more mound-lore, but found only excited gossip and opposition. It was really flattering to see how solicitous the people were about my safety, but I had to set their almost frantic remonstrances aside. I shewed them Grey Eagle's charm, but none of them had ever heard of it before, or seen anything even remotely like it. They agreed that it could not be an Indian relic, and imagined that the old chief's ancestors must have obtained it from some trader.

When they saw they could not deter me from my trip, the Binger citizens sadly did what they could to aid my outfitting. Having known before my arrival the sort of work to be done, I had most of my supplies already with me—machete and trench-knife for shrub-clearing and excavating, electric torches for any underground phase which might develop, rope, field-glasses, tape-measure, microscope, and incidentals for emergencies—as much, in fact, as might be comfortably stowed in a convenient handbag. To this equipment I added only the heavy revolver which the sheriff forced upon me, and the pick and shovel which I thought might expedite my work.

I decided to carry these latter things slung over my shoulder with a stout cord—for I soon saw that I could not hope for any helpers or fellow-explorers. The village would watch me, no doubt, with all its available telescopes and field-glasses; but it would not send any citizen so much as a yard over the flat plain toward the lone hillock. My start was timed for early the next morning, and all the rest of that day I was treated with the awed and uneasy respect which people give to a man about to set out for certain doom.

When morning came—a cloudy though not a threatening morning—the whole village turned out to see me start across the dust-blown plain. Binoculars shewed the lone man at his usual pacing on the mound, and I resolved to keep him in sight as steadily as possible during my approach. At the last moment a vague sense of dread oppressed me, and I was just weak and whimsical enough to let Grey Eagle's talisman swing on my chest in full view of any beings or ghosts who might be inclined to heed it. Bidding au revoir to Compton and his mother, I started off at a brisk stride despite the bag in my left hand and the clanking pick and shovel strapped to my back; holding my field-glass in my right hand and taking a glance at the silent pacer from time to time. As I neared the mound I saw the man very clearly, and fancied I could trace an expression of infinite evil and decadence on his seamed, hairless features. I was startled, too, to see that his goldenly gleaming weapon-case bore hieroglyphs very similar to those on the unknown talisman I wore. All the creature's costume and trappings bespoke exquisite workmanship and cultivation. Then, all too abruptly, I saw him start down the farther side of the mound and out of sight. When I reached the place, about ten minutes after I set out, there was no one there.

There is no need of relating how I spent the early part of my search in surveying and circumnavigating the mound, taking measurements, and stepping back to view the thing from different angles. It had impressed me tremendously as I approached it, and there seemed to be a kind of latent menace in its too regular outlines. It was the only elevation of any sort on the wide, level plain; and I could not doubt for a moment that it was an artificial tumulus. The steep sides seemed wholly unbroken, and without marks of human tenancy or passage. There were no signs of a path toward the top; and, burdened as I was, I managed to scramble up only with considerable difficulty. When I reached the summit I found a roughly level elliptical plateau about 300 by 50 feet in dimensions; uniformly covered with rank grass and dense underbrush, and utterly incompatible with the constant presence of a pacing sentinel. This condition gave me a real shock, for it shewed beyond question that the "Old Indian", vivid though he seemed, could not be other than a collective hallucination.

I looked about with considerable perplexity and alarm, glancing wistfully back at the village and the mass of black dots which I knew was the watching crowd. Training my glass upon them, I saw that they were studying me avidly with their glasses; so to reassure them I waved my cap in the air with a show of jauntiness which I was far from feeling. Then, settling to my work I flung down pick, shovel, and bag; taking my machete from the latter and commencing to clear away underbrush. It was a weary task, and now and then I felt a curious shiver as some perverse gust of wind arose to hamper my motion with a skill approaching deliberateness. At times it seemed as if a half-tangible force were pushing me back as I worked—almost as if the air thickened in front of me, or as if formless hands tugged at my wrists. My energy seemed used up without producing adequate results, yet for all that I made some progress.

By afternoon I had clearly perceived that, toward the northern end of the mound, there was a slight bowl-like depression in the root-tangled earth. While this might mean nothing, it would be a good place to begin when I reached the digging stage, and I made a mental note of it. At the same time I noticed another and very peculiar thing—namely, that the Indian talisman swinging from my neck seemed to behave oddly at a point about seventeen feet southeast of the suggested bowl. Its gyrations were altered whenever I happened to stoop around that point, and it tugged downward as if attracted by some magnetism in the soil. The more I noticed this, the more it struck me, till at length I decided to do a little preliminary digging there without further delay.

As I turned up the soil with my trench-knife I could not help wondering at the relative thinness of the reddish regional layer. The country as a whole was all red sandstone earth, but here I found a strange black loam less than a foot down. It was such soil as one finds in the strange, deep valleys farther west and south, and must surely have been brought from a considerable distance in the prehistoric age when the mound was reared. Kneeling and digging, I felt the leathern cord around my neck tugged harder and harder, as something in the soil seemed to draw the heavy metal talisman more and more. Then I felt my implements strike a hard surface, and wondered if a rock layer rested beneath. Prying about with the trench-knife, I found that such was not the case. Instead, to my intense surprise and feverish interest, I brought up a mould-clogged, heavy object of cylindrical shape—about a foot long and four inches in diameter—to which my hanging talisman clove with glue-like tenacity. As I cleared off the black loam my wonder and tension increased at the bas-reliefs revealed by that process. The whole cylinder, ends and all, was covered with figures and hieroglyphs; and I saw with growing excitement that these things were in the same unknown tradition as those on Grey Eagle's charm and on the yellow metal trappings of the ghost I had seen through my binoculars.

Sitting down, I further cleaned the magnetic cylinder against the rough corduroy of my knickerbockers, and observed that it was made of the same heavy, lustrous unknown metal as the charm—hence, no doubt, the singular attraction. The carvings and chasings were very strange and very horrible—nameless monsters and designs fraught with insidious evil—and all were of the highest finish and craftsmanship. I could not at first make head or tail of the thing, and handled it aimlessly until I spied a cleavage near one end. Then I sought eagerly for some mode of opening, discovering at last that the end simply unscrewed.

The cap yielded with difficulty, but at last it came off, liberating a curious aromatic odour. The sole contents was a bulky roll of a yellowish, paper-like substance inscribed in greenish characters, and for a second I had the supreme thrill of fancying that I held a written key to unknown elder worlds and abysses beyond time. Almost immediately, however, the unrolling of one end shewed that the manuscript was in Spanish—albeit the formal, pompous Spanish of a long-departed day. In the golden sunset light I looked at the heading and the opening paragraph, trying to decipher the wretched and ill-punctuated script of the vanished writer. What manner of relic was this? Upon what sort of a discovery had I stumbled? The first words set me in a new fury of excitement and curiosity, for instead of diverting me from my original quest they startlingly confirmed me in that very effort.

The yellow scroll with the green script began with a bold, identifying caption and a ceremoniously desperate appeal for belief in incredible revelations to follow:

> RELACIÓN DE PÁNFILO DE ZAMACONA
> Y NUÑEZ, HIDALGO DE LUARCA EN
> ASTURIAS, TOCANTE AL MUNDO SOTERRÁNEO
> DE XINAIÁN, A. D. MDXLV

> En el nombre de la santísima Trinidad, Padre, Hijo, y Espíritu-Santo, tres personas distintas y un solo. Dios verdadero, y de la santísima Virgen muestra Señora, YO, PÁNFILO DE ZAMACONA, HIJO DE PEDRO GUZMAN Y ZAMACONA, HIDALGO, Y DE LA DOÑA YNÉS ALVARADO Y NUÑEZ, DE LUARCA EN ASTURIAS, juro para que todo que deco está verdadero como sacramento. . . .

I paused to reflect on the portentous significance of what I was reading. "The Narrative of Pánfilo de Zamacona y Nuñez, gentleman, of Luarca in Asturias, *Concerning the Subterranean World of Xinaián, A. D. 1545*" . . . Here, surely, was too much for any mind to absorb all at once. A subterranean world—again that persistent idea which filtered through all the Indian tales and through all the utterances of those who had come back from the mound. And the date—1545—what could this mean? In 1540 Coronado and his men had gone north from Mexico into the wilderness, but had they not turned back in 1542? My eye ran questingly down the opened part of the scroll, and almost at once seized on the name *Francisco Vásquez de Coronado*. The writer of this thing, clearly, was one of Coronado's men—but what had he been doing in this remote realm three years after his party had gone back? I must read further, for another glance told me that what was now unrolled was merely a summary of Coronado's northward march, differing in no essential way from the account known to history.

It was only the waning light which checked me before I could unroll and read more, and in my impatient bafflement I almost forgot to be frightened at the onrush of night in this sinister place. Others, however, had not forgotten the lurking terror, for I heard a loud distant hallooing from a knot of men who had gathered at the edge of the town. Answering the anxious hail, I restored the manuscript to its strange cylinder—to which the disc around my neck still clung until I pried it off and packed it and my smaller implements for departure. Leaving the pick and shovel for the next day's work, I took up my handbag, scrambled down the steep side of the mound, and in another quarter-hour was back in the village explaining and exhibiting my curious find. As darkness drew on, I glanced back at the mound I had so lately left, and saw with a shudder that the faint bluish torch of the nocturnal squaw-ghost had begun to glimmer.

It was hard work waiting to get at the bygone Spaniard's narrative; but I knew I must have quiet and leisure for a good translation, so reluctantly saved the task for the later hours of night. Promising the townsfolk a clear account of my findings in the morning, and giving them an ample opportunity to examine the bizarre and provocative cylinder, I accompanied Clyde Compton home and ascended to my room for the translating process as soon as I possibly could. My host and his mother were intensely eager to hear the tale, but I thought they had better wait till I could thoroughly absorb the text myself and give them the gist concisely and unerringly.

Opening my handbag in the light of a single electric bulb, I again took out the cylinder and noted the instant magnetism which pulled the Indian talisman to its carven surface. The designs glimmered evilly on the richly lustrous and unknown metal, and I could not help shivering as I studied the abnormal and blasphemous forms that leered at me with such exquisite workmanship. I wish now that I had carefully photographed all these designs—though perhaps it is just as well that I did not. Of one thing I am really glad, and that is that I could not then identify the squatting octopus-headed thing which dominated most of the ornate cartouches, and which the manuscript called "Tulu". Recently I have associated it, and the legends in the manuscript connected with it, with some new-found folklore of monstrous and unmentioned Cthulhu, a horror which seeped down from the stars while the young earth was still half-formed; and had I known of the connexion then, I could not have stayed in the same room with the thing. The secondary motif, a semi-anthropomorphic serpent, I did quite readily place as a prototype of the Yig, Quetzalcoatl, and Kukulcan conceptions. Before opening the cylinder I tested its magnetic powers on metals other than that of Grey Eagle's disc, but found that no attraction existed. It was no common magnetism which pervaded this morbid fragment of unknown worlds and linked it to its kind.

At last I took out the manuscript and began translating—jotting down a synoptic outline in English as I went, and now and then regretting the absence of a Spanish dictionary when I came upon some especially obscure or archaic word or construction. There was a sense of ineffable strangeness in thus being thrown back nearly four centuries in the midst of my continuous quest—thrown back to a year when my own forbears were settled, homekeeping gentlemen of Somerset and Devon under Henry the Eighth, with never a thought of the adventure that was to take their blood to Virginia and the New World; yet when that new world possessed, even as now, the same brooding mystery of the mound which formed my present sphere and horizon. The sense of a throwback was all the stronger because I felt instinctively that the common problem of the Spaniard and myself was one of such abysmal timelessness—of such unholy and unearthly eternity—that the scant four hundred years between us bulked as nothing in comparison. It took no more than a single look at that monstrous and insidious cylinder to make me realise the dizzying gulfs that yawned between all men of the known earth and the primal mysteries it represented. Before that gulf Pánfilo de Zamacona and I stood side by side; just as Aristotle and I, or Cheops and I, might have stood.

III.

Of his youth in Luarca, a small, placid port on the Bay of Biscay, Zamacona told little. He had been wild, and a younger son, and had come to New Spain in 1532, when only twenty years old. Sensitively imaginative, he had listened spellbound to the floating rumours of rich cities and unknown worlds to the north—and especially to the tale of the Franciscan friar Marcos de Niza, who came back from a trip in 1539 with glowing accounts of fabulous

Cíbola and its great walled towns with terraced stone houses. Hearing of Coronado's contemplated expedition in search of these wonders—and of the greater wonders whispered to lie beyond them in the land of buffaloes—young Zamacona managed to join the picked party of 300, and started north with the rest in 1540.

History knows the story of that expedition—how Cíbola was found to be merely the squalid Pueblo village of Zuñi, and how de Niza was sent back to Mexico in disgrace for his florid exaggerations; how Coronado first saw the Grand Canyon, and how at Cicuyé, on the Pecos, he heard from the Indian called El Turco of the rich and mysterious land of Quivira, far to the northeast, where gold, silver, and buffaloes abounded, and where there flowed a river two leagues wide. Zamacona told briefly of the winter camp at Tiguex on the Pecos, and of the northward start in April, when the native guide proved false and led the party astray amidst a land of prairie-dogs, salt pools, and roving, bison-hunting tribes.

When Coronado dismissed his larger force and made his final forty-two-day march with a very small and select detachment, Zamacona managed to be included in the advancing party. He spoke of the fertile country and of the great ravines with trees visible only from the edge of their steep banks; and of how all the men lived solely on buffalo-meat. And then came mention of the expedition's farthest limit—of the presumable but disappointing land of Quivira with its villages of grass houses, its brooks and rivers, its good black soil, its plums, nuts, grapes, and mulberries, and its maize-growing and copper-using Indians. The execution of El Turco, the false native guide, was casually touched upon, and there was a mention of the cross which Coronado raised on the bank of a great river in the autumn of 1541—a cross bearing the inscription, "Thus far came the great general, Francisco Vásquez de Coronado".

This supposed Quivira lay at about the fortieth parallel of north latitude, and I see that quite lately the New York archaeologist Dr. Hodge has identified it with the course of the Arkansas River through Barton and Rice Counties, Kansas. It is the old home of the Wichitas, before the Sioux drove them south into what is now Oklahoma, and some of the grass-house village sites have been found and excavated for artifacts. Coronado did considerable exploring hereabouts, led hither and thither by the persistent rumours of rich cities and hidden worlds which floated fearfully around on the Indians' tongues. These northerly natives seemed more afraid and reluctant to talk about the rumoured cities and worlds than the

Mexican Indians had been; yet at the same time seemed as if they could reveal a good deal more than the Mexicans had they been willing or dared to do so. Their vagueness exasperated the Spanish leader, and after many disappointing searches he began to be very severe toward those who brought him stories. Zamacona, more patient than Coronado, found the tales especially interesting; and learned enough of the local speech to hold long conversations with a young buck named Charging Buffalo, whose curiosity had led him into much stranger places than any of his fellow-tribesmen had dared to penetrate.

It was Charging Buffalo who told Zamacona of the queer stone doorways, gates, or cave-mouths at the bottom of some of those deep, steep, wooded ravines which the party had noticed on the northward march. These openings, he said, were mostly concealed by shrubbery; and few had entered them for untold aeons. Those who went to where they led, never returned—or in a few cases returned mad or curiously maimed. But all this was legend, for nobody was known to have gone more than a limited distance inside any of them within the memory of the grandfathers of the oldest living men. Charging Buffalo himself had probably been farther than anyone else, and he had seen enough to curb both his curiosity and his greed for the rumoured gold below.

Beyond the aperture he had entered there was a long passage running crazily up and down and round about, and covered with frightful carvings of monsters and horrors that no man had ever seen. At last, after untold miles of windings and descents, there was a glow of terrible blue light; and the passage opened upon a shocking nether world. About this the Indian would say no more, for he had seen something that had sent him back in haste. But the golden cities must be somewhere down there, he added, and perhaps a white man with the magic of the thunder-stick might succeed in getting to them. He would not tell the big chief Coronado what he knew, for Coronado would not listen to Indian talk any more. Yes—he could shew Zamacona the way if the white man would leave the party and accept his guidance. But he would not go inside the opening with the white man. It was bad in there.

The place was about a five days' march to the south, near the region of great mounds. These mounds had something to do with the evil world down there—they were probably ancient closed-up passages to it, for once the Old Ones below had had colonies on the surface and had traded with men everywhere, even in the lands that had sunk under the big waters. It was when those lands had sunk that the Old Ones closed themselves up below and refused to deal with surface people. The refugees from the sinking places had told them that the gods of outer earth were against men, and that no men could survive on the outer earth unless they were daemons in league with the evil gods. That is why they shut out all surface folk, and did fearful things to any who ventured down where they dwelt. There had been sentries once at the various openings, but after ages they were no longer needed. Not many people cared to talk about the hidden Old Ones, and the legends about them would probably have died out but for certain ghostly reminders of their presence now and then. It seemed that the infinite ancientness of these creatures had brought them strangely near to the borderline of spirit, so that their ghostly emanations were more commonly frequent and vivid. Accordingly the region of the great mounds was often convulsed with spectral nocturnal battles reflecting those which had been fought in the days before the openings were closed.

The Old Ones themselves were half-ghost—indeed, it was said that they no longer grew old or reproduced their kind, but flickered eternally in a state between flesh and spirit. The change was not complete, though, for they had to breathe. It was because the underground world needed air that the openings in the deep valleys were not blocked up as the mound-openings on the plains had been. These openings, Charging Buffalo added, were probably based on natural fissures in the earth. It was whispered that the Old Ones had come down from the stars to the world when it was very young, and had gone inside to build their cities of solid gold because the surface was not then fit to live on. They were the ancestors of all men, yet none could guess from what star—or what place beyond the stars—they came. Their hidden cities were still full of gold and silver, but men had better let them alone unless protected by very strong magic.

They had frightful beasts with a faint strain of human blood, on which they rode, and which they employed for other purposes. The things, so people hinted, were carnivorous, and like their masters, preferred human flesh; so that although the Old Ones themselves did not breed, they had a sort of half-human slave-class which also served to nourish the human and animal population. This had been very oddly recruited, and was supplemented by a second slave-class of reanimated corpses. The Old Ones knew how to make a corpse into an automaton which would last almost indefinitely and perform any sort of work when directed by streams of thought. Charging Buffalo said that the people had all come to talk by means of thought only; speech having been found crude and needless, except for religious devotions and emotional expression, as aeons of discovery and study rolled by. They worshipped Yig, the great father of serpents, and Tulu, the octopus-headed entity that had brought them down from the stars; appeasing both of these hideous monstrosities by means of human sacrifices offered up in a very curious manner which Charging Buffalo did not care to describe.

Zamacona was held spellbound by the Indian's tale, and at once resolved to accept his guidance to the cryptic doorway in the ravine. He did not believe the accounts of strange ways attributed by legend to the hidden people, for the experiences of the party had been such as to disillusion one regarding native myths of unknown lands; but he did feel that some sufficiently marvellous field of riches and adventure must indeed lie beyond the weirdly carved passages in the earth. At first he thought of persuading Charging Buffalo to tell his story to Coronado—offering to shield him against any effects of the leader's testy scepticism—but later he decided that a lone adventure would be better. If he had no aid, he would not have to share anything he found; but might perhaps become a great discoverer and owner of fabulous riches. Success would make him a greater figure than Coronado himself—perhaps a greater figure than anyone else in New Spain, including even the mighty viceroy Don Antonio de Mendoza.

On October 7, 1541, at an hour close to midnight, Zamacona stole out of the Spanish camp near the grass-house village and met Charging Buffalo for the long southward journey. He travelled as lightly as possible, and did not wear his heavy helmet and breastplate. Of the details of the trip the manuscript told very little, but Zamacona records his arrival at the great ravine on October 13th. The descent of the thickly wooded slope took no great time; and though the Indian had trouble in locating the shrubbery-hidden stone door again amidst the twilight of that deep gorge, the place was finally found. It was a very small aperture as doorways go, formed of monolithic sandstone jambs and lintel, and bearing signs of nearly effaced and now undecipherable carvings. Its height was perhaps seven feet, and its width not more than four. There were drilled places in the jambs which argued the bygone presence of a hinged door or gate, but all other traces of such a thing had long since vanished.

At sight of this black gulf Charging Buffalo displayed considerable fear, and threw down his pack of supplies with signs of haste. He had provided Zamacona with a good stock of resinous torches and provisions, and had guided him honestly and well; but refused to share in the venture that lay ahead. Zamacona gave him the trinkets he had kept for such an occasion, and obtained his promise to return to the region in a month; afterward shewing the way southward to the Pecos Pueblo villages. A prominent rock on the plain above them was chosen as a meeting-place; the one arriving first to pitch camp until the other should arrive.

In the manuscript Zamacona expressed a wistful wonder as to the Indian's length of waiting at the rendezvous—for he himself could never keep that tryst. At the last moment Charging Buffalo tried to dissuade him from his plunge into the darkness, but soon saw it was futile, and gestured a stoical farewell. Before lighting his first torch and entering the opening with his ponderous pack, the Spaniard watched the lean form of the Indian scrambling hastily and rather relievedly upward among the trees. It was the cutting of his last link with the world; though he did not know that he was never to see a human being—in the accepted sense of that term—again.

Zamacona felt no immediate premonition of evil upon entering that ominous doorway, though from the first he was surrounded by a bizarre and unwholesome atmosphere. The passage, slightly taller and wider than the aperture, was for many yards a level tunnel of Cyclopean masonry, with heavily worn flagstones under foot, and grotesquely carved granite and sandstone blocks in sides and ceiling. The carvings must have been loathsome and terrible indeed, to judge from Zamacona's description; according to which most of them revolved around the monstrous beings Yig and Tulu. They were unlike anything the adventurer had ever seen before, though he added that the native architecture of Mexico came closest to them of all things in the outer world. After some distance the tunnel began to dip abruptly, and irregular natural rock appeared on all sides. The passage seemed only partly artificial, and decorations were limited to occasional cartouches with shocking bas-reliefs.

Following an enormous descent, whose steepness at times produced an acute danger of slipping and tobogganing, the passage became exceedingly uncertain in its direction and variable in its contour. At times it narrowed almost to a slit or grew so low that stooping and even crawling were necessary, while at other times it broadened out into sizeable caves or chains of caves. Very little human construction, it was plain, had gone into this part of the tunnel; though occasionally a sinister cartouche or hieroglyphic on the wall, or a blocked-up lateral passageway, would remind Zamacona that this was in truth the aeon-forgotten high-road to a primal and unbelievable world of living things.

For three days, as best he could reckon, Pánfilo de Zamacona scrambled down, up, along, and around, but always predominately downward, through this dark region of palaeogean night. Once in a while he heard some secret being of darkness patter or flap out of his way, and on just one occasion he half glimpsed a great, bleached thing that set him trembling. The quality of the air was mostly very tolerable; though foetid zones were now and then met with, while one great cavern of stalactites and stalagmites afforded a depressing dampness. This latter, when Charging Buffalo had come upon it, had quite seriously barred the way; since the limestone deposits of ages had built fresh pillars in the path of the primordial abyss-denizens. The Indian, however, had broken through these; so that Zamacona did not find his course impeded. It was an unconscious comfort to him to reflect that someone else from the outside world had been there before—and the Indian's careful descriptions had removed the element of surprise and unexpectedness. More—Charging Buffalo's knowledge of the tunnel had led him to provide so good a torch supply for the journey in and out, that there would be no danger of becoming stranded in darkness. Zamacona camped twice, building a fire whose smoke seemed well taken care of by the natural ventilation.

At what he considered the end of the third day—though his cocksure guesswork chronology is not at any time to be given the easy faith that he gave it—Zamacona encountered the prodigious descent and subsequent prodigious climb which Charging Buffalo had described as the tunnel's last phase. As at certain earlier points, marks of artificial improvement were here discernible; and several times the steep gradient was eased by a flight of rough-hewn steps. The torch shewed more and more of the monstrous carvings on the walls, and finally the resinous flare seemed mixed with a fainter and more diffusive light as Zamacona climbed up and up after the last downward stairway. At length the ascent ceased, and a level passage of artificial masonry with dark, basaltic blocks led straight ahead. There was no need for a torch now, for all the air was glowing with a bluish, quasi-electric radiance that flickered like an aurora. It was the strange light of the inner world that the Indian had described—and in another moment Zamacona emerged from the tunnel upon a bleak, rocky hillside which climbed above him to a seething, impenetrable sky of bluish coruscations, and descended dizzily below him to an apparently illimitable plain shrouded in bluish mist.

He had come to the unknown world at last, and from his manuscript it is clear that he viewed the formless landscape as proudly and exaltedly as ever his fellow-countryman Balboa viewed the new-found Pacific from that unforgettable peak in Darien. Charging Buffalo had turned back at this point, driven by fear of something which he would only describe vaguely and evasively as a herd of bad cattle, neither horse nor buffalo, but like the things the mound-spirits rode at night—but Zamacona could not be deterred by any such trifle. Instead of fear, a strange sense of glory filled him; for he had imagination enough to know what it meant to stand alone in an inexplicable nether world whose existence no other white man suspected.

The soil of the great hill that surged upward behind him and spread steeply downward below him was dark grey, rock-strown, without vegetation, and probably basaltic in origin; with an unearthly cast which made him feel like an intruder on an alien planet. The vast distant plain, thousands of feet below, had no features he could distinguish; especially since it appeared to be largely veiled in a curling, bluish vapour. But more than hill or plain or cloud, the bluely luminous, coruscating sky impressed the adventurer with a sense of supreme wonder and mystery. What created this sky within a world he could not tell; though he knew of the northern lights, and had even seen them once or twice. He concluded that this subterraneous light was something vaguely akin to the aurora; a view which moderns may well endorse, though it seems likely that certain phenomena of radio-activity may also enter in.

At Zamacona's back the mouth of the tunnel he had traversed yawned darkly; defined by a stone doorway very like the one he had entered in the world above, save that it was of greyish-black basalt instead of red sandstone. There were hideous sculptures, still in good preservation and perhaps corresponding to those on the outer portal which time had largely weathered away. The absence of weathering here argued a dry, temperate climate; indeed, the Spaniard already began to note the delightfully spring-like stability of temperature which marks the air of the north's interior. On the stone jambs were works proclaiming the bygone presence of hinges, but of any actual door or gate no trace remained. Seating himself for rest and thought, Zamacona lightened his pack by removing an amount of food and torches sufficient to take him back through the tunnel. These he proceeded to cache at the opening, under a cairn hastily formed of the rock fragments which everywhere lay around. Then, readjusting his lightened pack, he commenced his descent toward the distant plain; preparing to invade a region which no living thing of outer earth had penetrated in a century or more, which no white man had ever penetrated, and from which, if legend were to be believed, no organic creature had ever returned sane.

Zamacona strode briskly along down the steep, interminable slope; his progress checked at times by the bad walking that came from loose rock fragments, or by the excessive precipitousness of the grade. The distance of the mist-shrouded plain must have been enormous, for many hours' walking brought him apparently no closer to it than he had been before. Behind him was always the great hill stretching upward into a bright aërial sea of bluish coruscations. Silence was universal; so that his own footsteps, and the fall of stones that he dislodged, struck on his ears with startling distinctness. It was at what he regarded as about noon that he first saw the abnormal footprints which set him to thinking of Charging Buffalo's terrible hints, precipitate flight, and strangely abiding terror.

The rock-strown nature of the soil gave few opportunities for tracks of any kind, but at one point a rather level interval had caused the loose detritus to accumulate in a ridge, leaving a considerable area of dark-grey loam absolutely bare. Here, in a rambling confusion indicating a large herd aimlessly wandering, Zamacona found the abnormal prints. It is to be regretted that he could not describe them more exactly, but the manuscript displayed far more vague fear than accurate observation. Just what it was that so frightened the Spaniard can only be inferred from his later hints regarding the beasts. He referred to the prints as 'not hooves, nor hands, nor feet, nor precisely paws—nor so large as to cause alarm on that account'. Just why or how long ago the things had been there, was not easy to guess. There was no vegetation visible, hence grazing was out of the question; but of course if the beasts were carnivorous they might well have been hunting smaller animals, whose tracks their own would tend to obliterate.

Glancing backward from this plateau to the heights above, Zamacona thought he detected traces of a great winding road which had once led from the tunnel downward to the plain. One could get the impression of this former highway only from a broad panoramic view, since a trickle of loose rock fragments had long ago obscured it; but the adventurer felt none the less certain that it had existed. It had not, probably, been an elaborately paved trunk route; for the small tunnel it reached seemed scarcely like a main avenue to the outer world. In choosing a straight path of descent Zamacona had not followed its curving course, though he must have crossed it once or twice. With his attention now called to it, he looked ahead to see if he could trace it downward toward the plain; and this he finally thought he could do. He resolved to investigate its surface when next he crossed it, and perhaps to pursue its line for the rest of the way if he could distinguish it.

Having resumed his journey, Zamacona came some time later upon what he thought was a bend of the ancient road. There were signs of grading and of some primal attempt at rock-surfacing, but not enough was left to make the route worth following. While rummaging about in the soil with his sword, the Spaniard turned up something that glittered in the eternal blue daylight, and was thrilled at beholding a kind of coin or medal of a dark, unknown, lustrous metal, with hideous designs on each side. It was utterly and bafflingly alien to him, and from his description I have no doubt but that it was a duplicate of the talisman given me by Grey Eagle almost four centuries afterward. Pocketing it after a long and curious examination, he strode onward; finally pitching camp at an hour which he guessed to be the evening of the outer world.

The next day Zamacona rose early and resumed his descent through this blue-litten world of mist and desolation and preternatural silence. As he advanced, he at last became able to distinguish a few objects on the distant plain below—trees, bushes, rocks, and a small river that came into view from the right and curved forward at a point to the left of his contemplated course. This river seemed to be spanned by a bridge connected with the descending roadway, and with care the explorer could trace the route of the road beyond it in a straight line over the plain. Finally he even thought he could detect towns scattered along the rectilinear ribbon; towns whose left-hand edges reached the river and sometimes crossed it. Where such crossings occurred, he saw as he descended, there were always signs of bridges either ruined or surviving. He was now in the midst of a sparse grassy vegetation, and saw that below him the growth became thicker and thicker. The road was easier to define now, since its surface discouraged the grass which the looser soil supported. Rock fragments were less frequent, and the barren upward vista behind him looked bleak and forbidding in contrast to his present milieu.

It was on this day that he saw the blurred mass moving over the distant plain. Since his first sight of the sinister footprints he had met with no more of these, but something about that slowly and deliberately moving mass peculiarly sickened him. Nothing but a herd of grazing animals could move just like that, and after seeing the footprints he did not wish to meet the things which had made them. Still, the moving mass was not near the road—and his curiosity and greed for fabled gold were great. Besides, who could really judge things from vague, jumbled footprints or from the panic-twisted hints of an ignorant Indian?

In straining his eyes to view the moving mass Zamacona became aware of several other interesting things. One was that certain parts of the now unmistakable towns glittered oddly in the misty blue light. Another was that, besides the towns, several similarly glittering structures of a more isolated sort were scattered here and there along the road and over the plain. They seemed to be embowered in clumps of vegetation, and those off the road had small avenues leading to the highway. No smoke or other signs of life could be discerned about any of the towns or buildings. Finally Zamacona saw that the plain was not infinite in extent, though the half-concealing blue mists had hitherto made it seem so. It was bounded in the remote distance by a range of low hills, toward a gap in which the river and roadway seemed to lead. All this—especially the glittering of certain pinnacles in the towns—had become very vivid when Zamacona pitched his second camp amidst the endless blue day. He likewise noticed the flocks of high-soaring birds, whose nature he could not clearly make out.

The next afternoon—to use the language of the outer world as the manuscript did at all times—Zamacona reached the silent plain and crossed the soundless, slow-running river on a curiously carved and fairly well-preserved bridge of black basalt. The water was clear, and contained large fishes of a wholly strange aspect. The roadway was now paved and somewhat overgrown with weeds and creeping vines, and its course was occasionally outlined by small pillars bearing obscure symbols. On every side the grassy level extended, with here and there a clump of trees or shrubbery, and with unidentifiable bluish flowers growing irregularly over the whole area. Now and then some spasmodic motion of the grass indicated the presence of serpents. In the course of several hours the traveller reached a grove of old and alien-looking evergreen-trees which he knew, from distant viewing, protected one of the glittering-roofed isolated structures. Amidst the encroaching vegetation he saw the hideously sculptured pylons of a stone gateway leading off the road, and was presently forcing his way through briers above a moss-crusted tessellated walk lined with huge trees and low monolithic pillars.

At last, in this hushed green twilight, he saw the crumbling and ineffably ancient facade of the building—a temple, he had no doubt. It was a mass of nauseous bas-reliefs; depicting scenes and beings, objects and ceremonies, which could certainly have no place on this or any sane planet. In hinting of these things Zamacona displays for the first time that shocked and pious hesitancy which impairs the informative value of the rest of his manuscript. We cannot help regretting that the Catholic ardour of Renaissance Spain had so thoroughly permeated his thought and feeling. The door of the place stood wide open, and absolute darkness filled the windowless interior. Conquering the repulsion which the mural sculptures had excited, Zamacona took out flint and steel, lighted a resinous torch, pushed aside curtaining vines, and sallied boldly across the ominous threshold.

For a moment he was quite stupefied by what he saw. It was not the all-covering dust and cobwebs of immemorial aeons, the fluttering winged things, the shriekingly loathsome sculptures on the walls, the bizarre form of the many basins and braziers, the sinister pyramidal altar with the hollow top, or the monstrous, octopus-headed abnormality in some strange, dark metal leering and squatting broodingly on its hieroglyphed pedestal, which robbed him of even the power to give a startled cry. It was nothing so unearthly as this—but merely the fact that, with the exception of the dust, the cobwebs, the winged things, and the gigantic emerald-eyed idol, every particle of substance in sight was composed of pure and evidently solid gold.

Even the manuscript, written in retrospect after Zamacona knew that gold is the most common structural metal of a nether world containing limitless lodes and veins of it, reflects the frenzied excitement which the traveller felt upon suddenly finding the real source of all the Indian legends of golden cities. For a time the power of detailed observation left him, but in the end his faculties were recalled by a peculiar tugging sensation in the pocket of his doublet. Tracing the feeling, he realised that the disc of strange metal he had found in the abandoned road was being attracted strongly by the vast octopus-headed, emerald-eyed idol on the pedestal, which he now saw to be composed of the same unknown exotic metal. He was later to learn that this strange magnetic substance—as alien to the inner world as to the outer world of men—is the one precious metal of the blue-lighted abyss. None knows what it is or where it occurs in Nature, and the amount of it on this planet came down from the stars with the people when great Tulu, the octopus-headed god, brought them for the first time to this earth. Certainly, its only known source was a stock of pre-existing artifacts, including multitudes of Cyclopean idols. It could never be placed or analysed, and even its magnetism was exerted only on its own kind. It was the supreme ceremonial metal of the hidden people, its use being regulated by custom in such a way that its magnetic properties might cause no inconvenience. A very weakly magnetic alloy of it with such base metals as iron, gold, silver, copper, or zinc, had formed the sole monetary standard of the hidden people at one period of their history.

Zamacona's reflections on the strange idol and its magnetism were disturbed by a tremendous wave of fear as, for the first time in this silent world, he heard a rumble of very definite and obviously approaching sound. There was no mistaking its nature. It was a thunderously charging herd of large animals; and, remembering the Indian's panic, the footprints, and the moving mass distantly seen, the Spaniard shuddered in terrified anticipation. He did not analyse his position, or the significance of this onrush of great lumbering beings, but merely responded to an elemental urge toward self-protection. Charging herds do not stop to find victims in obscure places, and on the outer earth Zamacona would have felt little or no alarm in such a massive, grove-girt edifice. Some instinct, however, now bred a deep and peculiar terror in his soul; and he looked about frantically for any means of safety.

There being no available refuge in the great, gold-patined interior, he felt that he must close the long-disused door; which still hung on its ancient hinges, doubled back against the inner wall. Soil, vines, and moss had entered the opening from outside, so that he had to dig a path for the great gold portal with his sword; but he managed to perform this work very swiftly under the frightful stimulus of the approaching noise. The hoofbeats had grown still louder and more menacing by the time he began tugging at the heavy door itself; and for a while his fears reached a frantic height, as hope of starting the age-clogged metal grew faint. Then, with a creak, the thing responded to his youthful strength, and a frenzied siege of pulling and pushing ensued. Amidst the roar of unseen stampeding feet success came at last, and the ponderous golden door clanged shut, leaving Zamacona in darkness but for the single lighted torch he had wedged between the pillars of a basin-tripod. There was a latch, and the frightened man blessed his patron saint that it was still effective.

Sound alone told the fugitive the sequel. When the roar grew very near it resolved itself into separate footfalls, as if the evergreen grove had made it necessary for the herd to slacken speed and disperse. But feet continued to approach, and it became evident that the beasts were advancing among the trees and circling the hideously carven temple walls. In the curious deliberation of their tread Zamacona found something very alarming and repulsive, nor did he like the scuffling sounds which were audible even through the thick stone walls and heavy golden door. Once the door rattled ominously on its archaic hinges, as if under a heavy impact, but fortunately it still held. Then, after a seemingly endless interval, he heard retreating steps and realised that his unknown visitors were leaving. Since the herds did not seem to be very numerous, it would have perhaps been safe to venture out within a half-hour or less; but Zamacona took no chances. Opening his pack, he prepared his camp on the golden tiles of the temple's floor, with the great door still securely latched against all comers; drifting eventually into a sounder sleep than he could have known in the blue-litten spaces outside. He did not even mind the hellish, octopus-headed bulk of great Tulu, fashioned of unknown metal and leering with fishy, sea-green eyes, which squatted in the blackness above him on its monstrously hieroglyphed pedestal.

Surrounded by darkness for the first time since leaving the tunnel, Zamacona slept profoundly and long. He must have more than made up the sleep he had lost at his two previous camps, when the ceaseless glare of the sky had kept him awake despite his fatigue, for much distance was covered by other living feet while he lay in his healthily dreamless rest. It is well that he rested deeply, for there were many strange things to be encountered in his next period of consciousness.

IV.

What finally roused Zamacona was a thunderous rapping at the door. It beat through his dreams and dissolved all the lingering mists of drowsiness as soon as he knew what it was. There could be no mistake about it—it was a definite, human, and peremptory rapping; performed apparently with some metallic object, and with all the measured quality of conscious thought or will behind it. As the awakening man rose clumsily to his feet, a sharp vocal note was added to the summons—someone calling out, in a not unmusical voice, a formula which the manuscript tries to represent as *"oxi, oxi, giathcán ycá relex"*. Feeling sure that his visitors were men and not daemons, and arguing that they could have no reason for considering him an enemy, Zamacona decided to face them openly and at once; and accordingly fumbled with the ancient latch till the golden door creaked open from the pressure of those outside.

As the great portal swung back, Zamacona stood facing a group of about twenty individuals of an aspect not calculated to give him alarm. They seemed to be Indians; though their tasteful robes and trappings and swords were not such as he had seen among any of the tribes of the outer world, while their faces had many subtle differences from the Indian type. That they did not mean to be irresponsibly hostile, was very clear; for instead of menacing him in any way they merely probed him attentively and significantly with their eyes, as if they expected their gaze to open up some sort of communication. The longer they gazed, the more he seemed to know about them and their mission; for although no one had spoken since the vocal summons before the opening of the door, he found himself slowly realising that they had come from the great city beyond the low hills, mounted on animals, and that they had been summoned by animals who had reported his presence; that they were not sure what kind of person he was or just where he had come from, but that they knew he must be associated with that dimly remembered outer world which they sometimes visited in curious dreams. How he read all this in the gaze of the two or three leaders he could not possibly explain; though he learned why a moment later.

As it was, he attempted to address his visitors in the Wichita dialect he had picked up from Charging Buffalo; and after this failed to draw a vocal reply he successively tried the Aztec, Spanish, French, and Latin tongues—adding as many scraps of lame Greek, Galician, and Portuguese, and of the Bable peasant patois of his native Asturias, as his memory could recall. But not even this polyglot array—his entire linguistic stock—could bring a reply in kind. When, however, he paused in perplexity, one of the visitors began speaking in an utterly strange and rather fascinating language whose sounds the Spaniard later had much difficulty in representing on paper. Upon his failure to understand this, the speaker pointed first to his own eyes, then to his forehead, and then to his eyes again, as if commanding the other to gaze at him in order to absorb what he wanted to transmit.

Zamacona, obeying, found himself rapidly in possession of certain information. The people, he learned, conversed nowadays by means of unvocal radiations of thought; although they had formerly used a spoken language which still survived as the written tongue, and into which they still dropped orally for tradition's sake, or when strong feeling demanded a spontaneous outlet. He could understand them merely by concentrating his attention upon their eyes; and could reply by summoning up a mental image of what he wished to say, and throwing the substance of this into his glance. When the thought-speaker paused, apparently inviting a response, Zamacona tried his best to follow the prescribed pattern, but did not appear to succeed very well. So he nodded, and tried to describe himself and his journey by signs. He pointed upward, as if to the outer world, then closed his eyes and made signs as of a mole burrowing. Then he opened his eyes again and pointed downward, in order to indicate his descent of the great slope. Experimentally he blended a spoken word or two with his gestures—for example, pointing successively to himself and to all of his visitors and saying *"un hombre"*, and then pointing to himself alone and very carefully pronouncing his individual name, *Pánfilo de Zamacona*.

Before the strange conversation was over, a good deal of data had passed in both directions. Zamacona had begun to learn how to throw his thoughts, and had likewise picked up several words of the region's archaic spoken language. His visitors, moreover, had absorbed many beginnings of an elementary Spanish vocabulary. Their own old language was utterly unlike anything the Spaniard had ever heard, though there were times later on when he was to fancy an infinitely remote linkage with the Aztec, as if the latter represented some far stage of corruption, or some very thin infiltration of loan-words. The underground world, Zamacona learned, bore an ancient name which the manuscript records as *"Xinaián"*, but which, from the writer's supplementary explanations and diacritical marks, could probably be best represented to Anglo-Saxon ears by the phonetic arrangement *K'n-yan.*

It is not surprising that this preliminary discourse did not go beyond the merest essentials, but those essentials were highly important. Zamacona learned that the people of K'n-yan were almost infinitely ancient, and that they had come from a distant part of space where physical conditions are much like those of the earth. All this, of course, was legend now; and one could not say how much truth was in it, or how much worship was really due to the octopus-headed being Tulu who had traditionally brought them hither and whom they still reverenced for aesthetic reasons. But they knew of the outer world, and were indeed the original stock who had peopled it as soon as its crust was fit to live on. Between glacial ages they had had some remarkable surface civilisations, especially one at the South Pole near the mountain Kadath.

At some time infinitely in the past most of the outer world had sunk beneath the ocean, so that only a few refugees remained to bear the news to K'n-yan. This was undoubtedly due to the wrath of space-devils hostile alike to men and to men's gods—for it bore out rumours of a primordially earlier sinking which had submerged the gods themselves, including great Tulu, who still lay prisoned and dreaming in the watery vaults of the half-cosmic city Relex. No man not a slave of the space-devils, it was argued, could live long on the outer earth; and it was decided that all beings who remained there must be evilly connected. Accordingly traffic with the lands of sun and starlight abruptly ceased. The subterraneous approaches to K'n-yan, or such as could be remembered, were either blocked up or carefully guarded; and all encroachers were treated as dangerous spies and enemies.

But this was long ago. With the passing of ages fewer and fewer visitors came to K'n-yan, and eventually sentries ceased to be maintained at the unblocked approaches. The mass of the people forgot, except through distorted memories and myths and some very singular dreams, that an outer world existed; though educated folk never ceased to recall the essential facts. The last visitors ever recorded—centuries in the past—had not even been treated as devil-spies; faith in the old legendry having long before died out. They had been questioned eagerly about the fabulous outer regions; for scientific curiosity in K'n-yan was keen, and the myths, memories, dreams, and historical fragments relating to the earth's surface had often tempted scholars to the brink of an external expedition which they had not quite dared to attempt. The only thing demanded of such visitors was that they refrain from going back and informing the outer world of K'n-yan's positive existence; for after all, one could not be sure about these outer lands. They coveted gold and silver, and might prove highly troublesome intruders. Those who had obeyed the injunction had lived happily, though regrettably briefly, and had told all they could about their world—little enough, however, since their accounts were all so fragmentary and conflicting that one could hardly tell what to believe and what to doubt. One wished that more of them would come. As for those who disobeyed and tried to escape—it was very unfortunate about them. Zamacona himself was very welcome, for he appeared to be a higher-grade man, and to know much more about the outer world, than anyone else who had come down within memory. He could tell them much—and they hoped he would be reconciled to his life-long stay.

Many things which Zamacona learned about K'n-yan in that first colloquy left him quite breathless. He learned, for instance, that during the past few thousand years the phenomena of old age and death had been conquered; so that men no longer grew feeble or died except through violence or will. By regulating the system, one might be as physiologically young and immortal as he wished; and the only reason why any allowed themselves to age, was that they enjoyed the sensation in a world where stagnation and commonplaceness reigned. They could easily become young again when they felt like it. Births had ceased, except for experimental purposes, since a large population had been found needless by a master-race which controlled Nature and organic rivals alike. Many, however, chose to die after a while; since despite the cleverest efforts to invent new pleasures, the ordeal of consciousness became too dull for sensitive souls—especially those in whom time and satiation had blinded the primal instincts and emotions of self-preservation. All the members of the group before Zamacona were from 500 to 1500 years old; and several had seen surface visitors before, though time had blurred the recollection. These visitors, by the way, had often tried to duplicate the longevity of the underground race; but had been able to do so only fractionally, owing to evolutionary differences developing during the million or two years of cleavage.

These evolutionary differences were even more strikingly shewn in another particular—one far stranger than the wonder of immortality itself. This was the ability of the people of K'n-yan to regulate the balance between matter and abstract energy, even where the bodies of living organic beings were concerned, by the sheer force of the technically trained will. In other words, with suitable effort a learned man of K'n-yan could dematerialise and rematerialise himself—or, with somewhat greater effort and subtler technique, any other object he chose; reducing solid matter to free external particles and recombining the particles again without damage. Had not Zamacona answered his visitors' knock when he did, he would have discovered this accomplishment in a highly puzzling way; for only the strain and bother of the process prevented the twenty men from passing bodily through the golden door without pausing for a summons. This art was much older than the art of perpetual life; and it could be taught to some extent, though never perfectly, to any intelligent person. Rumours of it had reached the outer world in past aeons; surviving in secret traditions and ghostly legendry. The men of K'n-yan had been amused by the primitive and imperfect spirit tales brought down by outer-world stragglers. In practical life this principle had certain industrial applications, but was generally suffered to remain neglected through lack of any particular incentive to its use. Its chief surviving form was in connexion with sleep, when for excitement's sake many dream-connoisseurs resorted to it to enhance the vividness of their visionary wanderings. By the aid of this method certain dreamers even paid half-material visits to a strange, nebulous realm of mounds and valleys and varying light which some believed to be the forgotten outer world. They would go thither on their beasts, and in an age of peace live over the old, glorious battles of their forefathers. Some philosophers thought that in such cases they actually coalesced with immaterial forces left behind by these warlike ancestors themselves.

The people of K'n-yan all dwelt in the great, tall city of Tsath beyond the mountains. Formerly several races of them had inhabited the entire underground world, which stretched down to unfathomable abysses and which included besides the blue-litten region a red-litten region called Yoth, where relics of a still older and non-human race were found by archaeologists. In the course of time, however, the men of Tsath had conquered and enslaved the rest; interbreeding them with certain horned and four-footed animals of the red-litten region, whose semi-human leanings were very peculiar, and which, though containing a certain artificially created element, may have been in part the degenerate descendants of those peculiar entities who had left the relics. As aeons passed, and mechanical discoveries made the business of life extremely easy, a concentration of the people of Tsath took place; so that all the rest of K'n-yan became relatively deserted.

It was easier to live in one place, and there was no object in maintaining a population of overflowing proportions. Many of the old mechanical devices were still in use, though others had been abandoned when it was seen that they failed to give pleasure, or that they were not necessary for a race of reduced numbers whose mental force could govern an extensive array of inferior and semi-human industrial organisms. This extensive slave-class was highly composite, being bred from ancient conquered enemies, from outer-world stragglers, from dead bodies curiously galvanised into effectiveness, and from the naturally inferior members of the ruling race of Tsath. The ruling type itself had become highly superior through selective breeding and social evolution—the nation having passed through a period of idealistic industrial democracy which gave equal opportunities to all, and thus, by raising the naturally intelligent to power, drained the masses of all their brains and stamina. Industry, being found fundamentally futile except for the supplying of basic needs and the gratification of inescapable yearnings, had become very simple. Physical comfort was ensured by an urban mechanisation of standardised and easily maintained pattern, and other elemental needs were supplied by scientific agriculture and stock-raising. Long travel was abandoned, and people went back to using the horned, half-human beasts instead of maintaining the profusion of gold, silver, and steel transportation machines which had once threaded land, water, and air. Zamacona could scarcely believe that such things had ever existed outside dreams, but was told he could see specimens of them in museums. He could also see the ruins of other vast magical devices by travelling a day's journey to the valley of Do-Hna, to which the race had spread during its period of greatest numbers. The cities and temples of this present plain were of a far more archaic period, and had never been other than religious and antiquarian shrines during the supremacy of the men of Tsath.

In government, Tsath was a kind of communistic or semi-anarchical state; habit rather than law determining the daily order of things. This was made possible by the age-old experience and paralysing ennui of the race, whose wants and needs were limited to physical fundamentals and to new sensations. An aeon-long tolerance not yet undermined by growing reaction had abolished all illusions of values and principles, and nothing but an approximation to custom was ever sought or expected. To see that the mutual encroachments of pleasure-seeking never crippled the mass life of the community—this was all that was desired. Family organisation had long ago perished, and the civil and social distinction of the sexes had disappeared. Daily life was organised in ceremonial patterns; with games, intoxication, torture of slaves, day-dreaming, gastronomic and emotional orgies, religious exercises, exotic experiments, artistic and philosophical discussions, and the like, as the principal occupations. Property—chiefly land, slaves, animals, shares in the common city enterprise of Tsath, and ingots of magnetic Tulu-metal, the former universal money standard—was allocated on a very complex basis which included a certain amount equally divided among all the freemen. Poverty was unknown, and labour consisted only of certain administrative duties imposed by an intricate system of testing and selection. Zamacona found difficulty in describing conditions so unlike anything he had previously known; and the text of his manuscript proved unusually puzzling at this point.

Art and intellect, it appeared, had reached very high levels in Tsath; but had become listless and decadent. The dominance of machinery had at one time broken up the growth of normal aesthetics, introducing a lifelessly geometrical tradition fatal to sound expression. This had soon been outgrown, but had left its mark upon all pictorial and decorative attempts; so that except for conventionalised religious designs, there was little depth or feeling in any later work. Archaistic reproductions of earlier work had been found much preferable for general enjoyment. Literature was all highly individual and analytical, so much so as to be wholly incomprehensible to Zamacona. Science had been profound and accurate, and all-embracing save in the one direction of astronomy. Of late, however, it was falling into decay, as people found it increasingly useless to tax their minds by recalling its maddening infinitude of details and ramifications. It was thought more sensible to abandon the deepest speculations and to confine philosophy to conventional forms. Technology, of course, could be carried on by rule of thumb. History was more and more neglected, but exact and copious chronicles of the past existed in the libraries. It was still an interesting subject, and there would be a vast number to rejoice at the fresh outer-world knowledge brought in by Zamacona. In general, though, the modern tendency was to feel rather than to think; so that men were now more highly esteemed for inventing new diversions than for preserving old facts or pushing back the frontier of cosmic mystery.

Religion was a leading interest in Tsath, though very few actually believed in the supernatural. What was desired was the aesthetic and emotional exaltation bred by the mystical moods and sensuous rites which attended the colourful ancestral faith. Temples to Great Tulu, a spirit of universal harmony anciently symbolised as the octopus-headed god who had brought all men down from the stars, were the most richly constructed objects in all K'n-yan; while the cryptic shrines of Yig, the principle of life symbolised as the Father of all Serpents, were almost as lavish and remarkable. In time Zamacona learned much of the orgies and sacrifices connected with this religion, but seemed piously reluctant to describe them in his manuscript. He himself never participated in any of the rites save those which he mistook for perversions of his own faith; nor did he ever lose an opportunity to try to convert the people to that faith of the Cross which the Spaniards hoped to make universal.

Prominent in the contemporary religion of Tsath was a revived and almost genuine veneration for the rare, sacred metal of Tulu—that dark, lustrous, magnetic stuff which was nowhere found in Nature, but which had always been with men in the form of idols and hieratic implements. From the earliest times any sight of it in its unalloyed form had impelled respect, while all the sacred archives and litanies were kept in cylinders wrought of its purest substance. Now, as the neglect of science and intellect was dulling the critically analytical spirit, people were beginning to weave around the metal once more that same fabric of awestruck superstition which had existed in primitive times.

Another function of religion was the regulation of the calendar, born of a period when time and speed were regarded as prime fetiches in man's emotional life. Periods of alternate waking and sleeping, prolonged, abridged, and inverted as mood and convenience dictated, and timed by the tail-beats of Great Yig, the Serpent, corresponded very roughly to terrestrial days and nights; though Zamacona's sensations told him they must actually be almost twice as long. The year-unit, measured by Yig's annual shedding of his skin, was equal to about a year and a half of the outer world. Zamacona thought he had mastered this calendar very well when he wrote his manuscript, whence the confidently given date of 1545; but the document failed to suggest that his assurance in this matter was fully justified.

As the spokesman of the Tsath party proceeded with his information, Zamacona felt a growing repulsion and alarm. It was not only what was told, but the strange, telepathic manner of telling, and the plain inference that return to the outer world would be impossible, that made the Spaniard wish he had never descended to this region of magic, abnormality, and decadence. But he knew that nothing but friendly acquiescence would do as a policy, hence decided to coöperate in all his visitors' plans and furnish all the information they might desire. They, on their part, were fascinated by the outer-world data which he managed haltingly to convey.

It was really the first draught of reliable surface information they had had since the refugees straggled back from Atlantis and Lemuria aeons before, for all their subsequent emissaries from outside had been members of narrow and local groups without any knowledge of the world at large—Mayas, Toltecs, and Aztecs at best, and mostly ignorant tribes of the plains. Zamacona was the first European they had ever seen, and the fact that he was a youth of education and brilliancy made him of still more emphatic value as a source of knowledge. The visiting party shewed their breathless interest in all he contrived to convey, and it was plain that his coming would do much to relieve the flagging interest of weary Tsath in matters of geography and history.

The only thing which seemed to displease the men of Tsath was the fact that curious and adventurous strangers were beginning to pour into those parts of the upper world where the passages to K'n-yan lay. Zamacona told them of the founding of Florida and New Spain, and made it clear that a great part of the world was stirring with the zest of adventure—Spanish, Portuguese, French, and English. Sooner or later Mexico and Florida must meet in one great colonial empire—and then it would be hard to keep outsiders from the rumoured gold and silver of the abyss. Charging Buffalo knew of Zamacona's journey into the earth. Would he tell Coronado, or somehow let a report get to the great viceroy, when he failed to find the traveller at the promised meeting-place? Alarm for the continued secrecy and safety of K'n-yan shewed in the faces of the visitors, and Zamacona absorbed from their minds the fact that from now on sentries would undoubtedly be posted once more at all the unblocked passages to the outside world which the men of Tsath could remember.

V.

The long conversation of Zamacona and his visitors took place in the green-blue twilight of the grove just outside the temple door. Some of the men reclined on the weeds and moss beside the half-vanished walk, while others, including the Spaniard and the chief spokesman of the Tsath party, sat on the occasional low monolithic pillars that lined the temple approach. Almost a whole terrestrial day must have been consumed in the colloquy, for Zamacona felt the need of food several times, and ate from his well-stocked pack while some of the Tsath party went back for provisions to the roadway, where they had left the animals on which they had ridden. At length the prime leader of the party brought the discourse to a close, and indicated that the time had come to proceed to the city.

There were, he affirmed, several extra beasts in the cavalcade, upon one of which Zamacona could ride. The prospect of mounting one of those ominous hybrid entities whose fabled nourishment was so alarming, and a single sight of which had set Charging Buffalo into such a frenzy of flight, was by no means reassuring to the traveller. There was, moreover, another point about the things which disturbed him greatly—the apparently preternatural intelligence with which some members of the previous day's roving pack had reported his presence to the men of Tsath and brought out the present expedition. But Zamacona was not a coward, hence followed the men boldly down the weed-grown walk toward the road where the things were stationed.

And yet he could not refrain from crying out in terror at what he saw when he passed through the great vine-draped pylons and emerged upon the ancient road. He did not wonder that the curious Wichita had fled in panic, and had to close his eyes a moment to retain his sanity. It is unfortunate that some sense of pious reticence prevented him from describing fully in his manuscript the nameless sight he saw. As it is, he merely hinted at the shocking morbidity of these great floundering white things, with black fur on their backs, a rudimentary horn in the centre of their foreheads, and an unmistakable trace of human or anthropoid blood in their flat-nosed, bulging-lipped faces. They were, he declared later in his manuscript, the most terrible objective entities he ever saw in his life, either in K'n-yan or in the outer world. And the specific quality of their supreme terror was something apart from any easily recognisable or describable feature. The main trouble was that they were not wholly products of Nature.

The party observed Zamacona's fright, and hastened to reassure him as much as possible. The beasts or *gyaa-yothn,* they explained, surely were curious things; but were really very harmless. The flesh they ate was not that of intelligent people of the master-race, but merely that of a special slave-class which had for the most part ceased to be thoroughly human, and which indeed was the principal meat stock of K'n-yan. They—or their principal ancestral element—had first been found in a wild state amidst the Cyclopean ruins of the deserted red-litten world of Yoth which lay below the blue-litten world of K'n-yan. That part of them was human, seemed quite clear; but men of science could never decide whether they were actually the descendants of the bygone entities who had lived and reigned in the strange ruins. The chief ground for such a supposition was the well-known fact that the vanished inhabitants of Yoth had been quadrupedal. This much was known from the very few manuscripts and carvings found in the vaults of Zin, beneath the largest ruined city of Yoth. But it was also known from these manuscripts that the beings of Yoth had possessed the art of synthetically creating life, and had made and destroyed several efficiently designed races of industrial and transportational animals in the course of their history—to say nothing of concocting all manner of fantastic living shapes for the sake of amusement and new sensations during the long period of decadence. The beings of Yoth had undoubtedly been reptilian in affiliations, and most physiologists of Tsath agreed that the present beasts had been very much inclined toward reptilianism before they had been crossed with the mammal slave-class of K'n-yan.

It argues well for the intrepid fire of those Renaissance Spaniards who conquered half the unknown world, that Pánfilo de Zamacona y Nuñez actually mounted one of the morbid beasts of Tsath and fell into place beside the leader of the cavalcade—the man named

Gll'-Hthaa-Ynn, who had been most active in the previous exchange of information. It was a repulsive business; but after all, the seat was very easy, and the gait of the clumsy *gyaa-yoth* surprisingly even and regular. No saddle was necessary, and the animal appeared to require no guidance whatever. The procession moved forward at a brisk gait, stopping only at certain abandoned cities and temples about which Zamacona was curious, and which Gll'-Hthaa-Ynn was obligingly ready to display and explain. The largest of these towns, B'graa, was a marvel of finely wrought gold, and Zamacona studied the curiously ornate architecture with avid interest. Buildings tended toward height and slenderness, with roofs bursting into a multitude of pinnacles. The streets were narrow, curving, and occasionally picturesquely hilly, but Gll'-Hthaa-Ynn said that the later cities of K'n-yan were far more spacious and regular in design. All these old cities of the plain shewed traces of levelled walls—reminders of the archaic days when they had been successively conquered by the now dispersed armies of Tsath.

There was one object along the route which Gll'-Hthaa-Ynn exhibited on his own initiative, even though it involved a detour of about a mile along a vine-tangled side path. This was a squat, plain temple of black basalt blocks without a single carving, and containing only a vacant onyx pedestal. The remarkable thing about it was its story, for it was a link with a fabled elder world compared to which even cryptic Yoth was a thing of yesterday. It had been built in imitation of certain temples depicted in the vaults of Zin, to house a very terrible black toad-idol found in the red-litten world and called Tsathoggua in the Yothic manuscripts. It had been a potent and widely worshipped god, and after its adoption by the people of K'n-yan had lent its name to the city which was later to become dominant in that region. Yothic legend said that it had come from a mysterious inner realm beneath the red-litten world—a black realm of peculiar-sensed beings which had no light at all, but which had had great civilisations and mighty gods before ever the reptilian quadrupeds of Yoth had come into being. Many images of Tsathoggua existed in Yoth, all of which were alleged to have come from the black inner realm, and which were supposed by Yothic archaeologists to represent the aeon-extinct race of that realm. The black realm called N'kai in the Yothic manuscripts had been explored as thoroughly as possible by these archaeologists, and singular stone troughs or burrows had excited infinite speculation.

When the men of K'n-yan discovered the red-litten world and deciphered its strange manuscripts, they took over the Tsathoggua cult and brought all the frightful toad images up to the land of blue light—housing them in shrines of Yoth-quarried basalt like the one Zamacona now saw. The cult flourished until it almost rivalled the ancient cults of Yig and Tulu, and one branch of the race even took it to the outer world, where the smallest of the images eventually found a shrine at Olathoë, in the land of Lomar near the earth's north pole. It was rumoured that this outer-world cult survived even after the great ice-sheet and the hairy Gnophkehs destroyed Lomar, but of such matters not much was definitely known in K'n-yan. In that world of blue light the cult came to an abrupt end, even though the name of Tsath was suffered to remain.

What ended the cult was the partial exploration of the black realm of N'kai beneath the red-litten world of Yoth. According to the Yothic manuscripts, there was no surviving life in N'kai, but something must have happened in the aeons between the days of Yoth and the coming of men to the earth; something perhaps not unconnected with the end of Yoth. Probably it had been an earthquake, opening up lower chambers of the lightless world which had been closed against the Yothic archaeologists; or perhaps some more frightful juxtaposition of energy and electrons, wholly inconceivable to any sort of vertebrate minds, had taken place. At any rate, when the men of K'n-yan went down into N'kai's black abyss with their great atom-power searchlights they found living things—living things that oozed along stone channels and worshipped onyx and basalt images of Tsathoggua. But they were not toads like Tsathoggua himself. Far worse—they were amorphous lumps of viscous black slime that took temporary shapes for various purposes. The explorers of K'n-yan did not pause for detailed observations, and those who escaped alive sealed the passage leading from red-litten Yoth down into the gulfs of nether horror. Then all the images of Tsathoggua in the land of K'n-yan were dissolved into the ether by disintegrating rays, and the cult was abolished forever.

Aeons later, when naive fears were outgrown and supplanted by scientific curiosity, the old legends of Tsathoggua and N'kai were recalled, and a suitably armed and equipped exploring party went down to Yoth to find the closed gate of the black abyss and see what might still lie beneath. But they could not find the gate, nor could any man ever do so in all the ages that followed. Nowadays there were those who doubted that any abyss had ever existed, but the few scholars who could still decipher the Yothic manuscripts believed that the evidence for such a thing was adequate, even though the middle records of K'n-yan, with accounts of the one frightful expedition into N'kai, were more open to question. Some of the later religious cults tried to suppress remembrance of N'kai's existence, and attached severe penalties to its mention; but these had not begun to be taken seriously at the time of Zamacona's advent to K'n-yan.

As the cavalcade returned to the old highway and approached the low range of mountains, Zamacona saw that the river was very close on the left. Somewhat later, as the terrain rose, the stream entered a gorge and passed through the hills, while the road traversed the gap at a rather higher level close to the brink. It was about this time that light rainfall came. Zamacona noticed the occasional drops and drizzle, and looked up at the coruscating blue air, but there was no diminution of the strange radiance. Gll'-Hthaa-Ynn then told him that such condensations and precipitations of water-vapour were not uncommon, and that they never dimmed the glare of the vault above. A kind of mist, indeed, always hung about the lowlands of K'n-yan, and compensated for the complete absence of true clouds.

The slight rise of the mountain pass enabled Zamacona, by looking behind, to see the ancient and deserted plain in panorama as he had seen it from the other side. He seems to have appreciated its strange beauty, and to have vaguely regretted leaving it; for he speaks of being urged by Gll'-Hthaa-Ynn to drive his beast more rapidly. When he faced frontward again he saw that the crest of the road was very near; the weed-grown way leading starkly up and ending against a blank void of blue light. The scene was undoubtedly highly impressive—a steep green mountain wall on the right, a deep river-chasm on the left with another green mountain wall beyond it, and ahead, the churning sea of bluish coruscations into which the upward path dissolved. Then came the crest itself, and with it the world of Tsath outspread in a stupendous forward vista.

Zamacona caught his breath at the great sweep of peopled landscape, for it was a hive of settlement and activity beyond anything he had ever seen or dreamed of. The downward slope of the hill itself was relatively thinly strown with small farms and occasional temples; but beyond it lay an enormous plain covered like a chessboard with planted trees, irrigated by narrow canals cut from the river, and threaded by wide, geometrically precise roads of gold or basalt blocks. Great silver cables borne aloft on golden pillars linked the low, spreading buildings and clusters of buildings which rose here and there, and in some places one could see lines of partly ruinous pillars without cables. Moving objects shewed the fields to be under tillage, and in some cases Zamacona saw that men were ploughing with the aid of the repulsive, half-human quadrupeds.

But most impressive of all was the bewildering vision of clustered spires and pinnacles which rose afar off across the plain and shimmered flower-like and spectral in the coruscating blue light. At first Zamacona thought it was a mountain covered with houses and temples, like some of the picturesque hill cities of his own Spain, but a second glance shewed him that it was not indeed such. It was a city of the plain, but fashioned of such heaven-reaching towers that its outline was truly that of a mountain. Above it hung a curious greyish haze, through which the blue light glistened and took added overtones of radiance from the million golden minarets. Glancing at Gll'-Hthaa-Ynn, Zamacona knew that this was the monstrous, gigantic, and omnipotent city of Tsath.

As the road turned downward toward the plain, Zamacona felt a kind of uneasiness and sense of evil. He did not like the beast he rode, or the world that could provide such a beast, and he did not like the atmosphere that brooded over the distant city of Tsath. When the cavalcade began to pass occasional farms, the Spaniard noticed the forms that worked in the fields; and did not like their motions and proportions, or the mutilations he saw on most of them. Moreover, he did not like the way that some of these forms were herded in corrals, or the way they grazed on the heavy verdure. Gll'-Hthaa-Ynn indicated that these beings were members of the slave-class, and that their acts were controlled by the master of the farm, who gave them hypnotic impressions in the morning of all they were to do during the day. As semi-conscious machines, their industrial efficiency was nearly perfect. Those in the corrals were inferior specimens, classified merely as livestock.

Upon reaching the plain, Zamacona saw the larger farms and noted the almost human work performed by the repulsive horned *gyaa-yothn*. He likewise observed the more manlike shapes that toiled along the furrows, and felt a curious fright and disgust toward certain of them whose motions were more mechanical than those of the rest. These, Gll'-Hthaa-Ynn explained, were what men called the *y'm-bhi*—organisms which had died, but which had been mechanically reanimated for industrial purposes by means of atomic energy and thought-power. The slave-class did not share the immortality of the freemen of Tsath, so that with time the number of *y'm-bhi* had become very large. They were dog-like and faithful, but not so readily amenable to thought-commands as were living slaves. Those which most repelled Zamacona were those whose mutilations were greatest; for some were wholly headless, while others had suffered singular and seemingly capricious subtractions, distortions, transpositions, and graftings in various places. The Spaniard could not account for this condition, but Gll'-Hthaa-Ynn made it clear that these were slaves who had been used for the amusement of the people in some of the vast arenas; for the men of Tsath were connoisseurs of delicate sensation, and required a constant supply of fresh and novel stimuli for their jaded impulses. Zamacona, though by no means squeamish, was not favourably impressed by what he saw and heard.

Approached more closely, the vast metropolis became dimly horrible in its monstrous extent and inhuman height. Gll'-Hthaa-Ynn explained that the upper parts of the great towers were no longer used, and that many had been taken down to avoid the bother of maintenance. The plain around the original urban area was covered with newer and smaller dwellings, which in many cases were preferred to the ancient towers. From the whole mass of gold and stone a monotonous roar of activity droned outward over the plain, while cavalcades and streams of wagons were constantly entering and leaving over the great gold- or stone-paved roads.

Several times Gll'-Hthaa-Ynn paused to shew Zamacona some particular object of interest, especially the temples of Yig, Tulu, Nug, Yeb, and the Not-to-Be-Named One which lined the road at infrequent intervals, each in its embowering grove according to the custom of K'n-yan. These temples, unlike those of the deserted plain beyond the mountains, were still in active use; large parties of mounted worshippers coming and going in constant streams. Gll'-Hthaa-Ynn took Zamacona into each of them, and the Spaniard watched the subtle orgiastic rites with fascination and repulsion. The ceremonies of Nug and Yeb sickened him especially—so much, indeed, that he refrained from describing them in his manuscript. One squat, black temple of Tsathoggua was encountered, but it had been turned into a shrine of Shub-Niggurath, the All-Mother and wife of the Not-to-Be-Named One. This deity was a kind of sophisticated Astarte, and her worship struck the pious Catholic as supremely obnoxious. What he liked least of all were the emotional sounds emitted by the celebrants—jarring sounds in a race that had ceased to use vocal speech for ordinary purposes.

Close to the compact outskirts of Tsath, and well within the shadow of its terrifying towers, Gll'-Hthaa-Ynn pointed out a monstrous circular building before which enormous crowds were lined up. This, he indicated, was one of the many amphitheatres where curious sports and sensations were provided for the weary people of K'n-yan. He was about to pause and usher Zamacona inside the vast curved facade, when the Spaniard, recalling the mutilated forms he had seen in the fields, violently demurred. This was the first of those friendly clashes of taste which were to convince the people of Tsath that their guest followed strange and narrow standards.

Tsath itself was a network of strange and ancient streets; and despite a growing sense of horror and alienage, Zamacona was enthralled by its intimations of mystery and cosmic wonder. The dizzy giganticism of its overawing towers, the monstrous surge of teeming life through its ornate avenues, the curious carvings on its doorways and windows, the odd vistas glimpsed from balustraded plazas and tiers of titan terraces, and the enveloping grey haze which seemed to press down on the gorge-like streets in low ceiling-fashion, all combined to produce such a sense of adventurous expectancy as he had never known before. He was taken at once to a council of executives which held forth in a gold-and-copper palace behind a gardened and fountained park, and was for some time subjected to close, friendly questioning in a vaulted hall frescoed with vertiginous arabesques. Much was expected of him, he could see, in the way of historical information about the outside earth; but in return all the mysteries of K'n-yan would be unveiled to him. The one great drawback was the inexorable ruling that he might never return to the world of sun and stars and Spain which was his.

A daily programme was laid down for the visitor, with time apportioned judiciously among several kinds of activities. There were to be conversations with persons of learning in various places, and lessons in many branches of Tsathic lore. Liberal periods of research were allowed for, and all the libraries of K'n-yan both secular and sacred were to be thrown open to him as soon as he might master the written languages. Rites and spectacles were to be attended—except when he might especially object—and much time would be left for the enlightened pleasure-seeking and emotional titillation which formed the goal and nucleus of daily life. A house in the suburbs or an apartment in the city would be assigned him, and he would be initiated into one of the large affection-groups, including many noblewomen of the most extreme and art-enhanced beauty, which in latter-day K'n-yan took the place of family units. Several horned *gyaa-yothn* would be provided for his transportation and errand-running, and ten living slaves of intact body would serve to conduct his establishment and protect him from thieves and sadists and religious orgiasts on the public highways. There were many mechanical devices which he must learn to use, but Gll'-Hthaa-Ynn would instruct him immediately regarding the principal ones.

Upon his choosing an apartment in preference to a suburban villa, Zamacona was dismissed by the executives with great courtesy and ceremony, and was led through several gorgeous streets to a cliff-like carven structure of some seventy or eighty floors. Preparations for his arrival had already been instituted, and in a spacious ground-floor suite of vaulted rooms slaves were busy adjusting hangings and furniture. There were lacquered and inlaid tabourets, velvet and silk reclining-corners and squatting-cushions, and infinite rows of teakwood and ebony pigeon-holes with metal cylinders containing some of the manuscripts he was soon to read—standard classics which all urban apartments possessed. Desks with great stacks of membrane-paper and pots of the prevailing green pigment were in every room—each with graded sets of pigment brushes and other odd bits of stationery. Mechanical writing devices stood on ornate golden tripods, while over all was shed a brilliant blue light from energy-globes set in the ceiling. There were windows, but at this shadowy ground-level they were of scant illuminating value. In some of the rooms were elaborate baths, while the kitchen was a maze of technical contrivances. Supplies were brought, Zamacona was told, through the network of underground passages which lay beneath Tsath, and which had once accommodated curious mechanical transports. There was a stable on that underground level for the beasts, and Zamacona would presently be shewn how to find the nearest runway to the street. Before his inspection was finished, the permanent staff of slaves arrived and were introduced; and shortly afterward there came some half-dozen freemen and noblewomen of his future affection-group, who were to be his companions for several days, contributing what they could to his instruction and amusement. Upon their departure, another party would take their place, and so onward in rotation through a group of about fifty members.

VI.

Thus was Pánfilo de Zamacona y Nuñez absorbed for four years into the life of the sinister city of Tsath in the blue-litten nether world of K'n-yan. All that he learned and saw and did is clearly not told in his manuscript; for a pious reticence overcame him when he began to write in his native Spanish tongue, and he dared not set down everything. Much he consistently viewed with repulsion, and many things he steadfastly refrained from seeing or doing or eating. For other things he atoned by frequent countings of the beads of his rosary. He explored the entire world of K'n-yan, including the deserted machine-cities of the middle period on the gorse-grown plain of Nith, and made one descent into the red-litten world of Yoth to see the Cyclopean ruins. He witnessed prodigies of craft and machinery which left him breathless, and beheld human metamorphoses, dematerialisations, rematerialisations, and reanimations which made him cross himself again and again. His very capacity for astonishment was blunted by the plethora of new marvels which every day brought him.

But the longer he stayed, the more he wished to leave, for the inner life of K'n-yan was based on impulses very plainly outside his radius. As he progressed in historical knowledge, he understood more; but understanding only heightened his distaste. He felt that the people of Tsath were a lost and dangerous race—more dangerous to themselves than they knew—and that their growing frenzy of monotony-warfare and novelty-quest was leading them rapidly toward a precipice of disintegration and utter horror. His own visit, he could see, had accelerated their unrest; not only by introducing fears of outside invasion, but by exciting in many a wish to sally forth and taste the diverse external world he described. As time progressed, he noticed an increasing tendency of the people to resort to dematerialisation as an amusement; so that the apartments and amphitheatres of Tsath became a veritable Witches' Sabbath of transmutations, age-adjustments, death-experiments, and projections. With the growth of boredom and restlessness, he saw, cruelty and subtlety and revolt were growing apace. There was more and more cosmic abnormality, more and more curious sadism, more and more ignorance and superstition, and more and more desire to escape out of physical life into a half-spectral state of electronic dispersal.

All his efforts to leave, however, came to nothing. Persuasion was useless, as repeated trials proved; though the mature disillusion of the upper classes at first prevented them from resenting their guest's open wish for departure. In a year which he reckoned as 1543 Zamacona made an actual attempt to escape through the tunnel by which he had entered K'n-yan, but after a weary journey across the deserted plain he encountered forces in the dark passage which discouraged him from future attempts in that direction. As a means of sustaining hope and keeping the image of home in mind, he began about this time to make rough draughts of the manuscript relating his adventures; delighting in the loved, old Spanish words and the familiar letters of the Roman alphabet. Somehow he fancied he might get the manuscript to the outer world; and to make it convincing to his fellows he resolved to enclose it in one of the Tulu-metal cylinders used for sacred archives. That alien, magnetic substance could not but support the incredible story he had to tell.

But even as he planned, he had little real hope of ever establishing contact with the earth's surface. Every known gate, he knew, was guarded by persons or forces that it were better not to oppose. His attempt at escape had not helped matters, for he could now see a growing hostility to the outer world he represented. He hoped that no other European would find his way in; for it was possible that later comers might not fare as well as he. He himself had been a cherished fountain of data, and as such had enjoyed a privileged status. Others, deemed less necessary, might receive rather different treatment. He even wondered what would happen to him when the sages of Tsath considered him drained dry of fresh facts; and in self-defence began to be more gradual in his talks on earth-lore, conveying whenever he could the impression of vast knowledge held in reserve.

One other thing which endangered Zamacona's status in Tsath was his persistent curiosity regarding the ultimate abyss of N'kai, beneath red-litten Yoth, whose existence the dominant religious cults of K'n-yan were more and more inclined to deny. When exploring Yoth he had vainly tried to find the blocked-up entrance; and later on he experimented in the arts of dematerialisation and projection, hoping that he might thereby be able to throw his consciousness downward into the gulfs which his physical eyes could not discover. Though never becoming truly proficient in these processes, he did manage to achieve a series of monstrous and portentous dreams which he believed included some elements of actual projection into N'kai; dreams which greatly shocked and perturbed the leaders of Yig and Tulu-worship when he related them, and which he was advised by friends to conceal rather than exploit. In time those dreams became very frequent and maddening; containing things which he dared not record in his main manuscript, but of which he prepared a special record for the benefit of certain learned men in Tsath.

It may have been unfortunate—or it may have been mercifully fortunate—that Zamacona practiced so many reticences and reserved so many themes and descriptions for subsidiary manuscripts. The main document leaves one to guess much about the detailed manners, customs, thoughts, language, and history of K'n-yan, as well as to form any adequate picture of the visual aspect and daily life of Tsath. One is left puzzled, too, about the real motivations of the people; their strange passivity and craven unwarlikeness, and their almost cringing fear of the outer world despite their possession of atomic and dematerialising powers which would have made them unconquerable had they taken the trouble to organise armies as in the old days. It is evident that K'n-yan was far along in its decadence—reacting with mixed apathy and hysteria against the standardised and time-tabled life of stultifying regularity which machinery had brought it during its middle period. Even the grotesque and repulsive customs and modes of thought and feeling can be traced to this source; for in his historical research Zamacona found evidence of bygone eras in which K'n-yan had held ideas much like those of the classic and renaissance outer world, and had possessed a national character and art full of what Europeans regard as dignity, kindness, and nobility.

The more Zamacona studied these things, the more apprehensive about the future he became; because he saw that the omnipresent moral and intellectual disintegration was a tremendously deep-seated and ominously accelerating movement. Even during his stay the signs of decay multiplied. Rationalism degenerated more and more into fanatical and orgiastic superstition, centring in a lavish adoration of the magnetic Tulu-metal, and tolerance steadily dissolved into a series of frenzied hatreds, especially toward the outer world of which the scholars were learning so much from him.

At times he almost feared that the people might some day lose their age-long apathy and brokenness and turn like desperate rats against the unknown lands above them, sweeping all before them by virtue of their singular and still-remembered scientific powers. But for the present they fought their boredom and sense of emptiness in other ways; multiplying their hideous emotional outlets and increasing the mad grotesqueness and abnormality of their diversions. The arenas of Tsath must have been accursed and unthinkable places—Zamacona never went near them. And what they would be in another century, or even in another decade, he did not dare to think. The pious Spaniard crossed himself and counted his beads more often than usual in those days.

In the year 1545, as he reckoned it, Zamacona began what may well be accepted as his final series of attempts to leave K'n-yan. His fresh opportunity came from an unexpected source—a female of his affection-group who conceived for him a curious individual infatuation based on some hereditary memory of the days of monogamous wedlock in Tsath. Over this female—a noblewoman of moderate beauty and of at least average intelligence named T'la-yub—Zamacona acquired the most extraordinary influence; finally inducing her to help him in an escape, under the promise that he would let her accompany him. Chance proved a great factor in the course of events, for T'la-yub came of a primordial family of gate-lords who had retained oral traditions of at least one passage to the outer world which the mass of people had forgotten even at the time of the great closing; a passage to a mound on the level plains of earth which had, in consequence, never been sealed up or guarded. She explained that the primordial gate-lords were not guards or sentries, but merely ceremonial and economic proprietors, half-feudal and baronial in status, of an era preceding the severance of surface-relations. Her own family had been so reduced at the time of the closing that their gate had been wholly overlooked; and they had ever afterward preserved the secret of its existence as a sort of hereditary secret—a source of pride, and of a sense of reserve power, to offset the feeling of vanished wealth and influence which so constantly irritated them.

Zamacona, now working feverishly to get his manuscript into final form in case anything should happen to him, decided to take with him on his outward journey only five beast-loads of unalloyed gold in the form of the small ingots used for minor decorations—enough, he calculated, to make him a personage of unlimited power in his own world. He had become somewhat hardened to the sight of the monstrous *gyaa-yothn* during his four years of residence in Tsath, hence did not shrink from using the creatures; yet he resolved to kill and bury them, and cache the gold, as soon as he reached the outer world, since he knew that even a glimpse of one of the things would drive any ordinary Indian mad. Later he could arrange for a suitable expedition to transport the treasure to Mexico. T'la-yub he would perhaps allow to share his fortunes, for she was by no means unattractive; though possibly he would arrange for her sojourn amongst the plains Indians, since he was not overanxious to preserve links with the manner of life in Tsath. For a wife, of course, he would choose a lady of Spain—or at worst, an Indian princess of normal outer-world descent and a regular and approved past. But for the present T'la-yub must be used as a guide. The manuscript he would carry on his own person, encased in a book-cylinder of the sacred and magnetic Tulu-metal.

The expedition itself is described in the addendum to Zamacona's manuscript, written later, and in a hand shewing signs of nervous strain. It set out amidst the most careful precautions, choosing a rest-period and proceeding as far as possible along the faintly lighted passages beneath the city. Zamacona and T'la-yub, disguised in slaves' garments, bearing provision-knapsacks, and leading the five laden beasts on foot, were readily taken for commonplace workers; and they clung as long as possible to the subterranean way—using a long and little-frequented branch which had formerly conducted the mechanical transports to the now ruined suburb of L'thaa. Amidst the ruins of L'thaa they came to the surface, thereafter passing as rapidly as possible over the deserted, blue-litten plain of Nith toward the Grh-yan range of low hills. There, amidst the tangled underbrush, T'la-yub found the long disused and half-fabulous entrance to the forgotten tunnel; a thing she had seen but once before—aeons in the past, when her father had taken her thither to shew her this monument to their family pride. It was hard work getting the laden *gyaa-yothn* to scrape through the obstructing vines and briers, and one of them displayed a rebelliousness destined to bear dire consequences—bolting away from the party and loping back toward Tsath on its detestable pads, golden burden and all.

It was nightmare work burrowing by the light of blue-ray torches upward, downward, forward, and upward again through a dank, choked tunnel that no foot had trodden since ages before the sinking of Atlantis; and at one point T'la-yub had to practice the fearsome art of dematerialisation on herself, Zamacona, and the laden beasts in order to pass a point wholly clogged by shifting earth-strata. It was a terrible experience for Zamacona; for although he had often witnessed dematerialisation in others, and even practiced it himself to the extent of dream-projection, he had never been fully subjected to it before. But T'la-yub was skilled in the arts of K'n-yan, and accomplished the double metamorphosis in perfect safety.

Thereafter they resumed the hideous burrowing through stalactited crypts of horror where monstrous carvings leered at every turn; alternately camping and advancing for a period which Zamacona reckoned as about three days, but which was probably less. At last they came to a very narrow place where the natural or only slightly hewn cave-walls gave place to walls of wholly artificial masonry, carved into terrible bas-reliefs. These walls, after about a mile of steep ascent, ended with a pair of vast niches, one on each side, in which monstrous, nitre-encrusted images of Yig and Tulu squatted, glaring at each other across the passage as they had glared since the earliest youth of the human world. At this point the passage opened into a prodigious vaulted and circular chamber of human construction; wholly covered with horrible carvings, and revealing at the farther end an arched passageway with the foot of a flight of steps. T'la-yub knew from family tales that this must be very near the earth's surface, but she could not tell just how near. Here the party camped for what they meant to be their last rest-period in the subterraneous world.

It must have been hours later that the clank of metal and the padding of beasts' feet awakened Zamacona and T'la-yub. A bluish glare was spreading from the narrow passage between the images of Yig and Tulu, and in an instant the truth was obvious. An alarm had been given at Tsath—as was later revealed, by the returning *gyaa-yoth* which had rebelled at the brier-choked tunnel-entrance —and a swift party of pursuers had come to arrest the fugitives. Resistance was clearly useless, and none was offered. The party of twelve beast-riders proved studiously polite, and the return commenced almost without a word or thought-message on either side.

It was an ominous and depressing journey, and the ordeal of dematerialisation and rematerialisation at the choked place was all the more terrible because of the lack of that hope and expectancy which had palliated the process on the outward trip. Zamacona heard his captors discussing the imminent clearing of this choked place by intensive radiations, since henceforward sentries must be maintained at the hitherto unknown outer portal. It would not do to let outsiders get within the passage, for then any who might escape without due treatment would have a hint of the vastness of the inner world and would perhaps be curious enough to return in greater strength. As with the other passages since Zamacona's coming, sentries must be stationed all along, as far as the very outermost gate; sentries drawn from amongst all the slaves, the dead-alive *y'm-bhi,* or the class of discredited freemen. With the overrunning of the American plains by thousands of Europeans, as the Spaniard had predicted, every passage was a potential source of danger; and must be rigorously guarded until the technologists of Tsath could spare the energy to prepare an ultimate and entrance-hiding obliteration as they had done for many passages in earlier and more vigorous times.

Zamacona and T'la-yub were tried before three *gn'agn* of the supreme tribunal in the gold-and-copper palace behind the gardened and fountained park, and the Spaniard was given his liberty because of the vital outer-world information he still had to impart. He was told to return to his apartment and to his affection-group; taking up his life as before, and continuing to meet deputations of scholars according to the latest schedule he had been following. No restrictions would be imposed upon him so long as he might remain peacefully in K'n-yan—but it was intimated that such leniency would not be repeated after another attempt at escape. Zamacona had felt that there was an element of irony in the parting words of the chief *gn'ag*—an assurance that all of his *gyaa-yothn,* including the one which had rebelled, would be returned to him.

The fate of T'la-yub was less happy. There being no object in retaining her, and her ancient Tsathic lineage giving her act a greater aspect of treason than Zamacona's had possessed, she was ordered to be delivered to the curious diversions of the amphitheatre; and afterward, in a somewhat mutilated and half-dematerialised form, to be given the functions of a *y'm-bhi* or animated corpse-slave and stationed among the sentries guarding the passage whose existence she had betrayed. Zamacona soon heard, not without many pangs of regret he could scarcely have anticipated, that poor T'la-yub had emerged from the arena in a headless and otherwise incomplete state, and had been set as an outermost guard upon the mound in which the passage had been found to terminate. She was, he was told, a night-sentinel, whose automatic duty was to warn off all comers with a torch; sending down reports to a small garrison of twelve dead slave *y'm-bhi* and six living but partly dematerialised freemen in the vaulted, circular chamber if the approachers did not heed her warning. She worked, he was told, in conjunction with a day-sentinel—a living freeman who chose this post in preference to other forms of discipline for other offences against the state. Zamacona, of course, had long known that most of the chief gate-sentries were such discredited freemen.

It was now made plain to him, though indirectly, that his own penalty for another escape-attempt would be service as a gate-sentry—but in the form of a dead-alive *y'm-bhi* slave, and after amphitheatre-treatment even more picturesque than that which T'la-yub was reported to have undergone. It was intimated that he —or parts of him—would be reanimated to guard some inner section of the passage; within sight of others, where his abridged person might serve as a permanent symbol of the rewards of treason. But, his informants always added, it was of course inconceivable that he would ever court such a fate. So long as he remained peaceably in K'n-yan, he would continue to be a free, privileged, and respected personage.

Yet in the end Pánfilo de Zamacona did court the fate so direfully hinted to him. True, he did not really expect to encounter it; but the nervous latter part of his manuscript makes it clear that he was prepared to face its possibility. What gave him a final hope of scatheless escape from K'n-yan was his growing mastery of the art of dematerialisation. Having studied it for years, and having learned still more from the two instances in which he had been subjected to it, he now felt increasingly able to use it independently and effectively. The manuscript records several notable experiments in this art—minor successes accomplished in his apartment—and reflects Zamacona's hope that he might soon be able to assume the spectral form in full, attaining complete invisibility and preserving that condition as long as he wished.

Once he reached this stage, he argued, the outward way lay open to him. Of course he could not bear away any gold, but mere escape was enough. He would, though, dematerialise and carry away with him his manuscript in the Tulu-metal cylinder, even though it cost additional effort; for this record and proof must reach the outer world at all hazards. He now knew the passage to follow; and if he could thread it in an atom-scattered state, he did not see how any person or force could detect or stop him. The only trouble would be if he failed to maintain his spectral condition at all times. That was the one ever-present peril, as he had learned from his experiments. But must one not always risk death and worse in a life of adventure? Zamacona was a gentleman of Old Spain; of the blood that faced the unknown and carved out half the civilisation of the New World.

For many nights after his ultimate resolution Zamacona prayed to St. Pamphilus and other guardian saints, and counted the beads of his rosary. The last entry in the manuscript, which toward the end took the form of a diary more and more, was merely a single sentence—*"Es más tarde de lo que pensaba—tengo que marcharme"*. . . . "It is later than I thought; I must go." After that, only silence and conjecture—and such evidence as the presence of the manuscript itself, and what that manuscript could lead to, might provide.

VII.

When I looked up from my half-stupefied reading and note-taking the morning sun was high in the heavens. The electric bulb was still burning, but such things of the real world—the modern outer world—were far from my whirling brain. I knew I was in my room at Clyde Compton's at Binger—but upon what monstrous vista had I stumbled? Was this thing a hoax or a chronicle of madness? If a hoax, was it a jest of the sixteenth century or of to-day? The manuscript's age looked appallingly genuine to my not wholly unpracticed eyes, and the problem presented by the strange metal cylinder I dared not even think about.

Moreover, what a monstrously exact explanation it gave of all the baffling phenomena of the mound—of the seemingly meaningless and paradoxical actions of diurnal and nocturnal ghosts, and of the queer cases of madness and disappearance! It was even an accursedly *plausible* explanation—evilly *consistent*—if one could adopt the incredible. It must be a shocking hoax devised by someone who knew all the lore of the mound. There was even a hint of social satire in the account of that unbelievable nether world of horror and decay. Surely this was the clever forgery of some learned cynic—something like the leaden crosses in New Mexico, which a jester once planted and pretended to discover as a relique of some forgotten Dark Age colony from Europe.

Upon going down to breakfast I hardly knew what to tell Compton and his mother, as well as the curious callers who had already begun to arrive. Still in a daze, I cut the Gordian Knot by giving a few points from the notes I had made, and mumbling my belief that the thing was a subtle and ingenious fraud left there by some previous explorer of the mound—a belief in which everybody seemed to concur when told of the substance of the manuscript. It is curious how all that breakfast group—and all the others in Binger to whom the discussion was repeated—seemed to find a great clearing of the atmosphere in the notion that somebody was playing a joke on somebody. For the time we all forgot that the known, recent history of the mound presented mysteries as strange as any in the manuscript, and as far from acceptable solution as ever.

The fears and doubts began to return when I asked for volunteers to visit the mound with me. I wanted a larger excavating party—but the idea of going to that uncomfortable place seemed no more attractive to the people of Binger than it had seemed on the previous day. I myself felt a mounting horror upon looking toward the mound and glimpsing the moving speck which I knew was the daylight sentinel; for in spite of all my scepticism the morbidities of that manuscript stuck by me and gave everything connected with the place a new and monstrous significance. I absolutely lacked the resolution to look at the moving speck with my binoculars. Instead, I set out with the kind of bravado we display in nightmares—when, knowing we are dreaming, we plunge desperately into still thicker horrors, for the sake of having the whole thing over the sooner. My pick and shovel were already out there, so I had only my handbag of smaller paraphernalia to take. Into this I put the strange cylinder and its contents, feeling vaguely that I might possibly find something worth checking up with some part of the green-lettered Spanish text. Even a clever hoax might be founded on some actual attribute of the mound which a former explorer had discovered—and that magnetic metal was damnably odd! Grey Eagle's cryptic talisman still hung from its leathern cord around my neck.

I did not look very sharply at the mound as I walked toward it, but when I reached it there was nobody in sight. Repeating my upward scramble of the previous day, I was troubled by thoughts of what *might* lie close at hand *if,* by any miracle, any part of the manuscript *were* actually half-true. In such a case, I could not help reflecting, the hypothetical Spaniard Zamacona must have barely reached the outer world when overtaken by some disaster—perhaps an involuntary rematerialisation. He would naturally, in that event, have been seized by whichever sentry happened to be on duty at the time—either the discredited freeman, or, as a matter of supreme irony, the very T'la-yub who had planned and aided his first attempt at escape—and in the ensuing struggle the cylinder with the manuscript might well have been dropped on the mound's summit, to be neglected and gradually buried for nearly four centuries. But, I added, as I climbed over the crest, one must not think of extravagant things like that. Still, if there *were* anything in the tale, it must have been a monstrous fate to which Zamacona had been dragged back . . . the amphitheatre . . . mutilation . . . duty somewhere in the dank, nitrous tunnel as a dead-alive slave . . . a maimed corpse-fragment as an automatic interior sentry. . . .

It was a very real shock which chased this morbid speculation from my head, for upon glancing around the elliptical summit I saw at once that my pick and shovel had been stolen. This was a highly provoking and disconcerting development; baffling, too, in view of the seeming reluctance of all the Binger folk to visit the mound. Was this reluctance a pretended thing, and had the jokers of the village been chuckling over my coming discomfiture as they solemnly saw me off ten minutes before? I took out my binoculars and scanned the gaping crowd at the edge of the village. No—they did not seem to be looking for any comic climax; yet was not the whole affair at bottom a colossal joke in which all the villagers and reservation people were concerned—legends, manuscript, cylinder, and all? I thought of how I had seen the sentry from a distance, and then found him unaccountably vanished; thought also of the conduct of old Grey Eagle, of the speech and expressions of Compton and his mother, and of the unmistakable fright of most of the Binger people. On the whole, it could not very well be a village-wide joke. The fear and the problem were surely real, though obviously there were one or two jesting daredevils in Binger who had stolen out to the mound and made off with the tools I had left.

Everything else on the mound was as I had left it—brush cut by my machete, slight, bowl-like depression toward the north end, and the hole I had made with my trench-knife in digging up the magnetism-revealed cylinder. Deeming it too great a concession to the unknown jokers to return to Binger for another pick and shovel, I resolved to carry out my programme as best I could with the machete and trench-knife in my handbag; so extracting these, I set to work excavating the bowl-like depression which my eye had picked as the possible site of a former entrance to the mound. As I proceeded, I felt again the suggestion of a sudden wind blowing against me which I had noticed the day before—a suggestion which seemed stronger, and still more reminiscent of unseen, formless, opposing hands laid on my wrists, as I cut deeper and deeper through the root-tangled red soil and reached the exotic black loam beneath. The talisman around my neck appeared to twitch oddly in the breeze—not in any one direction, as when attracted by the buried cylinder, but vaguely and diffusely, in a manner wholly unaccountable.

Then, quite without warning, the black, root-woven earth beneath my feet began to sink cracklingly, while I heard a faint sound of sifting, falling matter far below me. The obstructing wind, or forces, or hands now seemed to be operating from the very seat of the sinking, and I felt that they aided me by pushing as I leaped back out of the hole to avoid being involved in any cave-in. Bending down over the brink and hacking at the mould-caked root-tangle with my machete, I felt that they were against me again—but at no time were they strong enough to stop my work. The more roots I severed, the more falling matter I heard below. Finally the hole began to deepen of itself toward the centre, and I saw that the earth was sifting down into some large cavity beneath, so as to leave a good-sized aperture when the roots that had bound it were gone. A few more hacks of the machete did the trick, and with a parting cave-in and uprush of curiously chill and alien air the last barrier gave way. Under the morning sun yawned a huge opening at least three feet square, and shewing the top of a flight of stone steps down which the loose earth of the collapse was still sliding. My quest had come to something at last! With an elation of accomplishment almost overbalancing fear for the nonce, I replaced the trench-knife and machete in my handbag, took out my powerful electric torch, and prepared for a triumphant, lone, and utterly rash invasion of the fabulous nether world I had uncovered.

It was rather hard getting down the first few steps, both because of the fallen earth which had choked them and because of a sinister up-pushing of a cold wind from below. The talisman around my neck swayed curiously, and I began to regret the disappearing square of daylight above me. The electric torch shewed dank, water-stained, and salt-encrusted walls fashioned of huge basalt blocks, and now and then I thought I descried some trace of carving beneath the nitrous deposits. I gripped my handbag more tightly, and was glad of the comforting weight of the sheriff's heavy revolver in my right-hand coat pocket. After a time the passage began to wind this way and that, and the staircase became free from obstructions. Carvings on the walls were now definitely traceable, and I shuddered when I saw how clearly the grotesque figures resembled the monstrous bas-reliefs on the cylinder I had found. Winds and forces continued to blow malevolently against me, and at one or two bends I half fancied the torch gave glimpses of thin, transparent shapes not unlike the sentinel on the mound as my binoculars had shewed him. When I reached this stage of visual chaos I stopped for a moment to get a grip on myself. It would not do to let my nerves get the better of me at the very outset of what would surely be a trying experience, and the most important archaeological feat of my career.

But I wished I had not stopped at just that place, for the act fixed my attention on something profoundly disturbing. It was only a small object lying close to the wall on one of the steps below me, but that object was such as to put my reason to a severe test, and bring up a line of the most alarming speculations. That the opening above me had been closed against all material forms for generations was utterly obvious from the growth of shrub-roots and accumulation of drifting soil; yet the object before me was most distinctly *not* many generations old. For it was an electric torch much like the one I now carried—warped and encrusted in the tomb-like dampness, but none the less perfectly unmistakable. I descended a few steps and picked it up, wiping off the evil deposits on my rough coat. One of the nickel bands bore an engraved name and address, and I recognised it with a start the moment I made it out. It read "Jas. C. Williams, 17 Trowbridge St., Cambridge, Mass."—and I knew that it had belonged to one of the two daring college instructors who had disappeared on June 28, 1915. Only thirteen years ago, and yet I had just broken through the sod of centuries! How had the thing got there? Another entrance—or was there something after all in this mad idea of dematerialisation and rematerialisation?

Doubt and horror grew upon me as I wound still farther down the seemingly endless staircase. Would the thing never stop? The carvings grew more and more distinct, and assumed a narrative pictorial quality which brought me close to panic as I recognised many unmistakable correspondences with the history of K'n-yan as sketched in the manuscript now resting in my handbag. For the first time I began seriously to question the wisdom of my descent, and to wonder whether I had not better return to the upper air before I came upon something which would never let me return as a sane man. But I did not hesitate long, for as a Virginian I felt the blood of ancestral fighters and gentlemen-adventurers pounding a protest against retreat from any peril known or unknown.

My descent became swifter rather than slower, and I avoided studying the terrible bas-reliefs and intaglios that had unnerved me. All at once I saw an arched opening ahead, and realised that the prodigious staircase had ended at last. But with that realisation came horror in mounting magnitude, for before me there yawned a vast vaulted crypt of all-too-familiar outline—a great circular space answering in every least particular to the carving-lined chamber described in the Zamacona manuscript.

It was indeed the place. There could be no mistake. And if any room for doubt yet remained, that room was abolished by what I saw directly across the great vault. It was a second arched opening, commencing a long, narrow passage and having at its mouth two huge opposite niches bearing loathsome and titanic images of shockingly familiar pattern. There in the dark unclean Yig and hideous Tulu squatted eternally, glaring at each other across the passage as they had glared since the earliest youth of the human world.

From this point onward I ask no credence for what I tell—for what I *think* I saw. It is too utterly unnatural, too utterly monstrous and incredible, to be any part of sane human experience or objective reality. My torch, though casting a powerful beam ahead, naturally could not furnish any general illumination of the Cyclopean crypt; so I now began moving it about to explore the giant walls little by little. As I did so, I saw to my horror that the space was by no means vacant, but was instead littered with odd furniture and utensils and heaps of packages which bespoke a populous recent occupancy—no nitrous reliques of the past, but queerly shaped objects and supplies in modern, every-day use. As my torch rested on each article or group of articles, however, the distinctness of the outlines soon began to grow blurred; until in the end I could scarcely tell whether the things belonged to the realm of matter or to the realm of spirit.

All this while the adverse winds blew against me with increasing fury, and the unseen hands plucked malevolently at me and snatched at the strange magnetic talisman I wore. Wild conceits surged through my mind. I thought of the manuscript and what it said about the garrison stationed in this place—twelve dead slave *y'm-bhi* and six living but partly dematerialised freemen—that was in 1545—three hundred and eighty-three years ago. . . . What since then? Zamacona had predicted change . . . subtle disintegration . . . more dematerialisation . . . weaker and weaker . . . was it Grey Eagle's talisman that held them at bay—their sacred Tulu-metal—and were they feebly trying to pluck it off so that they might do to me what they had done to those who had come before? . . . It occurred to me with shuddering force that I was building my speculations out of a full belief in the Zamacona manuscript—this must not be—I must get a grip on myself—

But, curse it, every time I tried to get a grip I saw some fresh sight to shatter my poise still further. This time, just as my will power was driving the half-seen paraphernalia into obscurity, my glance and torch-beam had to light on two things of very different nature; two things of the eminently real and sane world; yet they did more to unseat my shaky reason than anything I had seen before—because I knew what they were, and knew how profoundly, in the course of Nature, they ought not to be there. *They were my own missing pick and shovel, side by side, and leaning neatly against the blasphemously carved wall of that hellish crypt.* God in heaven—and I had babbled to myself about daring jokers from Binger!

That was the last straw. After that the cursed hypnotism of the manuscript got at me, and I actually *saw* the half-transparent shapes of the things that were pushing and plucking; pushing and plucking—those leprous palaeogean things with something of humanity still clinging to them—the *complete* forms, and the forms that were morbidly and perversely *incomplete* . . . all these, and hideous *other entities*—the four-footed blasphemies with ape-like face and projecting horn . . . and not a sound so far in all that nitrous hell of inner earth. . . .

Then there *was* a sound—a flopping; a padding; a dull, advancing sound which heralded beyond question a being as structurally material as the pickaxe and the shovel—something wholly unlike the shadow-shapes that ringed me in, yet equally remote from any sort of life as life is understood on the earth's wholesome surface. My shattered brain tried to prepare me for what was coming, but could not frame any adequate image. I could only say over and over again to myself, "It is of the abyss, but it is *not* dematerialised." The padding grew more distinct, and from the mechanical cast of the tread I knew it was a dead thing that stalked in the darkness. Then

—oh, God, *I saw it in the full beam of my torch; saw it framed like a sentinel in the narrow passage between the nightmare idols of the serpent Yig and the octopus Tulu. . . .*

Let me collect myself enough to hint at what I saw; to explain why I dropped torch and handbag and fled empty-handed in the utter blackness, wrapped in a merciful unconsciousness which did not wear off until the sun and the distant yelling and the shouting from the village roused me as I lay gasping on the top of the accursed mound. I do not yet know what guided me again to the earth's surface. I only know that the watchers in Binger saw me stagger up into sight three hours after I had vanished; saw me lurch up and fall flat on the ground as if struck by a bullet. None of them dared to come out and help me; but they knew I must be in a bad state, so tried to rouse me as best they could by yelling in chorus and firing off revolvers.

It worked in the end, and when I came to I almost rolled down the side of the mound in my eagerness to get away from that black aperture which still yawned open. My torch and tools, and the handbag with the manuscript, were all down there; but it is easy to see why neither I nor anyone else ever went after them. When I staggered across the plain and into the village I dared not tell what I had seen. I only muttered vague things about carvings and statues and snakes and shaken nerves. And I did not faint again until somebody mentioned that the ghost-sentinel had reappeared about the time I had staggered half way back to town. I left Binger that evening, and have never been there since, though they tell me the ghosts still appear on the mound as usual.

But I have resolved to hint here at last what I dared not hint to the people of Binger on that terrible August afternoon. I don't know yet just how I can go about it—and if in the end you think my reticence strange, just remember that to imagine such a horror is one thing, *but to see it is another thing*. I saw it. I think you'll recall my citing early in this tale the case of a bright young man named Heaton who went out to that mound one day in 1891 and came back at night as the village idiot, babbling for eight years about horrors and then dying in an epileptic fit. What he used to keep moaning was "*That white man—oh, my God, what they did to him. . . .*"

Well, I saw the same thing that poor Heaton saw—and I saw it after reading the manuscript, so I know more of its history than he did. That makes it worse—for I know all that it *implies;* all that must be still brooding and festering and waiting down there. I told you it had padded mechanically toward me out of the narrow passage and had stood sentry-like at the entrance between the frightful eidola of Yig and Tulu. That was very natural and inevitable—because the thing *was* a sentry. It had been made a sentry for punishment, and it was quite dead—besides lacking head, arms, lower legs, and other customary parts of a human being. Yes—it had been a very human being once; and what is more, it had been *white.* Very obviously, if that manuscript was as true as I think it was, this being had been used for the *diversions of the amphitheatre* before its life had become wholly extinct and supplanted by automatic impulses controlled from outside.

On its white and only slightly hairy chest some letters had been gashed or branded—I had not stopped to investigate, but had merely noted that they were in an awkward and fumbling Spanish; an awkward Spanish implying a kind of ironic use of the language by an alien inscriber familiar neither with the idiom nor the Roman letters used to record it. The inscription had read *"Secuestrado a la voluntad de Xinaián en el cuerpo decapitado de Tlayúb"—"Seized by the will of K'n-yan in the headless body of T'la-yub."*

Zealia Bishop

Medusa's Coil

I.

The drive toward Cape Girardeau had been through unfamiliar country; and as the late afternoon light grew golden and half-dreamlike I realised that I must have directions if I expected to reach the town before night. I did not care to be wandering about these bleak southern Missouri lowlands after dark, for roads were poor and the November cold rather formidable in an open roadster. Black clouds, too, were massing on the horizon; so I looked about among the long, grey and blue shadows that streaked the flat, brownish fields, hoping to glimpse some house where I might get the needed information.

It was a lonely and deserted country, but at last I spied a roof among a clump of trees near the small river on my right; perhaps a full half-mile from the road, and probably reachable by some path or drive which I would presently come upon. In the absence of any nearer dwelling, I resolved to try my luck there; and was glad when the bushes by the roadside revealed the ruin of a carved stone gateway, covered with dry, dead vines and choked with undergrowth which explained why I had not been able to trace the path across the fields in my first distant view. I saw that I could not drive the car in, so I parked it very carefully near the gate—where a thick evergreen would shield it in case of rain—and got out for the long walk to the house.

Traversing that brush-grown path in the gathering twilight I was conscious of a distinct sense of foreboding, probably induced by the air of sinister decay hovering about the gate and the former driveway. From the carvings on the old stone pillars I inferred that this place was once an estate of manorial dignity; and I could clearly see that the driveway had originally boasted guardian lines of linden trees, some of which had died, while others had lost their special identity among the wild scrub growths of the region.

As I ploughed onward, cockleburrs and stickers clung to my clothes, and I began to wonder whether the place could be inhabited after all. Was I tramping on a vain errand? For a moment I was tempted to go back and try some farm farther along the road, when a view of the house ahead aroused my curiosity and stimulated my venturesome spirit.

There was something provocatively fascinating in the tree-girt, decrepit pile before me, for it spoke of the graces and spaciousness of a bygone era and a far more southerly environment. It was a typical wooden plantation house of the classic, early nineteenth-century pattern, with two and a half stories and a great Ionic portico whose pillars reached up as far as the attic and supported a triangular pediment. Its state of decay was extreme and obvious; one of the vast columns having rotted and fallen to the ground, while the upper piazza or balcony had sagged dangerously low. Other buildings, I judged, had formerly stood near it.

As I mounted the broad stone steps to the low porch and the carved and fanlighted doorway I felt distinctly nervous, and started to light a cigarette—desisting when I saw how dry and inflammable everything about me was. Though now convinced that the house was deserted, I nevertheless hesitated to violate its dignity without knocking; so tugged at the rusty iron knocker until I could get it to move, and finally set up a cautious rapping which seemed to make the whole place shake and rattle. There was no response, yet once more I plied the cumbrous, creaking device—as much to dispel the sense of unholy silence and solitude as to arouse any possible occupant of the ruin.

Somewhere near the river I heard the mournful note of a dove, and it seemed as if the coursing water itself were faintly audible. Half in a dream, I seized and rattled the ancient latch, and finally gave the great six-panelled door a frank trying. It was unlocked, as

I could see in a moment; and though it stuck and grated on its hinges I began to push it open, stepping through it into a vast shadowy hall as I did so.

But the moment I took this step I regretted it. It was not that a legion of spectres confronted me in that dim and dusty hall with the ghostly Empire furniture; but that I knew all at once that the place was not deserted at all. There was a creaking on the great curved staircase, and the sound of faltering footsteps slowly descending. Then I saw a tall, bent figure silhouetted for an instant against the great Palladian window on the landing.

My first start of terror was soon over, and as the figure descended the final flight I was ready to greet the householder whose privacy I had invaded. In the semi-darkness I could see him reach in his pocket for a match. There came a flare as he lighted a small kerosene lamp which stood on a rickety console table near the foot of the stairs. In the feeble glow was revealed the stooping figure of a very tall, emaciated old man; disordered as to dress and unshaved as to face, yet for all that with the bearing and expression of a gentleman.

I did not wait for him to speak, but at once began to explain my presence.

"You'll pardon my coming in like this, but when my knocking didn't raise anybody I concluded that no one lived here. What I wanted originally was to know the right road to Cape Girardeau—the shortest road, that is. I wanted to get there before dark, but now, of course—"

As I paused, the man spoke; in exactly the cultivated tone I had expected, and with a mellow accent as unmistakably Southern as the house he inhabited.

"Rather, you must pardon me for not answering your knock more promptly. I live in a very retired way, and am not usually expecting visitors. At first I thought you were a mere curiosity-seeker. Then when you knocked again I started to answer, but I am not well and have to move very slowly. Spinal neuritis—very troublesome case.

"But as for your getting to town before dark—it's plain you can't do that. The road you are on—for I suppose you came from the gate—isn't the best or shortest way. What you must do is to take your first left after you leave the gate—that is, the first real road to your left. There are three or four cart paths you can ignore, but you can't mistake the real road because of the extra large willow tree on the right just opposite it. Then when you've turned, keep on past two roads and turn to the right along the third. After that—"

Perplexed by these elaborate directions—confusing things indeed to a total stranger—I could not help interrupting.

"Please wait a moment! How can I follow all these clues in pitch darkness, without ever having been near here before, and with only an indifferent pair of headlights to tell me what is and what isn't a road? Besides, I think it's going to storm pretty soon, and my car is an open one. It looks as if I were in a bad fix if I want to get to Cape Girardeau tonight. The fact is, I don't think I'd better try to make it. I don't like to impose burdens, or anything like that—but in view of the circumstances, do you suppose you could put me up for the night? I won't be any trouble—no meals or anything. Just let me have a corner to sleep in till daylight, and I'm all right. I can leave the car in the road where it is—a bit of wet weather won't hurt it if worst comes to worst."

As I made my sudden request I could see the old man's face lose its former expression of quiet resignation and take on an odd, surprised look.

"Sleep—*here?*"

He seemed so astonished at my request that I repeated it.

"Yes, why not? I assure you I won't be any trouble. What else *can* I do? I'm a stranger hereabouts, these roads are a labyrinth in the dark, and I'll wager it'll be raining torrents outside of an hour—"

This time it was my host's turn to interrupt, and as he did so I could feel a peculiar quality in his deep, musical voice.

"A stranger—of course you must be, else you wouldn't think of sleeping here; wouldn't think of coming here at all. People don't come here nowadays."

He paused, and my desire to stay was increased a thousandfold by the sense of mystery his laconic words seemed to evoke. There was surely something alluringly queer about this place, and the pervasive musty smell seemed to cloak a thousand secrets. Again I noticed the extreme decrepitude of everything about me; manifest even in the feeble rays of the single small lamp. I felt woefully chilly, and saw with regret that no heating seemed to be provided; yet so great was my curiosity that I still wished most ardently to stay and learn something of the recluse and his dismal abode.

"Let that be as it may," I replied. "I can't help about other people. But I surely would like to have a spot to stop till daylight. Still—if people don't relish this place, mayn't it be because it's getting so run-down? Of course I suppose it would take a fortune to keep such an estate up, but if the burden's too great why don't you look for smaller quarters? Why try to stick it out here in this way—with all the hardships and discomforts?"

The man did not seem offended, but answered me very gravely. "Surely you may stay if you really wish to—*you* can come to no harm that I know of. But others claim there are certain peculiarly undesirable influences here. As for me—I stay here because I have to. There is something I feel it a duty to guard—something that holds me. I wish I had the money and health and ambition to take decent care of the house and grounds."

With my curiosity still more heightened, I prepared to take my host at his word; and followed him slowly upstairs when he motioned me to do so. It was very dark now, and a faint pattering outside told me that the threatened rain had come. I would have been glad of any shelter, but this was doubly welcome because of the hints of mystery about the place and its master. For an incurable lover of the grotesque, no more fitting haven could have been provided.

II.

There was a second-floor corner room in less unkempt shape than the rest of the house, and into this my host led me; setting down his small lamp and lighting a somewhat larger one. From the cleanliness and contents of the room, and from the books ranged along the walls, I could see that I had not guessed amiss in thinking the man a gentleman of taste and breeding. He was a hermit and eccentric, no doubt, but he still had standards and intellectual interests. As he waved me to a seat I began a conversation on general topics, and was pleased to find him not at all taciturn. If anything, he seemed glad of someone to talk to, and did not even attempt to swerve the discourse from personal topics.

He was, I learned, one Antoine de Russy, of an ancient, powerful, and cultivated line of Louisiana planters. More than a century ago his grandfather, a younger son, had migrated to southern Missouri and founded a new estate in the lavish ancestral manner; building this pillared mansion and surrounding it with all the accessories of a great plantation. There had been, at one time, as many as 200 negroes in the cabins which stood on the flat ground in the rear—ground that the river had now invaded—and to hear them singing and laughing and playing the banjo at night was to know the fullest charm of a civilisation and social order now sadly extinct. In front of the house, where the great guardian oaks and willows stood, there had been a lawn like a broad green carpet, always watered and trimmed and with flagstoned, flower-bordered walks curving through it. "Riverside"—for such the place was called—had been a lovely and idyllic homestead in its day; and my host could recall it when many traces of its best period still lingered.

It was raining hard now, with dense sheets of water beating against the insecure roof, walls, and windows, and sending in drops through a thousand chinks and crevices. Moisture trickled down to the floor from unsuspected places, and the mounting wind rattled the rotting, loose-hinged shutters outside. But I minded none of this, nor even thought of my roadster outside beneath the trees, for I saw that a story was coming. Incited to reminiscence, my host made a move to shew me to sleeping-quarters; but kept on recalling the older, better days. Soon, I saw, I would receive an inkling of why he lived alone in that ancient place, and why his neighbours thought it full of undesirable influences. His voice was very musical as he spoke on, and his tale soon took a turn which left me no chance to grow drowsy.

"Yes—Riverside was built in 1816, and my father was born here in 1828. He'd be over a century old now if he were alive, but he died young—so young I can just barely remember him. In '64 that was—he was killed in the war, Seventh Louisiana Infantry C.S.A., for he went back to the old home to enlist. My grandfather was too old to fight, yet he lived on to be ninety-five, and helped my mother bring me up. A good bringing-up, too—I'll give them credit. We always had strong traditions—high notions of honour—and my grandfather saw to it that I grew up the way de Russys have grown up, generation after generation, ever since the Crusades. We weren't quite wiped out financially, but managed to get on very comfortably after the war. I went to a good school in Louisiana, and later to Princeton. Later on I was able to get the plantation on a fairly profitable basis—though you see what it's come to now.

"My mother died when I was twenty, and my grandfather two years later. It was rather lonely after that; and in '85 I married a distant cousin in New Orleans. Things might have been different if she'd lived, but she died when my son Denis was born. Then I had only Denis. I didn't try marriage again, but gave all my time to the boy. He was like me—like all the de Russys—darkish and tall and thin, and with the devil of a temper. I gave him the same training my grandfather had given me, but he didn't need much training when it came to points of honour. It was in him, I reckon. Never saw such high spirit—all I could do to keep him from running away to the Spanish War when he was eleven! Romantic young devil, too—full of high notions—you'd call 'em Victorian, now—no trouble at all to make him let the nigger wenches alone. I sent him to the same school I'd gone to, and to Princeton, too. He was Class of 1909.

"In the end he decided to be a doctor, and went a year to the Harvard Medical School. Then he hit on the idea of keeping to the old French tradition of the family, and argued me into sending him across to the Sorbonne. I did—and proudly enough, though I knew how lonely I'd be with him so far off. Would to God I hadn't! I thought he was the safest kind of a boy to be in Paris. He had a room in the Rue St. Jacques—that's near the University in the 'Latin Quarter'—but according to his letters and his friends he didn't cut up with the gayer dogs at all. The people he knew were mostly young fellows from home—serious students and artists who thought more of their work than of striking attitudes and painting the town red.

"But of course there were lots of fellows who were on a sort of dividing line between serious studies and the devil. The aesthetes—the decadents, you know. Experimenters in life and sensation—the Baudelaire kind of a chap. Naturally Denis ran up against a good many of these, and saw a good deal of their life. They had all sorts of crazy circles and cults—imitation devil-worship, fake Black Masses, and the like. Doubt if it did them much harm on the whole—probably most of 'em forgot all about it in a year or two. One of the deepest in this queer stuff was a fellow Denis had known at school—for that matter, whose father I'd known myself. Frank Marsh, of New Orleans. Disciple of Lafcadio Hearn and Gauguin and Van Gogh—regular epitome of the yellow 'nineties. Poor devil—he had the makings of a great artist, at that.

"Marsh was the oldest friend Denis had in Paris, so as a matter of course they saw a good deal of each other—to talk over old times at St. Clair Academy, and all that. The boy wrote me a good deal about him, and I didn't see any especial harm when he spoke of the group of mystics Marsh ran with. It seems there was some cult of prehistoric Egyptian and Carthaginian magic having a rage among the Bohemian element on the left bank—some nonsensical thing that pretended to reach back to forgotten sources of hidden truth in lost African civilisations—the great Zimbabwe, the dead Atlantean cities in the Hoggar region of the Sahara—and that had a lot of gibberish connected with snakes and human hair. At least, I called it gibberish, then. Denis used to quote Marsh as saying odd things about the veiled facts behind the legend of Medusa's snaky locks—and behind the later Ptolemaic myth of Berenice, who offered up her hair to save her husband-brother, and had it set in the sky as the constellation Coma Berenices.

"I don't think this business made much impression on Denis until the night of the queer ritual at Marsh's rooms when he met the priestess. Most of the devotees of this cult were young fellows, but the head of it was a young woman who called herself 'Tanit-Isis'—letting it be known that her real name—her name in this latest incarnation, as she put it—was Marceline Bedard. She claimed to be the left-handed daughter of Marquis de Chameaux, and seemed to have been both a petty artist and an artist's model before adopting this more lucrative magical game. Someone said she had lived for a time in the West Indies—Martinique, I think—but she was very reticent about herself. Part of her pose was a great show of austerity and holiness, but I don't think the more experienced students took that very seriously.

"Denis, though, was far from experienced, and wrote me fully ten pages of slush about the goddess he had discovered. If I'd only realised his simplicity I might have done something, but I never thought a puppy infatuation like that could mean much. I felt absurdly sure that Denis' touchy personal honour and family pride would always keep him out of the most serious complications.

"As time went on, though, his letters began to make me nervous. He mentioned this Marceline more and more, and his friends less and less; and began talking about the 'cruel and silly way' they declined to introduce her to their mothers and sisters. He seems to have asked her no questions about herself, and I don't doubt but that she filled him full of romantic legendry concerning her origin and divine revelations and the way people slighted her. At length I could see that Denis was altogether cutting his own crowd and spending the bulk of his time with this alluring priestess. At her especial request he never told the old crowd of their continual meetings; so nobody over there tried to break the affair up.

"I suppose she thought he was fabulously rich; for he had the air of a patrician, and people of a certain class think all aristocratic

Americans are wealthy. In any case, she probably thought this a rare chance to contract a genuine right-handed alliance with a really eligible young man. By the time my nervousness burst into open advice, it was too late. The boy had lawfully married her, and wrote that he was dropping his studies and bringing the woman home to Riverside. He said she had made a great sacrifice and resigned her leadership of the magical cult, and that henceforward she would be merely a private gentlewoman—the future mistress of Riverside, and mother of de Russys to come.

"Well, sir, I took it the best way I could. I knew that sophisticated Continentals have different standards from our old American ones—and anyway, I really knew nothing against the woman. A charlatan, perhaps, but why necessarily any worse? I suppose I tried to keep as naive as possible about such things in those days, for the boy's sake. Clearly, there was nothing for a man of sense to do but to let Denis alone so long as his new wife conformed to de Russy ways. Let her have a chance to prove herself—perhaps she wouldn't hurt the family as much as some might fear. So I didn't raise any objections or ask any penitence. The thing was done, and I stood ready to welcome the boy back, whatever he brought with him.

"They got here three weeks after the telegram telling of the marriage. Marceline was beautiful—there was no denying that—and I could see how the boy might very well get foolish about her. She did have an air of breeding, and I think to this day she must have had some strains of good blood in her. She was apparently not much over twenty; of medium size, fairly slim, and as graceful as a tigress in posture and motions. Her complexion was a deep olive—like old ivory—and her eyes were large and very dark. She had small, classically regular features—though not quite clean-cut enough to suit my taste—and the most singular head of jet black hair that I ever saw.

"I didn't wonder that she had dragged the subject of hair into her magical cult, for with that heavy profusion of it the idea must have occurred to her naturally. Coiled up, it made her look like some Oriental princess in a drawing of Aubrey Beardsley's. Hanging down her back, it came well below her knees and shone in the light as if it had possessed some separate, unholy vitality of its own. I would almost have thought of Medusa or Berenice myself—without having such things suggested to me—upon seeing and studying that hair.

"Sometimes I thought it moved slightly of itself, and tended to arrange itself in distinct ropes or strands, but this may have been sheer illusion. She brushed it incessantly, and seemed to use some sort of preparation on it. I got the notion once—a curious, whimsical notion—that it was a living thing which she had to feed in some strange way. All nonsense—but it added to my feeling of constraint about her and her hair.

"For I can't deny that I failed to like her wholly, no matter how hard I tried. I couldn't tell what the trouble was, but it was there. Something about her repelled me very subtly, and I could not help weaving morbid and macabre associations about everything connected with her. Her complexion called up thoughts of Babylon, Atlantis, Lemuria, and the terrible forgotten dominations of an elder world; her eyes struck me sometimes as the eyes of some unholy forest creature or animal-goddess too immeasurably ancient to be fully human; and her hair—that dense, exotic, overnourished growth of oily inkiness—made one shiver as a great black python might have done. There was no doubt but that she realised my involuntary attitude—though I tried to hide it, and she tried to hide the fact that she noticed it.

"Yet the boy's infatuation lasted. He positively fawned on her, and overdid all the little gallantries of daily life to a sickening degree. She appeared to return the feeling, though I could see it took a conscious effort to make her duplicate his enthusiasms and extravagances. For one thing, I think she was piqued to learn that we weren't as wealthy as she had expected.

"It was a bad business all told. I could see that sad undercurrents were arising. Denis was half-hypnotised with puppy-love, and began to grow away from me as he felt my shrinking from his wife. This kind of thing went on for months, and I saw that I was losing my only son—the boy who had formed the centre of all my thoughts and acts for the past quarter century. I'll own that I felt bitter about it—what father wouldn't? And yet I could do nothing.

"Marceline seemed to be a good wife enough in those early months, and our friends received her without any quibbling or questioning. I was always nervous, though, about what some of the young fellows in Paris might write home to their relatives after the news of the marriage spread around. Despite the woman's love of secrecy, it couldn't remain hidden forever—indeed, Denis had written a few of his closest friends, in strict confidence, as soon as he was settled with her at Riverside.

"I got to staying alone in my room more and more, with my failing health as an excuse. It was about that time that my present spinal neuritis began to develop—which made the excuse a pretty good one. Denis didn't seem to notice the trouble, or take any interest in me and my habits and affairs; and it hurt me to see how callous he was getting. I began to get sleepless, and often racked my brain in the night to try to find out what really was the matter—what it really was that made my new daughter-in-law so repulsive and even dimly horrible to me. It surely wasn't her old mystical nonsense, for she had left all the past behind her and never mentioned it once. She didn't even do any painting, although I understood that she had once dabbled in art.

"Oddly, the only ones who seemed to share my uneasiness were the servants. The darkies around the house seemed very sullen in their attitude toward her, and in a few weeks all save the few who were strongly attached to our family had left. These few—old Scipio and his wife Sarah, the cook Delilah, and Mary, Scipio's daughter—were as civil as possible; but plainly revealed that their new mistress commanded their duty rather than their affection. They stayed in their own remote part of the house as much as possible. McCabe, our white chauffeur, was insolently admiring rather than hostile; and another exception was a very old Zulu woman, said to have come from Africa over a hundred years before, who had been a sort of leader in her small cabin as a kind of family pensioner. Old Sophonisba always shewed reverence whenever Marceline came near her, and one time I saw her kiss the ground where her mistress had walked. Blacks are superstitious animals, and I wondered whether Marceline had been talking any of her mystical nonsense to our hands in order to overcome their evident dislike."

III.

"Well, that's how we went on for nearly half a year. Then, in the summer of 1916, things began to happen. Toward the middle of June Denis got a note from his old friend Frank Marsh, telling of a sort of nervous breakdown which made him want to take a rest in the country. It was postmarked New Orleans—for Marsh had gone home from Paris when he felt the collapse coming on—and seemed a very plain though polite bid for an invitation from us. Marsh, of course, knew that Marceline was here; and asked very courteously after her. Denis was sorry to hear of his trouble and told him at once to come along for an indefinite visit.

"Marsh came—and I was shocked to notice how he had changed since I had seen him in his earlier days. He was a smallish, lightish fellow, with blue eyes and an undecided chin; and now I could see the effects of drink and I don't know what else in his puffy eyelids, enlarged nose-pores, and heavy lines around the mouth. I reckon he had taken his pose of decadence pretty seriously, and set out to be as much of a Rimbaud, Baudelaire, or Lautréamont as he could. And yet he was delightful to talk to—for like all decadents he was exquisitely sensitive to the colour and atmosphere and names of things; admirably, thoroughly alive, and with whole records of conscious experience in obscure, shadowy fields of living and feeling which most of us pass over without knowing they exist. Poor young devil—if only his father had lived longer and taken him in hand! There was great stuff in the boy!

"I was glad of the visit, for I felt it would help to set up a normal atmosphere in the house again. And that's what it really seemed to do at first; for as I said, Marsh was a delight to have around. He was as sincere and profound an artist as I ever saw in my life, and I certainly believe that nothing on earth mattered to him except the perception and expression of beauty. When he saw an exquisite thing, or was creating one, his eyes would dilate until the light irises went nearly out of sight—leaving two mystical black pits in that weak, delicate, chalk-like face; black pits opening on strange worlds which none of us could guess about.

"When he reached here, though, he didn't have many chances to shew this tendency; for he had, as he told Denis, gone quite stale. It seems he had been very successful as an artist of a bizarre kind—like Fuseli or Goya or Sime or Clark Ashton Smith—but had suddenly become played out. The world of ordinary things around him had ceased to hold anything he could recognise as beauty—beauty, that is, of enough force and poignancy to arouse his creative faculty. He had often been this way before—all decadents are—but this time he could not invent any new, strange, or outré sensation or experience which would supply the needed illusion of fresh beauty or stimulatingly adventurous expectancy. He was like a Durtal or a des Esseintes at the most jaded point of his curious orbit.

"Marceline was away when Marsh arrived. She hadn't been enthusiastic about his coming, and had refused to decline an invitation from some of our friends in St. Louis which came about that time for her and Denis. Denis, of course, stayed to receive his guest;

but Marceline had gone on alone. It was the first time they had ever been separated, and I hoped the interval would help to dispel the sort of daze that was making such a fool of the boy. Marceline shewed no hurry to get back, but seemed to me to prolong her absence as much as she could. Denis stood it better than one would have expected from such a doting husband, and seemed more like his old self as he talked over other days with Marsh and tried to cheer the listless aesthete up.

"It was Marsh who seemed most impatient to see the woman; perhaps because he thought her strange beauty, or some phase of the mysticism which had gone into her one-time magical cult, might help to reawaken his interest in things and give him another start toward artistic creation. That there was no baser reason, I was absolutely certain from what I knew of Marsh's character. With all his weaknesses, he was a gentleman—and it had indeed relieved me when I first learned that he wanted to come here because his willingness to accept Denis' hospitality proved that there was no reason why he shouldn't.

"When, at last, Marceline did return, I could see that Marsh was tremendously affected. He did not attempt to make her talk of the bizarre thing which she had so definitely abandoned, but was unable to hide a powerful admiration which kept his eyes—now dilated in that curious way for the first time during his visit—riveted to her every moment she was in the room. She, however, seemed uneasy rather than pleased by his steady scrutiny—that is, she seemed so at first, though this feeling of hers wore away in a few days, and left the two on a basis of the most cordial and voluble congeniality. I could see Marsh studying her constantly when he thought no one was watching; and I wondered how long it would be that only the artist, and not the primitive man, would be aroused by her mysterious graces.

"Denis naturally felt some irritation at this turn of affairs; though he realised that his guest was a man of honour and that, as kindred mystics and aesthetes, Marceline and Marsh would naturally have things and interests to discuss in which a more or less conventional person could have no part. He didn't hold anything against anybody, but merely regretted that his own imagination was too limited and traditional to let him talk with Marceline as Marsh talked. At this stage of things I began to see more of the boy. With his wife otherwise busy, he had time to remember that he had a father—and a father who was ready to help him in any sort of perplexity or difficulty.

"We often sat together on the veranda watching Marsh and Marceline as they rode up or down the drive on horseback, or played tennis on the court that used to stretch south of the house. They talked mostly in French, which Marsh, though he hadn't more than a quarter-portion of French blood, handled more glibly than either Denis or I could speak it. Marceline's English, always academically correct, was rapidly improving in accent; but it was plain that she relished dropping back into her mother-tongue. As we looked at the congenial couple they made, I could see the boy's cheek and throat muscles tighten—though he wasn't a whit less ideal a host to Marsh, or a whit less considerate a husband to Marceline.

"All this was generally in the afternoon; for Marceline rose very late, had breakfast in bed, and took an immense amount of time preparing to come downstairs. I never knew of anyone so wrapped up in cosmetics, beauty exercises, hair-oils, unguents, and everything of that kind. It was in these morning hours that Denis and Marsh did their real visiting, and exchanged the close confidences which kept their friendship up despite the strain that jealousy imposed.

"Well, it was in one of those morning talks on the veranda that Marsh made the proposition which brought on the end. I was laid up with some of my neuritis, but had managed to get downstairs and stretch out on the front parlour sofa near the long window. Denis and Marsh were just outside; so I couldn't help hearing all they said. They had been talking about art, and the curious, capricious environmental elements needed to jolt an artist into producing the real article, when Marsh suddenly swerved from abstractions to the personal application he must have had in mind from the start.

"'I suppose,' he was saying, 'that nobody can tell just what it is in some scenes or objects that makes them aesthetic stimuli for certain individuals. Basically, of course, it must have some reference to each man's background of stored-up mental associations, for no two people have the same scale of sensitiveness and responses. We decadents are artists for whom all ordinary things have ceased to have any emotional or imaginative significance, but no one of us responds in the same way to exactly the same extraordinary thing. Now take me, for instance. . . .'

"He paused and resumed.

"'I know, Denny, that I can say these things to you because you have such a preternaturally unspoiled mind—clean, fine, direct, objective, and all that. You won't misunderstand as an oversubtilised, effete man of the world might.'

"He paused once more.

"'The fact is, I think I know what's needed to set my imagination working again. I've had a dim idea of it ever since we were in Paris, but I'm sure now. It's Marceline, old chap—that face and that hair, and the train of shadowy images they bring up. Not merely visible beauty—though God knows there's enough of that—but something peculiar and individualised, that can't exactly be explained. Do you know, in the last few days I've felt the existence of such a stimulus so keenly that I honestly think I could outdo myself—break into the real masterpiece class if I could get hold of paint and canvas at just the time when her face and hair set my fancy stirring and weaving. There's something weird and other-worldly about it—something joined up with the dim ancient thing Marceline represents. I don't know how much she's told you about that side of her, but I can assure you there's plenty of it. She has some marvellous links with the outside. . . .'

"Some change in Denis' expression must have halted the speaker here, for there was a considerable spell of silence before the words went on. I was utterly taken aback, for I'd expected no such overt development like this; and I wondered what my son could be thinking. My heart began to pound violently, and I strained my ears in the frankest of intentional eavesdropping. Then Marsh resumed.

"'Of course you're jealous—I know how a speech like mine must sound—but I can swear to you that you needn't be.'

"Denis did not answer, and Marsh went on.

"'To tell the truth, I could never be in love with Marceline—I couldn't even be a cordial friend of hers in the warmest sense. Why, damn it all, I felt like a hypocrite talking with her these days as I've been doing.

"'The case simply is, that one phase of her half hypnotises me in a certain way—a very strange, fantastic, and dimly terrible way—just as another phase half hypnotises you in a much more normal way. I see something in her—or to be psychologically exact, something through her or beyond her—that you don't see at all. Something that brings up a vast pageantry of shapes from forgotten abysses, and makes me want to paint incredible things whose outlines vanish the instant I try to envisage them clearly. Don't mistake, Denny, your wife is a magnificent being, a splendid focus of cosmic forces who has a right to be called divine if anything on earth has!'

"I felt a clearing of the situation at this point, for the abstract strangeness of Marsh's expressed statement, plus the flattery he was now heaping on Marceline, could not fail to disarm and mollify one as fondly proud of his consort as Denis always was. Marsh evidently caught the change himself, for there was more confidence in his tone as he continued.

"'I must paint her, Denny—must paint that hair—and you won't regret it. There's something more than mortal about that hair—something more than beautiful—'

"He paused, and I wondered what Denis could be thinking. I wondered, indeed, what I was really thinking myself. Was Marsh's interest actually that of the artist alone, or was he merely infatuated as Denis had been? I had thought, in their schooldays, that he had envied my boy; and I dimly felt that it might be the same now. On the other hand, something in that talk of artistic stimulus had rung amazingly true; so that the more I pondered, the more I was inclined to take the stuff at face value. Denis seemed to do so, too, for although I could not catch his low-spoken reply, I could tell by the effect it produced that it must have been affirmative.

"There was a sound of someone slapping another on the back, and then a grateful speech from Marsh that I was long to remember.

"'That's great, Denny; and just as I told you, you'll never regret it. In a sense, I'm half doing it for you. You'll be a different man when you see it. I'll put you back where you used to be—give you a waking-up and a sort of salvation—but you can't see what I mean as yet. Just remember old friendship, and don't get the idea that I'm not the same old bird!'

"I rose perplexedly as I saw the two stroll off across the lawn, arm in arm, and smoking in unison. What could Marsh have meant by his strange and almost ominous reassurance? The more my fears were quieted in one direction, the more they were aroused in another. Look at it in any way I could, it seemed to be rather a bad business.

"But matters got started just the same. Denis fixed up an attic room with skylights, and Marsh sent for all sorts of painting equipment. Everyone was rather excited about the new venture, and I was at least glad that something was on foot to break the brooding tension. Soon the sittings began, and we all took them quite seriously—for we could see that Marsh regarded them as important artistic events. Denny and I used to go quietly about the house as though something sacred were occurring, and we knew that it was sacred so far as Marsh was concerned.

"With Marceline, though, it was a different matter, as I began to see at once. Whatever Marsh's reactions to the sittings may have been, hers were painfully obvious. Every possible way she betrayed a frank and commonplace infatuation for the artist, and would repulse Denis' marks of affection whenever she dared. Oddly, I noticed this more vividly than Denis himself, and tried to devise some plan for keeping the boy's mind easy until the matter could be straightened out. There was no use in having him excited about it if it could be helped.

"In the end I decided that Denis had better be away while the disagreeable situation existed. I could represent his interests well enough at this end, and sooner or later Marsh would finish the picture and go. My view of Marsh's honour was such that I did not look for any worse developments. When the matter had blown over, and Marceline had forgotten about her new infatuation, it would be time enough to have Denis on hand again.

"So I wrote a long letter to my marketing and financial agent in New York, and cooked up a plan to have the boy summoned there for an indefinite time. I had the agent write him that our affairs absolutely required one of us to go East, and of course my illness made it clear that I could not be the one. It was arranged that when Denis got to New York he would find enough plausible matters to keep him busy as long as I thought he ought to be away.

"The plan worked perfectly, and Denis started for New York without the least suspicion; Marceline and Marsh going with him in the car to Cape Girardeau, where he caught the afternoon train to St. Louis. They returned about dark, and as McCabe drove the car back to the stables I could hear them talking on the veranda—in those same chairs near the long parlour window where Marsh and Denis had sat when I overheard them talk about the portrait. This time I resolved to do some intentional eavesdropping, so quietly went down to the front parlour and stretched out on the sofa near the window.

"At first I could not hear anything, but very shortly there came a sound as of a chair being shifted, followed by a short, sharp breath and a sort of inarticulately hurt exclamation from Marceline. Then I heard Marsh speaking in a strained, almost formal voice.

"'I'd enjoy working tonight if you're not too tired.'

"Marceline's reply was in the same hurt tone which had marked her exclamation. She used English as he had done.

"'Oh, Frank, is that really all you care about? Forever working! Can't we just sit out in this glorious moonlight?'

"He answered impatiently, his voice shewing a certain contempt beneath the dominant quality of artistic enthusiasm.

"'Moonlight! Good God, what cheap sentimentality! For a supposedly sophisticated person you surely do hang on to some of the crudest claptrap that ever escaped from the dime novels! With art at your elbow, you have to think of the moon—cheap as a spotlight at the varieties! Or perhaps it makes you think of the Roodmas dance around the stone pillars at Auteuil. Hell, how you used to make those goggle-eyed yaps stare! But no—I suppose you've dropped all that now. No more Atlantean magic or hair-snake rites for Madame de Russy! I'm the only one to remember the old things—the things that came down through the temples of Tanit and echoed on the ramparts of Zimbabwe. But I won't be cheated of that remembrance—all that is weaving itself into the thing on my canvas—the thing that is going to capture wonder and crystallise the secrets of 75,000 years. . . .'

"Marceline interrupted in a voice full of mixed emotions.

"'It's you who are cheaply sentimental now! You know well that the old things had better be let alone. All of you had better look out if ever I chant the old rites or try to call up what lies hidden in Yuggoth, Zimbabwe, and R'lyeh. I thought you had more sense!

"'You lack logic. You want me to be interested in this precious painting of yours, yet you never let me see what you're doing. Always that black cloth over it! It's of me—I shouldn't think it would matter if I saw it. . . .'

"Marsh was interrupting this time, his voice curiously hard and strained.

"'No. Not now. You'll see it in due course of time. You say it's of you—yes, it's that, but it's more. If you knew, you mightn't be so impatient. Poor Denis! My God, it's a shame!'

"My throat went suddenly dry as the words rose to an almost febrile pitch. What could Marsh mean? Suddenly I saw that he had stopped and was entering the house alone. I heard the front door slam, and listened as his footsteps ascended the stairs. Outside on the veranda I could still hear Marceline's heavy, angry breathing. I crept away sick at heart, feeling that there were grave things to ferret out before I could safely let Denis come back.

"After that evening the tension around the place was even worse than before. Marceline had always lived on flattery and fawning, and the shock of those few blunt words from Marsh was too much for her temperament. There was no living in the house with her any more, for with poor Denis gone she took out her abusiveness on everybody. When she could find no one indoors to quarrel with she would go out to Sophonisba's cabin and spend hours talking with the queer old Zulu woman. Aunt Sophy was the only person who would fawn abjectly enough to suit her, and when I tried once to overhear their conversation I found Marceline whispering about 'elder secrets' and 'unknown Kadath' while the negress rocked to and fro in her chair, making inarticulate sounds of reverence and admiration every now and then.

"But nothing could break her dog-like infatuation for Marsh. She would talk bitterly and sullenly to him, yet was getting more and more obedient to his wishes. It was very convenient for him, since he now became able to make her pose for the picture whenever he felt like painting. He tried to shew gratitude for this willingness, but I thought I could detect a kind of contempt or even loathing beneath his careful politeness. For my part, I frankly hated Marceline! There was no use in calling my attitude anything as mild as mere dislike these days. Certainly, I was glad Denis was away. His letters, not nearly so frequent as I wished, shewed signs of strain and worry.

"As the middle of August went by I gathered from Marsh's remarks that the portrait was nearly done. His mood seemed increasingly sardonic, though Marceline's temper improved a bit as the prospect of seeing the thing tickled her vanity. I can still recall the day when Marsh said he'd have everything finished within a week. Marceline brightened up perceptibly, though not without a venomous look at me. It seemed as if her coiled hair visibly tightened about her head.

"'I'm to be the first to see it!' she snapped. Then, smiling at Marsh, she said, 'And if I don't like it I shall slash it to pieces!'

"Marsh's face took on the most curious look I have ever seen it wear as he answered her.

"'I can't vouch for your taste, Marceline, but I swear it will be magnificent! Not that I want to take much credit—art creates itself—and this thing had to be done. Just wait!'

"During the next few days I felt a queer sense of foreboding, as if the completion of the picture meant a kind of catastrophe instead of a relief. Denis, too, had not written me, and my agent in New York said he was planning some trip to the country. I wondered what the outcome of the whole thing would be. What a queer mixture of elements—Marsh and Marceline, Denis and I! How would all these ultimately react on one another? When my fears grew too great I tried to lay them all to my infirmity, but that explanation never quite satisfied me."

IV.

"Well, the thing exploded on Tuesday, the twenty-sixth of August. I had risen at my usual time and had breakfast, but was not good for much because of the pain in my spine. It had been troubling me badly of late, and forcing me to take opiates when it got too unbearable; nobody else was downstairs except the servants, though I could hear Marceline moving about in her room. Marsh slept in the attic next his studio, and had begun to keep such late hours that he was seldom up till noon. About ten o'clock the pain got the better of me, so that I took a double dose of my opiate and lay down on the parlour sofa. The last I heard was Marceline's pacing overhead. Poor creature—if I had known! She must have been walking before the long mirror admiring herself. That was like her. Vain from start to finish—revelling in her own beauty, just as she revelled in all the little luxuries Denis was able to give her.

"I didn't wake up till near sunset, and knew instantly how long I had slept from the golden light and long shadows outside the long window. Nobody was about, and a sort of unnatural stillness seemed to be hovering over everything. From afar, though, I thought I could sense a faint howling, wild and intermittent, whose quality had a slight but baffling familiarity about it. I'm not much for psychic premonitions, but I was frightfully uneasy from the start. There had been dreams—even worse than the ones I had been dreaming in the weeks before—and this time they seemed hideously linked to some black and festering reality. The whole place had a poisonous air. Afterward I reflected that certain sounds must have filtered through to my unconscious brain during those hours of drugged sleep. My pain, though, was very much eased; and I rose and walked without difficulty.

"Soon enough I began to see that something was wrong. Marsh and Marceline might have been riding, but someone ought to have been getting dinner in the kitchen. Instead, there was only silence, except for that faint distant howl or wail; and nobody answered when I pulled the old-fashioned bell-cord to summon Scipio. Then, chancing to look up, I saw the spreading stain on the ceiling—the bright red stain, that must have come through the floor of Marceline's room.

"In an instant I forgot my crippled back and hurried upstairs to find out the worst. Everything under the sun raced through my mind as I struggled with the dampness-warped door of that silent chamber, and most hideous of all was a terrible sense of malign fulfilment and fatal expectedness. I had, it struck me, known all along that nameless horrors were gathering; that something profoundly and cosmically evil had gained a foot-hold under my roof from which only blood and tragedy could result.

"The door gave at last, and I stumbled into the large room beyond—all dim from the branches of the great trees outside the windows. For a moment I could do nothing but flinch at the faint evil odour that immediately struck my nostrils. Then, turning on the electric light and glancing around, I glimpsed a nameless blasphemy on the yellow and blue rug.

"It lay face down in a great pool of dark, thickened blood, and had the gory print of a shod human foot in the middle of its naked back. Blood was spattered everywhere—on the walls, furniture, and floor. My knees gave way as I took in the sight, so that I had to stumble to a chair and slump down. The thing had obviously been a human being, though its identity was not easy to establish at first; since it was without clothes, and had most of its hair hacked and torn from the scalp in a very crude way. It was of a deep ivory colour, and I knew that it must have been Marceline. The shoe-print on the back made the thing seem all the more hellish. I could not even picture the strange, loathsome tragedy which must have taken place while I slept in the room below. When I raised my hand to wipe my dripping forehead I saw that my fingers were sticky with blood. I shuddered, then realised that it must have come from the knob of the door which the unknown murderer had forced shut behind him as he left. He had taken his weapon with him, it seemed, for no instrument of death was visible here.

"As I studied the floor I saw that a line of sticky footprints like the one on the body led away from the horror to the door. There was another blood-trail, too, and of a less easily explainable kind; a broadish, continuous line, as if marking the path of some huge snake. At first I concluded it must be due to something the murderer had dragged after him. Then, noting the way some of the footprints seemed to be superimposed on it, I was forced to believe that it had been there when the murderer left. But what crawling entity could have been in that room with the victim and her assassin, leaving before the killer when the deed was done? As I asked myself this question I thought I heard fresh bursts of that faint, distant wailing.

"Finally, rousing myself from a lethargy of horror, I got on my feet again and began following the footprints. Who the murderer was, I could not even faintly guess, nor could I try to explain the absence of the servants. I vaguely felt that I ought to go up to Marsh's attic quarters, but before I had fully formulated the idea I saw that the bloody trail was indeed taking me there. Was he himself the murderer? Had he gone mad under the strain of the morbid situation and suddenly run amok?

"In the attic corridor the trail became faint, the prints almost ceasing as they merged with the dark carpet. I could still, however, discern the strange single path of the entity who had gone first; and this led straight to the closed door of Marsh's studio, disappearing beneath it at a point about half way from side to side. Evidently it had crossed the threshold at a time when the door was wide open.

"Sick at heart, I tried the knob and found the door unlocked. Opening it, I paused in the waning north light to see what fresh nightmare might be awaiting me. There was certainly something human on the floor, and I reached for the switch to turn on the chandelier.

"But as the light flashed up my gaze left the floor and its horror—that was Marsh, poor devil—to fix itself frantically and incredulously upon the living thing that cowered and stared in the open doorway leading to Marsh's bedroom. It was a tousled, wild-eyed thing, crusted with dried blood and carrying in its hand a wicked machete which had been one of the ornaments of the studio wall. Yet even in that awful moment I recognised it as one whom I had thought more than a thousand miles away. It was my own boy Denis—or the maddened wreck which had once been Denis.

"The sight of me seemed to bring back a trifle of sanity—or at least of memory—in the poor boy. He straightened up and began to toss his head about as if trying to shake free from some enveloping influence. I could not speak a word, but moved my lips in an effort to get back my voice. My eyes wandered for a moment to the figure on the floor in front of the heavily draped easel—the figure toward which the strange blood-trail led, and which seemed to be tangled in the coils of some dark, ropy object. The shifting of my glance apparently produced some impression in the twisted brain of the boy, for suddenly he began to mutter in a hoarse whisper whose purport I was soon able to catch.

"'I had to exterminate her—she was the devil—the summit and high-priestess of all evil—the spawn of the pit—Marsh knew, and tried to warn me. Good old Frank—I didn't kill him, though I was ready to before I realised. But I went down there and killed her—then that cursed hair—'

"I listened in horror as Denis choked, paused, and began again.

"'You didn't know—her letters got queer and I knew she was in love with Marsh. Then she nearly stopped writing. He never mentioned her—I felt something was wrong, and thought I ought to come back and find out. Couldn't tell you—your manner would have given it away. Wanted to surprise them. Got here about noon today—came in a cab and sent the house-servants all off—let the field hands alone, for their cabins are all out of earshot. Told McCabe to get me some things in Cape Girardeau and not bother to come back till tomorrow. Had all the niggers take the old car and let Mary drive them to Bend Village for a vacation—told 'em we were all going on some sort of outing and wouldn't need help. Said they'd better stay all night with Uncle Scip's cousin, who keeps that nigger boarding-house.'

"Denis was getting very incoherent now, and I strained my ears to grasp every word. Again I thought I heard that wild, far-off wail, but the story had first place for the present.

"'Saw you sleeping in the parlour, and took a chance you wouldn't wake up. Then went upstairs on the quiet to hunt up Marsh and . . . that woman!'

"The boy shuddered as he avoided pronouncing Marceline's name. At the same time I saw his eyes dilate in unison with a bursting of the distant crying, whose vague familiarity had now become very great.

"'She was not in her room, so I went up to the studio. Door was shut, and I could hear voices inside. Didn't knock—just burst in and found her posing for the picture. Nude, but with that hellish hair all draped around her. And making all sorts of sheep's eyes at Marsh. He had the easel turned half away from the door, so I couldn't see the picture. Both of them were pretty well jolted when I shewed up, and Marsh dropped his brush. I was in a rage and told him he'd have to shew me the portrait, but he got calmer every minute. Told me it wasn't quite done, but would be in a day or two—said I could see it then—she—hadn't seen it.

"'But that didn't go with me. I stepped up, and he dropped a velvet curtain over the thing before I could see it. He was ready to fight before letting me see it, but that—that—she—stepped up and sided with me. Said we ought to see it. Frank got horribly worked up, and gave me a punch when I tried to get at the curtain. I punched back and seemed to have knocked him out. Then I was almost knocked out myself by the shriek that—that creature—gave. She'd drawn aside the hangings herself, and had caught a look at what Marsh had been painting. I wheeled around and saw her rushing like mad out of the room—*then I saw the picture.*'

"Madness flared up in the boy's eyes again as he got to this place, and I thought for a minute he was going to spring at me with his machete. But after a pause he partly steadied himself.

"'Oh, God—that thing! Don't ever look at it! Burn it with the hangings around it and throw the ashes into the river! Marsh knew—and was warning me. He knew what it was—what that woman—that leopardess, or gorgon, or lamia, or whatever she was—actually represented. He'd tried to hint to me ever since I met her in his Paris studio, but it couldn't be told in words. I thought they all wronged her when they whispered horrors about her—she had me hypnotised so that I couldn't believe the plain facts—but this picture has caught the whole secret—the whole monstrous background!

"'God, but Frank is an artist! That thing is the greatest piece of work any living soul has produced since Rembrandt! It's a crime to burn it—but it would be a greater crime to let it exist—just as it would have been an abhorrent sin to let—that she-daemon—exist any longer. The minute I saw it I understood what—she—was, and what part she played in the frightful secret that has come down from the days of Cthulhu and the Elder Ones—the secret that was nearly wiped out when Atlantis sank, but that kept half alive in hidden traditions and allegorical myths and furtive, midnight cult-practices. For you know she was the real thing. It wasn't any fake. It would have been merciful if it had been a fake. It was the old, hideous shadow that philosophers never dared mention—the thing hinted at in the *Necronomicon* and symbolised in the Easter Island colossi.

"'She thought we couldn't see through—that the false front would hold till we had bartered away our immortal souls. And she was half right—she'd have got me in the end. She was only—waiting. But Frank—good old Frank—was too much for me. *He knew what it all meant, and painted it.* I don't wonder she shrieked and ran off when she saw it. It wasn't quite done, but God knows *enough was there.*

"'Then I knew I'd got to kill her—kill her, and everything connected with her. It was a taint that wholesome human blood couldn't bear. There was something else, too—but you'll never know that if you burn the picture without looking. I staggered down to her room with this machete that I got off the wall here, leaving Frank still knocked out. He was breathing, though, and I knew and thanked heaven that I hadn't killed him.

"'I found her in front of the mirror braiding that accursed hair. She turned on me like a wild beast, and began spitting out her hatred of Marsh. The fact that she'd been in love with him—and I knew she had—only made it worse. For a minute I couldn't move, and she came within an ace of completely hypnotising me. Then I thought of the picture, and the spell broke. She saw the breaking in my eyes, and must have noticed the machete, too. I never saw anything give such a wild jungle beast look as she did then. She sprang for me with claws out like a leopard's, but I was too quick. I swung the machete, and it was all over.'

"Denis had to stop again there, and I saw the perspiration running down his forehead through the spattered blood. But in a moment he hoarsely resumed.

"'I said it was all over—but God! some of it had only just begun! I felt I had fought the legions of Satan, and put my foot on the back of the thing I had annihilated. *Then I saw that blasphemous braid of coarse black hair begin to twist and squirm of itself.*

"'I might have known it. It was all in the old tales. That damnable hair had a life of its own, that couldn't be ended by killing the creature itself. I knew I'd have to burn it, so I started to hack it off with the machete. God, but it was devilish work! Tough—like iron wires—but I managed to do it. And it was loathsome the way the big braid writhed and struggled in my grasp.

"'About the time I had the last strand cut or pulled off I heard that eldritch wailing from behind the house. You know—it's still going off and on. I don't know what it is, but it must be something springing from this hellish business. It half seems like something I ought to know but can't quite place. It got my nerves the first time I heard it, and I dropped the severed braid in my fright. Then, I got a worse fright—for in another second the braid had turned on me and began to strike venomously with one of its ends which had knotted itself up like a sort of grotesque head. I struck out with the machete, and it turned away. Then, when I had my breath again, I saw that the monstrous thing was crawling along the floor by itself like a great black snake. I couldn't do anything for a while, but when it vanished through the door I managed to pull myself together and stumble after it. I could follow the broad, bloody trail, and I saw it led upstairs. It brought me here—and may heaven curse me if I didn't see it through the doorway, striking at poor dazed Marsh like a maddened rattler as it had struck at me, finally coiling around him as a python would. He had begun to come to, but that abominable serpent thing got him before he was on his feet. I knew that all of that woman's hatred was behind it, but I hadn't the power to pull it off. I tried, but it was too much for me. Even the machete was no good—I couldn't swing it freely or it would have slashed Frank to pieces. So I saw those monstrous coils tighten—saw poor Frank crushed to death before my eyes—and all the time that awful faint howling came from somewhere beyond the fields.

"'That's all. I pulled the velvet cloth over the picture and hope it'll never be lifted. The thing must be burnt. I couldn't pry the coils off poor, dead Frank—they cling to him like a leach, and seem to have lost their motion altogether. It's as if that snaky rope of hair has a kind of perverse fondness for the man it killed—it's clinging to him—embracing him. You'll have to burn poor Frank with it—but for God's sake don't forget to see it in ashes. That and the picture. They must both go. The safety of the world demands that they go.'

"Denis might have whispered more, but a fresh burst of distant wailing cut us short. For the first time we knew what it was, for a westerly veering wind brought articulate words at last. We ought to have known long before, since sounds much like it had often come from the same source. It was wrinkled Sophonisba, the ancient Zulu witch-woman who had fawned on Marceline, keening from her cabin in a way which crowned the horrors of this nightmare tragedy. We could both hear some of the things she howled, and knew that secret and primordial bonds linked this savage sorceress with that other inheritor of elder secrets who had just been extirpated. Some of the words she used betrayed her closeness to daemonic and palaeogean traditions.

"'*Iä! Iä! Shub-Niggurath! Ya-R'lyeh! N'gagi n'bulu bwana n'lolo!* Ya, yo, pore Missy Tanit, pore Missy Isis! Marse Clooloo, come up outen de water an' git yo chile—she done daid! She done daid! De hair ain' got no missus no mo', Marse Clooloo. Ol' Sophy, she know! Ol' Sophy, she done got de black stone outen Big Zimbabwe in ol' Affriky! Ol' Sophy, she done dance in de moonshine roun' de crocodile-stone befo' de N'bangus cotch her and sell her to de ship folks! No mo' Tanit! No mo' Isis! No mo' witch-woman to keep de fire a-goin' in de big stone place! Ya, yo! *N'gagi n'bulu bwana n'lolo! Iä! Shub-Niggurath!* She daid! Ol' Sophy know!'

"That wasn't the end of the wailing, but it was all I could pay attention to. The expression on my boy's face shewed that it had reminded him of something frightful, and the tightening of his hand on the machete boded no good. I knew he was desperate, and sprang to disarm him if possible before he could do anything more.

"But I was too late. An old man with a bad spine doesn't count for much physically. There was a terrible struggle, but he had done for himself before many seconds were over. I'm not sure yet but that he tried to kill me, too. His last panting words were something about the need of wiping out everything that had been connected with Marceline, either by blood or marriage."

V.

"I wonder to this day that I didn't go stark mad in that instant—or in the moments and hours afterward. In front of me was the slain body of my boy—the only human being I had to cherish—and ten feet away, in front of that shrouded easel, was the body of his best friend, with a nameless coil of horror wound around it. Below was the scalped corpse of that she-monster, about whom I was half-ready to believe anything. I was too dazed to analyse the probability of the hair story—and even if I had not been, that dismal howling from Aunt Sophy's cabin would have been enough to quiet doubt for the nonce.

"If I'd been wise, I'd have done just what poor Denis told me to—burned the picture and the body-grasping hair at once and without curiosity—but I was too shaken to be wise. I suppose I muttered foolish things over my boy—and then I remembered that the night was wearing on and that the servants would be back in the morning. It was plain that a matter like this could never be explained, and I knew that I must cover things up and invent a story.

"That coil of hair around Marsh was a monstrous thing. As I poked at it with a sword which I took from the wall I almost thought I felt it tighten its grip on the dead man. I didn't dare touch it—and the longer I looked at it the more horrible things I noticed about it. One thing gave me a start. I won't mention it—but it partly explained the need for feeding the hair with queer oils as Marceline had always done.

"In the end I decided to bury all three bodies in the cellar—with quicklime, which I knew we had in the storehouse. It was a night of hellish work. I dug three graves—my boy's a long way from the other two, for I didn't want him to be near either the woman's body or her hair. I was sorry I couldn't get the coil from around poor Marsh. It was terrible work getting them all down to the cellar. I used blankets in carting the woman and the poor devil with the coil around him. Then I had to get two barrels of lime from the storehouse. God must have given me strength, for I not only moved them both but filled all three graves without a hitch.

"Some of the lime I made into whitewash. I had to take a stepladder and fix over the parlour ceiling where the blood had oozed through. And I burned nearly everything in Marceline's room, scrubbing the walls and floor and heavy furniture. I washed up the attic studio, too, and the trail and footprints that led there. And all the time I could hear old Sophy's wailing in the distance. The devil must have been in that creature to let her voice go on like that. But she always was howling queer things. That's why the field niggers didn't get scared or curious that night. I locked the studio door and took the key to my room. Then I burned all my stained clothes in the fireplace. By dawn the whole house looked quite normal so far as any casual eye could tell. I hadn't dared touch the covered easel, but meant to attend to that later.

"Well, the servants came back next day, and I told them all the young folks had gone to St. Louis. None of the field hands seemed to have seen or heard anything, and old Sophonisba's wailing had stopped at the instant of sunrise. She was like a sphinx after that, and never let out a word of what had been on her brooding witch-brain the day and night before.

"Later on I pretended that Denis and Marsh and Marceline had gone back to Paris and had a certain discreet agency mail me letters from there—letters I had fixed up in forged handwriting. It took a good deal of deceit and reticence to explain things to various friends, and I know people have secretly suspected me of holding something back. I had the deaths of Marsh and Denis reported during the war, and later said Marceline had entered a convent. Fortunately Marsh was an orphan whose eccentric ways had alienated him from his people in Louisiana. Things might have been patched up a good deal better for me if I had had the sense to burn the picture, sell the plantation, and give up trying to manage things with a shaken and overstrained mind. You see what my folly has brought me to. Failing crops—hands discharged one by one—place falling to ruin—and myself a hermit and a target for dozens of queer countryside stories. Nobody will come around here after dark nowadays —or any other time if it can be helped. That's why I knew you must be a stranger.

"And why do I stay here? I can't wholly tell you that. It's bound up too closely with things at the very rim of sane reality. It wouldn't have been so, perhaps, if I hadn't looked at the picture. I ought to have done as poor Denis told me. I honestly meant to burn it when I went up to that locked studio a week after the horror, but I looked first—and that changed everything.

"No—there's no use telling what I saw. You can, in a way, see for yourself presently; though time and dampness have done their work. I don't think it can hurt you if you want to take a look, but it was different with me. I knew too much of what it all meant.

"Denis had been right—it was the greatest triumph of human art since Rembrandt, even though still unfinished. I grasped that at the start, and knew that poor Marsh had justified his decadent philosophy. He was to painting what Baudelaire was to poetry—and Marceline was the key that had unlocked his inmost stronghold of genius.

"The thing almost stunned me when I pulled aside the hangings —stunned me before I half knew what the whole thing was. You know, it's only partly a portrait. Marsh had been pretty literal when he hinted that he wasn't painting Marceline alone, but what he saw through her and beyond her.

"Of course she was in it—was the key to it, in a sense—but her figure only formed one point in a vast composition. She was nude except for that hideous web of hair spun around her, and was half-seated, half-reclining on a sort of bench or divan, carved in patterns unlike those of any known decorative tradition. There was a monstrously shaped goblet in one hand, from which was spilling fluid whose colour I haven't been able to place or classify to this day— I don't know where Marsh even got the pigments.

"The figure and the divan were in the left-hand foreground of the strangest sort of scene I ever saw in my life. I think there was a faint suggestion of its all being a kind of emanation from the woman's brain, yet there was also a directly opposite suggestion—as if she were just an evil image or hallucination conjured up by the scene itself.

"I can't tell you now whether it's an exterior or an interior—whether those hellish Cyclopean vaultings are seen from the outside or the inside, or whether they are indeed carven stone and not merely a morbid fungous arborescence. The geometry of the whole thing is crazy—one gets the acute and obtuse angles all mixed up.

"And God! The shapes of nightmare that float around in that perpetual daemon twilight! The blasphemies that lurk and leer and hold a Witches' Sabbat with that woman as a high-priestess! The black shaggy entities that are not quite goats—the crocodile-headed beast with three legs and a dorsal row of tentacles—and the flat-nosed aegipans dancing in a pattern that Egypt's priests knew and called accursed!

"But the scene wasn't Egypt—it was *behind* Egypt; behind even Atlantis; behind fabled Mu, and myth-whispered Lemuria. It was the ultimate fountain-head of all horror on this earth, and the symbolism shewed only too clearly how integral a part of it Marceline was. I think it must be the unmentionable R'lyeh, that was not built by any creatures of this planet—the thing Marsh and Denis used to talk about in the shadows with hushed voices. In the picture it appears that the whole scene is deep under water—though everybody seems to be breathing freely.

"Well—I couldn't do anything but look and shudder, and finally I saw that Marceline was watching me craftily out of those monstrous, dilated eyes on the canvas. It was no mere superstition—Marsh had actually caught something of her horrible vitality in his symphonies of line and colour, so that she still brooded and stared and hated, just as if most of her weren't down in the cellar under quicklime. *And it was worst of all when some of those Hecate-born snaky strands of hair began to lift themselves up from the surface and grope out into the room toward me.*

"Then it was that I knew the last final horror, and realised I was a guardian and a prisoner forever. She was the thing from which the first dim legends of Medusa and the Gorgons had sprung, and something in my shaken will had been captured and turned to stone at last. Never again would I be safe from those coiling snaky strands—the strands in the picture, and those that lay brooding under the lime near the wine casks. All too late I recalled the tales of the virtual indestructibility, even through centuries of burial, of the hair of the dead.

"My life since has been nothing but horror and slavery. Always there had lurked the fear of what broods down in the cellar. In less than a month the niggers began whispering about the great black snake that crawled around near the wine casks after dark, and about the curious way its trail would lead to another spot six feet away. Finally I had to move everything to another part of the cellar, for not a darky could be induced to go near the place where the snake was seen.

"Then the field hands began talking about the black snake that visited old Sophonisba's cabin every night after midnight. One of them shewed me its trail—and not long afterward I found out that Aunt Sophy herself had begun to pay strange visits to the cellar of the big house, lingering and muttering for hours in the very spot where none of the other blacks would go near. God, but I was glad when that old witch died! I honestly believe she had been a priestess of some ancient and terrible tradition back in Africa. She must have lived to be almost a hundred and fifty years old.

"Sometimes I think I hear something gliding around the house at night. There will be a queer noise on the stairs, where the boards are loose, and the latch of my room will rattle as if with an inward pressure. I always keep my door locked, of course. Then there are certain mornings when I seem to catch a sickish musty odour in the corridors, and notice a faint, ropy trail through the dust of the floors. I know I must guard the hair in the picture, for if anything were to happen to it, there are entities in this house which would take a sure and terrible revenge. I don't even dare to die—for life and death are all one to those in the clutch of what came out of R'lyeh. Something would be on hand to punish my neglect. Medusa's coil has got me, and it will always be the same. Never mix up with secret and ultimate horror, young man, if you value your immortal soul."

VI.

As the old man finished his story I saw that the small lamp had long since burned dry, and that the large one was nearly empty. It must, I knew, be near dawn; and my ears told me that the storm was over. The tale had held me in a half-daze, and I almost feared to glance at the door lest it reveal an inward pressure from some unnamable source. It would be hard to say which had the greatest hold on me—stark horror, incredulity, or a kind of morbid fantastic curiosity. I was wholly beyond speech and had to wait for my strange host to break the spell.

"Do you want to see—the thing?"

His voice was very low and hesitant, and I saw he was tremendously in earnest. Of my various emotions, curiosity gained the upper hand; and I nodded silently. He rose, lighting a candle on a nearby table and holding it high before him as he opened the door.

"Come with me—upstairs."

I dreaded to brave those musty corridors again, but fascination downed all my qualms. The boards creaked beneath our feet, and I trembled once when I thought I saw a faint, rope-like line traced in the dust near the staircase.

The steps of the attic were noisy and rickety, with several of the treads missing. I was just glad of the need of looking sharply to my footing, for it gave me an excuse not to glance about. The attic corridor was pitch-black and heavily cobwebbed, and inch-deep with dust except where a beaten trail led to a door on the left at the farther end. As I noticed the rotting remains of a thick carpet I thought of the other feet which had pressed it in bygone decades—of these, and of one thing which did not have feet.

The old man took me straight to the door at the end of the beaten path, and fumbled a second with the rusty latch. I was acutely frightened now that I knew the picture was so close, yet dared not retreat at this stage. In another moment my host was ushering me into the deserted studio.

The candle light was very faint, yet served to shew most of the principal features. I noticed the low, slanting roof, the huge enlarged dormer, the curios and trophies hung on the walls—and most of all, the great shrouded easel in the centre of the floor. To that easel de Russy now walked, drawing aside the dusty velvet hangings on the side turned away from me, and motioning me silently to approach. It took a good deal of courage to make me obey, especially when I saw how my guide's eyes dilated in the wavering candle light as he looked at the unveiled canvas. But again curiosity conquered everything, and I walked around to where de Russy stood. Then I saw the damnable thing.

I did not faint—though no reader can possibly realise the effort it took to keep me from doing so. I did cry out, but stopped short when I saw the frightened look on the old man's face. As I had expected, the canvas was warped, mouldy, and scabrous from dampness and neglect; but for all that I could trace the monstrous hints of evil cosmic outsideness that lurked all through the nameless scene's morbid content and perverted geometry.

It was as the old man had said—a vaulted, columned hell of mingled Black Masses and Witches' Sabbaths—and what perfect completion could have added to it was beyond my power to guess. Decay had only increased the utter hideousness of its wicked symbolism and diseased suggestion, for the parts most affected by time were just those parts of the picture which in Nature—or in that extra-cosmic realm that mocked Nature—would be apt to decay or disintegrate.

The utmost horror of all, of course, was Marceline—and as I saw the bloated, discoloured flesh I formed the odd fancy that perhaps the figure on the canvas had some obscure, occult linkage with the figure which lay in quicklime under the cellar floor. Perhaps the lime had preserved the corpse instead of destroying it—but could it have preserved those black, malign eyes that glared and mocked at me from their painted hell?

And there was something else about the creature which I could not fail to notice—something which de Russy had not been able to put into words, but which perhaps had something to do with Denis' wish to kill all those of his blood who had dwelt under the same roof with her. Whether Marsh knew, or whether the genius in him painted it without his knowing, none could say. But Denis and his father could not have known till they saw the picture.

Surpassing all in horror was the streaming black hair—which covered the rotting body, *but which was itself not even slightly decayed.* All I had heard of it was amply verified. It was nothing human, this ropy, sinuous, half-oily, half-crinkly flood of serpent darkness. Vile, independent life proclaimed itself at every unnatural twist and convolution, and the suggestion of numberless *reptilian heads* at the out-turned ends was far too marked to be illusory or accidental.

The blasphemous thing held me like a magnet. I was helpless, and did not wonder at the myth of the gorgon's glance which turned all beholders to stone. Then I thought I saw a change come over the thing. The leering features perceptibly moved, so that the rotting jaw fell, allowing the thick, beast-like lips to disclose a row of pointed yellow fangs. The pupils of the fiendish eyes dilated, and the eyes themselves seemed to bulge outward. And the hair—that accursed hair! *It had begun to rustle and wave perceptibly, the snake-heads all turning toward de Russy and vibrating as if to strike!*

Reason deserted me altogether, and before I knew what I was doing I drew my automatic and sent a shower of twelve steel-jacketed bullets through the shocking canvas. The whole thing at once fell to pieces, even the frame toppling from the easel and clattering to the dust-covered floor. But though this horror was shattered, another had risen before me in the form of de Russy himself, whose maddened shrieks as he saw the picture vanish were almost as terrible as the picture itself had been.

With a half-articulate scream of "God, now you've done it!" the frantic old man seized me violently by the arm and commenced to drag me out of the room and down the rickety stairs. He had dropped the candle in his panic; but dawn was near, and some faint grey light was filtering in through the dust-covered windows. I tripped and stumbled repeatedly, but never for a moment would my guide slacken his pace.

"Run!" he shrieked, "run for your life! You don't know what you've done! I never told you the whole thing! There were things I had to do—*the picture talked to me and told me*. I had to guard and keep it—now the worst will happen! *She and that hair will come up out of their graves, for God knows what purpose!*

"Hurry, man! For God's sake let's get out of here while there's time. If you have a car take me along to Cape Girardeau with you. It may get me in the end, anywhere, but I'll give it a run for its money. Out of here—quick!"

As we reached the ground floor I became aware of a slow, curious thumping from the rear of the house, followed by a sound of a door shutting. De Russy had not heard the thumping, but the other noise caught his ear and drew from him the most terrible shriek that ever sounded in human throat.

"Oh, God—great God—that was the cellar door—she's coming—"

By this time I was desperately wrestling with the rusty latch and sagging hinges of the great front door—almost as frantic as my host now that I heard the slow, thumping tread approaching from the unknown rear rooms of the accursed mansion. The night's rain had warped the oaken planks, and the heavy door stuck and resisted even more strongly than it had when I forced an entrance the evening before.

Somewhere a plank creaked beneath the foot of whatever was walking, and the sound seemed to snap the last cord of sanity in the poor old man. With a roar like that of a maddened bull he released his grip on me and made a plunge to the right, through the open door of a room which I judged had been a parlour. A second later, just as I got the front door open and was making my own escape, I heard the tinkling clatter of broken glass and knew he had leapt through a window. And as I bounded off the sagging porch to commence my mad race down the long, weed-grown drive I thought I could catch the thud of dead, dogged footfalls which did not follow me, but which kept leadenly on through the door of the cobwebbed parlour.

I looked backward only twice as I plunged heedlessly through the burrs and briers of that abandoned drive, past the dying lindens and grotesque scrub-oaks, in the grey pallor of a cloudy November dawn. The first time was when an acrid smell overtook me, and I thought of the candle de Russy had dropped in the attic studio. By then I was comfortably near the road, on the high place from which the roof of the distant house was clearly visible above its encircling trees; and just as I expected, thick clouds of smoke were billowing out of the attic dormers and curling upward into the leaden heavens. I thanked the powers of creation that an immemorial curse was about to be purged by fire and blotted from the earth.

But in the next instant came that second backward look in which I glimpsed two other things—things that cancelled most of the relief and gave me a supreme shock from which I shall never recover. I have said that I was on a high part of the drive, from which much of the plantation behind me was visible. This vista included not only the house and its trees but some of the abandoned and partly flooded flat land beside the river, and several bends of the weed-choked drive I had been so hastily traversing. In both of these latter places I now beheld sights—or suspicions of sights—which I wish devoutly I could deny.

It was a faint, distant scream which made me turn back again, and as I did so I caught a trace of motion on the dull grey marshy plain behind the house. At that distance human figures are very small, yet I thought the motion resolved itself into two of these—pursuer and pursued. I even thought I saw the dark-clothed leading figure overtaken and seized by the bald, naked figure in the rear—overtaken, seized, and dragged violently in the direction of the now burning house.

But I could not watch the outcome, for at once a nearer sight obtruded itself—a suggestion of motion among the underbrush at a point some distance back along the deserted drive. *Unmistakably, the weeds and bushes and briers were swaying as no wind could sway them; swaying as if some large, swift serpent were wriggling purposefully along on the ground in pursuit of me.*

That was all I could stand. I scrambled along madly for the gate, heedless of torn clothing and bleeding scratches, and jumped into the roadster parked under the great evergreen tree. It was a bedraggled, rain-drenched sight; but the works were unharmed and I had no trouble in starting the thing. I went on blindly in the direction the car was headed for; nothing was in my mind but to get away from that frightful region of nightmares and cacodaemons—to get away as quickly and as far as gasoline could take me.

About three or four miles along the road a farmer hailed me—a kindly, drawling fellow of middle age and considerable native intelligence. I was glad to slow down and ask directions, though I knew I must present a strange enough aspect. The man readily told me the way to Cape Girardeau, and inquired where I had come from in such a state at such an early hour. Thinking it best to say little, I merely mentioned that I had been caught in the night's rain and had taken shelter at a nearby farmhouse, afterward losing my way in the underbrush trying to find my car.

"At a farmhouse, eh? Wonder whose it could a ben. Ain't nothin' standin' this side o' Jim Ferris' place acrost Barker's Crick, an' that's all o' twenty miles by the rud."

I gave a start, and wondered what fresh mystery this portended. Then I asked my informant if he had overlooked the large ruined plantation house whose ancient gate bordered the road not far back.

"Funny ye sh'd recolleck that, stranger! Must a ben here afore some time. But that house ain't there now. Burnt down five or six years ago—and they did tell some queer stories about it."

I shuddered.

"You mean Riverside—ol' man de Russy's place. Queer goin's on there fifteen or twenty years ago. Ol' man's boy married a gal from abroad, and some folks thought she was a mighty odd sort. Didn't like the looks of her. Then she and the boy went off sudden, and later on the ol' man said he was kilt in the war. But some o' the niggers hinted queer things. Got around at last that the ol' fellow fell in love with the gal himself and kilt her and the boy. That place was sure enough haunted by a black snake, mean that what it may.

"Then five or six years ago the ol' man disappeared and the house burned down. Some do say he was burnt up in it. It was a mornin' after a rainy night just like this, when lots o' folks heard an awful yellin' acrost the fields in old de Russy's voice. When they stopped and looked, they see the house goin' up in smoke quick as a wink—that place was all like tinder anyhow, rain or no rain. Nobody never seen the ol' man agin, but onct in a while they tell of the ghost of that big black snake glidin' aroun'.

"What d'ye make of it, anyhow? You seem to hev knowed the place. Didn't ye ever hear tell of the de Russys? What d'ye reckon was the trouble with that gal young Denis married? She kinder made everybody shiver and feel hateful, though ye couldn't never tell why."

I was trying to think, but that process was almost beyond me now. The house burned down years ago? Then where, and under what conditions, had I passed the night? And why did I know what I knew of these things? Even as I pondered I saw a hair on my coat sleeve—the short, grey hair of an old man.

In the end I drove on without telling anything. But I did hint that gossip was wronging the poor old planter who had suffered so much. I made it clear—as if from distant but authentic reports wafted among friends—that if anyone was to blame for the trouble at Riverside it was the woman, Marceline. She was not suited to Missouri ways, I said, and it was too bad that Denis had ever married her.

More I did not intimate, for I felt that the de Russys, with their proudly cherished honour and high, sensitive spirits, would not wish me to say more. They had borne enough, God knows, without the countryside guessing what a daemon of the pit—what a gorgon of the elder blasphemies—had come to flaunt their ancient and stainless name.

Nor was it right that the neighbours should know that other horror which my strange host of the night could not bring himself to tell me—that horror which he must have learned, as I learned it, from details in the lost masterpiece of poor Frank Marsh.

It would be too hideous if they knew that the one-time heiress of Riverside—the accursed gorgon or lamia whose hateful crinkly coil of serpent-hair must even now be brooding and twining vampirically around an artist's skeleton in a lime-packed grave beneath a charred foundation—was faintly, subtly, yet to the eyes of genius unmistakably the scion of Zimbabwe's most primal grovellers. No wonder she owned a link with that old witch-woman Sophonisba—for, though in deceitfully slight proportion, Marceline was a negress.

Hazel Heald

The Man of Stone

Ben Hayden was always a stubborn chap, and once he had heard about those strange statues in the upper Adirondacks, nothing could keep him from going to see them. I had been his closest acquaintance for years, and our Damon and Pythias friendship made us inseparable at all times. So when Ben firmly decided to go—well, I had to trot along too, like a faithful collie.

"Jack," he said, "you know Henry Jackson, who was up in a shack beyond Lake Placid for that beastly spot in his lung? Well, he came back the other day nearly cured, but had a lot to say about some devilish queer conditions up there. He ran into the business all of a sudden and can't be sure yet that it's anything more than a case of bizarre sculpture; but just the same his uneasy impression sticks.

"It seems he was out hunting one day, and came across a cave with what looked like a dog in front of it. Just as he was expecting the dog to bark he looked again, and saw that the thing wasn't alive at all. It was a stone dog—such a perfect image, down to the smallest whisker, that he couldn't decide whether it was a supernaturally clever statue or a petrified animal. He was almost afraid to touch it, but when he did he realised it was surely made of stone.

"After a while he nerved himself up to go into the cave—and there he got a still bigger jolt. Only a little way in there was another stone figure—or what looked like it—but this time it was a man's. It lay on the floor, on its side, wore clothes, and had a peculiar smile on its face. This time Henry didn't stop to do any touching, but beat it straight for the village, Mountain Top, you know. Of course he asked questions—but they did not get him very far. He found he was on a ticklish subject, for the natives only shook their heads, crossed their fingers, and muttered something about a 'Mad Dan'—whoever he was.

"It was too much for Jackson, so he came home weeks ahead of his planned time. He told me all about it because he knows how fond I am of strange things—and oddly enough, I was able to fish up a recollection that dovetailed pretty neatly with his yarn. Do you remember Arthur Wheeler, the sculptor who was such a realist that people began calling him nothing but a solid photographer? I think you knew him slightly. Well, as a matter of fact, he ended up in that part of the Adirondacks himself. Spent a lot of time there, and then dropped out of sight. Never heard from again. Now if stone statues that look like men and dogs are turning up around there, it looks to me as if they might be his work—no matter what the rustics say, or refuse to say, about them. Of course a fellow with Jackson's nerves might easily get flighty and disturbed over things like that; but I'd have done a lot of examining before running away.

"In fact, Jack, I'm going up there now to look things over—and you're coming along with me. It would mean a lot to find Wheeler—or any of his work. Anyhow, the mountain air will brace us both up."

So less than a week later, after a long train ride and a jolting bus trip through breathlessly exquisite scenery, we arrived at Mountain Top in the late, golden sunlight of a June evening. The village comprised only a few small houses, a hotel, and the general store at which our bus drew up; but we knew that the latter would probably prove a focus for such information. Surely enough, the usual group of idlers was gathered around the steps; and when we represented ourselves as health-seekers in search of lodgings they had many recommendations to offer.

Though we had not planned to do any investigating till the next day, Ben could not resist venturing some vague, cautious questions when he noticed the senile garrulousness of one of the ill-clad loafers. He felt, from Jackson's previous experience, that it would be useless to begin with references to the queer statues; but decided to mention Wheeler as one whom we had known, and in whose fate we consequently had a right to be interested.

The crowd seemed uneasy when Sam stopped his whittling and started talking, but they had slight occasion for alarm. Even this barefoot old mountain decadent tightened up when he heard Wheeler's name, and only with difficulty could Ben get anything coherent out of him.

"Wheeler?" he had finally wheezed. "Oh, yeh—that feller as was all the time blastin' rocks and cuttin' 'em up into statues. So yew knowed him, hey? Wal, they ain't much we kin tell ye, and mebbe that's too much. He stayed out to Mad Dan's cabin in the hills—but not so very long. Got so he wa'nt wanted no more . . . by Dan, that is. Kinder soft-spoken and got around Dan's wife till the old devil took notice. Pretty sweet on her, I guess. But he took the trail sudden, and nobody's seen hide nor hair of him since. Dan must a told him sumthin' pretty plain—bad feller to get agin ye, Dan is! Better keep away from thar, boys, for they ain't no good in that part of the hills. Dan's ben workin' up a worse and worse mood, and ain't seen about no more. Nor his wife, neither. Guess he's penned her up so's nobody else kin make eyes at her!"

As Sam resumed his whittling after a few more observations, Ben and I exchanged glances. Here, surely, was a new lead which deserved intensive following up. Deciding to lodge at the hotel, we settled ourselves as quickly as possible; planning for a plunge into the wild hilly country on the next day.

At sunrise we made our start, each bearing a knapsack laden with provisions and such tools as we thought we might need. The day before us had an almost stimulating air of invitation—through which only a faint undercurrent of the sinister ran. Our rough mountain road quickly became steep and winding, so that before long our feet ached considerably.

After about two miles we left the road—crossing a stone wall on our right near a great elm and striking off diagonally toward a steeper slope according to the chart and directions which Jackson had prepared for us. It was rough and briery travelling, but we knew that the cave could not be far off. In the end we came upon the aperture quite suddenly—a black, bush-grown crevice where the ground shot abruptly upward, and beside it, near a shallow rock pool, a small, still figure stood rigid—as if rivalling its own uncanny petrification.

It was a grey dog—or a dog's statue—and as our simultaneous gasp died away we scarcely knew what to think. Jackson had exaggerated nothing, and we could not believe that any sculptor's hand had succeeded in producing such perfection. Every hair of the animal's magnificent coat seemed distinct, and those on the back were bristled up as if some unknown thing had taken him unaware. Ben, at last half-kindly touching the delicate stony fur, gave vent to an exclamation.

"Good God, Jack, but this can't be any statue! Look at it—all the little details, and the way the hair lies! None of Wheeler's technique here! This is a real dog—though heaven only knows how he ever got in this state. Just like stone—feel for yourself. Do you suppose there's any strange gas that sometimes comes out of the cave and does this to animal life? We ought to have looked more into the local legends. And if this is a real dog—or was a real dog—then that man inside must be the real thing too."

It was with a good deal of genuine solemnity—almost dread—that we finally crawled on hands and knees through the cave-mouth, Ben leading. The narrowness looked hardly three feet, after which the grotto expanded in every direction to form a damp, twilight chamber floored with rubble and detritus. For a time we could make out very little, but as we rose to our feet and strained our eyes we began slowly to descry a recumbent figure amidst the greater darkness ahead. Ben fumbled with his flashlight, but hesitated for a moment before turning it on the prostrate figure. We had little doubt that the stony thing was what had once been a man, and something in the thought unnerved us both.

When Ben at last sent forth the electric beam we saw that the object lay on its side, back toward us. It was clearly of the same material as the dog outside, but was dressed in the mouldering and unpetrified remains of rough sport clothing. Braced as we were for a shock, we approached quite calmly to examine the thing; Ben going around to the other side to glimpse the averted face. Neither could possibly have been prepared for what Ben saw when he flashed the light on those stony features. His cry was wholly excusable, and I could not help echoing it as I leaped to his side and shared the sight. Yet it was nothing hideous or intrinsically terrifying. It was merely a matter of recognition, for beyond the least shadow of a doubt this chilly rock figure with its half-frightened, half-bitter expression had at one time been our old acquaintance, Arthur Wheeler.

Some instinct sent us staggering and crawling out of the cave, and down the tangled slope to a point whence we could not see the ominous stone dog. We hardly knew what to think, for our brains were churning with conjectures and apprehensions. Ben, who had known Wheeler well, was especially upset; and seemed to be piecing together some threads I had overlooked.

Again and again as we paused on the green slope he repeated "Poor Arthur, poor Arthur!" but not till he muttered the name "Mad Dan" did I recall the trouble into which, according to old Sam Poole, Wheeler had run just before his disappearance. Mad Dan, Ben implied, would doubtless be glad to see what had happened. For a moment it flashed over both of us that the jealous host might have been responsible for the sculptor's presence in this evil cave, but the thought went as quickly as it came.

The thing that puzzled us most was to account for the phenomenon itself. What gaseous emanation or mineral vapour could have wrought this change in so relatively short a time was utterly beyond us. Normal petrification, we know, is a slow chemical replacement process requiring vast ages for completion; yet here were two stone images which had been living things—or at least Wheeler had—only a few weeks before. Conjecture was useless. Clearly, nothing remained but to notify the authorities and let them guess what they might; and yet at the back of Ben's head that notion about Mad Dan still persisted. Anyhow, we clawed our way back to the road, but Ben did not turn toward the village, but looked along upward toward where old Sam had said Dan's cabin lay. It was the second house from the village, the ancient loafer had wheezed, and lay on the left far back from the road in a thick copse of scrub oaks. Before I knew it Ben was dragging me up the sandy highway past a dingy farmstead and into a region of increasing wildness.

It did not occur to me to protest, but I felt a certain sense of mounting menace as the familiar marks of agriculture and civilisation grew fewer and fewer. At last the beginning of a narrow, neglected path opened up on our left, while the peaked roof of a squalid, unpainted building shewed itself beyond a sickly growth of half-dead trees. This, I knew, must be Mad Dan's cabin; and I wondered that Wheeler had ever chosen so unprepossessing a place for his headquarters. I dreaded to walk up that weedy, uninviting path, but could not lag behind when Ben strode determinedly along and began a vigorous rapping at the rickety, musty-smelling door.

There was no response to the knock, and something in its echoes sent a series of shivers through one. Ben, however, was quite unperturbed; and at once began to circle the house in quest of unlocked windows. The third that he tried—in the rear of the dismal cabin—proved capable of opening, and after a boost and a vigorous spring he was safely inside and helping me after him.

The room in which we landed was full of limestone and granite blocks, chiselling tools and clay models, and we realised at once that it was Wheeler's erstwhile studio. So far we had not met with any sign of life, but over everything hovered a damnably ominous dusty odour. On our left was an open door evidently leading to a kitchen on the chimney side of the house, and through this Ben started, intent on finding anything he could concerning his friend's last habitat. He was considerably ahead of me when he crossed the threshold, so that I could not see at first what brought him up short and wrung a low cry of horror from his lips.

In another moment, though, I did see—and repeated his cry as instinctively as I had done in the cave. For here in this cabin—far from any subterranean depths which could breed strange gases and work strange mutations—were two stony figures which I knew at once were no products of Arthur Wheeler's chisel. In a rude armchair before the fireplace, bound in position by the lash of a long rawhide whip, was the form of a man—unkempt, elderly, and with a look of fathomless horror on its evil, petrified face.

On the floor beside it lay a woman's figure; graceful, and with a face betokening considerable youth and beauty. Its expression seemed to be one of sardonic satisfaction, and near its outflung right hand was a large tin pail, somewhat stained on the inside, as with a darkish sediment.

We made no move to approach those inexplicably petrified bodies, nor did we exchange any but the simplest conjectures. That this stony couple had been Mad Dan and his wife we could not well doubt, but how to account for their present condition was another matter. As we looked horrifiedly around we saw the suddenness with which the final development must have come—for everything about us seemed, despite a heavy coating of dust, to have been left in the midst of commonplace household activities.

The only exception to this rule of casualness was on the kitchen table; in whose cleared centre, as if to attract attention, lay a thin, battered, blank-book weighted down by a sizeable tin funnel. Crossing to read the thing, Ben saw that it was a kind of diary or set of dated entries, written in a somewhat cramped and none too practiced hand. The very first words riveted my attention, and before ten seconds had elapsed he was breathlessly devouring the halting text—I avidly following as I peered over his shoulder. As we read on—moving as we did so into the less loathsome atmosphere of the adjoining room—many obscure things became terribly clear to us, and we trembled with a mixture of complex emotions.

This is what we read—and what the coroner read later on. The public has seen a highly twisted and sensationalised version in the cheap newspapers, but not even that has more than a fraction of the genuine terror which the simple original held for us as we puzzled it out alone in that musty cabin among the wild hills, with two monstrous stone abnormalities lurking in the death-like silence of the next room. When we had finished Ben pocketed the book with a gesture half of repulsion, and his first words were "Let's get out of here."

Silently and nervously we stumbled to the front of the house, unlocked the door, and began the long tramp back to the village. There were many statements to make and questions to answer in the days that followed, and I do not think that either Ben or I can ever shake off the effects of the whole harrowing experience. Neither can some of the local authorities and city reporters who flocked around—even though they burned a certain book and many papers found in attic boxes, and destroyed considerable apparatus in the deepest part of that sinister hillside cave. But here is the text itself:

"Nov. 5—My name is Daniel Morris. Around here they call me 'Mad Dan' because I believe in powers that nobody else believes in nowadays. When I go up on Thunder Hill to keep the Feast of the Foxes they think I am crazy—all except the back country folks that are afraid of me. They try to stop me from sacrificing the Black Goat at Hallow Eve, and always prevent my doing the Great Rite that would open the gate. They ought to know better, for they know I am a Van Kauran on my mother's side, and anybody this side of the Hudson can tell what the Van Kaurans have handed down. We come from Nicholas Van Kauran, the wizard, who was hanged in Wijtgaart in 1587, and everybody knows he had made the bargain with the Black Man.

"The soldiers never got his *Book of Eibon* when they burned his house, and his grandson, William Van Kauran, brought it over when he came to Rensselaerwyck and later crossed the river to Esopus. Ask anybody in Kingston or Hurley about what the

William Van Kauran line could do to people that got in their way. Also, ask them if my Uncle Hendrik didn't manage to keep hold of the *Book of Eibon* when they ran him out of town and he went up the river to this place with his family.

"I am writing this—and am going to keep writing this—because I want people to know the truth after I am gone. Also, I am afraid I shall really go mad if I don't set things down in plain black and white. Everything is going against me, and if it keeps up I shall have to use the secrets in the *Book* and call in certain Powers. Three months ago that sculptor Arthur Wheeler came to Mountain Top, and they sent him up to me because I am the only man in the place who knows anything except farming, hunting, and fleecing summer boarders. The fellow seemed to be interested in what I had to say, and made a deal to stop here for $13.00 a week with meals. I gave him the back room beside the kitchen for his lumps of stone and his chiselling, and arranged with Nate Williams to tend to his rock blasting and haul his big pieces with a drag and yoke of oxen.

"That was three months ago. Now I know why that cursed son of hell took so quick to the place. It wasn't my talk at all, but the looks of my wife Rose, that is Osborne Chandler's oldest girl. She is sixteen years younger than I am, and is always casting sheep's eyes at the fellows in town. But we always managed to get along fine enough till this dirty rat shewed up, even if she did balk at helping me with the Rites on Roodmas and Hallowmass. I can see now that Wheeler is working on her feelings and getting her so fond of him that she hardly looks at me, and I suppose he'll try to elope with her sooner or later.

"But he works slow like all sly, polished dogs, and I've got plenty of time to think up what to do about it. They don't either of them know I suspect anything, but before long they'll both realise it doesn't pay to break up a Van Kauran's home. I promise them plenty of novelty in what I'll do.

"Nov. 25—Thanksgiving Day! That's a pretty good joke! But at that I'll have something to be thankful for when I finish what I've started. No question but that Wheeler is trying to steal my wife. For the time being, though, I'll let him keep on being a star boarder. Got the *Book of Eibon* down from Uncle Hendrik's old trunk in the attic last week, and am looking up something good which won't require sacrifices that I can't make around here. I want something that'll finish these two sneaking traitors, and at the same time get me into no trouble. If it has a twist of drama in it, so much the better. I've thought of calling in the emanation of Yoth, but that needs a child's blood and I must be careful about the neighbours. The Green Decay looks promising, but that would be a bit unpleasant for me as well as for them. I don't like certain sights and smells.

"Dec. 10—*Eureka!* I've got the very thing at last! Revenge is sweet—and this is the perfect climax! Wheeler, the sculptor—this is too good! Yes, indeed, that damned sneak is going to produce a statue that will sell quicker than any of the things he's been carving these past weeks! A realist, eh? Well—the new statuary won't lack any realism! I found the formula in a manuscript insert opposite page 679 of the *Book*. From the handwriting I judge it was put there by my great-grandfather Bareut Picterse Van Kauran—the one who disappeared from New Paltz in 1839. *Iä! Shub-Niggurath!* The Goat with a Thousand Young!

"To be plain, I've found a way to turn those wretched rats into stone statues. It's absurdly simple, and really depends more on plain chemistry than on the Outer Powers. If I can get hold of the right stuff I can brew a drink that'll pass for home-made wine, and one swig ought to finish any ordinary being short of an elephant. What it amounts to is a kind of petrification infinitely speeded up. Shoots the whole system full of calcium and barium salts and replaces living cells with mineral matter so fast that nothing can stop it. It must have been one of those things great-grandfather got at the Great Sabbat on Sugar-Loaf in the Catskills. Queer things used to go on there. Seems to me I heard of a man in New Paltz—Squire Hasbrouck—turned to stone or something like that in 1834. He was an enemy of the Van Kaurans. First thing I must do is order the five chemicals I need from Albany and Montreal. Plenty of time later to experiment. When everything is over I'll round up all the statues and sell them as Wheeler's work to pay for his overdue board bill! He always was a realist and an egoist—wouldn't it be natural for him to make a self-portrait in stone, and to use my wife for another model—as indeed he's really been doing for the past fortnight? Trust the dull public not to ask *what quarry* the queer stone came from!

"Dec. 25—Christmas. Peace on earth, and so forth! These two swine are goggling at each other as if I didn't exist. They must think I'm deaf, dumb, and blind! Well, the barium sulphate and calcium chloride came from Albany last Thursday, and the acids, catalytics, and instruments are due from Montreal any day now. The mills of the gods—and all that! I'll do the work in Allen's Cave near the lower wood lot, and at the same time will be openly making some wine in the cellar here. There ought to be some excuse for offering a new drink—though it won't take much planning to fool those moonstruck nincompoops. The trouble will be to make Rose take wine, for she pretends not to like it. Any experiments that I make on animals will be down at the cave, and nobody ever thinks of going there in winter. I'll do some wood-cutting to account for my time away. A small load or two brought in will keep him off the track.

"Jan. 20—It's harder work than I thought. A lot depends on the exact proportions. The stuff came from Montreal, but I had to send again for some better scales and an acetylene lamp. They're getting curious down at the village. Wish the express office weren't in Steenwyck's store. Am trying various mixtures on the sparrows that drink and bathe in the pool in front of the cave—when it's melted. Sometimes it kills them, but sometimes they fly away. Clearly, I've missed some important reaction. I suppose Rose and that upstart are making the most of my absence—but I can afford to let them. There can be no doubt of my success in the end.

"Feb. 11—Have got it at last! Put a fresh lot in the little pool—which is well melted today—and the first bird that drank toppled over as if he were shot. I picked him up a second later, and he was a perfect piece of stone, down to the smallest claws and feather. Not a muscle changed since he was poised for drinking, so he must have died the instant any of the stuff got to his stomach. I didn't expect the petrification to come so soon. But a sparrow isn't a fair test of the way the thing would act with a large animal. I must get something bigger to try it on, for it must be the right strength when I give it to those swine. I guess Rose's dog Rex will do. I'll take him along the next time and say a timber wolf got him. She thinks a lot of him, and I shan't be sorry to give her something to sniffle over before the big reckoning. I must be careful where I keep this book. Rose sometimes pries around in the queerest places.

"Feb. 15—Getting warm! Tried it on Rex and it worked like a charm with only double the strength. I fixed the rock pool and got him to drink. He seemed to know something queer had hit him, for he bristled and growled, but he was a piece of stone before he could turn his head. The solution ought to have been stronger, and for a human being ought to be very much stronger. I think I'm getting the hang of it now, and am about ready for that cur Wheeler. The stuff seems to be tasteless, but to make sure I'll flavour it with the new wine I'm making up at the house. Wish I were surer about the tastelessness, so I could give it to Rose in water without trying to urge wine on her. I'll get the two separately—Wheeler out here and Rose at home. Have just fixed a strong solution and cleared away all strange objects in front of the cave. Rose whimpered like a puppy when I told her a wolf had got Rex, and Wheeler gurgled a lot of sympathy.

"March 1—*Iä R'lyeh!* Praise the Lord Tsathoggua! I've got the son of hell at last! Told him I'd found a new ledge of friable limestone down this way, and he trotted after me like the yellow cur he is! I had the wine-flavoured stuff in a bottle on my hip, and he was glad of a swig when we got here. Gulped it down without a wink—and dropped in his tracks before you could count three. But he knows I've had my vengeance, for I made a face at him that he couldn't miss. I saw the look of understanding come into his face as he keeled over. In two minutes he was solid stone.

"I dragged him into the cave and put Rex's figure outside again. That bristling dog shape will help to scare people off. It's getting time for the spring hunters, and besides, there's a damned 'lunger' named Jackson in a cabin over the hill who does a lot of snooping around in the snow. I wouldn't want my laboratory and storeroom to be found just yet! When I got home I told Rose that Wheeler had found a telegram at the village summoning him suddenly home. I don't know whether she believed me or not but it doesn't matter. For form's sake, I packed Wheeler's things and took them down the hill, telling her I was going to ship them after him. I put them in the dry well at the abandoned Rapelye place. Now for Rose!

"March 3—Can't get Rose to drink any wine. I hope that stuff is tasteless enough to go unnoticed in water. I tried it in tea and coffee, but it forms a precipitate and can't be used that way. If I use it in water I'll have to cut down the dose and trust to a more gradual action. Mr. and Mrs. Hoog dropped in this noon, and I had hard work keeping the conversation away from Wheeler's departure. It mustn't get around that we say he was called back to New York when everybody at the village knows no telegram came, and that he didn't leave on the bus. Rose is acting damned queer about the whole thing. I'll have to pick a quarrel with her and keep her locked in the attic. The best way is to try to make her drink that doctored wine—and if she does give in, so much better.

"March 7—Have started in on Rose. She wouldn't drink the wine so I took a whip to her and drove her up in the attic. She'll never come down alive. I pass her a platter of salty bread and salt meat, and a pail of slightly doctored water, twice a day. The salt food ought to make her drink a lot, and it can't be long before the action sets in. I don't like the way she shouts about Wheeler when I'm at the door. The rest of the time she is absolutely silent.

"March 9—It's damned peculiar how slow that stuff is in getting hold of Rose. I'll have to make it stronger—probably she'll never taste it with all the salt I've been feeding her. Well, if it doesn't get her there are plenty of other ways to fall back on. But I would like to carry this neat statue plan through! Went to the cave this morning and all is well there. I sometimes hear Rose's steps on the ceiling overhead, and I think they're getting more and more dragging. The stuff is certainly working, but it's too slow. Not strong enough. From now on I'll rapidly stiffen up the dose.

"March 11—It is very queer. She is still alive and moving. Tuesday night I heard her piggling with a window, so went up and gave her a rawhiding. She acts more sullen than frightened, and her eyes look swollen. But she could never drop to the ground from that height and there's nowhere she could climb down. I have had dreams at night, for her slow, dragging pacing on the floor above gets on my nerves. Sometimes I think she works at the lock on the door.

"March 15—Still alive, despite all the strengthening of the dose. There's something queer about it. She crawls now, and doesn't pace very often. But the sound of her crawling is horrible. She rattles the windows, too, and fumbles with the door. I shall have to finish her off with the rawhide if this keeps up. I'm getting very sleepy. Wonder if Rose has got on her guard somehow. But she must be drinking the stuff. This sleepiness is abnormal—I think the strain is telling on me. I'm sleepy. . . ."

(Here the cramped handwriting trails out in a vague scrawl, giving place to a note in a firmer, evidently feminine handwriting, indicative of great emotional tension.)

"March 16—4 a.m.—This is added by Rose C. Morris, about to die. Please notify my father, Osborne E. Chandler, Route 2, Mountain Top, N.Y. I have just read what the beast has written. I felt sure he had killed Arthur Wheeler, but did not know how till I read this terrible notebook. Now I know what I escaped. I noticed the water tasted queer, so took none of it after the first sip. I threw it all out of the window. That one sip has half paralysed me, but I can still get about. The thirst was terrible, but I ate as little as possible of the salty food and was able to get a little water by setting some old pans and dishes that were up here under places where the roof leaked.

"There were two great rains. I thought he was trying to poison me, though I didn't know what the poison was like. What he has written about himself and me is a lie. We were never happy together and I think I married him only under one of those spells that he was able to lay on people. I guess he hypnotised both my father and me, for he was always hated and feared and suspected of dark dealings with the devil. My father once called him The Devil's Kin, and he was right.

"No one will ever know what I went through as his wife. It was not simply common cruelty—though God knows he was cruel enough, and beat me often with a leather whip. It was more—more than anyone in this age can ever understand. He was a monstrous creature, and practiced all sorts of hellish ceremonies handed down by his mother's people. He tried to make me help in the rites—and I don't dare even hint what they were. I would not, so he beat me. It would be blasphemy to tell what he tried to make me do. I can say he was a murderer even then, for I know what he sacrificed one night on Thunder Hill. He was surely the Devil's Kin. I tried four times to run away, but he always caught and beat me. Also, he had a sort of hold over my mind, and even over my father's mind.

"About Arthur Wheeler I have nothing to be ashamed of. We did come to love each other, but only in an honourable way. He gave me the first kind treatment I had ever had since leaving my father's, and meant to help me get out of the clutches of that fiend. He had several talks with my father, and was going to help me get out west. After my divorce we would have been married.

"Ever since that brute locked me in the attic I have planned to get out and finish him. I always kept the poison overnight in case I could escape and find him asleep and give it to him somehow. At first he waked easily when I worked on the lock of the door and tested the conditions at the windows, but later he began to get more tired and sleep sounder. I could always tell by his snoring when he was asleep.

"Tonight he was so fast asleep I forced the lock without waking him. It was hard work getting downstairs with my partial paralysis, but I did. I found him here with the lamp burning—asleep at the table, where he had been writing in this book. In the corner was the long rawhide whip he had so often beaten me with. I used it to tie him to the chair so he could not move a muscle. I lashed his neck so that I could pour anything down his throat without his resisting.

"He waked up just as I was finishing and I guess he saw right off that he was done for. He shouted frightful things and tried to chant mystical formulas, but I choked him off with a dish towel from the sink. Then I saw this book he had been writing in, and stopped to read it. The shock was terrible, and I almost fainted four or five times. My mind was not ready for such things. After that I talked to that fiend for two or three hours steady. I told him everything I had wanted to tell him through all the years I had been his slave, and a lot of other things that had to do with what I had read in this awful book.

"He looked almost purple when I was through, and I think he was half delirious. Then I got a funnel from the cupboard and jammed it into his mouth after taking out the gag. He knew what I was going to do, but was helpless. I had brought down the pail of poisoned water, and without a qualm, I poured a good half of it into the funnel.

"It must have been a very strong dose, for almost at once I saw that brute begin to stiffen and turn a dull stony grey. In ten minutes I knew he was solid stone. I could not bear to touch him, but the tin funnel *clinked* horribly when I pulled it out of his mouth. I wish I could have given that Kin of the Devil a more painful, lingering death, but surely this was the most appropriate he could have had.

"There is not much more to say. I am half-paralysed, and with Arthur murdered I have nothing to live for. I shall make things complete by drinking the rest of the poison after placing this book where it will be found. In a quarter of an hour I shall be a stone statue. My only wish is to be buried beside the statue that was Arthur—when it is found in that cave where the fiend left it. Poor trusting Rex ought to lie at our feet. I do not care what becomes of the stone devil tied in the chair. . . ."

Hazel Heald

The Horror in the Museum

It was languid curiosity which first brought Stephen Jones to Rogers' Museum. Someone had told him about the queer underground place in Southwark Street across the river, where waxen things so much more horrible than the worst effigies at Madame Tussaud's were shewn, and he had strolled in one April day to see how disappointing he would find it. Oddly, he was not disappointed. There was something different and distinctive here, after all. Of course, the usual gory commonplaces were present—Landru, Dr. Crippen, Madame Demers, Rizzio, Lady Jane Grey, endless maimed victims of war and revolution, and monsters like Gilles de Rais and Marquis de Sade—but there were other things which had made him breathe faster and stay till the ringing of the closing bell. The man who had fashioned this collection could be no ordinary mountebank. There was imagination—even a kind of diseased genius—in some of this stuff.

Later he had learned about George Rogers. The man had been on the Tussaud staff, but some trouble had developed which led to his discharge. There were aspersions on his sanity and tales of his crazy forms of secret worship—though latterly his success with his own basement museum had dulled the edge of some criticisms while sharpening the insidious point of others. Teratology and the iconography of nightmare were his hobbies, and even he had had the prudence to screen off some of his worst effigies in a special alcove for adults only. It was this alcove which had fascinated Jones so much. There were lumpish hybrid things which only fantasy could spawn, moulded with devilish skill, and coloured in a horribly life-like fashion.

Some were the figures of well-known myth—gorgons, chimaeras, dragons, cyclops, and all their shuddersome congeners. Others were drawn from darker and more furtively whispered cycles of subterranean legend—black, formless Tsathoggua, many-tentacled Cthulhu, proboscidian Chaugnar Faugn, and other rumoured blasphemies from forbidden books like the *Necronomicon,* the *Book of Eibon,* or the *Unaussprechlichen Kulten* of von Junzt. But the worst were wholly original with Rogers, and represented shapes which no tale of antiquity had ever dared to suggest. Several were hideous parodies on forms of organic life we know, while others seemed taken from feverish dreams of other planets and other galaxies. The wilder paintings of Clark Ashton Smith might suggest a few—but nothing could suggest the effect of poignant, loathsome terror created by their great size and fiendishly cunning workmanship, and by the diabolically clever lighting conditions under which they were exhibited.

Stephen Jones, as a leisurely connoisseur of the bizarre in art, had sought out Rogers himself in the dingy office and workroom behind the vaulted museum chamber—an evil-looking crypt lighted dimly by dusty windows set slit-like and horizontal in the brick wall on a level with the ancient cobblestones of a hidden courtyard. It was here that the images were repaired—here, too, where some of them had been made. Waxen arms, legs, heads, and torsos lay in grotesque array on various benches, while on high tiers of shelves matted wigs, ravenous-looking teeth, and glassy, staring eyes were indiscriminately scattered. Costumes of all sorts hung from hooks, and in one alcove were great piles of flesh-coloured wax-cakes and shelves filled with paint-cans and brushes of every description. In the centre of the room was a large melting-furnace used to prepare the wax for moulding, its fire-box topped by a huge iron container on hinges, with a spout which permitted the pouring of melted wax with the merest touch of a finger.

Other things in the dismal crypt were less describable—isolated parts of problematical entities whose assembled forms were the phantoms of delirium. At one end was a door of heavy plank, fastened by an unusually large padlock and with a very peculiar symbol painted over it. Jones, who had once had access to the dreaded *Necronomicon,* shivered involuntarily as he recognised that symbol. This showman, he reflected, must indeed be a person of disconcertingly wide scholarship in dark and dubious fields.

Nor did the conversation of Rogers disappoint him. The man was tall, lean, and rather unkempt, with large black eyes which gazed combustively from a pallid and usually stubble-covered face. He did not resent Jones's intrusion, but seemed to welcome the chance of unburdening himself to an interested person. His voice was of singular depth and resonance, and harboured a sort of repressed intensity bordering on the feverish. Jones did not wonder that many had thought him mad.

With every successive call—and such calls became a habit as the weeks went by—Jones had found Rogers more communicative and confidential. From the first there had been hints of strange faiths and practices on the showman's part, and later on these hints expanded into tales—despite a few odd corroborative photographs—whose extravagance was almost comic. It was some time in June, on a night when Jones had brought a bottle of good whiskey and plied his host somewhat freely, that the really demented talk first appeared. Before that there had been wild enough stories—accounts of mysterious trips to Thibet, the African interior, the Arabian desert, the Amazon valley, Alaska, and certain little-known islands of the South Pacific, plus claims of having read such monstrous and half-fabulous books as the prehistoric Pnakotic fragments and the Dhol chants attributed to malign and non-human Leng—but nothing in all this had been so unmistakably insane as what had cropped out that June evening under the spell of the whiskey.

To be plain, Rogers began making vague boasts of having found certain things in Nature that no one had found before, and of having brought back tangible evidences of such discoveries. According to his bibulous harangue, he had gone farther than anyone else in interpreting the obscure and primal books he studied, and had been directed by them to certain remote places where strange survivals are hidden—survivals of aeons and life-cycles earlier than mankind, and in some cases connected with other dimensions and other worlds, communication with which was frequent in the forgotten pre-human days. Jones marvelled at the fancy which could conjure up such notions, and wondered just what Rogers' mental history had been. Had his work amidst the morbid grotesqueries of Madame Tussaud's been the start of his imaginative flights, or was the tendency innate, so that his choice of occupation was merely one of its manifestations? At any rate, the man's work was very closely linked with his notions. Even now there was no mistaking the trend of his blackest hints about the nightmare monstrosities in the screened-off "Adults only" alcove. Heedless of ridicule, he was trying to imply that not all of these daemoniac abnormalities were artificial.

It was Jones's frank scepticism and amusement at these irresponsible claims which broke up the growing cordiality. Rogers, it was clear, took himself very seriously; for he now became morose and resentful, continuing to tolerate Jones only through a dogged urge to break down his wall of urbane and complacent incredulity. Wild tales and suggestions of rites and sacrifices to nameless elder gods continued, and now and then Rogers would lead his guest to one of the hideous blasphemies in the screened-off alcove and point out features difficult to reconcile with even the finest human craftsmanship. Jones continued his visits through sheer fascination, though he knew he had forfeited his host's regard. At times he would try to humour Rogers with pretended assent to some mad hint or assertion, but the gaunt showman was seldom to be deceived by such tactics.

The tension came to a head later in September. Jones had casually dropped into the museum one afternoon, and was wandering through the dim corridors whose horrors were now so familiar, when he heard a very peculiar sound from the general direction of Rogers' workroom. Others heard it, too, and started nervously as the echoes reverberated through the great vaulted basement. The three attendants exchanged odd glances; and one of them, a dark, taciturn, foreign-looking fellow who always served Rogers as a repairer and assistant designer, smiled in a way which seemed to puzzle his colleagues and which grated very harshly on some facet of Jones's sensibilities. It was the yelp or scream of a dog, and was such a sound as could be made only under conditions of the utmost fright and agony combined. Its stark, anguished frenzy was appalling to hear, and in this setting of grotesque abnormality it held a double hideousness. Jones remembered that no dogs were allowed in the museum.

He was about to go to the door leading into the workroom, when the dark attendant stopped him with a word and a gesture. Mr. Rogers, the man said in a soft, somewhat accented voice at once apologetic and vaguely sardonic, was out, and there were standing orders to admit no one to the workroom during his absence. As for that yelp, it was undoubtedly something out in the courtyard behind the museum. This neighbourhood was full of stray mongrels, and their fights were sometimes shockingly noisy. There were no dogs in any part of the museum. But if Mr. Jones wished to see Mr. Rogers he might find him just before closing-time.

After this Jones climbed the old stone steps to the street outside and examined the squalid neighbourhood curiously. The leaning, decrepit buildings—once dwellings but now largely shops and warehouses—were very ancient indeed. Some of them were of a gabled type seeming to go back to Tudor times, and a faint miasmatic stench hung subtly about the whole region. Beside the dingy house whose basement held the museum was a low archway pierced by a dark cobbled alley, and this Jones entered in a vague wish to find the courtyard behind the workroom and settle the affair of the dog more comfortably in his mind. The courtyard was dim in the late afternoon light, hemmed in by rear walls even uglier and more intangibly menacing than the crumbling street facades of the evil old houses. Not a dog was in sight, and Jones wondered how the aftermath of such a frantic turmoil could have completely vanished so soon.

Despite the assistant's statement that no dog had been in the museum, Jones glanced nervously at the three small windows of the basement workroom—narrow, horizontal rectangles close to the grass-grown pavement, with grimy panes that stared repulsively and incuriously like the eyes of dead fish. To their left a worn flight of steps led to an opaque and heavily bolted door. Some impulse urged him to crouch low on the damp, broken cobblestones and peer in, on the chance that the thick green shades, worked by long cords that hung down to a reachable level, might not be drawn. The outer surfaces were thick with dirt, but as he rubbed them with his handkerchief he saw there was no obscuring curtain in the way of his vision.

So shadowed was the cellar from the inside that not much could be made out, but the grotesque working paraphernalia now and then loomed up spectrally as Jones tried each of the windows in turn. It seemed evident at first that no one was within; yet when he peered through the extreme right-hand window—the one nearest the entrance alley—he saw a glow of light at the farther end of the apartment which made him pause in bewilderment. There was no reason why any light should be there. It was an inner side of the room, and he could not recall any gas or electric fixture near that point. Another look defined the glow as a large vertical rectangle, and a thought occurred to him. It was in that direction that he had always noticed the heavy plank door with the abnormally large padlock—the door which was never opened, and above which was crudely smeared that hideous cryptic symbol from the fragmentary records of forbidden elder magic. It must be open now—and there was a light inside. All his former speculations as to where that door led, and as to what lay behind it, were now renewed with trebly disquieting force.

Jones wandered aimlessly around the dismal locality till close to six o'clock, when he returned to the museum to make the call on Rogers. He could hardly tell why he wished so especially to see the man just then, but there must have been some subconscious misgivings about that terribly unplaceable canine scream of the afternoon, and about the glow of light in that disturbing and usually unopened inner doorway with the heavy padlock. The attendants were leaving as he arrived, and he thought that Orabona—the dark foreign-looking assistant—eyed him with something like sly, repressed amusement. He did not relish that look—even though he had seen the fellow turn it on his employer many times.

The vaulted exhibition room was ghoulish in its desertion, but he strode quickly through it and rapped at the door of the office and workroom. Response was slow in coming, though there were footsteps inside. Finally, in response to a second knock, the lock rattled, and the ancient six-panelled portal creaked reluctantly open to reveal the slouching, feverish-eyed form of George Rogers. From the first it was clear that the showman was in an unusual mood. There was a curious mixture of reluctance and actual gloating in his welcome, and his talk at once veered to extravagances of the most hideous and incredible sort.

Surviving elder gods—nameless sacrifices—the other than artificial nature of some of the alcove horrors—all the usual boasts, but uttered in a tone of peculiarly increasing confidence. Obviously, Jones reflected, the poor fellow's madness was gaining on him. From time to time Rogers would send furtive glances toward the heavy, padlocked inner door at the end of the room, or toward a piece of coarse burlap on the floor not far from it, beneath which some small object appeared to be lying. Jones grew more nervous as the moments passed, and began to feel as hesitant about mentioning the afternoon's oddities as he had formerly been anxious to do so.

Rogers' sepulchrally resonant bass almost cracked under the excitement of his fevered rambling.

"Do you remember," he shouted, "what I told you about that ruined city in Indo-China where the Tcho-Tchos lived? You had to admit I'd been there when you saw the photographs, even if you did think I made that oblong swimmer in darkness out of wax. If you'd seen it writhing in the underground pools as I did. . . .

"Well, this is bigger still. I never told you about this, because I wanted to work out the later parts before making any claim. When you see the snapshots you'll know the geography couldn't have been faked, and I fancy I have another way of proving that *It* isn't any waxed concoction of mine. You've never seen it, for the experiments wouldn't let me keep It on exhibition."

The showman glanced queerly at the padlocked door.

"It all comes from that long ritual in the eighth Pnakotic fragment. When I got it figured out I saw it could have only one meaning. There were things in the north before the land of Lomar—before mankind existed—and this was one of them. It took us all the way to Alaska, and up the Noatak from Fort Morton, but the thing was there as we knew it would be. Great Cyclopean ruins, acres of them. There was less left than we had hoped for, but after three million years what could one expect? And weren't the Esquimau legends all in the right direction? We couldn't get one of the beggars to go with us, and had to sledge all the way back to Nome for Americans. Orabona was no good up in that climate—it made him sullen and hateful.

"I'll tell you later how we found It. When we got the ice blasted out of the pylons of the central ruin the stairway was just as we knew it would be. Some carvings still there, and it was no trouble keeping the Yankees from following us in. Orabona shivered like a leaf—you'd never think it from the damned insolent way he struts around here. He knew enough of the Elder Lore to be properly afraid. The eternal light was gone, but our torches shewed enough. We saw the bones of others who had been before us—aeons ago, when the climate was warm. Some of these bones were of things you couldn't even imagine. At the third level down we found the ivory throne the fragments said so much about—and I may as well tell you it wasn't empty.

"The thing on that throne didn't move—and we knew then that It needed the nourishment of sacrifice. But we didn't want to wake It then. Better to get It to London first. Orabona and I went to the surface for the big box, but when we had packed it we couldn't get

It up the three flights of steps. These steps weren't made for human beings, and their size bothered us. Anyway, it was devilish heavy. We had to have the Americans down to get It out. They weren't anxious to go into the place, but of course the worst thing was safely inside the box. We told them it was a batch of ivory carvings—archaeological stuff; and after seeing the carved throne they probably believed us. It's a wonder they didn't suspect hidden treasure and demand a share. They must have told queer tales around Nome later on; though I doubt if they ever went back to those ruins, even for the ivory throne."

Rogers paused, felt around in his desk, and produced an envelope of good-sized photographic prints. Extracting one and laying it face down before him, he handed the rest to Jones. The set was certainly an odd one: ice-clad hills, dog sledges, men in furs, and vast tumbled ruins against a background of snow—ruins whose bizarre outlines and enormous stone blocks could hardly be accounted for. One flashlight view shewed an incredible interior chamber with wild carvings and a curious throne whose proportion could not have been designed for a human occupant. The carvings on the gigantic masonry—high walls and peculiar vaulting overhead—were mainly symbolic, and involved both wholly unknown designs and certain hieroglyphs darkly cited in obscene legends. Over the throne loomed the same dreadful symbol which was now painted on the workroom wall above the padlocked plank door. Jones darted a nervous glance at the closed portal. Assuredly, Rogers had been to strange places and had seen strange things. Yet this mad interior picture might easily be a fraud—taken from a very clever stage setting. One must not be too credulous. But Rogers was continuing:

"Well, we shipped the box from Nome and got to London without any trouble. That was the first time we'd ever brought back anything that had a chance of coming alive. I didn't put It on display, because there were more important things to do for It. It needed the nourishment of sacrifice, for It was a god. Of course I couldn't get It the sort of sacrifices which It used to have in It's day, for such things don't exist now. But there were other things which might do. The blood is the life, you know. Even the lemurs and elementals that are older than the earth will come when the blood of men or beasts is offered under the right conditions."

The expression on the narrator's face was growing very alarming and repulsive, so that Jones fidgeted involuntarily in his chair.

Rogers seemed to notice his guest's nervousness, and continued with a distinctly evil smile.

"It was last year that I got It, and ever since then I've been trying rites and sacrifices. Orabona hasn't been much help, for he was always against the idea of waking It. He hates It—probably because he's afraid of what It will come to mean. He carries a pistol all the time to protect himself—fool, as if there were human protection against It! If I ever see him draw that pistol, I'll strangle him. He wanted me to kill It and make an effigy of It. But I've stuck by my plans, and I'm coming out on top in spite of all the cowards like Orabona and damned sniggering sceptics like you, Jones! I've chanted the rites and made certain sacrifices, *and last week the transition came*. The sacrifice was—received and enjoyed!"

Rogers actually licked his lips, while Jones held himself uneasily rigid. The showman paused and rose, crossing the room to the piece of burlap at which he had glanced so often. Bending down, he took hold of one corner as he spoke again.

"You've laughed enough at my work—now it's time for you to get some facts. Orabona tells me you heard a dog screaming around here this afternoon. *Do you know what that meant?*"

Jones started. For all his curiosity he would have been glad to get out without further light on the point which had so puzzled him. But Rogers was inexorable, and began to lift the square of burlap. Beneath it lay a crushed, almost shapeless mass which Jones was slow to classify. Was it a once-living thing which some agency had flattened, sucked dry of blood, punctured in a thousand places, and wrung into a limp, broken-boned heap of grotesqueness? After a moment Jones realised what it must be. It was what was left of a dog—a dog, perhaps of considerable size and whitish colour. Its breed was past recognition, for distortion had come in nameless and hideous ways. Most of the hair was burned off as by some pungent acid, and the exposed, bloodless skin was riddled by innumerable circular wounds or incisions. The form of torture necessary to cause such results was past imagining.

Electrified with a pure loathing which conquered his mounting disgust, Jones sprang up with a cry.

"You damned sadist—you madman—you do a thing like this and dare to speak to a decent man!"

Rogers dropped the burlap with a malignant sneer and faced his oncoming guest. His words held an unnatural calm.

"Why, you fool, do you think *I* did this? Let us admit that the results are unbeautiful from our limited human standpoint. What of it? It is not human and does not pretend to be. To sacrifice is merely to offer. I gave the dog to *It.* What happened is It's work, not mine. It needed the nourishment of the offering, and took it in It's own way. But let me shew you what It looks like."

As Jones stood hesitating, the speaker returned to his desk and took up the photograph he had laid face down without shewing. Now he extended it with a curious look. Jones took it and glanced at it in an almost mechanical way. After a moment the visitor's glance became sharper and more absorbed, for the utterly satanic force of the object depicted had an almost hypnotic effect. Certainly, Rogers had outdone himself in modelling the eldritch nightmare which the camera had caught. The thing was a work of sheer, infernal genius, and Jones wondered how the public would react when it was placed on exhibition. So hideous a thing had no right to exist—probably the mere contemplation of it, after it was done, had completed the unhinging of its maker's mind and led him to worship it with brutal sacrifices. Only a stout sanity could resist the insidious suggestion that the blasphemy was—or had once been—some morbid and exotic form of actual life.

The thing in the picture squatted or was balanced on what appeared to be a clever reproduction of the monstrously carved throne in the other curious photograph. To describe it with any ordinary vocabulary would be impossible, for nothing even roughly corresponding to it has ever come within the imagination of sane mankind. It represented something meant perhaps to be roughly connected with the vertebrates of this planet—though one could not be too sure of that. Its bulk was Cyclopean, for even squatted it towered to almost twice the height of Orabona, who was shewn beside it. Looking sharply, one might trace its approximations toward the bodily features of the higher vertebrates.

There was an almost globular torso, with six long, sinuous limbs terminating in crab-like claws. From the upper end a subsidiary globe bulged forward bubble-like; its triangle of three staring, fishy eyes, its foot-long and evidently flexible proboscis, and a distended lateral system analogous to gills, suggesting that it was a head. Most of the body was covered with what at first appeared to be fur, but which on closer examination proved to be a dense growth of dark, slender tentacles or sucking filaments, each tipped with a mouth suggesting the head of an asp. On the head and below the proboscis the tentacles tended to be longer and thicker, and marked with spiral stripes—suggesting the traditional serpent-locks of Medusa. To say that such a thing could have an *expression* seems paradoxical; yet Jones felt that that triangle of bulging fish-eyes and that obliquely poised proboscis all bespoke a blend of hate, greed, and sheer cruelty incomprehensible to mankind because mixed with other emotions not of the world or this solar system. Into this bestial abnormality, he reflected, Rogers must have poured at once all his malignant insanity and all his uncanny sculptural genius. The thing was incredible—and yet the photograph proved that it existed.

Rogers interrupted his reveries.

"Well—what do you think of It? Now do you wonder what crushed the dog and sucked it dry with a million mouths? It needed nourishment— and It will need more. It is a god, and I am the first priest of It's latter-day hierarchy. Iä! Shub-Niggurath! The Goat with a Thousand Young!"

Jones lowered the photograph in disgust and pity.

"See here, Rogers, this won't do. There are limits, you know. It's a great piece of work, and all that, but it isn't good for you. Better not see it any more—let Orabona break it up, and try to forget about it. And let me tear this beastly picture up, too."

With a snarl, Rogers snatched the photograph and returned it to the desk.

"Idiot—you—and you still think It's all a fraud! You still think I made It, and you still think my figures are nothing but lifeless wax! Why, damn you, you're a worse clod than a wax image yourself! But I've got proof this time, and you're going to know! Not just now, for It is resting after the sacrifice—but later. Oh, yes—you will not doubt the power of It then."

As Rogers glanced toward the padlocked inner door Jones retrieved his hat and stick from a nearby bench.

"Very well, Rogers, let it be later. I must be going now, but I'll call around tomorrow afternoon. Think my advice over and see if it doesn't sound sensible. Ask Orabona what he thinks, too."

Rogers actually bared his teeth in wild-beast fashion.

"Must be going now, eh? Afraid, after all! Afraid, for all your bold talk! You say the effigies are only wax, and yet you run away when I begin to prove that they aren't. You're like the fellows who take my standing bet that they daren't spend the night in the museum—they come boldly enough, but after an hour they shriek and hammer to get out! Want me to ask Orabona, eh? You two—

always against me! You want to break down the coming earthly reign of It!"

Jones preserved his calm.

"No, Rogers—there's nobody against you. And I'm not afraid of your figures, either, much as I admire your skill. But we're both a bit nervous tonight, and I fancy some rest will do us good."

Again Rogers checked his guest's departure.

"Not afraid, eh?—then why are you so anxious to go? Look here —do you or don't you dare to stay alone here in the dark? What's your hurry if you don't believe in It?"

Some new idea seemed to have struck Rogers, and Jones eyed him closely.

"Why, I've no special hurry—but what would be gained by my staying here alone? What would it prove? My only objection is that it isn't very comfortable for sleeping. What good would it do either of us?"

This time it was Jones who was struck with an idea. He continued in a tone of conciliation.

"See here, Rogers—I've just asked you what it would prove if I stayed, when we both know. It would prove that your effigies are just effigies, and that you oughtn't to let your imagination go the way it's been going lately. Suppose I *do* stay. If I stick it out till morning, will you agree to take a new view of things—go on a vacation for three months or so and let Orabona destroy that new thing of yours? Come, now—isn't that fair?"

The expression on the showman's face was hard to read. It was obvious that he was thinking quickly, and that of sundry conflicting emotions, malign triumph was getting the upper hand. His voice held a choking quality as he replied.

"Fair enough! *If you do stick it out,* I'll take your advice. But stick you must. We'll go out for dinner and come back. I'll lock you in the display room and go home. In the morning I'll come down ahead of Orabona—he comes half an hour before the rest—and see how you are. But don't try it unless you are *very* sure of your scepticism. Others have backed out—you have that chance. And I suppose a pounding on the outer door would always bring a constable. You may not like it so well after a while—you'll be in the same building, though not in the same room with It."

As they left the rear door into the dingy courtyard, Rogers took with him the piece of burlap—weighted with a gruesome burden. Near the centre of the court was a manhole, whose cover the showman lifted quietly, and with a shuddersome suggestion of familiarity. Burlap and all, the burden went down to the oblivion of a cloacal labyrinth. Jones shuddered, and almost shrank from the gaunt figure at his side as they emerged into the street.

By unspoken mutual consent, they did not dine together, but agreed to meet in front of the museum at eleven.

Jones hailed a cab, and breathed more freely when he had crossed Waterloo Bridge and was approaching the brilliantly lighted Strand. He dined at a quiet café, and subsequently went to his home in Portland Place to bathe and get a few things. Idly he wondered what Rogers was doing. He had heard that the man had a vast, dismal house in the Walworth Road, full of obscure and forbidden books, occult paraphernalia, and wax images which he did not choose to place on exhibition. Orabona, he understood, lived in separate quarters in the same house.

At eleven Jones found Rogers waiting by the basement door in Southwark Street. Their words were few, but each seemed taut with a menacing tension. They agreed that the vaulted exhibition room alone should form the scene of the vigil, and Rogers did not insist that the watcher sit in the special adult alcove of supreme horrors. The showman, having extinguished all the lights with switches in the workroom, locked the door of that crypt with one of the keys on his crowded ring. Without shaking hands he passed out the street door, locked it after him, and stamped up the worn steps to the sidewalk outside. As his tread receded, Jones realised that the long, tedious vigil had commenced.

II.

Later, in the utter blackness of the great arched cellar, Jones cursed the childish naiveté which had brought him there. For the first half-hour he had kept flashing on his pocket-light at intervals, but now just sitting in the dark on one of the visitors' benches had become a more nerve-racking thing. Every time the beam shot out it lighted up some morbid, grotesque object—a guillotine, a nameless hybrid monster, a pasty-bearded face crafty with evil, a body with red torrents streaming from a severed throat. Jones knew that no sinister reality was attached to these things, but after that first half-hour he preferred not to see them.

Why he had bothered to humour that madman he could scarcely imagine. It would have been much simpler merely to have let him alone, or to have called in a mental specialist. Probably, he reflected, it was the fellow-feeling of one artist for another. There was so much genius in Rogers that he deserved every possible chance to be helped quietly out of his growing mania. Any man who could imagine and construct the incredibly life-like things that he had produced was surely not far from actual greatness. He had the fancy of a Sime or a Doré joined to the minute, scientific craftsmanship of a Blatschka. Indeed, he had done for the world of nightmare what the Blatschkas with their marvellously accurate plant models of finely wrought and coloured glass had done for the world of botany.

At midnight the strokes of a distant clock filtered through the darkness, and Jones felt cheered by the message from a still-surviving outside world. The vaulted museum chamber was like a tomb—ghastly in its utter solitude. Even a mouse would be cheering company; yet Rogers had once boasted that—for "certain reasons", as he said—no mice or even insects ever came near the place. That was very curious, yet it seemed to be true. The deadness and silence were virtually complete. If only something would make a sound! He shuffled his feet, and the echoes came spectrally out of the absolute stillness. He coughed, but there was something mocking in the staccato reverberations. He could not, he vowed, begin talking to himself. That meant nervous disintegration. Time seemed to pass with abnormal and disconcerting slowness. He could have sworn that hours had elapsed since he last flashed the light on his watch, yet here was only the stroke of midnight.

He wished that his senses were not so preternaturally keen. Something in the darkness and stillness seemed to have sharpened them, so that they responded to faint intimations hardly strong enough to be called true impressions. His ears seemed at times to catch a faint, elusive susurrus which could not *quite* be identified with the nocturnal hum of the squalid streets outside, and he thought of vague, irrelevant things like the music of the spheres and the unknown, inaccessible life of alien dimensions pressing on our own. Rogers often speculated about such things.

The floating specks of light in his blackness-drowned eyes seemed inclined to take on curious symmetries of pattern and motion. He had often wondered about those strange rays from the unplumbed abyss which scintillate before us in the absence of all earthly illumination, but he had never known any that behaved just as these were behaving. They lacked the restful aimlessness of ordinary light-specks—suggesting some will and purpose remote from any terrestrial conception.

Then there was that suggestion of odd stirrings. Nothing was open, yet in spite of the general draughtlessness Jones felt that the air was not uniformly quiet. There were intangible variations in pressure—not quite decided enough to suggest the loathsome pawings of unseen elementals. It was abnormally chilly, too. He did not like any of this. The air tasted salty, as if it were mixed with the brine of dark subterrene waters, and there was a bare hint of some odour of ineffable mustiness. In the daytime he had never noticed that the waxen figures had an odour. Even now that half-received hint was not the way wax figures ought to smell. It was more like the faint smell of specimens in a natural-history museum. Curious, in view of Rogers' claims that his figures were not all artificial—indeed, it was probably that claim which made one's imagination conjure up the olfactory suspicion. One must guard against excesses of the imagination—had not such things driven poor Rogers mad?

But the utter loneliness of this place was frightful. Even the distant chimes seemed to come from across cosmic gulfs. It made Jones think of that insane picture which Rogers had shewed him—the wildly carved chamber with the cryptic throne which the fellow had claimed was part of a three-million-year-old ruin in the shunned and inaccessible solitudes of the Arctic. Perhaps Rogers had been to Alaska, but that picture was certainly nothing but stage scenery. It couldn't normally be otherwise, with all that carving and those terrible symbols. And that monstrous shape supposed to have been found on that throne—what a flight of diseased fancy! Jones wondered just how far he actually was from the insane masterpiece in wax—probably it was kept behind that heavy, padlocked plank door leading somewhere out of the workroom. But it would never do to brood about a waxen image. Was not the present room full of such things, some of them scarcely less horrible than the dreadful "IT"? And beyond a thin canvas screen on the left was the "Adults only" alcove with its nameless phantoms of delirium.

The proximity of the numberless waxen shapes began to get on Jones's nerves more and more as the quarter-hours wore on. He knew the museum so well that he could not get rid of their usual images even in the total darkness. Indeed, the darkness had the effect of adding to the remembered images certain very disturbing imaginative overtones. The guillotine seemed to creak, and the bearded face of Landru—slayer of his fifty wives—twisted itself into expressions of monstrous menace. From the severed throat of Madame Demers a hideous bubbling sound seemed to emanate, while the headless, legless victim of a trunk murder tried to edge closer and closer on its gory stumps. Jones began shutting his eyes to see if that would dim the images, but found it was useless. Besides, when he shut his eyes the strange, purposeful patterns of light-specks became more disturbingly pronounced.

Then suddenly he began trying to keep the hideous images he had formerly been trying to banish. He tried to keep them because they were giving place to still more hideous ones. In spite of himself his memory began reconstructing the utterly non-human blasphemies that lurked in the obscurer corners, and these lumpish hybrid growths oozed and wriggled toward him as though hunting him down in a circle. Black Tsathoggua moulded itself from a toad-like gargoyle to a long, sinuous line with hundreds of rudimentary feet, and a lean, rubbery night-gaunt spread its wings as if to advance and smother the watcher. Jones braced himself to keep from screaming. He knew he was reverting to the traditional terrors of his childhood, and resolved to use his adult reason to keep the phantoms at bay. It helped a bit, he found, to flash the light again. Frightful as were the images it shewed, these were not as bad as what his fancy called out of the utter blackness.

But there were drawbacks. Even in the light of his torch he could not help suspecting a slight, furtive trembling on the part of the canvas partition screening off the terrible "Adults only" alcove. He knew what lay beyond, and shivered. Imagination called up the shocking form of fabulous Yog-Sothoth—only a congeries of iridescent globes, yet stupendous in its malign suggestiveness. What was this accursed mass slowly floating toward him and bumping on the partition that stood in the way? A small bulge in the canvas far to the right suggested the sharp horn of Gnoph-keh, the hairy myth-thing of the Greenland ice, that walked sometimes on two legs, sometimes on four, and sometimes on six. To get this stuff out of his head Jones walked boldly toward the hellish alcove with torch burning steadily. Of course, none of his fears was true. Yet were not the long, facial tentacles of great Cthulhu actually swaying, slowly and insidiously? He knew they were flexible, but he had not realised that the draught caused by his advance was enough to set them in motion.

Returning to his former seat outside the alcove, he shut his eyes and let the symmetrical light-specks do their worst. The distant clock boomed a single stroke. Could it be only one? He flashed the light on his watch and saw that it was precisely that hour. It would be hard indeed waiting for morning. Rogers would be down at about eight o'clock, ahead of even Orabona. It would be light outside in the main basement long before that, but none of it could penetrate here. All the windows in this basement had been bricked up but the three small ones facing the court. A pretty bad wait, all told.

His ears were getting most of the hallucinations now—for he could swear he heard stealthy, plodding footsteps in the workroom beyond the closed and locked door. He had no business thinking of that unexhibited horror which Rogers called "It". The thing was a contamination—it had driven its maker mad, and now even its picture was calling up imaginative terrors. It could not be in the workroom—it was very obviously beyond that padlocked door of heavy planking. Those steps were certainly pure imagination.

Then he thought he heard the key turn in the workroom door. Flashing on his torch, he saw nothing but the ancient six-panelled portal in its proper position. Again he tried darkness and closed eyes, but there followed a harrowing illusion of creaking—not the guillotine this time, but the slow, furtive opening of the workroom door. He would not scream. Once he screamed, he would be lost. There was a sort of padding or shuffling audible now, and it was slowly advancing toward him. He must retain command of himself. Had he not done so when the nameless brain-shapes tried to close in on him? The shuffling crept nearer, and his resolution failed. He did not scream but merely gulped out a challenge.

"Who goes there? Who are you? What do you want?"

There was no answer, but the shuffling kept on. Jones did not know which he feared most to do—turn on his flashlight or stay in the dark while the thing crept upon him. This thing was different, he felt profoundly, from the other terrors of the evening. His fingers and throat worked spasmodically. Silence was impossible, and the suspense of utter blackness was beginning to be the most intolerable of all conditions. Again he cried out hysterically—"Halt! Who goes there?"—as he switched on the revealing beams of his torch. Then, paralysed by what he saw, he dropped the flashlight and screamed—not once but many times.

Shuffling toward him in the darkness was the gigantic, blasphemous form of a black thing not wholly ape and not wholly insect. Its hide hung loosely upon its frame, and its rugose, dead-eyed rudiment of a head swayed drunkenly from side to side. Its fore paws were extended, with talons spread wide, and its whole body was taut with murderous malignity despite its utter lack of facial expression. After the screams and the final coming of darkness it leaped, and in a moment had Jones pinned to the floor. There was no struggle, for the watcher had fainted.

Jones's fainting spell could not have lasted more than a moment, for the nameless thing was apishly dragging him through the darkness when he began recovering consciousness. What started him fully awake were the sounds which the thing was making—or rather, the voice with which it was making them. That voice was human, and it was familiar. Only one living being could be behind the hoarse, feverish accents which were chanting to an unknown horror.

"Iä! Iä!" it was howling. "I am coming, O Rhan-Tegoth, coming with the nourishment. You have waited long and fed ill, but now you shall have what was promised. That and more, for instead of Orabona it will be one of high degree who had doubted you. You shall crush and drain him, with all his doubts, and grow strong thereby. And ever after among men he shall be shewn as a monument to your glory. Rhan-Tegoth, infinite and invincible, I am your slave and high-priest. You are hungry, and I provide. I read the sign and have led you forth. I shall feed you with blood, and you shall feed me with power. Iä! Shub-Niggurath! The Goat with a Thousand Young!"

In an instant all the terrors of the night dropped from Jones like a discarded cloak. He was again master of his mind, for he knew the very earthly and material peril he had to deal with. This was no monster of fable, but a dangerous madman. It was Rogers, dressed in some nightmare covering of his own insane designing, and about to make a frightful sacrifice to the devil-god he had fashioned out of wax. Clearly, he must have entered the workroom from the rear courtyard, donned his disguise, and then advanced to seize his neatly trapped and fear-broken victim. His strength was prodigious, and if he was to be thwarted, one must act quickly. Counting on the madman's confidence in his unconsciousness he determined to take him by surprise, while his grasp was relatively lax. The feel of a threshold told him he was crossing into the pitch-black workroom.

With the strength of mortal fear Jones made a sudden spring from the half-recumbent posture in which he was being dragged. For an instant he was free of the astonished maniac's hands, and in another instant a lucky lunge in the dark had put his own hands at his captor's weirdly concealed throat. Simultaneously Rogers gripped him again, and without further preliminaries the two were locked in a desperate struggle of life and death. Jones's athletic training, without doubt, was his sole salvation; for his mad assailant, freed from every inhibition of fair play, decency, or even self-preservation, was an engine of savage destruction as formidable as a wolf or panther.

Guttural cries sometimes punctured the hideous tussle in the dark. Blood spurted, clothing ripped, and Jones at last felt the actual throat of the maniac, shorn of its spectral mask. He spoke not a word, but put every ounce of energy into the defence of his life. Rogers kicked, gouged, butted, bit, clawed, and spat—yet found strength to yelp out actual sentences at times. Most of his speech was in a ritualistic jargon full of references to "It" or "Rhan-Tegoth", and to Jones's overwrought nerves it seemed as if the cries echoed from an infinite distance of daemoniac snortings and bayings. Toward the last they were rolling on the floor, overturning benches or striking against the walls and the brick foundations of the central melting-furnace. Up to the very end Jones could not be certain of saving himself, but chance finally intervened in his favour. A jab of his knee against Rogers' chest produced a general relaxation, and a moment later he knew he had won.

Though hardly able to hold himself up, Jones rose and stumbled about the walls seeking the light-switch—for his flashlight was gone, together with most of his clothing. As he lurched along he dragged his limp opponent with him, fearing a sudden attack when the madman came to. Finding the switch-box, he fumbled till he had the right handle. Then, as the wildly disordered workroom burst into sudden radiance, he set about binding Rogers with such cords and belts as he could easily find. The fellow's disguise—or what was left of it—seemed to be made of a puzzlingly queer sort of leather. For some reason it made Jones's flesh crawl to touch it, and there seemed to be an alien, rusty odour about it. In the normal clothes beneath it was Rogers' key-ring, and this the exhausted victor seized as his final passport to freedom. The shades at the small, slit-like windows were all securely drawn, and he let them remain so.

Washing off the blood of battle at a convenient sink, Jones donned the most ordinary-looking and least ill-fitting clothes he could find on the costume hooks. Testing the door to the courtyard, he found it fastened with a spring-lock which did not require a key from the inside. He kept the key-ring, however, to admit him on his return with aid—for plainly, the thing to do was to call in an alienist. There was no telephone in the museum, but it would not take long to find an all-night restaurant or chemist's shop where one could be had. He had almost opened the door to go when a torrent of hideous abuse from across the room told him that Rogers—whose visible injuries were confined to a long, deep scratch down the left cheek—had regained consciousness.

"Fool! Spawn of Noth-Yidik and effluvium of K'thun! Son of the dogs that howl in the maelstrom of Azathoth! You would have been sacred and immortal, and now you are betraying It and It's priest! Beware—for It is hungry! It would have been Orabona—that damned treacherous dog ready to turn against me and It—but I give you the first honour instead. Now you must both beware, for It is not gentle without It's priest.

"Iä! Iä! Vengeance is at hand! Do you know you would have been immortal? Look at the furnace! There is a fire ready to light, and there is wax in the kettle. I would have done with you as I have done with other once-living forms. Hei! You, who have vowed all my effigies are waxen, would have become a waxen effigy yourself! The furnace was all ready! When It had had It's fill, and you were like that dog I shewed you, I would have made your flattened, punctured fragments immortal! Wax would have done it. Haven't you said I'm a great artist? Wax in every pore—wax over every square inch of you—Iä! Iä! And ever after the world would have looked at your mangled carcass and wondered how I ever imagined and made such a thing! Hei! And Orabona would have come next, and others after him—and thus would my waxen family have grown!

"Dog—do you still think I *made* all my effigies? Why not say *preserved?* You know by this time the strange places I've been to, and the strange things I've brought back. Coward—you could never face the dimensional shambler whose hide I put on to scare you—the mere sight of it alive, or even the full-fledged thought of it, would kill you instantly with fright! Iä! Iä! It waits hungry for the blood that is the life!"

Rogers, propped against the wall, swayed to and fro in his bonds.

"See here, Jones—if I let you go will you let me go? It must be taken care of by It's high-priest. Orabona will be enough to keep It alive—and when he is finished I will make his fragments immortal in wax for the world to see. It could have been you, but you have rejected the honour. I won't bother you again. Let me go, and I will share with you the power that It will bring me. Iä! Iä! Great is Rhan-Tegoth! Let me go! Let me go! It is starving down there beyond that door, and if It dies the Old Ones can never come back. Hei! Hei! Let me go!"

Jones merely shook his head, though the hideousness of the showman's imaginings revolted him. Rogers, now staring wildly at the padlocked plank door, thumped his head again and again against the brick wall and kicked with his tightly bound ankles. Jones was afraid he would injure himself, and advanced to bind him more firmly to some stationary object. Writhing, Rogers edged away from him and set up a series of frenetic ululations whose utter, monstrous unhumanness was appalling, and whose sheer volume was almost incredible. It seemed impossible that any human throat could produce noises so loud and piercing, and Jones felt that if this continued there would be no need to telephone for aid. It could not be long before a constable would investigate, even granting that there were no listening neighbours in this deserted warehouse district.

"Wza-y'ei! Wza-y'ei!" howled the madman. *"Y'kaa haa bho—ii, Rhan-Tegoth—Cthulhu fhtagn—Ei! Ei! Ei! Ei!—Rhan-Tegoth, Rhan-Tegoth, Rhan-Tegoth!"*

The tautly trussed creature, who had started squirming his way across the littered floor, now reached the padlocked plank door and commenced knocking his head thunderously against it. Jones dreaded the task of binding him further, and wished he were not so exhausted from the previous struggle. This violent aftermath was getting hideously on his nerves, and he began to feel a return of the nameless qualms he had felt in the dark. Everything about Rogers and his museum was so hellishly morbid and suggestive of black vistas beyond life! It was loathsome to think of the waxen masterpiece of abnormal genius which must at this very moment be lurking close at hand in the blackness beyond the heavy, padlocked door.

And now something happened which sent an additional chill down Jones's spine, and caused every hair—even the tiny growth on the backs of his hands—to bristle with a vague fright beyond classification. Rogers had suddenly stopped screaming and beating his head against the stout plank door, and was straining up to a sitting posture, head cocked on one side as if listening intently for something. All at once a smile of devilish triumph overspread his face, and he began speaking intelligibly again—this time in a hoarse whisper contrasting oddly with his former stentorian howling.

"Listen, fool! Listen hard! *It* has heard me, and is coming. Can't you hear It splashing out of It's tank down there at the end of the runway? I dug it deep, because there was nothing too good for It. It is amphibious, you know—you saw the gills in the picture. It came to the earth from lead-grey Yuggoth, where the cities are under the warm deep sea. It can't stand up in there—too tall—has to sit or crouch. Let me get my keys—we must let It out and kneel down before It. Then we will go out and find a dog or cat—or perhaps a drunken man—to give It the nourishment It needs."

It was not what the madman said, but the way he said it, that disorganised Jones so badly. The utter, insane confidence and sincerity in that crazed whisper were damnably contagious. Imagination, with such a stimulus, could find an active menace in the devilish wax figure that lurked unseen just beyond the heavy planking. Eyeing the door in unholy fascination, Jones noticed that it bore several distinct cracks, though no marks of violent treatment were visible on this side. He wondered how large a room or closet lay behind it, and how the waxen figure was arranged. The maniac's idea of a tank and runway was as clever as all his other imaginings.

Then, in one terrible instant, Jones completely lost the power to draw a breath. The leather belt he had seized for Rogers' further strapping fell from his limp hands, and a spasm of shivering convulsed him from head to foot. He might have known the place would drive him mad as it had driven Rogers—and now he *was* mad. He was mad, for he now harboured hallucinations more weird than any which had assailed him earlier that night. The madman was bidding him hear the splashing of a mythical monster in a tank beyond the door—and now, God help him, *he did hear it!*

Rogers saw the spasm of horror reach Jones's face and transform it to a staring mask of fear. He cackled.

"At last, fool, you believe! At last you know! You hear It and It comes! Get me my keys, fool—we must do homage and serve It!"

But Jones was past paying attention to any human words, mad or sane. Phobic paralysis held him immobile and half-conscious, with wild images racing phantasmagorically through his helpless imagination. There *was* a splashing. There *was* a padding or shuffling, as of great wet paws on a solid surface. Something *was* approaching. Into his nostrils, from the cracks in that nightmare plank door, poured a noisome animal stench like and yet unlike that of the mammal cages at the zoölogical gardens in Regent's Park.

He did not know now whether Rogers was talking or not. Everything real had faded away, and he was a statue obsessed with dreams and hallucinations so unnatural that they became almost objective and remote from him. He thought he heard a sniffing or snorting from the unknown gulf beyond the door, and when a sudden baying, trumpeting noise assailed his ears he could not feel sure that it came from the tightly bound maniac whose image swam uncertainly in his shaken vision. The photograph of that accursed, unseen wax thing persisted in floating through his consciousness. Such a thing had no right to exist. Had it not driven him mad?

Even as he reflected, a fresh evidence of madness beset him. Something, he thought, was fumbling with the latch of the heavy padlocked door. It was patting and pawing and pushing at the planks. There was a thudding on the stout wood, which grew louder and louder. The stench was horrible. And now the assault on that door from the inside was a malign, determined pounding like the strokes of a battering-ram. There was an ominous cracking —a splintering—a welling foetor—a falling plank—*a black paw ending in a crab-like claw. . . .*

"Help! Help! God help me! . . . Aaaaaaa! . . ."

With intense effort Jones is today able to recall a sudden bursting of his fear-paralysis into the liberation of frenzied automatic flight. What he evidently did must have paralleled curiously the wild, plunging flights of maddest nightmares; for he seems to have leaped across the disordered crypt at almost a single bound, yanked open the outside door, which closed and locked itself after him with a clatter, sprung up the worn stone steps three at a time, and raced frantically and aimlessly out of that dank cobblestoned court and through the squalid streets of Southwark.

Here the memory ends. Jones does not know how he got home, and there is no evidence of his having hired a cab. Probably he raced all the way by blind instinct—over Waterloo Bridge, along the Strand and Charing Cross, and up Haymarket and Regent Street to his own neighbourhood. He still had on the queer mélange of museum costumes when he grew conscious enough to call the doctor.

A week later the nerve specialists allowed him to leave his bed and walk in the open air.

But he had not told the specialists much. Over his whole experience hung a pall of madness and nightmare, and he felt that silence was the only course. When he was up, he scanned intently all the papers which had accumulated since that hideous night, but found no reference to anything queer at the museum. How much, after all, had been reality? Where did reality end and morbid dream begin? Had his mind gone wholly to pieces in that dark exhibition chamber, and had the whole fight with Rogers been a phantasm of fever? It would help to put him on his feet if he could settle some of these maddening points. He *must* have seen that damnable photograph of the wax image called "It", for no brain but Rogers' could ever have conceived such a blasphemy.

It was a fortnight before he dared to enter Southwark Street again. He went in the middle of the morning, when there was the greatest amount of sane, wholesome activity around the ancient, crumbling shops and warehouses. The museum's sign was still there, and as he approached he saw that the place was open. The gateman nodded in a pleasant recognition as he summoned up the courage to enter, and in the vaulted chamber below an attendant touched his cap cheerfully. Perhaps everything had been a dream. Would he dare to knock at the door of the workroom and look for Rogers?

Then Orabona advanced to greet him. His dark, sleek face was a trifle sardonic, but Jones felt that he was not unfriendly. He spoke with a trace of accent.

"Good morning, Mr. Jones. It is some time since we have seen you here. Did you wish Mr. Rogers? I'm sorry, but he is away. He had word of business in America, and had to go. Yes, it was very sudden. I am in charge now—here, and at the house. I try to maintain Mr. Rogers' high standard—till he is back."

The foreigner smiled—perhaps from affability alone. Jones scarcely knew how to reply, but managed to mumble out a few inquiries about the day after his last visit. Orabona seemed greatly amused by the questions, and took considerable care in framing his replies.

"Oh, yes, Mr. Jones—the twenty-eighth of last month. I remember it for many reasons. In the morning—before Mr. Rogers got here, you understand—I found the workroom in quite a mess. There was a great deal of—cleaning up—to do. There had been—

late work, you see. Important new specimen given its secondary baking process. I took complete charge when I came.

"It was a hard specimen to prepare—but of course Mr. Rogers has taught me a great deal. He is, as you know, a very great artist. When he came he helped me complete the specimen—helped very materially, I assure you—but he left soon without even greeting the men. As I tell you, he was called away suddenly. There were important chemical reactions involved. They made loud noises—in fact, some teamsters in the court outside fancy they heard several pistol shots—very amusing idea!

"As for the new specimen—that matter is very unfortunate. It is a great masterpiece—designed and made, you understand, by Mr. Rogers. He will see about it when he gets back."

Again Orabona smiled.

"The police, you know. We put it on display a week ago, and there were two or three faintings. One poor fellow had an epileptic fit in front of it. You see, it is a trifle—stronger—than the rest. Larger, for one thing. Of course, it was in the adult alcove. The next day a couple of men from Scotland Yard looked it over and said it was too morbid to be shewn. Said we'd have to remove it. It was a tremendous shame—such a masterpiece of art—but I didn't feel justified in appealing to the courts in Mr. Rogers' absence. He would not like so much publicity with the police now—but when he gets back—when he gets back—"

For some reason or other Jones felt a mounting tide of uneasiness and repulsion. But Orabona was continuing.

"You are a connoisseur, Mr. Jones. I am sure I violate no law in offering you a private view. It may be—subject, of course, to Mr. Rogers' wishes—that we shall destroy the specimen some day—but that would be a crime."

Jones had a powerful impulse to refuse the sight and flee precipitately, but Orabona was leading him forward by the arm with an artist's enthusiasm. The adult alcove, crowded with nameless horrors, held no visitors. In the farther corner a large niche had been curtained off, and to this the smiling assistant advanced.

"You must know, Mr. Jones, that the title of this specimen is 'The Sacrifice to Rhan-Tegoth'."

Jones started violently, but Orabona appeared not to notice.

"The shapeless, colossal god is a feature in certain obscure legends which Mr. Rogers has studied. All nonsense, of course, as you've so often assured Mr. Rogers. It is supposed to have come from outer space, and to have lived in the Arctic three million years ago. It treated its sacrifices rather peculiarly and horribly, as you shall see. Mr. Rogers had made it fiendishly life-like—even to the face of the victim."

Now trembling violently, Jones clung to the brass railing in front of the curtained niche. He almost reached out to stop Orabona when he saw the curtain beginning to swing aside, but some conflicting impulse held him back. The foreigner smiled triumphantly.

"Behold!"

Jones reeled in spite of his grip on the railing.

"God!—great God!"

Fully ten feet high despite a shambling, crouching attitude expressive of infinite cosmic malignancy, a monstrosity of unbelievable horror was shewn starting forward from a Cyclopean ivory throne covered with grotesque carvings. In the central pair of its six legs it bore a crushed, flattened, distorted, bloodless thing, riddled with a million punctures, and in places seared as with some pungent acid. Only the mangled head of the victim, lolling upside down at one side, revealed that it represented something once human.

The monster itself needed no title for one who had seen a certain hellish photograph. That damnable print had been all too faithful; yet it could not carry the full horror which lay in the gigantic actuality. The globular torso—the bubble-like suggestion of a head—the three fishy eyes—the foot-long proboscis—the bulging gills—the monstrous capillation of asp-like suckers—the six sinuous limbs with their black paws and crab-like claws—God! the familiarity of that black paw ending in a crab-like claw! . . .

Orabona's smile was utterly damnable. Jones choked, and stared at the hideous exhibit with a mounting fascination which perplexed and disturbed him. What half-revealed horror was holding and forcing him to look longer and search out details? This had driven Rogers mad . . . Rogers, supreme artist . . . said they weren't artificial. . . .

Then he localised the thing that held him. It was the crushed waxen victim's lolling head, and something that it implied. This head was not entirely devoid of a face, and that face was familiar. It was like the mad face of poor Rogers. Jones peered closer, hardly knowing why he was driven to do so. Wasn't it natural for a mad egotist to mould his own features into his masterpiece? Was there anything more that subconscious vision had seized on and suppressed in sheer terror?

The wax of the mangled face had been handled with boundless dexterity. Those punctures—how perfectly they reproduced the myriad wounds somehow inflicted on that poor dog! But there was something more. On the left cheek one could trace an irregularity which seemed outside the general scheme—as if the sculptor had sought to cover up a defect of his first modelling. The more Jones looked at it, the more mysteriously it horrified him—and then, suddenly, he remembered a circumstance which brought his horror to a head. That night of hideousness—the tussle—the bound madman *—and the long, deep scratch down the left cheek of the actual living Rogers. . . .*

Jones, releasing his desperate clutch on the railing, sank in a total faint.

Orabona continued to smile.

Hazel Heald

Winged Death

The Orange Hotel stands in High Street near the railway station in Bloemfontein, South Africa. On Sunday, January 24, 1932, four men sat shivering from terror in a room on its third floor. One was George C. Titteridge, proprietor of the hotel; another was police constable Ian De Witt of the Central Station; a third was Johannes Bogaert, the local coroner; the fourth, and apparently the least disorganised of the group, was Dr. Cornelius Van Keulen, the coroner's physician.

On the floor, uncomfortably evident amidst the stifling summer heat, was the body of a dead man—but this was not what the four were afraid of. Their glances wandered from the table, on which lay a curious assortment of things, to the ceiling overhead, across whose smooth whiteness a series of huge, faltering alphabetical characters had somehow been scrawled in ink; and every now and then Dr. Van Keulen would glance half-furtively at a worn leather blank-book which he held in his left hand. The horror of the four seemed about equally divided among the blank-book, the scrawled words on the ceiling, and a dead fly of peculiar aspect which floated in a bottle of ammonia on the table. Also on the table were an open inkwell, a pen and writing-pad, a physician's medical case, a bottle of hydrochloric acid, and a tumbler about a quarter full of black oxide of manganese.

The worn leather book was the journal of the dead man on the floor, and had at once made it clear that the name "Frederick N. Mason, Mining Properties, Toronto, Canada", signed in the hotel register, was a false one. There were other things—terrible things—which it likewise made clear; and still other things of far greater terror at which it hinted hideously without making them clear or even fully believable. It was the half-belief of the four men, fostered by lives spent close to the black, settled secrets of brooding Africa, which made them shiver so violently in spite of the searing January heat.

The blank-book was not a large one, and the entries were in a fine handwriting, which, however, grew careless and nervous-looking toward the last. It consisted of a series of jottings at first rather irregularly spaced, but finally becoming daily. To call it a diary would not be quite correct, for it chronicled only one set of its writer's activities. Dr. Van Keulen recognised the name of the dead man the moment he opened the cover, for it was that of an eminent member of his own profession who had been largely connected with African matters. In another moment he was horrified to find this name linked with a dastardly crime, officially unsolved, which had filled the newspapers some four months before. And the farther he read, the deeper grew his horror, awe, and sense of loathing and panic.

Here, in essence, is the text which the doctor read aloud in that sinister and increasingly noisome room while the three men around him breathed hard, fidgeted in their chairs, and darted frightened glances at the ceiling, the table, the thing on the floor, and one another:

JOURNAL OF THOMAS SLAUENWITE, M.D.

Touching punishment of Henry Sargent Moore, Ph.D., of Brooklyn, New York, Professor of Invertebrate Biology in Columbia University, New York, N.Y. Prepared to be read after my death, for the satisfaction of making public the accomplishment of my revenge, which may otherwise never be imputed to me even if it succeeds.

January 5, 1929—I have now fully resolved to kill Dr. Henry Moore, and a recent incident has shewn me how I shall do it. From now on, I shall follow a consistent line of action; hence the beginning of this journal.

It is hardly necessary to repeat the circumstances which have driven me to this course, for the informed part of the public is familiar with all the salient facts. I was born in Trenton, New Jersey, on April 12, 1885, the son of Dr. Paul Slauenwite, formerly of Pretoria, Transvaal, South Africa. Studying medicine as part of my family tradition, I was led by my father (who died in 1916, while I was serving in France in a South African regiment) to specialise in African fevers; and after my graduation from Columbia spent much time in researches which took me from Durban, in Natal, up to the equator itself.

In Mombasa I worked out my new theory of the transmission and development of remittent fever, aided only slightly by the papers of the late government physician, Sir Norman Sloane, which I found in the house I occupied. When I published my results I became at a single stroke a famous authority. I was told of the probability of an almost supreme position in the South African health service, and even a probable knighthood, in the event of my becoming a naturalised citizen, and accordingly I took the necessary steps.

Then occurred the incident for which I am about to kill Henry Moore. This man, my classmate and friend of years in America and Africa, chose deliberately to undermine my claim to my own theory; alleging that Sir Norman Sloane had anticipated me in every essential detail, and implying that I had probably found more of his papers than I had stated in my account of the matter. To buttress this absurd accusation he produced certain personal letters from Sir Norman which indeed shewed that the older man had been over my ground, and that he would have published his results very soon but for his sudden death. This much I could only admit with regret. What I could not excuse was the jealous suspicion that I had stolen the theory from Sir Norman's papers. The British government, sensibly enough, ignored these aspersions, but withheld the half-promised appointment and knighthood on the ground that my theory, while original with me, was not in fact new.

I could soon see that my career in Africa was perceptibly checked; though I had placed all my hopes on such a career, even to the point of resigning American citizenship. A distinct coolness toward me had arisen among the Government set in Mombasa, especially among those who had known Sir Norman. It was then that I resolved to be even with Moore sooner or later, though I did not know how. He had been jealous of my early celebrity, and had taken advantage of his old correspondence with Sir Norman to ruin me. This from the friend whom I had myself led to take an interest in Africa—whom I had coached and inspired till he achieved his present moderate fame as an authority on African entomology. Even now, though, I will not deny that his attainments are profound. I made him, and in return he has ruined me. Now—some day—I shall destroy him.

When I saw myself losing ground in Mombasa, I applied for my present situation in the interior—at M'gonga, only fifty miles from the Uganda line. It is a cotton and ivory trading-post, with only eight white men besides myself. A beastly hole, almost on the equator, and full of every sort of fever known to mankind. Poisonous snakes and insects everywhere, and niggers with diseases nobody ever heard of outside medical college. But my work is not hard, and I have always had plenty of time to plan things to do to Henry Moore. It amuses me to give his *Diptera of Central and Southern Africa* a prominent place on my shelf. I suppose it actually is a standard manual—they use it at Columbia, Harvard, and the U. of Wis.—but my own suggestions are really responsible for half its strong points.

Last week I encountered the thing which decided me how to kill Moore. A party from Uganda brought in a black with a queer illness which I can't yet diagnose. He was lethargic, with a very low temperature, and shuffled in a peculiar way. Most of the others were afraid of him and said he was under some kind of witch-doctor spell; but Gobo, the interpreter, said he had been bitten by an insect. What it was, I can't imagine—for there is only a slight puncture on the arm. It is bright red, though, with a purple ring around it. Spectral-looking—I don't wonder the boys lay it to black magic. They seem to have seen cases like it before, and say there's really nothing to do about it.

Old N'Kuru, one of the Galla boys at the post, says it must be the bite of a devil-fly, which makes its victim waste away gradually and die, and then takes hold of his soul and personality if it is still alive itself—flying around with all his likes, dislikes, and consciousness. A queer legend—and I don't know of any local insect deadly enough to account for it. I gave this sick black—his name is Mevana—a good shot of quinine and took a sample of his blood for testing, but haven't made much progress. There is certainly a strange germ present, but I can't even remotely identify it. The nearest thing to it is the bacillus one finds in oxen, horses, and dogs that the tsetse-fly has bitten; but tsetse-flies don't infect human beings, and this is too far north for them anyway.

However—the important thing is that I've decided how to kill Moore. If this interior region has insects as poisonous as the natives say, I'll see that he gets a shipment of them from a source he won't suspect, and with plenty of assurances that they are harmless. Trust him to throw overboard all caution when it comes to studying an unknown species—and then we'll see how Nature takes its course! It ought not to be hard to find an insect that scares the blacks so much. First to see how poor Mevana turns out—and then to find my envoy of death.

Jan. 7—Mevana is no better, though I have injected all the antitoxins I know of. He has fits of trembling, in which he rants affrightedly about the way his soul will pass when he dies into the insect that bit him, but between them he remains in a kind of half-stupor. Heart action still strong, so I may pull him through. I shall try to, for he can probably guide me better than anyone else to the region where he was bitten.

Meanwhile I'll write to Dr. Lincoln, my predecessor here, for Allen, the head factor, says he had a profound knowledge of the local sicknesses. He ought to know about the death-fly if any white man does. He's at Nairobi now, and a black runner ought to get me a reply in a week—using the railway for half the trip.

Jan. 10—Patient unchanged, but I have found what I want! It was in an old volume of the local health records, which I've been going over diligently while waiting to hear from Lincoln. Thirty years ago there was an epidemic that killed off thousands of natives in Uganda, and it was definitely traced to a rare fly called *Glossina palpalis*—a sort of cousin of the *Glossina marsitans,* or tsetse. It lives in the bushes on the shores of lakes and rivers, and feeds on the blood of crocodiles, antelopes, and large mammals. When these food animals have the germ of trypanosomiasis, or sleeping-sickness, it picks it up and develops acute infectivity after an incubation period of thirty-one days. Then for seventy-five days it is sure death to anyone or anything it bites.

Without doubt, this must be the "devil-fly" the niggers talk about. Now I know what I'm heading for. Hope Mevana pulls through. Ought to hear from Lincoln in four or five days—he has a great reputation for success in things like this. My worst problem will be to get the flies to Moore without his recognising them. With his cursed plodding scholarship it would be just like him to know all about them since they're actually on record.

Jan. 15—Just heard from Lincoln, who confirms all that the records say about *Glossina palpalis.* He has a remedy for sleeping-sickness which has succeeded in a great number of cases when not given too late. Intermuscular injections of tryparsamide. Since Mevana was bitten about two months ago, I don't know how it will work—but Lincoln says that cases have been known to drag on eighteen months, so possibly I'm not too late. Lincoln sent over some of his stuff, so I've just given Mevana a stiff shot. In a stupor now. They've brought his principal wife from the village, but he doesn't even recognise her. If he recovers, he can certainly shew me where the flies are. He's a great crocodile hunter, according to report, and knows all Uganda like a book. I'll give him another shot tomorrow.

Jan. 16—Mevana seems a little brighter today, but his heart action is slowing up a bit. I'll keep up the injections, but not overdo them.

Jan. 17—Recovery really pronounced today. Mevana opened his eyes and shewed signs of actual consciousness, though dazed, after the injection. Hope Moore doesn't know about tryparsamide. There's a good chance he won't, since he never leaned much toward medicine. Mevana's tongue seemed paralysed, but I fancy that will pass off if I can only wake him up. Wouldn't mind a good sleep myself, but not of this kind!

Jan. 25—Mevana nearly cured! In another week I can let him take me into the jungle. He was frightened when he first came to—about having the fly take his personality after he died—but brightened up finally when I told him he was going to get well. His wife, Ugowe, takes good care of him now, and I can rest a bit. Then for the envoys of death!

Feb. 3—Mevana is well now, and I have talked with him about a hunt for flies. He dreads to go near the place where they got him, but I am playing on his gratitude. Besides, he has an idea that I can ward off disease as well as cure it. His pluck would shame a white man—there's no doubt that he'll go. I can get off by telling the head factor the trip is in the interest of local health work.

March 12—In Uganda at last! Have five boys besides Mevana, but they are all Gallas. The local blacks couldn't be hired to come near the region after the talk of what had happened to Mevana. This jungle is a pestilential place—steaming with miasmal vapours. All the lakes look stagnant. In one spot we came upon a trace of Cyclopean ruins which made even the Gallas run past in a wide circle. They say these megaliths are older than man, and that they used to be a haunt or outpost of "The Fishers from Outside"—whatever that means—and of the evil gods Tsadogwa and Clulu.

To this day they are said to have a malign influence, and to be connected somehow with the devil-flies.

March 15—Struck Lake Mlolo this morning—where Mevana was bitten. A hellish, green-scummed affair, full of crocodiles, Mevana has fixed up a fly-trap of fine wire netting baited with crocodile meat. It has a small entrance, and once the quarry get in, they don't know enough to get out. As stupid as they are deadly, and ravenous for fresh meat or a bowl of blood. Hope we can get a good supply. I've decided that I must experiment with them—finding a way to change their appearance so that Moore won't recognise them. Possibly I can cross them with some other species, producing a strange hybrid whose infection-carrying capacity will be undiminished. We'll see. I must wait, but am in no hurry now. When I get ready I'll have Mevana get me some infected meat to feed my envoys of death—and then for the post-office. Ought to be no trouble getting infection, for this country is a veritable pest-hole.

March 16—Good luck. Two cages full. Five vigorous specimens with wings glistening like diamonds. Mevana is emptying them into a large can with a tightly meshed top, and I think we caught them in the nick of time. We can get them to M'gonga without trouble. Taking plenty of crocodile meat for their food. Undoubtedly all or most of it is infected.

April 20—Back at M'gonga and busy in the laboratory. Have sent to Dr. Joost in Pretoria for some tsetse-flies for hybridisation experiments. Such a crossing, if it will work at all, ought to produce something pretty hard to recognise yet at the same time just as deadly as the *palpalis*. If this doesn't work, I shall try certain other diptera from the interior, and I have sent to Dr. Vandervelde at Nyangwe for some of the Congo types. I shan't have to send Mevana for more tainted meat after all; for I find I can keep cultures of the germ *Trypanosoma gambiense,* taken from the meat we got last month, almost indefinitely in tubes. When the time comes, I'll taint some fresh meat and feed my winged envoys a good dose—then *bon voyage* to them!

June 18—My tsetse-flies from Joost came today. Cages for breeding were all ready long ago, and I am now making selections. Intend to use ultra-violet rays to speed up the life-cycle. Fortunately I have the needed apparatus in my regular equipment. Naturally I tell no one what I'm doing. The ignorance of the few men here makes it easy for me to conceal my aims and pretend to be merely studying existing species for medical reasons.

June 29—The crossing is fertile! Good deposits of eggs last Wednesday, and now I have some excellent larvae. If the mature insects look as strange as these do, I need do nothing more. Am preparing separate numbered cages for the different specimens.

July 7—New hybrids are out! Disguise is excellent as to shape, but sheen of wings still suggests *palpalis*. Thorax has faint suggestions of the stripes of the tsetse. Slight variation in individuals. Am feeding them all on tainted crocodile meat, and after infectivity develops will try them on some of the blacks—apparently, of course, by accident. There are so many mildly venomous flies around here that it can easily be done without exciting suspicion. I shall loose an insect in my tightly screened dining-room when Batta, my house-boy, brings in breakfast—keeping well on guard myself. When it has done its work I'll capture or swat it—an easy thing because of its stupidity—or asphyxiate it by filling the room with chlorine gas. If it doesn't work the first time, I'll try again until it does. Of course, I'll have the tryparsamide handy in case I get bitten myself—but I shall be careful to avoid biting, for no antidote is really certain.

Aug. 10—Infectivity mature, and managed to get Batta stung in fine shape. Caught the fly on him, returning it to its cage. Eased up the pain with iodine, and the poor devil is quite grateful for the service. Shall try a variant specimen on Gamba, the factor's messenger, tomorrow. That will be all the tests I shall dare to make here, but if I need more I shall take some specimens to Ukala and get additional data.

Aug. 11—Failed to get Gamba, but recaptured the fly alive. Batta still seems as well as usual, and has no pain in the back where he was stung. Shall wait before trying to get Gamba again.

Aug. 14—Shipment of insects from Vandervelde at last. Fully seven distinct species, some more or less poisonous. Am keeping them well fed in case the tsetse crossing doesn't work. Some of these fellows look very unlike the *palpalis*, but the trouble is that they may not make a fertile cross with it.

Aug. 17—Got Gamba this afternoon, but had to kill the fly on him. It nipped him in the left shoulder. I dressed the bite, and Gamba is as grateful as Batta was. No change in Batta.

Aug. 20—Gamba unchanged so far—Batta too. Am experimenting with a new form of disguise to supplement the hybridisation—some sort of dye to change the telltale glitter of the *palpalis'* wings. A bluish tint would be best—something I could spray on a whole batch of insects. Shall begin by investigating things like Prussian and Turnbull's blue—iron and cyanogen salts.

Aug. 25—Batta complained of a pain in his back today—things may be developing.

Sept. 3—Have made fair progress in my experiments. Batta shews signs of lethargy, and says his back aches all the time. Gamba beginning to feel uneasy in his bitten shoulder.

Sept. 24—Batta worse and worse, and beginning to get frightened about his bite. Thinks it must be a devil-fly, and entreated me to kill it—for he saw me cage it—until I pretended to him that it had died long ago. Said he didn't want his soul to pass into it upon his death. I give him shots of plain water with a hypodermic to keep his morale up. Evidently the fly retains all the properties of the *palpalis*. Gamba down, too, and repeating all of Batta's symptoms. I may decide to give him a chance with tryparsamide, for the effect of the fly is proved well enough. I shall let Batta go on, however, for I want a rough idea of how long it takes to finish a case.

Dye experiments coming along finely. An isomeric form of ferrous ferrocyanide, with some admixture of potassium salts, can be dissolved in alcohol and sprayed on the insects with splendid effect. It stains the wings blue without affecting the dark thorax much, and doesn't wear off when I sprinkle the specimens with water. With this disguise, I think I can use the present tsetse hybrids and avoid bothering with any more experiments. Sharp as he is, Moore couldn't recognise a blue-winged fly with a half-tsetse thorax. Of course, I keep all this dye business strictly under cover. Nothing must ever connect me with the blue flies later on.

Oct. 9—Batta is lethargic and has taken to his bed. Have been giving Gamba tryparsamide for two weeks, and fancy he'll recover.

Oct. 25—Batta very low, but Gamba nearly well.

Nov. 18—Batta died yesterday, and a curious thing happened which gave me a real shiver in view of the native legends and Batta's own fears. When I returned to the laboratory after the death I heard the most singular buzzing and thrashing in cage 12, which contained the fly that bit Batta. The creature seemed frantic, but stopped still when I appeared—lighting on the wire netting and looking at me in the oddest way. It reached its legs through the wires as if it were bewildered. When I came back from dining with Allen, the thing was dead. Evidently it had gone wild and beaten its life out on the sides of the cage.

It certainly is peculiar that this should happen just as Batta died. If any black had seen it, he'd have laid it at once to the absorption of the poor devil's soul. I shall start my blue-stained hybrids on their way before long now. The hybrid's rate of killing seems a little ahead of the pure *palpalis'* rate, if anything. Batta died three months and eight days after infection—but of course there is always a wide margin of uncertainty. I almost wish I had let Gamba's case run on.

Dec. 5—Busy planning how to get my envoys to Moore. I must have them appear to come from some disinterested entomologist who has read his *Diptera of Central and Southern Africa* and believes he would like to study this "new and unidentifiable species". There must also be ample assurances that the blue-winged fly is harmless, as proved by the natives' long experience. Moore will be off his guard, and one of the flies will surely get him sooner or later—though one can't tell just when.

I'll have to rely on the letters of New York friends—they still speak of Moore from time to time—to keep me informed of early results, though I dare say the papers will announce his death. Above all, I must shew no interest in his case. I shall mail the flies while on a trip, but must not be recognised when I do it. The best plan will be to take a long vacation in the interior, grow a beard, mail the package at Ukala while passing as a visiting entomologist, and return here after shaving off the beard.

April 12, 1930—Back in M'gonga after my long trip. Everything has come off finely—with clockwork precision. Have sent the flies to Moore without leaving a trace. Got a Christmas vacation Dec. 15th, and set out at once with the proper stuff. Made a very good mailing container with room to include some germ-tainted crocodile meat as food for the envoys. By the end of February I had beard enough to shape into a close Vandyke.

Shewed up at Ukala March 9th and typed a letter to Moore on the trading-post machine. Signed it "Nevil Wayland-Hall"—supposed to be an entomologist from London. Think I took just the right tone—interest of a brother-scientist, and all that. Was artistically casual in emphasising the "complete harmlessness" of the specimens. Nobody suspected anything. Shaved the beard as soon as I hit the bush, so that there wouldn't be any uneven tanning by the time I got back here. Dispensed with native bearers except for one small stretch of swamp—I can do wonders with one knapsack, and my sense of direction is good. Lucky I'm used to such travelling. Explained my protracted absence by pleading a touch of fever and some mistakes in direction when going through the bush.

But now comes the hardest part psychologically—waiting for news of Moore without shewing the strain. Of course, he may possibly escape a bite until the venom is played out—but with his recklessness the chances are one hundred to one against him. I have no regrets; after what he did to me, he deserves this and more.

June 30, 1930—Hurrah! The first step worked! Just heard casually from Dyson of Columbia that Moore had received some new blue-winged flies from Africa, and that he is badly puzzled over them! No word of any bite—but if I know Moore's slipshod ways as I think I do, there'll be one before long!

August 27, 1930—Letter from Morton in Cambridge. He says Moore writes of feeling very run-down, and tells of an insect bite on the back of his neck—from a curious new specimen that he received about the middle of June. Have I succeeded? Apparently Moore doesn't connect the bite with his weakness. If this is the real stuff, then Moore was bitten well within the insect's period of infectivity.

Sept. 12, 1930—Victory! Another line from Dyson says that Moore is really in an alarming shape. He now traces his illness to the bite, which he received around noon on June 19, and is quite bewildered about the identity of the insect. Is trying to get in touch with the "Nevil Wayland-Hall" who sent him the shipment. Of the hundred-odd that I sent, about twenty-five seem to have reached him alive. Some escaped at the time of the bite, but several larvae have appeared from eggs laid since the time of mailing. He is, Dyson says, carefully incubating these larvae. When they mature I suppose he'll identify the tsetse-*palpalis* hybridisation—but that won't do him much good now. He'll wonder, though, why the blue wings aren't transmitted by heredity!

Nov. 8, 1930—Letters from half a dozen friends tell of Moore's serious illness. Dyson's came today. He says Moore is utterly at sea about the hybrids that came from the larvae and is beginning to think that the parents got their blue wings in some artificial way. Has to stay in bed most of the time now. No mention of using tryparsamide.

Feb. 13, 1931—Not so good! Moore is sinking, and seems to know no remedy, but I think he suspects me. Had a very chilly letter from Morton last month, which told nothing of Moore; and now Dyson writes—also rather constrainedly—that Moore is forming theories about the whole matter. He's been making a search for "Wayland-Hall" by telegraph—at London, Ukala, Nairobi, Mombasa, and other places—and of course finds nothing. I judge that he's told Dyson whom he suspects, but that Dyson doesn't believe it yet. Fear Morton does believe it.

I see that I'd better lay plans for getting out of here and effacing my identity for good. What an end to a career that started out so well! More of Moore's work—but this time he's paying for it in advance! Believe I'll go back to South Africa—and meanwhile will quietly deposit funds there to the credit of my new self—"Frederick Nasmyth Mason of Toronto, Canada, broker in mining properties". Will establish a new signature for identification. If I never have to take the step, I can easily re-transfer the funds to my present self.

Aug. 15, 1931—Half a year gone, and still suspense. Dyson and Morton—as well as several other friends—seem to have stopped writing me. Dr. James of San Francisco hears from Moore's friends now and then, and says Moore is in an almost continuous coma. He hasn't been able to walk since May. As long as he could talk he complained of being cold. Now he can't talk, though it is thought he still has glimmers of consciousness. His breathing is short and quick, and can be heard some distance away. No question but that *Trypanosoma gambiense* is feeding on him—but he holds out better than the niggers around here. Three months and eight days finished Batta, and here Moore is alive over a year after his biting. Heard rumours last month of an intensive search around Ukala for "Wayland-Hall". Don't think I need to worry yet, though, for there's absolutely nothing in existence to link me with this business.

Oct. 7, 1931—It's over at last! News in the *Mombasa Gazette*. Moore died September 20 after a series of trembling fits and with a temperature vastly below normal. So much for that! I said I'd get him, and I did! The paper had a three-column report of his long illness and death, and of the futile search for "Wayland-Hall". Obviously, Moore was a bigger character in Africa than I had realised. The insect that bit him has now been fully identified from the surviving specimens and developed larvae, and the wing-staining is also detected. It is universally realised that the flies were prepared and shipped with intent to kill. Moore, it appears, communicated certain suspicions to Dyson, but the latter—and the police—are maintaining secrecy because of absence of proof. All of Moore's enemies are being looked up, and the Associated Press hints that "an investigation, possibly involving an eminent physician now abroad, will follow".

One thing at the very end of the report—undoubtedly, the cheap romancing of a yellow journalist—gives me a curious shudder in view of the legends of the blacks and the way the fly happened to go wild when Batta died. It seems that an odd incident occurred on the night of Moore's death; Dyson having been aroused by the buzzing of a blue-winged fly—which immediately flew out the window—just before the nurse telephoned the death news from Moore's home, miles away in Brooklyn.

But what concerns me most is the African end of the matter. People at Ukala remember the bearded stranger who typed the letter and sent the package, and the constabulary are combing the country for any blacks who may have carried him. I didn't use many, but if officers question the Ubandes who took me through N'Kini jungle belt I'll have more to explain than I like. It looks as if the time has come for me to vanish; so tomorrow I believe I'll resign and prepare to start for parts unknown.

Nov. 9, 1931—Hard work getting my resignation acted on, but release came today. I didn't want to aggravate suspicion by decamping outright. Last week I heard from James about Moore's death—but nothing more than is in the papers. Those around him in New York seem rather reticent about details, though they all talk about a searching investigation. No word from any of my friends in the East. Moore must have spread some dangerous suspicions around before he lost consciousness—but there isn't an iota of proof he could have adduced.

Still, I am taking no chances. On Thursday I shall start for Mombasa, and when there will take a steamer down the coast to Durban. After that I shall drop from sight—but soon afterward the mining properties' broker Frederick Nasmyth Mason, from Toronto, will turn up in Johannesburg.

Let this be the end of my journal. If in the end I am not suspected, it will serve its original purpose after my death and reveal what would otherwise not be known. If, on the other hand, these suspicions do materialise and persist, it will confirm and clarify the vague charges, and fill in many important and puzzling gaps. Of course, if danger comes my way I shall have to destroy it.

Well, Moore is dead—as he amply deserves to be. Now Dr. Thomas Slauenwite is dead, too. And when the body formerly belonging to Thomas Slauenwite is dead, the public may have this record.

II.

Jan. 15, 1932—A new year—and a reluctant reopening of this journal. This time I am writing solely to relieve my mind, for it would be absurd to fancy that the case is not definitely closed. I am settled in the Vaal Hotel, Johannesburg, under my new name, and no one has so far challenged my identity. Have had some inconclusive business talks to keep up my part as a mine broker, and believe I may actually work myself into that business. Later I shall go to Toronto and plant a few evidences for my fictitious past.

But what is bothering me is an insect that invaded my room around noon today. Of course I have had all sorts of nightmares about blue flies of late, but those were only to be expected in view of my prevailing nervous strain. This thing, however, was a waking actuality, and I am utterly at a loss to account for it. It buzzed around my bookshelf for fully a quarter of an hour, and eluded every attempt to catch or kill it. The queerest thing was its colour and aspect—for it had blue wings and was in every way a duplicate of my hybrid envoys of death. How it could possibly be one of these, in fact, I certainly don't know. I disposed of all the hybrids—stained and unstained—that I didn't send to Moore, and can't recall any instance of escape.

Can this be wholly an hallucination? Or could any of the specimens that escaped in Brooklyn when Moore was bitten have found their way back to Africa? There was that absurd story of the blue fly that waked Dyson when Moore died—but after all, the survival and return of some of the things is not impossible. It is perfectly plausible that the blue should stick to their wings, too, for the pigment I devised was almost as good as tattooing for permanence. By elimination, that would seem to be the only rational explanation for this thing; though it is very curious that the fellow has come as far south as this. Possibly it's some hereditary homing instinct inherent in the tsetse strain. After all, that side of him belongs to South Africa.

I must be on my guard against a bite. Of course the original venom—if this is actually one of the flies that escaped from Moore—was worn out ages ago; but the fellow must have fed as he flew back from America, and he may well have come through Central Africa and picked up a fresh infectivity. Indeed, that's more probable than not; for the *palpalis* half of his heredity would naturally take him back to Uganda, and all the trypanosomiasis germs. I still have some of the tryparsamide left—I couldn't bear to destroy my medicine case, incriminating though it may be—but since reading up on the subject I am not so sure about the drug's action as I was. It gives one a fighting chance—certainly it saved Gamba—but there's always a large probability of failure.

It's devilish queer that this fly should have happened to come into my room—of all places in the wide expanse of Africa! Seems to strain coincidence to the breaking-point. I suppose that if it comes again, I shall certainly kill it. I'm surprised that it escaped me today, for ordinarily these fellows are extremely stupid and easy to catch. Can it be a pure illusion after all? Certainly the heat is getting me of late as it never did before—even up around Uganda.

Jan. 16—Am I going insane? The fly came again this noon, and acted so anomalously that I can't make head or tail of it. Only delusion on my part could account for what that buzzing pest seemed to do. It appeared from nowhere, and went straight to my bookshelf—circling again and again to front a copy of Moore's *Diptera of Central and Southern Africa*. Now and then it would light on top or back of the volume, and occasionally it would dart forward toward me and retreat before I could strike at it with a folded paper. Such cunning is unheard of among the notoriously stupid African diptera. For nearly half an hour I tried to get the cursed thing, but at last it darted out the window through a hole in the screen that I hadn't noticed. At times I fancied it deliberately mocked me by coming within reach of my weapon and then skilfully sidestepping as I struck out. I must keep a tight hold of my consciousness.

Jan. 17—Either I am mad or the world is in the grip of some sudden suspension of the laws of probability as we know them. That damnable fly came in from somewhere just before noon and commenced buzzing around the copy of Moore's *Diptera* on my shelf. Again I tried to catch it, and again yesterday's experience was repeated. Finally the pest made for the open inkwell on my table and dipped itself in—just the legs and thorax, keeping its wings clear. Then it sailed up to the ceiling and lit—beginning to crawl around in a curved patch and leaving a trail of ink. After a time it hopped a bit and made a single ink spot unconnected with the trail—then it dropped squarely in front of my face, and buzzed out of sight before I could get it.

Something about this whole business struck me as monstrously sinister and abnormal—more so than I could explain to myself. When I looked at the ink-trail on the ceiling from different angles, it seemed more and more familiar to me, and it dawned on me suddenly that it formed an absolutely perfect question-mark. What device could be more malignly appropriate? It is a wonder that I did not faint. So far the hotel attendants have not noticed it. Have not seen the fly this afternoon and evening, but am keeping my inkwell securely closed. I think my extermination of Moore must be preying on me, and giving me morbid hallucinations. Perhaps there is no fly at all.

Jan. 18—Into what strange hell of living nightmare am I plunged? What occurred today is something which could not normally happen—*and yet an hotel attendant has seen the marks on the ceiling and concedes their reality.* About eleven o'clock this morning, as I was writing on a manuscript, something darted down to the inkwell for a second and flashed aloft again before I could see what it was. Looking up, I saw that hellish fly on the ceiling as it had been before—crawling along and tracing another trail of curves and turns. There was nothing I could do, but I folded a newspaper in readiness to get the creature if it should fly near enough. When it had made several turns on the ceiling it flew into a dark corner and disappeared, and as I looked upward at the doubly defaced plastering I saw that the new ink-trail was that of a huge and unmistakable figure 5!

For a time I was almost unconscious from a wave of nameless menace for which I could not fully account. Then I summoned up my resolution and took an active step. Going out to a chemist's shop I purchased some gum and other things necessary for preparing a sticky trap—also a duplicate inkwell. Returning to my room, I filled the new inkwell with the sticky mixture and set it where the old one had been, leaving it open. Then I tried to concentrate my mind on some reading. About three o'clock I heard the accursed insect again, and saw it circling around the new inkwell. It descended to the sticky surface but did not touch it, and afterward sailed straight toward me—retreating before I could hit it. Then it went to the bookshelf and circled around Moore's treatise. There is something profound and diabolic about the way the intruder hovers near that book.

The worst part was the last. Leaving Moore's book, the insect flew over to the open window and began beating itself rhythmically against the wire screen. There would be a series of beats and then a series of equal length and another pause, and so on. Something about this performance held me motionless for a couple of moments, but after that I went over to the window and tried to kill the noxious thing. As usual, no use. It merely flew across the room to a lamp and began beating the same tattoo on the stiff cardboard shade. I felt a vague desperation, and proceeded to shut all the doors as well as the window whose screen had the imperceptible hole. It seemed very necessary to kill this persistent being, whose hounding was rapidly unseating my mind. Then, unconsciously counting, I began to notice that each of its series of beatings contained just *five* strokes.

Five—the same number that the thing had traced in ink on the ceiling in the morning! Could there be any conceivable connexion? The notion was maniacal, for that would argue a human intellect and a knowledge of written figures in the hybrid fly. A human intellect—did not that take one back to the most primitive legends of the Uganda blacks? And yet there was that infernal cleverness in eluding me as contrasted with the normal stupidity of the breed. As I laid aside my folded paper and sat down in growing horror, the insect buzzed aloft and disappeared through a hole in the ceiling where the radiator pipe went to the room above.

The departure did not soothe me, for my mind had started on a train of wild and terrible reflections. If this fly had a human intelligence, where did that intelligence come from? Was there any truth in the native notion that these creatures acquire the personality of their victims after the latter's death? If so, whose personality did this fly bear? I had reasoned out that it must be one of those which escaped from Moore at the time he was bitten. *Was this the envoy of death which had bitten Moore? If so, what did it want with me?* What did it want with me anyway? In a cold perspiration I remembered the actions of the fly that had bitten Batta when Batta died. Had its own personality been displaced by that of its dead victim? Then there was that sensational news account of the fly that waked Dyson when Moore died. As for that fly that was hounding me—could it be that a vindictive human personality drove it on? How it hovered around Moore's book!—I refused to think any farther than that. All at once I began to feel sure that the creature was indeed infected, and in the most virulent way. With a malign deliberation so evident in every act, it must surely have charged itself on purpose with the deadliest bacilli in all Africa. My mind, thoroughly shaken, was now taking the thing's human qualities for granted.

I now telephoned the clerk and asked for a man to stop up the radiator pipehole and other possible chinks in my room. I spoke of being tormented by flies, and he seemed to be quite sympathetic. When the man came, I shewed him the ink-marks on the ceiling, which he recognised without difficulty. So they are real! The resemblance to a question-mark and a figure 5 puzzled and fascinated him. In the end he stopped up all the holes he could find, and mended the window-screen, so that I can now keep both windows open. He evidently thought me a bit eccentric, especially since no insects were in sight while he was here. But I am past minding that.

So far the fly has not appeared this evening. God knows what it is, what it wants, or what will become of me!

Jan. 19—I am utterly engulfed in horror. *The thing has touched me.* Something monstrous and daemoniac is at work around me, and I am a helpless victim. In the morning, when I returned from breakfast, that winged fiend from hell brushed into the room over my head, and began beating itself against the window-screen as it did yesterday. This time, though, each series of beats contained only *four* strokes. I rushed to the window and tried to catch it, but it escaped as usual and flew over to Moore's treatise, where it buzzed around mockingly. Its vocal equipment is limited, but I noticed that its spells of buzzing came in groups of four.

By this time I was certainly mad, for I called out to it, "*Moore, Moore, for God's sake, what do you want?*" When I did so, the creature suddenly ceased its circling, flew toward me, and made a low, graceful dip in the air, somehow suggestive of a bow. Then it flew back to the book. At least, I seemed to see it do all this—though I am trusting my senses no longer.

And then the worst thing happened. I had left my door open, hoping the monster would leave if I could not catch it; but about 11:30 I shut the door, concluding it had gone. Then I settled down to read. Just at noon I felt a tickling on the back of my neck, but when I put my hand up nothing was there. In a moment I felt the tickling again—and before I could move, that nameless spawn of hell sailed into view from behind, did another of those mocking, graceful dips in the air, and flew out through the keyhole—which I had never dreamed was large enough to allow its passage.

That the thing had touched me, I could not doubt. It had touched me without injuring me—and then I remembered in a sudden cold fright that Moore had been bitten *on the back of the neck at noon.* No invasion since then—but I have stuffed all the keyholes with paper and shall have a folded paper ready for use whenever I open the door to leave or enter.

Jan. 20—I cannot yet believe fully in the supernatural, yet I fear none the less that I am lost. The business is too much for me. Just before noon today that devil appeared *outside* the window and repeated its beating operations; but this time in series of *three.* When I went to the window it flew off out of sight. I still have resolution enough to take one more defensive step. Removing both window-screens, I coated them with my sticky preparation—the one I used in the inkwell—outside and inside, and set them back in place. If that creature attempts another tattoo, it will be its last!

Rest of the day in peace. Can I weather this experience without becoming a maniac?

Jan. 21—On board train for Bloemfontein.

I am routed. The thing is winning. It has a diabolic intelligence against which all my devices are powerless. It appeared outside the window this morning, *but did not touch the sticky screen.* Instead, it sheered off without lighting and began buzzing around in circles —*two at a time,* followed by a pause in the air. After several of these performances it flew off out of sight over the roofs of the city. My nerves are just about at the breaking-point, for these *suggestions of numbers* are capable of a hideous interpretation. Monday the thing dwelt on the figure *five;* Tuesday it was *four;* Wednesday it was *three;* and now today it is *two. Five, four, three, two*—what can this be save some monstrous and unthinkable *counting-off of days?* For what purpose, only the evil powers of the universe can know. I spent all the afternoon packing and arranging about my trunks, and now I have taken the night express for Bloemfontein. Flight may be useless, but what else can one do?

Jan. 22—Settled at the Orange Hotel, Bloemfontein—a comfortable and excellent place—but the horror followed me. I had shut all the doors and windows, stopped all the keyholes, looked for any possible chinks, and pulled down all the shades—but just before noon I heard a dull tap on one of the window-screens. I waited—and after a long pause another tap came. A second pause, and still another single tap. Raising the shade, I saw that accursed fly, as I had expected. It described one large, slow circle in the air, and then flew out of sight. I was left as weak as a rag, and had to rest on the couch. *One!* This was clearly the burden of the monster's present message. *One* tap, *one* circle. Did this mean *one* more day for me before some unthinkable doom? Ought I to flee again, or entrench myself here by sealing up the room?

After an hour's rest I felt able to act, and ordered a large reserve supply of canned and packaged food—also linen and towels—sent in. Tomorrow I shall not under any circumstances open any crevice of door or window. When the food and linen came the black looked at me queerly, but I no longer care how eccentric—or insane —I may appear. I am hounded by powers worse than the ridicule of mankind. Having received my supplies, I went over every square millimeter of the walls, and stopped up every microscopic opening I could find. At last I feel able to get real sleep.

[*Handwriting here becomes irregular, nervous, and very difficult to decipher.*]

Jan. 23—It is just before noon, and I feel that something very terrible is about to happen. Didn't sleep as late as I expected, even though I got almost no sleep on the train the night before. Up early, and have had trouble getting concentrated on anything—reading or writing. That slow, deliberate counting-off of days is too much for me. I don't know which has gone wild—Nature or my head. Until about eleven I did very little except walk up and down the room.

Then I heard a rustle among the food packages brought in yesterday, and that daemoniac fly crawled out before my eyes. I grabbed something flat and made passes at the thing despite my panic fear, but with no more effect than usual. As I advanced, that blue-winged horror retreated as usual to the table where I had piled my books, and lit for a second on Moore's *Diptera of Central and Southern Africa*. Then as I followed, it flew over to the mantel clock and lit on the dial near the figure 12. Before I could think up another move it had begun to crawl around the dial very slowly and deliberately—in the direction of the hands. It passed under the minute hand, curved down and up, passed under the hour hand, and finally came to a stop exactly at the figure 12. As it hovered there it fluttered its wings with a buzzing noise.

Is this a portent of some sort? I am getting as superstitious as the blacks. The hour is now a little after eleven. Is twelve the end? I have just one last resort, brought to my mind through utter desperation. Wish I had thought of it before. Recalling that my medicine case contains both of the substances necessary to generate chlorine gas, I have resolved to fill the room with that lethal vapour—asphyxiating the fly while protecting myself with an ammonia-sealed handkerchief tied over my face. Fortunately I have a good supply of ammonia. This crude mask will probably neutralise the acrid chlorine fumes till the insect is dead—or at least helpless enough to crush. But I must be quick. How can I be sure that the thing will not suddenly dart for me before my preparations are complete? I ought not to be stopping to write in this journal.

Later—Both chemicals—hydrochloric acid and manganese dioxide—on the table all ready to mix. I've tied the handkerchief over my nose and mouth, and have a bottle of ammonia ready to keep it soaked until the chlorine is gone. Have battened down both windows. But I don't like the actions of that hybrid daemon. It stays on the clock, but is very slowly crawling around backward from the 12 mark to meet the gradually advancing minute-hand.

Is this to be my last entry in this journal? It would be useless to try to deny what I suspect. Too often a grain of incredible truth lurks behind the wildest and most fantastic of legends. Is the personality of Henry Moore trying to get at me through this blue-winged devil? Is this the fly that bit him, and that in consequence absorbed his consciousness when he died? If so, and if it bites me, will my own personality displace Moore's and enter that buzzing body when I die of the bite later on? Perhaps, though, I need not die even if it gets me. There is always a chance with tryparsamide. And I regret nothing. Moore had to die, be the outcome what it will.

Slightly later.

The fly has paused on the clock-dial near the 45-minute mark. It is now 11:30. I am saturating the handkerchief over my face with ammonia, and keeping the bottle handy for further applications. This will be the final entry before I mix the acid and manganese and liberate the chlorine. I ought not to be losing time, but it steadies me to get things down on paper. But for this record, I'd have lost all my reason long ago. The fly seems to be getting restless, and the minute-hand is approaching it. Now for the chlorine. . . .

[*End of the journal*]

On Sunday, Jan. 24, 1932, after repeated knocking had failed to gain any response from the eccentric man in Room 303 of the Orange Hotel, a black attendant entered with a pass key and at once fled shrieking downstairs to tell the clerk what he had found. The clerk, after notifying the police, summoned the manager; and the latter accompanied Constable De Witt, Coroner Bogaert, and Dr. Van Keulen to the fatal room.

The occupant lay dead on the floor—his face upward, and bound with a handkerchief which smelled strongly of ammonia. Under this covering the features shewed an expression of stark, utter fear which transmitted itself to the observers. On the back of the neck Dr. Van Keulen found a virulent insect bite—dark red, with a purple ring around it—which suggested a tsetse-fly or something less innocuous. An examination indicated that death must be due to heart-failure induced by sheer fright rather than to the bite—though a subsequent autopsy indicated that the germ of trypanosomiasis had been introduced into the system.

On the table were several objects—a worn leather blank-book containing the journal just described, a pen, writing-pad, and open inkwell, a doctor's medicine case with the initials "T. S." marked in gold, bottles of ammonia and hydrochloric acid, and a tumbler about a quarter full of black manganese dioxide. The ammonia bottle demanded a second look because something besides the fluid seemed to be in it. Looking closer, Coroner Bogaert saw that the alien occupant was a fly.

It seemed to be some sort of hybrid with vague tsetse affiliations, but its wings—shewing faintly blue despite the action of the strong ammonia—were a complete puzzle. Something about it waked a faint memory of newspaper reading in Dr. Van Keulen—a memory which the journal was soon to confirm. Its lower parts seemed to have been stained with ink, so thoroughly that even the ammonia had not bleached them. Possibly it had fallen at one time into the inkwell, though the wings were untouched. But how had it managed to fall into the narrow-necked ammonia bottle? It was as if the creature had deliberately crawled in and committed suicide!

But the strangest thing of all was what Constable De Witt noticed on the smooth white ceiling overhead as his eyes roved about curiously. At his cry the other three followed his gaze—even Dr. Van Keulen, who had for some time been thumbing through the worn leather book with an expression of mixed horror, fascination, and incredulity. The thing on the ceiling was a series of shaky, straggling ink-tracks, such as might have been made by the crawling of some ink-drenched insect. At once everyone thought of the stains on the fly so oddly found in the ammonia bottle.

But these were no ordinary ink-tracks. Even a first glance revealed something hauntingly familiar about them, and closer inspection brought gasps of startled wonder from all four observers. Coroner Bogaert instinctively looked around the room to see if there were any conceivable instrument or arrangement of piled-up furniture which could make it possible for those straggling marks to have been drawn by human agency. Finding nothing of the sort, he resumed his curious and almost awestruck upward glance.

For beyond a doubt these inky smudges formed definite letters of the alphabet—letters coherently arranged in English words. The doctor was the first to make them out clearly, and the others listened breathlessly as he recited the insane-sounding message so incredibly scrawled in a place no human hand could reach:

> "SEE MY JOURNAL—*IT* GOT ME FIRST—I DIED—THEN I SAW I WAS IN *IT*—THE BLACKS ARE RIGHT—STRANGE POWERS IN NATURE—NOW I WILL DROWN WHAT IS LEFT—"

Presently, amidst the puzzled hush that followed, Dr. Van Keulen commenced reading aloud from the worn leather journal.

Hazel Heald

Out of the Aeons

(Ms. found among the effects of the late Richard H. Johnson, Ph.D., curator of the Cabot Museum of Archaeology, Boston, Mass.)

It is not likely that anyone in Boston—or any alert reader elsewhere—will ever forget the strange affair of the Cabot Museum. The newspaper publicity given to that hellish mummy, the antique and terrible rumours vaguely linked with it, the morbid wave of interest and cult activities during 1932, and the frightful fate of the two intruders on December 1st of that year, all combined to form one of those classic mysteries which go down for generations as folklore and become the nuclei of whole cycles of horrific speculation.

Everyone seems to realise, too, that something very vital and unutterably hideous was suppressed in the public accounts of the culminant horrors. Those first disquieting hints as to the *condition* of one of the two bodies were dismissed and ignored too abruptly—nor were the singular *modifications* in the mummy given the following-up which their news value would normally prompt. It also struck people as queer that the mummy was never restored to its case. In these days of expert taxidermy the excuse that its disintegrating condition made exhibition impracticable seemed a peculiarly lame one.

As curator of the museum I am in a position to reveal all the suppressed facts, but this I shall not do during my lifetime. There are things about the world and universe which it is better for the majority not to know, and I have not departed from the opinion in which all of us—museum staff, physicians, reporters, and police—concurred at the period of the horror itself. At the same time it seems proper that a matter of such overwhelming scientific and historic importance should not remain wholly unrecorded—hence this account which I have prepared for the benefit of serious students. I shall place it among various papers to be examined after my death, leaving its fate to the discretion of my executors. Certain threats and unusual events during the past weeks have led me to believe that my life—as well as that of other museum officials—is in some peril through the enmity of several widespread secret cults of Asiatics, Polynesians, and heterogeneous mystical devotees; hence it is possible that the work of the executors may not be long postponed. [Executor's note: Dr. Johnson died suddenly and rather mysteriously of heart-failure on April 22, 1933. Wentworth Moore, taxidermist of the museum, disappeared around the middle of the preceding month. On February 18 of the same year Dr. William Minot, who superintended a dissection connected with the case, was stabbed in the back, dying the following day.]

The real beginning of the horror, I suppose, was in 1879—long before my term as curator—when the museum acquired that ghastly, inexplicable mummy from the Orient Shipping Company. Its very discovery was monstrous and menacing, for it came from a crypt of unknown origin and fabulous antiquity on a bit of land suddenly upheaved from the Pacific's floor.

On May 11, 1878, Capt. Charles Weatherbee of the freighter *Eridanus,* bound from Wellington, New Zealand, to Valparaiso, Chile, had sighted a new island unmarked on any chart and evidently of volcanic origin. It projected quite boldly out of the sea in the form of a truncated cone. A landing-party under Capt. Weatherbee noted evidences of long submersion on the rugged slopes which they climbed, while at the summit there were signs of recent destruction, as by an earthquake. Among the scattered rubble were massive stones of manifestly artificial shaping, and a little examination disclosed the presence of some of that prehistoric Cyclopean masonry found on certain Pacific islands and forming a perpetual archaeological puzzle.

Finally the sailors entered a massive stone crypt—judged to have been part of a much larger edifice, and to have originally lain far underground—in one corner of which the frightful mummy crouched. After a short period of virtual panic, caused partly by certain carvings on the walls, the men were induced to move the mummy to the ship, though it was only with fear and loathing that they touched it. Close to the body, as if once thrust into its clothes, was a cylinder of an unknown metal containing a roll of thin, bluish-white membrane of equally unknown nature, inscribed with peculiar characters in a greyish, indeterminable pigment. In the centre of the vast stone floor was a suggestion of a trap-door, but the party lacked apparatus sufficiently powerful to move it.

The Cabot Museum, then newly established, saw the meagre reports of the discovery and at once took steps to acquire the mummy and the cylinder. Curator Pickman made a personal trip to Valparaiso and outfitted a schooner to search for the crypt where the thing had been found, though meeting with failure in this matter. At the recorded position of the island nothing but the sea's unbroken expanse could be discerned, and the seekers realised that the same seismic forces which had suddenly thrust the island up had carried it down again to the watery darkness where it had brooded for untold aeons. The secret of that immovable trap-door would never be solved. The mummy and the cylinder, however, remained —and the former was placed on exhibition early in November, 1879, in the museum's hall of mummies.

The Cabot Museum of Archaeology, which specialises in such remnants of ancient and unknown civilisations as do not fall within the domain of art, is a small and scarcely famous institution, though one of high standing in scientific circles. It stands in the heart of Boston's exclusive Beacon Hill district—in Mt. Vernon Street, near Joy—housed in a former private mansion with an added wing in the rear, and was a source of pride to its austere neighbours until the recent terrible events brought it an undesirable notoriety.

The hall of mummies on the western side of the original mansion (which was designed by Bulfinch and erected in 1819), on the second floor, is justly esteemed by historians and anthropologists as harbouring the greatest collection of its kind in America. Here may be found typical examples of Egyptian embalming from the earliest Sakkarah specimens to the last Coptic attempts of the eighth century; mummies of other cultures, including the prehistoric Indian specimens recently found in the Aleutian Islands; agonised Pompeian figures moulded in plaster from tragic hollows in the ruin-choking ashes; naturally mummified bodies from mines and other excavations in all parts of the earth—some surprised by their terrible entombment in the grotesque postures caused by their last, tearing death-throes—everything, in short, which any collection of the sort could well be expected to contain. In 1879, of course, it was much less ample than it is now; yet even then it was remarkable. But that shocking thing from the primal Cyclopean crypt on an ephemeral sea-spawned island was always its chief attraction and most impenetrable mystery.

The mummy was that of a medium-sized man of unknown race, and was cast in a peculiar crouching posture. The face, half shielded by claw-like hands, had its under jaw thrust far forward, while the shrivelled features bore an expression of fright so hideous that few spectators could view them unmoved. The eyes were closed, with lids clamped down tightly over eyeballs apparently bulging and prominent. Bits of hair and beard remained, and the colour of the whole was a sort of dull neutral grey. In texture the thing was half leathery and half stony, forming an insoluble enigma to those experts who sought to ascertain how it was embalmed. In places bits of its substance were eaten away by time and decay. Rags of some peculiar fabric, with suggestions of unknown designs, still clung to the object.

Just what made it so infinitely horrible and repulsive one could hardly say. For one thing, there was a subtle, indefinable sense of limitless antiquity and utter alienage which affected one like a view from the brink of a monstrous abyss of unplumbed blackness—but mostly it was the expression of crazed fear on the puckered, prognathous, half-shielded face. Such a symbol of infinite, inhuman, cosmic fright could not help communicating the emotion to the beholder amidst a disquieting cloud of mystery and vain conjecture.

Among the discriminating few who frequented the Cabot Museum this relic of an elder, forgotten world soon acquired an unholy fame, though the institution's seclusion and quiet policy prevented it from becoming a popular sensation of the "Cardiff Giant" sort. In the last century the art of vulgar ballyhoo had not invaded the field of scholarship to the extent it has now succeeded in doing. Naturally, savants of various kinds tried their best to classify the frightful object, though always without success. Theories of a bygone Pacific civilisation, of which the Easter Island images and the megalithic masonry of Ponape and Nan-Matol are conceivable vestiges, were freely circulated among students, and learned journals carried varied and often conflicting speculations on a possible former continent whose peaks survive as the myriad islands of Melanesia and Polynesia. The diversity in dates assigned to the hypothetical vanished culture—or continent—was at once bewildering and amusing; yet some surprisingly relevant allusions were found in certain myths of Tahiti and other islands.

Meanwhile the strange cylinder and its baffling scroll of unknown hieroglyphs, carefully preserved in the museum library, received their due share of attention. No question could exist as to their association with the mummy; hence all realised that in the unravelling of their mystery the mystery of the shrivelled horror would in all probability be unravelled as well. The cylinder, about four inches long by seven-eighths of an inch in diameter, was of a queerly iridescent metal utterly defying chemical analysis and seemingly impervious to all reagents. It was tightly fitted with a cap of the same substance, and bore engraved figurings of an evidently decorative and possibly symbolic nature—conventional designs which seemed to follow a peculiarly alien, paradoxical, and doubtfully describable system of geometry.

Not less mysterious was the scroll it contained—a neat roll of some thin, bluish-white, unanalysable membrane, coiled round a slim rod of metal like that of the cylinder, and unwinding to a length of some two feet. The large, bold hieroglyphs, extending in a narrow line down the centre of the scroll and penned or painted with a grey pigment defying analysis, resembled nothing known to linguists and palaeographers, and could not be deciphered despite the transmission of photographic copies to every living expert in the given field.

It is true that a few scholars, unusually versed in the literature of occultism and magic, found vague resemblances between some of the hieroglyphs and certain primal symbols described or cited in two or three very ancient, obscure, and esoteric texts such as the *Book of Eibon,* reputed to descend from forgotten Hyperborea; the Pnakotic fragments, alleged to be pre-human; and the monstrous and forbidden *Necronomicon* of the mad Arab Abdul Alhazred. None of these resemblances, however, was beyond dispute; and because of the prevailing low estimation of occult studies, no effort was made to circulate copies of the hieroglyphs among mystical specialists. Had such circulation occurred at this early date, the later history of the case might have been very different; indeed, a glance at the hieroglyphs by any reader of von Junzt's horrible

Nameless Cults would have established a linkage of unmistakable significance. At this period, however, the readers of that monstrous blasphemy were exceedingly few; copies having been incredibly scarce in the interval between the suppression of the original Düsseldorf edition (1839) and of the Bridewell translation (1845) and the publication of the expurgated reprint by the Golden Goblin Press in 1909. Practically speaking, no occultist or student of the primal past's esoteric lore had his attention called to the strange scroll until the recent outburst of sensational journalism which precipitated the horrible climax.

II.

Thus matters glided along for a half-century following the installation of the frightful mummy at the museum. The gruesome object had a local celebrity among cultivated Bostonians, but no more than that; while the very existence of the cylinder and scroll—after a decade of futile research—was virtually forgotten. So quiet and conservative was the Cabot Museum that no reporter or feature writer ever thought of invading its uneventful precincts for rabble-tickling material.

The invasion of ballyhoo commenced in the spring of 1931, when a purchase of somewhat spectacular nature—that of the strange objects and inexplicably preserved bodies found in crypts beneath the almost vanished and evilly famous ruins of Château Faussesflammes, in Averoigne, France—brought the museum prominently into the news columns. True to its "hustling" policy, the *Boston Pillar* sent a Sunday feature writer to cover the incident and pad it with an exaggerated general account of the institution itself; and this young man—Stuart Reynolds by name—hit upon the nameless mummy as a potential sensation far surpassing the recent acquisitions nominally forming his chief assignment. A smattering of theosophical lore, and a fondness for the speculations of such writers as Colonel Churchward and Lewis Spence concerning lost continents and primal forgotten civilisations, made Reynolds especially alert toward any aeonian relic like the unknown mummy.

At the museum the reporter made himself a nuisance through constant and not always intelligent questionings and endless demands for the movement of encased objects to permit photographs from unusual angles. In the basement library room he pored endlessly over the strange metal cylinder and its membraneous scroll, photographing them from every angle and securing pictures of every bit of the weird hieroglyphed text. He likewise asked to see all books with any bearing whatever on the subject of primal cultures and sunken continents—sitting for three hours taking notes, and leaving only in order to hasten to Cambridge for a sight (if permission were granted) of the abhorred and forbidden *Necronomicon* at the Widener Library.

On April 5th the article appeared in the Sunday *Pillar,* smothered in photographs of mummy, cylinder, and hieroglyphed scroll, and couched in the peculiarly simpering, infantile style which the *Pillar* affects for the benefit of its vast and mentally immature clientele. Full of inaccuracies, exaggerations, and sensationalism, it was precisely the sort of thing to stir the brainless and fickle interest of the herd—and as a result the once quiet museum began to be swarmed with chattering and vacuously staring throngs such as its stately corridors had never known before.

There were scholarly and intelligent visitors, too, despite the puerility of the article—the pictures had spoken for themselves—and many persons of mature attainments sometimes see the *Pillar* by accident. I recall one very strange character who appeared during November—a dark, turbaned, and bushily bearded man with a laboured, unnatural voice, curiously expressionless face, clumsy hands covered with absurd white mittens, who gave a squalid West End address and called himself "Swami Chandraputra". This fellow was unbelievably erudite in occult lore and seemed profoundly and solemnly moved by the resemblance of the hieroglyphs on the scroll to certain signs and symbols of a forgotten elder world about which he professed vast intuitive knowledge.

By June, the fame of the mummy and scroll had leaked far beyond Boston, and the museum had inquiries and requests for photographs from occultists and students of arcana all over the world. This was not altogether pleasing to our staff, since we are a scientific institution without sympathy for fantastic dreamers; yet we answered all questions with civility. One result of these catechisms was a highly learned article in *The Occult Review* by the famous New Orleans mystic Etienne-Laurent de Marigny, in which was asserted the complete identity of some of the odd geometrical designs on the iridescent cylinder, and of several of the hieroglyphs on the membraneous scroll, with certain ideographs of horrible significance (transcribed from primal monoliths or from the secret rituals of hidden bands of esoteric students and devotees) reproduced in the hellish and suppressed *Black Book* or *Nameless Cults* of von Junzt.

De Marigny recalled the frightful death of von Junzt in 1840, a year after the publication of his terrible volume at Düsseldorf, and commented on his blood-curdling and partly suspected sources of information. Above all, he emphasised the enormous relevance of the tales with which von Junzt linked most of the monstrous ideographs he had reproduced. That these tales, in which a cylinder and scroll were expressly mentioned, held a remarkable suggestion of relationship to the things at the museum, no one could deny; yet they were of such breath-taking extravagance—involving such unbelievable sweeps of time and such fantastic anomalies of a forgotten elder world—that one could much more easily admire than believe them.

Admire them the public certainly did, for copying in the press was universal. Illustrated articles sprang up everywhere, telling or purporting to tell the legends in the *Black Book,* expatiating on the horror of the mummy, comparing the cylinder's designs and the scroll's hieroglyphs with the figures reproduced by von Junzt, and indulging in the wildest, most sensational, and most irrational theories and speculations. Attendance at the museum was trebled, and the widespread nature of the interest was attested by the plethora of mail on the subject—most of it inane and superfluous—received at the museum. Apparently the mummy and its origin formed—for imaginative people—a close rival to the depression as chief topic of 1931 and 1932. For my own part, the principal effect of the furore was to make me read von Junzt's monstrous volume in the Golden Goblin edition—a perusal which left me dizzy and nauseated, yet thankful that I had not seen the utter infamy of the unexpurgated text.

III.

The archaic whispers reflected in the *Black Book,* and linked with designs and symbols so closely akin to what the mysterious scroll and cylinder bore, were indeed of a character to hold one spellbound and not a little awestruck. Leaping an incredible gulf of time—behind all the civilisations, races, and lands we know—they clustered round a vanished nation and a vanished continent of the misty, fabulous dawn-years . . . that to which legend has given the name of Mu, and which old tablets in the primal Naacal tongue speak of as flourishing 200,000 years ago, when Europe harboured only hybrid entities, and lost Hyperborea knew the nameless worship of black amorphous Tsathoggua.

There was mention of a kingdom or province called K'naa in a very ancient land where the first human people had found monstrous ruins left by those who had dwelt there before—vague waves of unknown entities which had filtered down from the stars and lived out their aeons on a forgotten, nascent world. K'naa was a sacred place, since from its midst the bleak basalt cliffs of Mount Yaddith-Gho soared starkly into the sky, topped by a gigantic fortress of Cyclopean stone, infinitely older than mankind and built by the alien spawn of the dark planet Yuggoth, which had colonised the earth before the birth of terrestrial life.

The spawn of Yuggoth had perished aeons before, but had left behind them one monstrous and terrible living thing which could never die—their hellish god or patron daemon Ghatanothoa, which lowered and brooded eternally though unseen in the crypts beneath that fortress on Yaddith-Gho. No human creature had ever climbed Yaddith-Gho or seen that blasphemous fortress except as a distant and geometrically abnormal outline against the sky; yet most agreed that Ghatanothoa was still there, wallowing and burrowing in unsuspected abysses beneath the megalithic walls. There were always those who believed that sacrifices must be made to Ghatanothoa, lest it crawl out of its hidden abysses and waddle horribly through the world of men as it had once waddled through the primal world of the Yuggoth-spawn.

People said that if no victims were offered, Ghatanothoa would ooze up to the light of day and lumber down the basalt cliffs of Yaddith-Gho bringing doom to all it might encounter. For no living thing could behold Ghatanothoa, or even a perfect graven image of Ghatanothoa, however small, without suffering a change more horrible than death itself. Sight of the god, or its image, as all the legends of the Yuggoth-spawn agreed, meant paralysis and petrifaction of a singularly shocking sort, in which the victim was turned to stone and leather on the outside, while the brain within remained perpetually alive—horribly fixed and prisoned through the ages, and maddeningly conscious of the passage of interminable epochs of helpless inaction till chance and time might complete the decay of the petrified shell and leave it exposed to die. Most brains, of course, would go mad long before this aeon-deferred release could arrive. No human eyes, it was said, had ever glimpsed

Ghatanothoa, though the danger was as great now as it had been for the Yuggoth-spawn.

And so there was a cult in K'naa which worshipped Ghatanothoa and each year sacrificed to it twelve young warriors and twelve young maidens. These victims were offered up on flaming altars in the marble temple near the mountain's base, for none dared climb Yaddith-Gho's basalt cliffs or draw near to the Cyclopean pre-human stronghold on its crest. Vast was the power of the priests of Ghatanothoa, since upon them alone depended the preservation of K'naa and of all the land of Mu from the petrifying emergence of Ghatanothoa out of its unknown burrows.

There were in the land an hundred priests of the Dark God, under Imash-Mo the High-Priest, who walked before King Thabon at the Nath-feast, and stood proudly whilst the King knelt at the Dhoric shrine. Each priest had a marble house, a chest of gold, two hundred slaves, and an hundred concubines, besides immunity from civil law and the power of life and death over all in K'naa save the priests of the King. Yet in spite of these defenders there was ever a fear in the land lest Ghatanothoa slither up from the depths and lurch viciously down the mountain to bring horror and petrification to mankind. In the latter years the priests forbade men even to guess or imagine what its frightful aspect might be.

It was in the Year of the Red Moon (estimated as B. C. 173,148 by von Junzt) that a human being first dared to breathe defiance against Ghatanothoa and its nameless menace. This bold heretic was T'yog, High-Priest of Shub-Niggurath and guardian of the copper temple of the Goat with a Thousand Young. T'yog had thought long on the powers of the various gods, and had had strange dreams and revelations touching the life of this and earlier worlds. In the end he felt sure that the gods friendly to man could be arrayed against the hostile gods, and believed that Shub-Niggurath, Nug, and Yeb, as well as Yig the Serpent-god, were ready to take sides with man against the tyranny and presumption of Ghatanothoa.

Inspired by the Mother Goddess, T'yog wrote down a strange formula in the hieratic Naacal of his order, which he believed would keep the possessor immune from the Dark God's petrifying power. With this protection, he reflected, it might be possible for a bold man to climb the dreaded basalt cliffs and—first of all human beings—enter the Cyclopean fortress beneath which Ghatanothoa reputedly brooded. Face to face with the god, and with the power of Shub-Niggurath and her sons on his side, T'yog believed that he might be able to bring it to terms and at last deliver mankind from its brooding menace. With humanity freed through his efforts, there would be no limits to the honours he might claim. All the honours of the priests of Ghatanothoa would perforce be transferred to him; and even kingship or godhood might conceivably be within his reach.

So T'yog wrote his protective formula on a scroll of *pthagon* membrane (according to von Junzt, the inner skin of the extinct yakith-lizard) and enclosed it in a carven cylinder of *lagh* metal—the metal brought by the Elder Ones from Yuggoth, and found in no mine of earth. This charm, carried in his robe, would make him proof against the menace of Ghatanothoa—it would even restore the Dark God's petrified victims if that monstrous entity should ever emerge and begin its devastations. Thus he proposed to go up the shunned and man-untrodden mountain, invade the alien-angled citadel of Cyclopean stone, and confront the shocking devil-entity in its lair. Of what would follow, he could not even guess; but the hope of being mankind's saviour lent strength to his will.

He had, however, reckoned without the jealousy and self-interest of Ghatanothoa's pampered priests. No sooner did they hear of his plan than—fearful for their prestige and privilege in case the Daemon-God should be dethroned—they set up a frantic clamour against the so-called sacrilege, crying that no man might prevail against Ghatanothoa, and that any effort to seek it out would merely provoke it to a hellish onslaught against mankind which no spell or priestcraft could hope to avert. With those cries they hoped to turn the public mind against T'yog; yet such was the people's yearning for freedom from Ghatanothoa, and such their confidence in the skill and zeal of T'yog, that all the protestations came to naught. Even the King, usually a puppet of the priests, refused to forbid T'yog's daring pilgrimage.

It was then that the priests of Ghatanothoa did by stealth what they could not do openly. One night Imash-Mo, the High-Priest, stole to T'yog in his temple chamber and took from his sleeping form the metal cylinder; silently drawing out the potent scroll and putting in its place another scroll of great similitude, yet varied enough to have no power against any god or daemon. When the cylinder was slipped back into the sleeper's cloak Imash-Mo was content, for he knew T'yog was little likely to study that cylinder's contents again. Thinking himself protected by the true scroll, the heretic would march up the forbidden mountain and into the Evil Presence—and Ghatanothoa, unchecked by any magic, would take care of the rest.

It would no longer be needful for Ghatanothoa's priests to preach against the defiance. Let T'yog go his way and meet his doom. And secretly, the priests would always cherish the stolen scroll—the true and potent charm—handing it down from one High-Priest to another for use in any dim future when it might be needful to contravene the Devil-God's will. So the rest of the night Imash-Mo slept in great peace, with the true scroll in a new cylinder fashioned for its harbourage.

It was dawn on the Day of the Sky-Flames (nomenclature undefined by von Junzt) that T'yog, amidst the prayers and chanting of the people and with King Thabon's blessing on his head, started up the dreaded mountain with a staff of tlath-wood in his right hand. Within his robe was the cylinder holding what he thought to be the true charm—for he had indeed failed to find out the imposture. Nor did he see any irony in the prayers which Imash-Mo and the other priests of Ghatanothoa intoned for his safety and success.

All that morning the people stood and watched as T'yog's dwindling form struggled up the shunned basalt slope hitherto alien to men's footsteps, and many stayed watching long after he had vanished where a perilous ledge led round to the mountain's hidden side. That night a few sensitive dreamers thought they heard a faint tremor convulsing the hated peak; though most ridiculed them for the statement. Next day vast crowds watched the mountain and prayed, and wondered how soon T'yog would return. And so the next day, and the next. For weeks they hoped and waited, and then they wept. Nor did anyone ever see T'yog, who would have saved mankind from fears, again.

Thereafter men shuddered at T'yog's presumption, and tried not to think of the punishment his impiety had met. And the priests of Ghatanothoa smiled to those who might resent the god's will or challenge its right to the sacrifices. In later years the ruse of Imash-Mo became known to the people; yet the knowledge availed not to change the general feeling that Ghatanothoa were better left alone. None ever dared to defy it again. And so the ages rolled on, and King succeeded King, and High-Priest succeeded High-Priest, and nations rose and decayed, and lands rose above the sea and returned into the sea. And with many millennia decay fell upon K'naa—till at last on a hideous day of storm and thunder, terrific rumbling, and mountain-high waves, all the land of Mu sank into the sea forever.

Yet down the later aeons thin streams of ancient secrets trickled. In distant lands there met together grey-faced fugitives who had survived the sea-fiend's rage, and strange skies drank the smoke of altars reared to vanished gods and daemons. Though none knew to what bottomless deep the sacred peak and Cyclopean fortress of dreaded Ghatanothoa had sunk, there were still those who mumbled its name and offered to it nameless sacrifices lest it bubble up through leagues of ocean and shamble among men spreading horror and petrifaction.

Around the scattered priests grew the rudiments of a dark and secret cult—secret because the people of the new lands had other gods and devils, and thought only evil of elder and alien ones—and within that cult many hideous things were done, and many strange objects cherished. It was whispered that a certain line of elusive priests still harboured the true charm against Ghatanothoa which Imash-Mo stole from the sleeping T'yog; though none remained who could read or understand the cryptic syllables, or who could even guess in what part of the world the lost K'naa, the dreaded peak of Yaddith-Gho, and the titan fortress of the Devil-God had lain.

Though it flourished chiefly in those Pacific regions around which Mu itself had once stretched, there were rumours of the hidden and detested cult of Ghatanothoa in ill-fated Atlantis, and on the abhorred plateau of Leng. Von Junzt implied its presence in the fabled subterrene kingdom of K'n-yan, and gave clear evidence that it had penetrated Egypt, Chaldaea, Persia, China, the forgotten Semite empires of Africa, and Mexico and Peru in the New World. That it had a strong connexion with the witchcraft movement in Europe, against which the bulls of popes were vainly directed, he more than strongly hinted. The West, however, was never favourable to its growth; and public indignation—aroused by glimpses of hideous rites and nameless sacrifices—wholly stamped out many of its branches. In the end it became a hunted, doubly furtive underground affair—yet never could its nucleus be quite exterminated. It always survived somehow, chiefly in the Far East and on the Pacific Islands, where its teachings became merged into the esoteric lore of the Polynesian *Areoi*.

Von Junzt gave subtle and disquieting hints of actual contact with the cult; so that as I read I shuddered at what was rumoured about his death. He spoke of the growth of certain ideas regarding the appearance of the Devil-God—a creature which no human being (unless it were the too-daring T'yog, who had never returned) had ever seen—and contrasted this habit of speculation with the taboo prevailing in ancient Mu against any attempt to imagine what the horror looked like. There was a peculiar fearfulness about the devotees' awed and fascinated whispers on this subject—whispers heavy with morbid curiosity concerning the precise nature of what T'yog might have confronted in that frightful pre-human edifice on the dreaded and now-sunken mountains before the end (if it was an end) finally came—and I felt oddly disturbed by the German scholar's oblique and insidious references to this topic.

Scarcely less disturbing were von Junzt's conjectures on the whereabouts of the stolen scroll of cantrips against Ghatanothoa, and on the ultimate uses to which this scroll might be put. Despite all my assurance that the whole matter was purely mythical, I could not help shivering at the notion of a latter-day emergence of the monstrous god, and at the picture of an humanity turned suddenly to a race of abnormal statues, each encasing a living brain doomed to inert and helpless consciousness for untold aeons of futurity. The old Düsseldorf savant had a poisonous way of suggesting more than he stated, and I could understand why his damnable book was suppressed in so many countries as blasphemous, dangerous, and unclean.

I writhed with repulsion, yet the thing exerted an unholy fascination; and I could not lay it down till I had finished it. The alleged reproductions of designs and ideographs from Mu were marvellously and startlingly like the markings on the strange cylinder and the characters on the scroll, and the whole account teemed with details having vague, irritating suggestions of resemblance to things connected with the hideous mummy. The cylinder and scroll—the Pacific setting—the persistent notion of old Capt. Weatherbee that the Cyclopean crypt where the mummy was found had once lain under a vast building . . . somehow I was vaguely glad that the volcanic island had sunk before that massive suggestion of a trap-door could be opened.

IV.

What I read in the *Black Book* formed a fiendishly apt preparation for the news items and closer events which began to force themselves upon me in the spring of 1932. I can scarcely recall just when the increasingly frequent reports of police action against the odd and fantastical religious cults in the Orient and elsewhere commenced to impress me; but by May or June I realised that there was, all over the world, a surprising and unwonted burst of activity on the part of bizarre, furtive, and esoteric mystical organisations ordinarily quiescent and seldom heard from.

It is not likely that I would have connected these reports with either the hints of von Junzt or the popular furore over the mummy and cylinder in the museum, but for certain significant syllables and persistent resemblances—sensationally dwelt upon by the press—in the rites and speeches of the various secret celebrants brought to public attention. As it was, I could not help remarking with disquiet the frequent recurrence of a name—in various corrupt forms—which seemed to constitute a focal point of all the cult worship, and which was obviously regarded with a singular mixture of reverence and terror. Some of the forms quoted were G'tanta, Tanotah, Than-Tha, Gatan, and Ktan-Tah—and it did not require the suggestions of my now numerous occultist correspondents to make me see in these variants a hideous and suggestive kinship to the monstrous name rendered by von Junzt as Ghatanothoa.

There were other disquieting features, too. Again and again the reports cited vague, awestruck references to a "true scroll"—something on which tremendous consequences seemed to hinge, and which was mentioned as being in the custody of a certain "Nagob", whoever and whatever he might be. Likewise, there was an insistent repetition of a name which sounded like Tog, Tiok, Yog, Zob, or Yob, and which my more and more excited consciousness involuntarily linked with the name of the hapless heretic T'yog as given in the *Black Book*. This name was usually uttered in connexion with such cryptical phrases as "It is none other than he", "He had looked upon its face", "He knows all, though he can neither see nor feel", "He has brought the memory down through the aeons", "The true scroll will release him", "Nagob has the true scroll", "He can tell where to find it".

Something very queer was undoubtedly in the air, and I did not wonder when my occultist correspondents, as well as the sensational Sunday papers, began to connect the new abnormal stirrings with the legends of Mu on the one hand, and with the frightful mummy's recent exploitation on the other hand. The widespread articles in the first wave of press publicity, with their insistent linkage of the mummy, cylinder, and scroll with the tale in the *Black Book,* and their crazily fantastic speculations about the whole matter, might very well have roused the latent fanaticism in hundreds of those furtive groups of exotic devotees with which our complex world abounds. Nor did the papers cease adding fuel to the flames—for the stories on the cult-stirrings were even wilder than the earlier series of yarns.

As the summer drew on, attendants noticed a curious new element among the throngs of visitors which—after a lull following the first burst of publicity—were again drawn to the museum by the second furore. More and more frequently there were persons of strange and exotic aspect—swarthy Asiatics, long-haired nondescripts, and bearded brown men who seemed unused to European clothes—who would invariably inquire for the hall of mummies and would subsequently be found staring at the hideous Pacific specimen in a veritable ecstasy of fascination. Some quiet, sinister undercurrent in this flood of eccentric foreigners seemed to impress all the guards, and I myself was far from undisturbed. I could not help thinking of the prevailing cult-stirrings among just such exotics as these—and the connexion of those stirrings with myths all too close to the frightful mummy and its cylinder scroll.

At times I was half tempted to withdraw the mummy from exhibition—especially when an attendant told me that he had several times glimpsed strangers making odd obeisances before it, and had overheard sing-song mutterings which sounded like chants or rituals addressed to it at hours when the visiting throngs were somewhat thinned. One of the guards acquired a queer nervous hallucination about the petrified horror in the lone glass case, alleging that he could see from day to day certain vague, subtle, and infinitely slight changes in the frantic flexion of the bony claws, and in the fear-crazed expression of the leathery face. He could not get rid of the loathsome idea that those horrible, bulging eyes were about to pop suddenly open.

It was early in September, when the curious crowds had lessened and the hall of mummies was sometimes vacant, that the attempt to get at the mummy by cutting the glass of its case was made. The culprit, a swarthy Polynesian, was spied in time by a guard, and was overpowered before any damage occurred. Upon investigation the fellow turned out to be an Hawaiian notorious for his activity in certain underground religious cults, and having a considerable police record in connexion with abnormal and inhuman rites and sacrifices. Some of the papers found in his room were highly puzzling and disturbing, including many sheets covered with hieroglyphs closely resembling those on the scroll at the museum and in the *Black Book* of von Junzt; but regarding these things he could not be prevailed upon to speak.

Scarcely a week after this incident, another attempt to get at the mummy—this time by tampering with the lock of his case—resulted in a second arrest. The offender, a Cingalese, had as long and unsavoury a record of loathsome cult activities as the Hawaiian had possessed, and displayed a kindred unwillingness to talk to the police. What made this case doubly and darkly interesting was that a guard had noticed this man several times before, and had heard him addressing to the mummy a peculiar chant containing unmistakable repetitions of the word "T'yog". As a result of this affair I doubled the guards in the hall of mummies, and ordered them never to leave the now notorious specimen out of sight, even for a moment.

As may well be imagined, the press made much of these two incidents, reviewing its talk of primal and fabulous Mu, and claiming boldly that the hideous mummy was none other than the daring heretic T'yog, petrified by something he had seen in the pre-human citadel he had invaded, and preserved intact through 175,000 years of our planet's turbulent history. That the strange devotees represented cults descended from Mu, and that they were worshipping the mummy—or perhaps even seeking to awaken it to life by spells and incantations—was emphasised and reiterated in the most sensational fashion.

Writers exploited the insistence of the old legends that the *brain* of Ghatanothoa's petrified victims remained conscious and unaffected—a point which served as a basis for the wildest and most improbable speculations. The mention of a "true scroll" also received due attention—it being the prevailing popular theory that T'yog's stolen charm against Ghatanothoa was somewhere in existence, and that cult-members were trying to bring it into contact with T'yog himself for some purpose of their own. One result of this exploitation was that a third wave of gaping visitors began flooding the museum and staring at the hellish mummy which served as a nucleus for the whole strange and disturbing affair.

It was among this wave of spectators—many of whom made repeated visits—that talk of the mummy's vaguely changing aspect first began to be widespread. I suppose—despite the disturbing notion of the nervous guard some months before—that the museum's personnel was too well used to the constant sight of odd shapes to pay close attention to details; in any case, it was the excited whispers of visitors which at length aroused the guards to the subtle mutation which was apparently in progress. Almost simultaneously the press got hold of it—with blatant results which can well be imagined.

Naturally, I gave the matter my most careful observation, and by the middle of October decided that a definite disintegration of the mummy was under way. Through some chemical or physical influence in the air, the half-stony, half-leathery fibres seemed to be gradually relaxing, causing distinct variations in the angles of the limbs and in certain details of the fear-twisted facial expression. After a half-century of perfect preservation this was a highly disconcerting development, and I had the museum's taxidermist, Dr. Moore, go carefully over the gruesome object several times. He reported a general relaxation and softening, and gave the thing two or three astringent sprayings, but did not dare to attempt anything drastic lest there be a sudden crumbling and accelerated decay.

The effect of all this upon the gaping crowds was curious. Heretofore each new sensation sprung by the press had brought fresh waves of staring and whispering visitors, but now—though the papers blathered endlessly about the mummy's changes—the public seemed to have acquired a definite sense of fear which outranked even its morbid curiosity. People seemed to feel that a sinister aura hovered over the museum, and from a high peak the attendance fell to a level distinctly below normal. This lessened attendance gave added prominence to the stream of freakish foreigners who continued to infest the place, and whose numbers seemed in no way diminished.

On November 18th a Peruvian of Indian blood suffered a strange hysterical or epileptic seizure in front of the mummy, afterward shrieking from his hospital cot, "It tried to open its eyes!—T'yog tried to open his eyes and stare at me!" I was by this time on the point of removing the object from exhibition, but permitted myself to be overruled at a meeting of our very conservative directors. However, I could see that the museum was beginning to acquire an unholy reputation in its austere and quiet neighbourhood. After this incident I gave instructions that no one be allowed to pause before the monstrous Pacific relic for more than a few minutes at a time.

It was on November 24th, after the museum's five o'clock closing, that one of the guards noticed a minute opening of the mummy's eyes. The phenomenon was very slight—nothing but a thin crescent of cornea being visible in either eye—but it was none the less of the highest interest. Dr. Moore, having been summoned hastily, was about to study the exposed bits of eyeball with a magnifier when his handling of the mummy caused the leathery lids to fall tightly shut again. All gentle efforts to open them failed, and the taxidermist did not dare to apply drastic measures. When he notified me of all this by telephone I felt a sense of mounting dread hard to reconcile with the apparently simple event concerned. For a moment I could share the popular impression that some evil, amorphous blight from unplumbed deeps of time and space hung murkily and menacingly over the museum.

Two nights later a sullen Filipino was trying to secrete himself in the museum at closing time. Arrested and taken to the station, he refused even to give his name, and was detained as a suspicious person. Meanwhile the strict surveillance of the mummy seemed to discourage the odd hordes of foreigners from haunting it. At least, the number of exotic visitors distinctly fell off after the enforcement of the "move along" order.

It was during the early morning hours of Thursday, December 1st, that a terrible climax developed. At about one o'clock horrible screams of mortal fright and agony were heard issuing from the museum, and a series of frantic telephone calls from neighbours brought to the scene quickly and simultaneously a squad of police and several museum officials, including myself. Some of the policemen surrounded the building while others, with the officials, cautiously entered. In the main corridor we found the night watchman strangled to death—a bit of East Indian hemp still knotted around his neck—and realised that despite all precautions some darkly evil intruder or intruders had gained access to the place. Now, however, a tomb-like silence enfolded everything and we almost feared to advance upstairs to the fateful wing where we knew the core of the trouble must lurk. We felt a bit more steadied after flooding the building with light from the central switches in the corridor, and finally crept reluctantly up the curving staircase and through a lofty archway to the hall of mummies.

V.

It is from this point onward that reports of the hideous case have been censored—for we have all agreed that no good can be accomplished by a public knowledge of those terrestrial conditions implied by the further developments. I have said that we flooded the whole building with light before our ascent. Now beneath the beams that beat down on the glistening cases and their gruesome contents, we saw outspread a mute horror whose baffling details testified to happenings utterly beyond our comprehension. There were two intruders—who we afterward agreed must have hidden in the building before closing time—but they would never be executed for the watchman's murder. They had already paid the penalty.

One was a Burmese and the other a Fiji-Islander—both known to the police for their share in frightful and repulsive cult activities. They were dead, and the more we examined them the more utterly monstrous and unnamable we felt their manner of death to be. On both faces was a more wholly frantic and inhuman look of fright than even the oldest policeman had ever seen before; yet in the state of the two bodies there were vast and significant differences.

The Burmese lay collapsed close to the nameless mummy's case, from which a square of glass had been neatly cut. In his right hand was a scroll of bluish membrane which I at once saw was covered with greyish hieroglyphs—almost a duplicate of the scroll in the strange cylinder in the library downstairs, though later study brought out subtle differences. There was no mark of violence on the body, and in view of the desperate, agonised expression on the twisted face we could only conclude that the man died of sheer fright.

It was the closely adjacent Fijian, though, that gave us the profoundest shock. One of the policemen was the first to feel of him, and the cry of fright he emitted added another shudder to that neighbourhood's night of terror. We ought to have known from the lethal greyness of the once-black, fear-twisted face, and of the bony hands—one of which still clutched an electric torch—that something was hideously wrong; yet every one of us was unprepared for what that officer's hesitant touch disclosed. Even now I can think of it only with a paroxysm of dread and repulsion. To be brief—the hapless invader, who less than an hour before had been a sturdy living Melanesian bent on unknown evils, was now a rigid, ash-grey figure of stony, leathery petrification, in every respect identical with the crouching, aeon-old blasphemy in the violated glass case.

Yet that was not the worst. Crowning all other horrors, and indeed seizing our shocked attention before we turned to the bodies on the floor, was the state of the frightful mummy. No longer could its changes be called vague and subtle, for it had now made radical shifts of posture. It had sagged and slumped with a curious loss of rigidity; its bony claws had sunk until they no longer even partly covered its leathery, fear-crazed face; and—God help us!—*its hellish bulging eyes had popped wide open, and seemed to be staring directly at the two intruders who had died of fright or worse.*

That ghastly, dead-fish stare was hideously mesmerising, and it haunted us all the time we were examining the bodies of the invaders. Its effect on our nerves was damnably queer, for we somehow felt a curious rigidity creeping over us and hampering our simplest motions—a rigidity which later vanished very oddly when we passed the hieroglyphed scroll around for inspection. Every now and then I felt my gaze drawn irresistibly toward those horrible bulging eyes in the case, and when I returned to study them after viewing the bodies I thought I detected something very singular about the glassy surface of the dark and marvellously well-preserved pupils. The more I looked, the more fascinated I became; and at last I went down to the office—despite that strange stiffness in my limbs—and brought up a strong multiple magnifying glass. With this I commenced a very close and careful survey of the fishy pupils, while the others crowded expectantly around.

I had always been rather sceptical of the theory that scenes and objects become photographed on the retina of the eye in cases of death or coma; yet no sooner did I look through the lens than I realised the presence of some sort of image other than the room's reflection in the glassy, bulging optics of this nameless spawn of the aeons. Certainly, there was a dimly outlined scene on the age-old retinal surface, and I could not doubt that it formed the last thing on which those eyes had looked in life—countless millennia ago. It seemed to be steadily fading, and I fumbled with the magnifier in order to shift another lens into place. Yet it must have been accurate and clear-cut; even if infinitesimally small, when—in response to some evil spell or act connected with their visit—it had confronted those intruders who were frightened to death. With the extra lens I could make out many details formerly invisible, and the awed group around me hung on the flood of words with which I tried to tell what I saw.

For here, in the year 1932, a man in the city of Boston was looking on something which belonged to an unknown and utterly alien world—a world that vanished from existence and normal memory aeons ago. There was a vast room—a chamber of Cyclopean masonry—and I seemed to be viewing it from one of its corners. On the walls were carvings so hideous that even in this imperfect image their stark blasphemousness and bestiality sickened me. I could not believe that the carvers of these things were human, or that they had ever seen human beings when they shaped the frightful outlines which leered at the beholder. In the centre of the chamber was a colossal trap-door of stone, pushed upward to permit the emergence of some object from below. The object should have been clearly visible—indeed, must have been when the eyes first opened before the fear-stricken intruders—though under my lenses it was merely a monstrous blur.

As it happened, I was studying the right eye only when I brought the extra magnification into play. A moment later I wished fervently that my search had ended there. As it was, however, the zeal of discovery and revelation was upon me, and I shifted my powerful lenses to the mummy's left eye in the hope of finding the image less faded on that retina. My hands, trembling with excitement and unnaturally stiff from some obscure influence, were slow in bringing the magnifier into focus, but a moment later I realised that the image was less faded than in the other eye. I saw in a morbid flash of half-distinctness the insufferable thing which was welling up through the prodigious trap-door in that Cyclopean, immemorially archaic crypt of a lost world—and fell fainting with an inarticulate shriek of which I am not even ashamed.

By the time I revived there was no distinct image of anything in either eye of the monstrous mummy. Sergeant Keefe of the police looked with my glass, for I could not bring myself to face that abnormal entity again. And I thanked all the powers of the cosmos that I had not looked earlier than I did. It took all my resolution, and a great deal of solicitation, to make me relate what I had glimpsed in the hideous moment of revelation. Indeed, I could not speak till we had all adjourned to the office below, out of sight of that daemoniac thing which could not be. For I had begun to harbour the most terrible and fantastic notions about the mummy and its glassy, bulging eyes—that it had a kind of hellish consciousness, seeing all that occurred before it and trying vainly to communicate some frightful message from the gulfs of time. That meant madness —but at last I thought I might be better off if I told what I had half seen.

After all, it was not a long thing to tell. Oozing and surging up out of that yawning trap-door in the Cyclopean crypt I had glimpsed such an unbelievable behemothic monstrosity that I could not doubt the power of its original to kill with its mere sight. Even now I cannot begin to suggest it with any words at my command. I might call it gigantic—tentacled—proboscidian—octopus-eyed—semi-amorphous—plastic—partly squamous and partly rugose—ugh! But nothing I could say could even adumbrate the loathsome, unholy, non-human, extra-galactic horror and hatefulness and unutterable evil of that forbidden spawn of black chaos and illimitable night. As I write these words the associated mental image causes me to lean back faint and nauseated. As I told of the sight to the men around me in the office, I had to fight to preserve the consciousness I had regained.

Nor were my hearers much less moved. Not a man spoke above a whisper for a full quarter-hour, and there were awed, half-furtive references to the frightful lore in the *Black Book,* to the recent newspaper tales of cult-stirrings, and to the sinister events in the museum. Ghatanothoa . . . Even its smallest perfect image could petrify—T'yog—the false scroll—he never came back—the true scroll which could fully or partly undo the petrification—did it survive?—the hellish cults—the phrases overheard—"It is none other than he"—"He had looked upon its face"—"He knows all, though he can neither see nor feel"—"He had brought the memory down through the aeons"—"The true scroll will release him"—"Nagob has the true scroll"—"He can tell where to find it." Only the healing greyness of the dawn brought us back to sanity; a sanity which made of that glimpse of mine a closed topic—something not to be explained or thought of again.

We gave out only partial reports to the press, and later on coöperated with the papers in making other suppressions. For example, when the autopsy shewed the brain and several other internal organs of the petrified Fijian to be fresh and unpetrified, though hermetically sealed by the petrification of the exterior flesh—an anomaly about which physicians are still guardedly and bewilderedly debating—we did not wish a furore to be started. We knew too well what the yellow journals, remembering what was said of the intact-brained and still-conscious state of Ghatanothoa's stony-leathery victims, would make of this detail.

As matters stood, they pointed out that the man who had held the hieroglyphed scroll—and who had evidently thrust it at the mummy through the opening in the case—was not petrified, while the man who had *not* held it was. When they demanded that we make certain experiments—applying the scroll both to the stony-leathery body of the Fijian and to the mummy itself—we indignantly refused to abet such superstitious notions. Of course, the mummy was withdrawn from public view and transferred to the museum laboratory awaiting a really scientific examination before some suitable medical authority. Remembering past events, we kept it under a strict guard; but even so, an attempt was made to enter the museum at 2:25 a.m. on December 5th. Prompt working of the burglar alarm frustrated the design, though unfortunately the criminal or criminals escaped.

That no hint of anything further ever reached the public, I am profoundly thankful. I wish devoutly that there were nothing more to tell. There will, of course, be leaks, and if anything happens to me I do not know what my executors will do with this manuscript; but at least the case will not be painfully fresh in the multitude's memory when the revelation comes. Besides, no one will believe the facts when they are finally told. That is the curious thing about the multitude. When their yellow press makes hints, they are ready to swallow anything; but when a stupendous and abnormal revelation is actually made, they laugh it aside as a lie. For the sake of general sanity it is probably better so.

I have said that a scientific examination of the frightful mummy was planned. This took place on December 8th, exactly a week after the hideous culmination of events, and was conducted by the eminent Dr. William Minot, in conjunction with Wentworth Moore, Sc.D., taxidermist of the museum. Dr. Minot had witnessed the autopsy of the oddly petrified Fijian the week before. There were also present Messrs. Lawrence Cabot and Dudley Saltonstall of the museum's trustees, Drs. Mason, Wells, and Carver of the museum staff, two representatives of the press, and myself. During the week the condition of the hideous specimen had not visibly changed, though some relaxation of its fibres caused the position of the glassy, open eyes to shift slightly from time to time. All of the staff dreaded to look at the thing—for its suggestion of quiet, conscious watching had become intolerable—and it was only with an effort that I could bring myself to attend the examination.

Dr. Minot arrived shortly after 1:00 p.m., and within a few minutes began his survey of the mummy. Considerable disintegration took place under his hands, and in view of this—and of what we told him concerning the gradual relaxation of the specimen since the first of October—he decided that a thorough dissection ought to be made before the substance was further impaired. The proper instruments being present in the laboratory equipment, he began at once; exclaiming aloud at the odd, fibrous nature of the grey, mummified substance.

But his exclamation was still louder when he made the first deep incision, for out of that cut there slowly trickled a thick crimson stream whose nature—despite the infinite ages dividing this hellish mummy's lifetime from the present—was utterly unmistakable. A few more deft strokes revealed various organs in astonishing degrees of non-petrified preservation—all, indeed, being intact except where injuries to the petrified exterior had brought about malformation or destruction. The resemblance of this condition to that found in the fright-killed Fiji-Islander was so strong that the eminent physician gasped in bewilderment. The perfection of those ghastly bulging eyes was uncanny, and their exact state with respect to petrification was very difficult to determine.

At 3:30 p.m. the brain-case was opened—and ten minutes later our stunned group took an oath of secrecy which only such guarded documents as this manuscript will ever modify. Even the two reporters were glad to confirm the silence. *For the opening had revealed a pulsing, living brain.*

Hazel Heald

The Horror in the Burying-Ground

When the state highway to Rutland is closed, travellers are forced to take the Stillwater road past Swamp Hollow. The scenery is superb in places, yet somehow the route has been unpopular for years. There is something depressing about it, especially near Stillwater itself. Motorists feel subtly uncomfortable about the tightly shuttered farmhouse on the knoll just north of the village, and about the white-bearded half-wit who haunts the old burying-ground on the south, apparently talking to the occupants of some of the graves.

Not much is left of Stillwater, now. The soil is played out, and most of the people have drifted to the towns across the distant river or to the city beyond the distant hills. The steeple of the old white church has fallen down, and half of the twenty-odd straggling houses are empty and in various stages of decay. Normal life is found only around Peck's general store and filling-station, and it is here that the curious stop now and then to ask about the shuttered house and the idiot who mutters to the dead.

Most of the questioners come away with a touch of distaste and disquiet. They find the shabby loungers oddly unpleasant and full of unnamed hints in speaking of the long-past events brought up. There is a menacing, portentous quality in the tones which they use to describe very ordinary events—a seemingly unjustified tendency to assume a furtive, suggestive, confidential air, and to fall into awesome whispers at certain points—which insidiously disturbs the listener. Old Yankees often talk like that; but in this case the melancholy aspect of the half-mouldering village, and the dismal nature of the story unfolded, give these gloomy, secretive mannerisms an added significance. One feels profoundly the quintessential horror that lurks behind the isolated Puritan and his strange repressions—feels it, and longs to escape precipitately into clearer air.

The loungers whisper impressively that the shuttered house is that of old Miss Sprague—Sophie Sprague, whose brother Tom was buried on the seventeenth of June, back in '86. Sophie was never the same after that funeral—that and the other thing which happened the same day—and in the end she took to staying in all the time. Won't even be seen now, but leaves notes under the back-door mat and has her things brought from the store by Ned Peck's boy. Afraid of something—the old Swamp Hollow burying-ground most of all. Never could be dragged near there since her brother—and the other one—were laid away. Not much wonder, though, seeing the way crazy Johnny Dow rants. He hangs around the burying-ground all day and sometimes at night, and claims he talks with Tom—and the other. Then he marches by Sophie's house and shouts things at her—that's why she began to keep the shutters closed. He says things are coming from somewhere to get her sometime. Ought to be stopped, but one can't be too hard on poor Johnny. Besides, Steve Barbour always had his opinions.

Johnny does his talking to two of the graves. One of them is Tom Sprague's. The other, at the opposite end of the graveyard, is that of Henry Thorndike, who was buried on the same day. Henry was the village undertaker—the only one in miles—and never liked around Stillwater. A city fellow from Rutland—been to college and full of book learning. Read queer things nobody else ever heard of, and mixed chemicals for no good purpose. Always trying to invent something new—some new-fangled embalming-fluid or some foolish kind of medicine. Some folks said he had tried to be a doctor but failed in his studies and took to the next best profession. Of course, there wasn't much undertaking to do in a place like Stillwater, but Henry farmed on the side.

Mean, morbid disposition—and a secret drinker if you could judge by the empty bottles in his rubbish heap. No wonder Tom Sprague hated him and blackballed him from the Masonic lodge, and warned him off when he tried to make up to Sophie. The way he experimented on animals was against Nature and Scripture. Who could forget the state that collie dog was found in, or what happened to old Mrs. Akeley's cat? Then there was the matter of Deacon Leavitt's calf, when Tom had led a band of the village boys to demand an accounting. The curious thing was that the calf came alive after all in the end, though Tom had found it as stiff as a poker. Some said the joke was on Tom, but Thorndike probably thought otherwise, since he had gone down under his enemy's fist before the mistake was discovered.

Tom, of course, was half drunk at the time. He was a vicious brute at best, and kept his poor sister half cowed with threats. That's probably why she is such a fear-racked creature still. There were only the two of them, and Tom would never let her leave because that meant splitting the property. Most of the fellows were too afraid of him to shine up to Sophie—he stood six feet one in his stockings—but Henry Thorndike was a sly cuss who had ways of doing things behind folk's backs. He wasn't much to look at, but Sophie never discouraged him any. Mean and ugly as he was, she'd have been glad if anybody could have freed her from her brother. She may not have stopped to wonder how she could get clear of him after he got her clear of Tom.

Well, that was the way things stood in June of '86. Up to this point, the whispers of the loungers at Peck's store are not so unbearably portentous; but as they continue, the element of secretiveness and malign tension grows. Tom Sprague, it appears, used to go to Rutland on periodic sprees, his absences being Henry Thorndike's great opportunities. He was always in bad shape when he got back, and old Dr. Pratt, deaf and half blind though he was, used to warn him about his heart, and about the danger of delirium tremens. Folks could always tell by the shouting and cursing when he was home again.

It was on the ninth of June—on a Wednesday, the day after young Joshua Goodenough finished building his new-fangled silo—that Tom started out on his last and longest spree. He came back the next Tuesday morning and folks at the store saw him lashing his bay stallion the way he did when whiskey had a hold of him. Then there came shouts and shrieks and oaths from the Sprague house, and the first thing anybody knew Sophie was running over to old Dr. Pratt's at top speed.

The doctor found Thorndike at Sprague's when he got there, and

Tom was on the bed in his room, with eyes staring and foam around his mouth. Old Pratt fumbled around and gave the usual tests, then shook his head solemnly and told Sophie she had suffered a great bereavement—that her nearest and dearest had passed through the pearly gates to a better land, just as everybody knew he would if he didn't let up on his drinking.

Sophie kind of sniffled, the loungers whisper, but didn't seem to take on much. Thorndike didn't do anything but smile—perhaps at the ironic fact that he, always an enemy, was now the only person who could be of any use to Thomas Sprague. He shouted something in old Dr. Pratt's half-good ear about the need of having the funeral early on account of Tom's condition. Drunks like that were always doubtful subjects, and any extra delay—with merely rural facilities—would entail consequences, visual and otherwise, hardly acceptable to the deceased's loving mourners. The doctor had muttered that Tom's alcoholic career ought to have embalmed him pretty well in advance, but Thorndike assured him to the contrary, at the same time boasting of his own skill, and of the superior methods he had devised through his experiments.

It is here that the whispers of the loungers grow acutely disturbing. Up to this point the story is usually told by Ezra Davenport, or Luther Fry, if Ezra is laid up with chilblains, as he is apt to be in winter; but from there on old Calvin Wheeler takes up the thread, and his voice has a damnably insidious way of suggesting hidden horror. If Johnny Dow happens to be passing by there is always a pause, for Stillwater does not like to have Johnny talk too much with strangers.

Calvin edges close to the traveller and sometimes seizes a coat-lapel with his gnarled, mottled hand while he half shuts his watery blue eyes.

"Well, sir," he whispers, "Henry he went home an' got his undertaker's fixin's—crazy Johnny Dow lugged most of 'em, for he was always doin' chores for Henry—an' says as Doc Pratt an' crazy Johnny should help lay out the body. Doc always did say as how he thought Henry talked too much—a-boastin' what a fine workman he was, an' how lucky it was that Stillwater had a reg'lar undertaker instead of buryin' folks jest as they was, like they do over to Whitby.

"'Suppose,' says he, 'some fellow was to be took with some of them paralysin' cramps like you read about. How'd a body like it when they lowered him down and begun shovelin' the dirt back?

How'd he like it when he was chokin' down there under the new headstone, scratchin' an' tearin' if he chanced to get back the power, but all the time knowin' it wasn't no use? No, sir, I tell you it's a blessin' Stillwater's got a smart doctor as knows when a man's dead and when he ain't, and a trained undertaker who can fix a corpse so he'll stay put without no trouble.'

"That was the way Henry went on talkin', most like he was talkin' to poor Tom's remains; and old Doc Pratt he didn't like what he was able to catch of it, even though Henry did call him a smart doctor. Crazy Johnny kept watchin' of the corpse, and it didn't make it none too pleasant the way he'd slobber about things like, 'He ain't cold, Doc,' or 'I see his eyelids move,' or 'There's a hole in his arm jest like the ones I git when Henry gives me a syringe full of what makes me feel good.' Thorndike shut him up on that, though we all knowed he'd been givin' poor Johnny drugs. It's a wonder the poor fellow ever got clear of the habit.

"But the worst thing, accordin' to the doctor, was the way the body jerked up when Henry begun to shoot it full of embalmin'-fluid. He'd been boastin' about what a fine new formula he'd got practicin' on cats and dogs, when all of a sudden Tom's corpse began to double up like it was alive and fixin' to wrassle. Land of Goshen, but Doc says he was scared stiff, though he knowed the way corpses act when the muscles begin to stiffen. Well, sir, the long and short of it is, that the corpse sat up an' grabbed a holt of Thorndike's syringe so that it got stuck in Henry hisself, an' give him as neat a dose of his own embalmin'-fluid as you'd wish to see. That got Henry pretty scared, though he yanked the point out and managed to get the body down again and shot full of the fluid. He kept measurin' more of the stuff out as though he wanted to be sure there was enough, and kept reassurin' himself as not much had got into him, but crazy Johnny begun singin' out, 'That's what you give Lige Hopkins's dog when it got all dead an' stiff an' then waked up agin. Now you're a-going to get dead an' stiff like Tom Sprague be! Remember it don't set to work till after a long spell if you don't get much.'

"Sophie, she was downstairs with some of the neighbours—my wife Matildy, she that's dead an' gone this thirty year, was one of them. They were all tryin' to find out whether Thorndike was over when Tom came home, and whether findin' him there was what set poor Tom off. I may as well say as some folks thought it mighty funny that Sophie didn't carry on more, nor mind the way Thorndike had smiled. Not as anybody was hintin' that Henry helped Tom off with some of his queer cooked-up fluids and syringes, or that Sophie would keep still if she thought so—but you know how folks will guess behind a body's back. We all knowed the nigh crazy way Thorndike had hated Tom—not without reason, at that—and Emily Barbour says to my Matildy as how Henry was lucky to have ol' Doc Pratt right on the spot with a death certificate as didn't leave no doubt for nobody."

When old Calvin gets to this point he usually begins to mumble indistinguishably in his straggling, dirty white beard. Most listeners try to edge away from him, and he seldom appears to heed the gesture. It is generally Fred Peck, who was a very small boy at the time of the events, who continues the tale.

Thomas Sprague's funeral was held on Thursday, June 17th, only two days after his death. Such haste was thought almost indecent in remote and inaccessible Stillwater, where long distances had to be covered by those who came, but Thorndike had insisted that the peculiar condition of the deceased demanded it. The undertaker had seemed rather nervous since preparing the body, and could be seen frequently feeling his pulse. Old Dr. Pratt thought he must be worrying about the accidental dose of embalming-fluid. Naturally, the story of the "laying out" had spread, so that a double zest animated the mourners who assembled to glut their curiosity and morbid interest.

Thorndike, though he was obviously upset, seemed intent on doing his professional duty in magnificent style. Sophie and others who saw the body were most startled by its utter lifelikeness, and the mortuary virtuoso made doubly sure of his job by repeating certain injections at stated intervals. He almost wrung a sort of reluctant admiration from the townsfolk and visitors, though he tended to spoil that impression by his boastful and tasteless talk. Whenever he administered to his silent charge he would repeat that eternal rambling about the good luck of having a first-class undertaker. What—he would say as if directly addressing the body—if Tom had had one of those careless fellows who bury their subjects alive? The way he harped on the horrors of premature burial was truly barbarous and sickening.

Services were held in the stuffy best room—opened for the first time since Mrs. Sprague died. The tuneless little parlour organ groaned disconsolately, and the coffin, supported on trestles near the hall door, was covered with sickly-smelling flowers. It was obvious that a record-breaking crowd was assembling from far and near, and Sophie endeavoured to look properly grief-stricken for their benefit. At unguarded moments she seemed both puzzled and uneasy, dividing her scrutiny between the feverish-looking undertaker and the life-like body of her brother. A slow disgust at Thorndike seemed to be brewing within her, and neighbours whispered freely that she would soon send him about his business now that Tom was out of the way—that is, if she could, for such a slick customer was sometimes hard to deal with. But with her money and remaining looks she might be able to get another fellow, and he'd probably take care of Henry well enough.

As the organ wheezed into *Beautiful Isle of Somewhere* the Methodist church choir added their lugubrious voices to the gruesome cacophony, and everyone looked piously at Deacon Leavitt—everyone, that is, except crazy Johnny Dow, who kept his eyes glued to the still form beneath the glass of the coffin. He was muttering softly to himself.

Stephen Barbour—from the next farm—was the only one who noticed Johnny. He shivered as he saw that the idiot was talking directly to the corpse, and even making foolish signs with his fingers as if to taunt the sleeper beneath the plate glass. Tom, he reflected, had kicked poor Johnny around on more than one occasion, though probably not without provocation. Something about this whole event was getting on Stephen's nerves. There was a suppressed tension and brooding abnormality in the air for which he could not account. Johnny ought not to have been allowed in the house—and it was curious what an effort Thorndike seemed to be making not to look at the body. Every now and then the undertaker would feel his pulse with an odd air.

The Reverend Silas Atwood droned on in a plaintive monotone about the deceased—about the striking of Death's sword in the midst of this little family, breaking the earthly tie between this loving brother and sister. Several of the neighbours looked furtively at one another from beneath lowered eyelids, while Sophie actually began to sob nervously. Thorndike moved to her side and tried to reassure her, but she seemed to shrink curiously away from him. His motions were distinctly uneasy, and he seemed to feel acutely the abnormal tension permeating the air. Finally, conscious of his duty as master of ceremonies, he stepped forward and announced in a sepulchral voice that the body might be viewed for the last time.

Slowly the friends and neighbours filed past the bier, from which Thorndike roughly dragged crazy Johnny away. Tom seemed to be resting peacefully. That devil had been handsome in his day. A few genuine sobs—and many feigned ones—were heard, though most of the crowd were content to stare curiously and whisper afterward. Steve Barbour lingered long and attentively over the still face, and moved away shaking his head. His wife, Emily, following after him, whispered that Henry Thorndike had better not boast so much about his work, for Tom's eyes had come open. They had been shut when the services began, for she had been up and looked. But they certainly looked natural—not the way one would expect after two days.

When Fred Peck gets this far he usually pauses as if he did not like to continue. The listener, too, tends to feel that something unpleasant is ahead. But Peck reassures his audience with the statement that what happened isn't as bad as folks like to hint. Even Steve never put into words what he may have thought, and crazy Johnny, of course, can't be counted at all.

It was Luella Morse—the nervous old maid who sang in the choir—who seems to have touched things off. She was filing past the coffin like the rest, but stopped to peer a little closer than anyone else except the Barbours had peered. And then, without warning, she gave a shrill scream and fell in a dead faint.

Naturally, the room was at once a chaos of confusion. Old Dr. Pratt elbowed his way to Luella and called for some water to throw in her face, and others surged up to look at her and at the coffin. Johnny Dow began chanting to himself, "He knows, he knows, he kin hear all we're a-sayin' and see all we're a-doin', and they'll bury him that way"—but no one stopped to decipher his mumbling except Steve Barbour.

In a very few moments Luella began to come out of her faint, and could not tell exactly what had startled her. All she could whisper was, "The way he looked—the way he looked." But to other eyes the body seemed exactly the same. It was a gruesome sight, though, with those open eyes and that high colouring.

And then the bewildered crowd noticed something which put both Luella and the body out of their minds for a moment. It was Thorndike—on whom the sudden excitement and jostling crowd seemed to be having a curiously bad effect. He had evidently been knocked down in the general bustle, and was on the floor trying to drag himself to a sitting posture. The expression on his face was terrifying in the extreme, and his eyes were beginning to take on a glazed, fishy expression. He could scarcely speak aloud, but the husky rattle of his throat held an ineffable desperation which was obvious to all.

"Get me home, quick, and let me be. That fluid I got in my arm by mistake . . . heart action . . . this damned excitement . . . too much . . . wait . . . wait . . . don't think I'm dead if I seem to . . . only the fluid—just get me home and wait . . . I'll come to later, don't know how long . . . all the time I'll be conscious and know what's going on . . . don't be deceived. . . ."

As his words trailed off into nothingness old Dr. Pratt reached him and felt his pulse—watching a long time and finally shaking his head. "No use doing anything—he's gone. Heart no good—and that fluid he got in his arm must have been bad stuff. I don't know what it is."

A kind of numbness seemed to fall on all the company. New death in the chamber of death! Only Steve Barbour thought to bring up Thorndike's last choking words. Was he surely dead, when he himself had said he might falsely seem so? Wouldn't it be better to wait a while and see what would happen? And for that matter, what harm would it do if Doc Pratt were to give Tom Sprague another looking over before burial?

Crazy Johnny was moaning, and had flung himself on Thorndike's body like a faithful dog. "Don't ye bury him, don't ye bury him! He ain't dead no more nor Lige Hopkins's dog nor Deacon Leavitt's calf was when he shot 'em full. He's got some stuff he puts into ye to make ye seem like dead when ye ain't! Ye seem like dead but ye know everything what's a-goin' on, and the next day ye come to as good as ever. Don't ye bury him—he'll come to under the earth an' he can't scratch up! He's a good man, an' not like Tom Sprague. Hope to Gawd Tom scratches an' chokes for hours an' hours. . . ."

But no one save Barbour was paying any attention to poor Johnny. Indeed, what Steve himself had said had evidently fallen on deaf ears. Uncertainty was everywhere. Old Doc Pratt was applying final tests and mumbling about death certificate blanks, and unctuous Elder Atwood was suggesting that something be done about a double interment. With Thorndike dead there was no undertaker this side of Rutland, and it would mean a terrible expense if one were to be brought from there, and if Thorndike were not embalmed in this hot June weather—well, one couldn't tell.

And there were no relatives or friends to be critical unless Sophie chose to be—but Sophie was on the other side of the room, staring silently, fixedly, and almost morbidly into her brother's coffin.

Deacon Leavitt tried to restore a semblance of decorum, and had poor Thorndike carried across the hall to the sitting-room, meanwhile sending Zenas Wells and Walter Perkins over to the undertaker's house for a coffin of the right size. The key was in Henry's trousers pocket. Johnny continued to whine and paw at the body, and Elder Atwood busied himself with inquiring about Thorndike's denomination—for Henry had not attended local services. When it was decided that his folks in Rutland—all dead now—had been Baptists, the Reverend Silas decided that Deacon Leavitt had better offer the brief prayer.

It was a gala day for the funeral-fanciers of Stillwater and vicinity. Even Luella had recovered enough to stay. Gossip, murmured and whispered, buzzed busily while a few composing touches were given to Thorndike's cooling, stiffening form. Johnny had been cuffed out of the house, as most agreed he should have been in the first place, but his distant howls were now and then wafted gruesomely in.

When the body was encoffined and laid out beside that of Thomas Sprague, the silent, almost frightening-looking Sophie gazed intently at it as she had gazed at her brother's. She had not uttered a word for a dangerously long time, and the mixed expression on her face was past all describing or interpreting. As the others withdrew to leave her alone with the dead she managed to find a sort of mechanical speech, but no one could make out the words, and she seemed to be talking first to one body and then the other.

And now, with what would seem to an outsider the acme of gruesome unconscious comedy, the whole funeral mummery of the afternoon was listlessly repeated. Again the organ wheezed, again the choir screeched and scraped, again a droning incantation arose, and again the morbidly curious spectators filed past a macabre object—this time a dual array of mortuary repose. Some of the more sensitive people shivered at the whole proceeding, and again Stephen Barbour felt an underlying note of eldritch horror and daemoniac abnormality. God, how life-like both of those corpses were . . . and how in earnest poor Thorndike had been about not wanting to be judged dead . . . and how he hated Tom Sprague . . . but what could one do in the face of common sense—a dead man was a dead man, and there was old Doc Pratt with his years of experience . . . if nobody else bothered, why should one bother oneself? . . . Whatever Tom had got he had probably deserved . . . and if Henry had done anything to him, the score was even now . . . well, Sophie was free at last. . . .

As the peering procession moved at last toward the hall and the outer door, Sophie was alone with the dead once more. Elder Atwood was out in the road talking to the hearse-driver from Lee's livery stable, and Deacon Leavitt was arranging for a double quota of pall-bearers. Luckily the hearse would hold two coffins. No hurry—Ed Plummer and Ethan Stone were going ahead with shovels to dig the second grave. There would be three livery hacks and any number of private rigs in the cavalcade—no use trying to keep the crowd away from the graves.

Then came that frantic scream from the parlour where Sophie and the bodies were. Its suddenness almost paralysed the crowd and brought back the same sensation which had surged up when Luella had screamed and fainted. Steve Barbour and Deacon Leavitt started to go in, but before they could enter the house Sophie was bursting forth, sobbing and gasping about "That face at the window! . . . that face at the window! . . ."

At the same time a wild-eyed figure rounded the corner of the house, removing all mystery from Sophie's dramatic cry. It was, very obviously, the face's owner—poor crazy Johnny, who began to leap up and down, pointing at Sophie and shrieking, "She knows! She knows! I seen it in her face when she looked at 'em and talked to 'em! She knows, and she's a-lettin' 'em go down in the earth to scratch an' claw for air. . . . But they'll talk to her so's she kin hear 'em . . . they'll talk to her, an' appear to her . . . and some day they'll come back an' git her!"

Zenas Wells dragged the shrieking half-wit to a woodshed behind the house and bolted him in as best he could. His screams and poundings could be heard at a distance, but nobody paid him any further attention. The procession was made up, and with Sophie in the first hack it slowly covered the short distance past the village to the Swamp Hollow burying-ground.

Elder Atwood made appropriate remarks as Thomas Sprague was laid to rest, and by the time he was through, Ed and Ethan had finished Thorndike's grave on the other side of the cemetery—to which the crowd presently shifted. Deacon Leavitt then spoke ornamentally, and the lowering process was repeated. People had begun to drift off in knots, and the clatter of receding buggies and carryalls was quite universal, when the shovels began to fly again. As the earth thudded down on the coffin-lids, Thorndike's first, Steve Barbour noticed the queer expressions flitting over Sophie Sprague's face. He couldn't keep track of them all, but behind the rest there seemed to lurk a sort of wry, perverse, half-suppressed look of vague triumph. He shook his head.

Zenas had run back and let crazy Johnny out of the woodshed before Sophie got home, and the poor fellow at once made frantically for the graveyard. He arrived before the shovelmen were through, and while many of the curious mourners were still lingering about. What he shouted into Tom Sprague's partly filled grave, and how he clawed at the loose earth of Thorndike's freshly finished mound across the cemetery, surviving spectators still shudder to recall. Jotham Blake, the constable, had to take him back to the town farm by force, and his screams waked dreadful echoes.

This is where Fred Peck usually leaves off the story. What more, he asks, is there to tell? It was a gloomy tragedy, and one can scarcely wonder that Sophie grew queer after that. That is all one hears if the hour is so late that old Calvin Wheeler has tottered home, but when he is still around he breaks in again with that damnably suggestive and insidious whisper. Sometimes those who hear him dread to pass either the shuttered house or the graveyard afterward, especially after dark.

"Heh, heh . . . Fred was only a little shaver then, and don't remember no more than half of what was goin' on! You want to know why Sophie keeps her house shuttered, and why crazy Johnny still keeps a-talkin' to the dead and a-shoutin' at Sophie's windows? Well, sir, I don't know's I know all there is to know, but I hear what I hear."

Here the old man ejects his cud of tobacco and leans forward to buttonhole the listener.

"It was that same night, mind ye—toward mornin', and just eight hours after them burials—when we heard the first scream from Sophie's house. Woke us all up—Steve and Emily Barbour and me and Matildy goes over hot-footin', all in night gear, and finds Sophie all dressed and dead fainted on the settin'-room floor. Lucky she hadn't locked the door. When we got her to she was shakin' like a leaf, and wouldn't let on by so much as a word what was ailin' her. Matildy and Emily done what they could to quiet her down, but Steve whispered things to me as didn't make me none too easy. Come about an hour when we allowed we'd be goin' home soon, that Sophie she begun to tip her head on one side like she was a-listenin' to somethin'. Then on a sudden she screamed again, and keeled over in another faint.

"Well, sir, I'm tellin' what I'm tellin', and won't do no guessin' like Steve Barbour would a done if he dared. He always was the greatest hand for hintin' things . . . died ten years ago of pneumony. . . .

"What we heard so faint-like was just poor crazy Johnny, of course. 'Taint more than a mile to the buryin'-ground, and he must a got out of the window where they'd locked him up at the town farm—even if Constable Blake says he didn't get out that night. From that day to this he hangs around them graves a-talkin' to the both of them—cussin' and kickin' at Tom's mound, and puttin' posies and things on Henry's. And when he ain't a-doin' that he's hangin' around Sophie's shuttered windows howlin' about what's a-comin' soon to git her.

"She wouldn't never go near the buryin'-ground, and now she won't come out of the house at all nor see nobody. Got to sayin' there was a curse on Stillwater—and I'm dinged if she ain't half right, the way things is a-goin' to pieces these days. There certainly was somethin' queer about Sophie right along. Once when Sally Hopkins was a-callin' on her—in '97 or '98, I think it was—there was an awful rattlin' at her winders—and Johnny was safe locked up at the time—at least, so Constable Dodge swore up and down. But I ain't takin' no stock in their stories about noises every seventeenth of June, or about faint shinin' figures a-tryin' Sophie's door and winders every black mornin' about two o'clock.

"You see, it was about two o'clock in the mornin' that Sophie heard the sounds and keeled over twice that first night after the buryin'. Steve and me, and Matildy and Emily, heard the second lot, faint as it was, just like I told you. And I'm a-tellin' you again as how it must a been crazy Johnny over to the buryin'-ground, let Jotham Blake claim what he will. There ain't no tellin' the sound of a man's voice so far off, and with our heads full of nonsense it ain't no wonder we thought there was two voices—and voices that hadn't ought to be speakin' at all.

"Steve, he claimed to have heard more than I did. I verily believe he took some stock in ghosts. Matildy and Emily was so scared they didn't remember what they heard. And curious enough, nobody else in town—if anybody was awake at the ungodly hour—never said nothin' about hearin' no sounds at all.

"Whatever it was, was so faint it might have been the wind if there hadn't been words. I made out a few, but don't want to say as I'd back up all Steve claimed to have caught. . . .

"'She-devil' . . . 'all the time' . . . 'Henry' . . . and 'alive' was plain . . . and so was 'you know' . . . 'said you'd stand by' . . . 'get rid of him' and 'bury me' . . . in a kind of changed voice. . . . Then there was that awful 'comin' again some day'—in a death-like squawk . . . but you can't tell me Johnny couldn't have made those sounds. . . .

"Hey, you! What's takin' you off in such a hurry? Mebbe there's more I could tell you if I had a mind. . . ."

William Lumley

The Diary of Alonzo Typer

EDITOR'S NOTE: Alonzo Hasbrouck Typer of Kingston, N.Y., was last seen and recognised on April 17, 1908, around noon, at the Hotel Richmond in Batavia. He was the only survivor of an ancient Ulster County family, and was fifty-three years old at the time of his disappearance.

Mr. Typer was educated privately and at Columbia and Heidelberg Universities. All his life was spent as a student; the field of his researches including many obscure and generally feared borderlands of human knowledge. His papers on vampirism, ghouls, and poltergeist phenomena were privately printed after rejection by many publishers. He resigned from the Society for Psychical Research in 1902 after a series of peculiarly bitter controversies.

At various times Mr. Typer travelled extensively, sometimes dropping out of sight for long periods. He is known to have visited obscure spots in Nepal, India, Thibet, and Indo-China, and passed most of the year 1899 on mysterious Easter Island. The extensive search for Mr. Typer after his disappearance yielded no results, and his estate was divided among distant cousins in New York City.

The diary herewith presented was allegedly found in the ruins of a large country house near Attica, N.Y., which had borne a curiously sinister reputation for generations before its collapse. The edifice was very old, antedating the general white settlement of the region, and had formed the home of a strange and secretive family named van der Heyl, which had migrated from Albany in 1746 under a curious cloud of witchcraft suspicion. The structure probably dated from about 1760.

Of the history of the van der Heyls very little is known. They remained entirely aloof from their normal neighbours, employed negro servants brought directly from Africa and speaking little English, and educated their children privately and at European colleges. Those of them who went out into the world were soon lost to sight, though not before gaining evil repute for association with Black Mass groups and cults of even darker significance.

Around the dreaded house a straggling village arose, populated by Indians and later by renegades from the surrounding country, which bore the dubious name of Chorazin. Of the singular hereditary strains which afterward appeared in the mixed Chorazin villagers, several monographs have been written by ethnologists. Just behind the village, and in sight of the van der Heyl house, is a steep hill crowned with a peculiar ring of ancient standing stones which the Iroquois always regarded with fear and loathing. The origin and nature of the stones, whose date, according to archaeological and climatological evidence, must be fabulously early, is a problem still unsolved.

From about 1795 onward, the legends of the incoming pioneers and later population have much to say about strange cries and chants proceeding at certain seasons from Chorazin and from the great house and hill of standing stones; though there is reason to suppose that the noises ceased about 1872, when the entire van der Heyl household—servants and all—suddenly and simultaneously disappeared.

Thenceforward the house was deserted; for other disastrous events—including three unexplained deaths, five disappearances, and four cases of sudden insanity—occurred when later owners and interested visitors attempted to stay in it. The house, village, and extensive rural areas on all sides reverted to the state and were auctioned off in the absence of discoverable van der Heyl heirs. Since about 1890 the owners (successively the late Charles A. Shields and his son Oscar S. Shields, of Buffalo) have left the entire property in a state of absolute neglect, and have warned all inquirers not to visit the region.

Of those known to have approached the house during the last forty years, most were occult students, police officers, newspaper men, and odd characters from abroad. Among the latter was a mysterious Eurasian, probably from Cochin-China, whose later appearance with blank mind and bizarre mutilations excited wide press notice in 1903.

Mr. Typer's diary—a book about 6 × 3½ inches in size, with tough paper and an oddly durable binding of thin sheet metal—was discovered in the possession of one of the decadent Chorazin villagers on Nov. 16, 1935, by a state policeman sent to investigate the rumoured collapse of the deserted van der Heyl mansion. The house had indeed fallen, obviously from sheer age and decrepitude, in the severe gale of Nov. 12. Disintegration was peculiarly complete, and no thorough search of the ruins could be made for several weeks. John Eagle, the swarthy, simian-faced, Indian-like villager who had the diary, said that he found the book quite near the surface of the debris, in what must have been an upper front room.

Very little of the contents of the house could be identified, though an enormous and astonishingly solid brick vault in the cellar (whose ancient iron door had to be blasted open because of the strangely figured and perversely tenacious lock) remained intact and presented several puzzling features. For one thing, the walls were covered with still undeciphered hieroglyphs roughly incised in the brickwork. Another peculiarity was a huge circular aperture in the rear of the vault, blocked by a cave-in evidently caused by the collapse of the house.

But strangest of all was the apparently *recent* deposit of some foetid, slimy, pitch-black substance on the flagstoned floor, extending in a yard-broad, irregular line with one end at the blocked circular aperture. Those who first opened the vault declared that the place smelled like the snake-house at a zoo.

The diary, which was apparently designed solely to cover an investigation of the dreaded van der Heyl house by the vanished Mr. Typer, has been proved by handwriting experts to be genuine. The script shews signs of increasing nervous strain as it progresses toward the end, in places becoming almost illegible. Chorazin villagers—whose stupidity and taciturnity baffle all students of the region and its secrets—admit no recollection of Mr. Typer as distinguished from other rash visitors to the dreaded house.

The text of the diary is here given verbatim and without comment. How to interpret it, and what, other than the writer's madness, to infer from it, the reader must decide for himself. Only the future can tell what its value may be in solving a generation-old mystery. It may be remarked that genealogists confirm Mr. Typer's belated memory in the matter of *Adriaen Sleght.*

THE DIARY

April 17, 1908

Arrived here about 6 p.m. Had to walk all the way from Attica in the teeth of an oncoming storm, for no one would rent me a horse or rig, and I can't run an automobile. This place is even worse than I had expected, and I dread what is coming, even though I long at the same time to learn the secret. All too soon will come the night—the old Walpurgis Sabbat horror—and after that time in Wales I know what to look for. Whatever comes, I shall not flinch. Prodded by some unfathomable urge, I have given my whole life to the quest of unholy mysteries. I came here for nothing else, and will not quarrel with fate.

It was very dark when I got here, though the sun had by no means set. The storm-clouds were the densest I had ever seen, and I could not have found my way but for the lightning flashes. The village is a hateful little backwater, and its few inhabitants no better than idiots. One of them saluted me in a queer way, as if he knew me. I could see very little of the landscape—just a small, swampy valley of strange brown weed-stalks and dead fungi surrounded by scraggly, evilly twisted trees with bare boughs. But behind the village is a dismal-looking hill on whose summit is a circle of great stones with another stone at the centre. That, without question, is the vile primordial thing V—— told me about at the N——estbat.

The great house lies in the midst of a park all overgrown with curious-looking briers. I could scarcely break through, and when I did the vast age and decrepitude of the building almost stopped me from entering. The place looked filthy and diseased, and I wondered how so leprous a bulk could hang together. It is wooden; and though its original lines are hidden by a bewildering tangle of wings added at various dates, I think it was first built in the square colonial fashion of New England. Probably that was easier to build than a Dutch stone house—and then, too, I recall that Dirck van der Heyl's wife was from Salem, a daughter of the unmentionable Abaddon Corey. There was a small pillared porch, and I got under it just as the storm burst. It was a fiendish tempest—black as midnight, with rain in sheets, thunder and lightning like the day of general dissolution, and a wind that actually clawed at me. The door was unlocked, so I took out my electric torch and went inside. Dust was inches thick on floor and furniture, and the place smelled like a mould-caked tomb. There was a hall reaching all the way through, and a curving staircase on the right. I ploughed a way upstairs and selected this front room to camp out in. The whole place seems fully furnished, though most of the furniture is breaking down. This is written at eight o'clock, after a cold meal from my travelling-case. After this the village people will bring me supplies—though they won't agree to come any closer than the ruins of the park gate until (as they say) later. I wish I could get rid of an unpleasant feeling of familiarity with this place.

Later

I am conscious of several presences in this house. One in particular is decidedly hostile toward me—a malevolent will which is seeking to break down my own and overcome me. I must not countenance this for an instant, but must use all my forces to resist it. It is appallingly evil, and definitely non-human. I think it must be allied to powers outside earth—powers in the spaces behind time and beyond the universe. It towers like a colossus, bearing out what is said in the Aklo writings. There is such a feeling of vast size connected with it that I wonder these chambers can contain its bulk—and yet it has no visible bulk. Its age must be unutterably vast—shockingly, indescribably so.

April 18

Slept very little last night. At 3 a.m. a strange, creeping wind began to pervade the whole region—ever rising until the house rocked as if in a typhoon. As I went down the staircase to see to the rattling front door the darkness took half-visible forms in my imagination. Just below the landing I was pushed violently from behind—by the wind, I suppose, though I could have sworn I saw the dissolving outlines of a gigantic black paw as I turned quickly about. I did not lose my footing, but safely finished the descent and shot the heavy bolt of the dangerously shaking door.

I had not meant to explore the house till dawn; yet now, unable to sleep again and fired with mixed terror and curiosity, I felt reluctant to postpone my search. With my powerful torch I ploughed through the dust to the great south parlour, where I knew the portraits would be. There they were, just as V—— had said, and as I seemed to know from some obscurer source as well. Some were so blackened, mouldy, and dust-clouded that I could make little or nothing of them, but from those I could trace I recognised that they were indeed of the hateful line of the van der Heyls. Some of the paintings seemed to suggest faces I had known; but just *what* faces, I could not recall.

The outlines of that frightful hybrid Joris—spawned in 1773 by old Dirck's youngest daughter—were clearest of all, and I could trace the green eyes and the serpent look in his face. Every time I shut off the flashlight that face would seem to glow in the dark until I half fancied it shone with a faint, greenish light of its own. The more I looked, the more evil it seemed, and I turned away to avoid hallucinations of changing expression.

But that to which I turned was even worse. The long, dour face, small, closely set eyes, and swine-like features identified it at once, even though the artist had striven to make the snout look as human as possible. This was what V—— had whispered about. As I stared in horror, I thought the eyes took on a reddish glow—and for a moment the background seemed replaced by an alien and seemingly irrelevant scene—a lone, bleak moor beneath a dirty yellow sky, whereon grew a wretched-looking blackthorn bush. Fearing for my sanity, I rushed from that accursed gallery to the dust-cleared corner upstairs where I have my "camp".

Later

Decided to explore some of the labyrinthine wings of the house by daylight. I cannot get lost, for my footprints are distinct in the ankle-deep dust—and I can trace other identifying marks when necessary. It is curious how easily I learn the intricate windings of the corridors. Followed a long, outflung northerly "ell" to its extremity, and came to a locked door, which I forced. Beyond was a very small room quite crowded with furniture, and with the panelling badly worm-eaten. On the outer wall I spied a black space behind the rotting woodwork, and discovered a narrow secret passage leading downward to unknown black depths. It was a steeply inclined chute or tunnel without steps or hand-holds, and I wondered what its use could have been.

Above the fireplace was a mouldy painting, which I found on close inspection to be that of a young woman in the dress of the late eighteenth century. The face is of classic beauty, yet with the most fiendishly evil expression which I have ever known the human countenance to bear. Not merely callousness, greed, and cruelty, but some quality hideous beyond human comprehension seems to sit upon those finely carved features. And as I looked it seemed to me that the artist—or the slow processes of mould and decay—had imparted to that pallid complexion a sickly greenish cast, and the least suggestion of an almost imperceptibly scaly texture. Later I ascended to the attic, where I found several chests of strange books—many of utterly alien aspect in letters and in physical form alike. One contained variants of the Aklo formulae which I had never known to exist. I have not yet examined the books on the dusty shelves downstairs.

April 19

There are certainly unseen presences here, even though the dust as yet bears no footprints but my own. Cut a path through the briers yesterday to the park gate where my supplies are left, but this morning I found it closed. Very odd, since the bushes are hardly stirring with spring sap. Again I had that feeling of something at hand so colossal that the chambers can scarcely contain it. This time I feel more than one of the presences is of such a size, and I know now that the third Aklo ritual—which I found in that book in the attic yesterday—would make such beings solid and visible. Whether I shall dare to try this materialisation remains to be seen. The perils are great.

Last night I began to glimpse evanescent shadow-faces and forms in the dim corners of the halls and chambers—faces and forms so hideous and loathsome that I dare not describe them. They seem allied in substance to that titanic paw which tried to push me down the stairs night before last—and must of course be phantoms of my disturbed imagination. What I am seeking would not be quite like these things. I have seen the paw again—sometimes alone and sometimes with its mate—but I have resolved to ignore all such phenomena.

Early this afternoon I explored the cellar for the first time—descending by a ladder found in a storeroom, since the wooden steps had rotted away. The whole place is a mass of nitrous encrustations, with amorphous mounds marking the spots where various objects have disintegrated. At the farther end is a narrow passage which seems to extend under the northerly "ell" where I found the little locked room, and at the end of this is a heavy brick wall with a locked iron door. Apparently belonging to a vault of some sort, this wall and door bear evidences of eighteenth-century workmanship and must be contemporary with the oldest additions to the house—clearly pre-Revolutionary. On the lock—which is obviously older than the rest of the ironwork—are engraved certain symbols which I cannot decipher.

V—— had not told me about this vault. It fills me with a greater disquiet than anything else I have seen, for every time I approach it I have an almost irresistible impulse to *listen* for something. Hitherto no untoward *sounds* have marked my stay in this malign place. As I left the cellar I wished devoutly that the steps were still there—for my progress up the ladder seemed maddeningly slow. I do not want to go down there again—and yet some evil genius urges me to try it *at night* if I would learn what is to be learned.

April 20

I have sounded the depths of horror—only to be made aware of still lower depths. Last night the temptation was too strong, and in the black small hours I descended once more into that nitrous, hellish cellar with my flashlight—tiptoeing among the amorphous heaps to that terrible brick wall and locked door. I made no sound, and refrained from whispering any of the incantations I knew, but I listened—listened with mad intentness.

At last I heard the sounds from beyond those barred plates of sheet iron—the menacing padding and muttering, as of gigantic night-things within. Then, too, there was a damnable slithering, as of a vast serpent or sea-beast dragging its monstrous folds over a paved floor. Nearly paralysed with fright, I glanced at the huge rusty lock, and at the alien, cryptic hieroglyphs graven upon it. They were signs I could not recognise, and something in their vaguely Mongoloid technique hinted at a blasphemous and indescribable antiquity. At times I fancied I could see them glowing with a greenish light.

I turned to flee, but found that vision of the titan paws before me—the great talons seeming to swell and become more tangible as I gazed. Out of the cellar's evil blackness they stretched, with shadowy hints of scaly wrists beyond them, and with a waxing, malignant will guiding their horrible gropings. Then I heard from behind me—within that abominable vault—a fresh burst of muffled reverberations which seemed to echo from far horizons like distant thunder. Impelled by this greater fear, I advanced toward the shadowy paws with my flashlight and saw them vanish before the full force of the electric beam. Then up the ladder I raced, torch between my teeth, nor did I rest till I had regained my upstairs "camp".

What is to be my ultimate end, I dare not imagine. I came as a seeker, but now I know that something is seeking me. I could not leave if I wished. This morning I tried to go to the gate for my supplies, but found the briers twisted tightly in my path. It was the same in every direction—behind and on all sides of the house. In places the brown, barbed vines had uncurled to astonishing heights —forming a steel-like hedge against my egress. The villagers are connected with all this. When I went indoors I found my supplies in the great front hall, though without any clue to how they came there. I am sorry now that I swept the dust away. I shall scatter some more and see what prints are left.

This afternoon I read some of the books in the great shadowy library at the rear of the ground floor, and formed certain suspicions which I cannot bear to mention. I had never seen the text of Pnakotic Manuscripts or of the Eltdown Shards before, and would not have come here had I known what they contain. I believe it is too late now—for the awful Sabbat is only ten days away. It is for that night of horror that *they* are saving me.

April 21

I have been studying the portraits again. Some have names attached, and I noticed one—of an evil-faced woman, painted some two centuries ago—which puzzled me. It bore the name of Trintje van der Heyl Sleght, and I have a distinct impression that I once met the name of Sleght before, in some significant connexion. It was not horrible then, though it becomes so now. I must rack my brain for the clue.

The *eyes* of these pictures haunt me. Is it possible that some of them are emerging more distinctly from their shrouds of dust and decay and mould? The serpent-faced and swine-faced warlocks stare horribly at me from their blackened frames, and a score of other hybrid faces are beginning to peer out of shadowy backgrounds. There is a hideous look of family resemblance in them all —and that which is human is more horrible than that which is non-human. I wish they reminded me less of other faces—faces I have known in the past. They were an accursed line, and Cornelis of Leyden was the worst of them. It was *he* who broke down the barrier after his father had found that other key. I am sure that V—— knows only a fragment of the horrible truth, so that I am indeed unprepared and defenceless. What of the line before old Claes? What he did in 1591 could never have been done without generations of evil heritage, or some link with the outside. And what of the branches this monstrous line has sent forth? Are they scattered over the world, all awaiting their common heritage of horror? I must recall the place where I once so particularly noticed the name of Sleght.

I wish I could be sure that these pictures stay always in their frames. For several hours now I have been seeing momentary presences like the earlier paws and shadow-faces and forms, but closely duplicating some of the ancient portraits. Somehow I can never glimpse a presence and the portrait it resembles at the same time—the light is always wrong for one or the other, or else the presence and the portrait are in different rooms.

Perhaps, as I have hoped, the presences are mere figments of imagination; but I cannot be sure now. Some are female, and of the same hellish beauty as the picture in the little locked room. Some are like no portrait I have seen, yet make me feel that their painted features lurk unrecognised beneath the mould and soot of canvases I cannot decipher. A few, I desperately fear, have approached materialisation in solid or semi-solid form—and some have a dreadful and unexplained familiarity.

There is one woman who in fell loveliness excels all the rest. Her poisonous charms are like a honeyed flower growing on the brink of hell. When I look at her closely she vanishes, only to reappear later. Her face has a greenish cast, and now and then I fancy I can spy a suspicion of the squamose in its smooth texture. Who is she? Is she that being who must have dwelt in the little locked room a century and more ago?

My supplies were again left in the front hall—that, clearly, is to be the custom. I had sprinkled dust about to catch footprints, but this morning the whole hall was swept clean by some unknown agency.

April 22

This has been a day of horrible discovery. I explored the cobwebbed attic again, and found a carved, crumbling chest—plainly from Holland—full of blasphemous books and papers far older than any hitherto encountered here. There was a Greek *Necronom-*

icon, a Norman-French *Livre d'Eibon,* and a first edition of old Ludvig Prinn's *De Vermis Mysteriis.* But the old bound manuscript was the worst. It was in low Latin, and full of the strange, crabbed handwriting of Claes van der Heyl—being evidently the diary or notebook kept by him between 1560 and 1580. When I unfastened the blackened silver clasp and opened the yellowed leaves a coloured drawing fluttered out—the likeness of a monstrous creature resembling nothing so much as a squid, beaked and tentacled, with great yellow eyes, and with certain abominable approximations to the human form in its contours.

I had never before seen so utterly loathsome and nightmarish a form. On the paws, feet, and head-tentacles were curious claws—reminding me of the colossal shadow-shapes which have groped so horribly in my path—while the entity as a whole sat upon a great throne-like pedestal inscribed with unknown hieroglyphs of vaguely Chinese cast. About both writing and image there hung an air of sinister evil so profound and pervasive that I could not think it the product of any one world or age. Rather must that monstrous shape be a focus for all the evil in unbounded space, throughout the aeons past and to come—and those eldritch symbols be vile sentient eikons endowed with a morbid life of their own and ready to wrest themselves from the parchment for the reader's destruction. To the meaning of that monster and of those hieroglyphs I had no clue, but I knew that both had been traced with a hellish precision and for no namable purpose. As I studied the leering characters, their kinship to the symbols on that ominous lock in the cellar became more and more manifest. I left the picture in the attic, for never could sleep come to me with such a thing nearby.

All the afternoon and evening I read in the manuscript book of old Claes van der Heyl, and what I read will cloud and make horrible whatever period of life lies ahead of me. The genesis of the world, and of previous worlds, unfolded itself before my eyes. I learned of the city Shamballah, built by the Lemurians fifty million years ago, yet inviolate still behind its walls of psychic force in the eastern desert. I learned of the Book of Dzyan, whose first six chapters antedate the earth, and which was old when the lords of Venus came through space in their ships to civilise our planet. And I saw recorded in writing for the first time that name which others had spoken to me in whispers, and which I had known in a closer and more horrible way—the shunned and dreaded name of *Yian-Ho.*

In several places I was held up by passages requiring a key. Eventually, from various allusions, I gathered that old Claes had not dared to embody all his knowledge in one book, but had left certain points for another. Neither volume can be wholly intelligible without its fellow; hence I have resolved to find the second one if it lies anywhere within this accursed house. Though plainly a prisoner, I have not lost my lifelong zeal for the unknown; and am determined to probe the cosmos as deeply as possible before doom comes.

April 23

Searched all the morning for the second diary, and found it about noon in a desk in the little locked room. Like the first, it is in Claes van der Heyl's barbarous Latin; and it seems to consist of disjointed notes referring to various sections of the other. Glancing through the leaves, I spied at once the abhorred name of Yian-Ho—of Yian-Ho, that lost and hidden city wherein brood aeon-old secrets, and of which dim memories older than the body lurk behind the minds of all men. It was repeated many times, and the text around it was strown with crudely drawn hieroglyphs plainly akin to those on the pedestal in that hellish drawing I had seen. Here, clearly, lay the key to that monstrous tentacled shape and its forbidden message. With this knowledge I ascended the creaking stairs to the attic of cobwebs and horror.

When I tried to open the attic door it stuck as never before. Several times it resisted every effort to open it, and when at last it gave way I had a distinct feeling that some colossal, unseen shape had suddenly released it—a shape that soared away on non-material but audibly beating wings. When I found the horrible drawing I felt that it was not precisely where I had left it. Applying the key in the other book, I soon saw that the latter was no instant guide to the secret. It was only a clue—a clue to a secret too black to be left lightly guarded. It would take hours—perhaps days—to extract the awful message.

Shall I live long enough to learn the secret? The shadowy black arms and paws haunt my vision more and more now, and seem even more titanic than at first. Nor am I ever long free from those vague, unhuman presences whose nebulous bulk seems too vast for the chambers to contain. And now and then the grotesque, evanescent faces and forms, and the mocking portrait-shapes, troop before me in bewildering confusion.

Truly, there are terrible primal arcana of earth which had better be left unknown and unevoked; dread secrets which have nothing to do with man, and which man may learn only in exchange for peace and sanity; cryptic truths which make the knower evermore an alien among his kind, and cause him to walk alone on earth. Likewise are there dread survivals of things older and more potent than man; things that have blasphemously straggled down through the aeons to ages never meant for them; monstrous entities that have lain sleeping endlessly in incredible crypts and remote caverns, outside the laws of reason and causation, and ready to be waked by such blasphemers as shall know their dark forbidden signs and furtive passwords.

April 24

Studied the picture and the key all day in the attic. At sunset I heard strange sounds, of a sort not encountered before and seeming to come from far away. Listening, I realised that they must flow from that queer abrupt hill with the circle of standing stones, which lies behind the village and some distance north of the house. I had heard that there was a path from the house leading up that hill to the primal cromlech, and had suspected that at certain seasons the van der Heyls had much occasion to use it; but the whole matter had hitherto lain latent in my consciousness. The present sounds consisted of a shrill piping intermingled with a peculiar and hideous sort of hissing or whistling—a bizarre, alien kind of music, like nothing which the annals of earth describe. It was very faint, and soon faded, but the matter has set me thinking. It is toward the hill that the long, northerly "ell" with the secret chute, and the locked brick vault under it, extend. Can there be any connexion which has so far eluded me?

April 25

I have made a peculiar and disturbing discovery about the nature of my imprisonment. Drawn toward the hill by a sinister fascination, I found the briers giving way before me, *but in that direction only.* There is a ruined gate, and beneath the bushes the traces of the old path no doubt exist. The briers extend part way up and all around the hill, though the summit with the standing stones bears only a curious growth of moss and stunted grass. I climbed the hill and spent several hours there, noticing a strange wind which seems always to sweep around the forbidding monoliths and which sometimes seems to whisper in an oddly articulate though darkly cryptic fashion.

These stones, both in colour and in texture, resemble nothing I have seen elsewhere. They are neither brown nor grey, but rather of a dirty yellow merging into an evil green and having a suggestion of chameleon-like variability. Their texture is queerly like that of a scaled serpent, and is inexplicably nauseous to the touch—being as cold and clammy as the skin of a toad or other reptile. Near the central menhir is a singular stone-rimmed hollow which I cannot explain, but which may possibly form the entrance to a long-choked well or tunnel. When I sought to descend the hill at points away from the house I found the briers intercepting me as before, though the path toward the house was easily retraceable.

April 26

Up on the hill again this evening, and found that windy whispering much more distinct. The almost angry humming came close to actual speech—of a vague sibilant sort—and reminded me of the strange piping chant I had heard from afar. After sunset there came a curious flash of premature summer lightning on the northern horizon, followed almost at once by a queer detonation high in the fading sky. Something about this phenomenon disturbed me greatly, and I could not escape the impression that the noise ended in a kind of unhuman hissing speech which trailed off into guttural cosmic laughter. Is my mind tottering at last, or has my unwarranted curiosity evoked unheard-of horrors from the twilight spaces? The Sabbat is close at hand now. What will be the end?

April 27

At last my dreams are to be realised! Whether or not my life or spirit or body will be claimed, I shall enter the gateway! Progress in deciphering those crucial hieroglyphs in the picture has been slow, but this afternoon I hit upon the final clue. By evening I knew their meaning—and that meaning can apply in only one way to the things I have encountered in this house.

There is beneath this house—sepulchred I know not where—an ancient forgotten One who will shew me the gateway I would enter, and give me the lost signs and words I shall need. How long It has lain buried here—forgotten save by those who reared the stones on the hill, and by those who later sought out this place and built this house—I cannot conjecture. It was in search of this Thing, beyond question, that Hendrik van der Heyl came to New-Netherland in 1638. Men of this earth know It not, save in the secret whispers of the fear-shaken few who have found or inherited the key. No human eye has even yet glimpsed It—unless, perhaps, the vanished wizards of this house delved farther than has been guessed.

With knowledge of the symbols came likewise a mastery of the Seven Lost Signs of Terror—and a tacit recognition of the hideous and unutterable Words of Fear. All that remains for me to accomplish is the Chant which will transfigure that Forgotten One who is Guardian of the Ancient Gateway. I marvel much at the Chant. It is composed of strange and repellent gutturals and disturbing sibilants resembling no language I have ever encountered—even in the blackest chapters of the *Livre d'Eibon.* When I visited the hill at sunset I tried to read it aloud, but evoked in response only a vague, sinister rumbling on the far horizon, and a thin cloud of elemental dust that writhed and whirled like some evil living thing. Perhaps I do not pronounce the alien syllables correctly, or perhaps it is only on the Sabbat—that hellish Sabbat for which the Powers in this house are without question holding me—that the great Transfiguration can occur.

Had an odd spell of fright this morning. I thought for a moment that I recalled where I had seen that baffling name of Sleght before, and the prospect of realisation filled me with unutterable horror.

April 28

Today dark ominous clouds have hovered intermittently over the circle on the hill. I have noticed such clouds several times before, but their contours and arrangements now hold a fresh significance. They are snake-like and fantastic, and curiously like the evil shadow-shapes I have seen in the house. They float in a circle around the primal cromlech—revolving repeatedly as though endowed with a sinister life and purpose. I could swear, too, that they give forth an angry murmuring. After some fifteen minutes they sail slowly away, ever to the eastward, like the units of a straggling battalion. Are they indeed those dread Ones whom Solomon knew of old—those giant black beings whose number is legion and whose tread doth shake the earth?

I have been rehearsing the Chant that will transfigure the Nameless Thing, yet strange fears assail me even when I utter the syllables under my breath. Piecing all evidence together, I have now discovered that the only way to It is through the locked cellar vault. That vault was built with a hellish purpose, and must cover the hidden burrow leading to the Immemorial Lair. What guardians live endlessly within, flourishing from century to century on an unknown nourishment, only the mad may conjecture. The warlocks of this house, who called them out of inner earth, have known them only too well, as the shocking portraits and memories of the place reveal.

What troubles me most is the limited nature of the Chant. It evokes the Nameless One, yet provides no method for the control of That Which is evoked. There are, of course, the general signs and gestures, but whether they will prove effective toward such an One remains to be seen. Still, the rewards are great enough to justify any danger—and I could not retreat if I would, since an unknown force plainly urges me on.

I have discovered one more obstacle. Since the locked cellar vault must be traversed, the key to that place must be found. The lock is infinitely too strong for forcing. That the key is somewhere hereabouts cannot be doubted, but the time before the Sabbat is very short. I must search diligently and thoroughly. It will take courage to unlock that iron door, for what prisoned horrors may not lurk within?

Later

I have been shunning the cellar for the past day or two, but late this afternoon I again descended to those forbidding precincts. At first all was silent, but within five minutes the menacing padding and muttering began once more beyond the iron door. This time it was loud and more terrifying than on any previous occasion, and I likewise recognised the slithering that bespoke some monstrous sea-beast—now swifter and nervously intensified, as if the thing were striving to force its way through the portal to where I stood.

As the pacing grew louder, more restless, and more sinister, there began to pound through it those hellish and unidentifiable reverberations which I had heard on my second visit to the cellar—those muffled reverberations which seemed to echo from far horizons like distant thunder. Now, however, their volume was magnified an hundredfold, and their timbre freighted with new and terrifying implications. I can compare the sound to nothing more aptly than to the roar of some dread monster of the vanished saurian age, when primal horrors roamed the earth, and Valusia's serpent-men laid the foundation-stones of evil magic. To such a roar—but swelled to deafening heights reached by no known organic throat—was this shocking sound akin. Dare I unlock the door and face the onslaught of what lies beyond?

April 29

The key to the vault is found. I came upon it this noon in the little locked room—buried beneath rubbish in a drawer of the ancient desk, as if some belated effort to conceal it had been made. It was wrapped in a crumbling newspaper dated Oct. 31, 1872; but there was an inner wrapping of dried skin—evidently the hide of some unknown reptile—which bore a Low Latin message in the same crabbed writing as that of the notebooks I found. As I had thought, the lock and key were vastly older than the vault. Old Claes van der Heyl had them ready for something he or his descendants meant to do—and how much older than he they were I could not estimate. Deciphering the Latin message, I trembled in a fresh access of clutching terror and nameless awe.

"The secrets of the monstrous primal Ones," ran the crabbed text, "whose cryptic words relate the hidden things that were before man; the things no one of earth should learn, lest peace be forever forfeited; shall by me never suffer revelation. To Yian-Ho, that lost and forbidden city of countless aeons whose place may not be told, I have been in the veritable flesh of this body, as none other among the living has been. Therein have I found, and thence have I borne away, that knowledge which I would gladly lose, though I may not. I have learnt to bridge a gap that should not be bridged, and must call out of the earth That Which should not be waked or called. And what is sent to follow me will not sleep till I or those after me have found and done what is to be found and done.

"That which I have awaked and borne away with me, I may not part with again. So is it written in the Book of Hidden Things. That which I have willed to be has twined its dreadful shape around me, and—if I live not to do the bidding—around those children born and unborn who shall come after me, until the bidding be done. Strange may be their joinings, and awful the aid they may summon till the end be reached. Into lands unknown and dim must the seeking go, and a house must be built for the outer Guardians.

"This is the key to that lock which was given me in the dreadful, aeon-old, and forbidden city of Yian-Ho; the lock which I or mine must place upon the vestibule of That Which is to be found. And may the Lords of Yaddith succour me—or him—who must set that lock in place or turn the key thereof."

Such was the message—a message which, once I had read it, I seemed to have known before. Now, as I write these words, the key is before me. I gaze on it with mixed dread and longing, and cannot find words to describe its aspect. It is of the same unknown, subtly greenish frosted metal as the lock; a metal best compared to brass tarnished with verdigris. Its design is alien and fantastic, and the coffin-shaped end of the ponderous bulk leaves no doubt of the lock it was meant to fit. The handle roughly forms a strange, non-human image, whose exact outlines and identity cannot now be traced. Upon holding it for any length of time I seem to feel an alien, anomalous *life* in the cold metal—a quickening or pulsing too feeble for ordinary recognition. Below the eidolon is graven a faint, aeon-worn legend in those blasphemous, Chinese-like hieroglyphs I have come to know so well. I can make out only the beginning—the words "my vengeance lurks"—before the text fades to indistinctness. There is some fatality in this timely finding of the key—*for tomorrow night comes the hellish Sabbat.* But strangely enough, amidst all this hideous expectancy, that question of the Sleght name bothers me more and more. Why should I dread to find it linked with the van der Heyls?

Walpurgis-Eve—April 30

The time has come. I waked last night to see the sky glowing with a lurid greenish radiance—that same morbid green which I have seen in the eyes and skin of certain portraits here, on the shocking lock and key, on the monstrous menhirs of the hill, and in a thousand other recesses of my consciousness. There were strident whispers in the air—sibilant whistlings like those of the wind around that dreadful cromlech. Something spoke to me out of the frore aether of space, and it said, "The hour falls." It is an omen, and I laugh at my own fears. Have I not the dread words and the Seven Lost Signs of Terror—the power coercive of any Dweller in the cosmos or in the unknown darkened spaces? I will no longer hesitate.

The heavens are very dark, as if a terrific storm were coming on—a storm even greater than that of the night when I reached here, nearly a fortnight ago. From the village—less than a mile away—I hear a queer and unwonted babbling. It is as I thought—these poor degraded idiots are within the secret, and keep the awful Sabbat on the hill. Here in the house the shadows gather densely. In the darkness the key before me almost glows with a greenish light of its own. I have not yet been to the cellar. It is better that I wait, lest the sound of that muttering and padding—those slitherings and muffled reverberations—unnerve me before I can unlock the fateful door.

Of what I shall encounter, and what I must do, I have only the most *general* idea. Shall I find my task in the vault itself, or must I burrow deeper into the nighted heart of our planet? There are things I do not yet understand—or at least, prefer not to understand—despite a dreadful, increasing, and inexplicable sense of bygone familiarity with this fearsome house. That chute, for instance, leading down from the little locked room. But I think I know why the wing with the vault extends toward the hill.

6 p.m.

Looking out the north windows, I can see a group of villagers on the hill. They seem unaware of the lowering sky, and are digging near the great central menhir. It occurs to me that they are working on that stone-rimmed hollow place which looks like a long-choked tunnel entrance. What is to come? How much of the olden Sabbat rites have these people retained? That key glows horribly—it is not imagination. Dare I use it as it must be used? Another matter has greatly disturbed me. Glancing nervously through a book in the library I came upon an ampler form of the name that has teased my memory so sorely: Trintje, wife of Adriaen Sleght. The *Adriaen* leads me to the very brink of recollection.

Midnight

Horror is unleashed, but I must not weaken. The storm has broken with pandaemoniac fury, and lightning has struck the hill three times, yet the hybrid, malformed villagers are gathering within the cromlech. I can see them in the almost constant flashes. The great standing stones loom up shockingly, and have a dull green luminosity that reveals them even when the lightning is not there. The peals of thunder are deafening, and every one seems to be horribly *answered* from some indeterminate direction. As I write, the creatures on the hill have begun to chant and howl and scream in a degraded, half-simian version of the ancient ritual. Rain pours down like a flood, yet they leap and emit sounds in a kind of diabolic ecstasy.

"Iä! Shub-Niggurath! The Goat with a Thousand Young!"

But the worst thing is within the house. Even at this height, I have begun to hear sounds from the cellar. *It is the padding and muttering and slithering and muffled reverberations within the vault. . . .*

Memories come and go. That name of Adriaen Sleght pounds oddly at my consciousness. Dirck van der Heyl's son-in-law—his child old Dirck's granddaughter and Abaddon Corey's great-granddaughter. . . .

Later

Merciful God! *At last I know where I saw that name.* I know, and am transfixed with horror. All is lost. . . .

The key has begun to feel warm as my left hand nervously clutches it. At times that vague quickening or pulsing is so distinct that I can almost feel the living metal move. It came from Yian-Ho for a terrible purpose, and to me—who all too late know the thin stream of van der Heyl blood that trickles down through the Sleghts into my own lineage—has descended the hideous task of fulfilling that purpose. . . .

My courage and curiosity wane. I know the horror that lies beyond that iron door. What if Claes van der Heyl was my ancestor—need I expiate his nameless sin? *I will not—I swear I will not!* . . .

[*Writing here grows indistinct*]

Too late—cannot help self—black paws materialise—am dragged away toward the cellar. . . .

Secondary Revisions

Sonia H. Greene

The Horror at Martin's Beach

I have never heard an even approximately adequate explanation of the horror at Martin's Beach. Despite the large number of witnesses, no two accounts agree; and the testimony taken by local authorities contains the most amazing discrepancies.

Perhaps this haziness is natural in view of the unheard-of character of the horror itself, the almost paralytic terror of all who saw it, and the efforts made by the fashionable Wavecrest Inn to hush it up after the publicity created by Prof. Alton's article "Are Hypnotic Powers Confined to Recognized Humanity?"

Against all these obstacles I am striving to present a coherent version; for I beheld the hideous occurrence, and believe it should be known in view of the appalling possibilities it suggests. Martin's Beach is once more popular as a watering-place, but I shudder when I think of it. Indeed, I cannot look at the ocean at all now without shuddering.

Fate is not always without a sense of drama and climax, hence the terrible happening of August 8, 1922, swiftly followed a period of minor and agreeably wonder-fraught excitement at Martin's Beach. On May 17 the crew of the fishing smack *Alma* of Gloucester, under Capt. James P. Orne, killed, after a battle of nearly forty hours, a marine monster whose size and aspect produced the greatest possible stir in scientific circles and caused certain Boston naturalists to take every precaution for its taxidermic preservation.

The object was some fifty feet in length, of roughly cylindrical shape, and about ten feet in diameter. It was unmistakably a gilled fish in its major affiliations; but with certain curious modifications, such as rudimentary forelegs and six-toed feet in place of pectoral fins, which prompted the widest speculation. Its extraordinary mouth, its thick and scaly hide, and its single, deep-set eye were wonders scarcely less remarkable than its colossal dimensions; and when the naturalists pronounced it an infant organism, which could not have been hatched more than a few days, public interest mounted to extraordinary heights.

Capt. Orne, with typical Yankee shrewdness, obtained a vessel large enough to hold the object in its hull, and arranged for the exhibition of his prize. With judicious carpentry he prepared what amounted to an excellent marine museum, and, sailing south to the wealthy resort district of Martin's Beach, anchored at the hotel wharf and reaped a harvest of admission fees.

The intrinsic marvelousness of the object, and the importance which it clearly bore in the minds of many scientific visitors from near and far, combined to make it the season's sensation. That it was absolutely unique—unique to a scientifically revolutionary degree—was well understood. The naturalists had shown plainly that it radically differed from the similarly immense fish caught off the Florida coast; that, while it was obviously an inhabitant of almost incredible depths, perhaps thousands of feet, its brain and principal organs indicated a development startlingly vast, and out of all proportion to anything hitherto associated with the fish tribe.

On the morning of July 20 the sensation was increased by the loss of the vessel and its strange treasure. In the storm of the preceding night it had broken from its moorings and vanished forever from the sight of man, carrying with it the guard who had slept aboard despite the threatening weather. Capt. Orne, backed by extensive scientific interests and aided by large numbers of fishing boats from Gloucester, made a thorough and exhaustive searching cruise, but with no result other than the prompting of interest and conversation. By August 7 hope was abandoned, and Capt. Orne had returned to the Wavecrest Inn to wind up his business affairs at Martin's Beach and confer with certain of the scientific men who remained there. The horror came on August 8.

It was in the twilight, when grey sea-birds hovered low near the shore and a rising moon began to make a glittering path across the waters. The scene is important to remember, for every impression counts. On the beach were several strollers and a few late bathers; stragglers from the distant cottage colony that rose modestly on a green hill to the north, or from the adjacent cliff-perched Inn whose imposing towers proclaimed its allegiance to wealth and grandeur.

Well within viewing distance was another set of spectators, the loungers on the Inn's high-ceiled and lantern-lighted veranda, who appeared to be enjoying the dance music from the sumptuous ballroom inside. These spectators, who included Capt. Orne and his group of scientific confreres, joined the beach group before the horror progressed far; as did many more from the Inn. Certainly there was no lack of witnesses, confused though their stories be with fear and doubt of what they saw.

There is no exact record of the time the thing began, although a majority say that the fairly round moon was "about a foot" above the low-lying vapors of the horizon. They mention the moon because what they saw seemed subtly connected with it—a sort of stealthy, deliberate, menacing ripple which rolled in from the far skyline along the shimmering lane of reflected moonbeams, yet which seemed to subside before it reached the shore.

Many did not notice this ripple until reminded by later events; but it seems to have been very marked, differing in height and motion from the normal waves around it. Some called it *cunning* and *calculating*. And as it died away craftily by the black reefs afar out, there suddenly came belching up out of the glitter-streaked brine a cry of death; a scream of anguish and despair that moved pity even while it mocked it.

First to respond to the cry were the two life guards then on duty; sturdy fellows in white bathing attire, with their calling proclaimed in large red letters across their chests. Accustomed as they were to rescue work, and to the screams of the drowning, they could find nothing familiar in the unearthly ululation; yet with a trained sense of duty they ignored the strangeness and proceeded to follow their usual course.

Hastily seizing an air-cushion, which with its attached coil of rope lay always at hand, one of them ran swiftly along the shore to the scene of the gathering crowd; whence, after whirling it about to gain momentum, he flung the hollow disc far out in the direction from which the sound had come. As the cushion disappeared in the waves, the crowd curiously awaited a sight of the hapless being whose distress had been so great; eager to see the rescue made by the massive rope.

But that rescue was soon acknowledged to be no swift and easy matter; for, pull as they might on the rope, the two muscular guards could not move the object at the other end. Instead, they found that object pulling with equal or even greater force in the very opposite direction, till in a few seconds they were dragged off their feet and into the water by the strange power which had seized on the proffered life-preserver.

One of them, recovering himself, called immediately for help from the crowd on the shore, to whom he flung the remaining coil of rope; and in a moment the guards were seconded by all the hardier men, among whom Capt. Orne was foremost. More than a dozen strong hands were now tugging desperately at the stout line, yet wholly without avail.

Hard as they tugged, the strange force at the other end tugged harder; and since neither side relaxed for an instant, the rope became rigid as steel with the enormous strain. The struggling participants, as well as the spectators, were by this time consumed with curiosity as to the nature of the force in the sea. The idea of a drowning man had long been dismissed; and hints of whales, submarines, monsters, and demons now passed freely around. Where humanity had first led the rescuers, wonder kept them at their task; and they hauled with a grim determination to uncover the mystery.

It being decided at last that a whale must have swallowed the air-cushion, Capt. Orne, as a natural leader, shouted to those on shore that a boat must be obtained in order to approach, harpoon, and land the unseen leviathan. Several men at once prepared to scatter in quest of a suitable craft, while others came to supplant the captain at the straining rope, since his place was logically with whatever boat party might be formed. His own idea of the situation was very broad, and by no means limited to whales, since he had to do with a monster so much stranger. He wondered what might be the acts and manifestations of an adult of the species of which the fifty-foot creature had been the merest infant.

And now there developed with appalling suddenness the crucial fact which changed the entire scene from one of wonder to one of horror, and dazed with fright the assembled band of toilers and onlookers. Capt. Orne, turning to leave his post at the rope, found his hands held in their place with unaccountable strength; and in a moment he realized that he was unable to let go of the rope. His plight was instantly divined, and as each companion tested his own situation the same condition was encountered. The fact could not be denied—every struggler was irresistibly held in some mysterious bondage to the hempen line which was slowly, hideously, and relentlessly pulling them out to sea.

Speechless horror ensued; a horror in which the spectators were petrified to utter inaction and mental chaos. Their complete demoralization is reflected in the conflicting accounts they give, and the sheepish excuses they offer for their seemingly callous inertia. I was one of them, and know.

Even the strugglers, after a few frantic screams and futile groans, succumbed to the paralyzing influence and kept silent and fatalistic in the face of unknown powers. There they stood in the pallid moonlight, blindly pulling against a spectral doom and swaying monotonously backward and forward as the water rose first to their knees, then to their hips. The moon went partly under a cloud, and in the half-light the line of swaying men resembled some sinister and gigantic centipede, writhing in the clutch of a terrible creeping death.

Harder and harder grew the rope, as the tug in both directions increased, and the strands swelled with the undisturbed soaking of the rising waves. Slowly the tide advanced, till the sands so lately peopled by laughing children and whispering lovers were now swallowed by the inexorable flow. The herd of panic-stricken watchers surged blindly backward as the water crept above their feet, while the frightful line of strugglers swayed hideously on, half submerged, and now at a substantial distance from their audience. Silence was complete.

The crowd, having gained a huddling-place beyond reach of the tide, stared in mute fascination; without offering a word of advice or encouragement, or attempting any kind of assistance. There was in the air a nightmare fear of impending evils such as the world had never before known.

Minutes seemed lengthened into hours, and still that human snake of swaying torsos was seen above the fast rising tide. Rhythmically it undulated; slowly, horribly, with the seal of doom upon it. Thicker clouds now passed over the ascending moon, and the glittering path on the waters faded nearly out.

Very dimly writhed the serpentine line of nodding heads, with now and then the livid face of a backward-glancing victim gleaming pale in the darkness. Faster and faster gathered the clouds, till at length their angry rifts shot down sharp tongues of febrile flame. Thunders rolled, softly at first, yet soon increasing to a deafening, maddening intensity. Then came a culminating crash—a shock whose reverberations seemed to shake land and sea alike—and on its heels a cloudburst whose drenching violence overpowered the darkened world as if the heavens themselves had opened to pour forth a vindictive torrent.

The spectators, instinctively acting despite the absence of conscious and coherent thought, now retreated up the cliff steps to the hotel veranda. Rumors had reached the guests inside, so that the refugees found a state of terror nearly equal to their own. I think a few frightened words were uttered, but cannot be sure.

Some, who were staying at the Inn, retired in terror to their rooms; while others remained to watch the fast sinking victims as the line of bobbing heads showed above the mounting waves in the fitful lightning flashes. I recall thinking of those heads, and the bulging eyes they must contain; eyes that might well reflect all the fright, panic, and delirium of a malignant universe—all the sorrow, sin, and misery, blasted hopes and unfulfilled desires, fear, loathing and anguish of the ages since time's beginning; eyes alight with all the soul-racking pain of eternally blazing infernos.

And as I gazed out beyond the heads, my fancy conjured up still another eye; a single eye, equally alight, yet with a purpose so revolting to my brain that the vision soon passed. Held in the clutches of an unknown vise, the line of the damned dragged on; their silent screams and unuttered prayers known only to the demons of the black waves and the night-wind.

There now burst from the infuriate sky such a mad cataclysm of satanic sound that even the former crash seemed dwarfed. Amidst a blinding glare of descending fire the voice of heaven resounded with the blasphemies of hell, and the mingled agony of all the lost reverberated in one apocalyptic, planet-rending peal of Cyclopean din. It was the end of the storm, for with uncanny suddenness the rain ceased and the moon once more cast her pallid beams on a strangely quieted sea.

There was no line of bobbing heads now. The waters were calm and deserted, and broken only by the fading ripples of what seemed to be a whirlpool far out in the path of the moonlight whence the strange cry had first come. But as I looked along that treacherous lane of silvery sheen, with fancy fevered and senses overwrought, there trickled upon my ears from some abysmal sunken waste the faint and sinister echoes of a laugh.

C. M. Eddy, Jr.

Ashes

"Hello, Bruce. Haven't seen you in a dog's age. Come in."

I threw open the door, and he followed me into the room. His gaunt, ungainly figure sprawled awkwardly into the chair I indicated, and he twirled his hat between nervous fingers. His deepset eyes wore a worried, hunted look, and he glanced furtively around the room as if searching for a hidden something which might unexpectedly pounce upon him. His face was haggard and colorless. The corners of his mouth twitched spasmodically.

"What's the matter, old man? You look as if you'd seen a ghost. Brace up!" I crossed to the buffet, and poured a small glass of wine from the decanter. "Drink this!"

He downed it with a hasty gulp, and took to toying with his hat again.

"Thanks, Prague—I don't feel quite myself tonight."

"You don't look it, either! What's wrong?"

Malcolm Bruce shifted uneasily in his chair.

I eyed him in silence for a moment, wondering what could possibly affect the man so strongly. I knew Bruce as a man of steady nerves and iron will. To find him so visibly upset was, in itself, unusual. I passed cigars, and he selected one, automatically.

It was not until the second cigar had been lighted that Bruce broke the silence. His nervousness was apparently gone. Once more he was the dominant, self-reliant figure I knew of old.

"Prague," he began, "I've just been through the most devilish, gruesome experience that ever befell a man. I don't know whether I dare tell it or not, for fear you'll think I've gone crazy—and I wouldn't blame you if you did! But it's true, every word of it!"

He paused, dramatically, and blew a few rings of smoke in the air.

I smiled. Many a weird tale I had listened to over that self-same table. There must have been some kink in my personality that inspired confidence, for I had been told stories that some men would have given years of their life to have heard. And yet, despite my love of the bizarre and the dangerous, and my longing to explore far reaches of little-known lands, I had been doomed to a life of prosaic, flat, uneventful business.

"Do you happen to have heard of Professor Van Allister?" asked Bruce.

"You don't mean Arthur Van Allister?"

"The same! Then you *know* him?"

"I should say so! Known him for years. Ever since he resigned as Professor of Chemistry at the College so he could have more time for his experiments. Why, I even helped him choose the plans for that sound-proof laboratory of his, on the top floor of his home. Then he got so busy with his confounded experiments he couldn't find time to be chummy!"

"You may recall, Prague, that when we were in college together, I used to dabble quite a bit in chemistry?"

I nodded, and Bruce continued:

"About four months ago I found myself out of a job. Van Allister advertised for an assistant, and I answered. He remembered me from college days, and I managed to convince him I knew enough about chemistry to warrant a trial.

"He had a young lady doing his secretarial work—a Miss Marjorie Purdy. She was one of these strict-attention-to-business types, and as good-looking as she was efficient. She had been helping Van Allister a bit in his laboratory, and I soon discovered she took a genuine interest in puttering around, making experiments of her own. Indeed, she spent nearly all her spare time with us in the laboratory.

"It was only natural that such companionship should result in a close friendship, and it wasn't long before I began to depend on her to help me in difficult experiments when the Professor was busy. I never could seem to stump her. That girl took to chemistry as a duck takes to water!

"About two months ago Van Allister had the laboratory partitioned off, and made a separate workroom for himself. He told us that he was about to enter upon a series of experiments which, if successful, would bring him everlasting fame. He flatly refused to make us his confidants in any way, shape, or manner.

"From that time on, Miss Purdy and I were left alone more and more. For days at a time the Professor would retire to the seclusion of his new workshop, sometimes not even appearing for his meals.

"That meant, too, that we had more spare time on our hands. Our friendship ripened. I felt a growing admiration for the trim young woman who seemed perfectly content to fuss around smelly bottles and sticky messes, gowned in white from head to foot, even to the rubber gloves she wore.

"Day before yesterday Van Allister invited us into his workshop.

"'At last I have achieved success,' he announced, holding up for our inspection a small bottle containing a colorless liquid. 'I have here what will rank as the greatest chemical discovery ever known. I am going to prove its efficacy right before your eyes. Bruce, will you bring me one of the rabbits, please?'

"I went back into the other room and brought him one of the rabbits we kept, together with guinea pigs, for experimental purposes.

"He put the little animal into a small glass box just large enough to hold it, and closed the cover. Then he set a glass funnel in a hole in the top of the box, and we drew nearer to watch the experiment.

"He uncorked the bottle, and poised it above the rabbit's prison.

"'Now to prove whether my weeks of effort have resulted in success or failure!'

"Slowly, methodically, he emptied the contents of the bottle into the funnel, and we watched it trickle into the compartment with the frightened animal.

"Miss Purdy uttered a suppressed cry, and I rubbed my eyes to make sure that they had not deceived me. For, in the case where but a moment before there had been a live, terrified rabbit, *there was now nothing but a pile of soft, white ashes!*

"Professor Van Allister turned to us with an air of supreme satisfaction. His face radiated ghoulish glee and his eyes were alight with a weird, insane gleam. When he spoke, his voice took on a tone of mastery.

"'Bruce—and you, too, Miss Purdy—it has been your privilege to witness the first successful trial of a preparation that will revolutionize the world. It will instantaneously reduce to a fine ash anything with which it comes into contact, except glass! Just think what that means. An army equipped with glass bombs filled with my compound could annihilate the world! Wood, metal, stone, brick—*everything*—swept away before them; leaving no more trace than the rabbit I have just experimented upon—just a pile of soft, white ashes!'

"I glanced at Miss Purdy. Her face had gone as white as the apron she wore.

"We watched Van Allister as he transferred all that was left of the bunny to a small bottle, and neatly labeled it. I'll admit that I was suffering a mental chill myself by the time he dismissed me, and we left him alone behind the tightly closed doors of his workshop.

"Once safely outside, Miss Purdy's nerves gave way completely. She reeled, and would have fallen had I not caught her in my arms.

"The feel of her soft, yielding body held close to my own was the last straw. I cast prudence to the winds and crushed her tightly to my breast. Kiss after kiss I pressed upon her full red lips, until her eyes opened and I saw the lovelight reflected in them.

"After a delicious eternity we came back to earth again—long enough to realize that the laboratory was no place for such ardent demonstrations. At any moment Van Allister might come out of his retreat, and if he should discover our love-making—in his present state of mind—we dared not think of what might happen.

"For the rest of the day I was like a man in a dream. It's a wonder to me that I succeeded in accomplishing anything at all. My body was merely an automaton, a well-trained machine, going about its appointed tasks, while my mind soared into far-away realms of delightful day-dreaming.

"Marjorie kept busy with her secretarial work for the rest of the day, and not once did I lay eyes upon her until my tasks in the laboratory were completed.

"That night we gave over to the joys of our new-found happiness. Prague, I shall remember that night as long as I live! The happiest moment I have ever known was when Marjorie Purdy promised to become my wife.

"Yesterday was another day of unalloyed bliss. All day long my sweetheart and I worked side by side. Then followed another night of love-making. If you've never been in love with the only girl in the world, Prague, you can't understand the delirious joy that comes from the very thought of her! And Marjorie returned my devotion a hundred-fold. She gave herself unreservedly into my keeping.

"Along about noontime, today, I needed something to complete an experiment, and I stepped over to the drug store for it.

"When I returned I missed Marjorie. I looked for her hat and coat, and they were gone. The Professor had not shown himself since the experiment upon the rabbit, and was locked in his workshop.

"I asked the servants, but none of them had seen her leave the house, nor had she left any message for me.

"As the afternoon wore on I grew frantic. Evening came, and still no sign of my dear little girl.

"All thought of work was forgotten. I paced the floor of my room like a caged lion. Every jangle of the 'phone or ring at the door bolstered up my faltering hopes of some word from her, but each time I was doomed to disappointment. Each minute seemed an hour; each hour an eternity!

"Good God, Prague! You can't imagine how I suffered! From the heights of sublime love I mentally plunged to the darkest depths of despair. I conjured visions of all sorts of terrible fates overtaking her. Still, not a word did I hear.

"It seemed to me that I had lived a lifetime, but my watch told me it was only half-past seven when the butler told me that Van Allister wanted me in the laboratory.

"I was in no mood for experiments, but while I was under his roof he was my master, and it was for me to obey.

"The Professor was in his workshop, the door slightly ajar. He called to me to close the door of the laboratory and join him in the little room.

"In my present state of mind my brain photographed every minute detail of the scene which met my eyes. In the center of the room, on a marble-top table, was a glass case about the shape and size of a coffin. It was filled almost to the brim with that same colorless liquid which the small bottle had contained, two days before.

"At the left, on a glass-top tabourette, was a newly labeled glass jar. I could not repress an involuntary shudder as I realized that it was filled with soft, white ashes. Then I saw something that almost made my heart stop beating!

"On a chair, in a far corner of the workshop, was the hat and coat of the girl who had pledged her life to mine—the girl whom I had vowed to cherish and protect while life should last!

"My senses were numbed, my soul surcharged with horror, as realization flashed over me. There could be but one explanation. *The ashes in that jar were the ashes of Marjorie Purdy!*

"The world stood still for one long, terrible moment, and then I went mad—stark, staring mad!

"The next I can remember, the Professor and I were locked in a desperate struggle. Old as he was, he still possessed a strength nearly equal to mine, and he had the added advantage of calm self-possession.

"Closer and closer he forced me to the glass coffin. A few moments more and my ashes would join those of the girl I had loved. I stumbled against the tabourette, and my fingers closed over the jar of ashes. With one, last, superhuman effort, I raised it high above my head, and brought it down with crushing force upon the skull of my antagonist! His arm relaxed, his limp form dropped in a senseless heap to the floor.

"Still acting upon impulse, I raised the silent form of the Professor and carefully, lest I should spill some of it on the floor, lowered the body into the casket of death!

"A moment, and it was over. Professor and liquid, both, were gone, and in their place was a little pile of soft, white ashes!

"As I gazed at my handiwork the brainstorm passed away, and I came face to face with the cold, hard truth that I had killed a fellow-being. An unnatural calm possessed me. I knew that there was not a single shred of evidence against me, barring the fact that I was the last one known to be alone with the Professor. Nothing remained but ashes!

"I put on my hat and coat, told the butler that the Professor had left word he was not to be disturbed, and that I was going out for the evening. Once outside, all my self-possession vanished. My nerves were shot to pieces. I don't know where I went—only that I wandered aimlessly, here and there, until I found myself outside your apartment just a little while ago.

"Prague, I felt as if I must talk with someone; that I must unburden my tortured mind. I knew that I could trust you, old pal, so I've told you the whole story. Here I am—do with me as you will. Life holds nothing more for me, now that—Marjorie—is gone!"

Bruce's voice trembled with emotion and broke as he mentioned the name of the girl he loved.

I leaned across the table, and gazed searchingly into the eyes of the abject figure that slouched dejectedly in the big chair. Then I rose, put on my hat and coat, crossed to Bruce, who had buried his head in his hands, and was shaking with silent sobs.

"Bruce!"

Malcolm Bruce raised his eyes.

"Bruce, listen to me. *Are you sure Marjorie Purdy is dead?*"

"Am I sure that—" His eyes widened at the suggestion, and he sat erect with a sudden start.

"Exactly," I went on. "Are you positive that the ashes in that jar were the ashes of Marjorie Purdy?"

"Why—I—see here, Prague! What are you driving at?"

"Then you're *not* sure. You saw the girl's hat and coat in that chair, and in your state of mind you jumped at conclusions. 'The ashes must be those of the missing girl. . . . The Professor must have made away with her. . . .' and all that. Come now, did Van Allister *tell* you anything—"

"I don't know what he said. I tell you I went *berserk*—mad!"

"Then you come along with me. If she's not dead, she must be somewhere in that house, and if she *is* there, we're going to find her!"

On the street we hailed a taxi, and in a few moments the butler admitted us to Van Allister's home. Bruce let us into the laboratory with his key. The door of the workshop was still ajar.

My eyes swept the room in a comprehensive survey. At the left, over near the window, was a closed door. I strode across the room and tried the knob, but it refused to yield.

"Where does that lead?"

"Just an anteroom, where the Professor keeps his apparatus."

"All the same, that door's coming open," I returned, grimly. Stepping back a pace or two, I planted a well-directed kick upon the door. Another, and still another, and the frame-work around the lock gave way.

Bruce, with an inarticulate cry, sped across the room to a huge mahogany chest. He selected one of the keys on his ring, inserted it in the lock, and flung back the cover with trembling hands.

"Here she is, Prague—quick! Get her out where there's air!"

Together we bore the limp figure of the girl into the laboratory. Bruce hastily mixed a concoction which he forced between her lips. A second dose, and her eyes slowly opened.

Her bewildered glance traveled around the room, at last resting on Bruce, and her eyes lighted with sudden, happy recognition. Later, after the first few moments of reunion, the girl told us her story:

"After Malcolm went out, this afternoon, the Professor sent word to me to come into the workshop. As he often summoned me to do some errand or other, I thought nothing of it, and to save time, took my hat and coat along. He closed the door of the little room, and, without warning, attacked me from behind. He overpowered me, tied me hand and foot. It was needless to gag me. As you know, the laboratory is absolutely sound-proof.

"Then he produced a huge Newfoundland dog he had secured from somewhere or other, reduced it to ashes before my very eyes, and put the ashes in a glass jar that was on a tabourette in the workshop.

"He went into the anteroom and, from the chest where you found me, took out the glass casket. At least, it seemed a casket to my terror-stricken eyes! He mixed enough of his horrible liquid to fill it almost to the brim.

"Then he told me that but one thing remained. That was—to perform the experiment upon a human being!" She shuddered at the recollection. "He dilated at length upon what a privilege it would be for anyone to sacrifice his life in such a manner, for such a cause. Then he calmly informed me that he had selected you as the subject of his experiment, and that I was to play the role of witness! I fainted.

"The Professor must have feared some sort of intrusion, for the next I remember is waking inside the chest where you discovered me. It was stifling! Every breath I took came harder and harder. I thought of you, Malcolm—thought of the wonderful, happy hours we had spent together the last few days. I wondered what I would do when you were gone! I even prayed that he would kill me, too! My throat grew parched and dry—everything went black before my eyes.

"Next, I opened them to find myself here—with you, Malcolm," her voice sank to a hoarse, nervous whisper. "Where—where is the Professor?"

Bruce silently led her into the workshop. She shivered as the coffin of glass came within her range of vision. Still silently, he crossed directly to the casket, and, taking up a handful of the soft, white ashes, let them sift slowly through his fingers!

C. M. Eddy, Jr.

The Ghost-Eater

I.

Moon-madness? A touch of fever? I wish I could think so! But when I am alone after dark in the waste places where my wanderings take me, and hear across infinite voids the demon echoes of those screams and snarls, and that detestable crunching of bones, I shudder again at the memory of that eldritch night.

I knew less of woodcraft in those days, though the wilderness called just as strongly to me as it does now. Up to that night I had always been careful to employ a guide, but circumstances now suddenly forced me to a trial of my own skill. It was midsummer in Maine, and, despite my great need to get from Mayfair to Glendale by the next noon, I could find no person willing to pilot me. Unless I took the long route through Potowisset, which would not bring me to my goal in time, there would be dense forests to penetrate; yet whenever I asked for a guide I was met with refusal and evasion.

Stranger that I was, it seemed odd that everyone should have glib excuses. There was too much "important business" on hand for such a sleepy village, and I knew that the natives were lying. But they all had "imperative duties", or said that they had; and would do no more than assure me that the trail through the woods was very plain, running due north, and not in the least difficult for a vigorous young fellow. If I started while the morning was still early, they averred, I could get to Glendale by sundown and avoid a night in the open. Even then I suspected nothing. The prospect seemed good, and I resolved to try it alone, let the lazy villagers hang back as they might. Probably I would have tried it even if I had suspected; for youth is stubborn, and from childhood I had only laughed at superstition and old wives' tales.

So before the sun was high I had started off through the trees at a swinging stride, lunch in my hand, guardian automatic in my pocket, and belt filled with crisp bills of large denominations. From the distances given me and a knowledge of my own speed, I had figured on making Glendale a little after sunset; but I knew that even if detained over night through some miscalculation, I had plenty of camping experience to fall back on. Besides, my presence at my destination was not really necessary till the following noon.

It was the weather that set my plans awry. As the sun rose higher, it scorched through even the thickest of the foliage, and burned up my energy at every step. By noon my clothes were soaking with perspiration, and I felt myself faltering in spite of all my resolution. As I pushed deeper into the woods I found the trail greatly obstructed with underbrush, and at many points nearly effaced. It must have been weeks—perhaps months—since anyone had broken his way through; and I began to wonder if I could, after all, live up to my schedule.

At length, having grown very hungry, I looked for the deepest patch of shade I could find, and proceeded to eat the lunch which the hotel had prepared for me. There were some indifferent sandwiches, a piece of stale pie, and a bottle of very light wine; by no means sumptuous fare, but welcome enough to one in my state of overheated exhaustion.

It was too hot for smoking to be of any solace, so I did not take out my pipe. Instead, I stretched myself at full length under the trees when my meal was done, intent on stealing a few moments' rest before commencing the last lap of my journey. I suppose I was a fool to drink that wine; for, light though it was, it proved just enough to finish the work the sultry, oppressive day had begun. My plan called for the merest momentary relaxation, yet, with scarcely a warning yawn, I dropped off into a sound slumber.

II.

When I opened my eyes twilight was closing in about me. A wind fanned my cheeks, restoring me quickly to full perception; and as I glanced up at the sky I saw with apprehension that black racing clouds were leading on a solid wall of darkness prophetic of violent thunderstorm. I knew now that I could not reach Glendale before morning, but the prospect of a night in the woods—my first night of lone forest camping—became very repugnant under these trying conditions. In a moment I decided to push along for a while at least, in the hope of finding some shelter before the tempest should break.

Darkness spread over the woods like a heavy blanket. The lowering clouds grew more threatening, and the wind increased to a veritable gale. A flash of distant lightning illuminated the sky, followed by an ominous rumble that seemed to hint of malign pursuit. Then I felt a drop of rain on my outstretched hand; and though still walking on automatically, resigned myself to the inevitable. Another moment and I had seen the light; the light of a window through the trees and the darkness. Eager only for shelter, I hastened toward it—would to God I had turned and fled!

There was a sort of imperfect clearing, on the farther side of which, with its back against the primeval wood, stood a building. I had expected a shanty or log-cabin, but stopped short in surprise when I beheld a neat and tasteful little house of two stories; some seventy years old by its architecture, yet still in a state of repair betokening the closest and most civilized attention. Through the small panes of one of the lower windows a bright light shone, and toward this—spurred by the impact of another raindrop—I presently hurried across the clearing, rapping loudly on the doors as soon as I gained the steps.

With startling promptness my knock was answered by a deep, pleasant voice which uttered the single syllable, "Come!"

Pushing open the unlocked door, I entered a shadowy hall lighted by an open doorway at the right, beyond which was a book-lined room with the gleaming window. As I closed the outer door behind me I could not help noticing a peculiar odor about the house; a faint, elusive, scarcely definable odor which somehow suggested animals. My host, I surmised, must be a hunter or trapper, with his business conducted on the premises.

The man who had spoken sat in a capacious easy-chair beside a marble-topped center table, a long lounging-robe of gray swathing his lean form. The light from a powerful argand lamp threw his features into prominence, and as he eyed me curiously I studied him in no less detail. He was strikingly handsome, with thin, clean-shaven face, glossy, flaxen hair neatly brushed, long, regular eyebrows that met in a slanting angle above the nose, shapely ears set low and well back on the head, and large expressive gray eyes almost luminous in their animation. When he smiled a welcome he showed a magnificently even set of firm white teeth, and as he waved me to a chair I was struck by the fineness of his slender hands, with their long, tapering fingers whose ruddy, almond-shaped nails were slightly curved and exquisitely manicured. I could not help wondering why a man of such engaging personality should choose the life of a recluse.

"Sorry to intrude," I ventured, "but I've given up the hope of making Glendale before morning, and there's a storm coming on which sent me looking for cover." As if to corroborate my words, there came at this point a vivid flash, a crashing reverberation, and the first breaking of a torrential downpour that beat maniacally against the windows.

My host seemed oblivious to the elements, and flashed me another smile when he answered. His voice was soothing and well modulated, and his eyes held a calmness almost hypnotic.

"You're welcome to whatever hospitality I can offer, but I'm afraid it won't be much. I've a game leg, so you'll have to do most of the waiting on yourself. If you're hungry you'll find plenty in the kitchen—plenty of food, if not of ceremony!" It seemed to me that I could detect the slightest trace of a foreign accent in his tone, though his language was fluently correct and idiomatic.

Rising to an impressive height, he headed for the door with long, limping steps, and I noticed the huge hairy arms that hung at his side in such curious contrast with his delicate hands.

"Come," he suggested. "Bring the lamp along with you. I might as well sit in the kitchen as here."

I followed him into the hall and the room across it, and at his direction ransacked the woodpile in the corner and the cupboard on the wall. A few moments later, when the fire was going nicely, I asked him if I might not prepare food for both; but he courteously declined.

"It's too hot to eat," he told me. "Besides, I had a bite before you came."

After washing the dishes left from my lone meal, I sat down for a while, smoking my pipe contentedly. My host asked a few questions about the neighboring villages, but lapsed into sullen taciturnity when he learned I was an outsider. As he brooded there silently I could not help feeling a quality of strangeness in him; some subtle alienage that could hardly be analyzed. I was quite certain, for one thing, that he was tolerating me because of the storm rather than welcoming me with genuine hospitality.

As for the storm, it seemed almost to have spent itself. Outside, it was already growing lighter—for there was a full moon behind the clouds—and the rain had dwindled to a trivial drizzle. Perhaps, I thought, I could now resume my journey after all; an idea which I suggested to my host.

"Better wait till morning," he remarked. "You say you're afoot, and it's a good three hours to Glendale. I've two bedrooms upstairs, and you're welcome to one of them if you care to stay."

There was a sincerity in his invitation which dispelled any doubts I had held regarding his hospitality, and I now concluded that his silences must be the result of long isolation from his fellows in this wilderness. After sitting without a word through three fillings of my pipe, I finally began to yawn.

"It's been rather a strenuous day for me," I admitted, "and I guess I'd better be making tracks for bed. I want to be up at sunrise, you know, and on my way."

My host waved his arm toward the door, through which I could see the hall and the staircase.

"Take the lamp with you," he instructed. "It's the only one I have, but I don't mind sitting in the dark, really. Half the time I don't light it at all when I'm alone. Oil is so hard to get out here, and I go to the village so seldom. Your room is the one on the right, at the head of the stairs."

Taking the lamp and turning in the hall to say good-night, I could see his eyes glowing almost phosphorescently in the darkened room I had left; and I was half reminded for a moment of the jungle, and the circles of eyes that sometimes glow just beyond the radius of the campfire. Then I started upstairs.

As I reached the second floor I could hear my host limping across the hall to the other room below, and perceived that he moved with owlish sureness despite the darkness. Truly, he had but little need of the lamp. The storm was over, and as I entered the room assigned me I found it bright with the rays of a full moon that streamed on the bed from an uncurtained south window. Blowing out the lamp and leaving the house in darkness but for the moonbeams, I sniffed at the pungent odor that rose above the scent of the kerosene—the quasi-animal odor I had noticed on first entering the place. I crossed to the window and threw it wide, breathing deep of the cool, fresh night air.

When I started to undress I paused almost instantly, recalling my money belt, still in its place about my waist. Possibly, I reflected, it would be well not to be too hasty or unguarded; for I had read of men who seized just such an opportunity to rob and even to murder the stranger within their dwelling. So, arranging the bedclothes to look as if they covered a sleeping figure, I drew the room's only chair into the concealing shadows, filled and lighted my pipe again, and sat down to rest or watch, as the occasion might demand.

III.

I could not have been sitting there long when my sensitive ears caught the sound of footsteps ascending the stairs. All the old lore of robber landlords rushed on me afresh, when another moment revealed that the steps were plain, loud, and careless, with no attempt at concealment; while my host's tread, as I had heard it from the head of the staircase, was a soft limping stride. Shaking the ashes from my pipe, I slipped it in my pocket. Then, seizing and drawing my automatic, I rose from the chair, tiptoed across the room, and crouched tensely in a spot which the opening door would cover.

The door opened, and into the shaft of moonlight stepped a man I had never seen before. Tall, broad-shouldered, and distinguished, his face half hidden by a heavy square-cut beard and his neck buried in a high black stock of a pattern long obsolete in America, he was indubitably a foreigner. How he could have entered the house without my knowledge was quite beyond me, nor could I believe for an instant that he had been concealed in either of the two rooms or the hall below me. As I gazed intently at him in the insidious moonbeams it seemed to me that I could see directly through his sturdy form; but perhaps this was only an illusion that came from my shock of surprise.

Noticing the disarray of the bed, but evidently missing the intended effect of occupancy, the stranger muttered something to himself in a foreign tongue and proceeded to disrobe. Flinging his clothes into the chair I had vacated, he crept into bed, pulled the covers over him, and in a moment or two was breathing with the regular respiration of a sound sleeper.

My first thought was to seek out my host and demand an explanation, but a second later I deemed it better to make sure that the whole incident was not a mere delusive after-effect of my wine-drugged sleep in the woods. I still felt weak and faint, and despite my recent supper was as hungry as if I had not eaten since that noonday lunch.

I crossed to the bed, reached out, and grasped at the shoulder of the sleeping man. Then, barely checking a cry of mad fright and dizzy astonishment, I fell back with pounding pulses and dilated eyes. *For my clutching fingers had passed directly through the sleeping form, and seized only the sheet below!*

A complete analysis of my jarred and jumbled sensations would be futile. The man was intangible, yet I could still see him there, hear his regular breathing, and watch his figure as it half turned beneath the clothes. And then, as I was quite certain of my own madness or hypnosis, I heard other footsteps on the stairs; soft, padded, doglike, limping footsteps, pattering up, up, up. . . . And again that pungent animal smell, this time in redoubled volume. Dazed and dream-drowsed, I crept once more behind the protecting opened door, shaken to the marrow, but now resigned to any fate known or nameless.

Then into that shaft of eerie moonlight stepped the gaunt form of a great gray wolf. Limped, I should have said, for one hind foot was held in the air, as though wounded by some stray shot. The beast turned its head in my direction, and as it did so the pistol dropped from my twitching fingers and clattered unheeded to the floor. The ascending succession of horrors was fast paralyzing my will and consciousness, *for the eyes that now glared toward me from that hellish head were the gray phosphorescent eyes of my host as they had peered at me through the darkness of the kitchen.*

I do not yet know whether it saw me. The eyes turned from my direction to the bed, and gazed gluttonously on the spectral sleeping form there. Then the head tilted back, and from that demon throat came the most shocking ululation I have ever heard; a thick, nauseous, lupine howl that made my heart stand still. The form on the bed stirred, opened his eyes, and shrank from what he saw. The animal crouched quivering, and then—as the ethereal figure uttered a shriek of mortal human anguish and terror that no ghost of legend could counterfeit—sprang straight for its victim's throat, its white, firm, even teeth flashing in the moonlight as they closed on the jugular vein of the screaming phantasm. The scream ended in a blood-choked gurgle, and the frightened human eyes turned glassy.

That scream had roused me to action, and in a second I had retrieved my automatic and emptied its entire contents into the wolfish monstrosity before me. *But I heard the unhindered thud of each bullet as it imbedded itself in the opposite wall.*

My nerves gave way. Blind fear hurled me toward the door, and blind fear prompted the one backward glance in which I saw that the wolf had sunk its teeth into the body of its quarry. Then came that culminating sensory impression and the devastating thought to which it gave birth. This was the same body I had thrust my hand *through* a few moments before . . . and yet as I plunged down that black nightmare staircase *I could hear the crunching of bones.*

IV.

How I found the trail to Glendale, or how I managed to traverse it, I suppose I shall never know. I only know that sunrise found me on the hill at the edge of the woods, with the steepled village outspread below me, and the blue thread of the Cataqua sparkling in the distance. Hatless, coatless, ashen-faced, and as soaked with perspiration as if I had spent the night abroad in the storm, I hesitated to enter the village till I had recovered at least some outward semblance of composure. At last I picked my way down hill and through the narrow streets with their flagstone sidewalks and Colonial doorways till I reached the Lafayette House, whose proprietor eyed me askance.

"Where from so early, son? And why the wild look?"

"I've just come through the woods from Mayfair."

"You—came—through—the Devil's Woods—*last night*—and—*alone?*" The old man stared with a queer look of alternate horror and incredulity.

"Why not?" I countered. "I couldn't have made it in time through Potowisset, and I had to be here not later than this noon."

"And last night was *full moon!* . . . My Gawd!" He eyed me curiously. "See anything of Vasili Oukranikov or the Count?"

"Say, do I look that simple? What are you trying to do—jolly me?"

But his tone was as grave as a priest's as he replied. "You must be new to these parts, sonny. If you weren't you'd know all about Devil's Woods and the full moon and Vasili and the rest."

I felt anything but flippant, yet knew I must not seem serious after my earlier remarks. "Go on—I know you're dying to tell me. I'm like a donkey—all ears."

Then he told the legend in his dry way, stripping it of vitality and convincingness through lack of coloring, detail, and atmosphere. But for me it needed no vitality or convincingness that any poet could have given. Remember what I had witnessed, and remember that I had never heard of the tale until *after* I had had the experience and fled from the terror of those crunched phantom bones.

"There used to be quite a few Russians scattered betwixt here and Mayfair—they came after one of their nihilist troubles back in Russia. Vasili Oukranikov was one of 'em—a tall, thin, handsome chap with shiny yellow hair and a wonderful manner. They said, though, that he was a servant of the devil—a werewolf and eater of men.

"He built him a house in the woods about a third of the way from here to Mayfair and lived all alone. Every once in a while a traveler would come out of the woods with some pretty strange tale about being chased by a big wolf with shining human eyes—like Oukranikov's. One night somebody took a pot shot at the wolf, and the next time the Russian came into Glendale he walked with a limp. That settled it. There wasn't any mere suspicion now, but hard facts.

"Then he sent to Mayfair for the Count—his name was Feodor Tchernevsky and he had bought the old gambrel-roofed Fowler place up State Street—to come out and see him. They all warned the Count, for he was a fine man and a splendid neighbor, but he said he could take care of himself all right. It was the night of the full moon. He was brave as they make 'em, and all he did was to tell some men he had around the place to follow him to Vasili's if he didn't show up in decent time. They did—and you tell me, sonny, that you've been through those woods at night?"

"Sure I tell you"—I tried to appear nonchalant—"I'm no Count, and here I am to tell the tale! . . . But what did the men find at Oukranikov's house?"

"They found the Count's mangled body, sonny, and a gaunt gray wolf hovering over it with blood-slavering jaws. You can guess who the wolf was. And folks do say that at every full moon—but sonny, didn't you see or hear anything?"

"Not a thing, pop! And say, what became of the wolf—or Vasili Oukranikov?"

"Why, son, they killed it—filled it full of lead and buried it in the house, and then burned the place down—you know all this was sixty years ago when I was a little shaver, but I remember it as if 'twas yesterday."

I turned away with a shrug of my shoulders. It was all so quaint and silly and artificial in the full light of day. But sometimes when I am alone after dark in waste places, and hear the demon echoes of those screams and snarls, and that detestable crunching of bones, I shudder again at the memory of that eldritch night.

C. M. Eddy, Jr.

The Loved Dead

It is midnight. Before dawn they will find me and take me to a black cell where I shall languish interminably, while insatiable desires gnaw at my vitals and wither up my heart, till at last I become one with the dead that I love.

My seat is the foetid hollow of an aged grave; my desk is the back of a fallen tombstone worn smooth by devastating centuries; my only light is that of the stars and a thin-edged moon, yet I can see as clearly as though it were mid-day. Around me on every side, sepulchral sentinels guarding unkempt graves, the tilting, decrepit headstones lie half-hidden in masses of nauseous, rotting vegetation. Above the rest, silhouetted against the livid sky, an august monument lifts its austere, tapering spire like the spectral chieftain of a lemurian horde. The air is heavy with the noxious odors of fungi and the scent of damp, mouldy earth, but to me it is the aroma of Elysium. It is still—terrifyingly still—with a silence whose very profundity bespeaks the solemn and the hideous. Could I choose my habitation it would be in the heart of some such city of putrefying flesh and crumbling bones; for their nearness sends ecstatic thrills through my soul, causing the stagnant blood to race through my veins and my torpid heart to pound with delirious joy—for the presence of death is life to me!

My early childhood was one long, prosaic, and monotonous apathy. Strictly ascetic, wan, pallid, undersized, and subject to protracted spells of morbid moroseness, I was ostracized by the healthy, normal youngsters of my own age. They dubbed me a spoil-sport, an "old woman", because I had no interest in the rough, childish games they played, or any stamina to participate in them, had I so desired.

Like all rural villages, Fenham had its quota of poison-tongued gossips. Their prying imaginations hailed my lethargic temperament as some abhorrent abnormality; they compared me with my parents and shook their heads in ominous doubt at the vast difference. Some of the more superstitious openly pronounced me a changeling, while others who knew something of my ancestry called attention to the vague mysterious rumors concerning a great-great-grand uncle who had been burned at the stake as a necromancer.

Had I lived in some larger town, with greater opportunities for congenial companionship, perhaps I could have overcome this early tendency to be a recluse. As I reached my teens I grew even more sullen, morbid, and apathetic. My life lacked motivation. I seemed in the grip of something that dulled my senses, stunted my development, retarded my activities, and left me unaccountably dissatisfied.

I was sixteen when I attended my first funeral. A funeral in Fenham was a pre-eminent social event, for our town was noted for the longevity of its inhabitants. When, moreover, the funeral was that of such a well-known character as my grandfather, it was safe to assume that the townspeople would turn out en masse to pay due homage to his memory. Yet I did not view the approaching ceremony with even latent interest. Anything that tended to lift me out of my habitual inertia held for me only the promise of physical and mental disquietude. In deference to my parents' importunings, mainly to give myself relief from their caustic condemnations of what they chose to call my unfilial attitude, I agreed to accompany them.

There was nothing out of the ordinary about my grandfather's funeral unless it was the voluminous array of floral tributes; but this, remember, was my initiation to the solemn rites of such an occasion. Something about the darkened room, the oblong coffin with its somber drapings, the banked masses of fragrant blooms, the dolorous manifestations of the assembled villagers, stirred me from my normal listlessness and arrested my attention. Roused from my momentary reverie by a nudge from my mother's sharp elbow, I followed her across the room to the casket where the body of my grandparent lay.

For the first time I was face to face with Death. I looked down upon the calm placid face lined with its multitudinous wrinkles, and saw nothing to cause so much of sorrow. Instead, it seemed to me that grandfather was immeasurably content, blandly satisfied. I felt swayed by some strange discordant sense of elation. So slowly, so stealthily had it crept over me, that I could scarcely define its coming. As I mentally review that portentous hour it seems that it must have originated with my first glimpse of that funeral scene, silently strengthening its grip with subtle insidiousness. A baleful malignant influence that seemed to emanate from the corpse itself held me with magnetic fascination. My whole being seemed charged with some ecstatic electrifying force, and I felt my form straighten without conscious volition. My eyes were trying to burn beneath the closed lids of the dead man's and read some secret message they concealed. My heart gave a sudden leap of unholy glee, and pounded against my ribs with demoniacal force as if to free itself from the confining walls of my frail frame. Wild, wanton, soul-satisfying sensuality engulfed me. Once more the vigorous prod of a maternal elbow jarred me into activity. I had made my way to the sable-shrouded coffin with leaden tread; I walked away with new-found animation.

I accompanied the cortege to the cemetery, my whole physical being permeated with this mystic enlivening influence. It was as if I had quaffed deep draughts of some exotic elixir—some abominable concoction brewed from blasphemous formulae in the archives of Belial.

The townsfolk were so intent upon the ceremony that the radical change in my demeanor passed unnoticed by all save my father and my mother; but in the fortnight that followed, the village busybodies found fresh material for their vitriolic tongues in my altered bearing. At the end of the fortnight, however, the potency of the stimulus began to lose its effectiveness. Another day or two and I had completely reverted to my old-time languor, though not to the complete and engulfing insipidity of the past. Before, there had been an utter lack of desire to emerge from the enervation; now vague and indefinable unrest disturbed me. Outwardly I had become myself again, and the scandal-mongers turned to some more engrossing subject. Had they even so much as dreamed the true cause of my exhilaration they would have shunned me as if I were a filthy, leprous thing. Had I visioned the execrable power behind my brief period of elation I would have locked myself forever from the rest of the world and spent my remaining years in penitent solitude.

Tragedy often runs in trilogies, hence despite the proverbial longevity of our townspeople the next five years brought the death of both parents. My mother went first, in an accident of the most unexpected nature; and so genuine was my grief that I was honestly surprised to find its poignancy mocked and contradicted by that almost forgotten feeling of supreme and diabolical ecstasy. Once more my heart leaped wildly within me, once more it pounded at trip-hammer speed and sent the hot blood coursing through my veins with meteoric fervor. I shook from my shoulders the harassing cloak of stagnation only to replace it with the infinitely more horrible burden of loathsome, unhallowed desire. I haunted the death-chamber where the body of my mother lay, my soul athirst for the devilish nectar that seemed to saturate the air of the darkened room. Every breath strengthened me, lifted me to towering heights of seraphic satisfaction. I knew, now, that it was but a sort of drugged delirium which must soon pass and leave me correspondingly weakened by its malign power, yet I could no more control my longing than I could untwist the Gordian knots in the already tangled skein of my destiny.

I knew, too, that through some strange Satanic curse my life depended upon the dead for its motive force; that there was a singularity in my makeup which responded only to the awesome presence of some lifeless clod. A few days later, frantic for the bestial intoxicant on which the fullness of my existence depended, I interviewed Fenham's sole undertaker and talked him into taking me on as a sort of apprentice.

The shock of my mother's demise had visibly affected my father. I think that if I had broached the idea of such outré employment at any other time he would have been emphatic in his refusal. As it was he nodded acquiescence after a moment's sober thought. How little did I dream that he would be the object of my first practical lesson!

He, too, died suddenly; developing some hitherto unsuspected heart affliction. My octogenarian employer tried his best to dissuade me from the unthinkable task of embalming his body, nor did he detect the rapturous glint in my eyes as I finally won him over to my damnable point of view. I cannot hope to express the reprehensible, the unutterable thoughts that swept in tumultuous waves of passion through my racing heart as I labored over the lifeless clay. Unsurpassed love was the keynote of these concepts, a love greater—far greater—than any I had ever borne him while he was alive.

My father was not a rich man, but he had possessed enough of worldly goods to make him comfortably independent. As his sole heir I found myself in rather a paradoxical position. My early youth had totally failed to fit me for contact with the modern world, yet the primitive life of Fenham with its attendant isolation palled upon me. Indeed, the longevity of the inhabitants defeated my sole motive in arranging my indenture.

After settling the estate it proved an easy matter to secure my release and I headed for Bayboro, a city some fifty miles away. Here my year of apprenticeship stood me in good stead. I had no trouble in establishing a favorable connection as an assistant with the Gresham Corporation, a concern that maintained the largest funeral parlors in the city. I even prevailed upon them to let me sleep upon the premises—for already the proximity of the dead was becoming an obsession.

I applied myself to my task with unwonted zeal. No case was too gruesome for my impious sensibilities, and I soon became master at my chosen vocation. Every fresh corpse brought into the establishment meant a fulfilled promise of ungodly gladness, of irreverent gratification; a return of that rapturous tumult of the arteries which transformed my grisly task into one of beloved devotion—yet every carnal satiation exacted its toll. I came to dread the days that brought no dead for me to gloat over, and prayed to all the obscene gods of the nethermost abysses to bring swift, sure death upon the residents of the city.

Then came the nights when a skulking figure stole surreptitiously through the shadowy streets of the suburbs; pitch-dark nights when the midnight moon was obscured by heavy lowering clouds. It was a furtive figure that blended with the trees and cast fugitive glances over its shoulder; a figure bent on some malignant mission. After one of these prowlings the morning papers would scream to their sensation-mad clientele the details of some nightmare crime; column on column of lurid gloating over abominable atrocities; paragraph on paragraph of impossible solutions and extravagant, conflicting suspicions. Through it all I felt a supreme sense of security, for who would for a moment suspect an employee in an undertaking establishment, where Death was supposedly an every-day affair, of seeking surcease from unnamable urgings in the cold-blooded slaughter of his fellow-beings? I planned each crime with maniacal cunning, varying the manner of my murders so that no one would even dream that all were the work of one blood-stained pair of hands. The aftermath of each nocturnal venture was an ecstatic hour of pleasure, pernicious and unalloyed; a pleasure always heightened by the chance that its delicious source might later be assigned to my gloating administrations in the course of my regular occupation. Sometimes that double and ultimate pleasure did occur—O rare and delicious memory!

During long nights when I clung to the shelter of my sanctuary, I was prompted by the mausolean silence to devise new and unspeakable ways of lavishing my affections upon the dead that I loved—the dead that gave me life!

One morning Mr. Gresham came much earlier than usual—came to find me stretched out upon a cold slab deep in ghoulish slumber, my arms wrapped about the stark, stiff, naked body of a foetid corpse! He roused me from my salacious dreams, his eyes filled with mingled detestation and pity. Gently but firmly he told me that I must go, that my nerves were unstrung, that I needed a long rest from the repellent tasks my vocation required, that my impressionable youth was too deeply affected by the dismal atmosphere of my environment. How little did he know of the demoniacal desires that spurred me on in my disgusting infirmities! I was wise enough to see that argument would only strengthen his belief in my potential madness—it was far better to leave than to invite discovery of the motive underlying my actions.

After this I dared not stay long in one place for fear some overt act would bare my secret to an unsympathetic world. I drifted from city to city, from town to town. I worked in morgues, around cemeteries, once in a crematory—anywhere that afforded me an opportunity to be near the dead that I so craved.

Then came the world war. I was one of the first to go across, one of the last to return. Four years of blood-red charnel Hell . . . sickening slime of rain-rotten trenches . . . deafening bursting of hysterical shells . . . monotonous droning of sardonic bullets . . . smoking frenzies of Phlegethon's fountains . . . stifling fumes of murderous gases . . . grotesque remnants of smashed and shredded bodies . . . four years of transcendent satisfaction.

In every wanderer there is a latent urge to return to the scenes of his childhood. A few months later found me making my way through the familiar byways of Fenham. Vacant dilapidated farm houses lined the adjacent roadsides, while the years had brought equal retrogression to the town itself. A mere handful of the houses were occupied, but among these was the one I had once called home. The tangled, weed-choked driveway, the broken window panes, the uncared-for acres that stretched behind, all bore mute confirmation of the tales that guarded inquiries had elicited—that it now sheltered a dissolute drunkard who eked out a meager existence from the chores his few neighbors gave him out of sympathy for the mistreated wife and undernourished child who shared his lot. All in all, the glamour surrounding my youthful environment was entirely dispelled; so, prompted by some errant foolhardy thought, I next turned my steps toward Bayboro.

Here, too, the years had brought changes, but in reverse order. The small city I remembered had almost doubled in size despite its wartime depopulation. Instinctively I sought my former place of employment, finding it still there but with an unfamiliar name and "Successor to" above the door, for the influenza epidemic had claimed Mr. Gresham, while the boys were overseas. Some fateful mood impelled me to ask for work. I referred to my tutelage under Mr. Gresham with some trepidation, but my fears were groundless —my late employer had carried the secret of my unethical conduct with him to the grave. An opportune vacancy insured my immediate re-installation.

Then came vagrant haunting memories of scarlet nights of impious pilgrimages, and an uncontrollable desire to renew those illicit joys. I cast caution to the winds and launched upon another series of damnable debaucheries. Once more the yellow sheets found welcome material in the devilish details of my crimes, comparing them to the red weeks of horror that had appalled the city years before. Once more the police sent out their dragnet and drew into its enmeshing folds—nothing!

My thirst for the noxious nectar of the dead grew to a consuming fire, and I began to shorten the periods between my odious exploits. I realized that I was treading on dangerous ground, but demoniac desire gripped me in its torturing tentacles and urged me on.

All this time my mind was becoming more and more benumbed to any influence except the satiation of my insane longings. Little details vitally important to one bent on such evil escapades escaped me. Somehow, somewhere, I left a vague trace, an elusive clue, behind—not enough to warrant my arrest, but sufficient to turn the tide of suspicion in my direction. I sensed this espionage, yet was helpless to stem the surging demand for more dead to quicken my enervated soul.

Then came the night when the shrill whistle of the police roused me from my fiendish gloating over the body of my latest victim, a gory razor still clutched tightly in my hand. With one dexterous motion I closed the blade and thrust it into the pocket of the coat I wore. Nightsticks beat a lusty tattoo upon the door. I crashed the window with a chair, thanking Fate I had chosen one of the cheaper tenement districts for my locale. I dropped into a dingy alley as blue-coated forms burst through the shattered door. Over shaky fences, through filthy back yards, past squalid ramshackle houses, down dimly lighted narrow streets I fled. I thought at once of the wooded marshes that lay beyond the city and stretched for half a hundred miles till they touched the outskirts of Fenham. If I could reach this goal I would be temporarily safe. Before dawn I was plunging headlong through the foreboding wasteland, stumbling over the rotting roots of half-dead trees whose naked branches stretched out like grotesque arms striving to encumber me with mocking embraces.

The imps of the nefarious gods to whom I offered my idolatrous prayers must have guided my footsteps through that menacing morass. A week later, wan, bedraggled, and emaciated, I lurked in the woods a mile from Fenham. So far I had eluded my pursuers, yet I dared not show myself, for I knew that the alarm must have been sent broadcast. I vaguely hoped I had thrown them off the trail. After that first frenetic night I had heard no sound of alien voices, no crashing of heavy bodies through the underbrush. Perhaps they had concluded that my body lay hidden in some stagnant pool or had vanished forever in the tenacious quagmire.

Hunger gnawed at my vitals with poignant pangs, thirst left my throat parched and dry. Yet far worse was the unbearable hunger of my starving soul for the stimulus I found only in the nearness of the dead. My nostrils quivered in sweet recollection. No longer could I delude myself with the thought that this desire was a mere whim of the heated imagination. I knew now that it was an integral part of life itself; that without it I should burn out like an empty lamp. I summoned all my remaining energy to fit me for the task of satisfying my accursed appetite. Despite the peril attending my move I set out to reconnoiter, skirting the sheltering shadows like an obscene wraith. Once more I felt that strange sensation of being led by some unseen satellite of Satan. Yet even my sin-steeped soul revolted for a moment when I found myself before my native abode, the scene of my youthful hermitage.

Then these disquieting memories faded. In their place came overwhelming lustful desire. Behind the rotting walls of this old house lay my prey. A moment later I had raised one of the shattered windows and climbed over the sill. I listened for a moment, every sense alert, every muscle tensed for action. The silence reassured me. With cat-like tread I stole through the familiar rooms until stertorous snores indicated the place where I was to find surcease from my sufferings. I allowed myself a sigh of anticipatory ecstasy as I pushed open the door of the bedchamber. Panther-like I made my way to the supine form stretched out in drunken stupor. The wife and child—where were they?—well, they could wait. My clutching fingers groped for his throat. . . .

Hours later I was again the fugitive, but a new-found stolen strength was mine. Three silent forms slept to wake no more. It was not until the garish light of day penetrated my hiding-place that I visualized the certain consequences of my rashly purchased relief. By this time the bodies must have been discovered. Even the most obtuse of the rural police must surely link the tragedy with my flight from the nearby city. Besides, for the first time I had been careless enough to leave some tangible proof of my identity—my fingerprints on the throats of the newly dead. All day I shivered in nervous apprehension. The mere crackling of a dry twig beneath my feet conjured mental images that appalled me. That night, under cover of the protecting darkness I skirted Fenham and made for the woods that lay beyond. Before dawn came the first definite hint of renewed pursuit—the distant baying of hounds.

Through the long night I pressed on, but by morning I could feel my artificial strength ebbing. Noon brought once more the insistent call of the contaminating curse, and I knew I must fall by the way unless I could once more experience that exotic intoxication that came only with the proximity of the loved dead. I had traveled in a wide semicircle. If I pushed steadily ahead, midnight would bring me to the cemetery where I had laid away my parents years before. My only hope, I felt certain, lay in reaching this goal before I was overtaken. With a silent prayer to the devils that dominated my destiny I turned leaden feet in the direction of my last stronghold.

God! Can it be that a scant twelve hours have passed since I started for my ghostly sanctuary? I have lived an eternity in each leaden hour. But I have reached a rich reward. The noxious odors of this neglected spot are frankincense to my suffering soul!

The first streaks of dawn are graying the horizon. They are coming! My sharp ears catch the far-off howling of the dogs! It is but a matter of minutes before they find me and shut me away forever from the rest of the world, to spend my days in ravaging yearnings till at last I join the dead I love!

They shall not take me! A way of escape is open! A coward's choice, perhaps, but better—far better—than endless months of nameless misery. I will leave this record behind me that some soul may perhaps understand why I make this choice.

The razor! It has nestled forgotten in my pocket since my flight from Bayboro. Its blood-stained blade gleams oddly in the waning light of the thin-edged moon. One slashing stroke across my left wrist and deliverance is assured. . . .

Warm, fresh blood spatters grotesque patterns on dingy, decrepit slabs . . . phantasmal hordes swarm over the rotting graves . . . spectral fingers beckon me . . . ethereal fragments of unwritten melodies rise in celestial crescendo . . . distant stars dance drunkenly in demoniac accompaniment . . . a thousand tiny hammers beat hideous dissonances on anvils inside my chaotic brain . . . gray ghosts of slaughtered spirits parade in mocking silence before me . . . scorching tongues of invisible flame sear the brand of Hell upon my sickened soul . . . I can—write—no—more. . . .

C. M. Eddy, Jr.

Deaf, Dumb, and Blind

A little after noon on the twenty-eighth day of June, 1924, Dr. Morehouse stopped his machine before the Tanner place and four men alighted. The stone building, in perfect repair and freshness, stood near the road, and but for the swamp in the rear it would have possessed no trace of dark suggestion. The spotless white doorway was visible across a trim lawn for some distance down the road; and as the doctor's party approached, it could be seen that the heavy portal yawned wide open. Only the screen door was closed. The proximity of the house had imposed a kind of nervous silence on the four men, for what lurked therein could only be imagined with vague terror. This terror underwent a marked abatement when the explorers heard distinctly the sound of Richard Blake's typewriter.

Less than an hour before, a grown man had fled from that house, hatless, coatless, and screaming, to fall upon the doorstep of his nearest neighbor, half a mile away, babbling incoherently of "house", "dark", "swamp", and "room". Dr. Morehouse had needed no further spur to excited action when told that a slavering, maddened creature had burst out of the old Tanner home by the edge of the swamp. He had known that something would happen when the two men had taken the accursed stone house—the man who had fled; and his master, Richard Blake, the author-poet from Boston, the genius who had gone into the war with every nerve and sense alert and had come out as he was now; still debonair though half a paralytic, still walking with song among the sights and sounds of living fantasy though shut forever from the physical world, deaf, dumb, and blind!

Blake had reveled in the weird traditions and shuddering hints about the house and its former tenants. Such eldritch lore was an imaginative asset from whose enjoyment his physical state might not bar him. He had smiled at the prognostications of the superstitious natives. Now, with his sole companion fled in a mad ecstasy of panic fright, and himself left helpless with whatever had caused that fright, Blake might have less occasion to revel and smile! This, at least, was Dr. Morehouse's reflection as he had faced the problem of the fugitive and called on the puzzled cottager to help him track the matter down. The Morehouses were an old Fenham family, and the doctor's grandfather had been one of those who burned the hermit Simeon Tanner's body in 1819. Not even at this distance could the trained physician escape a spinal tingle at what was recorded of that burning—at the naive inferences drawn by ignorant countrymen from a slight and meaningless conformation of the deceased. That tingle he knew to be foolish, for trifling bony protuberances on the fore part of the skull are of no significance, and often observable in bald-headed men.

Among the four men who ultimately set resolute faces toward that abhorrent house in the doctor's car, there occurred a singularly awed exchange of vague legends and half-furtive scraps of gossip handed down from curious grandmothers—legends and hints seldom repeated and almost never systematically compared. They extended as far back as 1692, when a Tanner had perished on Gallows Hill in Salem after a witchcraft trial, but did not grow intimate till the time the house was built—1747, though the ell was more recent. Not even then were the tales very numerous, for queer though the Tanners all were, it was only the last of them, old Simeon, whom people desperately feared. He added to what he had inherited—added horribly, everyone whispered—and bricked up the windows of the southeast room, whose east wall gave on the swamp. That was his study and library, and it had a door of double thickness with braces. It had been chopped through with axes that terrible winter night in 1819 when the stinking smoke had poured from the chimney and they found Tanner's body in there—with that expression on its face. It was because of that expression—not because of the two bony protuberances beneath the bushy white hair—that they had burned the body and the books and manuscripts it had had in that room. However, the short distance to the Tanner place was covered before much important historical matter could be correlated.

As the doctor, at the head of the party, opened the screen door and entered the arched hallway, it was noticed that the sound of typewriting had suddenly ceased. At this point two of the men also thought they noticed a faint effusion of cold air strangely out of keeping with the great heat of the day, though they afterward refused to swear to this. The hall was in perfect order, as were the various rooms entered in quest of the study where Blake was presumably to be found. The author had furnished his home in exquisite Colonial taste; and though having no help but the one manservant, he had succeeded in maintaining it in a state of commendable neatness.

Dr. Morehouse led his men from room to room through the wide-open doors and archways, at last finding the library or study which he sought—a fine southerly room on the ground floor adjoining the once-dreaded study of Simeon Tanner, lined with the books which the servant communicated through an ingenious alphabet of touches, and the bulky Braille volumes which the author himself read with sensitive finger-tips. Richard Blake, of course, was there, seated as usual before his typewriter with a draft-scattered stack of newly written pages on the table and floor, and one sheet still in the machine. He had stopped work, it appeared, with some suddenness; perhaps because of a chill which had caused him to draw together the neck of his dressing-gown; and his head was turned toward the doorway of the sunny adjoining room in a manner quite singular for one whose lack of sight and hearing shuts out all sense of the external world.

On drawing nearer and crossing to where he could see the author's face, Dr. Morehouse turned very pale and motioned to the others to stand back. He needed time to steady himself, and to dispel all possibility of hideous illusion. No longer did he need to speculate why they had burned old Simeon Tanner's body on that wintry night because of the *expression* it wore, for here was something only a well-disciplined mind could confront. The late Richard Blake, whose typewriter had ceased its nonchalant clicking only as the men had entered the house, had seen something despite his blindness, and had been affected by it. Humanity had nothing to do with the look that was on his face, or with the glassy morbid vision that blazed in great, blue, bloodshot eyes shut to this world's images for six years. Those eyes were fixed with an ecstasy of clear-sighted horror on the doorway leading to Simeon Tanner's old study, where the sun blazed on walls once shrouded in bricked-up blackness. And Dr. Arlo Morehouse reeled dizzily when he saw that for all the dazzling daylight the inky pupils of those eyes were dilated as cavernously as those of a cat's eyes in the dark.

The doctor closed the staring blind eyes before he let the others view the face of the corpse. Meanwhile he examined the lifeless form with feverish diligence, using scrupulous technical care, despite his throbbing nerves and almost shaking hands. Some of his results he communicated from time to time to the awed and inquisitive trio around him; other results he judiciously withheld, lest they lead to speculations more disquieting than human speculations should be. It was not from any word of his, but from shrewd independent observation, that one of the men muttered about the body's tousled black hair and the way the papers were scattered. This man said it was as if a strong breeze had blown through the open doorway which the dead man faced; whereas, although the once-bricked windows beyond were indeed fully open to the warm June air, there had been scarcely a breath of wind during the entire day.

When one of the men began to gather the sheets of newly written manuscript as they lay on floor and table, Dr. Morehouse stopped him with an alarmed gesture. He had seen the sheet that remained in the machine, and had hastily removed and pocketed it after a sentence or two blanched his face afresh. This incident prompted him to collect the scattered sheets himself, and stuff them bulkily into an inside pocket without stopping to arrange them. And not even what he had read terrified him half so much as what he now noticed—the subtle difference in touch and heaviness of typing which distinguished the sheets he picked up from the one he had found on the typewriter. This shadowy impression he could not divorce from that other horrible circumstance which he was so zealously concealing from the men who had heard the machine's clicking not ten minutes before—the circumstance he was trying to exclude from even his own mind till he could be alone and resting in the merciful depths of his Morris chair. One may judge of the fear he felt at that circumstance by considering what he braved to keep it suppressed. In more than thirty years of professional practice he had never regarded a medical examiner as one from whom a fact might be withheld; yet through all the formalities which now followed, no man ever knew that when he examined this staring, contorted, blind man's body he had seen at once *that death must have occurred at least half an hour before discovery.*

Dr. Morehouse presently closed the outer door and led the party through every corner of the ancient structure in search of any evidence which might directly illuminate the tragedy. Never was a result more completely negative. He knew that the trap-door of old Simeon Tanner had been removed as soon as that recluse's books and body had been burnt, and that the sub-cellar and the sinuous tunnel under the swamp had been filled up as soon as they were discovered, some thirty-five years later. Now he saw that no fresh abnormalities had come to replace them, and that the whole establishment exhibited only the normal neatness of modern restoration and tasteful care.

Telephoning for the sheriff at Fenham and for the county medical examiner at Bayboro, he awaited the arrival of the former, who, when he came, insisted on swearing in two of the men as deputies until the examiner should arrive. Dr. Morehouse, knowing the mystification and futility confronting the officials, could not help smiling wryly as he left with the villager whose house still sheltered the man who had fled.

They found the patient exceedingly weak, but conscious and fairly composed. Having promised the sheriff to extract and transmit all possible information from the fugitive, Dr. Morehouse began some calm and tactful questioning, which was received in a rational and compliant spirit and baffled only by effacement of memory. Much of the man's quiet must have come from merciful inability to recollect, for all he could now tell was that he had been in the study with his master and had seemed to see the next room suddenly grow dark—the room where sunshine had for more than a hundred years replaced the gloom of bricked-up windows. Even this memory, which indeed he half doubted, greatly disturbed the unstrung nerves of the patient, and it was with the utmost gentleness and circumspection that Dr. Morehouse told him his master was dead—a natural victim of the cardiac weakness which his terrible wartime injuries must have caused. The man was grieved, for he had been devoted to the crippled author; but he promised to show fortitude in taking the body back to the family in Boston after the close of the medical examiner's formal inquiry.

The physician, after satisfying as vaguely as possible the curiosity of the householder and his wife, and urging them to shelter the patient and keep him from the Tanner house until his departure with the body, next drove home in a growing tremble of excitement. At last he was free to read the typed manuscript of the dead man, and to gain at least an inkling of what hellish thing had defied those shattered senses of sight and sound and penetrated so disastrously to the delicate intelligence that brooded in external darkness and silence. He knew it would be a grotesque and terrible perusal, and he did not hasten to begin it. Instead, he very deliberately put his car in the garage, made himself comfortable in a dressing-gown, and placed a stand of sedative and restorative medicines beside the great chair he was to occupy. Even after that he obviously wasted time as he slowly arranged the numbered sheets, carefully avoiding any comprehensive glance at their text.

What the manuscript did to Dr. Morehouse we all know. It would never have been read by another had his wife not picked it up as he lay inert in his chair an hour later, breathing heavily and unresponsive to a knocking which one would have thought violent enough to arouse a mummied Pharaoh. Terrible as the document is, particularly in the obvious *change of style* near the end, we cannot avoid the belief that to the folklore-wise physician it presented some *added and supreme horror* which no other will ever be so unfortunate as to receive. Certainly, it is the general opinion of Fenham that the doctor's wide familiarity with the mutterings of old people and the tales his grandfather told him in youth furnished him some special information, in the light of which Richard Blake's hideous chronicle acquired a new, clear, and devastating significance nearly insupportable to the normal human mind. That would explain the slowness of his recovery on that June evening, the reluctance with which he permitted his wife and son to read the manuscript, the singular ill-grace with which he acceded to their determination not to burn a document so darkly remarkable, and most of all, the peculiar rashness with which he hastened to purchase the old Tanner property, destroy the house with dynamite, and cut down the trees of the swamp for a substantial distance from the road. Concerning the whole subject he now maintains an inflexible reticence, and it is certain that there will die with him a knowledge without which the world is better off.

The manuscript, as here appended, was copied through the courtesy of Floyd Morehouse, Esq., son of the physician. A few omissions, indicated by asterisks, have been made in the interest of the public peace of mind; still others have been occasioned by the indefiniteness of the text, where the stricken author's lightning-like touch-typing seems shaken into incoherence or ambiguity. In three places, where lacunae are fairly well elucidated by the context, the task of recension has been attempted. Of the *change in style* near the end it were best to say nothing. Surely it is plausible enough to attribute the phenomenon, as regards both content and physical aspect of typing, to the racked and tottering mind of a victim whose former handicaps had paled to nothing before that which he now faced. Bolder minds are at liberty to supply their own deductions.

Here, then, is the document, written in an accursed house by a brain closed to the world's sights and sounds—a brain left alone and unwarned to the mercies and mockeries of powers that no seeing, hearing man has ever stayed to face. Contradictory as it is to all that we know of the universe through physics, chemistry, and biology, the logical mind will classify it as a singular product of dementia—a dementia communicated in some sympathetic way to the man who burst out of that house in time. And thus, indeed, may it very well be regarded so long as Dr. Arlo Morehouse maintains his silence.

THE MANUSCRIPT

Vague misgivings of the last quarter hour are now becoming definite fears. To begin with, I am thoroughly convinced that something must have happened to Dobbs. For the first time since we have been together he has failed to answer my summons. When he did not respond to my repeated ringing I decided that the bell must be out of order, but I have pounded on the table with vigor enough to rouse a charge of Charon. At first I thought he might have slipped out of the house for a breath of fresh air, for it has been hot and sultry all the forenoon, but it is not like Dobbs to stay away so long without first making sure that I would want nothing. It is, however, the unusual occurrence of the last few minutes which confirms my suspicion that Dobbs's absence is a matter beyond his control. It is this same happening which prompts me to put my impressions and conjectures on paper in the hope that the mere act of recording them may relieve a certain sinister suggestion of impending tragedy. Try as I will, I cannot free my mind from the legends connected with this old house—mere superstitious fol-de-rol for dwarfed brains to revel in, and on which I would not even waste a thought if Dobbs were here.

Through the years that I have been shut away from the world I used to know, Dobbs has been my sixth sense. Now, for the first time since my incapacitation, I realize the full extent of my impotency. It is Dobbs who had compensated for my sightless eyes, my useless ears, my voiceless throat, and my crippled legs. There is a glass of water on my typewriter table. Without Dobbs to fill it when it has been emptied, my plight will be like that of Tantalus. Few have come to this house since we have lived here—there is little in common between garrulous country folk and a paralytic who cannot see, hear, or speak to them—it may be days before anyone else appears. Alone . . . with only my thoughts to keep me company; disquieting thoughts which have been in no wise assuaged by the sensations of the last few minutes. I do not like these sensations, either, for more and more they are converting mere village gossip into a fantastic imagery which affects my emotions in a most peculiar and almost unprecedented manner.

It seems hours since I started to write this, but I know it can be only a few minutes, for I have just inserted this fresh page into the machine. The mechanical action of switching the sheets, brief though it was, has given me a fresh grip on myself. Perhaps I can shake off this sense of approaching danger long enough to recount that which has already happened.

At first it was no more than a mere tremor, somewhat similar to the shivering of a cheap tenement block when a heavy truck rumbles close by the curb—but this is no loosely built frame structure. Perhaps I am supersensitive to such things, and it may be that I am allowing my imagination to play tricks; but it seemed to me that the disturbance was more pronounced directly in front of me—and my chair faces the southeast wing; away from the road, directly in line with the swamp at the rear of the dwelling! Delusion though this may have been, there is no denying what followed. I was reminded of moments when I have felt the ground tremble beneath my feet at the bursting of giant shells; times when I have seen ships tossed like chaff before the fury of a typhoon. The house shook like a Dweurgarian cinder in the sieves of Niflheim. Every timber in the floor beneath my feet quivered like a suffering thing. My typewriter trembled till I could imagine that the keys were chattering of their fear.

A brief moment and it was over. Everything is as calm as before. Altogether too calm! It seems impossible that such a thing could happen and yet leave everything exactly as it was before. No, not exactly—I am thoroughly convinced that something has happened to Dobbs! It is this conviction, added to this unnatural calm, which accentuates the premonitory fear that persists in creeping over me.

Fear? Yes—though I am trying to reason sanely with myself that there is nothing of which to be afraid. Critics have both praised and condemned my poetry because of what they term a vivid imagination. At such a time as this I can heartily agree with those who cry "too vivid". Nothing can be very much amiss or. . . .

Smoke! Just a faint sulfurous trace, but one which is unmistakable to my keenly attuned nostrils. So faint, indeed, that it is impossible for me to determine whether it comes from some part of the house or drifts through the window of the adjoining room, which opens on the swamp. The impression is rapidly becoming more clearly defined. I am sure, now, that it does not come from outside. Vagrant visions of the past, somber scenes of other days, flash before me in stereoscopic review. A flaming factory . . . hysterical screams of terrified women penned in by walls of fire; a blazing schoolhouse . . . pitiful cries of helpless children trapped by collapsing stairs, a theatre fire . . . frantic babel of panic-stricken people fighting to freedom over blistering floors; and, over all, impenetrable clouds of black, noxious, malicious smoke polluting the peaceful sky. The air of the room is saturated with thick, heavy, stifling waves . . . at any moment I expect to feel hot tongues of flame lick eagerly at my useless legs . . . my eyes smart . . . my ears throb . . . I cough and choke to rid my lungs of the Ocypetean fumes . . . smoke such as is associated only with appalling catastrophes . . . acrid, stinking, mephitic smoke permeated with the revolting odor of burning flesh***

Once more I am alone with this portentous calm. The welcome breeze that fans my cheeks is fast restoring my vanished courage. Clearly, the house cannot be on fire, for every vestige of the torturous smoke is gone. I cannot detect a single trace of it, though I have been sniffing like a bloodhound. I am beginning to wonder if I am going mad; if the years of solitude have unhinged my mind—but the phenomenon has been too definite to permit me to class it as mere hallucination. Sane or insane, I cannot conceive these things as aught but actualities—and the moment I catalogue them as such I can come to only one logical conclusion. The inference in itself is enough to upset one's mental stability. To concede this is to grant the truth of the superstitious rumors which Dobbs compiled from the villagers and transcribed for my sensitive finger-tips to read—unsubstantial hearsay that my materialistic mind instinctively condemns as asininity!

I wish the throbbing in my ears would stop! It is as if mad spectral players were beating a duet upon the aching drums. I suppose it is merely a reaction to the suffocating sensations I have just experienced. A few more deep drafts of this refreshing air . . .

Something—someone is in the room! I am as sure I am no longer alone as if I could see the presence I sense so infallibly. It is an impression quite similar to one which I have had while elbowing my way through a crowded street—the definite notion that eyes were singling me out from the rest of the throng with a gaze intense enough to arrest my subconscious attention—the same sensation, only magnified a thousandfold. Who—what—can it be? After all, my fears may be groundless, perhaps it means only that Dobbs has returned. No . . . it is not Dobbs. As I anticipated, the tattoo upon my ears has ceased and a low whisper has caught my attention . . . the overwhelming significance of the thing has just registered itself upon my bewildered brain . . . *I can hear!*

It is not a single whispering voice, but many! *** Lecherous buzzing of bestial blowflies . . . Satanic humming of libidinous bees . . . sibilant hissing of obscene reptiles . . . a whispering chorus no human throat could sing! It is gaining in volume . . . the room rings with demoniacal chanting; tuneless, toneless, and grotesquely grim . . . a diabolical choir rehearsing unholy litanies . . . paeans of Mephistophelian misery set to music of wailing souls . . . a hideous crescendo of pagan pandemonium ***

The voices that surround me are drawing closer to my chair. The chanting has come to an abrupt end and the whispering has resolved itself into intelligible sounds. I strain my ears to distinguish the words. Closer . . . and still closer. They are clear, now—too clear! Better had my ears been blocked forever than forced to listen to their hellish mouthings ***

Impious revelations of soul-sickening Saturnalia *** ghoulish conceptions of devastating debaucheries *** profane bribes of Cabirian orgies *** malevolent threats of unimagined punishments ***

It is cold. Unseasonably cold! As if inspired by the cacodemoniacal presences that harass me, the breeze that was so friendly a few minutes ago growls angrily about my ears—an icy gale that rushes in from the swamp and chills me to the bone.

If Dobbs has deserted me I do not blame him. I hold no brief for cowardice or craven fear, but there are some things *** I only hope his fate has been nothing worse than to have departed in time!

My last doubt is swept away. I am doubly glad, now, that I have held to my resolve to write down my impressions . . . not that I expect anyone to understand . . . or believe . . . it has been a relief from the maddening strain of idly waiting for each new manifestation of psychic abnormality. As I see it, there are but three courses that may be taken: to flee from this accursed place and spend the torturous years that lie ahead in trying to forget—but flee I *cannot;* to yield to an abominable alliance with forces so malign that Tartarus to them would seem but an alcove of Paradise—but yield I *will not;* to die—far rather would I have my body torn limb from limb than to contaminate my soul in barbarous barter with such emissaries of Belial ***

I have had to pause for a moment to blow upon my fingers. The room is cold with the foetid frigor of the tomb . . . a peaceful numbness is creeping over me . . . I must fight off this lassitude; it is undermining my determination to die rather than give in to the insidious importunings . . . I vow, anew, to resist until the end . . . the end that I know cannot be far away ***

The wind is colder than ever, if such a thing be possible . . . a wind freighted with the stench of dead-alive things *** O merciful God Who took my sight! *** a wind so cold it burns where it should freeze . . . it has become a blistering sirocco ***

Unseen fingers grip me . . . ghost fingers that lack the physical strength to force me from my machine . . . icy fingers that force me into a vile vortex of vice . . . devil-fingers that draw me down into a cesspool of eternal iniquity . . . death fingers that shut off my breath and make my sightless eyes feel they must burst with the pain *** frozen points press against my temples *** hard, bony knobs, akin to horns *** boreal breath of some long-dead thing kisses my fevered lips and sears my hot throat with frozen flame ***

It is dark *** not the darkness that is part of years of blindness *** the impenetrable darkness of sin-steeped night *** the pitch-black darkness of Purgatory ***

I see *** *spes mea Christus!* *** it is the end ***

****

Not for mortal mind is any resisting of force beyond human imagination. Not for immortal spirit is any conquering of that which hath probed the depths and made of immortality a transient moment. The end? Nay! It is but the blissful beginning. . . .

Wilfred Blanch Talman

Two Black Bottles

Not all of the few remaining inhabitants of Daalbergen, that dismal little village in the Ramapo Mountains, believe that my uncle, old Dominie Vanderhoof, is really dead. Some of them believe he is suspended somewhere between heaven and hell because of the old sexton's curse. If it had not been for that old magician, he might still be preaching in the little damp church across the moor.

After what has happened to me in Daalbergen, I can almost share the opinion of the villagers. I am not sure that my uncle is dead, but I am very sure that he is not alive upon this earth. There is no doubt that the old sexton buried him once, but he is not in that grave now. I can almost feel him behind me as I write, impelling me to tell the truth about those strange happenings in Daalbergen so many years ago.

It was the fourth day of October when I arrived at Daalbergen in answer to a summons. The letter was from a former member of my uncle's congregation, who wrote that the old man had passed away and that there should be some small estate which I, as his only living relative, might inherit. Having reached the secluded little hamlet by a wearying series of changes on branch railways, I found my way to the grocery store of Mark Haines, writer of the letter, and he, leading me into a stuffy back room, told me a peculiar tale concerning Dominie Vanderhoof's death.

"Y' should be careful, Hoffman," Haines told me, "when y' meet that old sexton, Abel Foster. He's in league with the devil, sure's you're alive. 'Twa'n't two weeks ago Sam Pryor, when he passed the old graveyard, heared him mumblin' t' the dead there. 'Twa'n't right he should talk that way—an' Sam does vow that there was a voice answered him—a kind o' half-voice, hollow and muffled-like, as though it come out o' th' ground. There's others, too, as could tell y' about seein' him standin' afore old Dominie Slott's grave—that one right agin' the church wall—a-wringin' his hands an' a-talkin' t' th' moss on th' tombstone as though it was the old Dominie himself."

Old Foster, Haines said, had come to Daalbergen about ten years before, and had been immediately engaged by Vanderhoof to take care of the damp stone church at which most of the villagers worshipped. No one but Vanderhoof seemed to like him, for his presence brought a suggestion almost of the uncanny. He would sometimes stand by the door when the people came to church, and the men would coldly return his servile bow while the women brushed past in haste, holding their skirts aside to avoid touching him. He could be seen on week days cutting the grass in the cemetery and tending the flowers around the graves, now and then crooning and muttering to himself. And few failed to notice the particular attention he paid to the grave of the Reverend Guilliam Slott, first pastor of the church in 1701.

It was not long after Foster's establishment as a village fixture that disaster began to lower. First came the failure of the mountain mine where most of the men worked. The vein of iron had given out, and many of the people moved away to better localities, while those who had large holdings of land in the vicinity took to farming and managed to wrest a meager living from the rocky hillsides. Then came the disturbances in the church. It was whispered about that the Reverend Johannes Vanderhoof had made a compact with the devil, and was preaching his word in the house of God. His sermons had become weird and grotesque—redolent with sinister things which the ignorant people of Daalbergen did not understand. He transported them back over ages of fear and superstition to regions of hideous, unseen spirits, and peopled their fancy with night-haunting ghouls. One by one the congregation dwindled, while the elders and deacons vainly pleaded with Vanderhoof to change the subject of his sermons. Though the old man continually promised to comply, he seemed to be enthralled by some higher power which forced him to do its will.

A giant in stature, Johannes Vanderhoof was known to be weak and timid at heart, yet even when threatened with expulsion he continued his eerie sermons, until scarcely a handful of people remained to listen to him on Sunday morning. Because of weak finances, it was found impossible to call a new pastor, and before long not one of the villagers dared venture near the church or the parsonage which adjoined it. Everywhere there was fear of those spectral wraiths with whom Vanderhoof was apparently in league.

My uncle, Mark Haines told me, had continued to live in the parsonage because there was no one with sufficient courage to tell him to move out of it. No one ever saw him again, but lights were visible in the parsonage at night, and were even glimpsed in the church from time to time. It was whispered about the town that Vanderhoof preached regularly in the church every Sunday morning, unaware that his congregation was no longer there to listen. He had only the old sexton, who lived in the basement of the church, to take care of him, and Foster made a weekly visit to what remained of the business section of the village to buy provisions. He no longer bowed servilely to everyone he met, but instead seemed to harbor a demoniac and ill-concealed hatred. He spoke to no one except as was necessary to make his purchases, and glanced from left to right out of evil-filled eyes as he walked the street with his cane tapping the uneven pavements. Bent and shriveled with extreme age, his presence could actually be felt by anyone near him, so powerful was that personality which, said the townspeople, had made Vanderhoof accept the devil as his master. No person in Daalbergen doubted that Abel Foster was at the bottom of all the town's ill luck, but not a one dared lift a finger against him, or could even approach him without a tremor of fear. His name, as well as Vanderhoof's, was never mentioned aloud. Whenever the matter of the church across the moor was discussed, it was in whispers; and if the conversation chanced to be nocturnal, the whisperers would keep glancing over their shoulders to make sure that nothing shapeless or sinister crept out of the darkness to bear witness to their words.

The churchyard continued to be kept just as green and beautiful as when the church was in use, and the flowers near the graves in the cemetery were tended just as carefully as in times gone by. The old sexton could occasionally be seen working there, as if still being paid for his services, and those who dared venture near said that he maintained a continual conversation with the devil and with those spirits which lurked within the graveyard walls.

One morning, Haines went on to say, Foster was seen digging a grave where the steeple of the church throws its shadow in the afternoon, before the sun goes down behind the mountain and puts the entire village in semi-twilight. Later, the church bell, silent for months, tolled solemnly for a half-hour. And at sundown those who were watching from a distance saw Foster bring a coffin from the parsonage on a wheelbarrow, dump it into the grave with slender ceremony, and replace the earth in the hole.

The sexton came to the village the next morning, ahead of his usual weekly schedule, and in much better spirits than was customary. He seemed willing to talk, remarking that Vanderhoof had died the day before, and that he had buried his body beside that of Dominie Slott near the church wall. He smiled from time to time, and rubbed his hands in an untimely and unaccountable glee. It was apparent that he took a perverse and diabolic delight in Vanderhoof's death. The villagers were conscious of an added uncanniness in his presence, and avoided him as much as they could. With Vanderhoof gone they felt more insecure than ever, for the old sexton was now free to cast his worst spells over the town from the church across the moor. Muttering something in a tongue which no one understood, Foster made his way back along the road over the swamp.

It was then, it seems, that Mark Haines remembered having heard Dominie Vanderhoof speak of me as his nephew. Haines accordingly sent for me, in the hope that I might know something which would clear up the mystery of my uncle's last years. I assured my summoner, however, that I knew nothing about my uncle or his past, except that my mother had mentioned him as a man of gigantic physique but with little courage or power of will.

Having heard all that Haines had to tell me, I lowered the front legs of my chair to the floor and looked at my watch. It was late afternoon.

"How far is it out to the church?" I inquired. "Think I can make it before sunset?"

"Sure, lad, y' ain't goin' out there t'night! Not t' that place!" The old man trembled noticeably in every limb and half rose from his chair, stretching out a lean, detaining hand. "Why, it's plumb foolishness!" he exclaimed.

I laughed aside his fears and informed him that, come what may, I was determined to see the old sexton that evening and get the whole matter over as soon as possible. I did not intend to accept the superstitions of ignorant country folk as truth, for I was convinced that all I had just heard was merely a chain of events which the over-imaginative people of Daalbergen had happened to link with their ill-luck. I felt no sense of fear or horror whatever.

Seeing that I was determined to reach my uncle's house before nightfall, Haines ushered me out of his office and reluctantly gave me the few required directions, pleading from time to time that I change my mind. He shook my hand when I left, as though he never expected to see me again.

"Take keer that old devil, Foster, don't git ye!" he warned, again and again. "I wouldn't go near him after dark fer love n'r money. No siree!" He re-entered his store, solemnly shaking his head, while I set out along a road leading to the outskirts of the town.

I had walked barely two minutes before I sighted the moor of which Haines had spoken. The road, flanked by a whitewashed fence, passed over the great swamp, which was overgrown with clumps of underbrush dipping down into the dank, slimy ooze. An odor of deadness and decay filled the air, and even in the sunlit afternoon little wisps of vapor could be seen rising from the unhealthful spot.

On the opposite side of the moor I turned sharply to the left, as I had been directed, branching from the main road. There were several houses in the vicinity, I noticed; houses which were scarcely more than huts, reflecting the extreme poverty of their owners. The road here passed under the drooping branches of enormous willows which almost completely shut out the rays of the sun. The miasmal odor of the swamp was still in my nostrils, and the air was damp and chilly. I hurried my pace to get out of that dismal tunnel as soon as possible.

Presently I found myself in the light again. The sun, now hanging like a red ball upon the crest of the mountain, was beginning to dip low, and there, some distance ahead of me, bathed in its bloody iridescence, stood the lonely church. I began to sense that uncanniness which Haines had mentioned; that feeling of dread which made all Daalbergen shun the place. The squat, stone hulk of the church itself, with its blunt steeple, seemed like an idol to which the tombstones that surrounded it bowed down and worshipped, each with an arched top like the shoulders of a kneeling person, while over the whole assemblage the dingy, gray parsonage hovered like a wraith.

I had slowed my pace a trifle as I took in the scene. The sun was disappearing behind the mountain very rapidly now, and the damp air chilled me. Turning my coat collar up about my neck, I plodded on. Something caught my eye as I glanced up again. In the shadow of the church wall was something white—a thing which seemed to have no definite shape. Straining my eyes as I came nearer, I saw that it was a cross of new timber, surmounting a mound of freshly turned earth. The discovery sent a new chill through me. I realized that this must be my uncle's grave, but something told me that it was not like the other graves near it. It did not seem like a *dead* grave. In some intangible way it appeared to be *living,* if a grave can be said to live. Very close to it, I saw as I came nearer, was another grave; an old mound with a crumbling stone about it. Dominie Slott's tomb, I thought, remembering Haines's story.

There was no sign of life anywhere about the place. In the semi-twilight I climbed the low knoll upon which the parsonage stood, and hammered upon the door. There was no answer. I skirted the house and peered into the windows. The whole place seemed deserted.

The lowering mountains had made night fall with disarming suddenness the minute the sun was fully hidden. I realized that I could see scarcely more than a few feet ahead of me. Feeling my way carefully, I rounded a corner of the house and paused, wondering what to do next.

Everything was quiet. There was not a breath of wind, nor were there even the usual noises made by animals in their nocturnal ramblings. All dread had been forgotten for a time, but in the presence of that sepulchral calm my apprehensions returned. I imagined the air peopled with ghastly spirits that pressed around me, making the air almost unbreathable. I wondered, for the hundredth time, where the old sexton might be.

As I stood there, half expecting some sinister demon to creep from the shadows, I noticed two lighted windows glaring from the belfry of the church. I then remembered what Haines had told me about Foster's living in the basement of the building. Advancing cautiously through the blackness, I found a side door of the church ajar.

The interior had a musty and mildewed odor. Everything I touched was covered with a cold, clammy moisture. I struck a match and began to explore, to discover, if I could, how to get into the belfry. Suddenly I stopped in my tracks.

A snatch of song, loud and obscene, sung in a voice that was guttural and thick with drink, came from above me. The match burned my fingers, and I dropped it. Two pin-points of light pierced the darkness of the farther wall of the church, and below them, to one side, I could see a door outlined where light filtered through its cracks. The song stopped as abruptly as it had commenced, and there was absolute silence again. My heart was thumping and blood racing through my temples. Had I not been petrified with fear, I should have fled immediately.

Not caring to light another match, I felt my way among the pews until I stood in front of the door. So deep was the feeling of depression which had come over me that I felt as though I were acting in a dream. My actions were almost involuntary.

The door was locked, as I found when I turned the knob. I hammered upon it for some time, but there was no answer. The silence was as complete as before. Feeling around the edge of the door, I found the hinges, removed the pins from them, and allowed the door to fall toward me. Dim light flooded down a steep flight of steps. There was a sickening odor of whisky. I could now hear someone stirring in the belfry room above. Venturing a low halloo, I thought I heard a groan in reply, and cautiously climbed the stairs.

My first glance into that unhallowed place was indeed startling. Strewn about the little room were old and dusty books and manuscripts—strange things that bespoke almost unbelievable age. On rows of shelves which reached to the ceiling were horrible things in glass jars and bottles—snakes and lizards and bats. Dust and mold and cobwebs encrusted everything. In the center, behind a table upon which was a lighted candle, a nearly empty bottle of whisky, and a glass, was a motionless figure with a thin, scrawny, wrinkled face and wild eyes that stared blankly through me. I recognized Abel Foster, the old sexton, in an instant. He did not move or speak as I came slowly and fearfully toward him.

"Mr. Foster?" I asked, trembling with unaccountable fear when I heard my voice echo within the close confines of the room. There was no reply, and no movement from the figure behind the table. I wondered if he had not drunk himself to insensibility, and went behind the table to shake him.

At the mere touch of my arm upon his shoulder, the strange old man started from his chair as though terrified. His eyes, still having in them that same blank stare, were fixed upon me. Swinging his arms like flails, he backed away.

"Don't!" he screamed. "Don't touch me! Go back—go back!"

I saw that he was both drunk and struck with some kind of a

nameless terror. Using a soothing tone, I told him who I was and why I had come. He seemed to understand vaguely and sank back into his chair, sitting limp and motionless.

"I thought ye was him," he mumbled. "I thought ye was him come back fer it. He's been a-tryin' t' get out—a-tryin' t' get out sence I put him in there." His voice again rose to a scream and he clutched his chair. "Maybe he's got out now! Maybe he's out!"

I looked about, half expecting to see some spectral shape coming up the stairs.

"Maybe who's out?" I inquired.

"Vanderhoof!" he shrieked. "Th' cross over his grave keeps fallin' down in th' night! Every morning the earth is loose, and gets harder t' pat down. He'll come out an' I won't be able t' do nothin'."

Forcing him back into the chair, I seated myself on a box near him. He was trembling in mortal terror, with the saliva dripping from the corners of his mouth. From time to time I felt that sense of horror which Haines had described when he told me of the old sexton. Truly, there was something uncanny about the man. His head had now sunk forward upon his breast, and he seemed calmer, mumbling to himself.

I quietly arose and opened a window to let out the fumes of whisky and the musty odor of dead things. Light from a dim moon, just risen, made objects below barely visible. I could just see Dominie Vanderhoof's grave from my position in the belfry, and blinked my eyes as I gazed at it. That cross *was* tilted! I remembered that it had been vertical an hour ago. Fear took possession of me again. I turned quickly. Foster sat in his chair watching me. His glance was saner than before.

"So ye're Vanderhoof's nephew," he mumbled in a nasal tone. "Waal, ye might's well know it all. He'll be back arter me afore long, he will—jus' as soon as he can get out o' that there grave. Ye might's well know all about it now."

His terror appeared to have left him. He seemed resigned to some horrible fate which he expected any minute. His head dropped down upon his chest again, and he went on muttering in that nasal monotone.

"Ye see all them there books and papers? Waal, they was once Dominie Slott's—Dominie Slott, who was here years ago. All them things is got t' do with magic—black magic that th' old Dominie knew afore he come t' this country. They used t' burn 'em an' boil 'em in oil fer knowin' that over there, they did. But old Slott knew, and he didn't go fer t' tell nobody. No sir, old Slott used to preach here generations ago, an' he used to come up here an' study them books, an' use all them dead things in jars, an' pronounce magic curses an' things, but he didn't let nobody know it. No, nobody knowed it but Dominie Slott an' me."

"You?" I ejaculated, leaning across the table toward him.

"That is, me after I learned it." His face showed lines of trickery as he answered me. "I found all this stuff here when I come t' be church sexton, an' I used t' read it when I wa'n't at work. An' I soon got t' know all about it."

The old man droned on, while I listened, spellbound. He told about learning the difficult formulae of demonology, so that, by means of incantations, he could cast spells over human beings. He had performed horrible occult rites of his hellish creed, calling down anathema upon the town and its inhabitants. Crazed by his desires, he tried to bring the church under his spell, but the power of God was too strong. Finding Johannes Vanderhoof very weak-willed, he bewitched him so that he preached strange and mystic sermons which struck fear into the simple hearts of the country folk. From his position in the belfry room, he said, behind a painting of the temptation of Christ which adorned the rear wall of the church, he would glare at Vanderhoof while he was preaching, through holes which were the eyes of the Devil in the picture. Terrified by the uncanny things which were happening in their midst, the congregation left one by one, and Foster was able to do what he pleased with the church and with Vanderhoof.

"But what did you do with him?" I asked in a hollow voice as the old sexton paused in his confession. He burst into a cackle of laughter, throwing back his head in drunken glee.

"I took his soul!" he howled in a tone that set me trembling. "I took his soul and put it in a bottle—in a little black bottle! And I buried him! But he ain't got his soul, an' he cain't go neither t' heaven n'r hell! But he's a-comin' back after it. He's a-tryin' t' get out o' his grave now. I can hear him pushin' his way up through the ground, he's that strong!"

As the old man had proceeded with his story, I had become more and more convinced that he must be telling me the truth, and not merely gibbering in drunkenness. Every detail fitted what Haines had told me. Fear was growing upon me by degrees. With the old wizard now shouting with demoniac laughter, I was tempted to bolt down the narrow stairway and leave that accursed neighborhood. To calm myself, I rose and again looked out of the window. My eyes nearly started from their sockets when I saw that the cross above Vanderhoof's grave had fallen perceptibly since I had last looked at it. It was now tilted to an angle of forty-five degrees!

"Can't we dig up Vanderhoof and restore his soul?" I asked almost breathlessly, feeling that something must be done in a hurry. The old man rose from his chair in terror.

"No, no, no!" he screamed. "He'd kill me! I've fergot th' formula, an' if he gets out he'll be alive, without a soul. He'd kill us both!"

"Where is the bottle that contains his soul?" I asked, advancing threateningly toward him. I felt that some ghastly thing was about to happen, which I must do all in my power to prevent.

"I won't tell ye, ye young whelp!" he snarled. I felt, rather than saw, a queer light in his eyes as he backed into a corner. "An' don't ye touch me, either, or ye'll wish ye hadn't!"

I moved a step forward, noticing that on a low stool behind him there were two black bottles. Foster muttered some peculiar words in a low, singsong voice. Everything began to turn gray before my eyes, and something within me seemed to be dragged upward, trying to get out at my throat. I felt my knees become weak.

Lurching forward, I caught the old sexton by the throat, and with my free arm reached for the bottles on the stool. But the old man fell backward, striking the stool with his foot, and one bottle fell to the floor as I snatched the other. There was a flash of blue flame, and a sulfurous smell filled the room. From the little heap of broken glass a white vapor rose and followed the draft out the window.

"Curse ye, ye rascal!" sounded a voice that seemed faint and far away. Foster, whom I had released when the bottle broke, was crouching against the wall, looking smaller and more shriveled than before. His face was slowly turning greenish-black.

"Curse ye!" said the voice again, hardly sounding as though it came from his lips. "I'm done fer! That one in there was mine! *Dominie Slott took it out two hundred years ago!*"

He slid slowly toward the floor, gazing at me with hatred in eyes that were rapidly dimming. His flesh changed from white to black, and then to yellow. I saw with horror that his body seemed to be crumbling away and his clothing falling into limp folds.

The bottle in my hand was growing warm. I glanced at it, fearfully. It glowed with a faint phosphorescence. Stiff with fright, I set it upon the table, but could not keep my eyes from it. There was an ominous moment of silence as its glow became brighter, and then there came distinctly to my ears the sound of sliding earth. Gasping for breath, I looked out of the window. The moon was now well up in the sky, and by its light I could see that the fresh cross above Vanderhoof's grave had completely fallen. Once again there came the sound of trickling gravel, and no longer able to control myself, I stumbled down the stairs and found my way out of doors. Falling now and then as I raced over the uneven ground, I ran on in abject terror. When I had reached the foot of the knoll, at the entrance to that gloomy tunnel beneath the willows, I heard a horrible roar behind me. Turning, I glanced back toward the church. Its wall reflected the light of the moon, and silhouetted against it was a gigantic, loathsome, black shadow climbing from my uncle's grave and floundering gruesomely toward the church.

I told my story to a group of villagers in Haines's store the next morning. They looked from one to the other with little smiles during my tale, I noticed, but when I suggested that they accompany me to the spot, gave various excuses for not caring to go. Though there seemed to be a limit to their credulity, they cared to run no risks. I informed them that I would go alone, though I must confess that the project did not appeal to me.

As I left the store, one old man with a long, white beard hurried after me and caught my arm.

"I'll go wi' ye, lad," he said. "It do seem that I once heared my gran'pap tell o' su'thin' o' the sort concernin' old Dominie Slott. A queer old man I've heared he were, but Vanderhoof's been worse."

Dominie Vanderhoof's grave was open and deserted when we arrived. Of course it could have been grave-robbers, the two of us agreed, and yet. . . . In the belfry the bottle which I had left upon the table was gone, though the fragments of the broken one were found on the floor. And upon the heap of yellow dust and crumpled clothing that had once been Abel Foster were certain immense footprints.

After glancing at some of the books and papers strewn about the belfry room, we carried them down the stairs and burned them, as something unclean and unholy. With a spade which we found in the church basement we filled in the grave of Johannes Vanderhoof, and, as an afterthought, flung the fallen cross upon the flames.

Old wives say that now, when the moon is full, there walks about the churchyard a gigantic and bewildered figure clutching a bottle and seeking some unremembered goal.

Henry S. Whitehead

The Trap

It was on a certain Thursday morning in December that the whole thing began with that unaccountable motion I thought I saw in my antique Copenhagen mirror. Something, it seemed to me, stirred—something reflected in the glass, though I was alone in my quarters. I paused and looked intently, then, deciding that the effect must be a pure illusion, resumed the interrupted brushing of my hair.

I had discovered the old mirror, covered with dust and cobwebs, in an outbuilding of an abandoned estate-house in Santa Cruz's sparsely settled Northside territory, and had brought it to the United States from the Virgin Islands. The venerable glass was dim from more than two hundred years' exposure to a tropical climate, and the graceful ornamentation along the top of the gilt frame had been badly smashed. I had had the detached pieces set back into the frame before placing it in storage with my other belongings.

Now, several years later, I was staying half as a guest and half as a tutor at the private school of my old friend Browne on a windy Connecticut hillside—occupying an unused wing in one of the dormitories, where I had two rooms and a hallway to myself. The old mirror, stowed securely in mattresses, was the first of my possessions to be unpacked on my arrival; and I had set it up majestically in the living-room, on top of an old rosewood console which had belonged to my great-grandmother.

The door of my bedroom was just opposite that of the living-room, with a hallway between; and I had noticed that by looking into my chiffonier glass I could see the larger mirror through the two doorways—which was exactly like glancing down an endless, though diminishing, corridor. On this Thursday morning I thought I saw a curious suggestion of motion down that normally empty corridor—but, as I have said, soon dismissed the notion.

When I reached the dining-room I found everyone complaining of the cold, and learned that the school's heating-plant was temporarily out of order. Being especially sensitive to low temperatures, I was myself an acute sufferer; and at once decided not to brave any freezing schoolroom that day. Accordingly I invited my class to come over to my living-room for an informal session around my grate-fire—a suggestion which the boys received enthusiastically.

After the session one of the boys, Robert Grandison, asked if he might remain; since he had no appointment for the second morning period. I told him to stay, and welcome. He sat down to study in front of the fireplace in a comfortable chair.

It was not long, however, before Robert moved to another chair somewhat farther away from the freshly replenished blaze, this change bringing him directly opposite the old mirror. From my own chair in another part of the room I noticed how fixedly he began to look at the dim, cloudy glass, and, wondering what so greatly interested him, was reminded of my own experience earlier that morning. As time passed he continued to gaze, a slight frown knitting his brows.

At last I quietly asked him what had attracted his attention. Slowly, and still wearing the puzzled frown, he looked over and replied rather cautiously:

"It's the corrugations in the glass—or whatever they are, Mr. Canevin. I was noticing how they all seem to run from a certain point. Look—I'll show you what I mean."

The boy jumped up, went over to the mirror, and placed his finger on a point near its lower left-hand corner.

"It's right here, sir," he explained, turning to look toward me and keeping his finger on the chosen spot.

His muscular action in turning may have pressed his finger against the glass. Suddenly he withdrew his hand as though with some slight effort, and with a faintly muttered "Ouch." Then he looked at the glass in obvious mystification.

"What happened?" I asked, rising and approaching.

"Why—it—" He seemed embarrassed. "It—I—felt—well, as

though it were pulling my finger into it. Seems—er—perfectly foolish, sir, but—well—it was a most peculiar sensation." Robert had an unusual vocabulary for his fifteen years.

I came over and had him show me the exact spot he meant.

"You'll think I'm rather a fool, sir," he said shamefacedly, "but—well, from right here I can't be absolutely sure. From the chair it seemed to be clear enough."

Now thoroughly interested, I sat down in the chair Robert had occupied and looked at the spot he selected on the mirror. Instantly the thing "jumped out at me." Unmistakably, from that particular angle, all the many whorls in the ancient glass appeared to converge like a large number of spread strings held in one hand and radiating out in streams.

Getting up and crossing to the mirror, I could no longer see the curious spot. Only from certain angles, apparently, was it visible. Directly viewed, that portion of the mirror did not even give back a normal reflection—for I could not see my face in it. Manifestly I had a minor puzzle on my hands.

Presently the school gong sounded, and the fascinated Robert Grandison departed hurriedly, leaving me alone with my odd little problem in optics. I raised several window-shades, crossed the hallway, and sought for the spot in the chiffonier mirror's reflection. Finding it readily, I looked very intently and thought I again detected something of the "motion." I craned my neck, and at last, at a certain angle of vision, the thing again "jumped out at me."

The vague "motion" was now positive and definite—an appearance of torsional movement, or of whirling; much like a minute yet intense whirlwind or waterspout, or a huddle of autumn leaves dancing circularly in an eddy of wind along a level lawn. It was, like the earth's, a double motion—around and around, and at the same time *inward,* as if the whorls poured themselves endlessly toward some point inside the glass. Fascinated, yet realizing that the thing must be an illusion, I grasped an impression of quite distinct *suction,* and thought of Robert's embarrassed explanation: *"I felt as though it were pulling my finger into it."*

A kind of slight chill ran suddenly up and down my backbone. There was something here distinctly worth looking into. And as the idea of investigation came to me, I recalled the rather wistful expression of Robert Grandison when the gong called him to class. I remembered how he had looked back over his shoulder as he walked obediently out into the hallway, and resolved that he should be included in whatever analysis I might make of this little mystery.

Exciting events connected with that same Robert, however, were soon to chase all thoughts of the mirror from my consciousness for a time. I was away all that afternoon, and did not return to the school until the five-fifteen "Call-Over"—a general assembly at which the boys' attendance was compulsory. Dropping in at this function with the idea of picking Robert up for a session with the mirror, I was astonished and pained to find him absent—a very unusual and unaccountable thing in his case. That evening Browne told me that the boy had actually disappeared, a search in his room, in the gymnasium, and in all other accustomed places being unavailing, though all his belongings—including his outdoor clothing—were in their proper places.

He had not been encountered on the ice or with any of the hiking groups that afternoon, and telephone calls to all the school-catering merchants of the neighborhood were in vain. There was, in short, no record of his having been seen since the end of the lesson periods at two-fifteen; when he had turned up the stairs toward his room in Dormitory Number Three.

When the disappearance was fully realized, the resulting sensation was tremendous throughout the school. Browne, as headmaster, had to bear the brunt of it; and such an unprecedented occurrence in his well-regulated, highly organized institution left him quite bewildered. It was learned that Robert had not run away to his home in western Pennsylvania, nor did any of the searching-parties of boys and masters find any trace of him in the snowy countryside around the school. So far as could be seen, he had simply vanished.

Robert's parents arrived on the afternoon of the second day after his disappearance. They took their trouble quietly, though, of course, they were staggered by this unexpected disaster. Browne looked ten years older for it, but there was absolutely nothing that could be done. By the fourth day the case had settled down in the opinion of the school as an insoluble mystery. Mr. and Mrs. Grandison went reluctantly back to their home, and on the following morning the ten days' Christmas vacation began.

Boys and masters departed in anything but the usual holiday spirit; and Browne and his wife were left, along with the servants, as my only fellow-occupants of the big place. Without the masters and boys it seemed a very hollow shell indeed.

That afternoon I sat in front of my grate-fire thinking about Robert's disappearance and evolving all sorts of fantastic theories to account for it. By evening I had acquired a bad headache, and ate a light supper accordingly. Then, after a brisk walk around the massed buildings, I returned to my living-room and took up the burden of thought once more.

A little after ten o'clock I awakened in my armchair, stiff and chilled, from a doze during which I had let the fire go out. I was physically uncomfortable, yet mentally aroused by a peculiar sensation of expectancy and possible hope. Of course it had to do with the problem that was harassing me. For I had started from that inadvertent nap with a curious, persistent idea—the odd idea that a tenuous, hardly recognizable Robert Grandison had been trying desperately to communicate with me. I finally went to bed with one conviction unreasoningly strong in my mind. Somehow I was sure that young Robert Grandison was still alive.

That I should be receptive of such a notion will not seem strange to those who know my long residence in the West Indies and my close contact with unexplained happenings there. It will not seem strange, either, that I fell asleep with an urgent desire to establish some sort of mental communication with the missing boy. Even the most prosaic scientists affirm, with Freud, Jung, and Adler, that the subconscious mind is most open to external impressions in sleep; though such impressions are seldom carried over intact into the waking state.

Going a step further and granting the existence of telepathic forces, it follows that such forces must act most strongly on a sleeper; so that if I were ever to get a definite message from Robert, it would be during a period of profoundest slumber. Of course, I might lose the message in waking; but my aptitude for retaining such things has been sharpened by types of mental discipline picked up in various obscure corners of the globe.

I must have dropped asleep instantaneously, and from the vividness of my dreams and the absence of wakeful intervals I judge that my sleep was a very deep one. It was six-forty-five when I awakened, and there still lingered with me certain impressions which I knew were carried over from the world of somnolent cerebration. Filling my mind was the vision of Robert Grandison strangely transformed to a boy of a dull greenish dark-blue color; Robert desperately endeavoring to communicate with me by means of speech, yet finding some almost insuperable difficulty in so doing. A wall of curious spatial separation seemed to stand between him and me—a mysterious, invisible wall which completely baffled us both.

I had seen Robert as though at some distance, yet queerly enough he seemed at the same time to be just beside me. He was both larger and smaller than in real life, his apparent size varying *directly,* instead of *inversely,* with the distance as he advanced and retreated in the course of conversation. That is, he grew larger instead of smaller to my eye when he stepped away or backwards, and vice versa; as if the laws of perspective in his case had been wholly reversed. His aspect was misty and uncertain—as if he lacked sharp or permanent outlines; and the anomalies of his coloring and clothing baffled me utterly at first.

At some point in my dream Robert's vocal efforts had finally crystallized into audible speech—albeit speech of an abnormal thickness and dullness. I could not for a time understand anything he said, and even in the dream racked my brain for a clue to where he was, what he wanted to tell, and why his utterance was so clumsy and unintelligible. Then little by little I began to distinguish words and phrases, the very first of which sufficed to throw my dreaming self into the wildest excitement and to establish a certain mental connection which had previously refused to take conscious form because of the utter incredibility of what it implied.

I do not know how long I listened to those halting words amidst my deep slumber, but hours must have passed while the strangely remote speaker struggled on with his tale. There was revealed to me such a circumstance as I cannot hope to make others believe without the strongest corroborative evidence, yet which I was quite ready to accept as truth—both in the dream and after waking—because of my former contacts with uncanny things. The boy was obviously watching my face—mobile in receptive sleep—as he choked along; for about the time I began to comprehend him, his own expression brightened and gave signs of gratitude and hope.

Any attempt to hint at Robert's message, as it lingered in my ears after a sudden awakening in the cold, brings this narrative to a point where I must choose my words with the greatest care. Everything involved is so difficult to record that one tends to flounder helplessly. I have said that the revelation established in my mind a certain connection which reason had not allowed me to formulate consciously before. This connection, I need no longer hesitate to hint, had to do with the old Copenhagen mirror whose suggestions of motion had so impressed me on the morning of the disappearance, and whose whorl-like contours and apparent illusions of suction had later exerted such a disquieting fascination on both Robert and me.

Resolutely, though my outer consciousness had previously rejected what my intuition would have liked to imply, it could reject that stupendous conception no longer. What was fantasy in the tale of "Alice" now came to me as a grave and immediate reality. That looking-glass had indeed possessed a malign, abnormal suction; and the struggling speaker in my dream made clear the extent to which it violated all the known precedents of human experience and all the age-old laws of our three sane dimensions. It was more than a mirror—it was a gate; a trap; a link with spatial recesses not meant for the denizens of our visible universe, and realizable only in terms of the most intricate non-Euclidean mathematics. *And in some outrageous fashion Robert Grandison had passed out of our ken into the glass and was there immured, waiting for release.*

It is significant that upon awakening I harbored no genuine doubt of the reality of the revelation. That I had actually held conversation with a trans-dimensional Robert, rather than evoked the whole episode from my broodings about his disappearance and about the old illusions of the mirror, was as certain to my utmost instincts as any of the instinctive certainties commonly recognized as valid.

The tale thus unfolded to me was of the most incredibly bizarre character. As had been clear on the morning of his disappearance, Robert was intensely fascinated by the ancient mirror. All through the hours of school, he had it in mind to come back to my living-room and examine it further. When he did arrive, after the close of the school day, it was somewhat later than two-twenty, and I was absent in town. Finding me out and knowing that I would not mind, he had come into my living-room and gone straight to the mirror; standing before it and studying the place where, as we had noted, the whorls appeared to converge.

Then, quite suddenly, there had come to him an overpowering urge to place his hand upon this whorl-center. Almost reluctantly, against his better judgment, he had done so; and upon making the contact had felt at once the strange, almost painful suction which had perplexed him that morning. Immediately thereafter—quite without warning, but with a wrench which seemed to twist and tear every bone and muscle in his body and to bulge and press and cut at every nerve—he had been abruptly *drawn through* and found himself *inside.*

Once through, the excruciatingly painful stress upon his entire system was suddenly released. He felt, he said, as though he had just been born—a feeling that made itself evident every time he tried to do anything; walk, stoop, turn his head, or utter speech. Everything about his body seemed a misfit.

These sensations wore off after a long while, Robert's body becoming an organized whole rather than a number of protesting parts. Of all the forms of expression, speech remained the most difficult; doubtless because it is complicated, bringing into play a number of different organs, muscles, and tendons. Robert's feet, on the other hand, were the first members to adjust themselves to the new conditions within the glass.

During the morning hours I rehearsed the whole reason-defying problem; correlating everything I had seen and heard, dismissing the natural scepticism of a man of sense, and scheming to devise possible plans for Robert's release from his incredible prison. As I did so a number of originally perplexing points became clear—or at least, clearer—to me.

There was, for example, the matter of Robert's coloring. His face and hands, as I have indicated, were a kind of dull greenish dark-blue; and I may add that his familiar blue Norfolk jacket had turned to a pale lemon-yellow while his trousers remained a neutral gray as before. Reflecting on this after waking, I found the circumstance closely allied to the reversal of perspective which made Robert seem to grow larger when receding and smaller when approaching. Here, too, was a physical *reversal*—for every detail of his coloring in the unknown dimension was the exact reverse or complement of the corresponding color detail in normal life. In physics the typical complementary colors are blue and yellow, and red and green. These pairs are opposites, and when mixed yield gray. Robert's natural color was a pinkish-buff, the opposite of which is the greenish-blue I saw. His blue coat had become yellow, while the gray trousers remained gray. This latter point baffled me until I remembered that gray is itself a mixture of opposites. There is no opposite for gray—or rather, it is its own opposite.

Another clarified point was that pertaining to Robert's curiously dulled and thickened speech—as well as to the general awkwardness and sense of misfit bodily parts of which he complained. This, at the outset, was a puzzle indeed; though after long thought the clue occurred to me. Here again was the same *reversal* which affected perspective and coloration. Anyone in the fourth dimension must necessarily be reversed in just this way—hands and feet, as well as colors and perspectives, being changed about. It would be the same with all the other dual organs, such as nostrils, ears, and eyes. Thus Robert had been talking with a reversed tongue, teeth, vocal cords, and kindred speech-apparatus; so that his difficulties in utterance were little to be wondered at.

As the morning wore on, my sense of the stark reality and maddening urgency of the dream-disclosed situation increased rather than decreased. More and more I felt that something must be done, yet realized that I could not seek advice or aid. Such a story as mine —a conviction based upon mere dreaming—could not conceivably bring me anything but ridicule or suspicions as to my mental state. And what, indeed, could I do, aided or unaided, with as little working data as my nocturnal impressions had provided? I must, I finally recognized, have more information before I could even think of a possible plan for releasing Robert. This could come only through the receptive conditions of sleep, and it heartened me to reflect that according to every probability my telepathic contact would be resumed the moment I fell into deep slumber again.

I accomplished sleeping that afternoon, after a midday dinner at which, through rigid self-control, I succeeded in concealing from Browne and his wife the tumultuous thoughts that crashed through my mind. Hardly had my eyes closed when a dim telepathic image began to appear; and I soon realized to my infinite excitement that it was identical with what I had seen before. If anything, it was more distinct; and when it began to speak I seemed able to grasp a greater proportion of the words.

During this sleep I found most of the morning's deductions confirmed, though the interview was mysteriously cut off long prior to my awakening. Robert had seemed apprehensive just before communication ceased, but had already told me that in his strange fourth-dimensional prison colors and spatial relationships were indeed reversed—black being white, distance increasing apparent size, and so on.

He had also intimated that, notwithstanding his possession of full physical form and sensations, most human vital properties seemed curiously suspended. Nutriment, for example, was quite unnecessary—a phenomenon really more singular than the omnipresent reversal of objects and attributes, since the latter was a reasonable and mathematically indicated state of things. Another significant piece of information was that the only exit from the glass to the world was the entrance-way, and that this was permanently barred and impenetrably sealed, so far as egress was concerned.

That night I had another visitation from Robert; nor did such impressions, received at odd intervals while I slept receptively minded, cease during the entire period of his incarceration. His efforts to communicate were desperate and often pitiful; for at times the telepathic bond would weaken, while at other times fatigue, excitement, or fear of interruption would hamper and thicken his speech.

I may as well narrate as a continuous whole all that Robert told me throughout the whole series of transient mental contacts—perhaps supplementing it at certain points with facts directly related after his release. The telepathic information was fragmentary and often nearly inarticulate, but I studied it over and over during the waking intervals of three intense days; classifying and cogitating with feverish diligence, since it was all that I had to go upon if the boy were to be brought back into our world.

The fourth-dimensional region in which Robert found himself was not, as in scientific romance, an unknown and infinite realm of strange sights and fantastic denizens; but was rather a projection of certain limited parts of our own terrestrial sphere within an alien and normally inaccessible aspect or direction of space. It was a curiously fragmentary, intangible, and heterogeneous world—a series of apparently dissociated scenes merging indistinctly one into the other; their constituent details having an obviously different status from that of an object drawn into the ancient mirror as Robert had been drawn. These scenes were like dream-vistas or magic-lantern images—elusive visual impressions of which the boy was not really a part, but which formed a sort of panoramic background or ethereal environment against which or amidst which he moved.

He could not touch any of the parts of these scenes—walls, trees, furniture, and the like—but whether this was because they were truly non-material, or because they always receded at his approach, he was singularly unable to determine. Everything seemed fluid, mutable, and unreal. When he walked, it appeared to be on whatever lower surface the visible scene might have—floor, path, greensward, or such; but upon analysis he always found that the contact was an illusion. There was never any difference in the resisting force met by his feet—and by his hands when he would stoop experimentally—no matter what changes of apparent surface might be involved. He could not describe this foundation or limiting plane on which he walked as anything more definite than a virtually abstract pressure balancing his gravity. Of definite tactile distinctiveness it had none, and supplementing it there seemed to be a kind of restricted levitational force which accomplished transfers of altitude. He could never actually climb stairs, yet would gradually walk up from a lower level to a higher.

Passage from one definite scene to another involved a sort of gliding through a region of shadow or blurred focus where the details of each scene mingled curiously. All the vistas were distinguished by the absence of transient objects, and the indefinite or ambiguous appearance of such semi-transient objects as furniture or details of vegetation. The lighting of every scene was diffuse and perplexing, and of course the scheme of reversed colors—bright red grass, yellow sky with confused black and gray cloud-forms, white tree-trunks, and green brick walls—gave to everything an air of unbelievable grotesquerie. There was an alteration of day and night, which turned out to be a reversal of the normal hours of light and darkness at whatever point on the earth the mirror might be hanging.

This seemingly irrelevant diversity of the scenes puzzled Robert until he realized that they comprised merely such places as had been reflected for long continuous periods in the ancient glass. This also explained the odd absence of transient objects, the generally arbitrary boundaries of vision, and the fact that all exteriors were framed by the outlines of doorways or windows. The glass, it appeared, had power to store up these intangible scenes through long exposure; though it could never absorb anything corporeally, as Robert had been absorbed, except by a very different and particular process.

But—to me at least—the most incredible aspect of the mad phenomenon was the monstrous subversion of our known laws of space involved in the relation of various illusory scenes to the actual terrestrial regions represented. I have spoken of the glass as storing up the images of these regions, but this is really an inexact definition. In truth, each of the mirror scenes formed a true and quasi-permanent fourth-dimensional projection of the corresponding mundane region; so that whenever Robert moved to a certain part of a certain scene, as he moved into the image of my room when sending his telepathic messages, *he was actually in that place itself, on earth*—though under spatial conditions which cut off all sensory communication, in either direction, between him and the present tri-dimensional aspect of the place.

Theoretically speaking, a prisoner in the glass could in a few moments go anywhere on our planet—into any place, that is, which had ever been reflected in the mirror's surface. This probably applied even to places where the mirror had not hung long enough to produce a clear illusory scene; the terrestrial region being then represented by a zone of more or less formless shadow. Outside the definite scenes was a seemingly limitless waste of neutral gray shadow about which Robert could never be certain, and into which he never dared stray far lest he become hopelessly lost to the real and mirror worlds alike.

Among the earliest particulars which Robert gave, was the fact that he was not alone in his confinement. Various others, all in antique garb, were in there with him—a corpulent middle-aged gentleman with tied queue and velvet knee-breeches who spoke English fluently though with a marked Scandinavian accent; a rather beautiful small girl with very blonde hair which appeared a glossy dark blue; two apparently mute Negroes whose features contrasted grotesquely with the pallor of their reversed-colored skins; three young men; one young woman; a very small child, almost an infant; and a lean, elderly Dane of extremely distinctive aspect and a kind of half-malign intellectuality of countenance.

This last-named individual—Axel Holm, who wore the satin small-clothes, flared-skirted coat, and voluminous full-bottomed periwig of an age more than two centuries in the past—was notable among the little band as being the one responsible for the presence of them all. He it was who, skilled equally in the arts of magic and glass working, had long ago fashioned this strange dimensional prison in which himself, his slaves, and those whom he chose to invite or allure thither were immured unchangingly for as long as the mirror might endure.

Holm was born early in the seventeenth century, and had followed with tremendous competence and success the trade of a glass-blower and molder in Copenhagen. His glass, especially in the form of large drawing-room mirrors, was always at a premium. But the same bold mind which had made him the first glazier of Europe also served to carry his interests and ambitions far beyond the sphere of mere material craftsmanship. He had studied the world around him, and chafed at the limitations of human knowledge and capability. Eventually he sought for dark ways to overcome those limitations, and gained more success than is good for any mortal.

He had aspired to enjoy something like eternity, the mirror being his provision to secure this end. Serious study of the fourth dimension was far from beginning with Einstein in our own era; and Holm, more than erudite in all the methods of his day, knew that a bodily entrance into that hidden phase of space would prevent him from dying in the ordinary physical sense. Research showed him that the principle of reflection undoubtedly forms the chief gate to all dimensions beyond our familiar three; and chance placed in his hands a small and very ancient glass whose cryptic properties he believed he could turn to advantage. Once "inside" this mirror according to the method he had envisaged, he felt that "life" in the sense of form and consciousness would go on virtually forever, provided the mirror could be preserved indefinitely from breakage or deterioration.

Holm made a magnificent mirror, such as would be prized and carefully preserved; and in it deftly fused the strange whorl-configured relic he had acquired. Having thus prepared his refuge and his trap, he began to plan his mode of entrance and conditions of tenancy. He would have with him both servitors and companions; and as an experimental beginning he sent before him into the glass two dependable Negro slaves brought from the West Indies. What his sensations must have been upon beholding this first concrete demonstration of his theories, only imagination can conceive.

Undoubtedly a man of his knowledge realized that absence from the outside world, if deferred beyond the natural span of life of those within, must mean instant dissolution at the first attempt to return to that world. But, barring that misfortune or accidental breakage, those within would remain forever as they were at the time of entrance. They would never grow old, and would need neither food nor drink.

To make his prison tolerable he sent ahead of him certain books and writing materials, a chair and table of stoutest workmanship, and a few other accessories. He knew that the images which the glass would reflect or absorb would not be tangible, but would merely extend around him like a background of dream. His own transition in 1687 was a momentous experience; and must have been attended by mixed sensations of triumph and terror. Had anything gone wrong, there were frightful possibilities of being lost in dark and inconceivable multiple dimensions.

For over fifty years he had been unable to secure any additions to the little company of himself and slaves, but later on he had perfected his telepathic method of visualizing small sections of the outside world close to the glass, and attracting certain individuals in those areas through the mirror's strange entrance. Thus Robert, influenced into a desire to press upon the "door," had been lured within. Such visualizations depended wholly on telepathy, since no one inside the mirror could see out into the world of men.

It was, in truth, a strange life that Holm and his company had lived inside the glass. Since the mirror had stood for fully a century with its face to the dusty stone wall of the shed where I found it, Robert was the first being to enter this limbo after all that interval. His arrival was a gala event, for he brought news of the outside world which must have been of the most startling impressiveness to the more thoughtful of those within. He, in his turn—young though he was—felt overwhelmingly the weirdness of meeting and talking with persons who had been alive in the seventeenth and eighteenth centuries.

The deadly monotony of life for the prisoners can only be vaguely conjectured. As mentioned, its extensive spatial variety was limited to localities which had been reflected in the mirror for long periods; and many of these had become dim and strange as tropical climates had made inroads on the surface. Certain localities were bright and beautiful, and in these the company usually gathered. But no scene could be fully satisfying; since the visible objects were all unreal and intangible, and often of perplexingly indefinite outline. When the tedious periods of darkness came, the general custom was to indulge in memories, reflections, or conversations. Each one of that strange, pathetic group had retained his or her personality unchanged and unchangeable, since becoming immune to the time effects of outside space.

The number of inanimate objects within the glass, aside from the clothing of the prisoners, was very small; being largely limited to the accessories Holm had provided for himself. The rest did without even furniture, since sleep and fatigue had vanished along with most other vital attributes. Such inorganic things as were present, seemed as exempt from decay as the living beings. The lower forms of animal life were wholly absent.

Robert derived most of his information from Herr Thiele, the gentleman who spoke English with a Scandinavian accent. This portly Dane had taken a fancy to him, and talked at considerable length. The others, too, had received him with courtesy and goodwill; Holm himself, seeming well-disposed, had told him about various matters including the door of the trap.

The boy, as he told me later, was sensible enough never to attempt communication with me when Holm was nearby. Twice, while thus engaged, he had seen Holm appear; and had accordingly ceased at once. At no time could I see the world behind the mirror's surface. Robert's visual image, which included his bodily form and the clothing connected with it, was—like the aural image of his halting voice and like his own visualization of myself—a case of purely telepathic transmission; and did not involve true inter-dimensional sight. However, had Robert been as trained a telepathist as Holm, he might have transmitted a few strong images apart from his immediate person.

Throughout this period of revelation I had, of course, been desperately trying to devise a method for Robert's release. On the fourth day—the ninth after the disappearance—I hit on a solution. Everything considered, my laboriously formulated process was not a very complicated one; though I could not tell beforehand how it would work, while the possibility of ruinous consequences in case of a slip was appalling. This process depended, basically, on the fact that there was no possible exit from inside the glass. If Holm and his prisoners were permanently sealed in, then release must come wholly from outside. Other considerations included the disposal of the other prisoners, if any survived, and especially of Axel Holm. What Robert had told me of him was anything but reassuring; and I certainly did not wish him loose in my apartment, free once more to work his evil will upon the world. The telepathic messages had not made fully clear the effect of liberation on those who had entered the glass so long ago.

There was, too, a final though minor problem in case of success—that of getting Robert back into the routine of school life without having to explain the incredible. In case of failure, it was highly inadvisable to have witnesses present at the release operations—and lacking these, I simply could not attempt to relate the actual facts if I should succeed. Even to me the reality seemed a mad one whenever I let my mind turn from the data so compellingly presented in that tense series of dreams.

When I had thought these problems through as far as possible, I procured a large magnifying-glass from the school laboratory and studied minutely every square millimeter of that whorl-center which presumably marked the extent of the original ancient mirror used by Holm. Even with this aid I could not quite trace the exact boundary between the old area and the surface added by the Danish wizard; but after a long study decided on a conjectural oval boundary which I outlined very precisely with a soft blue pencil. I then made a trip to Stamford, where I procured a heavy glass-cutting tool; for my primary idea was to remove the ancient and magically potent mirror from its later setting.

My next step was to figure out the best time of day to make the crucial experiment. I finally settled on two-thirty a.m.—both because it was a good season for uninterrupted work, and because it was the "opposite" of two-thirty p.m., the probable moment at which Robert had entered the mirror. This form of "oppositeness" may or may not have been relevant, but I knew at least that the chosen hour was as good as any—and perhaps better than most.

I finally set to work in the early morning of the eleventh day after the disappearance, having drawn all the shades of my living-room and closed and locked the door into the hallway. Following with breathless care the elliptical line I had traced, I worked around the whorl-section with my steel-wheeled cutting tool. The ancient glass, half an inch thick, crackled crisply under the firm, uniform pressure; and upon completing the circuit I cut around it a second time, crunching the roller more deeply into the glass.

Then, very carefully indeed, I lifted the heavy mirror down from its console and leaned it face-inward against the wall; prying off two of the thin, narrow boards nailed to the back. With equal caution I smartly tapped the cut-around space with the heavy wooden handle of the glass-cutter.

At the very first tap the whorl-containing section of glass dropped out on the Bokhara rug beneath. I did not know what might happen, but was keyed up for anything, and took a deep involuntary breath. I was on my knees for convenience at the moment, with my face quite near the newly made aperture; and as I breathed there poured into my nostrils a powerful *dusty* odor—a smell not comparable to any other I have ever encountered. Then everything within my range of vision suddenly turned to a dull gray before my failing eyesight as I felt myself overpowered by an invisible force which robbed my muscles of their power to function.

I remember grasping weakly and futilely at the edge of the nearest window drapery and feeling it rip loose from its fastening. Then I sank slowly to the floor as the darkness of oblivion passed over me.

When I regained consciousness I was lying on the Bokhara rug with my legs held unaccountably up in the air. The room was full of that hideous and inexplicable dusty smell—and as my eyes began to take in definite images I saw that Robert Grandison stood in front of me. It was he—fully in the flesh and with his coloring normal—who was holding my legs aloft to bring the blood back to my head as the school's first-aid course had taught him to do with persons who had fainted. For a moment I was struck mute by the stifling odor and by a bewilderment which quickly merged into a sense of triumph. Then I found myself able to move and speak collectedly.

I raised a tentative hand and waved feebly at Robert.

"All right, old man," I murmured, "you can let my legs down now. Many thanks. I'm all right again, I think. It was the smell—I imagine—that got me. Open that farthest window, please—wide—from the bottom. That's it—thanks. No—leave the shade down the way it was."

I struggled to my feet, my disturbed circulation adjusting itself in waves, and stood upright hanging to the back of a big chair. I was still "groggy," but a blast of fresh, bitterly cold air from the window revived me rapidly. I sat down in the big chair and looked at Robert, now walking toward me.

"First," I said hurriedly, "tell me, Robert—those others—Holm? What happened to *them,* when I—opened the exit?"

Robert paused half-way across the room and looked at me very gravely.

"I saw them fade away—into nothingness—Mr. Canevin," he said with solemnity; "and with them—everything. There isn't any more 'inside,' sir—thank God, and you, sir!"

And young Robert, at last yielding to the sustained strain which he had borne through all those terrible eleven days, suddenly broke down like a little child and began to weep hysterically in great, stifling, dry sobs.

I picked him up and placed him gently on my davenport, threw a rug over him, sat down by his side, and put a calming hand on his forehead.

"Take it easy, old fellow," I said soothingly.

The boy's sudden and very natural hysteria passed as quickly as it had come on as I talked to him reassuringly about my plans for his quiet restoration to the school. The interest of the situation and the need of concealing the incredible truth beneath a rational explanation took hold of his imagination as I had expected; and at last he sat up eagerly, telling the details of his release and listening to the instructions I had thought out. He had, it seems, been in the "projected area" of my bedroom when I opened the way back, and had emerged in that actual room—hardly realizing that he was "out." Upon hearing a fall in the living-room he had hastened thither, finding me on the rug in my fainting spell.

I need mention only briefly my method of restoring Robert in a seemingly normal way—how I smuggled him out of the window in an old hat and sweater of mine, took him down the road in my quietly started car, coached him carefully in a tale I had devised, and returned to arouse Browne with the news of his discovery. He had, I explained, been walking alone on the afternoon of his disappearance; and had been offered a motor ride by two young men who, as a joke and over his protests that he could go no farther than Stamford and back, had begun to carry him past that town. Jumping from the car during a traffic stop with the intention of hitch-hiking back before Call-Over, he had been hit by another car just as the traffic was released—awakening ten days later in the Greenwich home of the people who had hit him. On learning the date, I added, he had immediately telephoned the school; and I, being the only one awake, had answered the call and hurried after him in my car without stopping to notify anyone.

Browne, who at once telephoned to Robert's parents, accepted my story without question; and forbore to interrogate the boy because of the latter's manifest exhaustion. It was arranged that he should remain at the school for a rest, under the expert care of Mrs. Browne, a former trained nurse. I naturally saw a good deal of him during the remainder of the Christmas vacation, and was thus enabled to fill in certain gaps in his fragmentary dream-story.

Now and then we would almost doubt the actuality of what had occurred; wondering whether we had not both shared some monstrous delusion born of the mirror's glittering hypnotism, and whether the tale of the ride and accident were not after all the real truth. But whenever we did so we would be brought back to belief by some monstrous and haunting memory; with me, of Robert's dream-figure and its thick voice and inverted colors; with him, of the whole fantastic pageantry of ancient people and dead scenes that he had witnessed. And then there was that joint recollection of that damnable dusty odor. . . . We knew what it meant: the instant dissolution of those who had entered an alien dimension a century and more ago.

There are, in addition, at least two lines of rather more positive evidence; one of which comes through my researches in Danish annals concerning the sorcerer, Axel Holm. Such a person, indeed, left many traces in folklore and written records; and diligent library sessions, plus conferences with various learned Danes, have shed much more light on his evil fame. At present I need say only that the Copenhagen glass-blower—born in 1612—was a notorious Luciferian whose pursuits and final vanishing formed a matter of awed debate over two centuries ago. He had burned with a desire to know all things and to conquer every limitation of mankind—to which end he had delved deeply into occult and forbidden fields ever since he was a child.

He was commonly held to have joined a coven of the dreaded witch-cult, and the vast lore of ancient Scandinavian myth—with its Loki the Sly One and the accursed Fenris-Wolf—was soon an open book to him. He had strange interests and objectives, few of which were definitely known, but some of which were recognized as intolerably evil. It is recorded that his two Negro helpers, originally slaves from the Danish West Indies, had become mute soon after their acquisition by him; and that they had disappeared not long before his own disappearance from the ken of mankind.

Near the close of an already long life the idea of a glass of immortality appears to have entered his mind. That he had acquired an enchanted mirror of inconceivable antiquity was a matter of common whispering; it being alleged that he had purloined it from a fellow-sorcerer who had entrusted it to him for polishing.

This mirror—according to popular tales a trophy as potent in its way as the better-known Aegis of Minerva or Hammer of Thor—was a small oval object called "Loki's Glass," made of some polished fusible mineral and having magical properties which included the divination of the immediate future and the power to show the possessor his enemies. That it had deeper potential properties, realizable in the hands of an erudite magician, none of the common people doubted; and even educated persons attached much fearful importance to Holm's rumored attempts to incorporate it in a larger glass of immortality. Then had come the wizard's disappearance in 1687, and the final sale and dispersal of his goods amidst a growing cloud of fantastic legendry. It was, altogether, just such a story as one would laugh at if possessed of no particular key; yet to me, remembering those dream messages and having Robert Grandison's corroboration before me, it formed a positive confirmation of all the bewildering marvels that had been unfolded.

But as I have said, there is still another line of rather positive evidence—of a very different character—at my disposal. Two days after his release, as Robert, greatly improved in strength and appearance, was placing a log on my living-room fire, I noticed a certain awkwardness in his motions and was struck by a persistent idea. Summoning him to my desk I suddenly asked him to pick up an ink-stand—and was scarcely surprised to note that, despite lifelong right-handedness, he obeyed unconsciously with his left hand. Without alarming him, I then asked that he unbutton his coat and let me listen to his cardiac action. What I found upon placing my ear to his chest—and what I did not tell him for some time afterward—was that *his heart was beating on his right side.*

He had gone into the glass right-handed and with all organs in their normal positions. Now he was left-handed and with organs reversed, and would doubtless continue so for the rest of his life. Clearly, the dimensional transition had been no illusion—for this physical change was tangible and unmistakable. Had there been a natural exit from the glass, Robert would probably have undergone a thorough re-reversal and emerged in perfect normality—as indeed the color-scheme of his body and clothing did emerge. The forcible nature of his release, however, undoubtedly set something awry; so that dimensions no longer had a chance to right themselves as chromatic wave-frequencies still did.

I had not merely *opened* Holm's trap; I had *destroyed* it; and at the particular stage of destruction marked by Robert's escape some of the reversing properties had perished. It is significant that in escaping Robert had felt no pain comparable to that experienced in entering. Had the destruction been still more sudden, I shiver to think of the monstrosities of color the boy would always have been forced to bear. I may add that after discovering Robert's reversal I examined the rumpled and discarded clothing he had worn in the glass, and found, as I had expected, a complete reversal of pockets, buttons, and all other corresponding details.

At this moment Loki's Glass, just as it fell on my Bokhara rug from the now patched and harmless mirror, weighs down a sheaf of papers on my writing-table here in St. Thomas, venerable capital of the Danish West Indies—now the American Virgin Islands. Various collectors of old Sandwich glass have mistaken it for an odd bit of that early American product—but I privately realize that my paper-weight is an antique of far subtler and more paleogean craftsmanship. Still, I do not disillusion such enthusiasts.

Duane W. Rimel

The Tree on the Hill

I.

Southeast of Hampden, near the tortuous Salmon River gorge, is a range of steep, rocky hills which have defied all efforts of sturdy homesteaders. The canyons are too deep and the slopes too precipitous to encourage anything save seasonal livestock grazing. The last time I visited Hampden the region—known as Hell's Acres—was part of the Blue Mountain Forest Reserve. There are no roads linking this inaccessible locality with the outside world, and the hillfolk will tell you that it is indeed a spot transplanted from his Satanic Majesty's front yard. There is a local superstition that the area is haunted—but by what or by whom no one seems to know. Natives will not venture within its mysterious depths, for they believe the stories handed down to them by the Nez Perce Indians, who have shunned the region for untold generations, because, according to them, it is a playground of certain giant devils from the Outside. These suggestive tales made me very curious.

My first excursion—and my last, thank God!—into those hills occurred while Constantine Theunis and I were living in Hampden the summer of 1938. He was writing a treatise on Egyptian mythology, and I found myself alone much of the time, despite the fact that we shared a modest cabin on Beacon Street, within sight of the infamous Pirate House, built by Exer Jones over sixty years ago.

The morning of June 23rd found me walking in those oddly shaped hills, which had, since seven o'clock, seemed very ordinary indeed. I must have been about seven miles south of Hampden before I noticed anything unusual. I was climbing a grassy ridge overlooking a particularly deep canyon, when I came upon an area totally devoid of the usual bunch-grass and greaseweed. It extended southward, over numerous hills and valleys. At first I thought the spot had been burned over the previous fall, but upon examining the turf, I found no signs of a blaze. The nearby slopes and ravines looked terribly scarred and seared, as if some gigantic torch had blasted them, wiping away all vegetation. And yet there was no evidence of fire. . . .

I moved on over rich, black soil in which no grass flourished. As I headed for the approximate center of this desolate area, I began to notice a strange silence. There were no larks, no rabbits, and even the insects seemed to have deserted the place. I gained the summit of a lofty knoll and tried to guess at the size of that bleak, inexplicable region. Then I saw the lone tree.

It stood on a hill somewhat higher than its companions, and attracted the eye because it was so utterly unexpected. I had seen no trees for miles: thorn and hackberry bushes clustered the shallower ravines, but there had been no mature trees. Strange to find one standing on the crest of the hill.

I crossed two steep canyons before I came to it; and a surprise awaited me. It was not a pine tree, nor a fir tree, nor a hackberry tree. I had never, in all my life, seen one to compare with it—and I never have to this day, for which I am eternally thankful!

More than anything it resembled an oak. It had a huge, twisted trunk, fully a yard in diameter, and the large limbs began spreading outward scarcely seven feet from the ground. The leaves were round, and curiously alike in size and design. It might have been a tree painted on a canvas, but I will swear that it was real. I shall always know that it *was* real, despite what Theunis said later.

I recall that I glanced at the sun and judged the time to be about ten o'clock a.m., although I did not look at my watch. The day was becoming warm, and I sat for a while in the welcome shade of the huge tree. Then I regarded the rank grass that flourished beneath it—another singular phenomenon when I remembered the bleak terrain through which I had passed. A wild maze of hills, ravines, and bluffs hemmed me in on all sides, although the rise on which I sat was rather higher than any other within miles. I looked far to the east—and I jumped to my feet, startled and amazed. Shimmering through a blue haze of distance were the Bitterroot Mountains! There is no other range of snow-capped peaks within three hundred miles of Hampden; and I knew—at this altitude—that I shouldn't be seeing them at all. For several minutes I gazed at the marvel; then I became drowsy. I lay in the rank grass, beneath the tree. I unstrapped my camera, took off my hat, and relaxed, staring skyward through the green leaves. I closed my eyes.

Then a curious phenomenon began to assail me—a vague, cloudy sort of vision—glimpsing or day-dreaming seemingly without relevance to anything familiar. I thought I saw a great temple by a sea of ooze, where three suns gleamed in a pale red sky. The vast tomb, or temple, was an anomalous color—a nameless blue-violet shade. Large beasts flew in the cloudy sky, and I seemed to hear the pounding of their scaly wings. I went nearer the stone temple, and a huge doorway loomed in front of me. Within that portal were swirling shadows that seemed to dart and leer and try to snatch me inside that awful darkness. I thought I saw three flaming eyes in the shifting void of a doorway, and I screamed with mortal fear. In that noisome depth, I knew, lurked utter destruction—a living hell even worse than death. I screamed again. The vision faded.

I saw the round leaves and the sane earthly sky. I struggled to rise. I was trembling; cold perspiration beaded my brow. I had a mad impulse to flee; run insanely from that sinister tree on the hill—but I checked the absurd intuition and sat down, trying to collect my senses. Never had I dreamed anything so realistic; so horrifying. What had caused the vision? I had been reading several of Theunis' tomes on ancient Egypt. . . . I mopped my forehead, and decided that it was time for lunch. But I did not feel like eating.

Then I had an inspiration. I would take a few snapshots of the tree, for Theunis. They might shock him out of his habitual air of unconcern. Perhaps I would tell him about the dream. . . . Opening my camera, I took half a dozen shots of the tree, and every aspect of the landscape as seen from the tree. Also, I included one of the gleaming, snow-crested peaks. I might want to return, and these photos would help. . . .

Folding the camera, I returned to my cushion of soft grass. Had that spot beneath the tree a certain alien enchantment? I know that I was reluctant to leave it. . . .

I gazed upward at the curious round leaves. I closed my eyes. A breeze stirred the branches, and their whispered music lulled me into tranquil oblivion. And suddenly I saw again the pale red sky and the three suns. The land of three shadows! Again the great temple came into view. I seemed to be floating on the air—a disembodied spirit exploring the wonders of a mad, multi-dimensional world! The temple's oddly angled cornices frightened me, and I knew that this place was one that no man on earth had ever seen in his wildest dreams.

Again the vast doorway yawned before me; and I was sucked within that black, writhing cloud. I seemed to be staring at space unlimited. I saw a void beyond my vocabulary to describe; a dark, bottomless gulf teeming with nameless shapes and entities—things of madness and delirium, as tenuous as a mist from Shamballah.

My soul shrank. I was terribly afraid. I screamed and screamed, and felt that I would soon go mad. Then in my dream I ran and ran in a fever of utter terror, but I did not know what I was running from. . . . I left that hideous temple and that hellish void, yet I knew I must, barring some miracle, return. . . .

At last my eyes flew open. I was not beneath the tree. I was sprawled on a rocky slope, my clothing torn and disordered. My hands were bleeding. I stood up, pain stabbing through me. I recognized the spot—the ridge where I had first seen the blasted area! I must have walked miles—unconscious! The tree was not in sight, and I was glad. . . . Even the knees of my trousers were torn, as if I had crawled part of the way. . . .

I glanced at the sun. Late afternoon! *Where* had I been? I snatched out my watch. It had stopped at 10:34. . . .

II.

"So you have the snapshots?" Theunis drawled. I met his gray eyes across the breakfast table. Three days had slipped by since my return from Hell's Acres. I had told him about the dream beneath the tree, and he had laughed.

"Yes," I replied. "They came last night. Haven't had a chance to open them yet. Give 'em a good, careful study—if they aren't all failures. Perhaps you'll change your mind."

Theunis smiled; sipped his coffee. I gave him the unopened envelope and he quickly broke the seal and withdrew the pictures. He glanced at the first one, and the smile faded from his leonine face. He crushed out his cigarette.

"My God, man! Look at this!"

I seized the glossy rectangle. It was the first picture of the tree, taken at a distance of fifty feet or so. The cause of Theunis' excitement escaped me. There it was, standing boldly on the hill, while below it grew the jungle of grass where I had lain. In the distance were my snow-capped mountains!

"There you are," I cried. "The proof of my story—"

"Look at it!" Theunis snapped. "The shadows—there are three for every rock, bush, and tree!"

He was right. . . . Below the tree, spread in fanlike incongruity, lay three overlapping shadows. Suddenly I realized that the picture held an abnormal and inconsistent element. The leaves on the thing were too lush for the work of sane nature, while the trunk was bulged and knotted in the most abhorrent shapes. Theunis dropped the picture on the table.

"There is something wrong," I muttered. "The tree I saw didn't look as repulsive as that—"

"Are you sure?" Theunis grated. "The fact is, you may have seen many things not recorded on this film."

"It shows more than I saw!"

"That's the point. There is something damnably out of place in this landscape; something I can't understand. The tree seems to suggest a thought—beyond my grasp. . . . It is too misty; too uncertain; too unreal to be natural!" He rapped nervous fingers on the table. He snatched the remaining films and shuffled through them, rapidly.

I reached for the snapshot he had dropped, and sensed a touch of bizarre uncertainty and strangeness as my eyes absorbed its every detail. The flowers and weeds pointed at varying angles, while some of the grass grew in the most bewildering fashion. The tree seemed too veiled and clouded to be readily distinguished, but I noted the huge limbs and the half-bent flower stems that were ready to fall over, yet did not fall. And the many, overlapping shadows. . . . They were, altogether, very disquieting shadows—too long or short when compared to the stems they fell below to give one a feeling of comfortable normality. The landscape hadn't shocked me the day of my visit. . . . There was a dark familiarity and mocking suggestion in it; something tangible, yet distant as the stars beyond the galaxy.

Theunis came back to earth. "Did you mention *three* suns in your dreaming orgy?"

I nodded, frankly puzzled. Then it dawned on me. My fingers trembled slightly as I stared at the picture again. My dream! Of course—

"The others are just like it," Theunis said. "That same uncertainness; that *suggestion*. I should be able to catch the mood of the thing; see it in its real light, but it is too. . . . Perhaps later I shall find out, if I look at it long enough."

We sat in silence for some time. A thought came to me, suddenly, prompted by a strange, inexplicable longing to visit the tree again. "Let's make an excursion. I think I can take you there in half a day."

"You'd better stay away," replied Theunis, thoughtfully. "I doubt if you could find the place again if you wanted to."

"Nonsense," I replied. "Surely, with these photos to guide us—"

"Did you see any familiar landmarks in them?"

His observation was uncanny. After looking through the remaining snaps carefully, I had to admit that there were none.

Theunis muttered under his breath and drew viciously on his cigarette. "A perfectly normal—or nearly so—picture of a spot apparently dropped from nowhere. Seeing mountains at this low altitude is preposterous . . . but wait!"

He sprang from the chair as a hunted animal and raced from the room. I could hear him moving about in our makeshift library, cursing volubly. Before long he reappeared with an old, leather-bound volume. Theunis opened it reverently, and peered over the odd characters.

"What do you call that?" I inquired.

"This is an early English translation of the *Chronicle of Nath,* written by Rudolf Yergler, a German mystic and alchemist who borrowed some of his lore from Hermes Trismegistus, the ancient Egyptian sorcerer. There is a passage here that might interest you—might make you understand why this business is even further from the natural than you suspect. Listen."

> "So in the year of the Black Goat there came unto Nath a shadow that should not be on Earth, and that had no form known to the eyes of Earth. And it fed on the souls of men; they that it gnawed being lured and blinded with dreams till the horror and the endless night lay upon them. Nor did they see that which gnawed them; for the shadow took false shapes that men know or dream of, and only freedom seemed waiting in the Land of the Three Suns. But it was told by priests of the Old Book that he who could see the shadow's true shape, and live after the seeing, might shun its doom and send it back to the starless gulf of its spawning. This none could do save through the Gem; wherefore did Ka-Nefer the High-Priest keep that gem sacred in the temple. And when it was lost with Phrenes, he who braved the hor-

> ror and was never seen more, there was weeping in Nath. Yet did the Shadow depart sated at last, nor shall it hunger again till the cycles roll back to the year of the Black Goat."

Theunis paused while I stared, bewildered. Finally he spoke. "Now, Single, I suppose you can guess how all this links up. There is no need of going deep into the primal lore behind this business, but I may as well tell you that according to the old legends this is the so-called 'Year of the Black Goat'—when certain horrors from the fathomless Outside are supposed to visit the earth and do infinite harm. We don't know how they'll be manifest, but there's reason to think that strange mirages and hallucinations will be mixed up in the matter. I don't like the thing you've run up against—the story or the pictures. It may be pretty bad, and I warn you to look out. But first I must try to do what old Yergler says—to see if I can glimpse the matter as it is. Fortunately the old Gem he mentions has been rediscovered—I know where I can get at it. We must use it on the photographs and see what we see.

"It's more or less like a lens or prism, though one can't take photographs with it. Someone of peculiar sensitiveness might look through and sketch what he sees. There's a bit of danger, and the looker may have his consciousness shaken a trifle; for the real shape of the shadow isn't pleasant and doesn't belong on this earth. But it would be a lot more dangerous not to do anything about it. Meanwhile, if you value your life and sanity, keep away from that hill—and from the thing you think is a tree on it."

I was more bewildered than ever. "How can there be organized beings from the Outside in our midst?" I cried. "How do we know that such things exist?"

"You reason in terms of this tiny earth," Theunis said. "Surely you don't think that the world is a rule for measuring the universe. There are entities we never dream of floating under our very noses. Modern science is thrusting back the borderland of the unknown and proving that the mystics were not so far off the track—"

Suddenly I knew that I did not want to look at the picture again; I wanted to destroy it. I wanted to run from it. Theunis was suggesting something beyond. . . . A trembling, cosmic fear gripped me and drew me away from the hideous picture, for I was afraid I would recognize some object in it. . . .

I glanced at my friend. He was poring over the ancient book, a strange expression on his face. He sat up straight. "Let's call the thing off for today. I'm tired of this endless guessing and wondering. I must get the loan of the gem from the museum where it is, and do what is to be done."

"As you say," I replied. "Will you have to go to Croydon?"

He nodded.

"Then we'll both go home," I said decisively.

III.

I need not chronicle the events of the fortnight that followed. With me they formed a constant and enervating struggle between a mad longing to return to the cryptic tree of dreams and freedom, and a frenzied dread of that selfsame thing and all connected with it. That I did not return is perhaps less a matter of my own will than a matter of pure chance. Meanwhile I knew that Theunis was desperately active in some investigation of the strangest nature—something which included a mysterious motor trip and a return under circumstances of the greatest secrecy. By hints over the telephone I was made to understand that he had somewhere borrowed the obscure and primal object mentioned in the ancient volume as "The Gem," and that he was busy devising a means of applying it to the photographs I had left with him. He spoke fragmentarily of "refraction," "polarization," and "unknown angles of space and time," and indicated that he was building a kind of box or camera obscura for the study of the curious snapshots with the gem's aid.

It was on the sixteenth day that I received the startling message from the hospital in Croydon. Theunis was there, and wanted to see me at once. He had suffered some odd sort of seizure; being found prone and unconscious by friends who found their way into his house after hearing certain cries of mortal agony and fear. Though still weak and helpless, he had now regained his senses and seemed frantic to tell me something and have me perform certain important duties. This much the hospital informed me over the wire; and within half an hour I was at my friend's bedside, marveling at the inroads which worry and tension had made on his features in so brief a time. His first act was to move away the nurses in order to speak in utter confidence.

"Single—I saw it!" His voice was strained and husky. "You must destroy them all—those pictures. I sent it back by seeing it, but the pictures had better go. That tree will never be seen on the hill again

—at least, I hope not—till thousands of eons bring back the Year of the Black Goat. You are safe now—mankind is safe." He paused, breathing heavily, and continued.

"Take the Gem out of the apparatus and put it in the safe—you know the combination. It must go back where it came from, for there's a time when it may be needed to save the world. They won't let me leave here yet, but I can rest if I know it's safe. Don't look through the box as it is—it would fix you as it's fixed me. And burn those damned photographs . . . the one in the box and the others. . . ." But Theunis was exhausted now, and the nurses advanced and motioned me away as he leaned back and closed his eyes.

In another half-hour I was at his house and looking curiously at the long black box on the library table beside the overturned chair. Scattered papers blew about in a breeze from the open window, and close to the box I recognized with a queer sensation the envelope of pictures I had taken. It required only a moment for me to examine the box and detach at one end my earliest picture of the tree, and at the other end a strange bit of amber-colored crystal, cut in devious angles impossible to classify. The touch of the glass fragment seemed curiously warm and electric, and I could scarcely bear to put it out of sight in Theunis' wall safe. The snapshot I handled with a disconcerting mixture of emotions. Even after I had replaced it in the envelope with the rest I had a morbid longing to save it and gloat over it and rush out and up the hill toward its original. Peculiar line-arrangements sprang out of its details to assault and puzzle my memory . . . pictures behind pictures . . . secrets lurking in half-familiar shapes. . . . But a saner contrary instinct, operating at the same time, gave me the vigor and avidity of unplaceable fear as I hastily kindled a fire in the grate and watched the problematic envelope burn to ashes. Somehow I felt that the earth had been purged of a horror on whose brink I had trembled, and which was none the less monstrous because I did not know what it was.

Of the source of Theunis' terrific shock I could form no coherent guess, nor did I dare to think too closely about it. It is notable that I did not at any time have the least impulse to look through the box before removing the gem and photograph. What was shown in the picture by the antique crystal's lens or prism-like power was not, I felt curiously certain, anything that a normal brain ought to be called upon to face. Whatever it was, I had myself been close to it—had been completely under the spell of its allurement—as it brooded on that remote hill in the form of a tree and an unfamiliar landscape. And I did not wish to know what I had so narrowly escaped.

Would that my ignorance might have remained complete! I could sleep better at night. As it was, my eye was arrested before I left the room by the pile of scattered papers rustling on the table beside the black box. All but one were blank, but that one bore a crude drawing in pencil. Suddenly recalling what Theunis had once said about sketching the horror revealed by the gem, I strove to turn away; but sheer curiosity defeated my sane design. Looking again almost furtively, I observed the nervous haste of the strokes, and the unfinished edge left by the sketcher's terrified seizure. Then, in a burst of perverse boldness, I looked squarely at the dark and forbidden design—and fell in a faint.

I shall never describe fully what I saw. After a time I regained my senses, thrust the sheet into the dying fire, and staggered out through the quiet streets to my home. I thanked God that I had not looked through the crystal at the photograph, and prayed fervently that I might forget the drawing's terrible hint of what Theunis had beheld. Since then I have never been quite the same. Even the fairest scenes have seemed to hold some vague, ambiguous hint of the nameless blasphemies which may underlie them and form their masquerading essence. And yet the sketch was so slight—so little indicative of all that Theunis, to judge from his guarded accounts later on, must have discerned!

Only a few basic elements of the landscape were in the thing. For the most part a cloudy, exotic-looking vapor dominated the view. Every object that might have been familiar was seen to be part of something vague and unknown and altogether un-terrestrial—something infinitely vaster than any human eye could grasp, and infinitely alien, monstrous, and hideous as guessed from the fragment within range.

Where I had, in the landscape itself, seen the twisted, half-sentient tree, there was here visible only a gnarled, terrible hand or talon with fingers or feelers shockingly distended and evidently groping toward something on the ground or in the spectator's direction. And squarely below the writhing, bloated digits I thought I saw an outline in the grass where a man had lain. But the sketch was hasty, and I could not be sure.

Duane W. Rimel

The Disinterment

I awoke abruptly from a horrible dream and stared wildly about. Then, seeing the high, arched ceiling and the narrow stained windows of my friend's room, a flood of uneasy revelation coursed over me; and I knew that all of Andrews' hopes had been realized. I lay supine in a large bed, the posts of which reared upward in dizzy perspective; while on vast shelves about the chamber were the familiar books and antiques I was accustomed to seeing in that secluded corner of the crumbling and ancient mansion which had formed our joint home for many years. On a table by the wall stood a huge candelabrum of early workmanship and design, and the usual light window-curtains had been replaced by hangings of somber black, which took on a faint, ghostly luster in the dying light.

I recalled forcibly the events preceding my confinement and seclusion in this veritable medieval fortress. They were not pleasant, and I shuddered anew when I remembered the couch that had held me before my tenancy of the present one—the couch that everyone supposed would be my last. Memory burned afresh regarding those hideous circumstances which had compelled me to choose between a true death and a hypothetical one—with a later re-animation by therapeutic methods known only to my comrade, Marshall Andrews. The whole thing had begun when I returned from the Orient a year before and discovered, to my utter horror, that I had contracted leprosy while abroad. I had known that I was taking grave chances in caring for my stricken brother in the Philippines, but no hint of my own affliction appeared until I returned to my native land. Andrews himself had made the discovery, and kept it from me as long as possible; but our close acquaintance soon disclosed the awful truth.

At once I was quartered in our ancient abode atop the crags overlooking crumbling Hampden, from whose musty halls and quaint, arched doorways I was never permitted to go forth. It was a terrible existence, with the yellow shadow hanging constantly over me; yet my friend never faltered in his faith, taking care not to contract the dread scourge, but meanwhile making life as pleasant and comfortable as possible. His widespread though somewhat sinister fame as a surgeon prevented any authority from discovering my plight and shipping me away.

It was after nearly a year of this seclusion—late in August—that Andrews decided on a trip to the West Indies—to study "native" medical methods, he said. I was left in care of venerable Simes, the household factotum. So far no outward signs of the disease had developed, and I enjoyed a tolerable though almost completely private existence during my colleague's absence. It was during this time that I read many of the tomes Andrews had acquired in the course of his twenty years as a surgeon, and learned why his reputation, though locally of the highest, was just a bit shady. For the volumes included any number of fanciful subjects hardly related to modern medical knowledge: treatises and unauthoritative articles on monstrous experiments in surgery; accounts of the bizarre effects of glandular transplantation and rejuvenation in animals and men alike; brochures on attempted brain transference, and a host of other fanatical speculations not countenanced by orthodox physicians. It appeared, too, that Andrews was an authority on obscure medicaments; some of the few books I waded through revealing that he had spent much time in chemistry and in the search for new drugs which might be used as aids in surgery. Looking back at those studies now, I find them hellishly suggestive when associated with his later experiments.

Andrews was gone longer than I expected, returning early in November, almost four months later; and when he did arrive, I was quite anxious to see him, since my condition was at last on the brink of becoming noticeable. I had reached a point where I must seek absolute privacy to keep from being discovered. But my anxiety was slight as compared with his exuberance over a certain new plan he had hatched while in the Indies—a plan to be carried out with the aid of a curious drug he had learned of from a native "doctor" in Haiti. When he explained that his idea concerned me, I became somewhat alarmed; though in my position there could be little to make my plight worse. I had, indeed, considered more than once the oblivion that would come with a revolver or a plunge from the roof to the jagged rocks below.

On the day after his arrival, in the seclusion of the dimly lit study, he outlined the whole grisly scheme. He had found in Haiti a drug, the formula for which he would develop later, which induced a state of profound sleep in anyone taking it; a trance so deep that death was closely counterfeited—with all muscular reflexes, even the respiration and heart-beat, completely stilled for the time being. Andrews had, he said, seen it demonstrated on natives many times. Some of them remained somnolent for days at a time, wholly immobile and as much like death as death itself. This suspended animation, he explained further, would even pass the closest examination of any medical man. He himself, according to all known laws, would have to report as dead a man under the influence of such a drug. He stated, too, that the subject's body assumed the precise appearance of a corpse—even a slight *rigor mortis* developing in prolonged cases.

For some time his purpose did not seem wholly clear, but when the full import of his words became apparent I felt weak and nauseated. Yet in another way I was relieved; for the thing meant at least a partial escape from my curse, an escape from the banishment and shame of an ordinary death of the dread leprosy. Briefly, his plan was to administer a strong dose of the drug to me and call the local authorities, who would immediately pronounce me dead, and see that I was buried within a very short while. He felt assured that with their careless examination they would fail to notice my leprosy symptoms, which in truth had hardly appeared. Only a trifle over fifteen months had passed since I had caught the disease, whereas the corruption takes seven years to run its entire course.

Later, he said, would come resurrection. After my interment in the family graveyard—beside my centuried dwelling and barely a quarter-mile from his own ancient pile—the appropriate steps would be taken. Finally, when my estate was settled and my decease widely known, he would secretly open the tomb and bring me to his own abode again, still alive and none the worse for my adventure. It seemed a ghastly and daring plan, but to me it offered the only hope for even a partial freedom; so I accepted his proposition, but not without a myriad of misgivings. What if the effect of the drug should wear off while I was in my tomb? What if the coroner should discover the awful ruse, and fail to inter me? These were some of the hideous doubts which assailed me before the experiment. Though death would have been a release from my curse, I feared it even worse than the yellow scourge; feared it even when I could see its black wings constantly hovering over me.

Fortunately I was spared the horror of viewing my own funeral and burial rites. They must, however, have gone just as Andrews had planned, even to the subsequent disinterment; for after the initial dose of the poison from Haiti I lapsed into a semi-paralytic state and from that to a profound, night-black sleep. The drug had been administered in my room, and Andrews had told me before giving it that he would recommend to the coroner a verdict of heart failure due to nerve strain. Of course, there was no embalming—Andrews saw to that—and the whole procedure, leading up to my secret transportation from the graveyard to his crumbling manor, covered a period of three days. Having been buried late in the afternoon of the third day, my body was secured by Andrews that very night. He had replaced the fresh sod just as it had been when the workmen left. Old Simes, sworn to secrecy, had helped Andrews in his ghoulish task.

Later I had lain for over a week in my old familiar bed. Owing to some unexpected effect of the drug, my whole body was completely paralyzed, so that I could move my head only slightly. All my senses, however, were fully alert, and by another week's time I was able to take nourishment in good quantities. Andrews explained that my body would gradually regain its former sensibilities; though owing to the presence of the leprosy it might take considerable time. He seemed greatly interested in analyzing my daily symptoms, and always asked if there was any feeling present in my body.

Many days passed before I was able to control any part of my anatomy, and much longer before the paralysis crept from my enfeebled limbs so that I could feel the ordinary bodily reactions. Lying and staring at my numb hulk was like having it injected with a perpetual anesthetic. There was a total alienation I could not understand, considering that my head and neck were quite alive and in good health.

Andrews explained that he had revived my upper half first and could not account for the complete bodily paralysis; though my condition seemed to trouble him little considering the damnably intent interest he centered upon my reactions and stimuli from the very beginning. Many times during lulls in our conversation I would catch a strange gleam in his eyes as he viewed me on the couch—a glint of victorious exultation which, queerly enough, he never voiced aloud; though he seemed to be quite glad that I had run the gauntlet of death and had come through alive. Still, there was that horror I was to meet in less than six years, which added to my desolation and melancholy during the tedious days in which I awaited the return of normal bodily functions. But I would be up and about, he assured me, before very long, enjoying an existence few men had ever experienced. The words did not, however, impress me with their true and ghastly meaning until many days later.

During that awful siege in bed Andrews and I became somewhat estranged. He no longer treated me so much like a friend as like an implement in his skilled and greedy fingers. I found him possessed of unexpected traits—little examples of baseness and cruelty, apparent even to the hardened Simes, which disturbed me in a most unusual manner. Often he would display extraordinary cruelty to live specimens in his laboratory, for he was constantly carrying on various hidden projects in glandular and muscular transplantation on guinea-pigs and rabbits. He had also been employing his newly discovered sleeping-potion in curious experiments with suspended animation. But of these things he told me very little; though old Simes often let slip chance comments which shed some light on the proceedings. I was not certain how much the old servant knew, but he had surely learned considerable, being a constant companion to both Andrews and myself.

With the passage of time, a slow but consistent feeling began creeping into my disabled body; and at the reviving symptoms Andrews took a fanatical interest in my case. He still seemed more coldly analytical than sympathetic toward me, taking my pulse and heart-beat with more than usual zeal. Occasionally, in his fevered examinations, I saw his hands tremble slightly—an uncommon sight with so skilled a surgeon—but he seemed oblivious of my scrutiny. I was never allowed even a momentary glimpse of my full body, but with the feeble return of the sense of touch, I was aware of a bulk and heaviness which at first seemed awkward and unfamiliar.

Gradually I regained the use of my hands and arms; and with the passing of the paralysis came a new and terrible sensation of physical estrangement. My limbs had difficulty in following the commands of my mind, and every movement was jerky and uncertain. So clumsy were my hands, that I had to become accustomed to them all over again. This must, I thought, be due to my disease and the advance of the contagion in my system. Being unaware of how the early symptoms affected the victim (my brother's being a more advanced case), I had no means of judging; and since Andrews shunned the subject, I deemed it better to remain silent.

One day I asked Andrews—I no longer considered him a friend—if I might try rising and sitting up in bed. At first he objected strenuously, but later, after cautioning me to keep the blankets well up around my chin so that I would not be chilled, he permitted it. This seemed strange, in view of the comfortable temperature. Now that late autumn was slowly turning into winter, the room was always well heated. A growing chilliness at night, and occasional glimpses of a leaden sky through the window, had told me of the changing season; for no calendar was ever in sight upon the dingy walls. With the gentle help of Simes I was eased to a sitting position, Andrews coldly watching from the door to the laboratory. At my success a slow smile spread across his leering features, and he turned to disappear from the darkened doorway. His mood did nothing to improve my condition. Old Simes, usually so regular and consistent, was now often late in his duties, sometimes leaving me alone for hours at a time.

The terrible sense of alienation was heightened by my new position. It seemed that the legs and arms inside my gown were hardly able to follow the summoning of my mind, and it became mentally exhausting to continue movement for any length of time. My fingers, woefully clumsy, were wholly unfamiliar to my inner sense of touch, and I wondered vaguely if I were to be accursed the rest of my days with an awkwardness induced by my dread malady.

It was on the evening following my half-recovery that the dreams began. I was tormented not only at night but during the day as well. I would awaken, screaming horribly, from some frightful nightmare I dared not think about outside the realm of sleep. These dreams consisted mainly of ghoulish things; graveyards at night, stalking corpses, and lost souls amid a chaos of blinding light and shadow. The terrible *reality* of the visions disturbed me most of all: it seemed that some *inside* influence was inducing the grisly vistas of moonlit tombstones and endless catacombs of the restless dead. I could not place their source; and at the end of a week I was quite frantic with abominable thoughts which seemed to obtrude themselves upon my unwelcome consciousness.

By that time a slow plan was forming whereby I might escape the living hell into which I had been propelled. Andrews cared less and less about me, seeming intent only on my progress and growth and recovery of normal muscular reactions. I was becoming every day more convinced of the nefarious doings going on in that laboratory across the threshold—the animal cries were shocking, and rasped hideously on my overwrought nerves. And I was gradually beginning to think that Andrews had not saved me from deportation solely for my own benefit, but for some accursed reason of his own. Simes's attention was slowly becoming slighter and slighter, and I was convinced that the aged servitor had a hand in the deviltry somewhere. Andrews no longer eyed me as a friend, but as an object of experimentation; nor did I like the way he fingered his scalpel when he stood in the narrow doorway and stared at me with crafty alertness. I had never before seen such a transformation come over any man. His ordinarily handsome features were now lined and whisker-grown, and his eyes gleamed as if some imp of Satan were staring from them. His cold, calculating gaze made me shudder horribly, and gave me a fresh determination to free myself from his bondage as soon as possible.

I had lost track of time during my dream-orgy, and had no way of knowing how fast the days were passing. The curtains were often drawn in the daytime, the room being lit by waxen cylinders in the large candelabrum. It was a nightmare of living horror and unreality; though through it all I was gradually becoming stronger. I always gave careful responses to Andrews' inquiries concerning my returning physical control, concealing the fact that a new life was vibrating through me with every passing day—an altogether strange sort of strength, but one which I was counting on to serve me in the coming crisis.

Finally, one chilly evening when the candles had been extinguished, and a pale shaft of moonlight fell through the dark curtains upon my bed, I determined to rise and carry out my plan of action. There had been no movement from either of my captors for several hours, and I was confident that both were asleep in adjoining bedchambers. Shifting my cumbersome weight carefully, I rose to a sitting position and crawled cautiously out of bed, down upon the floor. A vertigo gripped me momentarily, and a wave of weakness flooded my entire being. But finally strength returned, and by clutching at a bed-post I was able to stand upon my feet for the first time in many months. Gradually a new strength coursed through me, and I donned the dark robe which I had seen hanging on a nearby chair. It was quite long, but served as a cloak over my nightdress. Again came that feeling of awful unfamiliarity which I had experienced in bed; that sense of alienation, and of difficulty in making my limbs perform as they should. But there was need for haste before my feeble strength might give out. As a last precaution in dressing, I slipped some old shoes over my feet; but though I could have sworn they were my own, they seemed abnormally loose, so that I decided they must belong to the aged Simes.

Seeing no other heavy objects in the room, I seized from the table the huge candelabrum, upon which the moon shone with a pallid glow, and proceeded very quietly toward the laboratory door.

My first steps came jerkily and with much difficulty, and in the semi-darkness I was unable to make my way very rapidly. When I reached the threshold, a glance within revealed my former friend seated in a large overstuffed chair; while beside him was a smoking-stand upon which were assorted bottles and a glass. He reclined half-way in the moonlight through the large window, and his greasy features were creased in a drunken smirk. An opened book lay in his lap—one of the hideous tomes from his private library.

For a long moment I gloated over the prospect before me, and then, stepping forward suddenly, I brought the heavy weapon down upon his unprotected head. The dull crunch was followed by a spurt of blood, and the fiend crumpled to the floor, his head laid half open. I felt no contrition at taking the man's life in such a manner. In the hideous, half-visible specimens of his surgical wizardry scattered about the room in various stages of completion and preservation, I felt there was enough evidence to blast his soul without my aid. Andrews had gone too far in his practices to continue living, and as one of his monstrous specimens—of that I was now hideously certain—it was my duty to exterminate him.

Simes, I realized, would be no such easy matter; indeed, only unusual good fortune had caused me to find Andrews unconscious.

When I finally reeled up to the servant's bedchamber door, faint from exhaustion, I knew it would take all my remaining strength to complete the ordeal.

The old man's room was in utmost darkness, being on the north side of the structure, but he must have seen me silhouetted in the doorway as I came in. He screamed hoarsely, and I aimed the candelabrum at him from the threshold. It struck something soft, making a sloughing sound in the darkness; but the screaming continued. From that time on events became hazy and jumbled together, but I remember grappling with the man and choking the life from him little by little. He gibbered a host of awful things before I could lay hands on him—cried and begged for mercy from my clutching fingers. I hardly realized my own strength in that mad moment which left Andrews' associate in a condition like his own.

Retreating from the darkened chamber, I stumbled for the stairway door, sagged through it, and somehow reached the landing below. No lamps were burning, and my only light was a filtering of moonbeams coming from the narrow windows in the hall. But I made my jerky way over the cold, damp slabs of stone, reeling from the terrible weakness of my exertion, and reached the front door after ages of fumbling and crawling about in the darkness.

Vague memories and haunting shadows came to taunt me in that ancient hallway; shadows once friendly and understandable, but now grown alien and unrecognizable, so that I stumbled down the worn steps in a frenzy of something more than fear. For a moment I stood in the shadow of the giant stone manor, viewing the moonlit trail down which I must go to reach the home of my forefathers, only a quarter of a mile distant. But the way seemed long, and for a while I despaired of ever traversing the whole of it.

At last I grasped a piece of dead wood as a cane and set out down the winding road. Ahead, seemingly only a few rods away in the moonlight, stood the venerable mansion where my ancestors had lived and died. Its turrets rose spectrally in the shimmering radiance, and the black shadow cast on the beetling hillside appeared to shift and waver, as if belonging to a castle of unreal substance. There stood the monument of half a century; a haven for all my family old and young, which I had deserted many years ago to live with the fanatical Andrews. It stood empty on that fateful night, and I hope that it may always remain so.

In some manner I reached the aged place; though I do not remember the last half of the journey at all. It was enough to be near the family cemetery, among whose moss-covered and crumbling stones I would seek the oblivion I had desired. As I approached the moonlit spot the old familiarity—so absent during my abnormal existence—returned to plague me in a wholly unexpected way. I drew close to my own tombstone, and the feeling of homecoming grew stronger; with it came a fresh flood of that awful sense of alienation and disembodiment which I knew so well. I was satisfied that the end was drawing near; nor did I stop to analyze emotions till a little later, when the full horror of my position burst upon me.

Intuitively I knew my own tombstone; for the grass had scarcely begun to grow between the pieces of sod. With feverish haste I began clawing at the mound, and scraping the wet earth from the hole left by the removal of the grass and roots. How long I worked in the nitrous soil before my fingers struck the coffin-lid, I can never say; but sweat was pouring from me and my nails were but useless, bleeding hooks.

At last I threw out the last bit of loose earth, and with trembling fingers tugged on the heavy lid. It gave a trifle; and I was prepared to lift it completely open when a fetid and nauseous odor assailed my nostrils. I started erect, horrified. Had some idiot placed my tombstone on the wrong grave, causing me to unearth another body? For surely there could be no mistaking that awful stench. Gradually a hideous uncertainty came over me and I scrambled from the hole. One look at the newly made headpiece was enough. This was indeed my own grave . . . but what fool had buried within it another corpse?

All at once a bit of the unspeakable truth propelled itself upon my brain. The odor, in spite of its putrescence, seemed somehow familiar—horribly *familiar*. . . . Yet I could not credit my senses with such an idea. Reeling and cursing, I fell into the black cavity once more, and by the aid of a hastily lit match, lifted the long lid completely open. Then the light went out, as if extinguished by a malignant hand, and I clawed my way out of that accursed pit, screaming in a frenzy of fear and loathing.

When I regained consciousness I was lying before the door of my own ancient manor, where I must have crawled after that hideous rendezvous in the family cemetery. I realized that dawn was close at hand, and rose feebly, opening the aged portal before me and entering the place which had known no footsteps for over a decade. A fever was ravaging my weakened body, so that I was hardly able to stand, but I made my way slowly through the musty, dimly lit chambers and staggered into my own study—the study I had deserted so many years before.

When the sun has risen, I shall go to the ancient well beneath the old willow tree by the cemetery and cast my deformed *self* into it. No other man shall ever view this blasphemy which has survived life longer than it should have. I do not know what people will say when they see my disordered grave, but this will not trouble me if I can find oblivion from that which I beheld amidst the crumbling, moss-crusted stones of the hideous place.

I know now why Andrews was so secretive in his actions; so damnably gloating in his attitude toward me after my artificial death. He had meant me for a specimen all the time—a specimen of his greatest feat of surgery, his masterpiece of unclean witchery . . . an example of perverted artistry for him alone to see. Where Andrews obtained that *other* with which I lay accursed in his moldering mansion I shall probably never know; but I am afraid that it was brought from Haiti along with his fiendish medicine. At least these long hairy arms and horrible short legs are alien to me . . . alien to all natural and sane laws of mankind. The thought that I shall be tortured with that *other* during the rest of my brief existence is another hell.

Now I can but wish for that which once was mine; that which every man blessed of God ought to have at death; that which I saw in that awful moment in the ancient burial ground when I raised the lid on the coffin—my own shrunken, decayed, and headless body.

R. H. Barlow

"Till A' the Seas"

Upon an eroded cliff-top rested the man, gazing far across the valley. Lying thus, he could see a great distance, but in all the sere expanse there was no visible motion. Nothing stirred the dusty plain, the disintegrated sand of long-dry river-beds, where once coursed the gushing streams of Earth's youth. There was little greenery in this ultimate world, this final stage of mankind's prolonged presence upon the planet. For unnumbered aeons the drought and sandstorms had ravaged all the lands. The trees and bushes had given way to small, twisted shrubs that persisted long through their sturdiness; but these, in turn, perished before the onslaught of coarse grasses and stringy, tough vegetation of strange evolution.

The ever-present heat, as Earth drew nearer to the sun, withered and killed with pitiless rays. It had not come at once; long aeons had gone before any could feel the change. And all through those first ages man's adaptable form had followed the slow mutation and modelled itself to fit the more and more torrid air. Then the day had come when men could bear their hot cities but ill, and a gradual recession began, slow yet deliberate. Those towns and settlements closest to the equator had been first, of course, but later there were others. Man, softened and exhausted, could cope no longer with the ruthlessly mounting heat. It seared him as he was, and evolution was too slow to mould new resistances in him.

Yet not at first were the great cities of the equator left to the spider and the scorpion. In the early years there were many who stayed on, devising curious shields and armours against the heat and the deadly dryness. These fearless souls, screening certain buildings against the encroaching sun, made miniature worlds of refuge wherein no protective armour was needed. They contrived marvellously ingenious things, so that for a while men persisted in the rusting towers, hoping thereby to cling to old lands till the searing should be over. For many would not believe what the astronomers said, and looked for a coming of the mild olden world again. But one day the men of Dath, from the new city of Niyara, made signals to Yuanario, their immemorially ancient capital, and gained no answer from the few who remained therein. And when explorers reached that millennial city of bridge-linked towers they found only silence. There was not even the horror of corruption, for the scavenger lizards had been swift.

Only then did the people fully realize that these cities were lost to them; know that they must forever abandon them to nature. The other colonists in the hot lands fled from their brave posts, and total silence reigned within the high basalt walls of a thousand empty towns. Of the dense throngs and multitudinous activities of the past, nothing finally remained. There now loomed against the rainless deserts only the blistered towers of vacant houses, factories, and structures of every sort, reflecting the sun's dazzling radiance and parching in the more and more intolerable heat.

Many lands, however, had still escaped the scorching blight, so that the refugees were soon absorbed in the life of a newer world. During strangely prosperous centuries the hoary deserted cities of the equator grew half-forgotten and entwined with fantastic fables. Few thought of those spectral, rotting towers . . . those huddles of shabby walls and cactus-choked streets, darkly silent and abandoned. . . .

Wars came, sinful and prolonged, but the times of peace were greater. Yet always the swollen sun increased its radiance as Earth drew closer to its fiery parent. It was as if the planet meant to return to that source whence it was snatched, aeons ago, through the accidents of cosmic growth.

After a time the blight crept outward from the central belt. Southern Yarat burned as a tenantless desert—and then the north.

In Perath and Baling, those ancient cities where brooding centuries dwelt, there moved only the scaly shapes of the serpent and the salamander, and at last Loton echoed only to the fitful falling of tottering spires and crumbling domes.

Steady, universal, and inexorable was the great eviction of man from the realms he had always known. No land within the widening stricken belt was spared; no people left unrouted. It was an epic, a titan tragedy whose plot was unrevealed to the actors—this wholesale desertion of the cities of men. It took not years or even centuries, but millennia of ruthless change. And still it kept on—sullen, inevitable, savagely devastating.

Agriculture was at a standstill, the world fast became too arid for crops. This was remedied by artificial substitutes, soon universally used. And as the old places that had known the great things of mortals were left, the loot salvaged by the fugitives grew smaller and smaller. Things of the greatest value and importance were left in dead museums—lost amid the centuries—and in the end the heritage of the immemorial past was abandoned. A degeneracy both physical and cultural set in with the insidious heat. For man had so long dwelt in comfort and security that this exodus from past scenes was difficult. Nor were these events received phlegmatically; their very slowness was terrifying. Degradation and debauchery were soon common; government was disorganized, and the civilizations aimlessly slid back toward barbarism.

When, forty-nine centuries after the blight from the equatorial belt, the whole western hemisphere was left unpeopled, chaos was complete. There was no trace of order or decency in the last scenes of this titanic, wildly impressive migration. Madness and frenzy stalked through them, and fanatics screamed of an Armageddon close at hand.

Mankind was now a pitiful remnant of the elder races, a fugitive not only from the prevailing conditions, but from his own degeneracy. Into the northland and the antarctic went those who could; the rest lingered for years in an incredible saturnalia, vaguely doubting the forthcoming disasters. In the city of Borligo a wholesale execution of the new prophets took place, after months of unfulfilled expectations. They thought the flight to the northland unnecessary, and looked no longer for the threatened ending.

How they perished must have been terrible indeed—those vain, foolish creatures who thought to defy the universe. But the blackened, scorched towns are mute. . . .

These events, however, must not be chronicled—for there are larger things to consider than this complex and unhastening downfall of a lost civilization. During a long period morale was at lowest ebb among the courageous few who settled upon the alien arctic and antarctic shores, now mild as were those of southern Yarat in the long-dead past. But here there was respite. The soil was fertile, and forgotten pastoral arts were called into use anew. There was, for a long time, a contented little epitome of the lost lands; though here were no vast throngs or great buildings. Only a sparse remnant of humanity survived the aeons of change and peopled those scattered villages of the later world.

How many millennia this continued is not known. The sun was slow in invading this last retreat; and as the eras passed there developed a sound, sturdy race, bearing no memories or legends of the old, lost lands. Little navigation was practiced by this new people, and the flying machine was wholly forgotten. Their devices were of the simplest type, and their culture was simple and primitive. Yet they were contented, and accepted the warm climate as something natural and accustomed.

But unknown to these simple peasant-folk, still further rigours of nature were slowly preparing themselves. As the generations passed, the waters of the vast and unplumbed ocean wasted slowly away; enriching the air and the desiccated soil, but sinking lower and lower each century. The splashing surf still glistened bright, and the swirling eddies were still there, but a doom of dryness hung over the whole watery expanse. However, the shrinkage could not have been detected save by instruments more delicate than any then known to the race. Even had the people realized the ocean's contraction, it is not likely that any vast alarm or great disturbance would have resulted, for the losses were so slight, and the seas so great. . . . Only a few inches during many centuries—but in many centuries; increasing—

* * *

So at last the oceans went, and water became a rarity on a globe of sun-baked drought. Man had slowly spread over all the arctic and antarctic lands; the equatorial cities, and many of later habitation, were forgotten even to legend.

And now again the peace was disturbed, for water was scarce, and found only in deep caverns. There was little enough, even of this; and men died of thirst wandering in far places. Yet so slow were these deadly changes, that each new generation of man was loath to believe what it heard from its parents. None would admit that the heat had been less or the water more plentiful in the old days, or take warning that days of bitterer burning and drought were to come. Thus it was even at the end, when only a few hundred human creatures panted for breath beneath the cruel sun; a piteous huddled handful out of all the unnumbered millions who had once dwelt on the doomed planet.

And the hundreds became small, till man was to be reckoned only in tens. These tens clung to the shrinking dampness of the caves, and knew at last that the end was near. So slight was their range that none had ever seen the tiny, fabled spots of ice left close to the planet's poles—if such indeed remained. Even had they existed and been known to man, none could have reached them across the trackless and formidable deserts. And so the last pathetic few dwindled. . . .

It cannot be described, this awesome chain of events that depopulated the whole Earth; the range is too tremendous for any to picture or encompass. Of the people of Earth's fortunate ages, billions of years before, only a few prophets and madmen could have conceived that which was to come—could have grasped visions of the still, dead lands, and long-empty sea-beds. The rest would have doubted . . . doubted alike the shadow of change upon the planet and the shadow of doom upon the race. For man has always thought himself the immortal master of natural things. . . .

II.

When he had eased the dying pangs of the old woman, Ull wandered in a fearful daze out into the dazzling sands. She had been a fearsome thing, shrivelled and so dry; like withered leaves. Her face had been the colour of the sickly yellow grasses that rustled in the hot wind, and she was loathsomely old.

But she had been a companion; someone to stammer out vague fears to, to talk to about this incredible thing; a comrade to share one's hopes for succour from those silent other colonies beyond the mountains. He could not believe none lived elsewhere, for Ull was young, and not certain as are the old.

For many years he had known none but the old woman—her name was Mladdna. She had come that day in his eleventh year, when all the hunters went to seek food, and did not return. Ull had no mother that he could remember, and there were few women in the tiny group. When the men vanished, those three women, the young one and the two old, had screamed fearfully, and moaned long. Then the young one had gone mad, and killed herself with a sharp stick. The old ones buried her in a shallow hole dug with their nails, so Ull had been alone when this still older Mladdna came.

She walked with the aid of a knotty pole, a priceless relique of the old forests, hard and shiny with years of use. She did not say whence she came, but stumbled into the cabin while the young suicide was being buried. There she waited till the two returned, and they accepted her incuriously.

That was the way it had been for many weeks, until the two fell sick, and Mladdna could not cure them. Strange that those younger two should have been stricken, while she, infirm and ancient, lived on. Mladdna had cared for them many days, and at length they died, so that Ull was left with only the stranger. He screamed all the night, so she became at length out of patience, and threatened to die too. Then, hearkening, he became quiet at once; for he was not desirous of complete solitude. After that he lived with Mladdna and they gathered roots to eat.

Mladdna's rotten teeth were ill suited to the food they gathered, but they contrived to chop it up till she could manage it. This weary routine of seeking and eating was Ull's childhood.

Now he was strong, and firm, in his nineteenth year, and the old woman was dead. There was naught to stay for, so he determined at once to seek out those fabled huts beyond the mountains, and live with the people there. There was nothing to take on the journey. Ull closed the door of his cabin—why, he could not have told, for no animals had been there for many years—and left the dead woman within. Half-dazed, and fearful at his own audacity, he walked long hours in the dry grasses, and at length reached the first of the foothills. The afternoon came, and he climbed until he was weary, and lay down on the grasses. Sprawled there, he thought of many things. He wondered at the strange life, passionately anxious to seek out the lost colony beyond the mountains; but at last he slept.

When he awoke there was starlight on his face, and he felt refreshed. Now that the sun was gone for a time, he travelled more quickly, eating little, and determining to hasten before the lack of water became difficult to bear. He had brought none; for the last people, dwelling in one place and never having occasion to bear their precious water away, made no vessels of any kind. Ull hoped to reach his goal within a day, and thus escape thirst; so he hurried on beneath the bright stars, running at times in the warm air, and at other times lapsing into a dogtrot.

So he continued until the sun arose, yet still he was within the small hills, with three great peaks looming ahead. In their shade he rested again. Then he climbed all the morning, and at mid-day surmounted the first peak, where he lay for a time, surveying the space before the next range.

Upon an eroded cliff-top rested the man, gazing far across the valley. Lying thus he could see a great distance, but in all the sere expanse there was no visible motion. . . .

The second night came, and found Ull amid the rough peaks, the valley and the place where he had rested far behind. He was nearly out of the second range now, and hurrying still. Thirst had come upon him that day, and he regretted his folly. Yet he could not have stayed there with the corpse, alone in the grasslands. He sought to convince himself thus, and hastened ever on, tiredly straining.

And now there were only a few steps before the cliff wall would part and allow a view of the land beyond. Ull stumbled wearily down the stony way, tumbling and bruising himself even more. It was nearly before him, this land where men were rumoured to have dwelt; this land of which he had heard tales in his youth. The way was long, but the goal was great. A boulder of giant circumference cut off his view; upon this he scrambled anxiously. Now at last he could behold by the sinking orb his long-sought destination, and his thirst and aching muscles were forgotten as he saw joyfully that a small huddle of buildings clung to the base of the farther cliff.

Ull rested not; but, spurred on by what he saw, ran and staggered and crawled the half mile remaining. He fancied that he could detect forms among the rude cabins. The sun was nearly gone; the hateful, devastating sun that had slain humanity. He could not be sure of details, but soon the cabins were near.

They were very old, for clay blocks lasted long in the still dryness of the dying world. Little, indeed, changed but the living things—the grasses and these last men.

Before him an open door swung upon rude pegs. In the fading light Ull entered, weary unto death, seeking painfully the expected faces.

Then he fell upon the floor and wept, for at the table was propped a dry and ancient skeleton.

* * *

He rose at last, crazed by thirst, aching unbearably, and suffering the greatest disappointment any mortal could know. He was, then, the last living thing upon the globe. His the heritage of the Earth . . . all the lands, and all to him equally useless. He staggered up, not looking at the dim white form in the reflected moonlight, and went through the door. About the empty village he wandered, searching for water and sadly inspecting this long-empty place so spectrally preserved by the changeless air. Here there was a dwelling, there a rude place where things had been made—clay vessels holding only dust, and nowhere any liquid to quench his burning thirst.

Then, in the centre of the little town, Ull saw a well-curb. He knew what it was, for he had heard tales of such things from Mladdna. With pitiful joy, he reeled forward and leaned upon the edge. There, at last, was the end of his search. Water—slimy, stagnant, and shallow, but water—before his sight.

Ull cried out in the voice of a tortured animal, groping for the chain and bucket. His hand slipped on the slimy edge; and he fell upon his chest across the brink. For a moment he lay there—then soundlessly his body was precipitated down the black shaft.

There was a slight splash in the murky shallowness as he struck some long-sunken stone, dislodged aeons ago from the massive coping. The disturbed water subsided into quietness.

And now at last the Earth was dead. The final, pitiful survivor had perished. All the teeming billions; the slow aeons; the empires and civilizations of mankind were summed up in this poor twisted form—and how titanically meaningless it all had been! Now indeed had come an end and climax to all the efforts of humanity—how monstrous and incredible a climax in the eyes of those poor complacent fools of the prosperous days! Not ever again would the planet know the thunderous tramping of human millions—or even the crawling of lizards and the buzz of insects, for they, too, had gone. Now was come the reign of sapless branches and endless fields of tough grasses. Earth, like its cold, imperturbable moon, was given over to silence and blackness forever.

The stars whirred on; the whole careless plan would continue for infinities unknown. This trivial end of a negligible episode mattered not to distant nebulae or to suns new-born, flourishing, and dying. The race of man, too puny and momentary to have a real function or purpose, was as if it had never existed. To such a conclusion the aeons of its farcically toilsome evolution had led.

But when the deadly sun's first rays darted across the valley, a light found its way to the weary face of a broken figure that lay in the slime.

R. H. Barlow

The Night Ocean

I went to Ellston Beach not only for the pleasures of sun and ocean, but to rest a weary mind. Since I knew no person in the little town, which thrives on summer vacationists and presents only blank windows during most of the year, there seemed no likelihood that I might be disturbed. This pleased me, for I did not wish to see anything but the expanse of pounding surf and the beach lying before my temporary home.

My long work of the summer was completed when I left the city, and the large mural design produced by it had been entered in the contest. It had taken me the bulk of the year to finish the painting, and when the last brush was cleaned I was no longer reluctant to yield to the claims of health and find rest and seclusion for a time. Indeed, when I had been a week on the beach I recalled only now and then the work whose success had so recently seemed all-important. There was no longer the old concern with a hundred complexities of colour and ornament; no longer the fear and mistrust of my ability to render a mental image actual, and turn by my own skill alone the dim-conceived idea into the careful draught of a design. And yet that which later befell me by the lonely shore may have grown solely from the mental constitution behind such concern and fear and mistrust. For I have always been a seeker, a dreamer, and a ponderer on seeking and dreaming; and who can say that such a nature does not open latent eyes sensitive to unsuspected worlds and orders of being?

Now that I am trying to tell what I saw I am conscious of a thousand maddening limitations. Things seen by the inward sight, like those flashing visions which come as we drift into the blankness of sleep, are more vivid and meaningful to us in that form than when we have sought to weld them with reality. Set a pen to a dream, and the colour drains from it. The ink with which we write seems diluted with something holding too much of reality, and we find that after all we cannot delineate the incredible memory. It is as if our inward selves, released from the bonds of daytime and objectivity, revelled in prisoned emotions which are hastily stifled when we translate them. In dreams and visions lie the greatest creations of man, for on them rests no yoke of line or hue. Forgotten scenes, and lands more obscure than the golden world of childhood, spring into the sleeping mind to reign until awakening puts them to rout. Amid these may be attained something of the glory and contentment for which we yearn; some image of sharp beauties suspected but not before revealed, which are to us as the Grail to holy spirits of the medieval world. To shape these things on the wheel of art, to seek to bring some faded trophy from that intangible realm of shadow and gossamer, requires equal skill and memory. For although dreams are in all of us, few hands may grasp their moth-wings without tearing them.

Such skill this narrative does not have. If I might, I would reveal to you the hinted events which I perceived dimly, like one who peers into an unlit realm and glimpses forms whose motion is concealed. In my mural design, which then lay with a multitude of others in the building for which they were planned, I had striven equally to catch a trace of this elusive shadow-world, and had perhaps succeeded better than I shall now succeed. My stay in Ellston was to await the judging of that design; and when days of unfamiliar leisure had given me perspective, I discovered that—in spite of those weaknesses which a creator always detects most clearly—I had indeed managed to retain in line and colour some fragments snatched from the endless world of imagining. The difficulties of the process, and the resulting strain on all my powers, had undermined my health and brought me to the beach during this period of waiting. Since I wished to be wholly alone, I rented (to the delight of the incredulous owner) a small house some distance from the village of Ellston—which, because of the waning season, was alive with a moribund bustle of tourists, uniformly uninteresting to me. The house, dark from the sea-wind though it had not been painted, was not even a satellite of the village; but swung below it on the coast like a pendulum beneath a still clock, quite alone upon a hill of weed-grown sand. Like a solitary warm animal it crouched facing the sea, and its inscrutable dirty windows stared upon a lonely realm of earth and sky and enormous sea. It will not do to use too much imagining in a narrative whose facts, could they be augmented and fitted into a mosaic, would be strange enough in themselves; but I thought the little house was lonely when I saw it, and that like myself, it was conscious of its meaningless nature before the great sea.

I took the place in late August, arriving a day before I was expected, and encountering a van and two workingmen unloading the furniture provided by the owner. I did not know then how long I would stay, and when the truck that brought the goods had left I settled my small luggage and locked the door (feeling very proprietary about having a house after months of a rented room) to go down the weedy hill and on the beach. Since it was quite square and had but one room, the house required little exploration. Two windows in each side provided a great quantity of light, and somehow a door had been squeezed in as an after-thought on the oceanward wall. The place had been built about ten years previously, but on account of its distance from Ellston village was difficult to rent even during the active summer season. There being no fireplace, it stood empty and alone from October until far into the spring. Though actually less than a mile below Ellston, it seemed more remote; since a bend in the coast caused one to see only grassy dunes in the direction of the village.

The first day, half-gone when I was installed, I spent in the enjoyment of sun and restless water—things whose quiet majesty made the designing of murals seem distant and tiresome. But this was the natural reaction to a long concern with one set of habits and activities. I was through with my work and my vacation was begun. This fact, while elusive for the moment, showed in everything which surrounded me that afternoon of my arrival, and in the utter change from old scenes. There was an effect of bright sun upon a shifting sea of waves whose mysteriously impelled curves were strewn with what appeared to be rhinestone. Perhaps a water-colour might have caught the solid masses of intolerable light which lay upon the beach where the sea mingled with the sand. Although the ocean bore her own hue, it was dominated wholly and incredibly by the enormous glare. There was no other person near me, and I enjoyed the spectacle without the annoyance of any alien object upon the stage. Each of my senses was touched in a different way, but sometimes it seemed that the roar of the sea was akin to that great brightness, or as if the waves were glaring instead of the sun, each of these being so vigorous and insistent that impressions coming from them were mingled. Curiously, I saw no one bathing near my little square house during that or succeeding afternoons, although the curving shore included a wide beach even more inviting than that at the village, where the surf was dotted with random figures. I supposed that this was because of the distance and because there had never been other houses below the town. Why this unbuilt stretch existed, I could not imagine; since many dwellings straggled along the northward coast, facing the sea with aimless eyes.

I swam until the afternoon had gone, and later, having rested, walked into the little town. Darkness hid the sea from me as I entered, and I found in the dingy lights of the streets tokens of a life which was not even conscious of the great, gloom-shrouded thing lying so close. There were painted women in tinsel adornments, and bored men who were no longer young—a throng of foolish marionettes perched on the lip of the ocean-chasm; unseeing, unwilling to see what lay above them and about, in the multitudinous grandeur of the stars and the leagues of the night ocean. I walked along that darkened sea as I went back to the bare little house, sending the beams of my flashlight out upon the naked and impenetrable void. In the absence of the moon, this light made a solid bar athwart the walls of the uneasy tide; and I felt an indescribable emotion born of the noise of the waters and the perception of my smallness as I cast that tiny beam upon a realm immense in itself, yet only the black border of the earthly deep. That nighted deep, upon which ships were moving alone in the darkness where I could not see them, gave off the murmur of a distant, angry rabble.

When I reached my high residence I knew that I had passed no one during the mile's walk from the village, and yet there somehow lingered an impression that I had been all the while accompanied by the spirit of the lonely sea. It was, I thought, personified in a shape which was not revealed to me, but which moved quietly about beyond my range of comprehension. It was like those actors who wait behind darkened scenery in readiness for the lines which will shortly call them before our eyes to move and speak in the sudden revelation of the footlights. At last I shook off this fancy and sought my key to enter the place, whose bare walls gave a sudden feeling of security.

My cottage was entirely free of the village, as if it had wandered down the coast and was unable to return; and there I heard nothing of the disturbing clamour when I returned each night after supper. I generally stayed but a short while upon the streets of Ellston, though sometimes I went into the place for the sake of the walk it provided. There were all the multitude of curio-shops and falsely regal theatre fronts that clutter vacation towns, but I never went into these; and the place seemed useful only for its restaurants. It was astonishing the number of useless things people found to do.

There was a succession of sun-filled days at first. I rose early, and beheld the grey sky agleam with promise of sunrise; a prophecy fulfilled as I stood witness. Those dawns were cold and their colours faint in comparison to that uniform radiance of day which gives to every hour the quality of white noon. That great light, so apparent the first day, made each succeeding day a yellow page in the book of time. I noticed that many of the beach people were displeased by the inordinate sun, whereas I sought it. After grey months of toil the lethargy induced by a physical existence in a region governed by the simple things—the wind and light and water—had a prompt effect upon me, and since I was anxious to continue this healing process, I spent all my time outdoors in the sunlight. This induced a state at once impassive and submissive, and gave me a feeling of security against the ravenous night. As darkness is akin to death, so is light to vitality. Through the heritage of a million years ago, when men were closer to the mother sea, and when the creatures of which we are born lay languid in the shallow, sun-pierced water; we still seek today the primal things when we are tired, steeping ourselves within their lulling security like those early half-mammals which had not yet ventured upon the oozy land.

The monotony of the waves gave repose, and I had no other occupation than witnessing a myriad ocean moods. There is a ceaseless change in the waters—colours and shades pass over them like the insubstantial expressions of a well-known face; and these are at once communicated to us by half-recognized senses. When the sea is restless, remembering old ships that have gone over her chasms, there comes up silently in our hearts the longing for a vanished horizon. But when she forgets, we forget also. Though we know her a lifetime, she must always hold an alien air, as if something too vast to have shape were lurking in the universe to which she is a door. The morning ocean, glimmering with a reflected mist of blue-white cloud and expanding diamond foam, has the eyes of one who ponders on strange things; and her intricately woven webs, through which dart a myriad coloured fishes, hold the air of some great idle thing which will arise presently from the hoary immemorial chasms and stride upon the land.

I was content for many days, and glad that I had chosen the lonely house which sat like a small beast upon those rounded cliffs of sand. Among the pleasantly aimless amusements fostered by such a life, I took to following the edge of the tide (where the waves left a damp, irregular outline rimmed with evanescent foam) for long distances; and sometimes I found curious bits of shell in the chance litter of the sea. There was an astonishing lot of debris on that inward-curving coast which my bare little house overlooked, and I judged that currents whose courses diverge from the village beach must reach that spot. At any rate, my pockets—when I had any—generally held vast stores of trash; most of which I threw away an hour or two after picking it up, wondering why I had kept it. Once, however, I found a small bone whose nature I could not identify, save that it was certainly nothing out of a fish; and I kept this, along with a large metal bead whose minutely carven design was rather unusual. This latter depicted a fishy thing against a patterned background of seaweed instead of the usual floral or geometrical designs, and was still clearly traceable though worn with years of tossing in the surf. Since I had never seen anything like it, I judged that it represented some fashion, now forgotten, of a previous year at Ellston, where similar fads were common.

I had been there perhaps a week when the weather began a gradual change. Each stage of this progressive darkening was followed by another subtly intensified, so that in the end the entire atmosphere surrounding me had shifted from day to evening. This was more obvious to me in a series of mental impressions than in what I actually witnessed, for the small house was lonely under the grey skies, and there was sometimes a beating wind that came out of the ocean bearing moisture. The sun was displaced by long intervals of cloudiness—layers of grey mist beyond whose unknown depth the sun lay cut off. Though it might glare with the old intensity above that enormous veil, it could not penetrate. The beach was a prisoner in a hueless vault for hours at a time, as if something of the night were welling into other hours.

Although the wind was invigorating and the ocean whipped into little churning spirals of activity by the vagrant flapping, I found the water growing chill, so that I could not stay in it as long as I had done previously, and thus I fell into the habit of long walks, which—when I was unable to swim—provided the exercise that I was so careful to obtain. These walks covered a greater range of sea-edge than my previous wanderings, and since the beach extended in a stretch of miles beyond the tawdry village, I often found myself wholly isolated upon an endless area of sand as evening drew close. When this occurred, I would stride hastily along the whispering sea-border, following the outline so that I should not wander inland and lose my way. And sometimes, when these walks were late (as they grew increasingly to be) I would come upon the crouching house that looked like a harbinger of the village. Insecure upon the wind-gnawed cliffs, a dark blot upon the morbid hues of the ocean sunset, it was more lonely than by the full light of either orb; and seemed to my imagination like a mute, questioning face turned toward me expectant of some action. That the place was isolated I have said, and this at first pleased me; but in that brief evening hour when the sun left a gore-splattered decline and darkness lumbered on like an expanding shapeless blot, there was an alien presence about the place: a spirit, a mood, an impression that came from the surging wind, the gigantic sky, and that sea which drooled blackening waves upon a beach grown abruptly strange. At these times I felt an uneasiness which had no very definite cause, although my solitary nature had made me long accustomed to the ancient silence and the ancient voice of nature. These misgivings, to which I could have put no sure name, did not affect me long, yet I think now that all the while a gradual consciousness of the ocean's immense loneliness crept upon me, a loneliness that was made subtly horrible by intimations—which were never more than such—of some animation or sentience preventing me from being wholly alone.

The noisy, yellow streets of the town, with their curiously unreal activity, were very far away, and when I went there for my evening meal (mistrusting a diet entirely of my own ambiguous cooking) I took increasing and quite unreasonable care that I should return to the cottage before the late darkness, though I was often abroad until ten or so. You will say that such action is unreasonable; that if I had feared the darkness in some childish way, I would have entirely avoided it. You will ask me why I did not leave the place since its loneliness was depressing me. To all this I have no reply, save that whatever unrest I felt, whatever of remote disturbance there was to me in brief aspects of the darkening sun or the eager salt-brittle wind or in the robe of the dark sea that lay crumpled like an enormous garment so close to me, was something which had an origin half in my own heart, which showed itself only at fleeting moments, and which had no very long effect upon me. In the recurrent days of diamond light, with sportive waves flinging blue peaks at the basking shore, the memory of dark moods seemed rather incredible, yet only an hour or two afterward I might again experience these moods once more, and descend to a dim region of despair.

Perhaps these inward emotions were only a reflection of the sea's own mood, for although half of what we see is coloured by the interpretation placed upon it by our minds, many of our feelings are shaped quite distinctly by external, physical things. The sea can bind us to her many moods, whispering to us by the subtle token of a shadow or a gleam upon the waves, and hinting in these ways of her mournfulness or rejoicing. Always she is remembering old things, and these memories, though we may not grasp them, are imparted to us, so that we share her gaiety or remorse. Since I was doing no work, seeing no person that I knew, I was perhaps susceptible to shades of her cryptic meaning which would have been overlooked by another. The ocean ruled my life during the whole of that late summer; demanding it as recompense for the healing she had brought me.

There were drownings at the beach that year; and while I heard of these only casually (such is our indifference to a death which does not concern us, and to which we are not witness), I knew that their details were unsavoury. The people who died—some of them swimmers of a skill beyond the average—were sometimes not found until many days had elapsed, and the hideous vengeance of the deep had scourged their rotten bodies. It was as if the sea had dragged them into a chasm-lair, and had mulled them about in the darkness until, satisfied that they were no longer of any use, she had floated them ashore in a ghastly state. No one seemed to know what had caused these deaths. Their frequency excited alarm among the timid, since the undertow at Ellston was not strong, and since there were known to be no sharks at hand. Whether the bodies showed marks of any attacks I did not learn, but the dread of a death which moves among the waves and comes on lone people from a lightless, motionless place is a dread which men know and do not like. They must quickly find a reason for such a death, even if there are no sharks. Since sharks formed only a suspected cause, and one never to my knowledge confirmed, the swimmers who continued during the rest of the season were on guard against treacherous tides rather than against any possible sea-animal. Autumn, indeed, was not a great distance off, and some people used this as an excuse for leaving the sea, where men were snared by death, and going to the security of inland fields, where one cannot even hear the ocean. So August ended, and I had been at the beach many days.

There had been a threat of storm since the fourth of the new month, and on the sixth, when I set out for a walk in the damp wind, there was a mass of formless cloud, colourless and oppressive, above the ruffled leaden sea. The motion of the wind, directed toward no especial goal but stirring uneasily, provided a sensation of coming animation—a hint of life in the elements which might be the long-expected storm. I had eaten my luncheon at Ellston, and though the heavens seemed the closing lid of a great casket, I ventured far down the beach and away from both the town and my no-longer-to-be-seen house. As the universal grey became spotted with a carrion purple—curiously brilliant despite its sombre hue—I found that I was several miles from any possible shelter. This, however, did not seem very important, for despite the dark skies with their added glow of unknown presage I was in a curious mood that flashed through a body grown suddenly alert and sensitive to the outline of shapes and meanings that were previously dim. Obscurely, a memory came to me; suggested by the likeness of the scene to one I had imagined when a story was read to me in childhood. That tale—of which I had not thought for many years—concerned a woman who was loved by the dark-bearded king of an underwater realm of blurred cliffs where fish-things lived; and who was taken from the golden-haired youth of her troth by a dark being crowned with a priest-like mitre and having the features of a withered ape. What had remained in the corner of my fancy was the image of cliffs beneath the water against the hueless, dusky no-sky of such a realm; and this, though I had forgotten most of the story, was recalled quite unexpectedly by the same pattern of cliff and sky which I then beheld. The sight was similar to what I had imagined in a year now lost save for random, incomplete impressions. Suggestions of this story may have lingered behind certain irritating unfinished memories, and in certain values hinted to my senses by scenes whose actual worth was bafflingly small. Frequently, in a momentary perception, we feel that a feathery landscape (for instance), a woman's dress along the curve of a road by afternoon, or the solidity of a century-defying tree against the pale morning sky (the conditions more than the object being significant) hold something precious, some golden virtue that we must grasp. And yet when such a scene or arrangement is viewed later, or from another point, we find that it has lost its value and meaning for us. Perhaps this is because the thing we see does not hold that elusive quality, but only suggests to the mind some very different thing which remains unremembered. The baffled mind, not wholly sensing the cause of its flashing appreciation, seizes on the object exciting it, and is surprised when there is nothing of worth therein. Thus it was when I beheld the purpling clouds. They held the stateliness and mystery of old monastery towers at twilight, but their aspect was also that of the cliffs in the old fairy-tale. Suddenly reminded of this lost image, I half expected to see, in the fine-spun dirty foam and among the waves which were now as if they had been poured of flawed black glass, the horrid figure of that ape-faced creature, wearing a mitre old with verdigris, advancing from its kingdom in some lost gulf to which those waves were sky.

I did not see any such creature from the realm of imagining, but as the chill wind veered, slitting the heavens like a rustling knife, there lay in the gloom of merging cloud and water only a grey object, like a piece of driftwood, tossing obscurely on the foam. This was a considerable distance out, and since it vanished shortly, may not have been wood, but a porpoise coming to the troubled surface.

I soon found that I had stayed too long contemplating the rising storm and linking my early fancies with its grandeur, for an icy rain began spotting down, bringing a more uniform gloom upon a scene already too dark for the hour. Hurrying along the grey sand, I felt the impact of cold drops upon my back, and before many moments my clothing was soaked throughout. At first I had run, put to flight by the colourless drops whose pattern hung in long linking strands from an unseen sky; but after I saw that refuge was too far to reach in anything like a dry state, I slackened my pace, and returned home as if I had walked under clear skies. There was not much reason to hurry, although I did not idle as upon previous occasions. The constraining wet garments were cold upon me, and with the gathering darkness, and the wind that rose endlessly from the ocean, I could not repress a shiver. Yet there was, beside the discomfort of the precipitous rain, an exhilaration latent in the purplish ravelled masses of cloud and the stimulated reactions of the body. In a mood half of exultant pleasure from resisting the rain (which streamed from me now, and filled my shoes and pockets) and half of strange appreciation of those morbid, dominant skies which hovered with dark wings above the shifting eternal sea, I tramped along the grey corridor of Ellston Beach. More rapidly than I had expected the crouching house showed in the oblique, flapping rain, and all the weeds of the sand cliff writhed in accompaniment to the frantic wind, as if they would uproot themselves to join the far-travelling element. Sea and sky had altered not at all, and the scene was that which had accompanied me, save that there was now painted upon it the hunching roof that seemed to bend from the assailing rain. I hurried up the insecure steps, and let myself into a dry room, where, unconsciously surprised that I was free of the nagging wind, I stood for a moment with water rilling from every inch of me.

There are two windows in the front of that house, one on each side, and these face nearly straight upon the ocean; which I now saw half obscured by the combined veils of the rain and the imminent night. From these windows I looked as I dressed myself in a motley array of dry garments seized from convenient hangers and from a chair too laden to sit upon. I was prisoned on all sides by an unnaturally increased dusk which had filtered down at some undefined hour under cover of the fostering storm. How long I had been on the reaches of wet grey sand, or what the real time was, I could not tell, though a moment's search produced my watch—fortunately left behind and thus avoiding the uniform wetness of my clothing. I half guessed the hour from the dimly seen hands, which were only slightly less indecipherable than the surrounding figures. In another moment my sight penetrated the gloom (greater in the house than beyond the bleared window) and saw that it was 6:45.

There had been no one upon the beach as I came in, and naturally I expected to see no further swimmers that night. Yet when I looked again from the window there appeared surely to be figures blotting the grime of the wet evening. I counted three moving about in some incomprehensible manner, and close to the house another—which may not have been a person but a wave-ejected log, for the surf was now pounding fiercely. I was startled to no little degree, and wondered for what purpose those hardy persons stayed out in such a storm. And then I thought that perhaps like myself they had been caught unintentionally in the rain and had surrendered to the watery gusts. In another moment, prompted by a certain civilized hospitality which overcame my love of solitude, I stepped to the door and emerged momentarily (at the cost of another wetting, for the rain promptly descended upon me in exultant fury) on the small porch, gesticulating toward the people. But whether they did not see me, or did not understand, they made no returning signal. Dim in the evening, they stood as if half-surprised, or as if they awaited some other action from me. There was in their attitude something of that cryptic blankness, signifying anything or nothing, which the house wore about itself as seen in the morbid sunset. Abruptly there came to me a feeling that a sinister quality lurked about those unmoving figures who chose to stay in the rainy night upon a beach deserted by all people, and I closed the door with a surge of annoyance which sought all too vainly to disguise a deeper emotion of fear; a consuming fright that welled up from the shadows of my consciousness. A moment later, when I had stepped to the window, there seemed to be nothing outside but the portentous night. Vaguely puzzled, and even more vaguely frightened—like one who has seen no alarming thing, but is apprehensive of what may be found in the dark street he is soon compelled to cross—I decided that I had very possibly seen no one; and that the murky air had deceived me.

The aura of isolation about the place increased that night, though just out of sight on the northward beach a hundred houses rose in the rainy darkness, their light bleared and yellow above streets of polished glass, like goblin-eyes reflected in an oily forest pool. Yet because I could not see them, or even reach them in bad weather—since I had no car nor any way to leave the crouching house except by walking in the figure-haunted darkness—I realized quite suddenly that I was, to all intents, alone with the dreary sea that rose and subsided unseen, unkenned, in the mist. And the voice of the sea had become a hoarse groan, like that of something wounded which shifts about before trying to rise.

Fighting away the prevalent gloom with a soiled lamp—for the darkness crept in at my windows and sat peering obscurely at me from the corners like a patient animal—I prepared my food, since I had no intentions of going to the village. The hour seemed incredibly advanced, though it was not yet nine o'clock when I went to bed. Darkness had come early and furtively, and throughout the remainder of my stay lingered evasively over each scene and action which I beheld. Something had settled out of the night—something forever undefined, but stirring a latent sense within me, so that I was like a beast expecting the momentary rustle of an enemy.

There were hours of wind, and sheets of the downpour flapped endlessly on the meagre walls barring it from me. Lulls came in which I heard the mumbling sea, and I could guess that large formless waves jostled one another in the pallid whine of the winds, and flung on the beach a spray bitter with salt. Yet in the very monotony of the restless elements I found a lethargic note, a sound that beguiled me, after a time, into slumber grey and colourless as the night. The sea continued its mad monologue, and the wind her nagging; but these were shut out by the walls of unconsciousness, and for a time the night ocean was banished from a sleeping mind.

Morning brought an enfeebled sun—a sun like that which men will see when the earth is old, if there are any men left; a sun more weary than the shrouded, moribund sky. Faint echo of its old image, Phoebus strove to pierce the ragged, ambiguous clouds as I awoke, at moments sending a wash of pale gold rippling across the northwestern interior of my house, at others waning till it was only a luminous ball, like some incredible plaything forgotten on the celestial lawn. After a while the falling rain—which must have continued throughout the previous night—succeeded in washing away those vestiges of purple cloud which had been like the ocean cliffs in an old fairy-tale. Cheated alike of the setting and rising sun, that day merged with the day before, as if the intervening storm had not ushered a long darkness into the world, but had swollen and subsided into one long afternoon. Gaining heart, the furtive sun exerted all his force in dispelling the old mist, streaked now like a dirty window, and cast it from his realm. The shallow blue day advanced as those grimy wisps retreated, and the loneliness which had encircled me welled back into a watchful place of retreat, whence it went no farther, but crouched and waited.

The ancient brightness was now once more upon the sun, and the old glitter on the waves, whose playful blue shapes had flocked upon that coast ere man was born, and would rejoice unseen when he was forgotten in the sepulchre of time. Influenced by these thin assurances, like one who believes the smile of friendship on an enemy's features, I opened my door, and as it swung outward, a black spot upon the inward burst of light, I saw the beach washed clean of any track, as if no foot before mine had disturbed the smooth sand. With the quick lift of spirit that follows a period of uneasy depression, I felt—in a purely yielding fashion and without volition—that my own memory was washed clean of all the mistrust and suspicion and disease-like fear of a lifetime, just as the filth of the water's edge succumbs to a particularly high tide and is carried out of sight. There was a scent of soaked, brackish grass, like the mouldy pages of a book, commingled with a sweet odour born of the hot sunlight upon inland meadows, and these were borne into me like an exhilarating drink, seeping and tingling through my veins as if they would convey to me something of their own impalpable nature, and float me dizzily in the aimless breeze. And conspiring with these things, the sun continued to shower upon me, like the rain of yesterday, an incessant array of bright spears; as if it also wished to hide that suspected background presence which moved beyond my sight and was betrayed only by a careless rustle on the borders of my consciousness, or by the aspect of blank figures staring out of an ocean void. That sun, a fierce ball solitary in the whirlpool of infinity, was like a horde of golden moths against my upturned face. A bubbling white grail of fire divine and incomprehensible, it withheld from me a thousand promised mirages where it granted one. For the sun did actually seem to indicate realms, secure and fanciful, where if I but knew the path I might wander in this curious exultation. Such things come of our own natures, for life has never yielded for one moment her secrets, and it is only in our interpretation of their hinted images that we may find ecstasy or dullness, according to a deliberately induced mood. Yet ever and again we must succumb to her deceptions, believing for the moment that we may this time find the withheld joy. And in this way the fresh sweetness of the wind, on a morning following the haunted darkness (whose evil intimations had given me a greater uneasiness than any menace to my body), whispered to me of ancient mysteries only half-linked with earth, and of pleasures that were the sharper because I felt that I might experience only a part of them. The sun and wind and that scent that rose upon them told me of festivals of gods whose senses are a millionfold more poignant than man's and whose joys are a millionfold more subtle and prolonged. These things, they hinted, could be mine if I gave myself wholly into their bright deceptive power; and the sun, a crouching god with naked celestial flesh, an unknown, too-mighty furnace upon which no eye might look, seemed almost sacred in the glow of my newly sharpened emotions. The ethereal thunderous light it gave was something before which all things must worship astonished. The slinking leopard in his green-chasmed forest must have paused briefly to consider its leaf-scattered rays, and all things nurtured by it must have cherished its bright message on such a day. For when it is absent in the far reaches of eternity, earth will be lost and black against an illimitable void. That morning, in which I shared the fire of life, and whose brief moment of pleasure is secure against the ravenous years, was astir with the beckoning of strange things whose elusive names can never be written.

As I made my way toward the village, wondering how it might look after a long-needed scrubbing by the industrious rain, I saw, tangled in a glimmer of sunlit moisture that was poured over it like a yellow vintage, a small object like a hand, some twenty feet ahead of me, and touched by the repetitious foam. The shock and disgust born in my startled mind when I saw that it was indeed a piece of rotten flesh overcame my new contentment, and engendered a shocked suspicion that it might actually be a hand. Certainly, no fish, or part of one, could assume that look, and I thought I saw mushy fingers wed in decay. I turned the thing over with my foot, not wishing to touch so foul an object, and it adhered stickily to the leather of the shoe, as if clutching with the grasp of corruption. The thing, whose shape was nearly lost, held too much resemblance to what I feared it might be, and I pushed it into the willing grasp of a seething wave, which took it from sight with an alacrity not often shown by those ravelled edges of the sea.

Perhaps I should have reported my find, yet its nature was too ambiguous to make action natural. Since it had been partly *eaten* by some ocean-dwelling monstrousness, I did not think it identifiable enough to form evidence of an unknown but possible tragedy. The numerous drownings, of course, came into my mind—as well as other things lacking in wholesomeness, some of which remained only as possibilities. Whatever the storm-dislodged fragment may have been, and whether it were fish or some animal akin to man, I have never spoken of it until now. And after all, there was no proof that it had not merely been distorted by rottenness into that shape.

I approached the town, sickened by the presence of such an object amid the apparent beauty of the clean beach, though it was horribly typical of the indifference of death in a nature which mingles rottenness with beauty, and perhaps loves the former more. In Ellston I heard of no recent drowning or other mishap of the sea, and found no reference to such in the columns of the local paper—the only one I read during my stay.

It is difficult to describe the mental state in which succeeding days found me. Always susceptible to morbid emotions whose dark anguish might be induced by things outside myself, or might spring from the abysses of my own spirit, I was ridden by a feeling which was not fear or despair, or anything akin to these, but was rather a perception of the brief hideousness and underlying filth of life—a feeling partly a reflection of my internal nature and partly a result of broodings induced by that gnawed rotten object which may have been a hand. In those days my mind was a place of shadowed cliffs and dark moving figures, like the ancient unsuspected realm which the fairy-tale recalled to me. I felt, in brief agonies of disillusionment, the gigantic blackness of this overwhelming universe, in which my days and the days of my race were as nothing to the shattered stars; a universe in which each action is vain and even the emotion of grief a wasted thing. The hours I had previously spent in something of regained health, contentment, and physical well-being were given now (as if those days of the previous week were something definitely ended) to an indolence like that of a man who no longer cares to live. I was engulfed by a piteous lethargic fear of some ineluctable doom which would be, I felt, the completed hate of the peering stars and of the black enormous waves that hoped to clasp my bones within them—the vengeance of all the indifferent, horrendous majesty of the night ocean.

Something of the darkness and restlessness of the sea had penetrated my heart, so that I lived in an unreasoning, unperceiving torment; a torment none the less acute because of the subtlety of its origin and the strange, unmotivated quality of its vampiric existence. Before my eyes lay the phantasmagoria of the purpling clouds, the strange silver bauble, the recurrent stagnant foam, the loneliness of that bleak-eyed house, and the mockery of the puppet town. I no longer went to the village, for it seemed only a travesty of life. Like my own soul, it stood upon a dark enveloping sea—a sea grown slowly hateful to me. And among these images, corrupt and festering, dwelt that of an object whose human contours left ever smaller the doubt of what it once had been.

These scribbled words can never tell of the hideous loneliness (something I did not even wish assuaged, so deeply was it embedded in my heart) which had insinuated itself within me, mumbling of terrible and unknown things stealthily circling nearer. It was not a madness: rather was it a too clear and naked perception of the darkness beyond this frail existence, lit by a momentary sun no more secure than ourselves; a realization of futility that few can experience and ever again touch the life about them; a knowledge that turn as I might, battle as I might with all the remaining power of my spirit, I could neither win an inch of ground from the inimical universe, nor hold for even a moment the life entrusted to me. Fearing death as I did life, burdened with a nameless dread, yet unwilling to leave the scene evoking it, I awaited whatever consummating horror was shifting itself in the immense region beyond the walls of consciousness.

Thus autumn found me, and what I had gained from the sea was lost back into it. Autumn on the beaches—a drear time betokened by no scarlet leaf nor any other accustomed sign. A frightening sea which changes not, though man changes. There was only a chilling of the waters, in which I no longer cared to enter—a further darkening of the pall-like sky, as if eternities of snow were waiting to descend upon the ghastly waves. Once that descent began, it would never cease, but would continue beneath the white and the yellow and the crimson sun, and beneath that ultimate small ruby which shall yield only to the futilities of night. The once friendly waters babbled meaningfully at me, and eyed me with a strange regard, yet whether the darkness of the scene were a reflection of my own broodings or whether the gloom within me were caused by what lay without, I could not have told. Upon the beach and me alike had fallen a shadow, like that of a bird which flies silently overhead—a bird whose watching eyes we do not suspect till the image on the ground repeats the image in the sky, and we look suddenly upward to find that something has been circling above us hitherto unseen.

The day was in late September, and the town had closed the resorts where mad frivolity ruled empty, fear-haunted lives, and where raddled puppets performed their summer antics. The puppets were cast aside, smeared with the painted smiles and frowns they had last assumed, and there were not a hundred people left in the town. Again the gaudy, stucco-fronted buildings lining the shore were permitted to crumble undisturbed in the wind. As the month advanced to the day of which I speak, there grew in me the light of a grey infernal dawn, wherein I felt some dark thaumaturgy would be completed. Since I feared such a thaumaturgy less than a continuance of my horrible suspicions—less than the too-elusive hints of something monstrous lurking behind the great stage—it was with more speculation than actual fear that I waited unendingly for the day of horror which seemed to be nearing. The day, I repeat, was late in September, though whether the 22nd or 23rd I am uncertain. Such details have fled before the recollection of those uncompleted happenings—episodes with which no orderly existence should be plagued, because of the damnable suggestions (and only suggestions) they contain. I knew the time with an intuitive distress of spirit—a recognition too deep for me to explain. Throughout those daylight hours I was expectant of the night; impatient, perhaps, so that the sunlight passed like a half-glimpsed reflection in rippled water—a day of whose events I recall nothing.

It was long since that portentous storm had cast a shadow over the beach, and I had determined, after hesitations caused by nothing tangible, to leave Ellston, since the year was chilling and there was no return to my earlier contentment. When a telegram came for me (lying two days in the Western Union office before I was located, so little was my name known) saying that my design had been accepted—winning above all others in the contest—I set a date for leaving. This news, which earlier in the year would have affected me strongly, I now received with a curious apathy. It seemed as unrelated to the unreality about me, as little pertinent to me, as if it were directed to another person whom I did not know, and whose message had come to me through some accident. None the less, it was that which forced me to complete my plans and leave the cottage by the shore.

There were only four nights of my stay remaining when there occurred the last of those events whose meaning lies more in the darkly sinister impression surrounding them than in anything obviously threatening. Night had settled over Ellston and the coast, and a pile of soiled dishes attested both to my recent meal and to my lack of industry. Darkness came as I sat with a cigarette before the seaward window, and it was a liquid which gradually filled the sky, washing in a floating moon, monstrously elevated. The flat sea bordering upon the gleaming sand, the utter absence of tree or figure or life of any sort, and the regard of that high moon made the vastness of my surroundings abruptly clear. There were only a few stars pricking through, as if to accentuate by their smallness the majesty of the lunar orb and of the restless shifting tide.

I had stayed indoors, fearing somehow to go out before the sea on such a night of shapeless portent, but I heard it mumbling secrets of an incredible lore. Borne to me on a wind out of nowhere was the breath of some strange palpitant life—the embodiment of all I had felt and of all I had suspected—stirring now in the chasms of the sky or beneath the mute waves. In what place this mystery turned from an ancient, horrible slumber I could not tell, but like one who stands by a figure lost in sleep, knowing that it will awake in a moment, I crouched by the window, holding a nearly burnt-out cigarette, and faced the rising moon.

Gradually there passed into that never-stirring landscape a brilliance intensified by the overhead glimmerings, and I seemed more and more under some compulsion to watch whatever might follow. The shadows were draining from the beach, and I felt that with them were all which might have been a harbour for my thoughts when the hinted thing should come. Where any of them did remain they were ebon and blank: still lumps of darkness sprawling beneath the cruel brilliant rays. The endless tableau of the lunar orb —dead now, whatever her past was, and cold as the unhuman sepulchres she bears amid the ruin of dusty centuries older than men —and the sea—astir, perhaps, with some unkenned life, some forbidden sentience—confronted me with a horrible vividness. I arose and shut the window; partly because of an inward prompting, but mostly, I think, as an excuse for transferring momentarily the stream of thought. No sound came to me now as I stood before the closed panes. Minutes or eternities were alike. I was waiting, like my own fearing heart and the motionless scene beyond, for the token of some ineffable life. I had set the lamp upon a box in the western corner of the room, but the moon was brighter, and her bluish rays invaded places where the lamplight was faint. The ancient glow of the round silent orb lay upon the beach as it had lain for aeons, and I waited in a torment of expectancy made doubly acute by the delay in fulfillment and the uncertainty of what strange completion was to come.

Outside the crouching hut a white illumination suggested vague spectral forms whose unreal, phantasmal motions seemed to taunt my blindness, just as unheard voices mocked my eager listening. For countless moments I was still, as if Time and the tolling of her great bell were hushed into nothingness. And yet there was nothing which I might fear: the moon-chiselled shadows were unnatural in no contour, and veiled nothing from my eyes. The night was silent —I knew that despite my closed window—and all the stars were fixed mournfully in a listening heaven of dark grandeur. No motion from me then, or word now, could reveal my plight, or tell of the fear-racked brain imprisoned in flesh which dared not break the silence, for all the torture it brought. As if expectant of death, and assured that nothing could serve to banish the soul-peril I confronted I crouched with a forgotten cigarette in my hand. A silent world gleamed beyond the cheap, dirty windows, and in one corner of the room a pair of dirty oars, placed there before my arrival, shared the vigil of my spirit. The lamp burned endlessly, yielding a sick light hued like a corpse's flesh. Glancing at it now and again for the desperate distraction it gave, I saw that many bubbles unaccountably rose and vanished in the kerosene-filled base. Curiously enough, there was no heat from the wick. And suddenly I became aware that the night as a whole was neither warm nor cold, but strangely neutral—as if all physical forces were suspended, and all the laws of a calm existence disrupted.

Then, with an unheard splash which sent from the silver water to the shore a line of ripples echoed in fear by my heart, a swimming thing emerged beyond the breakers. The figure may have been that of a dog, a human being, or something more strange. It could not have known that I watched—perhaps it did not care—but like a distorted fish it swam across the mirrored stars and dived beneath the surface. After a moment it came up again, and this time, since it was closer, I saw that it was carrying something across its shoulder. I knew, then, that it could be no animal, and that it was a man or something like a man, which came toward the land from a dark ocean. But it swam with a horrible ease.

As I watched, dread-filled and passive, with the fixed stare of one who awaits death in another yet knows he cannot avert it, the swimmer approached the shore—though too far down the southward beach for me to discern its outlines or features. Obscurely loping, with sparks of moonlit foam scattered by its quick gait, it emerged and was lost among the inland dunes.

Now I was possessed by a sudden recurrence of fear, which had died away in the previous moments. There was a tingling coldness all over me—though the room, whose window I dared not open now, was stuffy. I thought it would be very horrible if something were to enter a window which was not closed.

Now that I could no longer see the figure, I felt that it lingered somewhere in the close shadows, or peered hideously at me from whatever window I did not watch. And so I turned my gaze, eagerly and frantically, to each successive pane; dreading that I might indeed behold an intrusive regarding face, yet unable to keep myself from the terrifying inspection. But though I watched for hours, there was no longer anything upon the beach.

So the night passed, and with it began the ebbing of that strangeness—a strangeness which had surged up like an evil brew within a pot, had mounted to the very rim in a breathless moment, had paused uncertainly there, and had subsided, taking with it whatever unknown message it had borne. Like the stars that promise the revelation of terrible and glorious memories, goad us into worship by this deception, and then impart nothing, I had come frighteningly near to the capture of an old secret which ventured close to man's haunts and lurked cautiously just beyond the edge of the known. Yet in the end I had nothing. I was given only a glimpse of the furtive thing; a glimpse made obscure by the veils of ignorance. I cannot even conceive what might have shown itself had I been too close to that swimmer who went shoreward instead of into the ocean. I do not know what might have come if the brew had passed the rim of the pot and poured outward in a swift cascade of revelation. The night ocean withheld whatever it had nurtured. I shall know nothing more.

Even yet I do not know why the ocean holds such a fascination for me. But then, perhaps none of us can solve those things—they exist in defiance of all explanation. There are men, and wise men, who do not like the sea and its lapping surf on yellow shores; and they think us strange who love the mystery of the ancient and unending deep. Yet for me there is a haunting and inscrutable glamour in all the ocean's moods. It is in the melancholy silver foam beneath the moon's waxen corpse; it hovers over the silent and eternal waves that beat on naked shores; it is there when all is lifeless save for unknown shapes that glide through sombre depths. And when I behold the awesome billows surging in endless strength, there comes upon me an ecstasy akin to fear; so that I must abase myself before this mightiness, that I may not hate the clotted waters and their overwhelming beauty.

Vast and lonely is the ocean, and even as all things came from it, so shall they return thereto. In the shrouded depths of time none shall reign upon the earth, nor shall any motion be, save in the eternal waters. And these shall beat on dark shores in thunderous foam, though none shall remain in that dying world to watch the cold light of the enfeebled moon playing on the swirling tides and coarse-grained sand. On the deep's margin shall rest only a stagnant foam, gathering about the shells and bones of perished shapes that dwelt within the waters. Silent, flabby things will toss and roll along empty shores, their sluggish life extinct. Then all shall be dark, for at last even the white moon on the distant waves shall wink out. Nothing shall be left, neither above nor below the sombre waters. And until that last millennium, and beyond the perishing of all other things, the sea will thunder and toss throughout the dismal night.

H. P. Lovecraft: A Biographical Note

Howard Phillips Lovecraft, the visionary writer generally regarded as the mastermind of modern horror fiction, was born in Providence, Rhode Island, on August 20, 1890. The precocious only child of an ill-fated marriage, he endured a cloistered and traumatic upbringing. Lovecraft never knew his father, a traveling salesman of English ancestry who was institutionalized with syphilitic dementia in 1893. He was raised in his birthplace, the Victorian mansion of his maternal grandfather, by an overprotective mother and two maiden aunts. At the age of eight he discovered the stories of Edgar Allan Poe, whose aesthetics marked him forever.

Frequent illnesses disrupted the boy's formal schooling, but he devoured books on astronomy and Greek mythology and was enthralled by the poetry of Dryden and Pope. Financial reversals occasioned by his grandfather's death in 1904 forced the family to sell their ancestral home and seek lodgings in a nearby duplex. The move intensified an already claustrophobic relationship with his mother, who instilled in Lovecraft a profound conviction that he was different from other people.

Lovecraft suffered a nervous breakdown in 1908 and over the next five years became as reclusive as any of his eccentric fictional narrators. He gradually emerged from his depression through membership in the United Amateur Press Association (UAPA), a group of fledgling writers who published their own magazines. In addition to contributing poetry and essays to various journals, he put out thirteen issues of his own paper, *The Conservative* (1915–23), and began a prolific correspondence with colleagues. The five volumes of his posthumously issued *Selected Letters* (published 1965–76) represent some of Lovecraft's most substantial prose and reveal him to be an artist and philosopher of wide-ranging intellect. "Lovecraft [was] one of the most exhaustively self-chronicled individuals of his century," says his preeminent interpreter, S. T. Joshi. "His letters are the equivalent of a Pepys diary in the exhibition of the fluctuations of his mind and heart."

In 1921, while attending a convention of the UAPA in Boston, Lovecraft met Sonia Greene, a widowed Brooklyn milliner seven years his senior. Their brief, disastrous marriage took him to New York City for two years; his return to Providence in the spring of 1926 prompted the greatest creative outburst of his short career.

"The oldest and strongest emotion of mankind is fear, and the oldest and strongest kind of fear is fear of the unknown," observed Lovecraft in his pioneering essay *Supernatural Horror in Literature* (1925–27). Guided by this dictum, he produced a relatively small body of fiction: some sixty stories, most of which appeared in the newly founded pulp magazine *Weird Tales*. Three of them—*The Dream-Quest of Unknown Kadath* (1926–27), *The Case of Charles Dexter Ward* (1927), and *At the Mountains of Madness* (1931)—are generally classified as short novels. Many of Lovecraft's early pieces are innocuous, dreamlike creations heavily influenced by the Irish fantasist Lord Dunsany. In stark contrast are his harrowing tales of terror set against a meticulously described, historically grounded New England landscape. Lovecraft's most acclaimed stories are those in the cycle known as the "Cthulhu Mythos." Combining elements of horror and science fiction, they are an extended elaboration of Lovecraft's recurring fantasy that an entire alien civilization lurks on the underside of our known world. Included in the cycle is *At the Mountains of Madness,* in which an unsuspecting expedition uncovers a city of untold terror buried beneath an Antarctic wasteland. "*At the Mountains of Madness* ranks high among the horror stories of the English language," said *Time*. Joyce Carol Oates reflected: "There is a melancholy, operatic grandeur in Lovecraft's most passionate work, like *At the*

Mountains of Madness; a curious elegiac poetry of unspeakable loss, of adolescent despair and an existential loneliness so pervasive that it lingers in the reader's memory, like a dream, long after the rudiments of Lovecraftian plot have faded."

H. P. Lovecraft died of intestinal cancer in Providence on March 15, 1937. Fame accrued to him posthumously, owing chiefly to the efforts of Arkham House Publishers, which brought his writings to a wider audience. Beginning with *The Outsider and Others* (1939) and *Beyond the Wall of Sleep* (1943), the firm issued numerous collections of Lovecraft's work. Within a decade of his premature death, *Best Supernatural Stories of H. P. Lovecraft* (1945) would sell more than sixty-seven thousand hardcover copies in a single year.

"Lovecraft's fiction is one of the cornerstones of modern horror . . . a unique and visionary world of wonder, terror, and delirium," said Clive Barker. "[Lovecraft is] the American writer of the twentieth century most frequently compared with Poe, both in the quality of his art [and in] its thematic preoccupations," observed Joyce Carol Oates. "[He has] had an incalculable influence on succeeding generations of writers of horror fiction." And Stephen King concluded: "H. P. Lovecraft has yet to be surpassed as the twentieth century's greatest practitioner of the classic horror tale.

T0089065

PENGUIN BOOKS

AMERICAN DREAM

Jason DeParle is a senior writer for *The New York Times* and a frequent contributor to *The New York Times Magazine*. A graduate of Duke University, DeParle won a George Polk Award and was a two-time finalist for the Pulitzer Prize for his reporting on the welfare system. He lives in Washington, D.C., with his wife, Nancy-Ann, and their two sons.

Praise for *American Dream*

New York Public Library Helen Bernstein Award Winner
Sidney Hillman Award Winner
***Washington Monthly* Political Book Award Winner**

"Masterful . . . every bit the exhaustive and authoritative account we might expect from a *New York Times* reporter whose welfare coverage during the Clinton years twice made him a finalist for the Pulitzer Prize. What's startling is the gripping read DeParle provides along the way—an alchemy wrought by the fusion of his encyclopedic knowledge with his mischievous prose. The story of welfare reform turns out to be suspenseful, emotionally rich, rife with dramatic reversals and packed with enough ironies to keep Don DeLillo busy for several years. Who knew?"

—*The Nation*

"Fascinating . . . one of the best books on the American underclass ever written, a compelling account that is disturbing, yet hopeful."

—*National Review*

"Journalism doesn't get any better than this."
—Ellen Goodman, *The Boston Globe*

"DeParle connects the personal and the political . . . with a keen eye and an even more remarkable pen." —*American Prospect*

"Jason DeParle's *American Dream* is a singular achievement. He interweaves a fascinating discussion of the politics of the welfare reform movement with a poignant portrayal of the lives of three women in one extended family who move on and off the welfare rolls in a struggle to survive. This is must reading for anyone concerned about the limitations of American social policy in addressing the problems of the urban poor."
—William Julius Wilson, author of *The Truly Disadvantaged*, Lewis P. and Linda L. Geyser University Professor, Harvard University

"Beautifully written . . . important . . . the narrative really crackles." —*The New Republic*

"A significant book—clear-headed, deeply sensitive, and richly informative." —*San Jose Mercury News*

"DeParle . . . opens up the lives of his subjects in a way that . . . challenges easy left and right assumptions about them. . . . It's DeParle's achievement to detail all these impolite truths while catching you up in these women's lives and revealing their underlying strength. It helps that he's picked an appealing central character in Angie, the nurse's aide, who has a hilarious, no-B.S. mouth on her. . . . DeParle does a brilliant job."
—Mickey Kaus, *Slate*

"A panoramic view . . . starkly honest . . . a humorous, emotional story that is exhaustive in detail and scope."
—*The Boston Globe*

"A powerful bracing antidote . . . masterful detail."

—*Los Angeles Times*

"DeParle . . . shuns sentimentality and middle-class moralizing. His women are tough, profane and sad. They make wrong decisions, and you cringe. They hustle the system, and you shake your head. Then they surprise you by climbing out of bed in the middle of a frigid Wisconsin night to catch the van to suburban nursing homes in order to work double shifts. . . . It might even become an instant classic along the lines of Anthony Lukas' *Common Ground.*" —*The Times-Picayune*

"Reads like an epic novel." —*New York Post*

"With equal measure of compassion and dispassion, Jason DeParle confronts us inescapably with the reality of poverty in America. You cannot read this book and remain indifferent to those who are being left behind. This is one of the great works on social policy of this generation."

—Daniel Schorr, NPR senior news analyst

"A brilliant exercise that combines an honest but sensitive portrait of the women and their families with a larger look at the policy and the politics of welfare reform." —*The Economist*

"Superb and affecting . . . debunks many myths surrounding the old system." —*BusinessWeek*

"In this beautifully written, heartfelt book, Jason DeParle has pulled off a stunning feat of journalistic storytelling. Equally at home in the West Wing as he is on the inner-city streets of Milwaukee, DeParle chronicles the story behind the most important piece of social policy to come along in decades, and its impact on real lives. With a novelist's eye for irony and detail, he is unflinching in his reporting. What he finds will surprise you. It did me." —Alex Kotlowitz, author of *There Are No Children Here*

"Richly researched, beautifully written." —*Mother Jones*

"A superb book—honest, richly observed, and artfully written."
—*Commentary*

"A superb piece of reporting and narrative . . . his stories simmer on the page." —*Dissent*

"A dramatic and moving journey . . . told through three amazing women." —Townhall.com

"Convictions and prejudices of the left and the right all fall before this meticulously researched book; it will become a classic account of the lives of the American poor."
—Nathan Glazer, professor of sociology, Harvard University

"This is a book that will break your heart and open your mind. In the vividness of its characters and the sweep of its ambition, *American Dream* is the *Les Miserables* of our day. This book teems with humor, surprise, paradox, and redemption."
—Sister Helen Prejean, author of *Dead Man Walking*

American Dream

THREE WOMEN,
TEN KIDS,
AND A
NATION'S DRIVE
TO END WELFARE

Jason DeParle

PENGUIN BOOKS

To Nancy-Ann, Nicholas, and Zachary

PENGUIN BOOKS
Published by the Penguin Group
Penguin Group (USA) Inc., 375 Hudson Street, New York, New York 10014, U.S.A.
Penguin Group (Canada), 90 Eglinton Avenue East, Suite 700, Toronto,
Ontario, Canada M4P 2Y3 (a division of Pearson Penguin Canada Inc.)
Penguin Books Ltd, 80 Strand, London WC2R 0RL, England
Penguin Ireland, 25 St Stephen's Green, Dublin 2, Ireland (a division of Penguin Books Ltd)
Penguin Group (Australia), 250 Camberwell Road, Camberwell,
Victoria 3124, Australia (a division of Pearson Australia Group Pty Ltd)
Penguin Books India Pvt Ltd, 11 Community Centre, Panchsheel Park, New Delhi - 110 017, India
Penguin Group (NZ), 67 Apollo Drive, Rosedale, North Shore 0632, New Zealand
(a division of Pearson New Zealand Ltd)
Penguin Books (South Africa) (Pty) Ltd, 24 Sturdee Avenue, Rosebank, Johannesburg 2196, South Africa

Penguin Books Ltd, Registered Offices:
80 Strand, London WC2R 0RL, England

First published in the United States of America by Viking Penguin,
a member of Penguin Group (USA) Inc. 2004
Published in Penguin Books 2005

Copyright © Jason DeParle, 2004
All rights reserved

Excerpt from "What Does the Political Scientist Know" by Artur Miedzyrzecki from *Spoiling Cannibals' Fun: Polish Poetry from the Last Two Decades of Communist Rule,* edited and translated by Stanislaw Baranczak and Clare Cavanagh (Northwestern University Press). Used by permission.

THE LIBRARY OF CONGRESS HAS CATALOGUED THE HARDCOVER EDITION AS FOLLOWS:
DeParle, Jason.
American dream : three women, ten kids, and a nation's drive to end welfare / Jason DeParle.
p. cm.
Includes index.
ISBN 0-670-89275-0 (hc.)
ISBN 978-0-14-303437-7 (pbk.)
1. Public welfare—United States—Case studies. 2. Welfare recipients—Employment—United States—Case studies 3. Public welfare administration—United States—Case studies. I. Title.
HV95.D26 2004
362.5'568'0973—dc22 2004049494

Printed in the United States of America
Designed by Nancy Resnick

Except in the United States of America, this book is sold subject to the condition that it shall not, by way of trade or otherwise, be lent, resold, hired out, or otherwise circulated without the publisher's prior consent in any form of binding or cover other than that in which it is published and without a similar condition including this condition being imposed on the subsequent purchaser.

The scanning, uploading and distribution of this book via the Internet or via any other means without the permission of the publisher is illegal and punishable by law. Please purchase only authorized electronic editions, and do not participate in or encourage electronic piracy of copyrighted materials. Your support of the author's rights is appreciated.

147028622

I think all of us know in our heart of hearts America's biggest problem today is that too many of our people never got a shot at the American Dream.

—BILL CLINTON
FEBRUARY 2, 1993

I am born of black color
Descendant of slaves,
Who worked and cried so I can see better days
Who fought and ran
So I can be free to see better days.
Better days are here, so they say
So why am I still working, running, fighting and crying?
For my better days?
Or is it so my descendants can know of the work I'm putting in
For their better days?

—ANGELA JOBE
2003

CONTENTS

PART I

Welfare

ONE

The Pledge:
Washington and Milwaukee, 1991

Bruce Reed needed a better line.

A little-known speechwriter in a long-shot campaign, he was trapped in the office on a Saturday afternoon, staring at a flat phrase. A few weeks earlier, his boss, Bill Clinton, had stood on the steps of the Arkansas Capitol to announce he was running for president. One of the things Clinton had criticized that day was welfare. "We should insist that people move off the welfare rolls and onto the work rolls," he said. It wasn't the kind of thing most Democrats said, which was one reason Reed liked it; he thought the party carried too much liberal baggage, especially in its defense of the dole. But the phrase wasn't particularly memorable, either. With Clinton planning a big speech at Georgetown University, Reed tried again.

"If you can work, you'll have to do so," he wrote.

Mmmmm . . . still not right.

At thirty-one, Reed had a quick grin and an unlined face, but he was less of an innocent than he seemed. Five months earlier, when Clinton was still weighing the race, Reed had struck a hard-boiled pose. "A message has to fit on a bumpersticker," he wrote. "Sharpen those lines and you'll get noticed. Fuzz them and you'll disappear." Now the welfare rolls hit new highs with every passing month. And Reed lacked bumper-sticker stuff. At 5:00 p.m. he joined a conference call with a half-dozen other operatives in the fledgling campaign. Clinton wasn't on the line. He was in such a bad mood he wanted to cancel the speech. His voice was weak; he didn't feel ready. He wanted Mario Cuomo, the rival he most feared, to define his vision first. He was angry to hear that invitations had gone out and it was too late to turn back.

The group reviewed the latest draft, which outlined Clinton's domestic plans, and agreed the welfare section needed work. How about calling for an "end to permanent welfare"? Reed asked. That was better. Not quite right, but better. They swapped a few more lines, and the following morning Reed sent out a draft with a catchy new phrase. If Clinton spotted the change, he didn't say. On October 23, 1991, he delivered the words as drafted: "In a Clinton administration we're going to put an end to welfare as we know it." By the time it was clear the slogan mattered, no one could say who had coined it.

At first, no one noticed. *The New York Times* didn't cover the speech, and *The Washington Post* highlighted Clinton's promise to create a "New Covenant." But soon the power of the phrase made itself known. *End welfare as we know it*. "Pure heroin," one of the pollsters called it. When Reed reached the White House, he taped the words to his wall and called them his "guiding star." In time, they would send 9 million women and children streaming from the rolls.

One of those women was Angela Jobe. The month Bill Clinton announced that he was running for president, she stepped off a Greyhound bus in Milwaukee to start a new life. She was twenty-five years old and arrived from Chicago towing two large duffel bags and three young kids. Angie had a pretty milk-chocolate face and a fireplug build—her four-foot-eleven-inch frame carried 150 pounds—and the combination could make her look tender or tough, depending on her mood. She had never seen Milwaukee before and pronounced herself unimpressed. "Why they got all these old-ass houses!" she groused. "Where the brick at?" Irreverence was Angie's religion. She arrived in Milwaukee as she moved through the world, a short, stout fountain of exclamation points, half of them capping sentences that would peel paint from the bus station walls. Absent her animating humor, the transcript may sound off-putting. But up close her habit of excitable swearing, about her "cheap-ass jobs" and "crazy-ass friends" and her "too-cool, too-slick motherfucker" men, came off as something akin to charm. "I just express myself so accurately!" she laughed.

The cascade of off-color commentary, flowing alongside the late-night cans of Colt 45, could make Angie seem like a jaded veteran of ghetto life. Certainly she had plenty to feel jaded about. She grew up on the borders of Chicago's gangland. Her father was a drunk. She had her first baby at seventeen, dropped out of high school, and had two more in quick succession. She didn't have a diploma or a job, and the man she loved was in jail. By the time she arrived in Milwaukee, she had been on welfare for nearly eight years, the sum of her adult life. The hard face was real but also a mask. Her mother had worked two jobs to send her to parochial school, and though Angie tried to hide it, she still bore traces of the English student from Aquinas High. Lots of women came to Milwaukee looking for welfare checks. Not many then felt the need to start a poem about their efforts to discern God's will:

I'm tired
Of trying to understand
What God wants of me

Worried that was *too* irreverent, Angie substituted "the world" for "God" and stored the unfinished page in a bag so high in her closet she couldn't reach it with a chair. The old red nylon bag was filled with her yellowing treasures: love letters, journals, poems by Gwendolyn Brooks, the hospital bracelets that each of her kids had worn in the nursery. Stories of street fights Angie was happy to share, but the bag was so private that hardly anyone knew it existed. "Don't you know I like looking mean?" she said one day. While it sounded like one of her self-mocking jokes, Angie segued into a quiet confession. "If people think you're nice, they'll take your kindness for weakness. That's a side of me I don't want anybody to see. That way I don't have to worry about nobody hurting me." In welfare terms, Angie could pass as a paragon of "dependency": unmarried, uneducated, and unemployed. But Angie never thought of herself as depending on anything. She saw herself as a strong, self-reliant woman who did what it took to get by. She saw herself as a survivor.

No one survived on welfare alone, especially in Chicago, where benefits were modest but rents were not. Sometimes Angie worked, without telling welfare, at fast-food restaurants. Stints at Popeye's,

Church's, and KFC had marked her as a chicken-joint triathlete, a minimum-wage workhorse steeped in grease. She also relied on her children's father, Greg, a tall, soft-spoken man in braids who looked out at the world with seductive eyes. Greg, not welfare, marked the major border in Angie's life. Before Greg, she wore a plaid jumper and went to parochial school. After Greg, *right* after Greg, Angie was a teenage mother. Their relationship hadn't completely passed as a portrait of harmony. Once, when he went without feeding the kids, she tried to shoot him. But unlike most teen parents, they stayed together, and by the time their oldest child was entering school, Greg was making "beaucoup money" in the industry employing most men Angie knew. Greg was selling cocaine. His arrest, in the summer of 1991, hit her with the force of a sudden death. She had never even lived alone, never mind raised kids by herself. Without Greg, she couldn't pay the bills: rent was more than her entire welfare check. Ninety miles away, the economics were reversed. You could sign up for welfare, get an apartment, and have money left over. So many poor families were fleeing Chicago that taxpayers in southern Wisconsin griped about "Greyhound therapy." Higher welfare, lower rent—that's all Angie knew about Milwaukee when she stepped off the bus.

A few days later, Greg's sister arrived. Since Angie and Greg were all but married, Jewell was her all but sister-in-law. She was also Angie's closest friend. Jewell's boyfriend, Tony, had been caught in the same arrest, so Jewell faced a similar problem: she was twenty-two, with a three-year-old son, and unless she moved to the projects she couldn't live on welfare in Chicago. Plus she was six months pregnant. On the outside, they formed a study in contrasts. While Angie groomed herself for durability, Jewell arrived in cover-girl style. She was a half foot taller, with a curl in her hair, perfect teeth, and art gallery nails; with a gleaming pair of tennis shoes, she could turn sweatpants into high couture. She wasn't married, but Tony's letters from jail came addressed to "my sexy wife." Still, there was nothing brittle about her beauty or soft behind her reserve. While Angie swore away her frustrations and cried after too many beers, Jewell treated pain as a weakness best locked inside. Jewell was a survivor, too.

They went about settling down. Piling in with Angie's cousin for a week, they signed up for welfare at a three-story fortress of local fame known by its address, "Twelfth and Vliet." Like the shuttered homes around it, the building had traced the parabolic journey of American industrial life; launched as a department store near the century's start, it had sparkled with the city's blue-collar prosperity before being padlocked in 1961 and sold off to the county. By the time Angie and Jewell arrived, the building overlooked an eight-lane gash that funneled the prosperity to the suburbs north and west, and there was nothing left inside but long forms and hard chairs. The thirty-one-page application asked if they owned any stocks, bonds, trust funds, life insurance, farm equipment, livestock, snowmobiles, or boats. It asked nothing about the tragedy that had brought them to the county's door. Welfare dispensed money, not advice.

A few days later, they had their checks and started the apartment hunt. Jewell got a tip from a neighbor. If they moved into a homeless shelter first, the Red Cross would pay their security deposit and first month's rent. ("Getting your Red Cross" it was called.) "Homeless shelter" may conjure a vision of winos in a barracks, but the Family Crisis Center, in a converted monastery in the heart of the ghetto, had a cheerful air. It offered private rooms, a play area for the kids, and a chance to meet new people. From the shelter, they resumed the search for housing, and Angie found the perfect solution: adjacent apartments in a renovated Victorian complex on First Street, owned by an old woman who soon grew too senile to collect the rent.

On October 23, 1991—the day Clinton pledged to "end welfare"—two welfare mothers and four welfare kids awoke on a wooden floor. The apartment didn't have a refrigerator or stove, so they fashioned three meals from lunch meat. At five, Angie's middle child, Redd, still cried for his father. He was having a harder time accepting the arrest than Kesha, an openhearted, adaptable girl of seven, or Von, who, even at four, coolly distanced himself from family trouble; Redd was as hot as his name. Angie ached for Greg, too, but she was relieved to finish the move. There's something to having a place of your own, even when it's empty and hard.

As soon as he pledged to end welfare, Clinton had second thoughts. He needed the liberals, who turn out in primaries, but Cuomo, the liberals' philosopher-king, struck back by calling dependency a myth. Clinton feared his enemies might compare him to another white southerner who was criticizing welfare in the fall of 1991, the ex-Klansman David Duke. (Cuomo tried to do just that.) Looking ahead to the Super Tuesday ballot, Clinton chided his staff that "half this election is about winning the southern black vote." A black governor, Doug Wilder, was running, and Clinton feared Wilder might call him a racist. "This is a major, major deal," Clinton warned.

To protect himself, Clinton launched an attack against Duke even before the Georgetown speech. He also put out feelers to Jesse Jackson, who kept his guns quiet. But the best reassurance came from black voters themselves. In a focus group in North Carolina in the fall of 1991, they said they were all for cutting welfare, as long as they sensed an equal commitment to education and jobs. A campaign aide, Celinda Lake, flew home amazed. "The welfare message, worded correctly, plays extremely well in the black community," she reported. Indeed, far from alienating anyone, Clinton's welfare pledge roused voters everywhere. Clinton's main pollster, Stan Greenberg, was startled by the emotions it raised. Three-quarters of the people he probed in New Hampshire were impressed by Clinton's stance on welfare, while just a quarter cared he was a Rhodes Scholar. It was "by far, the single most important component of Clinton's biography," Greenberg wrote in a campaign memo. Voters were "stunned to hear a Democrat saying . . . 'Hey, you on the lower end can't abuse the welfare system any more.'"

As the scandal-a-day campaign rolled on, welfare emerged as its all-purpose elixir, there to cure what ailed. It reassured ethnic voters in Illinois, who found Clinton too slick. (They "were taken aback when Clinton talked about welfare," Greenberg wrote.) It soothed the reflexive distrust among Florida conservatives. ("The strongest media message was introduced by the 'welfare spot.'") It won Clinton a fresh look in Pennsylvania, where more than half the voters had character doubts. ("No other message comes close to this one on intensity and breadth of interest.") It was a values message, an economic message, and a policy message in one. It supplied his second-most popular line at the Democratic convention, and his most effective answer to the GOP's post-convention attacks. While the pledge to "end welfare" featured prominently in the barrage of late-season ads, the only mystery, given its force, was that Clinton didn't stress it even more.

The Republicans felt robbed—welfare was *their* issue. Sagging in the polls, President George H. W. Bush tried to copy the tune but sounded painfully off-key. "Get a job or get off the dole!" he screeched. On November 3, 1992, Clinton, the "end-welfare" candidate, became the end-welfare president-elect.

By then, Angie had spent another year in the system Clinton was pledging to end. When she arrived in the fall of 1991, the country already had a small welfare-to-work program called JOBS, and soon she got a letter. "Angela Jobe is a mandatory work program registrant," it began. "Work" was a bit of a euphemism, since the program mostly sent people to study for their high school diplomas, not to sweep the streets. "Mandatory" was euphemistic, too: Angie could have ignored the summons and kept more than 90 percent of her food stamps and cash. Still, she was happy to go. "I always worked!" Angie said. "What—I'm supposed to move up here and get lazy?" As a statement of fact, "I always worked" ignored some large résumé gaps. But as an assertion of identity it was revealing. Despite nearly eight years of welfare checks, Angie saw herself as a worker.

Arriving for the program, Angie discovered that six weeks of training could turn her into a certified nursing assistant. *Nursing assistant*: now that had a ring. She didn't know what nursing assistants did, but she figured they made good money. And it sounded better than frying chickens, "'cause 'chicken place' just ain't a nice career." She pictured her abridged frame draped in nursing whites and started to play with the words. "Nursing assistant . . . assisting a nurse . . . working in a hospital." Until the class began, Angie didn't realize that most nursing aides did scut work in nursing homes, a revelation that stole some of her excitement. ("Wiping butts" is how lots of welfare recipients described it.) She also felt intimidated to be back in a classroom, a place where she had known only failure. The bus stop was frigid in the depths of December. The blood pressure cuff gave her grief. More than half her classmates gave up. But if stubbornness was the stuff of many of her problems, it was also the start of her solutions. She forced herself to show up every day, and she was so proud at her graduation she had Jewell bring the kids. She went out that night to celebrate at a bar and started talking with the deejay.

Angie liked the class more than the work. She had understood, in a theoretical way, the physical strain involved: the lifting and pulling, the washing and feeding, the business of bedpans. But once she started at a nursing home, the sadness of it all set in. "I don't want to find no dead person!" was all she could think. She lasted eight days. Angie stayed home for a few months, then caught another break. She had thrown in an application at the post office, and an offer came through. The post office! A job for life! People look at you with respect when you work at the post office! It wasn't what she thought. She wasn't a full-fledged unionized worker, but a temporary employee at $6 an hour with no benefits or security. She didn't even work in the main post office. She caught a van to an airport annex, where she spent her time double-checking the presorted mail. All the same, it was a foot in the door, and she liked the routine. Since it was second-shift work, she could stay out late with the deejay and still have time to sleep. The welfare office didn't know she was working, so she kept her full benefits. Two more friends from Chicago had moved into the compound, which felt like a cross between a kibbutz and a sorority house; there was always someone to talk to or babysit the kids. Angie felt sufficiently good about herself to enroll in a GED class. A year after she arrived in Milwaukee, indigent and effectively widowed, she was reassembling a life.

The first sign of trouble was the Vienna sausage. The second was the naps. She'd drag herself to class, then stop by her girlfriend's house to munch potted pork and sleep on the couch. As the mound of empty weenie tins grew, so did her girlfriend's suspicions. "You need a pregnancy test," her friend said. Angie knew she wasn't pregnant. She had ditched the deejay months ago. She couldn't be pregnant. She had just had her period and she was taking birth control pills. She better not be pregnant. Von, her youngest child, just started school, and she wasn't going back to diapers. "I ain't," she said. "You is," said her friend. "You crazy!" Angie said. In November 1992, just after Clinton won the election, her friend ran an errand at a clinic. Along for the ride, Angie took a pregnancy test just to prove her wrong. "Miss Jobe, I need to speak with you," the nurse began. *Unh-uh,*

Angie thought. *Unh-uhhh!* She drank for a week and cried for a month. Then she quit the postal job. When you're too depressed to get out of bed, there's no sorting the mail.

Sorting the mail didn't cross Jewell's mind when she arrived in Milwaukee, no longer a girl yet not quite grown. Neither did making beds, mopping floors, frying chickens, or any of the other jobs she could land. Her adult work history consisted of a few months locked in the cashier's booth at an all-night Amoco station. Jobs weren't something that Jewell thought much about. Babies were.

Unlike Angie, Jewell was delighted to be pregnant. It didn't matter that her first son's father was long gone or that the new baby's father was in jail. Babies made Jewell feel alive. Like lots of girls who have a baby in high school, Jewell had gotten pregnant on purpose, thinking a child would bring her something to love. Unlike most, Jewell had found the theory worked. She loved everything about her first son, Terrell, from the moment he was born. His new baby smell. His miniature clothes. Even his middle-of-the-night cries. Ghetto life requires a hard face, but babies let Jewell smile. She went into labor in December 1991, two months after she arrived in Milwaukee. It was the middle of the night, but soon everyone in the compound was shouting. Angie stayed behind to watch the kids, while another friend rode with Jewell in the ambulance. By breakfast, Jewell had a second son, Tremmell. A few weeks later, Jewell swathed him against the Lake Michigan wind, got back on the bus, and carried him into the Cook County Jail, where father and son caught their first glimpse of each other through a partition of bulletproof glass. Jewell enjoyed showing Tony his son, but it was starting to sink in that Tony wasn't coming home.

Thrown into troubled waters, Angie and Jewell navigated in contrasting ways. Angie chugged ahead like a rusty tug, forming a wake of jettisoned plans: she was going to be a nurse or a postal clerk; she was going to get her high school degree; she was going to figure out what God wants of her; she was going to stop crying about Greg. Jewell was a sailboat without a sail, adrift with no plan at all. Passivity offered protection; when you don't get your hopes up, there's less to let you down. The new baby was almost four months old when one of her younger brother's friends floated into town—a wild, wiry street kid, barely out of his teens, whom everyone knew as Lucky. Or as one of the gang later said, "His name is Lucky but he's not." Lucky liked to drink, and drinking made him talk. He covered Jewell in verbal rainbows—Technicolor pledges of devotion, mixed with white lies and purple jokes. "Jewell! You want me to rob a bank? I'll rob it for you, Jewell!" "Jewell! I been wanting to talk to you ever since we was in grammar school! Man, you had a *big* ol' butt!" "Jewell! Can you be my lady?" They danced. She wasn't so much smitten as amused and lonelier than she knew. In Lucky, the court found its inebriated jester, and Jewell found a man.

Communal living got to Jewell—the noise, the gossip, the lack of privacy. She and Lucky moved away for a few months, but Lucky had problems with the neighborhood gang and they raced back after he got shot in the hand. Bored, restless, putting on weight, Jewell did something wildly out of character. She volunteered for JOBS, the same welfare-to-work program that had summoned Angie. "Dear Jewell M Reed," came the reply. "Please read the rights and responsibilities pamphlet." The dour bureaucratic response set the tone for what followed. Her case got handed to an inner-city group, the Opportunities Industrialization Center, whose renown lay more in winning state contracts than in finding poor people jobs. First she got parked in a motivation class. Then a caseworker urged her to forget about work and pursue her GED, though Jewell insisted that she wanted to make money. Finally she got herself referred to a course for nursing assistants, like the one that Angie had taken. She waited for two months, then learned that it was canceled. "They don't ever do much of nothing except take you through a lot of hassles," Jewell said. It was the last time she asked the welfare office for anything but a check.

Home soon after to visit Chicago, Jewell was catching up on family news when she learned that one of her favorite cousins was having problems. She had had another baby, split up with her husband, and moved in with her mother. Nearly a decade had passed since Jewell had seen Opal Caples, though as kids in the projects the two had been close. Even the big-city names chosen by their rural-born mothers had framed them as natural friends: Ruthie Mae and Hattie Mae had Opal and Jewell. Jewell wasn't one to act on impulse, but something made her pick up the phone, and the conversation clicked. Opal said she had three young daughters with rhyming names: Sierra, Kierra, and Tierra. *"F'real?"* Jewell said. "Yup!" Jewell had two preschool sons with rhyming names: Terrell and Tremmell. *"F'real?"* Opal said. "Yup!" Opal was drawing welfare, too, and her dilemma was the same one Jewell had faced: without help, she couldn't afford a place of her own in Chicago. Living with her churchy mother left Opal feeling caged. Jewell said her landlady had an empty apartment for $325, and welfare would pay more than $600. "Yahoo!" Opal said. "I'm coming."

Jewell didn't take her seriously—no one makes a decision like that in a few minutes on the phone. Yet something about Opal had always set her apart. She was probably the smartest of Jewell's childhood friends and definitely the wildest. Expelled from not one but two public schools, Opal, unlike Angie and Jewell, went on to graduate and even did a semester of community college. While Jewell didn't spend much time mulling life beyond the ghetto, Opal worked worldly allusions into her conversation. Her husband was so stuck on himself "he thinks he's the Prince of Wales." When their mothers made them go job hunting as teens, Opal got all the offers. "I have a personality that attracts people to me—I do!" she said. "Lotta people tell me that." With education, experience, and a gift for making friends, Opal could leave a welfare office voted most likely to succeed. But there was something that neither her caseworkers nor cousins knew. Opal had been smoking cocaine. A little at first, then a lot—off and on during her second pregnancy and constantly during her third. One reason she was living at home is that she had smoked up the rent money and fled before her husband found his stuff on the street. Opal's mother didn't want the extended family to know, and Opal wasn't about to tell. Among the hopes she held for Milwaukee was the hope of getting clean.

When she and Jewell met at the station there was no time for a reunion scene. They piled the kids and suitcases aboard and headed off for the two-hour ride up I-94. When Angie got home from work that night, she found a new resident of the compound—a short, dark, beguiling woman who told riotous stories of her life's escapades and was quick to swap Newports, insults, and beer. "That's my cousin!" Angie and Opal each would insist from then on. Biologically, they're not related (though through Greg their kids are), but that's a technicality that Angie indignantly dismissed. "What you mean?" she said. "We 'bout as biological as it gets!"

A few days later, a book of Jewell's food stamps disappeared. Soon Opal disappeared, too. "Damn, she must a met somebody already," Jewell thought. Her mother had heard a rumor that Opal was using drugs, but Jewell paid her no mind. Her mother said all kinds of crazy things. For years, her mother had said that the government was going to take welfare away. Jewell figured that was just something mothers liked to say.

Now and then at a social event, someone asks me what I do. If I don't feel like talking, I tell the truth. I say I cover "social policy" for *The New York Times,* and the conversation moves on. In a more adventurous mood, I tell the truth in a different way. I say I cover "welfare." That keeps the table boiling: say the word *welfare,* and there's no telling what might bubble up. Bill Clinton started one of those conversations on the fly in a campaign season, and what bubbled up was a free-for-all—and an "end" to welfare—more radical than anyone had imagined. This book represents a seven-year effort to find out what happened next.

Though I had spent years watching the welfare bill evolve, I realized why I found the subject so compelling as I listened, in the summer of 1996, to the final hours of Senate debate. The senators were talking about welfare the way people talk of it at dinner tables, in terms so ideological as to be virtually religious. They were talking of how their parents and grandparents had made it. (Or hadn't. Or couldn't.) They were talking of how their communities would care for the poor. (Or didn't. Or wouldn't.) At times, it seemed that the very idea of America was on trial. We live in a country rich beyond measure, yet one with unconscionable ghettos. We live in a country where anyone can make it; yet generation after generation, some families don't. To argue about welfare is to argue about why. I'll be pleased if this story challenges, and informs, the assumptions on both sides as much as it has challenged my own. "Ideas are interesting—people are boring," a welfare expert once told me. Ideas *are* interesting. But I proceeded on a broader faith, that what has occurred in the lives of the welfare poor is more interesting than either camp has assumed.

The story focuses on three women in one extended family, inseparable at the start but launched on differing arcs. Perhaps no three people can stand for 9 million. But with Angie's gumption, Jewell's reticence, and Opal's manipulative charm, the threesome cover a great deal of ground. A catalog of their collective lives would include everything from crack house to 401(k), with results that roughly reflect the experiences of welfare families nationwide. Two grabbed a toehold on the bottom of the employment ladder. One wound up with a journey through the new welfare system more tragic than I would have guessed possible.

Since welfare is a subject filled with biases, the reader may welcome a word about mine. At the time the president signed the law—the Personal Responsibility and Work Opportunity Reconciliation Act of 1996—I had been writing about inner-city life for more than a decade. Inevitably, I had opinions. I thought the harshness of the low-wage economy and the turmoil of poor people's lives required a federal safety net, not one torn by arbitrary time limits and handed to the states. I also thought the most constructive thing to do as a reporter was to clean my mental slate. With the welfare system starting over, I tried to do the same. To my relief, the first years brought reassurance: more work, less welfare, falling poverty rates. No signs of children "sleeping on grates," as Senator Daniel Patrick Moynihan had famously warned. Surely the vibrant economy helped, and tougher tests awaited. Still, after years on the poverty beat, there was something truly exotic to report: good news.

At the same time, I felt uneasy with the triumphal claims ringing through public life. The "greatest social policy change in this nation in sixty years," is how Tommy Thompson put it, after leaving his job as governor of Wisconsin to become the secretary of Health and Human Services. *The Wall Street Journal* did him one better: "the greatest advance for America's poor since the rise of capitalism." The very phrase "welfare-to-work" brims with implication: rising incomes, inspired kids, more hopeful lives. But the successes I witnessed were never so clear. Paradoxically, the closer I got to the welfare story, the less central welfare appeared. "Did it *work*?" people would ask about the landmark law. "That's your crazy stuff," Angie said, insisting the law was no landmark to her. "We don't be thinking 'bout that!"

In assembling this account, I have relied on years of discussions with the main characters. With their permission, I have also examined a decade's worth of welfare and earnings records and talked with others in their lives: relatives, boyfriends, caseworkers, bosses, and friends. Court records, tax returns, school transcripts, and letters have enhanced my understanding, and a trail of genealogical material extends the family history back six generations. In launching the project, I imagined, if only half-consciously, that it would follow a sleek narrative line of underdogs against the world. It is that story, but also a more complicated one—of adversity variously overcome, compounded, or merely endured. In that way, too, it embodies the story of welfare writ large.

Some readers may wonder why I focused on an African American family when nationally blacks and whites each accounted for about 40 percent of the rolls. I first chose to focus on Milwaukee, the epicenter of the antiwelfare crusade, and, as it happened, nearly 70 percent of the city's caseload was black. As the drive to end welfare began, the paradigmatic Milwaukee recipient was a black woman from Chicago whose mother or grandmother had started life in a Mississippi cotton field, a description that fits Angie, Opal, and Jewell. At the same time, there are advantages to seeing the rise and fall of welfare through African American eyes. Given their share of the national population, black families were more than six times as likely as whites to receive a welfare check. Among long-term recipients, the racial imbalance was even more pronounced: nearly seven of ten long-term recipients were African American. Considering our national history, that shouldn't be a surprise; for more than three centuries blacks were barred by violence and law from the full benefits of American life.

The story that follows is rooted in the racial past, a past much less distant than I first supposed. In understanding where it began, I got help from a regal woman named Hattie Mae Crenshaw. She is Jewell's mother, grandmother to Angie's kids, and an elder cousin whom Opal regards as an aunt. She was born beside a Mississippi bayou in 1937, in a shack without electricity or running water. By the time she reached late middle age, a job as a private nursing aide had carried her by Concorde to Paris. In between, she had lived much of the country's welfare history. Barely sixty when I met her, Hattie Mae wasn't old. But she was old enough to remember chopping cotton to pay the plantation store. She settled into her story from a white-tiger love seat in Jewell's living room. Family history bores Jewell; she left the room to do her nails. Hattie Mae smiled as she began: "I growed up on Senator Jim Eastland's plantation in Doddsville, Mississippi. That's when black peoples was just beginning to come out of slavery." Patient with my puzzled looks, Hattie Mae talked on, pointing me toward welfare's forgotten prequel.

The Caples Family

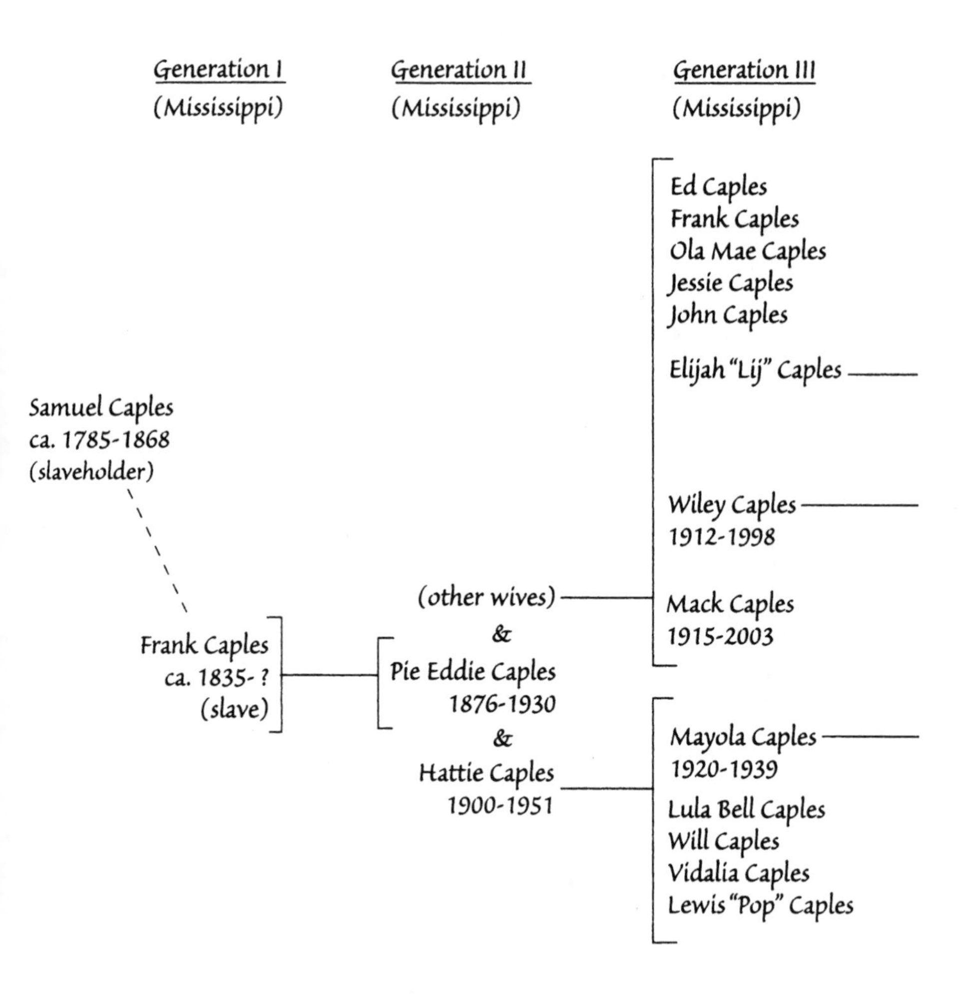

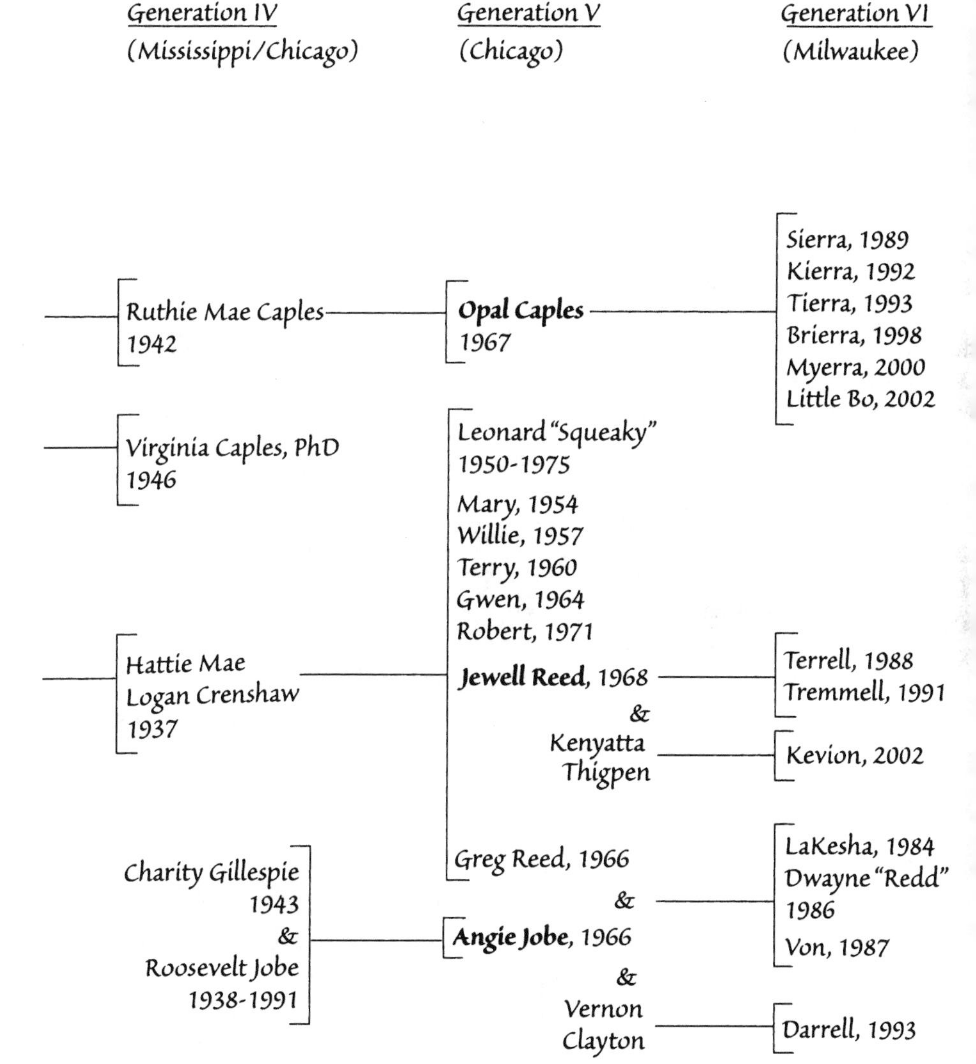

Generation IV
(Mississippi/Chicago)
Generation V
(Chicago)
Generation VI
(Milwaukee)
Ruthie Mae Caples
1942
Opal Caples
1967
Sierra, 1989
Kierra, 1992
Tierra, 1993
Brierra, 1998
Myerra, 2000
Little Bo, 2002
Virginia Caples, PhD
1946
Leonard "Squeaky"
1950-1975
Mary, 1954
Willie, 1957
Terry, 1960
Gwen, 1964
Robert, 1971
Hattie Mae
Logan Crenshaw
1937
Jewell Reed, 1968
Terrell, 1988
Tremmell, 1991
&
Kenyatta
Thigpen
Kevion, 2002
Greg Reed, 1966
&
LaKesha, 1984
Dwayne "Redd"
1986
Von, 1987
Charity Gillespie
1943
&
Roosevelt Jobe
1938-1991
Angie Jobe, 1966
&
Vernon
Clayton
Darrell, 1993

TWO

The Plantation: Mississippi, 1840–1960

It may sound strange to hear Hattie Mae say that at her birth in 1937 black people were "just beginning to come out of slavery." But her argument wasn't much different from those most modern historians make. And it was no different from what an improbable visitor found in the same fields a few years before she was born. Hortense Powdermaker must have caused quite a stir when she pulled into Sunflower County in 1932, explaining she had come in the depths of the Great Depression to conduct a scientific study of Negro life. She was a thirty-one-year-old Jewish academic, educated in London and just back from Melanesia—not a familiar figure in the cotton patch. It took the state's leading aristocrat, the poet and planter William Alexander Percy, to keep her from being run out of town. But soon she was traipsing through sharecropper shacks and sweating at church revivals, immersing herself in black life as no white Mississippian would dream. Though she struggled to get her study into print in 1939, *After Freedom* attained the status of a minor classic, praised by W. E. B. DuBois and reissued with each generation. The title is both chronological and ironic: it wasn't so long after slavery, and there wasn't much freedom. In a county where seven of ten residents were black, Powdermaker summarized white attitudes on the eve of Hattie Mae's birth:

> Negroes are innately inferior to white people, mentally and morally. Their place is in manual work.
>
> Any attempt at any kind of social equality would result in

> some disaster so overwhelming that it is dangerous even to talk about it. . . .
>
> Because the Whites are so seriously outnumbered, special means must be taken to keep the Negro in his place. . . .
>
> There may be good "niggers," and bad "niggers," but a "nigger" is a "nigger" and cannot escape the taint.

Powdermaker wrote as an optimist. While she didn't foresee anything like the northern migration or the civil rights revolution, two movements that would change the world of Hattie Mae, she did sense an impatience among younger blacks and presciently called it a force "capable of being mobilized." At the same time, she was attuned to an aspect of sharecropper life that would prove cause for less optimism: the widespread social chaos, in particular the fluid family structure. Outside a tiny black elite, formal marriages were rare. Most sharecroppers lived in unsteady common-law arrangements, "easily entered and easily dissolved." Nonmarital births prevailed: "Even if there is a man in the household, he is often not the child's father." Since women had broader access to jobs—they could work as field hands or domestics—black men were doubly marginalized. Domestic violence was epidemic ("It is something for a woman to boast about if her husband does not beat her"), and so were other forms of black-on-black violence, much of it ignored by the law. Among poor blacks, "it is more or less assumed that some member of any family will get into jail." Put differently, Powdermaker was describing many of the conditions later associated with a welfare underclass: single mothers, peripatetic men, an undertow of crime and violence. But welfare—that is, Aid to Families with Dependent Children—could scarcely be blamed. It didn't yet exist.

Charting the rise of the northern ghettos, Nicholas Lemann became the first contemporary writer to stress the ties to sharecropper life. "Every aspect of the underclass culture in the ghettos is directly traceable to roots in the South," he wrote in *The Atlantic* in 1986, "and not the South of slavery but . . . the nascent underclass of the sharecropper South." In the exchanges that followed, critics noted the many positive aspects of sharecropper society: the safety-net functions of the extended family, the vibrancy of the church, the yearning for education on display in the one-room schoolhouse. All true: countless black sharecroppers moved north and prospered, including some of Hattie Mae's kin. But the point as it pertains to welfare is simpler. Many of the problems blamed on "the liberal, welfare plantation" were flourishing decades before, on the not-so-liberal one.

To picture Hattie Mae's childhood, you have to picture the Mississippi Delta—endless, empty, mud-puddle flat, and stretching to the earth's very edge. The Eastland property runs about three miles west from the Sunflower River and three north and south. In other words, it is vast. To cross it on foot, as Hattie Mae used to do, is to be reminded daily of one's humble place in the scheme of things. The Eastlands lived on the eastern border, by the bridge to the wider world, in a house that spoke more of suburban comfort than antebellum grandeur. Across the river sat the crossroads "town" of Doddsville (1940 pop. 262), but with its own gin, shop, and store, the plantation was a town in itself. The commercial buildings clustered toward the front, near the Eastlands' home, while several hundred tenants spread out behind in places marked by informal names like "Sparkman" and "Sandy Ridge." Hattie Mae lived about two miles in, along a bayou behind Bob McLean Curve.

Even in the early 1940s, the plantation had a nineteenth-century feel. There were mules in the fields. Tenants did without electricity or running water. Some shacks barely had walls. "You could set on the inside and look at the outside," Hattie Mae said. With medical care rudimentary at best, anything from a mule kick to childbirth could prove life threatening. In the basic bargain of sharecropper life, the planter provided land, seed, tools, housing, and living expenses, often in the form of credit at an overpriced plantation store; think of it as a proto-welfare system. The tenant provided labor in exchange for half the profits. But since the accounting stayed in the planter's hands, so did the money. As a little girl, Hattie Mae would watch her uncles line up for the annual "settle." "Some would come out crying," she said. "Some would break even. If you came out with two hundred dollars, you were rich." James Eastland took over the plantation from his father, Woods, in 1934, and he ran it with unchecked power; the police were barred from crossing the bridge onto the property. "These are my niggers," Hattie Mae quoted him as saying. "If they keep themselves outta the grave, I'll keep 'em out of jail."

Hattie Mae's grandfather, Pie Eddie Caples, arrived on the plantation in 1927 with the kind of family tree that Hortense Powdermaker would have recognized. The wife he brought to the plantation was at least his fourth, and he had children with all of them. (The law firm handling the divorce was Eastland & Nichols.) One of the children he brought along was a six-year-old girl named Mayola, and a decade later she went into labor in the shack by the bayou and gave birth to Hattie Mae. The following year Mayola Caples got pregnant again, but this time the labor killed her. Not yet two, Hattie Mae was orphaned and not for the last time.

"My grandfather was a slave," Hattie Mae said, passing along the family legend as Jewell tended her nails. Family legend wasn't off by much. A bit of historical probing revealed that Pie Eddie Caples was a slave's son, whose father was first sent to the fields at the start of King Cotton's reign. With the expulsion of the Choctaw from central Mississippi in the early 1830s, 10 million acres of prime cotton land opened up, and a tide of white men rushed in to claim it. Squatters, settlers, gamblers, and thieves, they arrived hatching frontier schemes and dreaming of dollar signs. Among them in about 1843 was an aging Alabama saloonkeeper with a young wife and seven black slaves, including a boy about eight years old. The saloonkeeper's name was Samuel Caples. The boy's name was Frank. He was Pie Eddie's father, Hattie Mae's great-grandfather, and the person with whom the Caples story begins.

When the slaveholder Samuel Caples was young—he was born about 1785—black slaves had labored in American fields for more than 150 years, and it seemed the awful practice might die a natural death. Economically, it threw off shrinking rewards, since the soils of the upper South were spent. Philosophically, it posed discomfiting problems for a generation of Revolutionary leaders demanding their own freedom; they recognized, even though they didn't rectify, their hypocrisy at home. The slaveholder Thomas Jefferson called slavery a "detestable" institution. But by the time Samuel Caples arrived in Mississippi, no white southerner would say such a thing. Tantalized by cotton profits, a new generation embraced slavery not as a necessary evil but an outright social good, the burden a superior race endured to care for a lesser caste. Since the faith in white supremacy would outlive slavery itself, it was a development of some note.

Samuel Caples's life unfolded in eerie sync with the national tragedy. Born in Maryland around the time of the Constitutional Convention, he grew up with the new republic, impatiently pushing west in search of land and human property. By the 1830s, he had abandoned his life in middle Tennessee and settled in northwestern Alabama, where he seems to have prospered. He ran a tavern in the Fayette County courthouse; increased his slaveholdings to seven, from five; and had a son who served as constable. Then he packed up and lit out again. What dislodged a comfortable townsman isn't clear, but when he arrived in Scott County, Mississippi, in the early 1840s, he was a man approaching sixty and toting an eighteen-year-old bride. As a small slaveholder (one with fewer than twenty slaves), Caples was by far the most prevalent kind, though not one easily conjured by modern minds. His life was nothing like those of the grand planters along the Mississippi River, with hundreds of slaves, thousands of acres, and European books and clothes. Caples would have lived in frontier housing, probably a log cabin, and worked in the fields alongside his bondsmen. With virtually no savings—his wealth was tied up in his slaves—he was acutely vulnerable to market busts, a risk for the people he owned, since selling them was his easiest way to get cash. For Frank, bondage to a small slaveholder had some potential advantages; it spared him the mythic overseer, famed for his quick cruelty, and it may have brought a more varied workday. But it also deprived him of the communal life a large plantation afforded, like a broader potential choice in mates and the safety of numbers. What it really did was bind his fate to the whims of Samuel Caples, whose authority over his human possessions was all but absolute. The distance to free soil made escape nearly impossible.

There were two aspects of slavery its defenders preferred not to discuss: the sale and the lash. Whether Caples was quick with the lash is unknown, but he wasn't above the sale. In 1849, with prices for slaves and cotton rising, Caples disposed of "my Negro boy Hyram about fifteen years old" for $818.50, about $20,000 in contemporary terms. Hyram was about Frank's age, possibly his brother, perhaps even a twin. Though able to buy and sell men, Caples couldn't write his name, and he consummated the deal with an *X*. On the move again within a few years, Caples headed east into Newton County, where he had more kids, bought more land, and needed more cash. On April 16, 1855, he took out a loan of $833, offering as collateral one of the most valuable things he owned: Hattie Mae's great-grandfather. "Caples has this day executed his note," he acknowledged with his *X*,

> and . . . to secure full and punctual payment of said note . . . doth bargain, sell, and convey a certain negro boy slave for life named Frank in color black aged about twenty years to have and to hold the same unto himself, his heirs and assigns forever.

Amid the reverent "untos" and "doths," the note let Caples keep working his "slave for life" until the debt came due nine months later. But if he failed to repay, the lender was then free to take possession of Frank and sell him to the highest bidder. Whatever terrors he experienced in bondage, Frank Caples was spared that one. Cotton prices ticked up that year, and Samuel Caples repaid the debt.

What a strange sight the homestead must have made on the eve of Civil War—this old man, lord of 100-plus acres, thirteen kids, and nine slaves. At seventy-five, Samuel Caples had pushed his way across a succession of frontiers to an estate worth something like $200,000 in contemporary terms—nearly all in human property—and he lived just long enough to see a terrible war sweep it away. Surrendering to no one in martial fervor, he named his next son Jefferson Davis and joined a local militia formed, its founder proclaimed, "to aid in driving the enemy from our country." But no less an enemy than William T. Sherman entered the county a mile from Caples's farm, burning and looting in a practice run for his more infamous march to the sea. Chasing freedoms they had never known, thousands of slaves ran off to trail the conquering force—"ten miles of negros," "a grotesque crowd," a "remarkable hegira," Sherman and his entourage called them. Nothing if not prolific, Samuel Caples survived long enough to give his wife their sixteenth child, then died by the end of the decade. She lost the homestead in a tax sale, and much of the family left for Arkansas. Frank Caples, now a freedman, stayed.

Given the tragic history that followed, it's easy to forget the brief flowering of freedom that black Mississippians of his era enjoyed. Mississippi sent two black men to the United States Senate; black policemen patrolled the capital; and black letter carriers toted mail. Economically, progress halted with sharecropping, an impossibly rigged system close to slavery itself. Politically, blacks were driven from the polls first by violence and then by the law. As the future governor James Vardaman put it, the 1890 Mississippi constitution, with its poll taxes and literacy tests, was designed "for no other purpose than to eliminate the nigger from politics." With that, the Mississippi of modern legend emerged, in a tumult of lynchings, Jim Crow laws, and race-baiting politicians. No state entered the twentieth century with a larger ratio of black citizens—nearly six in ten Mississippians were black, and one in ten black Americans lived there—and no state went to greater lengths to insure black subjugation. Into this world of lost opportunity, the next three Caples generations were born, down to Hattie Mae. In 1876, Frank had a son, whom everyone called "Pie Eddie."

The red clay hills that Pie Eddie farmed would never yield an easy living. But one of the world's most fertile plains was a few hours away, running beside the Mississippi River for two hundred miles below Memphis. The Mississippi Delta was still mostly wilderness in antebellum days, but with the arrival of railroads and flood control it erupted in a speculative boom. Among those who began buying Delta land was a hill country pharmacist named Oliver Eastland, who in 1888 launched a giant cotton plantation that remains in the family today. He died a decade later and left it to his young sons, Woods and James.

The history of the Delta has only one theme: the need for cheap and abundant (in this case, black) labor. Without it the rich land was worthless, since cotton was an extremely labor-intensive crop. A plantation the size of the Eastlands' would need several hundred field hands, and planters went to extraordinary lengths to recruit and retain them. While *dependency* was a word typically tied to the region's poor blacks, dependency ran both ways; perhaps nowhere was the prosperity of the white elite as dependent on perpetuating a large black underclass. The corollary to the white need for black labor was the fear of black numbers in counties where blacks formed as much as a nine-to-one majority. Socially, an elaborate caste system evolved to underscore who was in charge. Of all the degradations of Hattie Mae's youth, none stung more than the prohibition on drinking from a white person's glass. Where caste failed, violence prevailed. In the first three decades of the twentieth century, the Delta was a national leader in lynchings, dispatching a black man, woman, or child to a mob death every 5.5 months. Whites knew they were guarding an island of privilege in a sea of potential black trouble.

Trouble came to the Eastland brothers early in their tenure as planters, after they recruited a field hand named Luther Holbert, who had worked for them back in the hills. What prompted the dispute with Holbert is unclear, but the outcome is not: on February 3, 1904, Holbert shot James Eastland dead. The murder of a planter by a black worker was no mere crime but a threat to the social and economic order. (The Memphis paper referred to James Eastland as Holbert's "young master.") Woods Eastland joined a rampaging posse that claimed at least three innocent blacks' lives before returning to the plantation with Holbert and his wife. By midday a crowd of a thousand assembled, and the accounts of what happened next, especially that of the *Vicksburg Evening Post,* made the case a touchstone in the literature of lynching:

> The blacks were forced to hold out their hands while one finger at a time was chopped off. The fingers were distributed as souvenirs. . . . one of his eyes, knocked out with a stick, hung by a shred from the socket. . . . The most excruciating form of punishment consisted in the use of a large corkscrew. . . . bored into the flesh of the man and the woman . . . and then pulled out, the spirals tearing out big pieces of raw, quivering flesh.

Holbert and his wife were then thrown on a pyre and burned to death.

Woods Eastland was indicted for murder—burning Holbert at the stake "was the intention of W. C. Eastland from the start," the Memphis paper noted with approval—but the case was thrown out before it reached a jury, and he was swept from the courthouse by a cheering crowd. He moved back to the hills, became the district attorney, and managed the plantation from afar. Nine months after the gruesome execution, his only child was born, and he named him for his slain brother: James Eastland. For much of the country, the younger Eastland would become the very symbol of southern defiance, the cigar-chomping Dixiecrat senator who boasted that he had a special suit pocket where civil rights bills went to die. For Hattie Mae, he was the man who owned all the land and made all the rules.

The two decades after the Holbert affair brought Delta planters their glory days. Rising cotton prices made Woods Eastland wealthy and kept him in need of more workers. One of the men he employed in the hills was Pie Eddie Caples, who was about fifty years old with a young wife and a passel of kids when "Mr. Woods" persuaded him to give the Delta a try. Climbing in the back of Woods Eastland's truck, the Caples clan rode out of the hills and onto the plantation in search of a better life, and when I found him three-quarters of a century later, Pie Eddie Caples's son Mack was still there. A strapping man of eighty-five, he had gnarled hands, bright eyes, and vivid memories of a twelve-year-old's first glimpse of the fertile land. "So much cotton in the field, look like it snowed!" he said. While the next generation, Hattie Mae's, despised plantation life, Mack spoke of it with the kind of vicarious pride a midcentury worker might have shown in GM or GE. The store shimmered with more stuff than he had seen, all offered on easy credit. While some planters plowed every acre, the Eastlands let tenants garden. And as patrons with influence, they could keep favored workers from jail. "Just as much money as Papa wanna borrow, Mr. Woods let him have it," Mack said. "I ain't never heard him cuss none of his hands. Mr. Woods was a mighty fine man!"

One cruelty of sharecropping was that the promise of prosperity almost always proved false. Another, as Nicholas Lemann has noted, was that the failure was subtly marked as the tenant's fault; he was, after all, ostensibly a partner in a profitable enterprise. If the system was meant to breed self-doubt, it also encouraged an ethos of "getting over," exacting your revenge on an unfair system by cheating it in return (an ethos that would reappear in dealings with the welfare system). Hortense Powdermaker found more than eight in ten sharecroppers worked all year, only to break even or sink further into debt. She was startled at how openly planters talked of cheating; they justified it by arguing that "the Negro is congenitally lazy and must be kept in debt in order to be made to work." Whatever disappointments Pie Eddie Caples suffered in the Delta, he didn't suffer them long. Three years after moving, he fell from a roof and injured his head. "Mr. Woods" sent him to a hospital in Jackson, and he died in surgery. Pie Eddie's widow and children stayed on the plantation, where seven years later, Hattie Mae was born to an unmarried teenage mother she would never know.

"I was a gorgeous little black child!" Hattie Mae told me one day. Though she started her life poor and orphaned, she didn't start it unhappily. Her saving grace was Pie Eddie's widow, the thirty-seven-year-old grandmother from whom she drew her home, her resilience, and her name. "I thought the sun rose and set in that old lady," she said. As a cheerful woman who could cook and sew, Mama Hattie had escaped the fields to make her living in white folks' homes, where the benefits to a cute granddaughter included a stream of hand-me-downs and "goo-gobs" of white girls' dolls. Early life had other comforts. With several acres to farm, there were fresh corn and peaches in season, jarred greens in winter, and smoked hogs year-round. The Gilfield Missionary Baptist Church was about a mile's hike across the fields, and the two Hatties regularly made the trek. Rounding out the household were Mama Hattie's kids—Will, Lula Bell, Vidalia, and Pop—who, a half generation ahead of Hattie Mae, were more like older siblings than aunts and uncles. Hattie Mae spent her days making mud pies and waiting for her grandmother to walk up the road. "Those were the happiest days of my life," she said.

Sharecropper society was not monolithic, and the Capleses had a reputation for inhabiting its tougher tiers. If you buy the notion that the social problems of northern ghettos had roots in the Jim Crow

South, the family history is one to explore. Among the children that Pie Eddie left behind, one (Frank) was shot and killed by his girlfriend. Another (Lula Bell) shot and killed her man. A third (Pop) did time in penitentiaries from Parchman to Joliet; among other things, he killed a man dating his ex-wife. Another, Vidalia, got involved with a man whose wife retaliated by torching Vidalia's house. A picture of Opal's grandfather, 'Lij, survives from the day the carnival came to town. Clenching a cigar between his teeth, he stares down the camera and thrusts open a wallet overflowing with bills, a portrait of the bravura that would fill his granddaughter's veins; the quickest way to get a laugh in the family is to ask how many times 'Lij married. Even Wiley, the stable homesteader of the group, kept a still. "They were known as a rough-riding group that stuck together," Hattie Mae said of her uncles and aunts. "If you mess with them you might as well kill them." Hattie Mae's father, Robert Logan, who was fifteen when she was born, came from a more prosperous and lighter-skinned plantation family that didn't approve of the Capleses; he left town for a long army career, and Hattie Mae's visits with him were confined to the occasional furlough.

As a stable, pious, hardworking woman with a bunch of hell-raising kids, Mama Hattie would scarcely be an unfamiliar figure in the contemporary ghetto. Nor would the crime that put an end to Hattie Mae's carefree years, sexual molestation. She was about seven when her grandmother's boyfriend, Clyde, started catching her alone and doing things she didn't want him to do. Afraid of retribution if she told, she kept the secret inside, as a source of confusion and pain. "Men back then didn't allow girls to have much a childhood," she said. Another calamity befell the family at about the same time, when her uncle Will got into a dispute with another plantation hand over a woman. Out playing one day, Hattie Mae ran home to say she had seen some men stuffing Will into a car. But no one listened to an excitable child until his body was found the next day. Bereft over her son's death, Mama Hattie briefly moved the family back to the hills, but Clyde came along, and in an argument he stabbed her. The boys gave him the kind of beating that insured he wouldn't return, and Mama Hattie moved back to the Doddsville plantation. Soon the household was going separate ways. With no one but young Hattie Mae at home, her grandmother landed a job as the Eastlands' cook, a privileged perch but one that required her to live in the cook's quarters near their house with no room for a child. Nine years old, Hattie Mae was effectively orphaned again, left to spend what remained of her childhood with whichever relative might take her in.

The life that followed would have extinguished a spirit less keen. At nine, she was old enough to pick cotton; at twelve, she could "chop," or weed, it. Both tasks took precedence over school, which let out when the cotton needed tending, and Hattie Mae made it no further than the eighth grade. As an abandoned girl whose beauty showed, she attracted more sexual predation. This time she told, but Aunt Vi accused her of lying about Uncle George and administered one of her infamous beatings. If black men were one source of Hattie Mae's grief, white folks were another. Unlike her grandmother, she had a hard time striking the pose of grateful deference that plantation life required. "I was the troublemaker," she said. Tired of snapping stalks in the cold, she led a group of younger cousins, including Opal's mother, Ruthie Mae, out of the field one day. When the overseer rode up on a horse and ordered them back to work, Hattie Mae snapped, "I'm not your child," which brought Uncle 'Lij racing to make peace before things got out of hand. Years later, as Congress debated the welfare bill, its proponents talked about work in transcendent terms, as a source of dignity, order, and hope. But the first thing Hattie Mae noticed about work was the unfairness of it all: "All the black people was out working for nothing." In picking season, she dragged a heavy sack across the field, bent or sometimes crawling, and pulled the fluffy fibers from the lacerating bolls. The bending made her back ache. The bolls made her fingers bleed. It felt like snatching thousands of eggs from nests of angry thorns.

As Hattie Mae took to the fields, James Eastland embarked on a long if accidental career in the United States Senate, one that like the plantation itself was bequeathed to him by his father. It began in 1941 when the incumbent senator died, leaving Mississippi governor Paul Johnson free to appoint a successor. For counsel, the governor turned to his old college roommate; the roommate was Woods Eastland. Declining his own chance to fill the seat, Woods persuaded his friend to send his son, who had served two terms in the state legislature but had been out of politics for nearly a decade. With that, at thirty-six Jim Eastland became the youngest senator in state history. War loomed and the Depression lingered when he arrived in Washington, but Eastland found fame with an issue of more limited interest: the price of cottonseed. The seed was an important byproduct of every farmer's harvest, and a federal official's talk of price controls had prices deeply depressed. With a fiery speech on the Senate floor, Eastland squelched the effort. Prices doubled, and Eastland, an unknown planter with a humorless style, became a statewide hero overnight. He left the Senate after eighty-eight days but went home and won the next year's race for the first of his six full terms.

If locally Eastland made his name with cotton, nationally it rested on race. One of the first battles of the civil rights age erupted midway through his first term, when President Truman sought permanent status for a wartime antidiscrimination agency, the Fair Employment Practices Commission. Segregationists rightly saw the move as a threat, and in the summer of 1945 Eastland helped kill it with a filibuster that marked him as no mean southern bigot but a truly distinctive one. The commission was a "Communist program" to "rape American justice," he said. "I assert that the Negro race is an inferior race. I say quite frankly that I am proud of the white race. I am proud that the purest of white blood flows through my veins. I know that the white race is a superior race. It has ruled the world. . . . It is responsible for all the progress on earth." Of would-be black voters, he later added: "The mental level of those people renders them incapable of suffrage." Reelected with no opposition, Eastland was rewarded with the chairmanship of the subcommittee on civil rights.

Eastland's turn on center stage arrived a few years later, when the Supreme Court decided the most important civil rights case of the century, *Brown vs. Board of Education*. The white South was divided as it groped for a response, with some segregationists seeing no choice but to give in and desegregate the schools. Eastland helped lead the opposite charge, condemning *Brown* as a "pro-Communist" decision and embracing the doctrine of massive resistance. As a prime supporter of the Citizens Council, he allied himself with a movement that all but explicitly endorsed the violence that terrorized the South. (J. W. Milam, one of the men who lynched Emmett Till not far from the Eastland plantation, explained he was acting in part to take a stand against school integration.) In 1956, Eastland's fervor landed him on the cover of *Time,* which argued that his aura of wealth and respectability made him a "far more dismaying phenomenon" than the usual southern demogogue. Amid this assault on Constitutional governance, Eastland got another promotion—to chairman of the full Judiciary Committee, through which all civil rights bills and judicial nominations passed.

To modern ears, he merely sounds cartoonish—a forgotten foil for a civil rights movement whose success in retrospect risks seeming preordained. But for the next twenty-two years, every legislative victory had to find a way around him, and by the 1970s, as Senate president pro tem, he stood third in line to the presidency. Long before that, he was for the Caples family a kind of feudal lord. To understand why there were holes in her roof or an ache in her back; why she couldn't vote or stay in school; why the field hand who shot her uncle Will was beyond the reach of the law, Hattie Mae had to look no farther than the other end of the cotton field. Even now, Ole Miss students study at the James O. Eastland Law Library, and justice is dispensed from the James O. Eastland Federal Courthouse. But one place visitors won't find his name is on the road to the Doddsville plantation, now run by his son, "Little Woods." Instead they find a sign celebrating the county's civil rights pioneer: "Home of Fannie Lou Hamer."

While one revolution was coming to politics, another was coming to the farm. Midway through Hattie Mae's childhood, the Delta greeted the awkward machine that would alter its way of life, the mechanical cotton picker. Rumbling across the heat-baked horizon, each of the pioneering contraptions could pick as much as fifty field hands. And no one would talk of giving them the vote. Suddenly the demographic logic of the Cotton Kingdom was upended. It no longer needed surplus labor; on the contrary, most whites were happy to see the black majority dwindle. Eastland's friends at the Citizens Council offered free tickets out. And with the postwar factories of the North humming, workers had places to go; a field hand could take a train to Chicago and quadruple his wages overnight. The black migration, which had started as a trickle, swelled to a flood. From 1940 to 1970, 5 million black southerners moved, filling the northern cities. Because it happened incrementally and seemed mostly to affect poor blacks, the migration never registered in white America as a momentous event, on par with war or depression. But there are few corners of American politics or culture it left unchanged. It gave rise to the modern black middle class, one of the great success stories of the century, and also to fearsome new ghettos whose problems would, for much of the public, become synonymous with welfare.

The Caples family split on Chicago. Most of Pie Eddie's kids gave it a try, but the older ones found it too fast; a few, like Mack, returned to the familiar rhythms of plantation life. Most stayed gone, and from Florida to California, their descendants now number in the hundreds, showcasing a level of black achievement that James Eastland couldn't have imagined. They are teachers, preachers, social workers, an air traffic controller, computer technicians, and a career navy man. But scores of others wound up in northern prisons or in long stays on the welfare rolls. As it happened, the family's biggest success grew on southern soil. Opting for the devil he knew, Pie Eddie's son Wiley Caples, the stable householder, gave up on Chicago and returned to the Eastland plantation. He got some ribbing from other field-workers by insisting that his daughter stay in school, but she took his faith in education to heart. After graduating from the county's Jim Crow schools, Virginia Caples went on to earn a PhD and became dean, provost, and acting president of Alabama A&M. Opal, who met her once as a child, boasted that her cousin Ginny was the "dean of Mississippi!" Like her father, Virginia Caples argued the family's obstacles only mounted with the transition to urban life. "I have always thanked my parents for moving back to Mississippi," she said. Among relatives who moved north, "You were always hearing about somebody killing and shooting."

For a long time, Hattie Mae shared the fear of Chicago. It sounded like a "big raggedy place that you could get lost in," and she felt lost enough. She was twelve years old and living with her aunt Vidalia when a man named Toot came to call. Toot was two decades older, and with Vidalia gone Hattie Mae had no way to stop him. She was nearly halfway through her pregnancy when Vidalia noticed and tried to beat the baby out with a switch. Four decades later, as Speaker of the House, Newt Gingrich would move to end welfare by citing "twelve-year-olds having babies" as one of its legacies. Hattie Mae is the rare woman who really did get pregnant at twelve. But she didn't know anything about welfare.

When the baby came in December 1950, the sharecropping system was falling apart, and the move to Chicago was well under way. Her grandmother died six months later, leaving Hattie Mae even more alone with the little boy she called Squeaky—Jewell's oldest brother. One of her aunts, Lula Bell, came home for the funeral, and saying, "You ain't nothing but a baby yourself," took the infant back to Chicago. There was a vague plan for Hattie Mae to follow, but she wouldn't catch up for nearly twenty years. She lived here and there until 1953; then, homeless, uneducated, alone, and abused, she sought shelter in her first marriage, to a young man named Willie Reed. He was twenty, she was fifteen.

Poor single mothers had plenty of problems, as welfare would later make clear. But so did reluctant teenage wives. Hattie Mae viewed her husband as little more than a housing program. They had the first of their three children when she was sixteen. She lost her next pregnancy a few days after one of Willie's attacks. She left him, returned, and followed his parents to a plantation in southern Missouri, where after years of Willie's explosive violence Hattie Mae decided to leave. Twenty-three years old, with two kids in her care and another on the way, she was scraping by as a field hand and domestic when someone told her she could get some help—a monthly welfare check. She had heard something about government checks a few years earlier. But it never occurred to her that a black woman could get one. Nervous, curious, she went to an office in Caruthersville, Missouri, in 1960 and enrolled in a small federal program called Aid to Families with Dependent Children. She became a welfare mother.

One thing to notice about Hattie Mae and welfare is that the check gave new powers. Rather than promote "dependency," which was later seen as a major failing, its effect was the opposite: it gave her a degree of independence she had never known. To begin with, it reduced her reliance on men, so it decreased the predatory violence in her life. It also bolstered her leverage in a rigged labor market designed for exploitation. Now she had options besides chopping cotton and washing white people's clothes. She said she didn't agree with friends who argued "the money is due you—your grandparents, they worked as slaves." But she certainly felt no qualms about getting paid for doing nothing. White folks had been doing it for years.

Another thing to notice is that Hattie Mae couldn't live on welfare alone. It reduced her dependence on her twin forms of grief, white folks and black men, but it eliminated neither. From the start, she juggled three sources of cash—welfare, boyfriends, and jobs—just as Jewell, Angie, and Opal would do. No single strategy assured a living, but you could survive by mixing all three. The problem was that to keep the welfare you had to hide the men and the jobs: you had to cheat. Fending off her caseworkers' questions made Hattie Mae feel that welfare was a seamy affair—impractical to avoid but a lot of work for a small piece of change. She doubted it had much of a future. Someday, she warned her daughters, the white folks would bring it to an end.

About the time she went on welfare, Hattie Mae met the first man she loved—Jewell's father, Isaac Johnson. He was tall, tough, and handsome, twenty years her senior, and considerably more prosperous than any black man she had known. He had a plumbing business and a corner store that he ran with a lady friend. When Hattie Mae stopped in to buy some pop, he made a point of driving her home. After they started going together, she ran into an old boyfriend, who slapped her outside the store; Isaac cut him from head to toe. That was but one of the protections he wrapped her in. He built her a comfortable house in the hamlet of Hayti, where she lived for seven years. In addition to the four children she had already had, she and Isaac had four more. Greg, her sixth, came in 1966 and grew up to father Angie's kids. Jewell, her seventh, followed in 1968.

Isaac could support the family, but Hattie Mae was in no rush to surrender the added security of her welfare check. Loving Isaac was one thing, but counting on him was another. She knew he had other women, and she never knew when he might leave. This was the age of the midnight raid, when caseworkers arrived unannounced to shine flashlights under the bed. Men and TVs were both forbidden, and Isaac had bought her a big one. When her caseworker knocked, she hid the television under a sheet and stuffed Isaac in a box. The caseworker wasn't fooled. "I know you can't make it on public aid alone," he said afterward. "You know how it is," she answered. That is, she admitted nothing. But when the caseworker didn't turn her in, she came to think of him as her first white friend. In time, he confided the reason for the raids. One of Isaac's other girlfriends kept calling the office to complain he was spending the night.

Hattie Mae never stopped loving Isaac. She just tired of his fooling around. She warned him she would leave, and she did in 1970, a few months before Jewell's second birthday. Thirty-three years old, pregnant with her eighth child, she waited for Isaac to go to work. Then she raced to the bus station, kids in tow, for the five-hundred-mile ride to Chicago. In arriving pregnant by bus in a new city after a problem with a man, Hattie Mae was writing the script that Jewell would follow with uncanny precision two decades later, when she stepped off a bus in Milwaukee. Hattie Mae never saw Isaac again, but he called every now and then. He said if any man raised a hand to her, he would *walk* to Chicago just to whip him. When the news arrived many years later that Isaac had died, Jewell, then a teenager, didn't care. She had never had any interest in meeting her father. But Hattie Mae felt like a piece of her heart had stopped beating.

THREE

The Crossroads: Chicago, 1966–1991

Much as Hattie Mae had feared, Chicago proved a "big raggedy place that you could get lost in," and countless people did. In the three decades before she arrived, Chicago's black population grew by eight hundred thousand. A city-within-a-city sprang up in its midst, and while it fostered a proud black middle class it also bred a destructive new street life, spreading havoc in the ghettos and fears far beyond. Just how it happened is still not fully understood. There had always been chaos in black southern life. But the stabilizing forces of the rural world—church, school, communal networks—carried less weight in the anonymous city, where someone looking to live the wild life could do it on a grander scale. Economics played a role. While the work paid better than picking cotton, many of the best jobs remained off-limits, and by the time Hattie Mae arrived in 1970, the blue-collar economy was dying. In two decades, Chicago would lose 60 percent of its manufacturing jobs, and with them the promise of a decent living on muscle alone. Plus, Chicago had its own segregationist passions, especially in housing and schools. Most tragically, it piled the poorest black migrants into monstrous public-housing towers, whose names would become synonymous with government folly: Henry Horner Homes (1957), Stateway Gardens (1958), Cabrini-Green (1958), the Robert Taylor Homes (1962).

In the early days, the ghetto was an eclectic place, with lawyers and preachers sandwiched beside porters and prostitutes. Fair-housing laws let much of the middle class escape, and those left behind grew not only poorer but socially set apart. Welfare rules loosened in the mid-1960s, and within a generation the nation's rolls quadrupled. From 1964 to 1976, the share of black children born to single mothers doubled to 50 percent. Crime, drugs—likewise up in startling fashion, especially after the mid-1980s onslaught of crack. In Chicago, a vicious gang culture appeared, filling the vacuum left by absent fathers. By the late 1980s, even left-of-center experts had broadened their concerns from poverty per se to self-defeating behaviors—to what William Julius Wilson, the country's preeminent black sociologist, called the "social pathologies of the inner city." That all this was happening after the triumphs in civil rights only lent the tableaux a more tragic cast. When Angie, Opal, and Jewell were born in the mid-1960s, the word *underclass* was obscure and distrusted; its suggestion of intransigence collided with the national faith in class mobility. By the time they reached high school, the word was widely used, however imprecisely, to describe people much like them.

Hattie Mae settled in more easily than she expected; she knew people everywhere. From the bus station, she took a taxi to the south-side projects where Aunt Lula Bell had a place. Hattie Mae's grown son, Squeaky, whom Lula Bell had raised, was in and out of the Stateway Gardens apartment, so among the reunions Hattie Mae enjoyed was that of mother and son. Her cousin from the Eastland plantation, Ruthie Mae Caples, lived in Stateway, too, with five kids and a factory job at Zenith. Ruthie's daughter Opal was a mischievous girl of four, two years older than Jewell, and both generations bonded. For all the hard living condensed in her years, Hattie was only thirty-three and still ready for some fun. Three decades later, a Polaroid of her and Ruthie in white go-go boots still crackled with danger. "We thought we was Miss Fine!" Hattie Mae said. Soon she had her own Stateway apartment and a version of her old survival plan: an unreported job, a boyfriend, and a monthly welfare check. The job, at a linens factory, didn't last. The boyfriend, Wesley, did, much to her children's chagrin.

The high-rise was tolerable for the first few years. But as Opal and Jewell were starting school, it was spinning out of control. The gangs frightened even Hattie Mae, who had witnessed more than her share of roughness. Coming home late from work one night, she barely out-raced some teenage boys intent, she presumed, on rape. Ruthie moved out first. Hattie Mae stayed, and a year later her son Squeaky was murdered—done in, she was told, by friends in a drug gang who suspected him of stealing their money. Hattie Mae was devastated, maybe all the more so because, as a thirteen-year-old mother, she had given him away. After two of her other sons were assaulted—Willie was shot at, and Greg was hit by a brick from a balcony—Hattie worried the whole family had become a target of gang reprisal. Vowing to salvage something from Squeaky's death, she promised she would get the rest of the kids out, and she found a job waiting tables at a bar.

The job, at the Marcellus Lounge, was a big break. The lounge drew a high-rolling crowd, including the drug baron Flukey Stokes, who would seal his place in Chicago lore (and a song by Stevie Ray Vaughn) by throwing himself a $200,000 anniversary party and burying his son, "Willie the Wimp," in a casket shaped like a Cadillac. Having traveled from Big Jim Eastland's plantation to Flukey Stokes's pool hall, Hattie Mae was living a kind of pulp fiction version of the underclass formation story. Flukey and his sidekicks liked Hattie. They called her "sister," bought clothes for her kids, and put out the word that she wasn't to be hurt. With $100 tips, she could net as much in a night at the lounge as she could in a month on welfare. As for where her friends got their money, she said, "I didn't get into their business, and they didn't get into mine." Hattie Mae kept the job (and since she didn't report it, her welfare check) well into Jewell's teens. She fled the projects when Jewell was eight. By then, the black belt had burst out of its historic confines and spread fifteen miles to the city's southern edge. Hattie Mae and the kids went with it, eventually landing in the far southeastern corner of the city, in a rough-and-tumble place called Jeffrey Manor.

Angie's mother had found her way to Jeffrey Manor, too—with her marriage dead and the neighborhood dying, Charity Jobe was trying to get out as Hattie Mae moved in. It was their children's lives that would converge in the Manor, much to Charity's dismay. Like Hattie Mae, Charity once picked Mississippi cotton. But while Hattie grew up orphaned and abused, Charity's roots were against-the-odds middle class, with her grandfather the rare sharecropper who made it. A son of emancipated slaves, Levi Gillespie was already an old man of sixty-eight in 1941, two years before Charity's birth, when he took out a contract to buy 110 acres in Egypt, Mississippi. He made the payments past the age of eighty, then transferred the mostly paid-for land to Charity's father. Henderson Gillespie retained his father's acreage and will. One family story celebrates the time a white store clerk called him a "nigger." "That'll be *Mister* Nigger," he said, and grabbed him in the groin until he said it. In contrast to Hattie Mae's childhood of violence and dislocation, Charity's was a model of order. She spent mornings in school and afternoons in the field. Meals didn't start without a blessing, and church on Sunday was an all-day affair. Her parents' marriage lasted nearly sixty years. When suitors called on his daughters, Henderson warned that if he saw them with a drink or a cigarette he would knock it down their throat. Walking four miles to the Jim Crow school, six of his eight kids earned high school degrees.

Charity hated the drudgery of fieldwork, and when she graduated in 1961, there was nothing else to do. One brother worked construction in Chicago and another parked cars at O'Hare; a sister ran a South Side bar. Charity followed them north and got an office job at a commercial laundry, where she met Angie's father. Roosevelt Jobe also came from northeastern Mississippi, but from a poorer, more troubled family; he told Charity his father had left when Roosevelt was still a boy and was never heard from again. "My daddy's family is really sometimey," Angie would say. "Sometime they like you, sometime they don't." At five foot three, Roosevelt compensated for size with flash; he talked smooth, dressed well, and courted Charity with candy and flowers. After two years, she went as far as applying for a marriage license, before deciding that a marriage wouldn't work. Then she found out she was pregnant. She couldn't face her father like that. She married Roosevelt on her lunch break in her pastor's living room.

Angie was born in 1966; her brother, Terrance, arrived the next year. Charity got a job as a hospital receptionist. Roosevelt moved to the Handy Button Company, where he made good money on the factory floor. Charity wanted to buy a house, and Jeffrey Manor, a ring of duplex townhomes with modest yards, was a place they could afford; they settled at 9807 South Clyde. Although Angie started first grade in the public system, Charity found the teachers indifferent—one said that she called in sick a lot because she didn't like the kids—and Charity transferred Angie to parochial school. When Charity wasn't at work, she was running to Scouts and Holy Cross Church, where, despite the family's Baptist roots, Angie was baptized as a Catholic and Terrance served as an altar boy. With Roosevelt scarcely around, her life was her kids.

Charity's brand of mothering was devoted but intense, at times overbearing. Loving and lecturing, caring and carping, combined with the force of a pressure hose. "Angela! The Lord don't play!" went one frequent refrain. A portrait of innocence in her plaid jumper, Angie had the kind of sweet streak that mothers prize in daughters, trusting Charity with confidences that others save for best friends. "My mother is the nicest person in my life," Angie wrote in grade school. "My mother's the best, if you ask me." But she also made an early practice of tugging against Charity's leash. While her younger brother feigned obedience and excelled in class, "I was the bad one," Angie said, "'cause I couldn't keep my mouth shut." An indifferent student, she did her homework with a knee in the chair and a foot out the door, convinced a freer, faster world beckoned just beyond. Few of the neighbors shared Charity's strictures, and Angie could look outside at midnight and see kids crowding the stoop. Charity's great fear was that Angie would somehow wind up with them; Angie's great fear was that she wouldn't. Mocking Charity's curfews, the neighborhood kids dubbed her "Mean Mama Lulu," and Mean Mama didn't spare the rod. Once, when some kids chased Angie home, Charity threatened to whip her if she didn't defend herself, a move she came to regret, as Angie found that despite her skinny schoolgirl frame fighting came naturally. A running routine of Angie's childhood involved Angie starting to say something smart, Charity warning her not to, and Angie saying it anyway—feeling empowered early on by her ability to take a blow. "I got slapped in the mouth a whole lot," Angie said. "The slap, sometime it felt good, 'cause I said what I wanted to say."

Years later, deep into a very different life, Angie would affectionately sum up her mother with a kind of spontaneous spoken poem. "My Mama is very different from me," she said.

My Mama don't drink,
My Mama don't smoke,
My Mama don't do nothing.
My Mama go to church.
That's all she do.

When the topic of her father arose, Angie began less lyrically. "My daddy was an asshole," she said. Growing up with Roosevelt Jobe wasn't much different, except in negative ways, than being raised by a single mom. She didn't see him much, and when she did he hardly spoke. His Cadillac had a rhinestone dash, and while Charity talked up the Ten Commandments, Roosevelt issued two: Don't Eat in My Car. Don't Fuck Up My Seats. For the most part, the family ignored him.

"You wanna marry my mama?" Angie asked a city bus driver one day. "I want a daddy!"

"Angela! You have a daddy!" Charity said.

"But he's never home!"

For a girl under her mother's thumb, Roosevelt modeled a looser way of life. Charity's friends warned her that he was messing around. Then a woman checked into the hospital where Charity worked and identified the father of her newborn son as Roosevelt Jobe. Angie wasn't old enough to understand what was going on, but she never forgot that fight. No matter how often Charity changed her unlisted number, the other woman continued to call, and Angie came to realize that her father had a second family. He also drank. Angie knew the extent of it before Charity did. She found vodka bottles hidden everywhere—inside the toilet tank, behind the dresser, underneath the couch. She would drain the bottles and refill them with water, but Roosevelt blamed Charity. As a grade school girl, Angie once rescued her mother by smashing an empty bottle against her father's head. One night when Roosevelt took a swing, Charity knocked him out with a flashlight, sending a terrified Angie racing from the house.

"Angela said you killed her daddy!" the neighbor said.

"I don't know if I killed him or not," Charity said. "If he isn't dead, he should be."

Angie's teachers at Holy Cross knew nothing of the turmoil at home. But they sensed that something was wrong. She was smart, popular, and sensitive; she wrote well. Still, she disliked school, and her grades languished in the low Cs. They couldn't understand why she didn't do better, and they urged Charity to hire a tutor. Although she found a kind one, he came to change Charity's life more than Angie's.

As Angie's family was coming apart, so was the neighborhood around her. The area known as Jeffrey Manor encompassed an eighty-acre subdivision called Merrionette Manor, which was built just after the Second World War and formed the neighborhood's core. The signature of its eponymous developer, Joseph E. Merrion, was the curving, mazelike streets, which isolated the enclave from the urban grid and lent it a leisurely feel. A small playground-park sat in the middle, and a school sprang up on the southern end. For a generation, the neighborhood worked as intended, providing a sheltered spot for raising kids. The 1968 graduates of Luella Elementary were left with so much nostalgia, they kept a Web site of memories three decades later: "pony league games," "the library bus," "Passover shopping at Hilman's." Not even Richard Speck's infamous slaughter of eight nursing students shattered the aura of innocence. But the arrival of black homeowners did. Across Chicago, whites fought housing integration with everything from rocks to full-blown riots; the first black family in Jeffrey Manor encountered a burning cross. A classic wave of panic selling followed, with realtors multiplying their commissions by urging white families to salvage what they could. In 1968, the Luella student body was nearly 90 percent white. Three years later, it was nearly 90 percent black.

Like Charity, who arrived in 1972, the first black families had a middle-class cast; some were more prosperous than the whites they replaced. But with an entire neighborhood up for sale, the Manor fell into disarray. Some of the newcomers came from rougher parts of town, trailing troubled relatives and friends. The labyrinthine streets, built for bikes, proved equally good for peddling drugs, since the police had no easy route in. Still on welfare and working at the bar, Hattie Mae arrived in 1979 with her boyfriend, Wesley, and four of her kids, the youngest of whom, Robert, at eight, was already proving a hellion. By the time Angie finished grade school in 1981, the playground was sprayed with a six-point star, marking the presence of the Gangster Disciples. Angie's first boyfriend, Jay, was shot at on the playground as a teen and later murdered outside a bar. "Our generation was terrible!" Angie said. "Everybody started losing they damn mind."

With its backdrop of gangs, guns, and drugs, the Manor of Angie's adolescence sounds like a familiar story of a big-city ghetto. Or it does until you take a closer look, when the facts of neighborhood life upend expectations. Jeffrey Manor wasn't even poor; the poverty rate of ten percent in Angie's census tract was two points below the national average. Nine of ten families owned their own homes. Seventy-three percent of the adults worked, well above the national average of 62 percent. Household income (about $47,000 in contemporary terms) ran a third higher than the average citywide. It certainly wasn't a welfare neighborhood; Hattie Mae aside, only one household in ten received cash aid. That was a bit more than the national average (8 percent) but much less than the Chicago norm (15 percent). In demographic terms, that is, the Manor defied the theories of decline canonized left and right. If it wasn't poor and jobless (left) or enervated by the dole (right)—then what was it? What made so many kids like Angie, "lose they damn mind"?

Despite decades of study, the honest answer may be that no one really knows. But one theory starts with race: black neighborhoods like Jeffrey Manor just seem like more precarious places to come of age than their white equivalents, even when they have similar incomes. The sociologist Mary Pattillo-McCoy spent three years studying a neighborhood just north of Jeffrey Manor for her book, *Black Picket Fences.* Like the Manor, the neighborhood she gave the pseudonym "Groveland" was filled with lower-middle- to middle-class homeowners and beset by drugs and gangs. She argued that the residents of such neighborhoods were caught in spatial buffer zones, trapped between the ghetto and prosperous white areas beyond. Given the recency of their middle-class status, black families lived in social buffer zones, too; they were more likely than whites to have relatives or friends who were poor or in jail. As a result, their kids grew up at what Pattillo-McCoy called a "crossroads," with as many ties leading back to the ghetto as leading away.

If the story was partly one of exclusion, from established social networks, it may also be one of seduction. Street culture can exert a downward pull even on would-be achievers. (The black student accused of "acting white" is a staple of inner-city life.) Southern black folklore paid special homage to tricksters and badmen, marginal figures skilled at overpowering or deceiving—"getting over" on—their white oppressors. Pattillo-McCoy, who was raised in a buffer-zone neighborhood in Milwaukee, warned that their modern equivalents, gangsta styles that "glamorize the hard life of poverty," carry special peril for buffer-zone teens. The Winnetka kid who wears baggy pants draws a reproving look from his mother; the Groveland kid draws a cop or a real gang. Lots of crossroads kids succeed, but with licit and illicit, gangsta and straight, so deeply intertwined, one Groveland resident could have been speaking for Angie when she said: "You could go any way any day."

There's another lens through which to see the Manor's problems: the abundance of single mothers. By 1980, a third of its children were being raised in female-headed households. That was less than the national average for African Americans (49 percent), but twice the rate for all kids nationwide. Indeed, it's the only piece of demographic data that makes the Manor look like an at-risk neighborhood; statistically the evidence is clear that children raised in single-parent homes face greater risks of educational failure, early pregnancy, unemployment, and crime. ("I wanted to join, 'cause I thought my father didn't love me," one Groveland gang member said.) In most Jeffrey Manor cases, the single moms were *working* moms, which may have meant they set an industrious example but also left their kids with lots of unsupervised time. "When we were in Jeffrey Manor, a lot of those kids out there didn't even have fathers," Charity said. "They were living with the aunties, staying with their grandmothers. They could stay out as late as they want." And Angie yearned to be with them.

While the marriage died nearly as soon as it started, Charity took her vows seriously enough to stay for a dozen years. The beginning of the end arrived one night when the kids ran out of food; Roosevelt told her to feed them bread and water and drove off in his Cadillac. Charity sent the kids to her brother's and went to bed with a butcher knife. This time, if he tried to hit her, she really would try to kill him. ("I had to pray on that, real hard," she said.) Charity enrolled in beauty school, and Angie, in the sixth grade, was old enough to crack the code: her mother was getting ready to leave. Angie was with her mother one night when Charity, exhausted from work and school, fell asleep behind the wheel and plowed into the neighbor's yard. "My mother was tired as hell," Angie said. "She was trying to get her life together; she didn't see ours drifting away."

The divorce hit Angie harder than anyone expected. It just seemed to shatter one of life's basic rules, that mothers and fathers come bundled together, however imperfectly. "He was an asshole, but he was still my daddy," Angie said. When Roosevelt refused to vacate the house, Charity and Angie were forced to move, violating a tenet of divorce management by leaving Angie further uprooted; her brother stayed with her dad. Even her body started to change. "Everything happened so fast," she said. As a young child, Angie had blended a winning innocence ("Wanna marry my mama?") with an insolent streak. Her mother had her pegged as a "follower," willing to abet whatever the worst kids wanted to do. After the divorce, the innocence faded and the insolence grew, to a level that would startle Angie herself.

As Angie finished eighth grade, Charity married Rodger Scott, the Holy Cross teacher she had hired to help Angie a few years earlier. Angie had liked Rodger as a tutor, finding him young, fun, and kind. But as a stepfather, even a mellow one, he inevitably formed a different identity in her mind. "It was like he was taking away my mama," she said. He, too, had been through a bitter divorce, and he brought his two young kids into the house, which left Angie feeling additionally invaded and burdened as a babysitter. Hugette, at six, was manageable enough, but even as a preschooler, Rodger's son, Jay, was beyond-the-pale wild. With Jay storming through the house, Angie was in no mood for her stepfather's discipline, however mild.

"How was school?"

"Where's your homework?"

Angie would mutter under her breath, "Who the hell are you?"

In her first year at Aquinas High, a Catholic girls' school that Charity struggled to afford, Angie still indulged her earnest streak. She joined the pep squad and gave an impassioned debate-team speech calling for temperance. ("Today I will persuade you that being a teenage drinker is not what you want to be.") She carried around four-by-six cards with poems by Jackie Earley ("Got up this morning / Feeling good & Black") and Langston Hughes ("I am the darker brother"). But as the year wore on, so did the tensions at home. She started tongue-lashing Rodger and smoking pot. She ran back to her father's house in Jeffrey Manor, where there were no rules. As her freshman year ended, Angie left to spend the summer with her father—or more to the point, without him, since Roosevelt was never around. In a sense, she never returned. After years of envying the kids on the stoop, Angie was free to join them. "I got a chance to be wild."

As an adolescent child of divorce staging a rebellion, Angie was scarcely an unfamiliar figure. With a caring if overbearing mother and a place in Catholic school, she did have a safety net. But it was thinner than it may seem. She struggled in class and had few close friends, an alcoholic father, and a gangland neighborhood. Charity grew so worried that she scraped up the money to send Angie to a psychologist, who certainly could have found much to explore. A little girl had grown up close to her mother, but close in a complicated way, relishing the attention but resenting the reins. Early on, she had found strength in defiance ("the slap, sometime it felt good"), and then everything had disappeared: her father, her brother, her home. A strange man had stolen her mother, too. Angry and abandoned, Angie responded as she would for decades, hiding her feelings behind a tart lip and quick fists. "Fighting I can deal with," she later said. "Emotions I can't deal with too good." At some level, Angie knew it even then, but she didn't tell the psychologist. Instead she spun fanciful tales of privation until Charity gave up. Her mother had bought her a dime-store journal, and it became the only therapist that Angie would trust. "Everything that bothers me, everything that hurts me, everything that's just not right—I write it down!" she said. "I write it down and I rise above it. That way I don't have to worry about nobody hurting me."

One night in high school, Angie smuggled in a forbidden girlfriend to sleep at the house. Charity confronted Angie. Angie said something smart. The next thing that Charity knew, she had dragged Angie into the kitchen, where she was beating her uncontrollably. "I went temporarily insane," Charity said. "I done grabbed her by the throat. I was banging her head against the refrigerator. I was so scared, I was shaking. I was sure I had killed her." Not long after, when Angie announced she was moving back to the Manor to stay with her father, Rodger and Charity felt powerless to stop her. Just a few years earlier, Angie had written a seventh-grade essay, singing her mother's virtues. "If she didn't love me, she wouldn't be out there working herself half to death trying to give me the best in life." By the end of her sophomore year, Angie was pretty much raising herself.

Angie was sixteen when she returned to Jeffrey Manor, and Hattie Mae was living down the block. Jewell was fourteen. Greg was sixteen. Both were warring with Hattie Mae's boyfriend, Wesley, a scowling presence in the house. The process of neighborhood change was more than a decade old, and the Manor's working-class homeowners contended with a rough street culture in their midst. Socially, the teenagers' world centered on Merrill Park, a small playground where they gathered after dark to smoke weed and get loud. That's what Angie was doing when she met Greg, a six-foot-tall manchild in braids, who towered over her by more than a foot and gazed down with his mother's soft eyes. Angie wasn't consciously focused on his looks. He had a girlfriend. She had a boyfriend. But Angie could tell Greg *anything*—the "crazy shit" her stepfather said, the way the weed made her giggle. Given Greg's feelings toward Wesley, they shared an easy solidarity on the stepfather question; then again, they shared an easy solidarity on everything. On the park benches filled with rowdy kids, Greg was both a leader and loner, a picture of competence. Half a lifetime later, Angie would still describe him as the strongest man she knew.

By the end of her sophomore year, her life swirled around him.

She woke up and went to bed with a joint; in between, she hung out with Greg. "Dear Diary," she confided, after they spent her seventeenth birthday drinking wine. "We got fucked up in the park tonight. But he made sure I got home all right. . . . We talked to each other all night." Not long after: "He seems to knows more about me than I know about myself." And then: "I think I'm falling in love." Over time, Angie's middle would thicken with matronly heft, but at seventeen her precocious build left Greg's older sisters alarmed; beside each other, Angie and Greg looked like they were about to combust. That summer, her father sold the house in Jeffrey Manor and moved a few miles away. Angie ran back to the Manor, where Hattie Mae found her in Greg's room and delivered a lecture about men: "All they want to do is screw ya." Angie brushed it off. She and Greg weren't sleeping together. He was her best friend. They were at his brother's house one night at the start of her junior year when Greg put on Michael Jackson's "Pretty Young Thing": "Where did you come from lady/and ooh won't you take me there." That's when Angie knew. Because her mother worked in a hospital, Angie had a pile of pamphlets about birth control. A month later, she was pregnant.

American life overlooks many things. But having a baby at age seventeen isn't one it overlooks easily. To most of the world, Angie presented a face of studied indifference. She didn't tell her mother for months, and she never did tell her father, who stayed too drunk to notice. But her worries ran deep. "I don't know what I'm going to do," she told her diary. "I just have to change my life. I have another life with me." After she fretted to her diary about how Greg would react, she found his response so comforting it bore recording twice. "He just said we will be all right," she wrote. "We will be all right." The relationship turned "wishy-washy" as the pregnancy advanced—she was moody, and he was tired from a job at Kentucky Fried Chicken—but Greg was with her when her water broke. They shared the ambulance to the hospital, where Greg fell asleep in his KFC clothes and in the early hours of May 7, 1984, Angie wept with relief at the sight of LaKesha Elaine Jobe. "Little tiny feet, little tiny hands," she wrote. "It's my baby girl."

About one American child in five was born outside marriage that year; among black children, the figure was three in five. Many people worried that mothers like Angie were organizing their lives around welfare—having babies to get a check. Angie's life suggests a competing view: it wasn't organized at all. It was rocketing forward on the adolescent fuel of anger, fear, hormones, and pot. Until she got pregnant, welfare was one of many things to which she had given no thought. (Charity, virulently antiwelfare, had briefly gotten food stamps during the divorce but was so embarrassed she gave them away.) Although Angie didn't get pregnant to get a check, a subtler welfare critique may hold more sway. Its easy availability may have played an enabling role, giving her a reason to set aside her appropriate alarm. "If we said how are you going to take care of this child, she could say I'll get on welfare," Rodger said. He and Charity resented it for reducing their leverage. Then again, they had no real leverage. With welfare or without it, chances are the outcome of Angie's teen rebellion would have been much the same. Hattie Mae helped with the forms, and Angie got the first in a string of checks that would last a dozen years.

Charity and Rodger could accept the fact that Angie had a baby. What they couldn't accept was Greg. He wouldn't look them in the eyes or come in the house. "He ain't nothing but a thug," Charity said, insisting that Angie stop seeing him. In Angie's mind, Greg's independence from the real thugs was part of his appeal. She considered him just streetwise enough to be interesting—"thug lite," she once said—and was proud when he bought Kesha diapers and milk. Tired of her father's drunken rages, Angie moved back to Charity's at the start of the school year and enrolled at a public school for teenage mothers. Angie lied and told her mother that she was hardly talking to Greg, a dodge belied by his late-night calls. Rodger would hang up, but Greg would call back and cuss him out. That's another thing Angie liked about Greg; he didn't take any guff. "Why can't they understand that we love each other and we gonna be together," Angie wrote in her diary. A few months into her senior year, Angie dropped out—another move that American life is slow to forgive. She said the school nursery wasn't changing Kesha's diaper. Charity thought she wanted more time with Greg.

One night Rodger found one of Greg's letters and started in again: Greg's no good. . . . You're a mother now. . . . You have to think of the future. When Rodger followed her into her room, Angie went off. "You ain't my daddy! Get away from me!" Greg had given her a switchblade, and she warned she was ready to use it. Amid the threats and accusations, Angie grabbed Kesha and raced back to her father's house. In retrospect, Rodger and Charity would blame themselves: if only they hadn't pushed so hard, maybe they could have retained some influence. Angie would look back and think of the fight as the night she regained her life. She and Greg were together. The sooner everyone accepted it, the better things would be.

Most relationships between teen parents quickly fall apart. Angie discovered why. Raising a child is hard work, even harder when you're poor and still partly a child yourself. Both she and Greg wanted to run the streets, and with a baby to care for they started to fight. After a few months at her father's house, Angie lowered her opinion of freedom and returned home to Charity and Rodger, where there was food in the fridge and a hand when a diaper needed changing. Her mother insisted she get a job, and as part of the truce she found one at Popeye's, working nights while Charity babysat. Angie liked going to work—it got her out of the house—and since she didn't tell the welfare office, she kept her whole welfare check. Greg had a job making pizzas. As Angie turned nineteen, they moved into their first apartment, a one-room kitchenette with a bed that folded out of the wall.

A life with Greg was what she had wanted, but poverty, youth, and a child in Pampers remained a combustible mix. Angie figured Greg saw other women; she saw other men. Popeye's provided an escape but left her muttering in her sleep about biscuits. She put herself out to cook Thanksgiving dinner, only to hear Greg call her potato salad nasty. (Worse, he was right.) By then, Angie was pregnant again, not quite on purpose but not purely by accident. Adding another child—a boy, Dwayne, they nicknamed Redd—did nothing to reduce the tension. At one point, Angie packed up and left, but she knew she wouldn't stay gone. No matter what she and Greg said to each other, they would quickly shrug it off. To others, not least her mother, Angie may have seemed a portrait of failure, another inner-city girl, out of school, coming of age as a welfare mother. But as Angie lived it—greasy biscuits, food stamps, and all—the story felt like one of overcoming the odds. She worked, kept her kids fed, and saw nothing to apologize for. "I was on my own, making it," she said. "I was with the guy I was in love with. We wasn't married by the courts, in God's eyes, but to me we was married. Married people have kids, married people take care of each other, even when they have problems. We was a family."

By the time Angie turned twenty-one, she was pregnant again, and the kitchenette would no longer do. They found a bigger place a few miles east in Chicago's South Shore, where their lives took a new turn. The apartment was in the middle of a drug market, and Greg, who'd had an on-and-off job hanging ceiling fans, discovered a gift for selling cocaine. Until then, Angie's finances had rested on the usual three-legged stool; she had welfare, a sporadic under-the-table job, and whatever money Greg brought in. No single income stream sufficed, but together they provided a living on the borders of just enough. Now Angie still had welfare and in time another job, at Kentucky Fried Chicken. But with the money that Greg brought in, her checks went uncashed for weeks. Chicken paid about $4 an hour, and welfare about $340 a month, but by Angie's guess Greg was pocketing $1,000 a week. He drove a Seville and kept the kids in brand-name clothes. For the first time as an adult (also the last), she didn't have to worry about money.

Crack was just arriving in Chicago, and the demand seemed insatiable. By the time their third child, DeVon, was born in 1987, Greg's customers were banging on the door day and night. One day she woke up with Greg in handcuffs and a cop over her bed, searching the room for drugs. But the only thing he found was Angie's .22. "I need a little protection," she explained, "'cause it's terrible around here!" With no drugs in the house, Greg was back by the afternoon. Sometimes Angie portrays herself as a mere observer of the chaos. In other tellings, she assigns herself a more active role. Once Greg handed her three sacks of cocaine to hide in the apartment; when he returned, there were only two left. With a frantic search, they found the missing parcel lying on the ground, like an unclaimed lottery ticket. One of their worst fights erupted when Angie came home from work to discover the kids hadn't eaten, though Greg was outside with money in his pocket, waiting for his supplier. She went out to get the kids' dinner and returned to see Greg still on the street—feeding himself. She got smart. He got smart. She chased him down the street, shooting. Stop playing, he screamed; you crazy? "You make me crazy!" Angie said.

Angie saw nothing wrong with selling drugs; no one forces anyone to buy, and if "you don't use it, you ain't got to worry about it." But she did sometimes worry about the danger, especially with the kids. As the business grew, Jewell moved in; she had gotten pregnant in her junior year of high school and Wesley had put her out. Until then Angie knew her only as Greg's younger sister, a long-legged teenager whose looks and reserve ran the risk of making her seem soft. Angie discovered that Jewell wasn't as reserved as she seemed, and she certainly wasn't soft. They quickly became best friends. The birth of Jewell's son, Terrell, left four young children in the house, and there was no telling what craziness Greg might attract. He mostly "served" from a nearby smoke house, but Angie dreamed that someone had broken in and killed them all. She couldn't sleep for a week.

Now and then, Angie would tell him to quit. But the money was good, and oh, that man could charm! One morning after a fight, Greg brought Angie roses; he sent them motoring across the floor in the arms of a robot the family named Robbie. A few years later, after Greg was gone, Angie would cry herself to sleep in Milwaukee, staring at the motorized toy and thinking of better times. "He did what he had to do to take care of his family, and I love him for it," she said. Life in Chicago was good.

It didn't strike her mother that way. Chicago had gotten Charity out of the fields, but its streets had stolen her kids. A decade later, the officials revamping the welfare laws would stress the potential of working mothers to serve as role models for their kids. For those with faith in the role-model theory, Charity gives reason to pause. She was the role model from central casting: hardworking, devout, zealously antiwelfare. But of the four kids she helped to raise, three took troubled turns. Angie chose a life with Greg. Angie's book-smart brother, Terrance, got twenty years for selling cocaine. Rodger's rebellious son, Jay, was murdered by his mother's boyfriend. Only Rodger's daughter, Hugette, navigated the passage to a stable adult life, with a four-year college degree and a job as a legal secretary. After a shooting beside the beauty parlor she ran, Charity moved back to Mississippi, where she and Rodger built a house on the land bought with her grandfather's sweat. She took a job at the welfare office and offered a stream of poor single mothers the lectures lost on Angie: stay in school, keep a job, commit yourself to marriage.

Hattie Mae's view of Chicago was more complex. In one light, her life seemed a grand dramatization of the underclass tragedy unfolding nationwide. All three of her daughters had gotten pregnant in high school and gone on welfare; two, including Jewell, would stay there for years. Of her five sons, only one held a steady job. Another was murdered; one would vanish for years at a time; and two were headed for long prison terms. But her life in Chicago didn't *feel* like a defeat, not to someone who started life in a shack by a cotton field. Between welfare and the Marcellus Lounge, her deep freeze had stayed full, and she didn't have to kowtow to white people. Compared to where she came from, her children lived "like millionaires." When Greg and Jewell were nearly grown, Hattie Mae, in her midforties, left welfare, went to school, and got certified as a nursing assistant. Her aura of cheerful kindness and midlife mellowing brought a job with a Chicago banker, who needed help for his mother. Born miles from paved roads, Hattie Mae entered late middle age accompanying the family on a European vacation. Her aunts had said a person could make it in Chicago. In time, she had proved them right.

As for the kids, she told herself to give them back to the Lord. "He can take care of them better than I can," she said. With some of the boys, she had seen trouble coming, but Greg surprised her. She considered him the "gentleman" of the house, the one who gave her no problems. But as he settled into life with Angie, Hattie Mae knew that something was wrong. He had nice cars and clothes but didn't keep a job, so she figured he was selling drugs. Hattie Mae didn't know it, but the police were catching on, too. In the seven months after his twenty-third birthday, Greg was arrested three times on drug-related charges. Two of the cases were dropped. The third earned him eighteen months probation for possessing a small amount of cocaine, which the police had found, along with a gun, after a traffic stop. His probation officer kept notes, warning of "His Tendency to Project Blame For His Action On Others." Still on probation, Greg was soon picked up again, on another drug-possession charge. The case was still pending as Greg and Angie approached their twenty-fifth birthdays in the spring of 1991.

One Sunday that June, Hattie Mae awoke with a start. It was one in the morning, and a spirit was talking: "Go see Greg," it said. "It's the last time you'll see him on the outside world." What a foolish dream, she thought. But as she tried to sleep, the spirit returned: "Get up and go see Greg." She found him the next afternoon and warned him that he was flirting with danger and three young children to feed. Greg assured her nothing was wrong, but that night she woke up again. She lit a cigarette and started to cry. "Lord, what is wrong with me?" she thought.

Angie quarreled with Greg that same night. Not long after Hattie Mae left, his friend George came by, and when George appeared, trouble usually followed. Eavesdropping as they stepped outside, Angie caught bits of the conversation. Some dudes had jumped George. He wanted revenge. He needed Greg's help. Jewell's boyfriend, Tony Nicholas, was in the living room watching the Bulls in the NBA finals. George promised him a new radiator and springs if he lent a hand. Another of Greg's friends, Dave Washington, left and returned with some guns. Angie took Greg aside. "You don't need to be involved!" she said. "Somebody's going to end up going to jail." Angie went to bed angry. George had other friends. Why bother them?

When the police banged on the door the following day, Greg was just waking up. Angie had been asleep when he had returned, so she hadn't yet talked to him. But the cops were talking about a wild shooting: a spray of bullets had wounded three men and killed a fourteen-year-old girl. "I know these motherfuckers ain't shot nobody," Angie told herself. She had seen Greg arrested before, but this time he looked worried, especially when police began to search his dresser drawers. After they left, Angie found what they missed, two guns in the secret compartment where Greg kept his drugs. She called Dave, who hid one in an abandoned house and threw the other in Lake Michigan. By then Greg had started talking, and soon the others fleshed out the story: Tony and Dave had opened fire while Greg had watched their backs. They missed the men they were looking for but hit the crowd out celebrating Michael Jordan's win. Dave led the police to the guns—they fished one from the lake—and a forensics lab identified the murder weapon as the one that Tony had fired.

Jewell was three months pregnant with Tony's baby, their first together, and she thought he would be home soon. He *couldn't* have shot that girl, he told her, and she saw no reason to doubt him. But Angie knew this kind of trouble was different from any that she had seen. While Greg hadn't fired a shot, he could still be charged with first-degree murder. The prosecutors offered a reduced sentence in exchange for his testimony, and Angie begged him to take it. With good behavior, he might be home in time to know his kids. Greg didn't want to testify against his friends, and he didn't consider himself guilty: he hadn't shot anyone. He recanted his statement and placed his bets on a trial. It was the one thing that Greg ever did that Angie would find hard to forgive.

Angie was twenty-five years old, and they had been together for eight years. Life with Greg was the only life she knew. Kesha would start second grade in the fall. Redd was ready for kindergarten, and Von about to turn four. Angie had children to raise, and without Greg she saw no way to support them. Frying chicken wouldn't pay the bills, and her welfare check wouldn't even cover the rent. Apartments in Milwaukee were cheaper and welfare paid more. Neither she nor Jewell knew anything else when they boarded the bus to go.

FOUR

The Survivors: Milwaukee, 1991–1995

The Milwaukee ghetto didn't look like a ghetto, at least not the kind that Angie had in mind when she stepped off the bus in September 1991. Its central city was strictly a low-rise affair. Tumbledown duplexes lined the streets, and corner stores announced themselves with hand-lettered "We Accept Food Stamps" signs. While ghettos once teemed, Milwaukee's vegetated, its vacant lots making the near north side feel almost pastoral. "Where Have All the Houses Gone?" the *Milwaukee Journal Sentinel* would ask, over an aerial shot of the vernal decay. Toward the ghetto's western edge, the padlocked factories on Thirty-fifth Street formed an industrial mausoleum. Three miles east, Third Street had died in the fifties and burned in the sixties; renamed Martin Luther King Jr. Drive, it now ran past a black holocaust museum. Between the district's rough borders, Thirty-fifth Street to a bit past Third, stretched the state's welfare belt: nine square miles, two shuttered breweries, and about fifteen thousand families drawing checks.

Angie harrumphed at the weedy vista, but it offered something that Chicago did not, an apartment of her own. From the Family Crisis Center, a shelter just off King Drive, she followed a lead to a "raggerly mansion" a few blocks east. The landlady, Rosalie Allen, had nine units in an old Victorian complex that were newly painted and by Chicago standards unbelievably cheap. Angie took one. Jewell took another. A friend from the shelter took a third. In Chicago, rent alone was $250 more than Angie's monthly check. In Milwaukee, Angie's check rose by two-thirds (to $617), while her rent fell in half. Now, she could pay the rent with $250 to spare. Proportionally, Jewell's welfare check rose even more, by almost three-quarters. She was sufficiently impressed that she called Chicago and told her friend Shon, who was pregnant with her third child and chafing at her mother's. Shon brought her cousin Lisa, who had just delivered her third child and was eager to escape the projects. Until Mrs. Allen could get the apartments ready, everyone slept at Jewell's: four women with nine kids and two more on the way. Jewell's brother Robert moved in. Robert's friend Lucky came, too. In time, the de facto economics grew even better than they appeared, since elderly Mrs. Allen forgot to collect the rent. While a strange new city might seem forbidding, the house on First Street felt like a freshman dorm: hardly anyone worked; everyone drank; and there were more people stirring at midnight than noon. "We just partied on First Street," Angie said. "Everybody partied."

Framed in docudrama clarity, this was just what Wisconsin feared: welfare families—*black* welfare families—racing in for higher benefits. The aid givers' fear of attracting aid seekers is a timeless one, or at least as old as the Elizabethan Poor Laws, which greeted migrating paupers with residency requirements nearly four centuries earlier. But the tensions in Wisconsin in the early 1990s were especially pronounced. A run-up in the state's benefits had left a stark imbalance along the Illinois line and roiled Wisconsin politics for decades. Angie and Jewell had no way to know that the very thing that had drawn them to town, larger welfare checks, was about to turn Milwaukee into the world's most famous welfare-eradication zone.

In Milwaukee, as in most American cities, the story of welfare was tangled in the story of race. One reason the city had almost no public housing was the belief, as one opponent put it in 1952, that the lack of affordable shelter was "the only thing that has kept ten thousand—aye, twenty thousand—Negroes from coming up here." A main champion of black interests, the white socialist mayor Frank Zeidler, survived a particularly ugly challenge in 1956 when his critics spread rumors that Zeidler was posting billboards across the South to lure more blacks to town. *Time* dubbed the campaign "the Shame of Milwaukee," and it bore a second distinction: forty years before Congress put time limits on welfare, Zeidler's opponent called for time-limiting stays in public housing, to keep black migrants away.

They came, anyway. As late as 1950, blacks composed as little as 3 percent of the city's population. Their numbers rose fivefold over the next two decades, though welfare was hardly involved. While Wisconsin's benefits were higher than those in the South, they were not much different from neighboring states, and the migrants mostly came for other reasons—for better jobs and schools, to join family, or to flee Jim Crow. Ironically, the racial conflict that ensued brought a liberal ascension—and with it, the rising benefits—that made Wisconsin a welfare magnet, after all. Some of the worst racial confrontations occurred on the city's south side, in blue-collar neighborhoods fiercely opposed to housing integration. After those precincts gave George Wallace his first strong northern showing in his 1964 presidential race, he said if he ever left Alabama he would settle on the south side of Milwaukee. Wallace stayed out, but a few years later the city's homegrown radical priest marched in. Organizing a band of black "youth commandos," Father James Groppi led a series of marches for six months, drawing rock-throwing crowds thousands strong and helping to win the city's first fair-housing laws. Next he turned to welfare.

The battle began in 1969, after conservative Republicans in the legislature pushed through a benefit cut of 15 percent. Groppi led what started as a small protest march and ended as a melee, as thousands of university students joined an impromptu occupation of the Capitol. The day played out like a carnival set piece. Groppi proclaimed a "war on the rich," while protesters flew a red flag and picnicked on the lawmakers' floor. Bloody clashes continued for a week. In the short run, the protest backfired. The moderate Republican governor, Warren Knowles, was trying to restore the cuts, but the trashing of the Capitol only hardened the conservatives' resolve. Yet the welfare cutters also suffered self-inflicted blows. Sneering about "virgin births," Assembly Speaker Harold Froehlich urged that recipients be prosecuted under antifornication laws. His ally, Ken Merkel, a John Bircher from the Milwaukee suburbs, suggested they trim their food budgets to twenty-two cents a meal, and his supporters called recipients "gorillas." The ugly racial subtext, coupled with the bloodied protesters, fed a broader rejection of the political right. In a landslide the following year, the Democrats captured the governorship and two-thirds of the assembly. Throughout the 1970s, the Democrats ruled Wisconsin.

The changes that followed made the state a lodestar of welfare liberalism: benefit increases, eligibility expansions, and streamlined applications. Benefits more than doubled in the 1970s. Caseloads tripled. In 1970, Wisconsin's grants per family ranked twenty-sixth nationwide. Five years later, among the lower forty-eight, only Connecticut paid more. The legislators who championed the benefit expansion saw it as an overdue bit of economic justice (and a hedge against further violence). But among the problems they created was a disparity along the southern border. Before the run-up, benefits in Wisconsin were 21 percent lower than those in Illinois. By 1980, Wisconsin's payments were 54 percent higher. The Chicago ghettos had horrific problems. Milwaukee offered safer streets, cheaper housing, and larger welfare checks—all just ninety miles up the road. Who wouldn't be tempted to move?

The notion that women like Angie and Jewell move for higher benefits has long been discounted by academics, and nationally the evidence was slight. But the Milwaukee-Chicago situation was unique, both in the proximity of the cities and the difference in what their benefits could buy. In 1986, a state-sponsored study concluded that migration played a "relatively small" part in the Wisconsin's caseload growth. Yet it also showed that nearly half the applicants in Milwaukee were newcomers from another state. In 1991, another study found that 21 percent of Milwaukee applicants had arrived in the previous three months. Surveyed by strangers, most migrants cited less stigmatized reasons for a move—family ties, better schools—but with people they knew, Angie and Jewell were blunt. "We came up here because the aid in Chicago wasn't nowhere as much as it was up here," Jewell said. Angie said the same: "We were figuring out how we were gonna pay our bills."

When they arrived in 1991, Milwaukee had the nation's fastest-growing ghetto. The number of high-poverty census tracts (those where two-fifths of the residents were poor) had tripled in just a decade. In 1970, only 1 percent of metro area residents lived in such areas of dense poverty, and nearly half were white; by 1990, 10 percent lived in the expanding poverty zone, and more than two-thirds were black. Half the black population of Milwaukee County was drawing a welfare check. Welfare was by no means the sole cause of the urban transformation; Milwaukee had lost nearly half of its manufacturing jobs in just twenty years (from 1967 to 1987). But welfare, compared to deindustrialization, was an issue politicians could more readily address, and voters were screaming for change. "Go back to Illinois," advised a letter published in the *Kenosha News*. "[A]ll you bring with you are more drugs, gangs, vandalism, murder, muggings, robberies and more rug rats for us to feed."

In 1986, advisers to the Democratic governor, Anthony Earl, approached him with a plan to trim benefits and impose work rules. Earl demurred; for many Democrats, the criticism of welfare still carried a racist taint. Earl's opponent in the fall election, Republican Tommy G. Thompson, made a similar welfare-cutting plan a cornerstone of his campaign. No one took Thompson seriously. Preternaturally ambitious, he had captured his assembly seat straight out of law school but was still stuck there twenty years later—the leader of a powerless minority, so reflexively negative he was known as "Dr. No." His opponent in the Republican primary had dismissed him as a "two-bit hack," and the head of the state Democratic Party declared her bra size larger than Thompson's IQ.

"Tommy Thompson wants to reform welfare and make Wisconsin like Mississippi," Earl complained.

"With you in charge," Thompson answered, "we're attracting all the people from Mississippi up here anyway."

Thompson rode the issue to an upset victory, cut benefits 5 percent, and put the savings in an early work program. Still, benefits remained comparatively high, and the work program weak. When Angie and Jewell arrived four years later, nothing much had changed.

Finding a house came easy for Angie. Living without Greg did not. She had been on her own for four months, so the shock of his arrest hovered in a strange middle distance, as raw as yesterday and as distant as a lifetime ago. She took so many of his collect calls she needed fake names to keep the phone turned on. They spent half their time telling each other he'd be home soon and half secretly wondering what to do if he wasn't. A month after Angie got to Milwaukee, her father died, bringing her something new to grieve. With everyone on First Street drinking, Angie drank, too: coolers, daiquiris, Tanqueray, beer. Drinking took her mind off Greg.

By the time Angie arrived, Thompson's early work initiative had been folded into a federal program called Job Opportunities and Basic Skills (JOBS), which for the first time required a part of the caseload to seek work, education, or training. When the appointment notice arrived, Angie met it with an open mind. She wanted to do something to let the kids know—to let herself know—that things would be all right. JOBS sent her to the nursing aides' course where graduation had conferred such pride, but once she quit the nursing home it lost track of her. After a few months, she pressed ahead on her own, finding work at the post office; taking up with the deejay, Vernon; and enrolling in a GED class. Her efforts to scramble onto her feet stood out, not least since she scrambled alone; no one else in the First Street compound was thinking about work or school. After a year in Milwaukee, Angie couldn't say just when her life there had come together. But she knew when it fell apart, the moment the nurse said the pregnancy test had come back positive. She went home and cried for a month.

She was much more upset to be pregnant at twenty-seven than she had been at seventeen. Then she had Greg. Now she had Vernon. Or actually, she didn't—she had already ditched him. Just getting her kids out the door some days was more than Angie could manage. Kesha had arrived in Milwaukee as a cheerful second-grader, surprisingly well-adjusted after what she had been through, but she was absent a third of the school year. Her asthma attacks were part of the problem, but so was everything else: the late-night parties, the winter cold, Angie's sadness over losing Greg. Kesha "tries very hard to do her work, even though all of the work that involves reading is difficult," her teachers wrote. At the end of the year, they called her a "pleasure" but held her back. Redd missed *half* his kindergarten year and struck his teachers as less of a pleasure. "Dwayne has to put forth more effort," one warned the next year, as he failed first grade. Having finally gained some forward momentum, Angie just couldn't see returning to bottles and diapers. Something about abortion made her hesitate, but survival was its own imperative: you do what you have to do. Angie bought a $350 money order and asked her cousin Adolph for a ride.

Adolph started up on the way—abortion's a sin, God don't play that—but Angie wasn't in the mood, particularly from a man. Adolph wouldn't be there to raise this child and neither would Vernon. "Just drive and shut up," she said. One of the protesters outside the clinic called her a "baby killer." A counselor asked if she'd considered other plans. She had considered them night and day. Finally she was in the examining room, with her feet up in stirrups, when a nurse explained what would follow. She would give Angie a pain pill, wait thirty minutes, and return to dilate her cervix. The aspiration would produce uterine cramps. To some women, it feels like labor.

Labor? As the words sank in, Angie couldn't believe what she had heard. "Labor" brought to her mind another word. *Baby.*

"Un-uhh," she thought. *"Un-uhh!"*

"Are you telling me I have to have my baby in order to kill my baby?" she said. "That's murder for real!"

Her legs flew out of the stirrups. Her feet hit the floor. "Gimme my money back," she said. "I'm fittin' to be gone."

To explain how much she wanted that abortion, Angie would later resort to quadruple adverbs; she "really, really, really, really" wanted it. She wanted it, literally, more than she could say. "My conscience just wouldn't let me," she said. In surrendering to biological chance, Angie surrendered more broadly. She quit school. She quit the post office. Too depressed to face the world, she stayed home drinking for months. If she couldn't control what was happening to her body, how could she pretend to control her larger fate? In June 1993, a miserable pregnancy peaked in an excruciating birth—a boy she named Darrell. She had been in Milwaukee for nearly two years, and she was in a deeper hole than when she had arrived.

Angie had summoned enough sentiment to put Darrell's sonogram in her photo album. But the flesh-and-blood presence of an infant did nothing to boost her spirits. Jewell didn't think she was coping very well and took over for a few days. Vernon dropped off some Pampers and clothes, but Angie didn't want to see him, and for years she more or less didn't. Angie sent the older kids to see her mom in Mississippi, and while they were gone, she heard the post office was hiring again. "It was time to get up off my ass," she said. She still had her welfare check, and the baby brought a two-year exemption from JOBS. But "I don't like sitting around no house," she said. "Some people's mind just ain't right for kids."

Angie's second tour at the post office is a story she tells with pride. It lasted a year and a half, long enough to earn her label as the First Street "workaholic." Sent downtown, rather than to the airport, Angie had a shorter commute. And as a handler, rather than a sorter, she could move around and talk with friends. Since no one else in the compound had a regular job, child care wasn't a problem. A romance with Lucky's uncle, Johnny, didn't work out, and Angie was more hurt than she liked to show. But she launched another, with a postal worker named Sherman. She bought her first car. Then she learned to drive. The kids had some good news, too. By the end of his kindergarten year, Von had learned to count to one hundred, and his report card swelled with superlatives: "A very good student and friend!" Kesha scored an even bigger triumph. After struggling through two years of second grade, she gained ground in third, and had a breakthrough year in fourth. Her attendance rate reached 90 percent, and, except for reading, she earned straight As; by the end of the year, even her reading had reached grade level. "Lakesha is a lovely young lady," her teacher wrote. "She has great potential for success."

But maintaining the momentum was hard, for Angie and the kids. Six months into her postal job, Angie found two Chicago police officers at her door, asking for Angela Jobe. "She ain't here," Angie said. The next thing she knew, she was in the back of their car, heading to Greg's trial. It had been nearly three years since Greg's arrest, and they each had reason to feel abandoned. Angie didn't write much anymore or bring the kids to see him; Greg couldn't do anything to help her raise them. Angie knew little about the shooting, and from the stand she shared as little as possible about what she did know. But she got a private visit with Greg before the trial began. The prosecutors were still offering a deal, and Angie urged him to take it. He wound up instead with sixty-five years.

Redd, still in first grade, turned eight the day after his father's sentencing. He still didn't know what his father had done, but among the kids he missed him the most. While Kesha missed Greg in a misty, little girl's way, sending him valentines, Redd missed him with raw fury. He put on weight as he repeated first grade, and classmates started to taunt him. Redd wasn't afraid to fight back, with his lip or with his fists. Academically he didn't meet the promotional requirements to get out of second grade, but at nine he was too old to stay back again, so his teacher passed him on to third. A lackluster student who had missed her own father, Angie identified with Redd. She also felt powerless to help him.

What she did was continue to work. Either from knowledge or canny sixth sense, Angie finally reported the job just before the state computer network probably would have caught her. "I have never had no friends tell them when they was working," she said. "Nobody but my dumb ass!" The fall-off in her benefits explains her reluctance: for every $100 she earned, her package of welfare and food stamps fell by $61, and she paid $7 in payroll taxes. She faced a higher marginal tax rate than Bill Gates did. With her take-home pay running about half the minimum wage, why bother? "'Cause I like working—that's why!" Angie said. "It makes me feel good, like I accomplish something. As long as I'm working, I can say 'I work,' doing what I can for my kids."

Angie's pride was real but hard to sustain, especially when the job left her with so little to show. Angie usually says her postal career ended with a layoff, a version she half believes. In truth, she quit. She quit because her "cool" supervisor was replaced by an autocrat. ("Everything went to hell! We was doing shit somebody else shoulda done.") She quit because the Christmas rush left her so tired, she was ready to go postal herself. ("Not one day off! You wonder why they crazy up in there?") She quit because she resented her temp-worker caste, while veterans could walk into union jobs at twice the pay. ("We ain't got no war—what makes you so special?") That is, she quit because the job market for low-skilled workers is stressful and exploitative. Yet quitting left her stuck at its lowest rungs. "If I was still working at the post office now, I'd be making about $12, $13 an hour," she said years later.

She also quit because she could: she had a welfare check. "I knew if I left the post office, I could still have money," she said. She told her caseworker she had stopped working months before she did, and with her full benefits restored, she bought a new living room set. For all her efforts, Angie was still stuck, and the welfare system let her stay that way.

Unlike Angie, Jewell wasn't thinking about jobs, and the JOBS program wasn't thinking about her. She was seven months pregnant when she got to Milwaukee, and the birth of her second son, Tremmell, left her exempt until he turned two. While Angie found refuge in the First Street parties, Jewell wearied of the commotion and made one of the modest bids for independence that subtly defined her. She moved away. The appearance of the letters *PZ* in her welfare file might have given her pause. In moving to Twentieth and Brown, she and her new boyfriend, Lucky, had moved to a "pickup zone," an area where checks got stolen so often the office made recipients come get them. With gunfire outside the window most nights, Jewell and the kids slept on the floor. Lucky had grown up a Gangster Disciple; Brown Street was Vice Lord ground. He got shot in the hand walking to the corner store, and Jewell raced back to First Street the next day. "I ain't no kicking-it type—I'm a home-bound type," she said. "But I ended up in the same place."

At twenty-four, Jewell had spent her life seeming to travel in circles. It took a second look to see the determination beneath the drift. The seventh of Hattie Mae's eight kids, Jewell was chubby as a little girl and painfully shy; as her oldest sister, Mary, put it, "If you didn't stop and pay attention, you wouldn't even know Jewell was around." She was just starting school when her oldest brother, Squeaky, was murdered. The killing quickened Hattie Mae's resolve to flee the projects but left her working nights at the Marcellus Lounge, with the kids home unsupervised. From the projects they moved to a house that Greg accidentally burned down. Their next apartment, lacking heat, got condemned, and it was from there they left for Jeffrey Manor. For a girl with an instinct to keep to herself, the frequent dislocations—new neighborhoods and schools—did nothing to diminish her reserve. "I didn't have no lotta friends," Jewell said. "Didn't nobody dislike me or anything. . . . I [just] wasn't the type to butt in on somebody's conversation." Reticence became her resilience.

Jewell's shyness never struck her as a problem, and neither did most of the other forces shaping her childhood: the absence of a father, the poverty of the projects, the series of here-and-there moves. What bothered Jewell was Wesley, Hattie Mae's boyfriend of nearly twenty years, and after that her husband. "Living with somebody you hate," is how Jewell describes it, a feeling her siblings shared. You can give the family tree a great shake without unloosing a kind word on his behalf. As a longtime worker at an aluminum factory, Wesley had money. But the kids complained he treated them like strangers in their own house, barring them from eating his food, accusing them of stealing things they hadn't stolen and doing things they hadn't done. For years on end, he and Jewell scarcely spoke.

As she reached her teens, Jewell started to thin out, and by eighth grade she had the kind of figure that made men notice. It was something that a shy girl enjoyed knowing about herself. "Guys would ride up and try to talk to me," she said. She was barely in her teens, and "they were like nineteen or twenty." Having started school late (because of a December birthday) and stayed back a year, Jewell entered high school nearly two years older than most students in her grade. Cutting classes and smoking weed, she failed ninth grade, which left her even farther behind—nearly eighteen by her sophomore year. Jewell had spent years dating her best friend's brother, Johnny. But in tenth grade she left him for a drug dealer named Otha, who ferried her around in an apple-red car with speakers that echoed blocks away. He presented her in public with a silent head-to-toe wave, a king presenting his queen. "Most women like a roughneck—a thug, if you want to call him that," she said. *Thug,* in her mind, meant nothing debased but *stylish* and *strong,* able to survive the ghetto unbowed. "I have a little thug in me," she said.

Soon, a bit of it showed. One day Jewell and Otha pulled up in front of Johnny and his new girlfriend, Dominique. The two men started to fight, and then the women did, too. The next day brought a rematch, and when Jewell bloodied her rival's face, Dominique vowed to raise a posse and exact her revenge. Everyone knew a big fight was coming. By the time Dominique appeared with four of her uncles and aunts, Jewell had smuggled Wesley's switchblade out of the house.

Surrounded as the fight began, she took two wild swings and carved a ravine through Dominique's arm. Jewell's family was stunned. Nice-and-quiet, keep-to-herself Jewell was the last person anyone expected to see arrested for battery. "I'm a nice person," Jewell said. "But I ain't gonna let nobody fuck over me." Including Otha. Tired of the king having too many queens, Jewell went back to Johnny. A few months later, Otha was murdered in a Manor feud, and Jewell was pregnant.

Mary, her oldest sister, urged her to get an abortion. Having been a teen mother herself, she had worked her way through community college and into a halfway decent job in a hospital billing office; she knew the struggles ahead. But Jewell had made up her mind. "I'd been thinking about it a long time," she said. "I just wanted something of my own, something that's mine, that I could love. I just wanted a baby, just *wanted* one. Even though I wasn't working, I didn't have my own place, whatever—I still wanted a baby." Wesley made Hattie Mae put her out, which was part of Jewell's hazy plan. She was tired of living in a habitat of hate. What may seem to others an act of self-destruction was to her one of self-preservation. On October 14, 1988, with the birth of Terrell Reed, Jewell had someone to love. She left school, went on welfare, moved in with Angie and Greg, and was neither surprised nor disturbed when Johnny drifted away. "I didn't feel like I needed anybody to help me take care of my baby," she said.

In Jewell's life, proximity often proved destiny. When Terrell was about six months old, a buddy of Greg's stopped by—a "big, tall chocolate man" named Tony Nicholas. Having had a baby with her best friend's brother, she took up with her brother's best friend. The next two years unfolded as a series of aborted plans. Tony was helping Greg sell drugs and would soon have a drug problem of his own. Jewell got partway through a dental hygienists' course and spent a few months as a gas station cashier. Wanting an apartment of her own, Jewell and Tony moved to Minneapolis, where they had heard welfare was high enough to cover the rent. But they didn't like being so far away and came back after eight months. Jewell had been trying to get pregnant again, and she had just told Tony she was having his baby when he joined the impromptu plot forming in Greg's kitchen. It was Tony's errant bullet that killed fourteen-year-old Kathryn Miles. A few months later, Jewell was back on the bus, this time to Milwaukee. She was a seasoned survivor, a woman half formed, and a prison widow at twenty-three.

It took Jewell two and a half years in Milwaukee just to apply for a job. Some efforts to explain why recipients languish focus on self-esteem. But Jewell liked herself just fine. Her real struggle was with something a psychologist might call self-efficacy: she just didn't think she could do much to shape the course of her life. And why would she? Her whole childhood can be read as a lesson in powerlessness. Shy by nature, often uprooted, subject to a stepfather she loathed, Jewell was raised in a world virtually designed to keep her feelings of self-efficacy low. She had seen nothing to suggest that cause brought effect, work brought results, or that risks would be rewarded. When it came to jobs, even her imagination was crimped. She was as close to Tony's mother as she was to anyone, but the only thing she knew about her work was that she "sat at a front desk." Jewell's only adult job, at the Amoco station, was one that Tony's mother had arranged. "I don't never think I'm going to get a job when I put in an application," she said. Especially if white people were involved. "I don't put myself in a place where there's a whole lotta white people," she said.

All of which makes Jewell's first encounter with the JOBS program especially disheartening. Tired of sitting around, Jewell finally called her caseworker and asked for help. In another context, this might be called a teachable moment. But the lesson it imparted was a familiar one of futility. Jewell sat through a two-week motivation course, signed up to train as a nursing aide, and heard nothing for two months. When she finally called in, she learned the course had been canceled. As bureaucratic runarounds go, this was exceedingly mundane. It just happened to reinforce one of her life's cruelest lessons: that things were the way they were and nothing she did would change them.

In time, she did something, anyway. The following year, Lucky's cousin Tiffany applied for a job at a factory that made airplane seats. Jewell tagged along and was startled when she got hired, too. "I guess they needed help that bad," she said. When Tiffany quit a few weeks later, Jewell lost her ride and the job. But not long after, Angie's cousin Adolph introduced her to his boss on an office-cleaning crew. "I didn't think I was going to get hired," Jewell said, though again she proved herself wrong. Since she didn't report the job, she kept her full welfare check. And after a few months, Jewell layered on a second job, as a postal temp for the Christmas season. That left her cleaning offices in the early evening, and sorting mail from midnight to six. About the same time, she started having terrible stomach pains. She was passing blood and making weekly trips to the emergency room, where for years her bleeding ulcers went undiagnosed. Feeling too weak to work two jobs, she left the cleaning crew. But the postal job, which paid better, ended after the holiday rush, and Jewell, now starting her fourth year in Milwaukee, was idle once again.

The JOBS program was supposed to do something about that. But having neglected to help her when she volunteered, it proved equally inept once Tremmell turned two and her exemption expired. It took eight months just to send her an appointment letter. By then she was secretly cleaning offices, so she threw the notice in the trash. Four more letters followed over the next five months, each of which she ignored. Then, about the time Jewell lost her job, the letters from the JOBS program ceased, and she sank back into bureaucratic oblivion. Like Angie, Jewell was stuck.

The taxpayers of Wisconsin, among many others, were wondering why. It's a big prosperous country out there—what kept women like Angie and Jewell from reaping its rewards? Just about everyone has given the subject at least a passing thought, the tragedy of the ghettos looming so large it can cast shadows on the whole national enterprise. One common liberal formulation was that welfare poor were "just like you and me"—generally trying their best—but held back by barriers beyond their control. They faced a shortage of jobs (or good-paying jobs); a lack of child care and transportation; the inability without welfare to get medical care. Parts of the First Street story can be read as vindicating this view. Angie left the post office largely because of its low pay. Jewell lost her job at the seat factory when she lost her ride;

her stomach pain made it harder to work. Still, it's hard to rest comfortably with the view that late-twentieth-century America was bereft of opportunity when so many penniless Ghanaians and Guatemalans were making their way. Years later, Bill Clinton would tell me that one of his aims in signing a welfare bill was to give recipients "the same piss and vinegar these immigrants have got." Another liberal body of thought (in muted conflict with the first) held that the poor weren't like you and me at all but beset by extraordinary problems. They were sick, addicted, depressed, and abused; they were stalked by violent men. This theory fits more easily with the evidence from First Street, where Angie fell into an immobilizing funk and the stacks of empty beer cans grew. But it omits the most prominent feature of Angie and Jewell's lives, their extraordinary resilience. While Jewell's stomach bled, she worked two jobs. From a terrible depression, Angie struggled back to work, while raising four kids. Lots of vastly more successful people would buckle under lighter loads. When I asked how they pictured themselves, Angie and Jewell each began with the same words: "I'm strong."

On the right, theories of the ghetto once began with talk of Easy Street, where happy idlers dined on food-stamp steaks. Ronald Reagan famously conjured the welfare cheat whose "tax-free cash income alone is over one hundred fifty thousand dollars." The Reaganesque talk of Welfare Queens was fading by the 1990s, and it was easy to see why. For all the parties, life on First Street was anything but happy. "We did a lot of crying," Angie said. "Maybe the drinking and the partying was a way just to escape." Another theory had recipients trapped in a subculture utterly isolated from work, in communities where alarm clocks never rang and no one learned the value of an honest day's pay. Though a staple of after-dinner speech, this view hardly described the world of Angie and Jewell. Both grew up with working mothers. And for all his drinking, Angie's father was a steady worker, too. Jewell's loathed quasi-stepfather worked. Angie had worked at three chicken joints, two post offices, and a nursing home. Even Jewell, despite her self-doubts, had found a succession of jobs, and she found them through a network of working ghetto friends. I once asked her if she had thought of her mother—a longtime AFDC recipient who was secretly employed—as a worker or a welfare recipient. The either-or formulation left her puzzled. "Both," she said. The thought that work and welfare were contrasting ways of life—a central premise of the public debate—was to her nonsensical.

The conservative critique that seems more on point concerns the absence of responsible fathers, a condition that had shaped the Caples family for at least three generations and that speaks more directly to the broader underclass dilemma. The lack of a father means the lack of the income, affection, and discipline that a father can provide. Kids can overcome it, and they do so all the time, but for someone growing up poor, having just one parent amounts to a double dose of disadvantage. Not too long ago, a statement like that would have been controversial; a generation of leftist and feminist scholars celebrated the strengths of single mothers and argued their children fared no worse on average than children with both parents at home. Several large-scale data sets have given subsequent scholars an empirical edge, and not many still argue that single parenthood carries no special risks. (They do argue over the risks' magnitude and the underlying causes of the fathers' absence.)

An illustrative figure here is Sara McLanahan of Princeton, a liberal sociologist (and then a single mother herself), who set out in the mid-1980s to disprove what she saw as the prejudice against the single-parent family. Toiling in the fields of multivariate analysis, she found the opposite of what she had expected. Her 1994 book with Gary Sandefur, *Growing Up with a Single Parent*, remains a definitive text.

> We have been studying this question for ten years, and in our opinion the evidence is quite clear: *Children who grow up in a household with only one biological parent are worse off, on average, than children who grow up in a household with both of their biological parents, regardless of the parents' race or educational background.* . . . [They] are twice as likely to drop out of high school, twice as likely to have a child before age twenty, and one and a half times as likely to be "idle"—out of school and out of work—in their late teens and early twenties. [italics in original]

They are also more likely to commit crimes. McLanahan didn't argue that all fatherless children would be better off with their *particular* father in the home; were he, say, violent or drunk, things could be worse with him nearby than gone. But on average at all tiers of society, having a father helps. It's true that troubled fathers are often the product of poverty and social disadvantage. But in turn, they become a cause.

Hattie Mae didn't grow up with her father (or, in her case, her mother, either), and she wound up a repeated victim of sexual abuse. Jewell, never knowing her father, despised his stand-in so much that she was relieved when he put her out. Angie did know her father—knew him as a drunk. Neither Greg nor Tony knew his father (they both had working mothers), and as they were serving a combined 150 years, their children faced a fatherless future, too. Among Angie's kids, the longing for a father was palpable. Angie saw Redd's grade-school fights as the product of his smoldering anger over the absence of Greg. Seven when she witnessed her father handcuffed and swept away, Kesha had processed the loss by airbrushing the memory. As she pictured it for the rest of her life, the police returned, removed the shackles, and let a father give his little girl a parting embrace.

The condition of central-city fathers was catastrophic—but was it welfare's doing? Fatherhood was a troubled institution in sharecropper society, too, as Hortense Powdermaker had found. ("Often there is no man in the household at all.") The conservative critique of the ghetto tended to blame welfare for all of its woes: poverty, crime, drugs, nonmarital births. Yet up close welfare's influence didn't seem so pervasive. Angie and Jewell moved just to get it. They received it for years. But that's different from saying they "depended" on it in any soul-altering sense. It was one way, among others, of hustling up some cash.

Angie and Jewell offered no theory about what stood between them and conventional success. But one striking part of the story they told is what they left out. They didn't talk of thwarted aspirations, of things they had sought but couldn't achieve. They certainly didn't talk of subjugation; they had no sense of victimhood. The real theme of their early lives was profound alienation—not of hopes discarded but of hopes that never took shape. In an unnoticed line in the first welfare speech of his presidency, Bill Clinton would say, "America's biggest problem today is that too many of our people never got a shot at the American Dream." He might have added that some people never even get the chance to dream it. The building blocks of middle-class life aren't hard to identify: finish school; keep a job; form a stable marriage. "We didn't think like that!" Angie erupted one day. "You think we just *had* to live in Milwaukee? So many opportunities for us here in Milwaukee? We got a nice job in Milwaukee! Nice home! We didn't come here because of that shit!" I started to ask what might have helped, when Angie cut me off. "If my *man* woulda come home! I just wanted my life to be back the way it was, happy or sad." Training, health insurance, wage subsidies—Angie could have used the programs the Left prescribed, as well as the prod sought by the Right. But she and Jewell also needed something more, something in which to believe. And that's something that any welfare office would find it hard to provide.

Just as no one expected Tommy Thompson to capture the governor's mansion, no one expected to him to keep it. He was a quirk, a fluke, a "two-bit hack"—and he went on to become the longest-serving governor in state history. One reason was his mastery of welfare politics. "It's a fantastic campaign issue," he told me in 1994, when the issue had reached such a boil that even Ted Kennedy ran workfare ads. One observer that year argued that "all the Republican candidates, and a good portion of the Democratic candidates, are copying Tommy Thompson." The observer was Tommy Thompson.

Thompson's early claims of success rested on a single statistic: caseload declines. From 1987 to 1993, the Wisconsin rolls fell 20 percent. Over the same years, caseloads rose in all but two states—nationally, they rose by a third. Thompson liked to say that he had moved more people off welfare than the rest of the country combined. *Res ipsa loquitor.* There was reason to be skeptical and not just because falling caseloads are value-neutral. (The question, of course, is what becomes of those not on the rolls.) Some of the declines simply came from his benefit cut, which also reduced eligibility; some came from the state's strong economy; and caseloads barely budged in Milwaukee, the only place where Thompson's efforts could be measured against the challenge of ghetto poverty.

As programs, Thompson's first efforts had flopped. Learnfare tried to keep kids in school by reducing the checks of families with teenage truants. Thompson said he got the idea while talking to his campaign driver, and it had that kind of commonsense appeal. But it assumed more control over their kids than many parents had, and bureaucratically it proved a nightmare, especially in Milwaukee where the schools were too disorganized to track attendance. In 1992, when researchers at the University of Wisconsin–Milwaukee found that it failed to boost school attendance, Thompson attacked them as liberal ideologues and canceled their contract. Then the new analysts found the same thing: "Learnfare had no detectable effect on school participation." The debate over Thompson's first work program ran a similar course. Work Experience and Job Training sent modest numbers of recipients into work or training programs. But when the evaluators (UW-M, again) found that it did little to move people into jobs, Thompson ended that contract, too, and ordered them to hand over their data to the state. They published their report, anyway, showing the earnings of recipients had risen in just two of twenty-nine counties.

Thompson was done with big messy programs and prominent evaluations. In his second term, he ramped down to pilot projects and focused on the press release. In the early nineties, Gerald Whitburn, Thompson's savvy welfare chief, ran the department like a unit of Procter & Gamble, rolling out a glossy new product each year, with maximum marketing oomph. "Bridefare," a four-county marriage project, won Thompson a Bush White House event. "Two-Tier," an effort to dissuade welfare migrants, staged a competition among prospective sites, a drawn-out process that kept the words *Thompson* and *welfare reform* in local headlines. It says something about Thompson's lens on welfare that Whitburn held a second cabinet portfolio. He was the governor's point man on polling.

Thompson's supporters make two plausible claims for his early record. By highlighting welfare's failures, they say, his programs helped build support for deeper change. "It's what I call the drip theory," Whitburn said. "Over and over, and pound and pound, and out of that comes more and more understanding and fewer and fewer opponents." To his credit, Thompson was also the rare governor who put up enough state matching funds to receive all his federal JOBS money. As a result, the modest percentage of the Wisconsin caseload enrolled in a welfare-to-work activity was two to three times the national average. That gave the bureaucracy some practice and probably helped trim the rolls. At the same time, Thompson had an advantage no other governor enjoyed, a special pipeline to federal aid. In one of his first acts in office, he cut a unique deal with the Reagan administration that eventually brought him a federal windfall of $148 million. Of that, $78 million ostensibly represented money the state had saved the feds by reducing its benefits, though no other state that cut benefits was allowed to make the same claim. The remaining $70 million was an even purer political gift. The embattled administration of George H. W. Bush, needing Thompson's active support, signed off on the figure a few months before the 1992 election, saying that it represented unspecified cost savings. As one White House negotiator explained: "Wisconsin was in play. It was an election year. You don't have to connect too many dots."

The "drip, drip, drip," the special deals, the outsized claims of success—it all made Wisconsin Democrats chafe. In early 1993, as Clinton took office with a pledge to "end welfare" through time limits, Thompson tried to upstage him by announcing his own time-limit plan. It would affect only one thousand people in two rural counties, but it captured national headlines and left the state Democrats an unappealing choice. They could go along and feed the Thompson publicity machine or be tagged as welfare apologists. (When I saw him afterward, Thompson bragged he made liberals feel like "their hearts had been cut out.") One thing that set Milwaukee apart from most big cities is that its leading Democrats were antiwelfare, too. Father Groppi notwithstanding, the idea of paying people *not* to work had never fit comfortably in its blue-collar culture; the focus of its famed socialist mayors had been clean government and rights for workers. As early as 1990, John Norquist, the Democratic mayor, had called for repealing AFDC and replacing it with public jobs. The mayor's chief of staff, David Riemer, a public jobs zealot, had written a book on the subject. Their ally, Representative Shirley Krug, had been pushing a bill to replace welfare with jobs.

In the fall of 1993, Norquist held a backyard picnic. A state legislator named Antonio Riley was there, complaining about Thompson's latest headline grab. Riemer, the mayor's aide, responded with a plea: end it. Answer Thompson's two-county tinkering with a plan to abolish AFDC statewide. Riley had grown up on welfare himself and considered it "a jailer of people." With the mayor's blessing, he and Riemer drafted a one-page bill to scrap AFDC and replace it with a system of public employment. As for the obvious questions—how would it work? what would it cost?—the sketchy bill left five years for future debate. It passed without a Republican vote. Now, in a bizarre inversion of politics, it was the GOP's turn to squirm: the Democrats had become the welfare repealers. The Republicans called it a publicity stunt, and they were largely right. Half the Democrats voted for the bill just to put Thompson in a bind. Whitburn, the welfare secretary, threatened a veto, and the effort seemed dead.

At breakfast the following morning, Thompson chewed him out. *Veto* a death sentence for AFDC? "It was like serving me up a filet mignon when I was only supposed to get a cheese sandwich," he later said. Wisconsin's unique partial veto let him excise the public-job guarantees, and as for the rest of the new system, he had until nearly the end of the decade to figure it out. The feds would have to sign off first. It probably wouldn't come to pass. If it did, no one had more than the vaguest idea of what would take the program's place.

As the backyard plot to end welfare hatched, Jewell recruited another recipient onto the Wisconsin rolls—her cousin Opal. They had been playmates in the projects two decades earlier, but until Jewell made a visit to Chicago and gave her a call, she hadn't heard Opal's voice in years. On the outs with her drug dealer husband and doubled up at her mother's with three young kids, Opal was dying for a place of her own. When Jewell told her she could get a place on First Street, she hung up and started to pack. Coming home from work a few days later, Angie found a kindred spirit in the compound and embraced her as "family." Opal had a knack for winning people over, and after five years of marriage she put it to quick use. She raced though a line of instant boyfriends with street names like "Smoke" and "Man." She fell for a preachy black Muslim named "Dre," whom Angie dubbed

"Me Don't Eat Pork," after she caught him sneaking bites of bacon. Opal seemed crushed when Dre moved on, but recovered to celebrate her twenty-eighth birthday with two suitors in her apartment, each unaware of the other. "Opal was crazy," Angie said. "Opal shoulda been caged!" The duo became a trio—not just real and fictive cousins, but closer than sisters. "We did just about everything together besides taking a bath," Angie said.

At about the time the three women were born in the mid-1960s, the anthropologist Carol Stack went to live among a group of poor black single mothers who, just like the trio's mothers, had migrated from the South to a midwestern city. A generation later, her famous study, *All Our Kin*, still reads as though it could have been written about Opal, Angie, and Jewell. Stack's women survived by creating a domestic network, across multiple households, of real and honorary kin, with few of the boundaries that characterize middle-class life. "They trade food stamps, rent money, a TV, hats, dice, a car, a nickel here, a cigarette there, food, milk, grits, and children." Life is a giant favor bank; letting someone move in with you today insures you can do the same tomorrow. While others had labeled the poor black family "broken" and "disorganized," Stack celebrated this cooperative living as "a profoundly creative adaptation to poverty."

And in part it was. But if the bond among the trio served its functions, it brought dysfunctions, too. Angie said she started to drink when her friend Lisa did; Jewell said she hung out and partied because Angie and Opal did. Even Stack found the networks discouraged work and marriage by casting them as "precarious" alternatives to the coop life. You don't travel very far in the ghetto without hearing a crab-pot story, of someone who tried to get ahead but was dragged down by family and friends—a resentful boyfriend, an addicted sister, a brother headed for jail. Stories of ghetto success often involve a moment of physically breaking away, to school, the army, or merely the asylum of an outside mentor. Stack argued that "survival demands the sacrifice of upward mobility." Maybe in 1968, but a generation later that was a high price to pay. While Angie denied feeling any downward pull, one noteworthy thing about her efforts to work is how little overt encouragement she received. "We ain't like, 'You go, girl!

Good!'" Angie said. "Who do shit like that? I don't need nobody to pat me on the back. I'm a grown woman." Looking back, Jewell would conclude that "everybody was too, too close."

And with Opal they grew closer still. She landed on First Street with charm, guile, a seductive smile, and a secret crack addiction. When Jewell's food stamps disappeared, Jewell suspected her brother Robert. When Opal disappeared, Jewell figured she had met a guy. Angie was clueless, too. But six months after Opal arrived, the child welfare bureau received an anonymous complaint: "Ms. Caples had minimal food, no beds or stove, and the children were sleeping on the floor. The caller indicated that Ms. Caples uses all of her AFDC on drugs." Sierra was four, Kierra was two, and Tierra was about to turn one. An investigator, unable to find Opal, let the matter drop. It wouldn't be the last time a bureaucracy would lose her trail.

Not long after, Opal brought Angie and Jewell along on a shopping trip to Kmart. Opal got into an argument with a security guard, and the three went to jail on shoplifting charges, only to emerge the following morning with another yarn. The case was dropped, but the episode lived on. One of their cellmates spent the night spinning tales about the crack house she ran. All three found Andrea's stories diverting, but Opal seemed especially engaged. She ran into Andrea shortly after her release, and when Andrea showed her where the drug house was, Opal knew all she needed to know. Jewell, by now aware of Opal's problem, began to chide her. "You need to leave that shit alone," she said. "I know what I'm doing," Opal would answer. "You ain't my mama. Shut up!" One thing Opal liked about Andrea is Andrea didn't lecture.

The First Street life sputtered to a close in the spring of 1995, after three and a half years. By then, Mrs. Allen was eighty years old, and she ceded control to her younger brother, who proclaimed himself the new sheriff in town. The metaphor was apt. Felmers O. Chaney had started his career in law enforcement by walking a ghetto beat, then gone on to become the city's first black police sergeant and the head of the local NAACP; soon he would have a Milwaukee prison named after him. Pay up or get out, he said. Jewell's tempestuous brother Robert knocked him to the ground, which sealed the end. Everyone decided to go.

As Angie and Jewell were making plans, Opal disappeared. In the past, she had straggled back after a day or two, fending off the lectures with a weary, "I know." This time, she never returned. Four days later, when the high wore off, Opal was sitting in Andrea's kitchen, too tired and ashamed to go home. She guessed, rightly, that Jewell had called her mother to come and get the kids; that was one lecture she didn't want to hear. Opal picked up a phone.

"Where are you now?" the drug counselor asked.

"In a smoke house," Opal said.

"Get in the car—don't stop, come straight here."

Frightened, crying, filled with dread, Opal did what she was told. Angie and Jewell found new apartments, and life on First Street ended as it began, with everyone still on public aid. At that point, something called the "Personal Responsibility Act" was making its way through Congress, though none of them paid it any mind. For decades, Hattie Mae had warned her kids that the white folks were going to stop giving out welfare checks. "When you're young," Jewell said, "you don't believe stuff like that."

PART II

Ending Welfare

FIVE

The Accidental Program: Washington, 1935–1991

The people who created Aid to Families with Dependent Children* weren't thinking about Angie, Opal, and Jewell. They had no idea their program would become the federal government's answer to ghetto poverty. They had no idea that ghetto poverty would demand a federal response. They thought they were excluding the two groups that came to dominate the rolls: unmarried women and racial minorities. Everything about welfare's trajectory—its size, its longevity, and the hostility it engendered—would have left them astonished.

The program began during the Depression as part of the Social Security Act. When the law passed in 1935, the main action revolved around programs of "social insurance" for working men, like unemployment insurance, old-age pensions, and survivors' benefits. With the whole capitalist system reeling, Edwin Witte, the economist Franklin Roosevelt tapped to draft the bill, took such little interest in the welfare provisions he farmed them out to the Children's Bureau of the Labor Department. Even there, they remained a secondary concern, behind a program to improve maternal and child health. AFDC was thrown in as a temporary measure, to tide over widowed mothers until Social Security matured. Over time, as workers paid into the system, their widows would qualify for death benefits, and welfare would wither away.

Impossible as it is to imagine now, a welfare check once conferred

*The program was originally called Aid to Dependent Children; "Families" was added in 1962. For simplicity's sake, I refer to AFDC throughout.

an element of prestige. AFDC essentially brought federal support to a system of underfinanced, state-run "Mothers' Pensions." Before the state programs arose in the 1910s, the care of destitute children was often left to charities, which dispatched them to orphanages or even leased them out as indentured servants. As concerns about abuse grew, Mothers' Pensions sought to keep poor children in their homes—but not just any homes. The payments were reserved for a small elite of "fit" mothers with so-called suitable homes. That typically excluded divorced mothers and those with children born outside marriage, and it almost always excluded racial minorities. The screening was so rigorous, those on the rolls were sometimes called "gilt-edged widows." Decades later, welfare would be condemned for encouraging poor women not to work. But that was precisely what it was created to do—in Edwin Witte's words, "to release from the wage-earning role the parent whose task is to raise children." Here's the dewy vision of one Arkansas congressman:

> I can see the careworn and dejected widow shout with joy . . . after having received assurance of financial aid for her children. I see her with the youngest child upon her knee and the others clustered by her, kissing the tears of joy from her pale cheek as she explains they can now obtain clothes and books, go to Sunday school, and attend the public school.

The "pale cheek" is telling: the last thing Congress intended in the thirties was to move black women out of the fields and onto the welfare rolls. The beneficiaries of the Mothers' Pensions were 96 percent white, and AFDC was meant to support the same population. Southern members of Congress controlled the presiding committees and made sure the law did nothing to interfere with the South's supply of cheap field labor. They let states set payments low, kept local discretion high, and rejected language seen as outlawing racial discrimination. The federal government shared in the costs, but states set benefits and many of the rules. As Witte later wrote, "No other federal aid legislation has ever gone to such lengths to deny the federal government supervisory power."

At the outset it worked as intended: black women like Hattie Mae were mostly barred from the rolls, especially in the South. Georgia went as far as establishing Negro quotas. After his tour of the South in the early 1940s, Gunnar Myrdal wondered how welfare discrimination had gone "to such extremes" and blamed state laws requiring "suitable homes." Since "practically all Negroes are believed to be 'immoral,' almost any discrimination against Negroes can be motivated on such grounds," he wrote. Another inspector, Mary S. Larabee, found southern officials approaching poor blacks with the "attitude that 'they have always gotten along' and 'all they'll do is have more children.'" The officials, Larabee wrote, "see no reason why the employable Negro mother should not continue her usually sketchy seasonal labor or indefinite domestic service rather than receive a public assistance grant." Covering about 2 percent of American children, welfare in 1940 was more or less what Congress intended: a small, predominantly white program.

But it didn't wither away. Between 1945 and 1960, caseloads nearly tripled. They grew partly from federal pressure to reduce racial discrimination. The size of the benefits also grew, which extended eligibility a bit farther up the income ladder. And as black families moved North, the racial barriers they faced, though significant, tended to be lower. More significant than the growth of the rolls was the shift in their composition. Congress accelerated the ability of widows to move into the more generous Social Security program. That creamed off the "worthy poor" that AFDC was meant to serve and left welfare with the stigmatized remains: the divorced, abandoned, and never-married mothers of out-of-wedlock children. At the program's start, five-sixths of its beneficiaries were widows. By 1960, when Hattie Mae first enrolled, almost two-thirds came from so-called broken families. By then, 40 percent of the caseload was black, triple the original rate.

Hostility was quick to arise. One of the iron laws of American life is that cash payments to the healthy nonworking poor breed suspicion. Mothers (or at least suitable white ones) were briefly deemed an exception only because society didn't expect them to work—their work was raising children. Yet even the Mothers' Pensions were carefully policed. At the time he created AFDC, Roosevelt himself was deeply concerned about dependency. The 1935 State of the Union

Address, which has been called the "founding document" of the modern welfare state, criticized the cash welfare strategy of the early New Deal and called for replacing it with a giant work program, the Works Progress Administration. In a passage much beloved by welfare's critics, Roosevelt warned that to give away cash "is to administer a narcotic, a subtle destroyer of the human spirit." The antigovernment conservatives who quote him today forget that Roosevelt wasn't just criticizing welfare; as the author Mickey Kaus has noted, he was creating as an alternative more than 3 million government jobs.

At first, the welfare expansion was incremental and bureaucratic—almost accidental. In the next stage, it was anything but. The welfare explosion of the 1960s proceeded from conscious design. Looking to wage a broader fight on poverty, a coterie of activists launched a remarkably successful crusade for something not previously known to exist: "welfare rights." They organized. They demonstrated. And above all they sued. *King vs. Smith* (1968) found in the statute an individual entitlement to benefits, meaning everyone who was eligible had to be served. (There could be no waiting lists.) *Shapiro vs. Thompson* (1969) struck down residency requirements. *Goldberg vs. Kelly* (1970) ruled that benefits couldn't be taken away without due process. From 1960 to 1973, the rolls more than quadrupled.

Though it has been much maligned in retrospect, it is easy to see in the context of the times the appeal of a welfare expansion. At the start of the sixties, poverty rates were twice what they are now; more than half of black Americans were poor. Mississippi had commissioned a study of families dropped from the rolls, and it inspires no nostalgia for the good old days. "Animals shouldn't live in such a place," investigators reported after visiting families left without aid. "There were six or seven little Negro children running freely through the shack and they were half-dressed, dirty and barefooted. . . . The older women seemed to accept their situation as if nothing mattered anymore. They seemed more like shells—defeated." In Sunflower County, where *90 percent* of the black people were poor, the millionaire James Eastland got welfare of a sort; the $170,000 a year he collected in cotton subsidies was nearly twice the county's annual school-lunch budget. As the civil rights leader Ralph Abernathy used to ask, if the country could pay Eastland not to grow food, couldn't it afford to help poor children eat?

As the sharecropping system fell apart, the poor flowed into cities looking for help, and welfare offices had endless tactics for turning them away. Some greeted migrants with bus tickets home. Others menacingly posted police outside their waiting rooms. Applications could be reclassified as "inquiries" and set aside instead of processed. Even in New York City, no more than half of the eligible population was enrolled in the early 1960s. Racial discrimination was rampant. Of the twenty-three thousand children purged from the Louisiana rolls, 95 percent were black. Under the famous "man in the house" rule, recipients also had to open their lives to degrading investigations. *King vs. Smith,* perhaps the most important welfare ruling of the age, reinstated benefits to a black woman dropped from the Alabama rolls for having sex with a weekend visitor. Under state law the relationship made the man a "substitute father," and she could regain her benefits only after two people swore the affair had ceased. The state offered a curious list of suitable sexual witnesses: "law-enforcement officials; ministers; neighbors; grocers." If welfare rights meant getting the grocer out of Mrs. Smith's bedroom—well, who could argue with that?

But a large, rights-oriented program would create problems, too—for poor people and the politics of poverty. The most audacious campaign for welfare rights occurred in New York City, where it was led by two Ivy League intellectuals, Richard Cloward and Frances Fox Piven. The spiraling rolls, the indignant protests, the saturation of welfare with due process rights—many of the movement's traits can be traced to the program that Cloward helped found and Piven helped staff on the Lower East Side of Manhattan, Mobilization for Youth. Though it quickly became the model for the war on poverty and the Legal Services program, poverty per se wasn't its focus when it started in 1962. Juvenile delinquency was. But no sooner did the program open its doors than it was overrun by families needing money. "The workers began focusing on getting these families on welfare," Cloward said. "It was something they could do." Their strategy can be summarized in a word: aggression. "They argued and cajoled;

they bluffed and threatened," Piven and Cloward later wrote. They also sued. By 1966, the city's rolls doubled to half a million, a figure not seen since the end of the Depression.

By then Cloward and Piven had glimpsed something bigger. In a 1966 article in *The Nation,* they called for a "massive drive to recruit the poor onto the rolls" nationwide. Arguing that aid only flows when the poor demand it, they urged "bureaucratic disruption in welfare agencies" and "demonstrations to create a climate of militancy." Requests for reprints ran thirty thousand strong. Soon after, the National Welfare Rights Organization was born, and the age of the welfare radical was officially under way. As Angie was born in the spring of 1966, demonstrations for welfare rights erupted in forty cities. "Harassment, giving ultimatums, overwhelming centers is our greatest tactic," wrote the NWRO. For some recipients, entitlement grew from a legal concept to a social one. In Brooklyn, welfare families jammed a Korvette's store, telling cashiers to "charge the goods to the welfare department." The classic exchange of the era involved Louisiana senator Russell Long, who dismissed the protesters as "brood mares" and "people who lay about all day making love and producing illegitimate babies." Referring to Long's complaint that he couldn't find anyone to iron his shirts, one welfare recipient warned: "We only want the kinds of jobs that pay ten thousand dollars or twenty thousand dollars! We aren't going to do anybody's laundry!" Another recipient pressed the thought to its logical conclusion: "You can't force me to work!"

Just as Cloward and Piven predicted, the bureaucracy responded by opening the tap. With ghetto riots quickening the impulse to placate the poor, New York reduced its application to a single page of self-declared need, and its welfare commissioner became known to detractors as Mitchell "Come and Get It" Ginsberg. Between 1966 and 1972, the New York City caseload doubled again. Nationally, the rolls nearly tripled. The creation of Medicaid in 1966 increased welfare's lure, since signing up for AFDC was the only way most families could enroll in the health insurance program. In pushing cities and states toward bankruptcy, Cloward and Piven had hoped to win local support for a federal bailout—preferably in the form of a guaranteed income. Astonishingly, the strategy nearly worked. Most leaders of the war on poverty embraced the idea, though the chief poverty warrior did not. It's ironic that the words *Lyndon Johnson* and *welfare* remained knotted in national memory, since Johnson hated the very word so much he sometimes called the Department of Health, Education, and Welfare "my department of health and education." Johnson thought the war on poverty would *cut* the rolls and predicted "the days of the dole in this country are numbered." It was Richard Nixon, of all people, who proposed a guaranteed income, after a Democratic adviser, Daniel Patrick Moynihan, helped persuade him of his chance to become a great Tory reformer, the American Disraeli. The Family Assistance Plan cleared the House in 1971, only to fail a year later in the Senate, where conservatives denounced it as a giveaway, and, in the strangest twist of all, liberals called it tight-fisted.

By 1973, when the welfare explosion finally slowed, there were 11 million Americans on the rolls, including one out of every nine kids. The program had reached a size it had never been expected to reach; served groups it hadn't been intended to serve; and armed them with rights it was never meant to confer. Over the next generation, nearly a third of the country's children would spend part of their childhood on welfare. For black children, the figure would approach 80 percent. Welfare had won in the streets and the courts. But it had lost in the broader culture. Even as a million people a year flowed onto the rolls in the late 1960s, Merle Haggard had topped the country charts with an anthem of blue-collar pride:

Hey, Hey, the working man
The working man like me
I ain't never been on welfare
And that's one place I won't be

Welfare. Did the American political dictionary contain a more loaded word?

As the smoke cleared, the program that remained combined the worst of both worlds: it offered the needy too little to live on and despised them for taking it. Even as benefits peaked in 1972, the average package of cash and food stamps left a mother with two children in poverty, and over the next two decades, the value of the typical check fell more than 40 percent. Despite some offsetting growth in food stamps, by 1992 the average package of cash and stamps came to just $7,600 a year, nearly $4,000 below the poverty threshold—hence the need for boyfriends and off-the-books work. As the program's benefits were fading, so was its original rationale: to let mothers stay home with their kids. When AFDC started, fewer than one married woman in ten worked outside the home. By the mid-1970s, half of American mothers worked; why, they asked, should they pay taxes to let poor mothers stay home? That a majority of recipients were minorities further eroded political support. While the program once conjured a West Virginia widow, it now brought to mind a black teen mother in a big-city ghetto; demographically, that was a death sentence.

Its costs posed problems, too. It's true that even when its federal costs peaked at $16 billion a year, AFDC accounted for only about 1 percent of the total federal budget. That was nothing like the $477 billion the country spent on Social Security and Medicare. But count the share of food stamps and Medicaid that went to poor mothers and children and you triple the cost. Plus AFDC and Medicaid required state matching funds, insuring constant conflict in state legislatures. In addition, there were dozens of other programs that critics could label "welfare." Half of recipients ate subsidized school lunches; a quarter lived in subsidized housing. Add Head Start, disability payments, and the like, and depending on who's doing the counting, the cost of welfare could range from negligible to more than $100 billion, or 15 percent of domestic spending. Its vague definition was one of its problems; welfare could be blamed for everything and typically was.

Among those who resented it the most were those receiving its aid. One of the country's leading welfare advocates, Mark Greenberg, got the ground-level view in 1978 when he left Harvard Law School for a legal-services job in Jacksonville, Florida. His clients couldn't live on welfare, but they couldn't live on work, either—not as maids or convenience-store clerks, where they earned little, lost jobs often, and received no benefits. The most industrious combined the two, often on the sly. "Many of the hardest-working people I met were at constant risk of being arrested for fraud," he said. "They hated welfare, but if they reported their jobs they would lose their children's Medicaid." One of Greenberg's clients was arrested in a dragnet after the Fernandina Beach police, looking for secret workers, canvassed the neighbors of *everyone* on food stamps as though they were criminal suspects. The client *had* reported her job, but one caseworker had failed to tell another. "While some people had made bad choices in their lives, the suffering they endured was vastly disproportionate," Greenberg said. "People were treated dismally by public bureaucracies."

It wasn't a sustainable situation—yet the striking thing is how long it was sustained. John Kennedy had promised sweeping reform and gotten an ineffective program of "rehabilitative services." Lyndon Johnson had signed the first work requirements in 1967, but they had little funding and no teeth. Richard Nixon had tried to marry a guaranteed income to modest work rules and fell in a hail of Left-Right recrimination. In Congress, the ruling Democrats were divided among themselves; liberals wanted to raise benefits, especially in the South, while conservatives wanted to cut costs. Substantively, the challenge involved preserving welfare's safety net functions while promoting work. But the outlook for low-skilled workers was increasingly precarious. From 1973 to 1989 unemployment averaged 7 percent, about 50 percent higher than the previous three decades; among black women it was *14 percent.* Wages were stagnant among women and eroding among men. At the end of the 1970s, *half* the black women in the labor force earned a wage that left a family of four in poverty, even if they worked full-time. With the American safety net already much smaller than its European counterparts, cuts seemed especially risky.

Where jobs did exist, it wasn't clear recipients could hold them. LaDonna Pavetti is perhaps the leading authority on recipients' personal attributes; she estimated that about half of the women on AFDC had problems that could interfere with the simplest jobs. A third had severely limited cognitive abilities. Thirteen percent reported near-daily bouts of depression. Ten percent had medical disabilities. Nine percent acknowledged heavy cocaine use. Some had multiple problems—depression *and* drug abuse. The good news is that even those with the worst problems worked. The bad news is that they didn't work steadily. They bounced around like the clients Mark Greenberg saw, making beds, cleaning offices, and drawing public aid.

Women who did leave welfare for work could count on little support. The system was filled with perverse incentives ("notches" and "cliffs"), meaning that recipients who increased their earnings often lost so much aid they wound up no better off. Sometimes they were worse off. Briefing Jimmy Carter on the problem, his welfare secretary, Joseph Califano, explained that if a Wisconsin woman doubled her earnings to $5,000, her net income would fall by $1,250 and she would lose Medicaid. Carter was appalled. "When people really understand this, I'm sure they will do something about it," he said. But any smoothing of the take-away rate would simply bring more people on the rolls, at a cost of billions. The other plausible solutions—creating government jobs, offering child care, expanding health insurance—likewise seemed prohibitively expensive. One reason the despised program endured so long is that it appeared to cost less than the alternatives. While Carter had promised a "complete overhaul," his plan never even came to a vote in a congressional committee. It did, however, produce a famous quote: welfare reform, Califano warned, was "the Middle East of domestic politics."

While welfare policy was immobilized as Angie came of age, ghetto life was entering a troubling new state. Poverty rates had plunged in the sixties and plateaued in the seventies, but they surged in the first half of the eighties—especially among children. One in five kids—and nearly half of black kids—lived below the poverty line. The post-industrial economy was one part of the story, but family structure was the other. The share of children born outside marriage, 5 percent in the fifties, reached 10 percent at the end of the sixties, 20 percent in the early eighties, and more than 25 percent at the decade's close. By 1990, two-thirds of African American children were born to single mothers. Half the nation's poor lived in single-mother households. The poor were growing not just in numbers but in social isolation. The number of slum and ghetto census tracts—those where at least two-fifths of the residents are poor—doubled in two decades. Then crack arrived, and with it shockwaves of violence. This wasn't just poverty but poverty of a new and disturbing sort: brutal, stigmatizing, self-destructive.

The disaster of the ghettos brought one thing disasters typically attract, journalists. In 1982, Ken Auletta published *The Underclass,* a book influential less for what it said than for popularizing the phrase. The *Chicago Tribune* followed a few years later with a book-length series on the city's ghetto poor. *The Washington Post* sent reporter Leon Dash to spend a year living in a poor District neighborhood; he returned with a startlingly candid look at teen pregnancy. Almost all the work on ghetto life was launched with sympathetic intent, but it inevitably covered some unflattering ground: school failure, nonmarital births, drugs, crime. The focus, that is, wasn't merely on poverty but also on behavior. One startling depiction of inner-city life came from Bill Moyers's 1986 documentary on the black family. Though the two-hour CBS special broadcast was titled *Crisis in Black America,* part of its power came from seeing how rarely those caught in the tragedy viewed their lives as a crisis. The most infamous of Moyers's characters was a man with six kids he didn't support, by four women, who crowed about his "strong sperm." "Well, the majority of the mothers are on welfare," he explained. "So what I'm not doing, the government does." His name was too fitting: Timothy McSeed.

While the state of the ghettos demanded redress, the problem of self-destructive behavior wasn't one that liberalism was programmed to confront: it smelled too much of blaming the victim. The phrase "blaming the victim" itself stems from what might be considered the protobattle over welfare reform: the outcry over Daniel Patrick Moynihan's 1965 report on the black family. In sounding an alarm about the percentage of black children born to single mothers, Moynihan didn't blame welfare. He blamed "three centuries of exploitation," from slavery to industrial unemployment. But with phrases like "tangle of pathology," the report drew famously bitter condemnations and left most liberals reluctant to discuss the social problems of the ghetto—welfare included. If anything, they romanticized the lives of poor single mothers, turning Angie Jobes into Tom Joads. With economists in control, most poverty academics had gotten out of the business of talking to poor people altogether; tenure passed through data sets, not inner-city streets. The experts spoke a desiccated, technical language, mostly to themselves.

Liberals further constrained their influence when they began to argue that mothers were right to stay on the rolls until they could land "good jobs"—no maid work and no Burger King. The quest for better jobs was generally a good thing, and for southern black women it had a special resonance, since they had been exploited for generations as field hands and domestics. But as it played out in the welfare debate, the good-jobs philosophy proved problematic. Substantively, it required long stays in training programs that typically proved ineffective. Politically, it made liberals look as though they had an inherently prowelfare bias. Even at the end of the Reagan era, prominent congressional Democrats were still denouncing modest work proposals as "slavefare." The silence about self-defeating behavior, combined with the rejection of entry-level jobs, left the liberals with an increasingly cramped message: Don't expect too much from people in the ghettos. In particular, don't expect them to work—at least not in the kind of jobs most could actually get. A common liberal move was not to talk about poor adults at all, but instead shift the locus to children, who were innocent. The leading advocacy group of the eighties was the Children's Defense Fund, whose logo featured a child's crayon drawing.

In 1984 an obscure social scientist named Charles Murray published a book called *Losing Ground,* which purported to explain what had gone wrong: welfare had ruined the poor. AFDC was one program that Murray had in mind, but also food stamps, Medicaid, subsidized housing, even workers' compensation, all of them skewing the normal incentives to work, marry, and form stable lives. Such suspicions were ancient ones, but Murray gave them fresh legs with a calm marshaling of statistics and a tone of abundant good intentions. He also pushed the logic to a radical new conclusion. Don't reform welfare; *abolish* it. The "lives of large numbers of poor people would be radically changed for the better." Elegant, accessible, in sync with its times, the book created a sensation. Within a few years when Hollywood wanted to cast a hip, tough-minded undergraduate, it showed him crossing Harvard Yard with a copy of *Losing Ground.* Pre-Murray, welfare's main critics had attacked on equity grounds: it was costly, wasteful, unfair to taxpayers. Post-Murray, the criticisms became much more profound: welfare was the evil from which all other evils flowed, from crime to family breakdown. To cut was to care.

Murray ignited a liberal revival. While some critics attacked on empirical grounds—if welfare drove poverty and nonmarital births, why had both conditions continued to rise as benefits declined?—others began working toward underclass theories of their own. Nicholas Lemann started his research on the ties to sharecropper life, bringing in a racial link that Murray had ignored. William Julius Wilson published a book of masterful sweep called *The Truly Disadvantaged,* which established the reigning explanation for the rise of the underclass. Where Murray pointed to welfare, Wilson described a complex interplay between industrial decline (which deprived inner-city men of decent jobs), desegregation (which allowed middle-class blacks to escape), and self-defeating cultural forces (which took on a life of their own in communities stripped of middle-class ballast). He put little emphasis on welfare, but he left no doubt that ghetto life had entered a tragic new state, defending the word *underclass* from those who found it too harsh and chiding fellow intellectuals on the Left to speak more bluntly about disturbing ghetto behaviors.

Another important writer to emerge post-Murray was the journalist Mickey Kaus, who called for saving the underclass with guaranteed government jobs. In a long essay in *The New Republic* in 1986, Kaus, a self-styled "neoliberal," attacked standard liberal positions that had emphasized voluntary training and education and produced modest results. "Our goal, in contrast, is to break the culture of poverty" through work requirements, he wrote. Kaus took an essentially Marxist version of work's centrality to life; his subsequent book, *The End of Equality,* quoted everyone from Eugene Debs to George Orwell on the dignity of menial labor. If welfare was replaced with government jobs, Kaus wrote,

> the ghetto-poor culture would be transformed. . . . Once work is the norm, and the subsidy of AFDC is removed, the natural incentives toward the formation of two-parent families will reassert themselves . . . if a mother has to set her alarm clock, she's likely to teach her children to set their alarm clocks as well. . . . It won't happen in one generation, necessarily, or even two. But it will happen. Underclass culture can't survive the end of welfare any more than feudal culture could survive the advent of capitalism.

Murray and Kaus hailed from opposite poles—one called for a radical constriction of government, the other, for several million government jobs. But they proceeded from a common assumption, that welfare was destroying American life.

Still, not much happened. Murray's plan was too radical even for Murray—he couched it as a "thought experiment," and even a politician as antiwelfare as Ronald Reagan wouldn't get close to it. Reagan praised workfare programs, but given the costs and complexity involved he didn't push for one. Instead, his first budget, in 1981, simply cut the existing program (trimming the rolls 7 percent) by making it harder for recipients to collect aid once they got jobs. The 1981 law also gave states greater latitude to experiment with mandatory work and training programs. More than half the states opted to do so, including Arkansas.

By 1983, as the experiments were starting, half the mothers of *preschool children* worked outside the house, further eroding the rationale for letting welfare recipients stay home. That year, a groundbreaking study by two Harvard professors raised new welfare concerns. Until then, the basic facts about program usage were subject to dispute. While conservatives warned of long-term dependency, liberals said the average recipient left within two years. Mary Jo Bane and David Ellwood proved them both right. Most people who entered the system did leave within two years. But a substantial minority stayed, and over time they came to dominate; the average woman on the rolls at any given moment would draw aid for ten years. To illustrate the concept, Bane and Ellwood used the analogy of a hospital ward, with two beds turning over daily and eight devoted to chronic care; though lots of people came and went, the typical occupant of the ward was in the middle of a long stay. While liberals continued to emphasize the turnover, it became impossible, in the light of the data, to dismiss long-term welfare receipt as a figment of conservative bias.

Not long after, the first results of the work experiments appeared, with an encouraging report. Out of eleven state programs studied, nine raised employment and earnings, albeit modestly. The studies were conducted by a prestigious nonprofit organization, the Manpower Demonstration Research Corporation, and they used control groups, which lent them the gloss of hard science. Critics had called mandatory programs ineffective and punitive, arguing that the money would be better spent on volunteers. But participants told MDRC they considered the work rules fair. Plus the programs saved money—while some up-front costs were involved, the investment more than paid for itself, usually within five years. As Jonah Edelman has written, if Ellwood and Bane showed long stays were a problem, the MDRC studies showed that "mandatory work and training programs were a viable solution." Soon blue-ribbon panels were hailing a "New Consensus." Conservatives would agree to "invest" more in welfare-to-work programs; liberals would agree to require some people to join. Spend more, demand more—it was a compelling idea.

It takes more than consensus to pass a bill. It takes politicians. After ignoring the issue for much of his presidency, Ronald Reagan was preparing his State of the Union speech in January 1986 just as Bill Moyers aired Timothy McSeed. Responding to the clamor, Reagan announced he would appoint a task force on welfare reform. The group's plan, unveiled at the end of the year, urged states to turn AFDC, food stamps, and Medicaid into a "block grant," with capped federal funding but expanded local control. It was an old Reagan idea, but deaf to the politics of the moment. It arrived DOA in a Democratic Congress, which regarded it as a stalking horse for more budget cuts—far from the spend-more, require-more "New Consensus." Congress had begun hearings, which emphasized the new theory of mutual obligation. The welfare commissioners put out a spend-more, ask-more plan, and so did the National Governors Association, led by the chairman of its welfare task force, Bill Clinton, who rejected block grants. The Clinton plan called for spending an extra $1 billion to $2 billion a year but emphasized the eventual savings. Getting the governors to endorse higher welfare spending wasn't easy, but Clinton was ambitious, intelligent, and charming, and he pressed hard. The vote was 49 to 1 (with Tommy Thompson the lone dissenter). Moynihan, by now a senator, took to calling a similar plan of his own "the governors' bill," and started his hearings by quoting a Clinton welfare speech. It would prove, in the years ahead, a rare moment of harmony for the two.

No freestanding welfare bill had passed Congress in twenty-six years, and before any plan became a law, it would have to find common ground between Ronald Reagan, who controlled the veto, and the liberal Democrats, who controlled the House. Liberals wanted to raise benefits, especially in the South. Conservatives wanted to hold down costs and ratchet up work demands. The safest bet was that nothing would happen, but the governors' involvement was an unprecedented plus and lent the effort a bipartisan air. And Clinton lobbied furiously, with calls to nervous southern Democrats, who worried about raising welfare costs. At one point, Clinton, by now chairman of the whole NGA (and visibly interested in higher office), virtually acted as a legislator himself, sitting in as House members drafted the bill. The bill still ran the risk of a veto as it sat in a House-Senate conference in the summer of 1988. But it got an unexpected boost from Vice President George Bush, who wanted to neutralize the issue for the fall elections, since his opponent, Governor Michael Dukakis of Massachusetts, had the more accomplished welfare record. Even with so many moons aligned, the bill had a near-death experience, squeezing through a crucial committee by a single vote.

The Family Support Act was signed in a Rose Garden ceremony on October 13, 1988. The next day, Jewell had her first child and went on the rolls; Angie by then had three. The law created the JOBS program—the one that sent Angie to nursing aides' school—and offered states up to $1 billion a year in matching funds. In exchange, when fully phased in, it required states to make sure that 20 percent of their eligible recipients enrolled. (About half the caseload was exempt.) Spend more, demand more—the law seemed the very embodiment of the "New Consensus," and its passage was celebrated as a historic breakthrough. Moynihan was especially ebullient, predicting it would "bring a generation of American women back into the mainstream." Instead, over the next few years, the caseloads swelled by a third. By then Clinton was back in the picture, and he had a new idea.

SIX

The Establishment Fails: Washington, 1992–1994

The speechwriter whose slogan ended welfare had never met anyone on welfare. That hardly disqualified him from a leading role in the spectacle about to unfold. Over the next five years, the drive to end welfare would attract an impassioned cast of the sort not found in civics class. There were the pollsters and admen of the primary season, awed by the power of the pledge to win votes, and the professors of the Clinton Camelot, vexed by its technical challenge. There was a grandiose Republican Speaker of the House, promising to liberate the poor, and his off-message troops likening them to "alligators" and "wolves." By turns surprisingly earnest and shamelessly cynical, the process swirled around an enigmatic president whose intentions were impossible to read. When the ink had dried, many would gripe the process was driven by expediency and bias rather than by a somber reading of the welfare literature. Which isn't to say that where it wound up was all wrong.

The speechwriter, Bruce Reed, came from a prosperous family in Idaho, a sparsely populated, overwhelmingly white state, and the one with the smallest percentage of children on public aid—Milwaukee alone had six times as many welfare recipients. With bookish parents who treated their children to European vacations, Reed couldn't have spent his formative years farther from the ghetto. After leaving Coeur d'Alene, he studied English literature at Princeton and Oxford (as a Rhodes Scholar), then made his way to Washington as a speechwriter and policy entrepreneur. He was trying to jump-start a struggling campaign when he set down the resonant phrase "end welfare as we know it." Reed's real interest wasn't welfare per se but the fate of liberalism. His parents had been stalwarts of a state Democratic party sliding toward extinction, and Reed had spent his childhood as a door knocker for increasingly doomed causes—"struggling," as he put it, "to defend every tenet of liberalism at the wrong end of the gun." The defining political moment of his youth came in 1980, when Ronald Reagan won the White House and Frank Church lost his seat in the United States Senate, depriving Idaho of its liberal icon and Reed of his boyhood hero. Reed's father felt so alienated he bought a shelf of books on the Middle Ages and repaired to the twelfth century. Reed, in his junior year of college, started to question his politics. One place where liberalism had erred, he decided, was in its defense of welfare.

In 1990, Reed took a job at the Democratic Leadership Council, a group formed in the Reagan years to rethink the party's liberal commitments. A few months later, the group appointed an exciting new chairman, Bill Clinton, whose distillation of his prolific interests into the twin themes of "opportunity" and "responsibility" seemed genuinely new. Clinton's tenure at the DLC reached its high-water mark in Cleveland in May 1991, when he warned that voters no longer trusted Democrats "to put their values into social policy" and used the example of welfare checks that came from "taxpayers' hides." "We should invest more money in people on welfare to give them the skills they need," Clinton said. "But we should demand that everybody who can go to work do it, for work is the best social program this country has ever devised."

Reed was dazzled. In person, he was boyish and smiling, littering his speech with pauses and "ums." But three weeks after the Cleveland event, Reed sent Clinton a fire-breathing memo, urging him to "build a mad as hell movement" and "say and do what it takes to win." When Clinton declared his candidacy in October 1991, his vague call to move families "off the welfare rolls and onto work rolls" wouldn't win the attention a dark horse needs. With a speech at Georgetown University, Clinton had another chance. It took Reed a half-dozen drafts, but he finally put down a phrase he liked: *End welfare as we know it.*

The slogan had arrived before the policy. What did it mean?

The next morning, Sunday, October 20, a colleague gave Reed a paper by a young Harvard professor named David Ellwood. The paper elaborated on ideas that Ellwood had laid out in his book *Poor Support,* which endorsed time limits on welfare but only as part of a larger expansion of aid. Ellwood pictured universal health care, job training, child care, and child support "assurance"—in effect, a guaranteed income for single mothers, since the government would make support payments if fathers did not. With those "poor supports" in place, Ellwood argued, the government could limit welfare to between eighteen and thirty-six months; then recipients would be offered a public job. Ignoring Ellwood's preconditions, Reed zeroed in on the most provocative issue—time limits—and chose a midpoint of two years. After that, he decided, welfare mothers should work.

The move from vague calls for work requirements (which Clinton had long supported) to time limits (which no prominent politician had endorsed) was a quantum leap. How would the government come up with the jobs? What would they cost? But Reed wasn't running a seminar. He gave Clinton the Ellwood paper the day before the speech, and Clinton signed off. On October 23, 1991, Clinton set forces in motion. "In a Clinton administration," he said,

> we're going to put an end to welfare as we know it. . . . We'll give them all the help they need for up to two years. But after that, if they're able to work, they'll have to take a job in the private sector or start earning their way through community service.

The pledge worked, in part, because of Clinton's credibility. As the son of a low-income single mother, he was no stranger to struggle. His friend-of-the-poor record was strong, and so were his calls for health care, child care, and wage supplements. And since Clinton had shown a long interest in welfare, both as the governors' point man and in Arkansas, he couldn't be accused, like his opponent, George Bush, of concocting the issue in a pollster's lab. But much of the electoral power radiated from the phrase itself. "End welfare" sounded definite and bold; most voters heard it as a cost-saving pledge; and as his fears about being likened to David Duke made clear, some whites welcomed it as an attack on blacks. "As we know it" offered an all-purpose hedge. After all, Clinton wasn't really proposing to end welfare; he was proposing that people work for it, in government-created jobs. Fiscally, his plan wasn't conservative at all. "I think we ought to end welfare as we know it by spending even more," Clinton said early in the race, even as his pollster, Stan Greenberg, argued that the plan "shows Clinton's skepticism about spending." While the unknowing took "end welfare" as a vow to end welfare, nervous elites detected a wink from a man they judged one of their own. Ending Welfare proved the perfect pledge for the perfectly protean candidate.

Among those unsettled by Clinton's plan was the man whose work helped inspire it, David Ellwood. Though he was sometimes described as Clinton's welfare adviser, they had met only in passing, and they never spoke during the campaign. As the architect of a mostly liberal plan with one conservative plank, Ellwood had often worried that time limits would be taken out of context. He wasn't for time limits at all unless they came wrapped in a much larger package of benefits and services. He thought the words "end welfare" sent all the wrong signals, and, as he feared, they set off an arms race. Outflanked, George Bush launched a shrill counterattack, and ten states accepted his offer to launch experiments, mostly with new penalties. Soon Ellwood was openly fretting. "I don't think these are issues that are best discussed under the klieg lights and sound bites of a presidential campaign," he said. A few weeks after Clinton's election, Ellwood wrote a paper rejecting a national overhaul, calling instead for experiments in a handful of states. "We simply do not have all the answers about how to transform the welfare system," he wrote. "For me, the greatest fear is that desperately needy people will be cut off welfare and hurt." Introduced at a meeting as the godfather of time limits, Ellwood said, "I deny paternity."

As he was leaving his office for Christmas break, Ellwood's phone rang. Donna Shalala, the incoming secretary of Health and Human Services, said she had spoken to the president-elect. Clinton wanted him to join the administration and help draft the welfare plan. Offered a once-in-a-lifetime chance, Ellwood set aside his doubts and sped to Washington, hoping the phrase "end welfare" would be forgotten. "Vacuous and incendiary," he later called it. His partner in drafting the president's plan was the slogan's author, Bruce Reed.

It is hard to conjure, at this remove, how captivating Clinton's election was to the small army of scholars, social workers, bureaucrats, and advocates who make social policy their lives. After twelve years, the words *antipoverty policy* had come to seem oxymoronic—the policy of Presidents Reagan and Bush had been not to have one. ("We fought a war on poverty and poverty won," Reagan had famously said.) Clinton raced into office like a grad student in overdrive. Universal health care! Empowerment Zones! Replicate the South Shore Bank! Out of exile to government they flowed—Harvard professors, Rhodes scholars, authors of the definitive books. It was, for its shining moment, a poverty nerd's Shangri-la.

Though it left much of the liberal establishment uneasy, the welfare plan (or what seemed like the plan) had many potential virtues. One has only to look at, say, Jewell's first years in Milwaukee to see how the themes of "opportunity" and "responsibility" might apply. The decrepit office at Twelfth and Vliet offered little of the former and demanded none of the latter. While politicians always pay lip service to work, part of what set Clinton apart was his apparent willingness to include community service jobs in the mix of welfare solutions. A term with no fixed definition, community service (or "workfare") jobs could involve scenarios with widely varying duties and pay, and it wasn't clear what Clinton had in mind. The Left feared punitive, make-work schemes, and the Right feared expensive boondoggles. But the subsidized posts had several possible sources of appeal (and might help different people in different ways): they might prompt the poor to find regular employment, polish their acculturation skills, or, if nothing else, create a safety net into which the principle of reciprocity is woven. The innovation in Clinton's formula was the conjunction: work rules *and* last-resort jobs. He didn't just talk of making work mandatory. He talked of making it possible.

Still, it seemed virtually certain that Clinton was raising expectations he couldn't fulfill. *End welfare?* No sooner had Congress passed the JOBS program than the rolls had surged to new highs. Of the 5 million families on AFDC, nearly 3 million had been on for more than two years. Putting them all in workfare posts would require an effort on a par with the WPA. While new services might move more people into private jobs before they hit the two-year wall, the first major study of a JOBS-like program had just appeared, and it had cut the rolls just 2 percent. Even if Clinton doubled or tripled that rate, enforcing a universal work requirement might still take several million community service jobs, at tremendous cost. By just mailing checks, the government spent an average of about $5,000 per family each year; a work slot (with child care for just one child) would cost about $11,700. The bill for 2 million of them would raise welfare's annual costs by more than $13 billion, nearly 50 percent. Nothing like that seemed remotely possible. Anyone armed with a pencil and napkin could see that Clinton had three likely options: start small, spend big, or riddle the rules with loopholes. There was a sense among the experts that a train wreck was coming.

The politics were as hard as the substance. Voters loved the abstract thought of "ending welfare." But Republicans wouldn't want to spend the money, and Democrats would rather spend it on other things. The public employees unions, an important part of Clinton's base, were adamantly opposed, rightly seeing an army of workfare warriors as a threat to their jobs. (Why pay someone to sweep the street if a welfare recipient will do it for free?) Shortly after his arrival in Washington, Ellwood visited some Democrats on the House Ways and Means Committee, where any bill's journey would begin. Representative Jim McDermott of Washington said, "It's stupid for the president to keep talking about ending welfare after two years." Robert Matsui of California warned, "You'll open a Pandora's box." Harold Ford, a machine boss from Memphis, summoned reporters to say that any workfare plan that failed to pay at least $9 an hour would be dead on arrival. Ford was known on the Hill as a flake, but not just any flake. He was chairman of the welfare subcommittee.

Outsiders weren't the only ones with doubts. Ellwood had come into office openly fretting. Donna Shalala, Ellwood's boss, had served as the chairwoman of the Children's Defense Fund, which had opposed even the weak work rules of the JOBS program. Shalala's predecessor at the advocacy group held an even loftier administration post. Her name was Hillary Rodham Clinton. Shalala barely mentioned welfare at her confirmation hearing, which left Moynihan ranting about the "clatter of campaign promises being tossed out the window." The biggest questions surrounded Clinton himself: did he really mean to "end welfare"? At times, he sounded surprisingly tough, like after the 1992 Los Angeles riots when he pledged to "break the culture of poverty." But when I talked to him during the campaign, he was citing the kinds of escape clauses that could render work rules meaningless. He talked of exempting people from the two-year limit if they were in "a meaningful training program," an exception of potentially vast proportions. And he said he wouldn't take away the checks of recipients who declined to work, merely reduce them—the same weak penalty that had hampered earlier welfare-to-work programs. "I don't think that you should punish the kids," he said. One likely outcome was that Clinton would send a few more people to the JOBS program, with a few workfare jobs at the end—JOBS Plus. It might be a small step in the right direction, but it wouldn't bring welfare's end.

Among the wild cards was the senior senator from New York, Daniel Patrick Moynihan, a dyspeptic skeptic and one whose support Clinton would sorely need. It would take a psychoanalytic society to fully explore the senator's feelings toward the end-welfare president. Personally he seemed to resent being upstaged as the Democrats' welfare thinker; politically he, perhaps alone, remained invested in the JOBS program, one of the few legislative triumphs of a career long on insight but short on laws; practically, he didn't see how time limits could work without an unaffordable work program (and even then he had doubts). Above all, he judged Clinton insincere, a man plying voters with promises he knew he couldn't fulfill. Moynihan spent half his time worrying that nothing would happen and half worrying that it would. As the new chairman of the Senate Finance Committee, he would have more power over Clinton's plans than any member of Congress. Upon arriving in Washington, Ellwood paid him a visit and found a gangly, snow-haired man in a bow tie, issuing a prophecy of doom. "So, you've come to do welfare reform," he said. "I'll look forward to reading your book about why it failed this time."

David Ellwood wasn't accustomed to failure. When he arrived in Washington at age thirty-nine he had already accomplished more than most scholars do in a lifetime. A tall, doughy math whiz who masked his young face with a scruffy beard, he was teaching at Harvard in his midtwenties and had tenure by the time he was thirty-five. His research on welfare caseloads was pathbreaking, and his 1988 book, *Poor Support,* became an instant antipoverty classic. As a Minnesotan who wore "Save the Children" neckties, Ellwood had the air of a do-gooder from Lake Wobegon. But he also had a habit of lapsing into lecture mode that often struck colleagues as arrogance. Professors are paid to think of themselves as the smartest people in the room. Ellwood had spent his life as a prodigy professor.

Like Bruce Reed, his bureaucratic rival, Ellwood came to welfare policy from an affluent childhood steeped in liberal politics. But while Reed heard the hoofbeats of Idaho's militant Right, Ellwood's sensibilities took hold in a pocket of splendid, benevolent isolation. The Ellwoods had their own wooded acre on Christmas Lake, a half hour away from downtown Minneapolis but a world away from its concerns. Even when he ventured overseas in high school, Ellwood wound up in Sweden. Thinking big ran in the family; just as Ellwood's embrace of time limits altered the welfare debate, his father upended the even larger world of health policy. As a pediatric neurologist, Paul Ellwood grew disenchanted with fee-for-service medicine and in the early 1970s he suggested an alternative model. He called it the "health maintenance organization," or HMO, only to grow anguished as it became a vehicle more for cutting costs than improving care. Vexed reformers, father and son, each would launch a revolutionary idea and despair as it gained a life of its own.

When Ellwood got to Washington shortly after the inauguration, welfare had already been relegated to the back burner, as Clinton turned to deficit reduction, a free-trade bill, and especially his promise of universal health care. The decision to elevate a health-care bill over his welfare plan has been endlessly second-guessed, not least by Clinton himself, who has called it one of the major errors of his presidency; some analysts think that in defining him as a big-government liberal, the decision may have cost him the Congress. Yet at the time Clinton had reasons to proceed as he did. There were 14 million people on welfare, but three times as many without health insurance.

Medical inflation was out of control, and if recipients were going to live decently as workers, they would need health care. One thing the second-guessers forget is that, given the hostility on Capitol Hill, a bill that passed in 1993 would have been a weak bill, "ending welfare" cosmetically. While the delay may have been necessary, Clinton did compound the damage by failing to provide any welfare timetable and letting the issue slip far from his view. To placate Moynihan, he promised in February 1993 to appoint a task force. But he didn't name its members for months, and the group was still doing its lost, lonely work a full year later.

Sometimes the action hides in plain sight. While he was stalling, Clinton made two moves that came to matter much more than his task force and his plan. In a speech to the National Governors Association a few weeks after taking office, he repeated a pledge to approve even those state experiments with which he disagreed. During the campaign, the stance had been attacked as a Clintonian fudge, but to the governors he defended it as federalism—letting various flowers bloom—especially if the experiments were evaluated. With everyone looking for a national bill, waivers seemed a small matter. But by the end of his first term, more than forty states were running experiments, one of which would sweep up Angie, Opal, and Jewell. While the waivers mattered substantively (long before the new law passed, the old one was coming apart a comma at a time), politically they mattered even more, since the governors' taste of state control whetted their appetite for new power. "I'm a big waiver guy," Clinton told his aides. "Let 'em rip."

In his talk to the governors, Clinton repeated another campaign pledge, to expand wage subsidies for low-income workers with kids. The "earned income tax credit" is an obscure name for an antipoverty program, and obscurity is part of its strength. While its bipartisan pedigree dates back to the Ford administration, most voters have scarcely heard of it. Because its benefits are reserved for workers, it doesn't get labeled welfare. But what the program does is send out checks—big checks, millions of them on a sliding scale to low-wage workers. In part to lure people off welfare, Clinton had promised to increase the payments so that anyone working full-time could lift a family of four out of poverty. "If you work, you shouldn't be poor," Clinton had said, in a phrase he cribbed from Ellwood. Unlike the phrase "end welfare," which was powerful because it was vague, this one was powerful because it was precise. There was an exact minimum wage and an exact poverty line, and Clinton had pledged to bridge them. When a draft plan came up short, Ellwood joined the effort to rewrite it, and a few weeks after landing in town he was summoned to the Oval Office, where the leader of the free world quizzed him on the phase-out rate. (The phase-out rate!) Clinton signed off on an expansion that nearly doubled the program's size, and with his first budget made the EITC the most important antipoverty program since the Great Society. The next year alone an additional four million families got checks of up to $2,500. Because it made it easier for women like Angie to survive on low-wage jobs, Clinton later cited the tax credit expansion as "one of the things that made welfare reform work." But because the details were technical and uncontroversial, and because it happened in an early rush of events, it attracted passing notice. The poverty reporter for *The New York Times* didn't even write about it. He—um, I—was busy looking for that national plan.

But there was no national plan. Four months after Clinton announced he was forming a task force, only its cochairs were clear: Reed, the keeper of the campaign flame; Ellwood, the academic; and Mary Jo Bane, another Harvard professor who had joined the administration. In June 1993, they were called to a meeting with Clinton, who was at his seductive best. Like Ellwood, he stressed that a welfare plan should appeal to "fundamental values." Like Ellwood, he acknowledged the complexity involved: "A certain humility dictates we should try different things." Like Ellwood, he knew the literature. Judith Gueron, the president of MDRC, briefed the group on a Learnfare experiment. While she cited its penalties, Clinton knew on his own that the program also paid bonuses to teen mothers who stayed in school; what most impressed him, he said, was the combination of carrots and sticks. The command of the data! The talk of values! The mix of urgency and restraint! Ellwood left the meeting enthralled. He wouldn't see Clinton again for nearly a year.

"Oh, that goddam task force!" Moynihan would say as, left to mark time, it grew beyond all manageable bounds, with thirty-six members splayed across seven "issue groups." For all the seeming specificity of Clinton's pledge—two years, then work—the central issues were unresolved. What would recipients do for the first two years? Would *everyone* then work? Doing what? For what kind of pay? Would their wages be matched by the EITC? Would those who broke the rules lose their whole check or only a part? The Hards were led by Reed, mindful of the campaign promise still taped to his wall. The Softs were led by Wendell Primus, Ellwood's deputy, who viewed ending welfare as a formula for increasing poverty. Ellwood was trapped in between, essentially a Soft trying to be Hard but torn and wanting consensus. They held hearings. They circulated drafts. They quarreled and leaked and quarreled about leaks. They became the butt of jokes. A series of field trips didn't resolve things, but they did prove eye-opening, even while underscoring that open eyes can see what they're trained to see. Some members had never set foot in a welfare office before. In New Jersey, Reed was struck by the bitterness between mothers and their children's absent dads, a problem he chalked up to AFDC. "It was so apparent what a destructive element the welfare check had become," he said. Primus focused on a Tennessee woman in an appalling shack, with holes in the roof and sewage in the yard. "What kind of program was really going to make her an independent, self-sufficient, taxpaying American?" he asked. Ellwood's epiphany came in a Chicago welfare office, where he watched a deaf applicant struggle with a caseworker who cared more about copying her utility bill than the details of her life. "The only reasonable reaction is to be very angry that this is not a system about helping these people," he said. Soon after, a new phrase cropped up in his talks. He started criticizing welfare as a giant, dysfunctional "check-writing machine."

In the spring of 1993, as the group was just getting started, MDRC published the most influential study of the end-welfare age. The study, of a welfare-to-work program called GAIN, compared six California counties, five of which had favored education and training, hoping to prepare recipients for higher-paying jobs. The sixth, Riverside County, had stressed basic job-search classes and encouraged most people to take the first job they could find. "Get a job, any job," was the Riverside mantra. After two years, Riverside had raised its participants' earnings by more than 50 percent, making the program about three times as effective as its rivals. Most states were still pushing education and training in their JOBS programs, so the study had the effect of turning the conventional wisdom—train first, then work—on its head. The idea of forsaking education in favor of "dead-end" jobs may sound cruel, and the thought can be taken too far (Riverside did have some education and training). But it's often what recipients want, at least initially. By the time they reached the welfare office, Angie and Jewell had already failed repeatedly in classroom settings; they wanted paychecks (or, at most, very brief training), not more open-ended classes. The Riverside philosophy quickly became the philosophy nationwide: work first.

Like many people in the welfare world, I made a pilgrimage to Riverside, where the county director, Lawrence Townsend, mixed indelicate asides ("every time I see a bag lady on the street, I wonder, 'was that an AFDC mother who hit the menopause wall?'") with odes to work's spiritual rewards. "Work is education in itself," he said, citing his own experiences unloading boxcars and shoveling manure. "It is inherently good. It is developmental. It brings hope." The notion that work is good for the soul runs deep in American life, and the talk of ending welfare revived it. Clinton, though no closer to a bill, was soon sounding similar themes. *Putting People First,* his campaign book, had mostly framed the needs of the poor in economic terms, but at a black Memphis church in November 1993, he recast the issue as one of a spiritual uplift. "Work organizes life," he said. "It gives structure and discipline to life. . . . It gives a role model to children." Elsewhere he told the story of an Arkansas woman named Lillie Harden, whom he had asked what she liked best about leaving the welfare rolls. "She looked me straight in the eye and said, 'When my boy goes to school and they say, "What does your mama do for a living?" he can give an answer.'" *That,* Clinton was saying, was success.

Years later, I had the chance to ask Clinton what got him thinking that way. "My *life,*" he began, with a force that seemed more than perfunctory:

> Because I used to get up in the morning and watch my mother get ready to go to work. And we had a lot of trouble in my home when I was a kid, and she still got up every day, no matter what the hell was going on, and she got herself ready and went to work. . . . It kept food on the table, but it gave us a sense of pride and meaning and direction. . . . I couldn't imagine what life would be like for a child to grow up in a home where the child never saw anybody go to work. . . . I know that it's sometimes hazardous to extrapolate your own experiences . . . but on *this* I don't think it is.

At some level, of course, Clinton was right: even drudge work can bring spiritual rewards. And a parent's work can set an example for kids (which is really a separate topic). The issue here involves the larger context: how much will low-wage work alone change the trajectory of underclass life? What if the mothers' jobs leave them poor? What if they're still stuck in the ghetto? What if their kids still lack fathers? For a gifted young boy in Hot Springs, a working mother was a source of inspiration. For Angie's kids (and for Angie as a kid), it was often a source of more unsupervised hours in a dangerous neighborhood. But "work first" was rising beyond program design to the realm of secular religion.

In December 1993, a month after his powerful Memphis speech, Clinton's task force sent him a confidential "draft discussion paper" that managed to be both complex and vague. It outlined nine "key features" with "five fundamental steps" plus an added "three features" to make sure the five steps are "only the beginning." Everyone got a line in. "We must guard against unrealistic expectations" (Softs). "But we must not be deterred" (Hards). The document said nothing of how many people would be involved, what the penalties would be, or how much the program would cost. "The whole question of how exactly the jobs will work is still very much under discussion," Ellwood said in an interview that day. That wasn't really his fault. No one was empowered to make a decision, and no one did. "We would like a signal from you," the cover memo asked of Clinton. The group never got a response.

"You let loose a lot of forces when you say 'End welfare as we know it,'" Moynihan complained one day. What Clinton let loose was a bidding war, with conservatives pushing ever-broader definitions of "welfare" and more literal plans to "end it." Clinton's stance on welfare had maddened the Republicans from the start, largely because he had stolen their issue but also because they judged him insincere. His incendiary verb of choice gave them the weapon they needed. Tommy Thompson made the first showy move, four months into Clinton's term. Looking to upstage the president, he proposed what sounded like a similar plan but was really the opposite. Clinton had called for two years of education and training followed by a "meaningful community service job." Thompson proposed two years followed by . . . nothing. Not "two years and work," but two years and have a nice life. The cold-turkey time limits were restricted to two counties, and Thompson needed federal permission to begin, which was part of the plan's appeal: it put Clinton on the spot. Clinton could accede and set a dangerous precedent or risk looking at odds with his own promises. After a protracted bureaucratic struggle, Clinton himself gave the green light.

The next move belonged to the House Republicans, who served up their own cold-turkey plan. Again, their idea sounded like Clinton's: two years followed by work. But once recipients spent three years in the work program, states could totally cut them off, not just in two counties but nationwide. A year earlier, some of the same GOP legislators had released a paper opposing a national time limit plan as an "untested" idea whose "feasibility . . . approaches zero." So what changed? "Clinton promised 'to end welfare as we know it,'" explained Representative Newt Gingrich, damp with mock sincerity. "Our bill gives him an opportunity to get the reform process moving." While Ellwood had come back from the field trips saluting "the great courage" of welfare families, the GOP press conference was thick with talk of drug addicts and cheats. As Representative Rick Santorum put it, "You can cut them off from AFDC permanently—end of story."

Then suddenly an attack emerged from a direction not found on most maps: Gingrich's right. Having rallied around a plan that could cut off more than half the nation's welfare recipients, the Republicans soon found it called . . . *soft*. "A cream puff." "Clinton Lite!" The unlikely force behind this assault was a dour analyst, with an undertaker's demeanor, who was about to push the debate into uncharted territory. In the welfare world, Robert Rector might be thought of as the anti-Ellwood, his polar opposite in ideology, credentials, and temperament. Ellwood came from a family of liberal intellectuals and hadn't left Harvard for twenty-one years. Rector was raised in Lynchburg, Virginia, the birthplace of the Moral Majority, and his résumé included a stint as a worker in a G.E. factory. Ellwood was famously fastidious with data. Rector once published a study saying tens of thousands of poor people had Jacuzzis and swimming pools, after extrapolating from a government survey that had found four. To the poverty establishment, Rector was a joke. But over the next two years, he would exercise far more influence than anyone in the more credentialed world. And remarkably, he proved to be the person who came closest to forecasting the law's signal result: the stunning caseload declines. Querulous, rigid, provincial, outrageous, Rector was weirdly prescient.

From his desk at the Heritage Foundation, Rector had something the academics didn't: troops. His standing with the Christian Coalition and other conservative grassroots groups made him the only welfare lobbyist who could light up the Capitol switchboard. The Gingrich plan spent too much money, he said, and didn't address the "real" welfare problem, the rise in nonmarital births. Finding two first-term Republicans to sponsor a bill, Rector produced something they called "the Real Welfare Reform Act." It would end all cash, food, and housing aid to any woman under age twenty-six who had a child outside of marriage. As one of the cosponsors, Representative James Talent of Missouri, put it, "The only way to 'end welfare as we know it' is to end welfare as we know it."

The idea of simply abolishing welfare had surfaced a decade earlier in Charles Murray's *Losing Ground*. But then no mainstream politician would touch it. Now two marquee names signed on, the former cabinet secretaries Jack Kemp and William Bennett, urging other conservatives to seize "an opportunity in the realm of politics" and "discredit the moderate pretensions of the president." Since conservatives had spent decades calling for workfare, there was a moving-the-goalposts quality to their claim that work wasn't the "real" issue. Gingrich, no stranger to cynical tactics, complained of "this stampede" to the right, but Democrats stampeded, too. The Republicans allowed states to drop people from the work rolls after three years. A group of conservative House Democrats wrote a bill that *required* it. Welfare was dead, said Nathan Deal of Georgia, and "the stench from its decaying carcass has filled the nostrils of every American."

To Ellwood's dismay, support for cold-turkey time limits was growing inside the task force, too. Clinton the campaigner had never contemplated any such thing. His template was two years of aid, followed by a community service job—not a limit on the job itself. The distinction may sound legalistic but philosophically it's profound: once you establish that even willing workers can be dropped from the rolls, you've stripped much of the safety from the safety net. But substantively, Reed argued that without a fixed time limit, people wouldn't have enough motivation to leave the work program for real jobs. And politically, he argued that "ending welfare" required a fixed end, not what he called a guaranteed job for life. About this time, Ellwood shared a draft of the plan with a dean of the poverty establishment, Henry Aaron of the Brookings Institution, who was so alarmed by the swing of events that he breached bureaucratic decorum. "I am impelled to write you," Aaron began in a letter to Ellwood, because conditions

> threaten disastrously bad welfare legislation with which you will forever be ashamed to have been associated. . . . A feral mood is loose on the Hill. . . . A Republican-conservative Democratic coalition is likely to send back legislation whose ferocity will confront the administration with a ghastly dilemma. Veto the bill and be labeled as defenders of the welfare status quo or sign a bill that betrays what you . . . stand for.

Aaron closed with an apology for being "presumptuous," but presumed a bit further. He suggested that Ellwood resign.

Rome wasn't quite burning, but Clinton was still fiddling around; after a full year in office, he was no closer to producing a plan. At the first cabinet meeting of 1994, he aired the political problem. Congressional leaders didn't want a welfare bill during the troubled heath care debate, but the longer he waited, the more he looked insincere. The group talked of how to seem committed while continuing the stall. I got an account of the discussion, and the *Times* ran the story under a provocative headline: "White House Seeks a Sleight-of-Hand Strategy on Welfare Reform." Moynihan erupted. All along he had complained that Clinton was merely playing a game—pledging to end welfare while "appointing people who have no intention of doing it." After reading of the latest delay, Moynihan walked into the *New York Post* and delivered the season's best line: Clinton, he told the tabloid, was using welfare as "boob bait for the Bubbas." As chairman of the Senate Finance Committee, Moynihan also warned that he "might just hold health care hostage" until the president sent up a welfare bill. Even by the erratic standards of Daniel Patrick Moynihan, this was a curious display of pique. After all, he *opposed* time limits, the idea behind the bill he was demanding. "Sometimes I do talk too much," Moynihan told me a few days later. But Clinton was stuck. In his 1994 State of the Union address, he agreed to produce a bill "this spring."

Friends' warnings notwithstanding, Ellwood felt a bloom of optimism. Though he had come into office alarmed at the talk of ending welfare, the field trips had quickened his criticisms of the status quo. Politically, he saw the outlines of a deal: Republicans would spend more to create the jobs, Democrats would demand that recipients take them, and voters would rally around a system that finally reflected their values—Minnesota style. It was a selective reading of the evidence, to be sure, but the Republicans *were* talking of creating workfare jobs. "I had a sense we were getting incredibly close," he said. Then he set off to find the money. As a professor, Ellwood hadn't had to confront such problems. "Many are willing to spend over $1 trillion to protect us from Soviet missiles," he had written. "Can we not spend a little for social policies?" As a candidate, Clinton hadn't fully confronted them either. "If you don't put money in there . . . you cannot crack the welfare problem," he had said. Gingrich had tackled the financing and addressed it in two ways. He would raise $20 billion by barring legal immigrants from most government programs, a non-starter for most Democrats. Even then, he had exempted about half the caseload, which sparked the wrath of the Right. Congress had just emptied its pockets twice, for the health-care and deficit-reduction bills, and none of the Democratic leaders wanted to dig in again, especially for a welfare plan. "There are things so much closer to members' hearts," warned Dan Rostenkowski, the Ways and Means chairman.

This was a bind, but a bind of Clinton's own making, obvious from the start. "There simply is no money. None!" Moynihan had warned Ellwood at their first meeting. Budget rules required that new spending come with offsetting cuts. The biggest programs—Social Security, Medicare, and Medicaid—were politically sacrosanct. That left Ellwood to forage among programs like food stamps and subsidized housing that mostly serve the poor. Substantively, this risked hurting the people he was trying to help. Politically, it gave the plan's liberal opponents something to attack: work rules were popular but budget cuts were not. In January 1994, Ellwood gave the White House a set of options, one of which would have raised billions by counting food stamps, welfare, and housing assistance as taxable income. After someone leaked it to me for a story in the *Times*, even Jay Leno got into the act: "If Clinton is going to raise taxes on the poor and cut benefits, what do we need the Republicans for?"

Politicians tend to be allergic to bad news, and Clinton was more allergic than most. It was March of his second year in office when he finally confronted the budget dilemma, summoning the three task force leaders to a meeting of the cabinet. The group offered him three options, costing from $10 billion to $18 billion over five years. "What's the least amount of money we could get away with?" Clinton asked. While the previous year he had urged them to be "bold," he now warned them about the "Tim Valentine problem." The North Carolina congressman, caught in an increasingly conservative district, had told the president he couldn't understand why ending welfare would cost money. "You have to meet the burdens of the Tim Valentines," he said. Ellwood reminded him that the welfare plan had never been designed to save money. But others in the room noticed Clinton getting that glassy-eyed look he gets when his mind has moved on.

The luxury version was out, but even paying for a Pinto was tough. There's a dissertation waiting to be written about the attempt to finance the Clinton plan, a process that pitted welfare recipients against half the gold-plated lobbies in town. Since proposed cuts in antipoverty programs had drawn flack, someone suggested "ending welfare for the wealthy" by capping the mortgage-interest deduction on multi-million-dollar homes. The Treasury secretary, Lloyd Bentsen, wasn't amused. How about financing virtue with vice, a new tax on gambling receipts? Standing on the White House lawn, Senator Harry Reid (Democrat of, hmmm, Nevada), pledged, "I will become the most negative, the most irresponsible, the most obnoxious person of anyone in the Senate." Cap the tax-free interest on annuities? The American Council of Life Insurance buried the White House in mailgrams. The embarrassing spectacle, which dragged on for months, didn't just delay the plan. It sealed its doom. It antagonized Congress. It created a blizzard of negative press. Above all, it forced Clinton into a glacial phase-in schedule. To keep down costs, he agreed to exclude from the whole program anyone then over twenty-two—about 85 percent of the caseload. Even by the end of the decade, only 8 percent of the women on welfare would be working for their checks.

At the time, the moral of the story seemed clear: presidents always forget how much welfare reform costs. So said many commentators (including me). It was only after witnessing what was yet to unfold that the deeper lesson appeared. Tough welfare-to-work programs didn't cost much, after all. They may even cost *less,* since they cut the rolls. In analyzing the Clinton plan, the Congressional Budget Office said it wouldn't cut caseloads at all, merely slow their rate of growth by 1.3 percentage points. In real life, the rolls fell more than 60 percent, and in Wisconsin the declines were about 90 percent. That's partly because the economy surged and because Congress passed a tougher law. But it's also because women like Angie responded in an unexpected way, shunning the new hassle-filled system to fend for themselves.

No one in Washington really saw it coming, but one person had a glimmer: Robert Rector, the anti-Ellwood, the uncredentialed provincial. Rector argued that the experiments predicting tiny caseload declines were flawed precisely because they were experimental. Small programs in which a few people did something modest couldn't predict large programs in which everyone did something substantial. Work requirements would have to reach a critical mass before people took them seriously, but then Rector predicted two things would happen. Fewer people would apply for aid. And those who did would leave more quickly. Rector made his case as early as 1993, in something called the *Journal of Labor Research*, where he cited three obscure studies in Washington State, Ohio, and Utah. The Utah work program had cut the caseload an astonishing 90 percent, but it only involved two-parent families, a tiny and less disadvantaged segment of the rolls. (Plus Utah is, well, *Utah.*) Even Rector had no idea how vast the caseload reductions would be. "I was off by a factor of three or four," he said.

The Clinton team paid Rector no mind, but it wouldn't have mattered if it did. The Congressional Budget Office made the binding estimates, and CBO's hands were tied, too. The analyst, John Tapogna, couldn't just guess; he had to have data, and a raft of more rigorous studies suggested that work programs did little to cut the rolls. It's tempting to see the failed forecasts as an indictment of the welfare establishment—Tapogna was Ellwood's former graduate student—but it's really a comment about establishments in general: sometimes the experts just don't know. "We were all captive of a self-limiting expertise," Tapogna said, looking back. Rector put it like this: "You've got somebody who's spent his whole life explaining why men can't fly . . . and there go the Wright brothers, taking off."

Short on money, long on delay, Clinton finally released his plan on June 14, 1994, late enough in the legislative session that there was little chance it would pass. He never did find the money; CBO later ruled that the $12 billion plan was still $5 billion short. Nor did he resolve the core issue of whether to time-limit the jobs. With Reed and Ellwood unable to agree, they took the issue to Clinton in a May Oval Office meeting. He sent them back to fashion a vague compromise, involving periodic reviews to make sure people in the work program were really looking for private jobs. Even as he released his plan, Clinton remained on both sides. "There has to be something at the end of the road for people who work hard and play by the rules," he said. But in a little-noticed exchange the next day, he defended his program by saying it had "absolute cutoffs. . . . You can just say, 'You're not eligible for benefits.'" As revealing as his nondecision was the way in which Clinton had made it—on the fly at a ten-minute meeting. Despite his fame as a policy wonk, the real surprise about Clinton and his plan was how little time he spent on it. He simply wasn't engaged. A year later, he would disown it himself, telling a columnist, "I wasn't pleased with it, either." That seemed like a typical dodge, but it may have expressed a deeper truth: he spent so little time working on it, it must not have seemed like his own.

So did it end welfare? At the time, for all the spectacle involved, there was a case to be made that it did. Yes, it had its share of loopholes and a glacial phase-in schedule. Still, if the law took effect as drafted, most recipients would eventually have to take a community service job or lose all cash aid. That was the crux of Clinton's end-welfare pledge, and in following through he'd proposed something tougher than any other president had. In retrospect, so much of the action was deferred, it was impossible to say what actually might have happened. Whatever the bill might have done later, there was something it couldn't do now—satisfy the outsized expectations the promise to end welfare had raised. "Tinkering," Tommy Thompson called it. At the rollout event, Clinton seemed subdued. The North Koreans were threatening to make nuclear arms; a showdown with Haiti's dictators was brewing; his health care plan was on life support; and the Whitewater prosecutor had just quizzed him under oath about the suicide of his friend and aide, Vincent Foster. In turning to welfare, Clinton spoke at the Kansas City bank that gave Harry S. Truman his first job—it now hired welfare recipients—and returned to his theme that work saves souls. "It gives hope and structure and meaning to our lives," he said. He repeated the story of Lillie Harden's son: when "they ask him 'what does your mama do for a living?' he can give an answer." But he also said, "Let us be honest—none of this will be easy to accomplish."

As Clinton's ebullience waned, Ellwood's grew. "I'm really proud of what we got," he said. "I really, really am." He began to imagine the plan might even catch fire before the fall elections. A few weeks later, the House held its first hearing, with Ellwood as the star witness. One of the interrogators was Bob Matsui, the California Democrat who had been skeptical of time limits all along and felt irritated by Ellwood's professorial air. Matsui thought it would be folly to debate welfare in a campaign season, when he feared the harshest measures would prevail. To make sure the administration got the message, he turned Ellwood into a piñata. *A giant check-writing machine?* Matsui declared himself offended: no one called Social Security a "check-writing machine"! *A two-year limit?* He demanded the evidence it would work. *Pass a bill this year?* Some people might say Ellwood was trying to "enhance his own résumé" before going back to Harvard. But "we would never suggest *that*!" The public flogging went on for two days, and the way congressional hearings are staged, there was little that Ellwood could do. Ellwood staggered away, knowing the bill was dead for the year. Matsui flew home to wait out the elections, figuring the climate the following year would be more conducive to temperate change.

SEVEN

Redefining Compassion: Washington, 1994–1995

On November 9, 1994, the country awoke to two words Democrats never dreamed they would hear: "Speaker Gingrich." Part emperor, part rock star, part talk-show host, he swept into town trailing spectacle and a dozen outlandish identities. He was the scorched-earth conservative who denounced his critics as "viciously hateful" and "totally sick." He was the wacky futurist who lunched with Alvin Toffler and mused about space aliens. He was a modern Moses, who delivered his flock from forty years in the minority wilderness. As he completed his rise from backbench bomb thrower to self-styled world leader, his triumph seemed absolute. Suddenly Gingrich, more than anyone else, had the power to define "ending welfare." It took Clinton seventeen months just to draft a plan; Gingrich, as leader of the Republican House, would write one and pass it in seventy-nine days.

It was a chance that Gingrich had chased throughout his congressional career. The very name of his original caucus, Conservative Opportunity Society, served as a semantic counterpoise to his favorite target: the liberal welfare state. Gingrich had looked on in disbelief in 1992, when Clinton had stolen the welfare issue from the napping Poppy Bush. Relishing the chance to steal it back, he declined to take Clinton's first call and vowed no compromise with the "left-wing elitists" in the White House. As long as the Democrats had controlled Congress, "ending welfare" had mostly seemed a rhetorical game. Now, wrote the GOP's leading welfare aide, Ron Haskins, "the time for the real Reagan revolution is at hand. . . . we can now do to the welfare state what we could not do in the early 1980s."

But beyond railing at the word *welfare,* it wasn't clear what Gingrich wanted to do. He had spent his career making trouble, not laws. He knew little about AFDC as a program, and he had never sat on the presiding committee, Ways and Means. Uncensored as ever, Gingrich ignited a furor after the election by rhapsodizing about orphanages, which his campaign document, the Contract with America, had mentioned as a welfare alternative. Yet he also showed more backroom savvy than is generally understood. In his new life as a legislative strategist, he soon hit upon the solution to virtually all his welfare woes. In policy terms, it was the equivalent of the girl next door, a vision of understated elegance that had been beckoning all along. The object of his newfound passion was something called a "block grant."

Every so often, an idea leaps from a list of perennial options and acquires the mystique of sacred doctrine. Republicans had favored block grants, like red ties and respectable cloth coats, since at least the Nixon days. One day, no one took them seriously as a welfare solution. The next day, doubts equaled heresy. In fact, someone *had* pushed block grants the previous year, an obscure Kansas congresswoman named Jan Meyers, who had badgered her GOP colleagues on the subject. But among those who had brushed her aside was Newt Gingrich. ("We thought it was too radical," he later said.) The Contract with America included a block-grant option, but as a throwaway line that commanded no attention.

Block grants differ from entitlement programs in two major ways. The first is financial. Entitlements guarantee aid to anyone who qualifies; spending automatically rises with need, and (in the case of AFDC) the states share the cost with the feds. They can't tell Angie, "Sorry, the program's broke—come back next year." Block grants offer fixed annual payments, regardless of need, and states manage as they see fit. Many housing and child-care programs are block grants, which is one reason they have long waiting lists. The second distinction is philosophical: since entitlements come with financial guarantees, they typically have more federal rules, whereas block grants set broad goals—"house the homeless"—and let states decide how to meet them. For Gingrich, the twin features of a block grant—limited federal funding and new state autonomy—combined to solve most of his problems. For one, it got him out of the financial bind that had always vexed welfare plans. As long as welfare remained an entitlement, the Congressional Budget Office would estimate work programs to cost billions and require Congress to find the money through tax hikes or budget cuts. But as soon as the program becomes a block grant, the cost-estimate game is over: Federal costs stay fixed by definition, no matter what states have to spend. Block grants also promised to bridge the ideological divide. Should the Republicans run work programs? Or just drop unmarried mothers from the rolls? With a new slogan, Gingrich could strike a posture at once radical and evasive: Let the states decide!

A state power agenda would also win Gingrich an important set of allies: the Republican governors. With their sweep of the 1994 elections, they controlled thirty statehouses, including those in eight of the nine largest states. Some, like Tommy Thompson in Wisconsin and John Engler in Michigan, were running experimental programs and could pose, with varying degrees of legitimacy, as veteran reformers. By contrast, the Gingrich "revolution" was powered by seventy-four freshmen legislators, all nationally unknown. ("We had a million freshmen who couldn't spell AFDC," Haskins, the welfare aide, said.) With Gingrich showing no signs of tempering his bombast, the governors could provide a reassuring front for an untested plan filled with risks for millions of poor women and children. "You could say to people, 'We're not talking theory here,'" Gingrich said. "Go visit Wisconsin."

One question remained: why would the governors sign on? Politically, Congress was taking the nation's toughest social problem and saying, "All yours!" Fiscally, the pact was just as perilous. The block grants wouldn't even rise with inflation, while historically caseloads had shown nothing but growth. Had the governors bought in five years earlier, they already would have lost $11 billion. Chris Henick, the director of the Republican Governors Association, wrote the chairman of the national party to warn that the governors might "resist publicly any transfers of programs, assuming these programs may be a burden to their own budgets." He added: "I wouldn't blame them." Governor George Voinovich of Ohio did resist, calling capped federal spending a "burdensome unfunded mandate." Block grants also raised doubts from a message point of view. As Ari Fleischer, a spokesman for the House Republicans, later said: "I couldn't understand how swapping one government entity for another was going to solve a very fundamental problem."

Yet just as Gingrich had hoped, most Republican governors couldn't wait for the chance to get their hands on the welfare program. Running small experiments with big press releases, Thompson and Engler had won national fame, an example not lost on ambitious rivals. Ego was also involved. While Clinton had approved virtually every experiment the states had requested, the governors bridled at having to ask—seeing no reason, as Thompson liked to say, "to come in on bended knee and kiss the ring" of a Washington bureaucrat. And while they never surrendered their financial fears (or demands), with caseloads at a record high, all they had to do to break even was to keep them from growing still higher. Even with modest programs, Wisconsin and Michigan had already begun reducing the rolls; others bet they could follow.

With Gingrich needing the governors, and the governors wanting power, the elements of a blockbuster deal were in place. It was sealed two weeks after the 1994 election at a meeting of the Republican Governors Association, which the GOP landslide transformed into a marquee event. Conveniently, the meeting in Williamsburg, Virginia, had already been designed, as an organizer wrote, for "a bit of gubernatorial spleen venting" at federal power. As a place to vent at central authority, colonial Williamsburg is hard to beat; tour guides in tricornered hats still walk the streets railing at George III. The host governor, George Allen, circulated an anti-Washington manifesto, which called for constitutional amendments to shift power back to the states. Everyone was quoting Patrick Henry. It was give-me-liberty-or-give-me-death time. Into this hyperbolic moment strode the hyperbolic Speaker-to-Be, peddling a vision of American greatness and the outline of a pact. Less federal money! More state control! Viva Patrick Henry! Welfare would only be the starting point for the block-grant revolution, with a hundred other programs to follow from health care to housing. As self-interest merged with true belief, the love fest went on for hours. The precepts were codified shortly after in a letter from Thompson, Engler, and Massachusetts governor William Weld: "We are willing to accept a reduction in funding if we are given the freedom to run these programs with few, if any, strings attached."

Would states' rights really rescue the poor? There was ample room for doubt. It was the states' failure to care for the needy that caused welfare to be federalized in the first place—their failure, in the 1920s and 1930s, to finance the Mothers' Pensions. As a creed, states' rights hadn't fully recovered from its Eastland-era service of segregation. And even as they enjoyed a renaissance as "laboratories of democracy," state bureaucracies could prove every bit as inept as federal ones. The child welfare systems of twenty-two states were in such disarray they had been placed under court supervision. While posing as reformist tigers, most governors hadn't done anything with the welfare authority they already had; they were barely meeting the minimal requirements of the JOBS program. The average state had just 13 percent of its caseload in welfare-to-work activities, which, as Jewell had discovered, often amounted to nothing more than a few weeks of motivation class. Although most conservatives celebrated the Federalist pact, the thought of governors as brave crusaders had Robert Rector of the Heritage Foundation feeling bilious again. He denounced the governors as "panhandlers," "sluggards," and "obstacles to reform rather than engines of reform." ("Rector has always been irritating," Gingrich said. "That's his major function in life.")

Leery of block grants, the Democrats prevented a bipartisan endorsement from the National Governors Association, at a meeting that turned into a showcase of frayed tempers and bad blood. Howard Dean of Vermont, the group's chairman, accused the GOP of trying "to starve children." Many critics feared a "race to the bottom," with states competing to keep services and tax burdens low. One way to think of AFDC was as a program of matching grants, since each dollar of state spending brought at least a dollar from the feds. Even in a program as unpopular as welfare, that helped sustain benefits: states could buy poor people a dollar of support for no more than fifty cents. Under block grants, the incentives are reversed; every dollar the state cuts is a dollar the state saves. And to those who said "Trust the states," critics had a retort—"What about Mississippi?"—where despite the feds paying most of the tab, the state offered a family of three just $120 a month.

But it was the Republicans whose votes counted, and among them the deal held. By the time Gingrich slammed down the Speaker's gavel in January 1995, he had united the party around a new vocabulary. "Ending welfare" meant packing it up and shipping it back to the states.

The bill shot through the House. Its secondary features would face revision in the long months ahead, but the core was set. There would be fixed federal funding. There would be vast state discretion. And there would be "hard" time limits (of no more than five years)—an idea that had sped from Ellwood's head through Clinton's mouth and into Gingrich's hands. There would also be an obscure bit of mischief around the concept of "work requirements"; the bill retained the rhetoric of work, while avoiding the substance of work programs. Work, after all, seemed expensive. While Gingrich solved the technical budgeting problem by moving to a block grant, the sums didn't seem large enough to run much of a work program on the ground. Wary of being left to foot the bill, the GOP governors wanted no federal work rules at all. As first proposed, the bill required the states to enroll just 2 percent of their recipients in "work activities," rising to 20 percent over time. And virtually anything could count as work, down to writing a résumé. That gave the Democrats a fresh line of attack—"Weak on work, tough on kids"—and earned Rector's scorn, too. "A major embarrassment," he said.

The Republicans found a solution: creative accounting. They greatly raised the percentage of families required to work. But they allowed states to count people as "working" whenever they left the rolls, whether they really were working or not. The obscure device at play is called the "caseload reduction credit." Think of it as giving states frequent-flier points every time they cut someone off welfare. Say a state is required to have 20 percent of its caseload in a welfare-to-work program and it cuts the rolls 15 percent; the new requirement becomes 5 percent. When fully phased in, the law required states to meet a work rate of 50 percent, a standard no state had ever met. But if they cut their rolls in half (as twenty states subsequently did), they wouldn't have to run a work program at all.

Oddly, it was Rector, a workfare zealot, who hatched the idea. He had visited a work program in Sheboygan, Wisconsin, where he expected to see a crowd of recipients sweeping floors and answering phones. But most people had responded to work assignments by surrendering their welfare checks. "And I started saying the real effect of a work program is to reduce the caseload—that's what you want to measure," he said. Rector had half a point: if work programs pushed women like Angie to leave welfare and find real jobs, that's the best result. But the credit doesn't distinguish between those leaving for jobs and those leaving for homeless shelters; states get "credit" either way. They could invest in troubled women and prepare them for work. (Some, like Oregon, would do just that.) Or they could cut them off for minor infractions. (Some, like Mississippi, would do that, too.) Indeed, nothing in the bill required states to provide services to anyone—not training, not child care, not transportation—none of the benefits typically cited by the bill's defenders. Putting people to work was a discretionary activity. The core curriculum was getting them off the rolls.

The Gingrich version of ending welfare bore another watermark: more and more programs risked being labeled "welfare" and subjected to deep cuts. A month after becoming Speaker, Gingrich startled his troops by announcing he would produce a balanced budget, which no Congress had done in decades. Since he had also promised large tax cuts (skewed to the wealthy), he would need spending reductions far beyond AFDC. That was part of his goal. Gingrich saw social spending as the spoils system that sustained the Democratic Party (through a network of advocates, beneficiaries, and bureaucrats). A balanced budget was the stake that he could drive through its heart. His targets included food stamps, school lunches, disability payments, foster care and adoption programs, and aid to immigrants. "You cannot sustain a welfare state inside a balanced budget," he said. The $12 billion increase that Clinton had proposed became a $65 billion cut.

To say the bill sped through the House makes its passage sound like a given. But Gingrich policed his precarious majority with a skillful mix of inspiration and fear; thirteen defectors could cost him the vote. One divisive issue involved how much freedom to give the states: should the money come with "strings" attached, or "no strings"?

Even more contentious were the fights over the so-called "illegitimacy provisions." Led by Rector, some conservatives favored a ban on aid to unwed teenage mothers that would last throughout their lives. Others with equally conservative credentials (like the National Right to Life Committee) worried an outright ban would prompt more teen abortions. With a scaled-down restriction still in place, it took an all-out effort by Gingrich himself to survive a crucial rules test by a margin of three votes. Having escaped a near-death experience, the bill passed in March 1995 on a vote of 234 to 199. Nine Democrats added their support, with just five Republicans opposed.

Democrats reacted with disbelief. An unthinkable leader ("Speaker Gingrich!") was doing unspeakable things. One Democrat suggested naming the law the "Make Americans Hungry Act." The Republican bill was *worse* than slavery, said Major Owens of Brooklyn, since at least on the plantation "everybody had a job." John Lewis, the civil rights hero, likened the Republicans to Nazis. The rancor was real, but the most notable sight wasn't the Democrats' resistance. It was the depths of their accommodation, as they found themselves surrendering ground they had defended tooth and nail. Having spent decades fending off work requirements ("slavefare"), liberals now attacked conservatives as insufficiently tough—"weak on work!" The world had changed so much so fast that even the Democratic leader, Dick Gephardt, would no longer say whether he supported something as basic as the federal entitlement. "You can't get hung up on that word," Gephardt said. "We're not trying to get people entitled. We're trying to get people to work." Worried that mutineers would give Gingrich a veto-proof majority, Gephardt managed to unite the Democrats around a substitute bill. But he kept conservatives on board only by embracing much of Gingrich's agenda: drop-dead time limits of four years and cuts totaling $9 billion. Liberals like Bob Matsui, who had thought the Clinton tonic too strong, were swallowing something incomparably stronger. The Democrats' main sponsor was Nathan Deal, the Georgian who had been railing about the "stench" from welfare's "carcass." A month after the caucus rallied around his plan, Deal joined the GOP. Now there were literally no Democratic alternatives. There were only competing Republican visions of what ending welfare would mean.

One night with the revolution in full raucous swing, I holed up in one of its marketing labs, the disheveled office of the pollster Frank Luntz. Fluorescent lights painted the air green, and all was silent except for Gingrich railing against the welfare state: "By creating a culture of poverty, we have destroyed the very people we are claiming to help." Colored lines crawled across his videotaped face—blue for Democrats, yellow for Republicans, and red for Independents. Hands on electronic dials, members of a focus group had weighed the Gingrich speech a syllable at a time. Luntz leaned forward and warned: "Here it comes—bang!" And bang it was. All three squiggles leapt in appreciation of a signature Gingrich line: "*Caring* for people is not synonymous with *caretaking* for people."

The squiggles, as much as the legislative fine print, measured the depths of what Gingrich achieved. He redefined compassion. Until roughly this point in the poverty debate, the arguments followed familiar lines. Claiming the mantle of social concern, liberals called for more programs and spending; calling for personal responsibility and fiscal restraint, conservatives resisted. Now and then conservatives managed to roll programs back, but by labeling reductions "punitive" or "mean," liberals could usually prevail. Gingrich set the old arguments on their head. While Reagan attacked poor people for abusing the programs, Gingrich attacked programs for abusing the poor. He didn't complain, as Reagan did, of high-living welfare queens; he reminded the public that poor children were suffering and said welfare was to blame. While Reagan talked of welfare recipients whose "tax-free cash income alone is over a hundred fifty thousand dollars," Gingrich talked of "twelve-year-olds having babies" and "seventeen-year-olds dying of AIDS." When I noted the change in tactics, Gingrich responded with the smile of a man well-pleased with his cleverness. "Congratulations!" he said. "You cracked the code!" The rhetoric did more than soften the message. It created a logic for deeper cuts: *The less we spend, the more we care!* As leader of the opposition, Moynihan decried the strategy as an "Orwellian perversion." But he acknowledged its reach. "You'll hear it in our Democratic caucus," he said. "'We are liberating you, breaking your chains!'" Even

Gingrich was surprised at his success. "I thought we'd be in more trouble on hurting the poor," he said.

The idea that ending welfare would liberate the poor was not wholly a Gingrich invention. Intellectually, Charles Murray had made the case a decade earlier in *Losing Ground.* Ending welfare won't mean that stingy people have won, Murray wrote, but that "generous people have stopped kidding themselves." Politically, caring conservatism found its first champion in Jack Kemp, the manic housing secretary who ran around promising to free the poor from "the government, liberal plantation." But where Kemp brought a seeming earnestness to the cause, Gingrich brought cunning and the pollsters' mad science. A management consultant named Morris Shechtman lent Gingrich the "caring-caretaking" line; in a daylong seminar for Gingrich and his staff, he called on recipients like Angie and Jewell to "grieve the unbundling of caretaking" and develop better "change-management skills." Another useful Gingrich ally was Richard Wirthlin, the former Reagan pollster, who distributed a memo about thirteen "power phrases" to "redefine compassion." "When Rep. Dunn"—Jennifer Dunn of Washington—"uses the word 'hope,'" he wrote, "her score moves up (+20)" points.

If hope was one part of the GOP message, fear was the other. Welfare may have been harming the poor, but most voters worried about the poor harming them: mugging them or bringing mayhem into their schools. Murray, the original welfare abolitionist, had moved on in *The Bell Curve* to warn of a dystopian future in which an underclass marked by low intelligence laid siege to a barricaded, cognitive elite. One reason the word *welfare* inspired so much loathing was the breadth of its reach: it conjured everything from crime to infectious disease. "You can't maintain civilization with twelve-year-olds having babies and fifteen-year-olds killing each other and seventeen-year-olds dying of AIDS," was the full text of the Gingrich refrain. Of all the allies that Gingrich summoned, the most important was the status quo, a circumstance that no one could defend. When the welfare bill moved to the floor, the leadership armed every Republican with a list of horrifying stories, including that of a four-month-old boy who "bled to death when bitten more than one hundred times by the family's pet rat." Let the Democrats defend that! What pet rats had to do with welfare, no one explained. Gingrich's point was simpler: anything's better than this.

Gingrich could operate as a breathtaking cynic, and for some of his followers the new compassion was just the old politics of race and class. In writing about welfare for *The New York Times,* I kept some of the mail I received. Some letters came in cramped grandmotherly script, with checks to pass along. Then there were notes like this: "Excuse me, but I think these little low-life scum on welfare should get exactly what life gave me, nothing. . . . They're human garbage." Or, "Dear Sir: What does it take before the liberal social reformers realize that 2000 years of civilziation [*sic*] has passed black people by." Or, "I as a middle class white person is paying for their children because the bloods can't keep it in their pants." One way to look at the billions in cuts is as what happens when a party controlled by southern white men gains power over a program that disproportionately aids black and Hispanic women. For all of Gingrich's efforts to prep his troops, some wound up with their wingtips in their mouths. Floridian John Mica made his case for ending welfare while holding a "Do Not Feed the Alligators" sign. Democrats jeered the reptilian reference, but the zoologists of the GOP pressed on. Barbara Cubin of Wyoming likened recipients to domesticated wolves.

Still, the House crusade wasn't particularly cynical or crude. Or at least it wasn't merely cynical or crude. The longer it went on, the more some members bought their lines. They didn't see themselves as people who cut school lunches to finance tax breaks for the rich. They were emancipators. Freedom riders! Liberators of the liberal plantation! After decades of predictable scripts, the debate turned downright avant-garde. Democrat Harold Ford was a black legislator from Memphis whose district abutted cotton fields and abounded with sharecroppers' children. "The bill . . . is mean-spirited, Mr. Chairman," he began. Mr. Chairman was Clay Shaw, a genial Fort Lauderdale accountant with no sharecroppers in his district—just sugar-white beaches and rich retirees. But he wasn't taking any guff. It is *your* party that defends the "last plantation in this country," Shaw erupted. "And for you to sit there and say that we are punishing kids—*we* are the ones that are going forward to try to break the cycle of poverty . . . ! No I do not believe it is the Republicans who are cruel. I think it's the Democrats!"

Long after the dust had settled, I had the chance to ask Clinton what he thought of all this. Had his nemesis, Gingrich, used the talk of liberating the poor as a fig leaf for budget cuts? "No," Clinton began, surprising me. "Well, I think the answer is yes and no. . . . I think it was a political strategy. But I believe Newt Gingrich believed in it. I think a lot of them did." Clinton warmed to the theme: "Some of the Republicans just thought, 'I'm going to make my conservative white folks happy.' . . . I think a lot of them thought most poor people were lazy. I think a lot of them thought poor people were undeserving. I think a lot of them had a different kind of conservative insight, which is the government can't help anybody, anyway, so why are we wasting money?" Nonetheless, Clinton continued, "there were a lot of conservative evangelicals, for example, who were for this who did it out of love . . . [who believed] that work could be liberating and responsibility was ennobling and empowering. . . . So I think you had a lot of things going on at once there."

Among the oddest converts to the Gingrich cause was Christopher Shays of Connecticut, a former Peace Corps volunteer and one of the most liberal members of the GOP. With a district that included the Bridgeport slums, he was also the rare Republican with ghetto constituents. After hearing Gingrich's speech about the horror of "twelve-year-olds having babies," Shays drove home and told his wife, "Oh my gosh, I agree with this guy." In corners of his own district he'd seen equally disturbing things. While he had some doubts about whether the GOP plan was "as well thought out as I'd like it to be," Shays said, "I'll take almost any alternative over what we have now." And on the day it passed the House, Shays was at Gingrich's side. "My Speaker came up to Connecticut and started talking about some issues I had been thinking about in my heart," he said. "About . . . how we could have twelve-year-olds having babies, and thirteen-year-olds selling drugs, and fifteen-year-olds killing each other. . . . In my heart I thought I was a caring person. But I realized I was a caretaking person." Then the unlikely convert concluded with some unlikely words: "My hero is Newt Gingrich."

The rise of Gingrich left Clinton in a funk. He needed to pass a welfare bill, but what kind of bill could he get? What cleared the House in March 1995 was the opposite of what he had proposed. Funding had been cut, not increased. The work program came with no jobs. Time limits were no longer a preface to a jobs program but an arbitrary ban on aid. Clinton's idea of a social contract had been: "We'll do more for you, and you'll do more for yourself." Gingrich had amputated it: "Do more for yourself."

Clinton's name hadn't been on the fall ballot, but from coast to coast his presidency had been the issue: his wife, his health plan, his tax increase. Republican ads had shown their Democratic opponents morphing into the president. He lost fifty-two House seats, eight in the Senate, and ten governorships. Operating furtively, Clinton's new strategist, Dick Morris, urged him to "fast forward the Gingrich agenda" and sign a welfare bill. The sooner he did, the sooner he would disarm the opposition. One of Clinton's new pollsters, Doug Schoen, told him voters had him pegged as a social liberal; he needed to "get welfare off the table," Schoen said. A widely read article by Mickey Kaus in *The New Republic* called Clinton's failure to end welfare "the fundamental strategic mistake of the Clinton presidency." That was an argument that Clinton later echoed. "I should have done welfare reform before we tried health care," he said. "The Democrats might have had something to run on."

As hard as the question of what Clinton could get was the question of what Clinton wanted. In the formative hours, no one knew, including he himself. "It wasn't really until the summer that he developed a clear position on what he would accept or not accept," Dick Morris said. "On anything, really." Echoing Gingrich, Clinton made three references in a six-day stretch to the need "to liberate" the poor. Speaking to county officials in March 1995, Clinton brought up Lillie Harden again: "She said, 'When my boy goes to school and they ask him, "What does your mama do for a living?" he can give an answer.'" But when conversation turned to what to do, Clinton got maddeningly dodgy. He praised his own bill. ("I still hope it will be the basis of what ultimately does pass.") Then he renounced his own bill. ("I wasn't pleased with it, either.") He praised block grants. ("I loved block grants . . . and I haven't changed just because I have become president.") Then he criticized block grants. ("It is not fair for the federal government to adopt a block-grant system, which flat funds big things that are very important.") He emphasized the importance of last-resort jobs. (If "these people can't find jobs in the private sector, how can we require them to work?") But he also praised bills without them. He criticized the House bill. He didn't say he would veto it. The evasions hit a peak in the fall, after the chief of staff, Leon Panetta, issued a veto threat. Was he speaking for the president? The White House talking points guided spokesmen: answer "yes and no."

Clinton's defenders say the hedging was strategic, and no doubt some of it was. "We called it the 'Modified Madman Theory,'" said Bruce Reed. "If they didn't know what it would take, we could get more." Others called it a rope-a-dope, conserving the powers of the presidency while Gingrich discredited himself with his most outlandish proposals. Some ambivalence, even expedience, is forgivable on Clinton's part. He'd suffered a blow, the politics were shifting, and many of the substantive orthodoxies would later be proved wrong. As a former governor, Clinton generally trusted the states (more so than most of his aides), and he didn't think the entitlement really mattered, given the disparity in state benefits. How crucial was it, he asked Morris, when Alaska paid a mother with two kids $923 a month and Mississippi gave her $120?

But Clinton wasn't evasive on some of the issues; he was evasive on all of them. And the more he hedged, the more Gingrich set the terms of debate. As the bill headed to the House floor in March 1995, what Clinton talked about most wasn't time limits or funding or community service jobs but an obscure tool of child-support enforcement—the Republicans' failure to take the "crucial" step of suspending the driver's licenses of deadbeat dads. With the entire safety net up for grabs, *that's* where he made his stand? Nearly half the states already had license-suspension laws, and most of the men that Angie knew didn't have licenses. But the issue had scored well in White House polls. "In no time in recent memory has there been a greater need for presidential leadership on this issue," wrote Donna Shalala, the secretary of Health and Human Services, betraying an impatience subordinates don't usually display toward presidents. "[U]ntil you make it clear what we believe in and stand for, Republicans will control the debate, and we may get a bad plan that the public does not understand."

With Clinton's fidelities unclear, the administration dissolved in palace intrigue. Operating in secret through the middle of the spring, Morris urged Clinton to "attack the bill only from the right," like calling for tougher work rules. Leon Panetta, the chief of staff, attacked from the left, on issues like the entitlement and budget cuts. Shorn of influence, David Ellwood lost heart for the fight. Just as his critics had warned, the Republicans had weaponized his concept of time limits and launched a counterstrike. He resigned in the summer of 1995 and returned to Harvard, where he spent the next few years in disillusioned exile, wondering where Clinton's core convictions lay. To be sure, the fog was thick. But a moment of subtle revelation arrived in May 1995, as the debate moved on to the Senate. Reuters called the White House one night, seeking comment on the latest GOP plan. Ginny Terzano, the spokeswoman on duty, checked with Panetta, then gave a response: if the Republicans "went to a block grant" and "did not provide a safety net for children, then the president would veto the bill." A few days later, she ran into Clinton. Who told you to say that? he asked. Terzano was taken aback. The chief of staff, she answered. "That's okay," she quotes Clinton as saying. "But I really want to sign a welfare reform bill."

EIGHT

The Elusive President: Washington, 1995–1996

In the end, Clinton got not just one but three chances to sign a bill. As welfare politics moved on to the Senate in the spring of 1995, no one knew that fifteen months of battle still lay ahead, with ambushes awaiting both sides. The Republican majority, so triumphant as the bill cleared the House, turned fractured and doubting, and Clinton, hard to read as ever, worked his way back into view. In retrospect, he called the bill a highlight of his presidency. But the only reason the final version made it to his desk was that his chief antagonist, Newt Gingrich, thought that signing it would politically destroy him.

Gingrich could push a bill through the House, but its prospects in the Senate were initially in doubt. The Senate is a graveyard for impetuous plans. The Republican majority was slimmer, and the rules gave obstructionists more sway. Bob Dole, the Republican leader, was no radical—Gingrich had once disparaged him as the "tax collector for the welfare state"—and neither was the chairman of the Finance Committee, Bob Packwood. Moynihan assured his staff that a body as august as the Finance Committee would never abolish AFDC. Then it did, just like that. Whatever affection Dole felt for the governors was quickened by his launch of a presidential campaign that needed their endorsements and mailing lists. Packwood had his own reasons to toe the party line. He was under investigation for sexual harassment and trying, in vain, to save his seat. The Left had looked for a Senate firewall. By the spring of 1995, the firewall was on fire, too.

Among Democrats, all eyes turned in one perplexing direction, toward that of Daniel Patrick Moynihan. He was the committee's ranking Democrat, and he had groomed an image as the very soul of social policy. Outside the Senate he was renowned for his mix of charm and erudition. Inside the Capitol, he was equally known for his thin record in the low art of passing bills. Aghast at the move to abolish AFDC, Moynihan had neither the instinct nor talent for a backroom fight to save it. It probably wouldn't have mattered, anyway, but it would take a dramatist to fully capture the ironies. He had spent decades demanding a national debate about fatherless families, only to despair when it finally occurred. He had spent decades feuding with the welfare Left, only to be left as its most prominent ally. Moynihan passed the spring in sputtering disbelief, then emerged in the fall of 1995 as the voice of national conscience. In speeches from the Senate floor, he was eloquent, learned, entertaining, and wholly ineffective. He may not have changed a single vote. But he did give the only speech published in *The New York Review of Books.* "Nothing I did connected," he later wrote, not without a trace of pride.

As a capstone to one of the great careers in public life, Moynihan's role in the welfare debate will be scrutinized for decades. Substantively, his worldview proceeded like this: "illegitimacy" (a normative term he preferred over "nonmarital births") was a profound new problem that the country had ignored at its peril. It was profound because it drove other problems, like crime, drugs, and indiscriminate rebellion against authority, especially among males. It was new in that it had exploded over the past four decades. But since it afflicted most industrialized countries, it couldn't have been driven by AFDC, one small American program. As a vast, disturbing condition, the rise of "dependency" deserved above all to be studied and discussed. "To ask questions. There it is," he had written, in praise of the thinker's life. As for what to do, Moynihan had never been sure. He had started his career pushing government jobs; embraced a guaranteed income; then turned to a more cautious services strategy, hoping that education and training would nudge poor mothers to work. Still, he had never been entirely convinced that single mothers ought to work, especially when their children were young; the jobs he had sought were for men. "I have spent much of my lifetime on this subject and have only grown more perplexed," he said.

One topic for future Moynihan studies concerns his gloom about the welfare poor. Not for him the polite talk that people on aid are "just like me and you." He referred to welfare recipients as "paupers—not a pretty word, but not a pretty condition"—or even "failed persons." Who knows what darkness from his ragged childhood shaded his views; his father deserted when Moynihan was ten, and the family fell from middle-class respectability to a series of cold-water flats. Moynihan would raise his hard-knocks past when it proved politically useful. But one knock he almost never mentioned was the Moynihans' own stay on welfare. What he really seemed to believe was that most welfare families would never be able to cope, and a mix of duty and self-interest demanded they be minimally maintained. "I just do what the Catholic bishops tell me," he snapped to a reporter one day. There was something refreshing about Moynihan's refusal to romanticize ghetto life. And something disturbing, too: the trio drawing checks on First Street weren't nearly as helpless as he believed. "To be dependent is to hang," he liked to say. Angie didn't think she was hanging by her check. Just cashing it.

After three decades of prescient forecasts, Moynihan was essentially left to argue that the country faced an earthshaking new problem, about which it should do nothing. With a bill speeding through Congress, that was an impossible stance to sustain. "Dear Senator," began a letter from an aide, Paul Offner. "I write to plead, even at this late date, for the introduction of a Moynihan welfare bill. . . . Democrats in the Senate are floundering. . . . you are the only one who can pull this together. . . . [W]ithout a proposal of our own—so members can say that they voted *for* welfare reform—we won't be able to hold our members. . . . the stakes are so high that we can't afford not to fight." Two weeks later, Moynihan unveiled the status-quo proposal Offner feared: more money for the JOBS program. There were no cosponsors.

That left the Senate Democrats like a lost school of fish—ready to bolt, but to where? With neither Clinton nor Moynihan to point the way, Tom Daschle, the Democratic leader, united the caucus, but he did so only with another move right (accepting "hard" time limits of five years). Clinton hailed the plan at a White House event, where Moynihan showed up, declared himself "on board," and warned it could prove "ruinous."

As the Democrats shambled toward their unity show, Republican unity suddenly collapsed, giving Clinton and the Democrats time to regroup. The bill seemed headed for quick passage when it cleared the Finance Committee in May. Within a few weeks, Dole was prepared to start debating it on the Senate floor. Then he lunched with the full caucus of Republican senators, and the next day he announced the floor debate was off: the conservatives were up in arms. "I absolutely intend to filibuster it," said Lauch Faircloth of North Carolina, with enough support for a credible threat. Chief among the conservatives' complaints was that the measure failed to combat the "real" welfare problem of "illegitimacy," since as a pure block grant, it let states decide what, if anything, to do. They wanted provisions like a mandatory "family cap," which would prohibit states from increasing grants when recipients had additional children. The uncivil war, which bogged the bill down for the rest of the summer, even featured as one of its unlikely sideshows a melee over the bill's preamble. Moderates wanted it to call marriage a foundation of society; conservatives wanted to call it *the* foundation. The "the" camp won, but only after Dole's centrist chief of staff, Sheila Burke, the "a" foundation leader, found herself pummeled in the conservative press as "Hillary Lite" and a font of "militant feminism." "Bring Me the Head of Sheila Burke" ran the *Time* account.

Once more in the thick of the fray was Robert Rector, who, operating from his office at the Heritage Foundation, staffed the illegitimacy debate as a one-man think tank and tactician. (He drafted the Faircloth alternative and his angry showdown with Sheila Burke helped spill the story into the press.) In seeking a debate over family structure, Rector had well-founded concerns; the problems of the inner city couldn't be solved by single mothers alone, even if they were working. The trouble was that no one had a clue of how to legislate a dad. The challenge of moving 5 million recipients to work was huge, but it proceeded from a template. Past programs. Evaluations. Offices and staff. In looking to deter nonmarital births, Congress had no place to start—not even any certainty that welfare played a causal role. Scholarly efforts to link welfare payments to birth rates had shown a faint influence at best; though welfare benefits had fallen for decades, nonmarital births had continued to rise. Maybe work itself would curb nonmarital births, by prompting women like Angie to demand more from their men. But even Rector made few claims for the additional measures he sought: a ban on aid to unmarried teens; an "illegitimacy bonus" (for states that cut nonmarital births); and the "family cap." "These moves were more to call attention to the issue than to provide a silver bullet," he said. "Because I don't think we know how to solve it."

The issue was politically perilous, too. Given the black-white disparities, a politician attacking nonmarital births still risked being called a racist. (Seventy percent of black children were born outside marriage in 1995, compared to 21 percent for whites.) Plus, the issue involved sexual responsibility—and how many politicians wanted to invite scrutiny of that? In demanding work, the authors of the "Personal Responsibility Act" practiced what they preached; some legislators worked so hard, they slept on their office couches. But someone charting the main players' sex lives would have found them having an affair with a junior staffer (Gingrich); having an affair with an intern (Clinton); fending off eighteen accusations of unwanted sexual advances (Packwood); or fondling a prostitute's toe (Dick Morris). That was part of Rector's gripe: without an effort by social conservatives, the issue would go ignored. He was looking for a "polemical beachhead"—a way to keep the subject in view—and with a handful of Senate allies making speeches all summer, he succeeded beyond his dreams. Faircloth: "The problem that is destroying this whole country is illegitimacy." John Ashcroft: "Illegitimacy is a threat to our nation and our culture." Phil Gramm: "We're going to end up losing America as we know it." There were other issues dividing the GOP, including child-care money and block-grant funding for high-growth Sunbelt states. But after a summer of marathan talks, Dole settled most of them. On the fractious subject of what to do about unmarried women having kids, all he could muster was a plan to take rival amendments to the floor. "We're just going to have a jump ball," he said. "But you still stay in the game if you lose."

When the Senate reconvened in September 1995, two things were clear: a bill would pass, and it would amount to a conservative revolution. After six decades of federal control, Congress would vote to hand welfare to the states, with capped funding, vast discretion, and lifetime limits of five years. The remaining disputes were secondary or symbolic. The only question was whether they would be settled in a way that mollified Democrats, giving the bill a bipartisan label and increasing the chances that Clinton would sign it. (On the "jump ball" over the illegitimacy issues, the conservatives mostly lost.) Roused from his torpor, Moynihan took to the Senate floor to remind colleagues that he owned a pen that President Kennedy had used to sign a bill deinstitutionalizing the mentally ill. That law, too, had bet on a local safety net, and it had left homeless schizophrenics wandering the streets. "In ten years' time we will wonder where these ragged children came from," he warned. "Why are they sleeping on grates?"

But the summer brought increasing signs that Clinton wanted a deal. In early August, his press secretary praised the emerging Senate plan. A few days later Clinton praised it, too, saying, "I cannot believe we can't reach an agreement here." That same day he met with his strategist, Dick Morris, who had written to advise him to "[b]rag about cuts in AFDC levels" and "never, never veto." At the White House, Bruce Reed gained control of the issue and embarked on a strategy one ally called "building a better block grant," accepting the states' rights approach with a few alterations. They entered the Senate debate with four priorities and quickly made progress on three: a "performance bonus" (to states that placed recipients in jobs); a "contingency fund" (that increased spending in a recession); and a "maintenance-of-effort" rule (that required states to keep up spending). As the debate spilled into its sixth day, September 14, the Democrats' fourth priority remained in doubt: more money for child care.

In any extended negotiation, minor matters can take on make-or-break weight. The disputed sums were small, in financial and policy terms. But the bigger issues had been resolved, and child care was something that voters could grasp. The Democrats demanded an extra $3 billion over five years: not a penny less. Republicans offered less: $3 billion over seven years. The Democrats' negotiator, Christopher Dodd, stood on the Senate floor and warned that within a few hours an agreement could be dead. With chances for a bill fading by the moment, Dole sprang a surprise: $3 billion, five years.

"That is the first time this Senator heard that offer," sputtered Dodd.

"My view is that this is what the Senator wanted," Dole said.

"We can put in a quorum call," Dodd replied.

Hardly a sound bite to ring in the new age. But next to "end welfare," those may have been the saga's most important words: a bill that Senate Democrats would support was a bill that Clinton would sign. Watching on C-Span from his White House office, a startled Bruce Reed called every Democratic office he could reach: *Take the deal!* When the Senate reconvened the following morning, Friday, September 15, the two sides had a pact. And twenty-four hours later, Clinton added his blessing in his weekly radio address. "We are now within striking distance," he said. "The Senate showed wisdom and courage." When the vote was tallied the following week—87 to 12—it brought high fives in the West Wing.

The Left came alive with panic: a Democratic president was about to achieve Ronald Reagan's welfare dream. Bishops wrote letters. Academics signed petitions. Marian Wright Edelman of the Children's Defense Fund published an "open letter," asking Clinton, "Do you think the Old Testament prophets . . . or Jesus Christ—would support such policies?" I shared the alarm, writing a piece in the form of a future encyclopedia entry that charted the suffering of the postwelfare poor. But the more telling sign is what didn't occur—no mass demonstrations, no Capitol sit-ins, no recipients with ardent demands. Nothing to suggest much political pain in signing the bill. A call from Robert Rector could get the Christian Coalition mobilized. A call from Marian Edelman was a call from Marian Edelman. It would be taken at the pinnacle of power and respectfully ignored.

The most notable challenge came from inside the administration and consisted not of placards but computer printouts. At the Department of Health and Human Services, Wendell Primus had revived an old habit from his career on Capitol Hill, of estimating how many children the proposed budget cuts would push into poverty. As the Senate reached its deal, his model spit out a number: 1.1 million. Analysts produce numbers all the time; the extraordinary thing is what happened next. Donna Shalala, the HHS secretary, raced to the White House, found Clinton in the hall, and stuck the study in his hand. She knew he was about to tape a radio address praising the Senate bill, and she wanted to head him off. "Clinton's tendency is to cut the deal too fast," she later said. "Anything I could hand him to make him slow down and think, I wanted to do." Clinton expressed surprise at the numbers but praised the bill anyway, citing the lawmakers' "wisdom and courage" for passing the "right kind" of reform. But when the study reached Bruce Reed a few hours later, he knew he had a problem—a piece of paper in presidential hands that made Clinton seem willing to impoverish kids. He assumed it would leak, and Primus did, too. (He later called the study "a stick of dynamite" lodged in the White Hall walls.) A month later Moynihan got a tip and demanded the study's release. With reporters giving chase, Reed orchestrated an absurd line—there is no poverty study—the idea being that since it hadn't passed clearance, it wasn't really a "study." Meanwhile, the nonexistent study appeared in the *Los Angeles Times*. While the lies were clumsy and bald, Reed had a substantive point: the study, for all its sophistication, was still a stab at the unknowable. It modeled the impact the law would have if past patterns of behavior remained. But the whole argument for the bill was that recipients would change: faced with unprecedented restrictions on aid, they would work more, earn more, perhaps even marry. No one could say for certain who was right. Not even an HHS computer. Trapped in its ruse, the White House agreed to redo the study and produced similar results. Yet the day the official numbers were released Clinton's press secretary said the president "may have to accept that bill anyway." To those who thought Clinton had abandoned principle, the affair only served to offer fresh evidence.

Yet Clinton didn't "accept that bill": he vetoed it, twice. It wasn't the advocates who changed his mind and it wasn't a study; it was, of all people, Newt Gingrich. With a spectacular meltdown in the fall of 1995, Gingrich did for the Left what it couldn't do for itself: he momentarily discredited the drive to end welfare. By the time the House and Senate reconciled their competing bills, welfare was caught up in a much larger fight, over whether to balance the budget. In their running battle, Gingrich appeared to be winning: Clinton had agreed in theory, while resisting specific assumptions and cuts. By mid-November 1995, federal spending authority gave out, and Gingrich tried to force Clinton's hand. He passed a bill to keep the government running, but only if Clinton made new concessions, including cuts in Medicare.

Clinton refused, and the government shut down. The Grand Canyon closed. Medical research ceased. The Pentagon stopped paying bills. Caught up in his antigovernment fervor, Gingrich had bet that voters wouldn't care, or would blame Clinton if they did. Wrong both times, he compounded his problems with a bizarre display of pique. Having cast the shutdown as a principled stand for fiscal discipline, he offered another reason: Clinton had ignored him on a trip aboard Air Force One. "This is petty: I'm going to say up front it's petty," he said at a reporters' breakfast. But when "nobody has talked to you and they ask you to get off the plane by the back ramp . . . [y]ou just wonder: Where is their sense of manners?" The New York *Daily News* drew Gingrich in diapers.

Epic fights can turn on less-than-epic events. The day Gingrich closed the government with a whine was the day Clinton won back his presidency. (And also the day he lost it: that night he met an intern named Monica Lewinsky.) The closure continued for six days, and the public blamed the Republicans two to one; Gingrich's job-approval rating sank to the depths of Nixon's during Watergate. Overwhelmed with frustration and fatigue, Gingrich broke down in an aide's office and sobbed. A second shutdown lasted three weeks, through the Christmas holidays, and Clinton looked like a sandlot hero who had faced down the bullies again. Until then, Clinton had sought political life by embracing Republican plans. He, too, favored block grants. He, too, was a balanced-budget man. Now the advantage lay in their differences, especially his refusal to accept the cuts in Medicare, a middle-class entitlement as popular as welfare was reviled. Welfare was, by contrast, a minor battleground, but this was no time for surrender. Give in to Gingrich on welfare? After a year of retreats, Clinton had a new answer: never!

He vetoed the GOP bill in December 1995 as part of the broader balanced budget. He vetoed it again in January 1996 as a stand-alone bill. Following his lead, the rest of the party reversed course, too. Thirty-five Senate Democrats had voted for the bill in September. By December, all but one changed their vote. In part, that's because a negotiation between the House and Senate had produced a significantly tougher bill. But it's also because the welfare zeitgeist had momentarily changed. The bill and the millions of lives it would touch were hostage to larger events.

Gingrich was slow to grasp his defeat. In marathon budget talks throughout December, Clinton charmed, chatted, winked, and smiled—and never surrendered an inch. "I've got a problem," Gingrich complained. "I get in those meetings and as a person I like the president. I melt when I'm around him." His wife said the gulling reminded her of a scene from *Leave It to Beaver.* Gingrich had been humiliated, but Clinton had a problem, too; having pledged to end welfare, he was approaching the 1996 election with two vetoes to defend. Gingrich swore to block any bill that would give Clinton a third chance. Dole, running for Clinton's job, was likewise opposed to a deal, since he wanted to make the vetoes a campaign issue. With Gingrich and Dole in control of Congress, their opposition to a third bill seemed to rule one out.

But among the GOP troops, other forces were taking hold, including an unlikely one: true belief. The chairman of the welfare subcommittee in the House, Clay Shaw, was a genial country-club Republican who had joined Ways and Means for the usual reasons, to work on taxes and raise campaign funds. But after a year of wielding the welfare gavel, Shaw had declared himself on "a rescue mission" to liberate the poor. ("This bill is about *hope*!" he barked, when another Republican tried to insert a measure Shaw considered punitive.) His staff director, Ron Haskins, a former U.S. Marine with a PhD in child development, was appalled to see Republicans blocking a welfare bill just to spite Clinton. "All of us are here to improve the nation's laws," he wrote to GOP members. "At the risk of seeming a little naive . . . [w]hen we reach age seventy-five and look back over our careers, will we feel we accomplished less because we didn't get full credit?" Operating outside the inner circle of power, Shaw and Haskins launched a long-shot effort to pass a new bill modeled after the Senate plan Clinton had already praised. They weren't total naifs. If Clinton signed, they would have a law. If he didn't, they would have an issue. "The politics were quite ravishing," Shaw said. "We'd win either way."

The dealmakers got a break in February, when the National Governors Association convened. In the partisan fervor of the previous year, block grants had failed to win the group's support. But by 1996, passions had cooled and self-interest had clarified: caseloads had already dropped 10 percent, so a block grant set at previous years' levels promised an immediate profit. With White House encouragement, the governors endorsed a block-grant plan much like the Senate's. Still, Gingrich and Dole remained opposed, and they found a new way to stop it: attaching a "poison pill" that would block grant Medicaid, imposing a huge health-care cut Clinton (and his wife) wouldn't abide. Shaw and Haskins couldn't believe it: *Republicans* were propping up the welfare status quo. A strategy memo from Representative Jennifer Dunn showcased a cynicism stark even by election-year standards. Emphasize "the tragedy of welfare and its crushing cruelty for the children," she wrote. But "draw opposition and, probably, a veto." Emphasize the suffering of children, and make sure they suffer some more.

By June, Republicans on the Ways and Means Committee were starting to rebel. If some worried about saving the poor, more were worried about saving their seats. They hadn't accomplished much, and Clinton was set to run against a "do-nothing Congress." The prospects for a bill improved when Dole resigned from the Senate to campaign full-time; now he could no longer block it. But Gingrich remained firmly opposed. "We're not going to give the president a bill he can sign," he told House Republicans. With that, the rebellion grew. "He doesn't care about us!" screamed Jim Bunning of Kentucky. "This is nuts!" said Dave Camp of Michigan, who collected one hundred Republican signatures urging a separate welfare bill. Perhaps Gingrich really believed what he said—that a welfare bill would save American civilization. That it would keep twelve-year-olds from having babies and seventeen-year-olds from dying of AIDS. He still wasn't willing to let one pass. Not if it might let Clinton out of a jam.

What finally swayed him wasn't a vision of liberating the needy but of something even more appealing: dividing the Democratic Party. The newest House Republican, a Louisiana party-switcher named Jimmy Hayes, clinched the case. Clinton was too skilled to be hurt by poison pills, Hayes told Gingrich. But sending him a clean welfare bill would leave him an impossible choice: damned (by his liberal party) if he signed, damned (by the public) if he didn't. The Democratic Party *loves* welfare, the ex-Democrat said. Imagine what would happen at the nominating convention if Clinton abolished AFDC. Picture the pickets; imagine the protests! Hayes thought Clinton wouldn't do it: he'd hand Dole a third veto. Gingrich thought Clinton *would* sign: he was too wired to public opinion to resist. But he was persuaded the price would be high. "We thought we would cause a split in their party," Gingrich later said. And on that, "We were just wrong." With Dole gone, momentum for a stand-alone bill had grown in the Senate, too. Party leaders made their decision in a July 9 conference call and announced it two days later: both houses would pass an unencumbered welfare bill. It was up to Clinton now.

What would he do? Even the most astute Clinton watchers could only guess. In January, he dismissed the Senate plan he once had lavishly praised. ("Moot.") Then he turned around and praised it again. ("A good bill.") In February, he hailed the governors' plan as "all any American could ever ask." The next day his spokesman criticized it. In June, Clinton praised a protest against time limits. Then he resumed his call for "tough time limits." A good negotiator uses ambiguity, and Clinton was a brilliant negotiator. But after nearly five years of pledging to end welfare, he owed the country a statement of first principles. There was lots of talk about the importance of training ("Government's going to have to train everybody"), but virtually no training in any of the bills. There was lots of talk about community service jobs ("what the Government's going to have to do is build a jobs program"), but nothing that made states provide them. There was, from start to finish, great confusion over time limits. Were they a precursor to a work program or an arbitrary ban on aid? As late as the spring of 1996, Clinton acted as if he opposed the latter: "I don't think it's a good idea to say, 'You can stay on welfare two years and then we're going to cut you off, no matter how young your children are or whether you have a job.'" But that is what hard time limits do. They cut people off *no matter* how young their children are. *Even* if they don't have a job.

To the end, Clinton clung to the pretense that it was possible to separate the economics of mother and child: "I say, 'tough on work, yes—tough on kids, no way!'" But you can't be "tough on work"—punish women who violate work rules—without the risk of being tough on their kids. Clay Shaw, less intellectual but more intellectually honest, acknowledged from the start that some families would be hurt, including some children. "We regret that there will be a certain negative side to what we're doing," he said. "Some people are going to fall through the cracks." His argument was that their numbers would be small and the long-term gains worth it—a risky stance but a coherent one. Clinton's position was no position at all: "I don't think it's a good thing to hurt children." Did anyone? Did Gingrich?

With his dodging and dashing, Clinton did himself a disservice. He left the impression he was merely playing a cynical game to win an election—an impression that still chafed him years later. "I was really steamed when everybody said, 'Oh, Bill Clinton just did this for the ninety-six election'!" he told me. "Hell, I didn't have to do this to win the election. . . . I was going to win the election in ninety-six on the economy. I did it 'cause I thought it was right." Indeed, for all his technocratic renown, a surprising thing about Clinton's approach to welfare was that his policy preferences weren't all that strong. Block grants or entitlements, hard time limits or soft ones—he could argue it either way. ("Frankly, I thought I knew more about it than people on both sides," he said.) The pledge to "end welfare" had let loose a storm, and Clinton was borne along like everyone else, albeit on waves of his own making.

Yet beneath the maddening evasions and elisions, he did have a more consistent vision and a less self-serving one—a vision of how welfare had poisoned the politics of poverty and race. Welfare cast poor people as shirkers. It discredited government. It aggravated the worst racial stereotypes. It left Democrats looking like the party of giveaways. In the speech in which Clinton first pledged to "end welfare," he also called for a rebirth of broader progressive traditions: "We've got to rebuild our political life before the demagogues and the racists, and those who pander to the worst in us, bring this country down." He clearly saw the two causes—ending welfare and reviving liberalism—as efforts that were linked.

More than most liberals, Clinton also showed an intuitive confidence in the welfare poor. "Part of it was being a governor for twelve years and going to the welfare office and meeting people on welfare," he told me. Plus, "I'd always known poor folks. I just never thought they were helpless." While Moynihan warned that without welfare, "the children are blown to the winds," Clinton, in my later talk with him, described recipients in the same way that Angie described herself. He called them "scrappy survivors." He had never adopted the apologetic tones of mainstream liberalism. Perhaps the best speech of his presidency was his 1993 homily in Memphis, urging the black underclass to stop destroying itself. Speaking from the pulpit where Martin Luther King Jr. had preached his last sermon, Clinton chided the congregation to imagine what King would say to them now. "I fought for freedom, he would say, but not for the freedom of people to kill each other," Clinton said. "Not for the freedom of children to have children and the fathers of those children to walk away from them as if they don't amount to anything. . . . I did not fight for the right of black people to murder other black people with reckless abandon." A black audience in a poor black city interrupted with applause eleven times.

While the Left saw the bill heading to his desk as an unthinkable surrender, Dick Morris plied him with the opposite argument, which was closer to what Clinton really believed. By signing a bill, even one with some problems, he wouldn't be abandoning the poor. He'd be setting the stage for a broader liberal resurgence. Once taxpayers saw the poor as workers, a more generous era would ensue. Stereotypes would fade. New benefits would flow. Eager for Clinton to sign, Morris bolstered the case with his ubiquitous polls. One survey split respondents into separate groups. The first was asked about spending on a set of antipoverty programs—Head Start, food stamps, housing, and the like. The second was asked about the same programs but told to assume that "the president has signed a bill requiring welfare recipients to work and setting time limits." Under that assumption, support for new spending rose ten to fifteen points. To Morris, that clinched the case: the country would do more for the poor once the poor did more for themselves.

He gave Clinton the results at a campaign meeting on July 18, 1996, the day the House passed the bill. The Morris critics in the room, of whom there were many, wondered if the numbers had been cooked. If so, they were cooked by someone who knew his clients' tastes. "I just instinctively knew it was true," Clinton told me, recalling the survey years later. "I really believed that if we passed welfare reform . . . we could diminish at least a lot of the overt racial stereotypes that I thought were paralyzing American politics." He would make the same case publicly at the signing ceremony: "After I sign my name to this bill, welfare will no longer be a political issue. . . . Every single person . . . who has ever said a disparaging word about the welfare system should now say, 'Okay, that's gone. What is my responsibility to make it better?' "

Morris didn't rely on an appeal to idealism alone. In the same meeting, he emphasized another poll: it showed that a veto would turn Clinton's fifteen-point lead into a three-point deficit. Morris's accompanying memo warned, "Welfare veto would be a disaster."

On July 31, 1996, Clinton ran out of time. The House was about to vote on the conference bill, and the Democrats demanded to know where he stood. Opponents had looked to Hillary Clinton to save the day, but the signals weren't reassuring. In July, her old friend Donna Shalala went to the White House to argue against the bill. Mrs. Clinton heard her out but warned that the president was in a political bind; Shalala came away certain that she wanted him to sign. About the same time, Mrs. Clinton reached out in an unlikely direction, arranging a visit with Doug Besharov, an analyst from the conservative American Enterprise Institute; with a sanguine view of the bill, Besharov was the kind of person likely to assuage any lingering doubts. Dick Morris quotes her saying at the time: "We have to do what we have to do, and I hope our friends understand it." That's not much different from how she put it in her memoir: "If he vetoed welfare a third time, Bill would be handing the Republicans a potential political windfall."

Still publicly unresolved, the president summoned the cabinet to a sudden meeting. Everyone filed in looking for clues. Mrs. Clinton was out of town. She must be distancing herself: a hint he would sign. Elaine Kamarck, a welfare hard-liner, had been invited to attend. Clinton must have wanted her support: another signal he would sign.

At one point, Clinton turned red with indignation, denouncing the unrelated cuts in programs for immigrants. He's overdoing it, one cabinet member thought; an additional clue. Conscious, no doubt, of being studied, Clinton told the group to focus on the merits, saying that with the Democratic convention coming he could argue the politics either way. Ken Apfel, a White House aide, walked the group through the specifics. AFDC would end, replaced by a block grant with fixed funding and vast new local control. The new program, Temporary Assistance for Needy Families, would limit recipients to no more than five years of federal aid, and states could set limits as short as they pleased. They would be required to enroll half their recipients in "work activities." But they could reduce that target point for point simply by cutting the rolls. Those were the bill's core features, and the Republicans had dictated them. At some point, Clinton had criticized them all.

Clinton did win two debates. The bills he vetoed would have made large cuts in food stamps and Medicaid. The one before him made lesser, though still considerable, food-stamp cuts, but (except for immigrants) left Medicaid in place. ("That's why I vetoed those first two bills," Clinton told me. "I thought there ought to be a national guarantee of health care and nutrition.") He also won some of the lesser debates over the welfare provisions themselves. He got assurances of continued state spending; exemptions from the time limits (for up to 20 percent of the caseload); and more money for child care. Because of the child-care money, the new program was actually projected to spend a bit more than the status quo, a remarkable concession from a Republican Congress. But the bill came with huge unrelated cuts—totaling $54 billion—in programs gratuitously labeled "welfare." About 40 percent of them were aimed at legal tax-paying immigrants, who in most cases were barred from food stamps and in some cases from Medicaid, too. Incensed at the budget cuts, Clinton told the group he had gotten "a good welfare bill, wrapped in a sack of shit."

Buying the second premise, though not the first, most cabinet members opposed both parts of the bill. The secretary of Health and Human Services said veto. The Labor secretary said veto. The Treasury secretary said veto. The Housing secretary said veto. The chief of staff said veto. David Ellwood, "the godfather of time limits," had left the administration a year earlier. But he dashed off a distressed op-ed, urging a veto, too. Clinton then turned to someone he knew would tell him to sign: the author of the end-welfare pledge, Bruce Reed. Reed had waited five years to make the case that followed. He argued that the central provisions would work as intended, moving recipients into jobs. He said the immigrant cuts could be restored later (about half of them were). He said that if Clinton vetoed a third bill, he might never get another chance. He even argued that President Roosevelt had faced a similar decision; before creating the WPA, his celebrated work program, Roosevelt had abolished a program of cash aid, throwing millions of people off the rolls. But above all, Reed said, you promised. Clinton had pledged to "end welfare," and the only way to do it was to sign.

Clinton ended the meeting without announcing a decision and returned to the Oval Office. With the cabinet milling in the cramped West Wing halls, he summoned a few people to run through it again. Leon Panetta, the chief of staff, was an immigrant's son who said the immigrant cuts were too deep: veto. Vice President Al Gore said the current system was just too damaged: sign. Then Clinton asked Reed once more: what had FDR done?

Given what was known at the time, there were plenty of reasons to veto. Time limits had morphed into arbitrary restrictions at odds with a safety net. "Work" had evolved into a game that could be played with accounting gimmicks. No one knew whether women like Angie would be able to find jobs, much less whether the jobs would bring "meaing" or "dignity" or "hope." The package came wrapped in extraneous budget cuts, and Clinton's lapses of leadership had let the process go astray. This wasn't at all what he had promised when he promised to end welfare. "I understand why they were scared of this," Clinton later said of his liberal critics. "I was scared of it, too." But there was also one good reason to sign, and it was the reason he would cite on television a few hours later: "I will sign this bill—first and foremost, because the current system is broken." Clinton's pledge to end welfare had been turned against him by a curious mix of idealists and rogues. But in at least one sense, the rogues were right. It was time to do something different. "All right, let's do it," Clinton said. "I want to sign this bill."

NINE

The Radical Cuts the Rolls: Milwaukee, 1995–1996

Imagine for a moment that you are Angela Jobe. You are twenty-nine years old with four kids to raise. You have just quit your job. Your landlord has tired of your crowd's wild parties and is throwing you out. If you need help, you know you won't get it from the men who fathered your kids. You'll be ninety when Greg gets out of jail, and Vernon (fortunately) isn't around. You've got a new man, but the kids resent him—they always do—and so far his main contribution to your finances has been to wreck your car. You know you're not on top of the kids the way you need to be, but it's hard to raise them all alone, even harder with no money, and at least you manage to keep everyone fed. One of the reasons is welfare. You've had it for nearly a dozen years. You've never raised children without it. While you don't like to admit it, welfare is one of the few sources of stability in your life: whether you're sick or healthy, depressed or inspired, you know that at the start of each month you'll get a $708 check. And now in the summer of 1995, the country's in a fever to take it away. You don't follow the details, of course, but you can't miss the talk in the air. Black leaders warn of slavery's return. The priests say your kids will starve.

What crosses your mind?

"I don't pay no attention to that crap!" Angie said, looking back. "I ain't thinking 'bout welfare!" Opal, the newshound of the group, wasn't thinking about it, either—she was busy in drug treatment. Jewell claimed to have noticed even less: "Didn't know, didn't care."

Even accounting for some false bravado, it is hard to square such studied indifference with the tenets of the national debate. From a distance, the threesome seemed the very definition of dependency. Together they had been on welfare for twenty-seven years; they had moved to Milwaukee just to get the benefits they now stood to lose. They appeared to embody the one assumption that the partisans on both sides shared—that the program was central to recipients' lives—which made conservatives so keen to restrict it and liberals so afraid of its loss. But as Angie and Jewell saw the world, if the money was there, they were happy to take it; if not, they would make other plans. With welfare or without it, Angie said, "you just learn how to survive."

The bill was still stalled in Congress in June 1995 when the trio left the First Street compound behind. They spent welfare's dying days apart, accumulating more of the misadventures that gave the system its bad name. If Angie felt anxious, it wasn't about welfare but the prospect of living alone. In Chicago, she had relied on Greg, and in Milwaukee she had forged a family out of Opal and Jewell. Now she was setting off on her own, with four kids between the ages of eleven and two and a loneliness she tried to ignore. A variety of men had come and gone in the four years since Greg's arrest. Angie had cared for some and tolerated others, but she sustained a relationship with none, and when she got to feeling empty inside she filled the hole with beer. Love, order, a father for her kids—there were lots of things missing from Angie's life. But, she figured, "I could always find me a job."

Just as Angie moved to her new place, another "old-ass" rental house on the near north side, the welfare office summoned her to a job-search class. Since Darrell had just turned two, she was no longer exempt, and the JOBS program was growing marginally more vigilant. Angie knew the routine: you sit through a week of pep talks, then make up a phony contact sheet listing all the employers you've called. "You think these people out here doing fifty million contacts and don't nobody hire 'em?" she said. "Come on!" She played along for two weeks, then decided it was time to go back to work. She had been off for five months.

While her dream of a postal career had faded away, the local branch was hiring, and Angie gave it a final try. This postal job, her third, was the worst. It only offered her five hours a day, and the shift began before dawn. "Who the hell want to be looking at mail that early in the morning?" she said. Since she was no longer living with Opal and Jewell, she left eleven-year-old Kesha in charge at home (with brothers ages nine, six, and two) and hoped for the best. Angie lasted six weeks until Kesha went back to school, and with that her hopes of postal glory—"a job for life"—sputtered to a close. Two months later, with the older kids in class, Angie took a job at a Budgetel. The 10:00 a.m. shift was more civilized (and Lucky's grandmother babysat Darrell). But motel maid work was nasty. Tampons, condoms, underwear—"You never know what you're going to find" in someone's sheets. With another five-hour shift, "I wasn't making crapola," Angie said. She hung on for nearly four months, but when she collected her tax money early the next year, she quit and took one of her breaks. As usual, she hadn't reported the jobs, so she still had her full welfare check.

For a year or so, Angie had thought of digging out her nursing smocks. She had lasted only three weeks in her first job at a nursing home. And lots of people made fun of a job that requires you to handle bedpans. But Angie was pushing thirty, and she had always told herself she would do something "professional" when she was grown. She practiced by taking Kesha's pulse and registered for the certification exam. In a nursing home, unlike a motel, "at least you know who peed in the bed."

While the end of group living left Angie lonely, Jewell welcomed the new privacy zone; as a homebody, she liked controlling her home. For her, the main drawback was the need to pay rent, something she never had done before. Greg's drug money had paid the rent in Chicago, and thanks to Mrs. Allen's deteriorating condition, no one had paid it in Milwaukee. At her new place, a duplex bungalow with a crack addict upstairs, Jewell discovered that she and Lucky had to pay "*all* our bills—had to pay rent and *every*-thing!" This struck her as somewhat unjust. Though welfare and food stamps totaled about $10,000 a year, rent and utilities consumed more than half, and Lucky drank too much to keep steady work. Jewell had dabbled in jobs before. Now she needed one.

Unlike Angie, who prided herself on her work history, Jewell had never given work much thought. She pictured herself doing something classy, like working in an office. But she couldn't type well enough. She did know a lot about hair and nails, and her skills as a kitchen-table beautician kept her in demand. But absurdly, the state required a high school degree to work in a beauty shop. The phone company was filling customer-service jobs; Lucky's cousin got one at $9 an hour. Jewell failed the reading test. Phone work didn't suit her, anyway, as she discovered a few months later in a telemarketing job. Talking on the phone was something Jewell excelled at. Talking to white people was not, and it proved to be the primary work of a Milwaukee telemarketer. White people made Jewell uneasy, and she avoided them when she could. Now she had a supervisor standing at her shoulder, coaching her to mimic their nasally Midwestern vowels. Jewell had a terrific telephone voice—a smooth, empathetic tone that lots of men found seductive. But she said "like-ded" for *liked* and "send-ded" for *sent,* and she had no luck getting strangers in Wauwatosa to give to the state police. Much of her shift was spent listening to them scream, "Don't call my damn house anymore!" She gave up after a couple weeks, wondering why the police needed money anyway: "Don't they make enough?"

As she scraped by on welfare over the summer, Jewell had other problems in mind. Tremmell, her four-year-old, was talking oddly, and an exam revealed he was deaf in one ear; he was going to need special help. Jewell had also taken in Opal's three girls, while Opal tried to get clean. That left her responsible for five young kids, and on some days Lucky made six. She returned to the job search in the fall of 1995 and discovered the post office was hiring temps for the holiday season. While Angie was eager to put postal work behind her, before she went postal herself, Jewell saw the vast downtown processing center as a temple of opportunity, even on a shift from midnight to six. It paid twice the minimum wage, and she could listen to headphones while she worked. Since she never even considered telling her caseworker about the job ("For *what?*"), she still had her full welfare and food stamps along with a paycheck. "Money was just coming in from everywhere," she said.

About the time she started the job, welfare resumed its lackluster efforts to push her into one. Jewell had been classified as a mandatory participant in the JOBS program for two years. But she had thrown the first nine appointment letters in the trash. When her tenth no-show finally triggered a penalty, it amounted to 6 percent of her combined welfare and food stamps, and she was flush with under-the-table earnings. Even so, she wandered in to set things straight. Lots of recipients had covert work, but Jewell now faced the special challenge of pretending to look for a job she already had. Soon, the awkwardness grew. Jewell was in the office one day when the computer spit out a list of her previous employers—all of them news to her caseworker. *Office cleaning . . . telemarketing . . . airplane seat factory*. Jewell tried to sound perplexed as her worker read off the list. "*Unh*-uhh," she said. "Somebody probably was using my Social Security card!" Technically, she could have been charged with fraud. But her current job was too recent to appear on the list, and like most caseworkers, Jewell's considered the old stuff more trouble than it was worth. Jewell was left to submit a fake job-search log, and when asked how she managed to find the only Milwaukee employers *not* hiring, she just shrugged. "Well, I went! They just didn't hire me." After two months of the obvious ruse, her caseworker put a note in the file: "Client not real motivated." "I wasn't," Jewell later laughed. "'Cause I was already working!"

Soon Opal was working, too, though as usual work occupied a place on the edge of her mental horizon. While Angie left First Street reluctantly and Jewell with a sense of relief, Opal left while coming unglued, racing to a rehab center. Medicaid financed a three-week stay, but after five years of smoking cocaine, even Opal knew she needed more than that; when her three weeks ran out, she left for a halfway house run by a storefront preacher. Pastor L. R. LeGrant required her residents to work, and Opal got hired at the Budgetel. She also started attending nightly meetings at Narcotics Anonymous, where a fellow twelve-stepper caught her eye. Within a few months, they were living together, and years later she talked of Kenny with a word she rarely applied to men. "I still love Kenny—I do," she said.

Opal was now twenty-eight—old enough to be getting herself together but young enough to rebuild a life. Kenny was a decade older and adamant about keeping them both off drugs, a welcome contrast to some of the men in her past. The kids came home from Jewell's, and as the makeshift family of five settled in, someone meeting Opal never would have surmised her problems. About then, the welfare office picked up the trail. Like Jewell, Opal was already working when she was summoned to her job-search class. Like Jewell, she ignored the notices until her caseworker reduced her check. Then, like Jewell, Opal had to master the art of the fake job search while already holding a job. Conning her caseworker was a skill Opal had; keeping a job was not. She missed too many days, and the Budgetel fired her.

Finding another job proved easy, even for a recovering addict with a trail of pink slips. Opal threw in an application at Target and charmed her way into a job as a cashier. Cash registers weren't good places for Opal; too much temptation lurked in the till. As a cashier at a Chicago Wendy's, she had taught herself to skim $100 from a single shift. The trick was keeping the math in her head—pocketing only the sales she didn't key in—and Opal, with a semester of community college, prided herself on her math. In the Target locker room, she caught wind of an easier scheme: cashiers would steer their friends through their lines, neglect to ring up most of the sale, and take a cut of the shoplifted goods. Opal sent Kenny through with a list: bathroom rug, garbage can, shower curtain, and clock—all in matching green and gold. "My bathroom was the prettiest room in the house," she said. Then Jewell and a friend gave it a try, and by the time the cart reached Opal's line it had the makings of a dumb-criminal joke. They grabbed twelve jackets, ten pairs of pants, eight shirts, six sets of pajamas, and a pile of underwear and gloves, along with a bottle of Batman soap and a jumbo pack of Charmin. The mountain of merchandise was worth more than $800. Watching on camera, the store detective noticed it heading toward Opal while bypassing shorter lines. When he saw her ring up a $90 sale, he called the cops. Jewell had nothing to say as the police took her away. But Opal went out in style. "If O. J. Simpson's innocent," she yelled, "so am I!"

The episode cost Jewell a morning in court and a $200 fine. No big deal. The real cost became clear a few months later, after her temp job at the post office ended. The postal service was hiring again, this time for *permanent* jobs. Jewell hurried to apply and with two successful stints as a temp worker she surprised herself by getting hired.

The starting pay was $11 an hour! Plus health insurance and paid vacations. She had already finished the orientation when a supervisor said they needed to talk—something about a court case had appeared on her background check. With that, the break of a lifetime vanished, done in by a cartful of shoplifted clothes. If part of the underclass dilemma wasn't just the lack of opportunity but the inability to answer when opportunity knocked, Jewell was now a walking example—and a particularly heartbroken one. She wasn't one to waste energy on regrets, but for years she talked of the post office in tones reserved for true love lost: "I would a *never* quit them. I would a *never* got fired. If they call me *now,* I'm going back."

As Opal and Jewell rode off in handcuffs in the fall of 1995, they were part of the tableau that made big-city welfare programs seem ungovernable. Tommy Thompson had been in office for nearly a decade and called himself the country's leading reformer. Outside Milwaukee, he had cut the rolls 45 percent. Inside city limits, the rolls had dropped just 7 percent, and even that was large by urban standards. Streetwise clients, incompetent staff, the undertow of crime and drugs—the sheer mass of the poverty and social disorder made the cities seem a world apart. At least by urban standards, Milwaukee's economy was strong; unemployment in Detroit and Cleveland ran nearly twice as high.

Onto this stage rambled a curious sight: an affable, paunchy, middle-aged bureaucrat in a leaky old Mercedes-Benz, convinced that he could make work programs work even in the heart of the ghetto. Nothing about Jason Turner suggested a figure about to make welfare history. He tangled his syntax and chewed cheap cigars. His shirttails were so chronically untucked that Thompson privately nicknamed him "Scruffy." But a few months before Congress passed the new law, Turner seized control of the Milwaukee program and set off the first urban exodus. In doing so, he turned an obscure patch of Midwestern blight into a policy lab that would draw visitors from around the globe. And he pioneered many of the methods that other states would use to cut the rolls.

Turner belongs to a welfare subgroup that confounds most stereotypes: the right-wing idealist. After decades of toil in conservative causes, he arrived in Milwaukee with two convictions. The first, in which he would be wholly vindicated, was that welfare recipients were much more capable of working than most experts had guessed. Even he didn't understand how many already had jobs. But he sensed that the number was high and trusted it could grow a lot higher. When Jewell said of welfare, "A lot of people was just getting it because they can get it—they know how to go out there and work," she was giving voice to the animating life-thought of Jason A. Turner.

Turner's second belief was that work—even tedious, low-wage work—had the power to save the soul. The idea that work would serve as a spiritual balm was one theme among many in the Washington debate; for Turner, it was a matter of lifelong faith. "Work is one's own gift to others," he said. "Work fulfills a basic human need." Without it, people suffer "spiritual harm." Once they became steady workers, Turner predicted, women like Angie would become happier, more self-fulfilled people, with more orderly homes, inspired children, healthier romantic relationships, and fewer problems with depression or drugs. Fumbling to make his point on television, Turner once exclaimed, "It's work that sets you free!" not realizing that he was quoting the motto on the gate to Auschwitz. He worked so late, he kept a bedroll in his office and often spent the night on the floor. The notion that, for some people, a job is just a job would not have occurred to him.

Turner's fascination with welfare began in a place where it didn't exist—the leafy precincts of Darien, Connecticut, where he grew up as the son of an advertising executive. Twelve years old in 1965, Turner was thumbing through *U.S. News & World Report* when he spotted an article on the welfare explosion. The news left him unsettled. "It hadn't occurred to me that there were whole classes of people who didn't work and who basically existed on government charity," he said. What if everyone tried that? Part of what fueled Turner's shock was his reverence for his grandfather, John Tufel, an orphan who had worked his way out of poverty and into a job as a Wall Street bond salesman; when he lost it in the Depression, he put on his suit and sold brushes door-to-door. In the moral universe of Turner's youth, nonwork was just a nonoption. While prep-school friends sat in class doodling football plays, Turner sketched workfare plans, blueprints of factories where welfare recipients would run the assembly lines. By his undergraduate years at Columbia University, he was sending them off to President Ford, hoping an over-the-transom plan to rescue the underclass might galvanize interest at the top. "One of the things that sustained me was I believed I had a solution: 'Hey guys, this is it!'"

Despite his fervor, it took Turner years to land his first welfare job. That may have been a blessing in disguise, for he used the delay in part to gain some exposure to the streets. In college, he drove a cab, mostly in the South Bronx, where he whisked around a captivating mix of drug dealers, hookers, grandmas, and kids. He also got robbed at gunpoint, twice—barely escaping the second time with his life. Having a gun stuck in his face reinforced his sense that social order was a fragile thing, not to be left untended. But it also quickened his curiosity: why run the risk of robbing someone, when a few hours of driving could earn just as much?

A second encounter with street life proved punishing in a different way. As a volunteer in the 1980 Reagan campaign, Turner had hoped to parlay his contacts into a welfare job but languished for years in the backwaters of the federal housing department. Deciding that if he couldn't save the poor, he would try to get rich, Turner cashed out his retirement plan, bought eleven cheap apartment buildings in the District of Columbia, and lost everything but his untucked shirt. The turning point came when he rented to a man who prepaid in cash and drove off in a new Bronco. Someone with a keener sense of property management might have spotted a drug dealer setting up shop. A few months later, half his tenants were smoking crack. Turner couldn't collect his rents, and District law made evictions nearly impossible. After three years of daily combat, Turner lost the buildings to foreclosure. "I got beaten," he said.

Life as a slumlord reinforced Turner's instinctive hostility toward welfare. But oddly enough, it also fortified his faith in the very people who had done him in. For all their problems, Turner regarded his tenants as a resilient lot. In a pinch, money would simply appear, from relatives, boyfriends, or God knows where. "There was nothing inherent in the people themselves that suggested they couldn't cope," he said. "They were able to support their families in a dysfunctional system. They'd do what they had to do to take care of their needs." Doing what they had to do is a phrase the Trio often use. That is, the man who was about to become their antagonist saw them much as they saw themselves; he saw them as "survivors," too.

Returning to Republican politics, Turner finally landed a welfare job, as a senior official under the first President Bush. But the Bush administration was no place for radical welfare schemes, and Turner departed four years later with his plans still on the shelf. Wisconsin offered him a second-tier post that most top feds would have found an affront. Even the title was opaque: director of capacity building. But his duties would include an overhaul of the Milwaukee program, meaning that at age forty, Turner would finally get his hands on a big-city welfare machine. He ignored the injury to bureaucratic pride and drove seventeen hours to the western shore of Lake Michigan. "I wanted to run an urban welfare-to-work program in the worst sort of way," he said.

Turner's timing was perfect. He got to Wisconsin in the spring of 1993, shortly before Tommy Thompson's showdown with the legislature's Democrats. First the governor accepted their dare to abolish AFDC. Then he had Turner lead a group to design its replacement—to do for real what he had been doing in his head since junior high school. The plan Turner proposed—Wisconsin Works, or "W-2"—was so radical that when Gerry Whitburn, the state welfare secretary, read it in his deer stand, he nearly fell out of the tree. *Everyone* would be forced to work in order to get a check: no exemptions, no exceptions, no delays. And work, not just join a job-search program. For those who couldn't find private employment, the state would create thousands of community service jobs. And it would offer subsidized child care and health care, not just to people on welfare but to a much broader class of needy workers. With its expansion of "opportunity" (child care, health care, and subsidized jobs) and "responsibility" (strict work rules), W-2 was a big, bold, serious plan, and in its broadest sense similar to what Clinton originally had in mind. Thompson, evolving from grandstander to innovator, signed off with surprisingly few changes, and Turner was as amazed as anyone in early 1996 when the proposal made it through the legislature intact. The obstacle of federal approval loomed, but when Clinton signed the welfare bill a few months later, handing authority to the states, Wisconsin was free to proceed. What started as a game of legislative chicken turned into what was, on paper at least, the boldest alternative to cash assistance since the WPA.

W-2 brought Wisconsin renown. But it is not really how the state ended welfare. By the time the program started in September 1997, the statewide caseload had already fallen nearly 60 percent, with Angie and Jewell among the first to tumble off the rolls. Indeed, Turner's success in cutting caseloads under AFDC is what made its expensive replacement affordable. In effect, he took a voluntary program that emphasized education and made it a mandatory program that emphasized work. Had someone done that to AFDC earlier, there wouldn't have been such fervor to end it.

Turner's first target wasn't the poor but the job-search bureaucracy. While the state set overall policy, and county caseworkers processed the checks, the motivation classes were mostly run by private contractors, like Goodwill Industries or the YWCA. And they got paid whether anyone got motivated or not. With a rudimentary form of performance-based contracting, Turner tied a small part of each group's pay to the number of people placed in jobs. The notion that they were *supposed* to be putting clients to work struck some of the groups as news. "I thought they wanted us to get people GEDs," the head of one agency said. As Turner put it: "Even though the program was called J-O-B-S, the message hadn't been absorbed, even by the chief executive." In each year from 1994 to 1996, the number of recipients placed in jobs rose by more than 30 percent. Since the baseline was low, and job loss high, the effect on the caseload was small. But Turner drew a lesson: "You can mobilize the bureaucracy a lot more than I had thought."

Focusing next on applicants, Turner swiped an idea from a hamlet two time zones away. He was making small talk at a conference one day when an Oregon official mentioned the news from an out-of-the-way place called LaGrande. Before opening a case, LaGrande made applicants meet with a "financial planner" to discuss alternatives: Could they move in with Mom? Had they looked for a job? New cases had plunged. "It turns out that people who apply for welfare have a lot more options than we think," the Oregon official said. The story was relayed as a curious backwoods development, not the makings of major new policy. But a light went on in Turner's head: the idea that the poor have other options was both an article of faith and the lesson of his days as a rent collector. Back in Wisconsin, Turner dialed up the "financial planner" herself, a former restaurant hostess named Sandy Steele, who was chosen for her welcoming persona; LaGrande wasn't at all trying to drive people away. Still, nearly a third of the applicants withdrew their forms rather than sit through the session. Never mind an hour of counseling, Turner thought: why not require every applicant to spend a few weeks looking for a job?

The idea clashed with the reigning administrative premise—that eligible families ought to get aid—and legislators wouldn't go along. But Turner found a loophole that allowed a pilot project. And to persuade local officials, he drove around Wisconsin with a giant speakerphone, piping in upbeat Sandy Steele to explain how she had done it. By the time he won permission to go statewide in March 1996, Turner required every applicant to spend a few weeks sitting in motivation class and filling out employer logs. Someone could always fake it, of course, but the more the hassle factor rose, the more the rolls went down; as soon as "Self-Sufficiency First" began, case openings fell by a third. Over time, the concept gained a new name—"diversion"—and variations were launched, amid significant controversy, in thirty states. In some cases, diversion *did* become a tool for driving the needy away; some of the most serious problems arose under a program later run by Turner himself as welfare commissioner in New York City.

Despite the ebbing applications, Turner still needed a program for those already on the rolls. For them came Turner's third initiative and his most potent: for the first time in the history of AFDC, he established a real work program in the heart of a major city. While the idea was one he had mulled all his life, he once again grabbed the details from an eccentric westerner, a Utah liberal named Bill Biggs, whose work had won a curious following on the Right. The Biggs story began in 1981, when Utah abolished the small, optional part of AFDC that served married couples. When the next year's recession left families sleeping in their cars, the legislature created a state relief program, but imposed a work requirement. Biggs took charge. The Emergency

Work Program, as he designed it, had two distinctive features. One, it really involved work; Biggs had recipients cleaning the highways, not sitting in motivation class. Even more unusual, it only paid people for the hours they logged on the job. This feature, known as "Pay for Performance," sounds exceedingly routine: you work, then you get paid. But most welfare-to-work programs took the opposite tack, sending recipients their monthly grants and threatening to reduce them later if they broke the rules. *Reduce,* not eliminate: on the rare occasions when penalties were imposed, they didn't amount to much. In practice, as Jewell had discovered, you got paid whether you showed up or not.

Biggs wasn't trying to cut the rolls. He was trying to help people get jobs, so he wanted to imitate a real workweek. Nonetheless, the caseload fell nearly 90 percent from the levels of the previous program; rather than work for welfare, most people quickly found regular jobs, even in Utah's down economy. Turner *was* trying to cut the rolls, and he proceeded in Milwaukee along similar lines. Through the county government and nonprofit groups, he lined up thousands of community service positions, where recipients could be sent to sweep floors, answer phones, or sort the mail. And he reduced their checks for every hour they missed. Wisconsin's version of Pay for Performance was even stricter than Utah's. The beleaguered Clinton administration, eager to look tough in the welfare wars of 1995, let Wisconsin punish those who didn't comply by taking away their food stamps, too. Under the old system, Jewell could ignore her work notices and still collect a cash and food stamp package worth more than $800 a month. Now if she failed to appear, $10 of food stamps was all she would have left. With the welfare world focused on the national bill, the experiment initially got little attention. But flying in below the radar in welfare's final hour, Turner put the whole safety net in play.

Turner launched Pay for Performance in March 1996, five months before Clinton signed the new federal law. With that, the city's caseloads collapsed. They fell 24 percent in the program's first year. They fell 66 percent in the two years until the transition to W-2 was complete. During that time, about twenty-two thousand Milwaukee families stopped getting welfare, meaning that about one city resident in ten was someone Turner had removed from the rolls. Nothing like it had ever been seen in a big-city welfare program. Outside Milwaukee, the rolls fell even faster, 93 percent over the two-year run-up to W-2. It didn't take a time limit to cut the rolls. It didn't take a surge in the economy. It simply took a work requirement, strictly enforced. "The numbers just blew me away," Turner said.

Why would so many ostensibly destitute people decline to work for welfare? One reason is that, as with Angie and Jewell, many were already working. Covert work is by definition hard to measure, but a Milwaukee researcher named John Pawasarat got a glimpse by comparing two state databases. One identified every city resident on welfare. The other showed everyone with earnings. Although only 12 percent of the recipients had said they were working, 31 percent appeared on the quarterly wage earners list—nearly a third had jobs. Over the course of a year, more than *half* of the people on welfare worked. And even that understates the amount of hidden work since the wage file omitted jobs in other states and informal jobs like babysitting or doing friends' hair. Many people didn't show up at the work program because they couldn't be in two places at once. For those who didn't already have a job, the work rules were a goad to get one. Working off her cash and food stamps, a woman on welfare would be earning the equivalent of the minimum wage—$5.15 an hour. Most entry-level jobs paid at least $6, and state and federal tax credits effectively raised that to about $9—offering at least the surface hopes of getting ahead. Plus, some of the jobs that Turner set up were transparently dull or dumb. In the most notorious case, women were sent to sort coin-sized toys called "pogs" into piles of different colors. When they finished, a supervisor dumped them, and the next crew started again. Faced with tedious or demeaning tasks, thousands of Milwaukee women had the same thought as Jewell: "I ain't gonna be doing that! I'll work and get my *own* money!"

Even those who piled the pogs weren't sure to get their checks. In his zeal to ferret out the guilty, Turner created a system that often punished the innocent, too, through an obscure change in the state's check-writing software. Let's say Jewell was assigned to work at a food bank but overslept. In the past, no penalties were imposed unless proof of her absence made a cumbersome trek—from the food bank to a work-program case manager (typically at a nonprofit agency like Goodwill) and then to a county eligibility worker, who had to go into the computer system and request a payment reduction. As long as the paperwork was missing, Jewell got her full check. Turner reversed the default mechanism. Now it was proof of Jewell's attendance that had to navigate the traffic jam. Until her eligibility worker got a time sheet and entered the hours she had actually worked, the computer wouldn't issue her payment. With that, the number of families penalized each month rose a dozenfold, to more than four thousand. This solved the problem that Turner had in mind: women who ignored the work rules no longer got paid. But thousands of women who did comply didn't get paid, either, simply because their paperwork was missing. Congressional investigators later found that 44 percent of the penalties were imposed in error. While the lost income was typically restored, it could take weeks just to get a caseworker on the line—and presumably the people who had agreed to work especially needed the cash. Unrepentant, Turner eventually retreated on tactical grounds, reverting to the old software. ("It just wasn't worth the advocates running around with a case of someone not getting their check," he said.) But in the collective mind of the city's poor, one thought seemed to be forming: *Why mess with these people?*

Not everyone who left, left for a job. Some turned to relatives, some to boyfriends. Some were too sick, depressed, or addicted to navigate the bureaucratic chaos. Even seeking a medical exemption demands an ability to function that some people didn't possess. One of the saddest sights I encountered in Milwaukee was that of Amber Peck, a fiftyish woman who lost her check, her apartment, and after a drug binge, her spot in a homeless shelter. We met on a snowy February night, and I gave her a ride to a cross-town church that had opened its floors to the dispossessed. She said that while she had understood the work rules, she couldn't bring herself to comply. "I stay depressed all the time." Then gripping two shopping bags filled with old clothes, she picked her way across an icy church lawn to lie on the hard, lonely floor.

In prosecuting his war, Turner was fully prepared to see such abject destitution rise. One of the failures of welfare, he argued, was that it papered over recipients' problems. By paying the rent, it let drug addicts ignore their addictions and the mentally ill postpone seeking help. "You want to get people into a situation where they have to resolve their issues," he said, a process he called "thrusting them into the public square." Whether much issue-resolution occurred is a matter of some doubt. A few years later, I went looking for Amber Peck, wondering whatever had become of her impossibly sad silhouette. The trail led to a low-income Samaritan named Eula Edwards, who answered the door in a torn housecoat and talked of having raised three dozen foster kids. She had taken in Amber after meeting her at a place called Power House Delivery Church. By the time I arrived, Amber was locked up on a drug charge, and Edwards was relieved. Before her arrest, Amber had been beaten on the streets and all but left for dead. "I used to be worried 'bout her all night," Edwards said. "At least now we know where she's at."

Still, Milwaukee saw nothing like the waves of dispossession that some people had feared—no children "sleeping on grates." (Amber Peck's teenage children had moved in with friends.) During the program's first winter, about forty-one additional families a night slept in the city's shelters. In the course of a year that translated into hundreds of additional homeless families, and in a shelter system as small as Milwaukee's they often exceeded the number of beds (hence the church floors). Nonetheless, by any reckoning, the homeless accounted for a tiny percentage of the ten thousand families who left welfare the first year. Food bank usage also rose that year, by 14 percent. Child welfare cases remained *lower* than they had been at welfare's peak. A smattering of critics still warned of "genocide." But Ramon Wagner of Community Advocates, a leading social services group, expressed surprise at the lack of more obvious distress. "We thought there'd be a more dramatic impact," he said.

Turner was amazed. He had never imagined that so many people would simply walk away. What he discovered in Milwaukee would soon become evident nationwide: welfare families depended on welfare less than anyone knew. "They must have had a lot more options than even I had realized," he said.

Angie received one of Jason Turner's first work notices. Two weeks later, she found her own job. She had already started to renew her nursing license when the Pay for Performance letter arrived, and a big nursing home was hiring. She timed her start to get a paycheck for Redd's tenth birthday. It was as easy as that.

Angie had landed plenty of jobs, and she resisted the notion that welfare hassled her into this one. "I ain't call that hassle—just 'cause they make you get up off your ass and look for a job," she said. "I was looking for a job, anyway." But this time several things were different. One is that she had to tell her caseworker right away; otherwise she would have been sent to sort pogs. Another is that when she got discouraged, she couldn't take one of her breaks; welfare would have made her work, too. In the long run, the aim was to mold her into the steady worker she imagined herself to be, with rising income and inspiration for the kids. But in the short run the rules just left her poorer, since she could no longer double-dip. Angie kept a partial welfare check during a brief transition. But after four months the payment dwindled to $11, and then it disappeared. With that, twelve years and about $60,000 worth of welfare payments ended, and she never received another. The state happened to process her final check on August 22, 1996, the day Clinton signed the new law.

In welfare theory, this would seem like a baccalaureate moment: she was off the welfare "plantation." After a lifetime of "dependency," she was fully, genuinely, that American hero, a working-class stiff—star of country music, socialist art, and beer ads everywhere. So how did it feel? Angie's smooth face puckered. "I never think about shit like that!" she said. "I always work, anyway." What did it mean? "It means I be a broke motherfucker for the rest of my life!"

Jewell, who had just lost her post office job, got the same letter as Angie. At first, she tried to beat the system. She was doing a little volunteer work at her son's school and passed it off as full-time community service. "I had got real cool with the teachers, so I just told them to say I was volunteering up there," she said. When that didn't work, she signed up for a course to become a nursing aide. Her mother was doing it; Angie was doing it; "Let me go ahead and have something under my belt," she decided. Six weeks later, she was on the job at a nursing home. As usual, Jewell didn't tell the welfare office she was working. But Sheriff Turner's new software tracked her down. Before issuing her next check, the computer tried to tabulate her hours on a workfare assignment. Finding none, it closed her case. The old system had sent Jewell a check every month for eight years. In five months, Turner pushed her off the rolls and into a full-time job. Like Angie, Jewell says the timing was pure coincidence. But on the bus to the nursing home each morning, she was astonished to find women heading to community service jobs—working for *welfare.* "Ain't no way I would wanna be working for free when I could be working somewhere and getting paid!" she said. Her contempt for the program happens to explain what made it so effective: "I didn't feel like going through all that; I just started working."

In Angie and Jewell, Turner's first theory found corroboration: lots of welfare recipients could work. Whether emptying bedpans would "set them free" was another matter. And Opal would pose the kind of challenge that Turner hadn't fully imagined. Within a few years, it would be hard to say whose failures were more disturbing—Opal's, with her self-destructive ways, or those of the celebrated system that squandered millions and did nothing to break her fall.

PART III

After Welfare

TEN

Angie and Jewell Go to Work: Milwaukee, 1996–1998

Nursing aides do difficult, dangerous work. They get hurt twice as often as coal miners and earn less than half the pay. They traffic in infectious fluids, in blood, urine, vomit, and poop. They handle corpses. They get attacked by patients. Above all, they lift. They lift people from beds and wheelchairs; they lift them from toilets and showers. They lift at awkward angles and times, and the people they lift can slip and resist. Nearly one in six nursing aides gets injured each year, and nearly half the incidents involve back injuries, where the risk of recurring problems is great. Coal mines and steel mills have grown safer with the years. Nursing homes have grown more dangerous. Science has prolonged patients' lives, while insurers have shortened hospital stays, sending ever-sicker patients into nursing-home care. In the decade before Angie started her job, the injury rate among nursing-home workers rose nearly 60 percent. Turnover is epidemic: a typical home often replaces nine of ten aides each year. Nationally, the job pays about $7.50 an hour, and one in five nursing aides lives in poverty. Although they are the foot soldiers of the health-care system, about a quarter have no health insurance.

Angie liked the job. She liked it more than lugging mail and a lot more than cleaning motels. She liked the bright, clean building. She liked break-room gossip and the teamwork of patient care. She liked the residents and the stories they told, especially the nursing-home rebels, who reminded her of herself. "Ain't no telling what might come outta they mouth!" she said. She liked her medical smocks. While others might call the job "wiping butts," Angie liked to look in the mirror and think of herself as a "nurse." Clinton and others had argued that work would bring new purpose and meaning. As a pioneer of postwelfare life, Angie offered an early test case and a promising one.

It didn't seem so at first. After renewing her license, she applied at a nursing home close to her house but was sent to a sister home eight miles south in the overwhelmingly white suburb of Greenfield. (The Greenfield population is 1 percent black.) "Wilderness," she fussed, making the trek in a $300 Oldsmobile as uncertain as her sense of direction. She found it strange that everyone at Clement Manor knew her name, then discovered that in a building with two hundred people, she was the only black worker on duty. Angie had never spent an entire day surrounded by white people and was surprised when "they didn't make you feel out of place." Soon, she made her first white friend, a coworker named April. Angie showed her how to put cornrows in her daughter's hair, and on Angie's thirtieth birthday April came along to a club. "She talked, she hung out—she just like she was black!" Angie said. Walking in to Clement Manor, Angie had wondered if she would last the day. But by the end of her first shift, "I knew when I woke up in the morning, I was going back."

With nursing aides in short supply, there's interest in what makes them tick—why suffer all that lifting and pulling when fast food pays as much? One theory is that aides are inherently drawn to the caregivers' role. "Often they have been caregivers of someone in their own family," said Robert Friedland, a nursing-home expert at Georgetown University. "They find something intrinsically valuable in doing the work itself." Angie's not one to put herself on the couch, but that's an insight she summoned on her own. "I think it was because of my Daddy," she volunteered one day. In her case, she *hadn't* taken care of him, which gnawed at her conscience. As Roosevelt Jobe drank himself to death, he hadn't looked after her, either. Angie was busy running the streets, and Roosevelt was too drunk to notice that his teenage daughter was pregnant. "I was mad at him, yeah, but that don't mean I don't love him," Angie said. "People make mistakes. He tried to mend it. He didn't have enough time." She saw her father for the last time just before she moved to Milwaukee, and after a separation of several years she was shocked by his decline. He couldn't even go to the bathroom on his own. "I had to hold his penis," Angie said. "That'll fuck up your head." They spent a tender two hours together in a park, the nicest father-daughter moment of their lives, and a month later he was dead. "I felt so guilty," Angie said. "I did not do nothing for him."

Five years later, Clement Manor gave her a second chance. The job tapped a vein of energy and imagination dormant in other parts of her life. She certainly had more patience for her patients than she did for her kids. Years later, she still laughed at the stories from the ward. "Okay, we had this man—he had dementia," Angie said. "He was always walking around with his pants down! He never kept 'em pulled up. *Never!"* Angie cackled. "He had a lady up there that liked him, *old* lady! She'd put makeup on her, dress in a little dress. If another resident sat next to him, *boooh,* she ready to fight! Even if they old and they can't remember nothing, they remember about sex. S-e-x! You'd catch him in somebody's bed in a minute!" A few weeks into the job, Angie's first patient died. "Scared-er than a motherfucker!" is how she felt when she had to clean him. She had never seen a corpse before. But after washing his body and combing his hair, she left the room thinking that dead people weren't so bad; unlike her kids, Angie would say, they can't talk back to her. In a less flippant mood, she put it this way: "It was easy, because he was suffering. And he just looked so much more at peace when he was dead." Another patient, as Angie moved to scrub her, barked, *"Get your hands off of me, you nigger!"* On the streets, that would have sent Angie's fists flying; on the ward, it made her laugh. ("Old people, sometimes they stuck in their ways. You overlook the things they say.") She smiled at the frightened old woman and, in the calmest voice she could muster, explained, "The nigger is cleaning your ass, 'cause you can't do it yourself—so you might as well let me."

The commute was harder to forgive, especially after her axle fell off. Then she had to get up at 4:00 a.m. and catch two buses to a 6:30 shift. Angie kept her enthusiasm for nursing homes but found a job closer to home, a place called the Mercy Residential & Rehabilitation Center. A 10 percent pay cut brought her down to $6.50 an hour. But it was "one bus, straight there."

By the end of 1996, the year she left welfare, Angie had worked nine months and earned $8,200, a pittance ideal in only one sense: it left her with an earned income tax credit about as large as anyone could get. As soon as her W-2s arrived, she hopped a bus to H&R Block and filed for a combined state-federal bonus of $4,700. The sum swelled her annual earnings by 57 percent. After a vast, if quiet, expansion at the start of the Clinton years, the $30 billion program became a pillar of post-welfare life. In Milwaukee, furniture stores ran annual tax-season sales, and car dealers brought bookkeepers to the lot, to help customers file. Despite the program's size (it spends more than AFDC did at its peak), not a lot is known about where the money goes. But one survey, of 650 workers in Chicago, offered some encouraging clues. While nearly a fifth spent the whole sum on what economists call consumption and Angie calls "surviving"—food, clothes, and overdue rent—more than 70 percent of the workers used at least some of the money for strategies to get ahead. They saved, moved, went back to school, or bought a reliable car. Angie had a foot in both camps. She bought the kids new beds and sank most of the rest, about $2,000, into another car. A "*nice* car." A car on the outer edges of what she could afford.

The salesman said he knew the previous owner and promised the car had been fastidiously maintained. It broke down five times in the first few weeks. Then it threw a rod. In the spring of 1997, Angie had the useless hulk towed back to the lot, where it sat as a smoldering monument to the salesman's empty assurances. "It was towed more than it was driven!" she said. A poor black woman with a melted engine is not one of society's more empowered figures. But what she lacked in automotive sophistication, Angie made up for with fury. She spent four hours in a waiting room standoff, listing all the people she would call—billboard lawyers, the television station, the "Bureau of Better Business." Then she drove away with a fine green Chevy and a feeling of vindication.

The car promised to change her life. Without it, she was stuck on an inner-city bus line, where wages ran the lowest. With it, she could "work the pool"; she could moonlight through a temp agency at short-staffed nursing homes. Pool work offered no job guarantees and often meant working at troubled sites. But it paid a premium, and pool work in the suburbs paid even more. After six months at Mercy,

Angie was earning $7 an hour. In South Milwaukee, fourteen miles away, she could earn more than $10. "Think I didn't find South Milwaukee?" she said. She found it in the morning, and she found it at night. She found it in manic double shifts that started before the sun rose and ended long after it set. Although the suburban cops made her nervous—"My black ass ain't supposed to be out there"—Angie's ambitions outran her fears. After a few months of juggling two jobs, she left Mercy to work the pool full-time. She made $1,600 in May; $1,300 in June; and $2,000 in July. Through six months of gyrating schedules and fatigue, she was on pace to earn nearly $20,000 a year.

Her success bolstered her confidence, much as the advocates of work had hoped. "You know how you might want to change your life around, do something different?" she said. What Angie wanted was her GED, for her pride above all else; she had been trying on and off for a dozen years. It's easy when you own a high school diploma to forget what it took to get one. Signing up for a class, Angie dragged home a workbook that ran a thousand pages. Square roots, onomatopoeia, the Pythagorean theorem, plate tectonics, cumulus clouds, the Townshend Acts, $2 \times (x^2+1)$—it was all there, a four-pound brick of stuff she should have long ago learned and forgotten. She was ten years older than most of the students and felt like the chaperone. As a onetime high school poet, she started with the literature review, huddling in the break room with "Sonnet 43": "I love thee to the depth and breadth and height / My soul can reach, when feeling out of sight." ("I always *liked* poetry," she said. "I just could never understand that shit.") In verse, as in person, Angie was more direct. Though with the move to Milwaukee her writing had waned—she wondered if she had run out of time or out of things to say—she responded with a poem about Roosevelt Jobe:

He was here now he is gone
Gone to a place where
the sky is blue
the wind is still
the trees and
the grass is green and bright
He is gone to a place to be at peace with life.

In the tradition of student crammers everywhere, Angie pulled an all-nighter before her first test. In the morning her heart was racing; what if people laughed? She felt no shame in being poor, but looking dumb she couldn't abide. What she suffered next hurt worse: the computer crashed and tests were canceled for the day. Remarkably resilient in most aspects of life—she could stare down corpses or used car salesmen—Angie didn't find the courage to return for another four years. "I was really, really hurt," she said.

She did keep working, and in the summer of 1997, she treated herself and the kids to their first family vacation—four days down South for the family reunion. The trip was not to be undersold as a marker of achievement. She bought each of the kids a new outfit and had Jewell do her hair. She fried up a cooler of chicken. Then she loaded a rental car and drove fourteen hours to Monroe County, Mississippi. Darrell had just turned four, and her mother had never seen him. Carloads of kin drove in from Chicago, and praying over the backyard feast they formed a portrait of mainstream achievement. Two of Angie's cousins were cops; another cousin worked for a bus company or airline—Angie was never sure which. One uncle parked rental cars at O'Hare. Another owned a beauty salon and a house with a swimming pool. No one asked Angie what she did for a living or whether she got welfare. They just fussed over her kids, teased her about her weight, and stuffed her with ribs and pie. Her presence said all that had to be said: Angie was making it.

Nursing homes didn't have the same effect on Jewell. She started at a place known for being rough on aides, the Bel Air Health Care and Alzheimer's Center, which had three hundred beds and a dementia ward that Jewell came to dread. Her patients threw food. They played in their poop. They moaned at phantom pains. "It was just like a big old crazy house!" she said. "Had to rassle with some of them." At $8.30 an hour, Bel Air paid more than most places outside the pool. But getting there involved a long bus ride, and Jewell was chronically late—"no special reason, just late." The average Bel Air aide stayed for eight months. Jewell lasted seven. "They terminated me because of my attendance."

She got fired two weeks before Christmas, 1996—her first without welfare—but Jewell wasn't worried. Lucky had wandered into a job at a rubber factory that paid nearly $10 an hour. Plus tax season was around the corner, and Jewell had $4,100 in credits coming, about as much as the average state paid out in welfare all year. She bought clothes and furniture for the kids and a Grand Am for herself. A few months later she got a job at Mercy Rehab, the nursing home where Angie was working. Mercy had a homier feel than Bel Air, but Jewell found it chronically short staffed, and she lost the Grand Am when a drunk driver hit her. (Neither of them had insurance.) One weekend, three months after she started, Jewell learned she was slated to cover a whole shift with just one other aide—the two of them would have to wash, dress, and feed sixty patients. "*Unh-uh,*'" she thought. "They're not fittin' to work me like that!" She didn't go in, and she didn't go back. After quitting in May, Jewell hardly worked the rest of the year. Her mind was on other things.

Life with Lucky wasn't happy and hadn't been for a while. She had lived with him for nearly five years, and he was the only father her two boys had known. But Lucky was always drunk. Screaming drunk. Obscene drunk. Falling-down-and-passing-out drunk. At twenty-eight, she thought she might like another baby, but Lucky had driven her to Norplant. As Jewell launched her nursing career, one of Lucky's best friends moved to town, with a story as vivid as his name: Kenyatta Q. Thigpen. The last time Jewell had seen him, a decade earlier, he was a mischievous kid in Jeffrey Manor, three years behind her and known by his graffiti *nom de guerre,* Mirf. Jewell hadn't paid much attention to Mirf. But Ken caught her eye. At twenty-five, he was a tall, muscular man with a dimpled smile, copper skin, and soft hair tied in a ponytail. They were playing Spades at her brother Robert's house when Jewell noticed the change. "Oh, he looks so nice," she thought. When Ken dropped in a few days later, Lucky got drunk and passed out; Ken and Jewell stayed up most of the night, playing video games. Soon after, she took him out for a hamburger. Then she gave him a call. "Should I *say* something?" Jewell asked herself. She decided it was too risky. Then she said it anyway: "What's up with you and me?" Ken pretended to be surprised. "What you want to be up?" he said. He left town to visit family in Mississippi, and needing a place to stay when he returned, he moved in with Lucky and Jewell. She had just started working on the Alzheimer's ward when their covert romance began.

After years with Lucky, Jewell found Ken an oasis of innocent fun. He didn't drink or do drugs; he liked kids; and while he didn't have any of his own he played the generous uncle with élan. He liked bowling, theme parks, and video games. He taught Jewell to drive a stick shift and took her to play miniature golf. He even liked to shop. He made her laugh with funny faces. Once when Jewell blew him a kiss, he leaped in the air to catch it. "He's silly!" she said. "We could talk about anything." Still, not many people leave Jeffrey Manor as innocents, and Ken certainly hadn't. His probation officer noted that he had "described his childhood as so-so, as both parents were addicted to cocaine." "So-so" was a generous view. Until he was twelve, Ken boasted of having the most popular, cookie-baking mother on the block. After she got addicted to drugs, he spent the rest of his childhood refereeing his parents' brawls and their smoke parties. Losing the house, the Thigpens split up, and his mother moved to a shelter. His father hung on to a steel-mill job, while Ken stole cars, lived here and there, and finished raising himself. As a high school linebacker with a vicious hit, he had hoped to play college ball. That didn't pan out, and a few weeks after graduation he started selling crack to his mother's friends. "I ain't qualified to do nothing else," he thought. "I ain't working in no McDonald's."

Ken soon discovered he had the qualities a good drug dealer needs. He was smart, personable, and hardworking. He was savvy about marketing; anyone who brought him five clients got a round on the house. And since he didn't consume his product, he didn't burn up his profits. Plus, he was tough. Because of his ponytailed good looks, some people called him "Pretty Boy." But his attitude toward collecting debts brought another nickname, "Batman." "I used to beat them niggers' ass down with a baseball bat," he said. He figured a reason that he didn't have kids is that one of his victims returned and blew off one of his balls. Among the talents that Ken seemed to lack was the knack of avoiding the cops. By the time he arrived in Milwaukee, he had spent half his adult life behind bars.

As their romance blossomed in the summer of 1996, Jewell and Ken were each making a new start. Jewell was leaving welfare for work. Ken was dabbling in modeling school and, despite passing thoughts of quitting the trade, building a new drug business. While traffic was slow for the first few months, he caught a break with a $10 sale to a "go-getter" of a woman named Tina. Among the things she knew how to go get were stolen checks; she had bribed someone at a currency exchange to cash them, and Ken soon had part of the take. Another thing Tina attracted were men willing to pay her for sex. "Once I got hooked up with her, I really took off," Ken said. "Not because of the drugs, but because she was a ho—and she became my ho."

In Ken's line of work, sex and drugs meet at an economic crossroads. What addicts demand are drugs. What they can supply is sex, even when their pockets are empty. Crack houses are filled with bingeing women eager to sell a $10 blow job to finance another high. "It don't make no sense to sell your body for a bag," Ken would say. "Come with me and I could make you a hundred dollars or two hundred dollars." Some people call this pimping, but that's a word Ken generally avoided. He saw himself more as a talent scout, a middleman in the great American tradition. In Tina he realized he had a star of unusual wattage. She had caramel skin, delicate braids, large breasts, and long legs. Plus, she could "conversate." Her escort service charged $225 and took a third for setting up the date. Ken provided drugs and protection—"the Be There"—and pocketed most of the rest.

As the enterprise grew, Ken found that coveted commercial force, "synergy." Selling drugs, he met women who wanted to sell sex. Selling sex helped him sell more drugs, since half the johns got high. His products went together "like Bonnie and Clyde," he said. Since the sex workers spent *their* earnings on crack, "no matter how the date goes, I'm gonna get all the money." Until he met Tina, Ken was scuffling by on about $200 a week. With her, his weekly take rose five- or sixfold, and since none of it went to the IRS, he had the take-home pay of someone making $100,000 a year. As the child of addicts, he knew the rap on dealers—parasites preying on the community, blah, blah. "That's a bunch of bullshit," he said. "If I turn my back on them, all they gonna do is go two houses down and get it from someone else." He'd sell to pregnant women as long as they had the cash. "I didn't make the rules, I just follow them."

In explaining how it worked, Ken sounded less like a ghetto badman than a middle manager. He set standards so that Tina would know "what I was going to expect out of her and what she could expect out of me." He pumped her up when her spirits were down: "I just told her if you gonna sell pussy, you gotta be the best at what you do. Ain't none of that selling pussy one day and laying up the next day." And when he had to, he made clear that poor performance brought repercussions. "You can pay me or you can pay the doctor"—so went a favorite refrain. "The first time I beat her up, she told me she wasn't going to work," he said. "*Smack!* 'What you mean, bitch, telling me you ain't going to work?'" Someone with a psychoanalytic bent might wonder if, in beating his whore, he was channeling the rage he felt toward another addict, the mother who had abandoned him. Ken didn't have such a bent. He just said he put in long hours and expected his subordinates to do the same. "It was like a job to me."

That Ken sold drugs was not something Jewell found notable. "That was every black man's job," she said. "I think if *I* could sell drugs and get away with it I would." The sex trade was something she knew less about. She was astonished, when Ken took her to a crack house, to find women ducking behind closed doors only to suddenly reappear, still working their lips and clutching their cash. "The shit these females would do!" Since she had never tried drugs, she couldn't fathom what made addicts act that way. She also thought, "I really don't care, since it ain't me." What she did care about, more than she expected, was Ken. At the start, she thought she was just having a fling, but the more it progressed, the more she saw "a match made in heaven." For months, people were talking. Then Lucky came home early from work and discovered the rumors were true. Too afraid to fight Ken, he turned his fury on Jewell. "Do what you gotta do," she said, refusing to deflect his blows. Ken left for Tina's, and Jewell stayed with Lucky. But she continued to see Ken whenever she could.

Jewell says the tumult had nothing to do with her flagging interest in a job. But she quit shortly after Lucky discovered the affair, and she hardly worked for the next seven months. She didn't have welfare. She didn't have work. She didn't even have food stamps or health insurance; like many former recipients, though she still qualified, she found the new bureaucracy so hard to deal with that she gave up. About a third of the families leaving welfare were in a similar position—

left for months without welfare or work—and their means of survival was a national mystery. Welfare-rights groups went as far as calling them "the disappeared." No one could see how they got by. Jewell's circumstance offers some clues: she had a private safety net. Lucky got fired from the rubber factory but found temp jobs here and there. Thigpen & Associates was throwing off cash. Opal gave Jewell a $65 book of food stamps each month. And after Angie returned from Mississippi, she and her kids moved in. That left nine people sharing a two-bedroom house, but Angie helped pay the rent. "If I got fired, there was always somebody else to help out," Jewell said. "So it really didn't matter."

Her mind told her that cheating on Lucky was wrong. But her heart had a mind of its own. In the summer of 1997, Lucky got locked up for driving without a license. Jewell threw a barbecue to welcome him home, and when Lucky got drunk and threw a beer bottle at Ken, Ken hit him so hard he broke his knuckle on Lucky's head. After the fight, Jewell delivered a harder blow. She told Lucky she wanted him gone.

Angie came home from Mississippi and raced back to work. The Chevy ran like a dream, and the nursing pool paid like one. "You could work seven days a week!" she said, and some weeks she did. In her first month back, she made another $1,800, two and a half times what the average person earned after leaving the Wisconsin rolls. Work made Angie feel useful. It bred empathy. At some level it really did become what Jason Turner had audaciously imagined, her "spiritual gift to others." What it didn't bring was any obvious social benefit to her kids. The most stirring case for putting mothers to work was the promise of planting new values and goals that would transform the next generation. Clinton had been so taken by Lillie Harden's story—"When my boy goes to school and they say 'what does your mama do for a living,' he can give an answer"—he flew her in from Arkansas to stand beside him as he signed the bill. Explanations of just how work would benefit kids were varied and a little vague. One theory emphasized new discipline: an alarm clock would act like a social metronome, imposing new order at home. Another stressed inspiration: watching their role-model mothers buckle down on the job, the kids would do the same in school. Their mothers' toil at indecent wages might even serve as an object lesson, warning children of the need to hone their skills and minds. In the storybook version, a bread-winning woman like Angie might meet a bread-winning man. You can almost picture the new house—small but neat, in a safe neighborhood, with better schools.

Angie's kids didn't live in that house. They squeezed in among the racy subplots at Jewell's. Angie's exit from welfare, a signal event in policy terms, barely registered on them. "Doesn't make no difference at all," said Redd a few years later. "She was working when she was on welfare." A change in family dynamics can take years, of course, and it can happen without children articulating it. But the kids' absences from school, alarming when Angie was on the rolls, grew even worse when she got off. During Angie's last five years on welfare, Kesha, Redd, and Von missed a combined 21 percent of their scheduled school days. Over the next three years, their absentee rate rose to 26 percent. In the course of an elementary school education, that's the equivalent of missing two full years. Angie valued education in an abstract way. She had even kept her notes from a high school debate about the importance of staying in school: "We as black women already has two strikes against us . . . if we don't have a good education, that may become another." But there were days when she just didn't have the energy to get the kids out the door. And days when she was already long out the door herself by the time the school bus came. While affluent parents endlessly complain of their kids' overscheduled lives, Angie's suffered from the opposite blight, long blocks of empty, unsupervised time, which grew longer the more she worked. Their childhoods passed on a sea of boredom, dotted by landfalls of chaos.

At fourteen, Kesha was an open, oddly innocent girl, who alone among the kids still poured out her thoughts in letters to her dad. She also had a severe case of asthma, which compounded her problems in school. With only one functioning lung, anything from cold weather to a whiff of cologne could bring a disabling attack; it was the rare day that passed without one. Landing in Milwaukee, Kesha had responded with courage, and not just physically. Failing second grade, barely able to read, she had struggled uphill to a fourth-grade report card that had shimmered with As. Kesha "has great potential for success," her teacher had written home. But with her transition to middle school two years later (Angie's first off the rolls), Kesha's progress slowed. She felt lost among the five hundred students. She didn't like switching classes or going to gym, and she wouldn't take her medicine in front of her classmates. (Her highest grade, a C, came in, of all things, sixth-grade Japanese.) As Angie moved in with Jewell, Kesha was starting seventh grade, and her schooling crashed: she was absent nearly half the year. Two weeks in the hospital set her back, but so did the unsteady housing, Angie's long hours, and Kesha's fights with Angie's new man. She ended the year with nearly straight Fs, and her education never really recovered.

Kesha felt especially close to her aunt Jewell, her great counselor in fashion and grooming. But Kesha soon had an unlikely new friend in Jewell's rival, Tina. Tina took Kesha shopping, paid for her to have her hair and nails done, and let her spend the night. Kesha understood she was being used as a pawn in Tina's rivalry with Jewell, but she didn't understand where Tina got the money. Or she didn't until Tina pulled out her slitted skirts and boasted that an evening's work could bring her $1,000. "If that's how she wants to make her money, that's on her," Kesha later said. "She was cool." Rather than bring Kesha a new role model, that is, Angie's first years off welfare left her passing time with a prostitute. Later I asked Angie what had gone through her mind. Was she just grateful to have someone buy Kesha things? Was she too tired to give it much thought? Did she genuinely have no qualms about Kesha's weekend visits with a call girl? Angie shot me one of her sour looks. "I'm not supposed to let my kids visit her 'cause that's her chosen profession?" she said. "I ain't got nothing against prostitutes. You don't judge people about stuff like that!" Whether her indignation reflected secret regrets or genuine belief, I never could tell.

Role-model theory took a curious bounce in Redd's life, too. If he had a role model, it wasn't Angie but Ken, the rare grown man who paid him any attention. "When I call him and wanna do something, he come gets me," Redd said. "Plus, he had that dust." Dust—money—loomed large to Redd, and even at twelve, he figured out where Ken got his. As a pudgy, picked-upon child, Redd was impressed by Ken's power over Tina and thought, "I got to find me a girl like that." For a school essay, he chose to write about Las Vegas, because "ho-ing is legal out there." Redd had always struggled in school, but by fourth grade, as Angie left welfare, his behavior grew as worrisome as his grades. His fifth-grade teacher could barely contain himself: "His disrespect toward authority is blatant . . . and demeaning to me as an adult." Redd got suspended for fighting so often that Angie told the school to stop calling her at work and asking her to come get him. "Keep him there!" she said. Equally unhappy in sixth grade and at home, Redd started smoking weed and got two pit bulls. The weed made him giggle. The animals made him feel safe.

Von was afraid of the dogs; in that, as in most things, the brothers formed a study in contrasts. Athletic where Redd was sedentary, even-keeled where Redd was explosive, Von was the only one of Angie's kids diligent about school. "School's fun," he said. "You benefit more from going to school than not going." Every inner-city school's got a kid like Von, an unmined gem waiting for someone to discover his shine. The question was whether anyone would notice before the mudslide of living swept him away. Riding the school bus one day, Von made a crack about a classmate's hair. She taunted him back, Von looked away, and Redd rushed over and punched her. Redd got suspended, but Von was the one whom Angie whipped, for walking away. Don't *ever* punk out on your brother when he's fighting your fight! Von was so mad when he got back to school he hit the girl himself. This time he got suspended. But he didn't get a whipping.

If there was a point on which the kids united, it was a resentment of Angie's boyfriends, who had wandered in and out of their lives since their father had gone to jail: Vernon, Johnny, Sherman, and then Johnny again. "I just really wanted them out," Von said. Angie often seemed to feel the same way: she once chased Sherman with a baseball bat until he jumped out the first-floor window. Kesha got so mad at Johnny, she threw a giant pickle jar from an attic window onto his head. "Every time we see a guy with Mama, we ready to fight him," Redd said. "We just real protective about Mama." About the time she left welfare, Angie finally sat down with the kids and explained what their father had done. He was helping his friends jump some guys, she said. The shooting was an accident. Though their father was serving time for murder, he hadn't even fired a shot. Kesha, at twelve, was quick to forgive. "It was an accident," she said. For Von, who was three at his father's arrest, it was a story about a virtual stranger. But Redd was disturbed. He could forgive his father's role in the shooting; what he couldn't forgive was his refusal to testify against his friends. He just couldn't understand why any child's father wouldn't do all he could to get home. "That's bogus," he said.

Soon after Angie moved in with Jewell, a friend brought her a message: the butcher at the corner store wanted to "talk." Marcus Robertson: big smile, shaved head, soft, dewy eyes like Greg's. "I don't want to talk to him!" she said. But she talked to him every time she stopped in for a loaf of bread. Her on-and-off relationship with Johnny had ended, and among the trio Angie missed congregate living the most. Opal had a boyfriend—Jewell had two—"and I was by myself, as usual." Marcus took Angie to a diner, and a few months later, when she moved to her own place, Marcus came along. Angie never said much about Marcus, then or in the years that followed. He brought home beer. He babysat. He was the rare man she knew who vacuumed and the only one the kids couldn't drive away. But he smoked too many blunts to keep up much of a conversation. And Angie's attitude spoiled early on, when she learned he was messing around. Twenty-three years old, eight years her junior, just out of jail for selling drugs, Marcus was in no settling-down way. The discovery of his infidelity didn't kill the relationship, only Angie's professed investment in it. "I like Marcus, but I don't like to be bothered like I'm his wife," she would say. She let him share her new house. But she never gave him a key.

One night soon after they met, Marcus borrowed Angie's car and headed out to party. He said he would stay at his mother's house, and he awoke there, hungover, the following morning to the blare of Angie's voice.

"Where the car at?"

"In the yard."

"Ain't no motherfucking car out there!"

Angie's green Chevy—literally and metaphorically her engine of progress—had vanished. Angie usually said it was stolen, as in a random crime. Once, she said the real story was that Marcus was selling a little crack, and his sister, seeing him asleep, drove off with his drugs and money. Opal and Jewell thought that Marcus lent it to another woman, who got it towed. Wherever the car went, she had no insurance, and its disappearance in November 1997 spelled the end of Angie's MVP season in the Welfare-to-Work League. She told it as a clear tale of cause and effect: without the car, she lost her job with the nursing pool and sank into a trough of discouragement and debt. The full story is more revealing. Angie found another job, with a pool that transported its workers in vans. The job paid the Christmas bills, but it offered fewer hours and lower pay, and she quit in January over a $10 charge for a van ride she didn't take. The driver said he honked and she didn't come out; Angie said he didn't show up. "Plus they try to talk to you smart," she said. "I got smart right back!" It was tax season. Three days later, she went to H&R Block and collected $5,200. That was twice what she needed to buy another car and return to the nursing pool. But she and Marcus had just moved into the new place on Concordia Street, and she wanted to fix it up. She bought a washer, dryer, refrigerator, and stove. She bought the boys new bedroom sets, since they had destroyed theirs again. And when the money ran out, she got on the bus and applied for a welfare check. Angela Jobe, working-class hero, was trying to get back on the dole!

One person who wouldn't be surprised is Toby Herr, who founded an employment program called Project Match in Chicago's Cabrini Green. Herr got her start as an employment expert in an unadorned way, piling some women in her car and driving off with the want ads. Her first surprise was how many found jobs. Her second was how quickly they lost them. Sick kids, drug problems, fights with the boss—the reasons ran the gamut of housing-project life. Only half her clients became steady workers, and on average it took them more than five years. Most programs stress their successes. Advertising her setbacks, Herr coined a phrase that became a maxim of the field: "Leaving welfare is a process, not an event."

While Herr's findings about job loss have been widely acknowledged, the causation is more complicated than it may seem. A large "barriers" literature has arisen, documenting impediments like depression, illiteracy, domestic violence, and especially the shortage of child care. But the focus on barriers goes only partway in explaining who works and who doesn't. The more barriers a poor mother has, the less likely she is to work; yet plenty of women work despite multiple obstacles, as Angie had. Depending on definitions, her barriers had at various times included shortages of child care and transportation, a severely asthmatic child, bouts of depression, and the lack of a high school diploma. Not to mention the Colt 45s. The barriers discussion also comes with an implicit logic: you fix the barriers and then go to work. Angie's back-and-forth moves (Jewell's, too) show the process to be more nuanced. All women leaving welfare have barriers. The challenge is learning to manage them without losing the job. Herr's training was in human development, not economics, which put her subtly at odds with others in the field. While services like child care and transportation are essential, she argued, new workers ultimately succeed by acquiring something else: a strong "work identity." Seasoned workers, when faced with personal turmoil, see the job as a pillar to cling to, rather than the thing to let go. "It's about making the psychological leap," Herr said. Cars and babysitters come and go. Work identities stay.

In her breakneck dash from the welfare rolls, Angie seemed to have the ultimate work identity. But liking a job isn't the same thing as internalizing the need for one. Angie also faced an especially immobilizing "barrier": troubled love. Conflicts with boyfriends get none of the attention reserved for child care and cars. But women leaving welfare are constantly undermined by the men in their lives, either deliberately, because the men resent their success, or simply because the lives of poor men are so infectiously troubled themselves. And a broken heart is debilitating in a way that a broken carburetor is not. To Herr, a woman with a tenuous work identity and an unfaithful man is behaving in wholly familiar ways when she turns from the job to focus on her home.

Angie didn't assemble the story like that. But the pieces are there. She applied for welfare the month that she and Marcus had their first big fight (one that landed her in the emergency room when she accidentally cut her own hand). She talked about wanting comfort at home ("I had to get my house together"). She talked about turning toward her children ("My kids really hadn't had nothing new"). She talked about being physically drained ("After a while, your body wear out—you need a break"). She said she didn't reject the notion of using her tax money to replace the lost car. She just didn't think of it. "I really wasn't thinking 'bout no car."

Angie had been losing jobs all her life. What happened next was new. She tried to get back on the welfare rolls in March 1998, just as Wisconsin completed its transition to W-2. A caseworker explained she could get a check. But first she had to sit through a self-esteem class. Then she would be assigned a community service job. The job would pay $673 a month, about half of what she could make in a nursing home even without a car. "Ain't nothing wrong with my damn self-esteem!" Angie said. The next day, she went back to Mercy Rehab and reclaimed her old job. Typically, when Angie tells the story, she supplies a negative spin, casting herself as a needy woman turned away. "They gave me a lot of yada, yada, yada. I said, 'Screw 'em,' and found me a job!" But that's mostly Angie's sardonic style. "They just did what they supposed to do," she said one day. "If they probably woulda gave me AFDC—who knows?—maybe I'd be on there, now."

Jewell became a steady worker, too—not with Angie's self-conscious pride, but simply because she had to. Her private safety net fell apart. Angie moved out, Lucky got fired, and Jewell was trying to put him out anyway. As stories of work identities go, Jewell's was disarmingly simple: when she had to work, she did. "It ain't like I had help no more," she said. "How the bills gonna get paid?" She tried a little more nursing home work, but old people continued to vex her. The want ads showed an opening at a large tool-making plant called G. B. Electric. As a "scanner," she worked the shipping line between the "pickers" and the "packers," making sure orders were properly filled. It didn't strike her as meaningful work, and it paid less than the Alzheimer's ward. But she showed up every day, and by the end of 1998 she had earned nearly $12,400. The average woman, in her second year off the Wisconsin rolls, earned about $8,100. Jewell was a sudden success.

Things grew even more complicated at home. Out of pity and

habit—and because she needed a babysitter—Jewell let Lucky back in the house. But she wouldn't let him back in her heart. Her life tumbled forward like a Nashville lyric: living with one man and loving his ex–best friend. Jewell felt so close to Ken that she sometimes pictured them as the same person: "He's the male version, I'm the female." But with Thigpen & Associates thriving, Ken's thoughts were on commerce, not love. "I wasn't in love with no woman—I was in love with the money," he said. "Jewell was like an escape for me." Ken's latest hire was a sixteen-year-old runaway. He brought her to Tina to learn the trade, then sent her to live with Jewell, explaining: "You know how to ho'. I want you to live with Jewell, so you'll know how to be a woman." Jewell took her in for a year. Around the same time, Ken gave Jewell a ring. He had it wrapped in paper and ribbons, and Jewell felt giddy as he guided it onto her hand. Opal made a big fuss and called it a "wedding ring." Jewell said it was just a "friendship ring" but hoped to be proven wrong.

Jewell had the ring, but Tina had the man—Ken lived with *her*—and neither wanted to share. As Jewell started her new job, she and Tina went to war. Jewell derided her as a hooker and an addict, but Tina was just as disdainful of Jewell for selling herself for $6.50 an hour. Over the phone, she called Jewell a "welfare recipient" and mocked her poverty. Jewell thanked her for whoring, laughing that through Ken she got a cut of the cash. When Jewell was hospitalized with bleeding ulcers, Tina woke her with a phone call at dawn to gloat about having Ken to herself. One of the rare times Jewell and Ken argued was after Jewell drove to Tina's and tried to beat her up. "Ain't nobody fittin' to jump on my whore, bruise up her face," Ken said. Through it all, Jewell continued to work. As inventories of work "barriers" go, Jewell had quite a list: a shortage of child care, chronic stomach pain, little work experience, and no high school diploma. And what category would Tina come under: "Hassles with Your Boyfriend's Hooker"? Maybe it helped that she didn't care about the substance of her job. Or maybe there wasn't much substance to care about; Jewell didn't think of her work as a "gift" to her fellow man, and with a teenage prostitute sleeping on her couch, it scarcely brought a storybook life to her kids. She wore her headphones, scanned her tools, and watched the clock. After six months as a temp worker, she got promoted to a regular job, with a raise to $7.50 an hour and a chance to buy into the health plan.

The turmoil around the house grew. Her hotheaded brother Robert shot at an undercover cop, sparking a two-week manhunt tracked on the local news. The police banged on Jewell's door with drawn guns, and helicopters circled her job. Robert got seven years, and Jewell took in his son, a happy-go-lucky three-year-old named Quinten. Jewell was barely scraping by herself, but she didn't hesitate. She said having three boys made her feel like the star of her own TV show. "*My Three Sons*—remember that?" she said. A few weeks later a new problem arose: a neighbor accused Lucky of rape. Lucky professed his innocence, and Jewell didn't know whom to believe. She also said, "I didn't really care." She had been trying to put Lucky out ever since she had let him back in, and the pending case of sexual assault (eventually dropped) was the final straw. The judge put him on house arrest, but that only caused Jewell new grief: it was her house. Now, he *couldn't* leave. It was the law.

Of the three old Jeffrey Manor friends, only Ken was free. One way he had avoided trouble was by refusing to set up a drug house; too many people come and go, and "that shit cause drama." But when a friend got arrested in the summer of 1998, Ken took over the lease. Business was lagging, and the house had a large client base. One day, Ken and Jewell made plans to hit the outlet mall. When she arrived at the crack house to meet him, Jewell's heart fell. Ken was in the back of a squad car, cuffed. The police had found a loaded rifle, a box of plastic bags, and about $400 worth of cocaine, some in the toilet and some in Ken's pocket. "Drama," just as he feared. Now Jewell's home life got *really* complicated. Awaiting trial, Ken was put on house arrest, too, but he didn't have a house. He couldn't keep staying with Tina: she had filed battery charges after one of their fights, so legally he was barred from her home. He couldn't go to Jewell's, either: even if he and Lucky weren't enemies, he figured you could only have one house arrest per house. For Jewell, that settled things: Lucky had to go. "Ooow, you making me *sick*," she told him. At ten and seven, Terrell and Tremmell cried and begged to go with him. Jewell felt awful, too; she knew that after six years he was the closest thing they had had to a father. But with Lucky finally out of the house, Ken was free to move in. And she had never wanted anything more.

Two years after leaving the welfare rolls, Jewell really did feel transformed—not by a job but by a gangster with dimples. She gave herself to Ken as she had never done before. She told him, "This is not just my house, it's *our* house: everything in here is *ours.*" She pledged "to keep everything honest" and "never lie." Straggling in at dawn, Ken woke her each morning to play video games. When she turned thirty, he made the weekend a rolling set of surprises: Friday, new coffee tables; Saturday, roses; Sunday, the cake. The family mostly sided with Lucky, and Angie grew especially caustic. "You ain't no good," she said, one night after too much beer. "I hope something bad happens to you!" *You hope something bad happens to me?* Angie's words got under Jewell's skin and festered there for years. Jewell had guilty feelings of her own. But that's different from having regrets.

One problem remained: possession of cocaine with intent to distribute. Ken had placed a bet he could beat it at trial, but he had already been convicted when he moved in with Jewell. With sentencing ahead, Jewell set her sights on probation. Ken figured he might draw a few months of work release. He felt confident enough to keep a hand in the business, even on house arrest. His first sentencing hearing was postponed, but something in the judge's tone left him spooked. He put $6,000 in the bank for Jewell and returned the next week, prepared for the worst. Jewell couldn't go with him; G. B. Electric was strict about missing days. She kissed him good-bye, borrowed his pager, and awaited the good news. It was night at the county jail when Ken was finally able to put through a call. "They gave me two years," he said.

ELEVEN

Opal's Hidden Addiction: Milwaukee, 1996–1998

One of the things I liked about Opal, the first few times we met, was her abundance of seeming candor. Stuck in a tedious job-search class in the presence of a reporter, most women on welfare would at least feign an earnest streak. They wouldn't saunter across the room, mock a practice job interview, and announce their delight in the dole. They wouldn't insist, as Opal did, "I *like* that welfare check!" She had the room roaring. We met in the summer of 1997, when Wisconsin's war on welfare was building to its peak. Jason Turner's first work program, Pay for Performance, had already cut Milwaukee's rolls by a third, with Angie and Jewell among the first to go. But it was an experiment grafted on to the old system, and in any given month it left more than half of the caseload untouched. Turner's new program—Wisconsin Works, or "W-2"—promised to extend the work rules to everyone: no work, no check, no exceptions. As the most ambitious of the new state programs, W-2 inspired lavish fears and praise, and with its rollout only weeks way, Milwaukee's welfare offices became an international media draw. Japanese television and *Le Monde* were on hand, and everyone was abuzz with sightings of "Maria!" (Shriver, that is) and the *Dateline NBC* crew.

The scene around Opal hardly conjured the words "Republican work program." Among the groups chosen to run W-2 was the Opportunities Industrialization Center, a social services agency with a black nationalist gloss and a talent for courting Tommy Thompson. Having agreed to run his first work program a decade before, when others had balked, OIC had banked his gratitude and a decade of subsequent contracts. With $57 million of W-2 money coming in, the group had renovated an abandoned theater on Martin Luther King Jr. Drive, where bow-tied Muslims glowered at the doors and recipients milled about, looking peevish and bored. I spent an hour in a room of corralled indigents, listening to a job counselor read from an almanac of occupations. It was social work as farce:

> *Mathematics:* reading graphs and stuff like that—it gets real deep when it comes to mathematics. . . . *Agriculture:* that thing with cows gets real deep—giving them those hormones? . . . *Social studies:* like socialization, only you studying it. . . . *Forestry:* why don't we see any more wolves? Somebody eating them?

As a showcase of private-sector efficiency, Opal's classroom was no more promising. One woman was eating chips for breakfast beneath the No Eating sign. Another was drunk. The instructor, Darlene Haines, was complaining to the class that she didn't feel qualified to teach. "It's kind of hard for me," she told the group. "They just kind of threw me into this." As she left the room, a chorus of operatic warnings rang out. "They're building orphanages and prisons!" the chip eater said. "It's going to be like Mississippi!" Haines returned with breaking news: Potawatomi Bingo would hire anyone who passed a drug test. Someone asked if marijuana was a drug. Things went downhill from there. "I can tell this isn't working," Haines sighed.

Needing a body for a practice interview, she called on a short, dark woman in the back wearing a look of boredom. Opal, inconspicuous until then, came forward with a mime of contempt. Head rolling, limbs flopping, she crossed the room in an arc of attitude and slouched into a chair. "I know how to *get* a job," she said. "I just don't know how to *keep* a job." Then as Haines launched into her role as the fictitious employer, Opal sprang to life. Her spine straightened. Her gaze locked in. "I am a courteous person," she began. "I am hardworking. I am dependable."

Haines looked startled. "What motivates you to work?" she asked.

"Being around smiling people," Opal said, smiling.

"What are your greatest achievements?"

"Well, I graduated from high school, and back in ninety-six, I completed a thirteen-week nurturing course."

"If I asked you, when could you start?"

"It would be next Monday, so I could arrange my babysitting situation."

"That won't be an issue?"

"No, I won't let it affect my job performance."

"*Girlfriend!*" the chip eater gasped. "And you said you wasn't motivated!"

Then Opal's limbs went limp. "I'm one of those women who don't *want* to work!" she said. Dragging herself back to her seat, she looked concerned that no one would believe her.

"The sister's gonna make it!" Haines said.

Opal, in fact, was working. Chased by the tightening rules, she had found a part-time job cleaning a hospital lab, and I joined her there the following night. Swabbing and scrubbing in a musical voice beneath posters of the digestive tract, Opal created a mood of easy intimacy. She didn't airbrush her wild adolescence ("I was out of control!"). She didn't disguise her motives for moving to town (welfare in Milwaukee "pays the most"). Her candor seemed the only aspect of her character she cared to defend. "I am an honest person!" she said. Though her formal education had stopped at a semester of community college, her account of welfare history could have been drawn from a grad-school text. AFDC was created in the 1930s for white widows, she said, "but with so many African American women on it" the politicians decided "it was just out of control." If the rolls were still predominantly white, "none of this W-2 would even be in effect."

In describing her streetwise past, Opal offered an unprompted aside. Lots of her friends had gotten high, but drugs had never tempted her. "Even though I fought and hung out with those people, I never did drugs," she said. When I visited her apartment, I noticed a sign that proclaimed it a "Drug-Free Zone." The man she introduced as her fiancé, Kenny Gross, was wearing a no-drugs pin. At that point, Opal had been smoking crack for seven years. And the drug was about to carve a destructive new path through her life.

"My Mama said I was bad since I was a baby," Opal was saying a few years later. We were driving around the South Side of Chicago on a survey of her youthful haunts: the projects where she had lived as a girl, the alleys where she had started to drink, the schools from which she had gotten expelled, the apartment where she had first smoked cocaine. Like her childhood, the trip began with the grim high rises of Stateway Gardens but passed through creditable working-class zones, and the accompanying narrative was equally eclectic, able to support multiple theories of her addiction. Opal began with biology. "I never knew my daddy, but he was a hard-core drug addict," she said. "Plus my Mama drank a lot, so I probably got it from both sides." One could add child psychology, wondering how much nurturing she got as the last of a young single mother's five kids. "It was like Viella raised us," Opal said of her oldest sister. In a later conversation, Kenny, her boyfriend, traced Opal's addiction to the murky realm of self-esteem: "Opal never thought she was attractive. She thought she was so dark." Mere proximity may have also played a role: she married a drug dealer. While the return to old streets and rebellions set her in high spirits—"Them was some *fun* days"—traces of loneliness showed. Three of her siblings had regular visits with their father, but Opal was left to speculate about hers, something she still did wistfully. He was so high the one time he came to visit, her mother wouldn't let her see him. "I always think, 'Would things be different if I had known my father?'"

One subject that doesn't arise in her childhood story is welfare: her mother was hardly on it. Half the time Opal was growing up, her mother worked two jobs. Like her cousin Hattie Mae, Ruthie Mae Caples was raised on the Eastland plantation, a granddaughter of Pie Eddie Caples, and she was still picking the Eastlands' cotton when she had her first child in her teens. After a detour to southern California, she joined the extended family in Chicago and found a job at a Zenith plant assembling TVs. Working her way out of the projects by the time Opal started school, Ruthie Mae settled at Fifty-ninth and Michigan—rough but not projects rough. That leaves Opal in that great class of troubled people often assumed to have been raised on welfare, who grew up with hardworking, single moms. "My Mama was at work *all* the time," Opal said.

Her siblings settled uneventfully into blue-collar lives. A brother made a navy career and another drove a truck. One sister worked as a medical clerk and the other in a bank. Yet "badness" acquired a power for Opal early on.

"I was just bad!"

"Man, we was bad!"

"We were some bad teenagers, boy."

"Bad as hell."

"Just *bad*!"

While Angie and Jewell saved their rebellions for adolescence, Opal got kicked out of sixth grade. "Running the halls, not going to my classes, talking back to the teachers . . . What didn't I do?" she said. She got caught spray painting a field house and trying to set it on fire. Corporal punishment didn't work; trips to Aunt Vidalia's brought the kind of rough-justice whippings honed in plantation days. The Jubilee CME Temple didn't work, either, though Opal liked singing in the choir. Trying to keep Opal out of trouble, her mother sent her to a public high school for girls. Opal got expelled in her sophomore year. In junior high school, she had started to drink—gin and juice, Wild Irish Rose, whatever she could find. "We used to get drunk and throw up all in the alley," Opal said. "Man, we used to trip!" She also found a protector. With a flashy wardrobe and a chassis for a chest, Robert Lee Johnson, her first boyfriend, made a fatherless girl feel safe. They stayed together throughout high school and married at City Hall two years after Opal's graduation, on her day off from Wendy's. Her mother wasn't there—she had to work—but she sponsored a reception shortly after, on Valentine's Day. Opal, at twenty-one, wore red and planned to stay with Robert Lee forever. For all her problems, Opal, unlike Angie and Jewell, entered adulthood with a diploma, a marriage, and a job.

Opal's mother got Robert Lee hired at Zenith, but third-shift work on an assembly line didn't hold his interest. One day he came home with what looked like a bag of soap chips. Crack was new to Chicago, and Opal was stunned to hear how much selling it would bring: $200 in an afternoon. "*Oowww*, we fittin' to have a *lot* of money!" she said. The ambience of the drug scene was ready-made for Opal's sense of adventure: the guns, the men, the scales, the cash, the pagers, the commotion. She and Robert Lee lived behind the Calumet Building, a high-rise filled with prospective clients, and Opal spent her nights on the back porch, drinking, watching the alleyway fights, and lending Robert Lee a hand. She had their first child at twenty-two, a girl they named Sierra. But that didn't slow them down, and neither did Robert Lee's arrests, one while Opal was still pregnant and another before Sierra turned one. With a single conviction for selling cocaine, he drew probation.

In Opal's tellings, the one letdown of married life was the discovery of Robert Lee's affairs. She was pregnant and visiting him in jail one day when she found a mysterious Tanya on his list. Stopping by McDonald's, she judged the cashier, Rene, too eager to slip him free food. Opal wasn't one to take betrayal passively. Slipping a suspicious key off his ring, she let herself into Rene's apartment and discovered Robert Lee in the living room, ironing his clothes. Opal found Rene and beat her up, and she swapped blows with Robert Lee, too, in knockdown, lamp-busting brawls. Opal doesn't scare easily, but at five foot eight, two hundred pounds, Robert Lee could scare her. Still, a decade after splitting up, she refused to get divorced. "I was in love with him," she said.

One thing that Opal couldn't understand was why people smoked cocaine. What could make them rob their families, neglect their kids, even sell their bodies to get it? "I saw how bad they looked and I said, 'Man, how could they do that?'" Robert Lee's brother had started smoking Primos, cigarettes laced with crack, and when Sierra was about a year old, he rolled one for Opal. She smoked it and felt nothing. She tried it again. "And you know what?" she said. "It didn't take no time at all to get hooked. But you don't *know* you're hooked." A few months later, Opal was pregnant with her second child and getting high constantly. "I used to think of all kinds of lies," she said, about why Robert Lee's drugs were missing. She said that his brother smoked them. Or a friend smoked them. Or she sold them and spent the money. One way to see Opal's theft of the drugs is as revenge for Robert Lee's affairs. (Enlisting his brother as a confederate gave her betrayal an incestuous edge.) Another is as pain relief: Opal had been medicating herself since her days of alleyway gin. When Robert Lee caught her rolling a Primo, she told him it was for a friend. "And he believed me!" she said. "Or he acted like he believed me—he was codependent."

But he wasn't blind. Opal smoked crack throughout the pregnancy, and shortly after the baby arrived, she burned through the rent money. Robert Lee sent her home to her mother, hoping that might set her straight. But "I was gonna do what I wanted to do, when I wanted to do it," Opal said. While the new baby, Kierra, was born free of cocaine, Opal grew so thin her relatives feared she had AIDS. Opal and Robert Lee reconciled, and soon she was pregnant again. So was Rene. Opal was back living with her mother when her third daughter, Tierra, was born in the spring of 1993. By then she was twenty-six years old, severely depressed, and she had been smoking crack for three years. That's when Jewell came home for a visit and happened to give a call.

The drug that captured Opal had ancient appeal—some cultures thought coca leaves a gift from the gods—but crack didn't make its American debut until the first half of the 1980s, appearing in Miami, Los Angeles, and New York, and exploding, by mid-decade, across the country. Crack is cocaine mixed with an additive, then cooked, cooled, and "cracked" into smokable pellets. Compared to powder, the champagne drug of the seventies, it had two advantages. Reaching the brain through the lungs, not the nose, it was much more efficient than snorting. It was also much cheaper. A gram of coke cost $100, but a crack vial could be bought for as little as $2.50. Suddenly, everyone could afford it. To say that crack makes you feel good hardly captures its appeal. People who smoke it resort to words like *euphoric* and *invincible,* describing a sensation that unites pleasure with power. "I felt I could handle anything, do anything," ran a women's magazine account. "Crack has you up and on the go," Opal said. "You on a *mission.*"

From the outside, the behavior of addicts defies explanation. In biochemical terms, the explanation is clear: the euphoria is a rush of dopamine, a neurotransmitter that tells the brain it is experiencing intense pleasure. Food and sex cause dopamine to surge, as do all drugs of abuse, from nicotine to heroin. Crack causes it to surge to mighty levels. It's a climax. A winning lottery ticket. The dunk that secures the championship ring. The problem is that the brain adjusts: it needs these new levels of dopamine just to feel normal and still more to feel high again. But chronic drug use actually causes it to get less. The body then inflicts a double whammy by activating a chemical, CRF, that suppresses the brain's sense of pleasure. With that, Mardi Gras is over, and the cops are on Bourbon Street swinging their sticks. Crashing, the crack addict grows paranoid, desperate for more dopamine. At the start, people smoke to get high, but over time they smoke to feel normal again. They smoke to "get straight."

As powerful as crack is, not everyone who tries it gets addicted. An addict develops a kind of brain disease, albeit one of her making. The drug hijacks the circuits that govern motivation and reorganizes them around the lone task of getting more crack. In the paradigmatic cocaine experiment, once a lab rat discovers that tapping a lever will deliver the drug, the tapping takes over her life. She doesn't eat, she doesn't sleep, she doesn't feed her young. She binges until she drops dead. While some people manage to stop on their own, most need the structured help a treatment program can provide. Even then about 80 percent relapse within a year, a figure that helps explain why public support for treatment programs is hard to sustain. For treatment to succeed, it literally has to change the brain.

Leaving a program, a drug user often feels a surge of well-being, a rush of health and competence for three to six months. But old cues can still trigger old cravings. Physical prompts, like a glimpse of a crack house, can do it. So can emotional ones: happiness, sadness, a song. Cues are so powerful that lab rats get a dopamine surge just by looking at their levers. When they relapse, addicts rarely relapse a little. They pick up where they left off. They binge, as if making up for lost time.

Two years after she got to Milwaukee, Opal got clean. Fleeing First Street after a four-day spree, she spent a few weeks in residential treatment before moving to the halfway house run by Pastor LeGrant. The preacher made three demands: get a job, pay the rent, and attend her storefront church. For all her earthly transgressions, Opal took pride in her spiritual roots—"I love sanctified churches"—and the

House of Faith made her feel at home. She was off to a good start in the Twelve Step world when a man at a recovery meeting captured her attention. He would have been hard to miss. If his purple pants didn't stand out, the spray of gold jewelry would. It was a look that said to Opal "sophisticated gentleman." Sitting beside her, Kenny Gross noticed Opal, too, noticed her short white shorts. Watching him eye her, another Twelve Stepper leaned over and warned, "Those shorts are going to get you in trouble." One rule of recovery, an emotionally fragile process, is to avoid the roller-coaster of romance for a year. And there was another reason for Opal to be wary. "He used to be one of the baddest pimps in Milwaukee!" her housemate said. But the image of Kenny in fur coats and feathered hats only piqued Opal's interest. As soon as she got an overnight pass, she took him to the Budgetel. "It was magic from then on," she said.

Kenny was a decade older than Opal and had been clean for three years. Still, even at thirty-eight, he radiated his old street vibes. He had a quick temper and a face that seemed angry even when he smiled, which wasn't often. He seldom kept a job for more than a few months, and with an aggressive sideline peddling rings and chains, he drew snickers from Opal's friends. Like Opal, he was raised by a working single mother, and like Opal he was drawn to the streets—nearly killing himself on a diet of heroin, coke, and pills. He got sober at the urging of a cousin dying of AIDS, and about sobriety he was deathly earnest. He wore his clean date on his NA medallion and defined his life's purpose as mentoring younger addicts. As Kenny once (inadvertently) put it, having once been a pimp, he was determined to become a "seductive member of society." Even at the Budgetel, all he wanted to talk about was The Program. "You on a *date,* nigger!" Opal said. "I don't wanna hear about no program!"

Opal was smitten. With the First Street family scattered about, she invited everyone to meet him at a sobriety picnic. Kenny arrived with a suit and Bible, offering temperance lectures. Lucky and Robert smuggled in beer and dubbed him "Preacher Man." Opal delivered an ultimatum: if Kenny wanted to keep seeing her, they had to move in together. Their first six months passed peacefully. He got a job as a short-order cook. She had welfare and some short-lived jobs. The girls came home from a stay at Jewell's—Sierra was six, Kierra, four, and

Tierra, two—and Opal enrolled in a nurturing program to improve her parenting skills. Kenny, seasoned at spotting cons, judged her to be sincere. "Her kids are her heart," he thought. They even talked of getting married someday.

Still, there were warning signs. Opal's rush toward romance was one, itself a form of addictive behavior. Her arrest for ripping off Target was another. One of the Twelve Steps requires people to take a "fearless moral inventory" of themselves, which is hard to do during a shoplifting scheme. Opal left the courtroom as her case was called—"I wasn't fittin' to admit I was guilty, even though I was"—which left her walking around with a warrant out for her arrest. Mindful of cues, Narcotics Anonymous tells addicts to avoid the "people, places, and things" they associate with getting high. But Opal wasn't about to avoid Angie and Jewell, even though there was usually a party nearby. She skipped NA meetings. She had a beer. Then, Kenny's special gold chain disappeared, the one with the abstinence medal. It took him a week to calm down, but when he did she told him what he already knew. She sold the chain, but not the medallion; no drug dealer wanted that. Opal's relapse, in the spring of 1996, occurred somewhere around the sixth month, toward the outer edge of what the statistics predict.

Kenny's sense of betrayal came in a double dose; his previous girlfriend had relapsed, too, and the last thing he wanted was another doomed affair. But he had slid back on his own first try. Hesitantly, he stayed, and Opal appeared to get clean, though he could never be sure. Kenny pushed her to get a job, and so for the first time did welfare. Opal made just enough effort to keep them both at bay. Jason Turner had just launched Pay for Performance, but by acknowledging her addiction, Opal managed to avoid a work assignment. Instead, she was sent to a brief outpatient program and told to look for a job on her own. It wouldn't have taken much of a sleuth to suspect she was stringing things along. In the logs she turned in over the next three months, she claimed she applied for 240 jobs, or about one every three hours, including six at the same Taco Bell, all without an offer. ("They don't check—come on.") Eventually she went back to the nurturing class and found a job at McDonald's, where she got fired for eating an apple pie and calling her boss "a fag." Someone at the nurturing program then helped her find the hospital job—with a path to full-time work at $10 an hour. However circuitous her path, Opal made her way into the best-paying job of her life.

She spent her first paycheck on crack. "I had been thinking about it a long time," she said. "I had wanted to do it so bad." Every addict's relapse is painful, but Opal's carried a special mix of guilt and defiance, since living with Kenny amounted to having a drug counselor at her side. Kenny's whole world was The Program—the nightly meetings, the sobriety club, the Twelve Steps as Ten Commandments. Kenny was drawn to the program's authority; Opal was programmed to defy it. "Why can't she just *get* it?" he would wonder. "Why don't you leave me?" she would say. She would binge. He would explode. She would cry and promise to quit. Despite himself, a part of him always believed her. He cheated on her; she caught him; they fought. When peace had been made, Opal would sometimes explain her thinking. "Opal looked at it like this," Kenny said. "If there's food, the rent's paid, kids took care of—she owed herself to get high." She told him—she told herself—she could handle it.

By the summer of 1997, Opal's brinksmanship with welfare was skating toward a new brink. She had slid past the JOBS program (with its weak penalties) and survived Pay for Performance (with luck), but the program the state was about to unveil, Wisconsin Works, called itself loophole free. The first thing that was radical about W-2 was its theory of "universal engagement": *everyone* was supposed to join in. The sick, the addicted, mothers with young kids—everyone was supposed to do something if they wanted a check. The second radical notion involved what they were supposed to do: work. Not just look for work or prepare for work, but spend at least part of the week in some sort of community service job. Most states avoided community service jobs, which were expensive, difficult to administer, and in the small-scale experiments of the past had shown a poor record of leading to private employment. In betting on them, Wisconsin hoped to achieve at least three things. One was diversion: forced to work for welfare, those with other options would leave. Another was acculturation: participants would learn the so-called soft skills, like grooming and punctuality. And a third was reciprocity: rather than getting something for nothing, the poor would give something back. The state promised to create the jobs by the tens of thousands.

If W-2 seemed unusually tough, it also seemed unusually generous. While the jobs would form the core of a "simulated workweek," they were supposed to be tailored to each recipient's needs. Other services could be layered on, like drug treatment or GED classes. And Wisconsin promised child care and health insurance, not only to families in W-2 but to a wider group of the working poor. Another distinctive element of W-2 lay in its administration: much of it would be privatized, with profit-seeking corporations invited to join nonprofits in submitting bids, in what the state called an effort to improve efficiency. Certainly there was much to worry about. Could everyone really work? Would the jobs prove useful, to recipients and society? Would the most vulnerable be driven from the rolls, like the miserable Amber Peck? Had the state gone too far in eliminating training—consigning people to a dead-end future of impossibly low wages? Still, by accompanying the rhetoric of work with the girders to support it—child care, health care, and the semblance of a last-resort job—Wisconsin's plan for "ending welfare" displayed a rare seriousness. To his credit, Thompson seemingly had created a program as big as his boasts.

And Opal seemed a good window through which to observe it. Though I didn't know she was using drugs as I watched her spoof the job-search class, I found her compellingly bilingual, fluent in the language of the streets and of the working-woman's world a notch above. With her disarming mix of intelligence and self-deprecation ("I *like* that welfare check"), she seemed just the kind of woman whose fortunes could swing either way. I included her in a preview of W-2 I wrote for *The New York Times Magazine*. Opal and the girls caught a bus downtown to a photo shoot, and a few weeks later a memorable cover appeared. In the back stood the serious, dark-suited men who had launched the welfare revolution, Tommy Thompson and Jason Turner. Across the front in pink shirts skipped Opal's girls, as if to a promising future. In the middle sat Opal, wearing a janitor's uniform, a finger wave from Jewell, and an enigmatic smile. Opal, of all people, was the W-2 poster child. "Has a job, but can she keep it?" the cover line asked.

TWELVE

Half a Safety Net: The United States, 1997–2003

As Opal swabbed hospital floors and slid back toward addiction, the new American safety net was appearing, one state at a time. Politically, the battle had been fought with glib slogans about trusting states over "arrogant federal bureaucrats." But the challenge at hand was immense. On one side stood 4.5 million poor single mothers with an unknowable mix of problems. Nine out of ten said they were jobless; nearly half had preschool kids; most got little (if any) help from their children's fathers; and about half lacked a high school diploma. Who could say how many like Opal were secretly smoking cocaine? On the other side were fifty state bureaucracies whose historical line of work had been limited to mailing them checks. They were operating in a politically charged atmosphere, with a low-paid, undertrained staff and substantial financial risks; if caseloads went up, they had billions to lose. The optimistic scenario was that states would undergo a vast "mission change," converting the old check-writing offices into job-placement machines. Federal law did allow another option: just kick people off the rolls.

Texas set some time limits as short as a year. Michigan set no time limits at all, pledging to use state funds for families who exhausted their federal aid. Oregon invested in casework, Rhode Island in child care. Mississippi placed its faith in the Lord, with Governor Kirk Fordice asking churches to pick up the charity load. "God, not government, will be the savior of welfare recipients," he said. While I started with doubts about state control, the effort brought much to admire. After decades in the check-writing trade, the average office was talking up jobs and however fumbling its ways—"that thing with cows, gets real deep"—moving people into them. Services expanded, especially child care, and for a surprising number of people, like Angie and Jewell, a small push or pull was all it took. At the same time, just as feared, many families got lost in the chaos—dropped from the rolls whether God proved their savior or not. And that's not to mention the bigger question framing the postwelfare years: how far would a low-wage job go in changing a poor family's life? Yet with caseloads plunging everywhere, the law had barely taken effect before it was crowned with claims of success. "The debate is over," Clinton said a year after signing the bill. "We know now that welfare reform works!" At that point, the average state program was about six months old. From the White House down, one trait most welfare abolishers shared was a weakness for their own PR.

For all its surface variety, the focus of the new system could be summarized in a word: work. The states pushed poor women to find it faster, keep it longer, and look for it as a condition of aid. Virtually every state regarded an entry-level job as preferable to the education and training efforts they had run in the past. And recipients who broke the rules risked big penalties, often the loss of all cash aid. Despite all the congressional talk of shoring up the two-parent family, no state made a serious attempt to reduce births to single mothers—a root cause of welfare but a socially charged one, and a problem to which there was no obvious solution. When word leaked that aides to New York City mayor Rudolph Giuliani planned "family-strengthening activities," the soon-to-be-divorced leader not only dropped the idea but publicly denounced it. Politicians like to do what they know how to do, and they more or less knew how to run job-search programs. From Harlem to Watts, waiting-room posters sounded a similar call: "Life works if you work first."

About three-quarters of the states made applicants do something before coming on the rolls, a process Jason Turner called "securing the front door." In some places, the requirement involved nothing more than sitting through a single orientation, though even that kept some people away. In New York City, where Turner became welfare commissioner, a required job search dragged on for four weeks, diverting about half of those who would have applied. With one missed day in a four-week program, a New York City applicant could be forced to start all over. One Harlem manager said the highlight of her career came the day she reopened the office as a "job center" that required applicants to complete a search for work. "Half the people said, '*Job center?* I didn't come for no job center!' This man said, 'No, no! *Ah-plee-ca-cion! Ah-plee-ca-cion!* No job, no job!'" She laughed so hard at the memory of her scattering clients she could barely finish the story. "I could not believe that those two little words—*job center*—could clear the area."

There's no doubt the hassles drove off people who had other ways to get by. But they also drove off people who needed help. The diversion effort in New York City involved not only the mandatory job search but aggressive attempts by front-line workers to verbally dissuade people from applying. In what a federal judge called a "culture of improper deterrence," many refused to even distribute applications during an aid-seeker's first visit to the office. "No matter how you phrase it," explained the newsletter of a Queens welfare office, "the goal . . . is the same: redirect the participant to another source." One consequence, in New York and beyond, was that eligible families stopped applying for other programs, such as Medicaid and food stamps, which were supposed to be part of the remaining safety net—at a cost of skipped meals and untreated disease. Nationwide, about two-thirds of the adults who left welfare lost Medicaid, even as the number of uninsured grew. Among children eligible for food stamps, the proportion of those who actually received them fell by about 20 percent. Scared, angry, or simply confused, all kinds of families stopped thinking of the welfare office as a place to get help.

For those who made it onto the rolls, states had to place a rising share in specified "work activities." A dozen activities qualified, from short-term training to sweeping the streets. By far the most common was the job-search class, which Riverside, California, among other sites, had shown the quickest and most cost-effective way of moving people off the rolls. Some classes left recipients to search on their own; others armed them with résumés, leads, and donated suits. Their quality ran from mediocre to downright awful. I once sat through a class in Riverside, California, at the peak of its job-placement fame. "Hopefully we can get you employed as soon as possible," the instructor began. "I shouldn't say hopefully. . . . I keep losing my train of thought." Down the hall, the recipients took upbeat, alliterative names—Kind Kathy, Willing Wanda, Dependable Dave. Then they gave themselves a round of applause and turned to a video that declared, "The employed lifestyle is better!"

There was no shortage of silliness involved. But among the early lessons was that that even silliness worked: requiring people to do *anything* was usually better than leaving them to do nothing. For Acerbic Angie or Jazzy Jewell, the hassle was a goad to make better plans. For some others, any activity offered a respite from lives stunted by terrible isolation. In Milwaukee, I spent two weeks at the YWCA's "Academy of Excellence," where one woman was so timid as it began she could barely speak her name. Another flamboyantly announced, "Ain't no such thing as bad sex, y'all!" then fled in tears when the talk turned to violent boyfriends. A certain esprit did evolve, even in such a care-worn group. The women wore mortarboards at their graduation, and some brought their kids to watch them collect the only diploma they might get.

While job-search class might not seem tough, the penalties for skipping it were. In nearly three-quarters of the states, recipients who missed an assignment could lose their whole check, a penalty known as a "full-family sanction." As a weapon of welfare reduction, time limits got much more attention, in part because the concept was easier to understand. But sanctions had a much bigger effect. By 1999, sanctions had eliminated a half-million families from the rolls—about six times the number cut off by time limits. Because of sanctions, between a quarter and a half of those enrolled in the typical program wound up losing all or part of their check.

At times, the tough penalties were all for the best. In Oregon I met a methamphetamine addict who said losing her check helped save her life. "That was part of the reason I went into treatment," Lori Furlow said. With weaker sanctions, New York found it harder to persuade troubled clients to get help. About a third of New York City's huge caseload was in the penalty process at any given time, and officials there griped about the "happily sanctioned"; able to ignore the work rules and still collect three-quarters of their cash and food stamps, some people did just that. But if weak penalties hurt some clients, so did strong ones—that's the dilemma of sanction policy. The goal should be to lure people in, not to drive them away. There was so much confusion in the system, however, many people who lost their checks didn't even know what they were supposed to be doing. Taking an in-depth look at one hundred sanctioned families, Utah found that about half had problems their caseworkers hadn't realized: illnesses, chronically sick kids, boyfriends who beat them if they left the house. "We were sanctioning people we shouldn't have been sanctioning," said Bill Biggs, the official in charge. It's natural to think that the plunging rolls followed a rational order, starting with the easy cases and proceeding to the hard ones. In truth, the process of "ending welfare" played out like a freak storm, hitting here and missing there. The sick, the addicted, the depressed and confused—all joined the employable and the secretly employed in a mass flight from the rolls.

For those unwilling or unable to hold jobs, the rules could be unforgiving. But the new system also brought needy workers new support, with child care, tax credits, and health insurance among the main examples. Overall spending on poor families *grew* in the postwelfare years, even as its focus shifted from nonworkers to the working poor. The expansion of the earned income tax credit is the obvious case in point. By the end of the decade, it offered workers up to $3,900 a year, a sum that went far in smoothing the transition from the rolls. For a typical woman leaving welfare, that turned a job that paid $6.50 an hour into one worth $8.35. Sixteen states, including Wisconsin, layered their own credits on top of the federal one. Not coincidentally, two days before he signed the welfare bill, Clinton also signed a law that raised the minimum wage (to a still-paltry $5.15)—another nod toward the notion that "people who work, shouldn't be poor."

There were other supports for new workers. The number of children in subsidized child care doubled in just three years. By the end of the decade, thirty-three states spent more on child care than they did on welfare checks. Although there were no formal guarantees, in practice everyone leaving welfare for work qualified for at least a year. In addition, all states expanded child-care programs for the broader population of low-income workers (not just those on the welfare rolls). In some states, the programs were modest and waiting lists long. Still, in general, child-care shortages kept fewer people from working than initially feared. Nearly all states loosened the asset rules that had made it hard for recipients to own reliable cars; some helped workers buy them. Nearly every state let recipients who found jobs keep more of their welfare checks during a transition (through something called an "earnings disregard"). The states also got much better at collecting child support, more than doubling the percentage of the cases in which the absent fathers paid. Even then, only about half the women leaving the rolls collected anything, but those who did averaged about $2,000 a year.

The health insurance story was less encouraging. Despite Clinton's hopes of a medical safety net, as Angie left welfare in 1996 about *half* the women streaming off the rolls wound up uninsured, as did nearly 30 percent of their kids. Medicaid's tight eligibility rules were part of the problem, but so was the unwelcoming bureaucracy; many families didn't get enrolled even when they qualified. In 1997, Congress took a step in the right direction by creating the State Children's Health Insurance Program, which spends about $4 billion a year to insure the children of needy workers. By the end of the decade, most states covered children up to twice the poverty line, meaning a family of three stayed eligible as its income approached $28,000. But adults remained out of luck, typically losing their Medicaid eligibility before their earnings reached $10,000. Even at the end of the decade, 37 percent of the adults leaving welfare had no health insurance. It's unconscionable that by staying on welfare, Opal could see a doctor for free while Angie and Jewell each lost coverage and went without needed care.

Nonetheless, despite its holes, the rise of a "work-based safety net" did ease the transition off welfare. A study by David Ellwood makes the point: in the mid-1980s, a typical mother of two leaving welfare for a minimum-wage job would have come out just $2,000 ahead, even with only modest work expenses, and the whole family would have lost health insurance. By the late 1990s, that same woman would have gained $7,000 and her kids could get Medicaid. As welfare (greatly) increased its hassles, work (modestly) increased its rewards.

What happened next astonished everyone. The welfare rolls collapsed. They collapsed in Boston and they collapsed in Phoenix. They collapsed in New York City. They fell fastest in states like Wisconsin and Florida, which made aggressive moves. But they also gave way in Texas and Illinois, which showed little bureaucratic zeal. They plunged where the economy boomed, and they plunged in stretches of the poverty belt, from New Mexico to West Virginia. Historically, the rolls had never fallen more than 8 percent in a year. By the time they leveled off in 2001, they had fallen for seven straight years by a total of 63 percent. Seven states cut the rolls by more than three-quarters. In Wisconsin, a half-dozen counties at some point in the year had a W-2 caseload of *zero*. Three million families—more than 9 million people—left the rolls nationwide.

Explaining what caused the rolls to vanish is harder than it seems. Certainly, the economy helped. Nationally, the unemployment rate fell to 4.0 percent, its lowest level in thirty years. Shorthanded employers who would have once shunned recipients all but begged them to apply. But previous booms hadn't cut the rolls. And the correlation between caseloads and state unemployment is faint at best. One study found that states with more unemployment had *greater* caseload declines, perhaps because they passed tougher laws. The tax-credit expansion also helped reduce welfare: the more work pays, the more people work. But the District of Columbia, with one of the largest local credits, had some of the smallest caseload declines. The auspicious economics surround the story like good weather—necessary, perhaps, for cutting the rolls but not sufficient.

Two prominent economists with contrasting politics—Rebecca M. Blank and June E. O'Neill—separately estimated that policy changes did three times as much to cut the rolls as the economy did. But which policy changes? In general, the places with the toughest sanctions had the steepest declines. But sanctions were tough in Tennessee, moderate in Oregon, and weak in Arkansas, and each cut its rolls similarly. Time limits may have encouraged families to leave welfare and bank their remaining time. But the rolls fell more in Michigan, with no time limits, than in Texas, Virginia, and Connecticut, with short ones. In general, the rolls fell faster under Republicans than Democrats. But they fell nearly as much in two of the most liberal states (California and Vermont) as they did in two conservative ones (Arizona and Tennessee).

Clearly something happened that neither economics nor policy fully explains. Rebecca Blank found that *half* of the caseload declines came from something her model couldn't detect. Part of what the era brought was a sudden cultural change, what social scientists sometimes call "message effects." From the TV news to waiting-room posters came the same strident message: "Get off the rolls!" In Creek County, Oklahoma, the rolls fell 30 percent even as the legislature was still debating the law, a decline officials largely attributed to the mere rumors of what was coming. In its mysteriously powerful convergence of events, the late 1990s can be thought of as a bookend to the 1960s. One era, branding welfare a right, sent the rolls to sudden highs; the other, deeming welfare wrong, shrank them equally fast.

The unexpected declines brought unintended effects. White families left welfare faster than blacks, and blacks left faster than Hispanics, who consequently composed a growing share of the rolls. The notion that most recipients are white, long misleading, grew plainly untrue. By the end of the decade, blacks and Hispanics outnumbered whites by a ratio of two to one. (The rolls were 39 percent black, 25 percent Hispanic, and 31 percent white.) As race changed, so did place: the caseload grew even more concentrated in big cities. In Wisconsin, where the trend was extreme, 85 percent of recipients lived in Milwaukee. Welfare, that is, increasingly became what most voters already assumed—a program for urban minorities.

At the same time, falling caseloads brought one problem that states welcomed: it left them rolling in dough. States literally had more money than they knew how to spend. The irony here should not be missed. The authors of the law set out to slash welfare budgets. Instead, by freezing federal payments at historic highs while caseloads fell, ardent conservatives achieved something that even liberals hadn't dared to propose: a huge rise in per capita welfare spending. Over six years, states collected $59 billion more than they could have under the previous system, when falling caseloads brought reduced federal dollars. By 1998, Wisconsin collected $22,000 for every family left on the rolls. Having promised to do more with less, the governors wound up with more—much more—than anyone had imagined.

Antipoverty windfalls are unheard of. Since the money came with few constraints, states had nearly unlimited reach to improve poor people's lives—not just those on the rolls but the broader working poor. They could have subsidized rents for needy workers or supplemented their wages. They could have helped entry-level workers like Angie and Jewell train for better jobs. The great expansion of child care largely stemmed from the welfare windfall. But in a perfectly legal maneuver, states also used billions just to sustain programs they had previously financed themselves. That freed funds for other uses but did nothing for the poor. Roads got paved, bridges painted, and taxes cut—all on the federal welfare nickel. In the first few years alone, New York diverted $1 billion into budget swaps. Wisconsin channeled $100 million into a property-tax cut. Most states tried to mask such schemes, but Minnesota spelled it out in the budget: "Replace state spending with federal dollars." In some states, huge sums simply gathered dust as officials bickered or dithered. Two years into the new welfare age, Wyoming had failed to spend 91 percent of its federal money. In New Mexico, the nation's poorest state, a third of the federal money went unspent as a defiant Republican governor, Gary E. Johnson, refused to implement a plan passed by Democratic legislators. He relented only after the state supreme court found him in contempt. But by then, he had already cut the rolls in half, mostly through eligibility cuts. With nearly $70 million of its welfare money unspent, New Mexico still had no job-placement agencies in counties where unemployment ran as high as 33 percent.

"What about Mississippi?" the skeptics had asked, when Congress insisted it could trust the states. Early in the new welfare age, I made a trip to the Delta, where Mack Caples, on the far side of eighty, still puttered in the Eastland fields. Nearby, things were proceeding about as feared: unemployment rates hit double digits for two hundred miles around, but the state was still purging the rolls. In Washington

County, where caseloads had fallen more than 30 percent, twice as many families had been sanctioned off the rolls as placed in jobs. Most of the jobs that did exist were distant or unappealing. The de facto capital of the Delta is Greenville, where twenty-seven recipients had moved from welfare to work in the month before I arrived. Of them, ten were packed off to a catfish plant an hour away. They left town at dawn on a company bus and spent their days severing fish heads in a jungle of conveyor belts and saws. The job paid the minimum wage, and annual turnover ran 300 percent. "You work in the cold, you work in the wet—and of course you're around guts," the manager, Donald Taylor, observed pleasantly. He praised the state for barring aid to anyone who quit. "If they can go back to Uncle Sam, you can't keep them in the plant."

A few years later, a study in the *American Journal of Political Science* tried to quantify the factors that shape state policy. The most important was race: the more blacks on the rolls, the tougher a state chose to be. That would come as no surprise in Mississippi, where Governor Fordice wore a tie with a Confederate flag to a meeting on minority set-asides. The racial rub was obvious in the Delta, where with few exceptions employers were white and welfare families black. Lured by a state subsidy, Kevin Cunningham, a gregarious Greenville insurance agent, hired a receptionist off the rolls. She was a well-spoken woman who played piano at her church, but he worried her friends might decide, "She knows where the cash drawer is." He warned her, as she started work, that "business language isn't Ebonics."

Hard luck stories were everywhere. Patricia Watson quit the catfish plant after coming home from work to find her six-year-old daughter missing and her teenage babysitter not even aware that the child was gone; for quitting, Watson was barred from all state aid. Curley Barron had rescued her nephews from foster care and was raising them with the help of a welfare check. But she gave them back when the state ordered her to stop caring for her disabled mother and join a work program. "It doesn't make any sense," she said. "The kids were a ward of the state—they weren't mine." Even by Delta standards, things were rough in Glendora, which made a cameo appearance in civil rights history as the place where Emmett Till was beaten before being dumped in the Tallahatchie River. All but three of its eighty-eight households had once gotten public aid. After being dropped from the rolls, a mother of four named Carrie Ann Bridges took a night job at a poultry plant seventy miles away. Coming home after midnight, she fell asleep and drove into a ditch, killing herself and her aunt.

The Delta would challenge any welfare plan. Two time zones away, Oregon presented a contrasting view of state autonomy. Of all the states, it probably worked hardest to help women like Opal, the so-called hard to serve. In Oregon City, a blue-collar suburb of Portland, caseworkers gave them a different name—"drawer people"—since under the old system, that's where their files had resided. With the rolls already cut in half, about three-quarters of those left on welfare had mental health problems. Half acknowledged drug or alcohol abuse, and 30 percent had criminal histories. Of the sixteen recipients I met in Oregon, eleven described incidents of childhood sexual abuse, a problem that gets no attention in the welfare literature but correlates with any number of problems that make it hard to keep a job. Women who were molested as children are more likely to abuse alcohol or drugs, suffer from depression, or become victims of domestic violence. In my conversations with welfare recipients over the years, talk of childhood molestation has arisen with eerie regularity. "I don't call it anything special," one Oregon woman told me, "because it seems like it happens to everybody."

While Oregon, like most places, pushed recipients to take entry-level jobs, it also offered a long list of services for those who didn't soon get one. With the caseload 80 percent white, it was the rare state where welfare hadn't figured in politics, and state spending was unusually high. Caseworkers could send addicts to treatment or depressed women to mental health clinics. They had job-placement counselors fluent in Russian and Vietnamese. Oregon made a special commitment to drug treatment, financing a residential program with a tax on beer and wine. Oregon had its problems, too. A system that emphasizes caseworkers' discretion rises and falls on their talents, which even in Oregon were often mediocre. Some applicants were just too troubled to find their way on the rolls, especially since they had to do a month of job search first. I met an indigent mother who was turned away even though her boyfriend had just beaten her, her landlord was evicting her, and she was scheduled for major surgery. She was told she couldn't get a check until she spent a month looking for a job.

Nevertheless, up and down the I-5 corridor, it was possible to glimpse what conscientious casework could achieve. There were few better examples than that of Rita Davis, who launched an earnest, vexed search for work after her husband left her. Sexually abused by her father in her teens, she had spent her adult life struggling with anxiety. She read at the seventh-grade level. And she weighed 325 pounds, one reason she was sent away jobless by a dozen temp agencies. Unremittingly earnest, she struggled to tell her story through deep, steadying breaths. "I'd call up on the phone and they'd say, 'Oh, you sound like the perfect person,'" she said. "Then they take one look at me and they blow it off." After months of rejection, she met a caseworker who spotted her hidden talent for numbers and persuaded an accounting agency to give her a job, with the state temporarily subsidizing her wage. That's when a new problem arose. Body odor. "I don't know what it is," Davis said. "I take a shower every day." Her doctor didn't know either. Her boss called the welfare office and complained that it was driving clients away. The caseworker rushed over with two sacks of deodorant and shampoo, and Davis experimented until something worked. Soon she won a promotion, from receptionist to bookkeeper. Poor, obese, abandoned, and abused, she had been relegated to a kind of nonexistence until—of all things—a welfare program came to her rescue. "I love this job," she said. "Somebody is able to look past my size and see me."

What happened with Rita Davis wasn't unique; every program, even Mississippi's, produced some inspired casework. In the new welfare age, someone really looking for help was much more likely to find it. Yet for all the talk about work requirements, the system harbored a strange little secret: many of the people left on the rolls weren't doing very much. The thought is sufficiently counterintuitive that it bears some explanation. After all, the new system was constantly called tough, and compared to the old one it was. But it was toughest in the application stage and during the first few months, when recipients risked losing their checks if they skipped the ubiquitous job-search class. After that, they could still be kicked off for failing to complete an assignment. But many people didn't have assignments, at least not consistent ones. When job-search class didn't lead to a job, it often led nowhere at all.

Seemingly the law prohibited this, by requiring states to place half their recipients in work activities. But the "caseload-reduction credit"—those frequent flier points for bureaucrats—cut the rate, point for point, for virtually every downtick in the rolls. By 2002, the rolls had fallen so far (60 percent) that twenty states could meet the work rate without putting a single recipient to work. Only ten states had to meet a work goal of 10 percent or more. In other words, to comply with the law, most states had to do . . . nothing.

Just how much they actually did became a topic of sharp dispute. Federal reports showed that in 2002 states enrolled a third of their caseload in eligible work activities. But the majority were recipients with regular jobs who collected some transitional welfare under the loosened earnings rules. Of the remaining caseload—in a sense, the core caseload—only 15 percent were participating in eligible welfare-to-work activities. Yet because of the caseload-reduction credit, every state met its participation requirement every year. The states argue that the federal numbers are misleading because they omit activities—like drug treatment or part-time work—that don't count toward the official rates. The states did their own survey and reported that 61 percent of recipients had some sort of assignment. But if there was underreporting in the federal numbers, there was overreporting, too; not everyone on the roster of a job-search class was actually looking for a job. In an odd inversion of welfare politics, the conservatives who had pushed the states-rights revolution began accusing the states of laxness, while liberals, fearful of onerous new rules, defended the states' judgment and skill. The truth is that no one really knows how much the average recipient was doing. But if my own travels were any indication, the answer was often "not much."

Why? Certainly the states had the funds. But keeping recipients productively engaged is hard work—much harder than it sounds. It's not as if women like Opal were lining up for help. You had to motivate people who didn't want to be motivated. You had to tailor programs to daunting needs. You had to penalize those who failed to comply, promptly and fairly. And you had to do it with a staff that was typically low-paid and poorly trained. Every state did some of this hard, creative work, more than in the past. But few sustained it on a wide scale. Nor did they have to. The mixture of hassle and help they offered was enough to cut the rolls. And cutting the rolls brought the sheen of success. It's easy to make a churlish complaint about people getting something for nothing. But the real concern is for the recipients themselves: hundreds of thousands of the most troubled families were left to idle on the rolls. That's especially worrisome in an age of time limits, when after five years, or in some places less, they could just be given the boot. With a booming economy, piles of cash, and vanishing caseloads, states had an unprecedented chance to help those left behind. What they managed to construct was at best half a safety net.

THIRTEEN

W-2 Buys the Crack: Milwaukee, 1998

Opal blew it. And in her case so did W-2. Having starred on the cover of *The New York Times Magazine,* she was fired by the time the issue hit the stands. It's not clear whether a binge caused the firing, but the firing, in the summer of 1997, gave way to more binges. "I *wanted* to go get high—I did," she said. "I was so scared to come home and face Kenny that I stayed gone for a day and a half." When she got back, Kenny said the police had taken the kids—though really he had left them with Jewell—and as Opal tried to leave for the police station, they started to fight. Kenny had his own demons raging. He demanded that Opal take him to confront the drug dealer, a stunt that could get someone shot. A few weeks later, she binged again. This time Kenny just acted hurt. "If you love me and the kids, why would you do that?" he asked. It was a question with no rational answer, only a chemical one.

Opal had lost lots of jobs, but none as promising as the one cleaning the hospital lab, with its path to a double-digit wage. In a three-page letter to her boss's boss, she pleaded for another chance. "I really, truly love my jobs," she wrote. "The choices I make now will be positive and aim at proving to myself and others that I am a strong bla"—she crossed out "black"—"woman who've had ups and downs in my life and is willing to live my Life to the fullest." The hospital manager didn't bother to read it. The timing seemed ominous. She was fired a month before the launch of W-2; in theory, cash welfare was finished. The only way anyone could get a check now was by working a community-service job, an option that Opal had ruled out. ("I don't work for free!") Opal had outlasted Angie and Jewell, but even she felt certain that her luck had come to an end. "I know I won't get no more cash from them."

Then she did. Opal's caseworker at the Opportunities Industrialization Center was Darlene Haines, the same woman Opal had dazzled in class with her spoof of the job interview. Haines was a blustery, gold-toothed woman with a hard-luck past, quick to boast of her savvy. "I don't play when it comes to gettin' people jobs," she said. Some of her clients called her a "hood rat," a ghetto woman putting on airs. But Opal liked her. Haines kept the cover of *The New York Times Magazine* on her wall—she was in the picture, too—and the sight of Opal posed with the governor made other clients gripe. "She's out there doing drugs," one said. With a few calls, Haines discovered that Opal's problems included a warrant for her arrest. Soon after, Opal showed up at OIC with an agitated look and a notice saying her benefits were slated to end. Haines took her into a private room. "They're goin' round saying you're using," she said. "They *who*?" Opal answered. Then she began to cry and admitted that she had been smoking cocaine.

This, in W-2 theory, was the perfect exchange. Among Jason Turner's complaints about the old welfare system was that it let recipients hide their real problems. He had talked of "thrusting them into the public square," where their needs could be addressed. With her tearful confession, Opal was accordingly thrust. But from there, theory and practice diverged in the hands of Darlene Haines. W-2 pictured addicts like Opal combining a community-service job with a drug-treatment program. Instead, Haines did the one thing the program expressly forbid: she simply sent Opal a check. She said she feared that if she cut Opal off, the kids would suffer. ("Women she likes, she gives them money," one of her coworkers complained.) A few months later, Haines herself was gone from OIC. She went on to jobs at rival agencies, Goodwill and Maximus, until her conviction for check forgery; she had a temp job at a bank where she altered a check and tried to cash it as though it was made out to her. Then Haines moved to the other side of the desk, as a W-2 client herself.

I saw Opal a few days after her encounter with Haines. Family life was in a fragile state. She was drinking beer and chain-smoking Newports, and she said she had been reading the Bible to ward off the urge to get high. With Opal spending her money on drugs, Kenny had pawned his jewelry to pay the rent, and the power company had shut off the lights. Despite her binges and depression, Opal had found a job in a factory that made diaper wipes—something she hadn't told Haines—and along with welfare she had an unemployment check: she was *triple*-dipping. "Drug addicts are some of the smartest people in the world," she said, more in sadness more than in pride. "'Cause we're able—I'm not gonna say me—to manipulate, to get whatever they want."

Two months later, when I saw her in January 1998, Opal was a different person. "I'm in better spirits—can you tell?" she said. She said she had stopped getting high. Kenny had given her a special Christmas present, a green Tommy Hilfiger coat, and she wore it with schoolgirl pride. Sierra, Kierra, and Tierra seemed better, too. Unprompted by Opal, they sat down to dinner and launched into a prayer. To make it to the factory, Opal had to get up at 5:00 a.m. and catch two buses across town. But she talked about packaging diaper wipes as though she'd found her calling. By now she had reported the job, so her W-2 benefits were about to end: her next check would be her last. She had just gone to H&R Block, and with a big check for tax credits coming, she had plans to refurnish the apartment. Opal, the unlikely poster child for welfare reform, was sounding like one. "Now I *have* to work," she said. "I'm better off."

Opal quit two weeks later, on her thirty-first birthday. With $4,000 of tax money in hand, a sunrise bus to an assembly line plant no longer held its allure. She decorated the apartment just as she had planned, with a green-striped sofa, matching love seats, and a new dining room set. It all wound up in the drug dealers' hands, with everything she owned. The most remarkable thing about Opal's collapse was its sheer velocity. It took about thirty days.

The first thing Kenny noticed was the air freshener. Then Opal started to chain-smoke again. They were supposed to be living in a drug-free building—the manager could demand a urine test—but there were people getting high on every floor. A neighbor had a drug-dealing son, so Opal no longer had to catch the bus to see Andrea, the crack-house proprietor she had met in jail. She could buy drugs down the hall. Kenny realized Opal had stopped wearing the Tommy Hilfiger coat. She told him she had lent it to Jewell, but he saw it on the drug dealer's back. "I was gonna *kill* him, not just shoot him," he said. "Not over the coat, over the fact that he was killing her and wouldn't care." A few weeks after Opal quit her job, Kenny went to Chicago for a sobriety convention and came home a few hours early. He found Opal as he'd never seen her, on the bed unable to speak. She had sold a television and a VCR and had another wrapped up to go. "She was looking crazy—it was like the devil," he said. Opal was so high, she later said, she felt like she was having an out-of-body experience, like she was watching a stranger's dream. She could hear Kenny storming around, demanding to know where she had sold their stuff. High as she was, she knew better than to say. Someone could get killed.

Though Kenny had five sober years behind him, no one's recovery is secure; if The Program had taught him anything, it should have taught him that. Having once put women on the street, he now found himself babysitting for a woman on the lam. He lost his job, which was nothing new. But blaming Opal was a more alarming sign, since it violated the ethic of personal responsibility at The Program's core. Out of work, out of money, and low on self-respect, Kenny walked into a liquor store and bought a miniature Courvoisier. It was his signature drink in his days as a pimp, and just staring at it made him stir. He could smell it. And taste it. He could feel its glow. The liquor store was next to a music shop, and Kenny used the rest of his money to buy a Gospel tape. He put the bottle on his dash and sat in the lot, letting the music play. *Should I?* he asked.

Most addicts who buy a bottle find a way to say yes. Kenny's first effort at sobriety had ended that way: six months clean, one sneaked drink, and he was back on the streets. In subsequent years, his counselors had urged him to answer temptation with a mental image. See the big picture beyond the small bottle, "Get something up under your feet." In the big picture, he wasn't homeless anymore. He wasn't stealing to get high. In the big picture, young guys trying to get sober looked up to him. Kenny stared down the bottle and delivered his verdict aloud: "I got a lot of people who depend on me, and I love myself today. So this is not the way out." When he went home shaken and told Opal what had happened, she drank the Courvoisier.

Kenny moved out a few weeks later, in the middle of March. "I looked at the Opal I met in the program, and she wasn't that Opal anymore," he said. "She chose drugs over me." With Kenny gone, Opal had no brakes at all. "Now I can just get high whenever I want," she figured. She wanted to every day. The next month passed in a blur. She got three bags of dope for the microwave and four for the end tables. She sold her jewelry, her clothes, her food stamps. With nothing to eat, she bummed milk from the neighbors for the girls. One day, she failed to pick them up from the day-care center that kept them after school. "I didn't forget—I was just high," she said. The center gave them to Kenny's mother, and Opal stayed gone two days. The girls started wetting their beds, and a social worker took them aside and asked if their mother used drugs. Sierra, at eight, knew enough to lie. But Kierra, six, felt trapped. "I don't think I want to tell you that," she said.

By the spring of 1998, as Opal hit the skids, the state's rolls had fallen about 85 percent. Whatever its shortcomings, the system had proved skilled at one thing: diverting people who were basically able into entry-level jobs. Opal, crazed with cocaine, posed a challenge of a different order. Everyone had known such cases existed, and W-2 had ambitiously promised them an individualized plan, one that combined a workfare job with services like drug treatment. Enthusiasts thought the rigor of work would itself have therapeutic value. Others feared the inordinate demands would drive the hardest cases away. What happened with Opal was a scenario neither side envisioned. First, W-2 ignored Opal's collapse. Then it abetted it.

As Opal started coming unglued, she called OIC to get back on the rolls. Darlene Haines was gone, and a new caseworker, Opal's third in a year, knew nothing of her addiction—though she would have had she looked in the computer. She told Opal not to bother coming in: just go look for a job. Instead, Opal spent the next few weeks selling off her possessions, until she grew so desperate she called back and confessed she was using drugs. On paper, what happened next went according to plan. The agency gave Opal an assignment that combined treatment with a community service job. But then it just forgot her. Special cases were supposed to be monitored by specialized workers; Opal's case wasn't monitored by anyone. It was assigned to a worker in a different department, Sonya Gordon, who waited two months just to schedule their first meeting. Opal fell into a bureaucratic black hole.

Looking to do just enough to reclaim her check, Opal showed up at the treatment program. But she mostly skipped the job, with a nonprofit agency that put people with disabilities to work at light assembly tasks. Treatment was a low-budget affair without urine tests, and she continued to get high every day. With no one at OIC handling her case, no one sent her a check. The treatment program ended. Out of food and facing eviction, Opal started calling OIC three times a day. But she couldn't even leave a message; her caseworker's voice mail was full. She couldn't reach a supervisor, either. OIC had a $57 million contract and about half the cases it had budgeted for. You'd think someone could answer the phones. (I once called an OIC worker and got a voice mail that advised, "Try to call only once a week.") Finally Opal just walked in, asking to talk to someone. Had a caseworker ever gone to her home, she could have seen all she needed to see: no food, no furniture, three frightened kids. Had the receptionist even looked in the file, she would have known that the thin, disheveled woman seeking help was a mother on drugs. Instead, she said the office didn't see walk-ins. She told her to make an appointment.

Sunday was Mother's Day. Opal and Jewell usually spent it together, but this year Opal didn't show. Jewell stopped by on Monday after work, and when Opal wouldn't answer the door, she waited outside, figuring Opal would come out soon to get the girls from day care. Opal emerged looking wild-eyed and wasted, and Jewell walked her to the day-care center. The girls looked terrible, too: hair uncombed, clothes askew. Back at the apartment, Jewell was shocked to discover that all the furniture was gone. She knew that Opal had been smoking Primos, but she had no idea things had gotten so bad. Jewell was furious: "How could you do this to the kids?"

"Fuck you, bitch!" Opal screamed.

"Fuck *you,* bitch," Jewell said.

Just then, Kenny pulled up. Though he had moved out two months earlier, he still came by every week or so to drop off cigarettes or milk. He hadn't gone back in the building, so he, too, didn't know she had sold everything. He arrived just in time to hear Opal telling Jewell that their days as cousins were through. Jewell went home, called Opal's mother, and told her to come get her grandchildren right away. Kenny gave Opal the news. "It's over," he said. "You don't have nothing left to sell but your body, if you haven't already started doing it." Opal put up a fight, but she knew she'd been beaten. She couldn't face her mother like that. She hated Kenny. She hated Jewell. "I should kill myself," she said. Kenny didn't take her seriously, but he didn't take any chances. He bought her a beer, made her drink half, and doused her with the rest. Once she smelled sufficiently drunk, he drove her to detox, one place he trusted to keep her safe. Her mother rushed up from Chicago for the kids, and Opal cried herself to sleep, a ward in a ward.

Detox was just an overnight solution; Opal had no place to go after that. The shelters were full, Medicaid wouldn't cover another residential program, and at forty, Kenny still lived with his mother; he couldn't take her there. He picked her up, cast in his conflicting roles—ex-lover, accuser, counselor, best friend—and they drove around so broke he had to stop by a friend's to bum gas money. They wound up at a sobriety meeting, Opal's first in a year, and a Program friend gave them a place to spend the night. In its bittersweet way, it felt like a date; they stayed up listening to recovery tapes and talking of better times. The next day Kenny pulled a rabbit from a hat. One of his old counselors ran a halfway house called Project HALT. Opal met none of the conditions to get in: she wasn't working, she couldn't pay the rent, and she hadn't stopped using drugs. But Kenny didn't see any other options. On top of all else, Opal was two months pregnant, with a child she claimed was his.

I caught up with her a few days after she arrived. She was fiddling with the blinds in a sad little room, trying to capture fading light through a dirty window. Opal recounted her collapse in matter-of-fact tones: the yearning for drugs, the good-bye to the girls, the thoughts of suicide. She was a woman in suspended animation, a detached observer of a shattered past and a future she felt powerless to change. The moment she sprang back to life was when she spit out her scorn for Jewell. "I ain't never gonna talk to her again!" she said. Yet Jewell may have kept her from losing the kids. A few days after she left her apartment, Opal returned to gather a few things. While she was there, an investigator arrived, saying someone had filed a child-welfare complaint. If Opal's mother hadn't gotten the girls, the state of Wisconsin might have had them.

From her dingy room in the halfway house, Opal started calling OIC again, pleading for a welfare check. Sonya Gordon, her caseworker, finally returned her call. If she was curious what Opal was doing in a place called Project HALT—"Hungry, Addicted, Lonely, and Tired"—she didn't say. She did say that nearly two months after inheriting the case she hadn't looked at it. She'd have to talk to a supervisor and call back. When she did, she compounded the errors: she agreed to send Opal $700 as back pay. There were any number of reasons Opal didn't qualify for a W-2 check. She hadn't worked for it, of course. Even more basic than that, she didn't have custody of her kids. But OIC didn't know.

Opal cashed the check and headed for Andrea's, telling herself she'd be back for dinner. She stayed for six months, making the crack house her home. Sonya Gordon transferred the case to yet another caseworker, Opal's fifth in a year, and the checks continued to flow. Pregnant addicts were a big concern in Wisconsin that year. Just as Opal moved in with Andrea, Tommy Thompson signed a "Cocaine Mom" law, authorizing courts to force pregnant women into treatment programs. "The unborn child is going to be preserved and protected and . . . healthy when born," he said. Meanwhile Opal was pregnant and living in a crack house—and Thompson's celebrated welfare program was buying the crack.

FOURTEEN

Golf Balls and Corporate Dreams: Milwaukee, 1997–1999

The Company's services are designed to make government operations more efficient and cost effective while improving the quality of the services provided to program beneficiaries.

—MAXIMUS, INC.

In theory, the people sending drug money to Opal had a motive to clean up their act: fear of the competition. After twenty-eight months, their contracts expired. If the Opportunities Industrialization Center wouldn't answer its phones, if it sent checks to pregnant women in crack houses, then it risked being replaced by its rivals. In practice, the agencies acted less like competitors than like members of a welfare cartel. With Milwaukee split into six exclusive regions, the contracting produced a kind of ethnic and ideological partition. One contract went to the black grassroots group (OIC). One went to its Hispanic counterpart (United Migrant Opportunities Services). Two blue chips of the public service world were dealt in (the YWCA and Goodwill Industries, which ran two regions). With a common consultant and common agenda—keeping state regulators at bay—the agencies showed more interest in sticking together than in raiding each other's turf. Think OPEC, not the Cola Wars.

The exception was the fifth agency, Maximus, Inc., which did want to take over the city. As a national, profit-seeking corporation, Maximus wasn't just the new face in town but the ultimate symbol of privatization: a welfare agency that traded on the New York Stock Exchange! The state saw a paragon of market-based virtues—efficiency, discipline, accountability—and considered letting Maximus run the whole Milwaukee program before bowing to the political imperative to include local groups. Critics saw a cold, distant corporation, looking to profit off the poor (and some just seized on any opportunity to attack W-2). When Opal moved to Andrea's, she didn't just land in a new service region. She landed in an ideological battle zone.

As a business, Maximus arrived in Milwaukee on a wave of spectacular success. In 1975, its founder, David Mastran, left a job at the Department of Health, Education, and Welfare to start a consulting firm in his basement. Two decades later he was master of an empire based in Reston, Virginia, with contracts in nearly every state. Along with consulting, Maximus ran programs itself; it collected child support in Tennessee, helped enroll Texans in Medicaid, and processed Connecticut's child-care payments. By allowing states to privatize their programs, the 1996 federal law set off a gold rush for similar contracts; one Wall Street analysis saw more than $2 billion a year coming up for grabs. Formidable rivals, like EDS and Lockheed Martin, the aerospace giant, were fighting for the business, but with its long record and tighter focus Maximus was thought to have an edge. The W-2 contract was a coup. No welfare experiment was followed more closely, and Maximus hoped to leverage the publicity and prestige into market share nationwide. The company went public on the eve of W-2's launch, and the share price rose by two-thirds over the next nine months. Mastran's stake was worth more than $100 million.

While W-2 brought special opportunity, it also posed a special challenge. The other W-2 agencies had run local programs for years; Maximus had to start from scratch, in a place where grassroots opinion ranged from suspicion to hostility. To lead the effort, the company hired a local Goodwill executive named George Leutermann, who had gained some national prominence a few years earlier with an employment program in nearby Kenosha. Leutermann brought Maximus instant connections: his family had run a Milwaukee grocery store for one hundred years, and he had spent a quarter century working in Wisconsin social services. For Leutermann, Maximus had an equal allure: one day, he was a cog in a bland bureaucracy, the next he was checking on his stock options as a corporate VP. With the chance to set up W-2, Leutermann, at fifty, wasn't just running a program but launching a new product line. "Over the next two years, we plan to replicate many of the systems we are testing in Milwaukee for use in other markets," he told the *Milwaukee Business Journal.*

Leutermann made a splash. Though his face sagged in a hangdog look, he held forth with the quick, glib rap of a man born to sell. Knowing the knock that Maximus faced—rapacious profiteers—he set out to soften the corporate image with an aggressive marketing campaign; there were billboards, bus ads, and CD-ROMS, even Maximus fanny packs. A succession of minority fetes and fairs wound up with a Maximus check. A team of "community outreach" specialists came on board, most of them local minority women, with generous salaries and vague promotional duties. Spin to the smooth jazz station, and you could hear the Maximus jingle:

People helping people
That's us
We're here at Maximus

In theory, the thing that made W-2 different was its stress on community service jobs: everyone was expected to work. But the heart of the program that Leutermann designed was another motivation class. Grandly reincarnated as "MaxAcademy," it grew into a weeks-long festival of assessment tests, Successory posters, and inspirational speakers, distinguished above all by empty seats. Attendance, though mandatory, was wretched. Leutermann called the class a way to polish the so-called soft skills, like punctuality and grooming, while getting to know clients more deeply than the usual office visits allowed. His detractors suspected he was equally drawn to its promotional qualities. Every visiting dignitary was routed to the class, and if enough clients didn't show up, employees would pose in their place. When *Nightline* came to town, MaxAcademy supplied the lead.

NIGHTLINE: "You are watching a revolution in progress."
INSPIRATIONAL SPEAKER: "You have to be aggressive when you're out in the workforce. . . ! You gotta want it!"
NIGHTLINE: "Twice a week, employers are here interviewing."

Cut to George Leutermann. For a VP looking to scale the ranks, it doesn't get much better than that. But no sooner was the program up and running than a group of disaffected managers began voicing a common complaint: the clients weren't doing anything. W-2 was built around the theory of "full engagement." As state officials described it, the average client would perform forty hours of weekly activity, of which thirty would involve real work. But the W-2 policy manual cast things in looser terms, demanding "up to" thirty hours of work. Or, actually, up to thirty hours of "work training activities," which could include the old job-search routine. The manual writers said that they were just trying to accommodate the occasional need for discretion, not create a big loophole. But the real-world practice of W-2 became much looser still. Many clients waited months for assignments. Others ignored them and got paid anyway. While Opal's ability to keep drawing a check may seem like a strange aberration, Maximus managers were busy swapping written complaints about clients in similar straits: "Job-seekers are essentially in limbo." "[M]any job seekers with W2 placements are not assigned activities." "The no show rate is high and we are losing people." "Today, Northwestern Mutual Life, a very important employer, is on site. . . . However there is one critical element missing, JOBSEEKERS." Six months after the program's start, Steve Perales, the second in charge, warned that "virtually no referrals are being made to the CSJ unit," the one that assigns community service jobs. While about 1,100 clients were supposed to have community service jobs, just 507 had gotten assignments, and "only about 88 are actually participating," he wrote. That is, in the country's most famous work program, only 8 percent of the clients were working. "What they were doing, I don't know," Leutermann later told me. "They were doing nothing."

One reason for the disarray was a shortage of caseworkers. Under state rules, each caseworker—a Financial and Employment Planner, or "Fep"—was supposed to manage no more than fifty-five clients. Some Maximus Feps had more than twice as many. The woman who would next handle Opal's case had 108. Four months after the program's launch, Mona Garland, a senior manager, wrote a memo warning that Maximus had thirteen caseworkers and needed twenty-eight. Leutermann argued that the state had placed too much emphasis on Feps. While W-2 had cast them as centralized problem-solvers, Leutermann pictured them as traffic cops, routing clients to more specialized services. But Garland, who became an embittered critic, suspected Leutermann had another thought in mind: caseworkers, unlike inspirational speakers, don't get you on *Nightline.*

In June 1998, ten months into W-2, the state produced its first quantitative look at the agencies' performance. The computerized audit, called a 740R report, examined what activities clients had been assigned. Of interest as a midterm report card, it also hinted at the criteria the state would use for contract renewals. A follow-up report would cover similar ground, and those who passed would gain the "right of first selection," a chance to keep running the program without another public bid. Agencies that failed could reenter the competitive fray, but they would be doing so under a cloud and could find themselves losing a lucrative contract in a particularly humiliating way. Since Maximus was using W-2 as a national exhibit, that would wreck the whole business plan. Failing wasn't an option.

Most of the Milwaukee agencies performed poorly, and Maximus looked especially bad. Sixty-seven percent of its clients had no work assignments. An internal Maximus analysis, a few months later, found that 46 percent of the clients had no assignments at all, work or otherwise. "I had no clue that we were in that kind of shape," Leutermann later said. "We were just out of whack all over the place." At the time, he exploded and blamed Garland. "[O]ur dismal performance" is "a major setback," and "our track record portends continued problems," he wrote. Garland responded with a blizzard of old memos, e-mails, and reports to say she had been warning him. The evidence of idle clients was kept from public view—neither Maximus nor the state had a motive to vet their failures—but amid the finger pointing, one issue got resolved. Maximus would hire more caseworkers.

As Opal lay around smoking Primos, Michael Steinborn sat at home, drinking vodka for breakfast. Sometimes he thought he *needed* a social worker. He had no clue he was about to become one. Some social-work careers begin in flights of youthful idealism; Michael's began at Ladies Night at a Milwaukee pickup joint. He was out with a high school friend, Jose Arteaga. They had both grown up in the inner city, sons of small-time landlords, and as classmates at the Jesuit high school, they used to have long, philosophical talks about how the ghetto had gotten so screwed up. Now at thirty, Michael was poor and screwed up himself, and Jose was a rising star at Maximus, director of case management. By the end of the night, Jose had an inspiration: Michael should come aboard as a Fep. *Yeah,* Michael thought. *Right.*

It was late and they were drinking, but they each had a reason to act like they were serious. Michael's reason was simple enough: he needed a job. In the decade since he had dropped out of Marquette, he had driven a taxi, delivered pizzas, swabbed toilets, attended fire fighters' school, rushed into a marriage, had a son, and gone through a bitter divorce. Joining a friend on the crew of a landscaping firm, Michael spent a few years mowing city lots, and then had a better idea—they should start a landscaping firm of their own. Michael's friend Alvin was black, so his 51 percent share gave them minority contractor status. It also gave Alvin the ability to cut Michael out, which he did, unsentimentally, once the business took off. Michael was devastated. It took a tackle from his sobbing girlfriend, Jai, to stop him as he tried to run after Alvin with a butcher knife. In the two years since, Michael had done some sheetrock and roofing jobs, but mostly he brooded and drank. By the summer of 1998, he owed ten months' worth of back child support and Jai was pregnant, due in a week. He needed some cash.

Jose's motives were more complex. In part, he wanted to help a friend, and as the chief of Feps he needed bodies. But he also thought that Michael would bring something to the job. Like all the agencies, Maximus had drawn most of its Feps from the old welfare program, prizing the veterans above all for their familiarity with the state computer system. Jose thought too many acted like data entry clerks, tidying their software screens but forgetting the client. "Their people skills weren't there," he said. Michael, on the other hand, had been doing protosocial work since his preteens, when his father first sent him out to collect rents. Jose saw him as a no-bullshit kind of guy, tough but empathetic. The kind the system needed. A few nights later, he showed up in Michael's kitchen with a bottle of tequila and a sheaf of paper. Taping flowcharts to the wall until 1:00 a.m., he offered a crash-course on W-2 as it existed in theory:

Point Number One: Only Work Pays. Free money was gone. Clients had to earn their checks in a simulated workweek. The bulk should be spent actually working, while the rest could be devoted to activities like training, treatment, or classes. For every hour clients missed, their checks got reduced by $5.15, the equivalent of the minimum wage. The idea was to model the workaday world.

Point Number Two: W-2 Provides the Jobs. The jobs progressed along a four-part ladder, with each a step up in difficulty and pay. At the bottom rung, W-2 Transitions, even the physically or mentally impaired might, say, perform light assembly tasks in a supervised setting. At the top was the ultimate goal, regular, unsubsidized employment. In between, most clients would be assigned to community service jobs—answering the phone at a food bank, perhaps, or sweeping a school. The bottom rung paid $628 a month, while regular community service paid $673. Grants no longer grew with family size, though for all but the largest families they paid more than the old system. In addition, the state provided child care, health care, and transportation, the support services that workers needed.

Point Number Three: Casework Is the Key. There *was* no casework in the old system, just a stream of checks. W-2 promised every client an individualized employment plan and a caseworker to help see her through. Quarreling with the boss? Drinking too much? Part sheriff, part shrink, the Fep was supposed to monitor progress and get to the bottom of things.

As the kitchen course came to its inebriated close, Michael liked the theory: he hadn't hung around the ghetto all his life without accumulating some disdain for welfare. But he wondered if the bureaucracy could pull it off. And for his own role as an agent of reform, he had no enthusiasm at all. As a high school student, he had taken a test of occupational interests and scoffed when it cast him as a future social worker. "You think I'm gonna be some underpaid, overworked *social worker?*" he had said. Office work dealt a blow to his muscular self-image. Office workers had soft hands. Still, though it pained him to admit it, the $28,000 salary was more than he had ever earned. Leaving for the first day of work, he kissed his baby, Christian, goodbye and headed off to log an office worker's day. "Your daddy's going to make some money," he said.

It started poorly and went downhill from there. His first battles weren't with clients but rather with the computer system that tracked them, a befuddling institution called CARES. The central nervous system of W-2, CARES had more than five hundred screens, each known by an opaque four-letter code. There was no doing the job without knowing the program, and despite three months of training, Michael thought he never would. Need to change someone's work assignment? Go to WPAS. Check her living arrangements? That's ANLA. Issue her check? Type "Y" in AGEC, but change the date in SFED, otherwise the check may not go out, even when AGEC said it did. For all the talk of making Feps bold new problem solvers, fluency in CARES was particularly prized, since it was the sole repository of the data that would govern contract renewal. It didn't matter when Michael used his lunch hour to drive clients to job interviews; there was no CARES screen for that. (He pictured one: SCKR, for "sucker.") What mattered was whether he had correctly coded their employability plans.

Facing a parade of addled clients, Michael found himself thinking more about keystrokes than the substance of what they said. Disabled child? Dying mother? "Shut up!" complained a voice in his head. "I'm trying to remember the transaction code!" His befuddlement reached its dark apogee with the arrival of a large, sobbing woman free-associating about her troubles. Michael entered the driver flow and dutifully posed the questions on his screen.

SOBBING WOMAN: I got into it with my sister's boyfriend. . . .
MICHAEL: What are your employment goals?

WOMAN: . . . he hit me in the head with a two-by-four . . .
MICHAEL: Foreign languages? Written or verbal?
WOMAN: . . . my brother's retarded . . .
MICHAEL: Distance from the nearest bus line?
WOMAN: . . . we're out of food . . .
MICHAEL: Volunteer work or hobbies?

Volunteer work or hobbies! "No, I don't want to hear that you've been at food pantries for the last two months," he thought. "What I want to know is whether you play volleyball!" A coworker suggested the information might help him guide clients to the right job, but Michael kept picturing a gnome in Madison darting out of the computer room: "A knitter! A knitter! We've got a knitter, folks!"

In its pitch to investors, Maximus had promised to outdo government with "a professional work environment that is more conducive to employee productivity." Michael had a different view: half the place was coming unglued. At least two of the caseworkers he came to know were addicted to crack. Another was hospitalized for job-related stress. A Fep with whom he shared an office went off on gambling jags, staying out at a casino all night, then sleeping at her desk. "Baby, I gotta take a little nap," she'd say as she locked the door. Another Fep walked off the job with a message on her screensaver: "God has something bigger and better for me than this place." Michael thought he might just be a magnet for office misfits. But the memo traffic inside the agency showed broader disarray. Leutermann warned that one caseworker was "going off the deep end lately," causing "all kinds of problems about his behavior in the bathroom." Another Maximus worker chased his supervisor from his office when she told him to clean up his files. "I am a Marine combat veteran that deals with Post Traumatic Stress Disorder," he wrote. "I lost my head." A flirtatious caseworker, rebuffed by a colleague, walked into his cubicle and bit him. As the incident report noted dryly: "He then told her to get her Monkey Ass away."

Given the power that caseworkers exert over poor, troubled women, welfare offices need to use special caution; predatory workers may pressure their clients for sex or drugs. Sometimes no pressure is needed. After Michael drove a client to a job interview, she sent him a card with a smiley face. "If you give me the chance, I'll ride you like a horse," she wrote. "Your voice just makes me melt!" Not everyone summoned Michael's self-control. A MaxAcademy teacher was quietly pushed out the door after a client complained that he was urging her and others to join a drug-peddling scheme. An internal report explained: "She said some of these women have told her that they have had sex with him because they are afraid he will cut off their benefits." A different caseworker resigned when his client announced she was carrying his baby. "Dumb ass . . . should have paid for the abortion like I asked him too!" she announced in the Maximus office. She went public only after another client told her MaxAcademy class that she was sleeping with him, too. Maximus kept the story out of the press, and the mordant office joke had it that the women were enrolled in "W-3," a program of lifelong checks for clients who kept their mouths shut. "Mike, you're a bright guy," one colleague said. "Get out while you can."

Maximus encouraged the hiring of family and friends, calling it an effective way to lure and keep talent. As head of the office, Leutermann certainly practiced what he preached. He put his wife, his son, and his niece on the payroll, along with his mistress and his mistress's mother. The gossip about the boss's affair reached the point that Leutermann urged subordinates not to mention it in front of his wife. In a memo titled "Rumors and Soap Operas," he wrote: "Our office continues to suffer through a problem of useless, superfluous, and often insidious rumormongering. . . . MAXIMUS does not have time to fixate on this type of drivel." Leutermann's girlfriend, a senior Maximus manager, was pregnant with his child when he hired her; at the time he circulated the memo, they had an eight-month-old son. The woman who rose to the number-two job in the Maximus office, Paula Lampley, had her son on the payroll, too, until he drew thirty years for reckless homicide; Romell Lampley, an employment counselor, got angry at his girlfriend's stepfather and ran him over with a car. "This project has had more than its share of complaints," wrote David Mastran, the CEO, ordering an investigation. "If we are doing nothing wrong, why are we receiving complaints?" The incident at hand involved an employee's complaint of racial discrimination, but Beverly Swann, the Maximus executive sent to the scene, warned that the problems went deeper. "I asked the question what message would you like to send the CEO and the response was clearly 'things are not what they appear to be,'" she wrote. "There is a perception that management are [*sic*] hiring friends, relatives, and former displaced associates." Years later, Mastran told me, "In all of our projects, we never had personnel problems like we had up there. It got out of control."

Perhaps he was thinking of Corey Daniels, the caseworker originally assigned to train Michael. Everything about him set off Michael's bullshit detector. He wore a platinum Dennis Rodman do and watched soap operas at his desk. He flashed wads of cash and boasted of his Cadillacs. Playing his voice mail on the speakerphone, he deleted clients' messages as soon as he heard their names. *Bo-rring! Heard that!* "The guy's a flipping goof," Michael said, demanding a new trainer. A background check would have shown that Daniels was also a convicted forger, with an arrest record that included kidnapping, battery, and impersonating a police officer. "You appear to be living a double life," a judge had warned, while giving him four years for passing forged checks. Maximus hired him while he was out on parole. A few months after his tutelage of Michael, Daniels was back in court, charged with extorting nearly $4,000 from his clients. Four of them brought similar complaints: that Daniels had threatened to reduce their checks if they didn't give him a share of the money. Michael, still new to office work, wondered what he had gotten into: "Drug abuse, check kiting, knocking up people—what is it about this place?"

He did find a Fep to admire. His new trainer, Elizabeth Matus, was a soft-spoken Nicaraguan immigrant who could do what Michael could not: talk and work CARES at the same time. For two months, he scarcely left her side. He wouldn't eat. He couldn't sleep. He stayed at the office until 9:00 at night, studying the CARES manual. "This isn't like putting up drywall," he told himself. "You're messing with people's lives." Then, ready or not, his password arrived: he was XMI28W, a full-fledged Fep. As if from a B movie, a clerk wheeled in seventy case files, some of them literally covered with dust. Most of the clients had been idle for months, while collecting checks. They needed appointment notices, work assignments, employability plans. With the state review approaching—and the corporate showcase at stake—Michael had two months to turn a pile of lost lives into CARES codes that could pass official muster.

One of those files was Opal's.

The crack house where Opal took refuge was a mustardy complex cast in an otherworldly light by the all-night gas station next door. The inside was otherworldly, too, a dark space of torn couches and acrid odors that slumbered until noon and buzzed until dawn. The building divided into four apartments, and discreet dealers operated from three. The fourth, where Opal lived with Andrea, was a rollicking bazaar, notorious enough to attract motorists off the nearby Interstate. Opal paid $250 a month to sleep there, pregnant, on the couch. No one knew where she was. Like a foreign trek, life at Andrea's combined adventure, escape, and a kind of liberating anonymity. It let her indulge her secret self, away from disapproving eyes.

W-2 kept paying the way. With her new address across district lines, OIC transferred the case, and Opal's introduction to Maximus had the makings of a dark spoof. Dragging herself in from the crack house, Opal discovered her case being reviewed by someone she knew from the recovery world as a fellow addict. The Maximus worker couldn't have been any happier to see Opal than Opal was to see her, especially if Opal was right in surmising that she was still snorting heroin. ("She had them blisters up her nose! You can tell!") "How you been doing?" the caseworker asked. Opal avoided an answer. She handed over an old drug-referral note and concocted a story about being in treatment. That bought her another month's check. Someone handed her a form asking about volunteer work and hobbies. "Reading, skating," Opal wrote.

More faux social work followed. When Opal missed her next appointment, Maximus arranged for a home visit, just what you'd want in the case of a pregnant woman on drugs. Except the home visitor never went in the home. He knocked on the crack house door and handed Opal an appointment notice. A look inside would have revealed a drug nest. A call to the police would have disclosed a warrant for Opal's arrest. A check with the Milwaukee public schools would have revealed that she didn't have her kids. Instead, Maximus sent

Opal to MaxAcademy. "That's wasteless," she said. "I been to so many motivation classes." She went one day and got another month's check.

As usual, welfare wasn't Opal's only way to get by. One of the dealers who hung around Andrea's was a small-timer in his late twenties, a rail-thin man with a pocked face and oversized nose, whom everyone called Bo. He wasn't much to look at, Opal thought, and he didn't have much to say. But she had a $300-a-day habit, and he had a pocketful of crack. Soon, Opal was calling him her "friend" and laughing behind his back about her ability to wheedle or steal his drugs.

Restless after four months in hiding, Opal finally walked to a pay phone and told Kenny where she was. A week later, I picked them up and the three of us headed off to a Red Lobster. Kenny looked dapper in a red turtleneck, with cubic zirconia sparkling in his ears and a No Drugs button on his chest. Six months pregnant, Opal was disconcertingly thin, with matted hair and bags beneath her eyes. But she sallied forth in gold lamé shoes, regal even in exile. Drugs were destroying her family and her health, but not her love of the fantastic tale. "I live in a crack house!" she began. It was a difficult sentence to parse—part apology, partly a boast. "That house is *booming.* I ain't never seen so many white people do drugs in my life! Doctors, bus drivers, men that own their own construction companies!" Andrea and her sister smoked cocaine, Opal said, and their daughters sold it. "It's like a family thing," she said. She griped about the rent Andrea charged her, but the dealers had to provide drugs to the house—and "now, I'm the house."

Kenny poured a dozen sugars in his tea and took it all in. "Daughter sells drugs to the mother, so you know she's going to hell," he said.

"So are you!" Opal said, raising the sore subject of his affairs. "You just fornicating."

"Thank you, Pope," he said.

Opal described her daily routine: sleep past noon and stay up till dawn, especially "if it's my day to watch the door." Kenny tried to sound more incredulous than he was. "Your day to open the door! What: they got your name on a refrigerator? 'Opal's day to open the door?' *I* used to work the door. The guy that works the door is the first to get hit upside the head when the robbers come through." Opal was thinking less of robbers than cops. The police had raided an adjacent apartment, and she couldn't understand why they hadn't burst into Andrea's yet. "The police don't want no white people doing drugs," she said. "They fittin' to raid it." Given the pending theft charges from Target, she seemed resigned to going to jail. "It seems like it's going to happen."

She said she had talked to her daughters several times "since I been AWOL." Kierra and Tierra had taken her absence in stride, but Sierra, the oldest at nine, had cried and asked when Opal would return. "I'm sick right now," Opal had told her. "When Mama gets better, I'm a come home and get y'all." She said she felt sad. She said she felt "self-pity." She said she felt "ashamed of what I'm doing." She didn't say she felt ready to stop. After dinner, she packed the leftovers in a box and stole a bottle of steak sauce. Then she rode back to Andrea's, where she was still living a couple months later when her case reached Michael's desk.

Whatever Maximus could blame for its failures with Opal, it couldn't blame a shortage of cash. As she spent her welfare money on Primos, Maximus went on a grander binge, showering the town with more than $1 million of billboards, TV ads, and corporate tchotchkes and financing the spree out of welfare funds. Like a Mafia wiretap or the Watergate tapes, the bookkeeping has the lurid appeal of shabby sin exposed to daylight. The company spent $100,000 of program funds on backpacks, coffee mugs, and other promotional fluff. It spent tens of thousands on employee entertainment, including meals, flowers, parties, and retreats. It spent $3,000 to take clients roller-skating at the zoo. In one of the more inventive uses of welfare funds, it doled out $2,600 for professional clowns to liven up Maximus events. Though Maximus later agreed to repay $500,000 to the state and donate another $500,000 to community groups, the true extent of the waste will never be known because the records were in such disarray. In nearly three-quarters of the transactions later examined by legislative auditors, Maximus either couldn't show what it had purchased or explain its relevance to W-2. Entries in the auditors' report literally read like this: Vendor: "Unknown." Item purchased: "Unknown." Welfare funds expended: "$5,302." For any welfare program to spend money like this defies comprehension. Why would a profit-seeking enterprise indulge such chaos and waste?

The answer starts with the financial incentives of W-2. It was designed as a risk-management system, much like an HMO. Each agency got a fixed payment to serve its region; in return, the agency financed everything from clients' benefits to caseworkers' telephone bills. Just as HMOs were supposed to profit by keeping people healthy (and out of hospitals), W-2 agencies were supposed to keep them employed (and off the welfare rolls). The more an agency cut its caseload, the more its profits would grow. Given those incentives, the most obvious fear was that the agencies would find ways to cut needy people off—*not* that they would pay women like Opal to sit around crack houses. But the rolls immediately fell so much that the financial pressures vanished. In offering the contracts, the state had budgeted for fifty thousand cases; when W-2 began, only twenty-three thousand people enrolled. Rather than rolling the dice, the agencies were rolling in dough.

The catch is that unrestricted profits were capped at 7 percent of the contract, or $4.2 million in Maximus's case. After that, the agencies kept only 10 percent of any leftover funds. Maximus knew its $4.2 million was in the bank. So it had little incentive to cut costs, since it would keep just a dime of each dollar it saved. In other words, it found itself with a big pot of someone else's money to spend. And spend it did, lavishly and foolishly, in a drive to burnish its corporate image. "I have permission to make seven percent on this contract, period," Leutermann said. "We're using it as a national exhibit."

Hoping to win over local skeptics, Leutermann hired a $60,000 PR chief with a half dozen $40,000 and $50,000 assistants for the "community outreach" team. Inside the agency, they were resented as deadwood, and Leutermann let most of them go as soon as the contract was renewed. He also tried to buy goodwill more directly. Lots of companies make charitable donations; Maximus made them with tens of thousands of program dollars that were supposed to be helping welfare recipients. Leutermann covered the ethnic bases, from the African American State Fair and the Black Holocaust Museum to the La Causa Celebrity Waiter Festival and Granny Shalom House. The Women in Public Policy Luncheon, the Hispanic Chamber of

Commerce, the Charlie Lagrew Fiddle and Jig Contest—likewise, all dealt in.

In the big scheme of things, Granny Shalom didn't cost taxpayers much. The advertising blitzkrieg did. State auditors estimated that Maximus spent $1.1 million on its marketing campaign. Bridgette Ridgeway, who spent two years overseeing the effort as a Maximus consultant and staff member, estimated the cost to be about twice as high, at $2.3 million. There were Maximus water bottles and Maximus visors. There were Maximus golf balls, towels, and tees, for all those golfers on the Maximus rolls. ("The golf balls were a bad idea," Leutermann later acknowledged.) There was a Maximus jingle. Make that *two* Maximus jingles; the first, rendered in a minor key, was recommissioned after a consultant warned that in "keeping with the Maximus image, the music should not reflect sad or dark tones." In one of Leutermann's wilder schemes, Maximus spent more than $23,000 to bring in Melba Moore, the once-upon-a-time Broadway star (and former welfare recipient), for what flyers called an "exclusive inspirational concert for Maximus families." She drew about two hundred people, putting the per-ticket cost at about $125.

Leutermann argued that as the new name in town, Maximus needed a PR campaign to counter the negative rumors spread by its critics and reassure wary clients. "Had we been given a fair shake from the start, that would never have been necessary," Leutermann later said. "But we were being painted from Day One as the for-profit, nasty assholes of the world." Advertising can be appropriate; the question is whom does it aid? It's one thing to leaflet poor neighborhoods, another to make sure that local pols tee off with Maximus balls. Among the expenses the state subsequently deemed *proper* was a share of the costs of hiring two of Tommy Thompson's cronies, for advice on how to target political donations and win new contracts. Much of the advertising occurred around the 1998 summer meeting of the National Governors Association, which was held in Milwaukee. Collectively, its members controlled a multi-billion-dollar welfare market, and Leutermann hit them with everything from TV ads to CD-ROMs; his goal, he wrote his boss, was "to put MAXIMUS on the lops [*sic*]"—lips? laps?—"of every one of the fifty-five governors who will attend" from Maine to Guam. Ridgeway, the former PR chief, became a Maximus critic after Leutermann let her go. "My department bought media on specific radio stations because we knew that politicians would listen," she said. "It wasn't what's best for the clients."

Maximus wasn't the only agency taking a joy ride on welfare funds. OIC spent $67,000 to sponsor the *Ray Rhodes Show,* the weekly football rundown hosted by the coach of the Green Bay Packers (a show more likely to be seen by legislators than welfare mothers). United Migrant Opportunity Services spent $23,000 from a different welfare contract to advertise at Milwaukee Brewers' games. A more disturbing report emerged when auditors looked at the Goodwill subsidiary, Employment Solutions, Inc., which ran two Milwaukee regions and therefore was the state's largest W-2 agency. Auditors found it spent more than $270,000 of program funds outside the state, mostly in an unsuccessful attempt to win a contract in Arizona; the contract went to Maximus. The audits didn't appear until 2000 and 2001, long after the money was spent. And the salient point is that they were done by the auditing branch of the legislature, not by Thompson or the subordinates he put in charge of his showcase program. On the day the legislative auditors released their findings, the state's top W-2 official, Linda Stewart, issued a competing press release. It complained the auditors had failed to credit her own "vigilant efforts at monitoring and oversight."

The waste, though concealed for years, finally came to light. Not so with the deeper problem of W-2, its neglect of so many clients. What George Leutermann called "our dismal performance" on the state's first client activity report, in June 1998, didn't tell Maximus anything its managers hadn't known: casework was weak to nonexistent, and most recipients were idle. If anything, the report understated the casework problems, since it only measured one aspect of the agency's performance, the assignment of work activities. In August, Maximus examined several hundred cases against a fuller list of state rules, such as proper caseworker ratios and employability plans; 78 percent failed. In truth, none of these measures got to the bottom of things. They focused on process, not results. They asked whether clients were told what to do, not whether they did it and certainly not whether doing it made sense. Keith Garland, the Maximus manager of quality control, studied attendance at MaxAcademy, the agency's signature effort. More than three-quarters of the people assigned to the class never showed up for a single day. Out of a caseload of nearly fifteen hundred, Garland said, "We had maybe one hundred people doing something." As for the rest: "We didn't know what people were doing. We didn't have a clue."

With so many people (like Opal) doing nothing, why did they still get checks? In a given month, Maximus reduced its payments to only about one client in four, and hardly anyone had her whole check taken away. That pattern was typical statewide. The bureaucratic chaos offers one explanation: people couldn't be punished for skipping assignments they hadn't received. Finances offer another: having maximized their profits, agencies had little self-interest in withholding benefits. Caseworkers disliked the sanctioning process, which was time-consuming and brought complaints from angry clients. But a subtle shift in welfare politics also played a role. By the end of 1998, Tommy Thompson was finishing his third term, and he had cut the rolls by 90 percent. Politically, he had nothing to gain by pushing more families off welfare. On the contrary, the new national concern was reaching "the hard to serve," and savvy officials were trying to show they had preserved a safety net. The entire history of W-2 reflects a move away from Jason Turner's Work or Else theory toward a more erratic and diffuse set of practices. In part that's because the original vision was too rigid (not every client was best served by a community service job) and in part because the bureaucracy never really tried to pull it off. For all those reasons, an unspoken assumption often prevailed: when in doubt, give 'em a check.

A few months after Maximus learned of its "dismal" results on the client activity report, the state announced the criteria it would use for contract renewal. There were, among other standards, three major measures of casework. The Feps could each handle no more than fifty-five clients at a time. They had to keep 95 percent of their employability plans up-to-date. And they had to make sure 80 percent of their clients had a full slate of assignments. This was more bureaucratic bunk. The state didn't ask whether Opal got a job—it asked whether she had an employability plan. Plus, it was easy to manipulate the data. In grading the agencies for contract renewal, the state's sole source of information was the computer system, CARES. The state had no way to know whether the assignments in the computer were real, much less whether clients were doing them. For months, Maximus tried to round up its clients and give them something to do. But if all else failed, the policy manual did permit another option: just type something in the system and send the client a copy. "It became a CARES game," says Mona Garland, the former operations manager. "You just go in there and code them this, this, and this to make CARES look right and ultimately meet the right of first selection. . . . They may not really be assigned to thirty hours, but you go into CARES and make it sound like they're assigned to thirty hours. The job-seeker may not even know." When I asked George Leutermann about this, he said: "I would imagine some of that did happen."

It happened to Opal. Finding her file in his dusty stack in November 1998, Michael Steinborn quickly sent her an appointment letter. As usual, she didn't show. One reason he needed to see her was to update her employability plan, since without one her case would fail to meet state standards. When she didn't appear, he simply went into CARES, wrote a plan, and stuck it in the mail. It showed her aspiring to become a teacher's assistant. And to get her started, he gave her the assignment he gave everyone. "Opal Caples?" he said to himself. "It's MaxAcademy for you!" He didn't know she was addicted to crack. He didn't know she was pregnant. He didn't know she was living in a drug house while her mother raised her kids. He had never met her. But with that, his casework was up to standards: Opal's case was now passing. "CARES is a fantasyland," he said.

The state took its computerized snapshot of the caseload on January 29, 1999. A few weeks later, Maximus, like all the Milwaukee agencies, learned that it had passed. Its "national exhibit" was safe. State officials were just as relieved. In scoring the agencies' performance, they were also scoring their own, and the last thing they wanted was any hint of failure. Thompson was mulling a run for president and pushing W-2 for a prestigious Innovations in American Government Award, which is cosponsored by the Ford Foundation and Harvard's John F. Kennedy School of Government. He won. In bestowing the $100,000 prize, award administrators called W-2 "one of the nation's best examples of government performance." One of the qualities they singled out was its financial efficiency. The other was the quality of its casework.

For Maximus, there was more good news. By the end of the year, with George Leutermann leading the charge, the company won a prized $100 million contract in New York City, where Jason Turner had gone on to serve as welfare commissioner; just as planned, W-2 proved a springboard to greater things. Six months later, the legislative auditors' report would appear, and the talk would shift to Melba Moore and clowns. But for a fleeting moment, more fleeting than he knew, Leutermann was on top of the world. "The company hired me because of the quality issue," he told a local business paper. "There is nothing worse than a pitch man not having substance to back him up."

Opal never read her employability plan. She had been missing for six months when Kenny ran into Angie and Jewell and told them where she was. A week later, the two of them knocked on her door. Opal came out, and they sat in the car, where the three women fell into the irreverent banter that marked them as family. Opal didn't say a word to Jewell about turning her in to her mother. Jewell didn't say anything to Opal about smoking cocaine. She just listened to Opal's spirited drug-house stories. "Girl," Opal said, "you see some tripped-out shit over there." More visits followed. Then Angie urged Opal to move in, and a few weeks before the baby was due, she finally did. With that, Angie achieved what W-2 had not; she got Opal out of the crack house.

Opal was miserable. She missed Andrea's, not just the drugs, but the rush of late-night excitement. There was nothing to do at Angie's but lie around, and lying around left her depressed. Angie and Marcus argued all the time, and Opal had never much liked Angie's kids, who didn't want her around. ("Opal's a *drug addict,*" whispered Darrell, Angie's five-year-old. "I don't talk to Opal.") The house smelled like the pit bulls that Marcus was raising, and the dogs had chewed up the top floor, forcing everyone into uncomfortably close quarters. Opal shared a bed with Kesha, who at fourteen felt an excitement about the baby that Opal didn't share. Kenny resisted Opal's claims that the baby was his, and he soon stopped coming by. Back in touch with her mother, Opal called one day and said she wanted to give the baby away. Her mother told her she was talking crazy; babies aren't something you give away. It was another thing to fight about.

As Angie came in one morning, Opal told her it was time. "Stop playin'," Angie said. Then Opal dropped her pants to show that her water had burst. "We fittin' to have a baby!" Angie screamed, jumping up and down. Angie went with Opal to the hospital, and Jewell joined them after work. Bo, Opal's new man, did not, seeing no reason, he said, to come out and "hear you holler." It was nearly midnight by the time Brierra Caples arrived, surrounded by her exhausted mother and two crying aunts. "What y'all crying for?" Opal fussed, pretending to be annoyed. But once the swaddled infant was laid on her chest, all that she could think about was what a beautiful daughter she had. The talk of adoption ceased. She told herself what she was soon telling others, it was time to start doing things right. "You ain't going nowhere, girl," Opal said in the delivery room. "You stayin' right here with me."

FIFTEEN

Caseworker XMI28W: Milwaukee, 1998–2000

Opal's return from the streets didn't register on Michael Steinborn, who had mailed off her employability plan a few weeks earlier but still hadn't met her. With his roster of "job seekers" fifty-something names long, Michael had other problems. One was now standing before him on the coldest day of the year, a candidate for hypothermia.

"Mi-ike!" she rasped. She stood so close it was all he could do to keep from backing away. She talked with such a loud lisp he thought she might be retarded. She had lost half her teeth, and her skin looked almost plastic. If she weren't so big in the butt, he would have guessed she was smoking crack. That's the thing he had noticed about addicts: their butts were the first thing to go. As her sandpaper voice silenced the room, the receptionists stopped to stare. "I need a coat, *Mi-ike*! You're my caseworker now, *Mi-ike*!" Michael felt his loathing for his job surge to new highs. "She's a mile a minute with the 'Mikes,'" he thought. "My new best friend."

Since inheriting her case months earlier, he had known her only as a computer code. She hadn't answered his appointment letters. (Typical.) She hadn't complained when he docked her check. (Not typical.) Now here she was in shirtsleeves with the wind-chill factor 24 below. Coats weren't part of Michael's job. That's what all those high-priced "community outreach" specialists were for. But given days to produce, the outreach team produced only excuses. Bunch of nail-filing bitches, he thought. The waste around this place. "They haven't gotten you a coat?" he said. "Look at me *Mi-ike*—does it look like I have a coat?" There was a thrift shop down the street. Michael promised her a coat.

Sometimes when Michael hatched a plan, his body moved faster than his brain. He was halfway out the door when he remembered he only had $4. He climbed back up the stairs, bummed a loan from a coworker, and ran four blocks through the snow. The drifts swallowed his office-worker shoes and buried his toes in ice. The thrift store was out of coats. There was another thrift store two blocks away, and after another frigid sprint Michael was surrounded by coats. There were blue coats and black coats, long coats and short coats; there were so many coats that he was losing his way when a voice came into his head. It was the familiar voice of self-reproach, his *You Idiot!* voice, and it reminded him that he wasn't there to make a fashion statement: just pick one, you idiot! He chose a blue ski jacket with a pink collar, nicer than anything he had expected to find. It cost $11. He had $9. His You Idiot! voice returned: Maximus has a $58 million contract, and you—idiot—can't afford a used coat. He humbled himself before the store clerk, who indulged herself in a show of disdain but let the difference slide.

It wasn't exactly a landmark in the annals of social work. But climbing the Maximus stairs, Michael allowed himself a frisson of satisfaction. The nail filers had sat around all week; Michael Steinborn, can-do guy, had gotten something done. She lifted her arms over her head and made a sour face. "Mi-ike! It's a little snug when I do this, Mi-ike!" The slapstick line came to mind: "Then don't do this!" But the coat had another problem. The zipper didn't work.

Back he went, six blocks through the snow. Back to the sign that warned: "No Exchanges. All Sales Final." What was he supposed to say? Special exceptions for guys like him, dumb-ass social workers with ice in their shoes? The clerk found him too pathetic to bother with; Michael walked out with a lined denim jacket and a zipper that zipped.

"Mi-ike!" she said. "The other one was better looking than this!"

Mi-ike wasn't going back in the cold. *Mi-ike* wasn't wearing a coat himself. He left his at home because his clients' kids kept wiping their Cheeto hands on it. *Mi-ike* said he was done talking about coats. "Okay, Mi-ike!" she said. How about a bus pass? Four days later, in shirtsleeves again, she told Michael's supervisor that no one had been willing to find her a coat.

A social worker! He couldn't believe he was a social worker! Six months earlier he was an unemployed jack of the building trades, drunk by noon and wondering how he and his pregnant girlfriend were going to get by. Now he was a "Financial and Employment Planner," dispensing career advice. He hated the grip of starched collars on his throat. He hated the new-carpet office smell. He hated the officious, self-satisfied talk of some of the senior staff. Above all, he hated feeling responsible for any part of ghetto life, just as he had as a kid collecting his father's rents. "Son, take it from me," his father had warned, after another tenant had trashed an apartment and skipped out owing a big debt. "They'll take and take, and then they'll spit you out." (When he wasn't griping about his tenants, Ted Steinborn was running them on errands and bringing them bags of used clothes.) Growing up in the family business, Michael took pride in never backing down from a fight and had his nose broken three times. The last thing he brought to his profession was a sentimental view of the poor. "I never wanted to be a sucker for a sob story," he said.

Yet as a caseworker Michael was surrounded by sob stories, and just like his father he believed some of them. He could carry on, and did, about his clients' bad-faith betrayals: their games, their evasions, their weak alibis. "You're lied to on a constant basis," he said. But sometimes he felt he was lying, too, talking up the promise in all these dead-end jobs. "People will call and say, 'I got a job!' I feel like saying, 'You're going to have a really fucked-up time living on $6.41 an hour.' But my job is to bullshit them, to say, 'Hey, that's great, it's a first step.'" Clients liked Michael. ("My guardian angel," one said.) Clients trusted Michael. ("Like a brother," said another.) Clients had crushes on Michael. To an extent rare among the city's 150 caseworkers, Michael's career served as a tutorial on what conscientious casework can (and can't) achieve.

Shortly after the coat debacle, Michael's supervisor caught him with an application for a job cutting plate glass. "Are you leaving us?" she asked. He was, sooner than he knew. The next day, when he got to work he just kept driving—nowhere, somewhere, anywhere but here. Resigning with his gas pedal, he spent thirty minutes feeling freed, and then he felt like a loser. He didn't get the plate glass job, and a no-call, no-show was a firing offense, the kind of stunt his clients would pull. Michael assumed he had burned his bridges until his buddy Jose, the manager, called and promised to smooth things over. Give it a second chance, he said. You owe yourself. What he didn't say was that, being shorthanded, Maximus couldn't afford to lose a caseworker, even one as disenchanted as XMI28W. "You fucker," Michael said. "You just want my XMI on the caseload." The next morning, he was back. "I had a new son," he said. "I had to feed him."

The promise of individualized casework—made lavishly in W-2, and echoed in many other programs—is more extraordinary than it sounds. Personalized attention, if it ever existed, was chased from the system two generations ago. Welfare-rights groups called it paternalistic and discriminatory: aid was a right, not a privilege. And budget offices deemed it frightfully expensive, especially as the rolls surged. By the late 1960s, the average caseworker was the equivalent of a postal clerk, a low-paid, rules-oriented cog. In his original proposal for W-2, Jason Turner wrote: "More of the success of Wisconsin Works will ride on the talents . . . [of the] 'financial planners,' than any other collective feature of the new design." He listed some of their ideal attributes: "Creative, intuitive, optimistic, a people person . . . a paradigm shifter, and a problem solver rather than an enabler." But having recruited heavily from the old system, W-2, like most programs, still mostly had postal clerks.

It wasn't as if most clients were eager for a stranger's help, especially when the stranger controlled her check. To Opal (or for that matter, Angie and Jewell), "personalized casework" was a euphemism for someone dipping in her business. Hoping to strengthen ties to their clients, officials in Oswego County, New York, tried an especially client-friendly program called Pathways. The *only* thing clients had to do to keep their checks was appear at a single monthly group meeting. Still more than a third either couldn't or wouldn't attend. "I was shocked," said Toby Herr, the Chicago social worker who designed the program. "They would give up their whole check rather than come. They wanted no part of it." In Milwaukee, the challenge was compounded by the balkanized private system, which ignored the fact that poor people constantly move. One in five clients changed regions each year, starting over with a new caseworker who knew nothing about them. Add the turnover *within* agencies, and you get what Opal got in her first year on W-2: six caseworkers at two agencies, of whom one was a fellow addict and another would be convicted of check forgery. And Wisconsin's bureaucracy was typically celebrated as among the country's best.

Yet shortly after Michael went AWOL, something strange occurred. He decided he might be good at the job and that the job might do some good. Casework requires a balance between inspiration and caution, hope and reality; balance wasn't Michael's forte. He skipped lunch to drive clients to job interviews. He brought them his son's used clothes. He stayed up past midnight to rewrite one woman's résumé. (She didn't show up the next day.) He offered to babysit while another enrolled in a training program. (She still didn't go.) When a client showed up desperate for diapers, he blew off his plan for an end-of-the-week beer and gave her his last $10; he knew he'd never get a voucher out of the bureaucracy on a Friday afternoon. Michael had a calculator routine. Follow along, he would say. W-2 pays $673 a month. There are 4.3 weeks in a month and forty hours in a week. Pivoting the calculator, he would show what welfare paid: $3.91 an hour. "Do you think you can do better?" He was waiting, as he put it, to see "the lightbulb go on inside someone's head."

Michael thought he had seen it all, but some things hit him afresh. One seemingly demure twenty-one-year-old always had new hairstyles and clothes. He wondered how she was getting by, especially since he'd been reducing her check. One day, she burst into tears and told him; an old man was paying to kiss her between the legs. He wasn't surprised at what she was doing, only at how much it upset him. Michael was stunned to discover that another client had a terminal liver disease. He had pegged her as a malingerer until the doctor warned she had five months to live. What's more, the county was threatening to drop her from Medicaid. The sick woman wanted to fax in her forms; the county worker told her to "fax your ass over here." Michael stood over the county supervisor's desk, ranting so wildly she started to call the security guard. "They just screw people left and right!" he said, sounding more like a welfare advocate than an agent of welfare repeal. In retrospect, Michael began to think of this period as a crazy jaunt, his SuperFep stage. "I came into this job because I needed money," he said. "Then, I started thinking, 'Maybe I could make a difference.'"

One afternoon, a nervous client named Kimberly Hansen told him she was ready to get out of the house. At twenty-five, she had been home for six years, caring for a daughter with cerebral palsy. But child care was going to be a problem: the girl needed a day-care center with transportation, wheelchair access, and someone who could feed her through a gastrointestinal tube. Previous caseworkers, following the book, had fobbed her off on an ineffective child-care referral service. Michael spent three hours calling around town and got her appointments to inspect two places. The next thing he knew, she filed a complaint with Legal Aid. The group dragged him to a refereed appeal. Absurdly, there was nothing to appeal. He hadn't reduced Hansen's check; he had pledged to keep sending it in full until she found child care. But the Legal Aid lawyer bore in. *You don't understand what you're dealing with here! This child has special needs!* Even Hansen was taken aback. "Michael really did try to help me," she protested. She had called the lawyers with a panic attack, not with a concrete complaint.

A few weeks later, she returned to his office, this time with her daughter, Mercedes. Any grudge Michael felt disappeared. Mercedes was in a wheelchair, paralyzed from the neck down. She had difficulty lifting her head or controlling her saliva flow. Still, she was immaculate, and Hansen hovered over her to keep her that way. Michael turned his head, fighting the impulse to cry. She was obviously a mother of unusual devotion; the last thing she needed was him giving her grief. "I didn't pity her as much as I respected her," he said. He went back to working the phone and helped her find the child care.

She got a job. She lost the job. She fell into a pit of depression. A doctor warned the depression stemmed from her fears of leaving Mercedes, but she wouldn't go to counseling. There are "perverts out there" in day-care centers, she told Michael. Since Mercedes can't talk, if someone tried to hurt her, Hansen wouldn't even know. Months passed until she felt ready to work again. When she did, the day-care center wouldn't let Mercedes return. Hansen owed $40 in late fees and "Ebenezer Day Care," as Michael dubbed it, wouldn't budge. Neither would W-2, which paid child-care bills but not late fees. Michael brokered a repayment plan: Hansen would pay $10 every other week. She missed the first payment. She was stuck at home, as paralyzed as Mercedes, when SuperFep leaped into the breach; he skipped lunch and drove across town to make the payment himself.

The effort went about as smoothly as his trips to the thrift store. Again, he had to borrow the money. Then the center wouldn't take cash. A money order alone wasn't good enough, either; the center demanded a signed agreement, pledging the balance. "She's really in a bad way," Michael pleaded. Rules are rules; blah-diddy-blah; your lack of planning isn't our emergency. He forged her signature and faxed the agreement. His supervisor warned him he was in too deep. Someone discovering that he gave Hansen money might imply he was expecting something in return. But Michael trusted her, and his trust was repaid. When I met her six months later, she described Michael as a "brother." Sometimes Michael felt good about that. Sometimes he reminded himself that she still didn't have a job.

Michael had just donned his SuperFep cape when Opal finally walked in, a few weeks after having Brierra. W-2 hadn't yet caught her attention. But with his gym-rat build and Marlon Brando eyes, Michael did. "He was fine!" she said. "Fine, fine, fine, *fine*-looking white man! I was flirting with him the whole time." Michael didn't notice. As a mother of a newborn, Opal was, for a rare moment, a caseworker's dream: he put her on maternity leave, and they were done for three months. When the leave expired and Michael insisted she do something for her check, he no longer looked so fine. "Michael Stein-some-shit," she would call him.

For now, he had another challenge: the Woman Without a Coat. She reappeared just after his meeting with Opal—loud, raspy, and coatless still. He tried to act indignant about her claim that he hadn't helped her. But his resolve melted in a hail of denials and her loud, sing-songy *Mi-ikes.* "I never said that, Mi-ike! I never told a lie about you!" She popped up in his office, talking gibberish: God is money, the Devil is deaf, beware the millennium bug. But in between her story trickled out. She was thirty-nine, with a grown daughter and a ten-year-old son. She was raised in the ghetto, but not on the streets; her mother was a church woman and her father kept a job. She played high school basketball, got her diploma, and landed a clerical job. Then a decade ago she went to a party where people were smoking a new drug. She figured it couldn't hurt to try it once. She stole, she whored, she slept in the gutter. Treatment programs couldn't keep her off of crack. Only her mother's death, two years ago, gave her the resolve to get clean. Her mother had been "about taking care of business," she would say, and now she was taking care of business, too. "I lost my soul on crack, Mi-ike. I'm about business now, Mi-ike, I'm about business."

At first Michael wasn't sure if he cared. But her stories had a morbid pull, and there was something obligating about her trust. Michael was particularly impressed with the impeccable manners of her son. Sit up straight, she would fuss. Look at the man when you speak. Oddly, he started feeling half pleased when the receptionist announced, with a sarcastic aside, that his train wreck of a client had arrived. While Michael didn't say so, she wasn't the only member of the tandem who often felt desperate about getting through the day. At one point, she brought him a crinkled sheet of greeting-card verse: "Obstacles are only what you see when you take your eye off the goal." He tacked it to his wall.

Bonding was one thing. Binding her to the scaffold of W-2 was another. In January, Michael assigned her a community service job, sorting clothes at the St. Vincent dePaul Society. She never showed up. In February, she called from a pay phone and announced she was going to be a nursing assistant. "Mi-ike, I'm in a training now!" Michael snapped at her: That's not how it works! You can't assign your own activities! "Why not, Mi-ike, if it'll help me get a job?" She didn't get her certificate, but Michael let her keep half her check. "I just didn't have the heart to cut her off," he said. In March, she got an eviction notice after falling four months behind on the rent. Michael grew newly concerned. Most landlords wouldn't carry her that long, and hers was no philanthropist. Michael asked if she had been having "rent dates," swapping sex for shelter, and her denials left him unconvinced. Maximus had a unit to deal with evictions; unfortunately, it was the same one that dealt with coats. She was still looking for a new place when the landlord removed her front door.

It took him weeks, but Michael found a solution. A nonprofit group, Community Advocates, would pay her security deposit. In exchange, it would become her "protective payee," cashing her W-2 check, paying the landlord, and giving her whatever remained. Most recipients balked at losing control of their money, but Michael's client quickly followed through, even putting down $10 for a key. All she had to do was to pick an apartment. SuperFep had gotten it done! But she didn't pick an apartment. She moved to a shelter. And the next thing Michael knew, she was sitting in his boss's office, complaining that no one would help her. He got her to a private room and lost his considerable temper. What was she doing in a homeless shelter? How could she do that to her son?

Her answers didn't make sense. All the vacant houses were on the south side, she said. She grew up on the north side. "I can't live on the south side, Mi-ike." Jesus, she was acting goofy; it was almost enough to make him think she was back on drugs. He was so pissed he started to taunt her: what, are your *connections* on the north side? She flared up and taunted him back: I walk by my connections all day! It took Michael a moment to grasp what she was saying. He hadn't been serious. She wasn't still using. She wasn't still smoking crack? "Yeah, I'm smoking crack!" When was the last time she smoked? Three days ago. She told him she had been clean two years. "I told you what you wanted to hear."

Michael felt the room spin. He felt like a total chump. He had poured some subconscious drive for redemption into a crackhead who had scammed him. "A small part of me knew it the whole time," he said. "I felt really stupid and really useless as somebody who was supposed to be helping her. And I felt very sad for her son." More shouting followed when Michael urged her to return to treatment. No way, she said; treatment programs tell you it's your fault. To some extent, Michael said, it *is* your fault. Don't you think I know that? Don't you think I hate myself every day? It more or less ended there, the conversation and the latest disillusioning chapter in the life of Super-

Fep. No hard feelings, he said with a parting embrace. But he needed to refer her to a more specialized caseworker. "Do what you got to do, Mi-ike. I always do."

A few weeks later, Michael was sitting at his desk, staring at the Excuse Woman. She never did *anything*, this one. The bus was late. The dog was sick. She lost the address. She forgot to call. Doing his best not to look like a man having a breakdown, he excused himself and crossed the hall to his supervisor's office. Question: who could he see about the company's counseling program? He was having a little problem with—how to put this?—managing his anger. He was having a problem with the idea that "financial and employment planners" were going to help "job seekers" scale the "work ladder" to achieve "self-sufficiency." In fact, he found the whole notion ridiculous, and he didn't want to be held responsible for the next calamity. He returned with a pamphlet for Employee Assistance and flashed the Excuse Woman a look of contempt. "What kind of fantasy world are you living in?" he asked.

He went home that night and told his girlfriend, Jai, he was looking for another job. They lie and cheat and lie some more. They bear out the cynic's adage: no good deed among Feps ever goes unpunished. He got no argument from Jai. Her own mother had spent years on welfare and left her for relatives to raise. "I'd tell them their sorry ass was always gonna be in the gutter," she said. "He calls them 'job seekers,' I call them 'money seekers.' I'd cuss 'em out and lose that job!" Michael was going back to hanging drywall. You nail it and it stays in place.

Who was he kidding with his calculator routine? Even his successes were emptying bedpans and swabbing hotel rooms. There's no such thing as a bad first job! Your kids are going to be proud! He'd been to a conference where Tommy Thompson had given that speech, and it had made him cringe. "I'm the guy the politicians hire to tell themselves they're doing something about the underbelly of society: 'Oh, we've got W-2! Isn't it a great program!' It's a farce. It's sickly comic. There's some delusion that we're going to take these people to the next level—that's not going to happen." Michael's midnight resolve faded with morning light. He couldn't quit; he had to pay the rent.

To boost his spirits, he hung up a MaxAcademy "Certificate of Completion" that belonged to a woman he hardly knew. Angiwetta Hills had walked in at closing hour, looking as ragged as her tale. She had lost her job, moved to a shelter, and gotten dropped from the rolls when Employment Solutions, the Goodwill subsidiary, failed to properly transfer the case. Here we go again, Michael thought, bracing for a tirade. Instead, she apologized for the way she looked; she had left her clean clothes at a relative's house and hadn't been able to change. Michael spent hours restoring her benefits. Then she surprised him with perfect attendance in Motivation Class. It wasn't exactly a new life. Or even a new job. But the surprise ran in both directions: she hadn't expected a caseworker to work so hard to straighten out her case or offer such reassurance. "He said, 'Everything's going to be all right, Angiwetta. You put in your half and I'll put in mine,'" she said.

His expectations of Dinah Doty ran just as low. At twenty-three, she was a high school dropout, pregnant with her fourth child, and about to be evicted. He rushed to get her a special grant, but she got evicted, anyway. She was pleasant enough, but very street, and Michael had her pegged as a lifer. Once her maternity leave expired, he gave her the calculator spiel: $3.91 an hour, can you beat it? The next week, she announced she had a job as a clerk at a homeless shelter for nearly $8 an hour. And she seemed so—Michael felt embarrassed to say it—*proud.* "Michael gave me that motivation to get up and basically open my eyes," she told me. "I have children to take care of. We conversate about it all the time. Michael understands where I'm coming from."

On that, she may have been more right than she knew. He had lost his business, wrecked his marriage, and wasted his shot at a college degree. There were days when he felt so disgusted with himself he couldn't look in a mirror. And he told that to some of his clients. "I say, 'I *know* what it's like to be down and out. I *know* what it's like to not even be able to get out of bed because you're drunk from the day before and you're too depressed.'" While Michael thought he had nothing to learn about the tragedy of ghetto life, he learned something, anyway. "They don't want to be perceived as vulnerable," he said of his clients. "But when you cut away the exterior, they're sad—sad for themselves, sad for their children, sad that they haven't done more with their lives. And they're just aching for you to listen. Not necessarily to solve their problem, just to listen. I'm not sure if I knew that before and chose to forget it or if I'm learning it for the first time."

The case he saw as his biggest success can be seen as a tribute to either his ample gifts or his slender expectations. In his first stack of dusty cases sat the file of Shelley Block, who had collected $6,000 the previous year without doing a thing. Michael sent letters. Michael made calls. Michael took away her check. That made his telephone ring. "What—you don't give out checks?" she said. He told her to come see him in the morning. "I don't *do* mornings," she said. Finally, she darkened his door. Literally. She weighed more than three hundred pounds. She had a pierced tongue and a tattooed neck, and she was as cynical in person as she was on the phone. Michael found her enchanting. "Everything she said made me laugh," he said. When she talked, vaguely, about becoming a nursing aide, Michael told her the truth: she was too fat to stand up all day. "I respected him for that," she told me. He lured her to MaxAcademy just to get her out of the house. Then he arranged a work assignment at Maximus, to keep her in sight. They talked—about her boyfriend, her boyfriend's crack problem, her days in a street gang. "He made me feel like he actually cared," she said.

One day, she arrived in his office especially depressed. She had dumped the crackhead boyfriend, who then broke in the house and beat her up. Michael responded with the best you-are-somebody lecture she had heard. "I see you as an authority figure," he said. "I can see you sitting behind a desk, making sound money. Don't ever let anybody put you down." When she got back to the car, her mother asked why she was crying. "Michael just makes me feel real good about myself," she said. Not long after, when Michael fell captive to one of his depressions and told her he wanted to leave, she turned the lecture around. "I told him, 'Don't quit! You're too good at what you do.'"

After a year on Michael's caseload, Shelley Block got a job. It was nothing that either one of them would mistake for a social triumph: a part-time job at an after-school program, driving a bus. It paid $7.25

an hour. It might lead to something better. But probably not. "Fep of the year," he said to himself. "A part-time bus driver. Big deal." Not long after, one of Michael's coworkers was down in the dumps, griping about the caseworker's lot. The clients don't listen. The system's a mess. The whole thing's a big con. Michael stunned himself with his response. "We do God's work here," he said. For a moment, he believed it.

SIXTEEN

Boyfriends: Milwaukee, Spring 1999

Angie did her share of God's work, too. She had been doing it now for three years: lifting, washing, dressing, and feeding the infirm. She did it before sunrise and after midnight. She did it when her feet were sore and her back had shooting pains. She did it in an old Polish neighborhood that once rioted to keep black people away. She did it without complaint. Stepping off a bus eight years earlier, looking for a welfare check, Angie was someone society carried. Now she carried those who couldn't carry themselves. "Angie has a sparkle," said her supervisor, Wendy Woolcott-Steele. "I think she's ace."

Angie's story had a special luster, but it conveyed a common theme: whatever the frustrations of SuperFeps or the failures of the bureaucracy, poor single mothers, defying predictions, went to work at unprecedented rates. Although they didn't all sparkle, about three-quarters of the women leaving the rolls in the late 1990s worked in the subsequent year. Six in ten worked at any given time, and those with jobs worked nearly full time, about thirty-five hours a week. No doubt the surging economy offered ideal conditions. Yet previous booms had largely left welfare families behind, and the gains were greatest among the most disadvantaged, which discounts the notion that a rising tide simply lifted all boats. The employment rates of never-married women rose nearly 50 percent, while those least affected by welfare policy (married, college educated, or childless) scarcely changed. In its curious mix of hassles ("They gave me a lot of yada, yada, yada. I said, 'Screw 'em' and found me a job") and help (child care and tax credits), the drive to end welfare created a singular employment machine. "It succeeded beyond, I think, what anybody could have rationally predicted," Clinton told me. And on one level he was right.

But the advocates of the law had talked on other levels, too—not just of putting poor people to work but of the rewards that work would bring. "Work organizes life," Clinton had said. "It gives meaning and self-esteem to people who are parents. It gives a role model to children." The celebrations of the law were celebrations of its social bequests—of *meaning* and *role models* and transformed kids. Of parables like that of Lillie Harden and her son. About the time Angie let Opal move in, Tommy Thompson invited another welfare-to-work success to tell her story during his State of the State Address. Michelle Crawford had gone from two decades of depression and drugs on welfare to a job at a plastics factory. Facing the legislature beside the man she nervously called "Government Thompson," she stole the show. "Today, I'm working as a machine operator, providing for my family," she said. Then, with flawless timing, she pointed toward the gallery where three of her children were watching. "Now, I tell my kids that this is what you get when you do your homework!"

The author Mickey Kaus went so far as to argue that the rising work rates presaged "The Ending of the Black Underclass."

> [B]y definition and in practice, working-poor mothers aren't in the "underclass." A maid changing sheets in a Marriott is no longer cut off from the world of work. . . . She can't afford to develop an attitude that sets itself in opposition to the mainstream culture. Her children will grow up knowing the discipline of a working home, and they will have at least one working "role model. . . ." If women know they . . . are going to have to work, they are apt to ask that men contribute by going to work. Young women will be less likely to have children out of wedlock.

Ordered lives, elevated hopes, inspired kids: it was a lot to hope for from a low-wage job. Three years into her postwelfare life, Angie Jobe—indefatigable worker, hard liver—offered one ground-level view.

Taking in Opal was God's work reprised, but there was a price to Angie's charity. With the pit bulls having destroyed the attic, Angie was out of space. The boys shared a foldout sofa in the living room, while Opal, Kesha, and Brierra squeezed into one bed and Angie and Marcus shared the other. The Concordia Street house was a shambles. The second-floor balcony dropped rails like rotted teeth, and so many roaches swarmed about that Opal lay awake worried that one would crawl in Brierra's ear. Angie blamed the landlord for not fixing things. The landlord blamed Angie for not paying the rent and tried to evict her twice. Before Marcus had gotten the pit bulls, someone had tried to break into Kesha's room. Two days after Opal moved in, there was a shooting in the abandoned apartment below. Opal's arrival settled things. Angie decided to move.

With tax time near, Angie had another windfall coming: $5,300, the equivalent of five months' pay. In truth, it was enough to subsidize a move to a better part of town. But Angie didn't know anyone in a better part of town. And she had neither a car nor the instincts of a housing pioneer. She found four bedrooms in a duplex on the near north side, at 2400 West Brown. The street took its name from Samuel Brown, the nineteenth-century settler who had turned his farm there into a stop on the Underground Railroad. By the time Angie arrived, the street cut through so many vacant lots it looked like it was being reclaimed by Farmer Brown's fields. Jewell had been living on Brown Street when gunfire had forced her to sleep on the floor and when Lucky had been shot in the hand. And a few years later, Brown Street would make the national news when a gang of boys, some as young as ten, armed themselves with shovels and bats and beat a neighborhood man to his death. Opal knew the area, too; Andrea's crack house was a short walk away. But at $450 a month, the price of Angie's new house was right. And Angie figured it wasn't much different from other places she had lived.

Just before the move, she and Opal stopped in for a look. The friendly new landlord was there, gluing down new living room carpet and throwing up a fresh coat of paint. "I want everything to be just right for you, Miss Jobe," he said. Opal thought that he might be a little too friendly. She noticed that without Marcus around Angie was friendly, too. "Oh, I want everything to be just right for you, Miss Jobe," she sang, as they got out of earshot. "Shut up, creep," Angie laughed. Angie worked the day of the move, so she missed most of the adventure. The kids packed their clothes in Hefty bags. The apartment had no appliances, so Marcus had to rent a trailer to tote the refrigerator and stove. His $500 Chevy broke down twice, bringing out Jewell in the snow to give him a jump. They finished at 1:30 in the morning. "We had a ghetto move," Kesha said.

The practical thing for Angie to do with the money that remained would have been to buy a car. Until she got one, Angie would be stuck with the lower wages along the bus line. Instead, she bought furniture again. Darrell got a new bedroom set, having destroyed his with more bed-jumping games. The living room got a new black-and-green couch, and the windows got window blinds. Angie didn't have a dining room, but she bought place settings for her dining room table and put it in the living room. Then she banned the kids from eating there. Sometimes when there's turmoil inside, you yearn to set appearances right.

Maybe it was her years in Catholic school, but Angie still believed in salvation, her own and that of others. Opal was pledging to kick the cocaine and get the girls back from her mother. Angie thought she could do it. The birth of Brierra had brought a surge of maternal diligence, to the point where Opal asked a hospital social worker about treatment programs. She didn't realize the social worker was attached to the county child welfare agency. When the conversation triggered a visit to Concordia Street, the caseworker grew so alarmed at the pit bulls and roaches that she threatened to take Brierra away. Opal beat a quick retreat to Jewell's and the incipient investigation fizzled. But so did Opal's talk of programs. "If I go to one of them, I got to cut the drinking out, too," she said.

Her short stay at Jewell's brought problems. Soon after Opal moved in, Jewell's car broke down. Jewell left Opal $100 to have it towed, and when she got home from work, Opal was gone. So was Jewell's money, along with a bunch of her video games and her pearl-handled .22. Jewell wasn't surprised that Opal would steal. But she was stunned that Opal would steal from her. From *family.* While Angie was trying to play Good Shepherd to Opal, Jewell's ethos was an eye for an eye: when Opal returned the following day, Jewell barred her from the house, kept her clothes, and temporarily took her food stamps. Jewell eventually let go of her anger but not her residential ban; Opal wasn't allowed in the house unless Jewell herself was there. Angie made a minor show of taking Opal back. "Let her come over here," she said. "I ain't got nothing to steal." It was a line that would make Jewell laugh.

Angie got a package deal. In taking in Opal, she not only got an infant, Brierra, she also got Opal's "friend" from the crack house, Bo. "I ain't fittin' to be Cuckoo for Cocoa Puffs," Opal said—not crazy for some man. But as her talk of sobriety faded, her talk of Bo increased. She said he made her feel "giddy-ish." Giddy was hard to understand—he was pitted, scraggy, dull, and dumb—but one could guess a source of his appeal. "Drugs!" Angie said. "'Cause he ain't no good-looking motherfucker!" What Bo saw in Opal was harder to say; most dealers didn't want a girlfriend consuming their goods. Her ability to win him over was both a tribute to her survival skills and his lack of alternatives. Mostly, they argued. On maternity leave from the work rules she had previously ignored, Opal had too much time on her hands, and she spent it in a jealous dudgeon. In a typical incident, she would accuse Bo of sleeping with his ex-girlfriend and threaten to leave; Bo would feign indifference but compensate with Pampers or a used VCR that someone had traded in for drugs. If Angie had misgivings about the soap opera in her living room, she kept them to herself. She figured it was Opal's business and nothing the kids hadn't seen.

Shortly after the move, Opal got $400 in tax credits from a month's work the previous year. The next morning, Jewell was standing in Angie's kitchen, bouncing a yo-yo. It was Saturday, and she had promised to take Opal shopping for baby clothes. Opal wasn't there. "Gone all night?" Jewell said.

"You shoulda gone yesterday!" Angie fussed.

"Oh, Opal," Jewell said.

Von arrived home from a fifth-grade basketball game, aiming a Sprite like a machine gun. "Y'all win?" Angie asked.

"We lost by five."

"Y'all always lose," she said. "Y'all the Bad News Bears."

"Opal, Opal, Opal!" Jewell said.

Darrell, who was five, chimed in. "She probably got lost over there," he said. Everyone knew where "over there" was. Andrea's house.

Bo walked in at midday, not knowing Opal was missing. "Where Brierra at?" he asked. Brierra was with Kesha (as usual), and Bo left on a scouting mission.

"Bring her back!" Jewell said.

"I mean put her on your back and carry her!" Angie said.

No one was going to find Opal until Opal was ready to be found. She had stayed at Andrea's until 4:00 in the morning, smoking up her tax money, when one of the night's big spenders told her he was tired of overpaying for dime bags. He wanted a quarter, a quantity the size of a Ping-Pong ball. It sells for $250, but not to an unknown white guy on Brown Street in the middle of the night. Opal knew a place to get one, and they got back to his house at sunrise on Saturday to celebrate their luck. By Sunday morning, when Opal came home, she had been partying for two nights and a day. Angie held her tongue. She had problems of her own.

One of them was Marcus. Like many poor black men, Marcus looked worse on paper than he did in person. On paper, he was a sporadically employed eleventh-grade dropout with a history of drug dealing and carrying illegal weapons—technically a habitual criminal. In person, he was an aimless but mostly placid soul who, lacking a father, had spent his youth seeking brotherhood in a gang. His twenty-five-year-old body was all hard edges—shaved head, tattooed biceps—but any air of menace was offset by a pair of basset hound eyes; he showed more interest in smoking blunts than in doing anyone harm. When they came to blows, Angie usually counted herself the aggressor. "I have a worse temper," she said. "He have to psyche hisself up to be mean."

The story of Angie and Marcus is, among other things, the story of the limits of a social reform that almost exclusively targets one gender.

In the end-welfare years, poor women went to work in record numbers. But poor men did not. And young, low-skilled black men—the sea in which women like Angie swim—continued to leave the job market at disconcerting rates. Despite the booming economy, the employment rates of young black men fell faster in the 1990s than they did the decade before. By the end of the nineties, only about half of young black men had jobs, compared with nearly 80 percent of Hispanics and whites. Theories abound: disheartening wages, high prison rates, the flight of urban jobs, employer discrimination even toward those with no record. (Does anyone draw more suspicion than a young black man?) Flooding the labor market with competition from women may even have made things marginally worse. It may be an exaggeration to say that behind every successful worker like Angie lurked a jealous, potentially disruptive man. But it's not a huge exaggeration.

David J. Pate Jr., a doctoral candidate at the University of Wisconsin, spent two years tracking black men in Milwaukee with children on welfare. On average they earned $8,800 a year and owed $6,500 in back support. Three-quarters had a high school diploma or less. Two-thirds had criminal convictions. Though their average age was thirty-four, many couldn't secure a badge of adulthood as basic as a driver's license or an apartment—a quarter still lived with their mothers. Where others have seen cavalier dereliction, Pate (who also runs a fatherhood program) viewed the men through sympathetic eyes. He saw wounded castaways—rejected by employers, chased by the courts, and exiled by the mothers of their kids. With the mothers in new relationships, some of the men couldn't see their children no matter how hard they tried. In the men's minds, the mothers' failures loomed large, especially when the mothers were on drugs: why should my money go to *her*? Pate may be right in arguing that "most of these men aspired to be good fathers." But the modesty of their gestures was revealing. "I buy diapers all that," boasted Deion, a jobless twenty-one-year-old. I once spent a day in a Milwaukee class that forced absent fathers like these to write their own obituaries through the eyes of the children they scarcely knew. "He really wasn't involved in our lives," stammered one man, imagining what his two-year-old twins might someday say over his coffin. He added a hopeful "but we respect him." By the time that Pate finished his study, two of the thirty-six men had been murdered.

If working mothers will save the underclass, having one hadn't saved Marcus. After stepping off a bus from Memphis, Mary Williams made a career slinging greens at Perkins, a Milwaukee soul-food palace. But Marcus's older brother was locked up for selling drugs, and his sister was strung out on drugs. "His mama real nice—I don't know how she got all them crazy-assed kids," Angie said. The same could be said about most people Angie knew. Like Opal, Marcus met his father just once, and his father was drunk at the time. "My mama was my daddy," he said. At fifteen, he joined the "Brothers of Struggle," neighborhood guys with bankrolls and loud cars. He tattooed a six-point star on one arm and put "Love Mom" on the other. Marcus thought the gang "stood for something," though he couldn't say just what. "You had all these guys behind you," he said. "Like a family." After dropping out of school, he cut meat in corner grocery stores and helped his guys sell weed and cocaine.

His twenty-third year was rough. He got caught in a drug house, selling crack. He got robbed at shotgun of two pounds of marijuana. Then his gang brothers accused him of stealing the weed and broke his arms with two-by-fours. Being hospitalized and sent to jail tempered his enthusiasm for the gang life, without quite extinguishing it: he would still earnestly recite the catechism of the six-point star: love, knowledge, wisdom, life, loyalty, understanding. He had been out of jail and working for two months, when Angie walked in the grocery store and Marcus saw more stars. "I just wanted to know her real bad," he said. She was eight years older, a woman of the world. She radiated class. On their first date, he took her to an all-night diner. "You can't just take Angie to McDonald's or Burger King," he said.

At the start, Angie may have cared for Marcus more than she liked to admit. She was lonely, he was handsome, and he introduced himself with a smile. He cooked and cleaned and watched the kids; occasionally he bought them clothes. On Mother's Day, he surprised Angie with flowers and balloons. There was one problem, Angie said: "Motherfucker just not faithful." As they got together, another woman spotted Marcus with Angie and dumped a pile of his clothes in the street. Angie knew there were others. "My day is coming," she would say. By the time she moved to Brown Street, it had come. Angie was staying out half the night, "talking" to a coworker named Tony. There were nights when Angie didn't come home; she'd say she stayed at Jewell's. One night Marcus confronted Tony, who assured him there was nothing going on. Opal thought Marcus had to know but was pretending that he didn't.

The kids viewed Marcus with a mixture of indifference and contempt. If Angie didn't respect him, why should they? But they also spent a lot of time alone with him—and a lot of time just alone. Angie worked the second shift, 2:00 to 10:00 p.m., which left her gone during most of their free hours. Just shy of fifteen, Kesha arrived on Brown Street with a wide smile, crooked canines, and the burdens and privileges of the oldest child. She was still enough of a little girl to dote on her kittens and keep a kitchen play set in her room. And enough of a teenager to always have a boy on her mind. "Dear Mom, I have a lot of questions about sex," she wrote after Marcus spotted her kissing one of her neighborhood suitors. "It's not like going to do anything elec because I'm not really. . . . You going to have to understand that I'm start to be a young lady." Hospitalized with asthma for weeks at a time the previous year, Kesha had missed half of seventh grade and failed nearly every course. Virtually raising Brierra, she was absent a good bit of eighth.

While Kesha had babies and boys on her mind, Redd seemed to have nothing in mind at all. Still, he would talk the paint off the wall in an effort to make himself heard. At thirteen, he spent his free time in the cramped living room, filibustering the walls, a portrait of growing, inchoate rage. "Apply yourself," Greg had written from prison. "Start going to the library at least twice a week." Instead Redd bought a CD and rapped to "I Don't Give a Fuck." His father was just another stranger. If Redd had troubles that were going unheeded, Von had potential that was going unshaped. At eleven, he was still a boy focused on boyhood stuff—cars, sports, and video games—and alone among Angie's kids, he felt invested in school. But Von "is always catching up, rather than being up," his fifth grade teacher warned. "Being up" was part of the problem. As Angie and Marcus had started to quarrel, Von had stopped going to bed; he waited until his mother was safely home, "'cause I knew they was gonna come in fighting when the bars closed." The semester that Marcus moved in, Von's school absences rose 50 percent. Darrell, at six, crawled in my lap whenever I walked in the door. He was all but walking through life with a sign that read Someone Hug Me.

I dropped in one night around the dinner hour. No one was talking about dinner. Angie was at the nursing home, feeding her patients. Marcus was gone. Opal was emitting operatic groans. Her three months of maternity leave had expired, and Michael Steinborn had promptly scheduled her for MaxAcademy. She was due there the next morning at 8:00. "I'm not going to be able to do it," she said. Von was practicing his pickup lines. "I'm a player, not a hater," he said.

But the real player was Kesha, who was mulling the problem with her latest boyfriend, Larry. They had met on a four-way telephone call and talked every day for a month before meeting face-to-face. Then one day, Kesha was at Jewell's, and Jewell said Larry could come by, and—

Darrell broke in. After a long absence, his father had started to visit again. "My daddy got a job, Kesha!"

"Mama told you that," Kesha said.

Darrell said he told his father, "I didn't know you had a job!"

Kesha wasn't interested in Darrell's daddy; Kesha was interested in Larry. So . . . Larry came over, and he was six-foot-one; and they played video games and put on some music; and Larry clapped and yelled, "Hit that note!" as Kesha sang along. Then they went to get some Tater Tots for Jewell, and Larry had to go. "And he was like, 'You ain't gonna give me no kiss?' And I said, 'Boy, what's your problem?'" This part of the story made her smile. "Then I gave him a hug and kiss!"

"*Ooow*, you *kissed* him!" Her brothers were listening in.

"Stop dippin'!" Kesha said, delighted with the audience.

The boys started to sing: "In the bedroom . . . In the hallway . . . We can do it anywhere."

Though nearly two months had passed, Kesha hadn't seen Larry again. He lived too far away, and she was wondering if they should break up. "I don't want no kids," she said. Then: "I want a daughter." Then: "I want to get married before I have a baby. My mama didn't ever get married. I want a big wedding. I never been to a wedding." Angie had never been to a wedding, either. "If it's in the summer I want to have it in a big old church," Kesha said. "I think it'd be a lot of fun if you be together a long time. My mama been with my dad for seven years before he went to jail—"

Kesha's vision of domestic bliss vanished as Marcus stormed in. "It smells like must through the whole house!" he said. It was 8:15 p.m. The breakfast dishes were still in the sink, and the boys' room was buried in clothing drifts three feet tall. Darrell added more bad news: Redd had skipped school. "Your ass is mine!" Marcus said. "My mama said it ain't!" Redd said, and ran to his room.

Kesha called Darrell a "tattletale punk" and slapped him on the head. Marcus was so angry—*this mess! these kids!*—he looked ready to charge the wall. "You were told to do the dishes last night!" he screamed.

"Last *night*?" The sarcasm dripped from Kesha's voice and pooled on the unswept floor. "This is a whole new day, Marcus."

Darrell bawled from Kesha's slap. Redd ran to the pay phone across the street and tried to reach Angie. But she was too busy with patients to come to the phone. "Go call your motherfucking mama," Marcus said, disappearing into his room. "And when you're done come deal with me!" Kesha rolled her eyes. It was almost 9:00 and no one had eaten. No wonder tempers flared. "We're all hungry," she said.

"Goal-setting is very important! . . . If you fail to plan, you plan to fail! . . . Getting a job is a full-time job!" The motivation lady was preaching the next morning, but Opal wasn't in the mood. She was slumped in a chair, eyes barely open, as the waves of aphorism crashed overhead. Angie had come home and fought with Marcus all night, then roused Opal and ordered her to class. "Last name, first name, Social Security number! This calendar is what you will follow each and every day while you're here at MaxAcademy. . . . Problem resolution, dressing for success—we'll have workshops! . . . We've had people from all over the world watching us, from Germany, Sweden! . . . It's all about children—that's why we're here!"

Two other people had shown up, neither with greater interest. Opal would give it one day. She had sat through so many motivation classes, she complained the curriculum was out of order: assessment tests belonged on the second day. "We changed it," the instructor said. As Opal played along with her number-two pencil (yes, she would like to "study ruins"; no, she wouldn't like to "grow grain"), Michael stopped by. "How's the baby doing?" he said. It was only their second meeting, and—now that he had stuck her in MaxAcademy—less pleasant than her first. Taking her aside, he noted she had missed her last appointment and said he didn't buy the excuse about babysitting problems. If she didn't attend the classes, he said, she couldn't get a check.

Opal glared. "I don't want to be here," she said.

"You really don't have any option," he said. "I take that back. You do have an option—you don't have to participate in the W-2 program." Caseworkers can sound nasty when they want but there was nothing nasty in Michael's voice. "I pulled your case history," he said. "You don't call, you don't show. I pulled your employment history. It's sketchy at best. . . . Do you have your GED?"

Opal clucked her tongue. "I have a high school diploma!" she said. "And some college!"

Michael looked skeptical. He told her to spend a few weeks in the class, to establish a morning routine. "Sometimes you need to be pushed in certain directions," he said.

"I don't."

"We'll see."

He gave her a week to find child care. After that, he warned, every hour's absence would be deducted from her check. Opal dragged herself back to class, leaving a trail of artificial braids on the rug. Even bodily she was coming unglued. "'Well you *say* you got a high school diploma,'" she fumed. "Like I was lying!"

Two days later, Mercy called in too many aides, and Angie got sent home. She figured it was just as well. Her feet were tired and she had errands to run, but she was waiting for Kesha to come home from school. In the morning's confusion, Redd hadn't been able to find the coat that Jewell had bought for his birthday. Angie was hoping that Kesha had worn it. Opal, who had been acting irritable all morning, came out of her room just before Kesha was due to arrive. Kesha didn't have the coat, she said. The crack house did.

Angie gasped. "You took Redd's birthday coat?" And the Play Station. And the CDs. And Kesha's radio and Von's new video game, Crash Bandicoot. Opal had been slipping in and out since dawn, auctioning off the kids' stuff. Angie was no stranger to fury, but Opal's betrayal propelled her to new heights: stealing's one thing, even stealing from me—but how could you steal from my *kids*? Opal started to pack and leave, but Angie demanded something more painful, a humiliating public confession as each of the kids walked in. Everyone yelled at Opal that day. Angie yelled, Bo yelled, Kesha, who was all but raising Opal's baby, yelled most of all: "You're a thief! You hurt people! You should leave that shit alone!" Marcus grabbed his gun and started toward the crack house until Angie reeled him in. "You don't go to no dope spot and tell 'em you want your stuff back," she said. "Marcus ain't wrapped too tight." Opal agreed to replace the items with her next welfare check and spent the afternoon looking contrite. Despite her anger, Angie, unlike Jewell, refused to put her out. "I wouldn't do that to Brierra," she said. Opal "would be in a shelter, just doing it again." At dinner, Opal asked Angie to go with her to a sobriety meeting, Opal's first in a year. When they got there, they found the meeting had moved. Looking back, Angie saw the trip as part of the con. "She knew they didn't have meetings no more," she said.

One good thing about the rhythm of the house was that it left no time to brood about old trouble; new trouble was always on the way. The next day, Opal's mother drove up from Chicago and left the girls for spring break. Eight kids, one bathroom, and a limited supply of food didn't make for a happy week. Opal's four daughters slept with her, piled in the bed with Bo. Redd tried to keep them from eating the cookies. Von put gum in Sierra's hair; Sierra put gum on Von. Opal locked Von out of the house, and when Von shook his finger in her face, Opal put him in a headlock and threw him to the floor. "When I got through with him, he was *real* hurt," she said.

The cocaine was playing tricks with Opal's eyes, highlighting the transgressions of everyone else, while blinding her to her own. She didn't approve of Angie's nagging: "She think she can be my mother!" She resented Angie's request for rent: "And spend all my food stamps? She is ripping me off." She didn't approve of Angie's parenting: "Them kids ain't never in school." She criticized Angie's consumption of beer: "I said, 'You ain't nothing but an alcoholic.'" Angie knew that Opal was busy cataloging her sins. But her refusal to put Opal out had grown to a point of pride. "You can't get angry any more," she said. "All you can do is pray now—just hope she find her way."

Jewell kept her distance from Angie and Opal, clucking her tongue at the antics. "Ain't neither one of them doing what they really supposed to," she said. By contrast, Jewell's house formed an oasis of tranquility. Jewell kept more regular hours than Angie; she didn't drink; and she kept her kids on a tighter leash. Like Angie, she had taken in a needy relative, but her nephew Quinten had just turned five, so she didn't have to worry about him pawning her stuff for drugs. The aura of order—or maybe just the big TV—made Jewell's place a favorite destination for Angie's kids. She had a white tiger-skin sofa and rug and a stack of G movies from *A Bug's Life* to *Babe.* Jewell's house felt like Jewell, racy yet domestic.

In some ways, Jewell's success on the job was even more impressive than Angie's, since she started with so little experience. After eight years on welfare, she was a 9-to-5 scanner of nameless objects on an industrial shipping line. But work was simply something she did. What she cared about was Ken, whose prominence in Jewell's post-welfare story was unlikely to get featured in a State of the State Address. Jewell's wages paid some of the bills. The remnants of Ken's drug and prostitution money paid others. While most of Jewell's friends might wait six months for an imprisoned man, they wouldn't wait two years, especially for one deftly promising nothing in return. Jewell decided the separation was a test—"to see if our love is strong enough"—and wrote him every other day. "That's all she talk about," giggled her seven-year-old, Tremmell. "Oh, I miss my boo-boo!"

Tina, Ken's hooker, missed Ken, too, and in his absence Jewell's conflicts with her grew. Jewell said Tina wrote Ken letters peddling the lie that Jewell was smoking crack. She said Tina called G. B. Electric and tried to get her fired by claiming that Jewell had threatened to beat her up. (After that, Jewell said, she *did* threaten to beat Tina up.) One day, Jewell emerged from work to find that the car that Ken had left her was gone. Jewell remembered that Tina had a key, and since

Jewell didn't have the title, the police said there was nothing they could do. Soon Jewell found a hospital bill collector at her door, seeking payment for treating her venereal disease. "I ain't got no gonorrhea!" she said. Then she realized she left some papers in the car. Tina had her Social Security number.

Ken and Jewell were together when he left, but not *together*. He didn't fully think of Jewell as his girlfriend, and he had Tina turning tricks. In person Jewell had stopped short of making demands, but in his absence her boldness grew. She told him to stop "waiting on some Miss America or Miss Hollywood to come to your life." She told him she wanted him to herself. Mail is everything to a man locked up, and Ken had nothing but time to ponder Jewell's devotion. She wrote him twenty times in the first month alone and sent him money and clothes. As Jewell grew more open, Ken did, too. "I really don't know what my problem is," he wrote. "[I]ts a man thing," he tried to explain. One letter said, "I'm willing to give it a try." Another called her a "soulmate."

> [Y]ou may not be that Miss hollywood or Miss America as you say but you are everything in a women that a man could want sense of humor, best friend, a sister I never had and a great Lover . . . you are like a dream. . . . I can't make any promises but I am willing to put effort into it. . . . I want to keep our relationship sacred.

"I couldn't stop reading it," Jewell said. At first, he signed off, "Okay, Ken" or "I'll holler at you." Then came a letter that said, "I love you" and one to "my gorgeous wife." How much was love, how much was loneliness, even he couldn't say. There were tensions, too; needing someone to watch Quinten, Jewell had let Lucky back in the house, and he intercepted Ken's mail. "I know he's your rent-a-dad," Ken fumed, routing his letters through a friend, but "make his Ass stand outside." Still, the sheer force of Jewell's devotion was one that Tina couldn't match. When Tina promised a package that she never sent, Ken wrote her to say they were through.

He had been gone for two months when Jewell got a letter that made her spirits soar. "Hello there my sexy wife," it began.

> I almost feel as you do. . . . I feel that we're so close in our love that when I'm not with you I'm just not where I want to be, everyday we spend apart is starting to feel like twenty-four more hours of lost, lonely time slowly ticking away. . . . So until you're in my arms please remember you are always, always on my mind; you are never, never out of my heart and you are needed more than ever in my life.

"Finally!" Jewell said. She strolled through the aisles of Sam's Club, pointing out the brand of diapers they'd wrap their baby in. She told him that her friends hadn't believed her when she said they were going to get married. *Married?* Whatever he felt toward his "sexy wife," a wedding was the last thing on Ken's mind. He was up for parole after six months and eager to get back to business, with Jewell or without her. "I said, 'Till death do us part,'" he wrote back. "So do that math."

Till death do we part—do the math. Ken started to say it all the time. Now and then, when her spirits sagged, Jewell wondered what it meant.

As Jewell chased her vision of the happy home, Angie's home life continued to fray. A week in April marked a calendar of chaos at 2400 West Brown. *Sunday:* Opal's tooth had been aching for weeks. Bo's Mama told her to spray it with perfume, and she vomited all over her room. *Monday:* Angie left for work after lunch and never came home. She called Marcus the next day to say that she had stayed at Jewell's. She didn't care if he believed her. *Tuesday:* Kesha was ready to fight Marcus, this time over a kitten. When her cat, Oreo, had gone into labor, Kesha had donned surgical gloves and stayed up all night, delivering the litter herself. Now the kittens were ready to be weaned, and Marcus had promised one to a friend. "Bet you ain't taking my kitten!" Kesha screamed, standing on the bed with her fists balled up. With Angie at work, it took Opal and Jewell to pull her away.

Wednesday: When morning arrived, Angie was home, and the fight was still in swing. "Jewell! Jewell!" Opal reported. "I tell you, if you woulda seen your niece, it woulda knocked you out! Angie told her fifteen times to get up and go to school. Kesha said, 'Mama, you make me sick—I ain't goin' nowhere!'"

Mama, you make me sick? "I woulda grabbed her by the collar!" Jewell said.

"Grab her by the collar?" Opal said. "I woulda grabbed her by the hair and dragged her out the house!"

"Wouldna been a crochet left in her hair!" Jewell said. "Redd, Kesha, and Von—they gonna whup her."

"If I was a man," Opal said, "I would not be living with Angie and putting up with her disrespectful-ass kids."

Thursday: Marcus was thinking along similar lines. Angie was gone—he wasn't sure where—and he and I were sitting in a bar. Angie gave him little time, he said. The kids gave him nothing but lip. He cooked and cleaned and ignored the snubs, but they stung more than he showed. "The kids don't listen to nothing I say—they don't respect me," he said. "But whenever they need a pair of shoes, who do they ask? Sometimes I'm like, 'Man, I should pack up and leave.'" Saying so only left him more melancholy; where would he go? "Deep down, each of them got they own way to love me, I guess."

Marcus got home at 1:00 a.m., full of Courvoisier. Angie rode up ninety minutes later, with Tony at the wheel. Marcus swore he saw her kissing him! He knew she had been messing with that man! Suddenly Marcus was banging on the car window and running for his shotgun. As Angie climbed the steps, Marcus was shooting at Tony's taillights. Angie brushed past him with a laugh. Hadn't she warned him that her day was coming? She taunted him with an R. Kelly song about feminine revenge—"When a Woman's Fed Up"—and locked herself in the bathroom. The next thing she knew, Marcus had blasted a hole in the ceiling outside the door.

"I was thinking, 'Damn! This motherfucker's trying to *kill* me!'" Angie said.

Kesha grabbed a skillet. Von used his fists. Marcus dropped the gun, and as Angie came out he grabbed her by the throat. "When a woman's fed up!" she sang again. Marcus sobbed with rage. Redd ran to the pay phone and called the police, who found Angie on the porch in the rain, swinging at Marcus with a broom. They wrote it off as a drunken lovers' squabble and sent Marcus on his way. Up all night, the kids stayed home from school the next day. Other than that, the only thing hurt was Marcus's pride and the friendly landlord's ceiling.

"Freedom!" Angie announced the next afternoon. "He can't come back no more. . . . That's *my* house. *I* pay the bills!" A few days later, Marcus was back, sweeping the kitchen as though nothing had happened.

SEVENTEEN

Money: Milwaukee, Summer 1999

"Who the hell is FICA?" Angie fumed. "They be eatin' my ass *up*." If Opal and Marcus were one source of frustration, her pay stub was another and closer to her heart. Leaving welfare, juggling multiple jobs, Angie had done all a welfare reformer could ask. And she had done it with a kind of willed faith that work would eventually pay. "I want my own house," she said, after some Brown Street kids tossed a rock through her window. "With a fence!"

On the surface, she was making good progress. Had she stayed on welfare, her cash and food stamps would have come to about $14,400 a year. In her first three years off welfare, her annual income (in constant dollars) averaged more than $24,900. On paper, she was up more than $10,000—a gain of nearly 75 percent.

Yet it didn't feel that way. Usually she said she has "a little more money, but it ain't that much." On a bleak day, she said, "No, I'm not better off economically—not yet."

While that may just sound like Angie grousing, it's a pretty fair read of the evidence. Like almost all recipients, Angie never lived on welfare alone; she had boyfriends of varying means and a series of (mostly) covert jobs. Quantifying the help from her boyfriends is hard. But through the tax returns lying in the bottom of her closet and her old welfare records, it's possible to see how Angie's part of the finances really worked. A comparison of her last four years on welfare with her first three years off produces a box score that looks like this:

	On Welfare	**Off Welfare**
Earnings:	$ 6,500	$16,100
Tax Credits:	$ 2,300	$ 5,600
Payroll Taxes:	$ -500	$-1,200
Cash Welfare:	$ 8,400	$ 0
Food Stamps:	$ 4,800	$ 4,400
Total Income:	$21,500	$24,900

As a strategy for promoting work, the law did its job: Angie's annual earnings more than doubled. Adding in tax credits (and subtracting FICA), the amount she brought home from the workplace rose by $12,200 a year. Yet the drop in welfare and food stamps cost her $8,800. On balance, she was up $3,400, a gain of 16 percent.

Or was she, really? The more she worked, the more her work expenses increased. There was bus fare, babysitting, work uniforms, and snacks from the vending machine. In Angie's case, the child-care costs were minimal, since the kids mostly minded themselves. But figure just $30 week for bus rides and the stolen car, a conservative estimate, and you wipe out nearly half the gain. In leaving welfare, Angie also lost her health insurance. The kids remained on Medicaid, which was crucial with Kesha's asthma attacks. But for twenty of her first thirty-six months off the rolls, Angie earned just enough to get disqualified. On welfare, she could call a cab and get driven to a doctor for free. But, with pains shooting down her back from lifting patients, Angie walked around uninsured.

Other than her back, Angie was healthy. Jewell was not. After she left welfare, her earnings rose *sixfold,* to nearly $13,000 a year. But her public aid fell 93 percent—she lost all of her welfare and most of her food stamps after she failed to file the monthly earnings reports required of people who work. While her overall income rose from about $14,700 to $16,600 (a gain of 13 percent), she also lost her health insurance for two years, and Jewell had bleeding ulcers. "I just dealt with that pain," she said. "I just got a lot of Tums, Rolaids, stuff like that." In the end, she was hospitalized and her wages were garnished to pay the bill, a circumstance that struck her as nothing unusual.

"Anybody that works is gonna get their check garnished," she said. "Everybody in Milwaukee owes a hospital bill."

In going to work, Angie and Jewell didn't just face new expenses. They also faced new uncertainty. Angie's income soared for a year, when she bought a car and worked two jobs. Then it crashed for three months after the car was stolen. So the experience registered less like a stable advance than a roller coaster ride. In Jewell's case, the ride was particularly steep. Her income leaped to $25,000 when she worked in the Alzheimer's ward, then fell to $8,000 the next year when she lost her job and focused on Ken. On welfare, they had a senile landlady who forgot to collect the rent. Off welfare, Jewell had rent to pay and her nephew Quinten to feed. Angie had Opal and Brierra.

So *did* they come out ahead in economic terms? Probably, a bit. And their earnings may grow with time, which wouldn't happen on welfare. Still, three years after they left the rolls, their material lives didn't *feel* much different. Their economic progress, such as it was, vanished in the noise of living.

To understand the economics of the postwelfare years, you have to juggle two competing ideas. The first is that most poor single mothers fared better than expected. The second is that they continued to lead terribly straitened lives. Earnings surged, welfare fell, and net incomes inched up—but not necessarily enough to keep the lights on. By national standards, Angie was a great success: she earned 50 percent to 75 percent more than the average woman leaving the rolls. Sifting through the piles of economic data, it's hard to know what to emphasize most—the amazing ability of poor mothers to work or the questions about what their work will achieve?

The case for encouragement starts with earnings trends: from 1994 to 2001, the poorest half of single mothers saw their annual earnings *double.* That universe includes most of the women who left welfare as well as many who might have gone on it absent the new law. (Among the poorest quarter of single mothers, the rise in earnings was proportionally even greater: 150 percent.) Mostly that's because the women worked more. But the wages of entry-level workers also rose. While it was common to talk of recipients being shoved into minimum-wage jobs, most earned in the range of $7.50 to $8.25 an hour (in today's terms)—well above the legal minimum.

Poverty rates brought more good news. Most of the conservatives who backed the law would have been happy to replace welfare with work, even if poverty levels didn't change. But poverty rates fell sharply—for some groups to record lows. Poverty rates are arbitrary and odd, and they generally undercount need. Crudely devised four decades ago as a multiple of food costs, the formula hasn't changed other than to grow with inflation. The numbers undercount poverty by ignoring work expenses and the increased costs of housing and health care (which have far outpaced inflation). But they also ignore billions distributed through certain programs like food stamps and tax credits. Their all-or-nothing quality is oblivious to nuance: the year she left welfare, Angie would have been poor with $18,437 and not poor with a dollar more. Nonetheless, the numbers retain an important symbolism, and since the methodology behind them hasn't changed, they can be useful in tracking trends.

Poverty rates didn't just fall; they plunged. And they plunged most among those groups targeted by the bill. America's child poverty rates, the highest in the industrial world, hadn't changed in fifteen years. Suddenly they dropped more than 20 percent. Poverty among blacks, Hispanics, and single mothers fell to all-time lows. Nearly *half* the country's black children were poor when Clinton first pledged to end welfare. By the time he left office the figure had fallen by more than a third, to 30 percent. The last president to preside over an economic expansion, Ronald Reagan, removed 290,000 Americans from poverty. The Clinton years multiplied that figure 22 times, moving 6.4 million people across the poverty line. More than half lived in families headed by single mothers. "This is the first recovery in three decades where everybody got better at the same time," Clinton said, just before leaving office. "I just think that's so important."

The bad news is that while incomes rose, they rose from distressingly low levels. Extrapolating from an hourly wage of $7.50, one would expect to see annual earnings of about $15,600. But most women leaving welfare earned much less. A few found only part-time work. Many more went months between jobs. In her first year and a half off the rolls, Jewell quit one nursing home (too much work), got fired at another (chronic tardiness), and ran through four temp jobs. Even Angie, a much more experienced worker, went jobless for two and a half months after her car was stolen and she fell into a funk. Only about a third of those leaving welfare nationwide held jobs in every quarter of the following year.

So what did former recipients really earn? In ballpark terms, if you count everyone leaving welfare (including those without jobs), the average woman earned less than $9,000 in her first year off the rolls. Count workers alone, and the figure grows to about $12,000. Count steady workers (excluding those who go back on welfare), and you can get to $14,500. Their paychecks did grow with time; in Wisconsin, the earnings of the average "leaver" rose 26 percent over three years. Still, their annual earnings over the three-year stretch averaged just $10,400 (even when you exclude those who didn't work at all). With earnings of $12,700, Jewell was well ahead of the pack. With $16,100 Angie was a star.

Nationally, most people leaving welfare did come out ahead, at least on paper. But that wasn't the case in Wisconsin. Maria Cancian and three colleagues at the University of Wisconsin examined the records of eight thousand of the state's former welfare families. Although their earnings and tax credits surged, their public aid dropped even faster, cutting their total income by about $2,600 in the first year, a loss of 20 percent. Even after three years, a minority of those leaving the rolls—40 percent—had incomes higher than when they were on welfare. Wisconsin had unusually high benefits, so families leaving welfare had more to lose, and in cutting the rolls so deeply the state pushed more marginal cases out the door. The before-after comparison might look different in, say, Chicago. Nonetheless, the Cancian study recorded something of note: the most celebrated welfare program in the world on average left poor people even poorer.

A focus on averages can leave things out. Even as poverty levels fell, the ranks of single mothers in "extreme poverty"—living below half the poverty line—rose by nearly 20 percent. Nationally, about one welfare mother in five earned nothing after leaving the rolls. How they survived remains unclear. There was no parallel rise in public destitution, no sidealk encampments of homeless families, as Daniel Patrick Moynihan had feared. *Spending* among the very poor rose, even as their incomes fell, suggesting they had more resources—boyfriends or relatives to take them in—than the Census Bureau could measure. While reliable data on the very poor are scarce, the best guess is that about 7 percent of single mothers grew poorer in the second half of the 1990s. The worst of them, like Amber Peck in Milwaukee, parceled out their kids, then trudged through the snow to sleep on church floors.

Opponents of the bill sometimes cite such families as evidence of its failure. But a policy that fails the most marginalized few isn't necessarily a failure overall, especially if it brings significant improvement to the lives of most others. What's more surprising is how much hardship persisted among the seeming winners, among workers like Angie and Jewell. By warning, as Senator Moynihan did, of "cholera epidemics," critics set the bar for suffering awfully high. Large numbers of welfare-to-work *successes* report problems in obtaining basic necessities—fewer problems, perhaps, than when they were on welfare, but not dramatically fewer. Depending how the question is asked, a quarter to a half of former recipients report shortages of food. Similar percentages cite an inability to pay rent and utilities. Half said they lacked health insurance at a given moment, meaning that many more experienced a period without insurance sometime in their first few years off the rolls. Sheldon Danziger and four academic colleagues tracked seven hundred Michigan families for four years. Those who moved from welfare to work had nearly twice the annual income of those who stayed on welfare but "similar levels of material hardship." They were less likely to go without food or shelter but much more likely to go without needed medical care.

In my own travels through postwelfare life, I was struck by how many working families complained about facing depleted cupboards—or about just plain going hungry. I spent some time with Michelle Crawford, the Milwaukee woman Tommy Thompson featured in his legislative address. ("I want to run for president," she remembered him telling her, "and I want you on my team.") While her pride in landing a job was real, so were her struggles to buy a commodity as basic as milk. To fool the kids, she sweetened a powdered mix and hid it in store-bought jugs. "Then we ran out of sugar," she said. Food wasn't on my mind when I stopped by Pulaski High School to talk to some students with welfare-to-work moms. But it was on the minds of the kids, who commandeered the conversation with macabre jokes about Ramen noodles and generic cereal. When I asked how many had recently gone to bed hungry, four out of five raised their hands. "Go to my house, look in the refrigerator—you'll be lucky if there's a gallon of milk," said a senior named Tiffany Fiegel. Then she burst into tears.

The persistence of so much hardship poses a paradox. If incomes were rising, and poverty falling, why did so many people skip meals and fall behind on the rent? The answer is that the near poor live only slightly better than the poor. The Economic Policy Institute, a Washington research and advocacy group, examined two databases that measure hardships like shortages of food or medical care. Material deprivation did fall once families crossed the poverty line. But it only fell a bit. Real freedom from grinding need didn't occur until families reached twice the poverty line—until a woman like Angie, with four kids, had an income of nearly $40,000. In Wisconsin, fewer than one former recipient in ten had an income of twice the poverty line the year after leaving the rolls. If past trends hold true, most never will: a decade after leaving AFDC, two-thirds of former welfare families still hadn't gotten that far.

One can quibble about the math, but the basic point is clear: there's a threshold that families have to cross to feel their lives have changed. And most haven't crossed it. Angie went from 103 percent of the poverty line during her last four years on welfare to 114 percent during her first three years as a worker. With an extra mouth to feed in Quinten, Jewell went the other way, from 98 percent of the poverty line on welfare to 93 percent off it. "How well am I doing?" Angie said one day. "I ain't gonna call me poor—but I *am* poor." The Census Bureau couldn't have put it any better.

To say that Angie lived on $25,000 makes her life sound more forgiving than it was. The tax money came just once a year and went mostly to big-ticket items—cars, refrigerators, bedroom sets. Food stamps went to food. Marcus pitched in, but his help was erratic and typically in-kind—a package of pork chops, a new coat—as opposed to something Angie could count on for the bills. (Help from Opal was similarly sporadic.) What Angie really lived on was her take-home pay, about $1,120 a month. The result was come-and-go economics: what comes, goes.

Nearly 60 percent went to shelter costs: $450 to rent and $200 to utilities.

Seventy-five dollars went to Walgreen's for items, like toothpaste and toilet paper, that food stamps wouldn't buy.

Seventy-five dollars went to Jewel-Osco, for groceries when the food stamps ran out.

Fifty dollars went to the Lorillard Tobacco Company, since Angie's body wouldn't function without a pack of Newports every other day.

What was left was about $270 a month, or $9 a day. With that, Angie had to buy the remaining stuff of her life: bus fare, haircuts, gerbil food, video games, winter coats, check-cashing fees, doctors' bills, Colt 45s, Halloween candy, Christmas presents, Kesha's color-guard uniform, Redd's rap discs, Von's basketball shoes, Darrell's birthday party at Chuck E. Cheese, and the occasional pizza supreme. It was a budget with no room for error. And a life with lots of error. "Cash money in my hands?" Angie said. "It's like the wind blows and it's gone."

The biweekly pay cycle had a rhythm all its own: two weeks of anticipation followed by the realization that the money had been spoken for twice. As a rule, food came before rent, and rent before utilities, which Angie relegated to the lower-order status of optional necessity. "If you ain't got no place to stay, all the gas and the lights in the world wouldn't make no difference," she said. In her first six months on Brown Street, she paid on the light bill once. "Paid on" is how she put it, since the bill was never fully paid. She owed more than $1,400, but with Kesha using a nebulizer the power company was slow to disconnect. The week after the fight with Marcus, Angie picked up a $490 paycheck, hoping to treat herself to an outfit and a plastic plant. Once she paid the rent and bought a bus pass, she had $23 and 12 days to go. Among Angie's coping skills was a healthy dose of denial: she refused to open the bills. "If I ain't got the money, I ain't got the money," she said. "No need to be worrying myself to death."

By the spring, the tax money was gone; Michael was cutting Opal's check; and Marcus lost his job when the corner grocery closed. To cap it off, a bureaucratic screwup cost Angie her food stamps. Angie was too proud to say that anyone in the house went hungry—"We survive! Ain't nobody starving in there!"—but it wasn't unusual at the end of the month to find the refrigerator reduced to a box of fish sticks and a bottle of ketchup. Half the household fights, it seemed, revolved around a shortage of food. Opal was supposed to help stock the fridge, but she sold some of her stamps for spending money and kept a cache of snacks locked in her room. One morning, after she beat Darrell to the last drop of milk for the cereal, the five-year-old flung himself to the floor.

"What you crying for, boy?" she said.

"I ain't got nothing to eat! I'm hungry!" he said.

"You need a good butt-whipping, Darrell!" Opal said.

Darrell wasn't the only one missing a meal. Called in to work on her thirty-third birthday, Angie was broke and didn't eat all day. The loss of her food stamps left her incensed. The program required an eligibility review every three months. Arriving for her most recent appointment, she discovered her caseworker had gone on a leave of absence. In welfare jargon, that had left Angie in a "vacant zone"; she no longer had a designated worker but could see whomever was free. No one was. A few weeks later, Angie got a notice saying she had been cut off for failing to complete the review.

"QUESTIONS: Ask your Worker," it said.

"Worker Name: VACANT."

It took two months of calling to get another appointment. When she did, the bus broke down, she got there late, and no one would see her again. Having worked until midnight the previous night, Angie was out of patience; she responded with an off-color tirade that nearly got her thrown out of the office. A supervisor calmed her down, but she still had to come back the following day, when ten minutes of paper pushing restored her stamps. The foul-ups had cost her $500, but she arrived home trying to pretend she didn't care. "Hell no, because I *work*!" she said. "I done got over all that, waiting on food stamps! I *hate* to be bothered with them. I wish I had a job that paid $10, $11 an hour—I wouldn't *have* to be bothered with them."

"That still ain't enough," Opal said.

"You could make it," Angie said. "You just have to budget."

But Angie didn't earn $11 an hour. She earned $7.82, and while her income placed her in the postwelfare elite, it still didn't pay the bills. She needed a pool job to make more money, and she needed a car to work the pool. With some of her friends moonlighting as home health aides, Angie put in an application. "I need two jobs to get me what I need!" she said. "One job ain't gonna make it."

A job was the last thing on Opal's mind. She hadn't slept in two days. She feared toothaches more than childbirth. Her head was exploding in pain. Pull 'em, she said. The dentist said her gums were infected. The infection could travel to her heart. The worst-case scenario, however remote, included the risk of death. Take an antibiotic; come back in a week. "Let's do it right," he said. Opal pleaded: *"Pull 'em!"*

The pain must have been extraordinary to lure her to a dentist's chair, a place she avoided even more than Motivation Class. She had been leaving her teeth in food for years, the latest in an Easter egg. She had tried aspirin, Chloroseptic, perfume, and Tanqueray; she had been sent home by the emergency room. There are thirty-two teeth in the human mouth. With a practice focused on indigent care, Dr. Celestino Perez had once pulled twenty-eight. Opal needed only ten teeth pulled. "You can take it awhile longer," he said. Blinking away silent tears, Opal disagreed. She was starting to sign a waiver, absolving him of liability if the procedure went awry, when I threw my thin influence behind the antibiotics, promising to rush her back if the pain didn't ebb. She climbed down from the chair and dragged herself home, a perfect portrait of wretchedness. If years of tooth rot couldn't get her attention, I wondered how W-2 stood a chance.

A week later, she was back in the chair, looking terrified. "I gotta shot with a needle?" she said. By the fourth shot, her chest was heaving. The sixth made her legs buck. By the tenth, she merely looked confused. Novocain was one drug she wasn't used to. "My nose numb," she said. Numbers twenty-eight and thirty popped right out, but thirteen, an upper-left bicuspid, put up a fight. It had broken off below the surface, so Dr. Perez had to peel back the gum. The root was so rotten it snapped in his pliers, startling everyone with its crack.

He grunted. She gurgled. Her head jerked around. "My hand's getting tired," he said. *"Unnhhhhh!"* As the bloody stump succumbed, the dentist smiled. Three down, seven to go; come back in a week. "God, I just love this stuff!" he said. Opal made her way to the door still searching for her nose.

Welfare was inflicting blows of its own. When she didn't return to MaxAcademy, Michael pulled the attendance sheets and docked her check. He hadn't figured out she was using drugs (though he should have, since it was noted in her case history). Still, she finally had a caseworker she couldn't completely con. She suddenly seemed like a textbook example of a tough case meeting a tough law. In theory, the possible outcomes appeared to be these: (a) Opal could surrender her resistance and work for a welfare check; (b) Opal could leave W-2 and find a job on her own; (c) Opal could get kicked off the rolls and sink into deeper destitution. The answer turned to be (d): the bureaucracy screwed up again.

As it happened, Maximus didn't have jurisdiction over Opal's case. In moving to Brown Street, she had moved to a region run by Employment Solutions, the Goodwill subsidiary. Once the error came to light, Michael transferred the case, and his dealings with Opal were done. In the name of private-sector efficiency, Opal was packed off to her third agency and seventh caseworker in less than two years. "I don't feel I did a damn thing for Opal," Michael said soon after. At Goodwill, Opal told her new caseworker, Darcy Cooper, that she had her high-school diploma and wanted to work as a teacher's assistant. Cooper was impressed. "Very intelligent—very highly intelligent," she told me afterward. "Very goal oriented." Cooper gave Opal some time to find child care. In the meantime, she sent her a full check.

"Thigpen, Kenyatta Q., # 362246. . . ." Jewell worked the eraserless pencil, looking too nervous to breathe. The Fox Lake Correctional Institution didn't tolerate mistakes. No hairpins, no wallets, no Spandex, no tube tops, no paper money. No more than one rosary per visitor. No exceptions. The reception area was clean, cold, quiet, and hard, like an autopsy room. While the prison was just eighty miles from Milwaukee, it lay across a landscape of one-stoplight towns that looked as though they had fallen off a feed-store calendar. Jewell didn't trust her car or her map-reading skills; she didn't trust the small-town police. The trip made her feel her blackness intensely. The only time she got to see Ken was when I could give her a ride. A few weeks earlier, I had picked her up when she got off work, and we drove two hours to arrive at 7:23 p.m.—thirty-seven minutes before visiting hours ended. A fat guard with a walrus mustache had barely looked up. No new visits after 7:15. No exceptions. This time, Jewell took the day off and spent $150 to have her hair done. Ken had just had his parole hearing, and she was coming for the news.

Jewell finished her form, removed her rings, and eyed another adversary. The Fox Lake metal detector was a tin-pot dictator, a court with no appeals. The wire in a bra, the button on a jean—anything could set it off. There was no follow-up scan; what the arch said, goes. Another visit nearly ended in defeat when her pants zipper made it buzz. Jewell was accustomed to feeling powerless when dealing with Authority; she had mutely turned to leave when I spotted an old woman with a friendly face coming from the visiting room. The woman went home in Jewell's Fubu jeans and Jewell cleared security in a rare out-of-style moment, in stranger's baggy yellow shorts. "Hands to the side. Walk slow. You've got three tries." The Walrus was working again. The arch buzzed. Jewell checked her hair for pins. The arch buzzed again. With the reception area empty, there were no shorts to be cadged. Jewell took one step back and two hopeful steps forward toward the visiting room. The arch acquiesced. "You've got three hours," the Walrus said. She looked like she had won the lottery.

Whether she was winning Ken was less clear. The drive to end welfare was, among other things, a drive to raise marriage rates; as a thirty-year-old mother of two, Jewell suddenly had her prospects, if not the kind the bill writers had in mind. While it had been eight years since her old boyfriend Tony had gone to prison for murder, he had just sent her a drawing of a wedding band. "Marry Me," he wrote. Ken's rival, Lucky, had moved out again, but he had sent Jewell a picture of clenched fists breaking free of their chains: "To my wife, I'm coming home." Ken, in his letters, sounded marriage-minded, too, referring to Jewell as "my wife," "my sexy wife," "my gorgeous wife," and "wifee." But the separated lovers had hit a low point the previous month, after Jewell promised to send money and clothes and failed to follow through. Having given her something he usually withholds—his trust—Ken got so angry he cursed out a guard, and his next letter came from the hole. "I blame you because if you wouldn't pissed me off I wouldn't have a fucking attitude," he wrote. "[T]hat came from trying to show you the soft side of me. . . . I will never look stupid again for no female. . . . I will be girl less." They weren't used to fights, and that one quickly passed. Yet now and then a trace of doubt crept into Jewell's voice. "If we stay together, it's just something to show us that we're meant to be together," she said one night. *If?* Does she ever have—"No—no doubts, no nothing!" she said.

Trends in family structure nationwide were similarly hard to assess. The welfare bill proved spectacularly successful in putting poor women to work, but that was only half of its stated purpose. Shoring up the two-parent family was the other. "Marriage is the foundation of a successful family," reads the first line of the Personal Responsibility Act, which goes on for three pages to chart the statistical correlations between single motherhood and social risk. Launching his attack on welfare in 1994, Newt Gingrich had warned that the growth of nonmarital births threatened American "civilization." That year, 32.6 percent of children were born outside of marriage. As Jewell was visiting Ken in prison, hoping to have his baby, the figure was up to 33.0 percent, and a few years later it hit 34.0 percent. There may be no statistic that said more about the prospects of the next generation. By 2002, 23.0 percent of whites, 43.5 percent of Hispanics, and 68.2 percent of African Americans were born outside of marriage—a total of 1.4 million kids. That doesn't mean that the welfare bill had *no* effect on childbearing. The increase in nonmarital births slowed to a crawl and did so just as the attacks on "illegitimacy" hit fever pitch. It would be remarkable if that were pure coincidence.

Looking beyond births, some researchers have found potentially good news in subsequent living arrangements: fewer children living with lone single mothers and more living with two adults. Examining the National Survey of America's Families, a database of 40,000 households, Gregory Acs and Sandi Nelson of the Urban Institute found a notable shift in family composition in the postwelfare years. In 1997, about 48 percent of low-income children lived with a lone single mother; five years later, the number had fallen to 42 percent. But just half of that reduction in single parenthood came from increased marriage between mothers and their children's biological fathers, which statistically produces the best outcomes for kids. Most of the rest came from cohabitation, which was less encouraging. On average, children raised in cohabiting homes fare no better than those raised by single mothers alone. (Kesha grabbing a skillet to defend Angie from Marcus is an example of a cohabiting home.) Examining a database from the Census Bureau, Wendell Primus found the decline in lone single motherhood especially pronounced among blacks and Hispanics. The share of low-income black children living with married parents rose from about 20 percent to 23 percent over five years. But the share with cohabiting mothers also rose. And the Census data don't specify whether the marriages brought biological fathers or stepfathers to the home. To the extent it was the latter, past studies predict a high risk of conflict with the kids. Both Angie and Jewell spent a good part of their adolescence warring with stepfathers.

If changes in family structure were unclear, the impact of welfare policy was even more so. Policies specifically aimed at reducing nonmarital births (like "family caps" that eliminate extra payments for additional kids) generally showed weak results. And there was no other obvious policy pattern. The District of Columbia had some of the most permissive welfare rules, and also the largest reduction in the share of children born to single moms. Even as Wisconsin was eradicating its welfare rolls, the share of children born to single mothers *rose*—at a pace more than twice the national average. For all the praise heaped on the two-parent families, the end-welfare years brought little new information about how to promote them.

Jewell was a marriage-promotion movement all her own, with a target audience of one. She reached the visiting room to find Ken in the clothes she had finally sent: tank top, jeans, new gym shoes. Elated just to see him, she waited awhile before asking what the parole board had done. "They played me," he said. "What?!" Jewell was crushed. At the hearing, he had stuck to his story: the drugs weren't his; he wanted to go home and take up a trade, maybe computers. The hearing officer had called his story "bullshit" and warned him to learn from his mistakes. Even with good behavior, he had nearly a year left to serve. He asked Jewell: can you wait? He said he knew it was hard. It *was* hard, harder than he knew. Jewell had never been alone before. But she'd never had a cause, either. "I'll be there for you now *and* when you get out," she said. The visit sped past. Ken joked that they should prick their fingers and seal a pact in blood. When Jewell said she already had a pact—her "friendship" ring—Ken said that whoever had given it to her must love her very much. "They do," Jewell said.

Despite the disappointing news, Jewell left the prison in an upbeat mood. In the distance from Ken she had found a new closeness, but at home an opposite dynamic was in play. For all her closeness to Opal and Angie, a new distance was creeping in. Opal's problems were obvious enough. But for reasons Jewell couldn't understand, Angie acted as though she didn't like Ken. Or maybe, Jewell thought, Angie didn't like the sight of her in love. She spent most of the ride back to Milwaukee airing her frustrations. "She's always saying little stuff. She told me once, 'You changed!' She said she never let a man come between me and her friendship. How did he come between our friendship?" With Opal, Jewell's conflicts had been out in the open; with Angie, they smoldered.

Even so, once we hit the city line, she made Brown Street her first stop. Family was family, and Jewell had news. "He got to do the remaining time," she said, sitting on Opal's bed.

"Girrl!" Opal oozed empathy. "Even if one person on your parole board say you can't be released?"

"It was only one," Jewell said.

"I thought it was four or five, like you see on TV!"

Angie had little to say about Ken or his parole. ("Whatever make her happy," she harrumphed later.) But standing beside Opal's dresser, she saw a flyer from the welfare office with a list of jobs and starting wages: "$8.25 an hour!" Angie said. That was more than she made after three years. They were all in places she couldn't get to without a car.

A second job was her way to get one. But six weeks after signing up with a home-health agency, Angie still didn't have a client. May brought birthdays, Kesha's and her own, and she came up empty on both. June brought graduation bills. With Von finishing fifth grade and Kesha eighth, Angie gave them each $100 for outfits and put off the rent. Two months after he shot up the ceiling, Marcus was adding to her woes. He was out of work and obsessively jealous, threatening to follow her wherever she went. Angie tried to send him home to his mother's, but he wouldn't go. Food was tight again; having fought to get her food stamps back, Angie still hadn't received them. When she called the office, she learned they had been sent by certified mail and signed for two weeks earlier, on Friday, June 4. Angie remembered the date. Mercy had been overstaffed and sent her home, and when she got there Opal was gone. Angie's heart sank: Opal and the food stamps had disappeared the same day. With Opal in Chicago, seeing the girls, Angie left for work, stopped by a friend's, and came home at midnight full of frustration and beer. Just then, her "friend" Tony drove up. Marcus spied him and climbed in the car. As they drove off to settle their differences, Tony had his gun; Marcus left his behind, afraid of what he might do.

Angie ignored them. Though it wasn't clear whether a felony or a peace talk was under way, Angie was brooding about the stamps. It could have been Marcus, she told herself. But Marcus doesn't steal. "The only thing he might a stole was my heart and broke it," she said. Maybe it was the upstairs neighbor; yeah, that was it. It *couldn't* have been Opal. It *wasn't* Opal. But what to do if it was? Angie mulled the question in a drunken soliloquy that was, by turns, angry, funny, wounded, and wise. "I love her, but drugs mess you up," she said. "It's not like she's a bad person—she's sweet as pie. . . . But she's tripped her kids to nothing and herself, mainly, to nothing. So what the hell would she care about coming over and tripping me to nothing? . . . All that shit I said, 'I'll never kick you out'—that don't mean shit. . . . I'll be unforgivable hurt."

She was still parsing moral codes an hour later, when she heard the front door rattle. After a half dozen Hennesseys on his rival's tab, Marcus was back. Angie laughed. "You're drunk!" she said. "You're fucked up!"

Marcus smiled and looked my way. "Did you tell him who Tony is?"

"Tony's my guy!"

Whatever had happened at the bar, Marcus wasn't ready to say. "Am I heartbroken?" he asked himself. "No, I'm not heartbroken."

"You all right?" Angie asked. "'Cause I want you to be all right."

"I'm not talking to you," Marcus said.

"I don't care. You think I care?"

It was 1:00 in the morning. She was out of food. Her men were facing off with cognac and pistols, and she was trying to decide whether to put Opal out. This struck Angie as just the time . . .

. . . to pick a portfolio of stocks. Eight years after arriving in Milwaukee, three years after she had left the rolls, Angie had climbed to a rarified height in postwelfare life. She had qualified for a 401(k). The enrollment deadline was the following day, and she wanted a hand in assessing her tolerance for risk. She foraged in her bedroom and returned with a booklet called *Help! Which Investment Options Are Right for Me?* "What would make you more upset?" it asked.

(a) Not owning stocks when the market goes up.
(b) Holding a stock when it drops.
(c) I have no experience and can't respond.

"I'm number two!" Angie said. "Hold the stock and it drops, I'll be *pissed*!"

"Angela, Miss Angela!" Marcus broke in. "How you doing?"

"Fine. Love ya!"

"Do you?"

Angie laughed. "I love *me*," she said. "Tired of you!" Tickled, she broke into song. "Love me, tired of you! Love me, tired of you!"

Marcus grinned and talked about getting a four-pack. "Get yourself a *job*, nigger!" Angie said.

"If you were invested in a stock and it suddenly declined 20 percent in value, what would you do?"

(a) I would never own a stock.
(b) Sell a portion to cut my losses.
(c) Sit tight, ride it out, maybe even buy some more.

"I ain't gonna buy no more!" Angie said. "But if my money already there, what the hell else can I do? I ain't got time to be calling them!"

Tallying her risk tolerance, the pamphlet judged Angie a "moderate" investor. "Yes, I *am*!" she said, giving it a toss. "I already know where I'm putting my money at—IBM computers and shit, cause that's the future, *computers*!" She would put in $6 out of every $100 she earned, and Mercy would add $1.50, to vest if she stayed seven years. "Marcus get outta my bed," she called. He'd gone off to sleep, but Angie removed him to the couch. It was 2:00 a.m., and Von warned her she was due to work the first shift, just a few hours away. "Won't be the first time," she said. She got to work at dawn and started buying computer stocks, shortly before the tech bubble burst.

Opal stayed in Chicago a week, warring with her mother. Opal wanted the girls for the summer. Granny wouldn't let them go. Little girls want to be with their mother no matter their mother's condition. When Granny finally took a poll, the vote was Milwaukee 3, Chicago 0. They were back at Angie's for all of two hours when the fights began. "This is my worst nightmare!" said Redd. "A house full of girls!" said Von. By day two, Opal and Angie were at odds. "Ain't no motherfucking food in the house," Opal fumed. While she denied any knowledge of the missing stamps, she had given Angie $200 out of her allotment to restock the cabinets. Now Angie was at work, and Opal was complaining that she hadn't bought enough groceries. "Ain't no meats in there!" she complained to Jewell. If Angie's charity toward Opal was admirable, it was also increasingly costly, for herself and her kids. But putting Opal out required a greater willingness to enforce boundaries than Angie yet possessed. Of the three, Angie had found the greatest comfort in the First Street family. Perhaps if she evicted Opal she would be telling herself that ultimately she was on her own, too.

On day three, Kesha had a fit. Her condom had disappeared. The romance with Larry had reignited, and everyone but Angie was worried. One of Angie's friends had tried to get Kesha on birth control pills. But Kesha, who had just turned fifteen, said she didn't need them. Then she spied a condom in Larry's wallet; wrote "Kesha-N-

Larry" on her bedroom mirror; and kept the condom on her dresser. "It's mine," she said. "He's going to use it on me!" After Opal's girls spent the night in her room, the prized packet vanished. They found it, beneath the bed, just in time to keep Kesha from meting out blows. "I ain't sexually active now," she said. "But I'm gonna be in the future. Maybe two months."

Perhaps Angie wasn't alarmed because she wasn't around very much. She had finally gotten an assignment as a home health aide. Angie had worried about working in a stranger's house, and her client, Karen, had worried, too; she was confined to a wheelchair with multiple sclerosis, and her last aide had stolen from her. But the two of them hit it off. After two hours with Karen in the morning, Angie headed to Mercy after lunch, stretching her workday from breakfast to 10:30 at night. But two weeks into the new routine, she got her first paycheck: $178.42. To celebrate, she bought the kids a pizza. No one was in the mood. "You found my mama?" Tierra, the six-year-old, asked everyone. Opal had gotten her welfare check on Wednesday, disappeared on Thursday, and left a message on Bo's pager Friday afternoon: "I know y'all mad at me, but I still got two hundred dollars, and I ain't coming back tonight." Angie raged. "I could think of a million and one things I coulda done with that money—paid on the light bill!" she said. Plaster fell from the gun blast to the ceiling. Newspaper still covered the broken window pane. And there on the table lay the pizza box, perched like a cardboard crown. Angie, God bless her, tried.

The job with Karen, months in the making, ended within a few weeks. Solving one problem (too little money) aggravated another (too much time away). Angie quit working for Karen and switched to the first shift at Mercy. Angie *hated* first-shift work. First shift made her alarm clock bleat at 4:30 a.m., it made her whole body rebel. But if she started at 6:00, she could leave at 2:00 p.m. and try to be home more. "I don't want Opal to be in the mood to take nothing, and I don't want Marcus in the house," she said. "I can kill two birds with one stone." Karen was facing a spinal operation and pleaded with Angie to stay. But Karen mostly needed help in the mornings. While she tried to create some dinner-hour work, Angie felt bad about sitting around and laid herself off. "Don't you let nobody take your money away like that," she warned Karen. "You might need that."

Shortly after, a friend told Angie there was an easier way to get a car. W-2 would loan her the money. This struck Angie as unlikely news, but it turned out to be true. To help people stay off welfare, the program offered "job access loans" (of up to $1,600) for cars, uniforms, or even rents. This was another example of what states could have done with their welfare windfalls, rather than siphoning them into suburban road projects, and Angie was a perfect candidate. She was also a mark for a used-car salesman, and she nearly got talked into a $7,000 Dodge that would have been destined for repossession. It was bright red. He offered financing. All she had to do was sign. Angie tried to believe the car man when he said she could afford it, then came to her senses just in time. "I'd be signing myself over to the Devil," she told him, pulling herself away. A few days later, she put a deposit on a rusty old Cutlass that wasn't half as pretty. But it cost only a quarter as much, and she figured it would run long enough to get her started at the pool.

Under the logic that ruled Angie's life, when something went right, something was about to go wrong. Marcus was losing his mind. While Angie and Marcus had always fought, she felt he had crossed a new line. She put him out every night and woke up to find him back: waiting on the porch, lying on the couch, using the shower. She rose before dawn to find him staring in her bedroom window. In the middle of car shopping, she had gotten a restraining order. But it wouldn't take effect until the police could put it in his hands. Following her to the bus stop a few days later, Marcus warned if she tried to evict him he would burn down the house. Angie had the worse temper of the two. "I think I'm gonna buy me a gun and blow his fucking head off," she said.

Angie came home from buying her car and went to bed early. The kids woke her up at 1:00 a.m. Marcus had been drinking; he was standing on the porch and somehow he had gotten a key. "Your door's open," he yelled. Angie had had enough. Enough double shifts and enough unpaid bills. Enough wounded male pride. "I'm a very violent person," she once said. "Not violent toward everybody—I'm violent toward people trying to hurt me." She picked up a screwdriver and told him to come in. He taunted her from the porch. She locked the door, and he opened it. Then she heard him drop the key. As he bent to grab it, she flew out the door in her nightgown and knocked him down the stairs. "You trying to hurt me?" Marcus laughed. "Trying to *kill* you," she said. Then she stabbed him in the back. Opal was in the middle, trying to pry them apart, and the screwdriver passed through her hand.

It took three calls to summon the police, but they arrived at 4:00 a.m., served the order, and drove Marcus away. Had he kept his wits about him, it would have ended there. Maybe he didn't realize how angry Angie was. Maybe he didn't understand that he was legally barred from the house. Maybe, as he said, he just wanted his clothes. But he was back at dawn, daring Angie to call the cops, and this time they kept him. He wasn't disturbing the peace anymore; he was violating a court order. And with his record as a chronic offender, he faced up to three years. "Marcus felt I wasn't going to go to this extreme," Angie said. "Wrong brother!" She spent the morning in bed, reading a romance novel. In a few days, she could pick up the car. And with the car, she tried to tell herself, there was no telling where she might get.

EIGHTEEN

A Shot at the American Dream: Milwaukee, Fall 1999

"I need a whole new life," Angie said, and for a moment she thought she had one. She lost a man, found a car, and glimpsed a vision of hourly wages climbing to double digits. She stopped drinking beer. She did her hair. She did jumping jacks in the living room. She got up early and cleaned the basement. With no one rattling her window at night, she let Opal's daughter Sierra sleep beside her. "I been sleeping heavenly," Angie said. She sensed a return to an earlier, idealized self: younger, stronger, lighter, free. With a week of vacation coming, she talked about driving to Mississippi. "If I don't go to Mississippi, I'm a get me a hotel room." She knew of one with a spa. "I deserve to romance myself."

Then the old life rushed back in: Angie was the only one working in a house with eight kids. Von and Kierra fought all day. Kesha's cats had fleas. Redd's summer-school teacher said he had an attitude. Kesha dumped Larry, the boy with the condom, and started dating the upstairs neighbor, Jermaine. One day, Opal's seven-year-old, Kierra, said, "I'm gonna get paid today!" She couldn't say why—or she wouldn't get paid—but the secret spilled: she had caught Jermaine in Kesha's bedroom, and they had tried to buy her silence. "She gonna be pregnant, Angie," Opal warned.

The week Angie picked up her car, she got her annual raise: 20 cents. "Cheap bastards!" she said. "I'm a damn good worker. I'm worth more than twenty cents!" A few weeks later, she came home from work to find her lights shut off. Opal had given her some money for the bill, but Angie had bought school clothes instead. The cutoff was her third in as many years. How the power got reconnected is a bit of a mystery. Angie said she got a note from the asthma doctor, reiterating Kesha's need for a breathing machine; Opal said Angie's cousin broke the lock and turned it on. When her vacation arrived, Angie got no farther than the neighborhood bar. She spent the night dancing alone.

One evening after the lights returned, Angie dragged in from a double shift. It was nearly midnight. She had worked sixteen hours. She was due back at dawn. Out of toilet paper, Angie had tried to swipe some from work, but even there she met defeat: the place had been picked clean. Angie usually treats her setbacks with mordant humor; this night she wasn't laughing. "Ain't got a pot to piss in or a window to throw it out of!" she spat.

"Why you working so hard?" her friend Barbara asked.

Angie shot her a withering look. "I got bills to pay!"

Kesha's face had swollen from the fleas, and Von worried that his would, too. "Mama, you sure there's no bugs in that blanket?" he said.

Angie didn't answer. "Gotta be back at 6:00 a.m.," she groaned. "I gotta get my ass in bed."

Two months after she got her car, Angie finally did it: she drove five miles west to the edge of town and applied for a nursing-pool job. At Mercy, she had just cleared $8 an hour. Top Techs Temporaries, Inc., paid up to $14 for some weekend shifts. Wendy, her Mercy supervisor, argued she was making a mistake. Lot of aides left for pool work only to return after months of canceled shifts. "They think they're going to be millionaires, but then they can't get the hours," she told me. But Angie wasn't quitting Mercy; she was just looking for extra pay. She filled out the Top Techs forms, got back in her car, and found it wouldn't start. She ate lunch and tried again; all that was driving was the autumn rain. Speeding past on an ugly afternoon, the commuters heading home for dinner had no way to know that the drenched woman trudging down the road was a welfare-to-work marvel trying to work two jobs. Angie had the car towed and caught a bus to a bar. "Three hundred and fifty-nine dollars and eighty-two cents!" she moaned when the bill came in. Still, her good humor was back. *Fourteen dollars an hour.*

Angie kept her thoughts about Marcus closer to her chest. Shortly after his arrest, she got a call from a prosecutor, asking if she wanted to press charges. "Look, I don't want the man to go to jail," she said. "I just want him to stay away from me." The prosecutor agreed to drop the case, and then reconsidered; this was a violation of a restraining order, and Marcus had a record. Marcus spent a week trying to make the $500 bail, and as soon as he did he headed to Angie's, this time with a police escort. Ostensibly there to collect his stuff, he was trying to collect his wits. He was no stalker—he was her man!—and now he could be facing three years. While the police gave them a few private minutes, Angie wouldn't engage. You chose your own way, she said. The next week, Angie went to a block party near Jewell's house. She disappeared into the crowd and when she emerged a few hours later Marcus was at her side. Opal and Jewell were stunned, and more surprised still when Angie let him come back to Brown Street for the night. The next weekend, he took her to a bar. When she ran out of hair gel not long after, Angie drove to the grocery store where Marcus had found a job, knowing he would get her a jar. "Oh, is the love coming back?" asked Marcus's boss. The kids were still applauding his absence when Marcus was back in the house.

Angie had little to say on the subject, but Opal and Jewell chewed it over good. Jewell stressed economics. "Us women that just got off W-2 can't make it out here by ourselves," she said. While Marcus didn't directly pay the bills, she noted that Angie had lost her lights just after she kicked him out. "Every little bit helps," she said. The difference between Marcus and no Marcus might be the difference between gel and no gel, beer and no beer, lights and a night in the dark. Opal, a student of both money and men, didn't slight fiscal concerns. She'd once heard Angie scream at Marcus, "I don't love you—if you ain't got no money, I don't want you around!" But Opal argued that Angie had feelings at the start. "It only got financial when they started having hard times." All Angie would say was that the restraining order, which remained in force, gave her a legal leash. "He have to go when I say go," since a call to the cops at any time would send him back to jail. One day, Marcus tried to bring her a microwave. Angie would have none of it. She didn't want anything to imply he had squatting rights.

Angie had no such leverage over Opal. No one did. Not her mother. Not her man. Not her lovely pigtailed daughters. And certainly not W-2, which had accomplished no more in Opal's life than the programs it had replaced. At the beginning of the year, Angie and Jewell had thought she could turn things around. She had gone to rehab once before and gotten clean. She was too smart, too strong, too much a *survivor* to squander her life on cocaine. "She's trying to get herself together," Jewell had said. No one would say that now. Opal, the woman who could light up a room, had vanished in a fog of listlessness and gloom. Most days, she didn't get up until dusk. On her feet, she exploded in fury. "I'll hit you so hard in the motherfucking mouth I'll knock your ass on the floor!" she screamed at Redd. They were fighting over a pancake. Opal wasn't Opal anymore but an imposter in her own skin.

As summer stretched into fall, the only one blind to Opal's problems was the woman being paid to address them: her new caseworker, Darcy Cooper. Months after she inherited Opal's case, I stopped in to see her, only to leave wondering which Opal Caples she claimed to have met. "She was out there looking for a job," Cooper said. "She did everything she was supposed to do." Opal had left ten teeth in the dentist's pliers just before they met. "Opal looked good, appearance-wise," Cooper said. "It seemed like her home life was intact." How she felt confident in Opal's home life wasn't clear, since Cooper had never visited her home. Opal did report that she had been stabbed, one hint that her home life wasn't "intact." In six months, Cooper had met with Opal twice, both times in her cubicle at Employment Solutions, the Goodwill subsidiary. Yet even at that, her cheerful credulousness must have been hard to sustain. Opal had given up. In the past, she had faked or flirted her way to a monthly check; when she had to, she pleaded. Now she had her own safety net—Angie and Bo—and W-2 could do what it pleased. A letter arrived, warning that she was halfway through the five-year federal limit—in welfare theory, a wake-up call. "I don't be reading that shit," she said. "I ain't trippin' about that check, long as I have my food stamps and medical card."

Still the checks kept coming. First, Cooper gave her a month to look for child care. Then, the stab wound bought more time. After that, Cooper had Opal fill out Employer Contact Sheets, the same forms she had been forging for years by thumbing through the Yellow Pages. Opal didn't even finish making up a list. She was literally too tired to fake it. "I told her 'Miss Cooper, I don't just be home sleeping'—which I do," Opal said. While some caseworkers acted callous or cavalier, Cooper just seemed myopically nice. She told me she had heard that clients sometimes fake the job search, but "to me, it seemed like she was actively doing it." She sent Opal another check. "We all have days when things don't go our own way," she said.

Others showed less understanding. To qualify for W-2, Opal had to identify Brierra's father, so the state could try to collect child support. Opal repeatedly missed her appointments, and the child-support office told Cooper to close the case. Cooper entered the case-closure codes. But even that didn't end Opal's aid. Across the country, hundreds of thousands of families were dropped from the rolls for minor infractions, or no infractions at all. In Opal's case, the computer seemed to have a gremlin inside: whenever it saw the words "Opal Caples" it churned out a welfare check. She got $673 for October; $673 for November; and $673 for December. By the end of the year, the tally of cash and food stamps topped $11,000. Even Opal was amazed. "I didn't do nothing," she said. "They just sent it."

Goodwill's incompetence was hardly unique, but it merits a moment of special attention, given the marker laid down by the program's aggressive young CEO. William Martin was barely thirty when he took charge of the $112 million contract, with one of his assets being his political ties to the administration that had awarded it; he had helped run Tommy Thompson's Milwaukee office. At the program's launch, Martin sounded like a business student on Nō-Dōz. W-2 was about "getting to yes" and finding "win-win opportunities." It was about "cutting-edge, private-sector, customer-centered growth." While welfare had left people "wards of the state," Martin, the descendant of a line of southern black preachers, said he had never met someone he couldn't put to work. "We start from a moral premise that it's simply unconscionable to leave somebody on welfare." Two years later, Opal looked like—well, a ward of the state—and Martin was articulating a new moral premise. "We try to give people the benefit of the doubt, rather than hold to the mechanics of everything," he said, when I asked about Opal's case. "If they had the wherewithal to make it on their own, they wouldn't be in the program."

Someone did "get to yes": William Martin. As Goodwill ignored Opal's downward slide, Martin collected $62,000 in performance bonuses, bringing his year's pay to more than $172,000. He also gave bonuses averaging nearly $10,000 to more than half his staff. In time, the project attracted the legislative auditors, who found some of what they had seen at Maximus: tens of thousands of welfare dollars spent on staff parties, embossed briefcases, and the like. They also found something that disturbed them more: Martin was using the W-2 contract as a marketing fund, spending money earmarked for client services to seek contracts in other states. This was not a "win-win" situation. State auditors deemed it a violation of the law. While Martin called it a bookkeeping error, among the expenses the auditors disallowed were nineteen first-class plane trips to Arizona, where Goodwill was battling Maximus for the next privatization prize. The day after they requested the agency's credit card records, Martin came forward to say he had discovered another $160,000 in unallowable costs. At Maximus, the auditors had found reckless extravagance; at Goodwill, they suspected a cover-up, and the headline in the Milwaukee paper soon read, "W-2 agency under FBI investigation." Martin was forced out of Goodwill, and after repaying a half million dollars, Goodwill was forced out of W-2, with its chief executive, John Miller, pleading "bumbling rather than trickiness." With that, Goodwill and Maximus, the two leading players in privatization, became the two leading emblems of waste and abuse. And they can scarcely be dismissed as an unrepresentative slice of the W-2 bureaucracy: together, they handled *half* the state's cases.

In the end, the real scandal was of the sort that financial auditors don't track: the scandalous absence of casework. With the rolls down 90 percent, the state was collecting more than $40,000 in federal payments for every family left on the rolls. Yet Opal had bounced between seven caseworkers at three agencies, at least two of whom had been on drugs themselves. And none of them had made the slightest difference in her life. There was another thing that Darcy Cooper didn't know about Opal: she was pregnant again. While Opal had urged Angie to take precautions with Kesha, she was too lost to heed her own advice, and another unwanted pregnancy, her second in two years, only added to the violence of her moods. "I'm gonna kick your motherfucking ass!" she screamed at Sierra one day. The girls had stayed in Milwaukee for the fall, still wanting to be with their mother, and the nine-year-old had taken a schoolbook from her room to read somewhere else in the house. While Opal kept saying she wanted an abortion, either she lacked the energy to pursue one or decided a baby would help her keep Bo. By October, her body started to swell. "Girl, just get ready," Jewell said, rubbing Opal's stomach.

At the end of the month, Angie lost her lights again, for the second time in three months. Opal ran an extension cord to the neighbor's outlet. Then she plugged in her boom box, and sat in the dark, listening to Al Green.

I'm so tiii-red *of being alone,*
I'm so tiii-red *of on-my-own.*

When Angie walked in at dinnertime, the only thing lit in the house was the tip of Opal's cigarette. Opal finished her smoke and left for Andrea's. "You know where to find me," she said.

Once Ken's drug money ran out, Jewell lost her lights, too. She owed only $500, a third of Angie's debt. But without an asthmatic child, she had to pay in full. That left her with no money for heating oil, and as the fall temperatures dipped to the 30s, she warmed the house with an oven. With her wages being garnished to satisfy her ulcer bills, Jewell was surrendering $99 out of each biweekly paycheck. At least Angie thought if she wrung enough shifts from her tired body, the system would reward her. Jewell bought no such notion. A supervisor called her off the floor at G. B. Electric one day to praise her work and add a quarter to her hourly pay. "He musta liked my eyes," Jewell laughed. The competing explanation—that work brings rewards—was one she didn't consider. "They don't care about no black person there!" she said. When a white coworker hurt her leg, the company gave the woman a desk job; when Jewell hurt her back, she had to miss four days without pay. "I wouldn't even want to go no further there," Jewell said one day. "They'll use you until they can't use you no more. That's what I think: they'll use you until they can't use you no more." Jewell had few convictions about the world. But she was adamant about that.

Her vision of the future boiled down to a vision of Ken. Jewell wanted him for herself, of course: for adventure, romance, and sunrise video games. But she also increasingly wanted him as a father for the boys. Although Terrell's father hadn't seen him since he was a baby, he had recently called to propose a visit. "He's not gonna come," Terrell said, and after encouraging him to give it a try, it pained Jewell when the eleven-year-old proved right. Tremmell's father, Tony, had sent a card calling him "the smartes, smoothes, handsomes the most educated son in the world." But the return address had an inmate number and would for another seventy-seven years. When she first had children, Jewell had thought fathers superfluous: "If they around, they around, if they not, they not—I'll do it by myself." Now she thought that boys got something special from a man. "It's financial *and* discipline," she said. "I think a male have a lotta effect on the kids when it comes to doing right and wrong. A mother could tell a child do something, and she'll have to holler or scream or spank 'em. I seen a lotta cases where the man can only say it one time and the child will do it." Though her sense of herself as a "strong black woman" was undiminished, a decade of raising her boys alone made her think "they need both of their parents."

Jewell was speaking off the cuff one day as we made another drive to the prison. But she was getting at the ultimate question about the postwelfare world: how much does having a working mother—a single, low-income working mother—enhance the life chances of the kids? Will it bring them a new shot at the American Dream? Bill Clinton, among others, saw working mothers as a source of inspiration; critics saw kids left in substandard care while the only parent they had was away. Either scenario—rising achievement or rising neglect—had a plausible logic. Now there is some data. Studies of a dozen programs have followed poor children as their mothers went to work, and collectively they have examined everything from changes in meal times and reading habits to criminal arrests. So it's possible to make some educated guesses about what difference a working mother makes. So far, the answer seems to be "not much." In one sense, that's reassuring: poor kids have suffered no obvious damage as their mothers left home to work. But they haven't inherited a new life trajectory, either. From the standpoint of child development, it hasn't much seemed to matter.

The small differences that have emerged are mostly counterintuitive. A few work programs have shown benefits to *younger* children. That's contrary to the conventional theory that young kids most need their moms. To the extent the programs helped, they appeared to do so not by turning mothers into role models but by getting more kids into formal day care. Reforming welfare, that is, didn't reform the house; it got the kids out. At the same time, there's a hint that adolescents did worse as their mothers left welfare for work. This, too, challenges the role model theory: presumably adolescents, contemplating their own passage to adult life, would be at just the right age to extract a positive lesson from the example of a working parent. Yet when Minnesota mothers joined a work program, their teenagers performed worse in school. In Canada, adolescents grew more likely to smoke, drink, and use drugs. In Florida, they grew more prone to school suspensions and criminal arrests. One theory is that the teens of working mothers get less supervision just when they need more: think Kesha and Jermaine. Another is that they inherit more burdens at home: think Kesha and Brierra.

But what's most striking aren't these small differences. It's the long list of things that don't seem to change when mothers leave welfare for work. As a leading review of the literature put it: "the list of 'dogs that didn't bark' is impressive and includes parental control, cognitive stimulation in the home, family routines, and harsh parenting." Another set of authors found "the children of current and former welfare recipients generally look similar" and identified "the role of poverty, more than welfare status per se, as a marker of risk in children's lives." A third researcher found that "[h]ome environments changed little." In wondering how far work will go to reorder poor women's lives, it's worth remembering the New Hope Project, a nationally renowned jobs program just down the street from Angie. New Hope was uniquely generous, offering guaranteed jobs, subsidized wages, health care, child care, and attentive casework. And it did achieve its main goal—putting more poor people to work. But it had little impact on the rest of family life. Psychologists found virtually no improvement in parents' mental health even under such ideal conditions. They found no rise in self-esteem. No improvement in feelings of "mastery." Even after two years in the program, the average participant still registered levels of depression considered cause for a clinical referral. The researchers came up with measures of parental "warmth," "control," "monitoring," "aspirations," and "cognitive stimulation." They asked whether New Hope families had dictionaries, magazines, or library cards; if they took trips to museums; if they went to church. Same result: families in the work program looked no different than families down the block. The program did have one outstanding finding; it significantly raised the school performance of six- to twelve-year-old boys. While researchers weren't positive why, the leading explanation stresses the program's success in getting children into after-school programs. Here, too, it seems, success came not from changing the home but from getting children out.

The studies are early and no doubt imperfect. Maybe working mothers convey something to their kids that social science can't measure. Or maybe they will with time. Women leaving welfare for work often *say* they feel better, even if their scores on mental-health tests don't rise. But it's one thing for a mother to feel some pride and another for her to alter the trajectory of her children's lives. Especially when the children are still growing up fatherless and poor. Angie, Opal, Jewell, Greg, Kenny Gross, Marcus—they all had mothers who worked. What none of them had was a functioning dad and the emotional and financial support that a second parent can bring.

Jewell was still talking of stand-in fathers when we reached the Fox Lake gate and hoping that the man inside would provide her boys with one. The denial of parole had left Ken shaken up; he was approaching his twenty-eighth birthday, and jail was getting old. With another nine months to serve, he enrolled in a masonry class. He hated it at first. He was used to making money by looking pretty, not by mixing mud. But he heard that masons make big bucks, and soon Jewell found puzzling words like mortar and trowel cluttering their conversations. Ken got straight As and became a teaching assistant. ("He does have the skills to go to work for a bricklaying company," Ken's instructor told me. "I wouldn't say he's a lost cause.") One morning Ken woke Jewell with a call. "He told me that when he get out, I ain't gonna have to work no more," she said. She got busy making plans. Maybe they'd move back to Chicago. Or maybe she'd go to school. She had always wanted to be a nurse—not an aide, but the real thing. If not a nurse a beautician, then. One with a real salon. They'd have a girl named Shavell. Or a boy named Travell. One thing certain was that her career as a scanner of industrial tools would end.

I waited while Jewell went inside.

"Till death do we part."

"Do that math."

"We ain't gonna rush things."

Jewell returned two hours later with a report of their conversation. "He said he want to spend the rest of his life with me. He said he wanna grow old with me. And if he was married, I'd be the woman he'd want to marry.

"But he never asked me," she said. "He never asked me to marry him."

It's a test, Jewell kept telling herself; the waiting is a test. Inside the prison, she fiddled with the ring that Ken had given her and told him that she would never take it off. His smile made his dimples stand out when he told her that a ring even more special might be hers someday.

Angie's nursing-pool plan was jinxed. The day she filed her Top Techs application, her car went dead; the day she finished her orientation, her lights got cut off. Her life had turned into allegory: literally, figuratively, she was a woman without power. At least there wasn't much food to spoil. Then again, there wasn't much food. The car bill had set her back on the rent, and she rolled into November still owing for October. The landlord winked and reduced the debt. So far Angie had only winked back. But "if I was by myself—whatever he wanted," she said.

Finally Top Techs called. She made it to the office by 5:00 a.m. and caught a van to Oconomowoc, thirty miles away, where the affluence of the nursing home seemed as exotic as the town's name. "Man, they closet is so big!" she said. At $11.50 an hour, Angie's wage was looking big, too. The next day was Saturday; she returned to the pool. She worked Sunday, as well. After just a few shifts, she got a raise of $1 an hour. She may have been running ragged to reach the next county by dawn, but she talked like a woman who had just glimpsed a future of boundless shimmering wealth. "I made $98—just for that one day!" she said. "Should I leave Mercy? Forget about my 401(k)?" She cut back to a seven-tenths' schedule at Mercy to make more time for the pool.

The next week, as Angie was walking out the door, Top Techs called to cancel. It was 4:30 a.m., pitch black, and bone-achingly cold. The scheduler offered her the second shift. But that wouldn't get her home until midnight, and she was due back the next day at dawn. Angie got back in bed. On Wednesday, Top Techs canceled again. Thursday made it three days in a row. This was just what Wendy, her supervisor at Mercy, had warned her about: big dollars, few hours. Everyone was looking for Christmas money, Angie figured. Things would look up soon. Not long after, Top Techs called three times in a day: we need you, we don't, we do. "I wish they'd make up their mind," Angie grumbled. One night she worked till 10:30 in the outer suburb of Waukesha. But the van didn't come for more than an hour, and she didn't get home until 1:00 a.m. "They leave you trapped out there!" she said. She could have driven herself, but she didn't know the way, she didn't trust her car, and she didn't trust the Waukesha police, especially at midnight. "My black ass ain't supposed to be out there."

As Angie started the Top Techs job, her old friend Lisa moved back to town, and Angie took her in. Lisa had been a core member of the First Street crew, and they instantly clicked again. But her arrival left seventeen people in the house, with enough kids to field a football team: Kesha, Redd, Von, Darrell, Sierra, Kierra, Tierra, Brierra—and now, for a month, Chaquita, Pierre, Chakiera, and Charlesha. Even Angie found it a bit much. The more time Angie spent at work, the more time the kids spent alone. At fifteen, Kesha had none of the rebel's instincts that Angie had shown at that age. She didn't drink, smoke weed, or hang in the streets. She even chose a crosstown high school for its prelaw program. "I always told my daddy that I was gonna be his lawyer and help get him out of jail," she said. But she was absent half her freshman year, and finished the second semester with Fs in every class but band. Kesha spent much of her time taking care of Brierra and the rest upstairs with her beau, Jermaine. At the other end of the age range, Darrell, at six, was so starved for attention that sometimes he called Angie a half dozen times in an eight-hour shift. Even Angie's boss, Wendy, noticed. "He just wants to talk to his mama," she said. One day Angie's cousin appeared at the house with a computer marked M.P.S., for Milwaukee Public Schools, to whom it seemingly belonged. Kesha used the graphics package to sketch pictures of a baby. Von used the machine to record his raps. Earlier in the year, his faux pickup lines had cited Fred Flintstone and Elmo. Now he went for the sixth-grade gangsta sound. "Fuck that, nigger!" he chanted to the hard drive. "Let's go get some weed. We fixing to bust somebody tonight. I ain't playin' no game."

Von *was* just playing, or so Angie thought. Her real worries centered on Redd. Though he was only thirteen, Angie could feel him slipping away. He never had taken an interest in school, and now in seventh grade he scarcely tried. When everyone in his class wrote Brett Favre, inviting the Packers star quarterback to visit, Redd alone refused; a summer-school teacher had called him a "dummy," and he was afraid of misspelling his words. His temper was worse than his spelling. Small setbacks, like a classmate's taunts, would leave him banging his head on the wall. He had a stack of suspension notices six inches deep. A single day's report had him "threatening a student, disruptive, hit another on the head, disrespectful, hiding in bathroom—a little bit out of control." Redd had been five when Greg went to jail, old enough to remember the loss, and scarcely a day went by when he and Marcus didn't fight. "He say [Marcus] ain't his daddy, he don't have to listen to him," Angie said. "He better listen to some damn body. That the only daddy he got. Gonna wind up in the same place his daddy at."

As the year progressed, so did Redd's problems. He cut school. He smoked a lot of weed. Like Kesha, he found someone three years older to "date." Though Angie didn't know it, Redd, not Kesha, was the first of her kids to become sexually active, at age thirteen. Angie worried that with his streetwise airs he was trying to emulate Greg. She also worried he didn't have the mettle to pull it off. "Redd is as sweet as pie, but *wanna* be bad," she said. "Redd is a kitten. Redd is a baby. . . . He's a ticking time bomb." Most of his teachers shared Angie's fears, and some just gave up on him. But at least one saw some promise, calling him "artistic," "thorough when you want to be," and praising his "sense of humor." Among the papers that survived in the bottom of his closet is a middle-school essay called "A Grimmer Mouse."

> He has small pointed ears and a big round body. . . . I found him in the woods crying in a box. I took him home and tried to feed him. . . . He was running around the house tring to find a place to sleep. So I built him a place to sleep in a bigger box with hay in the bottom of the box. He kicked the hay around + started to use it as a bath room. Then I notice he like to be under things, away from the light and people. I took another box and put a blanket in it and put it under my bed. There he sleeps and he is happy living under my bed. His predator is bright light and loud kids. The light because it hurts his eyes . . . The kids are because . . . loud nose inerfer with his hearing.

He came across it one day as he was showing me some school things. I asked him why the mouse had been crying.

"Cause he was just left out there by himself," Redd said. "Somebody who was supposed to be bathing him, feeding him, washing him, and stuff wasn't doing it."

Why not?

"Probably 'cause they didn't have no money to feed him and stuff."

How did that make him feel?

"He was crying, 'cause he was sad."

Was he angry, too?

"He had to be mad, 'cause he was chewing on a tree."

Redd suddenly stopped and looked up. Until then, he said, he hadn't realized that he had been writing about himself. "That's about my daddy," he said. "He wasn't here."

The more time I spent at Angie's, the more it felt like *everything* was about Greg. He had been gone for eight years, but his absence had left a hole that nothing had been able to fill—not welfare, not work, and certainly not the parade of men filing through Angie's life. Since moving to Milwaukee, Angie and the kids had seen him just three or four times. But he hung over the house like a private gravity field. Kesha wrote most often and treasured his typed responses. ("I miss you and love you babygirl.") She was now the same age as Kathryn Miles, the girl killed by Tony's wild shot as Greg watched his buddies' backs. Her father didn't mean to hurt the girl, Kesha said. "Can't hold it against him forever." But Von could hold it against him and did. "What's a grown man doing out shooting a little girl?" he said. "I don't care if it's an accident. You shouldn't a been there in the first place." That Greg had turned down a plea bargain only deepened Von's disdain: "Dude chose his friends over his family." Flipping through the family photo album, Von and I found a picture of a smiling Greg crouched behind one of his toddler sons; it could pass as a warm father-son moment—or it could have if they weren't holding a rifle. I asked what that was about. "Ask that crazy dude," he said, the crazy dude being his dad. Redd said if his father were around, Angie would benefit. "It wouldn't just be this guy, that guy—there'd be somebody to help Mama." But as for himself, Redd said, "I don't miss him. I don't think about him. I don't care that he's gone."

At the start of the school year, Greg had contacted the boys after a long silence and apologized "if I in any way made you feel unloved." He also offered his advice: stay out of the streets, listen to your mother, apply yourselves. When that didn't work, Angie asked me to arrange a visit. We needed the warden's permission for Greg to see Angie and three kids together, and once it came through, we piled in my car for the hundred-mile drive to Joliet, Illinois. The kids hadn't seen him in two years, but no one was talking about Greg. Redd slept, while Kesha and Von kept up an astonished commentary on the high cost of highway tolls. When the Stateville Correctional Center rolled into view, it looked like something that had wandered off the set of *Scared Straight*. It's a gloomy old fortress with thirty-foot walls and, until a few months earlier, a death chamber inside, obviously a much rougher place than where Ken was doing his time. The guards didn't thumb old magazines. They sat behind bulletproof glass.

While I had planned to wait outside, Greg had put me on his visiting list, and Angie invited me to meet him. He'd formed a dozen incongruous identities in my mind. He was a four-year-old boy, leaving Missouri on a bus, never to see his father again. He was a ten-year-old escaping the Chicago projects after someone dropped a brick on his head. He was Hattie Mae's "little gentleman" and Angie's soul mate. He was the charismatic street entrepreneur who'd commanded a crew of men. He was a letter writer of obvious intelligence and an affectionate, worried Dad. He was a drug dealer, a convicted murderer, a man whose crazy scheme had killed a teenage girl. We spent an hour in waiting-room limbo, then climbed the hill to the main cell block, passed through two sets of menacing doors, and entered a nicotine-dim room of hard chairs and vending machines. A handsome man in a denim shirt was standing there, slightly stooped from stomach surgery. He had a soft, polite voice and big, beautiful eyes. "Thanks for bringing the kids," he said. It was easy to see how Angie had fallen in love with him. And nearly impossible to picture him doing what he had done.

I left them to a private visit. When they emerged an hour later, Kesha and Von looked as though they'd come from a funeral, and Angie had her arm around Redd, who cried all the way to the car. A heavy silence fell over the drive home, and no one discussed what was said. "He really miss Greg—what can I say?" Angie later said about Redd. She didn't add—she didn't have to—how much she missed him, too.

Angie's day in prison was Marcus's day in court for violating the restraining order. I picked him up when we got back to town and encountered a portrait of defeat. While a guilty plea had limited his sentence to sixty days of work release, he worried less about going away than about what he would come back to. Ever since his arrest, Marcus had tried to make amends. He had cooked and cleaned and taken Angie out. He had left when she told him to go. But he realized he amounted to nothing more than an afterthought in the house. Angie "was like a gift—a gift I wasn't able to receive," he said. "I don't know how many times you could tell a person you're sorry. I mean, I'm *sorry*." That Angie and the kids had just returned from seeing

Greg completed his emotional rout; he knew he would never compare. We pulled up to the house, where he sat in the car pining so long the kids came out and stared. With the restraining order still in place, just walking through the door was a crime. Marcus finally mustered a weak smile and got out to break the law. "I'm a sucker for love," he said.

Marcus, Opal, the kids, the bills—Angie's problems never got solved. They orbited her like planets. They stuck to her like gum. A few weeks later, trying to gas up her car, she found that someone had stolen her last $20. Opal professed her innocence, and Angie had another suspect, her cousin's girlfriend. Still, she did something she had thought about for months: she told Opal it was time to go. What if, as usual, the shelters were full: would Angie really put her out? "Yes, yes, yes, yes, yes—I'm really tired!" she said. Opal called the shelters; the shelters were full; and Angie stopped bringing it up. As November turned to December, Opal had been there a year.

Angie's work plans turned circular, too. The money at Top Techs was great when she could get it, but she couldn't get it enough. She could get all the hours she wanted at Mercy, "but I don't make jack." Although Angie resented the Mercy pay, she did feel comfortable there. One day with her car in the shop, she woke Wendy at 4:00 a.m. to say she didn't have bus fare. Wendy got up and gave her a ride. ("Stuff happens to people," Wendy said.) On Thanksgiving, Angie cooked all night and slept through the morning shift. Wendy was less forgiving ("that little toad!"), but they had a history. While Angie had spent most of the year plotting her exit from Mercy, the pool felt too risky to count on full-time. She would hope for more pool hours later. For now she needed two jobs to earn one inadequate living.

Christmas was coming. Kesha wanted a VCR. Redd and Von wanted a weight-lifting set and Darrell, a Nintendo 64. Angie bought Marcus a coat, and she planned to treat herself at a male strip club on Christmas Eve. In all, she was facing bills of $500, or more, in a budget already in the red. She stormed through December like a one-woman nursing brigade, pulling doubles at Mercy and trekking to Oconomowoc whenever she could. "I wish you would tell Santa about me," she laughed one day. "I'm a good, hardworking woman who can't seem to get up off the ground."

In the middle of December, Angie and Opal had a new fight. Opal's food stamps arrived one morning, and by the time Angie dragged her out of the crack house she had burned through nearly $300 in a single afternoon. The house was out of groceries—again!—but Angie didn't have time to lecture; she was rushing to get Kesha to a color-guard show. The next day, Angie's friend Barbara called. She mentioned that she had lent Opal some money. But Opal said she couldn't pay her back because her food stamps hadn't come.

This, in the world of 2400 West Brown, was a minuscule lie, a transgression so slight that on another day Angie might not have noticed. It was a satellite sin, an outer-orbit derivative of the real dilemma: another month short on food. But it left Angie in a rage. She walked into Opal's room and said something she hadn't planned to say. *Get out.* Go. Leave within forty-eight hours. "I said, 'Why you keep *lyin'*?" Angie said. "Why you keep trying to *use* motherfuckers? Don't make no sense!" Opal wasn't surprised, just angry—angry at Angie, and though she couldn't admit it, angrier at herself. She threw back every accusation she could muster—calling Angie a drinker, a hypocrite, a bad mother. Angie was still simmering the following day. "She told me because I work all the time, that don't mean you're a better parent: 'Kids need their parents around them.' Yeah, they might do. But I buy my kids stuff when they need it. . . . You don't take care of nobody but yourself. . . . That girl crazy! But you know, it ain't nothing but the drugs—drugs make you say anything." Angie urged her to go back to rehab and offered to go with her. "Maybe I shouldn't drink as much beer." Opal had closed her ears.

Angie knew it was Christmas. She knew it was cold and the shelters were full. She knew that Opal's departure—to a room in Bo's cousin's house—would be freighted with sad symbolism: Opal would be hauling away her stuff on Brierra's first birthday. But "I ain't doing her no good here," she said. "She told me that a long time ago: I'm 'enabling' her—she learned that in rehab." Angie laughed. "Shoot! Why don't you take your ass back there and learn something else?" Yet underneath she was as earnest as could be. "If I don't put her out, she ain't never gonna get herself together," she said. "I love you," she told Opal. "When you get yourself together, I'll be there for you."

I stopped by on the eve of Opal's departure. Opal was packed and locked in her room, and Angie was propped up in bed at midnight with a Colt 45. Great heaps of stuff spilled everywhere: report cards, pay stubs, unopened bills, CDs, an iron, mounds of dirty clothes. A milk crate held a battered TV, and Marcus sprawled on the bedcovers. Having failed to report to the work-release program, he was a small-time fugitive. Despite the showdown with Opal, or perhaps because of it, Angie was in an expansive mood. All in all, she figured, it hadn't been a bad year. She had worked three jobs and bought a car. She had earned about $18,500, a personal record. She had started a retirement plan. She had been shot at by Marcus and ripped off by Opal. She had lost her lights twice and run low on food more times than she could count. Someone had just egged her car. Too bad the shelters were full, she laughed. She needed one.

So how had the new law changed her life? Had ending welfare worked? While I had posed versions of the question before, they never seemed to grab her, and I was starting to understand why. On welfare, Angie was a low-income single mother, raising her children in a dangerous neighborhood in a household roiled by chaos. She couldn't pay the bills. She drank lots of beer. And her kids needed a father. Off welfare, she was a low-income single mother, raising her children in a dangerous neighborhood in a household roiled by chaos. She couldn't pay the bills. She drank lots of beer. And her kids needed a father. "We're surviving!" is all Angie said. "'Cause that's what we have to do."

Were the kids proud that she works? It was a question that often arose when I talked about Angie with middle-class friends, most of whom took it as an article of faith that the answer had to be yes. Angie paused. "I don't think the kids think about that," she said. "They'd like it if I'd just sit around with them all day." She raised her voice to a mimicking squeal: "'Why you always at work?' Shoot! Why you think I gotta work? Ain't none a you got a job!" It was possible, of course, that the kids felt prouder than she knew and that the power of the example she set would become clearer with time. I asked if she thought her struggles to grind out a low-wage living would encourage the kids to stay in school. "Do I think they're going to finish high school? Hell, no!" Angie said. Watching her own mother struggle hadn't inspired her. "I just hope they understand what I'm doing, trying to make they life a little better. I ain't expecting nobody to be no rocket scientist. Just get up and make a life for yourself. And don't be selling no drugs."

Did she worry that Kesha would follow her path and become a teenage mom? "Sex ain't what's on Kesha's mind now," Angie said. "When she's ready, she'll let me know."

Marcus wasn't so sure. Kesha did spend a lot of time with that eighteen-year-old boy upstairs. . . .

Angie shot him a censuring look.

"No—I know she ain't having sex," he said. After a pause, he whispered, "She might as well move up there."

Angie yawned and talked on. In the hours between midnight and dawn, she found her sacred space, turning the jumble of junk and a flickering TV into her makeshift sanctuary. Finally, the beer cans were empty. The GED workbook was covered with dust. The kitchen clock flashed its usual time: 88:88. In the real world, it was almost 3:00 a.m., and in two hours Angie's alarm clock would drag her cussing from her sleep. She wasn't betting that an $8 or $9 an hour job would prove anyone's salvation, the kids' or her own. Still, by the time the sun rose over Milwaukee, she would be at the nursing home, complaining that she was broke and tired and desperate for a little sleep. Then she would get someone dressed and fed and ready for the day. Angie wasn't one to boast, but that did make her proud. "I work," she said.

Epilogue:

Washington and Milwaukee, 1999–2004

I started to write about ghetto poverty in the early 1980s, when the field felt as filled with defeat as Angie with her lights cut off. *Homelessness, the underclass, AIDS, crack*—the decade challenged dictionaries to keep pace as it redefined urban suffering. Whether I was writing about welfare or the broader fabric of inner-city life, I soon had the same formula reflexively in mind: things were bad and getting worse. Every reporter's early encounters leave indelible impressions. In St. Louis, poverty registered as a sound, the wails of teenagers mourning a gang murder. In Detroit, it arose as a scent: Lysol, body odor, and spaghetti sauce wafting through a homeless shelter. In Chicago, poverty was the menacing sight of high-rise projects stretching to the horizon; "American apartheid" it was sometimes called, and so it seemed. As dispiriting as the facts on the ground was the fatalism in the air, summarized (and spread) by Ronald Reagan's line: "We fought a war on poverty and poverty won." Appearing at a conference in the early 1990s, Robert Lampman, an architect of those early antipoverty efforts, celebrated the legacy of his life's work: soaring wages, full employment, vanishing need. Then the aging eminence delivered a line from *Saturday Night Live:* "Not!"

A few years later, Lampman's punch line would no longer work. Poverty plunged. Employment surged. Crime, teen pregnancy, crack use, AIDS—all saw substantial declines. By moving poor women into the workforce, the welfare bill contributed to that progress materially. And it symbolized it powerfully. Whatever hardships the bill left untouched, whatever corners of inner-city life it may never reach, the decade renewed a forgotten lesson: that progress is possible on problems that seem impervious to change. At the conference where Robert Lampman poked fun at himself, another participant tried to ward off the gloom with lines from a Polish poet, written as Solidarity was exposing the clefts in Soviet control. "What does the political scientist know?" the poem asks.

It doesn't occur to him
That no one knows when
Irrevocable changes may appear
Like an ice floe's sudden cracks

Change "political scientist" to "poverty expert" (or reporter) and you have the feeling of the postwelfare years.

Forced by the cracking ice to discard my formula, I struggled to find a new one. The upbeat statistical reports scarcely fit the hardships before my eyes. But which revealed the greater truth? Angie's 401(k), or her drunken stock-picking session among armed boyfriends? In the trio's lives, the layers of disadvantage ran even deeper than I first glimpsed—the garnished wages, the loss of heat and lights, the fights for the last drop of milk, Kesha's weekends with a prostitute, Opal's whole life. "That was every black man's job," Jewell said about selling crack, as if to say that one thing poverty can impoverish is one's sense of possibility. And, as steady workers with above-average earnings, Angie and Jewell were unusual *successes.*

Or maybe just usual ones. In getting to know Michelle Crawford, the welfare-to-work heroine championed by Tommy Thompson, I found a similar story of work mixed with woe. Michelle, too, had made an unlikely journey off the rolls—yet she was running out of food, coping with physical attacks from a jealous man (in her case, one she had married), and panicking over a teenage son's arrest, twice, for selling cocaine. In talking about Lillie Harden, Bill Clinton had stressed how much her move from welfare to work would mean to her kids: "She looked me straight in the eye and said, 'When my boy goes to school and they say, "What does your mama do for a living," he can give an answer.'" Harden did have a straight-A daughter who went on to college. But the son that Clinton was celebrating was better known for his rap sheet than his grades. Between the time Governor Clinton first told his story and the time President Clinton revived it, the teenage Carlton Harden had already served two years for shooting at some students outside a North Little Rock high school. In the past decade, he has been arrested twenty times, for offenses ranging from disorderly conduct to possession of crack cocaine with intent to deliver; he's gone to prison on drug charges twice. "Oh boy, it almost killed me," Lillie Harden told me, speaking of her son's problems. "He got out there and act like he don't have no brain." Harden had a stroke in 2002 and wanted me to ferry a message back to Clinton, asking if he could help her get on Medicaid. She had received it on welfare, but had been rejected now, and she couldn't afford her $450 monthly bill for prescription drugs. More sad than bitter, she said of her work: "It didn't pay off in the end." I used to imagine the story someone could tell from a few scraps of Angie's life. On the job. A 401(k). What a difference it must make to the kids!

Yet Angie and Jewell worked. They worked when their whole lives seemed like tutorials in the barriers to work. They worked when they didn't have enough to eat or didn't get to sleep. They worked through ulcers and depression and back pains. They worked when Marcus shot holes in the ceiling and Ken went to jail. With little education, experience, or encouragement—they worked. If one lesson was that their misfortunes ran deeper than typically imagined, another was that their resilience ran equally deep.

Skeptics viewed the rising work rates of poor single mothers as the ephemera of the economy. "Wait until a recession," they said (at times too eagerly). Downturns always hurt the needy, and the 2001 recession did, though not as much as feared. From 2000 to 2002, the incomes of disadvantaged single mothers fell about 2 percent, after rising 17 percent over the previous six years. Child poverty rates rose by a half percentage point, less than a fifth of the average rise inflicted by the previous three recessions. The employment rates of high school dropouts held up better than those of college graduates. In part this may have reflected the shape of the recession, which spread its pain further up the income ladder than recessions often do. But it also suggested that the work habits of women like Angie and Jewell outlasted the business cycle. From 2000 to 2003, even as unemployment rates rose, the welfare rolls fell another 7 percent, which may either show the enterprise of the needy or the failure of states to serve them—and probably shows some of both.

At the peak of the Milwaukee welfare wars, I took a drive around town with one of the city's premier eccentrics, John Gardner, a school board member and lefty labor organizer, who had long called for abolishing welfare and replacing it with public jobs. While he found much to criticize in the bureaucratic blunders of W-2—"It works despite itself," he said, an enviably succinct summation—he reveled at the sight of so many poor women groping their way into jobs. He likened the postwelfare years to the aftermath of slavery, when dispossessed families roamed the countryside wondering what, besides more hunger, their newfound freedom would bring. I silently dismissed the comparison as wild hyperbole; no welfare program ever administered the lash. I dismissed it but never forgot it, since it underscores the challenge of recognizing success when it first appears, cloaked in havoc and doubt. In the case of Emancipation, the trajectory of racial progress took roughly a century to come fully into view. In their first half dozen years off the rolls, it was easy to feel like nothing had changed in Angie and Jewell's lives. But *something* had.

The country knows now what it didn't know a decade ago: that antipoverty policy can enjoy a measure of success. To borrow a diplomatic term, that ought to serve as a "confidence-building" measure that encourages additional steps. Clinton predicted that ending welfare would transform the politics of poverty, and on the surface at least it has. No one runs for office, as Reagan did, deriding Welfare Queens. "Welfare mothers make responsible employees," claimed one public-service ad—unremarkable except for the pollster who helped design it, the former Reagan aide Richard Wirthlin. When I talked to Clinton in 2004, I asked whether his prediction of a new progressive politics had proved correct. "In some ways we'll never know," he said. "Because Al Gore didn't win the White House and because the economy turned down . . . and because the whole political focus of America changed after 9/11. But I will say this . . . [George W. Bush] thought in order to win the White House he had to run as a compassionate conservative. He had to run bragging on the religious programs that help poor people and inner-city kids. And he had to go out of his way to say that he wasn't a racist." Clinton didn't note, though he might have, what a contrast that had been from the 1988 campaign of the first George Bush, whose supporters sought to mobilize racial fears with images of the black murderer Willie Horton.

Yet it's hard to picture a radically new politics of poverty when politics remains so dominated by money and the poor so lacking in power. No matter how many double shifts Angie pulled, she couldn't close the growing income gaps that increasingly define American life. The rising inequality has grown so familiar that it has lost its ability to startle. In the salad days of the 1990s, the incomes of the poorest fifth of American households rose 8 percent; the top fifth gained 40 percent; and the richest 5 percent gained 72 percent, to $434,000 a year. That meant the top 5 percent of Americans received a greater share of the national income than the bottom 60 percent combined. It may seem as though it were ever so, but that particular milestone wasn't crossed until 1997, Angie's and Jewell's first full year off the rolls. Trading welfare checks for pay stubs, they staked a moral claim to a greater share of the nation's prosperity—and entered an economy that gave the common worker proportionally less and less.

"People who work shouldn't be poor," Clinton said. They shouldn't have their lights shut off. They shouldn't run out of food. They shouldn't have their wages garnished when their ulcers bleed. But low-wage workers have vanished from a domestic agenda that's been dominated by a tax-cutting frenzy, mostly aimed at the same upper-income families who have enjoyed such outsized gains. (Congress cut *dividend* taxes.) Health care, child care, wage supplements, transportation aid—the rudiments of a package of workers' aid aren't hard to imagine. Just hard to enact, and even harder with the deficits the tax cuts helped create. Angie and Jewell finally got health insurance, through a Wisconsin program called Badger Care. In subsidizing families up to twice the poverty line, it's an admirable example of helping needy workers and one that other states should follow. But the typical state Medicaid program cuts off adults well before they reach the poverty line. The number of child-care subsidies doubled, but between 50 percent and 85 percent of eligible families still receive no help. While Angie's tax credits kept her afloat, Wisconsin's state program was unusually generous; forty states have none. At $5.15 an hour, the real value of the minimum wage is lower than in 1950 when Hattie Mae was still picking cotton.

The remarkable thing about programs of workers' aid like these is how unremarkable they are: there's nothing untested, nothing (except a minimum-wage hike) even politically controversial. The major impediment is cost. In 2001, Isabel Sawhill and Adam Thomas of the Brookings Institution came up with a plan for more child care, larger tax credits, and a $1 an hour raise in the minimum wage. They estimated it would lower the poverty rate by 2 percentage points. It would reach *20 million* families. And since all the money would go to workers, it couldn't be derided as welfare. Was it unrealistically expensive? Yes and no: at $26 billion a year, it cost less than half of what Congress spent to eliminate the inheritance tax, a benefit that almost exclusively accrues to the families of multimillionaires.

The ultimate goal isn't a safety net but a reduced need for one—to give families like Angie's a chance at real upward mobility. Elevators are harder to design than safety nets, but there are obvious places to begin. The work-first emphasis on entry-level jobs outperformed earlier programs of lengthy, up-front study. But the bias against training has probably swung too far, especially in an economy that pays the unskilled so little. An Oregon program that mixed job search and training raised earnings twice as much as those that stressed immediate work. What if Mercy Rehab (which is owned by a chain, Extendicare, Inc., with 275 facilities and revenues of nearly $2 billion) let experienced aides spend part of the week training for better jobs? What if the government subsidized the cost? Another item for the mobility agenda involves literal mobility, helping inner-city residents physically get away—to the army, to Job Corps, to better neighborhoods. The famous Gautreaux program in Chicago quietly spirited inner-city families to subsidized homes in the suburbs, where their kids went on to college at twice the rate of those who stayed behind. Its successor, Moving to Opportunity, brought families better health, less crime, and improved behavior among girls. The success of the New Hope boys shows what a difference even a few hours of the right after-school program can make. A serious attempt to help the inner-city poor would also include the men. Some experimental programs have tried to raise their earnings and strengthen their ties with their children, and mostly the results have been disappointing. But so were those of welfare-to-work programs for women a generation ago. If calls to aid the ghettos once sounded dreamy, there's a difference now: something finally worked. Or at least worked enough to encourage new attempts.

Funding for the Personal Responsibility Act expired in 2002, setting up a long-awaited reauthorization debate. There were all sorts of fights that George W. Bush could have led as a "compassionate conservative," especially with the welfare surpluses gone and state budgets reeling. He could have brought health insurance to needy workers, increased on-the-job training, or extended a hand to inner-city men. He could have offered federal money for more after-school programs. (He tried to cut them.) If he was serious about helping the working poor, he could have created subsidies for states to create tax credits like Wisconsin's. Instead, the debate that unfolded was both rancorous and obscure. Concerned that too many people on the rolls were idle, the administration sought to increase the "participation rates," the share of recipients required to perform some sort of weekly activity. (Because of adjustments for caseload reduction, most states no longer had to meet a meaningful federal standard.) Idleness was certainly one problem, and federal standards may be part of the solution. But the Bush proposal was so extreme—with new caps on education and training and a 70 percent work rate that few states could meet—it left the debate paralyzed. Arguing, rightly, that more work would require more child care, the Democrats sought more money. The value of the block grant had eroded 30 percent, but the White House was adamantly opposed. As of 2004, the issues remained unresolved, and the states were operating on short-term extensions, adding uncertainty to their fiscal woes.

For the most part, the discussion has occurred off center stage, with the country understandably focused on war and terrorism. The one Bush proposal to gain broad attention was the "marriage initiative," a plan to redirect $300 million a year of welfare money into marriage-promotion efforts, ranging from advertising campaigns to courses on budgeting and conflict resolution. Much of the Left responded with derision, and the obvious criticisms were true: it was totally untested, the decision to marry is deeply personal, some communities lack marriageable men. But similar things could have been said about teenage pregnancy, which government and civic campaigns in the 1990s helped cut by 30 percent. Rather than dismiss it, why not see it and raise it one—with an equally large "fatherhood initiative" to help inner-city men find jobs and reconnect with their kids. One congressman did push such a bill a few years ago, and he was scarcely a starry-eyed liberal: Republican Clay Shaw, the House author of the 1996 welfare bill. (To skeptical Republican colleagues he asked, "Does anyone have a better idea?") The lives of poor single mothers are too hard, the prospects for their kids too bleak, to write off the low-income family like a chunk of bad debt.

The welfare revolution grew from the fear that the poor were mired in a culture of *entitlement*—stuck in a swamp of excessive demands, legal prerogative, social due. There certainly was a culture of entitlement in American life, but it was scarcely concentrated at the bottom (as anyone following the wave of corporate scandals now knows). What really stands out about Angie and Jewell is how little they felt they were owed. They went through life acting entitled to nothing. Not heat or lights. Not medical care. Not even three daily meals. And they scarcely complained. When welfare was there for the taking, they got on the bus and took it; when it wasn't, they made other plans. In ending welfare, the country took away their single largest source of income. They didn't lobby or sue. They didn't march or riot. They made their way against the odds into wearying, underpaid jobs. And that does now entitle them to something—to "a shot at the American Dream" more promising than the one they've received.

On a frigid afternoon in December 1999, Angie followed through with her plan to put Opal out. Opal's mother took in the three older girls, and Opal and Brierra moved to a room in Bo's cousin's house. While Angie and Opal patched up their friendship, Opal's luck expired. After an early labor, she delivered her fifth daughter, Myerra, and they both tested positive for cocaine. Opal acknowledged that she was essentially homeless and had been smoking crack for a decade, and the state took the kids. Myerra left the hospital for a foster home, and Angie took legal custody of Brierra to spare her the same fate.

Losing one's kids is the ultimate sanction, the death penalty of social work. So it held out the hope of shocking Opal straight, as her other calamities had not. The court told her that to regain her girls, she had to make regular visits, find a home, complete a treatment program, and pass drug tests. She failed on every score. Then she got pregnant again. Opal did go to an outpatient program, but the boy she dubbed "Little Bo" had cocaine in his blood, and Opal seemed especially dejected when the state took him away, too. In early 2004, the state was moving to sever her parental rights.

With the loss of her kids, Opal finally lost her welfare check. She still had $5,000 a year in food stamps and, until he got caught with a stash of cocaine, she had Bo. As a repeat offender, he drew four years, leaving Opal to drift here and there, staying with whoever would have her. She has withdrawn from everyone, including me, but we did talk briefly after the birth of her son. At her request, I contacted a residential program that specialized in central city women. The director pledged to find her a spot, saying that Opal fit the profile—mid-thirties, lost kids—of many clients who turned their lives around. But Opal didn't follow through. "I guess she's just gonna be out here"—on the streets—"till somebody kill her, or she overdose." Jewell said. "Is she hurting inside? If she's alone, do she cry about it? I don't know."

W-2 remained troubled, too. As the program imploded with scandal at Maximus and Goodwill, Tommy Thompson left for Washington and a job as secretary of Health and Human Services. Having shown so little oversight of his own program, he gained oversight of the welfare system nationwide. A commission arose to study the problems he left behind, but little became of its work. From 2000 to 2003, the unemployment rate in Milwaukee surged to 9.7 percent (compared with 5.3 percent when Angie and Jewell left the rolls), and the caseload nearly doubled to nine thousand—still just a quarter of what it had been a decade earlier. The agency heads demanded more money, amid the embarrassing news that they were paying themselves up to $200,000 a year. Despite the handsome pay, half the Milwaukee agencies failed to meet the modest new performance goal—moving 35 percent of clients into jobs—and a years-long academic study found that people who entered W-2 fared no better in earnings or employment than a similar group who did not. By its very presence, W-2 served as welfare deterrent. But for the average client, its services made no difference.

Bleeding red ink, one agency (the YWCA) exited W-2, and another (UMOS) ran up multiple fines for casework failures. With only three Milwaukee agencies left, the regions were redrawn, and the Opportunities Industrialization Center—where I first glimpsed Opal spoofing the job interview—became the largest in the state. Then $270,000 of its funds were traced to the bank account of a disgraced politician. Former state senator Gary George pleaded guilty to federal conspiracy charges after acknowledging that he took the money (disguised as legal fees and routed through an attorney) while serving in a position to influence the awarding of welfare contracts. In OIC's case, those contracts totaled about $140 million. In March 2004, the OIC president, Carl Gee, was indicted for his alleged role in the kickback scheme. Gee pleaded not guilty, and other OIC officials denied any wrongdoing, but the state stationed a full-time monitor on the premises. Like a gang-ridden school, Wisconsin's largest welfare agency was being run with a cop in the hall.

Jason Turner, W-2's designer, moved on to the top welfare job in New York City and contracting problems of his own. Eager to put his stamp on the city's giant system, he had the welfare agency issue a half-billion dollars in job-placement contracts through an expedited bidding procedure. The largest single piece, more than $100 million, went to Maximus, where George Leutermann was part of a corporate team that included one or two others with ties to Turner and that critics charged had gained an inside edge. The city comptroller challenged the contracts on the grounds of "corruption, favoritism, and cronyism," and, with the process tied up in court, *The New York Times* reported that Leutermann, while seeking the New York business, had put Turner's father-in-law on the Maximus payroll. (He was a contractor on an unrelated project.) Upholding the contracts, an appeals court found that the city had shown "no evidence of favoritism" toward Maximus. But in letting family ties develop with a corporate suitor, Turner damaged his reputation and added to a controversy that shadowed the rest of his term. Amid the outcry and delay, Maximus wound up with a diminished role and was eventually eased out of the city, and Leutermann soon left the company. Turner finished four years in office that cut the rolls in half but raised, even more pointedly than in Wisconsin, the concern that his tactics—diversion and strict work rules—drove the needy away. He is now a consultant based in Milwaukee, with clients as far away as Slovakia and Israel; the latter country is setting up a version of W-2 called "Israel Works."

Farther down the bureaucratic chain, Michael Steinborn remained at Maximus, though he stopped working directly with clients. Burned out on their crises, he moved into a job trying to line up prospective employers. With his personal life in disarray, Michael saw welfare from yet another angle. He split up with his girlfriend, Jai, after they had a second child, who was born with severe medical problems and needed months of hospitalization. As a single mother with a disabled infant, Jai no longer felt able to work, and she went on W-2 herself. Michael said he felt ashamed to have his own children on welfare. But he also said the checks, with his child-support payments, helped nurture their daughter to health. "The irony kills me: I'm telling people this isn't the way, and my own family ends up on the system," he said. It was a fittingly equivocal thought from a man so ambivalent about the program he helped run.

Home life took a happier turn for Jewell and Ken. True to her word, she waited for him—for 476 days. Then on a snowy dawn in April 2000, I picked her up for a last ride to the prison, where a ponytailed man with a duffel bag walked out, smiling a hundred-watt smile. I confess I had doubts; not much I knew recommended Ken as a candidate for domesticity. But after a week in seclusion, Jewell offered an upbeat report. "It's just like it was before he went in," she said, with late-night video games and excursions with the kids.

Ken was so proud of his bricklaying certificate he unpacked it before we left the prison parking lot. Back in Milwaukee, however, he couldn't find a masonry job. Emotionally, he was in the classic ex-con's state—frustrated, vulnerable, adrift—when a friend dropped off an ounce of cocaine. The scene played out like a temptation cartoon, with an elf on each shoulder. *Take it. Don't.* Ken had pictured the moment for months and had never known what he would do. He hated being broke. He hated prison more. He gave the drugs to a friend and declared himself retired from the trade. Ken found off-and-on work disposing of hazardous waste, then took a job delivering pizzas. The money is no good, but the nightly rhythm recalls his old ways: he can roam the city, flirt with clients, and get paid in cash. He has been free for nearly four years with no arrests. "It's still in my blood," he said of the hustler's life. "But I'm trying to get it out of my blood. When you got a positive influence"—Jewell—"you can't do nothing but positive things." Jewell's conquest of Ken is the rare event of which she can say: "It's just what I hoped for."

She wouldn't say that about work. After three years on the tool-scanning line, she grew so angry at her annual raise—25 cents an hour—that she walked out of G. B. Electric and never went back. "They're making millions of dollars a day, and here we is, making $8 and $9 an hour," she said. She landed a temp job at the post office but hurt her neck and shoulder toting the mail and got fired when investigators discovered her old shoplifting conviction. Seven years after leaving the rolls, Jewell is a nursing aide again, earning $10 an hour and feeling underpaid. "I wouldn't say I like it—I just do it," she said. Still, between her earnings, food stamps, and tax credits, Jewell brings home more than $20,000 a year, and Ken makes about as much hustling pizzas—together, they have a toehold on a lower-middle-class life. With a soft spot for electronics (and payment plans), Ken bought a computer to help him write raps, and Jewell plays dominoes online; calling, I often get a message that says, "The AOL customer . . . asked that you try to reach them on their cell phone." Though she is still "scuffling" to get by, Jewell said, "I ain't scuffling like I *used* to." She said Ken's presence has helped the boys, but it hasn't been a panacea. By the eighth grade, her oldest son, Terrell, was flirting with trouble—skipping class, hanging with the wrong friends—and Jewell grew alarmed.

Despite the basic domestic contentment, one thing was missing. "That should be us," Ken said, as a couple on television cuddled their baby. Their prospects weren't good. Jewell had fibroids on her uterine tissue, and Ken had never fathered a child. So they were astonished when Jewell emerged from the bathroom with a positive pregnancy test. The fibroids brought unbearable pain, and she put off seeing a doctor for a month until she could get health insurance. The growths finally forced a risky, first-trimester operation, with a 10 percent chance of saving the pregnancy. Nearly two months of bed rest and lost wages followed—then the baby shower. Looking every bit the proud father that Jewell had pictured, Ken prowled the event with a video camera and a button that said "Dad." Kevion Quatrell Thigpen arrived in March 2002. Continuing his evolution from bad man to homebody, Ken watches his son while Jewell is at work, then leaves for his nightly pizza rounds.

Jewell still hasn't gotten a wedding ring, though she raises the subject whenever she can. "Arrrghh," Ken says in mock consternation. Despite his display of commitment, marriage seems to conjure a standard of perfection—or at least to demand more money and trust than he feels able to command. "I still think it's gonna happen," Jewell said. Given her record of beating the odds, it would be a mistake to count her out.

While Jewell's bet on romance largely paid off, Angie's bet on work did not. She stayed at Mercy, where seven years of service have made her a fixture on the ward. But despite her "workaholic" pride, her earnings stalled. Actually, they fell. After her earnings peaked at $18,500, Angie cut back to three-quarters time and averaged less than $15,000 over the next four years. Jewell, the grudging worker, earned more. Several forces tempered Angie's drive, not the least of them fatigue. "People get tired!" she said. "I'm not no machine—and even they wear out." Her decision to raise Brierra made it harder to work long hours, and Angie gave up on the nursing pool she had pursued so purposefully. Some news she welcomed contributed to her decision to cut back: after years on a waiting list, she got a Section 8 housing subsidy, which, by reducing her rent by $3,000 a year, replaced the lost wages. But the bigger brake on Angie's drive was more dispiriting: having thrown herself into work, she lost faith that hard work pays. Angie finished a computer class and applied for a promotion to a medical records job. She didn't get it. She did get her semiannual raise: nine belittling cents. She was equally indignant about its size and symbolism: it left her at $8.99 an hour, priced like a Wal-Mart sale. Wanting to tell herself she earned "nine-something," Angie demanded (and got) the extra penny, but fumed at the missing respect. "That's just like an insult—I deserve way more than that," she said. "I like the work. I like the residents. But the money's just not right."

While Angie's earnings still rank her as a welfare-to-work success, she continues to draw heavily on government support: food stamps, tax credits, housing aid, and $215 a month in "kinship care" payments for Brierra. Those programs provide more than half of her income, and she also gets subsidized child care and health insurance. She would be a lot poorer without the help, but there is a downside to the generous layering of aid: every dollar of increased earnings cuts her benefits by 85 cents. With payroll taxes, she actually loses 93 cents, making the extra effort seem pointless—a fact she intuits without fully understanding the math. While the arithmetic of Angie's situation is extreme, her broader dilemma is common: absent a dramatic increase in skills, it's hard to see how she can work her way up to a significantly better standard of living. "Just treading water," she said. "Just making it, that's all."

After a few months on the lam, Marcus did his time in jail, then spent another two years at Angie's, feeling disrespected and warring with the kids. No longer a fugitive, he wasn't quite a boyfriend, either. "Just live together, that's it—barely talk," Angie said. She put him out after she caught him smoking pot with Redd but let him return after he grew mysteriously ill. Hospitalized with several bouts of pneumonia, Marcus was a phantom presence in the house—not there, not gone, not acknowledged. Then he got in a feud with one of his sister's friends, who broke into Angie's house and dropped a car battery on his head. Marcus never fully recovered, and died four months later, at age twenty-nine. Angie speculated that Marcus had cancer, but the word on the street—and on the death certificate—was that Marcus died of AIDS. With her housing voucher, Angie moved to a larger house, where other boarders still come and go. The kids sometimes criticized her drinking, but Angie no longer talked of swearing off beer, saying, "I need my peace of mind." On a happier front, she became a surprisingly enthusiastic parent to Brierra—"surprising" because Angie seemed to have had her fill of motherhood. Once worried that she would have to keep Brierra forever, she started the process of legal adoption to make sure that she does.

Her own kids continued to struggle. Darrell suffered from mysterious seizures for which the doctors could find no cause; one of Angie's friends thought they might be psychosomatic, a lonely boy's bid for attention. Von was Angie's most promising student ("School's fun"), but in high school he fell apart. Cutting classes, defying teachers, he finished his freshman year with a grade point average of 0.2. "It was just me being a knucklehead," he said. "Just trying to follow the crowd." If ever a kid needed some distance from the ghetto, it was Von, whose cerebral streak set him apart and left him lonely. Angie viewed his acting out as an effort to establish his street bona fides. "He don't want anybody to think he's weak," she said. Repeating his freshman year, Von talked of going to college and becoming a teen counselor, but his grades continued to lag.

After years of academic failure, Redd put on a brief but revealing display of ability. Determined to get out of eighth grade, he raised a D-minus average in the fall to a B-plus in the spring, putting the lie to the summer school teacher who had labeled him a "dummy." Then he lost interest again, failing ninth grade twice and dropping out. "It was boring," he said. Hitting his middle teens, Redd shed his doughboy build and gained a new confidence and charm, which may not have been all for the best. A neighbor showed him how to steal cars, and he had just bailed out of a joy ride when the police arrested his friends, finding them with several guns. At seventeen, Redd greeted most days with a joint and though he said he hadn't sold drugs, he added, "I'm ready to get out here and sell me some. . . . I'm tired of not having no money." Hattie Mae, his grandmother, came for a visit and burst into tears. With a headful of braids and his father's soulful eyes, Redd looked just like Greg. She felt like she was losing a son all over again.

For all the boys' problems, it was Kesha who gave Angie her first gray hairs. She continued to date Jermaine, the older boy upstairs. But his sexual pursuit led her to break things off, especially after he took her to a party where the other couples were taking Viagra. "Everybody wanted to do stuff, and I was like, 'You can take me home!' " she said. With her characteristic openness and poise, Kesha said she would know when she was ready; not long after, with a new boyfriend, she decided that she was. The birth control pills that Jewell helped her get ran out, and a few months shy of her seventeenth birthday, Kesha got pregnant. The baby's father was fourteen. She broke the news at his eighth-grade graduation and scarcely heard from him again.

Knowing the struggles ahead, Angie urged her to end the pregnancy, but Kesha wouldn't hear of it. "It's wrong to kill a baby," she said. "It's just so wrong. If you're grown enough to have sex, that's on you—you gotta take responsibility." It was the subject of their angriest fight. Still seventeen, repeating the ninth grade, Kesha had a daughter: LaNayia LaCherish Jobe. She was six months younger than Angie had been when she started down the incomparably hard path of poor single motherhood. Like Angie, Kesha dropped out of school. And like Angie she moved in with a boyfriend, a sporadically employed twenty-four-year-old who lives in his mother's house. But unlike Angie, she didn't go on welfare. "That's for people who really need it," she said. "I like to earn my own money." She took a job as a checkout clerk at a grocery store and spent most of her free time at home with her boyfriend and LaNayia. By all accounts a doting mother, much less wild at nineteen than Angie had been, Kesha had a second child, Latavia.

Angie said she's over the shock of becoming a thirty-five-year-old grandmother. But the ratio of hope to defeat in her life feels like it has shifted in a downward direction. Yet, for all the turmoil and need around her, and all her pure exhaustion, she continues to mine her life for scraps of optimism and meaning. Last year, she seized a moment to herself and wrote another poem, which she called "Better Days." It honors the ancestors "who worked and cried" to get her where she is, and like many chapters in her life it ends with some unanswered questions:

Better days are here, so they say
So why am I still working, running, fighting and crying?
For my better days?
Or is it so my descendants can know of the work I'm putting in
For their better days?

TIMELINE

Early 1840s	Frank Caples, a child slave, arrives in Mississippi. He is Jewell's and Opal's great-great-grandfather and the great-great-great-grandfather of Angie's oldest kids.
1876	Frank Caples has a son named Pie Eddie Caples.
1927	Woods Eastland recruits Pie Eddie Caples to sharecrop on his Delta plantation.
1934	Woods Eastland's son, James, begins running the family plantation.
1935	President Franklin D. Roosevelt signs the Social Security Act, creating AFDC.
1937	Pie Eddie's daughter Mayola gives birth to Hattie Mae.
1939	Mayola Caples dies, leaving Hattie Mae to be raised by her grandmother, "Mama" Hattie.
1941	James Eastland, 36, is appointed to the U.S. Senate; the following year, he wins the first of his six full terms.
1950	Hattie Mae, 13, has her first child, Squeaky.
1952	Hattie Mae, 15, marries Willie Reed, with whom she moves to Missouri and later has three children.
1960	Hattie Mae, 23, leaves Willie and goes on AFDC. Soon after, she meets Isaac Johnson.
1966	Greg Reed is born to Hattie Mae Reed and Isaac Johnson.
1966	Angela Jobe is born to Roosevelt and Charity Jobe.

1967	Opal Caples is born to Hattie Mae's cousin, Ruthie Mae Caples.
1968	Jewell Reed is born to Hattie Mae Reed and Isaac Johnson.
1970	Hattie Mae leaves Isaac and joins her family in the Chicago projects.
1972	Charity and Roosevelt Jobe move to a Chicago subdivision called Jeffrey Manor as Angie, 6, is starting school.
1979	Hattie Mae and her boyfriend, Wesley Crenshaw, move to Jeffrey Manor, now troubled by gangs and drugs.
1979	Charity leaves Roosevelt and moves from Jeffrey Manor.
1982–83	Angie, visiting her father's house, begins dating Greg.
1984	Angie and Greg have their first child, LaKesha. Angie leaves high school and goes on welfare.
1986	Angie and Greg have son, Dwayne, whom they nickname Redd. About this time, Greg starts selling drugs.
1987	Angie and Greg have a third child, DeVon.
1988	Jewell gets pregnant and moves in with Angie and Greg. After her son Terrell is born in October, she begins dating Tony Nicholas.
June 1991	Greg and Tony are arrested for murder.
September 1991	Angie and Jewell move to Milwaukee.
October 23, 1991	Bill Clinton, running for president, pledges to "end welfare as we know it."
December 1991	Jewell has her second son, Tremmell.
November 1992	Bill Clinton is elected president.
June 1993	Angie has her fourth child, Darrell. Soon after, she starts a post office job that lasts a year and a half.
September 1993	Jewell's cousin, Opal Caples, moves to Milwaukee.
December 1993	Wisconsin governor Tommy Thompson signs a bill pledging to replace AFDC within six years.
June 1994	Clinton proposes a welfare bill, which never reaches a congressional vote.

November 1994	Republicans capture the House and Senate. Newt Gingrich and GOP governors agree to make welfare a block grant, with capped federal funding but expanded state autonomy.
March 1995	The House passes a welfare bill, which Clinton criticizes.
April 1995	Jason Turner, a Wisconsin welfare official, drafts a plan for a new state welfare program called W-2. Governor Thompson signs it the following year.
June 1995	Angie, Opal, and Jewell leave the house on First Street.
September 1995	The Senate passes a welfare bill, with Clinton's praise.
December 1995	Clinton vetoes the welfare bill, which is attached to a GOP balanced budget plan.
January 1996	Clinton vetoes the welfare bill, this time as a separate measure.
March 1996	Jason Turner launches a Wisconsin work program called Pay for Performance; the rolls plummet.
Spring 1996	Angie and Jewell take jobs as nursing aides; Jewell begins seeing Ken Thigpen.
Spring 1996	GOP prepares a third welfare bill, tied to a "poison pill" of Medicaid cuts to force a third Clinton veto.
July 1996	The House and Senate drop the Medicaid cuts and pass a third welfare bill.
August 22, 1996	Clinton signs a bill abolishing AFDC and creating a new program, Temporary Assistance for Needy Families, with time limits, work requirements, and increased state control.
August 1996	After eight years on welfare, Jewell leaves the rolls.
September 1996	After twelve years on welfare, Angie leaves the rolls.
December 1996	Jewell gets fired and spends most of the next year with neither welfare nor work.
Spring 1997	Angie, thriving as a worker, buys a car.
August 1997	Angie meets Marcus Robertson, who soon moves in.
September 1997	Wisconsin launches W-2 a month after Opal appears on the cover of *The New York Times Magazine* with Thompson.
November 1997	Angie's car is stolen, sending her into a downward spiral.

January 1998	Jewell goes to work at G. B. Electric.
February to May 1998	Opal quits her job and sells off her furniture to buy cocaine. Her caseworkers at the Opportunities Industrialization Center, a W-2 agency, ignore her.
March 1998	Angie is deterred from returning to welfare and finds a job at Mercy Rehab.
May 1998	Opal's mother takes her kids, as Opal, who is pregnant, moves to a crack house and continues to get welfare.
November 1998	Michael Steinborn, a new W-2 caseworker at Maximus, Inc., inherits Opal's case. Opal moves in with Angie.
December 1998	Ken Thigpen is sentenced to two years for selling cocaine. Opal gives birth to Brierra.
April 1999	Maximus transfers Opal's case to Goodwill.
April 1999	Marcus shoots up Angie's ceiling.
June 1999	Angie gets a 401(k).
July 1999	Angie stabs Marcus, but soon lets him move back in.
October 1999	W-2 wins an award from Harvard and the Ford Foundation.
October 1999	Angie starts a second job, at a nursing pool.
December 1999	Angie evicts Opal.
March 2000	Opal has a fifth child, Myerra, and admits using cocaine. The state sends the baby to foster care, and Angie takes Brierra.
April 2000	Ken Thigpen is released from prison.
Summer 2000	Legislative auditors find financial abuses at Maximus.
January 2001	Tommy Thompson takes office as secretary of Health and Human Services under President George W. Bush.
Summer 2001	Legislative auditors find financial abuses at Goodwill, which is forced out of the W-2 program.
November 2001	Kesha, 17, has a baby and drops out of high school.
March 2002	Jewell and Ken have a son, Kevion Thigpen.
Fall 2002	Redd, 15, stops going to high school.
October 2003	Marcus dies of AIDS.
March 2004	The head of the Opportunities Industrialization Center is indicted on federal kickback charges.

NOTES

SOURCES AND METHODS

In telling this story, I have relied on years of discussions with the women at its heart, Angela Jobe, Jewell Reed, and Opal Caples. Their accounts have been indispensable, but I have not relied on their memories alone. With their permission, I have also had access to their complete welfare records for the past dozen years. This archive notes every check issued, letter sent, sanction imposed, and appointment kept or missed. It also includes the quarterly earnings reports that their employers filed with the state (to track their eligibility for unemployment insurance). This trove of data produced a much more complete picture of the trio's interactions with the welfare system than I could have assembled on my own. Unless noted differently, the reader can assume that references to their welfare cases were drawn from these files. Likewise, with the permission of Angie and her children, the Milwaukee Public Schools shared a decade's worth of report cards and attendance records. All three of the main characters shared their tax returns, and they and others shared portions of diaries, letters, school essays, and the like. In addition to consulting these private materials, I have foraged along a trail of public records that runs from the nineteenth century to the twenty-first, including deeds, birth and death certificates, decennial censuses, police reports, and records in civil and criminal court proceedings.

This is a reporter's endeavor: no names have been changed, characters melded, or quotes invented. Many scenes involving Angie, Jewell, and Opal are ones I witnessed firsthand. I have reconstructed others through interviews. In some places, I have included bits of dialogue from conversations where I wasn't present; these come from accounts by the people involved and represent their words verbatim. Likewise, I occasionally use quotes to describe what someone was thinking; the words between the quotes are his or her own. For the most part, the sourcing is obvious, but in places where multiple perspectives inform complicated events, I have cited the people on whose accounts I've drawn. A large academic literature exists on the history of welfare and poverty and the performance of the current law; to embed these women's story in a broader context, I've consulted it as much as possible and cited it selectively below.

In writing about the abolition of AFDC, I had the advantage of having covered much of the story for *The New York Times*, which allowed me to talk at length with many of the main players, some of whom generously shared their files after the bill was signed. Future scholars will likely have access to new materials, as the papers of Bill Clinton and other leaders are opened to public view; my envy of them is tempered by the hope that there was something to have been gained as well from seeing things firsthand. In the interests of economy, I've offered no citations for facts and figures routinely in the public realm. Unless otherwise noted, the figures on national caseloads come from the U.S. Department of Health and Human Services. The data on Wisconsin caseloads come from the Wisconsin Department of Workforce Development. Poverty rates are calculated annually by the U.S. Census Bureau. Figures on the share of children born outside marriage are kept by the National Center for Health Statistics, which is part of the Centers for Disease Control and Prevention. People writing about welfare in these years will also find themselves consulting the *Green Book*, a statistical compilation periodically published by the Ways and Means Committee of the U.S. House of Representatives.

In analyzing how Angie's and Jewell's incomes changed as they moved from welfare to work, I wound up with more material than the text of this book could accommodate. I've posted an expanded analysis at www.jasondeparle.com, where other information about this work and the people in it can be found.

ABBREVIATIONS

ADC: Winifred Bell, *Aid to Dependent Children* (New York: Columbia University Press, 1965)
Baseline: Department of Health and Human Services, "Aid to Families with Dependent Children: The Baseline," June 1998
BLS: Bureau of Labor Statistics
CBO: Congressional Budget Office
CHIPS: Petition for Determination of Status in Need of Protection or Services
CLASP: Center on Law and Social Policy
Cong. Rec.: *Congressional Record*
CQ: *Congressional Quarterly Weekly Report*
DWD: Wisconsin Department of Workforce Development
GAO: U.S. General Accounting Office
HHS: U.S. Department of Health and Human Services
LAB: Wisconsin Legislative Audit Bureau
MDRC: Manpower Demonstration Research Corporation
MJ: *The Milwaukee Journal*
MJS: *Milwaukee Journal Sentinel*

MS: *Milwaukee Sentinel*
NYP: *New York Post*
NYT: *The New York Times*
NYTM: *The New York Times Magazine*
PPP: *Public Papers of the Presidents of the United States—William J. Clinton* (Washington, DC: Government Printing Office)
USN: *U.S. News & World Report*
UW-M: University of Wisconsin–Milwaukee
WP: *The Washington Post*
WSJ: *The Wall Street Journal*

1. THE PLEDGE: WASHINGTON AND MILWAUKEE, 1991

3 **"We should insist":** Clinton speech in Little Rock, Oct. 3, 1991.
"If you can work": Account of the pledge to "end welfare as we know it" comes from interviews with Bruce Reed and Stan Greenberg, Clinton's pollster; Greenberg's notes; and drafts of the Clinton speech. See also David Whitman and Mathew Cooper, *USN,* June 20, 1994.
"fit on a bumpersticker": Memo from Bruce Reed to Bill Clinton, May 25, 1991.

4 **wanted to cancel:** Stan Greenberg diary, Oct. 19, 1991.
no one could say who had coined it: Greenberg said he may have done so; Reed said he didn't recall. Ironically, one prominent critic of the phrase, David Ellwood of Harvard University, had used it three years earlier, saying of some welfare experiments: "It's hard to believe that this spells the end of welfare as we know it." Bob Port, *St. Petersburg Times,* Nov. 21, 1988.
New Covenant: Spencer Rich, *WP,* Oct. 24, 1991.
"Pure heroin": Campaign memo from Celinda Lake, Oct. 1, 1992.
"guiding star": Jason DeParle, *NYT,* May 8, 1994.
"Greyhound therapy": Paul Peterson and Mark Rom, *Welfare Magnets: A New Case for a National Standard* (Washington, DC: Brookings Institution, 1990), 25.

6 **Twelfth and Vliet:** Carlen Hatala, City of Milwaukee Historic Preservation Commission, interview by the author. The department store was Schuster's.

7 **Cuomo struck back**: Joe Klein, *New York,* Nov. 18, 1991.
Clinton feared Duke: Greenberg diary, Oct. 20, 1991.

8 **"half this election," "major deal":** Greenberg diary, Dec. 1, 1991.
"The welfare message": Memo from Celinda Lake to Stan Greenberg, undated.
"single most important," voters "stunned"; Stan Greenberg, "Bill Clinton: New Hampshire, Exploratory Focus Groups," Sept. 27, 1991, 8.

8 **"taken aback":** Greenberg memo to Clinton, March 7, 1992, 3.
"The strongest media": Greenberg memo to Clinton, March 2, 1992, 4.
"No other message": Greenberg memo to Clinton, April 22, 1992, 4.
Democratic convention: Greenberg memo to Clinton, July 19, 1992, 6.
Most effective answer: Greenberg memo to Clinton, Aug. 18, 1992, 2.

9 **"Get a job":** Bush in Riverside, California, July 31, 1992. Clinton wasn't the first Democrat to get to Bush's right on welfare. In a 1970 Senate race, Lloyd Bentsen attacked Bush for voting for Nixon's Family Assistance Plan; in a statewide advertising campaign, Bentsen, who won, told Texas voters that a vote for Bush was "a vote for big welfare." Jonah Martin Edelman, " The Passage of the Family Support Act of 1988 and the Politics of Welfare Reform in the United States" (PhD dissertation, Balliol College, Oxford University, 1995), 211.

14 **"Biological as it gets":** Though Angie and Opal aren't related, Greg Logan, the father of Angie's first three children, is Opal's second cousin.

15 **children "sleeping on grates":** Moynihan, 104th Cong., 1st sess., *Cong. Rec.* 141 (Sept. 5, 1995): S 12705.
"greatest social policy": Thompson, HHS press release, Feb. 4, 2002.
"greatest advance . . . since capitalism": Editorial, *WSJ*, April 2, 2004.

16 **racial composition:** Nationally, in 1991 the rolls were 38 percent white, 39 percent black, and 17 percent Hispanic. *1993 Green Book,* 705.
nearly 70 percent of the city's caseload: John Pawasarat and Lois M. Quinn, "Demographics of Milwaukee County Populations Expected to Work Under Proposed Welfare Initiatives" (University of Wisconsin–Milwaukee, Employment & Training Institute, Nov. 1995), 1, 26.
six times as likely: In 1991, 2.3 percent of whites received Aid to Families with Dependent Children, compared to 15.5 percent of blacks and 9.3 percent of Hispanics. (Unpublished analysis by Wendell Primus, U.S. Congress Joint Economic Committee.)
nearly seven of ten long-term: Greg Duncan of Northwestern University calculated the number from the Panel Study of Income Dynamics, a longitudinal study of nearly eight thousand families. He defined "long term" as any recipient who, upon enrolling in AFDC, received payments in sixty of the following eighty-four months; among people in that category, 68 percent were black. Communication with Duncan by author.

2. THE PLANTATION: MISSISSIPPI, 1840–1960

20 **Percy kept her from being run out:** Hortense Powdermaker, *Stranger and Friend* (New York: W. W. Norton, 1966), 129.
"Negroes are innately inferior" to **"there may be good":** Hortense Powdermaker, *After Freedom* (1939; repr., Madison: University of Wisconsin Press, 1993), 22–23.

21 **"capable of being mobilized"** to **"it is more or less assumed":** Powdermaker, *After Freedom,* 68, 69, 208, 363.

welfare didn't exist: Powdermaker started her fieldwork in 1932; Aid to Dependent Children (later renamed Aid to Families with Dependent Children) was created in 1935 and didn't reach the rural South for years.

"Every aspect of underclass culture": Nicholas Lemann, "The Origins of the Underclass," *The Atlantic,* June 1986, 35.

In the exchanges that followed: Part of the controversy stemmed from Lemann's argument that there was a "strong correlation" between sharecropper experience in the South and underclass status in the North. Demographers have failed to show that sharecroppers fared worse than other black migrants (perhaps because the data are poor), and Lemann dropped the word *correlation* from *The Promised Land,* his acclaimed book on the black migration. There he presents the sharecropper thesis in a more diffuse form, arguing simply that black sharecropper society "was the equivalent of big-city ghetto society today in many ways." *The Promised Land: The Great Black Migration and How It Changed America* (New York: Knopf, 1991), 31.

22 **James Eastland took over:** *Current Biography,* vol. 10 (New York: H. W. Wilson Company, 1949), 184.

23 **Pie Eddie Caples arrived in 1927:** Interviews with Mack Caples (his son), Ruth V. Caples (his daughter-in-law), and Virginia Caples (his granddaughter).

Pie Eddie Caples's wives: Interviews with Mack Caples and Ruth V. Caples, along with decennial census records, identify three wives: Virgie Caples, Alice Caples, and Hattie Chapman Caples. An 1892 marriage certificate shows an earlier union to Savanah Watson Caples. Divorce papers in the Scott County, Miss., courthouse list Eastland & Nichols as his lawyers in his 1923 divorce from Alice. The Eastland in the law firm was Woods's brother Oliver, supporting Mack Caples's recollection that his father, Eddie, had ties to the Eastland family before moving to the Delta. (See main text page 28.)

labor killed her: Mayola Caples's death certificate, April 10, 1939.

Samuel Caples arrived in about 1843: The 1840 census has him still living in Fayette County, Alabama, a fifty- to sixty-year-old man with seven slaves. By 1843, he and his slaves appear on the tax rolls of Scott County, Mississippi. He is identified as a tavernkeeper in a genealogical reference book, *Looking Back: Fayette County, Alabama, 1824–1974* (Fayette, AL: Fayette County Historical Society, 1974), Part III, 68. Frank Caples's age can be deduced from the 1855 loan agreement (see below) that lists him as about twenty years old.

24 **"detestable":** John Chester Miller, *The Wolf by the Ears: Thomas Jefferson and Slavery* (New York: Free Press, 1977), 7.

24 **abandoned life in middle Tennessee:** In tracking Samuel Caples, I got help from two members of his descended family, Joyce McFarland and Kathe Hollingshaus. Their records show him as a "bondsman" in a Wilson County, Tenn., marriage in 1806 and selling land in Lincoln County, Tenn., in 1815 and 1821. The 1830 census places him in Fayette County, Alabama. A surviving log of a dry-goods store there shows him sending someone named Frank, presumably Hattie Mae's great-grandfather, to buy pins and tumblers on credit.

25 **"my Negro boy Hyram":** Bill of Sale, Samuel Caples to Bird Saffold, Jan. 1, 1849, on file at Scott County, Miss., Courthouse, Deed Book E, 38. The clerk of probate court who witnessed the sale happened to be Alfred Eastland, Senator James Eastland's great-great-grandfather.

"Caples has this day executed": Mortgage, Samuel Caples to A. J. Wright, April 17, 1855, on file at Scott County Courthouse, Deed Book F, 585–86.

Jefferson Davis Caples: He is listed as eight years old on the 1870 census.

joined a local militia: Service records at the Mississippi Department of Archives and History list Caples in "Capt. Thacker Vivion's Company, Mississippi Cavalry," a unit of volunteers whose members were all over fifty.

"ten miles of negros" to **"hegira":** Margie Riddle Bearss, *Sherman's Forgotten Campaign: The Meridian Expedition* (Baltimore: Gateway Press, 1987), 238–40.

26 **lost the homestead and family left:** Tax sale recorded in *Newton Weekly Ledger,* May 16, 1872, and referenced in Jean Strickland and Patricia Nicholson, *Newton County, Mississippi Newspaper Items 1872–1875 & W. P. A. Manuscript* (Moss Point, MS: self-published, 1998), 12; Arkansas, interviews with Kathe Hollingshaus and Joyce McFarland.

policemen, letter carriers, and "eliminate the nigger": Neil R. McMillen, *Dark Journey: Black Mississippians in the Age of Jim Crow* (Urbana: University of Illinois Press), 1989, 5, 43.

In 1876, Frank had a son: The 1890 Enumeration of Educable Children for Newton County, on file at the Mississippi Department of Archives and History (microfilm #14292) lists Eddie Caples as fourteen years old.

Oliver Eastland launched a plantation: Dan W. Smith Jr., "James O. Eastland: Early Life and Career, 1904–1942" (master's thesis, Mississippi College, 1978), 7.

27 **mob death every 5.5 months:** James C. Cobb, *The Most Southern Place on Earth: The Mississippi Delta and the Roots of Regional Identity* (New York: Oxford University Press, 1992), 114.

What prompted the dispute: White newspapers reported that Holbert was being evicted for harassing another worker over a woman. A black publication argued that "Holbert had persuaded a Negro whom Eastland held in involuntary servitude" over a debt "to leave the white planter." "The Doddsville Savagery," *The Voice of the Negro* 1, no. 3 (March 1904): 81. I am grateful to Todd Moye for pointing out these competing accounts.

27 **Holbert's "young master":** The Memphis *Commercial Appeal,* Feb. 4, 1904, which reported that the posse pursuing Holbert and his wife was "determined to burn the wretches at the stake."

"The blacks were forced": *Vicksburg Evening Post,* Feb. 13, 1904.

28 **"intention of W. C. Eastland":** *Commercial Appeal,* Feb. 8, 1904.

swept from the courthouse: New Orleans *Daily Picayune,* Sept. 22, 1904.

named for his slain brother, James: Although the Holbert lynching is often cited as a particularly gruesome example of the practice, its link to the Eastland family was largely forgotten at the height of Senator James Eastland's power, which is odd, since Eastland attracted a scathing liberal press.

civil rights bills went to die: Robert G. Sherrill, "James Eastland: Child of Scorn," *The Nation,* Oct. 4, 1965, 194.

"Mr. Woods" persuaded: Interview with Mack Caples.

29 **eight in ten, "congenitally lazy":** Powdermaker, *After Freedom,* 86, 88.

fell from a roof and died: Interview with Mack Caples; Ed Caples death certificate, Dec. 6, 1930.

drew her name: Oddly, at her birth, Hattie Mae was named Robert, for her father, Robert Logan. She grew up known as Hattie Mae, after her grandmother, but she didn't make the legal switch until the 1980s.

children that Pie Eddie left behind: Stories of Frank, Lula Bell, Pop, Vidalia, 'Lij, Wiley, and Will Caples from interviews with Hattie Mae Crenshaw, Mack Caples, Ruth V. Caples, and Virginia Caples.

31 **the Eastlands' cook:** Interviews with Hattie Mae Crenshaw and Ruth V. Caples. Woods Eastland, Senator James Eastland's son, was six when Mama Hattie died in 1951 but told me he recalls seeing a picture of himself as a young child with a housekeeper or cook named Hattie Mae.

"I was the troublemaker": Hattie Mae left the Eastland plantation for good smuggled out on the floor of a car; she had gotten some new dresses from a black boyfriend, but the wife of a white plantation boss, assuming only a white man could afford such goods, accused her of sleeping with her husband.

32 **Woods Eastland persuaded his friend:** Chris Myers, "Delta Obsession, World Power" (chapter in forthcoming PhD thesis), 21; Smith, "James O. Eastland," 37–39.

the price of cottonseed: Myers, "Delta Obsession, World Power," 24–26; Smith, "James O. Eastland," 48–54.

James Eastland helped kill FEPC: Chris Myers, "Reconstruction Revisited: James O. Eastland, Germany, and the Fair Employment Practices

Commission, 1945–1946," forthcoming in 2004, *Journal of Mississippi History.*

32 **"an inferior race":** 79th Cong., 1st sess., *Cong. Rec.* 91 (June 29, 1945): S 7000.

"mental level": Robert Sherrill, *Gothic Politics in the Deep South: Stars of the New Confederacy* (New York: Grossman, 1968), 211.

"pro-Communist" decision: Patricia Webb Robinson, "A Rhetorical Analysis of Senator James O. Eastland's Speeches, 1954–1959" (master's thesis, Louisiana State University, 1976), 29.

33 **J. W. Milam:** After his acquittal in the Till case, Milam said, "I just decided it was time a few people got put on notice. . . . Niggahs ain't gonna vote where I live. . . . They ain't gonna go to school with my kids." Cobb, *The Most Southern Place on Earth,* 219.

"far more dismaying phenomenon": *Time,* March 26, 1956, 26.

alter its way of life: For a fuller account of both the mechanical cotton-picker and the far-reaching effects of the black migration on American life, see Lemann, *The Promised Land,* from which I've drawn the references to fifty field hands, the Citizens Council's tickets, the quadrupling of wages, and the movement of five million southern blacks: 5, 95, 41, 6.

34 **"dean of Mississippi":** My interviews with Virginia Caples took place in the summer and fall of 2000 on the Eastland plantation, where her mother and her uncle Mack still lived. Virginia Caples was measured in her critique of plantation life, but she grew angry when her brother suggested that James Eastland had financed her education by loaning their father the money and forgiving the loan. "Senator Eastland didn't help my father do anything," she said. "Anything he did, my father earned ten times over. Anything Eastland had, my father and Uncle Mack helped him get."

35 **"twelve-year-olds having babies":** The line was part of Gingrich's stump speech in the mid-1990s; Katharine Q. Seelye, *NYT,* Oct. 27, 1994.

37 **midnight raid:** Under so-called man-in-the-house rules, a boyfriend, even the most casual one, could have been deemed a substitute father, rendering the family ineligible for aid.

3. THE CROSSROADS: CHICAGO, 1966–1991

38 **60 percent of manufacturing jobs:** William Julius Wilson, *When Work Disappears: The World of the Urban Poor* (New York: Knopf, 1996), 30.

Henry Horner Homes et al.: Lemann, *The Promised Land,* p. 92.

39 **rolls quadrupled:** From 984,000 cases in 1964 to 3.97 million in 1990. (Baseline, table 2.1.)

"social pathologies": William Julius Wilson, *The Truly Disadvantaged: The Inner City, the Underclass, and Public Policy* (Chicago: University of Chicago Press, 1987), vii.

39 **underclass:** Erol R. Ricketts and Isabel V. Sawhill proposed a four-part definition of underclass neighborhoods, as those with high levels of high school dropouts, nonworking men, welfare recipients, and single mothers. In 1980, 1 percent of the population lived in such census tracts. The difficulties of codification can be seen, however, in the case of Jeffrey Manor, the rough neighborhood where Angie and Jewell grew up; it fits only one of the four criteria—single-parent families. Ricketts and Sawhill, "Defining and Measuring the Underclass," *Journal of Policy Management and Analysis* 7, no. 2 (1988): 316–25.

41 **Levi Gillespie:** The 1880 Census lists Levi Gillespie, seven, as the son of Alfred Gillespie, forty-one, and his wife, Ella, twenty-seven.

contract to buy 110 acres: Deed on file at Monroe County Courthouse, Trust Book 1-Q, 167. The land was purchased on Nov. 24, 1941, and transferred to Levi's son Henderson for $1 on Jan. 25, 1954. Charity Scott said she grew up hearing "Papa Levi," her grandfather, urge his family to own land, warning that sharecroppers would always be in debt.

poorer, more troubled family: Angie and her mother both have a hazy, negative view of Roosevelt's family background. About Roosevelt's father, Charity said: "He might a got killed or just walked away—they don't know what happened." Angie recalls visiting the Mississippi Jobes as a child and encountering her first outhouse.

found out she was pregnant: Interview with Charity Scott.

42 **"My mother is the nicest":** Charity kept the May 6, 1980, essay, in which Angie describes her as the ultimate role model: "She is always telling me how much she loves me but she doesn't have to tell me because I can see it. I say if she didn't love me she wouldn't be out there working herself half to death trying to give me the best in life."

44 **signature of Joseph Merrion:** Interviews with his son, Jack Merrion, and grandson, Ed Merrion. Merrion built Jeffrey Manor shortly after serving as president of the National Association of Homebuilders.

1968 graduates of Luella: See www.netaxs.com/~jeff/luella.html (accessed May 25, 2004); also, Marja Mills, *Chicago Tribune,* Dec. 3, 1989.

whites fought housing integration: One of the most infamous battles was fought just a few blocks south of Jeffrey Manor, at Trumbull Park Homes, where the arrival of a single black family in white public housing set off a huge riot.

race of Luella students: Chicago Public Schools, annual student racial surveys, 1968–71.

45 **demographics of Jeffrey Manor:** The data cover Census Tract 5103 for 1980 and were supplied by Chuck Nelson and Marie Pees of the Census Bureau.

46 **"crossroads"** to **"merge styles":** Mary Pattillo-McCoy, *Black Picket Fences: Privilege and Peril Among the Black Middle Class* (Chicago: University of Chicago Press, 1999), 6, 11, 119. Elizabeth Fenn of Duke University points out to me that crossroads also had special meaning in black folklore, as dangerous, exciting places populated by badmen and tricksters.

46 **"any way any day":** Mary E. Pattillo, "Sweet Mothers and Gangbangers: Managing Crime in a Black Middle-Class Neighborhood," *Social Forces* 76, no. 3 (March 1998): 753.

a third in female-headed households: 1980 Census, Tract 5103.

statistical risks of single-parent homes: One example of the large social science literature is Sara McLanahan and Gary Sandefur, *Growing Up with a Single Parent: What Hurts, What Helps* (Cambridge, MA: Harvard University Press, 1994).

"I wanted to join": Pattillo-McCoy, *Black Picket Fences,* 145.

47 **beginning of the end:** Charity said that she prayed at length about her marriage. Then "the Lord just laid it out for me. 'Well, you're paying the house note; you're buying the groceries.' I was the one sending them to private school. What did I need him for? The next day I was at the lawyer's office, after saying 'thank you Lord' all night long." The property settlement gave Charity the "encyclopedia set," "china set with glasses," and "library books for Angela"; Roosevelt drove off with a late-model Lincoln and three other cars. Settlement agreement Feb. 4, 1981, *Charity Jobe v. Roosevelt Jobe,* case #80-4683, Circuit Court of Cook County, Illinois. I am grateful to Margaret Stapleton for her research assistance.

48 **psychologist:** Interviews with Angie Jobe, Rodger Scott, and Charity Scott.

50 **"Dear Diary"** to **"Little tiny feet":** Angie wrote these diary entries in 1983 and 1984 and read portions of them to me.

52 **switchblade:** Interviews with Angie Jobe and Rodger Scott.

53 **Angie still had welfare:** While the Chicago welfare office never asked Angie or Jewell to work or go to school, they did each enroll in a trade school on their own. Jewell signed up to be a dental hygienist, and Angie took a business school course. ("I got tired of working for chicken joints.") Neither finished, and Jewell wound up with an unpaid student loan for which bill collectors were still chasing her ten years later.

Terrance got twenty years: The long sentence, imposed by a federal judge in 1997, was required under mandatory sentencing laws, since Terrance had a prior drug conviction.

55 **Hattie Mae's children:** Mary, Gwen, and Jewell all became teen welfare mothers, but Mary quickly left the rolls. She worked her way through community college, eventually married, and landed a lower-lever managerial job at a Chicago hospital. In part, she credits her aspirations to the time she spent with Hattie Mae's father, Robert Logan, who reconnected with the family during her adolescence. (Jewell, fourteen years younger, knew him much less well.) "His side of the family was different," Mary said. "They were about education, schools, good jobs, having things." She

said her stepmother's family, whom Jewell likewise didn't know, played a similar role. Of Hattie Mae's sons, Squeaky was murdered, Terry is mostly out of touch with the family, and Greg and Robert both went to prison for violent crimes. But her second son, Willie, works with computers at DePaul University and his daughter Twanda recently graduated from Illinois State University.

55 **police catching on:** Arrests occurred on July 24, 1989, Nov. 30, 1989, Feb. 20, 1990, and Dec. 6, 1990.

"His Tendency to Project Blame": Notes of probation officer from Oct. 4, 1990, filed in *People vs. Gregory Reed,* case #91CR-16373, Circuit Court of Cook County, Illinois.

56 **a wild shooting:** The murder of fourteen-year-old Kathryn Miles is from interviews with Hattie Mae Crenshaw, Angie Jobe, and Jewell Reed, as well as the record in *People vs. Reed,* which includes the confessions of Greg Reed, Tony Nicholas, and David Washington.

4. THE SURVIVORS: MILWAUKEE, 1991–1995

58 **"Where Have All the Houses":** *MJS,* March 21, 1999.

fifteen thousand drawing checks: Author's communication with John Pawasarat, UW-M.

Angie's check rose: Angie's total monthly benefits rose 26 percent, from $709 in Chicago to $896 in Milwaukee. (AFDC rose from $373 to $617, while food stamps fell from $336 to $279.) Jewell's total package rose 41 percent, from $415 in Chicago to $586 in Milwaukee. (AFDC went from $286 to $496, in part due to a pregnancy allowance, while stamps fell from $147 to $90.)

59 **"only thing that has kept":** John Gurda, *The Making of Milwaukee* (Milwaukee: Milwaukee County Historical Society, 1999), 363.

"Shame of Milwaukee": *Time,* April 2, 1956.

time limits on public housing: After leaving office in 1960, Frank Zeidler produced a 1,022-page typescript, which awaits some future historian of urban change. In it, he writes that he stepped down after three terms because the "issue of my being too friendly to Negroes was again going to be raised" and tells of Alderman Milton J. McGuire calling for time limits on public housing. Frank P. Zeidler, "A Liberal in City Government: My Experiences as Mayor of Milwaukee" (typescript, Milwaukee Public Library), ch. 2, 59; ch. 4, 417.

60 **blacks composed 3 percent:** Gurda, *The Making of Milwaukee,* 361.

benefits not much different: In 1951, Wisconsin's average monthly benefit was slightly higher than that of its neighbors—$99 versus $96 in Illinois and $91 in Minnesota. (*Social Security Bulletin,* April 1951, table 13.) In 1967, it was lower: $175 in Wisconsin versus $178 in Minnesota and $195 in Illinois. (Department of Health, Education and Welfare, *Public Assistance Statistics,* June 1967, table 6.)

60 **if Wallace left Alabama:** Frank A. Aukofer, *City with a Chance: A Case History of the Civil Rights Revolution* (Milwaukee: Bruce Publishing, 1968), 56.

rock-throwing crowds: Ibid., 111–12.

welfare battle in 1969: benefit cut: *MJ,* Sept. 14, 1969; occupation of the Capitol: *MJ,* Sept. 30, 1969; antifornication laws, 22 cents a meal: *MJ,* Sept. 18, 1969; gorillas: *MJ,* Sept. 30, 1969.

61 **benefits more than doubled:** For a family of three, they rose from $184 in 1970 to $444 in 1980. *1993 Green Book,* 667.

Caseloads tripled: Excluding the small number of two-parent cases, the AFDC rolls rose from 23,000 cases in 1970 to 72,000 in 1980. Peter Tropman, "Wisconsin Works" (briefing paper for Gov. Anthony Earl, circa 1986).

among the lower forty-eight: *1993 Green Book,* 666–67.

hedge against violence: In calling for the restoration of the 1969 cuts, the Madison newspaper warned, "Unless we can figure out an economic system that will eliminate hunger in one of the world's most affluent nations, we are going to be faced with a radicalized poor who will demand a revolution." *The Capital Times,* May 12, 1971.

54 percent higher than Illinois: *1993 Green Book,* 666–67.

"relatively small," nearly half: Wisconsin Expenditure Commission, "Report of the Welfare Magnet Study Committee," Dec. 1986, 5, 104.

21 percent of Milwaukee applicants: "Prior Residence of Wisconsin Newly Opened AFDC Cases" (computer printout, prepared by Ed Mason and Chuck Brassington, Wisconsin Department of Health and Social Services, June 1991), copy provided by Gerald Whitburn. Of 695 new Milwaukee cases, 144 had come from out of state within the previous three months.

fastest-growing ghetto: Interview with Paul A. Jargowsky.

census tracts tripled: Paul A. Jargowsky, *Poverty and Place: Ghettos, Barrios, and the American City* (New York: Russell Sage Foundation, 1997), 225.

from 1 percent to 10 percent: Data provided to author by Jargowsky.

62 **half the black population:** Peter Tropman, "Wisconsin Works," 2. Tropman, a state welfare official, reported that 42 percent of Milwaukee's blacks were on AFDC and 7 percent on general relief, a state and local program.

lost manufacturing jobs: Julie Boatright Wilson, "Milwaukee: Industrial Metropolis on the Lake" (working paper, Wiener Center, Kennedy School of Government, Harvard University, April 1995), section IV, 2.

"Go back to Illinois": *Kenosha News,* March 16, 1986.

advisers to the Democratic governor: One of them, Peter Tropman, wanted to call the new program "Wisconsin Works," as Tommy Thompson named his a decade later.

62 **"two-bit hack," bra size:** Matt Pommer, *The Capital Times*, July 13, 1998.

"make Wisconsin like Mississippi": Norman Atkins, *NYTM*, Jan. 15, 1995.

64 **"baby killer":** Milwaukee was the site of large antiabortion protests in 1992, with more than one thousand arrests in four months. Tina Burnside, *MS*, Oct. 7, 1992.

66 **Angie reported the job:** Caseworkers had access to the quarterly earnings reports that employers file with state labor departments. But the records could lag as much as six months from an employee's starting date, and officials typically made criminal referrals for fraud only after discovering more than $3,000 of welfare or food stamp overpayments. Interview with Debra Bigler, Milwaukee County Department of Human Services. In practice, caseworkers sometimes ignored small amounts of unreported earnings, since recouping welfare overpayments could be a hassle.

for every $100: In the six months after she reported the job, Angie earned an average of $986 a month. But her AFDC and food stamps fell by $599, and she paid $75 in payroll taxes. That is, she effectively kept about $312, or 32 percent. That does not add in tax credits, but it doesn't subtract work expenses, either. Author's calculation based on 1994 monthly earnings reports.

68 **Hattie Mae's boyfriend, Wesley:** Although she and Wesley are now married, Hattie Mae said of his relationship with her kids: "If Wesley had been the type of father, man, he should have been and helped me to raise them, maybe—I'm saying maybe—some of the things that happened could have been prevented with Greg." Wesley told me he traced his anger to growing up black in the Delta, where a white boycott cost his father his dry-cleaning business after his father called for school desegregation. "I have a lot of hate and I'll always have a lot of hate," he said. "Hatred will not let you forget where you came from."

69 **battery:** Jewell, who had just turned eighteen, pleaded guilty and was sentenced to a year of supervision by the social services department.

Tony's drug problem; errant bullet: The presentencing report in the murder case says "he was snorting heroin and was spending up to $200 per day on the drug. . . . He did state . . . that he was under the influence of heroin at the time" of the shooting. A forensics expert identified the bullet as coming from Tony Nicholas's gun. In his closing argument, the prosecutor highlighted Tony's confession that he joined the plot after one of the coconspirators promised to fix his car: "He wanted used car parts to kill." *People vs. Antonio Nicholas*, case #91CR-16373, Circuit Court of Cook County, Illinois.

70 **self-efficacy:** See also Toby Herr and Suzanne L. Wagner, "Self-Efficacy as a Welfare-to-Work Goal: Emphasizing Both Psychology and Economics in Program Design" (Chicago: Project Match, Feb. 2003).

As bureaucratic runarounds go: Eight weeks after Jewell signed up for the course, her caseworker noted in the file that a letter had been sent, telling Jewell the course "has been placed on hold." Jewell said she never got the letter.

72 **"tax-free cash income alone":** While the Reagan story is sometimes called "apocryphal," he was referring to an actual case, albeit an atypical one whose known facts he exaggerated. The case involved a Chicago woman named Linda Taylor, whom an investigator initially described as having eighty aliases and a welfare income of $150,000; she was convicted of a more modest crime—using four aliases to steal $9,800. Reagan also told a New Hampshire audience that by moving to public housing in East Harlem, "you can get an apartment with eleven-foot ceilings, with a twenty-foot balcony, a swimming pool, laundry room, and play room." "'Welfare Queen' Becomes Issue in Reagan Campaign," *NYT,* Feb. 15, 1976; "Chicago Woman Sentenced in Welfare Fraud Cases," *NYT*, May 13, 1977.

73 **"We have been studying":** McLanahan and Sandefur, *Growing Up with a Single Parent,* 1–2.

74 **commit crimes:** Cynthia Harper and Sara McLanahan, "Father Absence and Youth Incarceration," *Journal of Adolescence,* forthcoming.

Tony's father: His presentencing report presents Tony Nicholas as another working mother's son disadvantaged by the absence of a father: "Deft. said his father was a heavy drug and alcohol abuser. Antonio stated he did not have much contact with his father. . . . Defts mother works as a secretary." *People vs. Nicholas,* case #91CR-16373, Circuit Court of Cook County, Illinois.

fatherhood in sharecropping society: In citing the disproportionate success she enjoyed, Virginia Caples, the university dean, cited two factors: her mother's stress on education and the presence of a stable father in the home. "My father was the centerpiece of the extended family," she said, in contrast to her uncles who "moved hither or yon—they would be lost for two, three years. . . . I'm not speaking in disparaging tones, but my father's brothers, you know, if it's a skirt tail they wanted to follow it. . . . They didn't seem to have that sense that 'I have five kids here and I need to do something for them.'" In tracing the Caples family history, I found many examples of hardworking mothers; this was a rare example I encountered of stable fatherhood.

"Often there is no man": Powdermaker, *After Freedom,* 146.

"America's biggest problem today": Clinton, speech to National Governors Association, Feb. 2, 1993.

75 **"fantastic campaign issue," one observer:** DeParle, *NYT*, Oct. 20, 1994.

75 **reason to be skeptical:** For the early Thompson record, see Michael Wiseman, "State Strategies for Welfare Reform: The Wisconsin Story," *Journal of Policy Analysis and Management* 15, no. 4 (1996): 515–46.

76 **campaign driver:** Tommy G. Thompson, *Power to the People: An American State at Work* (New York: HarperCollins, 1996), 42.

Learnfare failed to boost: John Pawasarat, Lois M. Quinn, and Frank Stetzer, "Evaluation of the Impact of Wisconsin's Learnfare Experiment on the School Attendance of Teenagers Receiving Aid to Families with Dependent Children" (Employment & Training Institute, UW-M, Feb. 1992). Some Learnfare critics warn the program can actually reduce parental control, since it gives rebellious teenagers power over their mothers' checks.

Thompson attacked researchers: Amy Rinard, *MS,* March 11, 1992.

the new analysts found: LAB, "An Evaluation of the Learnfare Program: Final Report," April 1997, 4.

hand over work program data: Dave Daley, *MJ,* Sept. 24, 1992.

published anyway: John Pawasarat and Lois M. Quinn, "Wisconsin Welfare Employment Experiments: An Evaluation of the WEJT and CWEP Programs" (Employment & Training Institute, UW-M, Sept. 1993). While Thompson accused the evaluators of slanting the data, an internal memo later surfaced arguing that the Thompson administration had done so itself. After collecting data on the program, a state researcher, Neil Gleason, complained the numbers in the state's published report "were taken so out of context that their meaning was reversed." Contrary to the state's claims of success, he wrote, the program had made families "less likely to leave AFDC" and had "increased AFDC costs." Memo from Neil Gleason to Fred Buhr, Aug. 18, 1988, provided to author by John Pawasarat. See also, Gregory D. Stanford, *MJ,* Oct. 13, 1993.

White House event: It was held on April 10, 1992.

point man on polling: Interview with Gerald Whitburn.

77 **percentage in welfare-to-work:** *1994 Green Book,* 357–59.

pipeline to federal aid: See Wiseman, "State Strategies for Welfare Reform," 524–25; Mark Greenberg, "Issues in Establishing a Distribution Formula for a Cash Assistance Block Grant" (CLASP, July 1995), 5–6. As Greenberg notes, if Wisconsin saved the feds money by cutting its grants to $517, imagine how much Mississippi saved by paying $120. Curious about the other $70 million, John Pawasarat of UW-M wrote federal officials asking how the figure was calculated. The response acknowledged they knew of no objective reason for giving Wisconsin the money: "No documentation can be found describing the basis for determining the specific amounts agreed upon." (Letter from Laurence J. Love, Acting Assistant Secretary for Children and Families, HSS, July 21, 1993.)

77 **Norquist called for repealing:** John O. Norquist, "The Future of America's Cities" (lecture, New York City, Nov. 12, 1990).

78 **Riemer responded with a plea:** My account of the Democrats' dare to abolish AFDC is drawn from interviews with John Gard, Walter Kunicki, John Norquist, David Riemer, Antonio Riley, Tommy Thompson, and Gerald Whitburn, as well as extensive notes kept by Riemer.

Thompson chewed out Whitburn: Interview with Gerald Whitburn.

"a filet mignon": DeParle, *NYT,* Oct. 20, 1994.

79 **"They trade food stamps"** to **"survival demands":** Carol Stack, *All Our Kin* (1974; repr., New York: Basic Books, 1997), 32, 43, 124.

80 **"Ms. Caples had minimal":** CHIPS, Wisconsin Circuit Court Children's Division, March 13, 2000.

investigator let the matter drop: Ibid.

Robert knocked down Felmers Chaney: Interviews with Jewell Reed, Angie Jobe, and Felmers Chaney.

5. THE ACCIDENTAL PROGRAM: WASHINGTON, 1935–1991

85 **AFDC:** The program became Aid to *Families* with Dependent Children because grants were extended to adults. That happened in 1952, though the name change followed a decade later.

farmed them out: Linda Gordon, *Pitied But Not Entitled: Single Mothers and the History of Welfare, 1890–1935* (Cambridge, MA: Harvard University Press, 1994), 256–57.

86 **Mothers' pensions, "gilt-edged widows":** Winifred Bell, *Aid to Dependent Children* (New York: Columbia University Press, 1965), 3–12.

"release from the wage-earning role": 1935 Report of the Committee on Economic Security; quoted in Jonah Martin Edelman, "The Passage of the Family Support Act of 1988 and the Politics of Welfare Reform in the United States" (PhD dissertation, Balliol College, Oxford University, 1995), 24. Edelman's unpublished dissertation is an especially rich source of information on the history and politics of AFDC.

"I can see the careworn": Gordon, *Pitied But Not Entitled,* 254–55.

96 percent white: Bell, *ADC,* 9.

Southern members of Congress: Frances Fox Piven and Richard Cloward, *Regulating the Poor: The Functions of Public Welfare* (1971; repr., New York: Vintage, 1993), 115–16; Gordon, *Pitied But Not Entitled,* 284–85. Gordon writes, "the fate of ADC was defined by the Civil War and Reconstruction," in that it was shaped by a Southern white political elite eager to preserve cheap black labor and hostile to federal authority.

"No other federal": Edwin Witte, "A Wild Dream or a Practical Plan?" in Robert J. Lampman, ed., *Social Security Perspectives: Essays by Ed-*

win E. Witte (Madison: University of Wisconsin Press, 1962), 6–7; cited in Edelman, "Family Support Act," 21.

87 **Negro quotas:** Bell, *ADC*, 35.

Myrdal wondered, "discrimination against Negroes": Gunnar Myrdal, *An American Dilemma: The Negro Problem and Modern Democracy* (1944; repr., New York: Pantheon, 1972), 359–60.

Mary S. Larabee: Bell, *ADC*, 34–35.

covering about 2 percent: Vincent J. Burke and Vee Burke, *Nixon's Good Deed: Welfare Reform* (New York: Columbia University Press, 1974), 9.

predominately white program: From 1937 to 1940, blacks composed 14 to 17 percent of the caseload. Bell, *ADC*, 34.

caseloads nearly tripled: From 274,000 cases in 1945 to 745,000 in 1960. Piven and Cloward, *Regulating the Poor*, appendix table 1.

widows, broken families: Edelman, "Family Support Act," 25.

40 percent black: Martin Gilens, *Why Americans Hate Welfare: Race, Media, and the Politics of Antipoverty Policy* (Chicago: University of Chicago Press, 1999), 106.

Pensions carefully policed: Even in 1914, a prominent social worker, Homer Folks, warned that "to pension desertion or illegitimacy would, undoubtedly, have the effect of a premium upon these crimes against society." Bell, *ADC*, 7.

88 **"founding document":** Mickey Kaus, *The End of Equality* (New York: Basic Books, 1992), 110.

caseloads more than quadrupled: From 745,000 cases in 1960 to 3.12 million in 1973. Piven and Cloward, *Regulating the Poor*, appendix table 1; Baseline, table 2.1.

"Animals shouldn't live in such": Bell, *ADC*, 103.

90 percent of blacks poor; Eastland's cotton subsidies: Nick Kotz examined the living conditions on the Eastland plantation in a four-part series for the *Des Moines Register and Tribune*, Feb. 25–28, 1968, from which this information comes. See also Kotz, *WP*, July 5, 1971.

89 **Ralph Abernathy:** Burke and Burke, *Nixon's Good Deed*, 44.

turning people away, half the eligible: Piven and Cloward, *Regulating the Poor*, 219.

of the 23,000 children purged: Bell, *ADC*, 137.

"a substitute father" to **"grocers":** *King vs. Smith*, 392 U.S. 309 (1968).

"workers began focusing": Cloward quote and background on welfare rights movement from interviews with Richard Cloward and Frances Fox Piven. In a sign of how quickly the spirit of the times changed, Cloward's proposal for Mobilization for Youth, the program that launched the welfare-rights age, included a boilerplate pledge to *cut* the welfare rolls. See also DeParle, *NYTM*, Dec. 29, 1998, and Frances Fox Piven and Richard A.

Cloward, *Poor People's Movements: Why They Succeed, How They Fail* (1977; repr., New York: Vintage, 1979), 264–361.

89 **"argued and cajoled":** Piven and Cloward, *Regulating the Poor,* 291.

90 **"massive drive to recruit the poor":** *The Nation,* May 2, 1966.

age of the welfare radical: Nick Kotz and Mary Lynn Kotz: *A Passion for Equality: George Wiley and the Movement* (New York: W.W. Norton, 1977), 40 cities, 307; Harassment, 234; Korvettes, 236; "brood mares," 251.

"people who lay about": Daniel Patrick Moynihan, *The Politics of a Guaranteed Income: The Nixon Administration and the Family Assistance Plan* (New York: Random House, 1973), 523.

iron his shirts: James T. Patterson, *America's Struggle Against Poverty 1900–1994* (Cambridge, MA: Harvard University Press, 1994), 194.

"jobs that pay ten thousand," "You can't force me": Burke and Burke, *Nixon's Good Deed,* 162.

New York City caseload doubled: From 502,000 recipients (as opposed to cases) in 1966 to 1.1 million in 1972, NYC, Human Resources Administration.

91 **"my department of health":** Burke and Burke, *Nixon's Good Deed,* 44.

"the days of the dole": Kaus, *The End of Equality,* 113.

one of every nine kids: Burke and Burke, *Nixon's Good Deed,* 9.

a third of children, 80 percent of black children: Daniel Patrick Moynihan, "Social Justice in the Next Century," *America,* Sept. 14, 1991, 134–35.

Merle Haggard: "Working Man Blues" reached number 1 in 1969.

average package of cash and food stamps: In 1972, a mother of two received an average of $10,370 (*1993 Green Book,* 1253, expressed in 1992 dollars); the poverty threshold in 1992 was $11,304 (Census Bureau); benefits for subsequent years in *1993 Green Book,* 1248–53.

92 **one in ten worked when AFDC started:** Kaus, *The End of Equality,* 111.

half worked by the mid-1970s: For mothers of minor children, the labor force participation rate (the share working or looking for work) was 49 percent in 1976 and 51 percent in 1977. Data provided to the author by Howard Hayghe, BLS.

triple the cost, 15 percent of domestic: Calculations by Adam Carasso of the Urban Institute, based on 1990 data.

school lunches, subsidized housing: *1993 Green Book,* p. 1604. The share with subsidized housing ranged from 19 percent in 1987 to 35 percent in 1990.

view in Jacksonville: Interview with Mark Greenberg. The case of Alice Roberts, the food stamp recipient arrested for fraud, wound up in the Fifth Circuit Court of Appeals, which barred the indiscriminate investigations. Quoting from a congressional report accompanying the food stamp law, the court warned of "the need to protect needy individuals from having their privacy bartered away in order to assuage their hunger." *Roberts vs. Austin,* 632, F2nd, 1202 (5th Cir. 1981), 9.

93 ***half* the black women:** Lawrence Mishel, Jared Bernstein, and Heather Boushey, *State of Working America 2002–03* (Ithaca, NY: ILR Press), 136.

problems that could interfere: Krista K. Olson and LaDonna Pavetti, "Personal and Family Challenges to the Successful Transition From Welfare to Work," The Urban Institute, May 17, 1996.

94 **Carter was appalled:** Laurence E. Lynn Jr., and David deF. Whitman, *The President as Policymaker: Jimmy Carter and Welfare Reform* (Philadelphia: Temple University Press, 1981), 88.

"Middle East": Joseph A. Califano Jr., *Governing America: An Insider's Report from the White House and the Cabinet* (New York: Simon & Schuster, 1981), 321.

slum and ghetto census tracts: Jargowsky, *Poverty and Place,* 35–41. Of the five million people who lived in high-poverty census tracts, 80 percent were members of racial minorities.

the disaster brought journalists: See Ken Auletta, *The Underclass* (New York: Random House, 1982); staff of the *Chicago Tribune, The American Millstone: An Examination of the Nation's Permanent Underclass* (Chicago: Contemporary Books, 1986); Leon Dash, *When Children Want Children: An Inside Look at the Crisis of Teenage Pregnancy* (1989; repr., New York: Penguin Books, 1990); Bill Moyers, "The Vanishing Family—Crisis in Black America," CBS, Jan. 25, 1986.

95 **"blaming the victim":** The phrase was coined by the psychologist William Ryan as part of his critique of the Moynihan report; see Ryan, *Blaming the Victim* (New York: Pantheon, 1971).

the Moynihan report: See Lee Rainwater and William L. Yancey, *The Moynihan Report and the Politics of Controversy* (Cambridge, MA: MIT Press, 1967), esp. 51, 75; also Lemann, *The Promised Land,* 171–76.

poverty academics: For an expanded discussion of academic research on poverty following the Moynihan report, see Alice O'Connor, *Poverty Knowledge: Social Science, Social Policy, and the Poor in Twentieth-Century U.S. History* (Princeton, NJ: Princeton University Press, 2001), especially chapters 8 and 9.

96 **"slavefare":** Edelman, "Family Support Act," 254, quoting Rep. Augustus Hawkins of California.

"lives of large numbers": Charles Murray, *Losing Ground* (New York: Basic Books, 1984), 229. Presciently, Murray foresaw a large element of his appeal. "Why can a publisher sell it?" he wrote in his book proposal. "Because a huge number of well-meaning whites fear that they are closet racists, and this book tells them they are not. It's going to make them feel better about things they already think but do not know how to say." DeParle, *NYTM,* Oct. 9, 1994. The film, *With Honors,* was released in 1994.

97 **reigning explanation:** William Julius Wilson, *The Truly Disadvantaged: The Inner City, the Underclass, and Public Policy* (Chicago: University of Chicago Press, 1987).

"Our goal": Mickey Kaus, "The Work Ethic State," *The New Republic,* July 7, 1986, 31.

"the ghetto-poor culture": Kaus, *The End of Equality,* 129.

98 **including Arkansas:** The Arkansas WORK program began in October 1982 under Governor Frank White. Having lost to White in 1980, Bill Clinton was reelected in Nov. 1982 and continued the program.

half the mothers of preschool: For women with children under six, the labor force participation rate was 50.5 percent in 1983. Data provided to the author by Howard Hayghe, BLS.

groundbreaking study: Mary Jo Bane and David T. Ellwood, "The Dynamics of Dependence: The Route to Self-Sufficiency," Report to HHS, 1983.

nine programs raised employment and earnings: Summarized in Edelman, "Family Support Act," 102. The modesty of some of the gains can be seen in the data on Arkansas, which raised the average recipient's earnings by a total of $78 over six months. Judith M. Gueron, "Reforming Welfare with Work" (Occasional Paper 2, Ford Foundation Project on Social Welfare and the American Future, 1987), 17.

99 **"viable solution":** Edelman, "Family Support Act," 104.

Reagan task force and events leading to the 1988 bill: Ibid., 100–147, 161, 262, 217.

6. THE ESTABLISHMENT FAILS: WASHINGTON, 1992–1994

101 **never met anyone on welfare:** Interview with Bruce Reed.

prosperous family: Interviews with Bruce Reed, Mary Lou Reed (his mother), and Tara Reed (his sister).

six times as many: In 1990, Idaho's average caseload was 6,100, and Milwaukee's was 36,200.

"We should invest": Clinton speech to Democratic Leadership Council in Cleveland, May 6, 1991.

"build a mad as hell": Reed memo to Bill Clinton, May 25, 1991.

"off the welfare rolls": Clinton speech in Little Rock, Oct. 3, 1991.

a half dozen drafts, The next morning: Interviews with Bruce Reed and Stan Greenberg.

103 **paper elaborated:** The paper, "Reducing Poverty by Replacing Welfare," was later printed in Mary Jo Bane and David T. Ellwood, *Welfare Realities: From Rhetoric to Reform* (Cambridge, MA: Harvard University Press, 1994), 143–62; it grew from David T. Ellwood, *Poor Support: Poverty in the American Family* (New York: Basic Books, 1988).

"end to welfare as we know it": Bill Clinton speech at Georgetown University, Oct. 23, 1991.

104 **"spending even more":** Clinton, interview by Paula Zahn, *CBS This Morning,* Nov. 14, 1991.

"skepticism about spending": Greenberg memo to Clinton, Aug. 16, 1992.

Among those unsettled: Interview with David Ellwood, DeParle, *NYTM*, Dec. 8, 1996.

met in passing: Ellwood tells the story of reintroducing himself to Clinton at a governors' meeting in the summer of 1991. Clinton lit up and told Ellwood he was carrying one of his papers. "Look, I've got it right here—all marked up," Ellwood recalls Clinton saying. Then fishing the paper from a notebook, Clinton said, "Oh wait, this is Hillary's copy." While the encounter fortified Ellwood's sense of Clinton's seriousness, it may also have laid a groundwork for subsequent disappointments; at their first White House meeting on welfare, Clinton passed a note to an aide suggesting he had Ellwood confused with his father, Paul Ellwood, a prominent health-care expert. (On the confusion with Paul Ellwood, see Whitman and Cooper, *USN*, June 20, 1994.)

klieg lights: 1992 interview with David Ellwood, in which he called child support assurance (a welfare *expansion* that Clinton had never mentioned) "the single most important" part of his plan and said of time limits, "You can do that last."

"We simply do not have": David T. Ellwood, "Major Issues in Time Limited Welfare" meeting (background paper prepared for meeting at the Urban Institute, Dec. 2, 1992), 20, 24.

"Vacuous and incendiary": David T. Ellwood, "From Social Science to Social Policy: The Fate of Intellectuals, Ideas, and Ideology in the Welfare Debate in the Mid-1990s" (lecture, Northwestern University, Jan. 9, 1996), 11.

105 **nearly 3 million:** Mark Greenberg, "The Devil Is in the Details: Key Questions in the Effort to 'End Welfare As We Know It,'" CLASP, July 1993, 11.

106 **cut the rolls 2 percent:** Stephen Freedman and others, "The GAIN Evaluation: Five-year Impacts on Employment, Earnings, and AFDC Receipt" (Working Paper 96.1, MDRC, July 1996), table 1.

By just mailing checks: Cost estimates come from CBO, "The Administration's Welfare Reform Proposals: A Preliminary Cost Estimate," Dec. 1994, and interviews with its coauthor John Tapogna.

The politics were hard: Early in their tenure, Ellwood and Reed convened a meeting of Democratic experts, many veterans of President Carter's failed reform. A sampling of their advice: "Start small." "Don't go national." "Be modest in goals and rhetoric." "A quarter of a loaf isn't so bad." "The planets could not be more misaligned. "What you want to do might be impossible." (Notes of one participant.)

106 **visited some Democrats:** McDermott, *USN,* June 20, 1994, 31; interviews with Robert Matsui and Harold Ford.

Children's Defense Fund opposed JOBS: Those wondering whether Clinton would really end welfare noted that his first stop in Washington as president-elect was a Children's Defense Fund event. For CDF's opposition to the Family Support Act, see letter from Marian Wright Edelman, the group's founder, on Sept. 28, 1988; cited in 100th Cong., 2nd sess., *Cong. Rec.* 134 (Sept. 30, 1988): H 9103.

107 **"clatter of campaign promises":** Pear, *NYT,* Jan. 15, 1993. Others voicing doubts included the housing secretary, Henry Cisneros ("I'm not a believer in artificial deadlines of that nature") and the domestic policy adviser, Carol Rasco (she warned workfare jobs would have to be part of a meaningful "piece on a career ladder. . . . I feel very strongly about that"); DeParle, *NYT,* June 21, 1993. Ellwood's deputy, Wendell Primus, was an ardent safety-net defender as a congressional aide; testifying a few months into office, he called for postponing a work rule already on the books; David E. Rosenbaum, *NYT,* May 5, 1993.

"break the culture": Clinton speech to American Newspaper Publishers Association, New York, May 6, 1992.

"punish the kids": Interview with Bill Clinton, Feb. 24, 1992.

JOBS Plus: "If you've done that, you've done a great thing," Moynihan told Reed, referring to an expanded JOBS program; interview with Bruce Reed.

a dyspeptic skeptic: "Need I say there is *no* commitment the campaign made that will so easily come to ruin," Moynihan wrote to Vernon Jordan, the head of the Clinton transition team, speaking of the pledge to end welfare. He was pushing an aide, Paul Offner, for a welfare job that instead went to Mary Jo Bane, a New York state official (and former Harvard professor), with whom he had clashed. The rebuff did nothing to ease Moynihan's distrust of the administration, which may have deepened when an anonymous Clinton aide told *Time,* "We'll roll right over him." (Moynihan letter to Jordan, Nov. 11, 1992; *Time,* Feb. 1, 1993.)

"I'll look forward": David T. Ellwood, "Welfare Reform As I Knew It," *The American Prospect,* May–June, 1996.

108 **an affluent childhood:** Interviews with David Ellwood, Ann Ellwood (his mother), Deborah Ellwood (his sister), Marilyn Ellwood (his wife), and Paul Ellwood (his father); see also DeParle, *NYTM,* Dec. 8, 1996.

putting health care before welfare: As a newcomer to Washington with few ties to the Hill, Clinton also may have hoped that starting with a health-care bill that Democrats wanted (as opposed to a welfare bill they disliked) would help him avoid Jimmy Carter's troubled relations with Congress.

109 **"Let 'em rip":** Clinton to leaders of welfare task force, June 18, 1993; interview with Bruce Reed. During my interviews with Reed, he sometimes consulted his records of meetings; any direct quotations of Clinton (or others) sourced to Reed stem from these written materials, rather than from his memory alone.

110 **Ellwood joined the effort:** Interviews with Ellwood and Bob Greenstein of the Center on Budget and Policy Priorities, who played an important behind-the-scenes role. Spotting the shortfall in the EITC, Greenstein sent a confidential memo to Melanne Verveer in Hillary Clinton's office. Mrs. Clinton passed it on to the president, who ordered the problem fixed. Among other things, the incident showed the rarefied access advocates like Greenstein momentarily enjoyed after twelve years of GOP control.

Clinton at his seductive best: Interviews with Bruce Reed, David Ellwood, and Judith Gueron.

111 **"that goddam task force":** Interview with Daniel Patrick Moynihan.

"destructive element": Interview with Bruce Reed.

"What kind of program": Interview with Wendell Primus.

"only reasonable reaction": Interview with David Ellwood.

112 **Riverside had raised earnings:** After two years, the counties that emphasized education and training raised their participants' earnings by 17 percent; Riverside's increase was 53 percent. For those who see this as complete vindication of the work-first model, several qualifications are worth noting. Even in Riverside about 60 percent of the participants got some education or training. Plus, the differences between Riverside and its rivals diminished with time, consistent with the notion that education is a long-term investment; over five years, recipients in Butte County earned more. And earnings in all sites remained low, on average just $3,800 in the fifth year. See Freedman and others, "The Gain Evaluation," table 1. See also Julie Strawn, "Beyond Job Search or Basic Education: Rethinking the Role of Skills in Welfare Reform," CLASP, April 1998.

"bag lady," "work is education": DeParle, *NYT,* May 16, 1993.

"Work organizes life": Clinton at Church of God in Christ, Memphis, Nov. 13, 1993, *PPP-1993,* vol. 2, 1985.

Lillie Harden: See, for instance, Clinton's State of the Union Address, Jan. 25, 1994 (*PPP-1994,* vol. 1, 129), where he told her story without using her name.

"My *life*": Interview with Bill Clinton, Jan. 30, 2004.

113 **task force sent him:** Working Group on Welfare Reform, Family Support, and Independence, "Draft Discussion Paper," Dec. 2, 1993.

114 **"You let loose":** Interview with Daniel Patrick Moynihan.

first showy move: Florida, with a Democratic governor, passed a time-limit bill first, in April 1993, but Thompson's move in May was much more public and political. Winking at those in the know, his handouts argued for time limits by citing the Bane-Ellwood data on dependency.

114 **"meaningful community service":** Gov. Bill Clinton and Sen. Al Gore, *Putting People First: How We Can All Change America* (New York: Times Books, 1992), 165.

Clinton gave the green light: Interview with Bruce Reed.

an "untested" idea: E. Clay Shaw, Nancy L. Johnson, Fred Grandy, "Moving Ahead: How America Can Reduce Poverty Through Work," June 1992, iii.

"You can cut them off": Rep. Rick Santorum at press conference, Nov. 10, 1993.

115 **Rector was raised:** Interview with Robert Rector.

Jacuzzis: DeParle, *The Washington Monthly* (July/Aug. 1991): 51–54.

"way to 'end welfare'": Rep. Jim Talent, press release, April 27, 1994.

116 **"realm of politics":** Memo from William Bennett, Jack Kemp, and Vin Weber, Empower America, April 13, 1994.

the "stench": DeParle, *NYT,* May 12, 1994.

"I am impelled": Henry Aaron to Ellwood, Jan. 14, 1994.

117 **"White House Seeks":** DeParle, *NYT,* Jan. 5, 1994.

"boob bait": Deborah Orin and Christopher Ruddy, *New York Post,* Jan. 7, 1994. While Moynihan's erratic behavior had many causes, his consumption of alcohol (an intermittent topic of conversation among his admirers and his critics) may have been among them. The night he told me "I talk too much," I had reached him at home, where he sounded like he'd been drinking.

"Many are willing": Ellwood, *Poor Support,* 241.

"If you don't put money": Clinton speech in Jonesboro, Georgia, Sept. 9, 1992.

118 **"things so much closer":** Interview with Bruce Reed.

This was a bind: For details on the attempt to finance the Clinton plan, see author's 1994 articles in the *NYT* on Feb. 13, 22, and 25; March 3, 10, 21, and 23; April 5; May 9, 16, and 19; and July 15.

"There simply is no money": Ellwood, "From Social Science to Social Policy," lecture, Jan. 9, 1996, 1.

"Tim Valentine problem": Interviews with Bruce Reed and David Ellwood.

119 **glassy-eyed look:** Robert Reich, *Locked in the Cabinet* (New York: Knopf, 1997), 156.

"the most negative": DeParle, *NYT,* May 9, 1994.

8 percent: DeParle, *NYT,* June 15, 1994.

slow the rate of growth: CBO, "The Administration's Welfare Reform Proposals," Dec. 1994, 10.

120 **Rector made his case:** Robert Rector, "Welfare Reform, Dependency Reduction, and Labor Market Entry," *Journal of Labor Research* 14, no. 3 (Summer 1993): 283–97.

120 **more rigorous studies:** The leading study of work (as opposed to education or job-search) programs was Thomas Brock, David Butler, and David Long, "Unpaid Work Experience for Welfare Recipients: Findings and Lessons from MDRC Research," MDRC, Sept. 1993. It examined programs in San Diego, Chicago, and West Virginia and concluded, "It is not clear from the limited evidence that unpaid work experience leads to reductions in welfare receipt or welfare payments," 3.

"self-limiting expertise": Interview with John Tapogna.

"there go the Wright brothers": Interview with Robert Rector.

$5 billion short: CBO, "The Administration's Welfare Reform Proposals," Dec. 1994, 2.

121 **Clinton on both sides:** "something at the end of the road," Clinton remarks in Kansas City, June 14, 1994, *PPP-1994,* vol. 1, 1078; "You're not eligible," Clinton exchange with reporters, June 15, 1994, *PPP-1994,* vol. 1, 1083.

"I wasn't pleased": Ben Wattenberg, *New York Post,* Nov. 3, 1995.

action was deferred: Clinton grasped the point that the future impact of a welfare bill was hard to predict, cautioning the cabinet on March 22, 1994, that "things depend entirely on how the welfare bureaucracy responds." Interview with Bruce Reed.

"hope and structure": Clinton remarks in Kansas City, June 14, 1994.

122 **turned Ellwood into a piñata:** DeParle, *NYT,* July 31, 1994.

7. REDEFINING COMPASSION: WASHINGTON, 1995

123 **"viciously hateful," "totally sick":** DeParle, *NYTM,* Jan. 28, 1996, 48.

declined Clinton's call: Maureen Dowd, *NYT,* Nov. 10, 1994.

"the real Reagan revolution": Memo from Ron Haskins to Bill Archer, Nov. 14, 1994.

124 **"it was too radical":** Interview with Newt Gingrich.

125 **"couldn't spell AFDC":** Interview with Ron Haskins.

" 'We're not talking theory' ": Interview with Newt Gingrich.

would have lost $11 billion: From 1989 through 1993, the federal government spent $63 billion on AFDC; had spending been frozen in 1988, the five-year total would have been $52 billion; *1996 Green Book,* 459. One reason Republicans had dismissed block grants the previous year, Rep. E. Clay Shaw Jr. told me, was that "we were afraid the governors would fight us." As governor in 1988, Bill Clinton opposed them. (See text, p. 99.)

"resist publicly": Memo from Henick to Haley Barbour, Nov. 11, 1994.

"burdensome unfunded mandate": George A. Voinovich, "The Need for a New Federalism: A State-Federal Legislative Agenda for the 104th Congress" (paper circulated at Republican Governors Association, Nov. 1994), 7.

126 **"I couldn't understand":** Interview with Ari Fleischer.
"come in on bended knee": A participant's notes from meeting with Thompson, Dec. 8, 1994.
meeting of Republican Governors: Interviews with Sheila Burke, Don Fierce, Chris Henick, Gerald Miller, LeAnne Redick, and others on background.
"**spleen-venting":** Memo from Chris Henick to Haley Barbour and others, Oct. 4, 1994.
"We are willing to accept": Letter from Engler, Weld, and Thompson to Rep. Clay Shaw, Dec. 12, 1994.

127 **child welfare systems:** Memo from Ray Scheppach, National Governors Association, to governors Thompson, Engler, and others, April 7, 1995.
average state had just 13 percent: *1996 Green Book,* 427.
Rector feeling bilious: "panhandlers": Rector, *National Review,* April 17, 1995; "sluggards," editorial, *National Review,* Feb. 6, 1995; "obstacles," Judith Havemann, *WP,* Feb. 19, 1995.
"**always been irritating":** Interview with Newt Gingrich.
"starve children": Dan Balz, *WP,* Jan. 9, 1995.
"A major embarrassment": *Charleston Gazette,* Feb. 14, 1995.

128 **twenty states wouldn't have to run a work program:** Temporary Assistance for Needy Families Program: Fourth Annual Report to Congress, May 2002, table 3:1:a.
Rector hatched the idea: Interviews with Robert Rector and Ron Haskins.

129 **"You cannot sustain":** Interview with Newt Gingrich.
$65 billion cut: Sharon Parrott, "Cash Assistance and Related Provisions in the Personal Responsibility Act," Center on Budget and Policy Priorities, April 6, 1995, 3.

130 **Democrats reacted:** "Make Americans Hungry," Rep. Harold Volkmer in *CQ,* March 11, 1995, 758; Rep. Major Owens in Robert Pear, *NYT,* March 23, 1995; Rep. John Lewis in Mary McGrory, *WP,* April 2, 1995.
"not trying to get people entitled": Robert Pear, *NYT,* March 9, 1995. The word does have unfortunate connotations, suggesting entitlements are by nature permissive. But in this context, "entitlement" refers only to the funding structure. A strict work program that cuts off recipients who fail to work could still be an entitlement, as long as those who do follow the rules are guaranteed the aid. The conflict between the word's formal and informal meanings was a source of constant confusion.

131 ***The less we spend:*** GOP senator Phil Gramm put on a particularly bald display of the New Compassion while campaigning before the Iowa caucuses in 1996. Around Washington, the Texan liked to say he was so tough he kept his heart in a jar, but when I asked why he wanted to end welfare, he said of recipients: "Because ahh *luvvvv* 'em!"

131 **"Orwellian perversion":** Interview with Daniel Patrick Moynihan.

132 **"I thought we'd be in more trouble":** Interview with Gingrich.
generous people have stopped: Murray, *Losing Ground,* p. 236.
Shechtman: DeParle, *NYTM,* Jan. 28, 1996.
thirteen "power phrases," "Rep. Dunn": The Wirthlin Group, "Pulseline Research on Welfare Reform Conducted on Behalf of the Republican National Committee & the National Republican Congressional Committee," March 1995, 3, 8.
dystopian future: *The Bell Curve* (coauthored with Richard Herrnstein) also marked a shift in Murray's treatment of race. When he first proposed ending welfare in *Losing Ground,* Murray took pains to stress his colorblind views. "It makes no difference whether Harold is white or black," he wrote, in his famous parable about the welfare couple Harold and Phyllis (p. 162). The main furor in *The Bell Curve* (New York: Free Press, 1994), however, was its stress on black-white differences in intelligence scores and especially his speculation about whether a genetic element was in play.
list of horrifying stories: Dick Armey, "Welfare Reform Debate Information," March 16, 1995.

133 **alligators and wolves:** 104th Cong., 1st sess., *Cong. Rec.* 141 (March 24, 1995): H 3766 (alligators), H 3722 (wolves).
After decades of predictable: Ford and Shaw traded barbs on Feb. 15, 1995, in the Ways and Means subcommittee on welfare.

134 **"Newt Gingrich believed":** Interview with Bill Clinton, Jan. 30, 2004.
Shays told his wife: Interview with Christopher Shays.
"My hero is Newt Gingrich": Christopher Shays press conference, Nov. 17, 1995.

135 **"fast-forward":** Dick Morris, *Behind the Oval Office: Getting Reelected Against All Odds* (1997; repr., Los Angeles: Renaissance Books), 37.
"get welfare off": Interview with Doug Schoen.
"strategic mistake": Mickey Kaus, "They Blew It," *The New Republic,* Dec. 5, 1994.
"I should have done welfare": Joe Klein, *The Natural: The Misunderstood Presidency of Bill Clinton* (New York: Doubleday, 2002), 81.
"It wasn't really until the summer": Interview with Dick Morris.
"liberate" the poor: Clinton State of the Union Address, Jan. 24, 1995, *PPP-1995,* vol. 1, 79; remarks at White House, Jan. 28, 1995, *PPP-1995,* vol. 1, 108; remarks at Democratic Governors Association dinner, Jan. 30, 1995, *PPP-1995,* vol. 1, 123.
Lillie Harden: Clinton remarks to National Association of Counties, March 7, 1995, *PPP-1995,* vol. 1, 321.
"I still hope it will be the basis": Clinton remarks to NACO, March 7, 1995, *PPP-1995,* vol. 1, 317.

136 **"I wasn't pleased":** *New York Post,* Nov. 3, 1995.

136 **"I loved block grants":** Clinton remarks to Florida Legislature, March 30, 1995, *PPP-1995,* vol. 1, 422.

"It is not fair": Ibid., p. 423.

If "these people can't find jobs": Clinton radio address, April 8, 1995, *PPP-1995,* vol. 1, 492.

praised bills without last-resort jobs: Clinton radio address, Sept. 16, 1995, *PPP-1995,* vol. 1, 1305.

answer "yes and no": Talking Points on Welfare Reform, Nov. 13, 1995, author's files.

Modified Madman: Interview with Bruce Reed.

didn't think the entitlement meant much: Interviews with Dick Morris, Bruce Reed, and Bill Clinton, who told me, "I didn't have a problem with block-granting to the states because we had already de facto done that" given the wide variation in state benefit levels; Jan. 30, 2004.

obscure tool of child support: Clinton radio address, March 18, 1995, *PPP-1995,* vol. 1, 373.

polled well: Interview with administration official on background.

"In no time in recent": Donna E. Shalala, Memorandum to the President, Jan. 19, 1995. Labor Secretary Robert Reich, an opponent of the bill, was another cabinet member impatient with Clinton's stance. "The big strategic error was to let things drift initially and not to signal what was acceptable and what wasn't," he told me. "Everything from that point on was about reducing the abomination."

137 **"only from the right":** Dick Morris memo to Bill Clinton, Feb. 17, 1995, excerpted in Morris, *Behind the Oval Office,* 353.

Panetta: Interview with Leon Panetta.

moment of subtle revelation: Reuters, May 23, 1995; interview with Ginny Terzano.

8. THE ELUSIVE PRESIDENT: WASHINGTON, 1995–1996

138 **Moynihan assured:** In an interview, Paul Offner, Moynihan's main welfare aide, said: "Dole and Packwood were probably his two closest friends on the Finance Committee. He thought there was no way in the world Dole was going to go along with this stuff. I think Moynihan was really blind-sided by those guys, whom he had such respect for, that they would fall in behind Gingrich. . . . They shut him out just as tight as could be."

affection Dole felt for the governors: Unlike Clinton, who portrayed his politicking as the essence of high-mindedness, Dole had an endearing habit of broadcasting his ulterior motives. He boasted his plan had the support of governors in New Hampshire, Iowa, and Arizona—"to name a few primary states." *CQ,* Aug. 12, 1995, 2444.

139 **only speech published:** Daniel Patrick Moynihan, "Congress Builds a Coffin," *The New York Review of Books,* Jan. 11, 1996.

"Nothing I did connected": Daniel Patrick Moynihan, *Miles to Go: A Personal History of Social Policy* (Cambridge, MA: Harvard University Press, 1996), 36.

drove other problems: Moynihan wrote, "From the wild Irish slums of the 19th-century Eastern Seaboard to the riot-torn suburbs of Los Angeles, there is one unmistakable lesson in American history: A community that allows a large number of young men to grow up in broken families, dominated by women, never acquiring any stable relationship to male authority, never acquiring any rational expectations about the future—that community asks for and gets chaos. Crime, violence, unrest, disorder—most particularly the furious, unrestrained lashing out at the whole social structure—that is not only to be expected; it is very near to inevitable." (*America,* Sept. 18, 1965, and repeated in *America,* Sept. 14, 1991)

"To ask questions": Mickey Kaus, a trenchant Moynihan observer, cites this quote in a book review in *The Washington Monthly,* Sept. 1986. The original is from Daniel Patrick Moynihan, *Family and Nation* (1986; repr., New York: Harcourt, Brace, Jovanovich, 1987), 187.

"grown more perplexed": 104th Cong., 1st sess., *Cong. Rec.* 141 (Dec. 21, 1995): S 19089.

gloom about the welfare poor: "paupers," Moynihan, letter to the editor, *NYT,* Dec. 26, 1991; "failed persons," Mickey Kaus, *NYT,* Nov. 19, 1996. At times, Moynihan wondered aloud whether the underclass had a biological basis in the falling age of female puberty. "You could find yourself talking about speciation here," he said in Senate hearing, a comment at once opaque and degrading (Senate Finance Committee, July 13, 1994). Once when an aide referred to welfare "clients," Moynihan flew into a rage: *Clients* pay and command respect! These are *recipients;* they take what they get.

140 **"I just do":** Robin Toner, *NYT,* June 18, 1995.

ragged childhood: Moynihan made his hard-knocks past part of his political persona, but one knock he rarely mentioned was his own family's stay on welfare. His father abandoned the family when he was ten, and his mother went on public aid before seeking refuge in a brief, unhappy second marriage to a well-to-do man. As a 1994 profile in *Vanity Fair* reported: "He doesn't talk about what happened. Even his daughter says she knows only the sketchiest outlines of the story." Elise O'Shaughnessy, *VF,* May 1994; see also Douglas Schoen, *Pat: A Biography of Daniel Patrick Moynihan* (New York: Harper & Row, 1974), 10–11.

"I write to plead": Letter from Offner to Moynihan, April 21, 1995.

"ruinous": Judith Havemann and John Harris, *WP,* June 15, 1995.

141 **"filibuster it":** Robert Pear, *NYT*, June 16, 1991.
bill's preamble: DeParle, *NYTM*, Nov. 12, 1995, 35.

142 **"These moves":** Interview with Robert Rector.
Senate allies: Faircloth, Judith Havemann, and John Harris in *WP,* June 15, 1995; Ashcroft in Robert Pear, *NYT,* Aug. 20, 1995; Gramm on CBS, *Face the Nation,* Aug. 6, 1995.
"jump ball": *CQ,* Aug. 12, 1995, 2444.

143 **"sleeping on grates":** 104th Cong., 1st sess., *Cong. Rec.* 141 (Sept. 6, 1995): S 12705.
"I cannot believe": Clinton news conference, Aug. 10, 1995, *PPP-1995,* vol. 2, 1245.
"[b]rag about cuts": Morris, *Behind the Oval Office,* 467. Morris told me he had been polling to see what message might win public support for a veto and found none.
Democrats demanded $3 billion: Interviews with Grace Reef, Laurie Rubiner, Cynthia Rice, and Helen Blank.
Dole, Dodd: In 104th Cong., 1st sess., *Cong. Rec.* 141 (Sept. 14, 1995): S 13581.

144 **"wisdom and courage":** Clinton radio address, Sept. 16, 1995, *PPP-1995,* vol. 2, 1366.
high fives in the West Wing: Alison Mitchell, *NYT,* Nov. 20, 1995.
open letter: Marian Wright Edelman, *WP,* Nov. 3, 1995.
encyclopedia entry: DeParle, *NYTM,* Dec. 17, 1995.
Primus revived: Interview with Wendell Primus. The study appears in 104th Cong., 1st sess., *Cong. Rec.,* 141 (Nov. 1, 1995): S 16466.
"Clinton's tendency": Interview with Donna Shalala.

145 **"right kind" of reform:** Clinton radio address, Sept. 16, 1995, *PPP-1995,* vol. 2, 1366.
"stick of dynamite": Interview with Wendell Primus.
nonexistent study: Elizabeth Shogren, *Los Angeles Times,* Oct. 27, 1995; also interviews with Wendell Primus, Bruce Reed, Donna Shalala, and Melissa Skolfield.
"may have to accept": Mike McCurry, White House briefing, Nov. 9, 1995.

146 **"This is petty":** David Maraniss and Michael Weisskopf, *"Tell Newt to Shut Up!"* (New York: Touchstone, 1996), 152.
job-approval rating: George Hager and Eric Pianin, *Mirage: Why Neither Democrats Nor Republicans Can Balance the Budget, End the Deficit, and Satisfy the Public* (New York: Times Books, 1997), 269.
Gingrich sobbed: Maraniss and Weisskopf, *"Tell Newt to Shut Up!"* 1.

147 **"I've got a problem,"** ***Leave It to Beaver:*** Ibid., 182, 190.
Clinton had a problem: Trent Lott, the second-ranking Senate Republican, sent around a bulletin asking, "Why take BC off the welfare hook?"

(*FaxNet,* Feb. 1, 1996), and the Republican National Committee began airing ads attacking Clinton's failure to end welfare.

147 **"All of us are here":** Ron Haskins, "A Potential Welfare Reform Agenda for the Second Session" (background paper for GOP members of the Ways and Means welfare subcommittee), Feb. 26, 1996, 1, 3. Ari Fleischer also worked to jump-start a bill, as did Mickey Kaus, who met with potential funders in the hopes of starting a nonprofit group to lobby for welfare legislation. Instead, he took on an informal role of ferrying messages between Haskins and Bruce Reed and working the press.

"politics were quite ravishing": Interview with Clay Shaw.

148 **block grant Medicaid:** In her memoir, Hillary Clinton wrote: "I made clear to Bill and his policy advisers in the West Wing that if I thought they were caving in . . . I would publicly oppose it . . . I would speak out against any bill that did not provide heath [*sic*] care through Medicaid." *Living History* (New York: Simon & Schuster, 2003), 326, 367.

Emphasize "the tragedy of welfare": Rep. Jennifer Dunn, Memorandum to GOP Welfare Reform Working Group, April 24, 1996.

"We're not going to give" to **"This is nuts!":** Notes from meeting of Ways and Means Republicans, June 12, 1996. A turning point in rank-and-file sentiment occurred on June 21, 1996, at a meeting of the whole House GOP. The Medicaid block grant was still in the bill, but the comments of Rep. Tillie Fowler of Florida brought rousing support for dropping it. She said her constituents weren't sure what Medicaid was; they confused it with Medicare. "But *welfare*—that they know! We have to pass that bill!" (Interviews with Tillie Fowler and Dave Camp.)

What finally swayed: Interviews with Newt Gingrich and Jimmy Hayes.

149 **"We thought we would cause a split":** Interview with Gingrich.

"Moot": Clinton exchange with reporters, Jan. 30, 1996, *PPP-1996,* vol. 1, 116.

"good bill": Clinton remarks to the National Governors Association, Feb. 6, 1996, *PPP-1996,* vol. 1, p. 177.

"all any American": Ibid.

spokesman criticized: Mike McCurry, White House briefing, Feb. 7, 1996.

praised a protest against time limits: Clinton remarks in radio address and exchange with reporters, June 1, 1996, *PPP-1996,* vol. 1, 848.

called for "tough time limits": Clinton remarks to the American Nurses Association, June 18, 1996, *PPP-1996,* vol. 1, 925.

negotiator uses ambiguity: Speaking to the NGA, Clinton called the latest bill "a real turning point" on July 16, 1996, but reversed himself a week later, dismissing it with a cornpone quip: "You can put wings on a pig but you don't make it an eagle." (Clinton remarks to the NGA, July 16,

1996, *PPP-1996,* vol. 2, 1129; remarks in Sacramento, July 23, 1996, *PPP-1996,* vol. 2, 1187.

149 **"Government's going to have to train everybody":** Clinton interview with Tom Brokaw, *NBC Nightly News,* Dec. 3, 1993.

"build a jobs program": Ibid.

"I don't think it's a good idea to say 'You can stay on welfare two years'": Clinton interview with the New Jersey media in Hackensack, March 11, 1996, *PPP-1996,* vol. 1, 419. In my 2004 interview with Clinton, he repeated his misgivings about time limits: "I think having a five-year lifetime limit, plus the cutoff after a certain time for able-bodied people, ignores the impact of having a sustained recession."

150 **"I say 'tough on work, yes'":** Clinton remarks to the NAACP, July 10, 1996, *PPP-1996,* vol. 2, 1106.

"We regret that there will be a certain negative side": Interview with Clay Shaw.

"I don't think it's a good thing to hurt children": Clinton interview with the New Jersey media in Hackensack, March 11, 1996, *PPP-1996,* vol. 1, 419.

"Bill Clinton just did this for the ninety-six election!": Interview with Bill Clinton, Jan. 30, 2004. The other Clinton quotes explaining his thinking come from the same interview.

"We've got to rebuild our political life": Clinton at Georgetown University, Oct. 23, 1991.

151 **"children are blown to the winds":** 104th Cong., 1st sess., *Cong. Rec.* 141 (Dec. 12, 1995): S 18436.

Clinton's 1993 homily: Clinton at Church of God in Christ, Memphis, Nov. 13, 1993.

Dick Morris plied him: Interviews with Morris, Bill Clinton, and Leon Panetta.

country would do more for the poor: Hillary Clinton makes the same argument in her memoir: "We also hoped to persuade the American public, now that the old welfare system had been replaced, to address the greater problem of poverty and its consequences. . . . I hoped welfare reform would be the beginning, not the end, of our concern for the poor." *Living History,* 369–70.

152 **"After I sign my name to this bill":** Clinton remarks in the Rose Garden, Aug. 22, 1996, *PPP-1996,* vol. 2, 1326.

three-point deficit, "veto would be a disaster": Morris, *Behind the Oval Office,* 596.

Hillary Clinton's signals: Interviews with Donna Shalala and Doug Besharov; Morris, *Behind the Oval Office,* 300; Hillary Clinton, *Living History,* 369.

Hillary Clinton was out of town: Hillary Clinton's role in the welfare bill has been the subject of great speculation and modest mystery. Her one-time ally, George Stephanopoulos, wrote: "In my last few phone calls with the first lady, I could tell she preferred a veto." *All Too Human* (New York: Little, Brown, 1999), 419. Joe Klein, a perceptive Clinton watcher, wrote: "Most of the President's staff, including his wife, were opposed." (*The Natural,* 151.) One White House aide told me he got a phone call from her shortly after the president endorsed the bill, in which she said something like: "Those of us who are opposed to it have to keep on fighting." But Melanne Verveer, her close aide and friend, told me: "If she were writing the bill, she might have nuanced it differently. But she was not opposing." Verveer said Clinton talked admiringly of a single mother she had met, who worked as an all-night waitress to stay off public aid. Verveer recalls Mrs. Clinton asking something along the lines of "How do you face a woman like that and not have others do the same?" Welfare, Verveer said, was "like a double standard for her." Bruce Reed said, "I had the sense that she was for it, or at least not against it. I had always been of the opinion that she was much more conservative on these issues than people thought. Her staff wasn't involved."

Certainly, like any politician, she was adept at letting different people hear what they wanted to hear. In 1996 with her liberal allies enraged, she had a motive to seem opposed. Now that she's an elected official, referring to a popular law, she has a motive to look like she was for it all along. But whether she was actively for it, or merely neutral, there's no evidence that she tried to stop the president from signing it. *Why* she lent it at least passive support is a separate question. The interesting thing about the account in her memoir is that it makes no attempts to hide the political considerations. Of critics like her old friend Marian Wright Edelman, she wrote: "They didn't have to negotiate with Newt Gingrich and Bob Dole or worry about maintaining a political balance in Congress." (*Living History,* 369.)

153 Clinton turned red with indignation: My account of the July 31, 1996, meeting comes from interviews with Henry Cisneros, Leon Panetta, Bruce Reed, Robert Reich, Donna Shalala, and George Stephanopoulos; Reich told me: "I began to suspect halfway through the meeting that it was not a sincere meeting. It was a show meeting. He wanted to show people he was sincere about their concerns, but he had already made up his mind." In an e-mail, Elaine Kamarck told me: "I was called in at the last minute by [Vice President Al] Gore personally, who said that Clinton had asked me to be there since he wanted some more people in the room who would argue in favor of the bill. I took it as a sign he'd made up his mind already."

Incensed at the budget cuts: Having agreed to give Clinton a third bill, the Republicans did what they could to maximize the political pain. In a memo to Gingrich, his legislative aide Jack Howard wrote: "I believe the

White House will sign just about anything we send them, so we should make them eat as much as we can" (memo, July 25, 1996).

153 **most cabinet members opposed:** One surprisingly strong argument for signing came from the Commerce secretary, Mickey Kantor, who had started his career as a legal aid lawyer; he argued to Clinton that the system was doing more harm than good. For the Ellwood op-ed opposing the bill, see *NYT*, July 22, 1996.

154 **Roosevelt had abolished:** The FDR story, which caught Clinton's notice, was part of the unusual campaign by Mickey Kaus, who was operating in the hybrid status of journalist and policy advocate. Kaus had called Reed from Los Angeles the night before the meeting and told him of FDR's end-welfare moment, which he had gotten from William Leuchtenburg's history, *Franklin D. Roosevelt and the New Deal, 1932–1940* (New York: Harper & Row, 1963). Reed asked him to fax the relevant pages. After racing around town in search of a copy, Kaus found one at Borders and got the passage to Reed at about midnight eastern time. It describes Roosevelt's decision to shut down the Civil Works Administration, a precursor to the WPA that had employed 4.5 million people in the winter of 1933–34. Leuchtenburg writes: "Alarmed at how much CWA was costing, Roosevelt ended it as quickly as he could. He feared he was creating a permanent class of reliefers whom he might never get off the government payroll." Leuchtenburg quotes Roosevelt telling his aides: "Nobody is going to starve in the warm weather." (See pp. 122–25.) In calling Clinton's attention to the story, Kaus said he was trying to make three points: (1) presidents used to do big, bold things; (2) it's impossible to overhaul welfare while holding every recipient harmless; (3) Clinton needed to "generally harden his heart" and accept that big policy changes toward the poor carry some costs.

"I want to sign this bill": Three Clinton welfare aides resigned in protest: Mary Jo Bane, Wendell Primus, and Peter Edelman, who aired his criticisms in a widely read article in *The Atlantic* (March 1997) called "The Worst Thing Bill Clinton Has Done."

9. THE RADICAL CUTS THE ROLLS: MILWAUKEE, 1995–1996

159 **penalty amounted to 6 percent:** Without the penalty, Jewell was getting $517 in AFDC and $340 in food stamps, for a total of $857. The penalty cut her cash to $440 but raised her food stamps to $363, for a total of $803.

160 **makings of a dumb-criminal joke:** Interviews with Opal Caples and Jewell Reed, and arrest report, Nov. 3, 1995.

161 **Milwaukee's economy:** From 1990 to 1994, the average unemployment rate in Milwaukee was 6.3 percent; by comparison, it was 12.3 percent in Detroit, 11.8 percent in Cleveland, and 8.8 percent in Chicago.

161 **right-wing idealist:** Interviews with Jason Turner; see also DeParle, *NYTM,* Aug. 24, 1997, and *NYTM,* Dec. 20, 1998.

162 **"It's work that sets you free!":** Robert Polner, *Newsday,* June 28, 1998.
welfare article: "How It Pays to Be Poor in America," *USN,* Nov. 1, 1965.

163 **robbed at gunpoint:** The second robbery occurred in Houston, where Turner was driving a cab on a college break.

165 **the statewide caseload had already fallen:** Some key caseload figures are these: 98,300 when Thompson took office (Jan. 1987); 81,300 when Turner arrived (April 1993); 31,500 when the transition to W-2 began (Sept. 1997); 13,400 when the transition to W-2 ended (March 1998); and 6,700 when Thompson left office (Jan. 2001). Turner took a lead role in designing W-2 but left the state government in the spring of 1997, so he played no role in running it.

While the caseload declines were extraordinary by anyone's accounting, these official data do modestly overstate its extent. Through 1996, AFDC included about 10,000 "child only" cases, in which the adult was not part of the case (often, for instance, a grandmother caring for a grandchild). With the conversion to W-2 in 1997, the state shifted those cases into two new programs, separate from W-2. So part of what appears as a welfare decline was really just a reshuffling of the existing caseload. By the state's official count, the rolls dropped 93 percent during Thompson's four terms (from 98,300 to 6,700). If one added back the child-only cases (as an apples-to-apples comparison should), the decline would equal 84 percent. For simplicity's sake (and because the child-only figures are unreliable for certain months), I use the official state numbers throughout the text unless otherwise noted.

recipients placed in jobs rose: Jason Turner, "Performance Contracting in Wisconsin" (unpublished paper, circa 1997), 2.

Oregon diversion program: Interviews with Jason Turner and with Verl T. Long and Sandy Steele, of the Oregon Department of Human Services; *AFSelf-Sufficiency* (newsletter, Division of Adult and Family Services, Dec. 1993), 6.

166 **case openings fell by a third:** Statewide, the annual number of case openings fell from 37,000 in 1995 to 24,200 in 1996. The decline was 21 percent in Milwaukee and 45 percent in the rest of the state. Author's analysis of DWD data.

The Emergency Work Program: Interview with Bill Biggs; testimony of Norman G. Angus, Director of Utah State Department of Social Services before the U.S. Senate Finance Committee, Sept. 1985.

167 **Utah caseload fell nearly 90 percent:** Frederick V. Jansen and Mary Jane Taylor, "Emergency Welfare Work and Employment: An Independent Evaluation of Utah's Emergency Work Program," June 13, 1991, 4. Three months after leaving the rolls, 76 percent of program participants were employed.

167 **Milwaukee's caseload collapsed:** In the two years beginning in March 1996, the Milwaukee caseload fell from 33,700 to 11,500. Outside Milwaukee, it dropped from 29,000 to 2,000. The total number of Milwaukee recipients, as opposed to cases, fell by 60,000 in a city of 611,000 residents. (As noted above, these official figures on caseload decline would look a bit smaller if they properly accounted for child-only cases.)

168 **nearly a third had jobs:** John Pawasarat and Lois M. Quinn, "Demographics of Milwaukee County Populations Expected to Work Under Proposed Welfare Initiatives" (UW-M, Employment & Training Institute, Nov. 1995), 33.

"pogs": Scott Sloan, *Shepherd Express,* July 10, 1997.

169 **sanctions rose a dozenfold:** In 1993, Turner's first year in Wisconsin, Milwaukee sanctioned about 360 people a month. (See State of Wisconsin, *JOBS Annual Report,* Dec. 1994, 60.) In the spring of 1996, under Pay for Performance, monthly sanctions averaged about 4,200. (Author's 1997 communication with Eva J. Davis, Milwaukee County Department of Human Services.) The penalties rose not only because of the default mechanism, of course, but also because the program had tougher rules with which few people would or could comply.

Congressional investigators: GAO, "States' Early Experience with Benefit Termination," May 1997, 7.

170 **homeless families, Ramon Wagner:** DeParle, *NYT,* May 7, 1997.

10. ANGIE AND JEWELL GO TO WORK: MILWAUKEE, 1996–1998

175 **difficult, dangerous work:** From 1995 to 1999, an average of 15.4 percent of nursing home workers were injured each year; among coal miners, the number was 7.6 percent (Bureau of Labor Statistics). In 1998, nursing aides earned an average of about $7.50 an hour, while coal miners earned $19.17. (The nursing aide figure is from author's communication with Joshua Wiener, Urban Institute; coal miners' data is from BLS.) Data on back injuries and rise in injury rates is from "Caring till It Hurts," Service Employees International Union, 1997, 2, 5. For turnover rates, poverty rates, and health insurance, see testimony of William A. Scanlon of the GAO before the Senate Finance Committee, May 17, 2001, 12–13.

176 **caregivers' role and background on nursing homes:** Interviews with Judith Feder, Robert Friedland, Robyn Stone, and Josh Wiener.

178 **650 Chicago workers:** Timothy M. Smeeding, Katherin Ross Phillips, and Michael O'Connor, "The EITC: Expectation, Knowledge, Use, and Economic and Social Mobility," *National Tax Journal* (Dec. 1, 2000).

180 **Bel Air turnover rate:** The annual turnover rate among Bel Air nursing aides was 144 percent versus a statewide average of 69 percent. *1999*

Consumer Information Report, Wisconsin Department of Health & Family Services, 6.

182 **probation officer noted:** J. Mulcrone, pretrial investigation in 93-CR 24020-02, filed Jan. 4, 1994, Circuit Court of Cook County.

186 **the kids' school absences rose:** Kesha's absentee rate rose from 19 percent when Angie was on welfare to 33 percent after she left the rolls. Redd's went from 27 percent to 29 percent, and Von's from 16 percent to 19 percent. The data cover the eight school years beginning in 1991–92; Kesha's eighth-grade attendance records are missing. (Author's analysis of attendance records supplied by Milwaukee Public Schools.)

190 **"Leaving welfare is a process":** Toby Herr and Robert Halpern with Aimee Conrad, "Changing What Counts: Re-thinking the Journey Out of Welfare" (Project Match, April 1991), 10.

191 **work despite multiple barriers:** One major study of W-2 bore out Herr's view that people with barriers can work. "Contrary to what one might expect, sample members who had at least a high school diploma were no more likely to have been employed than those who had not graduated from high school." People with high school diplomas did earn more. Irving Piliavin, Amy Dworsky, and Mark E. Courtney, "What Happens to Families Under W-2 in Milwaukee County, Wisconsin? Report from Wave 2 of the Milwaukee TANF Applicant Study," Chapin Hall Center for Children at the University of Chicago and Institute for Research on Poverty, University of Wisconsin, Madison, Sept. 2003, 58.

192 **$8,100:** See Maria Cancian and others, "Before and After TANF: The Economic Well-Being of Women on Welfare" (Institute for Research on Poverty, Special Report no. 77, May 2000), table 8. Among former recipients who worked, average earnings were $10,300. But only 79 percent worked. Counting all former recipients, employed and unemployed, lowers the figure to $8,100. (All figures, including Jewell's, in 1998 dollars.)

193 **Jewell took her in:** One peculiarity of the trio's experiences in the post-welfare years is that they each had a prostitute move in with them. After Ken's teenage associate left Jewell's, she stayed with Angie. The girl's sister, who was also occasionally employed as a sex worker by Ken, stayed with Opal and helped take care of her kids.

194 **two-week manhunt:** See *MJS,* Feb. 11, 12, 20, 21, and 26, 1998.

loaded rifle, $400 of cocaine: Arrest report, Sept. 19, 1998, on file in *State vs. Kenyatta Thigpen,* 98CF005103, Milwaukee County Circuit Court.

one house arrest per house: Actually, there is no ban on two accused felons sharing a residence on house arrest; decisions are made case by case.

11. OPAL'S HIDDEN ADDICTION: MILWAUKEE, 1996–1998

196 **cut Milwaukee's rolls by a third:** The city's caseload fell from 33,700 in March 1996, at the start of Pay for Performance, to 23,300 in July 1997.

more than half the caseload untouched: Of 55,000 cases statewide in June 1996, for instance, 20,400 were enrolled in welfare-to-work activities; author's communication with Paul Saeman, DWD.

sightings of "Maria!": At a motivation class in 1997 the instructor asked students for examples of how the program had helped. I thought: interview skills? self-esteem? A hand flew up: "It really helped me with the interview for *Dateline NBC*!"

197 **social work as farce:** OIC also marched Opal through something called the Harrington-O'Shea Career Decision-Making® System Revised, a list of ninety-six like-dislike questions compiled by two Boston psychologists. Opal reported that she would like to "write a novel," "perform scientific studies," or serve as "a mayor or senator." She would not like to "drive a large truck" or "carve animals out of wood." With that, the test detected an interest in social issues and suggested a future as a dean of students or probation officer. Opal wrote that she'd rather be a chemist.

201 **Robert Lee's arrests:** Interviews with Opal, Chicago court records.

202 **crack's American debut:** Michael Agar, "The Story of Crack: Towards a Theory of Illicit Drug Trends," *Addiction Research and Theory* 11, no. 1 (2003): 3–29; see also the history of crack on the Web site of the Drug Enforcement Administration.

"I could do anything": "My Secret Addiction," *Ladies' Home Journal*, Nov. 1994, 162.

behavior of addicts: Interviews with Ric Curtis, Francine Feinberg, Jerome Jaffe, George Koob, Michael Massing, Thomas McLellan, Anne Paczesny, Luigi Pulvirenti, and Pat Tucker. Also helpful is the 1998 Bill Moyers series on PBS, *Close to Home*, available at http:www.pbs.org/wnet/closetohome/home.html (accessed May 26, 2004).

paradigmatic cocaine experiment: Michael A. Bozarth and Roy A. Wise, "Toxicity Associated with Long-term Intravenous Heroin and Cocaine Self-Administration in the Rat," *Journal of the American Medical Association* (1985): 81–83.

206 **poor record of leading to employment:** Brock, Butler, and Long, "Unpaid Work Experience for Welfare Recipients," 3. One reason the early experiments failed to predict the later plunge of the rolls may have to do with scale; the declines came in part from changes in street and bureaucratic culture, which don't occur until the new rules are broadly applied.

207 **unusually generous:** Shortly before the program began, Tommy Thompson (who was first elected promising benefit cuts) pushed through a 20 percent hike, raising the community service jobs to $673 a month. In doing so, he overrode the objections of his aides and Republicans in the legislature. "It's brought in a lot of opponents and advocates to help make the system work," he said. Thompson's politically savvy move was one example of the kind of positive political dynamic Clinton had hoped the welfare bill would encourage. At the same time, W-2 drew some criticism on the Left for abandoning the practice of paying more to larger families. AFDC paid $440 a month to a mother with one child, and additional children raised the figure to $517, $617, and $708, up to $963 for a mother of ten. In paying a flat $673, the CSJs amounted to a pay raise for anyone with three kids or less—about 90 percent of the caseload. However, a few women with very large families lost significant ground.

207 **preview of W-2:** DeParle, "Getting Opal Caples to Work," *NYTM*, August 24, 1997.

12. HALF A SAFETY NET: THE UNITED STATES, 1997–2003

208 **Nine out of ten:** For jobs and children, *1996 Green Book*, 473; for fathers and education, interview with Donna Pavetti.

"God, not government": Joe Loconte, *WSJ*, Oct. 6, 1995.

209 **"The debate is over":** Clinton, remarks in St. Louis, Aug. 12, 1997, *PPP-1997*, vol. 2, 1087.

Rudolph Giuliani planned: Robert Polner, *Newsday*, May 12, 1998.

"Life works if you work": Thomas L. Gais and others, "Implementation of the Personal Responsibility Act of 1996," in Rebecca Blank and Ron Haskins, eds., *The New World of Welfare* (Washington, DC: Brookings Institution Press, 2001), 46.

About three-quarters made applicants look: Pamela A. Holcomb and Karin Martinson, "Putting Policy into Practice," in Alan Weil and Kenneth Finegold, eds., *Welfare Reform: The Next Act* (Washington, DC: The Urban Institute, 2002), 9. They found diversion programs in thirteen of seventeen sites studied.

210 **"culture of improper deterrence":** Shortly after becoming the New York City welfare commissioner, Jason Turner began converting the city's thirty-one welfare offices into so-called "job centers," with a heavy stress on diverting would-be applicants. City officials said that front-line workers merely were supposed to make sure that applicants had considered alternatives to welfare, like using food banks or soup kitchens. But city workers often refused to give out applications during a person's first visit to the office, in violation of the law; they did so not only for cash aid but for Medicaid and food stamps, too. While the city called such incidents isolated, District Judge William H. Pauley III found "system-wide failures" and wrote that the "evidence indicated that job centers were failing to timely process applications . . . erroneously denying food stamps and

Medicaid applications, [and] failing to allow individuals to apply for benefits on their first visit to a job center." Turner may not have helped his cause when he said in a deposition, "We acted first and worried about the consequences later." One of the plaintiffs was a homeless woman, pregnant with twins, who was skipping meals as she waited more than a month for food stamps. *Lakisha Reynolds vs. Rudolph Giuliani,* U.S. District Court, Southern District of New York, July 21, 2000.

210 **two-thirds of adults lost Medicaid:** Pamela Loprest, "How Are Families that Left Welfare Doing? A Comparison of Early and Recent Welfare Leavers," The Urban Institute, B-36, April 2001, 5. The data covers 1997, a low point in the health insurance story, which made modest improvements with time. The share of former recipients with Medicaid or other subsidized insurance rose from 36 percent in 1997 to 48 percent in 2002, in part because states did a better job of enrolling eligible families and in part because of the new state Children's Health Insurance Program, which in some states covered adults, too. (2002 data from author's communication with Loprest.)

Among children eligible for food stamps: Bob Greenstein and Jocelyn Guyer, "Supporting Work through Medicaid and Food Stamps," in Blank and Haskins, eds., *The New World of Welfare,* 347.

211 **three-quarters had full-family sanctions, half-million cut off:** Dan Bloom and Don Winstead, "Sanctions and Welfare Reform," in Isabel V. Sawhill and others, *Welfare Reform and Beyond: The Future of the Safety Net* (Washington, DC: Brookings Institution, 2002), 50–51. Some of those penalized ignored their assignments because they already had jobs. But on average, they had less education, less work experience, and more problems with domestic violence and physical and mental health than did other people leaving the rolls. They also wound up with lower employment rates. While sanctioned families can return to the rolls, often after a waiting period, the overwhelming majority do not. See also LaDonna Pavetti and Dan Bloom, "State Sanctions and Time Limits," in Blank and Haskins, *The New World of Welfare,* 261.

a third of New York City's caseload: Interviews with Seth Diamond, Swati Desai, NYC Human Resources Administration.

212 **Utah found half had problems:** DeParle, *NYT,* June 30, 1997.

thirty-three states spent more on child care: Mark H. Greenberg, CLASP, testimony before U.S. Senate Committee on Finance, March 19, 2002. Wisconsin spent *four* times as much on child care as it did on cash benefits.

213 **earnings disregards:** Wisconsin was the rare state that did *not* let recipients keep at least part of their checks once they got regular jobs.

collecting child support: Analysis of HHS data by Vicki Turetsky of CLASP. From 1996 to 2002, the share of child-support cases in which the government made a collection rose from 20 percent to 49 percent.

213 **half the adults, 30 percent of kids were uninsured:** Bowen Garrett and John Holahan, "Welfare Leavers, Medicaid Coverage, and Private Health Insurance," The Urban Institute, B-13, March 2000, 3.

eligibility for SCHIP and Medicaid: Author's communication with Edwin Park, Center on Budget and Policy Priorities.

37 percent adults uninsured: Author's communication with Pamela Loprest of the Urban Institute, who derived the data from the National Survey of America's Families.

mother of two leaving welfare: David T. Ellwood, "Anti-Poverty Policy for Families in the Next Century: From Welfare to Work—and Worries," *Journal of Economic Perspectives* (Winter 2000): 187–98.

214 **seven states cut the rolls by three-quarters:** It depends upon what years you choose, but from January 1993 to June 2000, they are Colorado, Florida, Idaho, Mississippi, Oklahoma, Wisconsin, and Wyoming.

states with more unemployment: Robert E. Rector and Sarah E. Youssef, "The Determinants of Welfare Caseload Decline," The Heritage Foundation, May 11, 1999.

prominent economists: June E. O'Neill and M. Anne Hill, "Gaining Ground? Measuring the Impact of Welfare Reform on Welfare and Work" (Manhattan Institute, July 2001); Rebecca M. Blank, "Declining Caseloads/Increased Work: What Can We Conclude About the Effects of Welfare Reform?" *Economic Policy Review* (Federal Reserve Bank of New York, Sept. 2001), table 2.

215 **Creek County:** Dana Milbank and Christopher Georges, *WSJ,* Feb. 11, 1997.

white families left faster, blacks and Hispanics outnumbered: DeParle, *NYT,* July 27, 1998; "Temporary Assistance for Needy Families Program: Fourth Annual Report to Congress," May 2002, ch. X, 190.

$59 billion more: Douglas J. Besharov and Peter Germanis, "Toughening TANF: How Much? And How Attainable?" University of Maryland School of Public Affairs, Welfare Reform Academy, March 23, 2004, 53.

216 **state spending, New York to New Mexico:** DeParle, *NYT,* August 29, 1999.

trip to the Delta: DeParle, *NYT,* Oct. 16, 1997.

217 **factors that shape state policy:** Joe Soss and others, "Setting the Terms of Relief: Explaining State Policy Choices in the Devolution Revolution," *American Journal of Political Science* 45, no. 2 (April 2001): 378–95

218 **Oregon presented a contrasting view:** DeParle, *NYT,* Nov. 20, 1997.

talk of childhood molestation: DeParle, *NYT,* Nov. 28, 1999.

220 **twenty states met the work rate:** HHS, Office of Family Assistance, "TANF Work Participation Rates, Fiscal Year 2002," April 25, 2003.

states reported that 61 percent: "Welfare Reform Reauthorization: State Impact of Proposed Changes in Work Requirements, April 2002

Survey Results," National Governors Association/American Public Human Services Association, 7.

13. W-2 BUYS THE CRACK: MILWAUKEE, 1998

223 **Opal admitted using cocaine:** Interviews with Opal Caples and Darlene Haines.

forgery: *State vs. Darlene Haines,* Case #2001CF000403, Milwaukee County Circuit Court; interview with Megan Carmody, assistant district attorney.

224 **Opal's collapse:** Interviews with Opal Caples, Jewell Reed, and Kenny Gross.

226 **failed to pick up the girls:** On April 15, 1998, someone filed a child-welfare complaint warning, "Ms. Caples had a cocaine addiction and had abandoned all her children at day care while on a crack binge." (CHIPS petition, March 13, 2000, 2.)

caseworker knew nothing of her addiction: Opal's computerized case notes, instantly available to any caseworker, contained three references to drug use over the previous eighteen months. There is "a conflict with her . . . treatment" (Aug. 19, 1996); she is "attending her treatment program" (Sept. 12, 1996); and "[s]he has just completed . . . her treatment program" (Dec. 23, 1996).

222 **Sonya Gordon:** In an interview, Gordon explained she was a "retention specialist," whose job was to prepare the case for the "AODA"—alcohol and other drug abuse—"specialist" by talking to Opal and her former employer about why she had lost her job. She spoke to neither. An additional note of folly entered the case when another OIC worker gave Opal a $400 "job access loan" under a program meant to help workers keep their jobs. "You really don't qualify for it if you're not working," Opal said. "It wasn't hard. I just went in and filled out my papers."

229 **an investigator arrived:** Interview with Opal Caples; CHIPS petition, March 13, 2000, 2. The investigation was triggered when Opal left the girls at day care, but a month passed before the social worker arrived.

"The unborn child": Sam Martino, *MJS,* June 17, 1998.

14. GOLF BALLS AND CORPORATE DREAMS: MILWAUKEE, 1997–1999

230 **"The Company's services":** Maximus, Inc., 1997 Form 10-K, Securities and Exchange Commission.

welfare cartel: In describing the agencies' cooperative spirit, the consultant, George Gerharz, told me: "This is the biggest small town in America—you don't screw each other."

230 **Goodwill Industries:** It ran the program through a subsidiary, Employment Solutions, Inc., which operated two Milwaukee regions and was therefore the state's largest W-2 agency. The agency run by the YWCA was called YW Works.

231 **Maximus thought to have an edge:** The Wall Street firm Donaldson, Lufkin & Jenrette, for instance, credited the bill with "creating vast opportunities for the private sector" and called Maximus "ideally positioned to benefit from the expected surge in outsourcing." (Maximus, Inc., Company Report, DL&J, Aug. 22, 1997, 14, 1.)

Mastran's stake: Adam Cohen, *Time,* March 23, 1998.

Maximus had to start from scratch: Among those Maximus employees who spoke on the record were Jose Arteaga, Keith Garland, Mona Garland, George Leutermann, David Mastran, Bridgette Ridgeway, and Michael Steinborn.

232 **"plan to replicate":** Pete Millard, *Milwaukee Business Journal,* July 7, 1997.

employees would pose: When CNN called to ask if the program offered clients tax advice, Maximus staged a class for the cameras. Keith Garland, the Maximus manager who conducted it, told me, "that's the only workshop I've ever done."

Nightline: Transcript, *ABC News,* Sept. 4, 1997.

233 **up to "thirty hours":** Even Jason Turner, who designed W-2 (and then left the state government), was unaware of the "up to" codicil until I pointed it out to him. "That wasn't the original plan," he said. "The counties were definitely not allowed to put people in twenty hours—that definitely wasn't permissible." Jean Shiel, the official who wrote the manual, said the language was meant to offer "a little bit of flexibility, but not much—we still emphasized it was thirty hours of work."

"limbo": Memorandum from Mona Garland to George Leutermann, March 3, 1998.

"[M]any job seekers": E-mail from Mona Garland to Jose Arteaga, April 30, 1998.

"The no-show rate": E-mail from Paula Lampley to Mona Garland, Oct. 29, 1997.

"Northwestern Mutual": E-mail from Mona Garland to caseworkers, March 24, 1998.

"virtually no referrals": E-mail from Steve Perales to Mona Garland, Feb. 11, 1998.

234 **more than twice as many:** "Distribution of Caseloads by FEP For the Week Ending June 5, 1998," data supplied by DWD at author's request.

13 Feps, needed 28: Mona Garland memo to Steve Perales, Jan. 14, 1998.

Sixty-seven percent had no work assignments: The comparable figures were 15 percent at Employment Solutions (Region 4); 21 percent at

Employment Solutions (Region 5); 33 percent at YW Works and OIC; and 52 percent at UMOS. The statewide average was 38 percent. "Full Participation Exceptions (740RC Report)," DWD, June 26, 1998.

234 **46 percent with no assignment:** E-mail from Jose Arteaga to four Maximus managers, Sept. 28, 1998.

"[O]ur dismal performance": George Leutermann memo to Mona Garland, June 30, 1998.

236 **W-2 Provides the Jobs:** The other tier on the W-2 ladder, rarely utilized, involved "Trial Jobs," in which the state used the welfare grant to subsidize work with a private employer. In January 2000, the breakdown of assignments statewide was 51 percent in Community Service Jobs; 35 percent in W-2 Transitions; 1 percent in Trial Jobs; and 13 percent on three months of paid maternity leave.

238 **"professional work environment":** Maximus, 1997 Form 10-K, 2.

Maximus work atmosphere: gambling jags and screensaver, interviews with Michael Steinborn; "off the deep end," e-mail from George Leutermann to Mona Garland, Feb. 23, 1998; "Marine combat veteran," e-mail from Maximus employee to his supervisor, Feb. 17, 1998; "Monkey Ass away," memo from Paula Lampley to Phyllis Kirk, Aug. 31, 1998; sex-and-drug peddling scheme, e-mail from Christine Brost to Steve Perales, March 17, 1998 and from interviews with Keith Garland and George Leutermann, who confirmed the credibility of the allegations; "dumb-ass . . . should have paid," a Maximus employee on the condition of anonymity.

239 **practiced what he preached:** Leutermann's wife, Barbara, ran literacy classes; his son, George Jr., had a summer job; his niece, Twila Hatzinger, worked in PR; his girlfriend was a senior manager; and her mother supervised receptionists. The "rumors and soap operas" memo is dated June 9, 1998. The talk of Leutermann's affair was so widespread it reached David Mastran, the CEO, who later said in an interview he considered it "a firing offense" but lacked evidence at the time; given the program's other problems, he said, it was a "peripheral issue in a bigger storm." Leutermann, in an interview, didn't deny the relationship with his subordinate (he is listed on a birth certificate as the father of her child) but said she was hired on merit. "She was basically a brilliant person," he said. Likewise, he said, "My wife was hired not because she was my wife but because she had a master's degree in computer education. . . . We didn't just hire people because they were relatives."

"more than its share of complaints": E-mail from David Mastran to George Leutermann and others, May 25, 1999; the Swann report, marked in a cover note as a "draft," is dated June 1, 1999, and was circulated to the senior corporate management.

"living a double life": Judge Diane S. Sykes, May 1, 1995; transcript of sentencing in *Wisconsin vs. Corey Daniels,* case #F-950959, Milwaukee

County Circuit Court, 14. At a trial that largely pitted his word against theirs, Daniels was acquitted of extorting money from Maximus clients. "I was a little, I wouldn't say surprised, but I wasn't sure I was going to come out of there with any acquittal," his attorney, Douglas Pachucki, told me.

242 **$300-a-day habit:** Opal Caples, CHIPS petition, March 13, 2000, 2.

243 **Maximus went on a grander binge:** Unless otherwise noted, spending details come from LAB, "Administration of the Wisconsin Works Program by Maximus, Inc.," and accompanying letter of transmittal, July 28, 2000. In yet another instance of governmental disarray, the audit citing program abuse was addressed to state senator Gary R. George, who later pleaded guilty to federal conspiracy charges after receiving kickbacks from OIC.

Maximus agreed to repay: DWD news release, Oct. 13, 2000.

244 **"I have permission":** 1998 interview with George Leutermann.

a $60,000 PR chief: Interview with Bridgette Ridgeway. One of the smiling kids in the Maximus ads was her son, for which he was paid a shoot fee. "The W-2 families didn't want to participate," she said.

Leutermann covered the bases: The fuller list of Maximus donations includes African World Festival ($5,000); Bastille Days Festival ($5,000); Black Education Hope Fund ($3,875); Black Excellence Awards ($500); The Charlie Lagrew Fiddle and Jig Contest at Indian Summer Festivals ($2,500); Juneteenth Day Street Festival ($1,100); Mary Church Terrell Club ($3,350); Milwaukee Minority Chamber of Commerce ($1,000); Milwaukee Urban League ($2,750); NAACP ($1,000); Project Equality of Wisconsin ($1,700), Spirit of Truth Worship Center ($2,000); Friends of Women's Studies ($500). (LAB audit, July 28, 2000.)

245 **golf balls:** The golf balls, though not in the auditors' reports, were cited by an anonymous Maximus employee interviewed by *The New York Times* and became a shorthand for the spending spree; Nina Bernstein, *NYT,* Feb. 22, 2000.

"sad or dark tones": Memo from Randle Jackson, Sykes Communications, May 19, 1998, in author's files.

Melba Moore: David Mastran, the Maximus CEO, defended the Moore concert as an example of the kind of unconventional activity privatization was meant to foster. "We were told, 'You guys in the private sector can do things that we can never do—we want you to think outside the box,'" he said in an interview. "Well, maybe it was stupid . . . [but] I thought it was a great idea." While legislative auditors found fault with it, he said, a state welfare official had given verbal approval ahead of time.

"painted from Day One": Interview with George Leutermann.

payment to Thompson's cronies: The consultants were Phil Prange, a longtime Thompson campaign fundraiser, and John Tries, a former cabinet member. While the consultants' invoices were not directly charged to W-2, state law allowed Maximus to recoup $8,500 in corporate overhead said to relate to their work. Steven Schultze, *MJS,* Aug. 15 and Oct. 14, 2000.

245 **"on the lops":** Memo from Leutermann to Holly Payne, July 7, 1998. For advice on how to work the convention, Leutermann also hired a publicist named Julie Jensen, whose husband, Scott, happened to be the Republican Speaker of the Assembly until his indictment a few years later on political corruption charges. Memo from Julie Jensen to Leutermann, May 20, 1998.

246 **"My department bought":** Interview with Bridgette Ridgeway.

OIC to Employment Solutions: LAB, "Administration of the Wisconsin Works Program by Employment Solutions Inc., and Other Selected Agencies," Feb. 16, 2001.

her own "vigilant efforts": Stewart resigned under fire three weeks later, but her successor, Jennifer Reinert, continued to defend Maximus. While auditors concluded that Maximus had overcharged the state $500,000, they also said the company failed to claim $1.6 million to which it was entitled—its disarray had cost it $1.1 million. Citing that finding, Reinert said of Maximus: "They were as much victims of sloppy bookkeeping as we were." Steve Schultze, *MJS,* Oct. 14, 2000.

78 percent failed: Memo from George Leutermann to Holly Payne, Oct. 11, 1998.

247 **attendance at MaxAcademy:** Interview with Keith Garland.

Maximus reduced payments: LAB, "Wisconsin Works (W-2) Program: An Evaluation," April 2001, 54–55. Statewide, only 4 percent of the caseload suffered full sanctions.

move away from Jason Turner's theory: The subtle philosophical shift even found doctrinal expression when the state scrapped a controversial policy known as "Light Touch." Reflecting Turner's zeal for deterrence, the policy told caseworkers to offer "only as much service as an eligible individual asks for or needs" rather than "every support available." In practice, the vague dictum encouraged caseworkers to withhold information about Medicaid and food stamps—both federal entitlements—and the food stamp rolls fell faster in Wisconsin than in any other state. Under fire from two federal investigations, the Thompson Administration eased its deterrence efforts. In 2002, Thompson's Republican successor, Scott McCallum, formally canceled "Light Touch," and by 2004, under a Democratic governor, Jim Doyle, the original W-2 philosophy had shifted 180 degrees. While Turner called for "securing the front door," the new program manual advised, "W-2 shall be participant friendly."

248 **just type something in the system:** In another sign of the distance between W-2 theory and practice, Turner was unaware that the policy manual allowed caseworkers to write employability plans and put them in the mail. "Is that what some of them were doing?" he said. "Making something up and putting them in the mail—that's crazy. That's not how it's supposed to happen. Oh shit, that's a surprise to me."

248 **the award administrators:** The Ford/Harvard evaluation shows how hard it is for outsiders to know what's really happening inside a program, and by extension how little reliable information there may be about welfare programs nationwide. To assess W-2, the Innovations program sent a respected researcher, Julie Boatright Wilson, on a two-day visit to Wisconsin. Wilson, a former New York state official, is a lecturer at the Kennedy School, and she had written a detailed economic and demographic study of Milwaukee. That is, she arrived with an experienced eye. In a whirlwind visit, she interviewed seventy-five to one hundred people, including George Leutermann, Paula Lampley, and Becky Redmond, the MaxAcademy speaker featured on *Nightline*. "I was struck by the extent to which the front-line workers believe in the program," she wrote in a confidential report. Citing W-2's "institutional culture" as its greatest strength, she praised caseworkers for their "problem-solving" and their "can-do attitude" and the state for "monitoring outcomes rather than process." Among her concerns was that the program might have too many people in community service jobs.

249 **"a pitch man":** Pete Millard, *Milwaukee Business Journal*, Feb. 14, 2000. Leutermann's problems began at the beginning of 2000 when Mona Garland, the manager he had blamed for the early casework problems, quit and filed a racial discrimination complaint with the Equal Employment Opportunity Commission. David Mastran, the Maximus CEO, told me the company paid to settle her case and those of four other Milwaukee employees. Garland also strafed the company in the press, calling its presence in Milwaukee a "travesty." Soon after, the New York City comptroller, Alan Hevesi, challenged the company's $100 million deal, saying that Maximus had gained an unfair political advantage in the contracting process. With that, storms were under way in both cities, with Leutermann caught in both. He stopped running the W-2 program in the summer of 2000 and left the company in 2001.

When I talked to Mastran, he offered what he called a "Yogi Berra" defense of the company's problems. "We made mistakes," he said, "but we didn't do anything wrong." That is, he conceded the problems in personnel ("In all our projects, we never had personnel problems like we had up there—it was out of control") and accounting ("guilty of being inept"), but stressed that none of its transgressions had reflected a conscious attempt to defraud the state. "I don't say we were looked at with a microscope," he said. "We were looked at with a proctoscope. And no one indicted us." In part, he blamed the problems on growing pains ("It's night and day now"); in part, on the lack of state oversight; and in part on Leutermann ("His head got too big"). He also argued that for all its problems Maximus performed as well as or better than the competition and sent along some data to make his case. The data covered later years, but my subjective sense is that he's probably right when he says, "relatively speaking, we were a top performer" from the start; on the surface the only place that elicited more confidence was YW Works. The numbers he sent showed the agencies with fairly similar outcomes, which is consistent with my sense that the operational differences between them were minor. To the extent W-2 "worked," it seemed to do so more as a general welfare deterrent than as a service delivery machine.

249 **Kenny resisted Opal's claims:** The following year, Kenny failed to appear at a paternity hearing, and the court issued a default judgment, naming him the father.

15. CASEWORKER XMI28W: MILWAUKEE, 1998–2000

253 **clients liked Michael:** Interviews with clients Shelley Block, Opal Caples, Juanita Dotts, Dinah Doty, Kim Hansen, Angiwetta Hills, Melina Scott, and Angela Wilkerson.

254 **"More of the success":** Jason Turner and others, "Wisconsin Works: Draft, April 1995," proposal to Secretary Carol Skornicka, 30–31.

Pathways: Suzanne L. Wagner, Charles Chang, and Toby Herr, "An Unanticipated Story of Caseload Declines: The First Two Years of the Pathways Case Management System in Oswego County, New York" (Chicago: Project Match, July 2002). Despite the shortage of personalized attention, people leaving the rolls often say they were treated fairly—in one Wisconsin survey, for instance, the ratio was 67 percent yes versus 32 percent no. DWD, "Survey of Those Leaving AFDC or W-2: January to March 1998: A Preliminary Report," Jan. 13, 1999, 11.

one in five changed regions: Caseload analysis from DWD, supplied at author's request.

255 **Wisconsin bureaucracy celebrated:** One prominent W-2 supporter, the political scientist Lawrence M. Mead, called the Wisconsin administrators "quite literally world statesmen and stateswomen" who exemplify "their state's intense faith in the public enterprise." Lawrence M. Mead, *Government Matters: Welfare Reform in Wisconsin* (Princeton, NJ: Princeton University Press, 2004), xi.

260 **refer to a more specialized:** It turned out that by moving to a shelter, Michael's client left the Maximus region, so her case was transferred to another agency. Checking CARES a few months later, Michael saw nothing that indicated her new caseworker knew she was using drugs.

"always gonna be in the gutter": Interview with Jai Marin.

16. BOYFRIENDS: MILWAUKEE, SPRING 1999

264 **three-quarters worked** to **thirty-five hours a week:** Gregory Acs and Pamela Loprest, with Tracy Roberts, "Final Synthesis Report of Findings from ASPE Leavers' Grants" (Washington, DC: The Urban Institute, Nov. 27, 2001), Executive Summary; hereafter "ASPE Leavers Study."

employment rates of never-married mothers: They grew from 44 percent in 1992 to 66 percent a decade later. Gary Burtless, "The Labor Force Status of Mothers Who Are Most Likely to Receive Welfare: Changes Following Reform," Brookings Institution Web site, March 30, 2004; for employment trends, see also Rebecca M. Blank and Lucie Schmidt, "Work, Wages, and Welfare," in Blank and Haskins, eds., *The New World of Work,* 70–102.

265 **"Work organizes life":** Clinton at Church of God in Christ in Memphis, Nov. 13, 1993, *PPP-1993,* vol. 2, 1985.

Michelle Crawford: DeParle, *NYT,* April 20, 1999.

"Ending of the Black Underclass": Mickey Kaus, "A Response to My Critics! The case for optimism about the underclass," www.kausfiles.com (accessed Nov. 8, 1999).

266 **Samuel Brown:** Carl Baehr, *Milwaukee Streets: The Stories Behind Their Names* (Milwaukee: Cream City Press, 1995), 33.

a gang of boys: The killing was the subject of dozens of articles in Milwaukee and beyond, starting with Leah Thorsen, *MJS,* Oct. 1, 2002.

267 **incipient investigation fizzled:** Opal's case file paints a less-than-vigilant picture of the child welfare bureaucracy. It notes that "Ms. Caples admitted to the hospital staff that she had a $300.00 a day cocaine habit and . . . that she had been bingeing two to three days at a time while staying at drug houses." A social worker met her at Angie's on Jan. 8, 1999, "but as of January 20, 1999, Ms. Caples had moved" and attempts "to locate Ms. Caples in February of 1999 were unsuccessful." CHIPS petition, March 13, 2000, 2.

270 **only half of young black men had jobs:** Harry J. Holzer and Paul Offner, "Trends in Employment Outcomes of Young Black Men, 1979–2000" (Institute for Research on Poverty: Discussion Paper 1247-02, Feb. 2002), table 1. The number fell from 59 percent in 1989 to 50 percent in 1999 before bouncing back to 54 percent in 2000, still far below its historical level at the peak of a business cycle.

black men in Milwaukee: David J. Pate Jr. "An Ethnographic Inquiry into the Life Experiences of African American Fathers with Children on W-2," in Daniel R. Meyer and Maria Cancian, *W-2 Child Support Demonstration Evaluation: Report on Nonexperimental Analyses* (Madison: Institute for Research on Poverty, March 2002), 2:29–118.

write their own obituaries: DeParle, *NYT,* Sept. 11, 1999.

271 **If working mothers:** Interviews with Marcus Robertson, Mary Williams.

Someone Hug Me: Darrell's first report cards showed a dismayingly familiar picture of uncultivated potential. "Darrell is such a joy to have in class. He works hard and does very well with others," wrote one teacher. But she pleaded: "Mom & Dad please help Darrell get to school." Another teacher warned: "Darell [*sic*] is having difficuties [*sic*] with all subject areas."

17. MONEY: MILWAUKEE, SUMMER 1999

282 **Had she stayed on welfare:** If Angie had gone on W-2 in 1999, she would have gotten $673 a month in cash and $417 in food stamps, or $13,080 a year. Expressed in 2003 dollars, the measure I use throughout this chapter unless otherwise noted, that's $14,400.

283 **how Angie's finances worked:** "On welfare" refers to Angie's last four-full years on AFDC, 1992 through 1995. "Off welfare" covers her first three years after leaving, 1997 through 1999. She left midway through 1996, making it a unique year that I placed in neither category. Earnings records are from tax returns and the state wage files kept to track eligibility for unemployment insurance; cash and food stamp figures come from state records. Angie's 1992 and 1993 earnings are estimates based on partial data; all other figures are actual. The numbers have been adjusted for inflation and expressed in constant 2003 dollars.

One thing to notice is that even when Angie was on AFDC, her welfare check accounted for only 38 percent of her income. Another 29 percent came from earnings (after taxes); 22 percent from food stamps; and 11 percent from tax credits. If that suggests she wasn't as "dependent" on AFDC as she seemed, it also explains why taking it away may do less, for good or ill, than either side assumed. A fuller picture of Angie's finances would have to quantify the contributions of boyfriends and relatives, which other research suggests typically add another 15 to 20 percent, further diminishing the role of AFDC. (See Kathryn Edin and Laura Lein, *Making Ends Meet* [New York: Russell Sage Foundation, 1997], 44.) Another thing to keep in mind is that Angie's monthly income was less stable than these multiyear averages suggest. Both of her peak-income years—$26,000 at the post office in 1994 and $27,400 at the nursing pool in 1997—were followed by years with steep losses. Her income fell nearly a third in 1995, when she got discouraged and quit, and by 20 percent in 1998, after her car got stolen. That is, the anxiety of living on sums like these is even greater than the numbers suggest. For more financial data see www.jasondeparle.com.

Jewell's earnings rose *sixfold*: Her box score looked like this:

	ON WELFARE	OFF WELFARE
Earnings	$1,900	$12,700
Tax credits	700	4,000
Payroll taxes	(-100)	(-1,000)
AFDC	7,800	0
Food stamps	4,400	900
TOTAL	$14,700	$16,600

Jewell's 1994 earnings and tax credits are estimates; all other numbers are actual. Amounts expressed in 2003 dollars.

283 **monthly earnings reports:** The state stopped requiring the reports in August 1997, a month after Jewell lost her stamps.

284 **earnings may grow with time:** For a later look at the finances of Angie and Jewell, see pages 403 and 404.

Angie earned at least 50 percent more: In her first three years off welfare, Angie's earnings averaged more than $16,100 a year. By contrast, a typical woman leaving the Wisconsin rolls earned between about $9,000 and $10,400, as discussed on page 286. Angie's first two jobs, at Clement Manor and Mercy Rehab, paid hourly wages of $8.33 and $7.46 (in 2003 dollars), placing her squarely in the middle of former recipients nationwide; her annual earnings were higher than average only because she worked more steadily.

case for encouragement: From 1994 to 2001, annual earnings among the poorest half of single mothers rose from $4,500 to $8,800; earnings among the poorest quarter rose from $1,500 to $3,900. Total income grew more modestly, rising 32 percent to $17,000 for the poorest half and rising 16 percent to $10,000 among the poorest quarter. Over the same years, hourly wages for women at the 20th percentile rose by 14 percent, to $7.79. (Author's communication with Jared Bernstein of the Economic Policy Institute.)

As for former recipients, Acs and Loprest found them earning about $8.25 an hour; Elise Richer and two colleagues produced an estimate of $8.20; Ron Haskins came up with about $7.50 (all in 2003 dollars). Converting a midpoint estimate of $7.85 back into late-nineties dollars suggests the average leaver earned about 35 percent above the minimum wage. (Acs and Loprest, "ASPE Leavers Study," table 3; Elise Richer, Steve Savner, and Mark Greenberg, "Frequently Asked Questions About Working Welfare Leavers," CLASP, Nov. 2001, 13; Ron Haskins, "Effects of Welfare Reform on Family Income and Poverty," in Blank and Haskins, *The New World of Welfare,* 109.)

285 **poverty rates plunged:** Among children, the poverty rate fell from 21.8 percent in 1994 to 16.3 percent in 2001; among blacks, from 30.6 percent to 22.5 percent; among Hispanics, 30.7 percent to 21.4 percent; and

among people living in single-mother homes, from 38.7 percent to 28.6 percent. In 2003, the poverty threshold was $12,682 for a mother with one child; $14,824 for a mother of two; $18,725 for a mother of three; and $21,623 for a mother of four.

285 **"first recovery in three decades":** Clinton interview with five reporters from *The New York Times,* Nov. 30, 2000.

286 **a third held jobs:** Acs and Loprest, "ASPE Leavers Study," Executive Summary and table 3.3.

average earnings: $9,000 and $12,000, Acs and Loprest, "ASPE Leavers Study," table 3.5. (The $9,000 includes an adjustment to account for non-workers.) $14,500 comes from the same study, table 3.7. All figures expressed in 2003 dollars.

Wisconsin earnings growth, three-year mean: Maria Cancian and others, "Before and After TANF: The Economic Well-Being of Women Leaving Welfare" (Madison: Institute for Research on Poverty, Special Report, no. 77), May 2000, table 8; figures in 2003 dollars.

poor people even poorer: The Cancian study examined eight thousand families who left the rolls in late 1995, just before Angie and Jewell. Over the next year, they gained $2,900 in earnings and tax credits but lost $5,500 in cash and food stamps. That reduced their total income from $13,600 on aid to $11,000 off it. (Ibid., fig. 2, in 2003 dollars.) The study appeared six months after W-2 won the Innovations Award and received almost no attention.

extreme poverty: Sheila R. Zedlewski and others, "Extreme Poverty Rising, Existing Government Programs Could Do More," Urban Institute, April 1, 2002; they use an alternate definition of poverty that includes food stamps.

Spending **among the very poor:** Ron Haskins, "Effects of Welfare Reform," in Blank and Haskins, *The New World of Welfare,* 116–19.

287 **about 7 percent grew poorer:** Analysis of Census Bureau data by Wendell Primus; Christopher Jencks and Joseph Swingle find the tipping point somewhere between the 5th and 10th percentile in "Without a Net," *The American Prospect,* Jan. 3, 2000.

basic necessities: Shortages of food, rent, Acs and Loprest, "ASPE Leavers Study," tables 6.2–3; half uninsured, Bowen Garrett and John Holahan, "Welfare Leavers, Medicaid Coverage, and Private Health Insurance," The Urban Institute, B-13, March 2000.

Michigan families: Sheldon Danziger and others, "Does It Pay to Move from Welfare to Work?" *Journal of Policy Analysis and Management* 21, no. 4 (2002): 671–92.

depleted cupboards: While I regularly encountered food shortages in my travels in Milwaukee, surveys by the United States Department of Agriculture indicated that food hardships declined in the late 1990s among the broader population, for some groups dramatically. One report found: "the prevalence of children's hunger declined by about half, from 1.1 percent of all households with children in 1995 to 0.6 percent in 1999." It's possible, of course, for both "food insecurity" and outright "hunger" (two different measures) to be declining yet still common among former welfare recipients. Mark Nord and Gary Bickel, "Measuring Children's Food Insecurity in U.S. Households, 1995–99," Economic Research Service, USDA, *Food Assistance and Nutrition Research Report,* Number 24, April 2002, Abstract.

288 **persistence of hardship:** Heather Boushey and others, *Hardships in America: The Real Story of Working Families* (Washington, DC: Economic Policy Institute, 2001), esp. table 4.

fewer than one in ten reach twice the poverty line: Maria Cancian and Daniel R. Meyer, "Alternative Measures of Economic Success Among TANF Participants," July 2003, table 2 (most but not all the of the families they surveyed had left the rolls).

most never will: Among former AFDC families, the share with incomes above 200 percent of the poverty line was 12 percent in the first year, 27 percent after five years, and 33 percent after ten years. Daniel R. Meyer and Maria Cancian, *Journal of Applied Social Sciences* 25, no. 1 (Winter/ Fall 2000–2001).

poverty status of Angie and Jewell: These numbers include food stamps and tax credits, which the official numbers omit. Angie's peak year rose from 121 percent of the poverty line on welfare to 127 percent off it—hardly any difference. Likewise, Jewell's rose from 117 percent on welfare to 121 percent off it. She did, however, experience more income fluctuation after leaving welfare. In her first full year off the rolls, when she mostly went jobless, her income fell to a new low of 54 percent of the poverty line.

289 **What Angie really lived on:** In her first three years off welfare, Angie's annual earnings after payroll taxes averaged $14,850 (in 2003 dollars), or $1,238 a month. To show how this fit her 1999 expenses on Brown Street, I converted it into 1999 dollars; that leaves her with monthly take-home pay of $1,121.

optional necessity: Angie's phone had long been cut off, but I had one installed in the summer of 1999, to make it easier to reach her.

291 **she earned $7.82:** That was her nominal wage in the spring of 1999, her third year off the rolls; the equivalent in 2003 dollars is $8.64.

292 **Michael didn't know Opal used drugs:** Along with notes from previous caseworkers indentifying her drug use, Michael had Opal's latest assessment test, which identified "substance use" as among her likely "work barriers." "To be honest, I don't pay any attention to it," Michael said. "I'm more interested in my interaction with them."

294 **nonmarital births:** From 1995 to 2002, the share of children born outside marriage dipped among blacks (from 69.9 percent to 68.2 percent), while it rose among Hispanics (from 40.8 percent to 43.5 percent) and whites (from 21.2 percent to 23.0 percent). Because of changes in reporting techniques in California, Michigan, and Texas, it's impossible to say when the national rate first slowed. The official numbers show a decline between 1994 and 1995, but most researchers think the trend lines changed a few years earlier.

294 **fewer children with lone single mothers:** Gregory Acs and Sandi Nelson, "Changes in Family Structure and Child Well-Being: Evidence from the 2002 National Survey of America's Families" (paper for University of Michigan, National Poverty Center), Aug. 15, 2003, table 3.

295 **more black children with married parents:** Wendell E. Primus, "Child Living Arrangements by Race and Income: A Supplementary Analysis," Center on Budget and Policy Priorities, Nov. 19, 2001, table 5. Since Primus had resigned from the government to protest the welfare bill, his public comment about an earlier version of this paper was widely noted: "In many ways, welfare reform is working better than I thought it would. . . . Whatever we have been doing over the last five years, we ought to keep going." With his willingness to reexamine a strongly held position in light of new evidence, Primus showed admirable intellectual integrity. (See Blaine Harden, *NYT,* Aug. 12, 2001.)

no obvious policy pattern: While doing little about welfare, the District of Columbia cut the share of children born outside marriage by 18 percent (68.8 percent in 1994 to 56.6 percent eight years later). Over the same years, as Wisconsin led the drive to end welfare, the share of its children born outside marriage rose 10 percent (from 27.2 percent to 30.0 percent). Nationally, the average rose 4.3 percent (from 32.6 percent in 1994 to 34 percent in 2002). (Author's communication with Stephanie Ventura, National Center for Health Statistics.)

296 **"$8.25 an hour":** The equivalent in 2003 dollars is $9.11.

18. A SHOT AT THE AMERICAN DREAM: MILWAUKEE, FALL 1999

308 **William Martin's performance bonuses:** LAB, audit of Employment Solutions, Inc., Feb. 16, 2001, 7.

Martin's total salary: Steve Schultze, *MJS,* Feb. 28, 2001.

staff parties to **$160,000 in unallowable costs:** LAB audit, 2–5, appendix 1.

"FBI investigation": Steve Schultze, *MJS,* June 23, 2001. No charges were filed as a result of the alleged investigation, which the FBI did not publicly confirm.

"bumbling rather than trickiness": Steve Schultze, *MJS,* June 8, 2001. David Mastran, the Maximus CEO, chose nearly the same words when describing the company's problems to me: "It was clearly ineptness on our part and lack of guidance on the state's part, rather than any mal intent." Once heralded as exemplars of efficiency, in other words, the state's two leading privatized agencies defended themselves by citing their own incompetence.

311 **benefits to *younger* children:** Johannes Bos and others, "How Welfare and Work Policies Affect Children: A Synthesis of Research," MDRC, March 2001, ES-4.

adolescents in Minnesota, Canada, and Florida: Jennifer L. Brooks, Elizabeth C. Hair, and Martha J. Zaslow, "Welfare Reform's Impact on Adolescents: Early Warning Signs," Child Trends, July 2001.

"dogs that didn't bark": Greg J. Duncan and P. Lindsay Chase-Lansdale, "Welfare Reform and Children's Well-Being," in Blank and Haskins, *The New World of Welfare,* 407.

"children of current and former recipients": Kathryn Tout, Juliet Scarpa, and Martha J. Zaslow, "Children of Current and Former Welfare Recipients: Similarly at Risk," Child Trends, March 2002.

"environments changed little": Bruce Fuller and others, "New Lives for Poor Families? Mothers and Young Children Move Through Welfare Reform," The Growing Up in Poverty Project—Wave 2 Findings, ES, 2.

312 **New Hope had little impact on family life:** Hans Bos and others, "New Hope for People with Low Incomes: Two-Year Results of a Program to Reduce Poverty and Reform Welfare," MDRC, 1999, tables 5.7, 6.1–6.3, 6.6–6.12. The evaluators concluded: "theory envisions that a program such as New Hope might have many more impacts than in fact emerged" (ch. 6, 14). By the five-year follow-up study, the depression rate among New Hope parents had slightly improved. Still, it remained high and was the only one of ten psychosocial measures in which researchers saw any improvement. Once again, they wrote, "the program had few impacts on the well-being of parents and families." Aletha C. Huston and others, "New Hope for Families and Children: Five-Year Results of a Program to Reduce Poverty and Reform Welfare," MDRC, June 2003, 89.

one outstanding finding: After two years, teachers ranked the New Hope boys as better behaved and more academically skilled than members of a control group, and the boys themselves were more likely to say they expected to attend college. The statistical magnitude was roughly equivalent to adding 100 points to an SAT score (Bos and others, table 7.2). Many of the positive effects for boys continued after five years (Huston and others, 146–59, 169).

314 **Lisa moved back:** After four years away, she was startled by the new hassle of getting a welfare check; she gave up and moved in with an old boyfriend, but not before spending two months crowded in at Angie's and Jewell's.

321 **earned about $18,500:** In 1999, Angie's nominal earnings were $16,800; the equivalent in 2003 dollars is $18,500.

EPILOGUE: WASHINGTON AND MILWAUKEE, 1999–2004

324 **"What does the political scientist":** The 1981 poem by Artur Miedzyzrecki was read by the political scientist Hugh Heclo at a conference at the University of Wisconsin in May 1992.

attacks from a jealous man: Donald Crawford described himself as an aspiring minister, but he was also a recovering addict who had been arrested a few years earlier for his role in torturing a man he suspected of stealing his drugs. Twice in the year before Michelle addressed the legislature, he had been led away in handcuffs for striking her; once, she had been arrested for hitting him and threatening him with a knife. DeParle, *NYT,* April 20 and Dec. 30, 1999.

Lillie Harden: Bill Clinton met her in Arkansas in 1986, and brought her to speak to the National Governors Association later that year. He retold her story often but didn't see her again until 1996, when she stood beside him in the Rose Garden as he talked about her inspired son and signed the new law. As he continued to tell the story during the 1996 campaign, the *Arkansas Democrat Gazette* published a Harden profile. It said Clinton had "bungled the resumes" of her four kids (one, whom Clinton had described as "studying to be a doctor," was working as a garbage collector); cited Carlton Harden's teenage imprisonment; and noted that during the years in which Clinton described Harden as an emblem of postwelfare success, she had gone back on welfare several times. (Frank Wolfe, *Arkansas Democrat Gazette,* Oct. 27, 1996.) In *My Life,* his memoir, Clinton called the story of Harden and her son "the best argument I've ever heard for welfare reform." He added: "I had been working on welfare reform for more than fifteen years. But I didn't consider it a Democratic issue. Or even a governors' issue. Welfare reform was about Lillie Hardin [*sic*] and her boy" (330).

When I talked to Harden, she seemed of two minds about whether working mothers have the ability to inspire their kids. She retold the story of Carlton saying, "Mama, I'm so proud of you," and warned that when mothers "sit around at home and don't do nothing it takes an effect on children." But later in the conversation she said, "Most of the time, these kids don't care about whether you work or scrape to take care of them. They just feel like it's something you have to do."

325 **the story someone could tell:** As too-tidy symbols of success, Crawford and Harden were scarcely unique. I was driving across Wisconsin with Jason Turner one day when he began raving about a woman named Jackie Muriel. As one of the first people off W-2, Muriel was the subject of a long profile in the *Milwaukee Journal Sentinel* that noted a moment in which she had run short on toilet paper. In the past, she had just resorted to theft, but this time she demurred, and Turner attributed the decision to the morally uplifting powers of work. "I was high on life for a week after I read that," Turner said. "It showed you that the system had the capability of transforming someone's life." A few months later, Muriel was in jail, and she went on to lose her kids. (Joel Dresang and Crocker Stephenson, *MJS*, May 18 and Sept. 28, 1997.) Another *Journal Sentinel* story making the rounds relied on a few Milwaukee bus drivers to argue that "a startling change" was under way in the city's poor neighborhoods. "I see more people with kids early in the morning," said one driver, William Love. Another, Pearlie Duncan, said, "You can look into their eyes; they're happy. The eyes tell no lies." A gift from the quote gods if ever there was one, "the eyes tell no lies" appeared in Thompson's application for the Harvard-Ford Foundation award, and Clinton cited the bus story in a radio address. Though I missed Duncan, I spent a morning riding the bus with William Love, whose fame as a social critic was news to him. As we rode around the central city, he said, "I can't say I see a noticeable change" from the welfare years. Then he thought of one: he owned some inner-city houses and had more tenants behind on their rent. (Michele Derus, *MJS*, June 28, 1998.)

For another cautionary welfare-to-work tale, see Peter Boyer's article in *The New Yorker* about the six-year-old Flint, Michigan, boy who took a gun to school and shot and killed a five-year-old girl. In the deluge of coverage, some noted that the little girl's mother, Veronica McQueen, was a welfare-to-work success. But so was the mother of the six-year-old gunman. Tamarla Owens was working not one but two jobs, and gone ten hours a day. Despite her long hours, she had gotten evicted, and sent her son to live with her drug-dealing brother, where he found the loaded gun. (Peter Boyer, *The New Yorker,* July 3, 2000.) In the recent literature of the ghetto, there is one role-model mother who stands out above the others, propelling her son to the Ivy League. But as Ron Suskind tells the story in his book *A Hope in the Unseen,* the moral isn't as clean as it might appear. When explaining what helped her son succeed, Barbara Jennings partly credited a decision she made when her son, Cedric, was two: she quit her job and went on welfare, so they could spend more time together. She lost income but gained time, and they spent it at church, libraries, and museums. In the preschool years, she explained, "a child either gets the love he needs or he doesn't." Then she went back to work. (New York: Broadway Books, 1998, 31.)

325 **incomes of disadvantaged single mothers:** Jared Bernstein of the Economic Policy Institute examined the incomes of all single mothers below twice the poverty threshold. From 1994 to 2000, their incomes rose 17 percent to $16,300, before surrendering 2 percent of the gains over the next two years. Bernstein, "Single Mothers Lose Ground in Weak Labor Market," EPI Web site, May 19, 2004. When I talked to Clinton, he, too, noted that the recession's effect on poor single mothers had been milder than feared: "The assumption was that since the welfare people were hired during the expansion, when the economy turned down, they'd be the first ones laid off, and that's not necessarily what's happened."

325 **child poverty rates:** Analysis by Gary Burtless of the Brookings Institution (presented at a briefing, Sept. 26, 2003).

employment of high school dropouts: Jared Bernstein and Lawrence Mishel, "Labor Markets Left Behind," Economic Policy Institute, Briefing Paper, Sept. 2003, 8–10.

unemployment rose: From 4.0 percent in 2000 to 6.0 percent in 2003.

326 **"works despite itself":** Gardner, who has spent more than two decades living and working in the central city of Milwaukee, said of W-2: "It is demonstrably, radically, unequivocally better than the old AFDC system, because it doesn't pay you not to work. And it's been implemented as badly as is humanly possible. . . . The moral is the right thing done badly is much better than the wrong thing, even when done well. . . . It is just staggering to me how many uneducated poor folks who I really didn't expect to work, are working."

327 **"compassionate conservative":** In noting that George W. Bush took pains "to say that he wasn't a racist," Clinton added: "Based on his appointments in Texas and his appointments in the White House, he's not. The only really unforgivably racist thing he's done is let his people call the white voters in South Carolina in the primary and tell them John McCain had a black baby. . . . But he has governed, at least, without apparent racial discrimination." The reference was to a phone campaign by anonymous Bush supporters, who spread the rumor that McCain's adopted Bangladeshi daughter was his illegitimate black child. The Bush campaign said it had nothing to do with the calls.

rising inequality: Data are from CBO, "Effective Federal Tax Rates, 1997–2000," Aug. 2003, table B1-C.

tax-cutting frenzy: *The Wall Street Journal* editorial page went as far as calling women like Angie and Jewell—people too poor to pay income taxes—"lucky duckies." Grover Norquist, Washington's leading antitax operative, told Terry Gross of the public radio show *Fresh Air* that inheritance taxes reflected the "morality of the Holocaust." (*WSJ*, Nov. 20, 2002; *Fresh Air*, Oct. 2, 2003.)

Medicaid eligibility: Matthew Broaddus and others, "Expanding Family Coverage: States' Medicaid Eligibility Policies for Working Families in the Year 2000," Center on Budget and Policy Priorities, Feb. 13, 2002.

child-care subsidies: Jennifer Mezey, Mark Greenberg, and Rachel

Schumacher, "The Vast Majority of Federally Eligible Children Did Not Receive Child Care Assistance in FY 2000," CLASP, Oct. 2, 2002.

327 **tax credits:** Nicholas Johnson, "A Hand Up: How State Earned Income Tax Credits Help Working Families Escape Poverty in 2001," Center on Budget and Policy Priorities, Dec. 2001.

328 **At $5.15 an hour:** The 1950 minimum wage of seventy-five cents is worth $5.85 in 2004 dollars, 70 cents more than today's minimum.

program of workers' aid: Isabel Sawhill and Adam Thomas, "A Hand Up for the Bottom Third: Toward a New Agenda for Low-Income Working Families," Brookings Institution, May 2001.

Oregon program: A study called the National Evaluation of Welfare to Work Strategies (NEWWS) examined 11 sites nationwide. Programs that stressed basic education achieved a five-year earnings gain of 7 percent. Job-search programs gained 12 percent. But with a "mixed-services" strategy of job search and training, Portland, Oregon, topped the list with a gain of nearly 25 percent. Nan Poppe, Julie Strawn, and Karin Martinson, "Whose Job Is It?" in Bob Giloth, ed., *Workforce Intermediaries for the 21st Century* (Philadelphia: Temple University Press, 2003), 39.

physically get away: For Gautreaux, see James E. Rosenbaum, "Changing the Geography of Opportunity by Expanding Residential Choice: Lessons from the Gautreaux Program," *Housing Policy Debate,* vol. 6, 1995, 231–69. For Moving to Opportunity, see Jeffrey R. Kling and Jeffrey B. Liebman, "Experimental Analysis of Neighborhood Effects on Youth," unpublished paper, May 2004.

329 **"marriage initiative":** When I talked to Clinton, he said: "If they shuffle a bunch of money to their political supporters and don't do anything but pontificate at people, well, I don't think it will have much impact. On the other hand, I think the central insight that children will be better off with two parents than one is true. . . . I didn't have any problem with him wanting to spend some money to help people build strong marriages and take care of kids." He suggested that Democrats support the initiative on the condition that some of the money be used to expand welfare eligibility and training for two-parent families, to keep more fathers in the home.

330 **Opal acknowledged crack use:** CHIPS petition, March 13, 2000.

331 **$200,000 a year:** Meg Kissinger, *MJS,* July 15, 2003.

half failed the performance goals: To succeed, agencies had to place 35 percent of their recipients in jobs. Maximus recorded a job-placement rate of 35.54 percent; YW Works had 35.25 percent; OIC had 28.55 percent; and UMOS had 24.38 percent. (Felicia Thomas-Lynn, *MJS,* July 31, 2003.)

332 **people in W-2 fared no better:** Irving Piliavin, Amy Dworksy, and Mark E. Courtney, "What Happens to Families Under W-2 in Milwaukee County, Wisconsin? Report from Wave 2 of the Milwaukee TANF Applicant Study," Chapin Hall Center for Children at the University of Chicago and Institute for Research on Poverty, University of Wisconsin, Madison, Sept. 2003, 43–58.

332 **Bleeding red ink:** The financial problems arose at YW Works, which had struck me as the most competent and creative of the five agencies. Its clients included Michelle Crawford, the woman whom Tommy Thompson had invited before the legislature, and the Y's handling of her case was one of the most skillful I've seen. Her caseworkers arranged for months of psychological counseling to address her depression, then put her through an on-the-job training program at a plastics factory the Y bought for that purpose. "They were like a family to me," Crawford said. But the factory failed in the recession, and the Y's longtime director, Julia Taylor, moved on, trailing board criticisms of her financial stewardship; in another venture, she used much of the agency's W-2 profits to create an unsuccessful software company in which, as a member of its two-person board of directors, she gave herself stock options. (See Bruce Murphy, *MJS*, May 30, 2004.) The penalty was assessed against the United Migrant Opportunity Society, after an audit found it had mishandled 86 of 110 cases. It was imposed in 2003 by a new Democratic governor, James Doyle. The original W-2 law allowed the state to penalize the agencies $5,000 for any instance of a "failure to serve" a client. But under Thompson and his Republican successor, Scott McCallum, no penalties were ever assessed.

"no evidence of favoritism": While a state appeals court rejected Comptroller Alan Hevesi's charges of "corruption," elements of the Maximus deal were cozy in a way that invited public distrust. Turner recruited a friend from Milwaukee, Tony Kearney, to work as a consultant on an ostensibly separate project, a "faith-based" initiative that tried to reach troubled recipients through the churches. But Kearney was also a consultant for Maximus, and his city work had him meeting with some of the same groups against whom Maximus would bid; some of them worried he was using his access to gather information about their proposals. Another element involved the role of Richard Schwartz, a former top aide to Mayor Rudolph Giuliani. In leaving City Hall, he founded a for-profit company, Opportunity America, to provide welfare-to-work services. The Maximus proposal pledged to give Schwartz a $30 million subcontract, which critics called a further way of seeking favor with the Giuliani administration. Turner had previously done some consulting work for Schwartz. In addition, *The Village Voice* later reported that, while seeking Turner's business, Leutermann also agreed to a request from Turner's wife, Angie, to contribute up to $60,000 to an abstinence program she had designed for the Milwaukee public schools. (She sought support from all five W-2 agencies, Turner told me, and Maximus and OIC agreed.)

When I asked Turner about the contracting dispute, he dismissed the criticisms as unfair attacks by interests wedded to the city's status quo. While he designed the bid process, he said, he didn't choose the seventeen vendors and therefore couldn't have favored Maximus or Schwartz even had he wanted to. He did say he hoped the process would bring in some for-profit companies, since he thought they would be more efficient. (At the time Maximus won the New York contract, its problems in Milwaukee were largely unknown.) Turner also stressed that multiple agencies—including the Manhattan district attorney and federal prosecutors—had investigated his conduct without finding any wrongdoing. The city conflict-of-interest board also found no breach of rules in the hiring of Turner's father-in-law. But it fined him $6,500 for two unrelated ethics violations: renting an apartment from a subordinate and having his city assistant help him for a few hours with a private consulting job. Leaving the welfare business, Schwartz sold his company to Maximus for $780,000 and became the editorial page editor of the *New York Daily News*.

334 **more than $20,000 a year:** For those betting that incomes of former welfare families will improve with time, Jewell's case is encouraging. She did much better in her second four years off the rolls than she did in her first three. She worked more regularly, at a rising wage, so her earnings in the second period rose 30 percent. She also straightened out her problems with the food stamp office (and, after having another child, spent six months getting W-2). Compared with her first years off the rolls, her total income grew nearly 40 percent, and she got out of poverty. The updated box score (in 2003 dollars) looks like this:

	FIRST 3 YEARS OFF WELFARE	NEXT 4 YEARS
Earnings	$12,700	$16,500
Tax credits	4,000	5,000
Payroll taxes	(-1,000)	(-1,300)
W-2	0	1,000
Food stamps	900	1,600
	$16,600	**$23,000**
% of poverty line	**93%**	**122%**

While the trend line is positive, on her own, Jewell is still in that near-poverty zone, in which material hardships abound. Or she would be if she were all alone. Counting Ken's income brings them to something like 185 percent of the poverty line, the level at which families usually start to feel better off. It's another bit of evidence pointing to the importance of men.

lower-middle-class life: The average married couple with kids has an annual income of about $65,000. With approximately $40,000 combined,

Jewell and Ken would rank at about the 25th percentile. (Author communication with Ed Welniak, Census Bureau.)

336 **"the money's just not right":** Here's Angie's updated box score (in 2003 dollars):

	FIRST 3 YEARS OFF WELFARE	NEXT 4 YEARS
Earnings:	$16,100	$14,900
Tax credits:	5,600	5,700
Payroll taxes:	(-1,200)	(-1,100)
W-2:	0	0
Food stamps:	4,400	4,600
Kinship care	0	2,400
	$24,900	**$26,500**
% of poverty line	**115%**	**116%**

Angie's summary—"just treading water"—is apt. Her earnings declined 7 percent, but her public subsidies grew, especially the kinship care payments for taking in Brierra. (In the old days, these were part of AFDC, so technically the household would have been back on the welfare rolls.) The payment raised her total income, but with Brierra her family size grew, so in relationship to the poverty line, Angie's circumstance hardly changed. She went from 103 percent of poverty (on welfare) to 115 percent (newly off) to 116 percent (in the next four years). On most days, it wasn't enough for her to notice the change.

ACKNOWLEDGMENTS

In doing this work, I've accumulated more debts than I can fully acknowledge, but it's gratifying to begin. This book wouldn't exist without *The New York Times,* which for more than a decade has let me go where I want and write what I wish about welfare and poverty. In an age of tight newsroom budgets, the *Times*'s commitment to a poverty beat is, in the literal sense, extraordinary. Joe Lelyveld, the executive editor through most of my tenure, made me feel empowered from the start, while Jack Rosenthal of the *Times Magazine* and Dean Baquet of the national desk—great editors and friends—offered extravagant support. Joe and Bill Keller let me spend a year in Milwaukee writing about welfare and also agreed to the leave with which I started the book. Howell Raines generously extended it, and Bill Keller, now the executive editor, patiently extended it again. Jon Landman has been a source of friendship and counsel since the day I walked in the door, and Gerry Marzorati helped make a magazine writer out of me. Other current or former employees of the *Times* to whom I'm indebted include Soma Golden Behr, Nicole Bengiveno, Doug Frantz, George Judson, Adam Moss, Matt Purdy, Andy Rosenthal, Bill Schmidt, and Arthur Sulzberger Jr.

Just as crucially, this book wouldn't exist without Angela Jobe, Jewell Reed, and Opal Caples, who along with their families have taught me a great deal about welfare and poverty and also about resilience. Kesha, Redd, and Von Jobe were always welcoming, and I'm grateful for the goodwill of Marcus Robertson, Kenny Gross, and especially Kenyatta Thigpen, a frank and articulate narrator of his past. In pointing me toward the Eastland plantation, Hattie Mae Crenshaw, Jewell's mother, gave this work a vital context. Listening to her tell her life story has been one of the great pleasures of my reporting career. Jewell's sister and niece, Mary Reed-Flowers and Monica Reed, greeted me warmly in Chicago and in subsequent interviews. Virginia Caples arranged two visits to the Eastland plantation and introduced me to her uncle, Mack Caples, Pie Eddie's son and a living link to the family's past. In the summer of 2000, Angie, the kids, and I made the drive from Milwaukee to Egypt, Mississippi, for her family's annual reunion, where Charity and Rodger Scott, Angie's mother and stepfather, greeted me as though I were real family. They've shown nothing but patience with my project ever since, even when it resurrected painful events in their past. Another person to whom I owe special thanks is Michael Steinborn, whose empathy and perseverance brightened an otherwise disheartening picture of the welfare bureaucracy. The relationship between a reporter and his subjects involves an odd mix of closeness and distance—closeness while gathering the material, distance while processing it. Virtually everyone listed above went through this cycle multiple times as I realized how much I still needed to understand and returned with more questions. They bore up with grace, for no reward other than my interest and gratitude. My interpretation of their lives is mine alone, offered in the reporter's vague faith that an important story, properly told, can help bring about "Better Days."

Writers need time. In getting it, I had the financial support of three generous institutions, which requested nothing in return and waited for years for the results. My gratitude goes to Mark Steinmeyer of the Smith Richardson Foundation and Drew Altman of the Henry J. Kaiser Family Foundation, which awarded me grants, and to Alex Jones of the Joan Shorenstein Center on the Press, Politics and Public Policy at the Kennedy School of Government at Harvard University, where I enjoyed a four-month fellowship in the fall of 2000. Gregg Easterbrook, Lyn Hogan, and Isabel Sawhill encouraged me to apply for the Smith Richardson grant. Judy Feder, dean of the Georgetown Public Policy Institute, put herself out to oversee the grants, as did her administrator, Sandy Fournier. As the hardcover edition was published in 2004, I benefited from another bit of unexpected good fortune—a travel grant from the Annie E. Casey Foundation, which allowed me to expand the book's reach through a series of talks across the country. For Casey's generous support, I am grateful to Doug Nelson, Ralph Smith, Patrick McCarthy, Mike Laracy, and Jane Dinse.

Writers also need readers, especially blunt ones. Nicholas Lemann was a crucial early supporter of this project, as he has been for much of my work; he was also at times a frank critic, who forced me to clarify my thoughts. Jack Rosenthal offered a similar mix of encouragement and critique as I mustered a first draft. Toby Herr and Mark Greenberg win Purple Hearts for reading multiple versions; Toby sometimes saw the story more clearly from a distance than I could up close, and Mark's inexhaustible patience was matched only by his command of the policy details. My father, James DeParle, in reading several drafts, was with me in the trenches, as he has been through every stretch of my life. (My mother, Joan DeParle, contributed to my writing in another way, working long hours to help pay for my education.) Others who helpfully read portions or full drafts include Nancy-Ann DeParle, Elizabeth Fenn, Lory Hough, Gerry Marzorati, Chris Myers, Mary Pattillo, Charles Peters, Nicholas Thompson, and Sam Verhovek. Finally, I'd like to thank Ann Hulbert, who signed on about two thirds of the way through as the book's de facto daily editor and has been improving it ever since. Her enthusiasm brought the effort new inspiration and her exquisite judgment, in matters big and small, gave it a safety net. Every author should be so lucky.

President Bill Clinton took time away from finishing his book to talk with me about mine; for making room on his crowded calendar, I'm grateful to him, Jim Kennedy, and Maggie Williams. Mickey Kaus first suggested I go to Milwaukee and has shared his time and insights over a number of years. Taylor Branch offered unexpected help at an important time. Debbie Bigler of the Milwaukee County Department of Human Services assembled the trio's welfare records and fielded years of follow-up questions with a conscientious good cheer that went well beyond the call of duty. Alex Nguyen, Marc Santora, and Seth Stern offered research assistance. I relied especially heavily on the research of Lory Hough, a tireless sleuth whose contributions touch every chapter. Her skill and enthusiasm allowed me to indulge my curiosity without sacrificing my time and therefore made this a much better book than it otherwise could have been. Charles Peters, my longtime mentor and friend, has contributed to my journalism in ways too numerous to list. His concern for social justice is as deep and informed as any I know, and in urging me to scrub my biases he offered a reporting principle that was particularly useful in tracking a story with so many surprises.

My forays into Mississippi's past were greatly aided by Chris Myers, a PhD candidate at the University of North Carolina–Chapel Hill, who is writing a dissertation about James Eastland; he not only shared early drafts of his thesis but conducted a series of tutorials on southern history. Elizabeth Fenn and Peter Wood of Duke University were two other generous history coaches. In my efforts as an amateur genealogist, I got invaluable assistance from a professional one, Jan Hillegas, who helped uncover pieces of the past in places that wouldn't have occurred to me. Historians Chris Waldrep and Todd Moye shared copies of the contemporaneous news coverage of the Luther Holbert affair. In my research on Chicago, I got help from Chuck Nelson and Marie Pees of the Census Bureau, who supplied the tract-level information on Jeffrey Manor. Conversations with Mary Pattillo helped me make sense of it.

Among those who helped me understand Wisconsin welfare politics, current and past, were John Gurda, Tom Kaplan, John Nichols, Peter Tropman, and Gerald Whitburn. David Riemer offered his time, shared his files, and wrote me a long memo about the events that led the Wisconsin legislature to abolish AFDC. Jason Turner welcomed me as a chronicler of his work, offered many useful introductions in Milwaukee, and spent a great deal of time responding to my questions. Coming to grips with Opal's story required me to learn about the effects of cocaine. I got helpful lessons from Ric Curtis, Francine Feinberg, Jerome Jaffe, Michael Massing, Thomas McLellan, Anne Paczesny, and Pat Tucker. Likewise, to understand the work lives of Angie and Jewell, I needed to know more about nursing homes, and got help from Judy Feder, Robert Friedland, Paul Kleyman, Robyn Stone, and Josh Wiener. I couldn't have told the full Maximus story without the interviews and documents provided by several company employees on the condition of anonymity.

A number of Washington figures involved in the welfare bill agreed to long sets of after-the-fact interviews, which, while quoted sparingly, greatly enhanced my ability to tell the story. My thanks to David Ellwood, Mark Greenberg, Stan Greenberg, Ron Haskins, Paul Offner, Wendell Primus, Robert Rector, Bruce Reed, Donna Shalala, and Melissa Skolfield. Among the social scientists on whose patience I regularly imposed were Greg Acs, Maria Cancian, Sheldon Danziger, Greg Duncan, Donna Pavetti, and especially Christopher Jencks, who guided me on several fronts. My talks with Jared Bernstein were particularly helpful as I thought through the economics of postwelfare life. Yulia Fungard helped me crunch the income numbers for Angie and Jewell. Several friends offered their encouragement and also their understanding when the work caused me to disappear; I drew on the support of Henry Brinton, Patti Cohen, E. J. Flynn, Tim Golden, Jon Rosenblum, and the Katy Varney–Dave Goetz clan. Liza Gorman and especially Allison Curran also did much to keep things on track.

Others to whom I owe thanks include: Jeff Aiken, Peggy Anderson, Ken Apfel, Jose Arteaga, Don Baer, Ruthie Mae Bailey, Hundley Batts, Richard Bavier, Jeremy Ben-Ami, Gordon Berlin, Doug Besharov, Bill Biggs, Helen Blank, Rebecca Blank, Tony Blankley, Andrew Bluth, Mary Bourdette, Heather Boushey, Sheila Burke, Vee Burke, Gary Burtless, Dick Buschmann, Adam Carasso, Felmers Chaney, Lindsay Chase-Lansdale, Henry Cisneros, Richard Cloward, James Cobb, Deborah Colton, Tom Corbett, Wesley Crenshaw, Ellen Dadisman, Kristina Daugirtas, Pat DeLessio, Seth Diamond, Jonah Edelman, Peter Edelman, James Fallows, Lester Feder, Pam Fendt, Don Fierce, Ari Fleischer, Tillie Fowler, Henry Freedman, Bruce Fuller, John Gardner, Keith Garland, Mona Garland, James Gibney, Ed Gillespie, Newt Gingrich, Karen Goldmeier, Marjorie Goldsborough, Linda Gordon, Peter Gottschalk, Bob Greenstein, Mary Gross, Jimmy Hayes, Chris Henick, Kathe Hollingshaus, Harry Holzer, Jack Howard, Paul Jargowsky, Chris Jennings, Julie Kerksick, Nick Kotz, Julie Sorrentino Kresge, Ed Kutler, Rachel Langenohl, Robert Lerman, John Lewis, Pamela Loprest, Ed Lorenzen, Tamara Stanton Luzzatto, Gary Mailman, Bob Matsui, Cindy Mann, Mary Kay Mantho, Jai Marin, Will Marshall, Joyce McFarland, Sara McLanahan, Lawrence Mead, Jan Meyers, Ron Mincy, Robert Moffitt, Kristin Moore, Dick Morris, Daniel Patrick Moynihan, Richard Nathan, Leon Panetta, David J. Pate Jr., John Pawasarat, Frances Fox Piven, Susan Pogodzinksi, LeAnne Redick, Mary Lou Reed, Tara Reed, Grace Reef, Robert Reich, Barbara Reinhold, Lou Richman, Cynthia Rice, Bridgette Ridgeway, Alice Rivlin, Laurie Rubiner, Paul Saeman, Isaac Shapiro, Doug Schoen, Clay Shaw, Ron Skarzenski, Margaret Stapleton, George Stephanopoulos, Gene Steurle, Julie Strawn, Paul Stuiber, James Talent, John Tapogna, Rich Tarplin, Julia Taylor, Barry Toiv, Vicki Turetsky, Jack Tweedie, Stephanie Ventura, Melanne Verveer, Barclay Walsh, John Wancheck, Kent Weaver, Jim Weill,

Marcus White, David Whitman, Julie Wilson, Michael Wiseman, and Wendy Woolcott-Steele.

Along with time and sources, a writer needs a publisher. At Viking, Wendy Wolf's enthusiasm for this project won me over eight years ago, and for her unflagging commitment I've been grateful many times since. A book that juggles dozens of characters across several centuries requires a special set of editing skills, and Wendy, a special editor, kept the narrative train moving. For her patience, and her impatience, I'm equally grateful. To her assistant, Cliff Corcoran, a word of thanks, too. My copy editor, Juli Barbato, gave the manuscript a careful read and saved me from several bad errors. Viking's production editor, Kate Griggs, showed great concern for getting things right, even as my last-minute revisions threw the schedule woefully off-course. For putting me in their good hands and goading me along, I'm grateful to my agent, Chuck Verrill, whose devotion to this book has run deep. Lastly, a special word of thanks to Katy Varney, Andrew Maraniss, and their associates at McNeely Pigott & Fox, for their spirit and skill in giving this book its launch. They give PR a good name.

I started this book on the verge of getting married and ended it as a father of two. My sons, Nicholas and Zachary, have never known a world in which their father wasn't in the room next to theirs, engaged in the mysteriously intense work they've come to call "making the book." They grew faster than it did, and one of the serendipitous rewards of this project was that it kept me nearby, where I could watch their young lives unfold. I can't imagine a writer's garret that offered a happier view. My friend Joe Lelyveld advises authors to eschew spousal encomia in print and indulge them in real life. I'll ignore his advice just long enough to say that Nancy-Ann DeParle is the best thing that ever happened to me.

INDEX